CW00521488

William Wilkie Collins (8 January 1824 – 23 September 1889) was an English novelist, playwright, and short story writer, best known for The Woman in White (1859), No Name (1862), Armadale (1866) and The Moonstone (1868). The last has been called the first modern English detective novel. Born to the family of painter William Collins in London, he grew up in Italy and France, learning French and Italian. He began work as a clerk for a tea merchant. After his first novel, Antonina, appeared in 1850, he met Charles Dickens, who became a close friend and mentor. Some of Collins's works appeared first in Dickens's journals All the Year Round and Household Words and they collaborated on drama and fiction. Collins published his best known works in the 1860s, achieving financial stability and an international following. However, he began suffering from gout. Taking opium for the pain developed into an addiction. In the 1870s and 1880s the quality of his writing declined along with his health. Collins was critical of the institution of marriage: he split his time between Caroline Graves, except for a two-year separation, and his common-law wife Martha Rudd, with whom he had three children. (Source: Wikipedia)

Literary works:

Basil (1852)
Hide and Seek (1854)
The Dead Secret (1856)
The Frozen Deep (1857)
"A House to Let" (1858)
"The Haunted House"
The Woman in White (1860)
No Name (1862)
Armadale (1866)
No Thoroughfare (1867)
The Moonstone (1868)
Man and Wife (1870)
Poor Miss Finch (1872)
The Law and the Lady (1875)
The Fallen Leaves (1879)

NO NAME
&
MAN AND WIFE

wilkie collins

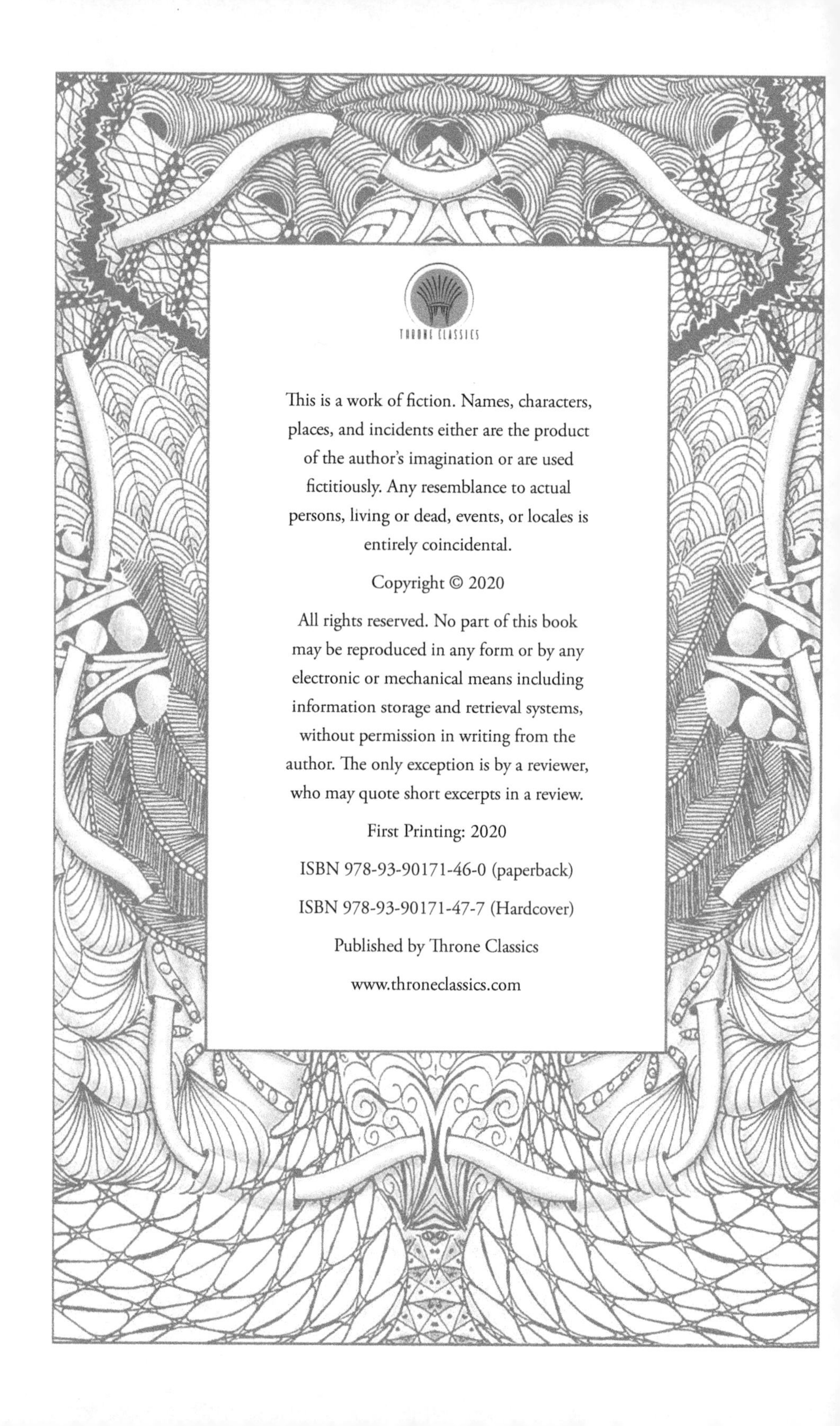

This is a work of fiction. Names, characters, places, and incidents either are the product of the author's imagination or are used fictitiously. Any resemblance to actual persons, living or dead, events, or locales is entirely coincidental.

First Printing: 2020

ISBN 978-93-90171-46-0 (paperback)

ISBN 978-93-90171-47-7 (Hardcover)

Published by Throne Classics

www.throneclassics.com

Contents

NO NAME
&
MAN AND WIFE

NO NAME

PREFACE.

THE main purpose of this story is to appeal to the reader's interest in a subject which has been the theme of some of the greatest writers, living and dead—but which has never been, and can never be, exhausted, because it is a subject eternally interesting to all mankind. Here is one more book that depicts the struggle of a human creature, under those opposing influences of Good and Evil, which we have all felt, which we have all known. It has been my aim to make the character of "Magdalen," which personifies this struggle, a pathetic character even in its perversity and its error; and I have tried hard to attain this result by the least obtrusive and the least artificial of all means—by a resolute adherence throughout to the truth as it is in Nature. This design was no easy one to accomplish; and it has been a great encouragement to me (during the publication of my story in its periodical form) to know, on the authority of many readers, that the object which I had proposed to myself, I might, in some degree, consider as an object achieved.

Round the central figure in the narrative other characters will be found grouped, in sharp contrast—contrast, for the most part, in which I have endeavored to make the element of humor mainly predominant. I have sought to impart this relief to the more serious passages in the book, not only because I believe myself to be justified in doing so by the laws of Art—but because experience has taught me (what the experience of my readers will doubtless confirm) that there is no such moral phenomenon as unmixed tragedy to be found in the world around us. Look where we may, the dark threads and the light cross each other perpetually in the texture of human life.

To pass from the Characters to the Story, it will be seen that the narrative related in these pages has been constructed on a plan which differs from the plan followed in my last novel, and in some other of my works published at an earlier date. The only Secret contained in this book is revealed midway in the first volume. From that point, all the main events of the story are purposely foreshadowed before they take place—my present design being to rouse the reader's interest in following the train of circumstances by which these foreseen events are brought about. In trying this new ground, I am not turning my back in doubt on the ground which I have passed over already. My one object in following a new course is to enlarge the range of my studies in the art of writing fiction, and to vary the form in which I make my appeal to the reader, as attractively as I can.

There is no need for me to add more to these few prefatory words than is here written. What I might otherwise have wished to say in this place, I have endeavored to make the book itself say for me.

TO FRANCIS CARR BEARD (FELLOW OF THE ROYAL COLLEGE OF SURGEONS OF ENGLAND), IN REMEMBRANCE OF THE TIME WHEN THE CLOSING SCENES OF THIS STORY WERE WRITTEN.

THE FIRST SCENE.

COMBE-RAVEN, SOMERSETSHIRE.

CHAPTER I.

THE hands on the hall-clock pointed to half-past six in the morning. The house was a country residence in West Somersetshire, called Combe-Raven. The day was the fourth of March, and the year was eighteen hundred and forty-six.

No sounds but the steady ticking of the clock, and the lumpish snoring of a large dog stretched on a mat outside the dining-room door, disturbed the mysterious morning stillness of hall and staircase. Who were the sleepers hidden in the upper regions? Let the house reveal its own secrets; and, one by one, as they descend the stairs from their beds, let the sleepers disclose themselves.

As the clock pointed to a quarter to seven, the dog woke and shook himself. After waiting in vain for the footman, who was accustomed to let him out, the animal wandered restlessly from one closed door to another on the ground-floor; and, returning to his mat in great perplexity, appealed to the sleeping family with a long and melancholy howl.

Before the last notes of the dog's remonstrance had died away, the oaken stairs in the higher regions of the house creaked under slowly-descending footsteps. In a minute more the first of the female servants made her appearance, with a dingy woolen shawl over her shoulders—for the March morning was bleak; and rheumatism and the cook were old acquaintances.

Receiving the dog's first cordial advances with the worst possible grace, the cook slowly opened the hall door and let the animal out. It was a wild morning. Over a spacious lawn, and behind a black plantation of firs, the rising sun rent its way upward through piles of ragged gray cloud; heavy drops of rain fell few and far between; the March wind shuddered round the corners of the house, and the wet trees swayed wearily.

Seven o'clock struck; and the signs of domestic life began to show themselves in more rapid succession.

The housemaid came down—tall and slim, with the state of the spring temperature written redly on her nose. The lady's-maid followed—young, smart, plump, and sleepy. The kitchen-maid came next—afflicted with the face-ache, and making no secret of her sufferings. Last of all, the footman appeared, yawning disconsolately; the living picture of a man who felt that he had been defrauded of his fair night's rest.

The conversation of the servants, when they assembled before the slowly lighting kitchen fire, referred to a recent family event, and turned at starting on this question: Had Thomas, the footman, seen anything of the concert at Clifton, at which his master and the two young ladies had been present on the previous night? Yes; Thomas had heard the concert; he had been paid for to go in at the back; it was a loud concert; it was a hot concert; it was described at the top of the bills as Grand; whether it was worth traveling sixteen miles to hear by railway, with the additional hardship of going back nineteen miles by road, at half-past one in the morning—was a question which he would leave his master and the young ladies to decide; his own opinion, in the meantime, being unhesitatingly, No. Further inquiries, on the part of all the female servants in succession, elicited no additional information of any sort. Thomas could hum none of the songs, and could describe none of the ladies' dresses. His audience, accordingly, gave him up in despair; and the kitchen small-talk flowed back into its ordinary channels, until the clock struck eight and startled the assembled servants into separating for their morning's work.

A quarter past eight, and nothing happened. Half-past—and more signs of life appeared from the bedroom regions. The next member of the family who came downstairs was Mr. Andrew Vanstone, the master of the house.

Tall, stout, and upright—with bright blue eyes, and healthy, florid complexion—his brown plush shooting-jacket carelessly buttoned awry; his vixenish little Scotch terrier barking unrebuked at his heels; one hand thrust into his waistcoat pocket, and the other smacking the banisters cheerfully as he came downstairs humming a tune—Mr. Vanstone showed his character on the surface of him freely to all men. An easy, hearty, handsome, good-humored gentleman, who walked on the sunny side of the way of life, and who asked nothing better than to meet all his fellow-passengers in this world on the sunny side, too. Estimating him by years, he had turned fifty. Judging him by lightness of heart, strength of constitution, and capacity for enjoyment, he was no older than most men who have only turned thirty.

"Thomas!" cried Mr. Vanstone, taking up his old felt hat and his thick walking stick from the hall table. "Breakfast, this morning, at ten. The young ladies are not likely to be down earlier after the concert last night.—By-the-by, how did you like the concert yourself, eh? You thought it was grand? Quite right; so it was. Nothing but crash-bang, varied now and then by bang-crash; all the women dressed within an inch of their lives; smothering heat, blazing gas, and no room for anybody—yes, yes, Thomas; grand's the word for it, and comfortable isn't." With that expression of opinion, Mr. Vanstone whistled to his vixenish terrier; flourished his stick at the hall door in cheerful defiance of the rain; and set off through wind and weather for his morning walk.

The hands, stealing their steady way round the dial of the clock, pointed to ten minutes to nine. Another member of the family appeared on the stairs—Miss Garth, the governess.

No observant eyes could have surveyed Miss Garth without seeing at once that she was a north-countrywoman. Her hard featured face; her masculine readiness and decision of movement; her obstinate honesty of look and manner, all proclaimed her border birth and border training. Though little more than forty years of age, her hair was quite gray; and she wore over it the plain cap of an old woman. Neither hair nor head-dress was out of harmony with her face—it looked older than her years: the hard handwriting of trouble had scored it heavily at some past time. The self-possession of her progress downstairs, and the air of habitual authority with which she looked about her, spoke well for her position in Mr. Vanstone's family. This was evidently not one of the forlorn, persecuted, pitiably dependent order of governesses. Here was a woman who lived on ascertained and honorable terms with her employers—a woman who looked capable of sending any parents in England to the right-about, if they failed to rate her at her proper value.

"Breakfast at ten?" repeated Miss Garth, when the footman had answered the bell, and had mentioned his master's orders. "Ha! I thought what would come of that concert last night. When people who live in the country patronize public amusements, public amusements return the compliment by upsetting the family afterward for days together. You're upset, Thomas, I can see your eyes are as red as a ferret's, and your cravat looks as if you had slept in it. Bring the kettle at a quarter to ten—and if you don't get better in the course of the day, come to me, and I'll give you a dose of physic. That's a well-meaning lad, if you only let him alone," continued Miss Garth, in soliloquy, when Thomas had retired; "but he's not strong enough for concerts twenty miles off. They wanted me to go with them last night. Yes: catch me!"

Nine o'clock struck; and the minute-hand stole on to twenty minutes past the hour, before any more footsteps were heard on the stairs. At the end of that time, two ladies appeared, descending to the breakfast-room together—Mrs. Vanstone and her eldest daughter.

If the personal attractions of Mrs. Vanstone, at an earlier period of life, had depended solely on her native English charms of complexion and freshness, she must have long since lost the last relics of her fairer self. But her beauty as a young woman had passed beyond the average national limits; and she still preserved the advantage of her more exceptional personal gifts. Although she was now in her forty-fourth year; although she had been tried, in bygone times, by the premature loss of more than one of her children, and by long attacks of illness which had followed those bereavements of former years—she still preserved the fair proportion and subtle delicacy of feature, once associated with the all-adorning brightness and freshness of beauty, which had left her never to return. Her eldest child, now descending the stairs by her side, was the mirror in which she could look back and see again the reflection of her own youth. There, folded thick on the daughter's head, lay the massive dark hair, which, on the mother's, was fast turning gray. There, in the daughter's cheek, glowed the lovely dusky red which had faded from the mother's to bloom again no more. Miss Vanstone had already reached the first maturity of womanhood; she had completed her six-and-twentieth year. Inheriting the dark majestic character of her mother's beauty, she had yet hardly inherited all its charms. Though the shape of her face was the same, the features were scarcely so delicate, their proportion was scarcely so true. She was not so tall. She had the dark-brown eyes of her mother—full and soft, with the steady luster in them which Mrs. Vanstone's eyes had lost—and yet there was less interest, less refinement and depth of feeling in her expression: it was gentle and feminine, but clouded by a certain quiet reserve, from which her mother's face was free. If we dare to look closely enough, may we not observe that the moral force of character and the higher intellectual capacities in parents seem often to wear out mysteriously in the course of transmission to children? In these days of insidious nervous exhaustion and subtly-spreading nervous malady, is it not possible that the same rule may apply, less rarely than we are willing to admit, to the bodily gifts as well?

The mother and daughter slowly descended the stairs together—the first dressed in dark brown, with an Indian shawl thrown over her shoulders; the second more simply attired in black, with a plain collar and cuffs, and a dark orange-colored ribbon over the bosom of her dress. As they crossed the hall and entered the breakfast-room, Miss Vanstone was full of the all-absorbing subject of the last night's concert.

"I am so sorry, mamma, you were not with us," she said. "You have been so strong and so well ever since last summer—you have felt so many years younger, as you said yourself—that I am sure the exertion would not have been too much for you."

"Perhaps not, my love—but it was as well to keep on the safe side."

"Quite as well," remarked Miss Garth, appearing at the breakfast-room door. "Look at Norah (good-morning, my dear)—look, I say, at Norah. A perfect wreck; a living proof of your wisdom and mine in staying at home. The vile gas, the foul air, the late hours—what can you expect? She's not made of iron, and she suffers accordingly. No, my dear, you needn't deny it. I see you've got a headache."

Norah's dark, handsome face brightened into a smile—then lightly clouded again with its accustomed quiet reserve.

"A very little headache; not half enough to make me regret the concert," she said, and walked away by herself to the window.

On the far side of a garden and paddock the view overlooked a stream, some farm buildings which lay beyond, and the opening of a wooded, rocky pass (called, in Somersetshire, a Combe), which here cleft its way through the hills that closed the prospect. A winding strip of road was visible, at no great distance, amid the undulations of the open ground; and along this strip the stalwart figure of Mr. Vanstone was now easily recognizable, returning to the house from his morning walk. He flourished his stick gayly, as he observed his eldest daughter at the window. She nodded and waved her hand in return, very gracefully and prettily—but with something of old-fashioned formality in her manner, which looked strangely in so young a woman, and which seemed out of harmony with a salutation addressed to her father.

The hall-clock struck the adjourned breakfast-hour. When the minute hand had recorded the lapse of five minutes more a door banged in the bedroom regions—a clear young voice was heard singing blithely—light, rapid footsteps pattered on the upper stairs, descended with a jump to the landing, and pattered again, faster than ever, down the lower flight. In another moment the youngest of Mr. Vanstone's two daughters (and two only surviving children) dashed into view on the dingy old oaken stairs, with the suddenness of a flash of light; and clearing the last three steps into the hall at a jump, presented herself breathless in the breakfast-room to make the family circle complete.

By one of those strange caprices of Nature, which science leaves still unexplained, the youngest of Mr. Vanstone's children presented no recognizable resemblance to either of her parents. How had she come by her hair? how had she come by her eyes? Even her father and mother had asked themselves those questions, as she grew up to girlhood, and had been sorely perplexed to answer them. Her hair was of that purely light-brown hue, unmixed with flaxen, or yellow, or red—which is oftener seen on the plumage of a bird than on the head of a human being. It was soft and plentiful, and waved downward from her low forehead in regular folds—but, to some tastes, it was dull and dead, in its absolute want of glossiness, in its monotonous purity of plain light color. Her eyebrows and eyelashes were just a shade darker than her hair, and seemed made expressly for those violet-blue eyes, which assert their most irresistible charm when associated with a fair complexion. But it was here exactly that the promise of her face failed of performance in the most startling manner. The eyes, which should have been dark, were incomprehensibly and discordantly light; they were of that nearly colorless gray which, though little attractive in itself, possesses the rare compensating merit of interpreting the finest gradations of thought, the gentlest changes of feeling, the deepest trouble of passion, with a subtle transparency of expression which no darker eyes can rival. Thus quaintly self-contradictory in the upper part of her face, she was hardly less at variance with established ideas of harmony in the lower. Her lips had the true feminine delicacy of form, her cheeks the lovely roundness and smoothness of youth—but the mouth was too large and firm, the chin too square and massive for her sex and age. Her complexion partook of the pure monotony of tint which characterized her hair—it was of the same soft, warm, creamy fairness all over, without a tinge of color in the cheeks, except on occasions of unusual bodily exertion or sudden mental disturbance. The whole countenance—so remarkable in its strongly opposed characteristics—was rendered additionally striking by its extraordinary mobility. The large, electric, light-gray eyes were hardly ever in repose; all varieties of expression followed each other over the plastic, ever-changing face, with a giddy rapidity which left sober analysis far behind in the race. The girl's exuberant vitality asserted itself all over her, from head to foot. Her figure—taller than her sister's, taller than the average of woman's height; instinct with such a seductive, serpentine suppleness, so lightly and playfully graceful, that its movements suggested, not unnaturally, the movements of a young cat—her figure was so perfectly developed already that no one who saw her could have supposed that she was only eighteen. She bloomed in the full physical maturity of twenty years or more—bloomed naturally and irresistibly, in right of her matchless health and strength. Here, in truth, lay the mainspring of this strangely-constituted organization. Her headlong course down the house stairs; the brisk activity of all her movements; the incessant sparkle of expression in her face; the enticing gayety which took the hearts of the quietest people by storm—even the reckless delight in bright colors which showed itself in her brilliantly-striped morning dress, in her fluttering ribbons, in the large scarlet rosettes on her smart little shoes—all sprang alike from the same source; from the overflowing physical health which strengthened every muscle, braced every nerve, and set the warm young blood tingling through her veins, like the blood of a growing child.

On her entry into the breakfast-room, she was saluted with the customary remonstrance which her flighty disregard of all punctuality habitually provoked from the long-suffering household authorities. In Miss Garth's favorite phrase, "Magdalen was born with all the senses—except a sense of order."

Magdalen! It was a strange name to have given her? Strange, indeed; and yet, chosen under no extraordinary circumstances. The name had been borne by one of Mr. Vanstone's sisters, who had died in early youth; and, in affectionate remembrance of her, he had called his second daughter by it—just as he had called his eldest daughter Norah, for his wife's sake. Magdalen! Surely, the grand old Bible name—suggestive of a sad and somber dignity; recalling, in its first association, mournful ideas of penitence and seclusion—had been here, as events had turned out, inappropriately bestowed? Surely, this self-contradictory girl had perversely accomplished one contradiction more, by developing into a character which was out of all harmony with her own Christian name!

"Late again!" said Mrs. Vanstone, as Magdalen breathlessly kissed her.

"Late again!" chimed in Miss Garth, when Magdalen came her way next. "Well?" she went on, taking the girl's chin familiarly in her hand, with a half-satirical, half-fond attention which betrayed that the youngest daughter, with all her faults, was the governess's favorite—"Well? and what has the concert done for you? What form of suffering has dissipation inflicted on your system this morning?"

"Suffering!" repeated Magdalen, recovering her breath, and the use of her tongue with it. "I don't know the meaning of the word: if there's anything the matter with me, I'm too well. Suffering! I'm ready for another concert to-night, and a ball to-morrow, and a play the day after. Oh," cried Magdalen, dropping into a chair and crossing her hands rapturously on the table, "how I do like pleasure!"

"Come! that's explicit at any rate," said Miss Garth. "I think Pope must have had you in his mind when he wrote his famous lines:

"'Men some to business, some to pleasure take, But every woman is at heart a rake.'"

"The deuce she is!" cried Mr. Vanstone, entering the room while Miss Garth was making her quotation, with the dogs at his heels. "Well; live and learn. If you're all rakes, Miss Garth, the sexes are turned topsy-turvy with a vengeance; and the men will have nothing left for it but to stop at home and darn the stockings.—Let's have some breakfast."

"How-d'ye-do, papa?" said Magdalen, taking Mr. Vanstone as boisterously round the neck as if he belonged to some larger order of Newfoundland dog, and was made to be romped with at his daughter's convenience. "I'm the rake Miss Garth means; and I want to go to another concert—or a play, if you like—or a ball, if you prefer it—or anything else in the way of amusement that puts me into a new dress, and plunges me into a crowd of people, and illuminates me with plenty of light, and sets me in a tingle of excitement all over, from head to foot. Anything will do, as long as it doesn't send us to bed at eleven o'clock."

Mr. Vanstone sat down composedly under his daughter's flow of language, like a man who was well used to verbal inundation from that quarter. "If I am to be allowed my choice of amusements next time," said the worthy gentleman, "I think a play will suit me better than a concert. The girls enjoyed themselves amazingly, my dear," he continued, addressing his wife. "More than I did, I must say. It was altogether above my mark. They played one piece of music which lasted forty minutes. It stopped three times, by-the-way; and we all thought it was done each time, and clapped our hands, rejoiced to be rid of it. But on it went again, to our great surprise and mortification, till we gave it up in despair, and all wished ourselves at Jericho. Norah, my dear! when we had crash-bang for forty minutes, with three stoppages by-the-way, what did they call it?"

"A symphony, papa," replied Norah.

"Yes, you darling old Goth, a symphony by the great Beethoven!" added Magdalen. "How can you say you were not amused? Have you forgotten the yellow-looking foreign woman, with the unpronounceable name? Don't you remember the faces she made when she sang? and the way she courtesied and courtesied, till she cheated the foolish people into crying encore? Look here, mamma—look here, Miss Garth!"

She snatched up an empty plate from the table, to represent a sheet of music, held it before her in the established concert-room position, and produced an imitation of the unfortunate singer's grimaces and courtesyings, so accurately and quaintly true to the original, that her father roared with laughter; and even the footman (who came in at that moment with the post-bag) rushed out of the room again, and committed the indecorum of echoing his master audibly on the other side of the door.

"Letters, papa. I want the key," said Magdalen, passing from the imitation at the breakfast-table to the post-bag on the sideboard with the easy abruptness which characterized all her actions.

Mr. Vanstone searched his pockets and shook his head. Though his youngest daughter might resemble him in nothing else, it was easy to see where Magdalen's unmethodical habits came from.

"I dare say I have left it in the library, along with my other keys," said Mr. Vanstone. "Go and look for it, my dear."

"You really should check Magdalen," pleaded Mrs. Vanstone, addressing her husband when her daughter had left the room. "Those habits of mimicry are growing on her; and she speaks to you with a levity which it is positively shocking to hear."

"Exactly what I have said myself, till I am tired of repeating it," remarked Miss Garth. "She treats Mr. Vanstone as if he was a kind of younger brother of hers."

"You are kind to us in everything else, papa; and you make kind allowances for Magdalen's high spirits—don't you?" said the quiet Norah, taking her father's part and her sister's with so little show of resolution on the surface that few observers would have been sharp enough to detect the genuine substance beneath it.

"Thank you, my dear," said good-natured Mr. Vanstone. "Thank you for a very pretty speech. As for Magdalen," he continued, addressing his wife and Miss Garth, "she's an unbroken filly. Let her caper and kick in the paddock to her heart's content. Time enough to break her to harness when she gets a little older."

The door opened, and Magdalen returned with the key. She unlocked the post-bag at the sideboard and poured out the letters in a heap. Sorting them gayly in less than a minute, she approached the breakfast-table with both hands full, and delivered the letters all round with the business-like rapidity of a London postman.

"Two for Norah," she announced, beginning with her sister. "Three for Miss Garth. None for mamma. One for me. And the other six all for papa. You lazy old darling, you hate answering letters, don't you?" pursued Magdalen, dropping the postman's character and assuming the daughter's. "How you will grumble and fidget in the study! and how you will wish there were no such things as letters in the world! and how red your nice old bald head will get at the top with the worry of writing the answers; and how many of the answers you will leave until tomorrow after all! The Bristol Theater's open, papa," she whispered, slyly and suddenly, in her father's ear; "I saw it in the newspaper when I went to the library to get the key. Let's go to-morrow night!"

While his daughter was chattering, Mr. Vanstone was mechanically sorting his letters. He turned over the first four in succession and looked carelessly at the addresses. When he came to the fifth his attention, which had hitherto wandered toward Magdalen, suddenly became fixed on the post-mark of the letter.

Stooping over him, with her head on his shoulder, Magdalen could see the post-mark as plainly as her father saw it—NEW ORLEANS.

"An American letter, papa!" she said. "Who do you know at New Orleans?"

Mrs. Vanstone started, and looked eagerly at her husband the moment Magdalen spoke those words.

Mr. Vanstone said nothing. He quietly removed his daughter's arm from his neck, as if he wished to be free from all interruption. She returned, accordingly, to her place at the breakfast-table. Her father, with the letter in his hand, waited a little before he opened it; her mother looking at him, the while, with an eager, expectant attention which attracted Miss Garth's notice, and Norah's, as well as Magdalen's.

After a minute or more of hesitation Mr. Vanstone opened the letter.

His face changed color the instant he read the first lines; his cheeks fading to a dull, yellow-brown hue, which would have been ashy paleness in a less florid man; and his expression becoming saddened and overclouded in a moment. Norah and Magdalen, watching anxiously, saw nothing but the change that passed over their father. Miss Garth alone observed the effect which that change produced on the attentive mistress of the house.

It was not the effect which she, or any one, could have anticipated. Mrs. Vanstone looked excited rather than alarmed. A faint flush rose on her cheeks—her eyes brightened—she stirred the tea round and round in her cup in a restless, impatient manner which was not natural to her.

Magdalen, in her capacity of spoiled child, was, as usual, the first to break the silence.

"What is the matter, papa?" she asked.

"Nothing," said Mr. Vanstone, sharply, without looking up at her.

"I'm sure there must be something," persisted Magdalen. "I'm sure there is bad news, papa, in that American letter."

"There is nothing in the letter that concerns you," said Mr. Vanstone.

It was the first direct rebuff that Magdalen had ever received from her father. She looked at him with an incredulous surprise, which would have been irresistibly absurd under less serious circumstances.

Nothing more was said. For the first time, perhaps, in their lives, the family sat round the breakfast-table in painful silence. Mr. Vanstone's hearty morning appetite, like his hearty morning spirits, was gone. He absently broke off some morsels of dry toast from the rack near him, absently finished his first cup of tea—then asked for a second, which he left before him untouched.

"Norah," he said, after an interval, "you needn't wait for me. Magdalen, my dear, you can go when you like."

His daughters rose immediately; and Miss Garth considerately followed their example. When an easy-tempered man does assert himself in his family, the rarity of the demonstration invariably has its effect; and the will of that easy-tempered man is Law.

"What can have happened?" whispered Norah, as they closed the breakfast-room door and crossed the hall.

"What does papa mean by being cross with Me?" exclaimed Magdalen, chafing under a sense of her own injuries.

"May I ask—what right you had to pry into your father's private affairs?" retorted Miss Garth.

"Right?" repeated Magdalen. "I have no secrets from papa—what business has papa to have secrets from me! I consider myself insulted."

"If you considered yourself properly reproved for not minding your own business," said the plain-spoken Miss Garth, "you would be a trifle nearer the truth. Ah! you are like all the rest of the girls in the present day. Not one in a hundred of you knows which end of her's uppermost."

The three ladies entered the morning-room; and Magdalen acknowledged Miss Garth's reproof by banging the door.

Half an hour passed, and neither Mr. Vanstone nor his wife left the breakfast-room. The servant, ignorant of what had happened, went in to clear the table—found his master and mistress seated close together in deep consultation—and immediately went out again. Another quarter of an hour elapsed before the breakfast-room door was opened, and the private conference of the husband and wife came to an end.

"I hear mamma in the hall," said Norah. "Perhaps she is coming to tell us something."

Mrs. Vanstone entered the morning-room as her daughter spoke. The color was deeper on her cheeks, and the brightness of half-dried tears glistened in her eyes; her step was more hasty, all her movements were quicker than usual.

"I bring news, my dears, which will surprise you," she said, addressing her daughters. "Your father and I are going to London to-morrow."

Magdalen caught her mother by the arm in speechless astonishment. Miss Garth dropped her work on her lap; even the sedate Norah started to her feet, and amazedly repeated the words, "Going to London!"

"Without us?" added Magdalen.

"Your father and I are going alone," said Mrs. Vanstone. "Perhaps, for as long as three weeks—but not longer. We are going"—she hesitated—"we are going on important family business. Don't hold me, Magdalen. This is a sudden necessity—I have a great deal to do to-day—many things to set in order before tomorrow. There, there, my love, let me go."

She drew her arm away; hastily kissed her youngest daughter on the forehead; and at once left the room again. Even Magdalen saw that her mother was not to be coaxed into hearing or answering any more questions.

The morning wore on, and nothing was seen of Mr. Vanstone. With the reckless curiosity of her age and character, Magdalen, in defiance of Miss Garth's prohibition and her sister's remonstrances, determined to go to the study and look for her father there. When she tried the door, it was locked on the inside. She said, "It's only me, papa;" and waited for the answer. "I'm busy now, my dear," was the answer. "Don't disturb me."

Mrs. Vanstone was, in another way, equally inaccessible. She remained in her own room, with the female servants about her, immersed in endless preparations for the approaching departure. The servants, little used in that family to sudden resolutions and unexpected orders, were awkward and confused in obeying directions. They ran from room to room unnecessarily, and lost time and patience in jostling each other on the stairs. If a stranger had entered the house that day, he might have imagined that an unexpected disaster had happened in it, instead of an unexpected necessity for a journey to London. Nothing proceeded in its ordinary routine. Magdalen, who was accustomed to pass the morning at the piano, wandered restlessly about the staircases and passages, and in and out of doors when there were glimpses of fine weather. Norah, whose fondness for reading had passed into a family proverb, took up book after book from table and shelf, and laid them down again, in despair of fixing her attention. Even Miss Garth felt the all-pervading influence of the household disorganization, and sat alone by the morning-room fire, with her head shaking ominously, and her work laid aside.

"Family affairs?" thought Miss Garth, pondering over Mrs. Vanstone's vague explanatory words. "I have lived twelve years at Combe-Raven; and these are the first family affairs which have got between the parents and the children, in all my experience. What does it mean? Change? I suppose I'm getting old. I don't like change."

CHAPTER II.

AT ten o'clock the next morning Norah and Magdalen stood alone in the hall at Combe-Raven watching the departure of the carriage which took their father and mother to the London train.

Up to the last moment, both the sisters had hoped for some explanation of that mysterious "family business" to which Mrs. Vanstone had so briefly alluded on the previous day. No such explanation had been offered. Even the agitation of the leave-taking, under circumstances entirely new in the home experience of the parents and children, had not shaken the resolute discretion of Mr. and Mrs. Vanstone. They had gone—with the warmest testimonies of affection, with farewell embraces fervently reiterated again and again—but without dropping one word, from first to last, of the nature of their errand.

As the grating sound of the carriage-wheels ceased suddenly at a turn in the road, the sisters looked one another in the face; each feeling, and each betraying in her own way, the dreary sense that she was openly excluded, for the first time, from the confidence of her parents. Norah's customary reserve strengthened into sullen silence—she sat down in one of the hall chairs and looked out frowningly through the open house door. Magdalen, as usual when her temper was ruffled, expressed her dissatisfaction in the plainest terms. "I don't care who knows it—I think we are both of us shamefully ill-used!" With those words, the young lady followed her sister's example by seating herself on a hall chair and looking aimlessly out through the open house door.

Almost at the same moment Miss Garth entered the hall from the morning-room. Her quick observation showed her the necessity for interfering to some practical purpose; and her ready good sense at once pointed the way.

"Look up, both of you, if you please, and listen to me," said Miss Garth. "If we are all three to be comfortable and happy together, now we are alone, we must stick to our usual habits and go on in our regular way. There is the state of things in plain words. Accept the situation—as the French say. Here am I to set you the example. I have just ordered an excellent dinner at the customary hour. I am going to the medicine-chest next, to physic the kitchen-maid—an unwholesome girl, whose face-ache is all stomach. In the meantime, Norah, my dear, you will find your work and your books, as usual, in the library. Magdalen, suppose you leave off tying your handkerchief into knots and use your fingers on the keys of the piano instead? We'll lunch at one, and take the dogs out afterward. Be as brisk and cheerful both of you as I am. Come, rouse up directly. If I see those gloomy faces any longer, as sure as my name's Garth, I'll give your mother written warning and go back to my friends by the mixed train at twelve forty."

Concluding her address of expostulation in those terms, Miss Garth led Norah to the library door, pushed Magdalen into the morning-room, and went on her own way sternly to the regions of the medicine-chest.

In this half-jesting, half-earnest manner she was accustomed to maintain a sort of friendly authority over Mr. Vanstone's daughters, after her proper functions as governess had necessarily come to an end. Norah, it is needless to say, had long since ceased to be her pupil; and Magdalen had, by this time, completed her education. But Miss Garth had lived too long and too intimately under Mr. Vanstone's roof to be parted with for any purely formal considerations; and the first hint at going away which she had thought it her duty to drop was dismissed with such affectionate warmth of protest that she never repeated it again, except in jest. The entire management of the household was, from that time forth, left in her hands; and to those duties she was free to add what companionable assistance she could render to Norah's reading, and what friendly superintendence she could still exercise over Magdalen's music. Such were the terms on which Miss Garth was now a resident in Mr. Vanstone's family.

Toward the afternoon the weather improved. At half-past one the sun was shining brightly; and the ladies left the house, accompanied by the dogs, to set forth on their walk.

They crossed the stream, and ascended by the little rocky pass to the hills beyond; then diverged to the left, and returned by a cross-road which led through the village of Combe-Raven.

As they came in sight of the first cottages, they passed a man, hanging about the road, who looked attentively, first at Magdalen, then at Norah. They merely observed that he was short, that he was dressed in black, and that he was a total stranger to them—and continued their homeward walk, without thinking more about the loitering foot-passenger whom they had met on their way back.

After they had left the village, and had entered the road which led straight to the house, Magdalen surprised Miss Garth by announcing that the stranger in black had turned, after they had passed him, and was now following them. "He keeps on Norah's side of the road," she said, mischievously. "I'm not the attraction—don't blame me."

Whether the man was really following them, or not, made little difference, for they were now close to the house. As they passed through the lodge-gates, Miss Garth looked round, and saw that the stranger was quickening his pace, apparently with the purpose of entering into conversation. Seeing this, she at once directed the young ladies to go on to the house with the dogs, while she herself waited for events at the gate.

There was just time to complete this discreet arrangement, before the stranger reached the lodge. He took off his hat to Miss Garth politely, as she turned round. What did he look like, on the face of him? He looked like a clergyman in difficulties.

Taking his portrait, from top to toe, the picture of him began with a tall hat, broadly encircled by a mourning band of crumpled crape. Below the hat was a lean, long, sallow face, deeply pitted with the smallpox, and characterized, very remarkably, by eyes of two different colors—one bilious green, one bilious brown, both sharply intelligent. His hair was iron-gray, carefully brushed round at the temples. His cheeks and chin were in the bluest bloom of smooth shaving; his nose was short Roman; his lips long, thin, and supple, curled up at the corners with a mildly-humorous smile. His white cravat was high, stiff, and dingy; the collar, higher, stiffer, and dingier, projected its rigid points on either side beyond his chin. Lower down, the lithe little figure of the man was arrayed throughout in sober-shabby black. His frock-coat was buttoned tight round the waist, and left to bulge open majestically at the chest. His hands were covered with black cotton gloves neatly darned at the fingers; his umbrella, worn down at the ferule to the last quarter of an inch, was carefully preserved, nevertheless, in an oilskin case. The front view of him was the view in which he looked oldest; meeting him face to face, he might have been estimated at fifty or more. Walking behind him, his back and shoulders were almost young enough to have passed for five-and-thirty. His manners were distinguished by a grave serenity. When he opened his lips, he spoke in a rich bass voice, with an easy flow of language, and a strict attention to the elocutionary claims of words in more than one syllable. Persuasion distilled from his mildly-curling lips; and, shabby as he was, perennial flowers of courtesy bloomed all over him from head to foot.

"This is the residence of Mr. Vanstone, I believe?" he began, with a circular wave of his hand in the direction of the house. "Have I the honor of addressing a member of Mr. Vanstone's family?"

"Yes," said the plain-spoken Miss Garth. "You are addressing Mr. Vanstone's governess."

The persuasive man fell back a step—admired Mr. Vanstone's governess—advanced a step again—and continued the conversation.

"And the two young ladies," he went on, "the two young ladies who were walking with you are doubtless Mr. Vanstone's daughters? I recognized the darker of the two, and the elder as I apprehend, by her likeness to her handsome mother. The younger lady—"

"You are acquainted with Mrs. Vanstone, I suppose?" said Miss Garth, interrupting the stranger's flow of language, which, all things considered, was beginning, in her opinion, to flow rather freely. The stranger acknowledged the interruption by one of his polite bows, and submerged Miss Garth in his next sentence as if nothing had happened.

"The younger lady," he proceeded, "takes after her father, I presume? I assure you, her face struck me. Looking at it with my friendly interest in the family, I thought it very remarkable. I said to myself—Charming, Characteristic, Memorable. Not like her sister, not like her mother. No doubt, the image of her father?"

Once more Miss Garth attempted to stem the man's flow of words. It was plain that he did not know Mr. Vanstone, even by sight—otherwise he would never have committed the error of supposing that Magdalen took after her father. Did he know Mrs. Vanstone any better? He had left Miss Garth's question on that point unanswered. In the name of wonder, who was he? Powers of impudence! what did he want?

"You may be a friend of the family, though I don't remember your face," said Miss Garth. "What may your commands be, if you please? Did you come here to pay Mrs. Vanstone a visit?"

"I had anticipated the pleasure of communicating with Mrs. Vanstone," answered this inveterately evasive and inveterately civil man. "How is she?"

"Much as usual," said Miss Garth, feeling her resources of politeness fast failing her.

"Is she at home?"

"No."

"Out for long?"

"Gone to London with Mr. Vanstone."

The man's long face suddenly grew longer. His bilious brown eye looked disconcerted, and his bilious green eye followed its example. His manner became palpably anxious; and his choice of words was more carefully selected than ever.

"Is Mrs. Vanstone's absence likely to extend over any very lengthened period?" he inquired.

"It will extend over three weeks," replied Miss Garth. "I think you have now asked me questions enough," she went on, beginning to let her temper get the better of her at last. "Be so good, if you please, as to mention your business and your name. If you have any message to leave for Mrs. Vanstone, I shall be writing to her by to-night's post, and I can take charge of it."

"A thousand thanks! A most valuable suggestion. Permit me to take advantage of it immediately."

He was not in the least affected by the severity of Miss Garth's looks and language—he was simply relieved by her proposal, and he showed it with the most engaging sincerity. This time his bilious green eye took the initiative, and set his bilious brown eye the example of recovered serenity. His curling lips took a new twist upward; he tucked his umbrella briskly under his arm; and produced from the breast of his coat a large old-fashioned black pocketbook. From this he took a pencil and a card—hesitated and considered for a moment—wrote rapidly on the card—and placed it, with the politest alacrity, in Miss Garth's hand.

"I shall feel personally obliged if you will honor me by inclosing that card in your letter," he said. "There is no necessity for my troubling you additionally with a message. My name will be quite sufficient to recall a little family matter to Mrs. Vanstone, which has no doubt escaped her memory. Accept my best thanks. This has been a day of agreeable surprises to me. I have found the country hereabouts remarkably pretty; I have seen Mrs. Vanstone's two charming daughters; I have become acquainted with an honored preceptress in Mr. Vanstone's family. I congratulate myself—I apologize for occupying your valuable time—I beg my renewed acknowledgments—I wish you good-morning."

He raised his tall hat. His brown eye twinkled, his green eye twinkled, his curly lips smiled sweetly. In a moment he turned on his heel. His youthful back appeared to the best advantage; his active little legs took him away trippingly in the direction of the village. One, two, three—and he reached the turn in the road. Four, five, six—and he was gone.

Miss Garth looked down at the card in her hand, and looked up again in blank astonishment. The name and address of the clerical-looking stranger (both written in pencil) ran as follows:

Captain Wragge. Post-office, Bristol.

CHAPTER III.

WHEN she returned to the house, Miss Garth made no attempt to conceal her unfavorable opinion of the stranger in black. His object was, no doubt, to obtain pecuniary assistance from Mrs. Vanstone. What the nature of his claim on her might be seemed less intelligible—unless it was the claim of a poor relation. Had Mrs. Vanstone ever mentioned, in the presence of her daughters, the name of Captain Wragge? Neither of them recollected to have heard it before. Had Mrs. Vanstone ever referred to any poor relations who were dependent on her? On the contrary she had mentioned of late years that she doubted having any relations at all who were still living. And yet Captain Wragge had plainly declared that the name on his card would recall "a family matter" to Mrs. Vanstone's memory. What did it mean? A false statement, on the stranger's part, without any intelligible reason for making it? Or a second mystery, following close on the heels of the mysterious journey to London?

All the probabilities seemed to point to some hidden connection between the "family affairs" which had taken Mr. and Mrs. Vanstone so suddenly from home and the "family matter" associated with the name of Captain Wragge. Miss Garth's doubts thronged back irresistibly on her mind as she sealed her letter to Mrs. Vanstone, with the captain's card added by way of inclosure.

By return of post the answer arrived.

Always the earliest riser among the ladies of the house, Miss Garth was alone in the breakfast-room when the letter was brought in. Her first glance at its contents convinced her of the necessity of reading it carefully through in retirement, before any embarrassing questions could be put to her. Leaving a message with the servant requesting Norah to make the tea that morning, she went upstairs at once to the solitude and security of her own room.

Mrs. Vanstone's letter extended to some length. The first part of it referred to Captain Wragge, and entered unreservedly into all necessary explanations relating to the man himself and to the motive which had brought him to Combe-Raven.

It appeared from Mrs. Vanstone's statement that her mother had been twice married. Her mother's first husband had been a certain Doctor Wragge—a widower with young children; and one of those children was now the unmilitary-looking captain, whose address was "Post-office, Bristol." Mrs. Wragge had left no family by her first husband; and had afterward married Mrs. Vanstone's father. Of that second marriage Mrs. Vanstone herself was the only issue. She had lost both her parents while she was still a young woman; and, in course of years, her mother's family connections (who were then her nearest surviving relatives) had been one after another removed by death. She was left, at the present writing, without a relation in the world—excepting, perhaps, certain cousins whom she had never seen, and of whose existence even, at the present moment, she possessed no positive knowledge.

Under these circumstances, what family claim had Captain Wragge on Mrs. Vanstone?

None whatever. As the son of her mother's first husband, by that husband's first wife, not even the widest stretch of courtesy could have included him at any time in the list of Mrs. Vanstone's most distant relations. Well knowing this (the letter proceeded to say), he had nevertheless persisted in forcing himself upon her as a species of family connection: and she had weakly sanctioned the intrusion, solely from the dread that he would otherwise introduce himself to Mr. Vanstone's notice, and take unblushing advantage of Mr. Vanstone's generosity. Shrinking, naturally, from allowing her husband to be annoyed, and probably cheated as well, by any person who claimed, however preposterously, a family connection with herself, it had been her practice, for many years past, to assist the captain from her own purse, on the condition that he should never come near the house, and that he should not presume to make any application whatever to Mr. Vanstone.

Readily admitting the imprudence of this course, Mrs. Vanstone further explained that she had perhaps been the more inclined to adopt it through having been always accustomed, in her early days, to see the captain living now upon one member, and now upon another, of her mother's family. Possessed of abilities which might have raised him to distinction in almost any career that he could have chosen, he had nevertheless, from his youth upward, been a disgrace to all his relatives. He had been expelled the militia regiment in which he once held a commission. He had tried one employment after another, and had discreditably failed in all. He had lived on his wits, in the lowest and basest meaning of the phrase. He had married a poor ignorant woman, who had served as a waitress at some low eating-house, who had unexpectedly come into a little money, and whose small inheritance he had mercilessly squandered to the last farthing. In plain terms, he was an incorrigible scoundrel; and he had now added one more to the list of his many misdemeanors by impudently breaking the conditions on which Mrs. Vanstone had hitherto assisted him. She had written at once to the address indicated on his card, in such terms and to such purpose as would prevent him, she hoped and believed, from ever venturing near the house again. Such were the terms in which Mrs. Vanstone concluded that first part of her letter which referred exclusively to Captain Wragge.

Although the statement thus presented implied a weakness in Mrs. Vanstone's character which Miss Garth, after many years of intimate experience, had never detected, she accepted the explanation as a matter of course; receiving it all the more readily inasmuch as it might, without impropriety, be communicated in substance to appease the irritated curiosity of the two young ladies. For this reason especially she perused the first half of the letter with an agreeable sense of relief. Far different was the impression produced on her when she advanced to the second half, and when she had read it to the end.

The second part of the letter was devoted to the subject of the journey to London.

Mrs. Vanstone began by referring to the long and intimate friendship which had existed between Miss Garth and herself. She now felt it due to that friendship to explain confidentially the motive which had induced her to leave home with her husband. Miss Garth had delicately refrained from showing it, but she must naturally have felt, and must still be feeling, great surprise at the mystery in which their departure had been involved; and she must doubtless have asked herself why Mrs. Vanstone should have been associated with family affairs which (in her independent position as to relatives) must necessarily concern Mr. Vanstone alone.

Without touching on those affairs, which it was neither desirable nor necessary to do, Mrs. Vanstone then proceeded to say that she would at once set all Miss Garth's doubts at rest, so far as they related to herself, by one plain acknowledgment. Her object in accompanying her husband to London was to see a certain celebrated physician, and to consult him privately on a very delicate and anxious matter connected with the state of her health. In plainer terms still, this anxious matter meant nothing less than the possibility that she might again become a mother.

When the doubt had first suggested itself she had treated it as a mere delusion. The long interval that had elapsed since the birth of her last child; the serious illness which had afflicted her after the death of that child in infancy; the time of life at which she had now arrived—all inclined her to dismiss the idea as soon as it arose in her mind. It had returned again and again in spite of her. She had felt the necessity of consulting the highest medical authority; and had shrunk, at the same time, from alarming her daughters by summoning a London physician to the house. The medical opinion, sought under the circumstances already mentioned, had now been obtained. Her doubt was confirmed as a certainty; and the result, which might be expected to take place toward the end of the summer, was, at her age and with her constitutional peculiarities, a subject for serious future anxiety, to say the least of it. The physician had done his best to encourage her; but she had understood the drift of his questions more clearly than he supposed, and she knew that he looked to the future with more than ordinary doubt.

Having disclosed these particulars, Mrs. Vanstone requested that they might be kept a secret between her correspondent and herself. She had felt unwilling to mention her suspicions to Miss Garth, until those suspicions had been confirmed—and she now recoiled, with even greater reluctance, from allowing her daughters to be in any way alarmed about her. It would be best to dismiss the subject for the present, and to wait hopefully till the summer came. In the meantime they would all, she trusted, be happily reunited on the twenty-third of the month, which Mr. Vanstone had fixed on as the day for their return. With this intimation, and with the customary messages, the letter, abruptly and confusedly, came to an end.

For the first few minutes, a natural sympathy for Mrs. Vanstone was the only feeling of which Miss Garth was conscious after she had laid the letter down. Ere long, however, there rose obscurely on her mind a doubt which perplexed and distressed her. Was the explanation which she had just read really as satisfactory and as complete as it professed to be? Testing it plainly by facts, surely not.

On the morning of her departure, Mrs. Vanstone had unquestionably left the house in good spirits. At her age, and in her state of health, were good spirits compatible with such an errand to a physician as the errand on which she was bent? Then, again, had that letter from New Orleans, which had necessitated Mr. Vanstone's departure, no share in occasioning his wife's departure as well? Why, otherwise, had she looked up so eagerly the moment her daughter mentioned the postmark. Granting the avowed motive for her journey—did not her manner, on the morning when the letter was opened, and again on the morning of departure, suggest the existence of some other motive which her letter kept concealed?

If it was so, the conclusion that followed was a very distressing one. Mrs. Vanstone, feeling what was due to her long friendship with Miss Garth, had apparently placed the fullest confidence in her, on one subject, by way of unsuspiciously maintaining the strictest reserve toward her on another. Naturally frank and straightforward in all her own dealings, Miss Garth shrank from plainly pursuing her doubts to this result: a want of loyalty toward her tried and valued friend seemed implied in the mere dawning of it on her mind.

She locked up the letter in her desk; roused herself resolutely to attend to the passing interests of the day; and went downstairs again to the breakfast-room. Amid many uncertainties, this at least was clear, Mr. and Mrs. Vanstone were coming back on the twenty-third of the month. Who could say what new revelations might not come back with them?

CHAPTER IV.

No new revelations came back with them: no anticipations associated with their return were realized. On the one forbidden subject of their errand in London, there was no moving either the master or the mistress of the house. Whatever their object might have been, they had to all appearance successfully accomplished it—for they both returned in perfect possession of their every-day looks and manners. Mrs. Vanstone's spirits had subsided to their natural quiet level; Mr. Vanstone's imperturbable cheerfulness sat as easily and indolently on him as usual. This was the one noticeable result of their journey—this, and no more. Had the household revolution run its course already? Was the secret thus far hidden impenetrably, hidden forever?

Nothing in this world is hidden forever. The gold which has lain for centuries unsuspected in the ground, reveals itself one day on the surface. Sand turns traitor, and betrays the footstep that has passed over it; water gives back to the tell-tale surface the body that has been drowned. Fire itself leaves the confession, in ashes, of the substance consumed in it. Hate breaks its prison-secrecy in the thoughts, through the doorway of the eyes; and Love finds the Judas who betrays it by a kiss. Look where we will, the inevitable law of revelation is one of the laws of nature: the lasting preservation of a secret is a miracle which the world has never yet seen.

How was the secret now hidden in the household at Combe-Raven doomed to disclose itself? Through what coming event in the daily lives of the father, the mother, and the daughters, was the law of revelation destined to break the fatal way to discovery? The way opened (unseen by the parents, and unsuspected by the children) through the first event that happened after Mr. and Mrs. Vanstone's return—an event which presented, on the surface of it, no interest of greater importance than the trivial social ceremony of a morning call.

Three days after the master and mistress of Combe-Raven had come back, the female members of the family happened to be assembled together in the morning-room. The view from the windows looked over the flower-garden and shrubbery; this last being protected at its outward extremity by a fence, and approached from the lane beyond by a wicket-gate. During an interval in the conversation, the attention of the ladies was suddenly attracted to this gate, by the sharp sound of the iron latch falling in its socket. Some one had entered the shrubbery from the lane; and Magdalen at once placed herself at the window to catch the first sight of the visitor through the trees.

After a few minutes, the figure of a gentleman became visible, at the point where the shrubbery path joined the winding garden-walk which led to the house. Magdalen looked at him attentively, without appearing, at first, to know who he was. As he came nearer, however, she started in astonishment; and, turning quickly to her mother and sister, proclaimed the gentleman in the garden to be no other than "Mr. Francis Clare."

The visitor thus announced was the son of Mr. Vanstone's oldest associate and nearest neighbor.

Mr. Clare the elder inhabited an unpretending little cottage, situated just outside the shrubbery fence which marked the limit of the Combe-Raven grounds. Belonging to the younger branch of a family of great antiquity, the one inheritance of importance that he had derived from his ancestors was the possession of a magnificent library, which not only filled all the rooms in his modest little dwelling, but lined the staircases and passages as well. Mr. Clare's books represented the one important interest of Mr. Clare's life. He had been a widower for many years past, and made no secret of his philosophical resignation to the loss of his wife. As a father, he regarded his family of three sons in the light of a necessary domestic evil, which perpetually threatened the sanctity of his study and the safety of his books. When the boys went to school, Mr. Clare said "good-by" to them—and "thank God" to himself. As for his small income, and his still smaller domestic establishment, he looked at them both from the same satirically indifferent point of view. He called himself a pauper with a pedigree. He abandoned the entire direction of his household to the slatternly old woman who was his only servant, on the condition that she was never to venture near his books, with a duster in her hand, from one year's end to the other. His favorite poets were Horace and Pope; his chosen philosophers, Hobbes and Voltaire. He took his exercise and his fresh air under protest; and always walked the same distance to a yard, on the ugliest high-road in the neighborhood. He was crooked of back, and quick of temper. He could digest radishes, and sleep after green tea. His views of human nature were the views of Diogenes, tempered by Rochefoucauld; his personal habits were slovenly in the last degree; and his favorite boast was that he had outlived all human prejudices.

Such was this singular man, in his more superficial aspects. What nobler qualities he might possess below the surface, no one had ever discovered. Mr. Vanstone, it is true, stoutly asserted that "Mr. Clare's worst side was his outside"—but in this expression of opinion he stood alone among his neighbors. The association between these two widely-dissimilar men had lasted for many years, and was almost close enough to be called a friendship. They had acquired a habit of meeting to smoke together on certain evenings in the week, in the cynic-philosopher's study, and of there disputing on every imaginable subject—Mr. Vanstone flourishing the stout cudgels of assertion, and Mr. Clare meeting him with the keen edged-tools of sophistry. They generally quarreled at night, and met on the neutral ground of the shrubbery to be reconciled together the next morning. The bond of intercourse thus curiously established between them was strengthened on Mr. Vanstone's side by a hearty interest in his neighbor's three sons—an interest by which those sons benefited all the more importantly, seeing that one of the prejudices which their father had outlived was a prejudice in favor of his own children.

"I look at those boys," the philosopher was accustomed to say, "with a perfectly impartial eye; I dismiss the unimportant accident of their birth from all consideration; and I find them below the average in every respect. The only excuse which a poor gentleman has for presuming to exist in the nineteenth century, is the excuse of extraordinary ability. My boys have been addle-headed from infancy. If I had any capital to give them, I should make Frank a butcher, Cecil a baker, and Arthur a grocer—those being the only human vocations I know of which are certain to be always in request. As it is, I have no money to help them with; and they have no brains to help themselves. They appear to me to be three human superfluities in dirty jackets and noisy boots; and, unless they clear themselves off the community by running away, I don't myself profess to see what is to be done with them."

Fortunately for the boys, Mr. Vanstone's views were still fast imprisoned in the ordinary prejudices. At his intercession, and through his influence, Frank, Cecil, and Arthur were received on the foundation of a well-reputed grammar-school. In holiday-time they were mercifully allowed the run of Mr. Vanstone's paddock; and were humanized and refined by association, indoors, with Mrs. Vanstone and her daughters. On these occasions, Mr. Clare used sometimes to walk across from his cottage (in his dressing-gown and slippers), and look at the boys disparagingly, through the window or over the fence, as if they were three wild animals whom his neighbor was attempting to tame. "You and your wife are excellent people," he used to say to Mr. Vanstone. "I respect your honest prejudices in favor of those boys of mine with all my heart. But you are so wrong about them—you are indeed! I wish to give no offense; I speak quite impartially—but mark my words, Vanstone: they'll all three turn out ill, in spite of everything you can do to prevent it."

In later years, when Frank had reached the age of seventeen, the same curious shifting of the relative positions of parent and friend between the two neighbors was exemplified more absurdly than ever. A civil engineer in the north of England, who owed certain obligations to Mr. Vanstone, expressed his willingness to take Frank under superintendence, on terms of the most favorable kind. When this proposal was received, Mr. Clare, as usual, first shifted his own character as Frank's father on Mr. Vanstone's shoulders—and then moderated his neighbor's parental enthusiasm from the point of view of an impartial spectator.

"It's the finest chance for Frank that could possibly have happened," cried Mr. Vanstone, in a glow of fatherly enthusiasm.

"My good fellow, he won't take it," retorted Mr. Clare, with the icy composure of a disinterested friend.

"But he shall take it," persisted Mr. Vanstone.

"Say he shall have a mathematical head," rejoined Mr. Clare; "say he shall possess industry, ambition, and firmness of purpose. Pooh! pooh! you don't look at him with my impartial eyes. I say, No mathematics, no industry, no ambition, no firmness of purpose. Frank is a compound of negatives—and there they are."

"Hang your negatives!" shouted Mr. Vanstone. "I don't care a rush for negatives, or affirmatives either. Frank shall have this splendid chance; and I'll lay you any wager you like he makes the best of it."

"I am not rich enough to lay wagers, usually," replied Mr. Clare; "but I think I have got a guinea about the house somewhere; and I'll lay you that guinea Frank comes back on our hands like a bad shilling."

"Done!" said Mr. Vanstone. "No: stop a minute! I won't do the lad's character the injustice of backing it at even money. I'll lay you five to one Frank turns up trumps in this business! You ought to be ashamed of yourself for talking of him as you do. What sort of hocus-pocus you bring it about by, I don't pretend to know; but you always end in making me take his part, as if I was his father instead of you. Ah yes! give you time, and you'll defend yourself. I won't give you time; I won't have any of your special pleading. Black's white according to you. I don't care: it's black for all that. You may talk nineteen to the dozen—I shall write to my friend and say Yes, in Frank's interests, by to-day's post."

Such were the circumstances under which Mr. Francis Clare departed for the north of England, at the age of seventeen, to start in life as a civil engineer.

From time to time, Mr. Vanstone's friend communicated with him on the subject of the new pupil. Frank was praised, as a quiet, gentleman-like, interesting lad—but he was also reported to be rather slow at acquiring the rudiments of engineering science. Other letters, later in date, described him as a little too ready to despond about himself; as having been sent away, on that account, to some new railway works, to see if change of scene would rouse him; and as having benefited in every respect by the experiment—except perhaps in regard to his professional studies, which still advanced but slowly. Subsequent communications announced his departure, under care of a trustworthy foreman, for some public works in Belgium; touched on the general benefit he appeared to derive from this new change; praised his excellent manners and address, which were of great assistance in facilitating business communications with the foreigners—and passed over in ominous silence the main question of his actual progress in the acquirement of knowledge. These reports, and many others which resembled them, were all conscientiously presented by Frank's friend to the attention of Frank's father. On each occasion, Mr. Clare exulted over Mr. Vanstone, and Mr. Vanstone quarreled with Mr. Clare. "One of these days you'll wish you hadn't laid that wager," said the cynic philosopher. "One of these days I shall have the blessed satisfaction of pocketing your guinea," cried the sanguine friend. Two years had then passed since Frank's departure. In one year more results asserted themselves, and settled the question.

Two days after Mr. Vanstone's return from London, he was called away from the breakfast-table before he had found time enough to look over his letters, delivered by the morning's post. Thrusting them into one of the pockets of his shooting-jacket, he took the letters out again, at one grasp, to read them when occasion served, later in the day. The grasp included the whole correspondence, with one exception—that exception being a final report from the civil engineer, which notified the termination of the connection between his pupil and himself, and the immediate return of Frank to his father's house.

While this important announcement lay unsuspected in Mr. Vanstone's pocket, the object of it was traveling home, as fast as railways could take him. At half-past ten at night, while Mr. Clare was sitting in studious solitude over his books and his green tea, with his favorite black cat to keep him company, he heard footsteps in the passage—the door opened—and Frank stood before him.

Ordinary men would have been astonished. But the philosopher's composure was not to be shaken by any such trifle as the unexpected return of his eldest son. He could not have looked up more calmly from his learned volume if Frank had been absent for three minutes instead of three years.

"Exactly what I predicted," said Mr. Clare. "Don't interrupt me by making explanations; and don't frighten the cat. If there is anything to eat in the kitchen, get it and go to bed. You can walk over to Combe-Raven tomorrow and give this message from me to Mr. Vanstone: 'Father's compliments, sir, and I have come back upon your hands like a bad shilling, as he always said I should. He keeps his own guinea, and takes your five; and he hopes you'll mind what he says to you another time.' That is the message. Shut the door after you. Good-night."

Under these unfavorable auspices, Mr. Francis Clare made his appearance the next morning in the grounds at Combe-Raven; and, something doubtful of the reception that might await him, slowly approached the precincts of the house.

It was not wonderful that Magdalen should have failed to recognize him when he first appeared in view. He had gone away a backward lad of seventeen; he returned a young man of twenty. His slim figure had now acquired strength and grace, and had increased in stature to the medium height. The small regular features, which he was supposed to have inherited from his mother, were rounded and filled out, without having lost their remarkable delicacy of form. His beard was still in its infancy; and nascent lines of whisker traced their modest way sparely down his cheeks. His gentle, wandering brown eyes would have looked to better advantage in a woman's face—they wanted spirit and firmness to fit them for the face of a man. His hands had the same wandering habit as his eyes; they were constantly changing from one position to another, constantly twisting and turning any little stray thing they could pick up. He was undeniably handsome, graceful, well-bred—but no close observer could look at him without suspecting that the stout old family stock had begun to wear out in the later generations, and that Mr. Francis Clare had more in him of the shadow of his ancestors than of the substance.

When the astonishment caused by his appearance had partially subsided, a search was instituted for the missing report. It was found in the remotest recesses of Mr. Vanstone's capacious pocket, and was read by that gentleman on the spot.

The plain facts, as stated by the engineer, were briefly these: Frank was not possessed of the necessary abilities to fit him for his new calling; and it was useless to waste time by keeping him any longer in an employment for which he had no vocation. This, after three years' trial, being the conviction on both sides, the master had thought it the most straightforward course for the pupil to go home and candidly place results before his father and his friends. In some other pursuit, for which he was more fit, and in which he could feel an interest, he would no doubt display the industry and perseverance which he had been too much discouraged to practice in the profession that he had now abandoned. Personally, he was liked by all who knew him; and his future prosperity was heartily desired by the many friends whom he had made in the North. Such was the substance of the report, and so it came to an end.

Many men would have thought the engineer's statement rather too carefully worded; and, suspecting him of trying to make the best of a bad case, would have entertained serious doubts on the subject of Frank's future. Mr. Vanstone was too easy-tempered and sanguine—and too anxious, as well, not to yield his old antagonist an inch more ground than he could help—to look at the letter from any such unfavorable point of view. Was it Frank's fault if he had not got the stuff in him that engineers were made of? Did no other young men ever begin life with a false start? Plenty began in that way, and got over it, and did wonders afterward. With these commentaries on the letter, the kind-hearted gentleman patted Frank on the shoulder. "Cheer up, my lad!" said Mr. Vanstone. "We will be even with your father one of these days, though he has won the wager this time!"

The example thus set by the master of the house was followed at once by the family—with the solitary exception of Norah, whose incurable formality and reserve expressed themselves, not too graciously, in her distant manner toward the visitor. The rest, led by Magdalen (who had been Frank's favorite playfellow in past times) glided back into their old easy habits with him without an effort. He was "Frank" with all of them but Norah, who persisted in addressing him as "Mr. Clare." Even the account he was now encouraged to give of the reception accorded to him by his father, on the previous night, failed to disturb Norah's gravity. She sat with her dark, handsome face steadily averted, her eyes cast down, and the rich color in her cheeks warmer and deeper than usual. All the rest, Miss Garth included, found old Mr. Clare's speech of welcome to his son quite irresistible. The noise and merriment were at their height when the servant came in, and struck the whole party dumb by the announcement of visitors in the drawing-room. "Mr. Marrable, Mrs. Marrable, and Miss Marrable; Evergreen Lodge, Clifton."

Norah rose as readily as if the new arrivals had been a relief to her mind. Mrs. Vanstone was the next to leave her chair. These two went away first, to receive the visitors. Magdalen, who preferred the society of her father and Frank, pleaded hard to be left behind; but Miss Garth, after granting five minutes' grace, took her into custody and marched her out of the room. Frank rose to take his leave.

"No, no," said Mr. Vanstone, detaining him. "Don't go. These people won't stop long. Mr. Marrable's a merchant at Bristol. I've met him once or twice, when the girls forced me to take them to parties at Clifton. Mere acquaintances, nothing more. Come and smoke a cigar in the greenhouse. Hang all visitors—they worry one's life out. I'll appear at the last moment with an apology; and you shall follow me at a safe distance, and be a proof that I was really engaged."

Proposing this ingenious stratagem in a confidential whisper, Mr. Vanstone took Frank's arm and led him round the house by the back way. The first ten minutes of seclusion in the conservatory passed without events of any kind. At the end of that time, a flying figure in bright garments flashed upon the two gentlemen through the glass—the door was flung open—flower-pots fell in homage to passing petticoats—and Mr. Vanstone's youngest daughter ran up to him at headlong speed, with every external appearance of having suddenly taken leave of her senses.

"Papa! the dream of my whole life is realized," she said, as soon as she could speak. "I shall fly through the roof of the greenhouse if somebody doesn't hold me down. The Marrables have come here with an invitation. Guess, you darling—guess what they're going to give at Evergreen Lodge!"

"A ball!" said Mr. Vanstone, without a moment's hesitation.

"Private Theatricals!!!" cried Magdalen, her clear young voice ringing through the conservatory like a bell; her loose sleeves falling back and showing her round white arms to the dimpled elbows, as she clapped her hands ecstatically in the air. "'The Rivals' is the play, papa—'The Rivals,' by the famous what's-his-name—and they want ME to act! The one thing in the whole universe that I long to do most. It all depends on you. Mamma shakes her head; and Miss Garth looks daggers; and Norah's as sulky as usual—but if you say Yes, they must all three give way and let me do as I like. Say Yes," she pleaded, nestling softly up to her father, and pressing her lips with a fond gentleness to his ear, as she whispered the next words. "Say Yes, and I'll be a good girl for the rest of my life."

"A good girl?" repeated Mr. Vanstone—"a mad girl, I think you must mean. Hang these people and their theatricals! I shall have to go indoors and see about this matter. You needn't throw away your cigar, Frank. You're well out of the business, and you can stop here."

"No, he can't," said Magdalen. "He's in the business, too."

Mr. Francis Clare had hitherto remained modestly in the background. He now came forward with a face expressive of speechless amazement.

"Yes," continued Magdalen, answering his blank look of inquiry with perfect composure. "You are to act. Miss Marrable and I have a turn for business, and we settled it all in five minutes. There are two parts in the play left to be filled. One is Lucy, the waiting-maid; which is the character I have undertaken—with papa's permission," she added, slyly pinching her father's arm; "and he won't say No, will he? First, because he's a darling; secondly, because I love him, and he loves me; thirdly, because there is never any difference of opinion between us (is there?); fourthly, because I give him a kiss, which naturally stops his mouth and settles the whole question. Dear me, I'm wandering. Where was I just now? Oh yes! explaining myself to Frank—"

"I beg your pardon," began Frank, attempting, at this point, to enter his protest.

"The second character in the play," pursued Magdalen, without taking the smallest notice of the protest, "is Falkland—a jealous lover, with a fine flow of language. Miss Marrable and I discussed Falkland privately on the window-seat while the rest were talking. She is a delightful girl—so impulsive, so sensible, so entirely unaffected. She confided in me. She said: 'One of our miseries is that we can't find a gentleman who will grapple with the hideous difficulties of Falkland.' Of course I soothed her. Of course I said: 'I've got the gentleman, and he shall grapple immediately.'—'Oh heavens! who is he?'—'Mr. Francis Clare.'—'And where is he?'—'In the house at this moment.'—'Will you be so very charming, Miss Vanstone, as to fetch him?'—'I'll fetch him, Miss Marrable, with the greatest pleasure.' I left the window-seat—I rushed into the morning-room—I smelled cigars—I followed the smell—and here I am."

"It's a compliment, I know, to be asked to act," said Frank, in great embarrassment. "But I hope you and Miss Marrable will excuse me—"

"Certainly not. Miss Marrable and I are both remarkable for the firmness of our characters. When we say Mr. So-and-So is positively to act the part of Falkland, we positively mean it. Come in and be introduced."

"But I never tried to act. I don't know how."

"Not of the slightest consequence. If you don't know how, come to me and I'll teach you."

"You!" exclaimed Mr. Vanstone. "What do you know about it?"

"Pray, papa, be serious! I have the strongest internal conviction that I could act every character in the play—Falkland included. Don't let me have to speak a second time, Frank. Come and be introduced."

She took her father's arm, and moved on with him to the door of the greenhouse. At the steps, she turned and looked round to see if Frank was following her. It was only the action of a moment; but in that moment her natural firmness of will rallied all its resources—strengthened itself with the influence of her beauty —commanded—and conquered. She looked lovely: the flush was tenderly bright in her cheeks; the radiant pleasure shone and sparkled in her eyes; the position of her figure, turned suddenly from the waist upward, disclosed its delicate strength, its supple firmness, its seductive, serpentine grace. "Come!" she said, with a coquettish beckoning action of her head. "Come, Frank!"

Few men of forty would have resisted her at that moment. Frank was twenty last birthday. In other words, he threw aside his cigar, and followed her out of the greenhouse.

As he turned and closed the door—in the instant when he lost sight of her—his disinclination to be associated with the private theatricals revived. At the foot of the house-steps he stopped again; plucked a twig from a plant near him; broke it in his hand; and looked about him uneasily, on this side and on that. The path to the left led back to his father's cottage—the way of escape lay open. Why not take it?

While he still hesitated, Mr. Vanstone and his daughter reached the top of the steps. Once more, Magdalen looked round—looked with her resistless beauty, with her all-conquering smile. She beckoned again; and again he followed her—up the steps, and over the threshold. The door closed on them.

So, with a trifling gesture of invitation on one side, with a trifling act of compliance on the other: so—with no knowledge in his mind, with no thought in hers, of the secret still hidden under the journey to London—they took the way which led to that secret's discovery, through many a darker winding that was yet to come.

CHAPTER V.

MR. VANSTONE'S inquiries into the proposed theatrical entertainment at Evergreen Lodge were answered by a narrative of dramatic disasters; of which Miss Marrable impersonated the innocent cause, and in which her father and mother played the parts of chief victims.

Miss Marrable was that hardest of all born tyrants—an only child. She had never granted a constitutional privilege to her oppressed father and mother since the time when she cut her first tooth. Her seventeenth birthday was now near at hand; she had decided on celebrating it by acting a play; had issued her orders accordingly; and had been obeyed by her docile parents as implicitly as usual. Mrs. Marrable gave up the drawing-room to be laid waste for a stage and a theater. Mr. Marrable secured the services of a respectable professional person to drill the young ladies and gentlemen, and to accept all the other responsibilities incidental to creating a dramatic world out of a domestic chaos. Having further accustomed themselves to the breaking of furniture and the staining of walls—to thumping, tumbling, hammering, and screaming; to doors always banging, and to footsteps perpetually running up and down stairs—the nominal master and mistress of the house fondly believed that their chief troubles were over. Innocent and fatal delusion! It is one thing in private society to set up the stage and choose the play—it is another thing altogether to find the actors. Hitherto, only the small preliminary annoyances proper to the occasion had shown themselves at Evergreen Lodge. The sound and serious troubles were all to come.

"The Rivals" having been chosen as the play, Miss Marrable, as a matter of course, appropriated to herself the part of "Lydia Languish." One of her favored swains next secured "Captain Absolute," and another laid violent hands on "Sir Lucius O'Trigger." These two were followed by an accommodating spinster relative, who accepted the heavy dramatic responsibility of "Mrs. Malaprop"—and there the theatrical proceedings came to a pause. Nine more speaking characters were left to be fitted with representatives; and with that unavoidable necessity the serious troubles began.

All the friends of the family suddenly became unreliable people, for the first time in their lives. After encouraging the idea of the play, they declined the personal sacrifice of acting in it—or, they accepted characters, and then broke down in the effort to study them—or they volunteered to take the parts which they knew were already engaged, and declined the parts which were waiting to be acted—or they were afflicted with weak constitutions, and mischievously fell ill when they were wanted at rehearsal—or they had Puritan relatives in the background, and, after slipping into their parts cheerfully at the week's beginning, oozed out of them penitently, under serious family pressure, at the week's end. Meanwhile, the carpenters hammered and the scenes rose. Miss Marrable, whose temperament was sensitive, became hysterical under the strain of perpetual anxiety; the family doctor declined to answer for the nervous consequences if something was not done. Renewed efforts were made in every direction. Actors and actresses were sought with a desperate disregard of all considerations of personal fitness. Necessity, which knows no law, either in the drama or out of it, accepted a lad of eighteen as the representative of "Sir Anthony Absolute"; the stage-manager undertaking to supply the necessary wrinkles from the illimitable resources of theatrical art. A lady whose age was unknown, and whose personal appearance was stout—but whose heart was in the right place—volunteered to act the part of the sentimental "Julia," and brought with her the dramatic qualification of habitually wearing a wig in private life. Thanks to these vigorous measures, the play was at last supplied with representatives—always excepting the two unmanageable characters of "Lucy" the waiting-maid, and "Falkland," Julia's jealous lover. Gentlemen came; saw Julia at rehearsal; observed her stoutness and her wig; omitted to notice that her heart was in the right place; quailed at the prospect, apologized, and retired. Ladies read the part of "Lucy"; remarked that she appeared to great advantage in the first half of the play, and faded out of it altogether in the latter half; objected to pass from the notice of the audience in that manner, when all the rest had a chance of distinguishing themselves to the end; shut up the book, apologized, and retired. In eight days more the night of performance would arrive; a phalanx of social martyrs two hundred strong had been convened to witness it; three full rehearsals were absolutely necessary; and two characters in the play were not filled yet. With this lamentable story, and with the humblest apologies for presuming on a slight acquaintance, the Marrables appeared at Combe-Raven, to appeal to the young ladies for a "Lucy," and to the universe for a "Falkland," with the mendicant pertinacity of a family in despair.

This statement of circumstances—addressed to an audience which included a father of Mr. Vanstone's disposition, and a daughter of Magdalen's temperament—produced the result which might have been anticipated from the first.

Either misinterpreting, or disregarding, the ominous silence preserved by his wife and Miss Garth, Mr. Vanstone not only gave Magdalen permission to assist the forlorn dramatic company, but accepted an invitation to witness the performance for Norah and himself. Mrs. Vanstone declined accompanying them on account of her health; and Miss Garth only engaged to make one among the audience conditionally on not being wanted at home. The "parts" of "Lucy" and "Falkland" (which the distressed family carried about with them everywhere, like incidental maladies) were handed to their representatives on the spot. Frank's faint remonstrances were rejected without a hearing; the days and hours of rehearsal were carefully noted down on the covers of the parts; and the Marrables took their leave, with a perfect explosion of thanks—father, mother, and daughter sowing their expressions of gratitude broadcast, from the drawing-room door to the garden-gates.

As soon as the carriage had driven away, Magdalen presented herself to the general observation under an entirely new aspect.

"If any more visitors call to-day," she said, with the profoundest gravity of look and manner, "I am not at home. This is a far more serious matter than any of you suppose. Go somewhere by yourself, Frank, and read over your part, and don't let your attention wander if you can possibly help it. I shall not be accessible before the evening. If you will come here—with papa's permission—after tea, my views on the subject of Falkland will be at your disposal. Thomas! whatever else the gardener does, he is not to make any floricultural noises under my window. For the rest of the afternoon I shall be immersed in study—and the quieter the house is, the more obliged I shall feel to everybody."

Before Miss Garth's battery of reproof could open fire, before the first outburst of Mr. Vanstone's hearty laughter could escape his lips, she bowed to them with imperturbable gravity; ascended the house-steps, for the first time in her life, at a walk instead of a run, and retired then and there to the bedroom regions. Frank's helpless astonishment at her disappearance added a new element of absurdity to the scene. He stood first on one leg and then on the other; rolling and unrolling his part, and looking piteously in the faces of the friends about him. "I know I can't do it," he said. "May I come in after tea, and hear Magdalen's views? Thank you—I'll look in about eight. Don't tell my father about this acting, please; I should never hear the last of it." Those were the only words he had spirit enough to utter. He drifted away aimlessly in the direction of the shrubbery, with the part hanging open in his hand—the most incapable of Falklands, and the most helpless of mankind.

Frank's departure left the family by themselves, and was the signal accordingly for an attack on Mr. Vanstone's inveterate carelessness in the exercise of his paternal authority.

"What could you possibly be thinking of, Andrew, when you gave your consent?" said Mrs. Vanstone. "Surely my silence was a sufficient warning to you to say No?"

"A mistake, Mr. Vanstone," chimed in Miss Garth. "Made with the best intentions—but a mistake for all that."

"It may be a mistake," said Norah, taking her father's part, as usual. "But I really don't see how papa, or any one else, could have declined, under the circumstances."

"Quite right, my dear," observed Mr. Vanstone. "The circumstances, as you say, were dead against me. Here were these unfortunate people in a scrape on one side; and Magdalen, on the other, mad to act. I couldn't say I had methodistical objections—I've nothing methodistical about me. What other excuse could I make? The Marrables are respectable people, and keep the best company in Clifton. What harm can she get in their house? If you come to prudence and that sort of thing—why shouldn't Magdalen do what Miss Marrable does? There! there! let the poor things act, and amuse themselves. We were their age once—and it's no use making a fuss—and that's all I've got to say about it."

With that characteristic defense of his own conduct, Mr. Vanstone sauntered back to the greenhouse to smoke another cigar.

"I didn't say so to papa," said Norah, taking her mother's arm on the way back to the house, "but the bad result of the acting, in my opinion, will be the familiarity it is sure to encourage between Magdalen and Francis Clare."

"You are prejudiced against Frank, my love," said Mrs. Vanstone.

Norah's soft, secret, hazel eyes sank to the ground; she said no more. Her opinions were unchangeable—but she never disputed with anybody. She had the great failing of a reserved nature—the failing of obstinacy; and the great merit—the merit of silence. "What is your head running on now?" thought Miss Garth, casting a sharp look at Norah's dark, downcast face. "You're one of the impenetrable sort. Give me Magdalen, with all her perversities; I can see daylight through her. You're as dark as night."

The hours of the afternoon passed away, and still Magdalen remained shut up in her own room. No restless footsteps pattered on the stairs; no nimble tongue was heard chattering here, there, and everywhere, from the garret to the kitchen—the house seemed hardly like itself, with the one ever-disturbing element in the family serenity suddenly withdrawn from it. Anxious to witness with her own eyes the reality of a transformation in which past experience still inclined her to disbelieve, Miss Garth ascended to Magdalen's room, knocked twice at the door, received no answer, opened it and looked in.

There sat Magdalen, in an arm-chair before the long looking-glass, with all her hair let down over her shoulders; absorbed in the study of her part and comfortably arrayed in her morning wrapper, until it was time to dress for dinner. And there behind her sat the lady's-maid, slowly combing out the long heavy locks of her young mistress's hair, with the sleepy resignation of a woman who had been engaged in that employment for some hours past. The sun was shining; and the green shutters outside the window were closed. The dim light fell tenderly on the two quiet seated figures; on the little white bed, with the knots of rose-colored ribbon which looped up its curtains, and the bright dress for dinner laid ready across it; on the gayly painted bath, with its pure lining of white enamel; on the toilet-table with its sparkling trinkets, its crystal bottles, its silver bell with Cupid for a handle, its litter of little luxuries that adorn the shrine of a woman's bed-chamber. The luxurious tranquillity of the scene; the cool fragrance of flowers and perfumes in the atmosphere; the rapt attitude of Magdalen, absorbed over her reading; the monotonous regularity of movement in the maid's hand and arm, as she drew the comb smoothly through and through her mistress's hair—all conveyed the same soothing impression of drowsy, delicious quiet. On one side of the door were the broad daylight and the familiar realities of life. On the other was the dream-land of Elysian serenity—the sanctuary of unruffled repose.

Miss Garth paused on the threshold, and looked into the room in silence.

Magdalen's curious fancy for having her hair combed at all times and seasons was among the peculiarities of her character which were notorious to everybody in the house. It was one of her father's favorite jokes that she reminded him, on such occasions, of a cat having her back stroked, and that he always expected, if the combing were only continued long enough, to hear her purr. Extravagant as it may seem, the comparison was not altogether inappropriate. The girl's fervid temperament intensified the essentially feminine pleasure that most women feel in the passage of the comb through their hair, to a luxury of sensation which absorbed her in enjoyment, so serenely self-demonstrative, so drowsily deep that it did irresistibly suggest a pet cat's enjoyment under a caressing hand. Intimately as Miss Garth was acquainted with this peculiarity in her pupil, she now saw it asserting itself for the first time, in association with mental exertion of any kind on Magdalen's part. Feeling, therefore, some curiosity to know how long the combing and the studying had gone on together, she ventured on putting the question, first to the mistress; and (receiving no answer in that quarter) secondly to the maid.

"All the afternoon, miss, off and on," was the weary answer. "Miss Magdalen says it soothes her feelings and clears her mind."

Knowing by experience that interference would be hopeless, under these circumstances, Miss Garth turned sharply and left the room. She smiled when she was outside on the landing. The female mind does occasionally—though not often—project itself into the future. Miss Garth was prophetically pitying Magdalen's unfortunate husband.

Dinner-time presented the fair student to the family eye in the same mentally absorbed aspect. On all ordinary occasions Magdalen's appetite would have terrified those feeble sentimentalists who affect to ignore the all-important influence which female feeding exerts in the production of female beauty. On this occasion she refused one dish after another with a resolution which implied the rarest of all modern martyrdoms—gastric martyrdom. "I have conceived the part of Lucy," she observed, with the demurest gravity. "The next difficulty is to make Frank conceive the part of Falkland. I see nothing to laugh at—you would all be serious enough if you had my responsibilities. No, papa—no wine to-day, thank you. I must keep my intelligence clear. Water, Thomas—and a little more jelly, I think, before you take it away."

When Frank presented himself in the evening, ignorant of the first elements of his part, she took him in hand, as a middle-aged schoolmistress might have taken in hand a backward little boy. The few attempts he made to vary the sternly practical nature of the evening's occupation by slipping in compliments sidelong she put away from her with the contemptuous self-possession of a woman of twice her age. She literally forced him into his part. Her father fell asleep in his chair. Mrs. Vanstone and Miss Garth lost their interest in the proceedings, retired to the further end of the room, and spoke together in whispers. It grew later and later; and still Magdalen never flinched from her task—still, with equal perseverance, Norah, who had been on the watch all through the evening, kept on the watch to the end. The distrust darkened and darkened on her face as she looked at her sister and Frank; as she saw how close they sat together, devoted to the same interest and working to the same end. The clock on the mantel-piece pointed to half-past eleven before Lucy the resolute permitted Falkland the helpless to shut up his task-book for the night. "She's wonderfully clever, isn't she?" said Frank, taking leave of Mr. Vanstone at the hall door. "I'm to come to-morrow, and hear more of her views—if you have no objection. I shall never do it; don't tell her I said so. As fast as she teaches me one speech, the other goes out of my head. Discouraging, isn't it? Goodnight."

The next day but one was the day of the first full rehearsal. On the previous evening Mrs. Vanstone's spirits had been sadly depressed. At a private interview with Miss Garth she had referred again, of her own accord, to the subject of her letter from London—had spoken self-reproachfully of her weakness in admitting Captain Wragge's impudent claim to a family connection with her—and had then reverted to the state of her health and to the doubtful prospect that awaited her in the coming summer in a tone of despondency which it was very distressing to hear. Anxious to cheer her spirits, Miss Garth had changed the conversation as soon as possible—had referred to the approaching theatrical performance—and had relieved Mrs. Vanstone's mind of all anxiety in that direction, by announcing her intention of accompanying Magdalen to each rehearsal, and of not losing sight of her until she was safely back again in her father's house. Accordingly, when Frank presented himself at Combe-Raven on the eventful morning, there stood Miss Garth, prepared—in the interpolated character of Argus—to accompany Lucy and Falkland to the scene of trial. The railway conveyed the three, in excellent time, to Evergreen Lodge; and at one o'clock the rehearsal began.

CHAPTER VI.

"I HOPE Miss Vanstone knows her part?" whispered Mrs. Marrable, anxiously addressing herself to Miss Garth, in a corner of the theater.

"If airs and graces make an actress, ma'am, Magdalen's performance will astonish us all." With that reply, Miss Garth took out her work, and seated herself, on guard, in the center of the pit.

The manager perched himself, book in hand, on a stool close in front of the stage. He was an active little man, of a sweet and cheerful temper; and he gave the signal to begin with as patient an interest in the proceedings as if they had caused him no trouble in the past and promised him no difficulty in the future. The two characters which opened the comedy of The Rivals, "Fag" and "The Coachman," appeared on the scene—looked many sizes too tall for their canvas background, which represented a "Street in Bath"—exhibited the customary inability to manage their own arms, legs, and voices—went out severally at the wrong exits—and expressed their perfect approval of results, so far, by laughing heartily behind the scenes. "Silence, gentlemen, if you please," remonstrated the cheerful manager. "As loud as you like on the stage, but the audience mustn't hear you off it. Miss Marrable ready? Miss Vanstone ready? Easy there with the 'Street in Bath'; it's going up crooked! Face this way, Miss Marrable; full face, if you please. Miss Vanstone—" he checked himself suddenly. "Curious," he said, under his breath—"she fronts the audience of her own accord!" Lucy opened the scene in these words: "Indeed, ma'am, I traversed half the town in search of it: I don't believe there's a circulating library in Bath I haven't been at." The manager started in his chair. "My heart alive! she speaks out without telling!" The dialogue went on. Lucy produced the novels for Miss Lydia Languish's private reading from under her cloak. The manager rose excitably to his feet. Marvelous! No hurry with the books; no dropping them. She looked at the titles before she announced them to her mistress; she set down "Humphrey Clinker" on "The Tears of Sensibility" with a smart little smack which pointed the antithesis. One moment—and she announced Julia's visit; another—and she dropped the brisk waiting-maid's courtesy; a third—and she was off the stage on the side set down for her in the book. The manager wheeled round on his stool, and looked hard at Miss Garth. "I beg your pardon, ma'am," he said. "Miss Marrable told me, before we began, that this was the young lady's first attempt. It can't be, surely!"

"It is," replied Miss Garth, reflecting the manager's look of amazement on her own face. Was it possible that Magdalen's unintelligible industry in the study of her part really sprang from a serious interest in her occupation—an interest which implied a natural fitness for it.

The rehearsal went on. The stout lady with the wig (and the excellent heart) personated the sentimental Julia from an inveterately tragic point of view, and used her handkerchief distractedly in the first scene. The spinster relative felt Mrs. Malaprop's mistakes in language so seriously, and took such extraordinary pains with her blunders, that they sounded more like exercises in elocution than anything else. The unhappy lad who led the forlorn hope of the company, in the person of "Sir Anthony Absolute," expressed the age and irascibility of his character by tottering incessantly at the knees, and thumping the stage perpetually with his stick. Slowly and clumsily, with constant interruptions and interminable mistakes, the first act dragged on, until Lucy appeared again to end it in soliloquy, with the confession of her assumed simplicity and the praise of her own cunning.

Here the stage artifice of the situation presented difficulties which Magdalen had not encountered in the first scene—and here, her total want of experience led her into more than one palpable mistake. The stage-manager, with an eagerness which he had not shown in the case of any other member of the company, interfered immediately, and set her right. At one point she was to pause, and take a turn on the stage—she did it. At another, she was to stop, toss her head, and look pertly at the audience—she did it. When she took out the paper to read the list of the presents she had received, could she give it a tap with her finger (Yes)? And lead off with a little laugh (Yes—after twice trying)? Could she read the different items with a sly look at the end of each sentence, straight at the pit (Yes, straight at the pit, and as sly as you please)? The manager's cheerful face beamed with approval. He tucked the play under his arm, and clapped his hands gayly; the gentlemen, clustered together behind the scenes, followed his example; the ladies looked at each other with dawning doubts whether they had not better have left the new recruit in the retirement of private life. Too deeply absorbed in the business of the stage to heed any of them, Magdalen asked leave to repeat the soliloquy, and make quite sure of her own improvement. She went all through it again without a mistake, this time, from beginning to end; the manager celebrating her attention to his directions by an outburst of professional approbation, which escaped him in spite of himself. "She can take a hint!" cried the little man, with a hearty smack of his hand on the prompt-book. "She's a born actress, if ever there was one yet!"

"I hope not," said Miss Garth to herself, taking up the work which had dropped into her lap, and looking down at it in some perplexity. Her worst apprehension of results in connection with the theatrical enterprise had foreboded levity of conduct with some of the gentlemen—she had not bargained for this. Magdalen, in the capacity of a thoughtless girl, was comparatively easy to deal with. Magdalen, in the character of a born actress, threatened serious future difficulties.

The rehearsal proceeded. Lucy returned to the stage for her scenes in the second act (the last in which she appears) with Sir Lucius and Fag. Here, again, Magdalen's inexperience betrayed itself—and here once more her resolution in attacking and conquering her own mistakes astonished everybody. "Bravo!" cried the gentlemen behind the scenes, as she steadily trampled down one blunder after another. "Ridiculous!" said the ladies, "with such a small part as hers." "Heaven forgive me!" thought Miss. Garth, coming round unwillingly to the general opinion. "I almost wish we were Papists, and I had a convent to put her in to-morrow." One of Mr. Marrable's servants entered the theater as that desperate aspiration escaped the governess. She instantly sent the man behind the scene with a message: "Miss Vanstone has done her part in the rehearsal; request her to come here and sit by me." The servant returned with a polite apology: "Miss Vanstone's kind love, and she begs to be excused—she's prompting Mr. Clare." She prompted him to such purpose that he actually got through his part. The performances of the other gentlemen were obtrusively imbecile. Frank was just one degree better—he was modestly incapable; and he gained by comparison. "Thanks to Miss Vanstone," observed the manager, who had heard the prompting. "She pulled him through. We shall be flat enough at night, when the drop falls on the second act, and the audience have seen the last of her. It's a thousand pities she hasn't got a better part!"

"It's a thousand mercies she's no more to do than she has," muttered Miss Garth, overhearing him. "As things are, the people can't well turn her head with applause. She's out of the play in the second act—that's one comfort!"

No well-regulated mind ever draws its inferences in a hurry; Miss Garth's mind was well regulated; therefore, logically speaking, Miss Garth ought to have been superior to the weakness of rushing at conclusions. She had committed that error, nevertheless, under present circumstances. In plainer terms, the consoling reflection which had just occurred to her assumed that the play had by this time survived all its disasters, and entered on its long-deferred career of success. The play had done nothing of the sort. Misfortune and the Marrable family had not parted company yet.

When the rehearsal was over, nobody observed that the stout lady with the wig privately withdrew herself from the company; and when she was afterward missed from the table of refreshments, which Mr. Marrable's hospitality kept ready spread in a room near the theater, nobody imagined that there was any serious reason for her absence. It was not till the ladies and gentlemen assembled for the next rehearsal that the true state of the case was impressed on the minds of the company. At the appointed hour no Julia appeared. In her stead, Mrs. Marrable portentously approached the stage, with an open letter in her hand. She was naturally a lady of the mildest good breeding: she was mistress of every bland conventionality in the English language—but disasters and dramatic influences combined, threw even this harmless matron off her balance at last. For the first time in her life Mrs. Marrable indulged in vehement gesture, and used strong language. She handed the letter sternly, at arms-length, to her daughter. "My dear," she said, with an aspect of awful composure, "we are under a Curse." Before the amazed dramatic company could petition for an explanation, she turned and left the room. The manager's professional eye followed her out respectfully—he looked as if he approved of the exit, from a theatrical point of view.

What new misfortune had befallen the play? The last and worst of all misfortunes had assailed it. The stout lady had resigned her part.

Not maliciously. Her heart, which had been in the right place throughout, remained inflexibly in the right place still. Her explanation of the circumstances proved this, if nothing else did. The letter began with a statement: She had overheard, at the last rehearsal (quite unintentionally), personal remarks of which she was the subject. They might, or might not, have had reference to her—Hair; and her—Figure. She would not distress Mrs. Marrable by repeating them. Neither would she mention names, because it was foreign to her nature to make bad worse. The only course at all consistent with her own self-respect was to resign her part. She inclosed it, accordingly, to Mrs. Marrable, with many apologies for her presumption in undertaking a youthful character, at—what a gentleman was pleased to term—her Age; and with what two ladies were rude enough to characterize as her disadvantages of—Hair, and—Figure. A younger and more attractive representative of Julia would no doubt be easily found. In the meantime, all persons concerned had her full forgiveness, to which she would only beg leave to add her best and kindest wishes for the success of the play.

In four nights more the play was to be performed. If ever any human enterprise stood in need of good wishes to help it, that enterprise was unquestionably the theatrical entertainment at Evergreen Lodge!

One arm-chair was allowed on the stage; and into that arm-chair Miss Marrable sank, preparatory to a fit of hysterics. Magdalen stepped forward at the first convulsion; snatched the letter from Miss Marrable's hand; and stopped the threatened catastrophe.

"She's an ugly, bald-headed, malicious, middle-aged wretch!" said Magdalen, tearing the letter into fragments, and tossing them over the heads of the company. "But I can tell her one thing—she shan't spoil the play. I'll act Julia."

"Bravo!" cried the chorus of gentlemen—the anonymous gentleman who had helped to do the mischief (otherwise Mr. Francis Clare) loudest of all.

"If you want the truth, I don't shrink from owning it," continued Magdalen. "I'm one of the ladies she means. I said she had a head like a mop, and a waist like a bolster. So she has."

"I am the other lady," added the spinster relative. "But I only said she was too stout for the part."

"I am the gentleman," chimed in Frank, stimulated by the force of example. "I said nothing—I only agreed with the ladies."

Here Miss Garth seized her opportunity, and addressed the stage loudly from the pit.

"Stop! Stop!" she said. "You can't settle the difficulty that way. If Magdalen plays Julia, who is to play Lucy?"

Miss Marrable sank back in the arm-chair, and gave way to the second convulsion.

"Stuff and nonsense!" cried Magdalen, "the thing's simple enough, I'll act Julia and Lucy both together."

The manager was consulted on the spot. Suppressing Lucy's first entrance, and turning the short dialogue about the novels into a soliloquy for Lydia Languish, appeared to be the only changes of importance necessary to the accomplishment of Magdalen's project. Lucy's two telling scenes, at the end of the first and second acts, were sufficiently removed from the scenes in which Julia appeared to give time for the necessary transformations in dress. Even Miss Garth, though she tried hard to find them, could put no fresh obstacles in the way. The question was settled in five minutes, and the rehearsal went on; Magdalen learning Julia's stage situations with the book in her hand, and announcing afterward, on the journey home, that she proposed sitting up all night to study the new part. Frank thereupon expressed his fears that she would have no time left to help him through his theatrical difficulties. She tapped him on the shoulder coquettishly with her part. "You foolish fellow, how am I to do without you? You're Julia's jealous lover; you're always making Julia cry. Come to-night, and make me cry at tea-time. You haven't got a venomous old woman in a wig to act with now. It's my heart you're to break—and of course I shall teach you how to do it."

The four days' interval passed busily in perpetual rehearsals, public and private. The night of performance arrived; the guests assembled; the great dramatic experiment stood on its trial. Magdalen had made the most of her opportunities; she had learned all that the manager could teach her in the time. Miss Garth left her when the overture began, sitting apart in a corner behind the scenes, serious and silent, with her smelling-bottle in one hand, and her book in the other, resolutely training herself for the coming ordeal, to the very last.

The play began, with all the proper accompaniments of a theatrical performance in private life; with a crowded audience, an African temperature, a bursting of heated lamp-glasses, and a difficulty in drawing up the curtain. "Fag" and "the Coachman," who opened the scene, took leave of their memories as soon as they stepped on the stage; left half their dialogue unspoken; came to a dead pause; were audibly entreated by the invisible manager to "come off"; and went off accordingly, in every respect sadder and wiser men than when they went on. The next scene disclosed Miss Marrable as "Lydia Languish," gracefully seated, very pretty, beautifully dressed, accurately mistress of the smallest words in her part; possessed, in short, of every personal resource—except her voice. The ladies admired, the gentlemen applauded.

Nobody heard anything but the words "Speak up, miss," whispered by the same voice which had already entreated "Fag" and "the Coachman" to "come off." A responsive titter rose among the younger spectators; checked immediately by magnanimous applause. The temperature of the audience was rising to Blood Heat—but the national sense of fair play was not boiled out of them yet.

In the midst of the demonstration, Magdalen quietly made her first entrance, as "Julia." She was dressed very plainly in dark colors, and wore her own hair; all stage adjuncts and alterations (excepting the slightest possible touch of rouge on her cheeks) having been kept in reserve to disguise her the more effectually in her second part. The grace and simplicity of her costume, the steady self-possession with which she looked out over the eager rows of faces before her, raised a low hum of approval and expectation. She spoke—after suppressing a momentary tremor—with a quiet distinctness of utterance which reached all ears, and which at once confirmed the favorable impression that her appearance had produced. The one member of the audience who looked at her and listened to her coldly, was her elder sister. Before the actress of the evening had been five minutes on the stage, Norah detected, to her own indescribable astonishment, that Magdalen had audaciously individualized the feeble amiability of "Julia's" character, by seizing no less a person than herself as the model to act it by. She saw all her own little formal peculiarities of manner and movement unblushingly reproduced—and even the very tone of her voice so accurately mimicked from time to time, that the accents startled her as if she was speaking herself, with an echo on the stage. The effect of this cool appropriation of Norah's identity to theatrical purposes on the audience—who only saw results—asserted itself in a storm of applause on Magdalen's exit. She had won two incontestable triumphs in her first scene. By a dexterous piece of mimicry, she had made a living reality of one of the most insipid characters in the English drama; and she had roused to enthusiasm an audience of two hundred exiles from the blessings of ventilation, all simmering together in their own animal heat. Under the circumstances, where is the actress by profession who could have done much more?

But the event of the evening was still to come. Magdalen's disguised re-appearance at the end of the act, in the character of "Lucy"—with false hair and false eyebrows, with a bright-red complexion and patches on her cheeks, with the gayest colors flaunting in her dress, and the shrillest vivacity of voice and manner—fairly staggered the audience. They looked down at their programmes, in which the representative of Lucy figured under an assumed name; looked up again at the stage; penetrated the disguise; and vented their astonishment in another round of applause, louder and heartier even than the last. Norah herself could not deny this time that the tribute of approbation had been well deserved. There, forcing its way steadily through all the faults of inexperience—there, plainly visible to the dullest of the spectators, was the rare faculty of dramatic impersonation, expressing itself in every look and action of this girl of eighteen, who now stood on a stage for the first time in her life. Failing in many minor requisites of the double task which she had undertaken, she succeeded in the one important necessity of keeping the main distinctions of the two characters thoroughly apart. Everybody felt that the difficulty lay here—everybody saw the difficulty conquered—everybody echoed the manager's enthusiasm at rehearsal, which had hailed her as a born actress.

When the drop-scene descended for the first time, Magdalen had concentrated in herself the whole interest and attraction of the play. The audience politely applauded Miss Marrable, as became the guests assembled in her father's house: and good-humoredly encouraged the remainder of the company, to help them through a task for which they were all, more or less, palpably unfit. But, as the play proceeded, nothing roused them to any genuine expression of interest when Magdalen was absent from the scene. There was no disguising it: Miss Marrable and her bosom friends had been all hopelessly cast in the shade by the new recruit whom they had summoned to assist them, in the capacity of forlorn hope. And this on Miss Marrable's own birthday! and this in her father's house! and this after the unutterable sacrifices of six weeks past! Of all the domestic disasters which the thankless theatrical enterprise had inflicted on the Marrable family, the crowning misfortune was now consummated by Magdalen's success.

Leaving Mr. Vanstone and Norah, on the conclusion of the play, among the guests in the supper-room, Miss Garth went behind the scenes; ostensibly anxious to see if she could be of any use; really bent on ascertaining whether Magdalen's head had been turned by the triumphs of the evening. It would not have surprised Miss Garth if she had discovered her pupil in the act of making terms with the manager for her forthcoming appearance in a public theater. As events really turned out, she found Magdalen on the stage, receiving, with gracious smiles, a card which the manager presented to her with a professional bow. Noticing Miss Garth's mute look of inquiry, the civil little man hastened to explain that the card was his own, and that he was merely asking the favor of Miss Vanstone's recommendation at any future opportunity.

"This is not the last time the young lady will be concerned in private theatricals, I'll answer for it," said the manager. "And if a superintendent is wanted on the next occasion, she has kindly promised to say a good word for me. I am always to be heard of, miss, at that address." Saying those words, he bowed again, and discreetly disappeared.

Vague suspicions beset the mind of Miss Garth, and urged her to insist on looking at the card. No more harmless morsel of pasteboard was ever passed from one hand to another. The card contained nothing but the manager's name, and, under it, the name and address of a theatrical agent in London.

"It is not worth the trouble of keeping," said Miss Garth.

Magdalen caught her hand before she could throw the card away—possessed herself of it the next instant—and put it in her pocket.

"I promised to recommend him," she said—"and that's one reason for keeping his card. If it does nothing else, it will remind me of the happiest evening of my life—and that's another. Come!" she cried, throwing her arms round Miss Garth with a feverish gayety—"congratulate me on my success!"

"I will congratulate you when you have got over it," said Miss Garth.

In half an hour more Magdalen had changed her dress; had joined the guests; and had soared into an atmosphere of congratulation high above the reach of any controlling influence that Miss Garth could exercise. Frank, dilatory in all his proceedings, was the last of the dramatic company who left the precincts of the stage. He made no attempt to join Magdalen in the supper-room—but he was ready in the hall with her cloak when the carriages were called and the party broke up.

"Oh, Frank!" she said, looking round at him as he put the cloak on her shoulders, "I am so sorry it's all over! Come to-morrow morning, and let's talk about it by ourselves."

"In the shrubbery at ten?" asked Frank, in a whisper.

She drew up the hood of her cloak and nodded to him gayly. Miss Garth, standing near, noticed the looks that passed between them, though the disturbance made by the parting guests prevented her from hearing the words. There was a soft, underlying tenderness in Magdalen's assumed gayety of manner—there was a sudden thoughtfulness in her face, a confidential readiness in her hand, as she took Frank's arm and went out to the carriage. What did it mean? Had her passing interest in him as her stage-pupil treacherously sown the seeds of any deeper interest in him, as a man? Had the idle theatrical scheme, now that it was all over, graver results to answer for than a mischievous waste of time?

The lines on Miss Garth's face deepened and hardened: she stood lost among the fluttering crowd around her. Norah's warning words, addressed to Mrs. Vanstone in the garden, recurred to her memory—and now, for the first time, the idea dawned on her that Norah had seen the consequences in their true light.

CHAPTER VII.

EARLY the next morning Miss Garth and Norah met in the garden and spoke together privately. The only noticeable result of the interview, when they presented themselves at the breakfast-table, appeared in the marked silence which they both maintained on the topic of the theatrical performance. Mrs. Vanstone was entirely indebted to her husband and to her youngest daughter for all that she heard of the evening's entertainment. The governess and the elder daughter had evidently determined on letting the subject drop.

After breakfast was over Magdalen proved to be missing, when the ladies assembled as usual in the morning-room. Her habits were so little regular that Mrs. Vanstone felt neither surprise nor uneasiness at her absence. Miss Garth and Norah looked at one another significantly, and waited in silence. Two hours passed—and there were no signs of Magdalen. Norah rose, as the clock struck twelve, and quietly left the room to look for her.

She was not upstairs dusting her jewelry and disarranging her dresses. She was not in the conservatory, not in the flower-garden; not in the kitchen teasing the cook; not in the yard playing with the dogs. Had she, by any chance, gone out with her father? Mr. Vanstone had announced his intention, at the breakfast-table, of paying a morning visit to his old ally, Mr. Clare, and of rousing the philosopher's sarcastic indignation by an account of the dramatic performance. None of the other ladies at Combe-Raven ever ventured themselves inside the cottage. But Magdalen was reckless enough for anything—and Magdalen might have gone there. As the idea occurred to her, Norah entered the shrubbery.

At the second turning, where the path among the trees wound away out of sight of the house, she came suddenly face to face with Magdalen and Frank: they were sauntering toward her, arm in arm, their heads close together, their conversation apparently proceeding in whispers. They looked suspiciously handsome and happy. At the sight of Norah both started, and both stopped. Frank confusedly raised his hat, and turned back in the direction of his father's cottage. Magdalen advanced to meet her sister, carelessly swinging her closed parasol from side to side, carelessly humming an air from the overture which had preceded the rising of the curtain on the previous night.

"Luncheon-time already!" she said, looking at her watch. "Surely not?"

"Have you and Mr. Francis Clare been alone in the shrubbery since ten o'clock?" asked Norah.

"Mr. Francis Clare! How ridiculously formal you are. Why don't you call him Frank?"

"I asked you a question, Magdalen."

"Dear me, how black you look this morning! I'm in disgrace, I suppose. Haven't you forgiven me yet for my acting last night? I couldn't help it, love; I should have made nothing of Julia, if I hadn't taken you for my model. It's quite a question of Art. In your place, I should have felt flattered by the selection."

"In your place, Magdalen, I should have thought twice before I mimicked my sister to an audience of strangers."

"That's exactly why I did it—an audience of strangers. How were they to know? Come! come! don't be angry. You are eight years older than I am—you ought to set me an example of good-humor."

"I will set you an example of plain-speaking. I am more sorry than I can say, Magdalen, to meet you as I met you here just now!"

"What next, I wonder? You meet me in the shrubbery at home, talking over the private theatricals with my old playfellow, whom I knew when I was no taller than this parasol. And that is a glaring impropriety, is it? 'Honi soit qui mal y pense.' You wanted an answer a minute ago—there it is for you, my dear, in the choicest Norman-French."

"I am in earnest about this, Magdalen—"

"Not a doubt of it. Nobody can accuse you of ever making jokes."

"I am seriously sorry—"

"Oh, dear!"

"It is quite useless to interrupt me. I have it on my conscience to tell you—and I will tell you—that I am sorry to see how this intimacy is growing. I am sorry to see a secret understanding established already between you and Mr. Francis Clare."

"Poor Frank! How you do hate him, to be sure. What on earth has he done to offend you?"

Norah's self-control began to show signs of failing her. Her dark cheeks glowed, her delicate lips trembled, before she spoke again. Magdalen paid more attention to her parasol than to her sister. She tossed it high in the air and caught it. "Once!" she said—and tossed it up again. "Twice!"—and she tossed it higher. "Thrice—" Before she could catch it for the third time, Norah seized her passionately by the arm, and the parasol dropped to the ground between them.

"You are treating me heartlessly," she said. "For shame, Magdalen—for shame!"

The irrepressible outburst of a reserved nature, forced into open self-assertion in its own despite, is of all moral forces the hardest to resist. Magdalen was startled into silence. For a moment, the two sisters—so strangely dissimilar in person and character—faced one another, without a word passing between them. For a moment the deep brown eyes of the elder and the light gray eyes of the younger looked into each other with steady, unyielding scrutiny on either side. Norah's face was the first to change; Norah's head was the first to turn away. She dropped her sister's arm in silence. Magdalen stooped and picked up her parasol.

"I try to keep my temper," she said, "and you call me heartless for doing it. You always were hard on me, and you always will be."

Norah clasped her trembling hands fast in each other. "Hard on you!" she said, in low, mournful tones—and sighed bitterly.

Magdalen drew back a little, and mechanically dusted the parasol with the end of her garden cloak.

"Yes!" she resumed, doggedly. "Hard on me and hard on Frank."

"Frank!" repeated Norah, advancing on her sister and turning pale as suddenly as she had turned red. "Do you talk of yourself and Frank as if your interests were One already? Magdalen! if I hurt you, do I hurt him? Is he so near and so dear to you as that?"

Magdalen drew further and further back. A twig from a tree near caught her cloak; she turned petulantly, broke it off, and threw it on the ground. "What right have you to question me?" she broke out on a sudden. "Whether I like Frank, or whether I don't, what interest is it of yours?" As she said the words, she abruptly stepped forward to pass her sister and return to the house.

Norah, turning paler and paler, barred the way to her. "If I hold you by main force," she said, "you shall stop and hear me. I have watched this Francis Clare; I know him better than you do. He is unworthy of a moment's serious feeling on your part; he is unworthy of our dear, good, kind-hearted father's interest in him. A man with any principle, any honor, any gratitude, would not have come back as he has come back, disgraced—yes! disgraced by his spiritless neglect of his own duty. I watched his face while the friend who has been better than a father to him was comforting and forgiving him with a kindness he had not deserved: I watched his face, and I saw no shame and no distress in it—I saw nothing but a look of thankless, heartless relief. He is selfish, he is ungrateful, he is ungenerous—he is only twenty, and he has the worst failings of a mean old age already. And this is the man I find you meeting in secret—the man who has taken such a place in your favor that you are deaf to the truth about him, even from my lips! Magdalen! this will end ill. For God's sake, think of what I have said to you, and control yourself before it is too late!" She stopped, vehement and breathless, and caught her sister anxiously by the hand.

Magdalen looked at her in unconcealed astonishment.

"You are so violent," she said, "and so unlike yourself, that I hardly know you. The more patient I am, the more hard words I get for my pains. You have taken a perverse hatred to Frank; and you are unreasonably angry with me because I won't hate him, too. Don't, Norah! you hurt my hand."

Norah pushed the hand from her contemptuously. "I shall never hurt your heart," she said; and suddenly turned her back on Magdalen as she spoke the words.

There was a momentary pause. Norah kept her position. Magdalen looked at her perplexedly—hesitated—then walked away by herself toward the house.

At the turn in the shrubbery path she stopped and looked back uneasily. "Oh, dear,

dear!" she thought to herself, "why didn't Frank go when I told him?" She hesitated, and went back a few steps. "There's Norah standing on her dignity, as obstinate as ever." She stopped again. "What had I better do? I hate quarreling: I think I'll make up." She ventured close to her sister and touched her on the shoulder. Norah never moved. "It's not often she flies into a passion," thought Magdalen, touching her again; "but when she does, what a time it lasts her!—Come!" she said, "give me a kiss, Norah, and make it up. Won't you let me get at any part of you, my dear, but the back of your neck? Well, it's a very nice neck—it's better worth kissing than mine—and there the kiss is, in spite of you!"

She caught fast hold of Norah from behind, and suited the action to the word, with a total disregard of all that had just passed, which her sister was far from emulating. Hardly a minute since the warm outpouring of Norah's heart had burst through all obstacles. Had the icy reserve frozen her up again already! It was hard to say. She never spoke; she never changed her position—she only searched hurriedly for her handkerchief. As she drew it out, there was a sound of approaching footsteps in the inner recesses of the shrubbery. A Scotch terrier scampered into view; and a cheerful voice sang the first lines of the glee in "As You Like It." "It's papa!" cried Magdalen. "Come, Norah—come and meet him."

Instead of following her sister, Norah pulled down the veil of her garden hat, turned in the opposite direction, and hurried back to the house. She ran up to her own room and locked herself in. She was crying bitterly.

CHAPTER VIII.

WHEN Magdalen and her father met in the shrubbery Mr. Vanstone's face showed plainly that something had happened to please him since he had left home in the morning. He answered the question which his daughter's curiosity at once addressed to him by informing her that he had just come from Mr. Clare's cottage; and that he had picked up, in that unpromising locality, a startling piece of news for the family at Combe-Raven.

On entering the philosopher's study that morning, Mr. Vanstone had found him still dawdling over his late breakfast, with an open letter by his side, in place of the book which, on other occasions, lay ready to his hand at meal-times. He held up the letter the moment his visitor came into the room, and abruptly opened the conversation by asking Mr. Vanstone if his nerves were in good order, and if he felt himself strong enough for the shock of an overwhelming surprise.

"Nerves!" repeated Mr. Vanstone. "Thank God, I know nothing about my nerves. If you have got anything to tell me, shock or no shock, out with it on the spot."

Mr. Clare held the letter a little higher, and frowned at his visitor across the breakfast-table. "What have I always told you?" he asked, with his sourest solemnity of look and manner.

"A great deal more than I could ever keep in my head," answered Mr. Vanstone.

"In your presence and out of it," continued Mr. Clare, "I have always maintained that the one important phenomenon presented by modern society is—the enormous prosperity of Fools. Show me an individual Fool, and I will show you an aggregate Society which gives that highly-favored personage nine chances out of ten—and grudges the tenth to the wisest man in existence. Look where you will, in every high place there sits an Ass, settled beyond the reach of all the greatest intellects in this world to pull him down. Over our whole social system, complacent Imbecility rules supreme—snuffs out the searching light of Intelligence with total impunity—and hoots, owl-like, in answer to every form of protest, See how well we all do in the dark! One of these days that audacious assertion will be practically contradicted, and the whole rotten system of modern society will come down with a crash."

"God forbid!" cried Mr. Vanstone, looking about him as if the crash was coming already.

"With a crash!" repeated Mr. Clare. "There is my theory, in few words. Now for the remarkable application of it which this letter suggests. Here is my lout of a boy—"

"You don't mean that Frank has got another chance?" exclaimed Mr. Vanstone.

"Here is this perfectly hopeless booby, Frank," pursued the philosopher. "He has never done anything in his life to help himself, and, as a necessary consequence, Society is in a conspiracy to carry him to the top of the tree. He has hardly had time to throw away that chance you gave him before this letter comes, and puts the ball at his foot for the second time. My rich cousin (who is intellectually fit to be at the tail of the family, and who is, therefore, as a matter of course, at the head of it) has been good enough to remember my existence; and has offered his influence to serve my eldest boy. Read his letter, and then observe the sequence of events. My rich cousin is a booby who thrives on landed property; he has done something for another booby who thrives on Politics, who knows a third booby who thrives on Commerce, who can do something for a fourth booby, thriving at present on nothing, whose name is Frank. So the mill goes. So the cream of all human rewards is sipped in endless succession by the Fools. I shall pack Frank off to-morrow. In course of time he'll come back again on our hands, like a bad shilling; more chances will fall in his way, as a necessary consequence of his meritorious imbecility. Years will go on—I may not live to see it, no more may you—it doesn't matter; Frank's future is equally certain either way—put him into the army, the Church, politics, what you please, and let him drift: he'll end in being a general, a bishop, or a minister of State, by dint of the great modern qualification of doing nothing whatever to deserve his place." With this summary of his son's worldly prospects, Mr. Clare tossed the letter contemptuously across the table and poured himself out another cup of tea.

Mr. Vanstone read the letter with eager interest and pleasure. It was written in a tone of somewhat elaborate cordiality; but the practical advantages which it placed at Frank's disposal were beyond all doubt. The writer had the means of using a friend's interest—interest of no ordinary kind—with a great Mercantile Firm in the City; and he had at once exerted this influence in favor of Mr. Clare's eldest boy. Frank would be received in the office on a very different footing from the footing of an ordinary clerk; he would be "pushed on" at every available opportunity; and the first "good thing" the House had to offer, either at home or abroad, would be placed at his disposal. If he possessed fair abilities and showed common diligence in exercising them, his fortune was made; and the sooner he was sent to London to begin the better for his own interests it would be.

"Wonderful news!" cried Mr. Vanstone, returning the letter. "I'm delighted—I must go back and tell them at home. This is fifty times the chance that mine was. What the deuce do you mean by abusing Society? Society has behaved uncommonly well, in my opinion. Where's Frank?"

"Lurking," said Mr. Clare. "It is one of the intolerable peculiarities of louts that they always lurk. I haven't seen my lout this morning. It you meet with him anywhere, give him a kick, and say I want him."

Mr. Clare's opinion of his son's habits might have been expressed more politely as to form; but, as to substance, it happened, on that particular morning, to be perfectly correct. After leaving Magdalen, Frank had waited in the shrubbery, at a safe distance, on the chance that she might detach herself from her sister's company, and join him again. Mr. Vanstone's appearance immediately on Norah's departure, instead of encouraging him to show himself, had determined him on returning to the cottage. He walked back discontentedly; and so fell into his father's clutches, totally unprepared for the pending announcement, in that formidable quarter, of his departure for London.

In the meantime, Mr. Vanstone had communicated his news—in the first place, to Magdalen, and afterward, on getting back to the house, to his wife and Miss Garth. He was too unobservant a man to notice that Magdalen looked unaccountably startled, and Miss Garth unaccountably relieved, by his announcement of Frank's good fortune. He talked on about it, quite unsuspiciously, until the luncheon-bell rang—and then, for the first time, he noticed Norah's absence. She sent a message downstairs, after they had assembled at the table, to say that a headache was keeping her in her own room. When Miss Garth went up shortly afterward to communicate the news about Frank, Norah appeared, strangely enough, to feel very little relieved by hearing it. Mr. Francis Clare had gone away on a former occasion (she remarked), and had come back. He might come back again, and sooner than they any of them thought for. She said no more on the subject than this: she made no reference to what had taken place in the shrubbery. Her unconquerable reserve seemed to have strengthened its hold on her since the outburst of the morning. She met Magdalen, later in the day, as if nothing had happened: no formal reconciliation took place between them. It was one of Norah's peculiarities to shrink from all reconciliations that were openly ratified, and to take her shy refuge in reconciliations that were silently implied. Magdalen saw plainly, in her look and manner, that she had made her first and last protest. Whether the motive was pride, or sullenness, or distrust of herself, or despair of doing good, the result was not to be mistaken—Norah had resolved on remaining passive for the future.

Later in the afternoon, Mr. Vanstone suggested a drive to his eldest daughter, as the best remedy for her headache. She readily consented to accompany her father; who thereupon proposed, as usual, that Magdalen should join them. Magdalen was nowhere to be found. For the second time that day she had wandered into the grounds by herself. On this occasion, Miss Garth—who, after adopting Norah's opinions, had passed from the one extreme of over-looking Frank altogether, to the other extreme of believing him capable of planning an elopement at five minutes' notice—volunteered to set forth immediately, and do her best to find the missing young lady. After a prolonged absence, she returned unsuccessful—with the strongest persuasion in her own mind that Magdalen and Frank had secretly met one another somewhere, but without having discovered the smallest fragment of evidence to confirm her suspicions. By this time the carriage was at the door, and Mr. Vanstone was unwilling to wait any longer. He and Norah drove away together; and Mrs. Vanstone and Miss Garth sat at home over their work.

In half an hour more, Magdalen composedly walked into the room. She was pale and depressed. She received Miss Garth's remonstrances with a weary inattention; explained carelessly that she had been wandering in the wood; took up some books, and put them down again; sighed impatiently, and went away upstairs to her own room.

"I think Magdalen is feeling the reaction, after yesterday," said Mrs. Vanstone, quietly. "It is just as we thought. Now the theatrical amusements are all over, she is fretting for more."

Here was an opportunity of letting in the light of truth on Mrs. Vanstone's mind, which was too favorable to be missed. Miss Garth questioned her conscience, saw her chance, and took it on the spot.

"You forget," she rejoined, "that a certain neighbor of ours is going away to-morrow. Shall I tell you the truth? Magdalen is fretting over the departure of Francis Clare."

Mrs. Vanstone looked up from her work with a gentle, smiling surprise.

"Surely not?" she said. "It is natural enough that Frank should be attracted by Magdalen; but I can't think that Magdalen returns the feeling. Frank is so very unlike her; so quiet and undemonstrative; so dull and helpless, poor fellow, in some things. He is handsome, I know, but he is so singularly unlike Magdalen, that I can't think it possible—I can't indeed."

"My dear good lady!" cried Miss Garth, in great amazement; "do you really suppose that people fall in love with each other on account of similarities in their characters? In the vast majority of cases, they do just the reverse. Men marry the very last women, and women the very last men, whom their friends would think it possible they could care about. Is there any phrase that is oftener on all our lips than 'What can have made Mr. So-and-So marry that woman?'—or 'How could Mrs. So-and-So throw herself away on that man?' Has all your experience of the world never yet shown you that girls take perverse fancies for men who are totally unworthy of them?"

"Very true," said Mrs. Vanstone, composedly. "I forgot that. Still it seems unaccountable, doesn't it?"

"Unaccountable, because it happens every day!" retorted Miss Garth, good-humoredly. "I know a great many excellent people who reason against plain experience in the same way—who read the newspapers in the morning, and deny in the evening that there is any romance for writers or painters to work upon in modern life. Seriously, Mrs. Vanstone, you may take my word for it—thanks to those wretched theatricals, Magdalen is going the way with Frank that a great many young ladies have gone before her. He is quite unworthy of her; he is, in almost every respect, her exact opposite—and, without knowing it herself, she has fallen in love with him on that very account. She is resolute and impetuous, clever and domineering; she is not one of those model women who want a man to look up to, and to protect them—her beau-ideal (though she may not think it herself) is a man she can henpeck. Well! one comfort is, there are far better men, even of that sort, to be had than Frank. It's a mercy he is going away, before we have more trouble with them, and before any serious mischief is done."

"Poor Frank!" said Mrs. Vanstone, smiling compassionately. "We have known him since he was in jackets, and Magdalen in short frocks. Don't let us give him up yet. He may do better this second time."

Miss Garth looked up in astonishment.

"And suppose he does better?" she asked. "What then?"

Mrs. Vanstone cut off a loose thread in her work, and laughed outright.

"My good friend," she said, "there is an old farmyard proverb which warns us not to count our chickens before they are hatched. Let us wait a little before we count ours."

It was not easy to silence Miss Garth, when she was speaking under the influence of a strong conviction; but this reply closed her lips. She resumed her work, and looked, and thought, unutterable things.

Mrs. Vanstone's behavior was certainly remarkable under the circumstances. Here, on one side, was a girl—with great personal attractions, with rare pecuniary prospects, with a social position which might have justified the best gentleman in the neighborhood in making her an offer of marriage—perversely casting herself away on a penniless idle young fellow, who had failed at his first start in life, and who even if he succeeded in his second attempt, must be for years to come in no position to marry a young lady of fortune on equal terms. And there, on the other side, was that girl's mother, by no means dismayed at the prospect of a connection which was, to say the least of it, far from desirable; by no means certain, judging her by her own words and looks, that a marriage between Mr. Vanstone's daughter and Mr. Clare's son might not prove to be as satisfactory a result of the intimacy between the two young people as the parents on both sides could possibly wish for!

It was perplexing in the extreme. It was almost as unintelligible as that past mystery—that forgotten mystery now—of the journey to London.

In the evening, Frank made his appearance, and announced that his father had mercilessly sentenced him to leave Combe-Raven by the parliamentary train the next morning. He mentioned this circumstance with an air of sentimental resignation; and listened to Mr. Vanstone's boisterous rejoicings over his new prospects with a mild and mute surprise. His gentle melancholy of look and manner greatly assisted his personal advantages. In his own effeminate way he was more handsome than ever that evening. His soft brown eyes wandered about the room with a melting tenderness; his hair was beautifully brushed; his delicate hands hung over the arms of his chair with a languid grace. He looked like a convalescent Apollo. Never, on any previous occasion, had he practiced more successfully the social art which he habitually cultivated—the art of casting himself on society in the character of a well-bred Incubus, and conferring an obligation on his fellow-creatures by allowing them to sit under him. It was undeniably a dull evening. All the talking fell to the share of Mr. Vanstone and Miss Garth. Mrs. Vanstone was habitually silent; Norah kept herself obstinately in the background; Magdalen was quiet and undemonstrative beyond all former precedent. From first to last, she kept rigidly on her guard. The few meaning looks that she cast on Frank flashed at him like lightning, and were gone before any one else could see them. Even when she brought him his tea; and when, in doing so, her self-control gave way under the temptation which no woman can resist—the temptation of touching the man she loves—even then, she held the saucer so dexterously that it screened her hand. Frank's self-possession was far less steadily disciplined: it only lasted as long as he remained passive. When he rose to go; when he felt the warm, clinging pressure of Magdalen's fingers round his hand, and the lock of her hair which she slipped into it at the same moment, he became awkward and confused. He might have betrayed Magdalen and betrayed himself, but for Mr. Vanstone, who innocently covered his retreat by following him out, and patting him on the shoulder all the way. "God bless you, Frank!" cried the friendly voice that never had a harsh note in it for anybody. "Your fortune's waiting for you. Go in, my boy—go in and win."

"Yes," said Frank. "Thank you. It will be rather difficult to go in and win, at first. Of course, as you have always told me, a man's business is to conquer his difficulties, and not to talk about them. At the same time, I wish I didn't feel quite so loose as I do in my figures. It's discouraging to feel loose in one's figures.—Oh, yes; I'll write and tell you how I get on. I'm very much obliged by your kindness, and very sorry I couldn't succeed with the engineering. I think I should have liked engineering better than trade. It can't be helped now, can it? Thank you, again. Good-by."

So he drifted away into the misty commercial future—as aimless, as helpless, as gentleman-like as ever.

CHAPTER IX.

THREE months passed. During that time Frank remained in London; pursuing his new duties, and writing occasionally to report himself to Mr. Vanstone, as he had promised.

His letters were not enthusiastic on the subject of mercantile occupations. He described himself as being still painfully loose in his figures. He was also more firmly persuaded than ever—now when it was unfortunately too late—that he preferred engineering to trade. In spite of this conviction; in spite of headaches caused by sitting on a high stool and stooping over ledgers in unwholesome air; in spite of want of society, and hasty breakfasts, and bad dinners at chop-houses, his attendance at the office was regular, and his diligence at the desk unremitting. The head of the department in which he was working might be referred to if any corroboration of this statement was desired. Such was the general tenor of the letters; and Frank's correspondent and Frank's father differed over them as widely as usual. Mr. Vanstone accepted them as proofs of the steady development of industrious principles in the writer. Mr. Clare took his own characteristically opposite view. "These London men," said the philosopher, "are not to be trifled with by louts. They have got Frank by the scruff of the neck—he can't wriggle himself free—and he makes a merit of yielding to sheer necessity."

The three months' interval of Frank's probation in London passed less cheerfully than usual in the household at Combe-Raven.

As the summer came nearer and nearer, Mrs. Vanstone's spirits, in spite of her resolute efforts to control them, became more and more depressed.

"I do my best," she said to Miss Garth; "I set an example of cheerfulness to my husband and my children—but I dread July." Norah's secret misgivings on her sister's account rendered her more than usually serious and uncommunicative, as the year advanced. Even Mr. Vanstone, when July drew nearer, lost something of his elasticity of spirit. He kept up appearances in his wife's presence—but on all other occasions there was now a perceptible shade of sadness in his look and manner. Magdalen was so changed since Frank's departure that she helped the general depression, instead of relieving it. All her movements had grown languid; all her usual occupations were pursued with the same weary indifference; she spent hours alone in her own room; she lost her interest in being brightly and prettily dressed; her eyes were heavy, her nerves were irritable, her complexion was altered visibly for the worse—in one word, she had become an oppression and a weariness to herself and to all about her. Stoutly as Miss Garth contended with these growing domestic difficulties, her own spirits suffered in the effort. Her memory reverted, oftener and oftener, to the March morning when the master and mistress of the house had departed for London, and then the first serious change, for many a year past, had stolen over the family atmosphere. When was that atmosphere to be clear again? When were the clouds of change to pass off before the returning sunshine of past and happier times?

The spring and the early summer wore away. The dreaded month of July came, with its airless nights, its cloudless mornings, and its sultry days.

On the fifteenth of the month, an event happened which took every one but Norah by surprise. For the second time, without the slightest apparent reason—for the second time, without a word of warning beforehand—Frank suddenly re-appeared at his father's cottage.

Mr. Clare's lips opened to hail his son's return, in the old character of the "bad shilling"; and closed again without uttering a word. There was a portentous composure in Frank's manner which showed that he had other news to communicate than the news of his dismissal. He answered his father's sardonic look of inquiry by at once explaining that a very important proposal for his future benefit had been made to him, that morning, at the office. His first idea had been to communicate the details in writing; but the partners had, on reflection, thought that the necessary decision might be more readily obtained by a personal interview with his father and his friends. He had laid aside the pen accordingly, and had resigned himself to the railway on the spot.

After this preliminary statement, Frank proceeded to describe the proposal which his employers had addressed to him, with every external appearance of viewing it in the light of an intolerable hardship.

The great firm in the City had obviously made a discovery in relation to their clerk, exactly similar to the discovery which had formerly forced itself on the engineer in relation to his pupil. The young man, as they politely phrased it, stood in need of some special stimulant to stir him up. His employers (acting under a sense of their obligation to the gentleman by whom Frank had been recommended) had considered the question carefully, and had decided that the one promising use to which they could put Mr. Francis Clare was to send him forthwith into another quarter of the globe.

As a consequence of this decision, it was now, therefore, proposed that he should enter the house of their correspondents in China; that he should remain there, familiarizing himself thoroughly on the spot with the tea trade and the silk trade for five years; and that he should return, at the expiration of this period, to the central establishment in London. If he made a fair use of his opportunities in China, he would come back, while still a young man, fit for a position of trust and emolument, and justified in looking forward, at no distant date, to a time when the House would assist him to start in business for himself. Such were the new prospects which—to adopt Mr. Clare's theory—now forced themselves on the ever-reluctant, ever-helpless and ever-ungrateful Frank. There was no time to be lost. The final answer was to be at the office on "Monday, the twentieth": the correspondents in China were to be written to by the mail on that day; and Frank was to follow the letter by the next opportunity, or to resign his chance in favor of some more enterprising young man.

Mr. Clare's reception of this extraordinary news was startling in the extreme. The glorious prospect of his son's banishment to China appeared to turn his brain. The firm pedestal of his philosophy sank under him; the prejudices of society recovered their hold on his mind. He seized Frank by the arm, and actually accompanied him to Combe-Raven, in the amazing character of visitor to the house!

"Here I am with my lout," said Mr. Clare, before a word could be uttered by the astonished family. "Hear his story, all of you. It has reconciled me, for the first time in my life, to the anomaly of his existence." Frank ruefully narrated the Chinese proposal for the second time, and attempted to attach to it his own supplementary statement of objections and difficulties. His father stopped him at the first word, pointed peremptorily southeastward (from Somersetshire to China); and said, without an instant's hesitation: "Go!" Mr. Vanstone, basking in golden visions of his young friend's future, echoed that monosyllabic decision with all his heart. Mrs. Vanstone, Miss Garth, even Norah herself, spoke to the same purpose. Frank was petrified by an absolute unanimity of opinion which he had not anticipated; and Magdalen was caught, for once in her life, at the end of all her resources.

So far as practical results were concerned, the sitting of the family council began and ended with the general opinion that Frank must go. Mr. Vanstone's faculties were so bewildered by the son's sudden arrival, the father's unexpected visit, and the news they both brought with them, that he petitioned for an adjournment before the necessary arrangements connected with his young friend's departure were considered in detail. "Suppose we all sleep upon it?" he said. "Tomorrow our heads will feel a little steadier; and to-morrow will be time enough to decide all uncertainties." This suggestion was readily adopted; and all further proceedings stood adjourned until the next day.

That next day was destined to decide more uncertainties than Mr. Vanstone dreamed of.

Early in the morning, after making tea by herself as usual, Miss Garth took her parasol and strolled into the garden. She had slept ill; and ten minutes in the open air before the family assembled at breakfast might help to compensate her, as she thought, for the loss of her night's rest.

She wandered to the outermost boundary of the flower-garden, and then returned by another path, which led back, past the side of an ornamental summer-house commanding a view over the fields from a corner of the lawn. A slight noise—like, and yet not like, the chirruping of a bird—caught her ear as she approached the summer-house. She stepped round to the entrance; looked in; and discovered Magdalen and Frank seated close together. To Miss Garth's horror, Magdalen's arm was unmistakably round Frank's neck; and, worse still, the position of her face, at the moment of discovery, showed beyond all doubt that she had just been offering to the victim of Chinese commerce the first and foremost of all the consolations which a woman can bestow on a man. In plainer words, she had just given Frank a kiss.

In the presence of such an emergency as now confronted her, Miss Garth felt instinctively that all ordinary phrases of reproof would be phrases thrown away.

"I presume," she remarked, addressing Magdalen with the merciless self-possession of a middle-aged lady, unprovided for the occasion with any kissing remembrances of her own— "I presume (whatever excuses your effrontery may suggest) you will not deny that my duty compels me to mention what I have just seen to your father?"

"I will save you the trouble," replied Magdalen, composedly. "I will mention it to him myself."

With those words, she looked round at Frank, standing trebly helpless in a corner of the summer-house. "You shall hear what happens," she said, with her bright smile. "And so shall you," she added for Miss Garth's especial benefit, as she sauntered past the governess on her way back to the breakfast-table. The eyes of Miss Garth followed her indignantly; and Frank slipped out on his side at that favorable opportunity.

Under these circumstances, there was but one course that any respectable woman could take—she could only shudder. Miss Garth registered her protest in that form, and returned to the house.

When breakfast was over, and when Mr. Vanstone's hand descended to his pocket in search of his cigar-case, Magdalen rose; looked significantly at Miss Garth; and followed her father into the hall.

"Papa," she said, "I want to speak to you this morning—in private."

"Ay! ay!" returned Mr. Vanstone. "What about, my dear!"

"About—" Magdalen hesitated, searching for a satisfactory form of expression, and found it. "About business, papa," she said.

Mr. Vanstone took his garden hat from the hall table—opened his eyes in mute perplexity—attempted to associate in his mind the two extravagantly dissimilar ideas of Magdalen and "business"—failed—and led the way resignedly into the garden.

His daughter took his arm, and walked with him to a shady seat at a convenient distance from the house. She dusted the seat with her smart silk apron before her father occupied it. Mr. Vanstone was not accustomed to such an extraordinary act of attention as this. He sat down, looking more puzzled than ever. Magdalen immediately placed herself on his knee, and rested her head comfortably on his shoulder.

"Am I heavy, papa?" she asked.

"Yes, my dear, you are," said Mr. Vanstone—"but not too heavy for me. Stop on your perch, if you like it. Well? And what may this business happen to be?"

"It begins with a question."

"Ah, indeed? That doesn't surprise me. Business with your sex, my dear, always begins with questions. Go on."

"Papa! do you ever intend allowing me to be married?"

Mr. Vanstone's eyes opened wider and wider. The question, to use his own phrase, completely staggered him.

"This is business with a vengeance!" he said. "Why, Magdalen! what have you got in that harum-scarum head of yours now?"

"I don't exactly know, papa. Will you answer my question?"

"I will if I can, my dear; you rather stagger me. Well, I don't know. Yes; I suppose I must let you be married one of these days—if we can find a good husband for you. How hot your face is! Lift it up, and let the air blow over it. You won't? Well—have your own way. If talking of business means tickling your cheek against my whisker I've nothing to say against it. Go on, my dear. What's the next question? Come to the point."

She was far too genuine a woman to do anything of the sort. She skirted round the point and calculated her distance to the nicety of a hair-breadth.

"We were all very much surprised yesterday—were we not, papa? Frank is wonderfully lucky, isn'the?"

"He's the luckiest dog I ever came across," said Mr. Vanstone "But what has that got to do with this business of yours? I dare say you see your way, Magdalen. Hang me if I can see mine!"

She skirted a little nearer.

"I suppose he will make his fortune in China?" she said. "It's a long way off, isn't it? Did you observe, papa, that Frank looked sadly out of spirits yesterday?"

"I was so surprised by the news," said Mr. Vanstone, "and so staggered by the sight of old Clare's sharp nose in my house, that I didn't much notice. Now you remind me of it—yes. I don't think Frank took kindly to his own good luck; not kindly at all."

"Do you wonder at that, papa?"

"Yes, my dear; I do, rather."

"Don't you think it's hard to be sent away for five years, to make your fortune among hateful savages, and lose sight of your friends at home for all that long time? Don't you think Frank will miss us sadly? Don't you, papa?—don't you?"

"Gently, Magdalen! I'm a little too old for those long arms of yours to throttle me in fun.—You're right, my love. Nothing in this world without a drawback. Frank will miss his friends in England: there's no denying that."

"You always liked Frank. And Frank always liked you."

"Yes, yes—a good fellow; a quiet, good fellow. Frank and I have always got on smoothly together."

"You have got on like father and son, haven't you?"

"Certainly, my dear."

"Perhaps you will think it harder on him when he has gone than you think it now?"

"Likely enough, Magdalen; I don't say no."

"Perhaps you will wish he had stopped in England? Why shouldn't he stop in England, and do as well as if he went to China?"

"My dear! he has no prospects in England. I wish he had, for his own sake. I wish the lad well, with all my heart."

"May I wish him well too, papa—with all my heart?"

"Certainly, my love—your old playfellow—why not? What's the matter? God bless my soul, what is the girl crying about? One would think Frank was transported for life. You goose! You know, as well as I do, he is going to China to make his fortune."

"He doesn't want to make his fortune—he might do much better."

"The deuce he might! How, I should like to know?"

"I'm afraid to tell you. I'm afraid you'll laugh at me. Will you promise not to laugh at me?"

"Anything to please you, my dear. Yes: I promise. Now, then, out with it! How might Frank do better?"

"He might marry Me."

If the summer scene which then spread before Mr. Vanstone's eyes had suddenly changed to a dreary winter view—if the trees had lost all their leaves, and the green fields had turned white with snow in an instant—his face could hardly have expressed greater amazement than it displayed when his daughter's faltering voice spoke those four last words. He tried to look at her—but she steadily refused him the opportunity: she kept her face hidden over his shoulder. Was she in earnest? His cheek, still wet with her tears, answered for her. There was a long pause of silence; she waited—with unaccustomed patience, she waited for him to speak. He roused himself, and spoke these words only: "You surprise me, Magdalen; you surprise me more than I can say."

At the altered tone of his voice—altered to a quiet, fatherly seriousness—Magdalen's arms clung round him closer than before.

"Have I disappointed you, papa?" she asked, faintly. "Don't say I have disappointed you! Who am I to tell my secret to, if not to you? Don't let him go—don't! don't! You will break his heart. He is afraid to tell his father; he is even afraid you might be angry with him. There is nobody to speak for us, except—except me. Oh, don't let him go! Don't for his sake—" she whispered the next words in a kiss—"Don't for Mine!"

Her father's kind face saddened; he sighed, and patted her fair head tenderly. "Hush, my love," he said, almost in a whisper; "hush!" She little knew what a revelation every word, every action that escaped her, now opened before him. She had made him her grown-up playfellow, from her childhood to that day. She had romped with him in her frocks, she had gone on romping with him in her gowns. He had never been long enough separated from her to have the external changes in his daughter forced on his attention. His artless, fatherly experience of her had taught him that she was a taller child in later years—and had taught him little more. And now, in one breathless instant, the conviction that she was a woman rushed over his mind. He felt it in the trouble of her bosom pressed against his; in the nervous thrill of her arms clasped around his neck. The Magdalen of his innocent experience, a woman—with the master-passion of her sex in possession of her heart already!

"Have you thought long of this, my dear?" he asked, as soon as he could speak composedly. "Are you sure—?"

She answered the question before he could finish it.

"Sure I love him?" she said. "Oh, what words can say Yes for me, as I want to say it? I love him—!" Her voice faltered softly; and her answer ended in a sigh.

"You are very young. You and Frank, my love, are both very young."

She raised her head from his shoulder for the first time. The thought and its expression flashed from her at the same moment.

"Are we much younger than you and mamma were?" she asked, smiling through her tears.

She tried to lay her head back in its old position; but as she spoke those words, her father caught her round the waist, forced her, before she was aware of it, to look him in the face—and kissed her, with a sudden outburst of tenderness which brought the tears thronging back thickly into her eyes. "Not much younger, my child," he said, in low, broken tones—"not much younger than your mother and I were." He put her away from him, and rose from the seat, and turned his head aside quickly. "Wait here, and compose yourself; I will go indoors and speak to your mother." His voice trembled over those parting words; and he left her without once looking round again.

She waited—waited a weary time; and he never came back. At last her growing anxiety urged her to follow him into the house. A new timidity throbbed in her heart as she doubtingly approached the door. Never had she seen the depths of her father's simple nature stirred as they had been stirred by her confession. She almost dreaded her next meeting with him. She wandered softly to and fro in the hall, with a shyness unaccountable to herself; with a terror of being discovered and spoken to by her sister or Miss Garth, which made her nervously susceptible to the slightest noises in the house. The door of the morning-room opened while her back was turned toward it. She started violently, as she looked round and saw her father in the hall: her heart beat faster and faster, and she felt herself turning pale. A second look at him, as he came nearer, re-assured her. He was composed again, though not so cheerful as usual. She noticed that he advanced and spoke to her with a forbearing gentleness, which was more like his manner to her mother than his ordinary manner to herself.

"Go in, my love," he said, opening the door for her which he had just closed. "Tell your mother all you have told me—and more, if you have more to say. She is better prepared for you than I was. We will take to-day to think of it, Magdalen; and to-morrow you shall know, and Frank shall know, what we decide."

Her eyes brightened, as they looked into his face and saw the decision there already, with the double penetration of her womanhood and her love. Happy, and beautiful in her happiness, she put his hand to her lips, and went, without hesitation, into the morning-room. There, her father's words had smoothed the way for her; there, the first shock of the surprise was past and over, and only the pleasure of it remained. Her mother had been her age once; her mother would know how fond she was of Frank. So the coming interview was anticipated in her thoughts; and—except that there was an unaccountable appearance of restraint in Mrs. Vanstone's first reception of her—was anticipated aright. After a little, the mother's questions came more and more unreservedly from the sweet, unforgotten experience of the mother's heart. She lived again through her own young days of hope and love in Magdalen's replies.

The next morning the all-important decision was announced in words. Mr. Vanstone took his daughter upstairs into her mother's room, and there placed before her the result of the yesterday's consultation, and of the night's reflection which had followed it. He spoke with perfect kindness and self-possession of manner—but in fewer and more serious words than usual; and he held his wife's hand tenderly in his own all through the interview.

He informed Magdalen that neither he nor her mother felt themselves justified in blaming her attachment to Frank. It had been in part, perhaps, the natural consequence of her childish familiarity with him; in part, also, the result of the closer intimacy between them which the theatrical entertainment had necessarily produced. At the same time, it was now the duty of her parents to put that attachment, on both sides, to a proper test—for her sake, because her happy future was their dearest care; for Frank's sake, because they were bound to give him the opportunity of showing himself worthy of the trust confided in him. They were both conscious of being strongly prejudiced in Frank's favor. His father's eccentric conduct had made the lad the object of their compassion and their care from his earliest years. He (and his younger brothers) had almost filled the places to them of those other children of their own whom they had lost. Although they firmly believed their good opinion of Frank to be well founded—still, in the interest of their daughter's happiness, it was necessary to put that opinion firmly to the proof, by fixing certain conditions, and by interposing a year of delay between the contemplated marriage and the present time.

During that year, Frank was to remain at the office in London; his employers being informed beforehand that family circumstances prevented his accepting their offer of employment in China. He was to consider this concession as a recognition of the attachment between Magdalen and himself, on certain terms only. If, during the year of probation, he failed to justify the confidence placed in him—a confidence which had led Mr. Vanstone to take unreservedly upon himself the whole responsibility of Frank's future prospects—the marriage scheme was to be considered, from that moment, as at an end. If, on the other hand, the result to which Mr. Vanstone confidently looked forward really occurred—if Frank's probationary year proved his claim to the most precious trust that could be placed in his hands—then Magdalen herself should reward him with all that a woman can bestow; and the future, which his present employers had placed before him as the result of a five years' residence in China, should be realized in one year's time, by the dowry of his young wife.

As her father drew that picture of the future, the outburst of Magdalen's gratitude could no longer be restrained. She was deeply touched—she spoke from her inmost heart. Mr. Vanstone waited until his daughter and his wife were composed again; and then added the last words of explanation which were now left for him to speak.

"You understand, my love," he said, "that I am not anticipating Frank's living in idleness on his wife's means? My plan for him is that he should still profit by the interest which his present employers take in him. Their knowledge of affairs in the City will soon place a good partnership at his disposal, and you will give him the money to buy it out of hand. I shall limit the sum, my dear, to half your fortune; and the other half I shall have settled upon yourself. We shall all be alive and hearty, I hope"—he looked tenderly at his wife as he said those words—"all alive and hearty at the year's end. But if I am gone, Magdalen, it will make no difference. My will—made long before I ever thought of having a son-in-law divides my fortune into two equal parts. One part goes to your mother; and the other part is fairly divided between my children. You will have your share on your wedding-day (and Norah will have hers when she marries) from my own hand, if I live; and under my will if I die. There! there! no gloomy faces," he said, with a momentary return of his every-day good spirits. "Your mother and I mean to live and see Frank a great merchant. I shall leave you, my dear, to enlighten the son on our new projects, while I walk over to the cottage—"

He stopped; his eyebrows contracted a little; and he looked aside hesitatingly at Mrs. Vanstone.

"What must you do at the cottage, papa?" asked Magdalen, after having vainly waited for him to finish the sentence of his own accord.

"I must consult Frank's father," he replied. "We must not forget that Mr. Clare's consent is still wanting to settle this matter. And as time presses, and we don't know what difficulties he may not raise, the sooner I see him the better."

He gave that answer in low, altered tones; and rose from his chair in a half-reluctant, half-resigned manner, which Magdalen observed with secret alarm.

She glanced inquiringly at her mother. To all appearance, Mrs. Vanstone had been alarmed by the change in him also. She looked anxious and uneasy; she turned her face away on the sofa pillow—turned it suddenly, as if she was in pain.

"Are you not well, mamma?" asked Magdalen.

"Quite well, my love," said Mrs. Vanstone, shortly and sharply, without turning round. "Leave me a little—I only want rest."

Magdalen went out with her father.

"Papa!" she whispered anxiously, as they descended the stairs; "you don't think Mr. Clare will say No?"

"I can't tell beforehand," answered Mr. Vanstone. "I hope he will say Yes."

"There is no reason why he should say anything else—is there?"

She put the question faintly, while he was getting his hat and stick; and he did not appear to hear her. Doubting whether she should repeat it or not, she accompanied him as far as the garden, on his way to Mr. Clare's cottage. He stopped her on the lawn, and sent her back to the house.

"You have nothing on your head, my dear," he said. "If you want to be in the garden, don't forget how hot the sun is—don't come out without your hat."

He walked on toward the cottage.

She waited a moment, and looked after him. She missed the customary flourish of his stick; she saw his little Scotch terrier, who had run out at his heels, barking and capering about him unnoticed. He was out of spirits: he was strangely out of spirits. What did it mean?

CHAPTER X.

ON returning to the house, Magdalen felt her shoulder suddenly touched from behind as she crossed the hall. She turned and confronted her sister. Before she could ask any questions, Norah confusedly addressed her, in these words: "I beg your pardon; I beg you to forgive me."

Magdalen looked at her sister in astonishment. All memory, on her side, of the sharp words which had passed between them in the shrubbery was lost in the new interests that now absorbed her; lost as completely as if the angry interview had never taken place. "Forgive you!" she repeated, amazedly. "What for?"

"I have heard of your new prospects," pursued Norah, speaking with a mechanical submissiveness of manner which seemed almost ungracious; "I wished to set things right between us; I wished to say I was sorry for what happened. Will you forget it? Will you forget and forgive what happened in the shrubbery?" She tried to proceed; but her inveterate reserve—or, perhaps, her obstinate reliance on her own opinions—silenced her at those last words. Her face clouded over on a sudden. Before her sister could answer her, she turned away abruptly and ran upstairs.

The door of the library opened, before Magdalen could follow her; and Miss Garth advanced to express the sentiments proper to the occasion.

They were not the mechanically-submissive sentiments which Magdalen had just heard. Norah had struggled against her rooted distrust of Frank, in deference to the unanswerable decision of both her parents in his favor; and had suppressed the open expression of her antipathy, though the feeling itself remained unconquered. Miss Garth had made no such concession to the master and mistress of the house. She had hitherto held the position of a high authority on all domestic questions; and she flatly declined to get off her pedestal in deference to any change in the family circumstances, no matter how amazing or how unexpected that change might be.

"Pray accept my congratulations," said Miss Garth, bristling all over with implied objections to Frank—"my congratulations, and my apologies. When I caught you kissing Mr. Francis Clare in the summer-house, I had no idea you were engaged in carrying out the intentions of your parents. I offer no opinion on the subject. I merely regret my own accidental appearance in the character of an Obstacle to the course of true-love—which appears to run smooth in summer-houses, whatever Shakespeare may say to the contrary. Consider me for the future, if you please, as an Obstacle removed. May you be happy!" Miss Garth's lips closed on that last sentence like a trap, and Miss Garth's eyes looked ominously prophetic into the matrimonial future.

If Magdalen's anxieties had not been far too serious to allow her the customary free use of her tongue, she would have been ready on the instant with an appropriately satirical answer. As it was, Miss Garth simply irritated her. "Pooh!" she said—and ran upstairs to her sister's room.

She knocked at the door, and there was no answer. She tried the door, and it resisted her from the inside. The sullen, unmanageable Norah was locked in.

Under other circumstances, Magdalen would not have been satisfied with knocking—she would have called through the door loudly and more loudly, till the house was disturbed and she had carried her point. But the doubts and fears of the morning had unnerved her already. She went downstairs again softly, and took her hat from the stand in the hall. "He told me to put my hat on," she said to herself, with a meek filial docility which was totally out of her character.

She went into the garden, on the shrubbery side; and waited there to catch the first sight of her father on his return. Half an hour passed; forty minutes passed—and then his voice reached her from among the distant trees. "Come in to heel!" she heard him call out loudly to the dog. Her face turned pale. "He's angry with Snap!" she exclaimed to herself in a whisper. The next minute he appeared in view; walking rapidly, with his head down and Snap at his heels in disgrace. The sudden excess of her alarm as she observed those ominous signs of something wrong rallied her natural energy, and determined her desperately on knowing the worst. She walked straight forward to meet her father.

"Your face tells your news," she said faintly. "Mr. Clare has been as heartless as usual—Mr. Clare has said No?"

Her father turned on her with a sudden severity, so entirely unparalleled in her experience of him that she started back in downright terror.

"Magdalen!" he said; "whenever you speak of my old friend and neighbor again, bear this in mind: Mr. Clare has just laid me under an obligation which I shall remember gratefully to the end of my life."

He stopped suddenly after saying those remarkable words. Seeing that he had startled her, his natural kindness prompted him instantly to soften the reproof, and to end the suspense from which she was plainly suffering. "Give me a kiss, my love," he resumed; "and I'll tell you in return that Mr. Clare has said—YES."

She attempted to thank him; but the sudden luxury of relief was too much for her. She could only cling round his neck in silence. He felt her trembling from head to foot, and said a few words to calm her. At the altered tones of his master's voice, Snap's meek tail re-appeared fiercely from between his legs; and Snap's lungs modestly tested his position with a brief, experimental bark. The dog's quaintly appropriate assertion of himself on his old footing was the interruption of all others which was best fitted to restore Magdalen to herself. She caught the shaggy little terrier up in her arms and kissed him next. "You darling," she exclaimed, "you're almost as glad as I am!" She turned again to her father, with a look of tender reproach. "You frightened me, papa," she said. "You were so unlike yourself."

"I shall be right again to-morrow, my dear. I am a little upset to-day."

"Not by me?"

"No, no."

"By something you have heard at Mr. Clare's?"

"Yes—nothing you need alarm yourself about; nothing that won't wear off by to-morrow. Let me go now, my dear; I have a letter to write; and I want to speak to your mother."

He left her and went on to the house. Magdalen lingered a little on the lawn, to feel all the happiness of her new sensations—then turned away toward the shrubbery to enjoy the higher luxury of communicating them. The dog followed her. She whistled, and clapped her hands. "Find him!" she said, with beaming eyes. "Find Frank!" Snap scampered into the shrubbery, with a bloodthirsty snarl at starting. Perhaps he had mistaken his young mistress and considered himself her emissary in search of a rat?

Meanwhile, Mr. Vanstone entered the house. He met his wife slowly descending the stairs, and advanced to give her his arm. "How has it ended?" she asked, anxiously, as he led her to the sofa.

"Happily—as we hoped it would," answered her husband. "My old friend has justified my opinion of him."

"Thank God!" said Mrs. Vanstone, fervently. "Did you feel it, love?" she asked, as her husband arranged the sofa pillows—"did you feel it as painfully as I feared you would?"

"I had a duty to do, my dear—and I did it."

After replying in those terms, he hesitated. Apparently, he had something more to say—something, perhaps, on the subject of that passing uneasiness of mind which had been produced by his interview with Mr. Clare, and which Magdalen's questions had obliged him to acknowledge. A look at his wife decided his doubts in the negative. He only asked if she felt comfortable; and then turned away to leave the room.

"Must you go?" she asked.

"I have a letter to write, my dear."

"Anything about Frank?"

"No: to-morrow will do for that. A letter to Mr. Pendril. I want him here immediately."

"Business, I suppose?"

"Yes, my dear—business."

He went out, and shut himself into the little front room, close to the hall door, which was called his study. By nature and habit the most procrastinating of letter-writers, he now inconsistently opened his desk and took up the pen without a moment's delay. His letter was long enough to occupy three pages of note-paper; it was written with a readiness of expression and a rapidity of hand which seldom characterized his proceedings when engaged over his ordinary correspondence. He wrote the address as follows: "Immediate—William Pendril, Esq., Serle Street, Lincoln's Inn, London"—then pushed the letter away from him, and sat at the table, drawing lines on the blotting-paper with his pen, lost in thought. "No," he said to himself; "I can do nothing more till Pendril comes." He rose; his face brightened as he put the stamp on the envelope. The writing of the letter had sensibly relieved him, and his whole bearing showed it as he left the room.

On the doorstep he found Norah and Miss Garth, setting forth together for a walk.

"Which way are you going?" he asked. "Anywhere near the post-office? I wish you would post this letter for me, Norah. It is very important—so important that I hardly like to trust it to Thomas, as usual."

Norah at once took charge of the letter.

"If you look, my dear," continued her father, "you will see that I am writing to Mr. Pendril. I expect him here to-morrow afternoon. Will you give the necessary directions, Miss Garth? Mr. Pendril will sleep here to-morrow night, and stay over Sunday.—Wait a minute! Today is Friday. Surely I had an engagement for Saturday afternoon?" He consulted his pocketbook and read over one of the entries, with a look of annoyance. "Grailsea Mill, three o'clock, Saturday. Just the time when Pendril will be here; and I must be at home to see him. How can I manage it? Monday will be too late for my business at Grailsea. I'll go to-day, instead; and take my chance of catching the miller at his dinner-time." He looked at his watch. "No time for driving; I must do it by railway. If I go at once, I shall catch the down train at our station, and get on to Grailsea. Take care of the letter, Norah. I won't keep dinner waiting; if the return train doesn't suit, I'll borrow a gig and get back in that way."

As he took up his hat, Magdalen appeared at the door, returning from her interview with Frank. The hurry of her father's movements attracted her attention; and she asked him where he was going.

"To Grailsea," replied Mr. Vanstone. "Your business, Miss Magdalen, has got in the way of mine—and mine must give way to it."

He spoke those parting words in his old hearty manner; and left them, with the old characteristic flourish of his trusty stick.

"My business!" said Magdalen. "I thought my business was done."

Miss Garth pointed significantly to the letter in Norah's hand. "Your business, beyond all doubt," she said. "Mr. Pendril is coming tomorrow; and Mr. Vanstone seems remarkably anxious about it. Law, and its attendant troubles already! Governesses who look in at summer-house doors are not the only obstacles to the course of true-love. Parchment is sometimes an obstacle. I hope you may find Parchment as pliable as I am—I wish you well through it. Now, Norah!"

Miss Garth's second shaft struck as harmless as the first. Magdalen had returned to the house, a little vexed; her interview with Frank having been interrupted by a messenger from Mr. Clare, sent to summon the son into the father's presence. Although it had been agreed at the private interview between Mr. Vanstone and Mr. Clare that the questions discussed that morning should not be communicated to the children until the year of probation was at an end—-and although under these circumstances Mr. Clare had nothing to tell Frank which Magdalen could not communicate to him much more agreeably—the philosopher was not the less resolved on personally informing his son of the parental concession which rescued him from Chinese exile. The result was a sudden summons to the cottage, which startled Magdalen, but which did not appear to take Frank by surprise. His filial experience penetrated the mystery of Mr. Clare's motives easily enough. "When my father's in spirits," he said, sulkily, "he likes to bully me about my good luck. This message means that he's going to bully me now."

"Don't go," suggested Magdalen.

"I must," rejoined Frank. "I shall never hear the last of it if I don't. He's primed and loaded, and he means to go off. He went off, once, when the engineer took me; he went off, twice, when the office in the City took me; and he's going off, thrice, now you've taken me. If it wasn't for you, I should wish I had never been born. Yes; your father's been kind to me, I know—and I should have gone to China, if it hadn't been for him. I'm sure I'm very much obliged. Of course, we have no right to expect anything else—still it's discouraging to keep us waiting a year, isn't it?"

Magdalen stopped his mouth by a summary process, to which even Frank submitted gratefully. At the same time, she did not forget to set down his discontent to the right side. "How fond he is of me!" she thought. "A year's waiting is quite a hardship to him." She returned to the house, secretly regretting that she had not heard more of Frank's complimentary complaints. Miss Garth's elaborate satire, addressed to her while she was in this frame of mind, was a purely gratuitous waste of Miss Garth's breath. What did Magdalen care for satire? What do Youth and Love ever care for except themselves? She never even said as much as "Pooh!" this time. She laid aside her hat in serene silence, and sauntered languidly into the morning-room to keep her mother company. She lunched on dire forebodings of a quarrel between Frank and his father, with accidental interruptions in the shape of cold chicken and cheese-cakes. She trifled away half an hour at the piano; and played, in that time, selections from the Songs of Mendelssohn, the Mazurkas of Chopin, the Operas of Verdi, and the Sonatas of Mozart—all of whom had combined together on this occasion and produced one immortal work, entitled "Frank." She closed the piano and went up to her room, to dream away the hours luxuriously in visions of her married future. The green shutters were closed, the easy-chair was pushed in front of the glass, the maid was summoned as usual; and the comb assisted the mistress's reflections, through the medium of the mistress's hair, till heat and idleness asserted their narcotic influences together, and Magdalen fell asleep.

It was past three o'clock when she woke. On going downstairs again she found her mother, Norah and Miss Garth all sitting together enjoying the shade and the coolness under the open portico in front of the house.

Norah had the railway time-table in her hand. They had been discussing the chances of Mr. Vanstone's catching the return train and getting back in good time. That topic had led them, next, to his business errand at Grailsea—an errand of kindness, as usual; undertaken for the benefit of the miller, who had been his old farm-servant, and who was now hard pressed by serious pecuniary difficulties. From this they had glided insensibly into a subject often repeated among them, and never exhausted by repetition—the praise of Mr. Vanstone himself. Each one of the three had some experience of her own to relate of his simple, generous nature. The conversation seemed to be almost painfully interesting to his wife. She was too near the time of her trial now not to feel nervously sensitive to the one subject which always held the foremost place in her heart. Her eyes overflowed as Magdalen joined the little group under the portico; her frail hand trembled as it signed to her youngest daughter to take the vacant chair by her side. "We were talking of your father," she said, softly. "Oh, my love, if your married life is only as happy—" Her voice failed her; she put her handkerchief hurriedly over her face and rested her head on Magdalen's shoulder. Norah looked appealingly to Miss Garth, who at once led the conversation back to the more trivial subject of Mr. Vanstone's return. "We have all been wondering," she said, with a significant look at Magdalen, "whether your father will leave Grailsea in time to catch the train—or whether he will miss it and be obliged to drive back. What do you say?"

"I say, papa will miss the train," replied Magdalen, taking Miss Garth's hint with her customary quickness. "The last thing he attends to at Grailsea will be the business that brings him there. Whenever he has business to do, he always puts it off to the last moment, doesn't he, mamma?"

The question roused her mother exactly as Magdalen had intended it should. "Not when his errand is an errand of kindness," said Mrs. Vanstone. "He has gone to help the miller in a very pressing difficulty—"

"And don't you know what he'll do?" persisted Magdalen. "He'll romp with the miller's children, and gossip with the mother, and hob-and-nob with the father. At the last moment when he has got five minutes left to catch the train, he'll say: 'Let's go into the counting-house and look at the books.' He'll find the books dreadfully complicated; he'll suggest sending for an accountant; he'll settle the business off hand, by lending the money in the meantime; he'll jog back comfortably in the miller's gig; and he'll tell us all how pleasant the lanes were in the cool of the evening."

The little character-sketch which these words drew was too faithful a likeness not to be recognized. Mrs. Vanstone showed her appreciation of it by a smile. "When your father returns," she said, "we will put your account of his proceedings to the test. I think," she continued, rising languidly from her chair, "I had better go indoors again now and rest on the sofa till he comes back."

The little group under the portico broke up. Magdalen slipped away into the garden to hear Frank's account of the interview with his father. The other three ladies entered the house together. When Mrs. Vanstone was comfortably established on the sofa, Norah and Miss Garth left her to repose, and withdrew to the library to look over the last parcel of books from London.

It was a quiet, cloudless summer's day. The heat was tempered by a light western breeze; the voices of laborers at work in a field near reached the house cheerfully; the clock-bell of the village church as it struck the quarters floated down the wind with a clearer ring, a louder melody than usual. Sweet odors from field and flower-garden, stealing in at the open windows, filled the house with their fragrance; and the birds in Norah's aviary upstairs sang the song of their happiness exultingly in the sun.

As the church clock struck the quarter past four, the morning-room door opened; and Mrs. Vanstone crossed the hall alone. She had tried vainly to compose herself. She was too restless to lie still and sleep. For a moment she directed her steps toward the portico—then turned, and looked about her, doubtful where to go, or what to do next. While she was still hesitating, the half-open door of her husband's study attracted her attention. The room seemed to be in sad confusion. Drawers were left open; coats and hats, account-books and papers, pipes and fishing-rods were all scattered about together. She went in, and pushed the door to—but so gently that she still left it ajar. "It will amuse me to put his room to rights," she thought to herself. "I should like to do something for him before I am down on my bed, helpless." She began to arrange his drawers, and found his banker's book lying open in one of them. "My poor dear, how careless he is! The servants might have seen all his affairs, if I had not happened to have looked in." She set the drawers right; and then turned to the multifarious litter on a side-table. A little old-fashioned music-book appeared among the scattered papers, with her name written in it, in faded ink. She blushed like a young girl in the first happiness of the discovery. "How good he is to me! He remembers my poor old music-book, and keeps it for my sake." As she sat down by the table and opened the book, the bygone time came back to her in all its tenderness. The clock struck the half-hour, struck the three-quarters—and still she sat there, with the music-book on her lap, dreaming happily over the old songs; thinking gratefully of the golden days when his hand had turned the pages for her, when his voice had whispered the words which no woman's memory ever forgets.

Norah roused herself from the volume she was reading, and glanced at the clock on the library mantel-piece.

"If papa comes back by the railway," she said, "he will be here in ten minutes."

Miss Garth started, and looked up drowsily from the book which was just dropping out of her hand.

"I don't think he will come by train," she replied. "He will jog back—as Magdalen flippantly expressed it—in the miller's gig."

As she said the words, there was a knock at the library door. The footman appeared, and addressed himself to Miss Garth.

"A person wishes to see you, ma'am."

"Who is it?"

"I don't know, ma'am. A stranger to me—a respectable-looking man—and he said he particularly wished to see you."

Miss Garth went out into the hall. The footman closed the library door after her, and withdrew down the kitchen stairs.

The man stood just inside the door, on the mat. His eyes wandered, his face was pale—he looked ill; he looked frightened. He trifled nervously with his cap, and shifted it backward and forward, from one hand to the other.

"You wanted to see me?" said Miss Garth.

"I beg your pardon, ma'am.—You are not Mrs. Vanstone, are you?"

"Certainly not. I am Miss Garth. Why do you ask the question?"

"I am employed in the clerk's office at Grailsea Station—"

"Yes?"

"I am sent here—"

He stopped again. His wandering eyes looked down at the mat, and his restless hands wrung his cap harder and harder. He moistened his dry lips, and tried once more.

"I am sent here on a very serious errand."

"Serious to me?"

"Serious to all in this house."

Miss Garth took one step nearer to him—took one steady look at his face. She turned cold in the summer heat. "Stop!" she said, with a sudden distrust, and glanced aside anxiously at the door of the morning-room. It was safely closed. "Tell me the worst; and don't speak loud. There has been an accident. Where?"

"On the railway. Close to Grailsea Station."

"The up-train to London?"

"No: the down-train at one-fifty—"

"God Almighty help us! The train Mr. Vanstone traveled by to Grailsea?"

"The same. I was sent here by the up-train; the line was just cleared in time for it. They wouldn't write—they said I must see 'Miss Garth,' and tell her. There are seven passengers badly hurt; and two—"

The next word failed on his lips; he raised his hand in the dead silence. With eyes that opened wide in horror, he raised his hand and pointed over Miss Garth's shoulder.

She turned a little, and looked back.

Face to face with her, on the threshold of the study door, stood the mistress of the house. She held her old music-book clutched fast mechanically in both hands. She stood, the specter of herself. With a dreadful vacancy in her eyes, with a dreadful stillness in her voice, she repeated the man's last words:

"Seven passengers badly hurt; and two—"

Her tortured fingers relaxed their hold; the book dropped from them; she sank forward heavily. Miss Garth caught her before she fell—caught her, and turned upon the man, with the wife's swooning body in her arms, to hear the husband's fate.

"The harm is done," she said; "you may speak out. Is he wounded, or dead?"

"Dead."

CHAPTER XI.

THE sun sank lower; the western breeze floated cool and fresh into the house. As the evening advanced, the cheerful ring of the village clock came nearer and nearer. Field and flower-garden felt the influence of the hour, and shed their sweetest fragrance. The birds in Norah's aviary sunned themselves in the evening stillness, and sang their farewell gratitude to the dying day.

Staggered in its progress for a time only, the pitiless routine of the house went horribly on its daily way. The panic-stricken servants took their blind refuge in the duties proper to the hour. The footman softly laid the table for dinner. The maid sat waiting in senseless doubt, with the hot-water jugs for the bedrooms ranged near her in their customary row. The gardener, who had been ordered to come to his master, with vouchers for money that he had paid in excess of his instructions, said his character was dear to him, and left the vouchers at his appointed time. Custom that never yields, and Death that never spares, met on the wreck of human happiness—and Death gave way.

Heavily the thunder-clouds of Affliction had gathered over the house—heavily, but not at their darkest yet. At five, that evening, the shock of the calamity had struck its blow. Before another hour had passed, the disclosure of the husband's sudden death was followed by the suspense of the wife's mortal peril. She lay helpless on her widowed bed; her own life, and the life of her unborn child, trembling in the balance.

But one mind still held possession of its resources—but one guiding spirit now moved helpfully in the house of mourning.

If Miss Garth's early days had been passed as calmly and as happily as her later life at Combe-Raven, she might have sunk under the cruel necessities of the time. But the governess's youth had been tried in the ordeal of family affliction; and she met her terrible duties with the steady courage of a woman who had learned to suffer. Alone, she had faced the trial of telling the daughters that they were fatherless. Alone, she now struggled to sustain them, when the dreadful certainty of their bereavement was at last impressed on their minds.

Her least anxiety was for the elder sister. The agony of Norah's grief had forced its way outward to the natural relief of tears. It was not so with Magdalen. Tearless and speechless, she sat in the room where the revelation of her father's death had first reached her; her face, unnaturally petrified by the sterile sorrow of old age—a white, changeless blank, fearful to look at. Nothing roused, nothing melted her. She only said, "Don't speak to me; don't touch me. Let me bear it by myself"—and fell silent again. The first great grief which had darkened the sisters' lives had, as it seemed, changed their everyday characters already.

The twilight fell, and faded; and the summer night came brightly. As the first carefully shaded light was kindled in the sick-room, the physician, who had been summoned from Bristol, arrived to consult with the medical attendant of the family. He could give no comfort: he could only say, "We must try, and hope. The shock which struck her, when she overheard the news of her husband's death, has prostrated her strength at the time when she needed it most. No effort to preserve her shall be neglected. I will stay here for the night."

He opened one of the windows to admit more air as he spoke. The view overlooked the drive in front of the house and the road outside. Little groups of people were standing before the lodge-gates, looking in. "If those persons make any noise," said the doctor, "they must be warned away." There was no need to warn them: they were only the laborers who had worked on the dead man's property, and here and there some women and children from the village. They were all thinking of him—some talking of him—and it quickened their sluggish minds to look at his house. The gentlefolks thereabouts were mostly kind to them (the men said), but none like him. The women whispered to each other of his comforting ways when he came into their cottages. "He was a cheerful man, poor soul; and thoughtful of us, too: he never came in and stared at meal-times; the rest of 'em help us, and scold us—all he ever said was, better luck next time." So they stood and talked of him, and looked at his house and grounds and moved off clumsily by twos and threes, with the dim sense that the sight of his pleasant face would never comfort them again. The dullest head among them knew, that night, that the hard ways of poverty would be all the harder to walk on, now he was gone.

A little later, news was brought to the bed-chamber door that old Mr. Clare had come alone to the house, and was waiting in the hall below, to hear what the physician said. Miss Garth was not able to go down to him herself: she sent a message. He said to the servant, "I'll come and ask again, in two hours' time"—and went out slowly. Unlike other men in all things else, the sudden death of his old friend had produced no discernible change in him. The feeling implied in the errand of inquiry that had brought him to the house was the one betrayal of human sympathy which escaped the rugged, impenetrable old man.

He came again, when the two hours had expired; and this time Miss Garth saw him.

They shook hands in silence. She waited; she nerved herself to hear him speak of his lost friend. No: he never mentioned the dreadful accident, he never alluded to the dreadful death. He said these words, "Is she better, or worse?" and said no more. Was the tribute of his grief for the husband sternly suppressed under the expression of his anxiety for the wife? The nature of the man, unpliably antagonistic to the world and the world's customs, might justify some such interpretation of his conduct as this. He repeated his question, "Is she better, or worse?"

Miss Garth answered him:

"No better; if there is any change, it is a change for the worse."

They spoke those words at the window of the morning-room which opened on the garden. Mr. Clare paused, after hearing the reply to his inquiry, stepped out on to the walk, then turned on a sudden, and spoke again:

"Has the doctor given her up?" he asked.

"He has not concealed from us that she is in danger. We can only pray for her."

The old man laid his hand on Miss Garth's arm as she answered him, and looked her attentively in the face.

"You believe in prayer?" he said.

Miss Garth drew sorrowfully back from him.

"You might have spared me that question sir, at such a time as this."

He took no notice of her answer; his eyes were still fastened on her face.

"Pray!" he said. "Pray as you never prayed before, for the preservation of Mrs. Vanstone's life."

He left her. His voice and manner implied some unutterable dread of the future, which his words had not confessed. Miss Garth followed him into the garden, and called to him. He heard her, but he never turned back: he quickened his pace, as if he desired to avoid her. She watched him across the lawn in the warm summer moonlight. She saw his white, withered hands, saw them suddenly against the black background of the shrubbery, raised and wrung above his head. They dropped—the trees shrouded him in darkness—he was gone.

Miss Garth went back to the suffering woman, with the burden on her mind of one anxiety more.

It was then past eleven o'clock. Some little time had elapsed since she had seen the sisters and spoken to them. The inquiries she addressed to one of the female servants only elicited the information that they were both in their rooms. She delayed her return to the mother's bedside to say her parting words of comfort to the daughters, before she left them for the night. Norah's room was the nearest. She softly opened the door and looked in. The kneeling figure by the bedside told her that God's help had found the fatherless daughter in her affliction. Grateful tears gathered in her eyes as she looked: she softly closed the door, and went on to Magdalen's room. There doubt stayed her feet at the threshold, and she waited for a moment before going in.

A sound in the room caught her ear—the monotonous rustling of a woman's dress, now distant, now near; passing without cessation from end to end over the floor—a sound which told her that Magdalen was pacing to and fro in the secrecy of her own chamber. Miss Garth knocked. The rustling ceased; the door was opened, and the sad young face confronted her, locked in its cold despair; the large light eyes looked mechanically into hers, as vacant and as tearless as ever.

That look wrung the heart of the faithful woman, who had trained her and loved her from a child. She took Magdalen tenderly in her arms.

"Oh, my love," she said, "no tears yet! Oh, if I could see you as I have seen Norah! Speak to me, Magdalen—try if you can speak to me."

She tried, and spoke:

"Norah," she said, "feels no remorse. He was not serving Norah's interests when he went to his death: he was serving mine."

With that terrible answer, she put her cold lips to Miss Garth's cheek.

"Let me bear it by myself," she said, and gently closed the door.

Again Miss Garth waited at the threshold, and again the sound of the rustling dress passed to and fro—now far, now near—to and fro with a cruel, mechanical regularity, that chilled the warmest sympathy, and daunted the boldest hope.

The night passed. It had been agreed, if no change for the better showed itself by the morning, that the London physician whom Mrs. Vanstone had consulted some months since should be summoned to the house on the next day. No change for the better appeared, and the physician was sent for.

As the morning advanced, Frank came to make inquiries from the cottage. Had Mr. Clare intrusted to his son the duty which he had personally performed on the previous day through reluctance to meet Miss Garth again after what he had said to her? It might be so. Frank could throw no light on the subject; he was not in his father's confidence. He looked pale and bewildered. His first inquiries after Magdalen showed how his weak nature had been shaken by the catastrophe. He was not capable of framing his own questions: the words faltered on his lips, and the ready tears came into his eyes. Miss Garth's heart warmed to him for the first time. Grief has this that is noble in it—it accepts all sympathy, come whence it may. She encouraged the lad by a few kind words, and took his hand at parting.

Before noon Frank returned with a second message. His father desired to know whether Mr. Pendril was not expected at Combe-Raven on that day. If the lawyer's arrival was looked for, Frank was directed to be in attendance at the station, and to take him to the cottage, where a bed would be placed at his disposal. This message took Miss Garth by surprise. It showed that Mr. Clare had been made acquainted with his dead friend's purpose of sending for Mr. Pendril. Was the old man's thoughtful offer of hospitality another indirect expression of the natural human distress which he perversely concealed? or was he aware of some secret necessity for Mr. Pendril's presence, of which the bereaved family had been kept in total ignorance? Miss Garth was too heart-sick and hopeless to dwell on either question. She told Frank that Mr. Pendril had been expected at three o'clock, and sent him back with her thanks.

Shortly after his departure, such anxieties on Magdalen's account as her mind was now able to feel were relieved by better news than her last night's experience had inclined her to hope for. Norah's influence had been exerted to rouse her sister; and Norah's patient sympathy had set the prisoned grief free. Magdalen had suffered severely—suffered inevitably, with such a nature as hers—in the effort that relieved her. The healing tears had not come gently; they had burst from her with a torturing, passionate vehemence—but Norah had never left her till the struggle was over, and the calm had come. These better tidings encouraged Miss Garth to withdraw to her own room, and to take the rest which she needed sorely. Worn out in body and mind, she slept from sheer exhaustion—slept heavily and dreamless for some hours. It was between three and four in the afternoon when she was roused by one of the female servants. The woman had a note in her hand—a note left by Mr. Clare the younger, with a message desiring that it might be delivered to Miss Garth immediately. The name written in the lower corner of the envelope was "William Pendril." The lawyer had arrived.

Miss Garth opened the note. After a few first sentences of sympathy and condolence, the writer announced his arrival at Mr. Clare's; and then proceeded, apparently in his professional capacity, to make a very startling request.

"If," he wrote, "any change for the better in Mrs. Vanstone should take place—whether it is only an improvement for the time, or whether it is the permanent improvement for which we all hope—in either case I entreat you to let me know of it immediately. It is of the last importance that I should see her, in the event of her gaining strength enough to give me her attention for five minutes, and of her being able at the expiration of that time to sign her name. May I beg that you will communicate my request, in the strictest confidence, to the medical men in attendance? They will understand, and you will understand, the vital importance I attach to this interview when I tell you that I have arranged to defer to it all other business claims on me; and that I hold myself in readiness to obey your summons at any hour of the day or night."

In those terms the letter ended. Miss Garth read it twice over. At the second reading the request which the lawyer now addressed to her, and the farewell words which had escaped Mr. Clare's lips the day before, connected themselves vaguely in her mind. There was some other serious interest in suspense, known to Mr. Pendril and known to Mr. Clare, besides the first and foremost interest of Mrs. Vanstone's recovery. Whom did it affect? The children? Were they threatened by some new calamity which their mother's signature might avert? What did it mean? Did it mean that Mr. Vanstone had died without leaving a will?

In her distress and confusion of mind Miss Garth was incapable of reasoning with herself, as she might have reasoned at a happier time. She hastened to the antechamber of Mrs. Vanstone's room; and, after explaining Mr. Pendril's position toward the family, placed his letter in the hands of the medical men. They both answered, without hesitation, to the same purpose. Mrs. Vanstone's condition rendered any such interview as the lawyer desired a total impossibility. If she rallied from her present prostration, Miss Garth should be at once informed of the improvement. In the meantime, the answer to Mr. Pendril might be conveyed in one word—Impossible.

"You see what importance Mr. Pendril attaches to the interview?" said Miss Garth.

Yes: both the doctors saw it.

"My mind is lost and confused, gentlemen, in this dreadful suspense. Can you either of you guess why the signature is wanted? or what the object of the interview may be? I have only seen Mr. Pendril when he has come here on former visits: I have no claim to justify me in questioning him. Will you look at the letter again? Do you think it implies that Mr. Vanstone has never made a will?"

"I think it can hardly imply that," said one of the doctors. "But, even supposing Mr. Vanstone to have died intestate, the law takes due care of the interests of his widow and his children—"

"Would it do so," interposed the other medical man, "if the property happened to be in land?"

"I am not sure in that case. Do you happen to know, Miss Garth, whether Mr. Vanstone's property was in money or in land?"

"In money," replied Miss Garth. "I have heard him say so on more than one occasion."

"Then I can relieve your mind by speaking from my own experience. The law, if he has died intestate, gives a third of his property to his widow, and divides the rest equally among his children."

"But if Mrs. Vanstone—"

"If Mrs. Vanstone should die," pursued the doctor, completing the question which Miss Garth had not the heart to conclude for herself, "I believe I am right in telling you that the property would, as a matter of legal course, go to the children. Whatever necessity there may be for the interview which Mr. Pendril requests, I can see no reason for connecting it with the question of Mr. Vanstone's presumed intestacy. But, by all means, put the question, for the satisfaction of your own mind, to Mr. Pendril himself."

Miss Garth withdrew to take the course which the doctor advised. After communicating to Mr. Pendril the medical decision which, thus far, refused him the interview that he sought, she added a brief statement of the legal question she had put to the doctors; and hinted delicately at her natural anxiety to be informed of the motives which had led the lawyer to make his request. The answer she received was guarded in the extreme: it did not impress her with a favorable opinion of Mr. Pendril. He confirmed the doctors' interpretation of the law in general terms only; expressed his intention of waiting at the cottage in the hope that a change for the better might yet enable Mrs. Vanstone to see him; and closed his letter without the slightest explanation of his motives, and without a word of reference to the question of the existence, or the non-existence, of Mr. Vanstone's will.

The marked caution of the lawyer's reply dwelt uneasily on Miss Garth's mind, until the long-expected event of the day recalled all her thoughts to her one absorbing anxiety on Mrs. Vanstone's account.

Early in the evening the physician from London arrived. He watched long by the bedside of the suffering woman; he remained longer still in consultation with his medical brethren; he went back again to the sick-room, before Miss Garth could prevail on him to communicate to her the opinion at which he had arrived.

When he called out into the antechamber for the second time, he silently took a chair by her side. She looked in his face; and the last faint hope died in her before he opened his lips.

"I must speak the hard truth," he said, gently. "All that can be done has been done. The next four-and-twenty hours, at most, will end your suspense. If Nature makes no effort in that time—I grieve to say it—you must prepare yourself for the worst."

Those words said all: they were prophetic of the end.

The night passed; and she lived through it. The next day came; and she lingered on till the clock pointed to five. At that hour the tidings of her husband's death had dealt the mortal blow. When the hour came round again, the mercy of God let her go to him in the better world. Her daughters were kneeling at the bedside as her spirit passed away. She left them unconscious of their presence; mercifully and happily insensible to the pang of the last farewell.

Her child survived her till the evening was on the wane and the sunset was dim in the quiet western heaven. As the darkness came, the light of the frail little life—faint and feeble from the first—flickered and went out. All that was earthly of mother and child lay, that night, on the same bed. The Angel of Death had done his awful bidding; and the two Sisters were left alone in the world.

CHAPTER XII.

EARLIER than usual on the morning of Thursday, the twenty-third of July, Mr. Clare appeared at the door of his cottage, and stepped out into the little strip of garden attached to his residence.

After he had taken a few turns backward and forward, alone, he was joined by a spare, quiet, gray-haired man, whose personal appearance was totally devoid of marked character of any kind; whose inexpressive face and conventionally-quiet manner presented nothing that attracted approval and nothing that inspired dislike. This was Mr. Pendril—this was the man on whose lips hung the future of the orphans at Combe-Raven.

"The time is getting on," he said, looking toward the shrubbery, as he joined Mr. Clare.

"My appointment with Miss Garth is for eleven o'clock: it only wants ten minutes of the hour."

"Are you to see her alone?" asked Mr. Clare.

"I left Miss Garth to decide—after warning her, first of all, that the circumstances I am compelled to disclose are of a very serious nature."

"And has she decided?"

"She writes me word that she mentioned my appointment, and repeated the warning I had given her to both the daughters. The elder of the two shrinks—and who can wonder at it?—from any discussion connected with the future which requires her presence so soon as the day after the funeral. The younger one appears to have expressed no opinion on the subject. As I understand it, she suffers herself to be passively guided by her sister's example. My interview, therefore, will take place with Miss Garth alone—and it is a very great relief to me to know it."

He spoke the last words with more emphasis and energy than seemed habitual to him. Mr. Clare stopped, and looked at his guest attentively.

"You are almost as old as I am, sir," he said. "Has all your long experience as a lawyer not hardened you yet?"

"I never knew how little it had hardened me," replied Mr. Pendril, quietly, "until I returned from London yesterday to attend the funeral. I was not warned that the daughters had resolved on following their parents to the grave. I think their presence made the closing scene of this dreadful calamity doubly painful, and doubly touching. You saw how the great concourse of people were moved by it—and they were in ignorance of the truth; they knew nothing of the cruel necessity which takes me to the house this morning. The sense of that necessity—and the sight of those poor girls at the time when I felt my hard duty toward them most painfully—shook me, as a man of my years and my way of life is not often shaken by any distress in the present or any suspense in the future. I have not recovered it this morning: I hardly feel sure of myself yet."

"A man's composure—when he is a man like you—comes with the necessity for it," said Mr. Clare. "You must have had duties to perform as trying in their way as the duty that lies before you this morning."

Mr. Pendril shook his head. "Many duties as serious; many stories more romantic. No duty so trying, no story so hopeless, as this."

With those words they parted. Mr. Pendril left the garden for the shrubbery path which led to Combe-Raven. Mr. Clare returned to the cottage.

On reaching the passage, he looked through the open door of his little parlor and saw Frank sitting there in idle wretchedness, with his head resting wearily on his hand.

"I have had an answer from your employers in London," said Mr. Clare. "In consideration of what has happened, they will allow the offer they made you to stand over for another month."

Frank changed color, and rose nervously from his chair.

"Are my prospects altered?" he asked. "Are Mr. Vanstone's plans for me not to be carried out? He told Magdalen his will had provided for her. She repeated his words to me; she said I ought to know all that his goodness and generosity had done for both of us. How can his death make a change? Has anything happened?"

"Wait till Mr. Pendril comes back from Combe-Raven," said his father. "Question him—don't question me."

The ready tears rose in Frank's eyes.

"You won't be hard on me?" he pleaded, faintly. "You won't expect me to go back to London without seeing Magdalen first?"

Mr. Clare looked thoughtfully at his son, and considered a little before he replied.

"You may dry your eyes," he said. "You shall see Magdalen before you go back."

He left the room, after making that reply, and withdrew to his study. The books lay ready to his hand as usual. He opened one of them and set himself to read in the customary manner. But his attention wandered; and his eyes strayed away, from time to time, to the empty chair opposite—the chair in which his old friend and gossip had sat and wrangled with him good-humoredly for many and many a year past. After a struggle with himself he closed the book. "D—n the chair!" he said: "it will talk of him; and I must listen." He reached down his pipe from the wall and mechanically filled it with tobacco. His hand shook, his eyes wandered back to the old place; and a heavy sigh came from him unwillingly. That empty chair was the only earthly argument for which he had no answer: his heart owned its defeat and moistened his eyes in spite of him. "He has got the better of me at last," said the rugged old man. "There is one weak place left in me still—and he has found it."

Meanwhile, Mr. Pendril entered the shrubbery, and followed the path which led to the lonely garden and the desolate house. He was met at the door by the man-servant, who was apparently waiting in expectation of his arrival.

"I have an appointment with Miss Garth. Is she ready to see me?"

"Quite ready, sir."

"Is she alone?"

"Yes, sir."

"In the room which was Mr. Vanstone's study?"

"In that room, sir."

The servant opened the door and Mr. Pendril went in.

The governess stood alone at the study window. The morning was oppressively hot, and she threw up the lower sash to admit more air into the room, as Mr. Pendril entered it.

They bowed to each other with a formal politeness, which betrayed on either side an uneasy sense of restraint. Mr. Pendril was one of the many men who appear superficially to the worst advantage, under the influence of strong mental agitation which it is necessary for them to control. Miss Garth, on her side, had not forgotten the ungraciously guarded terms in which the lawyer had replied to her letter; and the natural anxiety which she had felt on the subject of the interview was not relieved by any favorable opinion of the man who sought it. As they confronted each other in the silence of the summer's morning—both dressed in black; Miss Garth's hard features, gaunt and haggard with grief; the lawyer's cold, colorless face, void of all marked expression, suggestive of a business embarrassment and of nothing more—it would have been hard to find two persons less attractive externally to any ordinary sympathies than the two who had now met together, the one to tell, the other to hear, the secrets of the dead.

"I am sincerely sorry, Miss Garth, to intrude on you at such a time as this. But circumstances, as I have already explained, leave me no other choice."

"Will you take a seat, Mr. Pendril? You wished to see me in this room, I believe?"

"Only in this room, because Mr. Vanstone's papers are kept here, and I may find it necessary to refer to some of them."

After that formal interchange of question and answer, they sat down on either side of a table placed close under the window. One waited to speak, the other waited to hear. There was a momentary silence. Mr. Pendril broke it by referring to the young ladies, with the customary expressions of sympathy. Miss Garth answered him with the same ceremony, in the same conventional tone. There was a second pause of silence. The humming of flies among the evergreen shrubs under the window penetrated drowsily into the room; and the tramp of a heavy-footed cart-horse, plodding along the high-road beyond the garden, was as plainly audible in the stillness as if it had been night.

The lawyer roused his flagging resolution, and spoke to the purpose when he spoke next.

"You have some reason, Miss Garth," he began, "to feel not quite satisfied with my past conduct toward you, in one particular. During Mrs. Vanstone's fatal illness, you addressed a letter to me, making certain inquiries; which, while she lived, it was impossible for me to answer. Her deplorable death releases me from the restraint which I had imposed on myself, and permits—or, more properly, obliges me to speak. You shall know what serious reasons I had for waiting day and night in the hope of obtaining that interview which unhappily never took place; and in justice to Mr. Vanstone's memory, your own eyes shall inform you that he made his will."

He rose; unlocked a little iron safe in the corner of the room; and returned to the table with some folded sheets of paper, which he spread open under Miss Garth's eyes. When she had read the first words, "In the name of God, Amen," he turned the sheet, and pointed to the end of the next page. She saw the well-known signature: "Andrew Vanstone." She saw the customary attestations of the two witnesses; and the date of the document, reverting to a period of more than five years since. Having thus convinced her of the formality of the will, the lawyer interposed before she could question him, and addressed her in these words:

"I must not deceive you," he said. "I have my own reasons for producing this document."

"What reasons, sir?"

"You shall hear them. When you are in possession of the truth, these pages may help to preserve your respect for Mr. Vanstone's memory—"

Miss Garth started back in her chair.

"What do you mean?" she asked, with a stern straightforwardness.

He took no heed of the question; he went on as if she had not interrupted him.

"I have a second reason," he continued, "for showing you the will. If I can prevail on you to read certain clauses in it, under my superintendence, you will make your own discovery of the circumstances which I am here to disclose—circumstances so painful that I hardly know how to communicate them to you with my own lips."

Miss Garth looked him steadfastly in the face.

"Circumstances, sir, which affect the dead parents, or the living children?"

"Which affect the dead and the living both," answered the lawyer. "Circumstances, I grieve to say, which involve the future of Mr. Vanstone's unhappy daughters."

"Wait," said Miss Garth, "wait a little." She pushed her gray hair back from her temples, and struggled with the sickness of heart, the dreadful faintness of terror, which would have overpowered a younger or a less resolute woman. Her eyes, dim with watching, weary with grief, searched the lawyer's unfathomable face. "His unhappy daughters?" she repeated to herself, vacantly. "He talks as if there was some worse calamity than the calamity which has made them orphans." She paused once more; and rallied her sinking courage. "I will not make your hard duty, sir, more painful to you than I can help," she resumed. "Show me the place in the will. Let me read it, and know the worst."

Mr. Pendril turned back to the first page, and pointed to a certain place in the cramped lines of writing. "Begin here," he said.

She tried to begin; she tried to follow his finger, as she had followed it already to the signatures and the dates. But her senses seemed to share the confusion of her mind—the words mingled together, and the lines swam before her eyes.

"I can't follow you," she said. "You must tell it, or read it to me." She pushed her chair back from the table, and tried to collect herself. "Stop!" she exclaimed, as the lawyer, with visible hesitation and reluctance, took the papers in his own hand. "One question, first. Does his will provide for his children?"

"His will provided for them, when he made it."

"When he made it!" (Something of her natural bluntness broke out in her manner as she repeated the answer.) "Does it provide for them now?"

"It does not."

She snatched the will from his hand, and threw it into a corner of the room. "You mean well," she said; "you wish to spare me—but you are wasting your time, and my strength. If the will is useless, there let it lie. Tell me the truth, Mr. Pendril—tell it plainly, tell it instantly, in your own words!"

He felt that it would be useless cruelty to resist that appeal. There was no merciful alternative but to answer it on the spot.

"I must refer you to the spring of the present year, Miss Garth. Do you remember the fourth of March?"

Her attention wandered again; a thought seemed to have struck her at the moment when he spoke. Instead of answering his inquiry, she put a question of her own.

"Let me break the news to myself," she said—"let me anticipate you, if I can. His useless will, the terms in which you speak of his daughters, the doubt you seem to feel of my continued respect for his memory, have opened a new view to me. Mr. Vanstone has died a ruined man—is that what you had to tell me?"

"Far from it. Mr. Vanstone has died, leaving a fortune of more than eighty thousand pounds—a fortune invested in excellent securities. He lived up to his income, but never beyond it; and all his debts added together would not reach two hundred pounds. If he had died a ruined man, I should have felt deeply for his children: but I should not have hesitated to tell you the truth, as I am hesitating now. Let me repeat a question which escaped you, I think, when I first put it. Carry your mind back to the spring of this year. Do you remember the fourth of March?"

Miss Garth shook her head. "My memory for dates is bad at the best of times," she said. "I am too confused to exert it at a moment's notice. Can you put your question in no other form?"

He put it in this form:

"Do you remember any domestic event in the spring of the present year which appeared to affect Mr. Vanstone more seriously than usual?"

Miss Garth leaned forward in her chair, and looked eagerly at Mr. Pendril across the table. "The journey to London!" she exclaimed. "I distrusted the journey to London from the first! Yes! I remember Mr. Vanstone receiving a letter—I remember his reading it, and looking so altered from himself that he startled us all."

"Did you notice any apparent understanding between Mr. and Mrs. Vanstone on the subject of that letter?"

"Yes: I did. One of the girls—it was Magdalen—mentioned the post-mark; some place in America. It all comes back to me, Mr. Pendril. Mrs. Vanstone looked excited and anxious, the moment she heard the place named. They went to London together the next day; they explained nothing to their daughters, nothing to me. Mrs. Vanstone said the journey was for family affairs. I suspected something wrong; I couldn't tell what. Mrs. Vanstone wrote to me from London, saying that her object was to consult a physician on the state of her health, and not to alarm her daughters by telling them. Something in the letter rather hurt me at the time. I thought there might be some other motive that she was keeping from me. Did I do her wrong?"

"You did her no wrong. There was a motive which she was keeping from you. In revealing that motive, I reveal the painful secret which brings me to this house. All that I could do to prepare you, I have done. Let me now tell the truth in the plainest and fewest words. When Mr. and Mrs. Vanstone left Combe-Raven, in the March of the present year—"

Before he could complete the sentence, a sudden movement of Miss Garth's interrupted him. She started violently, and looked round toward the window. "Only the wind among the leaves," she said, faintly. "My nerves are so shaken, the least thing startles me. Speak out, for God's sake! When Mr. and Mrs. Vanstone left this house, tell me in plain words, why did they go to London?"

In plain words, Mr. Pendril told her:

"They went to London to be married."

With that answer he placed a slip of paper on the table. It was the marriage certificate of the dead parents, and the date it bore was March the twentieth, eighteen hundred and forty-six.

Miss Garth neither moved nor spoke. The certificate lay beneath her unnoticed. She sat with her eyes rooted on the lawyer's face; her mind stunned, her senses helpless. He saw that all his efforts to break the shock of the discovery had been efforts made in vain; he felt the vital importance of rousing her, and firmly and distinctly repeated the fatal words.

"They went to London to be married," he said. "Try to rouse yourself: try to realize the plain fact first: the explanation shall come afterward. Miss Garth, I speak the miserable truth! In the spring of this year they left home; they lived in London for a fortnight, in the strictest retirement; they were married by license at the end of that time. There is a copy of the certificate, which I myself obtained on Monday last. Read the date of the marriage for yourself. It is Friday, the twentieth of March—the March of this present year."

As he pointed to the certificate, that faint breath of air among the shrubs beneath the window, which had startled Miss Garth, stirred the leaves once more. He heard it himself this time, and turned his face, so as to let the breeze play upon it. No breeze came; no breath of air that was strong enough for him to feel, floated into the room.

Miss Garth roused herself mechanically, and read the certificate. It seemed to produce no distinct impression on her: she laid it on one side in a lost, bewildered manner. "Twelve years," she said, in low, hopeless tones—"twelve quiet, happy years I lived with this family. Mrs. Vanstone was my friend; my dear, valued friend—my sister, I might almost say. I can't believe it. Bear with me a little, sir, I can't believe it yet."

"I shall help you to believe it when I tell you more," said Mr. Pendril—"you will understand me better when I take you back to the time of Mr. Vanstone's early life. I won't ask for your attention just yet. Let us wait a little, until you recover yourself."

They waited a few minutes. The lawyer took some letters from his pocket, referred to them attentively, and put them back again. "Can you listen to me, now?" he asked, kindly. She bowed her head in answer. Mr. Pendril considered with himself for a moment, "I must caution you on one point," he said. "If the aspect of Mr. Vanstone's character which I am now about to present to you seems in some respects at variance with your later experience, bear in mind that, when you first knew him twelve years since, he was a man of forty; and that, when I first knew him, he was a lad of nineteen."

His next words raised the veil, and showed the irrevocable Past.

CHAPTER XIII.

"THE fortune which Mr. Vanstone possessed when you knew him" (the lawyer began) "was part, and part only, of the inheritance which fell to him on his father's death. Mr. Vanstone the elder was a manufacturer in the North of England. He married early in life; and the children of the marriage were either six or seven in number—I am not certain which. First, Michael, the eldest son, still living, and now an old man turned seventy. Secondly, Selina, the eldest daughter, who married in after-life, and who died ten or eleven years ago. After those two came other sons and daughters, whose early deaths make it unnecessary to mention them particularly. The last and by many years the youngest of the children was Andrew, whom I first knew, as I told you, at the age of nineteen. My father was then on the point of retiring from the active pursuit of his profession; and in succeeding to his business, I also succeeded to his connection with the Vanstones as the family solicitor.

"At that time, Andrew had just started in life by entering the army. After little more than a year of home-service, he was ordered out with his regiment to Canada. When he quitted England, he left his father and his elder brother Michael seriously at variance. I need not detain you by entering into the cause of the quarrel. I need only tell you that the elder Mr. Vanstone, with many excellent qualities, was a man of fierce and intractable temper. His eldest son had set him at defiance, under circumstances which might have justly irritated a father of far milder character; and he declared, in the most positive terms, that he would never see Michael's face again. In defiance of my entreaties, and of the entreaties of his wife, he tore up, in our presence, the will which provided for Michael's share in the paternal inheritance. Such was the family position, when the younger son left home for Canada.

"Some months after Andrew's arrival with his regiment at Quebec, he became acquainted with a woman of great personal attractions, who came, or said she came, from one of the Southern States of America. She obtained an immediate influence over him; and she used it to the basest purpose. You knew the easy, affectionate, trusting nature of the man in later life—you can imagine how thoughtlessly he acted on the impulse of his youth. It is useless to dwell on this lamentable part of the story. He was just twenty-one: he was blindly devoted to a worthless woman; and she led him on, with merciless cunning, till it was too late to draw back. In one word, he committed the fatal error of his life: he married her.

"She had been wise enough in her own interests to dread the influence of his brother-officers, and to persuade him, up to the period of the marriage ceremony, to keep the proposed union between them a secret. She could do this; but she could not provide against the results of accident. Hardly three months had passed, when a chance disclosure exposed the life she had led before her marriage. But one alternative was left to her husband—the alternative of instantly separating from her.

"The effect of the discovery on the unhappy boy—for a boy in disposition he still was—may be judged by the event which followed the exposure. One of Andrew's superior officers—a certain Major Kirke, if I remember right—found him in his quarters, writing to his father a confession of the disgraceful truth, with a loaded pistol by his side. That officer saved the lad's life from his own hand, and hushed up the scandalous affair by a compromise. The marriage being a perfectly legal one, and the wife's misconduct prior to the ceremony giving her husband no claim to his release from her by divorce, it was only possible to appeal to her sense of her own interests. A handsome annual allowance was secured to her, on condition that she returned to the place from which she had come; that she never appeared in England; and that she ceased to use her husband's name. Other stipulations were added to these. She accepted them all; and measures were privately taken to have her well looked after in the place of her retreat. What life she led there, and whether she performed all the conditions imposed on her, I cannot say. I can only tell you that she never, to my knowledge, came to England; that she never annoyed Mr. Vanstone; and that the annual allowance was paid her, through a local agent in America, to the day of her death. All that she wanted in marrying him was money; and money she got.

"In the meantime, Andrew had left the regiment. Nothing would induce him to face his brother-officers after what had happened. He sold out and returned to England. The first intelligence which reached him on his return was the intelligence of his father's death. He came to my office in London, before going home, and there learned from my lips how the family quarrel had ended.

"The will which Mr. Vanstone the elder had destroyed in my presence had not been, so far as I know, replaced by another. When I was sent for, in the usual course, on his death, I fully expected that the law would be left to make the customary division among his widow and his children. To my surprise, a will appeared among his papers, correctly drawn and executed, and dated about a week after the period when the first will had been destroyed. He had maintained his vindictive purpose against his eldest son, and had applied to a stranger for the professional assistance which I honestly believe he was ashamed to ask for at my hands.

"It is needless to trouble you with the provisions of the will in detail. There were the widow and three surviving children to be provided for. The widow received a life-interest only in a portion of the testator's property. The remaining portion was divided between Andrew and Selina—two-thirds to the brother; one-third to the sister. On the mother's death, the money from which her income had been derived was to go to Andrew and Selina, in the same relative proportions as before—five thousand pounds having been first deducted from the sum and paid to Michael, as the sole legacy left by the implacable father to his eldest son.

"Speaking in round numbers, the division of property, as settled by the will, stood thus. Before the mother's death, Andrew had seventy thousand pounds; Selina had thirty-five thousand pounds; Michael—had nothing. After the mother's death, Michael had five thousand pounds, to set against Andrew's inheritance augmented to one hundred thousand, and Selina's inheritance increased to fifty thousand.—Do not suppose that I am dwelling unnecessarily on this part of the subject. Every word I now speak bears on interests still in suspense, which vitally concern Mr. Vanstone's daughters. As we get on from past to present, keep in mind the terrible inequality of Michael's inheritance and Andrew's inheritance. The harm done by that vindictive will is, I greatly fear, not over yet.

"Andrew's first impulse, when he heard the news which I had to tell him, was worthy of the open, generous nature of the man. He at once proposed to divide his inheritance with his elder brother. But there was one serious obstacle in the way. A letter from Michael was waiting for him at my office when he came there, and that letter charged him with being the original cause of estrangement between his father and his elder brother. The efforts which he had made—bluntly and incautiously, I own, but with the purest and kindest intentions, as I know—to compose the quarrel before leaving home, were perverted, by the vilest misconstruction, to support an accusation of treachery and falsehood which would have stung any man to the quick. Andrew felt, what I felt, that if these imputations were not withdrawn before his generous intentions toward his brother took effect, the mere fact of their execution would amount to a practical acknowledgment of the justice of Michael's charge against him. He wrote to his brother in the most forbearing terms. The answer received was as offensive as words could make it. Michael had inherited his father's temper, unredeemed by his father's better qualities: his second letter reiterated the charges contained in the first, and declared that he would only accept the offered division as an act of atonement and restitution on Andrew's part. I next wrote to the mother to use her influence. She was herself aggrieved at being left with nothing more than a life interest in her husband's property; she sided resolutely with Michael; and she stigmatized Andrew's proposal as an attempt to bribe her eldest son into withdrawing a charge against his brother which that brother knew to be true. After this last repulse, nothing more could be done. Michael withdrew to the Continent; and his mother followed him there. She lived long enough, and saved money enough out of her income, to add considerably, at her death, to her elder son's five thousand pounds. He had previously still further improved his pecuniary position by an advantageous marriage; and he is now passing the close of his days either in France or Switzerland—a widower, with one son. We shall return to him shortly. In the meantime, I need only tell you that Andrew and Michael never again met—never again communicated, even by writing. To all intents and purposes they were dead to each other, from those early days to the present time.

"You can now estimate what Andrew's position was when he left his profession and returned to England. Possessed of a fortune, he was alone in the world; his future destroyed at the fair outset of life; his mother and brother estranged from him; his sister lately married, with interests and hopes in which he had no share. Men of firmer mental caliber might have found refuge from such a situation as this in an absorbing intellectual pursuit. He was not capable of the effort; all the strength of his character lay in the affections he had wasted. His place in the world was that quiet place at home, with wife and children to make his life happy, which he had lost forever. To look back was more than he dare. To look forward was more than he could. In sheer despair, he let his own impetuous youth drive him on; and cast himself into the lowest dissipations of a London life.

"A woman's falsehood had driven him to his ruin. A woman's love saved him at the outset of his downward career. Let us not speak of her harshly—for we laid her with him yesterday in the grave.

"You, who only knew Mrs. Vanstone in later life, when illness and sorrow and secret care had altered and saddened her, can form no adequate idea of her attractions of person and character when she was a girl of seventeen. I was with Andrew when he first met her. I had tried to rescue him, for one night at least, from degrading associates and degrading pleasures, by persuading him to go with me to a ball given by one of the great City Companies. There they met. She produced a strong impression on him the moment he saw her. To me, as to him, she was a total stranger. An introduction to her, obtained in the customary manner, informed him that she was the daughter of one Mr. Blake. The rest he discovered from herself. They were partners in the dance (unobserved in that crowded ball-room) all through the evening.

"Circumstances were against her from the first. She was unhappy at home. Her family and friends occupied no recognized station in life: they were mean, underhand people, in every way unworthy of her. It was her first ball—it was the first time she had ever met with a man who had the breeding, the manners and the conversation of a gentleman. Are these excuses for her, which I have no right to make? If we have any human feeling for human weakness, surely not!

"The meeting of that night decided their future. When other meetings had followed, when the confession of her love had escaped her, he took the one course of all others (took it innocently and unconsciously), which was most dangerous to them both. His frankness and his sense of honor forbade him to deceive her: he opened his heart and told her the truth. She was a generous, impulsive girl; she had no home ties strong enough to plead with her; she was passionately fond of him—and he had made that appeal to her pity which, to the eternal honor of women, is the hardest of all appeals for them to resist. She saw, and saw truly, that she alone stood between him and his ruin. The last chance of his rescue hung on her decision. She decided; and saved him.

"Let me not be misunderstood; let me not be accused of trifling with the serious social question on which my narrative forces me to touch. I will defend her memory by no false reasoning—I will only speak the truth. It is the truth that she snatched him from mad excesses which must have ended in his early death. It is the truth that she restored him to that happy home existence which you remember so tenderly—which he remembered so gratefully that, on the day when he was free, he made her his wife. Let strict morality claim its right, and condemn her early fault. I have read my New Testament to little purpose, indeed, if Christian mercy may not soften the hard sentence against her—if Christian charity may not find a plea for her memory in the love and fidelity, the suffering and the sacrifice, of her whole life.

"A few words more will bring us to a later time, and to events which have happened within your own experience.

"I need not remind you that the position in which Mr. Vanstone was now placed could lead in the end to but one result—to a disclosure, more or less inevitable, of the truth. Attempts were made to keep the hopeless misfortune of his life a secret from Miss Blake's family; and, as a matter of course, those attempts failed before the relentless scrutiny of her father and her friends. What might have happened if her relatives had been what is termed 'respectable' I cannot pretend to say. As it was, they were people who could (in the common phrase) be conveniently treated with. The only survivor of the family at the present time is a scoundrel calling himself Captain Wragge. When I tell you that he privately extorted the price of his silence from Mrs. Vanstone to the last; and when I add that his conduct presents no extraordinary exception to the conduct, in their lifetime, of the other relatives—you will understand what sort of people I had to deal with in my client's interests, and how their assumed indignation was appeased.

"Having, in the first instance, left England for Ireland, Mr. Vanstone and Miss Blake remained there afterward for some years. Girl as she was, she faced her position and its necessities without flinching. Having once resolved to sacrifice her life to the man she loved; having quieted her conscience by persuading herself that his marriage was a legal mockery, and that she was 'his wife in the sight of Heaven,' she set herself from the first to accomplish the one foremost purpose of so living with him, in the world's eye, as never to raise the suspicion that she was not his lawful wife. The women are few, indeed, who cannot resolve firmly, scheme patiently, and act promptly where the dearest interests of their lives are concerned. Mrs. Vanstone—she has a right now, remember, to that name—Mrs. Vanstone had more than the average share of a woman's tenacity and a woman's tact; and she took all the needful precautions, in those early days, which her husband's less ready capacity had not the art to devise—precautions to which they were largely indebted for the preservation of their secret in later times.

"Thanks to these safeguards, not a shadow of suspicion followed them when they returned to England. They first settled in Devonshire, merely because they were far removed there from that northern county in which Mr. Vanstone's family and connections had been known. On the part of his surviving relatives, they had no curious investigations to dread. He was totally estranged from his mother and his elder brother. His married sister had been forbidden by her husband (who was a clergyman) to hold any communication with him, from the period when he had fallen into the deplorable way of life which I have described as following his return from Canada. Other relations he had none. When he and Miss Blake left Devonshire, their next change of residence was to this house. Neither courting nor avoiding notice; simply happy in themselves, in their children, and in their quiet rural life; unsuspected by the few neighbors who formed their modest circle of acquaintance to be other than what they seemed—the truth in their case, as in the cases of many others, remained undiscovered until accident forced it into the light of day.

"If, in your close intimacy with them, it seems strange that they should never have betrayed themselves, let me ask you to consider the circumstances and you will understand the apparent anomaly. Remember that they had been living as husband and wife, to all intents and purposes (except that the marriage-service had not been read over them), for fifteen years before you came into the house; and bear in mind, at the same time, that no event occurred to disturb Mr. Vanstone's happiness in the present, to remind him of the past, or to warn him of the future, until the announcement of his wife's death reached him, in that letter from America which you saw placed in his hand. From that day forth—when a past which he abhorred was forced back to his memory; when a future which she had never dared to anticipate was placed within her reach—you will soon perceive, if you have not perceived already, that they both betrayed themselves, time after time; and that your innocence of all suspicion, and their children's innocence of all suspicion, alone prevented you from discovering the truth.

"The sad story of the past is now as well known to you as to me. I have had hard words to speak. God knows I have spoken them with true sympathy for the living, with true tenderness for the memory of the dead."

He paused, turned his face a little away, and rested his head on his hand, in the quiet, undemonstrative manner which was natural to him. Thus far, Miss Garth had only interrupted his narrative by an occasional word or by a mute token of her attention. She made no effort to conceal her tears; they fell fast and silently over her wasted cheeks, as she looked up and spoke to him. "I have done you some injury, sir, in my thoughts," she said, with a noble simplicity. "I know you better now. Let me ask your forgiveness; let me take your hand."

Those words, and the action which accompanied them, touched him deeply. He took her hand in silence. She was the first to speak, the first to set the example of self-control. It is one of the noble instincts of women that nothing more powerfully rouses them to struggle with their own sorrow than the sight of a man's distress. She quietly dried her tears; she quietly drew her chair round the table, so as to sit nearer to him when she spoke again.

"I have been sadly broken, Mr. Pendril, by what has happened in this house," she said, "or I should have borne what you have told me better than I have borne it to-day. Will you let me ask one question before you go on? My heart aches for the children of my love—more than ever my children now. Is there no hope for their future? Are they left with no prospect but poverty before them?"

The lawyer hesitated before he answered the question.

"They are left dependent," he said, at last, "on the justice and the mercy of a stranger."

"Through the misfortune of their birth?"

"Through the misfortunes which have followed the marriage of their parents."

With that startling answer he rose, took up the will from the floor, and restored it to its former position on the table between them.

"I can only place the truth before you," he resumed, "in one plain form of words. The marriage has destroyed this will, and has left Mr. Vanstone's daughters dependent on their uncle."

As he spoke, the breeze stirred again among the shrubs under the window.

"On their uncle?" repeated Miss Garth. She considered for a moment, and laid her hand suddenly on Mr. Pendril's arm. "Not on Michael Vanstone!"

"Yes: on Michael Vanstone."

Miss Garth's hand still mechanically grasped the lawyer's arm. Her whole mind was absorbed in the effort to realize the discovery which had now burst on her.

"Dependent on Michael Vanstone!" she said to herself. "Dependent on their father's bitterest enemy? How can it be?"

"Give me your attention for a few minutes more," said Mr. Pendril, "and you shall hear. The sooner we can bring this painful interview to a close, the sooner I can open communications with Mr. Michael Vanstone, and the sooner you will know what he decides on doing for his brother's orphan daughters. I repeat to you that they are absolutely dependent on him. You will most readily understand how and why, if we take up the chain of events where we last left it—at the period of Mr. and Mrs. Vanstone's marriage."

"One moment, sir," said Miss Garth. "Were you in the secret of that marriage at the time when it took place?"

"Unhappily, I was not. I was away from London—away from England at the time. If Mr. Vanstone had been able to communicate with me when the letter from America announced the death of his wife, the fortunes of his daughters would not have been now at stake."

He paused, and, before proceeding further, looked once more at the letters which he had consulted at an earlier period of the interview. He took one letter from the rest, and put it on the table by his side.

"At the beginning of the present year," he resumed, "a very serious business necessity, in connection with some West Indian property possessed by an old client and friend of mine, required the presence either of myself, or of one of my two partners, in Jamaica. One of the two could not be spared; the other was not in health to undertake the voyage. There was no choice left but for me to go. I wrote to Mr. Vanstone, telling him that I should leave England at the end of February, and that the nature of the business which took me away afforded little hope of my getting back from the West Indies before June. My letter was not written with any special motive. I merely thought it right—seeing that my partners were not admitted to my knowledge of Mr. Vanstone's private affairs—to warn him of my absence, as a measure of formal precaution which it was right to take. At the end of February I left England, without having heard from him. I was on the sea when the news of his wife's death reached him, on the fourth of March: and I did not return until the middle of last June."

"You warned him of your departure," interposed Miss Garth. "Did you not warn him of your return?"

"Not personally. My head-clerk sent him one of the circulars which were dispatched from my office, in various directions, to announce my return. It was the first substitute I thought of for the personal letter which the pressure of innumerable occupations, all crowding on me together after my long absence, did not allow me leisure to write. Barely a month later, the first information of his marriage reached me in a letter from himself, written on the day of the fatal accident. The circumstances which induced him to write arose out of an event in which you must have taken some interest—I mean the attachment between Mr. Clare's son and Mr. Vanstone's youngest daughter."

"I cannot say that I was favorably disposed toward that attachment at the time," replied Miss Garth. "I was ignorant then of the family secret: I know better now."

"Exactly. The motive which you can now appreciate is the motive that leads us to the point. The young lady herself (as I have heard from the elder Mr. Clare, to whom I am indebted for my knowledge of the circumstances in detail) confessed her attachment to her father, and innocently touched him to the quick by a chance reference to his own early life. He had a long conversation with Mrs. Vanstone, at which they both agreed that Mr. Clare must be privately informed of the truth, before the attachment between the two young people was allowed to proceed further. It was painful in the last degree, both to husband and wife, to be reduced to this alternative. But they were resolute, honorably resolute, in making the sacrifice of their own feelings; and Mr. Vanstone betook himself on the spot to Mr. Clare's cottage.—You no doubt observed a remarkable change in Mr. Vanstone's manner on that day; and you can now account for it?"

Miss Garth bowed her head, and Mr. Pendril went on.

"You are sufficiently acquainted with Mr. Clare's contempt for all social prejudices," he continued, "to anticipate his reception of the confession which his neighbor addressed to him. Five minutes after the interview had begun, the two old friends were as easy and unrestrained together as usual. In the course of conversation, Mr. Vanstone mentioned the pecuniary arrangement which he had made for the benefit of his daughter and of her future husband—and, in doing so, he naturally referred to his will here, on the table between us. Mr. Clare, remembering that his friend had been married in the March of that year, at once asked when the will had been executed: receiving the reply that it had been made five years since; and, thereupon, astounded Mr. Vanstone by telling him bluntly that the document was waste paper in the eye of the law. Up to that moment he, like many other persons, had been absolutely ignorant that a man's marriage is, legally as well as socially, considered to be the most important event in his life; that it destroys the validity of any will which he may have made as a single man; and that it renders absolutely necessary the entire re-assertion of his testamentary intentions in the character of a husband. The statement of this plain fact appeared to overwhelm Mr. Vanstone. Declaring that his friend had laid him under an obligation which he should remember to his dying day, he at once left the cottage, at once returned home, and wrote me this letter."

He handed the letter open to Miss Garth. In tearless, speechless grief, she read these words:

"MY DEAR PENDRIL—Since we last wrote to each other an extraordinary change has taken place in my life. About a week after you went away, I received news from America which told me that I was free. Need I say what use I made of that freedom? Need I say that the mother of my children is now my Wife?

"If you are surprised at not having heard from me the moment you got back, attribute my silence, in great part—if not altogether—to my own total ignorance of the legal necessity for making another will. Not half an hour since, I was enlightened for the first time (under circumstances which I will mention when me meet) by my old friend, Mr. Clare. Family anxieties have had something to do with my silence as well. My wife's confinement is close at hand; and, besides this serious anxiety, my second daughter is just engaged to be married. Until I saw Mr. Clare to-day, these matters so filled my mind that I never thought of writing to you during the one short month which is all that has passed since I got news of your return. Now I know that my will must be made again, I write instantly. For God's sake, come on the day when you receive this—come and relieve me from the dreadful thought that my two darling girls are at this moment unprovided for. If anything happened to me, and if my desire to do their mother justice, ended (through my miserable ignorance of the law) in leaving Norah and Magdalen disinherited, I should not rest in my grave! Come at any cost, to yours ever,

"A. V."

"On the Saturday morning," Mr. Pendril resumed, "those lines reached me. I instantly set aside all other business, and drove to the railway. At the London terminus, I heard the first news of the Friday's accident; heard it, with conflicting accounts of the numbers and names of the passengers killed. At Bristol, they were better informed; and the dreadful truth about Mr. Vanstone was confirmed. I had time to recover myself before I reached your station here, and found Mr. Clare's son waiting for me. He took me to his father's cottage; and there, without losing a moment, I drew out Mrs. Vanstone's will. My object was to secure the only provision for her daughters which it was now possible to make. Mr. Vanstone having died intestate, a third of his fortune would go to his widow; and the rest would be divided among his next of kin. As children born out of wedlock, Mr. Vanstone's daughters, under the circumstances of their father's death, had no more claim to a share in his property than the daughters of one of his laborers in the village. The one chance left was that their mother might sufficiently recover to leave her third share to them, by will, in the event of her decease. Now you know why I wrote to you to ask for that interview—why I waited day and night, in the hope of receiving a summons to the house. I was sincerely sorry to send back such an answer to your note of inquiry as I was compelled to write. But while there was a chance of the preservation of Mrs. Vanstone's life, the secret of the marriage was hers, not mine; and every consideration of delicacy forbade me to disclose it."

"You did right, sir," said Miss Garth; "I understand your motives, and respect them."

"My last attempt to provide for the daughters," continued Mr. Pendril, "was, as you know, rendered unavailing by the dangerous nature of Mrs. Vanstone's illness. Her death left the infant who survived her by a few hours (the infant born, you will remember, in lawful wedlock) possessed, in due legal course, of the whole of Mr. Vanstone's fortune. On the child's death—if it had only outlived the mother by a few seconds, instead of a few hours, the result would have been the same—the next of kin to the legitimate offspring took the money; and that next of kin is the infant's paternal uncle, Michael Vanstone. The whole fortune of eighty thousand pounds has virtually passed into his possession already."

"Are there no other relations?" asked Miss Garth. "Is there no hope from any one else?"

"There are no other relations with Michael Vanstone's claim," said the lawyer. "There are no grandfathers or grandmothers of the dead child (on the side of either of the parents) now alive. It was not likely there should be, considering the ages of Mr. and Mrs. Vanstone when they died. But it is a misfortune to be reasonably lamented that no other uncles or aunts survive. There are cousins alive; a son and two daughters of that elder sister of Mr. Vanstone's, who married Archdeacon Bartram, and who died, as I told you, some years since. But their interest is superseded by the interest of the nearer blood. No, Miss Garth, we must look facts as they are resolutely in the face. Mr. Vanstone's daughters are Nobody's Children; and the law leaves them helpless at their uncle's mercy."

"A cruel law, Mr. Pendril—a cruel law in a Christian country."

"Cruel as it is, Miss Garth, it stands excused by a shocking peculiarity in this case. I am far from defending the law of England as it affects illegitimate offspring. On the contrary, I think it a disgrace to the nation. It visits the sins of the parents on the children; it encourages vice by depriving fathers and mothers of the strongest of all motives for making the atonement of marriage; and it claims to produce these two abominable results in the names of morality and religion. But it has no extraordinary oppression to answer for in the case of these unhappy girls. The more merciful and Christian law of other countries, which allows the marriage of the parents to make the children legitimate, has no mercy on these children. The accident of their father having been married, when he first met with their mother, has made them the outcasts of the whole social community; it has placed them out of the pale of the Civil Law of Europe. I tell you the hard truth—it is useless to disguise it. There is no hope, if we look back at the past: there may be hope, if we look on to the future. The best service which I can now render you is to shorten the period of your suspense. In less than an hour I shall be on my way back to London. Immediately on my arrival, I will ascertain the speediest means of communicating with Mr. Michael Vanstone; and will let you know the result. Sad as the position of the two sisters now is, we must look at it on its best side; we must not lose hope."

"Hope?" repeated Miss Garth. "Hope from Michael Vanstone!"

"Yes; hope from the influence on him of time, if not from the influence of mercy. As I have already told you, he is now an old man; he cannot, in the course of nature, expect to live much longer. If he looks back to the period when he and his brother were first at variance, he must look back through thirty years. Surely, these are softening influences which must affect any man? Surely, his own knowledge of the shocking circumstances under which he has become possessed of this money will plead with him, if nothing else does?"

"I will try to think as you do, Mr. Pendril—I will try to hope for the best. Shall we be left long in suspense before the decision reaches us?"

"I trust not. The only delay on my side will be caused by the necessity of discovering the place of Michael Vanstone's residence on the Continent. I think I have the means of meeting this difficulty successfully; and the moment I reach London, those means shall be tried."

He took up his hat; and then returned to the table on which the father's last letter, and the father's useless will, were lying side by side. After a moment's consideration, he placed them both in Miss Garth's hands.

"It may help you in breaking the hard truth to the orphan sisters," he said, in his quiet, self-repressed way, "if they can see how their father refers to them in his will—if they can read his letter to me, the last he ever wrote. Let these tokens tell them that the one idea of their father's life was the idea of making atonement to his children. 'They may think bitterly of their birth,' he said to me, at the time when I drew this useless will; 'but they shall never think bitterly of me. I will cross them in nothing: they shall never know a sorrow that I can spare them, or a want which I will not satisfy.' He made me put those words in his will, to plead for him when the truth which he had concealed from his children in his lifetime was revealed to them after his death. No law can deprive his daughters of the legacy of his repentance and his love. I leave the will and the letter to help you: I give them both into your care."

He saw how his parting kindness touched her and thoughtfully hastened the farewell. She took his hand in both her own and murmured a few broken words of gratitude. "Trust me to do my best," he said—and, turning away with a merciful abruptness, left her. In the broad, cheerful sunshine he had come in to reveal the fatal truth. In the broad, cheerful sunshine—that truth disclosed—he went out.

CHAPTER XIV.

IT was nearly an hour past noon when Mr. Pendril left the house. Miss Garth sat down again at the table alone, and tried to face the necessity which the event of the morning now forced on her.

Her mind was not equal to the effort. She tried to lessen the strain on it—to lose the sense of her own position—to escape from her thoughts for a few minutes only. After a little, she opened Mr. Vanstone's letter, and mechanically set herself to read it through once more.

One by one, the last words of the dead man fastened themselves more and more firmly on her attention. The unrelieved solitude, the unbroken silence, helped their influence on her mind and opened it to those very impressions of past and present which she was most anxious to shun. As she reached the melancholy lines which closed the letter, she found herself—insensibly, almost unconsciously, at first—tracing the fatal chain of events, link by link backward, until she reached its beginning in the contemplated marriage between Magdalen and Francis Clare.

That marriage had taken Mr. Vanstone to his old friend, with the confession on his lips which would otherwise never have escaped them. Thence came the discovery which had sent him home to summon the lawyer to the house. That summons, again, had produced the inevitable acceleration of the Saturday's journey to Friday; the Friday of the fatal accident, the Friday when he went to his death. From his death followed the second bereavement which had made the house desolate; the helpless position of the daughters whose prosperous future had been his dearest care; the revelation of the secret which had overwhelmed her that morning; the disclosure, more terrible still, which she now stood committed to make to the orphan sisters. For the first time she saw the whole sequence of events—saw it as plainly as the cloudless blue of the sky and the green glow of the trees in the sunlight outside.

How—when could she tell them? Who could approach them with the disclosure of their own illegitimacy before their father and mother had been dead a week? Who could speak the dreadful words, while the first tears were wet on their cheeks, while the first pang of separation was at its keenest in their hearts, while the memory of the funeral was not a day old yet? Not their last friend left; not the faithful woman whose heart bled for them. No! silence for the present time, at all risks—merciful silence, for many days to come!

She left the room, with the will and the letter in her hand—with the natural, human pity at her heart which sealed her lips and shut her eyes resolutely to the future. In the hall she stopped and listened. Not a sound was audible. She softly ascended the stairs, on her way to her own room, and passed the door of Norah's bed-chamber. Voices inside, the voices of the two sisters, caught her ear. After a moment's consideration, she checked herself, turned back, and quickly descended the stairs again. Both Norah and Magdalen knew of the interview between Mr. Pendril and herself; she had felt it her duty to show them his letter making the appointment. Could she excite their suspicion by locking herself up from them in her room as soon as the lawyer had left the house? Her hand trembled on the banister; she felt that her face might betray her. The self-forgetful fortitude, which had never failed her until that day, had been tried once too often—had been tasked beyond its powers at last.

At the hall door she reflected for a moment again, and went into the garden; directing her steps to a rustic bench and table placed out of sight of the house among the trees. In past times she had often sat there, with Mrs. Vanstone on one side, with Norah on the other, with Magdalen and the dogs romping on the grass. Alone she sat there now—the will and the letter which she dared not trust out of her own possession, laid on the table—her head bowed over them; her face hidden in her hands. Alone she sat there and tried to rouse her sinking courage.

Doubts thronged on her of the dark days to come; dread beset her of the hidden danger which her own silence toward Norah and Magdalen might store up in the near future. The accident of a moment might suddenly reveal the truth. Mr. Pendril might write, might personally address himself to the sisters, in the natural conviction that she had enlightened them. Complications might gather round them at a moment's notice; unforeseen necessities might arise for immediately leaving the house. She saw all these perils—and still the cruel courage to face the worst, and speak, was as far from her as ever. Ere long the thickening conflict of her thoughts forced its way outward for relief, in words and actions. She raised her head and beat her hand helplessly on the table.

"God help me, what am I to do?" she broke out. "How am I to tell them?"

"There is no need to tell them," said a voice behind her. "They know it already."

She started to her feet and looked round. It was Magdalen who stood before her—Magdalen who had spoken those words.

Yes, there was the graceful figure, in its mourning garments, standing out tall and black and motionless against the leafy background. There was Magdalen herself, with a changeless stillness on her white face; with an icy resignation in her steady gray eyes.

"We know it already," she repeated, in clear, measured tones. "Mr. Vanstone's daughters are Nobody's Children; and the law leaves them helpless at their uncle's mercy."

So, without a tear on her cheeks, without a faltering tone in her voice, she repeated the lawyer's own words, exactly as he had spoken them. Miss Garth staggered back a step and caught at the bench to support herself. Her head swam; she closed her eyes in a momentary faintness. When they opened again, Magdalen's arm was supporting her, Magdalen's breath fanned her cheek, Magdalen's cold lips kissed her. She drew back from the kiss; the touch of the girl's lips thrilled her with terror.

As soon as she could speak she put the inevitable question. "You heard us," she said.

"Where?"

"Under the open window."

"All the time?"

"From beginning to end."

She had listened—this girl of eighteen, in the first week of her orphanage, had listened to the whole terrible revelation, word by word, as it fell from the lawyer's lips; and had never once betrayed herself! From first to last, the only movements which had escaped her had been movements guarded enough and slight enough to be mistaken for the passage of the summer breeze through the leaves!

"Don't try to speak yet," she said, in softer and gentler tones. "Don't look at me with those doubting eyes. What wrong have I done? When Mr. Pendril wished to speak to you about Norah and me, his letter gave us our choice to be present at the interview, or to keep away. If my elder sister decided to keep away, how could I come? How could I hear my own story except as I did? My listening has done no harm. It has done good—it has saved you the distress of speaking to us. You have suffered enough for us already; it is time we learned to suffer for ourselves. I have learned. And Norah is learning."

"Norah!"

"Yes. I have done all I could to spare you. I have told Norah."

She had told Norah! Was this girl, whose courage had faced the terrible necessity from which a woman old enough to be her mother had recoiled, the girl Miss Garth had brought up? the girl whose nature she had believed to be as well known to her as her own?

"Magdalen!" she cried out, passionately, "you frighten me!"

Magdalen only sighed, and turned wearily away.

"Try not to think worse of me than I deserve," she said. "I can't cry. My heart is numbed."

She moved away slowly over the grass. Miss Garth watched the tall black figure gliding away alone until it was lost among the trees. While it was in sight she could think of nothing else. The moment it was gone, she thought of Norah. For the first time in her experience of the sisters her heart led her instinctively to the elder of the two.

Norah was still in her own room. She was sitting on the couch by the window, with her mother's old music-book—the keepsake which Mrs. Vanstone had found in her husband's study on the day of her husband's death—spread open on her lap. She looked up from it with such quiet sorrow, and pointed with such ready kindness to the vacant place at her side, that Miss Garth doubted for the moment whether Magdalen had spoken the truth. "See," said Norah, simply, turning to the first leaf in the music-book—"my mother's name written in it, and some verses to my father on the next page. We may keep this for ourselves, if we keep nothing else." She put her arm round Miss Garth's neck, and a faint tinge of color stole over her cheeks. "I see anxious thoughts in your face," she whispered. "Are you anxious about me? Are you doubting whether I have heard it? I have heard the whole truth. I might have felt it bitterly, later; it is too soon to feel it now. You have seen Magdalen? She went out to find you—where did you leave her?"

"In the garden. I couldn't speak to her; I couldn't look at her. Magdalen has frightened me."

Norah rose hurriedly; rose, startled and distressed by Miss Garth's reply.

"Don't think ill of Magdalen," she said. "Magdalen suffers in secret more than I do. Try not to grieve over what you have heard about us this morning. Does it matter who we are, or what we keep or lose? What loss is there for us after the loss of our father and mother? Oh, Miss Garth, there is the only bitterness! What did we remember of them when we laid them in the grave yesterday? Nothing but the love they gave us—the love we must never hope for again. What else can we remember to-day? What change can the world, and the world's cruel laws make in our memory of the kindest father, the kindest mother, that children ever had!" She stopped: struggled with her rising grief; and quietly, resolutely, kept it down. "Will you wait here," she said, "while I go and bring Magdalen back? Magdalen was always your favorite: I want her to be your favorite still." She laid the music-book gently on Miss Garth's lap—and left the room.

"Magdalen was always your favorite."

Tenderly as they had been spoken, those words fell reproachfully on Miss Garth's ear. For the first time in the long companionship of her pupils and herself a doubt whether she, and all those about her, had not been fatally mistaken in their relative estimate of the sisters, now forced itself on her mind.

She had studied the natures of her two pupils in the daily intimacy of twelve years. Those natures, which she believed herself to have sounded through all their depths, had been suddenly tried in the sharp ordeal of affliction. How had they come out from the test? As her previous experience had prepared her to see them? No: in flat contradiction to it.

What did such a result as this imply?

Thoughts came to her, as she asked herself that question, which have startled and saddened us all.

Does there exist in every human being, beneath that outward and visible character which is shaped into form by the social influences surrounding us, an inward, invisible disposition, which is part of ourselves, which education may indirectly modify, but can never hope to change? Is the philosophy which denies this and asserts that we are born with dispositions like blank sheets of paper a philosophy which has failed to remark that we are not born with blank faces—a philosophy which has never compared together two infants of a few days old, and has never observed that those infants are not born with blank tempers for mothers and nurses to fill up at will? Are there, infinitely varying with each individual, inbred forces of Good and Evil in all of us, deep down below the reach of mortal encouragement and mortal repression—hidden Good and hidden Evil, both alike at the mercy of the liberating opportunity and the sufficient temptation? Within these earthly limits, is earthly Circumstance ever the key; and can no human vigilance warn us beforehand of the forces imprisoned in ourselves which that key may unlock?

For the first time, thoughts such as these rose darkly—as shadowy and terrible possibilities—in Miss Garth's mind. For the first time, she associated those possibilities with the past conduct and characters, with the future lives and fortunes of the orphan sisters.

Searching, as in a glass darkly, into the two natures, she felt her way, doubt by doubt, from one possible truth to another. It might be that the upper surface of their characters was all that she had, thus far, plainly seen in Norah and Magdalen. It might be that the unalluring secrecy and reserve of one sister, the all-attractive openness and high spirits of the other, were more or less referable, in each case, to those physical causes which work toward the production of moral results. It might be, that under the surface so formed—a surface which there had been nothing, hitherto, in the happy, prosperous, uneventful lives of the sisters to disturb—forces of inborn and inbred disposition had remained concealed, which the shock of the first serious calamity in their lives had now thrown up into view. Was this so? Was the promise of the future shining with prophetic light through the surface-shadow of Norah's reserve, and darkening with prophetic gloom, under the surface-glitter of Magdalen's bright spirits? If the life of the elder sister was destined henceforth to be the ripening ground of the undeveloped Good that was in her—was the life of the younger doomed to be the battle-field of mortal conflict with the roused forces of Evil in herself?

On the brink of that terrible conclusion, Miss Garth shrank back in dismay. Her heart was the heart of a true woman. It accepted the conviction which raised Norah higher in her love: it rejected the doubt which threatened to place Magdalen lower. She rose and paced the room impatiently; she recoiled with an angry suddenness from the whole train of thought in which her mind had been engaged but the moment before. What if there were dangerous elements in the strength of Magdalen's character—was it not her duty to help the girl against herself? How had she performed that duty? She had let herself be governed by first fears and first impressions; she had never waited to consider whether Magdalen's openly acknowledged action of that morning might not imply a self-sacrificing fortitude, which promised, in after-life, the noblest and the most enduring results. She had let Norah go and speak those words of tender remonstrance, which she should first have spoken herself. "Oh!" she thought, bitterly, "how long I have lived in the world, and how little I have known of my own weakness and wickedness until to-day!"

The door of the room opened. Norah came in, as she had gone out, alone.

"Do you remember leaving anything on the little table by the garden-seat?" she asked, quietly.

Before Miss Garth could answer the question, she held out her father's will and her father's letter.

"Magdalen came back after you went away," she said, "and found these last relics. She heard Mr. Pendril say they were her legacy and mine. When I went into the garden she was reading the letter. There was no need for me to speak to her; our father had spoken to her from his grave. See how she has listened to him!"

She pointed to the letter. The traces of heavy tear-drops lay thick over the last lines of the dead man's writing.

"Her tears," said Norah, softly.

Miss Garth's head drooped low over the mute revelation of Magdalen's return to her better self.

"Oh, never doubt her again!" pleaded Norah. "We are alone now—we have our hard way through the world to walk on as patiently as we can. If Magdalen ever falters and turns back, help her for the love of old times; help her against herself."

"With all my heart and strength—as God shall judge me, with the devotion of my whole life!" In those fervent words Miss Garth answered. She took the hand which Norah held out to her, and put it, in sorrow and humility, to her lips. "Oh, my love, forgive me! I have been miserably blind—I have never valued you as I ought!"

Norah gently checked her before she could say more; gently whispered, "Come with me into the garden—come, and help Magdalen to look patiently to the future."

The future! Who could see the faintest glimmer of it? Who could see anything but the ill-omened figure of Michael Vanstone, posted darkly on the verge of the present time—and closing all the prospect that lay beyond him?

CHAPTER XV.

ON the next morning but one, news was received from Mr. Pendril. The place of Michael Vanstone's residence on the Continent had been discovered. He was living at Zurich; and a letter had been dispatched to him, at that place, on the day when the information was obtained. In the course of the coming week an answer might be expected, and the purport of it should be communicated forthwith to the ladies at Combe-Raven.

Short as it was, the interval of delay passed wearily. Ten days elapsed before the expected answer was received; and when it came at last, it proved to be, strictly speaking, no answer at all. Mr. Pendril had been merely referred to an agent in London who was in possession of Michael Vanstone's instructions. Certain difficulties had been discovered in connection with those instructions, which had produced the necessity of once more writing to Zurich. And there "the negotiations" rested again for the present.

A second paragraph in Mr. Pendril's letter contained another piece of intelligence entirely new. Mr. Michael Vanstone's son (and only child), Mr. Noel Vanstone, had recently arrived in London, and was then staying in lodgings occupied by his cousin, Mr. George Bartram. Professional considerations had induced Mr. Pendril to pay a visit to the lodgings. He had been very kindly received by Mr. Bartram; but had been informed by that gentleman that his cousin was not then in a condition to receive visitors. Mr. Noel Vanstone had been suffering, for some years past, from a wearing and obstinate malady; he had come to England expressly to obtain the best medical advice, and he still felt the fatigue of the journey so severely as to be confined to his bed. Under these circumstances, Mr. Pendril had no alternative but to take his leave. An interview with Mr. Noel Vanstone might have cleared up some of the difficulties in connection with his father's instructions. As events had turned out, there was no help for it but to wait for a few days more.

The days passed, the empty days of solitude and suspense. At last, a third letter from the lawyer announced the long delayed conclusion of the correspondence. The final answer had been received from Zurich, and Mr. Pendril would personally communicate it at Combe-Raven on the afternoon of the next day.

That next day was Wednesday, the twelfth of August. The weather had changed in the night; and the sun rose watery through mist and cloud. By noon the sky was overcast at all points; the temperature was sensibly colder; and the rain poured down, straight and soft and steady, on the thirsty earth. Toward three o'clock, Miss Garth and Norah entered the morning-room, to await Mr. Pendril's arrival. They were joined shortly afterward by Magdalen. In half an hour more the familiar fall of the iron latch in the socket reached their ears from the fence beyond the shrubbery. Mr. Pendril and Mr. Clare advanced into view along the garden-path, walking arm-in-arm through the rain, sheltered by the same umbrella. The lawyer bowed as they passed the windows; Mr. Clare walked straight on, deep in his own thoughts—noticing nothing.

After a delay which seemed interminable; after a weary scraping of wet feet on the hall mat; after a mysterious, muttered interchange of question and answer outside the door, the two came in—Mr. Clare leading the way. The old man walked straight up to the table, without any preliminary greeting, and looked across it at the three women, with a stern pity for them in his ragged, wrinkled face.

"Bad news," he said. "I am an enemy to all unnecessary suspense. Plainness is kindness in such a case as this. I mean to be kind—and I tell you plainly—bad news."

Mr. Pendril followed him. He shook hands, in silence, with Miss Garth and the two sisters, and took a seat near them. Mr. Clare placed himself apart on a chair by the window. The gray rainy light fell soft and sad on the faces of Norah and Magdalen, who sat together opposite to him. Miss Garth had placed herself a little behind them, in partial shadow; and the lawyer's quiet face was seen in profile, close beside her. So the four occupants of the room appeared to Mr. Clare, as he sat apart in his corner; his long claw-like fingers interlaced on his knee; his dark vigilant eyes fixed searchingly now on one face, now on another. The dripping rustle of the rain among the leaves, and the clear, ceaseless tick of the clock on the mantel-piece, made the minute of silence which followed the settling of the persons present in their places indescribably oppressive. It was a relief to every one when Mr. Pendril spoke.

"Mr. Clare has told you already," he began, "that I am the bearer of bad news. I am grieved to say, Miss Garth, that your doubts, when I last saw you, were better founded than my hopes. What that heartless elder brother was in his youth, he is still in his old age. In all my unhappy experience of the worst side of human nature, I have never met with a man so utterly dead to every consideration of mercy as Michael Vanstone."

"Do you mean that he takes the whole of his brother's fortune, and makes no provision whatever for his brother's children?" asked Miss Garth.

"He offers a sum of money for present emergencies," replied Mr. Pendril, "so meanly and disgracefully insufficient that I am ashamed to mention it."

"And nothing for the future?"

"Absolutely nothing."

As that answer was given, the same thought passed, at the same moment, through Miss Garth's mind and through Norah's. The decision, which deprived both the sisters alike of the resources of fortune, did not end there for the younger of the two. Michael Vanstone's merciless resolution had virtually pronounced the sentence which dismissed Frank to China, and which destroyed all present hope of Magdalen's marriage. As the words passed the lawyer's lips, Miss Garth and Norah looked at Magdalen anxiously. Her face turned a shade paler—but not a feature of it moved; not a word escaped her. Norah, who held her sister's hand in her own, felt it tremble for a moment, and then turn cold—and that was all.

"Let me mention plainly what I have done," resumed Mr. Pendril; "I am very desirous you should not think that I have left any effort untried. When I wrote to Michael Vanstone, in the first instance, I did not confine myself to the usual formal statement. I put before him, plainly and earnestly, every one of the circumstances under which he has become possessed of his brother's fortune. When I received the answer, referring me to his written instructions to his lawyer in London—and when a copy of those instructions was placed in my hands—I positively declined, on becoming acquainted with them, to receive the writer's decision as final. I induced the solicitor, on the other side, to accord us a further term of delay; I attempted to see Mr. Noel Vanstone in London for the purpose of obtaining his intercession; and, failing in that, I myself wrote to his father for the second time. The answer referred me, in insolently curt terms, to the instructions already communicated; declared those instructions to be final; and declined any further correspondence with me. There is the beginning and the end of the negotiation. If I have overlooked any means of touching this heartless man—tell me, and those means shall be tried."

He looked at Norah. She pressed her sister's hand encouragingly, and answered for both of them.

"I speak for my sister, as well as for myself," she said, with her color a little heightened, with her natural gentleness of manner just touched by a quiet, uncomplaining sadness. "You have done all that could be done, Mr. Pendril. We have tried to restrain ourselves from hoping too confidently; and we are deeply grateful for your kindness, at a time when kindness is sorely needed by both of us."

Magdalen's hand returned the pressure of her sister's—withdrew itself—trifled for a moment impatiently with the arrangement of her dress—then suddenly moved the chair closer to the table. Leaning one arm on it (with the hand fast clinched), she looked across at Mr. Pendril. Her face, always remarkable for its want of color, was now startling to contemplate, in its blank, bloodless pallor. But the light in her large gray eyes was bright and steady as ever; and her voice, though low in tone, was clear and resolute in accent as she addressed the lawyer in these terms:

"I understood you to say, Mr. Pendril, that my father's brother had sent his written orders to London, and that you had a copy. Have you preserved it?"

"Certainly."

"Have you got it about you?"

"I have."

"May I see it?"

Mr. Pendril hesitated, and looked uneasily from Magdalen to Miss Garth, and from Miss Garth back again to Magdalen.

"Pray oblige me by not pressing your request," he said. "It is surely enough that you know the result of the instructions. Why should you agitate yourself to no purpose by reading them? They are expressed so cruelly; they show such abominable want of feeling, that I really cannot prevail upon myself to let you see them."

"I am sensible of your kindness, Mr. Pendril, in wishing to spare me pain. But I can bear pain; I promise to distress nobody. Will you excuse me if I repeat my request?"

She held out her hand—the soft, white, virgin hand that had touched nothing to soil it or harden it yet.

"Oh, Magdalen, think again!" said Norah.

"You distress Mr. Pendril," added Miss Garth; "you distress us all."

"There can be no end gained," pleaded the lawyer—"forgive me for saying so—there can really be no useful end gained by my showing you the instructions."

("Fools!" said Mr. Clare to himself. "Have they no eyes to see that she means to have her own way?")

"Something tells me there is an end to be gained," persisted Magdalen. "This decision is a very serious one. It is more serious to me—" She looked round at Mr. Clare, who sat closely watching her, and instantly looked back again, with the first outward betrayal of emotion which had escaped her yet. "It is even more serious to me," she resumed, "for private reasons—than it is to my sister. I know nothing yet but that our father's brother has taken our fortunes from us. He must have some motives of his own for such conduct as that. It is not fair to him, or fair to us, to keep those motives concealed. He has deliberately robbed Norah, and robbed me; and I think we have a right, if we wish it, to know why?"

"I don't wish it," said Norah.

"I do," said Magdalen; and once more she held out her hand.

At this point Mr. Clare roused himself and interfered for the first time.

"You have relieved your conscience," he said, addressing the lawyer. "Give her the right she claims. It is her right—if she will have it."

Mr. Pendril quietly took the written instructions from his pocket. "I have warned you," he said—and handed the papers across the table without another word. One of the pages of writing—was folded down at the corner; and at that folded page the manuscript opened, when Magdalen first turned the leaves. "Is this the place which refers to my sister and myself?" she inquired. Mr. Pendril bowed; and Magdalen smoothed out the manuscript before her on the table.

"Will you decide, Norah?" she asked, turning to her sister. "Shall I read this aloud, or shall I read it to myself?"

"To yourself," said Miss Garth; answering for Norah, who looked at her in mute perplexity and distress.

"It shall be as you wish," said Magdalen. With that reply, she turned again to the manuscript and read these lines:

".... You are now in possession of my wishes in relation to the property in money, and to the sale of the furniture, carriages, horses, and so forth. The last point left on which it is necessary for me to instruct you refers to the persons inhabiting the house, and to certain preposterous claims on their behalf set up by a solicitor named Pendril; who has, no doubt, interested reasons of his own for making application to me.

"I understand that my late brother has left two illegitimate children; both of them young women, who are of an age to earn their own livelihood. Various considerations, all equally irregular, have been urged in respect to these persons by the solicitor representing them. Be so good as to tell him that neither you nor I have anything to do with questions of mere sentiment; and then state plainly, for his better information, what the motives are which regulate my conduct, and what the provision is which I feel myself justified in making for the two young women. Your instructions on both these points you will find detailed in the next paragraph.

"I wish the persons concerned to know, once for all, how I regard the circumstances which have placed my late brother's property at my disposal. Let them understand that I consider those circumstances to be a Providential interposition which has restored to me the inheritance that ought always to have been mine. I receive the money, not only as my right, but also as a proper compensation for the injustice which I suffered from my father, and a proper penalty paid by my younger brother for the vile intrigue by which he succeeded in disinheriting me. His conduct, when a young man, was uniformly discreditable in all the relations of life; and what it then was it continued to be (on the showing of his own legal representative) after the time when I ceased to hold any communication with him. He appears to have systematically imposed a woman on Society as his wife who was not his wife, and to have completed the outrage on morality by afterward marrying her. Such conduct as this has called down a Judgment on himself and his children. I will not invite retribution on my own head by assisting those children to continue the imposition which their parents practiced, and by helping them to take a place in the world to which they are not entitled. Let them, as becomes their birth, gain their bread in situations. If they show themselves disposed to accept their proper position I will assist them to start virtuously in life by a present of one hundred pounds each. This sum I authorize you to pay them, on their personal application, with the necessary acknowledgment of receipt; and on the express understanding that the transaction, so completed, is to be the beginning and the end of my connection with them. The arrangements under which they quit the house I leave to your discretion; and I have only to add that my decision on this matter, as on all other matters, is positive and final."

Line by line—without once looking up from the pages before her —Magdalen read those atrocious sentences through, from beginning to end. The other persons assembled in the room, all eagerly looking at her together, saw the dress rising and falling faster and faster over her bosom—saw the hand in which she lightly held the manuscript at the outset close unconsciously on the paper and crush it, as she advanced nearer and nearer to the end—but detected no other outward signs of what was passing within her. As soon as she had done, she silently pushed the manuscript away, and put her hands on a sudden over her face. When she withdrew them, all the four persons in the room noticed a change in her. Something in her expression had altered, subtly and silently; something which made the familiar features suddenly look strange, even to her sister and Miss Garth; something, through all after years, never to be forgotten in connection with that day—and never to be described.

The first words she spoke were addressed to Mr. Pendril.

"May I ask one more favor," she said, "before you enter on your business arrangements?"

Mr. Pendril replied ceremoniously by a gesture of assent. Magdalen's resolution to possess herself of the Instructions did not appear to have produced a favorable impression on the lawyer's mind.

"You mentioned what you were so kind as to do, in our interests, when you first wrote to Mr. Michael Vanstone," she continued. "You said you had told him all the circumstances. I want—if you will allow me—to be made quite sure of what he really knew about us—when he sent these orders to his lawyer. Did he know that my father had made a will, and that he had left our fortunes to my sister and myself?"

"He did know it," said Mr. Pendril.

"Did you tell him how it happened that we are left in this helpless position?"

"I told him that your father was entirely unaware, when he married, of the necessity for making another will."

"And that another will would have been made, after he saw Mr. Clare, but for the dreadful misfortune of his death?"

"He knew that also."

"Did he know that my father's untiring goodness and kindness to both of us—"

Her voice faltered for the first time: she sighed, and put her hand to her head wearily. Norah spoke entreatingly to her; Miss Garth spoke entreatingly to her; Mr. Clare sat silent, watching her more and more earnestly. She answered her sister's remonstrance with a faint smile. "I will keep my promise," she said; "I will distress nobody." With that reply, she turned again to Mr. Pendril; and steadily reiterated the question—but in another form of words.

"Did Mr. Michael Vanstone know that my father's great anxiety was to make sure of providing for my sister and myself?"

"He knew it in your father's own words. I sent him an extract from your father's last letter to me."

"The letter which asked you to come for God's sake, and relieve him from the dreadful thought that his daughters were unprovided for? The letter which said he should not rest in his grave if he left us disinherited?"

"That letter and those words."

She paused, still keeping her eyes steadily fixed on the lawyer's face.

"I want to fasten it all in my mind," she said "before I go on. Mr. Michael Vanstone knew of the first will; he knew what prevented the making of the second will; he knew of the letter and he read the words. What did he know of besides? Did you tell him of my mother's last illness? Did you say that her share in the money would have been left to us, if she could have lifted her dying hand in your presence? Did you try to make him ashamed of the cruel law which calls girls in our situation Nobody's Children, and which allows him to use us as he is using us now?"

"I put all those considerations to him. I left none of them doubtful; I left none of them out."

She slowly reached her hand to the copy of the Instructions, and slowly folded it up again, in the shape in which it had been presented to her. "I am much obliged to you, Mr. Pendril." With those words, she bowed, and gently pushed the manuscript back across the table; then turned to her sister.

"Norah," she said, "if we both of us live to grow old, and if you ever forget all that we owe to Michael Vanstone—come to me, and I will remind you."

She rose and walked across the room by herself to the window. As she passed Mr. Clare, the old man stretched out his claw-like fingers and caught her fast by the arm before she was aware of him.

"What is this mask of yours hiding?" he asked, forcing her to bend to him, and looking close into her face. "Which of the extremes of human temperature does your courage start from—the dead cold or the white hot?"

She shrank back from him and turned away her head in silence. She would have resented that unscrupulous intrusion on her own thoughts from any man alive but Frank's father. He dropped her arm as suddenly as he had taken it, and let her go on to the window. "No," he said to himself, "not the cold extreme, whatever else it may be. So much the worse for her, and for all belonging to her."

There was a momentary pause. Once more the dripping rustle of the rain and the steady ticking of the clock filled up the gap of silence. Mr. Pendril put the Instructions back in his pocket, considered a little, and, turning toward Norah and Miss Garth, recalled their attention to the present and pressing necessities of the time.

"Our consultation has been needlessly prolonged," he sail, "by painful references to the past. We shall be better employed in settling our arrangements for the future. I am obliged to return to town this evening. Pray let me hear how I can best assist you; pray tell me what trouble and what responsibility I can take off your hands."

For the moment, neither Norah nor Miss Garth seemed to be capable of answering him. Magdalen's reception of the news which annihilated the marriage prospect that her father's own lips had placed before her not a month since, had bewildered and dismayed them alike. They had summoned their courage to meet the shock of her passionate grief, or to face the harder trial of witnessing her speechless despair. But they were not prepared for her invincible resolution to read the Instructions; for the terrible questions which she had put to the lawyer; for her immovable determination to fix all the circumstances in her mind, under which Michael Vanstone's decision had been pronounced. There she stood at the window, an unfathomable mystery to the sister who had never been parted from her, to the governess who had trained her from a child. Miss Garth remembered the dark doubts which had crossed her mind on the day when she and Magdalen had met in the garden. Norah looked forward to the coming time, with the first serious dread of it on her sister's account which she had felt yet. Both had hitherto remained passive, in despair of knowing what to do. Both were now silent, in despair of knowing what to say.

Mr. Pendril patiently and kindly helped them, by returning to the subject of their future plans for the second time.

"I am sorry to press any business matters on your attention," he said, "when you are necessarily unfitted to deal with them. But I must take my instructions back to London with me to night. With reference, in the first place, to the disgraceful pecuniary offer, to which I have already alluded. The younger Miss Vanstone having read the Instructions, needs no further information from my lips. The elder will, I hope, excuse me if I tell her (what I should be ashamed to tell her, but that it is a matter of necessity), that Mr. Michael Vanstone's provision for his brother's children begins and ends with an offer to each of them of one hundred pounds."

Norah's face crimsoned with indignation. She started to her feet, as if Michael Vanstone had been present in the room, and had personally insulted her.

"I see," said the lawyer, wishing to spare her; "I may tell Mr. Michael Vanstone you refuse the money."

"Tell him," she broke out passionately, "if I was starving by the roadside, I wouldn't touch a farthing of it!"

"Shall I notify your refusal also?" asked Mr. Pendril, speaking to Magdalen next.

She turned round from the window—but kept her face in shadow, by standing close against it with her back to the light.

"Tell him, on my part," she said, "to think again before he starts me in life with a hundred pounds. I will give him time to think." She spoke those strange words with a marked emphasis; and turning back quickly to the window, hid her face from the observation of every one in the room.

"You both refuse the offer," said Mr. Pendril, taking out his pencil, and making his professional note of the decision. As he shut up his pocketbook, he glanced toward Magdalen doubtfully. She had roused in him the latent distrust which is a lawyer's second nature: he had his suspicions of her looks; he had his suspicions of her language. Her sister seemed to have mere influence over her than Miss Garth. He resolved to speak privately to her sister before he went away.

While the idea was passing through his mind, his attention was claimed by another question from Magdalen.

"Is he an old man?" she asked, suddenly, without turning round from the window.

"If you mean Mr. Michael Vanstone, he is seventy-five or seventy-six years of age."

"You spoke of his son a little while since. Has he any other sons—or daughters?"

"None."

"Do you know anything of his wife?"

"She has been dead for many years."

There was a pause. "Why do you ask these questions?" said Norah.

"I beg your pardon," replied Magdalen, quietly; "I won't ask any more."

For the third time, Mr. Pendril returned to the business of the interview.

"The servants must not be forgotten," he said. "They must be settled with and discharged: I will give them the necessary explanation before I leave. As for the house, no questions connected with it need trouble you. The carriages and horses, the furniture and plate, and so on, must simply be left on the premises to await Mr. Michael Vanstone's further orders. But any possessions, Miss Vanstone, personally belonging to you or to your sister—jewelry and dresses, and any little presents which may have been made to you—are entirely at your disposal. With regard to the time of your departure, I understand that a month or more will elapse before Mr. Michael Vanstone can leave Zurich; and I am sure I only do his solicitor justice in saying—"

"Excuse me, Mr. Pendril," interposed Norah; "I think I understand, from what you have just said, that our house and everything in it belongs to—?" She stopped, as if the mere utterance of the man's name was abhorrent to her.

"To Michael Vanstone," said Mr. Pendril. "The house goes to him with the rest of the property."

"Then I, for one, am ready to leave it tomorrow!"

Magdalen started at the window, as her sister spoke, and looked at Mr. Clare, with the first open signs of anxiety and alarm which she had shown yet.

"Don't be angry with me," she whispered, stooping over the old man with a sudden humility of look, and a sudden nervousness of manner. "I can't go without seeing Frank first!"

"You shall see him," replied Mr. Clare. "I am here to speak to you about it, when the business is done."

"It is quite unnecessary to hurry your departure, as you propose," continued Mr. Pendril, addressing Norah. "I can safely assure you that a week hence will be time enough."

"If this is Mr. Michael Vanstone's house," repeated Norah; "I am ready to leave it tomorrow."

She impatiently quitted her chair and seated herself further away on the sofa. As she laid her hand on the back of it, her face changed. There, at the head of the sofa, were the cushions which had supported her mother when she lay down for the last time to repose. There, at the foot of the sofa, was the clumsy, old-fashioned arm-chair, which had been her father's favorite seat on rainy days, when she and her sister used to amuse him at the piano opposite, by playing his favorite tunes. A heavy sigh, which she tried vainly to repress, burst from her lips. "Oh," she thought, "I had forgotten these old friends! How shall we part from them when the time comes!"

"May I inquire, Miss Vanstone, whether you and your sister have formed any definite plans for the future?" asked Mr. Pendril. "Have you thought of any place of residence?"

"I may take it on myself, sir," said Miss Garth, "to answer your question for them. When they leave this house, they leave it with me. My home is their home, and my bread is their bread. Their parents honored me, trusted me, and loved me. For twelve happy years they never let me remember that I was their governess; they only let me know myself as their companion and their friend. My memory of them is the memory of unvarying gentleness and generosity; and my life shall pay the debt of my gratitude to their orphan children."

Norah rose hastily from the sofa; Magdalen impetuously left the window. For once, there was no contrast in the conduct of the sisters. For once, the same impulse moved their hearts, the same earnest feeling inspired their words. Miss Garth waited until the first outburst of emotion had passed away; then rose, and, taking Norah and Magdalen each by the hand, addressed herself to Mr. Pendril and Mr. Clare. She spoke with perfect self-possession; strong in her artless unconsciousness of her own good action.

"Even such a trifle as my own story," she said, "is of some importance at such a moment as this. I wish you both, gentlemen, to understand that I am not promising more to the daughters of your old friend than I can perform. When I first came to this house, I entered it under such independent circumstances as are not common in the lives of governesses. In my younger days,

I was associated in teaching with my elder sister: we established a school in London, which grew to be a large and prosperous one. I only left it, and became a private governess, because the heavy responsibility of the school was more than my strength could bear. I left my share in the profits untouched, and I possess a pecuniary interest in our establishment to this day. That is my story, in few words. When we leave this house, I propose that we shall go back to the school in London, which is still prosperously directed by my elder sister. We can live there as quietly as we please, until time has helped us to bear our affliction better than we can bear it now. If Norah's and Magdalen's altered prospects oblige them to earn their own independence, I can help them to earn it, as a gentleman's daughters should. The best families in this land are glad to ask my sister's advice where the interests of their children's home-training are concerned; and I answer, beforehand, for her hearty desire to serve Mr. Vanstone's daughters, as I answer for my own. That is the future which my gratitude to their father and mother, and my love for themselves, now offers to them. If you think my proposal, gentlemen, a fit and fair proposal—and I see in your faces that you do—let us not make the hard necessities of our position harder still, by any useless delay in meeting them at once. Let us do what we must do; let us act on Norah's decision, and leave this house to-morrow. You mentioned the servants just now, Mr. Pendril: I am ready to call them together in the next room, and to assist you in the settlement of their claims, whenever you please."

Without waiting for the lawyer's answer, without leaving the sisters time to realize their own terrible situation, she moved at once toward the door. It was her wise resolution to meet the coming trial by doing much and saying little. Before she could leave the room, Mr. Clare followed, and stopped her on the threshold.

"I never envied a woman's feelings before," said the old man. "It may surprise you to hear it; but I envy yours. Wait! I have something more to say. There is an obstacle still left—the everlasting obstacle of Frank. Help me to sweep him off. Take the elder sister along with you and the lawyer, and leave me here to have it out with the younger. I want to see what metal she's really made of."

While Mr. Clare was addressing these words to Miss Garth, Mr. Pendril had taken the opportunity of speaking to Norah. "Before I go back to town," he said, "I should like to have a word with you in private. From what has passed today, Miss Vanstone, I have formed a very high opinion of your discretion; and, as an old friend of your father's, I want to take the freedom of speaking to you about your sister."

Before Norah could answer, she was summoned, in compliance with Mr. Clare's request, to the conference with the servants. Mr. Pendril followed Miss Garth, as a matter of course. When the three were out in the hall, Mr. Clare re-entered the room, closed the door, and signed peremptorily to Magdalen to take a chair.

She obeyed him in silence. He took a turn up and down the room, with his hands in the side-pockets of the long, loose, shapeless coat which he habitually wore.

"How old are you?" he said, stopping suddenly, and speaking to her with the whole breadth of the room between them.

"I was eighteen last birthday," she answered, humbly, without looking up at him.

"You have shown extraordinary courage for a girl of eighteen. Have you got any of that courage left?"

She clasped her hands together, and wrung them hard. A few tears gathered in her eyes, and rolled slowly over her cheeks.

"I can't give Frank up," she said, faintly. "You don't care for me, I know; but you used to care for my father. Will you try to be kind to me for my father's sake?"

The last words died away in a whisper; she could say no more. Never had she felt the illimitable power which a woman's love possesses of absorbing into itself every other event, every other joy or sorrow of her life, as she felt it then. Never had she so tenderly associated Frank with the memory of her lost parents, as at that moment. Never had the impenetrable atmosphere of illusion through which women behold the man of their choice—the atmosphere which had blinded her to all that was weak, selfish, and mean in Frank's nature—surrounded him with a brighter halo than now, when she was pleading with the father for the possession of the son. "Oh, don't ask me to give him up!" she said, trying to take courage, and shuddering from head to foot. In the next instant, she flew to the opposite extreme, with the suddenness of a flash of lightning. "I won't give him up!" she burst out violently. "No! not if a thousand fathers ask me!"

"I am one father," said Mr. Clare. "And I don't ask you."

In the first astonishment and delight of hearing those unexpected words, she started to her feet, crossed the room, and tried to throw her arms round his neck. She might as well have attempted to move the house from its foundations. He took her by the shoulders and put her back in her chair. His inexorable eyes looked her into submission; and his lean forefinger shook at her warningly, as if he was quieting a fractious child.

"Hug Frank," he said; "don't hug me. I haven't done with you yet; when I have, you may shake hands with me, if you like. Wait, and compose yourself."

He left her. His hands went back into his pockets, and his monotonous march up and down the room began again.

"Ready?" he asked, stopping short after a while. She tried to answer. "Take two minutes more," he said, and resumed his walk with the regularity of clock-work. "These are the creatures," he thought to himself, "into whose keeping men otherwise sensible give the happiness of their lives. Is there any other object in creation, I wonder, which answers its end as badly as a woman does?"

He stopped before her once more. Her breathing was easier; the dark flush on her face was dying out again.

"Ready?" he repeated. "Yes; ready at last. Listen to me; and let's get it over. I don't ask you to give Frank up. I ask you to wait."

"I will wait," she said. "Patiently, willingly."

"Will you make Frank wait?"

"Yes."

"Will you send him to China?"

Her head drooped upon her bosom, and she clasped her hands again, in silence. Mr. Clare saw where the difficulty lay, and marched straight up to it on the spot.

"I don't pretend to enter into your feelings for Frank, or Frank's for you," he said. "The subject doesn't interest me. But I do pretend to state two plain truths. It is one plain truth that you can't be married till you have money enough to pay for the roof that shelters you, the clothes that cover you, and the victuals you eat. It is another plain truth that you can't find the money; that I can't find the money; and that Frank's only chance of finding it, is going to China. If I tell him to go, he'll sit in a corner and cry. If I insist, he'll say Yes, and deceive me. If I go a step further, and see him on board ship with my own eyes, he'll slip off in the pilot's boat, and sneak back secretly to you. That's his disposition."

"No!" said Magdalen. "It's not his disposition; it's his love for Me."

"Call it what you like," retorted Mr. Clare. "Sneak or Sweetheart —he's too slippery, in either capacity, for my fingers to hold him. My shutting the door won't keep him from coming back. Your shutting the door will. Have you the courage to shut it? Are you fond enough of him not to stand in his light?"

"Fond! I would die for him!"

"Will you send him to China?"

She sighed bitterly.

"Have a little pity for me," she said. "I have lost my father; I have lost my mother; I have lost my fortune—and now I am to lose Frank. You don't like women, I know; but try to help me with a little pity. I don't say it's not for his own interests to send him to China; I only say it's hard—very, very hard on me."

Mr. Clare had been deaf to her violence, insensible to her caresses, blind to her tears; but under the tough integument of his philosophy he had a heart—and it answered that hopeless appeal; it felt those touching words.

"I don't deny that your case is a hard one," he said. "I don't want to make it harder. I only ask you to do in Frank's interests what Frank is too weak to do for himself. It's no fault of yours; it's no fault of mine—but it's not the less true that the fortune you were to have brought him has changed owners."

She suddenly looked up, with a furtive light in her eyes, with a threatening smile on her lips.

"It may change owners again," she said.

Mr. Clare saw the alteration in her expression, and heard the tones of her voice. But the words were spoken low; spoken as if to herself—they failed to reach him across the breadth of the room. He stopped instantly in his walk and asked what she had said.

"Nothing," she answered, turning her head away toward the window, and looking out mechanically at the falling rain. "Only my own thoughts."

Mr. Clare resumed his walk, and returned to his subject.

"It's your interest," he went on, "as well as Frank's interest, that he should go. He may make money enough to marry you in China; he can't make it here. If he stops at home, he'll be the ruin of both of you. He'll shut his eyes to every consideration of prudence, and pester you to marry him; and when he has carried his point, he will be the first to turn round afterward and complain that you're a burden on him. Hear me out! You're in love with Frank—I'm not, and I know him. Put you two together often enough; give him time enough to hug, cry, pester, and plead; and I'll tell you what the end will be—you'll marry him."

He had touched the right string at last. It rung back in answer before he could add another word.

"You don't know me," she said, firmly. "You don't know what I can suffer for Frank's sake. He shall never marry me till I can be what my father said I should be—the making of his fortune. He shall take no burden, when he takes me; I promise you that! I'll be the good angel of Frank's life; I'll not go a penniless girl to him, and drag him down." She abruptly left her seat, advanced a few steps toward Mr. Clare, and stopped in the middle of the room. Her arms fell helpless on either side of her, and she burst into tears. "He shall go," she said. "If my heart breaks in doing it, I'll tell him to-morrow that we must say Good-by!"

Mr. Clare at once advanced to meet her, and held out his hand.

"I'll help you," he said. "Frank shall hear every word that has passed between us. When he comes to-morrow he shall know, beforehand, that he comes to say Good-by."

She took his hand in both her own—hesitated—looked at him—and pressed it to her bosom. "May I ask a favor of you, before you go?" she said, timidly. He tried to take his hand from her; but she knew her advantage, and held it fast. "Suppose there should be some change for the better?" she went on. "Suppose I could come to Frank, as my fat her said I should come to him—?"

Before she could complete the question, Mr. Clare made a second effort and withdrew his hand. "As your father said you should come to him?" he repeated, looking at her attentively.

"Yes," she replied. "Strange things happen sometimes. If strange things happen to me will you let Frank come back before the five years are out?"

What did she mean? Was she clinging desperately to the hope of melting Michael Vanstone's heart? Mr. Clare could draw no other conclusion from what she had just said to him. At the beginning of the interview he would have roughly dispelled her delusion. At the end of the interview he left her compassionately in possession of it.

"You are hoping against all hope," he said; "but if it gives you courage, hope on. If this impossible good fortune of yours ever happens, tell me, and Frank shall come back. In the meantime—"

"In the meantime," she interposed sadly, "you have my promise."

Once more Mr. Clare's sharp eyes searched her face attentively.

"I will trust your promise," he said. "You shall see Frank to-morrow."

She went back thoughtfully to her chair, and sat down again in silence. Mr. Clare made for the door before any formal leave-taking could pass between them. "Deep!" he thought to himself, as he looked back at her before he went out; "only eighteen; and too deep for my sounding!"

In the hall he found Norah, waiting anxiously to hear what had happened.

"Is it all over?" she asked. "Does Frank go to China?"

"Be careful how you manage that sister of yours," said Mr. Clare, without noticing the question. "She has one great misfortune to contend with: she's not made for the ordinary jog-trot of a woman's life. I don't say I can see straight to the end of the good or evil in her—I only warn you, her future will be no common one."

An hour later, Mr. Pendril left the house; and, by that night's post, Miss Garth dispatched a letter to her sister in London.

THE END OF THE FIRST SCENE.

BETWEEN THE SCENES.

PROGRESS OF THE STORY THROUGH THE POST.

I.

From Norah Vanstone to Mr. Pendril.

"Westmoreland House, Kensington,

"August 14th, 1846.

"DEAR MR. PENDRIL—The date of this letter will show you that the last of many hard partings is over. We have left Combe-Raven; we have said farewell to home.

"I have been thinking seriously of what you said to me on Wednesday, before you went back to town. I entirely agree with you that Miss Garth is more shaken by all she has gone through for our sakes than she is herself willing to admit; and that it is my duty, for the future, to spare her all the anxiety that I can on the subject of my sister and myself. This is very little to do for our dearest friend, for our second mother. Such as it is, I will do it with all my heart.

"But, forgive me for saying that I am as far as ever from agreeing with you about Magdalen. I am so sensible, in our helpless position, of the importance of your assistance; so anxious to be worthy of the interest of my father's trusted adviser and oldest friend, that I feel really and truly disappointed with myself for differing with you—and yet I do differ. Magdalen is very strange, very unaccountable, to those who don't know her intimately. I can understand that she has innocently misled you; and that she has presented herself, perhaps, under her least favorable aspect. But that the clew to her language and her conduct on Wednesday last is to be found in such a feeling toward the man who has ruined us, as the feeling at which you hinted, is what I can not and will not believe of my sister. If you knew, as I do, what a noble nature she has, you would not be surprised at this obstinate resistance of mine to your opinion. Will you try to alter it? I don't mind what Mr. Clare says; he believes in nothing. But I attach a very serious importance to what you say; and, kind as I know your motives to be, it distresses me to think you are doing Magdalen an injustice.

"Having relieved my mind of this confession, I may now come to the proper object of my letter. I promised, if you could not find leisure time to visit us to-day, to write and tell you all that happened after you left us. The day has passed without our seeing you. So I open my writing-case and perform my promise.

"I am sorry to say that three of the women-servants—the house-maid, the kitchen-maid, and even our own maid (to whom I am sure we have always been kind)—took advantage of your having paid them their wages to pack up and go as soon as your back was turned. They came to say good-by with as much ceremony and as little feeling as if they were leaving the house under ordinary circumstances. The cook, for all her violent temper, behaved very differently: she sent up a message to say that she would stop and help us to the last. And Thomas (who has never yet been in any other place than ours) spoke so gratefully of my dear father's unvarying kindness to him, and asked so anxiously to be allowed to go on serving us while his little savings lasted, that Magdalen and I forgot all formal considerations and both shook hands with him. The poor lad went out of the room crying. I wish him well; I hope he will find a kind master and a good place.

"The long, quiet, rainy evening out-of-doors—our last evening at Combe-Raven—was a sad trial to us. I think winter-time would have weighed less on our spirits; the drawn curtains and the bright lamps, and the companionable fires would have helped us. We were only five in the house altogether—after having once been so many! I can't tell you how dreary the gray daylight looked, toward seven o'clock, in the lonely rooms, and on the noiseless staircase. Surely, the prejudice in favor of long summer evenings is the prejudice of happy people? We did our best. We kept ourselves employed, and Miss Garth helped us. The prospect of preparing for our departure, which had seemed so dreadful earlier in the day, altered into the prospect of a refuge from ourselves as the evening came on. We each tried at first to pack up in our own rooms—but the loneliness was more than we could bear. We carried all our possessions downstairs, and heaped them on the large dining-table, and so made our preparations together in the same room. I am sure we have taken nothing away which does not properly belong to us.

"Having already mentioned to you my own conviction that Magdalen was not herself when you saw her on Wednesday, I feel tempted to stop here and give you an instance in proof of what I say. The little circumstance happened on Wednesday night, just before we went up to our rooms.

"After we had packed our dresses and our birthday presents, our books and our music, we began to sort our letters, which had got confused from being placed on the table together. Some of my letters were mixed with Magdalen's, and some of hers with mine. Among these last I found a card, which had been given to my sister early in the year by an actor who managed an amateur theatrical performance in which she took a part. The man had given her the card, containing his name and address, in the belief that she would be invited to many more amusements of the same kind, and in the hope that she would recommend him as a superintendent on future occasions. I only relate these trifling particulars to show you how little worth keeping such a card could be, in such circumstances as ours. Naturally enough, I threw it away from me across the table, meaning to throw it on the floor. It fell short, close to the place in which Magdalen was sitting. She took it up, looked at it, and immediately declared that she would not have had this perfectly worthless thing destroyed for the world. She was almost angry with me for having thrown it away; almost angry with Miss Garth for asking what she could possibly want with it! Could there be any plainer proof than this that our misfortunes—falling so much more heavily on her than on me—have quite unhinged her, and worn her out? Surely her words and looks are not to be interpreted against her, when she is not sufficiently mistress of herself to exert her natural judgment—when she shows the unreasonable petulance of a child on a question which is not of the slightest importance.

"A little after eleven we went upstairs to try if we could get some rest.

"I drew aside the curtain of my window and looked out. Oh, what a cruel last night it was: no moon, no stars; such deep darkness that not one of the dear familiar objects in the garden was visible when I looked for them; such deep stillness that even my own movements about the room almost frightened me! I tried to lie down and sleep, but the sense of loneliness came again and quite overpowered me. You will say I am old enough, at six-and-twenty, to have exerted more control over myself. I hardly know how it happened, but I stole into Magdalen's room, just as I used to steal into it years and years ago, when we were children. She was not in bed; she was sitting with her writing materials before her, thinking. I said I wanted to be with her the last night; and she kissed me, and told me to lie down, and promised soon to follow me. My mind was a little quieted and I fell asleep. It was daylight when I woke—and the first sight I saw was Magdalen, still sitting in the chair, and still thinking. She had never been to bed; she had not slept all through the night.

"'I shall sleep when we have left Combe-Raven,' she said. 'I shall be better when it is all over, and I have bid Frank good-by.' She had in her hand our father's will, and the letter he wrote to you; and when she had done speaking, she gave them into my possession. I was the eldest (she said), and those last precious relics ought to be in my keeping. I tried to propose to her that we should divide them; but she shook her head. 'I have copied for myself,' was her answer, 'all that he says of us in the will, and all that he says in the letter.' She told me this, and took from her bosom a tiny white silk bag, which she had made in the night, and in which she had put the extracts, so as to keep them always about her. 'This tells me in his own words what his last wishes were for both of us,' she said; 'and this is all I want for the future.'

"These are trifles to dwell on; and I am almost surprised at myself for not feeling ashamed to trouble you with them. But, since I have known what your early connection was with my father and mother, I have learned to think of you (and, I suppose, to write to you) as an old friend. And, besides, I have it so much at heart to change your opinion of Magdalen, that I can't help telling you the smallest things about her which may, in my judgment, end in making you think of her as I do.

"When breakfast-time came (on Thursday morning), we were surprised to find a strange letter on the table. Perhaps I ought to mention it to you, in case of any future necessity for your interference. It was addressed to Miss Garth, on paper with the deepest mourning-border round it; and the writer was the same man who followed us on our way home from a walk one day last spring—Captain Wragge. His object appears to be to assert once more his audacious claim to a family connection with my poor mother, under cover of a letter of condolence; which it is an insolence in such a person to have written at all. He expresses as much sympathy—on his discovery of our affliction in the newspaper—as if he had been really intimate with us; and he begs to know, in a postscript (being evidently in total ignorance of all that has really happened), whether it is thought desirable that he should be present, among the other relatives, at the reading of the will! The address he gives, at which letters will reach him for the next fortnight, is, 'Post-office, Birmingham.' This is all I have to tell you on the subject. Both the letter and the writer seem to me to be equally unworthy of the slightest notice, on our part or on yours.

"After breakfast Magdalen left us, and went by herself into the morning-room. The weather being still showery, we had arranged that Francis Clare should see her in that room, when he presented himself to take his leave. I was upstairs when he came; and I remained upstairs for more than half an hour afterward, sadly anxious, as you may well believe, on Magdalen's account.

"At the end of the half-hour or more, I came downstairs. As I reached the landing I suddenly heard her voice, raised entreatingly, and calling on him by his name—then loud sobs—then a frightful laughing and screaming, both together, that rang through the house. I instantly ran into the room, and found Magdalen on the sofa in violent hysterics, and Frank standing staring at her, with a lowering, angry face, biting his nails.

"I felt so indignant—without knowing plainly why, for I was ignorant, of course, of what had passed at the interview—that I took Mr. Francis Clare by the shoulders and pushed him out of the room. I am careful to tell you how I acted toward him, and what led to it; because I understand that he is excessively offended with me, and that he is likely to mention elsewhere what he calls my unladylike violence toward him. If he should mention it to you, I am anxious to acknowledge, of my own accord, that I forgot myself—not, I hope you will think, without some provocation.

"I pushed him into the hall, leaving Magdalen, for the moment, to Miss Garth's care. Instead of going away, he sat down sulkily on one of the hall chairs. 'May I ask the reason of this extraordinary violence?' he inquired, with an injured look. 'No,' I said. 'You will be good enough to imagine the reason for yourself, and to leave us immediately, if you please.' He sat doggedly in the chair, biting his nails and considering. 'What have I done to be treated in this unfeeling manner?' he asked, after a while. 'I can enter into no discussion with you,' I answered; 'I can only request you to leave us. If you persist in waiting to see my sister again, I will go to the cottage myself and appeal to your father.' He got up in a great hurry at those words. 'I have been infamously used in this business,' he said. 'All the hardships and the sacrifices have fallen to my share. I'm the only one among you who has any heart: all the rest are as hard as stones—Magdalen included. In one breath she says she loves me, and in another she tells me to go to China. What have I done to be treated with this heartless inconsistency? I am consistent myself—I only want to stop at home—and (what's the consequence?) you're all against me!' In that manner he grumbled his way down the steps, and so I saw the last of him. This was all that passed between us. If he gives you any other account of it, what he says will be false. He made no attempt to return. An hour afterward his father came alone to say good-by. He saw Miss Garth and me, but not Magdalen; and he told us he would take the necessary measures, with your assistance, for having his son properly looked after in London, and seen safely on board the vessel when the time came. It was a short visit, and a sad leave-taking. Even Mr. Clare was sorry, though he tried hard to hide it.

"We had barely two hours, after Mr. Clare had left us, before it would be time to go. I went back to Magdalen, and found her quieter and better, though terribly pale and exhausted, and oppressed, as I fancied, by thoughts which she could not prevail on herself to communicate. She would tell me nothing then—she has told me nothing since—of what passed between herself and Francis Clare. When I spoke of him angrily (feeling as I did that he had distressed and tortured her, when she ought to have had all the encouragement and comfort from him that man could give), she refused to hear me: she made the kindest allowances and the sweetest excuses for him, and laid all the blame of the dreadful state in which I had found her entirely on herself. Was I wrong in telling you that she had a noble nature? And won't you alter your opinion when you read these lines?

"We had no friends to come and bid us good-by; and our few acquaintances were too far from us—perhaps too indifferent about us—to call. We employed the little leisure left in going over the house together for the last time. We took leave of our old schoolroom, our bedrooms, the room where our mother died, the little study where our father used to settle his accounts and write his letters—feeling toward them, in our forlorn condition, as other girls might have felt at parting with old friends. From the house, in a gleam of fine weather, we went into the garden, and gathered our last nosegay; with the purpose of drying the flowers when they begin to wither, and keeping them in remembrance of the happy days that are gone. When we had said good-by to the garden, there was only half an hour left. We went together to the grave; we knelt down, side by side, in silence, and kissed the sacred ground. I thought my heart would have broken. August was the month of my mother's birthday; and, this time last year, my father and Magdalen and I were all consulting in secret what present we could make to surprise her with on the birthday morning.

"If you had seen how Magdalen suffered, you would never doubt her again. I had to take her from the last resting-place of our father and mother almost by force. Before we were out of the churchyard she broke from me and ran back. She dropped on her knees at the grave; tore up from it passionately a handful of grass; and said something to herself, at the same moment, which, though I followed her instantly, I did not get near enough to hear. She turned on me in such a frenzied manner, when I tried to raise her from the ground—she looked at me with such a fearful wildness in her eyes—that I felt absolutely terrified at the sight of her. To my relief, the paroxysm left her as suddenly as it had come. She thrust away the tuft of grass into the bosom of her dress, and took my arm and hurried with me out of the churchyard. I asked her why she had gone back—I asked what those words were which she had spoken at the grave. 'A promise to our dead father,' she answered, with a momentary return of the wild look and the frenzied manner which had startled me already. I was afraid to agitate her by saying more; I left all other questions to be asked at a fitter and a quieter time. You will understand from this how terribly she suffers, how wildly and strangely she acts under violent agitation; and you will not interpret against her what she said or did when you saw her on Wednesday last.

"We only returned to the house in time to hasten away from it to the train. Perhaps it was better for us so—better that we had only a moment left to look back before the turn in the road hid the last of Combe-Raven from our view. There was not a soul we knew at the station; nobody to stare at us, nobody to wish us good-by. The rain came on again as we took our seats in the train. What we felt at the sight of the railway—what horrible remembrances it forced on our minds of the calamity which has made us fatherless—I cannot, and dare not, tell you. I have tried anxiously not to write this letter in a gloomy tone; not to return all your kindness to us by distressing you with our grief. Perhaps I have dwelt too long already on the little story of our parting from home? I can only say, in excuse, that my heart is full of it; and what is not in my heart my pen won't write.

"We have been so short a time in our new abode that I have nothing more to tell you—except that Miss Garth's sister has received us with the heartiest kindness. She considerately leaves us to ourselves, until we are fitter than we are now to think of our future plans, and to arrange as we best can for earning our own living. The house is so large, and the position of our rooms has been so thoughtfully chosen, that I should hardly know—except when I hear the laughing of the younger girls in the garden—that we were living in a school.

"With kindest and best wishes from Miss Garth and my sister, believe me, dear Mr. Pendril, gratefully yours,

"NORAH VANSTONE."

II.

From Miss Garth to Mr. Pendril.

"Westmoreland House, Kensington,

"September 23d, 1846.

"MY DEAR SIR—I write these lines in such misery of mind as no words can describe. Magdalen has deserted us. At an early hour this morning she secretly left the house, and she has not been heard of since.

"I would come and speak to you personally; but I dare not leave Norah. I must try to control myself; I must try to write.

"Nothing happened yesterday to prepare me or to prepare Norah for this last—I had almost said, this worst—of all our afflictions. The only alteration we either of us noticed in the unhappy girl was an alteration for the better when we parted for the night. She kissed me, which she has not done latterly; and she burst out crying when she embraced her sister next. We had so little suspicion of the truth that we thought these signs of renewed tenderness and affection a promise of better things for the future.

"This morning, when her sister went into her room, it was empty, and a note in her handwriting, addressed to Norah, was lying on the dressing-table. I cannot prevail on Norah to part with the note; I can only send you the inclosed copy of it. You will see that it affords no clew to the direction she has taken.

"Knowing the value of time, in this dreadful emergency, I examined her room, and (with my sister's help) questioned the servants immediately on the news of her absence reaching me. Her wardrobe was empty; and all her boxes but one, which she has evidently taken away with her, are empty, too. We are of opinion that she has privately turned her dresses and jewelry into money; that she had the one trunk she took with her removed from the house yesterday; and that she left us this morning on foot. The answers given by one of the servants are so unsatisfactory that we believe the woman has been bribed to assist her; and has managed all those arrangements for her flight which she could not have safely undertaken by herself.

"Of the immediate object with which she has left us, I entertain no doubt.

"I have reasons (which I can tell you at a fitter time) for feeling assured that she has gone away with the intention of trying her fortune on the stage. She has in her possession the card of an actor by profession, who superintended an amateur theatrical performance at Clifton, in which she took part; and to him she has gone to help her. I saw the card at the time, and I know the actor's name to be Huxtable. The address I cannot call to mind quite so correctly; but I am almost sure it was at some theatrical place in Bow Street, Covent Garden. Let me entreat you not to lose a moment in sending to make the necessary inquiries; the first trace of her will, I firmly believe, be found at that address.

"If we had nothing worse to dread than her attempting to go on the stage, I should not feel the distress and dismay which now overpower me. Hundreds of other girls have acted as recklessly as she has acted, and have not ended ill after all. But my fears for Magdalen do not begin and end with the risk she is running at present.

"There has been something weighing on her mind ever since we left Combe-Raven—weighing far more heavily for the last six weeks than at first. Until the period when Francis Clare left England, I am persuaded she was secretly sustained by the hope that he would contrive to see her again. From the day when she knew that the measures you had taken for preventing this had succeeded; from the day when she was assured that the ship had really taken him away, nothing has roused, nothing has interested her. She has given herself up, more and more hopelessly, to her own brooding thoughts; thoughts which I believe first entered her mind on the day when the utter ruin of the prospects on which her marriage depended was made known to her. She has formed some desperate project of contesting the possession of her father's fortune with Michael Vanstone; and the stage career which she has gone away to try is nothing more than a means of freeing herself from all home dependence, and of enabling her to run what mad risks she pleases, in perfect security from all home control. What it costs me to write of her in these terms, I must leave you to imagine. The time has gone by when any consideration of distress to my own feelings can weigh with me. Whatever I can say which will open your eyes to the real danger, and strengthen your conviction of the instant necessity of averting it, I say in despite of myself, without hesitation and without reserve.

"One word more, and I have done.

"The last time you were so good as to come to this house, do you remember how Magdalen embarrassed and distressed us by questioning you about her right to bear her father's name? Do you remember her persisting in her inquiries, until she had forced you to acknowledge that, legally speaking, she and her sister had No Name? I venture to remind you of this, because you have the affairs of hundreds of clients to think of, and you might well have forgotten the circumstance. Whatever natural reluctance she might otherwise have had to deceiving us, and degrading herself, by the use of an assumed name, that conversation with you is certain to have removed. We must discover her by personal description—we can trace her in no other way.

"I can think of nothing more to guide your decision in our deplorable emergency. For God's sake, let no expense and no efforts be spared. My letter ought to reach you by ten o'clock this morning, at the latest. Let me have one line in answer, to say you will act instantly for the best. My only hope of quieting Norah is to show her a word of encouragement from your pen. Believe me, dear sir, yours sincerely and obliged,

"HARRIET GARTH."

III.

From Magdalen to Norah (inclosed in the preceding Letter).

"MY DARLING—Try to forgive me. I have struggled against myself till I am worn out in the effort. I am the wretchedest of living creatures. Our quiet life here maddens me; I can bear it no longer; I must go. If you knew what my thoughts are; if you knew how hard I have fought against them, and how horribly they have gone on haunting me in the lonely quiet of this house, you would pity and forgive me. Oh, my love, don't feel hurt at my not opening my heart to you as I ought! I dare not open it. I dare not show myself to you as I really am.

"Pray don't send and seek after me; I will write and relieve all your anxieties. You know, Norah, we must get our living for ourselves; I have only gone to get mine in the manner which is fittest for me. Whether I succeed, or whether I fail, I can do myself no harm either way. I have no position to lose, and no name to degrade. Don't doubt I love you—don't let Miss Garth doubt my gratitude. I go away miserable at leaving you; but I must go. If I had loved you less dearly, I might have had the courage to say this in your presence—but how could I trust myself to resist your persuasions, and to bear the sight of your distress? Farewell, my darling! Take a thousand kisses from me, my own best, dearest love, till we meet again.

"MAGDALEN."

IV.

From Sergeant Bulmer (of the Detective Police) to Mr. Pendril.

"Scotland Yard, September 29th, 1846.

"SIR—Your clerk informs me that the parties interested in our inquiry after the missing young lady are anxious for news of the same. I went to your office to speak to you about the matter to-day. Not having found you, and not being able to return and try again to-morrow, I write these lines to save delay, and to tell you how we stand thus far.

"I am sorry to say, no advance has been made since my former report. The trace of the young lady which we found nearly a week since, still remains the last trace discovered of her. This case seems a mighty simple one looked at from a distance. Looked at close, it alters very considerably for the worse, and becomes, to speak the plain truth—a Poser.

"This is how we now stand:

"We have traced the young lady to the theatrical agent's in Bow Street. We know that at an early hour on the morning of the twenty-third the agent was called downstairs, while he was dressing, to speak to a young lady in a cab at the door. We know that, on her production of Mr. Huxtable's card, he wrote on it Mr. Huxtable's address in the country, and heard her order the cabman to drive to the Great Northern terminus. We believe she left by the nine o'clock train. We followed her by the twelve o'clock train. We have ascertained that she called at half-past two at Mr. Huxtable's lodgings; that she found he was away, and not expected back till eight in the evening; that she left word she would call again at eight; and that she never returned. Mr. Huxtable's statement is—he and the young lady have never set eyes on each other. The first consideration which follows, is this: Are we to believe Mr. Huxtable? I have carefully inquired into his character; I know as much, or more, about him than he knows about himself; and my opinion is, that we are to believe him. To the best of my knowledge, he is a perfectly honest man.

"Here, then, is the hitch in the case. The young lady sets out with a certain object before her. Instead of going on to the accomplishment of that object, she stops short of it. Why has she stopped? and where? Those are, unfortunately, just the questions which we can't answer yet.

"My own opinion of the matter is, briefly, as follows: I don't think she has met with any serious accident. Serious accidents, in nine cases out of ten, discover themselves. My own notion is, that she has fallen into the hands of some person or persons interested in hiding her away, and sharp enough to know how to set about it. Whether she is in their charge, with or without her own consent, is more than I can undertake to say at present. I don't wish to raise false hopes or false fears; I wish to stop short at the opinion I have given already.

"In regard to the future, I may tell you that I have left one of my men in daily communication with the authorities. I have also taken care to have the handbills offering a reward for the discovery of her widely circulated. Lastly, I have completed the necessary arrangements for seeing the play-bills of all country theaters, and for having the dramatic companies well looked after. Some years since, this would have cost a serious expenditure of time and money. Luckily for our purpose, the country theaters are in a bad way. Excepting the large cities, hardly one of them is open, and we can keep our eye on them, with little expense and less difficulty.

"These are the steps which I think it needful to take at present. If you are of another opinion, you have only to give me your directions, and I will carefully attend to the same. I don't by any means despair of our finding the young lady and bringing her back to her friends safe and well. Please to tell them so; and allow me to subscribe myself, yours respectfully,

"ABRAHAM BULMER."

V.

Anonymous Letter addressed to Mr. Pendril.

"SIR—A word to the wise. The friends of a certain young lady are wasting time and money to no purpose. Your confidential clerk and your detective policeman are looking for a needle in a bottle of hay. This is the ninth of October, and they have not found her yet: they will as soon find the Northwest Passage. Call your dogs off; and you may hear of the young lady's safety under her own hand. The longer you look for her, the longer she will remain, what she is now—lost."

[The preceding letter is thus indorsed, in Mr. Pendril's handwriting: "No apparent means of tracing the inclosed to its source. Post-mark, 'Charing Cross.' Stationer's stamp cut off the inside of the envelope. Handwriting, probably a man's, in disguise. Writer, whoever he is, correctly informed. No further trace of the younger Miss Vanstone discovered yet."]

THE SECOND SCENE.

SKELDERGATE, YORK.

CHAPTER I.

IN that part of the city of York which is situated on the western bank of the Ouse there is a narrow street, called Skeldergate, running nearly north and south, parallel with the course of the river. The postern by which Skeldergate was formerly approached no longer exists; and the few old houses left in the street are disguised in melancholy modern costume of whitewash and cement. Shops of the smaller and poorer order, intermixed here and there with dingy warehouses and joyless private residences of red brick, compose the present aspect of Skeldergate. On the river-side the houses are separated at intervals by lanes running down to the water, and disclosing lonely little plots of open ground, with the masts of sailing-barges rising beyond. At its southward extremity the street ceases on a sudden, and the broad flow of the Ouse, the trees, the meadows, the public-walk on one bank and the towing-path on the other, open to view.

Here, where the street ends, and on the side of it furthest from the river, a narrow little lane leads up to the paved footway surmounting the ancient Walls of York. The one small row of buildings, which is all that the lane possesses, is composed of cheap lodging-houses, with an opposite view, at the distance of a few feet, of a portion of the massive city wall. This place is called Rosemary Lane. Very little light enters it; very few people live in it; the floating population of Skeldergate passes it by; and visitors to the Walk on the Walls, who use it as the way up or the way down, get out of the dreary little passage as fast as they can.

The door of one of the houses in this lost corner of York opened softly on the evening of the twenty-third of September, eighteen hundred and forty-six; and a solitary individual of the male sex sauntered into Skeldergate from the seclusion of Rosemary Lane.

Turning northward, this person directed his steps toward the bridge over the Ouse and the busy center of the city. He bore the external appearance of respectable poverty; he carried a gingham umbrella, preserved in an oilskin case; he picked his steps, with the neatest avoidance of all dirty places on the pavement; and he surveyed the scene around him with eyes of two different colors—a bilious brown eye on the lookout for employment, and a bilious green eye in a similar predicament. In plainer terms, the stranger from Rosemary Lane was no other than—Captain Wragge.

Outwardly speaking, the captain had not altered for the better since the memorable spring day when he had presented himself to Miss Garth at the lodge-gate at Combe-Raven. The railway mania of that famous year had attacked even the wary Wragge; had withdrawn him from his customary pursuits; and had left him prostrate in the end, like many a better man. He had lost his clerical appearance—he had faded with the autumn leaves. His crape hat-band had put itself in brown mourning for its own bereavement of black. His dingy white collar and cravat had died the death of old linen, and had gone to their long home at the paper-maker's, to live again one day in quires at a stationer's shop. A gray shooting-jacket in the last stage of woolen atrophy replaced the black frockcoat of former times, and, like a faithful servant, kept the dark secret of its master's linen from the eyes of a prying world. From top to toe every square inch of the captain's clothing was altered for the worse; but the man himself remained unchanged—superior to all forms of moral mildew, impervious to the action of social rust. He was as courteous, as persuasive, as blandly dignified as ever. He carried his head as high without a shirt-collar as ever he had carried it with one. The threadbare black handkerchief round his neck was perfectly tied; his rotten old shoes were neatly blacked; he might have compared chins, in the matter of smooth shaving, with the highest church dignitary in York. Time, change, and poverty had all attacked the captain together, and had all failed alike to get him down on the ground. He paced the streets of York, a man superior to clothes and circumstances—his vagabond varnish as bright on him as ever.

Arrived at the bridge, Captain Wragge stopped and looked idly over the parapet at the barges in the river. It was plainly evident that he had no particular destination to reach and nothing whatever to do. While he was still loitering, the clock of York Minster chimed the half-hour past five. Cabs rattled by him over the bridge on their way to meet the train from London, at twenty minutes to six. After a moment's hesitation, the captain sauntered after the cabs. When it is one of a man's regular habits to live upon his fellow-creatures, that man is always more or less fond of haunting large railway stations. Captain Wragge gleaned the human field, and on that unoccupied afternoon the York terminus was as likely a corner to look about in as any other.

He reached the platform a few minutes after the train had arrived. That entire incapability of devising administrative measures for the management of large crowds, which is one of the characteristics of Englishmen in authority, is nowhere more strikingly exemplified than at York. Three different lines of railway assemble three passenger mobs, from morning to night, under one roof; and leave them to raise a traveler's riot, with all the assistance which the bewildered servants of the company can render to increase the confusion. The customary disturbance was rising to its climax as Captain Wragge approached the platform. Dozens of different people were trying to attain dozens of different objects, in dozens of different directions, all starting from the same common point and all equally deprived of the means of information. A sudden parting of the crowd, near the second-class carriages, attracted the captain's curiosity. He pushed his way in; and found a decently-dressed man—assisted by a porter and a policeman—attempting to pick up some printed bills scattered from a paper parcel, which his frenzied fellow-passengers had knocked out of his hand.

Offering his assistance in this emergency, with the polite alacrity which marked his character, Captain Wragge observed the three startling words, "Fifty Pounds Reward," printed in capital letters on the bills which he assisted in recovering; and instantly secreted one of them, to be more closely examined at the first convenient opportunity. As he crumpled up the bill in the palm of his hand, his party-colored eyes fixed with hungry interest on the proprietor of the unlucky parcel. When a man happens not to be possessed of fifty pence in his own pocket, if his heart is in the right place, it bounds; if his mouth is properly constituted, it waters, at the sight of another man who carries about with him a printed offer of fifty pounds sterling, addressed to his fellow-creatures.

The unfortunate traveler wrapped up his parcel as he best might, and made his way off the platform, after addressing an inquiry to the first official victim of the day's passenger-traffic, who was sufficiently in possession of his senses to listen to it. Leaving the station for the river-side, which was close at hand, the stranger entered the ferryboat at the North Street Postern. The captain, who had carefully dogged his steps thus far, entered the boat also; and employed the short interval of transit to the opposite bank in a perusal of the handbill which he had kept for his own private enlightenment. With his back carefully turned on the traveler, Captain Wragge now possessed his mind of the following lines:

"FIFTY POUNDS REWARD.

"Left her home, in London, early on the morning of September 23d, 1846, A YOUNG LADY. Age—eighteen. Dress—deep mourning. Personal appearance—hair of a very light brown; eyebrows and eyelashes darker; eyes light gray; complexion strikingly pale; lower part of her face large and full; tall upright figure; walks with remarkable grace and ease; speaks with openness and resolution; has the manners and habits of a refined, cultivated lady. Personal marks—two little moles, close together, on the left side of the neck. Mark on the under-clothing—'Magdalen Vanstone.' Is supposed to have joined, or attempted to join, under an assumed name, a theatrical company now performing at York. Had, when she left London, one black box, and no other luggage. Whoever will give such information as will restore her to her friends shall receive the above Reward. Apply at the office of Mr. Harkness, solicitor, Coney Street, York. Or to Messrs. Wyatt, Pendril, and Gwilt, Serle Street, Lincoln's Inn, London."

Accustomed as Captain Wragge was to keep the completest possession of himself in all human emergencies, his own profound astonishment, when the course of his reading brought him to the mark on the linen of the missing young lady, betrayed him into an exclamation of surprise which even startled the ferryman. The traveler was less observant; his whole attention was fixed on the opposite bank of the river, and he left the boat hastily the moment it touched the landing-place. Captain Wragge recovered himself, pocketed the handbill, and followed his leader for the second time.

The stranger directed his steps to the nearest street which ran down to the river, compared a note in his pocketbook with the numbers of the houses on the left-hand side, stopped at one of them, and rang the bell. The captain went on to the next house; affected to ring the bell, in his turn, and stood with his back to the traveler—in appearance, waiting to be let in; in reality, listening with all his might for any scraps of dialogue which might reach his ears on the opening of the door behind him.

The door was answered with all due alacrity, and a sufficiently instructive interchange of question and answer on the threshold rewarded the dexterity of Captain Wragge.

"Does Mr. Huxtable live here?" asked the traveler.

"Yes, sir," was the answer, in a woman's voice.

"Is he at home?"

"Not at home now, sir; but he will be in again at eight to-night."

"I think a young lady called here early in the day, did she not?"

"Yes; a young lady came this afternoon."

"Exactly; I come on the same business. Did she see Mr. Huxtable?"

"No, sir; he has been away all day. The young lady told me she would come back at eight o'clock."

"Just so. I will call and see Mr. Huxtable at the same time."

"Any name, sir?"

"No; say a gentleman called on theatrical business—that will be enough. Wait one minute, if you please. I am a stranger in York; will you kindly tell me which is the way to Coney Street?"

The woman gave the required information, the door closed, and the stranger hastened away in the direction of Coney Street.

On this occasion Captain Wragge made no attempt to follow him. The handbill revealed plainly enough that the man's next object was to complete the necessary arrangements with the local solicitor on the subject of the promised reward.

Having seen and heard enough for his immediate purpose, the captain retraced his steps down the street, turned to the right, and entered on the Esplanade, which, in that quarter of the city, borders the river-side between the swimming-baths and Lendal Tower. "This is a family matter," said Captain Wragge to himself, persisting, from sheer force of habit, in the old assertion of his relationship to Magdalen's mother; "I must consider it in all its bearings." He tucked the umbrella under his arm, crossed his hands behind him, and lowered himself gently into the abyss of his own reflections. The order and propriety observable in the captain's shabby garments accurately typified the order and propriety which distinguished the operations of the captain's mind. It was his habit always to see his way before him through a neat succession of alternatives—and so he saw it now.

Three courses were open to him in connection with the remarkable discovery which he had just made. The first course was to do nothing in the matter at all. Inadmissible, on family grounds: equally inadmissible on pecuniary grounds: rejected accordingly. The second course was to deserve the gratitude of the young lady's friends, rated at fifty pounds. The third course was, by a timely warning to deserve the gratitude of the young lady herself, rated—at an unknown figure. Between these two last alternatives the wary Wragge hesitated; not from doubt of Magdalen's pecuniary resources—for he was totally ignorant of the circumstances which had deprived the sisters of their inheritance—but from doubt whether an obstacle in the shape of an undiscovered gentleman might not be privately connected with her disappearance from home. After mature reflection, he determined to pause, and be guided by circumstances. In the meantime, the first consideration was to be beforehand with the messenger from London, and to lay hands securely on the young lady herself.

"I feel for this misguided girl," mused the captain, solemnly strutting backward and forward by the lonely river-side. "I always have looked upon her—I always shall look upon her—in the light of a niece."

Where was the adopted relative at that moment? In other words, how was a young lady in Magdalen's critical position likely to while away the hours until Mr. Huxtable 's return? If there was an obstructive gentleman in the background, it would be mere waste of time to pursue the question. But if the inference which the handbill suggested was correct—if she was really alone at that moment in the city of York—where was she likely to be?

Not in the crowded thoroughfares, to begin with. Not viewing the objects of interest in the Minster, for it was now past the hour at which the cathedral could be seen. Was she in the waiting-room at the railway? She would hardly run that risk. Was she in one of the hotels? Doubtful, considering that she was entirely by herself. In a pastry-cook's shop? Far more likely. Driving about in a cab? Possible, certainly; but no more. Loitering away the time in some quiet locality, out-of-doors? Likely enough, again, on that fine autumn evening. The captain paused, weighed the relative claims on his attention of the quiet locality and the pastry-cook's shop; and decided for the first of the two. There was time enough to find her at the pastry-cook's, to inquire after her at the principal hotels, or, finally, to intercept her in Mr. Huxtable's immediate neighborhood from seven to eight. While the light lasted, the wise course was to use it in looking for her out-of-doors. Where? The Esplanade was a quiet locality; but she was not there—not on the lonely road beyond, which ran back by the Abbey Wall. Where next? The captain stopped, looked across the river, brightened under the influence of a new idea, and suddenly hastened back to the ferry.

"The Walk on the Walls," thought this judicious man, with a twinkle of his party-colored eyes. "The quietest place in York; and the place that every stranger goes to see."

In ten minutes more Captain Wragge was exploring the new field of search. He mounted to the walls (which inclose the whole western portion of the city) by the North Street Postern, from which the walk winds round until it ends again at its southernly extremity in the narrow passage of Rosemary Lane. It was then twenty minutes to seven. The sun had set more than half an hour since; the red light lay broad and low in the cloudless western heaven; all visible objects were softening in the tender twilight, but were not darkening yet. The first few lamps lit in the street below looked like faint little specks of yellow light, as the captain started on his walk through one of the most striking scenes which England can show.

On his right hand, as he set forth, stretched the open country beyond the walls—the rich green meadows, the boundary-trees dividing them, the broad windings of the river in the distance, the scattered buildings nearer to view; all wrapped in the evening stillness, all made beautiful by the evening peace. On his left hand, the majestic west front of York Minster soared over the city and caught the last brightest light of heaven on the summits of its lofty towers. Had this noble prospect tempted the lost girl to linger and look at it? No; thus far, not a sign of her. The captain looked round him attentively, and walked on.

He reached the spot where the iron course of the railroad strikes its way through arches in the old wall. He paused at this place—where the central activity of a great railway enterprise beats, with all the pulses of its loud-clanging life, side by side with the dead majesty of the past, deep under the old historic stones which tell of fortified York and the sieges of two centuries since—he stood on this spot, and searched for her again, and searched in vain. Others were looking idly down at the desolate activity on the wilderness of the iron rails; but she was not among them. The captain glanced doubtfully at the darkening sky, and walked on.

He stopped again where the postern of Micklegate still stands, and still strengthens the city wall as of old. Here the paved walk descends a few steps, passes through the dark stone guardroom of the ancient gate, ascends again, and continues its course southward until the walls reach the river once more. He paused, and peered anxiously into the dim inner corners of the old guard-room. Was she waiting there for the darkness to come, and hide her from prying eyes? No: a solitary workman loitered through the stone chamber; but no other living creature stirred in the place. The captain mounted the steps which led out from the postern and walked on.

He advanced some fifty or sixty yards along the paved footway; the outlying suburbs of York on one side of him, a rope-walk and some patches of kitchen garden occupying a vacant strip of ground on the other. He advanced with eager eyes and quickened step; for he saw before him the lonely figure of a woman, standing by the parapet of the wall, with her face set toward the westward view. He approached cautiously, to make sure of her before she turned and observed him. There was no mistaking that tall, dark figure, as it rested against the parapet with a listless grace. There she stood, in her long black cloak and gown, the last dim light of evening falling tenderly on her pale, resolute young face. There she stood—not three months since the spoiled darling of her parents; the priceless treasure of the household, never left unprotected, never trusted alone—there she stood in the lovely dawn of her womanhood, a castaway in a strange city, wrecked on the world!

Vagabond as he was, the first sight of her staggered even the dauntless assurance of Captain Wragge. As she slowly turned her face and looked at him, he raised his hat, with the nearest approach to respect which a long life of unblushing audacity had left him capable of making.

"I think I have the honor of addressing the younger Miss Vanstone?" he began. "Deeply gratified, I am sure—for more reasons than one."

She looked at him with a cold surprise. No recollection of the day when he had followed her sister and herself on their way home with Miss Garth rose in her memory, while he now confronted her, with his altered manner and his altered dress.

"You are mistaken," she said, quietly. "You are a perfect stranger to me."

"Pardon me," replied the captain; "I am a species of relation. I had the pleasure of seeing you in the spring of the present year. I presented myself on that memorable occasion to an honored preceptress in your late father's family. Permit me, under equally agreeable circumstances, to present myself to you. My name is Wragge."

By this time he had recovered complete possession of his own impudence; his party-colored eyes twinkled cheerfully, and he accompanied his modest announcement of himself with a dancing-master's bow.

Magdalen frowned, and drew back a step. The captain was not a man to be daunted by a cold reception. He tucked his umbrella under his arm and jocosely spelled his name for her further enlightenment. "W, R, A, double G, E—Wragge," said the captain, ticking off the letters persuasively on his fingers.

"I remember your name," said Magdalen. "Excuse me for leaving you abruptly. I have an engagement."

She tried to pass him and walk on northward toward the railway. He instantly met the attempt by raising both hands, and displaying a pair of darned black gloves outspread in polite protest.

"Not that way," he said; "not that way, Miss Vanstone, I beg and entreat!"

"Why not?" she asked haughtily.

"Because," answered the captain, "that is the way which leads to Mr. Huxtable's."

In the ungovernable astonishment of hearing his reply she suddenly bent forward, and for the first time looked him close in the face. He sustained her suspicious scrutiny with every appearance of feeling highly gratified by it. "H, U, X—Hux," said the captain, playfully turning to the old joke: "T, A—ta, Huxta; B, L, E—ble; Huxtable."

"What do you know about Mr. Huxtable?" she asked. "What do you mean by mentioning him to me?"

The captain's curly lip took a new twist upward. He immediately replied, to the best practical purpose, by producing the handbill from his pocket.

"There is just light enough left," he said, "for young (and lovely) eyes to read by. Before I enter upon the personal statement which your flattering inquiry claims from me, pray bestow a moment's attention on this Document."

She took the handbill from him. By the last gleam of twilight she read the lines which set a price on her recovery—which published the description of her in pitiless print, like the description of a strayed dog. No tender consideration had prepared her for the shock, no kind word softened it to her when it came. The vagabond, whose cunning eyes watched her eagerly while she read, knew no more that the handbill which he had stolen had only been prepared in anticipation of the worst, and was only to be publicly used in the event of all more considerate means of tracing her being tried in vain—than she knew it. The bill dropped from her hand; her face flushed deeply. She turned away from Captain Wragge, as if all idea of his existence had passed out of her mind.

"Oh, Norah, Norah!" she said to herself, sorrowfully. "After the letter I wrote you—after the hard struggle I had to go away! Oh, Norah, Norah!"

"How is Norah?" inquired the captain, with the utmost politeness.

She turned upon him with an angry brightness in her large gray eyes. "Is this thing shown publicly?" she asked, stamping her foot on it. "Is the mark on my neck described all over York?"

"Pray compose yourself," pleaded the persuasive Wragge. "At present I have every reason to believe that you have just perused the only copy in circulation. Allow me to pick it up."

Before he could touch the bill she snatched it from the pavement, tore it into fragments, and threw them over the wall.

"Bravo!" cried the captain. "You remind me of your poor dear mother. The family spirit, Miss Vanstone. We all inherit our hot blood from my maternal grandfather."

"How did you come by it?" she asked, suddenly.

"My dear creature, I have just told you," remonstrated the captain. "We all come by it from my maternal grandfather."

"How did you come by that handbill?" she repeated, passionately.

"I beg ten thousand pardons! My head was running on the family spirit.—How did I come by it? Briefly thus." Here Captain Wragge entered on his personal statement; taking his customary vocal exercise through the longest words of the English language, with the highest elocutionary relish. Having, on this rare occasion, nothing to gain by concealment, he departed from his ordinary habits, and, with the utmost amazement at the novelty of his own situation, permitted himself to tell the unmitigated truth.

The effect of the narrative on Magdalen by no means fulfilled Captain Wragge's anticipations in relating it. She was not startled; she was not irritated; she showed no disposition to cast herself on his mercy, and to seek his advice. She looked him steadily in the face; and all she said, when he had neatly rounded his last sentence, was—"Go on."

"Go on?" repeated the captain. "Shocked to disappoint you, I am sure; but the fact is, I have done."

"No, you have not," she rejoined; "you have left out the end of your story. The end of it is, you came here to look for me; and you mean to earn the fifty pounds reward."

Those plain words so completely staggered Captain Wragge that for the moment he stood speechless. But he had faced awkward truths of all sorts far too often to be permanently disconcerted by them. Before Magdalen could pursue her advantage, the vagabond had recovered his balance: Wragge was himself again.

"Smart," said the captain, laughing indulgently, and drumming with his umbrella on the pavement. "Some men might take it seriously. I'm not easily offended. Try again."

Magdalen looked at him through the gathering darkness in mute perplexity. All her little experience of society had been experience among people who possessed a common sense of honor, and a common responsibility of social position. She had hitherto seen nothing but the successful human product from the great manufactory of Civilization. Here was one of the failures, and, with all her quickness, she was puzzled how to deal with it.

"Pardon me for returning to the subject," pursued the captain. "It has just occurred to my mind that you might actually have spoken in earnest. My poor child! how can I earn the fifty pounds before the reward is offered to me? Those handbills may not be publicly posted for a week to come. Precious as you are to all your relatives (myself included), take my word for it, the lawyers who are managing this case will not pay fifty pounds for you if they can possibly help it. Are you still persuaded that my needy pockets are gaping for the money? Very good. Button them up in spite of me with your own fair fingers. There is a train to London at nine forty-five to-night. Submit yourself to your friend's wishes and go back by it."

"Never!" said Magdalen, firing at the bare suggestion, exactly as the captain had intended she should. "If my mind had not been made up before, that vile handbill would have decided me. I forgive Norah," she added, turning away and speaking to herself, "but not Mr. Pendril, and not Miss Garth."

"Quite right!" said Captain Wragge. "The family spirit. I should have done the same myself at your age. It runs in the blood. Hark! there goes the clock again—half-past seven. Miss Vanstone, pardon this seasonable abruptness! If you are to carry out your resolution—if you are to be your own mistress much longer, you must take a course of some kind before eight o'clock. You are young, you are inexperienced, you are in imminent danger. Here is a position of emergency on one side—and here am I, on the other, with an uncle's interest in you, full of advice. Tap me."

"Suppose I choose to depend on nobody, and to act for myself?" said Magdalen. "What then?"

"Then," replied the captain, "you will walk straight into one of the four traps which are set to catch you in the ancient and interesting city of York. Trap the first, at Mr. Huxtable's house; trap the second, at all the hotels; trap the third, at the railway station; trap the fourth, at the theater. That man with the handbills has had an hour at his disposal. If he has not set those four traps (with the assistance of the local solicitor) by this time, he is not the competent lawyer's clerk I take him for. Come, come, my dear girl! if there is somebody else in the background, whose advice you prefer to mine—"

"You see that I am alone," she interposed, proudly. "If you knew me better, you would know that I depend on nobody but myself."

Those words decided the only doubt which now remained in the captain's mind—the doubt whether the course was clear before him. The motive of her flight from home was evidently what the handbills assumed it to be—a reckless fancy for going on the stage. "One of two things," thought Wragge to himself, in his logical way. "She's worth more than fifty pounds to me in her present situation, or she isn't. If she is, her friends may whistle for her. If she isn't, I have only to keep her till the bills are posted." Fortified by this simple plan of action, the captain returned to the charge, and politely placed Magdalen between the two inevitable alternatives of trusting herself to him, on the one hand, or of returning to her friends, on the other.

"I respect independence of character wherever I find it," he said, with an air of virtuous severity. "In a young and lovely relative, I more than respect—I admire it. But (excuse the bold assertion), to walk on a way of your own, you must first have a way to walk on. Under existing circumstances, where is your way? Mr. Huxtable is out of the question, to begin with."

"Out of the question for to-night," said Magdalen; "but what hinders me from writing to Mr. Huxtable, and making my own private arrangements with him for to-morrow?"

"Granted with all my heart—a hit, a palpable hit. Now for my turn. To get to to-morrow (excuse the bold assertion, once more), you must first pass through to-night. Where are you to sleep?"

"Are there no hotels in York?"

"Excellent hotels for large families; excellent hotels for single gentlemen. The very worst hotels in the world for handsome young ladies who present themselves alone at the door without male escort, without a maid in attendance, and without a single article of luggage. Dark as it is, I think I could see a lady's box, if there was anything of the sort in our immediate neighborhood."

"My box is at the cloak-room. What is to prevent my sending the ticket for it?"

"Nothing—if you want to communicate your address by means of your box—nothing whatever. Think; pray think! Do you really suppose that the people who are looking for you are such fools as not to have an eye on the cloakroom? Do you think they are such fools—when they find you don't come to Mr. Huxtable's at eight to-night—as not to inquire at all the hotels? Do you think a young lady of your striking appearance (even if they consented to receive you) could take up her abode at an inn without becoming the subject of universal curiosity and remark? Here is night coming on as fast as it can. Don't let me bore you; only let me ask once more—Where are you to sleep?"

There was no answer to that question: in Magdalen's position, there was literally no answer to it on her side. She was silent.

"Where are you to sleep?" repeated the captain. "The reply is obvious—under my roof. Mrs. Wragge will be charmed to see you. Look upon her as your aunt; pray look upon her as your aunt. The landlady is a widow, the house is close by, there are no other lodgers, and there is a bedroom to let. Can anything be more satisfactory, under all the circumstances? Pray observe, I say nothing about to-morrow—I leave to-morrow to you, and confine myself exclusively to the night. I may, or may not, command theatrical facilities, which I am in a position to offer you. Sympathy and admiration may, or may not, be strong within me, when I contemplate the dash and independence of your character. Hosts of examples of bright stars of the British drama, who have begun their apprenticeship to the stage as you are beginning yours, may, or may not, crowd on my memory. These are topics for the future. For the present, I confine myself within my strict range of duty. We are within five minutes' walk of my present address. Allow me to offer you my arm. No? You hesitate? You distrust me? Good heavens! is it possible you can have heard anything to my disadvantage?"

"Quite possible," said Magdalen, without a moment's flinching from the answer.

"May I inquire the particulars?" asked the captain, with the politest composure. "Don't spare my feelings; oblige me by speaking out. In the plainest terms, now, what have you heard?"

She answered him with a woman's desperate disregard of consequences when she is driven to bay—she answered him instantly,

"I have heard you are a Rogue."

"Have you, indeed?" said the impenetrable Wragge. "A Rogue? Well, I waive my privilege of setting you right on that point for a fitter time. For the sake of argument, let us say I am a Rogue. What is Mr. Huxtable?"

"A respectable man, or I should not have seen him in the house where we first met."

"Very good. Now observe! You talked of writing to Mr. Huxtable a minute ago. What do you think a respectable man is likely to do with a young lady who openly acknowledges that she has run away from her home and her friends to go on the stage? My dear girl, on your own showing, it's not a respectable man you want in your present predicament. It's a Rogue—like me."

Magdalen laughed, bitterly.

"There is some truth in that," she said. "Thank you for recalling me to myself and my circumstances. I have my end to gain—and who am I, to pick and choose the way of getting to it? It is my turn to beg pardon now. I have been talking as if I was a young lady of family and position. Absurd! We know better than that, don't we, Captain Wragge? You are quite right. Nobody's child must sleep under Somebody's roof—and why not yours?"

"This way," said the captain, dexterously profiting by the sudden change in her humor, and cunningly refraining from exasperating it by saying more himself. "This way."

She followed him a few steps, and suddenly stopped.

"Suppose I am discovered?" she broke out, abruptly. "Who has any authority over me? Who can take me back, if I don't choose to go? If they all find me to-morrow, what then? Can't I say No to Mr. Pendril? Can't I trust my own courage with Miss Garth?"

"Can you trust your courage with your sister?" whispered the captain, who had not forgotten the references to Norah which had twice escaped her already.

Her head drooped. She shivered as if the cold night air had struck her, and leaned back wearily against the parapet of the wall.

"Not with Norah," she said, sadly. "I could trust myself with the others. Not with Norah."

"This way," repeated Captain Wragge. She roused herself; looked up at the darkening heaven, looked round at the darkening view. "What must be, must," she said, and followed him.

The Minster clock struck the quarter to eight as they left the Walk on the Wall and descended the steps into Rosemary Lane. Almost at the same moment the lawyer's clerk from London gave the last instructions to his subordinates, and took up his own position, on the opposite side of the river, within easy view of Mr. Huxtable's door.

CHAPTER II.

CAPTAIN WRAGGE stopped nearly midway in the one little row of houses composing Rosemary Lane, and let himself and his guest in at the door of his lodgings with his own key. As they entered the passage, a care-worn woman in a widow's cap made her appearance with a candle. "My niece," said the captain, presenting Magdalen; "my niece on a visit to York. She has kindly consented to occupy your empty bedroom. Consider it let, if you please, to my niece—and be very particular in airing the sheets? Is Mrs. Wragge upstairs? Very good. You may lend me your candle. My dear girl, Mrs. Wragge's boudoir is on the first floor; Mrs. Wragge is visible. Allow me to show you the way up."

As he ascended the stairs first, the care-worn widow whispered, piteously, to Magdalen, "I hope you'll pay me, miss. Your uncle doesn't."

The captain threw open the door of the front room on the first floor, and disclosed a female figure, arrayed in a gown of tarnished amber-colored satin, seated solitary on a small chair, with dingy old gloves on its hands, with a tattered old book on its knees, and with one little bedroom candle by its side. The figure terminated at its upper extremity in a large, smooth, white round face—like a moon—encircled by a cap and green ribbons, and dimly irradiated by eyes of mild and faded blue, which looked straightforward into vacancy, and took not the smallest notice of Magdalen's appearance, on the opening of the door.

"Mrs. Wragge!" cried the captain, shouting at her as if she was fast asleep. "Mrs. Wragge!"

The lady of the faded blue eyes slowly rose to an apparently interminable height. When she had at last attained an upright position, she towered to a stature of two or three inches over six feet. Giants of both sexes are, by a wise dispensation of Providence, created, for the most part, gentle. If Mrs. Wragge and a lamb had been placed side by side, comparison, under those circumstances, would have exposed the lamb as a rank impostor.

"Tea, captain?" inquired Mrs. Wragge, looking submissively down at her husband, whose head, when he stood on tiptoe, barely reached her shoulder.

"Miss Vanstone, the younger," said the captain, presenting Magdalen. "Our fair relative, whom I have met by fortunate accident. Our guest for the night. Our guest!" reiterated the captain, shouting once more as if the tall lady was still fast asleep, in spite of the plain testimony of her own eyes to the contrary.

A smile expressed itself (in faint outline) on the large vacant space of Mrs. Wragge's countenance. "Oh?" she said, interrogatively. "Oh, indeed? Please, miss, will you sit down? I'm sorry—no, I don't mean I'm sorry; I mean I'm glad—" she stopped, and consulted her husband by a helpless look.

"Glad, of course!" shouted the captain.

"Glad, of course," echoed the giantess of the amber satin, more meekly than ever.

"Mrs. Wragge is not deaf," explained the captain. "She's only a little slow. Constitutionally torpid—if I may use the expression. I am merely loud with her (and I beg you will honor me by being loud, too) as a necessary stimulant to her ideas. Shout at her—and her mind comes up to time. Speak to her—and she drifts miles away from you directly. Mrs. Wragge!"

Mrs. Wragge instantly acknowledged the stimulant. "Tea, captain?" she inquired, for the second time.

"Put your cap straight!" shouted her husband. "I beg ten thousand pardons," he resumed, again addressing himself to Magdalen. "The sad truth is, I am a martyr to my own sense of order. All untidiness, all want of system and regularity, cause me the acutest irritation. My attention is distracted, my composure is upset; I can't rest till things are set straight again. Externally speaking, Mrs. Wragge is, to my infinite regret, the crookedest woman I ever met with. More to the right!" shouted the captain, as Mrs. Wragge, like a well-trained child, presented herself with her revised head-dress for her husband's inspection.

Mrs. Wragge immediately pulled the cap to the left. Magdalen rose, and set it right for her. The moon-face of the giantess brightened for the first time. She looked admiringly at Magdalen's cloak and bonnet. "Do you like dress, miss?" she asked, suddenly, in a confidential whisper. "I do."

"Show Miss Vanstone her room," said the captain, looking as if the whole house belonged to him. "The spare-room, the landlady's spare-room, on the third floor front. Offer Miss Vanstone all articles connected with the toilet of which she may stand in need. She has no luggage with her. Supply the deficiency, and then come back and make tea."

Mrs. Wragge acknowledged the receipt of these lofty directions by a look of placid bewilderment, and led the way out of the room; Magdalen following her, with a candle presented by the attentive captain. As soon as they were alone on the landing outside, Mrs. Wragge raised the tattered old book which she had been reading when Magdalen was first presented to her, and which she had never let out of her hand since, and slowly tapped herself on the forehead with it. "Oh, my poor head!" said the tall lady, in meek soliloquy; "it's Buzzing again worse than ever!"

"Buzzing?" repeated Magdalen, in the utmost astonishment.

Mrs. Wragge ascended the stairs, without offering any explanation, stopped at one of the rooms on the second floor, and led the way in.

"This is not the third floor," said Magdalen. "This is not my room, surely?"

"Wait a bit," pleaded Mrs. Wragge. "Wait a bit, miss, before we go up any higher. I've got the Buzzing in my head worse than ever. Please wait for me till I'm a little better again."

"Shall I ask for help?" inquired Magdalen. "Shall I call the landlady?"

"Help?" echoed Mrs. Wragge. "Bless you, I don't want help! I'm used to it. I've had the Buzzing in my head, off and on—how many years?" She stopped, reflected, lost herself, and suddenly tried a question in despair. "Have you ever been at Darch's Dining-rooms in London?" she asked, with an appearance of the deepest interest.

"No," replied Magdalen, wondering at the strange inquiry.

"That's where the Buzzing in my head first began," said Mrs. Wragge, following the new clew with the deepest attention and anxiety. "I was employed to wait on the gentlemen at Darch's Dining-rooms—I was. The gentlemen all came together; the gentlemen were all hungry together; the gentlemen all gave their orders together—" She stopped, and tapped her head again, despondently, with the tattered old book.

"And you had to keep all their orders in your memory, separate one from the other?" suggested Magdalen, helping her out. "And the trying to do that confused you?"

"That's it!" said Mrs. Wragge, becoming violently excited in a moment. "Boiled pork and greens and pease-pudding, for Number One. Stewed beef and carrots and gooseberry tart, for Number Two. Cut of mutton, and quick about it, well done, and plenty of fat, for Number Three. Codfish and parsnips, two chops to follow, hot-and-hot, or I'll be the death of you, for Number Four. Five, six, seven, eight, nine, ten. Carrots and gooseberry tart—pease-pudding and plenty of fat—pork and beef and mutton, and cut 'em all, and quick about it—stout for one, and ale for t'other—and stale bread here, and new bread there—and this gentleman likes cheese, and that gentleman doesn't—Matilda, Tilda, Tilda, Tilda, fifty times over, till I didn't know my own name again—oh lord! oh lord!! oh lord!!! all together, all at the same time, all out of temper, all buzzing in my poor head like forty thousand million bees—don't tell the captain! don't tell the captain!" The unfortunate creature dropped the tattered old book, and beat both her hands on her head, with a look of blank terror fixed on the door.

"Hush! hush!" said Magdalen. "The captain hasn't heard you. I know what is the matter with your head now. Let me cool it."

She dipped a towel in water, and pressed it on the hot and helpless head which Mrs. Wragge submitted to her with the docility of a sick child.

"What a pretty hand you've got!" said the poor creature, feeling the relief of the coolness and taking Magdalen's hand, admiringly, in her own. "How soft and white it is! I try to be a lady; I always keep my gloves on—but I can't get my hands like yours. I'm nicely dressed, though, ain't I? I like dress; it's a comfort to me. I'm always happy when I'm looking at my things. I say—you won't be angry with me?—I should so like to try your bonnet on."

Magdalen humored her, with the ready compassion of the young. She stood smiling and nodding at herself in the glass, with the bonnet perched on the top of her head. "I had one as pretty as this, once," she said—"only it was white, not black. I wore it when the captain married me."

"Where did you meet with him?" asked Magdalen, putting the question as a chance means of increasing her scanty stock of information on the subject of Captain Wragge.

"At the Dining-rooms," said Mrs. Wragge. "He was the hungriest and the loudest to wait upon of the lot of 'em. I made more mistakes with him than I did with all the rest of them put together. He used to swear—oh, didn't he use to swear! When he left off swearing at me he married me. There was others wanted me besides him. Bless you, I had my pick. Why not? When you have a trifle of money left you that you didn't expect, if that don't make a lady of you, what does? Isn't a lady to have her pick? I had my trifle of money, and I had my pick, and I picked the captain—I did. He was the smartest and the shortest of them all. He took care of me and my money. I'm here, the money's gone. Don't you put that towel down on the table—he won't have that! Don't move his razors—don't, please, or I shall forget which is which. I've got to remember which is which to-morrow morning. Bless you, the captain don't shave himself! He had me taught. I shave him. I do his hair, and cut his nails—he's awfully particular about his nails. So he is about his trousers. And his shoes. And his newspaper in the morning. And his breakfasts, and lunches, and dinners, and teas—" She stopped, struck by a sudden recollection, looked about her, observed the tattered old book on the floor, and clasped her hands in despair. "I've lost the place!" she exclaimed helplessly. "Oh, mercy, what will become of me! I've lost the place."

"Never mind," said Magdalen; "I'll soon find the place for you again."

She picked up the book, looked into the pages, and found that the object of Mrs. Wragge's anxiety was nothing more important than an old-fashioned Treatise on the Art of Cookery, reduced under the usual heads of Fish, Flesh, and Fowl, and containing the customary series of recipes. Turning over the leaves, Magdalen came to one particular page, thickly studded with little drops of moisture half dry. "Curious!" she said. "If this was anything but a cookery-book, I should say somebody had been crying over it."

"Somebody?" echoed Mrs. Wragge, with a stare of amazement. "It isn't somebody—it's Me. Thank you kindly, that's the place, sure enough. Bless you, I'm used to crying over it. You'd cry, too, if you had to get the captain's dinners out of it. As sure as ever I sit down to this book the Buzzing in my head begins again. Who's to make it out? Sometimes I think I've got it, and it all goes away from me. Sometimes I think I haven't got it, and it all comes back in a heap. Look here! Here's what he's ordered for his breakfast to-morrow: 'Omelette with Herbs. Beat up two eggs with a little water or milk, salt, pepper, chives, and parsley. Mince small.'—There! mince small! How am I to mince small when it's all mixed up and running? 'Put a piece of butter the size of your thumb into the frying-pan.'—Look at my thumb, and look at yours! whose size does she mean? 'Boil, but not brown.'—If it mustn't be brown, what color must it be? She won't tell me; she expects me to know, and I don't. 'Pour in the omelette.'—There! I can do that. 'Allow it to set, raise it round the edge; when done, turn it over to double it.'—Oh, the number of times I turned it over and doubled it in my head, before you came in to-night! 'Keep it soft; put the dish on the frying-pan, and turn it over.' Which am I to turn over—oh, mercy, try the cold towel again, and tell me which—the dish or the frying-pan?"

"Put the dish on the frying-pan," said Magdalen; "and then turn the frying-pan over. That is what it means, I think."

"Thank you kindly," said Mrs. Wragge, "I want to get it into my head; please say it again."

Magdalen said it again.

"And then turn the frying-pan over," repeated Mrs. Wragge, with a sudden burst of energy. "I've got it now! Oh, the lots of omelettes all frying together in my head; and all frying wrong! Much obliged, I'm sure. You've put me all right again: I'm only a little tired with talking. And then turn the frying-pan, then turn the frying-pan, then turn the frying-pan over.

It sounds like poetry, don't it?"

Her voice sank, and she drowsily closed her eyes. At the same moment the door of the room below opened, and the captain's mellifluous bass notes floated upstairs, charged with the customary stimulant to his wife's faculties.

"Mrs. Wragge!" cried the captain. "Mrs. Wragge!"

She started to her feet at that terrible summons. "Oh, what did he tell me to do?" she asked, distractedly. "Lots of things, and I've forgotten them all!"

"Say you have done them when he asks you," suggested Magdalen. "They were things for me—things I don't want. I remember all that is necessary. My room is the front room on the third floor. Go downstairs and say I am coming directly."

She took up the candle and pushed Mrs. Wragge out on the landing. "Say I am coming directly," she whispered again—and went upstairs by herself to the third story.

The room was small, close, and very poorly furnished. In former days Miss Garth would have hesitated to offer such a room to one of the servants at Combe-Raven. But it was quiet; it gave her a few minutes alone; and it was endurable, even welcome, on that account. She locked herself in and walked mechanically, with a woman's first impulse in a strange bedroom, to the rickety little table and the dingy little looking-glass. She waited there for a moment, and then turned away with weary contempt. "What does it matter how pale I am?" she thought to herself. "Frank can't see me—what does it matter now!"

She laid aside her cloak and bonnet, and sat down to collect herself. But the events of the day had worn her out. The past, when she tried to remember it, only made her heart ache. The future, when she tried to penetrate it, was a black void. She rose again, and stood by the uncurtained window—stood looking out, as if there was some hidden sympathy for her own desolation in the desolate night.

"Norah!" she said to herself, tenderly; "I wonder if Norah is thinking of me? Oh, if I could be as patient as she is! If I could only forget the debt we owe to Michael Vanstone!"

Her face darkened with a vindictive despair, and she paced the little cage of a room backward and forward, softly. "No: never till the debt is paid!" Her thoughts veered back again to Frank. "Still at sea, poor fellow; further and further away from me; sailing through the day, sailing through the night. Oh, Frank, love me!"

Her eyes filled with tears. She dashed them away, made for the door, and laughed with a desperate levity, as she unlocked it again.

"Any company is better than my own thoughts," she burst out, recklessly, as she left the room. "I'm forgetting my ready-made relations—my half-witted aunt, and my uncle the rogue." She descended the stairs to the landing on the first floor, and paused there in momentary hesitation. "How will it end?" she asked herself. "Where is my blindfolded journey taking me to now? Who knows, and who cares?"

She entered the room.

Captain Wragge was presiding at the tea-tray with the air of a prince in his own banqueting-hall. At one side of the table sat Mrs. Wragge, watching her husband's eye like an animal waiting to be fed. At the other side was an empty chair, toward which the captain waved his persuasive hand when Magdalen came in. "How do you like your room?" he inquired; "I trust Mrs. Wragge has made herself useful? You take milk and sugar? Try the local bread, honor the York butter, test the freshness of a new and neighboring egg. I offer my little all. A pauper's meal, my dear girl—seasoned with a gentleman's welcome."

"Seasoned with salt, pepper, chives and parsley," murmured Mrs. Wragge, catching instantly at a word in connection with cookery, and harnessing her head to the omelette for the rest of the evening.

"Sit straight at the table!" shouted the captain. "More to the left, more still—that will do. During your absence upstairs," he continued, addressing himself to Magdalen, "my mind has not been unemployed. I have been considering your position with a view exclusively to your own benefit. If you decide on being guided to-morrow by the light of my experience, that light is unreservedly at your service. You may naturally say: 'I know but little of you, captain, and that little is unfavorable.' Granted, on one condition—that you permit me to make myself and my character quite familiar to you when tea is over. False shame is foreign to my nature. You see my wife, my house, my bread, my butter, and my eggs, all exactly as they are. See me, too, my dear girl, while you are about it."

When tea was over, Mrs. Wragge, at a signal from her husband, retired to a corner of the room, with the eternal cookery-book still in her hand. "Mince small," she whispered, confidentially, as she passed Magdalen. "That's a teaser, isn't it?"

"Down at heel again!" shouted the captain, pointing to his wife's heavy flat feet as they shuffled across the room. "The right shoe. Pull it up at heel, Mrs. Wragge—pull it up at heel! Pray allow me," he continued, offering his arm to Magdalen, and escorting her to a dirty little horse-hair sofa. "You want repose—after your long journey, you really want repose." He drew his chair to the sofa, and surveyed her with a bland look of investigation—as if he had been her medical attendant, with a diagnosis on his mind.

"Very pleasant! very pleasant!" said the captain, when he had seen his guest comfortable on the sofa. "I feel quite in the bosom of my family. Shall we return to our subject—the subject of my rascally self? No! no! No apologies, no protestations, pray. Don't mince the matter on your side—and depend on me not to mince it on mine. Now come to facts; pray come to facts. Who, and what am I? Carry your mind back to our conversation on the Walls of this interesting City, and let us start once more from your point of view. I am a Rogue; and, in that capacity (as I have already pointed out), the most useful man you possibly could have met with. Now observe! There are many varieties of Rogue; let me tell you my variety, to begin with. I am a Swindler."

His entire shamelessness was really super-human. Not the vestige of a blush varied the sallow monotony of his complexion; the smile wreathed his curly lips as pleasantly as ever his party-colored eyes twinkled at Magdalen with the self-enjoying frankness of a naturally harmless man. Had his wife heard him? Magdalen looked over his shoulder to the corner of the room in which she was sitting behind him. No the self-taught student of cookery was absorbed in her subject. She had advanced her imaginary omelette to the critical stage at which the butter was to be thrown in—that vaguely-measured morsel of butter, the size of your thumb. Mrs. Wragge sat lost in contemplation of one of her own thumbs, and shook her head over it, as if it failed to satisfy her.

"Don't be shocked," proceeded the captain; "don't be astonished. Swindler is nothing but a word of two syllables. S, W, I, N, D—swind; L, E, R—ler; Swindler. Definition: A moral agriculturist; a man who cultivates the field of human sympathy. I am that moral agriculturist, that cultivating man. Narrow-minded mediocrity, envious of my success in my profession, calls me a Swindler. What of that? The same low tone of mind assails men in other professions in a similar manner—calls great writers scribblers—great generals, butchers—and so on. It entirely depends on the point of view. Adopting your point, I announce myself intelligibly as a Swindler. Now return the obligation, and adopt mine. Hear what I have to say for myself, in the exercise of my profession.—Shall I continue to put it frankly?"

"Yes," said Magdalen; "and I'll tell you frankly afterward what I think of it."

The captain cleared his throat; mentally assembled his entire army of words—horse, foot, artillery, and reserves; put himself at the head; and dashed into action, to carry the moral intrenchments of Society by a general charge.

"Now observe," he began. "Here am I, a needy object. Very good. Without complicating the question by asking how I come to be in that condition, I will merely inquire whether it is, or is not, the duty of a Christian community to help the needy. If you say No, you simply shock me; and there is an end of it; if you say Yes, then I beg to ask, Why am I to blame for making a Christian community do its duty? You may say, Is a careful man who has saved money bound to spend it again on a careless stranger who has saved none? Why of course he is! And on what ground, pray? Good heavens! on the ground that he has got the money, to be sure. All the world over, the man who has not got the thing, obtains it, on one pretense or another, of the man who has—and, in nine cases out of ten, the pretense is a false one. What! your pockets are full, and my pockets are empty; and you refuse to help me? Sordid wretch! do you think I will allow you to violate the sacred obligations of charity in my person? I won't allow you—I say, distinctly, I won't allow you. Those are my principles as a moral agriculturist. Principles which admit of trickery? Certainly. Am I to blame if the field of human sympathy can't be cultivated in any other way? Consult my brother agriculturists in the mere farming line—do they get their crops for the asking? No! they must circumvent arid Nature exactly as I circumvent sordid Man. They must plow, and sow, and top-dress, and bottom-dress, and deep-drain, and surface-drain, and all the rest of it. Why am I to be checked in the vast occupation of deep-draining mankind? Why am I to be persecuted for habitually exciting the noblest feelings of our common nature? Infamous!—I can characterize it by no other word—infamous! If I hadn't confidence in the future, I should despair of humanity—but I have confidence in the future. Yes! one of these days (when I am dead and gone), as ideas enlarge and enlightenment progresses, the abstract merits of the profession now called swindling will be recognized. When that day comes, don't drag me out of my grave and give me a public funeral; don't take advantage of my having no voice to raise in my own defense, and insult me by a national statue. No! do me justice on my tombstone; dash me off, in one masterly sentence, on my epitaph. Here lies Wragge, embalmed in the tardy recognition of his species: he plowed, sowed, and reaped his fellow-creatures; and enlightened posterity congratulates him on the uniform excellence of his crops."

He stopped; not from want of confidence, not from want of words—purely from want of breath. "I put it frankly, with a dash of humor," he said, pleasantly. "I don't shock you—do I?" Weary and heart-sick as she was—suspicious of others, doubtful of herself—the extravagant impudence of Captain Wragge's defense of swindling touched Magdalen's natural sense of humor, and forced a smile to her lips. "Is the Yorkshire crop a particularly rich one just at present?" she inquired, meeting him, in her neatly feminine way, with his own weapons.

"A hit—a palpable hit," said the captain, jocosely exhibiting the tails of his threadbare shooting jacket, as a practical commentary on Magdalen's remark. "My dear girl, here or elsewhere, the crop never fails—but one man can't always gather it in. The assistance of intelligent co-operation is, I regret to say, denied me. I have nothing in common with the clumsy rank and file of my profession, who convict themselves, before recorders and magistrates, of the worst of all offenses—incurable stupidity in the exercise of their own vocation. Such as you see me, I stand entirely alone. After years of successful self-dependence, the penalties of celebrity are beginning to attach to me. On my way from the North, I pause at this interesting city for the third time; I consult my Books for the customary references to past local experience; I find under the heading, 'Personal position in York,' the initials, T. W. K., signifying Too Well Known. I refer to my Index, and turn to the surrounding neighborhood. The same brief marks meet my eye. 'Leeds. T. W. K.—Scarborough. T. W. K.—Harrowgate. T. W. K.'—and so on. What is the inevitable consequence? I suspend my proceedings; my resources evaporate; and my fair relative finds me the pauper gentleman whom she now sees before her."

"Your books?" said Magdalen. "What books do you mean?"

"You shall see," replied the captain. "Trust me, or not, as you like—I trust you implicitly. You shall see."

With those words he retired into the back room. While he was gone, Magdalen stole another look at Mrs. Wragge. Was she still self-isolated from her husband's deluge of words? Perfectly self-isolated. She had advanced the imaginary omelette to the last stage of culinary progress; and she was now rehearsing the final operation of turning it over—with the palm of her hand to represent the dish, and the cookery-book to impersonate the frying-pan. "I've got it," said Mrs. Wragge, nodding across the room at Magdalen. "First put the frying-pan on the dish, and then tumble both of them over."

Captain Wragge returned, carrying a neat black dispatch-box, adorned with a bright brass lock. He produced from the box five or six plump little books, bound in commercial calf and vellum, and each fitted comfortably with its own little lock.

"Mind!" said the moral agriculturist, "I take no credit to myself for this: it is my nature to be orderly, and orderly I am. I must have everything down in black and white, or I should go mad! Here is my commercial library: Daybook, Ledger, Book of Districts, Book of Letters, Book of Remarks, and so on. Kindly throw your eye over any one of them. I flatter myself there is no such thing as a blot, or a careless entry in it, from the first page to the last. Look at this room—is there a chair out of place? Not if I know it! Look at me. Am I dusty? am I dirty? am I half shaved? Am I, in brief, a speckless pauper, or am I not? Mind! I take no credit to myself; the nature of the man, my dear girl—the nature of the man!"

He opened one of the books. Magdalen was no judge of the admirable correctness with which the accounts inside were all kept; but she could estimate the neatness of the handwriting, the regularity in the rows of figures, the mathematical exactness of the ruled lines in red and black ink, the cleanly absence of blots, stains, or erasures. Although Captain Wragge's inborn sense of order was in him—as it is in others—a sense too inveterately mechanical to exercise any elevating moral influence over his actions, it had produced its legitimate effect on his habits, and had reduced his rogueries as strictly to method and system as if they had been the commercial transactions of an honest man.

"In appearance, my system looks complicated?" pursued the captain. "In reality, it is simplicity itself. I merely avoid the errors of inferior practitioners. That is to say, I never plead for myself; and I never apply to rich people—both fatal mistakes which the inferior practitioner perpetually commits. People with small means sometimes have generous impulses in connection with money—rich people, never. My lord, with forty thousand a year; Sir John, with property in half a dozen counties—those are the men who never forgive the genteel beggar for swindling them out of a sovereign; those are the men who send for the mendicity officers; those are the men who take care of their money. Who are the people who lose shillings and sixpences by sheer thoughtlessness? Servants and small clerks, to whom shillings and sixpences are of consequence. Did you ever hear of Rothschild or Baring dropping a fourpenny-piece down a gutter-hole? Fourpence in Rothschild's pocket is safer than fourpence in the pocket of that woman who is crying stale shrimps in Skeldergate at this moment. Fortified by these sound principles, enlightened by the stores of written information in my commercial library, I have ranged through the population for years past, and have raised my charitable crops with the most cheering success. Here, in book Number One, are all my Districts mapped out, with the prevalent public feeling to appeal to in each: Military District, Clerical District, Agricultural District; et cetera, et cetera. Here, in Number Two, are my cases that I plead: Family of an officer who fell at Waterloo; Wife of a poor curate stricken down by nervous debility; Widow of a grazier in difficulties gored to death by a mad bull; et cetera, et cetera. Here, in Number Three, are the people who have heard of the officer's family, the curate's wife, the grazier's widow, and the people who haven't; the people who have said Yes, and the people who have said No; the people to try again, the people who want a fresh case to stir them up, the people who are doubtful, the people to beware of; et cetera, et cetera. Here, in Number Four, are my Adopted Handwritings of public characters; my testimonials to my own worth and integrity; my Heartrending Statements of the officer's family, the curate's wife, and the grazier's widow, stained with tears, blotted with emotion; et cetera, et cetera. Here, in Numbers Five and Six, are my own personal subscriptions to local charities, actually paid in remunerative neighborhoods, on the principle of throwing a sprat to catch a herring; also, my diary of each day's proceedings, my personal reflections and remarks, my statement of existing difficulties (such as the difficulty of finding myself T. W. K. in this interesting city); my outgivings and incomings; wind and weather; politics and public events; fluctuations in my own health; fluctuations in Mrs. Wragge's head; fluctuations in our means and meals, our payments, prospects, and principles; et cetera, et cetera. So, my dear girl, the Swindler's Mill goes. So you see me exactly as I am. You knew, before I met you, that I lived on my wits. Well! have I, or have I not, shown you that I have wits to live on?"

"I have no doubt you have done yourself full justice," said Magdalen, quietly.

"I am not at all exhausted," continued the captain. "I can go on, if necessary, for the rest of the evening.—However, if I have done myself full justice, perhaps I may leave the remaining points in my character to develop themselves at future opportunities. For the present, I withdraw myself from notice. Exit Wragge. And now to business! Permit me to inquire what effect I have produced on your own mind? Do you still believe that the Rogue who has trusted you with all his secrets is a Rogue who is bent on taking a mean advantage of a fair relative?"

"I will wait a little," Magdalen rejoined, "before I answer that question. When I came down to tea, you told me you had been employing your mind for my benefit. May I ask how?"

"By all means," said Captain Wragge. "You shall have the net result of the whole mental process. Said process ranges over the present and future proceedings of your disconsolate friends, and of the lawyers who are helping them to find you. Their present proceedings are, in all probability, assuming the following form: the lawyer's clerk has given you up at Mr. Huxtable's, and has also, by this time, given you up, after careful inquiry, at all the hotels. His last chance is that you may send for your box to the cloak-room—you don't send for it—and there the clerk is to-night (thanks to Captain Wragge and Rosemary Lane) at the end of his resources. He will forthwith communicate that fact to his employers in London; and those employers (don't be alarmed!) will apply for help to the detective police. Allowing for inevitable delays, a professional spy, with all his wits about him, and with those handbills to help him privately in identifying you, will be here certainly not later than the day after tomorrow—possibly earlier. If you remain in York, if you attempt to communicate with Mr. Huxtable, that spy will find you out. If, on the other hand, you leave the city before he comes (taking your departure by other means than the railway, of course) you put him in the same predicament as the clerk—you defy him to find a fresh trace of you. There is my brief abstract of your present position. What do you think of it?"

"I think it has one defect," said Magdalen. "It ends in nothing."

"Pardon me," retorted the captain. "It ends in an arrangement for your safe departure, and in a plan for the entire gratification of your wishes in the direction of the stage. Both drawn from the resources of my own experience, and both waiting a word from you, to be poured forth immediately in the fullest detail."

"I think I know what that word is," replied Magdalen, looking at him attentively.

"Charmed to hear it, I am sure. You have only to say, 'Captain Wragge, take charge of me'—and my plans are yours from that moment."

"I will take to-night to consider your proposal," she said, after an instant's reflection. "You shall have my answer to-morrow morning."

Captain Wragge looked a little disappointed. He had not expected the reservation on his side to be met so composedly by a reservation on hers.

"Why not decide at once?" he remonstrated, in his most persuasive tones. "You have only to consider—"

"I have more to consider than you think for," she answered. "I have another object in view besides the object you know of."

"May I ask—?"

"Excuse me, Captain Wragge—you may not ask. Allow me to thank you for your hospitality, and to wish you good-night. I am worn out. I want rest."

Once more the captain wisely adapted himself to her humor with the ready self-control of an experienced man.

"Worn out, of course!" he said, sympathetically. "Unpardonable on my part not to have thought of it before. We will resume our conversation to-morrow. Permit me to give you a candle. Mrs. Wragge!"

Prostrated by mental exertion, Mrs. Wragge was pursuing the course of the omelette in dreams. Her head was twisted one way, and her body the other. She snored meekly. At intervals one of her hands raised itself in the air, shook an imaginary frying-pan, and dropped again with a faint thump on the cookery-book in her lap. At the sound of her husband's voice, she started to her feet, and confronted him with her mind fast asleep, and her eyes wide open.

"Assist Miss Vanstone," said the captain. "And the next time you forget yourself in your chair, fall asleep straight—don't annoy me by falling asleep crooked."

Mrs. Wragge opened her eyes a little wider, and looked at Magdalen in helpless amazement.

"Is the captain breakfasting by candle-light?" she inquired, meekly. "And haven't I done the omelette?"

Before her husband's corrective voice could apply a fresh stimulant, Magdalen took her compassionately by the arm and led her out of the room.

"Another object besides the object I know of?" repeated Captain Wragge, when he was left by himself. "Is there a gentleman in the background, after all? Is there mischief brewing in the dark that I don't bargain for?"

CHAPTER III.

TOWARD six o'clock the next morning, the light pouring in on her face awoke Magdalen in the bedroom in Rosemary Lane.

She started from her deep, dreamless repose of the past night with that painful sense of bewilderment, on first waking, which is familiar to all sleepers in strange beds. "Norah!" she called out mechanically, when she opened her eyes. The next instant her mind roused itself, and her senses told her the truth. She looked round the miserable room with a loathing recognition of it. The sordid contrast which the place presented to all that she had been accustomed to see in her own bed-chamber—the practical abandonment, implied in its scanty furniture, of those elegant purities of personal habit to which she had been accustomed from her childhood—shocked that sense of bodily self-respect in Magdalen which is a refined woman's second nature. Contemptible as the influence seemed, when compared with her situation at that moment, the bare sight of the jug and basin in a corner of the room decided her first resolution when she woke. She determined, then and there, to leave Rosemary Lane.

How was she to leave it? With Captain Wragge, or without him?

She dressed herself, with a dainty shrinking from everything in the room which her hands or her clothes touched in the process, and then opened the window. The autumn air felt keen and sweet; and the little patch of sky that she could see was warmly bright already with the new sunlight. Distant voices of bargemen on the river, and the chirping of birds among the weeds which topped the old city wall, were the only sounds that broke the morning silence. She sat down by the window; and searched her mind for the thoughts which she had lost, when weariness overcame her on the night before.

The first subject to which she returned was the vagabond subject of Captain Wragge.

The "moral agriculturist" had failed to remove her personal distrust of him, cunningly as he had tried to plead against it by openly confessing the impostures that he had practiced on others. He had raised her opinion of his abilities; he had amused her by his humor; he had astonished her by his assurance; but he had left her original conviction that he was a Rogue exactly where it was when he first met with her. If the one design then in her mind had been the design of going on the stage, she would, at all hazards, have rejected the more than doubtful assistance of Captain Wragge on the spot.

But the perilous journey on which she had now adventured herself had another end in view—an end, dark and distant—an end, with pitfalls hidden on the way to it, far other than the shallow pitfalls on the way to the stage. In the mysterious stillness of the morning, her mind looked on to its second and its deeper design, and the despicable figure of the swindler rose before her in a new view.

She tried to shut him out—to feel above him and beyond him again, as she had felt up to this time.

After a little trifling with her dress, she took from her bosom the white silk bag which her own hands had made on the farewell night at Combe-Raven. It drew together at the mouth with delicate silken strings. The first thing she took out, on opening it, was a lock of Frank's hair, tied with a morsel of silver thread; the next was a sheet of paper containing the extracts which she had copied from her father's will and her father's letter; the last was a closely-folded packet of bank-notes, to the value of nearly two hundred pounds—the produce (as Miss Garth had rightly conjectured) of the sale of her jewelry and her dresses, in which the servant at the boarding-school had privately assisted her. She put back the notes at once, without a second glance at them, and then sat looking thoughtfully at the lock of hair as it lay on her lap. "You are better than nothing," she said, speaking to it with a girl's fanciful tenderness. "I can sit and look at you sometimes, till I almost think I am looking at Frank. Oh, my darling! my darling!" Her voice faltered softly, and she put the lock of hair, with a languid gentleness, to her lips. It fell from her fingers into her bosom. A lovely tinge of color rose on her cheeks, and spread downward to her neck, as if it followed the falling hair. She closed her eyes, and let her fair head droop softly. The world passed from her; and, for one enchanted moment, Love opened the gates of Paradise to the daughter of Eve.

The trivial noises in the neighboring street, gathering in number as the morning advanced, forced her back to the hard realities of the passing time. She raised her head with a heavy sigh, and opened her eyes once more on the mean and miserable little room.

The extracts from the will and the letter—those last memorials of her father, now so closely associated with the purpose which had possession of her mind—still lay before her. The transient color faded from her face, as she spread the little manuscript open on her lap. The extracts from the will stood highest on the page; they were limited to those few touching words in which the dead father begged his children's forgiveness for the stain on their birth, and implored them to remember the untiring love and care by which he had striven to atone for it. The extract from the letter to Mr. Pendril came next. She read the last melancholy sentences aloud to herself: "For God's sake come on the day when you receive this—come and relieve me from the dreadful thought that my two darling girls are at this moment unprovided for. If anything happened to me, and if my desire to do their mother justice ended (through my miserable ignorance of the law) in leaving Norah and Magdalen disinherited, I should not rest in my grave!" Under these lines again, and close at the bottom of the page, was written the terrible commentary on that letter which had fallen from Mr. Pendril's lips: "Mr. Vanstone's daughters are Nobody's Children, and the law leaves them helpless at their uncle's mercy."

Helpless when those words were spoken—helpless still, after all that she had resolved, after all that she had sacrificed. The assertion of her natural rights and her sister's, sanctioned by the direct expression of her father's last wishes; the recall of Frank from China; the justification of her desertion of Norah—all hung on her desperate purpose of recovering the lost inheritance, at any risk, from the man who had beggared and insulted his brother's children. And that man was still a shadow to her! So little did she know of him that she was even ignorant at that moment of his place of abode.

She rose and paced the room with the noiseless, negligent grace of a wild creature of the forest in its cage. "How can I reach him in the dark?" she said to herself. "How can I find out—?" She stopped suddenly. Before the question had shaped itself to an end in her thoughts, Captain Wragge was back in her mind again.

A man well used to working in the dark; a man with endless resources of audacity and cunning; a man who would hesitate at no mean employment that could be offered to him, if it was employment that filled his pockets—was this the instrument for which, in its present need, her hand was waiting? Two of the necessities to be met, before she could take a single step in advance, were plainly present to her—the necessity of knowing more of her father's brother than she knew now; and the necessity of throwing him off his guard by concealing herself personally during the process of inquiry. Resolutely self-dependent as she was, the inevitable spy's work at the outset must be work delegated to another. In her position, was there any ready human creature within reach but the vagabond downstairs? Not one. She thought of it anxiously, she thought of it long. Not one! There the choice was, steadily confronting her: the choice of taking the Rogue, or of turning her back on the Purpose.

She paused in the middle of the room. "What can he do at his worst?" she said to herself. "Cheat me. Well! if my money governs him for me, what then? Let him have my money!" She returned mechanically to her place by the window. A moment more decided her. A moment more, and she took the first fatal step downward-she determined to face the risk, and try Captain Wragge.

At nine o'clock the landlady knocked at Magdalen's door, and informed her (with the captain's kind compliments) that breakfast was ready.

She found Mrs. Wragge alone, attired in a voluminous brown holland wrapper, with a limp cape and a trimming of dingy pink ribbon. The ex-waitress at Darch's Dining-rooms was absorbed in the contemplation of a large dish, containing a leathery-looking substance of a mottled yellow color, profusely sprinkled with little black spots.

"There it is!" said Mrs. Wragge. "Omelette with herbs. The landlady helped me. And that's what we've made of it. Don't you ask the captain for any when he comes in—don't, there's a good soul. It isn't nice. We had some accidents with it. It's been under the grate. It's been spilled on the stairs. It's scalded the landlady's youngest boy—he went and sat on it. Bless you, it isn't half as nice as it looks! Don't you ask for any. Perhaps he won't notice if you say nothing about it. What do you think of my wrapper? I should so like to have a white one. Have you got a white one? How is it trimmed? Do tell me!"

The formidable entrance of the captain suspended the next question on her lips. Fortunately for Mrs. Wragge, her husband was far too anxious for the promised expression of Magdalen's decision to pay his customary attention to questions of cookery. When breakfast was over, he dismissed Mrs. Wragge, and merely referred to the omelette by telling her that she had his full permission to "give it to the dogs."

"How does my little proposal look by daylight?" he asked, placing chairs for Magdalen and himself. "Which is it to be: 'Captain Wragge, take charge of me?' or, 'Captain Wragge, good-morning?'"

"You shall hear directly," replied Magdalen. "I have something to say first. I told you, last night, that I had another object in view besides the object of earning my living on the stage—"

"I beg your pardon," interposed Captain Wragge. "Did you say, earning your living?"

"Certainly. Both my sister and myself must depend on our own exertions to gain our daily bread."

"What!!!" cried the captain, starting to his feet. "The daughters of my wealthy and lamented relative by marriage reduced to earn their own living? Impossible—wildly, extravagantly impossible!" He sat down again, and looked at Magdalen as if she had inflicted a personal injury on him.

"You are not acquainted with the full extent of our misfortune," she said, quietly. "I will tell you what has happened before I go any further." She told him at once, in the plainest terms she could find, and with as few details as possible.

Captain Wragge's profound bewilderment left him conscious of but one distinct result produced by the narrative on his own mind. The lawyer's offer of Fifty Pounds Reward for the missing young lady ascended instantly to a place in his estimation which it had never occupied until that moment.

"Do I understand," he inquired, "that you are entirely deprived of present resources?"

"I have sold my jewelry and my dresses," said Magdalen, impatient of his mean harping on the pecuniary string. "If my want of experience keeps me back in a theater, I can afford to wait till the stage can afford to pay me."

Captain Wragge mentally appraised the rings, bracelets, and necklaces, the silks, satins, and laces of the daughter of a gentleman of fortune, at—say, a third of their real value. In a moment more, the Fifty Pounds Reward suddenly sank again to the lowest depths in the deep estimation of this judicious man.

"Just so," he said, in his most business-like manner. "There is not the least fear, my dear girl, of your being kept back in a theater, if you possess present resources, and if you profit by my assistance."

"I must accept more assistance than you have already offered—or none," said Magdalen. "I have more serious difficulties before me than the difficulty of leaving York, and the difficulty of finding my way to the stage."

"You don't say so! I am all attention; pray explain yourself!"

She considered her next words carefully before they passed her lips.

"There are certain inquiries," she said, "which I am interested in making. If I undertook them myself, I should excite the suspicion of the person inquired after, and should learn little or nothing of what I wish to know. If the inquiries could be made by a stranger, without my being seen in the matter, a service would be rendered me of much greater importance than the service you offered last night."

Captain Wragge's vagabond face became gravely and deeply attentive.

"May I ask," he said, "what the nature of the inquiries is likely to be?"

Magdalen hesitated. She had necessarily mentioned Michael Vanstone's name in informing the captain of the loss of her inheritance. She must inevitably mention it to him again if she employed his services. He would doubtless discover it for himself, by a plain process of inference, before she said many words more, frame them as carefully as she might. Under these circumstances, was there any intelligible reason for shrinking from direct reference to Michael Vanstone? No intelligible reason—and yet she shrank.

"For instance," pursued Captain Wragge, "are they inquiries about a man or a woman; inquiries about an enemy or a friend—?"

"An enemy," she answered, quickly.

Her reply might still have kept the captain in the dark—but her eyes enlightened him. "Michael Vanstone!" thought the wary Wragge. "She looks dangerous; I'll feel my way a little further."

"With regard, now, to the person who is the object of these inquiries," he resumed. "Are you thoroughly clear in your own mind about what you want to know?"

"Perfectly clear," replied Magdalen. "I want to know where he lives, to begin with."

"Yes. And after that?"

"I want to know about his habits; about who the people are whom he associates with; about what he does with his money—" She considered a little. "And one thing more," she said; "I want to know whether there is any woman about his house—a relation, or a housekeeper—who has an influence over him."

"Harmless enough, so far," said the captain. "What next?"

"Nothing. The rest is my secret."

The clouds on Captain Wragge's countenance began to clear away again. He reverted, with his customary precision, to his customary choice of alternatives. "These inquiries of hers," he thought, "mean one of two things—Mischief, or Money! If it's Mischief, I'll slip through her fingers. If it's Money, I'll make myself useful, with a view to the future."

Magdalen's vigilant eyes watched the progress of his reflections suspiciously. "Captain Wragge," she said, "if you want time to consider, say so plainly."

"I don't want a moment," replied the captain. "Place your departure from York, your dramatic career, and your private inquiries under my care. Here I am, unreservedly at your disposal. Say the word—do you take me?"

Her heart beat fast; her lips turned dry—but she said the word.

"I do."

There was a pause. Magdalen sat silent, struggling with the vague dread of the future which had been roused in her mind by her own reply. Captain Wragge, on his side, was apparently absorbed in the consideration of a new set of alternatives. His hands descended into his empty pockets, and prophetically tested their capacity as receptacles for gold and silver. The brightness of the precious metals was in his face, the smoothness of the precious metals was in his voice, as he provided himself with a new supply of words, and resumed the conversation.

"The next question," he said, "is the question of time. Do these confidential investigations of ours require immediate attention—or can they wait?"

"For the present, they can wait," replied Magdalen. "I wish to secure my freedom from all interference on the part of my friends before the inquiries are made."

"Very good. The first step toward accomplishing that object is to beat our retreat—excuse a professional metaphor from a military man—to beat our retreat from York to-morrow. I see my way plainly so far; but I am all abroad, as we used to say in the militia, about my marching orders afterward. The next direction we take ought to be chosen with an eye to advancing your dramatic views. I am all ready, when I know what your views are. How came you to think of the theater at all? I see the sacred fire burning in you; tell me, who lit it?"

Magdalen could only answer him in one way. She could only look back at the days that were gone forever, and tell him the story of her first step toward the stage at Evergreen Lodge. Captain Wragge listened with his usual politeness; but he evidently derived no satisfactory impression from what he heard. Audiences of friends were audiences whom he privately declined to trust; and the opinion of the stage-manager was the opinion of a man who spoke with his fee in his pocket and his eye on a future engagement.

"Interesting, deeply interesting," he said, when Magdalen had done. "But not conclusive to a practical man. A specimen of your abilities is necessary to enlighten me. I have been on the stage myself; the comedy of the Rivals is familiar to me from beginning to end. A sample is all I want, if you have not forgotten the words—a sample of 'Lucy,' and a sample of 'Julia.'"

"I have not forgotten the words," said Magdalen, sorrowfully; "and I have the little books with me in which my dialogue was written out. I have never parted with them; they remind me of a time—" Her lip trembled, and a pang of the heart-ache silenced her.

"Nervous," remarked the captain, indulgently. "Not at all a bad sign. The greatest actresses on the stage are nervous. Follow their example, and get over it. Where are the parts? Oh, here they are! Very nicely written, and remarkably clean. I'll give you the cues—it will all be over (as the dentists say) in no time. Take the back drawing-room for the stage, and take me for the audience. Tingle goes the bell; up runs the curtain; order in the gallery, silence in the pit—enter Lucy!"

She tried hard to control herself; she forced back the sorrow—the innocent, natural, human sorrow for the absent and the dead—pleading hard with her for the tears that she refused. Resolutely, with cold, clinched hands, she tried to begin. As the first familiar words passed her lips, Frank came back to her from the sea, and the face of her dead father looked at her with the smile of happy old times. The voices of her mother and her sister talked gently in the fragrant country stillness, and the garden-walks at Combe-Raven opened once more on her view. With a faint, wailing cry, she dropped into a chair; her head fell forward on the table, and she burst passionately into tears.

Captain Wragge was on his feet in a moment. She shuddered as he came near her, and waved him back vehemently with her hand. "Leave me!" she said; "leave me a minute by myself!" The compliant Wragge retired to the front room; looked out of the window; and whistled under his breath. "The family spirit again!" he said. "Complicated by hysterics."

After waiting a minute or two he returned to make inquiries.

"Is there anything I can offer you?" he asked. "Cold water? burned feathers? smelling salts? medical assistance? Shall I summon Mrs. Wragge? Shall we put it off till to-morrow?"

She started up, wild and flushed, with a desperate self-command in her face, with an angry resolution in her manner.

"No!" she said. "I must harden myself—and I will! Sit down again and see me act."

"Bravo!" cried the captain. "Dash at it, my beauty—and it's done!"

She dashed at it, with a mad defiance of herself—with a raised voice, and a glow like fever in her cheeks. All the artless, girlish charm of the performance in happier and better days was gone. The native dramatic capacity that was in her came, hard and bold, to the surface, stripped of every softening allurement which had once adorned it. She would have saddened and disappointed a man with any delicacy of feeling. She absolutely electrified Captain Wragge. He forgot his politeness, he forgot his long words. The essential spirit of the man's whole vagabond life burst out of him irresistibly in his first exclamation. "Who the devil would have thought it? She can act, after all!" The instant the words escaped his lips he recovered himself, and glided off into his ordinary colloquial channels. Magdalen stopped him in the middle of his first compliment. "No," she said; "I have forced the truth out of you for once. I want no more."

"Pardon me," replied the incorrigible Wragge. "You want a little instruction; and I am the man to give it you."

With that answer, he placed a chair for her, and proceeded to explain himself.

She sat down in silence. A sullen indifference began to show itself in her manner; her cheeks turned pale again; and her eyes looked wearily vacant at the wall before her. Captain Wragge noticed these signs of heart-sickness and discontent with herself, after the effort she had made, and saw the importance of rousing her by speaking, for once, plainly and directly to the point. She had set a new value on herself in his mercenary eyes. She had suggested to him a speculation in her youth, her beauty, and her marked ability for the stage, which had never entered his mind until he saw her act. The old militia-man was quick at his shifts. He and his plans had both turned right about together when Magdalen sat down to hear what he had to say.

"Mr. Huxtable's opinion is my opinion," he began. "You are a born actress. But you must be trained before you can do anything on the stage. I am disengaged—I am competent—I have trained others—I can train you. Don't trust my word: trust my eye to my own interests. I'll make it my interest to take pains with you, and to be quick about it. You shall pay me for my instructions from your profits on the stage. Half your salary for the first year; a third of your salary for the second year; and half the sum you clear by your first benefit in a London theater. What do you say to that? Have I made it my interest to push you, or have I not?"

So far as appearances went, and so far as the stage went, it was plain that he had linked his interests and Magdalen's together. She briefly told him so, and waited to hear more.

"A month or six weeks' study," continued the captain, "will give me a reasonable idea of what you can do best. All ability runs in grooves; and your groove remains to be found. We can't find it here—for we can't keep you a close prisoner for weeks together in Rosemary Lane. A quiet country place, secure from all interference and interruption, is the place we want for a month certain. Trust my knowledge of Yorkshire, and consider the place found. I see no difficulties anywhere, except the difficulty of beating our retreat to-morrow."

"I thought your arrangements were made last night?" said Magdalen.

"Quite right," rejoined the captain. "They were made last night; and here they are. We can't leave by railway, because the lawyer's clerk is sure to be on the lookout for you at the York terminus. Very good; we take to the road instead, and leave in our own carriage. Where the deuce do we get it? We get it from the landlady's brother, who has a horse and chaise which he lets out for hire. That chaise comes to the end of Rosemary Lane at an early hour to-morrow morning. I take my wife and my niece out to show them the beauties of the neighborhood. We have a picnic hamper with us, which marks our purpose in the public eye. You disfigure yourself in a shawl, bonnet, and veil of Mrs. Wragge's; we turn our backs on York; and away we drive on a pleasure trip for the day—you and I on the front seat, Mrs. Wragge and the hamper behind. Good again. Once on the highroad, what do we do? Drive to the first station beyond York, northward, southward, or eastward, as may be hereafter determined. No lawyer's clerk is waiting for you there. You and Mrs. Wragge get out—first opening the hamper at a convenient opportunity. Instead of containing chickens and Champagne, it contains a carpet-bag, with the things you want for the night. You take your tickets for a place previously determined on, and I take the chaise back to York. Arrived once more in this house, I collect the luggage left behind, and send for the woman downstairs. 'Ladies so charmed with such and such a place (wrong place of course), that they have determined to stop there. Pray accept the customary week's rent, in place of a week's warning. Good day.' Is the clerk looking for me at the York terminus? Not he. I take my ticket under his very nose; I follow you with the luggage along your line of railway—and where is the trace left of your departure? Nowhere. The fairy has vanished; and the legal authorities are left in the lurch."

"Why do you talk of difficulties?" asked Magdalen. "The difficulties seem to be provided for."

"All but ONE," said Captain Wragge, with an ominous emphasis on the last word. "The Grand Difficulty of humanity from the cradle to the grave—Money." He slowly winked his green eye; sighed with deep feeling; and buried his insolvent hands in his unproductive pockets.

"What is the money wanted for?" inquired Magdalen.

"To pay my bills," replied the captain, with a touching simplicity. "Pray understand! I never was—and never shall be—personally desirous of paying a single farthing to any human creature on the habitable globe. I am speaking in your interest, not in mine."

"My interest?"

"Certainly. You can't get safely away from York to-morrow without the chaise. And I can't get the chaise without money. The landlady's brother will lend it if he sees his sister's bill receipted, and if he gets his day's hire beforehand—not otherwise. Allow me to put the transaction in a business light. We have agreed that I am to be remunerated for my course of dramatic instruction out of your future earnings on the stage. Very good. I merely draw on my future prospects; and you, on whom those prospects depend, are naturally my banker. For mere argument's sake, estimate my share in your first year's salary at the totally inadequate value of a hundred pounds. Halve that sum; quarter that sum—"

"How much do you want?" said Magdalen, impatiently.

Captain Wragge was sorely tempted to take the Reward at the top of the handbills as his basis of calculation. But he felt the vast future importance of present moderation; and actually wanting some twelve or thirteen pounds, he merely doubled the amount, and said, "Five-and-twenty."

Magdalen took the little bag from her bosom, and gave him the money, with a contemptuous wonder at the number of words which he had wasted on her for the purpose of cheating on so small a scale. In the old days at Combe-Raven, five-and-twenty pounds flowed from a stroke of her father's pen into the hands of any one in the house who chose to ask for it.

Captain Wragge's eyes dwelt on the little bag as the eyes of lovers dwell on their mistresses. "Happy bag!" he murmured, as she put it back in her bosom. He rose; dived into a corner of the room; produced his neat dispatch-box; and solemnly unlocked it on the table between Magdalen and himself.

"The nature of the man, my dear girl—the nature of the man," he said, opening one of his plump little books bound in calf and vellum. "A transaction has taken place between us. I must have it down in black and white." He opened the book at a blank page, and wrote at the top, in a fine mercantile hand: "Miss Vanstone, the Younger: In account with Horatio Wragge, late of the Royal Militia. Dr.—Cr. Sept. 24th, 1846. Dr.: To estimated value of H. Wragge's interest in Miss V.'s first year's salary—say—200 pounds. Cr. By paid on account, 25 pounds." Having completed the entry—and having also shown, by doubling his original estimate on the Debtor side, that Magdalen's easy compliance with his demand on her had not been thrown away on him—the captain pressed his blotting-paper over the wet ink, and put away the book with the air of a man who had done a virtuous action, and who was above boasting about it.

"Excuse me for leaving you abruptly," he said. "Time is of importance; I must make sure of the chaise. If Mrs. Wragge comes in, tell her nothing—she is not sharp enough to be trusted. If she presumes to ask questions, extinguish her immediately. You have only to be loud. Pray take my authority into your own hands, and be as loud with Mrs. Wragge as I am!" He snatched up his tall hat, bowed, smiled, and tripped out of the room.

Sensible of little else but of the relief of being alone; feeling no more distinct impression than the vague sense of some serious change having taken place in herself and her position, Magdalen let the events of the morning come and go like shadows on her mind, and waited wearily for what the day might bring forth. After the lapse of some time, the door opened softly. The giant figure of Mrs. Wragge stalked into the room, and stopped opposite Magdalen in solemn astonishment.

"Where are your Things?" asked Mrs. Wragge, with a burst of incontrollable anxiety. "I've been upstairs looking in your drawers. Where are your night-gowns and night-caps? and your petticoats and stockings? and your hair-pins and bear's grease, and all the rest of it?"

"My luggage is left at the railway station," said Magdalen.

Mrs. Wragge's moon-face brightened dimly. The ineradicable female instinct of Curiosity tried to sparkle in her faded blue eyes—flickered piteously—and died out.

"How much luggage?" she asked, confidentially. "The captain's gone out. Let's go and get it!"

"Mrs. Wragge!" cried a terrible voice at the door.

For the first time in Magdalen's experience, Mrs. Wragge was deaf to the customary stimulant. She actually ventured on a feeble remonstrance in the presence of her husband.

"Oh, do let her have her Things!" pleaded Mrs. Wragge. "Oh, poor soul, do let her have her Things!"

The captain's inexorable forefinger pointed to a corner of the room—dropped slowly as his wife retired before it—and suddenly stopped at the region of her shoes.

"Do I hear a clapping on the floor!" exclaimed Captain Wragge, with an expression of horror. "Yes; I do. Down at heel again! The left shoe this time. Pull it up, Mrs. Wragge! pull it up!—The chaise will be here to-morrow morning at nine o'clock," he continued, addressing Magdalen. "We can't possibly venture on claiming your box. There is note-paper. Write down a list of the necessaries you want. I will take it myself to the shop, pay the bill for you, and bring back the parcel. We must sacrifice the box—we must, indeed."

While her husband was addressing Magdalen, Mrs. Wragge had stolen out again from her corner, and had ventured near enough to the captain to hear the words "shop" and "parcel." She clapped her great hands together in ungovernable excitement, and lost all control over herself immediately.

"Oh, if it's shopping, let me do it!" cried Mrs. Wragge. "She's going out to buy her Things! Oh, let me go with her—please let me go with her!"

"Sit down!" shouted the captain. "Straight! more to the right—more still. Stop where you are!"

Mrs. Wragge crossed her helpless hands on her lap, and melted meekly into tears.

"I do so like shopping," pleaded the poor creature; "and I get so little of it now!"

Magdalen completed her list; and Captain Wragge at once left the room with it. "Don't let my wife bore you," he said, pleasantly, as he went out. "Cut her short, poor soul—cut her short!"

"Don't cry," said Magdalen, trying to comfort Mrs. Wragge by patting her on the shoulder. "When the parcel comes back you shall open it."

"Thank you, my dear," said Mrs. Wragge, meekly, drying her eyes; "thank you kindly. Don't notice my handkerchief, please. It's such a very little one! I had a nice lot of them once, with lace borders. They're all gone now. Never mind! It will comfort me to unpack your Things. You're very good to me. I like you. I say—you won't be angry, will you? Give us a kiss."

Magdalen stooped over her with the frank grace and gentleness of past days, and touched her faded cheek. "Let me do something harmless!" she thought, with a pang at her heart—"oh let me do something innocent and kind for the sake of old times!"

She felt her eyes moistening, and silently turned away.

That night no rest came to her. That night the roused forces of Good and Evil fought their terrible fight for her soul—and left the strife between them still in suspense when morning came. As the clock of York Minster struck nine, she followed Mrs. Wragge to the chaise, and took her seat by the captain's side. In a quarter of an hour more York was in the distance, and the highroad lay bright and open before them in the morning sunlight.

THE END OF THE SECOND SCENE.

BETWEEN THE SCENES.

CHRONICLE OF EVENTS: PRESERVED IN CAPTAIN WRAGGE'S DISPATCH-BOX.

I.

Chronicle for October, 1846.

I HAVE retired into the bosom of my family. We are residing in the secluded village of Ruswarp, on the banks of the Esk, about two miles inland from Whitby. Our lodgings are comfortable, and we possess the additional blessing of a tidy landlady. Mrs. Wragge and Miss Vanstone preceded me here, in accordance with the plan I laid down for effecting our retreat from York. On the next day I followed them alone, with the luggage. On leaving the terminus, I had the satisfaction of seeing the lawyer's clerk in close confabulation with the detective officer whose advent I had prophesied. I left him in peaceable possession of the city of York, and the whole surrounding neighborhood. He has returned the compliment, and has left us in peaceable possession of the valley of the Esk, thirty miles away from him.

Remarkable results have followed my first efforts at the cultivation of Miss Vanstone's dramatic abilities.

I have discovered that she possesses extraordinary talent as a mimic. She has the flexible face, the manageable voice, and the dramatic knack which fit a woman for character-parts and disguises on the stage. All she now wants is teaching and practice, to make her sure of her own resources. The experience of her, thus gained, has revived an idea in my mind which originally occurred to me at one of the "At Homes" of the late inimitable Charles Mathews, comedian. I was in the Wine Trade at the time, I remember. We imitated the Vintage-processes of Nature in a back-kitchen at Brompton, and produced a dinner-sherry, pale and curious, tonic in character, round in the mouth, a favorite with the Court of Spain, at nineteen-and-sixpence a dozen, bottles included—Vide Prospectus of the period. The profits of myself and partners were small; we were in advance of the tastes of the age, and in debt to the bottle merchant. Being at my wits' end for want of money, and seeing what audiences Mathews drew, the idea occurred to me of starting an imitation of the great Imitator himself, in the shape of an "At Home," given by a woman. The one trifling obstacle in the way was the difficulty of finding the woman. From that time to this, I have hitherto failed to overcome it. I have conquered it at last; I have found the woman now. Miss Vanstone possesses youth and beauty as well as talent. Train her in the art of dramatic disguise; provide her with appropriate dresses for different characters; develop her accomplishments in singing and playing; give her plenty of smart talk addressed to the audience; advertise her as a Young Lady at Home; astonish the public by a dramatic entertainment which depends from first to last on that young lady's own sole exertions; commit the entire management of the thing to my care—and what follows as a necessary con sequence? Fame for my fair relative, and a fortune for myself.

I put these considerations, as frankly as usual, to Miss Vanstone; offering to write the Entertainment, to manage all the business, and to share the profits. I did not forget to strengthen my case by informing her of the jealousies she would encounter, and the obstacles she would meet, if she went on the stage. And I wound up by a neat reference to the private inquiries which she is interested in making, and to the personal independence which she is desirous of securing before she acts on her information. "If you go on the stage," I said, "your services will be bought by a manager, and he may insist on his claims just at the time when you want to get free from him. If, on the contrary, you adopt my views, you will be your own mistress and your own manager, and you can settle your course just as you like." This last consideration appeared to strike her. She took a day to consider it; and, when the day was over, gave her consent.

I had the whole transaction down in black and white immediately. Our arrangement is eminently satisfactory, except in one particular. She shows a morbid distrust of writing her name at the bottom of any document which I present to her, and roundly declares she will sign nothing. As long as it is her interest to provide herself with pecuniary resources for the future, she verbally engages to go on. When it ceases to be her interest, she plainly threatens to leave off at a week's notice. A difficult girl to deal with; she has found out her own value to me already. One comfort is, I have the cooking of the accounts; and my fair relative shall not fill her pockets too suddenly if I can help it.

My exertions in training Miss Vanstone for the coming experiment have been varied by the writing of two anonymous letters in that young lady's interests. Finding her too fidgety about arranging matters with her friends to pay proper attention to my instructions, I wrote anonymously to the lawyer who is conducting the inquiry after her, recommending him, in a friendly way, to give it up. The letter was inclosed to a friend of mine in London, with instructions to post it at Charing Cross. A week later I sent a second letter, through the same channel, requesting the lawyer to inform me, in writing, whether he and his clients had or had not decided on taking my advice. I directed him, with jocose reference to the collision of interests between us, to address his letter: "Tit for Tat, Post-office, West Strand."

In a few days the answer arrived—privately forwarded, of course, to Post-office, Whitby, by arrangement with my friend in London.

The lawyer's reply was short and surly: "SIR—If my advice had been followed, you and your anonymous letter would both be treated with the contempt which they deserve. But the wishes of Miss Magdalen Vanstone's eldest sister have claims on my consideration which I cannot dispute; and at her entreaty I inform you that all further proceedings on my part are withdrawn—on the express understanding that this concession is to open facilities for written communication, at least, between the two sisters. A letter from the elder Miss Vanstone is inclosed in this. If I don't hear in a week's time that it has been received, I shall place the matter once more in the hands of the police.—WILLIAM PENDRIL." A sour man, this William Pendril. I can only say of him what an eminent nobleman once said of his sulky servant—"I wouldn't have such a temper as that fellow has got for any earthly consideration that could be offered me!"

As a matter of course, I looked into the letter which the lawyer inclosed, before delivering it. Miss Vanstone, the elder, described herself as distracted at not hearing from her sister; as suited with a governess's situation in a private family; as going into the situation in a week's time; and as longing for a letter to comfort her, before she faced the trial of undertaking her new duties. After closing the envelope again, I accompanied the delivery of the letter to Miss

Vanstone, the younger, by a word of caution. "Are you more sure of your own courage now," I said, "than you were when I met you?" She was ready with her answer. "Captain Wragge, when you met me on the Walls of York I had not gone too far to go back. I have gone too far now."

If she really feels this—and I think she does—her corresponding with her sister can do no harm. She wrote at great length the same day; cried profusely over her own epistolary composition; and was remarkably ill-tempered and snappish toward me, when we met in the evening. She wants experience, poor girl—she sadly wants experience of the world. How consoling to know that I am just the man to give it her!

II.

Chronicle for November.

We are established at Derby. The Entertainment is written; and the rehearsals are in steady progress. All difficulties are provided for, but the one eternal difficulty of money. Miss Vanstone's resources stretch easily enough to the limits of our personal wants; including piano-forte hire for practice, and the purchase and making of the necessary dresses. But the expenses of starting the Entertainment are beyond the reach of any means we possess. A theatrical friend of mine here, whom I had hoped to interest in our undertaking, proves, unhappily, to be at a crisis in his career. The field of human sympathy, out of which I might have raised the needful pecuniary crop, is closed to me from want of time to cultivate it. I see no other resource left—if we are to be ready by Christmas—than to try one of the local music-sellers in this town, who is said to be a speculating man. A private rehearsal at these lodgings, and a bargain which will fill the pockets of a grasping stranger—such are the sacrifices which dire necessity imposes on me at starting. Well! there is only one consolation: I'll cheat the music-seller.

III.

Chronicle for December. First Fortnight.

The music-seller extorts my unwilling respect. He is one of the very few human beings I have met with in the course of my life who is not to be cheated. He has taken a masterly advantage of our helplessness; and has imposed terms on us, for performances at Derby and Nottingham, with such a business-like disregard of all interests but his own that—fond as I am of putting things down in black and white—I really cannot prevail upon myself to record the bargain. It is needless to say, I have yielded with my best grace; sharing with my fair relative the wretched pecuniary prospects offered to us. Our turn will come. In the meantime, I cordially regret not having known the local music-seller in early life.

Personally speaking, I have no cause to complain of Miss Vanstone. We have arranged that she shall regularly forward her address (at the post-office) to her friends, as we move about from place to place. Besides communicating in this way with her sister, she also reports herself to a certain Mr. Clare, residing in Somersetshire, who is to forward all letters exchanged between herself and his son. Careful inquiry has informed me that this latter individual is now in China. Having suspected from the first that there was a gentleman in the background, it is highly satisfactory to know that he recedes into the remote perspective of Asia. Long may he remain there!

The trifling responsibility of finding a name for our talented Magdalen to perform under has been cast on my shoulders. She feels no interest whatever in this part of the subject. "Give me any name you like," she said; "I have as much right to one as to another. Make it yourself." I have readily consented to gratify her wishes. The resources of my commercial library include a list of useful names to assume; and we can choose one at five minutes' notice, when the admirable man of business who now oppresses us is ready to issue his advertisements. On this point my mind is easy enough: all my anxieties center in the fair performer. I have not the least doubt she will do wonders if she is only left to herself on the first night. But if the day's post is mischievous enough to upset her by a letter from her sister, I tremble for the consequences.

IV.

Chronicle for December. Second Fortnight.

My gifted relative has made her first appearance in public, and has laid the foundation of our future fortunes.

On the first night the attendance was larger than I had ventured to hope. The novelty of an evening's entertainment, conducted from beginning to end by the unaided exertions of a young lady (see advertisement), roused the public curiosity, and the seats were moderately well filled. As good luck would have it, no letter addressed to Miss Vanstone came that day. She was in full possession of herself until she got the first dress on and heard the bell ring for the music. At that critical moment she suddenly broke down. I found her alone in the waiting-room, sobbing, and talking like a child. "Oh, poor papa! poor papa! Oh, my God, if he saw me now!" My experience in such matters at once informed me that it was a case of sal-volatile, accompanied by sound advice. We strung her up in no time to concert pitch; set her eyes in a blaze; and made her out-blush her own rouge. The curtain rose when we had got her at a red heat. She dashed at it exactly as she dashed at it in the back drawing-room at Rosemary Lane. Her personal appearance settled the question of her reception before she opened her lips. She rushed full gallop through her changes of character, her songs, and her dialogue; making mistakes by the dozen, and never stopping to set them right; carrying the people along with her in a perfect whirlwind, and never waiting for the applause. The whole thing was over twenty minutes sooner than the time we had calculated on. She carried it through to the end, and fainted on the waiting-room sofa a minute after the curtain was down. The music-seller having taken leave of his senses from sheer astonishment, and I having no evening costume to appear in, we sent the doctor to make the necessary apology to the public, who were calling for her till the place rang again. I prompted our medical orator with a neat speech from behind the curtain; and I never heard such applause, from such a comparatively small audience, before in my life. I felt the tribute—I felt it deeply. Fourteen years ago I scraped together the wretched means of existence in this very town by reading the newspaper (with explanatory comments) to the company at a public-house. And now here I am at the top of the tree.

It is needless to say that my first proceeding was to bowl out the music-seller on the spot. He called the next morning, no doubt with a liberal proposal for extending the engagement beyond Derby and Nottingham. My niece was described as not well enough to see him; and, when he asked for me, he was told I was not up. I happened to be at that moment engaged in putting the case pathetically to our gifted Magdalen. Her answer was in the highest degree satisfactory. She would permanently engage herself to nobody—least of all to a man who had taken sordid advantage of her position and mine. She would be her own mistress, and share the profits with me, while she wanted money, and while it suited her to go on. So far so good.

But the reason she added next, for her flattering preference of myself, was less to my taste. "The music-seller is not the man whom I employ to make my inquiries," she said. "You are the man." I don't like her steadily remembering those inquiries, in the first bewilderment of her success. It looks ill for the future; it looks infernally ill for the future.

V.

Chronicle for January, 1847.

She has shown the cloven foot already. I begin to be a little afraid of her.

On the conclusion of the Nottingham engagement (the results of which more than equaled the results at Derby), I proposed taking the entertainment next—now we had got it into our own hands—to Newark. Miss Vanstone raised no objection until we came to the question of time, when she amazed me by stipulating for a week's delay before we appeared in public again.

"For what possible purpose?" I asked.

"For the purpose of making the inquiries which I mentioned to you at York," she answered.

I instantly enlarged on the danger of delay, putting all the considerations before her in every imaginable form. She remained perfectly immovable. I tried to shake her on the question of expenses. She answered by handing me over her share of the proceeds at Derby and Nottingham—and there were my expenses paid, at the rate of nearly two guineas a day. I wonder who first picked out a mule as the type of obstinacy? How little knowledge that man must have had of women!

There was no help for it. I took down my instructions in black and white, as usual. My first exertions were to be directed to the discovery of Mr. Michael Vanstone's address: I was also expected to find out how long he was likely to live there, and whether he had sold Combe-Raven or not. My next inquiries were to inform me of his ordinary habits of life; of what he did with his money; of who his intimate friends were; and of the sort of terms on which his son, Mr. Noel Vanstone, was now living with him. Lastly, the investigations were to end in discovering whether there was any female relative, or any woman exercising domestic authority in the house, who was known to have an influence over either father or son.

If my long practice in cultivating the field of human sympathy had not accustomed me to private investigations into the affairs of other people, I might have found some of these queries rather difficult to deal with in the course of a week. As it was, I gave myself all the benefit of my own experience, and brought the answers back to Nottingham in a day less than the given time. Here they are, in regular order, for convenience of future reference:

(1.) Mr. Michael Vanstone is now residing at German Place, Brighton, and likely to remain there, as he finds the air suits him. He reached London from Switzerland in September last; and sold the Combe-Raven property immediately on his arrival.

(2.) His ordinary habits of life are secret and retired; he seldom visits, or receives company. Part of his money is supposed to be in the Funds, and part laid out in railway investments, which have survived the panic of eighteen hundred and forty-six, and are rapidly rising in value. He is said to be a bold speculator. Since his arrival in England he has invested, with great judgment, in house property. He has some houses in remote parts of London, and some houses in certain watering-places on the east coast, which are shown to be advancing in public repute. In all these cases he is reported to have made remarkably good bargains.

(3.) It is not easy to discover who his intimate friends are. Two names only have been ascertained. The first is Admiral Bartram; supposed to have been under friendly obligations, in past years, to Mr. Michael Vanstone. The second is Mr. George Bartram, nephew of the Admiral, and now staying on a short visit in the house at German Place. Mr. George Bartram is the son of the late Mr. Andrew Vanstone's sister, also deceased. He is therefore a cousin of Mr. Noel Vanstone's. This last—viz., Mr. Noel Vanstone—is in delicate health, and is living on excellent terms with his father in German Place.

(4.) There is no female relative in Mr. Michael Vanstone's family circle. But there is a housekeeper who has lived in his service ever since his wife's death, and who has acquired a strong influence over both father and son. She is a native of Switzerland, elderly, and a widow. Her name is Mrs. Lecount.

On placing these particulars in Miss Vanstone's hands, she made no remark, except to thank me. I endeavored to invite her confidence. No results; nothing but a renewal of civility, and a sudden shifting to the subject of the Entertainment. Very good. If she won't give me the information I want, the conclusion is obvious—I must help myself.

Business considerations claim the remainder of this page. Let me return to business.

_________________________Financial

Statement | Third Week in January

_________________________Place

Visited, | Perform ances, Newark. | Two

_________________________Net

Receipts, | Net Receipts, In black and white. |

Actually Realized. 25 pounds | 32 pounds 10s.

_________________________Apparent

Div. of Profits, | Actual Div. of Profits, |

Miss V............12 10 | Miss V...........12 10

Self..............12 10 | Self.............20 00

_________________________Private

Surplus on the Week, Or say, Self-presented

Testimonial. 7 pounds 10s.

_________________________Audited,

| Passed correct, | H. WRAGGE. |

H. WRAGGE

____

The next stronghold of British sympathy which we take by storm is Sheffield. We open the first week in February.

VI.

Chronicle for February.

Practice has now given my fair relative the confidence which I predicted would come with time. Her knack of disguising her own identity in the impersonation of different characters so completely staggers her audiences that the same people come twice over to find out how she does it. It is the amiable defect of the English public never to know when they have had enough of a good thing. They actually try to encore one of her characters—an old north-country lady; modeled on that honored preceptress in the late Mr. Vanstone's family to whom I presented myself at Combe-Raven. This particular performance fairly amazes the people. I don't wonder at it. Such an extraordinary assumption of age by a girl of nineteen has never been seen in public before, in the whole course of my theatrical experience.

I find myself writing in a lower tone than usual; I miss my own dash of humor. The fact is, I am depressed about the future. In the very height of our prosperity my perverse pupil sticks to her trumpery family quarrel. I feel myself at the mercy of the first whim in the Vanstone direction which may come into her head—I, the architect of her fortunes. Too bad; upon my soul, too bad.

She has acted already on the inquiries which she forced me to make for her. She has written two letters to Mr. Michael Vanstone.

To the first letter no answer came. To the second a reply was received. Her infernal cleverness put an obstacle I had not expected in the way of my intercepting it. Later in the day, after she had herself opened and read the answer, I laid another trap for her. It just succeeded, and no more. I had half a minute to look into the envelope in her absence. It contained nothing but her own letter returned. She is not the girl to put up quietly with such an insult as this. Mischief will come of it—Mischief to Michael Vanstone—which is of no earthly consequence: mischief to Me—which is a truly serious matter.

VII.

Chronicle for March.

After performing at Sheffield and Manchester, we have moved to Liverpool, Preston, and Lancaster. Another change in this weathercock of a girl. She has written no more letters to Michael Vanstone; and she has become as anxious to make money as I am myself. We are realizing large profits, and we are worked to death. I don't like this change in her: she has a purpose to answer, or she would not show such extraordinary eagerness to fill her purse. Nothing I can do—no cooking of accounts; no self-presented testimonials—can keep that purse empty. The success of the Entertainment, and her own sharpness in looking after her interests, literally force me into a course of comparative honesty. She puts into her pocket more than a third of the profits, in defiance of my most arduous exertions to prevent her. And this at my age! this after my long and successful career as a moral agriculturist! Marks of admiration are very little things; but they express my feelings, and I put them in freely.

VIII.

Chronicle for April and May.

We have visited seven more large towns, and are now at Birmingham. Consulting my books, I find that Miss Vanstone has realized by the Entertainment, up to this time, the enormous sum of nearly four hundred pounds. It is quite possible that my own profits may reach one or two miserable hundred more. But I was the architect of her fortunes—the publisher, so to speak, of her book—and, if anything, I am underpaid.

I made the above discovery on the twenty-ninth of the month—anniversary of the Restoration of my royal predecessor in the field of human sympathies, Charles the Second. I had barely finished locking up my dispatch-box, when the ungrateful girl, whose reputation I have made, came into the room and told me in so many words that the business connection between us was for the present at an end.

I attempt no description of my own sensations: I merely record facts. She informed me, with an appearance of perfect composure, that she needed rest, and that she had "new objects in view." She might possibly want me to assist those objects; and she might possibly return to the Entertainment. In either case it would be enough if we exchanged addresses, at which we could write to each other in case of need. Having no desire to leave me too abruptly, she would remain the next day (which was Sunday); and would take her departure on Monday morning. Such was her explanation, in so many words.

Remonstrance, as I knew by experience, would be thrown away. Authority I had none to exert. My one sensible course to take in this emergency was to find out which way my own interests pointed, and to go that way without a moment's unnecessary hesitation.

A very little reflection has since convinced me that she has a deep-laid scheme against Michael Vanstone in view. She is young, handsome, clever, and unscrupulous; she has made money to live on, and has time at her disposal to find out the weak side of an old man; and she is going to attack Mr. Michael Vanstone unawares with the legitimate weapons of her sex. Is she likely to want me for such a purpose as this? Doubtful. Is she merely anxious to get rid of me on easy terms? Probable. Am I the sort of man to be treated in this way by my own pupil? Decidedly not: I am the man to see my way through a neat succession of alternatives; and here they are:

First alternative: To announce my compliance with her proposal; to exchange addresses with her; and then to keep my eye privately on all her future movements. Second alternative: to express fond anxiety in a paternal capacity; and to threaten giving the alarm to her sister and the lawyer, if she persists in her design. Third alternative: to turn the information I already possess to the best account, by making it a marketable commodity between Mr. Michael Vanstone and myself. At present I incline toward the last of these three courses. But my decision is far too important to be hurried. To-day is only the twenty-ninth. I will suspend my Chronicle of Events until Monday.

May 31st.—My alternatives and her plans are both overthrown together.

The newspaper came in, as usual, after breakfast. I looked it over, and discovered this memorable entry among the obituary announcements of the day:

"On the 29th inst., at Brighton, Michael Vanstone, Esq., formerly of Zurich, aged 77."

Miss Vanstone was present in the room when I read those two startling lines. Her bonnet was on; her boxes were packed; she was waiting impatiently until it was time to go to the train.

I handed the paper to her, without a word on my side. Without a word on hers, she looked where I pointed, and read the news of Michael Vanstone's death.

The paper dropped out of her hand, and she suddenly pulled down her veil. I caught one glance at her face before she hid it from me. The effect on my mind was startling in the extreme. To put it with my customary dash of humor—her face informed me that the most sensible action which Michael Vanstone, Esq., formerly of Zurich, had ever achieved in his life was the action he performed at Brighton on the 29th instant.

Finding the dead silence in the room singularly unpleasant under existing circumstances, I thought I would make a remark. My regard for my own interests supplied me with a subject. I mentioned the Entertainment.

"After what has happened," I said, "I presume we go on with our performances as usual?"

"No," she answered, behind the veil. "We go on with my inquiries."

"Inquiries after a dead man?"

"Inquiries after the dead man's son."

"Mr. Noel Vanstone?"

"Yes; Mr. Noel Vanstone."

Not having a veil to put down over my own face, I stooped and picked up the newspaper. Her devilish determination quite upset me for the moment. I actually had to steady myself before I could speak to her again.

"Are the new inquiries as harmless as the old ones?" I asked.

"Quite as harmless."

"What am I expected to find out?"

"I wish to know whether Mr. Noel Vanstone remains at Brighton after the funeral."

"And if not?"

"If not, I shall want to know his new address wherever it may be."

"Yes. And what next?"

"I wish you to find out next if all the father's money goes to the son."

I began to see her drift. The word money relieved me; I felt quite on my own ground again.

"Anything more?" I asked.

"Only one thing more," she answered. "Make sure, if you please, whether Mrs. Lecount, the housekeeper, remains or not in Mr. Noel Vanstone's service."

Her voice altered a little as she mentioned Mrs. Lecount's name; she is evidently sharp enough to distrust the housekeeper already.

"My expenses are to be paid as usual?" I said.

"As usual."

"When am I expected to leave for Brighton?"

"As soon as you can."

She rose, and left the room. After a momentary doubt, I decided on executing the new commission. The more private inquiries I conduct for my fair relative the harder she will find it to get rid of hers truly, Horatio Wragge.

There is nothing to prevent my starting for Brighton to-morrow. So to-morrow I go. If Mr. Noel Vanstone succeeds to his father's property, he is the only human being possessed of pecuniary blessings who fails to inspire me with a feeling of unmitigated envy.

IX.

Chronicle for June.

9th.—I returned yesterday with my information. Here it is, privately noted down for convenience of future reference:

Mr. Noel Vanstone has left Brighton, and has removed, for the purpose of transacting business in London, to one of his late father's empty houses in Vauxhall Walk, Lambeth. This singularly mean selection of a place of residence on the part of a gentleman of fortune looks as if Mr. N. V. and his money were not easily parted.

Mr. Noel Vanstone has stepped into his father's shoes under the following circumstances: Mr. Michael Vanstone appears to have died, curiously enough, as Mr. Andrew Vanstone died—intestate. With this difference, however, in the two cases, that the younger brother left an informal will, and the elder brother left no will at all. The hardest men have their weaknesses; and Mr. Michael Vanstone's weakness seems to have been an insurmountable horror of contemplating the event of his own death. His son, his housekeeper, and his lawyer, had all three tried over and over again to get him to make a will; and had never shaken his obstinate resolution to put off performing the only business duty he was ever known to neglect. Two doctors attended him in his last illness; warned him that he was too old a man to hope to get over it; and warned him in vain. He announced his own positive determination not to die. His last words in this world (as I succeeded in discovering from the nurse who assisted Mrs. Lecount) were: "I'm getting better every minute; send for the fly directly and take me out for a drive." The same night Death proved to be the more obstinate of the two; and left his son (and only child) to take the property in due course of law. Nobody doubts that the result would have been the same if a will had been made. The father and son had every confidence in each other, and were known to have always lived together on the most friendly terms.

Mrs. Lecount remains with Mr. Noel Vanstone, in the same housekeeping capacity which she filled with his father, and has accompanied him to the new residence in Vauxhall Walk. She is acknowledged on all hands to have been a sufferer by the turn events have taken. If Mr. Michael Vanstone had made his will, there is no doubt she would have received a handsome legacy. She is now left dependent on Mr. Noel Vanstone's sense of gratitude; and she is not at all likely, I should imagine, to let that sense fall asleep for want of a little timely jogging. Whether my fair relative's future intentions in this quarter point toward Mischief or Money, is more than I can yet say. In either case, I venture to predict that she will find an awkward obstacle in Mrs. Lecount.

So much for my information to the present date. The manner in which it was received by Miss Vanstone showed the most ungrateful distrust of me. She confided nothing to my private ear but the expression of her best thanks. A sharp girl—a devilish sharp girl. But there is such a thing as bowling a man out once too often; especially when the name of that man happens to be Wragge.

Not a word more about the Entertainment; not a word more about moving from our present quarters. Very good. My right hand lays my left hand a wager. Ten to one, on her opening communications with the son as she opened them with the father. Ten to one, on her writing to Noel Vanstone before the month is out.

21st.—She has written by to-day's post. A long letter, apparently—for she put two stamps on the envelope. (Private memorandum, addressed to myself. Wait for the answer.)

22d, 23d, 24th.—(Private memorandum continued. Wait for the answer.)

25th.—The answer has come. As an ex-military man, I have naturally employed stratagem to get at it. The success which rewards all genuine perseverance has rewarded me—and I have got at it accordingly.

The letter is written, not by Mr. Noel Vanstone, but by Mrs. Lecount. She takes the highest moral ground, in a tone of spiteful politeness. Mr. Noel Vanstone's delicate health and recent bereavement prevent him from writing himself. Any more letters from Miss Vanstone will be returned unopened. Any personal application will produce an immediate appeal to the protection of the law. Mr. Noel Vanstone, having been expressly cautioned against Miss Magdalen Vanstone by his late lamented father, has not yet forgotten his father's advice. Considers it a reflection cast on the memory of the best of men, to suppose that his course of action toward the Misses Vanstone can be other than the course of action which his father pursued. This is what he has himself instructed Mrs. Lecount to say. She has endeavored to express herself in the most conciliatory language she could select; she had tried to avoid giving unnecessary pain, by addressing Miss Vanstone (as a matter of courtesy) by the family name; and she trusts these concessions, which speak for themselves, will not be thrown away.—Such is the substance of the letter, and so it ends.

I draw two conclusions from this little document. First—that it will lead to serious results. Secondly—that Mrs. Lecount, with all her politeness, is a dangerous woman to deal with. I wish I saw my way safe before me. I don't see it yet.

29th.—Miss Vanstone has abandoned my protection; and the whole lucrative future of the dramatic entertainment has abandoned me with her. I am swindled—I, the last man under heaven who could possibly have expected to write in those disgraceful terms of myself—I AM SWINDLED!

Let me chronicle the events. They exhibit me, for the time being, in a sadly helpless point of view. But the nature of the man prevails: I must have the events down in black and white.

The announcement of her approaching departure was intimated to me yesterday. After another civil speech about the information I had procured at Brighton, she hinted that there was a necessity for pushing our inquiries a little further. I immediately offered to undertake them, as before. "No," she said; "they are not in your way this time. They are inquiries relating to a woman; and I mean to make them myself!" Feeling privately convinced that this new resolution pointed straight at Mrs. Lecount, I tried a few innocent questions on the subject. She quietly declined to answer them. I asked next when she proposed to leave. She would leave on the twenty-eighth. For what destination? London. For long? Probably not. By herself? No.

With me? No. With whom then? With Mrs. Wragge, if I had no objection. Good heavens! for what possible purpose? For the purpose of getting a respectable lodging, which she could hardly expect to accomplish unless she was accompanied by an elderly female friend. And was I, in the capacity of elderly male friend, to be left out of the business altogether? Impossible to say at present. Was I not even to forward any letters which might come for her at our present address? No: she would make the arrangement herself at the post-office; and she would ask me, at the same time, for an address, at which I could receive a letter from her, in case of necessity for future communication. Further inquiries, after this last answer, could lead to nothing but waste of time. I saved time by putting no more questions.

It was clear to me that our present position toward each other was what our position had been previously to the event of Michael Vanstone's death. I returned, as before, to my choice of alternatives. Which way did my private interests point? Toward trusting the chance of her wanting me again? Toward threatening her with the interference of her relatives and friends? Or toward making the information which I possessed a marketable commodity between the wealthy branch of the family and myself? The last of the three was the alternative I had chosen in the case of the father. I chose it once more in the case of the son.

The train started for London nearly four hours since, and took her away in it, accompanied by Mrs. Wragge.

My wife is too great a fool, poor soul, to be actively valuable in the present emergency; but she will be passively useful in keeping up Miss Vanstone's connection with me—and, in consideration of that circumstance, I consent to brush my own trousers, shave my own chin, and submit to the other inconveniences of waiting on myself for a limited period. Any faint glimmerings of sense which Mrs. Wragge may have formerly possessed appear to have now finally taken their leave of her. On receiving permission to go to London, she favored us immediately with two inquiries. Might she do some shopping? and might she leave the cookery-book behind her? Miss Vanstone said Yes to one question, and I said Yes to the other—and from that moment, Mrs. Wragge has existed in a state of perpetual laughter. I am still hoarse with vainly repeated applications of vocal stimulant; and I left her in the railway carriage, to my inexpressible disgust, with both shoes down at heel.

Under ordinary circumstances these absurd particulars would not have dwelt on my memory. But, as matters actually stand, my unfortunate wife's imbecility may, in her present position, lead to consequences which we none of us foresee. She is nothing more or less than a grown-up child; and I can plainly detect that Miss Vanstone trusts her, as she would not have trusted a sharper woman, on that very account. I know children, little and big, rather better than my fair relative does; and I say—beware of all forms of human innocence, when it happens to be your interest to keep a secret to yourself.

Let me return to business. Here I am, at two o'clock on a fine summer's afternoon, left entirely alone, to consider the safest means of approaching Mr. Noel Vanstone on my own account. My private suspicions of his miserly character produce no discouraging effect on me. I have extracted cheering pecuniary results in my time from people quite as fond of their money as he can be. The real difficulty to contend with is the obstacle of Mrs. Lecount. If I am not mistaken, this lady merits a little serious consideration on my part. I will close my chronicle for to-day, and give Mrs. Lecount her due.

Three o'clock.—I open these pages again to record a discovery which has taken me entirely by surprise.

After completing the last entry, a circumstance revived in my memory which I had noticed on escorting the ladies this morning to the railway. I then remarked that Miss Vanstone had only taken one of her three boxes with her—and it now occurred to me that a private investigation of the luggage she had left behind might possibly be attended with beneficial results. Having, at certain periods of my life been in the habit of cultivating friendly terms with strange locks, I found no difficulty in establishing myself on a familiar footing with Miss Vanstone's boxes. One of the two presented nothing to interest me. The other—devoted to the preservation of the costumes, articles of toilet, and other properties used in the dramatic Entertainment—proved to be better worth examining: for it led me straight to the discovery of one of its owner's secrets.

I found all the dresses in the box complete—with one remarkable exception. That exception was the dress of the old north-country lady; the character which I have already mentioned as the best of all my pupil's disguises, and as modeled in voice and manner on her old governess, Miss Garth. The wig; the eyebrows; the bonnet and veil; the cloak, padded inside to disfigure her back and shoulders; the paints and cosmetics used to age her face and alter her complexion—were all gone. Nothing but the gown remained; a gaudily-flowered silk, useful enough for dramatic purposes, but too extravagant in color and pattern to bear inspection by daylight. The other parts of the dress are sufficiently quiet to pass muster; the bonnet and veil are only old-fashioned, and the cloak is of a sober gray color. But one plain inference can be drawn from such a discovery as this. As certainly as I sit here, she is going to open the campaign against Noel Vanstone and Mrs. Lecount in a character which neither of those two persons can have any possible reason for suspecting at the outset—the character of Miss Garth.

What course am I to take under these circumstances? Having got her secret, what am I to do with it? These are awkward considerations; I am rather puzzled how to deal with them.

It is something more than the mere fact of her choosing to disguise herself to forward her own private ends that causes my present perplexity. Hundreds of girls take fancies for disguising themselves; and hundreds of instances of it are related year after year in the public journals. But my ex-pupil is not to be confounded for one moment with the average adventuress of the newspapers. She is capable of going a long way beyond the limit of dressing herself like a man, and imitating a man's voice and manner. She has a natural gift for assuming characters which I have never seen equaled by a woman; and she has performed in public until she has felt her own power, and trained her talent for disguising herself to the highest pitch. A girl who takes the sharpest people unawares by using such a capacity as this to help her own objects in private life, and who sharpens that capacity by a determination to fight her way to her own purpose, which has beaten down everything before it, up to this time—is a girl who tries an experiment in deception, new enough and dangerous enough to lead, one way or the other, to very serious results. This is my conviction, founded on a large experience in the art of imposing on my fellow-creatures. I say of my fair relative's enterprise what I never said or thought of it till I introduced myself to the inside of her box. The chances for and against her winning the fight for her lost fortune are now so evenly balanced that I cannot for the life of me see on which side the scale inclines. All I can discern is, that it will, to a dead certainty, turn one way or the other on the day when she passes Noel Vanstone's doors in disguise.

Which way do my interests point now? Upon my honor, I don't know.

Five o'clock.—I have effected a masterly compromise; I have decided on turning myself into a Jack-on-both-sides.

By to-day's post I have dispatched to London an anonymous letter for Mr. Noel Vanstone. It will be forwarded to its destination by the same means which I successfully adopted to mystify Mr. Pendril; and it will reach Vauxhall Walk, Lambeth, by the afternoon of to-morrow at the latest.

The letter is short, and to the purpose. It warns Mr. Noel Vanstone, in the most alarming language, that he is destined to become the victim of a conspiracy; and that the prime mover of it is a young lady who has already held written communication with his father and himself. It offers him the information necessary to secure his own safety, on condition that he makes it worth the writer's while to run the serious personal risk which such a disclosure will entail on him. And it ends by stipulating that the answer shall be advertised in the Times; shall be addressed to "An Unknown Friend"; and shall state plainly what remuneration Mr. Noel Vanstone offers for the priceless service which it is proposed to render him.

Unless some unexpected complication occurs, this letter places me exactly in the position which it is my present interest to occupy. If the advertisement appears, and if the remuneration offered is large enough to justify me in going over to the camp of the enemy, over I go. If no advertisement appears, or if Mr. Noel Vanstone rates my invaluable assistance at too low a figure, here I remain, biding my time till my fair relative wants me, or till I make her want me, which comes to the same thing. If the anonymous letter falls by any accident into her hands, she will find disparaging allusions in it to myself, purposely introduced to suggest that the writer must be one of the persons whom I addressed while conducting her inquiries. If Mrs. Lecount takes the business in hand and lays a trap for me—I decline her tempting invitation by becoming totally ignorant of the whole affair the instant any second person appears in it. Let the end come as it may, here I am ready to profit by it: here I am, facing both ways, with perfect ease and security—a moral agriculturist, with his eye on two crops at once, and his swindler's sickle ready for any emergency.

For the next week to come, the newspaper will be more interesting to me than ever. I wonder which side I shall eventually belong to?

THE THIRD SCENE.

VAUXHALL WALK, LAMBETH.

CHAPTER I.

THE old Archiepiscopal Palace of Lambeth, on the southern bank of the Thames—with its Bishop's Walk and Garden, and its terrace fronting the river—is an architectural relic of the London of former times, precious to all lovers of the picturesque, in the utilitarian London of the present day. Southward of this venerable structure lies the street labyrinth of Lambeth; and nearly midway, in that part of the maze of houses which is placed nearest to the river, runs the dingy double row of buildings now, as in former days, known by the name of Vauxhall Walk.

The network of dismal streets stretching over the surrounding neighborhood contains a population for the most part of the poorer order. In the thoroughfares where shops abound, the sordid struggle with poverty shows itself unreservedly on the filthy pavement; gathers its forces through the week; and, strengthening to a tumult on Saturday night, sees the Sunday morning dawn in murky gaslight. Miserable women, whose faces never smile, haunt the butchers' shops in such London localities as these, with relics of the men's wages saved from the public-house clutched fast in their hands, with eyes that devour the meat they dare not buy, with eager fingers that touch it covetously, as the fingers of their richer sisters touch a precious stone. In this district, as in other districts remote from the wealthy quarters of the metropolis, the hideous London vagabond—with the filth of the street outmatched in his speech, with the mud of the street outdirtied in his clothes—lounges, lowering and brutal, at the street corner and the gin-shop door; the public disgrace of his country, the unheeded warning of social troubles that are yet to come. Here, the loud self-assertion of Modern Progress—which has reformed so much in manners, and altered so little in men—meets the flat contradiction that scatters its pretensions to the winds. Here, while the national prosperity feasts, like another Belshazzar, on the spectacle of its own magnificence, is the Writing on the Wall, which warns the monarch, Money, that his glory is weighed in the balance, and his power found wanting.

Situated in such a neighborhood as this, Vauxhall Walk gains by comparison, and establishes claims to respectability which no impartial observation can fail to recognize. A large proportion of the Walk is still composed of private houses. In the scattered situations where shops appear, those shops are not besieged by the crowds of more populous thoroughfares. Commerce is not turbulent, nor is the public consumer besieged by loud invitations to "buy." Bird-fanciers have sought the congenial tranquillity of the scene; and pigeons coo, and canaries twitter, in Vauxhall Walk. Second-hand carts and cabs, bedsteads of a certain age, detached carriage-wheels for those who may want one to make up a set, are all to be found here in the same repository. One tributary stream, in the great flood of gas which illuminates London, tracks its parent source to Works established in this locality. Here the followers of John Wesley have set up a temple, built before the period of Methodist conversion to the principles of architectural religion. And here—most striking object of all—on the site where thousands of lights once sparkled; where sweet sounds of music made night tuneful till morning dawned;

where the beauty and fashion of London feasted and danced through the summer seasons of a century—spreads, at this day, an awful wilderness of mud and rubbish; the deserted dead body of Vauxhall Gardens mouldering in the open air.

On the same day when Captain Wragge completed the last entry in his Chronicle of Events, a woman appeared at the window of one of the houses in Vauxhall Walk, and removed from the glass a printed paper which had been wafered to it announcing that Apartments were to be let. The apartments consisted of two rooms on the first floor. They had just been taken for a week certain by two ladies who had paid in advance—those two ladies being Magdalen and Mrs. Wragge.

As soon as the mistress of the house had left the room, Magdalen walked to the window, and cautiously looked out from it at the row of buildings opposite. They were of superior pretensions in size and appearance to the other houses in the Walk: the date at which they had been erected was inscribed on one of them, and was stated to be the year 1759. They stood back from the pavement, separated from it by little strips of garden-ground. This peculiarity of position, added to the breadth of the roadway interposing between them and the smaller houses opposite, made it impossible for Magdalen to see the numbers on the doors, or to observe more of any one who might come to the windows than the bare general outline of dress and figure. Nevertheless, there she stood, anxiously fixing her eyes on one house in the row, nearly opposite to her—the house she had looked for before entering the lodgings; the house inhabited at that moment by Noel Vanstone and Mrs. Lecount.

After keeping watch at the window in silence for ten minutes or more, she suddenly looked back into the room, to observe the effect which her behavior might have produced on her traveling companion.

Not the slightest cause appeared for any apprehension in that quarter. Mrs. Wragge was seated at the table absorbed in the arrangement of a series of smart circulars and tempting price-lists, issued by advertising trades-people, and flung in at the cab-windows as they left the London terminus. "I've often heard tell of light reading," said Mrs. Wragge, restlessly shifting the positions of the circulars as a child restlessly shifts the position of a new set of toys. "Here's light reading, printed in pretty colors. Here's all the Things I'm going to buy when I'm out shopping to-morrow. Lend us a pencil, please—you won't be angry, will you? I do so want to mark 'em off." She looked up at Magdalen, chuckled joyfully over her own altered circumstances, and beat her great hands on the table in irrepressible delight. "No cookery-book!" cried Mrs. Wragge. "No Buzzing in my head! no captain to shave to-morrow! I'm all down at heel; my cap's on one side; and nobody bawls at me. My heart alive, here is a holiday and no mistake!" Her hands began to drum on the table louder than ever, until Magdalen quieted them by presenting her with a pencil. Mrs. Wragge instantly recovered her dignity, squared her elbows on the table, and plunged into imaginary shopping for the rest of the evening.

Magdalen returned to the window. She took a chair, seated herself behind the curtain, and steadily fixed her eyes once more on the house opposite.

The blinds were down over the windows of the first floor and the second. The window of the room on the ground-floor was uncovered and partly open, but no living creature came near it. Doors opened, and people came and went, in the houses on either side; children by the dozen poured out on the pavement to play, and invaded the little strips of garden-ground to recover lost balls and shuttlecocks; streams of people passed backward and forward perpetually; heavy wagons piled high with goods lumbered along the road on their way to, or their way from, the railway station near; all the daily life of the district stirred with its ceaseless activity in every direction but one. The hours passed—and there was the house opposite still shut up, still void of any signs of human existence inside or out. The one object which had decided Magdalen on personally venturing herself in Vauxhall Walk—the object of studying the looks, manners and habits of Mrs. Lecount and her master from a post of observation known only to herself—was thus far utterly defeated. After three hours' watching at the window, she had not even discovered enough to show her that the house was inhabited at all.

Shortly after six o'clock, the landlady disturbed Mrs. Wragge's studies by spreading the cloth for dinner. Magdalen placed herself at the table in a position which still enabled her to command the view from the window. Nothing happened. The dinner came to an end; Mrs. Wragge (lulled by the narcotic influence of annotating circulars, and eating and drinking with an appetite sharpened by the captain's absence) withdrew to an arm-chair, and fell asleep in an attitude which would have caused her husband the acutest mental suffering; seven o'clock struck; the shadows of the summer evening lengthened stealthily on the gray pavement and the brown house-walls—and still the closed door opposite remained shut; still the one window open showed nothing but the black blank of the room inside, lifeless and changeless as if that room had been a tomb.

Mrs. Wragge's meek snoring deepened in tone; the evening wore on drearily; it was close on eight o'clock—when an event happened at last. The street door opposite opened for the first time, and a woman appeared on the threshold.

Was the woman Mrs. Lecount? No. As she came nearer, her dress showed her to be a servant. She had a large door-key in her hand, and was evidently going out to perform an errand. Roused partly by curiosity, partly by the impulse of the moment, which urged her impetuous nature into action after the passive endurance of many hours past, Magdalen snatched up her bonnet, and determined to follow the servant to her destination, wherever it might be.

The woman led her to the great thoroughfare of shops close at hand, called Lambeth Walk. After proceeding some little distance, and looking about her with the hesitation of a person not well acquainted with the neighborhood, the servant crossed the road and entered a stationer's shop. Magdalen crossed the road after her and followed her in.

The inevitable delay in entering the shop under these circumstances made Magdalen too late to hear what the woman asked for. The first words spoken, however, by the man behind the counter reached her ears, and informed her that the servant's object was to buy a railway guide.

"Do you mean a Guide for this month or a Guide for July?" asked the shopman, addressing his customer.

"Master didn't tell me which," answered the woman. "All I know is, he's going into the country the day after to-morrow."

"The day after to-morrow is the first of July," said the shopman. "The Guide your master wants is the Guide for the new month. It won't be published till to-morrow."

Engaging to call again on the next day, the servant left the shop, and took the way that led back to Vauxhall Walk.

Magdalen purchased the first trifle she saw on the counter, and hastily returned in the same direction. The discovery she had just made was of very serious importance to her; and she felt the necessity of acting on it with as little delay as possible.

On entering the front room at the lodgings she found Mrs. Wragge just awake, lost in drowsy bewilderment, with her cap fallen off on her shoulders, and with one of her shoes missing altogether. Magdalen endeavored to persuade her that she was tired after her journey, and that her wisest proceeding would be to go to bed. Mrs. Wragge was perfectly willing to profit by this suggestion, provided she could find her shoe first. In looking for the shoe, she unfortunately discovered the circulars, put by on a side-table, and forthwith recovered her recollection of the earlier proceedings of the evening.

"Give us the pencil," said Mrs. Wragge, shuffling the circulars in a violent hurry. "I can't go to bed yet—I haven't half done marking down the things I want. Let's see; where did I leave off? Try Finch's feeding-bottle for Infants. No! there's a cross against that: the cross means I don't want it. Comfort in the Field. Buckler's Indestructible Hunting-breeches. Oh dear, dear! I've lost the place. No, I haven't. Here it is; here's my mark against it. Elegant Cashmere Robes; strictly Oriental, very grand; reduced to one pound nineteen-and-sixpence. Be in time. Only three left. Only three! Oh, do lend us the money, and let's go and get one!"

"Not to-night," said Magdalen. "Suppose you go to bed now, and finish the circulars tomorrow? I will put them by the bedside for you, and you can go on with them as soon as you wake the first thing in the morning."

This suggestion met with Mrs. Wragge's immediate approval. Magdalen took her into the next room and put her to bed like a child—with her toys by her side. The room was so narrow, and the bed was so small; and Mrs. Wragge, arrayed in the white apparel proper for the occasion, with her moon-face framed round by a spacious halo of night-cap, looked so hugely and disproportionately large, that Magdalen, anxious as she was, could not repress a smile on taking leave of her traveling companion for the night.

"Aha!" cried Mrs. Wragge, cheerfully; "we'll have that Cashmere Robe to-morrow. Come here! I want to whisper something to you. Just you look at me—I'm going to sleep crooked, and the captain's not here to bawl at me!"

The front room at the lodgings contained a sofa-bedstead which the landlady arranged betimes for the night. This done, and the candles brought in, Magdalen was left alone to shape the future course as her own thoughts counseled her.

The questions and answers which had passed in her presence that evening at the stationer's shop led plainly to the conclusion that one day more would bring Noel Vanstone's present term of residence in Vauxhall Walk to an end. Her first cautious resolution to pass many days together in unsuspected observation of the house opposite before she ventured herself inside was entirely frustrated by the turn events had taken. She was placed in the dilemma of running all risks headlong on the next day, or of pausing for a future opportunity which might never occur. There was no middle course open to her. Until she had seen Noel Vanstone with her own eyes, and had discovered the worst there was to fear from Mrs. Lecount—until she had achieved this double object, with the needful precaution of keeping her own identity carefully in the dark—not a step could she advance toward the accomplishment of the purpose which had brought her to London.

One after another the minutes of the night passed away; one after another the thronging thoughts followed each other over her mind—and still she reached no conclusion; still she faltered and doubted, with a hesitation new to her in her experience of herself. At last she crossed the room impatiently to seek the trivial relief of unlocking her trunk and taking from it the few things that she wanted for the night. Captain Wragge's suspicions had not misled him. There, hidden between two dresses, were the articles of costume which he had missed from her box at Birmingham. She turned them over one by one, to satisfy herself that nothing she wanted had been forgotten, and returned once more to her post of observation by the window.

The house opposite was dark down to the parlor. There the blind, previously raised, was now drawn over the window: the light burning behind it showed her for the first time that the room was inhabited. Her eyes brightened, and her color rose as she looked at it.

"There he is!" she said to herself, in a low, angry whisper. "There he lives on our money, in the house that his father's warning has closed against me!" She dropped the blind which she had raised to look out, returned to her trunk, and took from it the gray wig which was part of her dramatic costume in the character of the North-country lady. The wig had been crumpled in packing; she put it on and went to the toilet-table to comb it out. "His father has warned him against Magdalen Vanstone," she said, repeating the passage in Mrs. Lecount's letter, and laughing bitterly, as she looked at herself in the glass. "I wonder whether his father has warned him against Miss Garth? To-morrow is sooner than I bargained for. No matter: to-morrow shall show."

CHAPTER II.

THE early morning, when Magdalen rose and looked out, was cloudy and overcast. But as time advanced to the breakfast hour the threatening of rain passed away; and she was free to provide, without hinderance from the weather, for the first necessity of the day—the necessity of securing the absence of her traveling companion from the house.

Mrs. Wragge was dressed, armed at all points with her collection of circulars, and eager to be away by ten o'clock. At an earlier hour Magdalen had provided for her being properly taken care of by the landlady's eldest daughter—a quiet, well-conducted girl, whose interest in the shopping expedition was readily secured by a little present of money for the purchase, on her own account, of a parasol and a muslin dress. Shortly after ten o'clock Magdalen dismissed Mrs. Wragge and her attendant in a cab. She then joined the landlady—who was occupied in setting the rooms in order upstairs—with the object of ascertaining, by a little well-timed gossip, what the daily habits might be of the inmates of the house.

She discovered that there were no other lodgers but Mrs. Wragge and herself. The landlady's husband was away all day, employed at a railway station. Her second daughter was charged with the care of the kitchen in the elder sister's absence. The younger children were at school, and would be back at one o'clock to dinner. The landlady herself "got up fine linen for ladies," and expected to be occupied over her work all that morning in a little room built out at the back of the premises. Thus there was every facility for Magdalen's leaving the house in disguise, and leaving it unobserved, provided she went out before the children came back to dinner at one o'clock.

By eleven o'clock the apartments were set in order, and the landlady had retired to pursue her own employments. Magdalen softly locked the door of her room, drew the blind over the window, and entered at once on her preparations for the perilous experiment of the day.

The same quick perception of dangers to be avoided and difficulties to be overcome which had warned her to leave the extravagant part of her character costume in the box at Birmingham now kept her mind fully alive to the vast difference between a disguise worn by gas-light for the amusement of an audience and a disguise assumed by daylight to deceive the searching eyes of two strangers. The first article of dress which she put on was an old gown of her own (made of the material called "alpaca"), of a dark-brown color, with a neat pattern of little star-shaped spots in white. A double flounce running round the bottom of this dress was the only milliner's ornament which it presented—an ornament not at all out of character with the costume appropriated to an elderly lady. The disguise of her head and face was the next object of her attention. She fitted and arranged the gray wig with the dexterity which constant practice had given her; fixed the false eyebrows (made rather large, and of hair darker than the wig) carefully in their position with the gum she had with her for the purpose, and stained her face with the customary stage materials, so as to change the transparent fairness of her complexion to the dull, faintly opaque color of a woman in ill health. The lines and markings of age followed next; and here the first obstacles presented themselves. The art which succeeded by gas-light failed by day: the difficulty of hiding the plainly artificial nature of the marks was almost insuperable. She turned to her trunk; took from it two veils; and putting on her old-fashioned bonnet, tried the effect of them in succession. One of the veils (of black lace) was too thick to be worn over the face at that summer season without exciting remark. The other, of plain net, allowed her features to be seen through it, just indistinctly enough to permit the safe introduction of certain lines (many fewer than she was accustomed to use in performing the character) on the forehead and at the sides of the mouth. But the obstacle thus set aside only opened the way to a new difficulty—the difficulty of keeping her veil down while she was speaking to other persons, without any obvious reason for doing so. An instant's consideration, and a chance look at her little china palette of stage colors, suggested to her ready invention the production of a visible excuse for wearing her veil. She deliberately disfigured herself by artificially reddening the insides of her eyelids so as to produce an appearance of inflammation which no human creature but a doctor—and that doctor at close quarters—could have detected as false. She sprang to her feet and looked triumphantly at the hideous transformation of herself reflected in the glass. Who could think it strange now if she wore her veil down, and if she begged Mrs. Lecount's permission to sit with her back to the light?

Her last proceeding was to put on the quiet gray cloak which she had brought from Birmingham, and which had been padded inside by Captain Wragge's own experienced hands, so as to hide the youthful grace and beauty of her back and shoulders. Her costume being now complete, she practiced the walk which had been originally taught her as appropriate to the character—a walk with a slight limp—and, returning to the glass after a minute's trial, exercised herself next in the disguise of her voice and manner. This was the only part of the character in which it had been possible, with her physical peculiarities, to produce an imitation of Miss Garth; and here the resemblance was perfect. The harsh voice, the blunt manner, the habit of accompanying certain phrases by an emphatic nod of the head, the Northumbrian burr expressing itself in every word which contained the letter "r"—all these personal peculiarities of the old North-country governess were reproduced to the life. The personal transformation thus completed was literally what Captain Wragge had described it to be—a triumph in the art of self-disguise. Excepting the one case of seeing her face close, with a strong light on it, nobody who now looked at Magdalen could have suspected for an instant that she was other than an ailing, ill-made, unattractive woman of fifty years old at least.

Before unlocking the door, she looked about her carefully, to make sure that none of her stage materials were exposed to view in case the landlady entered the room in her absence. The only forgotten object belonging to her that she discovered was a little packet of Norah's letters which she had been reading overnight, and which had been accidentally pushed under the looking-glass while she was engaged in dressing herself. As she took up the letters to put them away, the thought struck her for the first time, "Would Norah know me now if we met each other in the street?" She looked in the glass, and smiled sadly. "No," she said, "not even Norah."

She unlocked the door, after first looking at her watch. It was close on twelve o'clock. There was barely an hour left to try her desperate experiment, and to return to the lodging before the landlady's children came back from school.

An instant's listening on the landing assured her that all was quiet in the passage below. She noiselessly descended the stairs and gained the street without having met any living creature on her way out of the house. In another minute she had crossed the road, and had knocked at Noel Vanstone's door.

The door was opened by the same woman-servant whom she had followed on the previous evening to the stationer's shop. With a momentary tremor, which recalled the memorable first night of her appearance in public, Magdalen inquired (in Miss Garth's voice, and with Miss Garth's manner) for Mrs. Lecount.

"Mrs. Lecount has gone out, ma'am," said the servant.

"Is Mr. Vanstone at home?" asked Magdalen, her resolution asserting itself at once against the first obstacle that opposed it.

"My master is not up yet, ma'am."

Another check! A weaker nature would have accepted the warning. Magdalen's nature rose in revolt against it.

"What time will Mrs. Lecount be back?" she asked.

"About one o'clock, ma'am."

"Say, if you please, that I will call again as soon after one o'clock as possible. I particularly wish to see Mrs. Lecount. My name is Miss Garth."

She turned and left the house. Going back to her own room was out of the question. The servant (as Magdalen knew by not hearing the door close) was looking after her; and, moreover, she would expose herself, if she went indoors, to the risk of going out again exactly at the time when the landlady's children were sure to be about the house. She turned mechanically to the right, walked on until she recalled Vauxhall Bridge, and waited there, looking out over the river.

The interval of unemployed time now before her was nearly an hour. How should she occupy it?

As she asked herself the question, the thought which had struck her when she put away the packet of Norah's letters rose in her mind once more. A sudden impulse to test the miserable completeness of her disguise mixed with the higher and purer feeling at her heart, and strengthened her natural longing to see her sister's face again, though she dare not discover herself and speak. Norah's later letters had described, in the fullest details, her life as a governess—her hours for teaching, her hours of leisure, her hours for walking out with her pupils. There was just time, if she could find a vehicle at once, for Magdalen to drive to the house of Norah's employer, with the chance of getting there a few minutes before the hour when her sister would be going out. "One look at her will tell me more than a hundred letters!" With that thought in her heart, with the one object of following Norah on her daily walk, under protection of the disguise, Magdalen hastened over the bridge, and made for the northern bank of the river.

So, at the turning-point of her life—so, in the interval before she took the irrevocable step, and passed the threshold of Noel Vanstone's door—the forces of Good triumphing in the strife for her over the forces of Evil, turned her back on the scene of her meditated deception, and hurried her mercifully further and further away from the fatal house.

She stopped the first empty cab that passed her; told the driver to go to New Street, Spring Gardens; and promised to double his fare if he reached his destination by a given time. The man earned the money—more than earned it, as the event proved. Magdalen had not taken ten steps in advance along New Street, walking toward St. James's Park, before the door of a house beyond her opened, and a lady in mourning came out, accompanied by two little girls. The lady also took the direction of the Park, without turning her head toward Magdalen as she descended the house step. It mattered little; Magdalen's heart looked through her eyes, and told her that she saw Norah.

She followed them into St. James's Park, and thence (along the Mall) into the Green Park, venturing closer and closer as they reached the grass and ascended the rising ground in the direction of Hyde Park Corner. Her eager eyes devoured every detail in Norah's dress, and detected the slightest change that had taken place in her figure and her bearing. She had become thinner since the autumn—her head drooped a little; she walked wearily. Her mourning dress, worn with the modest grace and neatness which no misfortune could take from her, was suited to her altered station; her black gown was made of stuff; her black shawl and bonnet were of the plainest and cheapest kind. The two little girls, walking on either side of her, were dressed in silk. Magdalen instinctively hated them.

She made a wide circuit on the grass, so as to turn gradually and meet her sister without exciting suspicion that the meeting was contrived. Her heart beat fast; a burning heat glowed in her as she thought of her false hair, her false color, her false dress, and saw the dear familiar face coming nearer and nearer. They passed each other close. Norah's dark gentle eyes looked up, with a deeper light in them, with a sadder beauty than of old—rested, all unconscious of the truth, on her sister's face—and looked away from it again as from the face of a stranger. That glance of an instant struck Magdalen to the heart. She stood rooted to the ground after Norah had passed by. A horror of the vile disguise that concealed her; a yearning to burst its trammels and hide her shameful painted face on Norah's bosom, took possession of her, body and soul. She turned and looked back.

Norah and the two children had reached the higher ground, and were close to one of the gates in the iron railing which fenced the Park from the street. Drawn by an irresistible fascination, Magdalen followed them again, gained on them as they reached the gate, and heard the voices of the two children raised in angry dispute which way they wanted to walk next. She saw Norah take them through the gate, and then stoop and speak to them, while waiting for an opportunity to cross the road. They only grew the louder and the angrier for what she said. The youngest—a girl of eight or nine years old—flew into a child's vehement passion, cried, screamed, and even kicked at the governess. The people in the street stopped and laughed; some of them jestingly advised a little wholesome correction; one woman asked Norah if she was the child's mother; another pitied her audibly for being the child's governess. Before Magdalen could push her way through the crowd—before her all-mastering anxiety to help her sister had blinded her to every other consideration, and had brought her, self-betrayed, to Norah's side—an open carriage passed the pavement slowly, hindered in its progress by the press of vehicles before it. An old lady seated inside heard the child's cries, recognized Norah, and called to her immediately. The footman parted the crowd, and the children were put into the carriage. "It's lucky I happened to pass this way," said the old lady, beckoning contemptuously to Norah to take her place on the front seat; "you never could manage my daughter's children, and you never will." The footman put up the steps, the carriage drove on with the children and the governess, the crowd dispersed, and Magdalen was alone again.

"So be it!" she thought, bitterly. "I should only have distressed her. We should only have had the misery of parting to suffer again."

She mechanically retraced her steps; she returned, as in a dream, to the open space of the Park. Arming itself treacherously with the strength of her love for her sister, with the vehemence of the indignation that she felt for her sister's sake, the terrible temptation of her life fastened its hold on her more firmly than ever. Through all the paint and disfigurement of the disguise, the fierce despair of that strong and passionate nature lowered, haggard and horrible. Norah made an object of public curiosity and amusement; Norah reprimanded in the open street; Norah, the hired victim of an old woman's insolence and a child's ill-temper, and the same man to thank for it who had sent Frank to China!—and that man's son to thank after him! The thought of her sister, which had turned her from the scene of her meditated deception, which had made the consciousness of her own disguise hateful to her, was now the thought which sanctioned that means, or any means, to compass her end; the thought which set wings to her feet, and hurried her back nearer and nearer to the fatal house.

She left the Park again, and found herself in the streets without knowing where. Once more she hailed the first cab that passed her, and told the man to drive to Vauxhall Walk.

The change from walking to riding quieted her. She felt her attention returning to herself and her dress. The necessity of making sure that no accident had happened to her disguise in the interval since she had left her own room impressed itself immediately on her mind. She stopped the driver at the first pastry-cook's shop which he passed, and there obtained the means of consulting a looking-glass before she ventured back to Vauxhall Walk.

Her gray head-dress was disordered, and the old-fashioned bonnet was a little on one side. Nothing else had suffered. She set right the few defects in her costume, and returned to the cab. It was half-past one when she approached the house and knocked, for the second time, at Noel Vanstone's door. The woman-servant opened it as before.

"Has Mrs. Lecount come back?"

"Yes, ma'am. Step this way, if you please."

The servant preceded Magdalen along an empty passage, and, leading her past an uncarpeted staircase, opened the door of a room at the back of the house. The room was lighted by one window looking out on a yard; the walls were bare; the boarded floor was uncovered. Two bedroom chairs stood against the wall, and a kitchen-table was placed under the window. On the table stood a glass tank filled with water, and ornamented in the middle by a miniature pyramid of rock-work interlaced with weeds. Snails clung to the sides of the tank; tadpoles and tiny fish swam swiftly in the green water, slippery efts and slimy frogs twined their noiseless way in and out of the weedy rock-work; and on top of the pyramid there sat solitary, cold as the stone, brown as the stone, motionless as the stone, a little bright-eyed toad. The art of keeping fish and reptiles as domestic pets had not at that time been popularized in England; and Magdalen, on entering the room, started back, in irrepressible astonishment and disgust, from the first specimen of an Aquarium that she had ever seen.

"Don't be alarmed," said a woman's voice behind her. "My pets hurt nobody."

Magdalen turned, and confronted Mrs. Lecount. She had expected—founding her anticipations on the letter which the housekeeper had written to her—to see a hard, wily, ill-favored, insolent old woman. She found herself in the presence of a lady of mild, ingratiating manners, whose dress was the perfection of neatness, taste, and matronly simplicity, whose personal appearance was little less than a triumph of physical resistance to the deteriorating influence of time. If Mrs. Lecount had struck some fifteen or sixteen years off her real age, and had asserted herself to be eight-and-thirty, there would not have been one man in a thousand, or one woman in a hundred, who would have hesitated to believe her. Her dark hair was just turning to gray, and no more. It was plainly parted under a spotless lace cap, sparingly ornamented with mourning ribbons. Not a wrinkle appeared on her smooth white forehead, or her plump white cheeks. Her double chin was dimpled, and her teeth were marvels of whiteness and regularity. Her lips might have been critically considered as too thin, if they had not been accustomed to make the best of their defects by means of a pleading and persuasive smile. Her large black eyes might have looked fierce if they had been set in the face of another woman, they were mild and melting in the face of Mrs. Lecount; they were tenderly interested in everything she looked at—in Magdalen, in the toad on the rock-work, in the back-yard view from the window; in her own plump fair hands,—which she rubbed softly one over the other while she spoke; in her own pretty cambric chemisette, which she had a habit of looking at complacently while she listened to others. The elegant black gown in which she mourned the memory of Michael Vanstone was not a mere dress—it was a well-made compliment paid to Death. Her innocent white muslin apron was a little domestic poem in itself. Her jet earrings were so modest in their pretensions that a Quaker might have looked at them and committed no sin. The comely plumpness of her face was matched by the comely plumpness of her figure; it glided smoothly over the ground; it flowed in sedate undulations when she walked. There are not many men who could have observed Mrs. Lecount entirely from the Platonic point of view—lads in their teens would have found her irresistible—women only could have hardened their hearts against her, and mercilessly forced their way inward through that fair and smiling surface. Magdalen's first glance at this Venus of the autumn period of female life more than satisfied her that she had done well to feel her ground in disguise before she ventured on matching herself against Mrs. Lecount.

"Have I the pleasure of addressing the lady who called this morning?" inquired the housekeeper. "Am I speaking to Miss Garth?"

Something in the expression of her eyes, as she asked that question, warned Magdalen to turn her face further inward from the window than she had turned it yet. The bare doubt whether the housekeeper might not have seen her already under too strong a light shook her self-possession for the moment. She gave herself time to recover it, and merely answered by a bow.

"Accept my excuses, ma'am, for the place in which I am compelled to receive you," proceeded Mrs. Lecount in fluent English, spoken with a foreign accent. "Mr. Vanstone is only here for a temporary purpose. We leave for the sea-side to-morrow afternoon, and it has not been thought worth while to set the house in proper order. Will you take a seat, and oblige me by mentioning the object of your visit?"

She glided imperceptibly a step or two nearer to Magdalen, and placed a chair for her exactly opposite the light from the window. "Pray sit down," said Mrs. Lecount, looking with the tenderest interest at the visitor's inflamed eyes through the visitor's net veil.

"I am suffering, as you see, from a complaint in the eyes," replied Magdalen, steadily keeping her profile toward the window, and carefully pitching her voice to the tone of Miss Garth's. "I must beg your permission to wear my veil down, and to sit away from the light." She said those words, feeling mistress of herself again. With perfect composure she drew the chair back into the corner of the room beyond the window and seated herself, keeping the shadow of her bonnet well over her face. Mrs. Lecount's persuasive lips murmured a polite expression of sympathy; Mrs. Lecount's amiable black eyes looked more interested in the strange lady than ever. She placed a chair for herself exactly on a line with Magdalen's, and sat so close to the wall as to force her visitor either to turn her head a little further round toward the window, or to fail in politeness by not looking at the person whom she addressed. "Yes," said Mrs. Lecount, with a confidential little cough. "And to what circumstances am I indebted for the honor of this visit?"

"May I inquire, first, if my name happens to be familiar to you?" said Magdalen, turning toward her as a matter of necessity, but coolly holding up her handkerchief at the same time between her face and the light.

"No," answered Mrs. Lecount, with another little cough, rather harsher than the first. "The name of Miss Garth is not familiar to me."

"In that case," pursued Magdalen, "I shall best explain the object that causes me to intrude on you by mentioning who I am. I lived for many years as governess in the family of the late Mr. Andrew Vanstone, of Combe-Raven, and I come here in the interest of his orphan daughters."

Mrs. Lecount's hands, which had been smoothly sliding one over the other up to this time, suddenly stopped; and Mrs. Lecount's lips, self-forgetfully shutting up, owned they were too thin at the very outset of the interview.

"I am surprised you can bear the light out-of-doors without a green shade," she quietly remarked; leaving the false Miss Garth's announcement of herself as completely unnoticed as it she had not spoken at all.

"I find a shade over my eyes keeps them too hot at this time of the year," rejoined Magdalen, steadily matching the housekeeper's composure. "May I ask whether you heard what I said just now on the subject of my errand in this house?"

"May I inquire on my side, ma'am, in what way that errand can possibly concern me?" retorted Mrs. Lecount.

"Certainly," said Magdalen. "I come to you because Mr. Noel Vanstone's intentions toward the two young ladies were made known to them in the form of a letter from yourself."

That plain answer had its effect. It warned Mrs. Lecount that the strange lady was better informed than she had at first suspected, and that it might hardly be wise, under the circumstances, to dismiss her unheard.

"Pray pardon me," said the housekeeper, "I scarcely understood before; I perfectly understand now. You are mistaken, ma'am, in supposing that I am of any importance, or that I exercise any influence in this painful matter. I am the mouth-piece of Mr. Noel Vanstone; the pen he holds, if you will excuse the expression—nothing more. He is an invalid, and like other invalids, he has his bad days and his good. It was his bad day when that answer was written to the young person—shall I call her Miss Vanstone? I will, with pleasure, poor girl; for who am I to make distinctions, and what is it to me whether her parents were married or not? As I was saying, it was one of Mr. Noel Vanstone's bad days when that answer was sent, and therefore I had to write it; simply as his secretary, for want of a better. If you wish to speak on the subject of these young ladies—shall I call them young ladies, as you did just now? no, poor things, I will call them the Misses Vanstone.—If you wish to speak on the subject of these Misses Vanstone, I will mention your name, and your object in favoring me with this call, to Mr. Noel Vanstone. He is alone in the parlor, and this is one of his good days. I have the influence of an old servant over him, and I will use that influence with pleasure in your behalf. Shall I go at once?" asked Mrs. Lecount, rising, with the friendliest anxiety to make herself useful.

"If you please," replied Magdalen; "and if I am not taking any undue advantage of your kindness."

"On the contrary," rejoined Mrs. Lecount, "you are laying me under an obligation—you are permitting me, in my very limited way, to assist the performance of a benevolent action." She bowed, smiled, and glided out of the room.

Left by herself, Magdalen allowed the anger which she had suppressed in Mrs. Lecount's presence to break free from her. For want of a nobler object to attack, it took the direction of the toad. The sight of the hideous little reptile sitting placid on his rock throne, with his bright eyes staring impenetrably into vacancy, irritated every nerve in her body. She looked at the creature with a shrinking intensity of hatred; she whispered at it maliciously through her set teeth. "I wonder whose blood runs coldest," she said, "yours, you little monster, or Mrs. Lecount's? I wonder which is the slimiest, her heart or your back? You hateful wretch, do you know what your mistress is? Your mistress is a devil!"

The speckled skin under the toad's mouth mysteriously wrinkled itself, then slowly expanded again, as if he had swallowed the words just addressed to him. Magdalen started back in disgust from the first perceptible movement in the creature's body, trifling as it was, and returned to her chair. She had not seated herself again a moment too soon. The door opened noiselessly, and Mrs. Lecount appeared once more.

"Mr. Vanstone will see you," she said, "if you will kindly wait a few minutes. He will ring the parlor bell when his present occupation is at an end, and he is ready to receive you. Be careful, ma'am, not to depress his spirits, nor to agitate him in any way. His heart has been a cause of serious anxiety to those about him, from his earliest years. There is no positive disease; there is only a chronic feebleness—a fatty degeneration—a want of vital power in the organ itself. His heart will go on well enough if you don't give his heart too much to do—that is the advice of all the medical men who have seen him. You will not forget it, and you will keep a guard over your conversation accordingly. Talking of medical men, have you ever tried the Golden Ointment for that sad affliction in your eyes? It has been described to me as an excellent remedy."

"It has not succeeded in my case," replied Magdalen, sharply. "Before I see Mr. Noel Vanstone," she continued, "may I inquire—"

"I beg your pardon," interposed Mrs. Lecount. "Does your question refer in any way to those two poor girls?"

"It refers to the Misses Vanstone."

"Then I can't enter into it. Excuse me, I really can't discuss these poor girls (I am so glad to hear you call them the Misses Vanstone!) except in my master's presence, and by my master's express permission. Let us talk of something else while we are waiting here. Will you notice my glass Tank? I have every reason to believe that it is a perfect novelty in England."

"I looked at the tank while you were out of the room," said Magdalen.

"Did you? You take no interest in the subject, I dare say? Quite natural. I took no interest either until I was married. My dear husband—dead many years since—formed my tastes and elevated me to himself. You have heard of the late Professor Lecomte, the eminent Swiss naturalist? I am his widow. The English circle at Zurich (where I lived in my late master's service) Anglicized my name to Lecount. Your generous country people will have nothing foreign about them—not even a name, if they can help it. But I was speaking of my husband—my dear husband, who permitted me to assist him in his pursuits. I have had only one interest since his death—an interest in science. Eminent in many things, the professor was great at reptiles. He left me his Subjects and his Tank. I had no other legacy. There is the Tank. All the Subjects died but this quiet little fellow—this nice little toad. Are you surprised at my liking him? There is nothing to be surprised at. The professor lived long enough to elevate me above the common prejudice against the reptile creation. Properly understood, the reptile creation is beautiful. Properly dissected, the reptile creation is instructive in the last degree." She stretched out her little finger, and gently stroked the toad's back with the tip of it. "So refreshing to the touch," said Mrs. Lecount—"so nice and cool this summer weather!"

The bell from the parlor rang. Mrs. Lecount rose, bent fondly over the Aquarium, and chirruped to the toad at parting as if it had been a bird. "Mr. Vanstone is ready to receive you. Follow me, if you please, Miss Garth." With these words she opened the door, and led the way out of the room.

CHAPTER III.

"MISS GARTH, sir," said Mrs. Lecount, opening the parlor door, and announcing the visitor's appearance with the tone and manner of a well-bred servant.

Magdalen found herself in a long, narrow room, consisting of a back parlor and a front parlor, which had been thrown into one by opening the folding-doors between them. Seated not far from the front window, with his back to the light, she saw a frail, flaxen-haired, self-satisfied little man, clothed in a fair white dressing-gown many sizes too large for him, with a nosegay of violets drawn neatly through the button-hole over his breast. He looked from thirty to five-and-thirty years old. His complexion was as delicate as a young girl's, his eyes were of the lightest blue, his upper lip was adorned by a weak little white mustache, waxed and twisted at either end into a thin spiral curl. When any object specially attracted his attention he half closed his eyelids to look at it. When he smiled, the skin at his temples crumpled itself up into a nest of wicked little wrinkles. He had a plate of strawberries on his lap, with a napkin under them to preserve the purity of his white dressing-gown. At his right hand stood a large round table, covered with a collection of foreign curiosities, which seemed to have been brought together from the four quarters of the globe. Stuffed birds from Africa, porcelain monsters from China, silver ornaments and utensils from India and Peru, mosaic work from Italy, and bronzes from France, were all heaped together pell-mell with the coarse deal boxes and dingy leather cases which served to pack them for traveling. The little man apologized, with a cheerful and simpering conceit, for his litter of curiosities, his dressing-gown, and his delicate health; and, waving his hand toward a chair, placed his attention, with pragmatical politeness, at the visitor's disposal. Magdalen looked at him with a momentary doubt whether Mrs. Lecount had not deceived her. Was this the man who mercilessly followed the path on which his merciless father had walked before him? She could hardly believe it. "Take a seat, Miss Garth," he repeated, observing her hesitation, and announcing his own name in a high, thin, fretfully-consequential voice: "I am Mr. Noel Vanstone. You wished to see me—here I am!"

"May I be permitted to retire, sir?" inquired Mrs. Lecount.

"Certainly not!" replied her master. "Stay here, Lecount, and keep us company. Mrs. Lecount has my fullest confidence," he continued, addressing Magdalen. "Whatever you say to me, ma'am, you say to her. She is a domestic treasure. There is not another house in England has such a treasure as Mrs. Lecount."

The housekeeper listened to the praise of her domestic virtues with eyes immovably fixed on her elegant chemisette. But Magdalen's quick penetration had previously detected a look that passed between Mrs. Lecount and her master, which suggested that Noel Vanstone had been instructed beforehand what to say and do in his visitor's presence. The suspicion of this, and the obstacles which the room presented to arranging her position in it so as to keep her face from the light, warned Magdalen to be on her guard.

She had taken her chair at first nearly midway in the room. An instant's after-reflection induced her to move her seat toward the left hand, so as to place herself just inside, and close against, the left post of the folding-door. In this position she dexterously barred the only passage by which Mrs. Lecount could have skirted round the large table and contrived to front Magdalen by taking a chair at her master's side. On the right hand of the table the empty space was well occupied by the fireplace and fender, by some traveling-trunks, and a large packing-case. There was no alternative left for Mrs. Lecount but to place herself on a line with Magdalen against the opposite post of the folding-door, or to push rudely past the visitor with the obvious intention of getting in front of her. With an expressive little cough, and with one steady look at her master, the housekeeper conceded the point, and took her seat against the right-hand door-post. "Wait a little," thought Mrs. Lecount; "my turn next!"

"Mind what you are about, ma'am!" cried Noel Vanstone, as Magdalen accidentally approached the table in moving her chair. "Mind the sleeve of your cloak! Excuse me, you nearly knocked down that silver candlestick. Pray don't suppose it's a common candlestick. It's nothing of the sort—it's a Peruvian candlestick. There are only three of that pattern in the world. One is in the possession of the President of Peru; one is locked up in the Vatican; and one is on My table. It cost ten pounds; it's worth fifty. One of my father's bargains, ma'am. All these things are my father's bargains. There is not another house in England which has such curiosities as these. Sit down, Lecount; I beg you will make yourself comfortable. Mrs. Lecount is like the curiosities, Miss Garth—she is one of my father's bargains. You are one of my father's bargains, are you not, Lecount? My father was a remarkable man, ma'am. You will be reminded of him here at every turn. I have got his dressing-gown on at this moment. No such linen as this is made now—you can't get it for love or money. Would you like to feel the texture? Perhaps you're no judge of texture? Perhaps you would prefer talking to me about these two pupils of yours? They are two, are they not? Are they fine girls? Plump, fresh, full-blown English beauties?"

"Excuse me, sir," interposed Mrs. Lecount, sorrowfully. "I must really beg permission to retire if you speak of the poor things in that way. I can't sit by, sir, and hear them turned into ridicule. Consider their position; consider Miss Garth."

"You good creature!" said Noel Vanstone, surveying the housekeeper through his half-closed eyelids. "You excellent Lecount! I assure you, ma'am, Mrs. Lecount is a worthy creature. You will observe that she pities the two girls. I don't go so far as that myself, but I can make allowances for them. I am a large-minded man. I can make allowances for them and for you." He smiled with the most cordial politeness, and helped himself to a strawberry from the dish on his lap.

"You shock Miss Garth; indeed, sir, without meaning it, you shock Miss Garth," remonstrated Mrs. Lecount. "She is not accustomed to you as I am. Consider Miss Garth, sir. As a favor to me, consider Miss Garth."

Thus far Magdalen had resolutely kept silence. The burning anger, which would have betrayed her in an instant if she had let it flash its way to the surface, throbbed fast and fiercely at her heart, and warned her, while Noel Vanstone was speaking, to close her lips. She would have allowed him to talk on uninterruptedly for some minutes more if Mrs. Lecount had not interfered for the second time. The refined insolence of the housekeeper's pity was a woman's insolence; and it stung her into instantly controlling herself. She had never more admirably imitated Miss Garth's voice and manner than when she spoke her next words.

"You are very good," she said to Mrs. Lecount. "I make no claim to be treated with any extraordinary consideration. I am a governess, and I don't expect it. I have only one favor to ask. I beg Mr. Noel Vanstone, for his own sake, to hear what I have to say to him."

"You understand, sir?" observed Mrs. Lecount. "It appears that Miss Garth has some serious warning to give you. She says you are to hear her, for your own sake."

Mr. Noel Vanstone's fair complexion suddenly turned white. He put away the plate of strawberries among his father's bargains. His hand shook and his little figure twisted itself uneasily in the chair. Magdalen observed him attentively. "One discovery already," she thought; "he is a coward!"

"What do you mean, ma'am?" asked Noel Vanstone, with visible trepidation of look and manner. "What do you mean by telling me I must listen to you for my own sake? If you come her to intimidate me, you come to the wrong man. My strength of character was universally noticed in our circle at Zurich—wasn't it, Lecount?"

"Universally, sir," said Mrs. Lecount. "But let us hear Miss Garth. Perhaps I have misinterpreted her meaning."

"On the contrary," replied Magdalen, "you have exactly expressed my meaning. My object in coming here is to warn Mr. Noel Vanstone against the course which he is now taking."

"Don't!" pleaded Mrs. Lecount. "Oh, if you want to help these poor girls, don't talk in that way! Soften his resolution, ma'am, by entreaties; don't strengthen it by threats!" She a little overstrained the tone of humility in which she spoke those words—a little overacted the look of apprehension which accompanied them. If Magdalen had not seen plainly enough already that it was Mrs. Lecount's habitual practice to decide everything for her master in the first instance, and then to persuade him that he was not acting under his housekeeper's resolution but under his own, she would have seen it now.

"You hear what Lecount has just said?" remarked Noel Vanstone. "You hear the unsolicited testimony of a person who has known me from childhood? Take care, Miss Garth—take care!" He complacently arranged the tails of his white dressing-gown over his knees and took the plate of strawberries back on his lap.

"I have no wish to offend you," said Magdalen. "I am only anxious to open your eyes to the truth. You are not acquainted with the characters of the two sisters whose fortunes have fallen into your possession. I have known them from childhood; and I come to give you the benefit of my experience in their interests and in yours. You have nothing to dread from the elder of the two; she patiently accepts the hard lot which you, and your father before you, have forced on her. The younger sister's conduct is the very opposite of this. She has already declined to submit to your father's decision, and she now refuses to be silenced by Mrs. Lecount's letter. Take my word for it, she is capable of giving you serious trouble if you persist in making an enemy of her."

Noel Vanstone changed color once more, and began to fidget again in his chair. "Serious trouble," he repeated, with a blank look. "If you mean writing letters, ma'am, she has given trouble enough already. She has written once to me, and twice to my father. One of the letters to my father was a threatening letter—wasn't it, Lecount?"

"She expressed her feelings, poor child," said Mrs. Lecount. "I thought it hard to send her back her letter, but your dear father knew best. What I said at the time was, Why not let her express her feelings? What are a few threatening words, after all? In her position, poor creature, they are words, and nothing more."

"I advise you not to be too sure of that," said Magdalen. "I know her better than you do."

She paused at those words—paused in a momentary terror. The sting of Mrs. Lecount's pity had nearly irritated her into forgetting her assumed character, and speaking in her own voice.

"You have referred to the letters written by my pupil," she resumed, addressing Noel Vanstone as soon as she felt sure of herself again. "We will say nothing about what she has written to your father; we will only speak of what she has written to you. Is there anything unbecoming in her letter, anything said in it that is false? Is it not true that these two sisters have been cruelly deprived of the provision which their father made for them? His will to this day speaks for him and for them; and it only speaks to no purpose, because he was not aware that his marriage obliged him to make it again, and because he died before he could remedy the error. Can you deny that?"

Noel Vanstone smiled, and helped himself to a strawberry. "I don't attempt to deny it," he said. "Go on, Miss Garth."

"Is it not true," persisted Magdalen, "that the law which has taken the money from these sisters, whose father made no second will, has now given that very money to you, whose father made no will at all? Surely, explain it how you may, this is hard on those orphan girls?"

"Very hard," replied Noel Vanstone. "It strikes you in that light, too—doesn't it, Lecount?"

Mrs. Lecount shook her head, and closed her handsome black eyes. "Harrowing," she said; "I can characterize it, Miss Garth, by no other word—harrowing. How the young person—no! how Miss Vanstone, the younger—discovered that my late respected master made no will I am at a loss to understand. Perhaps it was put in the papers? But I am interrupting you, Miss Garth. Do have something more to say about your pupil's letter?" She noiselessly drew her chair forward, as she said these words, a few inches beyond the line of the visitor's chair. The attempt was neatly made, but it proved useless. Magdalen only kept her head more to the left, and the packing-case on the floor prevented Mrs. Lecount from advancing any further.

"I have only one more question to put," said Magdalen. "My pupil's letter addressed a proposal to Mr. Noel Vanstone. I beg him to inform me why he has refused to consider it."

"My good lady!" cried Noel Vanstone, arching his white eyebrows in satirical astonishment. "Are you really in earnest? Do you know what the proposal is? Have you seen the letter?"

"I am quite in earnest," said Magdalen, "and I have seen the letter. It entreats you to remember how Mr. Andrew Vanstone's fortune has come into your hands; it informs you that one-half of that fortune, divided between his daughters, was what his will intended them to have; and it asks of your sense of justice to do for his children what he would have done for them himself if he had lived. In plainer words still, it asks you to give one-half of the money to the daughters, and it leaves you free to keep the other half yourself. That is the proposal. Why have you refused to consider it?"

"For the simplest possible reason, Miss Garth," said Noel Vanstone, in high good-humor. "Allow me to remind you of a well-known proverb: A fool and his money are soon parted. Whatever else I may be, ma'am, I'm not a fool."

"Don't put it in that way, sir!" remonstrated Mrs. Lecount. "Be serious—pray be serious!"

"Quite impossible, Lecount," rejoined her master. "I can't be serious. My poor father, Miss Garth, took a high moral point of view in this matter. Lecount, there, takes a high moral point of view—don't you, Lecount? I do nothing of the sort. I have lived too long in the Continental atmosphere to trouble myself about moral points of view. My course in this business is as plain as two and two make four. I have got the money, and I should be a born idiot if I parted with it. There is my point of view! Simple enough, isn't it? I don't stand on my dignity; I don't meet you with the law, which is all on my side; I don't blame your coming here, as a total stranger, to try and alter my resolution; I don't blame the two girls for wanting to dip their fingers into my purse. All I say is, I am not fool enough to open it. Pas si bete, as we used to say in the English circle at Zurich. You understand French, Miss Garth? Pas si bete!" He set aside his plate of strawberries once more, and daintily dried his fingers on his fine white napkin.

Magdalen kept her temper. If she could have struck him dead by lifting her hand at that moment, it is probable she would have lifted it. But she kept her temper.

"Am I to understand," she asked, "that the last words you have to say in this matter are the words said for you in Mrs. Lecount's letter!"

"Precisely so," replied Noel Vanstone.

"You have inherited your own father's fortune, as well as the fortune of Mr. Andrew Vanstone, and yet you feel no obligation to act from motives of justice or generosity toward these two sisters? All you think it necessary to say to them is, you have got the money, and you refuse to part with a single farthing of it?"

"Most accurately stated! Miss Garth, you are a woman of business. Lecount, Miss Garth is a woman of business."

"Don't appeal to me, sir," cried Mrs. Lecount, gracefully wringing her plump white hands. "I can't bear it! I must interfere! Let me suggest—oh, what do you call it in English?—a compromise. Dear Mr. Noel, you are perversely refusing to do yourself justice; you have better reasons than the reason you have given to Miss Garth. You follow your honored father's example; you feel it due to his memory to act in this matter as he acted before you. That is his reason, Miss Garth—— I implore you on my knees to take that as his reason. He will do what his dear father did; no more, no less. His dear father made a proposal, and he himself will now make that proposal over again. Yes, Mr. Noel, you will remember what this poor girl says in her letter to you. Her sister has been obliged to go out as a governess; and she herself, in losing her fortune, has lost the hope of her marriage for years and years to come. You will remember this—and you will give the hundred pounds to one, and the hundred pounds to the other, which your admirable father offered in the past time? If he does this, Miss Garth, will he do enough? If he gives a hundred pounds each to these unfortunate sisters—?"

"He will repent the insult to the last hour of his life," said Magdalen.

The instant that answer passed her lips she would have given worlds to recall it. Mrs. Lecount had planted her sting in the right place at last. Those rash words of Magdalen's had burst from her passionately, in her own voice.

Nothing but the habit of public performance saved her from making the serious error that she had committed more palpable still, by attempting to set it right. Here her past practice in the Entertainment came to her rescue, and urged her to go on instantly in Miss Garth's voice as if nothing had happened.

"You mean well, Mrs. Lecount," she continued, "but you are doing harm instead of good. My pupils will accept no such compromise as you propose. I am sorry to have spoken violently just now; I beg you will excuse me." She looked hard for information in the housekeeper's face while she spoke those conciliatory words. Mrs. Lecount baffled the look by putting her handkerchief to her eyes. Had she, or had she not, noticed the momentary change in Magdalen's voice from the tones that were assumed to the tones that were natural? Impossible to say.

"What more can I do!" murmured Mrs. Lecount behind her handkerchief. "Give me time to think—give me time to recover myself. May I retire, sir, for a moment? My nerves are shaken by this sad scene. I must have a glass of water, or I think I shall faint. Don't go yet, Miss Garth. I beg you will give us time to set this sad matter right, if we can—I beg you will remain until I come back."

There were two doors of entrance to the room. One, the door into the front parlor, close at Magdalen's left hand. The other, the door into the back parlor, situated behind her. Mrs. Lecount politely retired—through the open folding-doors—by this latter means of exit, so as not to disturb the visitor by passing in front of her. Magdalen waited until she heard the door open and close again behind her, and then resolved to make the most of the opportunity which left her alone with Noel Vanstone. The utter hopelessness of rousing a generous impulse in that base nature had now been proved by her own experience. The last chance left was to treat him like the craven creature he was, and to influence him through his fears.

Before she could speak, Noel Vanstone himself broke the silence. Cunningly as he strove to hide it, he was half angry, half alarmed at his housekeeper's desertion of him. He looked doubtingly at his visitor; he showed a nervous anxiety to conciliate her until Mrs. Lecount's return.

"Pray remember, ma'am, I never denied that this case was a hard one," he began. "You said just now you had no wish to offend me—and I'm sure I don't want to offend you. May I offer you some strawberries? Would you like to look at my father's bargains? I assure you, ma'am, I am naturally a gallant man; and I feel for both these sisters—especially the younger one. Touch me on the subject of the tender passion, and you touch me on a weak place. Nothing would please me more than to hear that Miss Vanstone's lover (I'm sure I always call her Miss Vanstone, and so does Lecount)—I say, ma'am, nothing would please me more than to hear that Miss Vanstone's lover had come back and married her. If a loan of money would be likely to bring him back, and if the security offered was good, and if my lawyer thought me justified—"

"Stop, Mr. Vanstone," said Magdalen. "You are entirely mistaken in your estimate of the person you have to deal with. You are seriously wrong in supposing that the marriage of the younger sister—if she could be married in a week's time—would make any difference in the convictions which induced her to write to your father and to you. I don't deny that she may act from a mixture of motives. I don't deny that she clings to the hope of hastening her marriage, and to the hope of rescuing her sister from a life of dependence. But if both those objects were accomplished by other means, nothing would induce her to leave you in possession of the inheritance which her father meant his children to have. I know her, Mr. Vanstone! She is a nameless, homeless, friendless wretch. The law which takes care of you, the law which takes care of all legitimate children, casts her like carrion to the winds. It is your law—not hers. She only knows it as the instrument of a vile oppression, an insufferable wrong. The sense of that wrong haunts her like a possession of the devil. The resolution to right that wrong burns in her like fire. If that miserable girl was married and rich, with millions tomorrow, do you think she would move an inch from her purpose? I tell you she would resist, to the last breath in her body, the vile injustice which has struck at the helpless children, through the calamity of their father's death! I tell you she would shrink from no means which a desperate woman can employ to force that closed hand of yours open, or die in the attempt!"

She stopped abruptly. Once more her own indomitable earnestness had betrayed her. Once more the inborn nobility of that perverted nature had risen superior to the deception which it had stooped to practice. The scheme of the moment vanished from her mind's view; and the resolution of her life burst its way outward in her own words, in her own tones, pouring hotly and more hotly from her heart. She saw the abject manikin before her cowering, silent, in his chair. Had his fears left him sense enough to perceive the change in her voice? No: his face spoke the truth—his fears had bewildered him. This time the chance of the moment had befriended her. The door behind her chair had not opened again yet. "No ears but his have heard me," she thought, with a sense of unutterable relief. "I have escaped Mrs. Lecount."

She had done nothing of the kind. Mrs. Lecount had never left the room.

After opening the door and closing it again, without going out, the housekeeper had noiselessly knelt down behind Magdalen's chair. Steadying herself against the post of the folding-door, she took a pair of scissors from her pocket, waited until Noel Vanstone (from whose view she was entirely hidden) had attracted Magdalen's attention by speaking to her, and then bent forward, with the scissors ready in her hand. The skirt of the false Miss Garth's gown—the brown alpaca dress, with the white spots on it—touched the floor, within the housekeeper's reach. Mrs. Lecount lifted the outer of the two flounces which ran round the bottom of the dress one over the other, softly cut away a little irregular fragment of stuff from the inner flounce, and neatly smoothed the outer one over it again, so as to hide the gap. By the time she had put the scissors back in her pocket, and had risen to her feet (sheltering herself behind the post of the folding-door), Magdalen had spoken her last words. Mrs. Lecount quietly repeated the ceremony of opening and shutting the back parlor door; and returned to her place.

"What has happened, sir, in my absence?" she inquired, addressing her master with a look of alarm. "You are pale; you are agitated! Oh, Miss Garth, have you forgotten the caution I gave you in the other room?"

"Miss Garth has forgotten everything," cried Noel Vanstone, recovering his lost composure on the re-appearance of Mrs. Lecount. "Miss Garth has threatened me in the most outrageous manner. I forbid you to pity either of those two girls any more, Lecount—especially the younger one. She is the most desperate wretch I ever heard of! If she can't get my money by fair means, she threatens to have it by foul. Miss Garth has told me that to my face. To my face!" he repeated, folding his arms, and looking mortally insulted.

"Compose yourself, sir," said Mrs. Lecount. "Pray compose yourself, and leave me to speak to Miss Garth. I regret to hear, ma'am, that you have forgotten what I said to you in the next room. You have agitated Mr. Noel; you have compromised the interests you came here to plead; and you have only repeated what we knew before. The language you have allowed yourself to use in my absence is the same language which your pupil was foolish enough to employ when she wrote for the second time to my late master. How can a lady of your years and experience seriously repeat such nonsense? This girl boasts and threatens. She will do this;

she will do that. You have her confidence, ma'am. Tell me, if you please, in plain words, what can she do?"

Sharply as the taunt was pointed, it glanced off harmless. Mrs. Lecount had planted her sting once too often. Magdalen rose in complete possession of her assumed character and composedly terminated the interview. Ignorant as she was of what had happened behind her chair, she saw a change in Mrs. Lecount's look and manner which warned her to run no more risks, and to trust herself no longer in the house.

"I am not in my pupil's confidence," she said. "Her own acts will answer your question when the time comes. I can only tell you, from my own knowledge of her, that she is no boaster. What she wrote to Mr. Michael Vanstone was what she was prepared to do—-what, I have reason to think, she was actually on the point of doing, when her plans were overthrown by his death. Mr. Michael Vanstone's son has only to persist in following his father's course to find, before long, that I am not mistaken in my pupil, and that I have not come here to intimidate him by empty threats. My errand is done. I leave Mr. Noel Vanstone with two alternatives to choose from. I leave him to share Mr. Andrew Vanstone's fortune with Mr. Andrew Vanstone's daughters—or to persist in his present refusal and face the consequences." She bowed, and walked to the door.

Noel Vanstone started to his feet, with anger and alarm struggling which should express itself first in his blank white face. Before he could open his lips, Mrs. Lecount's plump hands descended on his shoulders, put him softly back in his chair, and restored the plate of strawberries to its former position on his lap.

"Refresh yourself, Mr. Noel, with a few more strawberries," she said, "and leave Miss Garth to me."

She followed Magdalen into the passage, and closed the door of the room after her.

"Are you residing in London, ma'am?" asked Mrs. Lecount.

"No," replied Magdalen. "I reside in the country."

"If I want to write to you, where can I address my letter?"

"To the post-office, Birmingham," said Magdalen, mentioning the place which she had last left, and at which all letters were still addressed to her.

Mrs. Lecount repeated the direction to fix it in her memory, advanced two steps in the passage, and quietly laid her right hand on Magdalen's arm.

"A word of advice, ma'am," she said; "one word at parting. You are a bold woman and a clever woman. Don't be too bold; don't be too clever. You are risking more than you think for." She suddenly raised herself on tiptoe and whispered the next words in Magdalen's ear. "I hold you in the hollow of my hand!" said Mrs. Lecount, with a fierce hissing emphasis on every syllable. Her left hand clinched itself stealthily as she spoke. It was the hand in which she had concealed the fragment of stuff from Magdalen's gown—the hand which held it fast at that moment.

"What do you mean?" asked Magdalen, pushing her back.

Mrs. Lecount glided away politely to open the house door.

"I mean nothing now," she said; "wait a little, and time may show. One last question, ma'am, before I bid you good-by. When your pupil was a little innocent child, did she ever amuse herself by building a house of cards?"

Magdalen impatiently answered by a gesture in the affirmative.

"Did you ever see her build up the house higher and higher," proceeded Mrs. Lecount, "till it was quite a pagoda of cards? Did you ever see her open her little child's eyes wide and look at it, and feel so proud of what she had done already that she wanted to do more? Did you ever see her steady her pretty little hand, and hold her innocent breath, and put one other card on the top, and lay the whole house, the instant afterward, a heap of ruins on the table? Ah, you have seen that. Give her, if you please, a friendly message from me. I venture to say she has built the house high enough already; and I recommend her to be careful before she puts on that other card."

"She shall have your message," said Magdalen, with Miss Garth's bluntness, and Miss Garth's emphatic nod of the head. "But I doubt her minding it. Her hand is rather steadier than you suppose, and I think she will put on the other card."

"And bring the house down," said Mrs. Lecount.

"And build it up again," rejoined Magdalen. "I wish you good-morning."

"Good-morning," said Mrs. Lecount, opening the door. "One last word, Miss Garth. Do think of what I said in the back room! Do try the Golden Ointment for that sad affliction in your eyes!"

As Magdalen crossed the threshold of the door she was met by the postman ascending the house steps with a letter picked out from the bundle in his hand. "Noel Vanstone, Esquire?" she heard the man say, interrogatively, as she made her way down the front garden to the street.

She passed through the garden gates little thinking from what new difficulty and new danger her timely departure had saved her. The letter which the postman had just delivered into the housekeeper's hands was no other than the anonymous letter addressed to Noel Vanstone by Captain Wragge.

CHAPTER IV.

MRS. LECOUNT returned to the parlor, with the fragment of Magdalen's dress in one hand, and with Captain Wragge's letter in the other.

"Have you got rid of her?" asked Noel Vanstone. "Have you shut the door at last on Miss Garth?"

"Don't call her Miss Garth, sir," said Mrs. Lecount, smiling contemptuously. "She is as much Miss Garth as you are. We have been favored by the performance of a clever masquerade; and if we had taken the disguise off our visitor, I think we should have found under it Miss Vanstone herself.—Here is a letter for you, sir, which the postman has just left."

She put the letter on the table within her master's reach. Noel Vanstone's amazement at the discovery just communicated to him kept his whole attention concentrated on the housekeeper's face. He never so much as looked at the letter when she placed it before him.

"Take my word for it, sir," proceeded Mrs. Lecount, composedly taking a chair. "When our visitor gets home she will put her gray hair away in a box, and will cure that sad affliction in her eyes with warm water and a sponge. If she had painted the marks on her face, as well as she painted the inflammation in her eyes, the light would have shown me nothing, and I should certainly have been deceived. But I saw the marks; I saw a young woman's skin under that dirty complexion of hers; I heard in this room a true voice in a passion, as well as a false voice talking with an accent, and I don't believe in one morsel of that lady's personal appearance from top to toe. The girl herself, in my opinion, Mr. Noel—and a bold girl too."

"Why didn't you lock the door and send for the police?" asked Mr. Noel. "My father would have sent for the police. You know, as well as I do, Lecount, my father would have sent for the police."

"Pardon me, sir," said Mrs. Lecount, "I think your father would have waited until he had got something more for the police to do than we have got for them yet. We shall see this lady again, sir. Perhaps she will come here next time with her own face and her own voice. I am curious to see what her own face is like. I am curious to know whether what I have heard of her voice in a passion is enough to make me recognize her voice when she is calm. I possess a little memorial of her visit of which she is not aware, and she will not escape me so easily as she thinks. If it turns out a useful memorial, you shall know what it is. If not, I will abstain from troubling you on so trifling a subject.—Allow me to remind you, sir, of the letter under your hand. You have not looked at it yet."

Noel Vanstone opened the letter. He started as his eye fell on the first lines—hesitated—and then hurriedly read it through. The paper dropped from his hand, and he sank back in his chair. Mrs. Lecount sprang to her feet with the alacrity of a young woman and picked up the letter.

"What has happened, sir?" she asked. Her face altered as she put the question, and her large black eyes hardened fiercely, in genuine astonishment and alarm.

"Send for the police," exclaimed her master. "Lecount, I insist on being protected. Send for the police!"

"May I read the letter, sir?"

He feebly waved his hand. Mrs. Lecount read the letter attentively, and put it aside on the table, without a word, when she had done.

"Have you nothing to say to me?" asked Noel Vanstone, staring at his housekeeper in blank dismay. "Lecount, I'm to be robbed! The scoundrel who wrote that letter knows all about it, and won't tell me anything unless I pay him. I'm to be robbed! Here's property on this table worth thousands of pounds—property that can never be replaced—property that all the crowned heads in Europe could not produce if they tried. Lock me in, Lecount, and send for the police!"

Instead of sending for the police, Mrs. Lecount took a large green paper fan from the chimney-piece, and seated herself opposite her master.

"You are agitated, Mr. Noel," she said, "you are heated. Let me cool you."

With her face as hard as ever—with less tenderness of look and manner than most women would have shown if they had been rescuing a half-drowned fly from a milk-jug—she silently and patiently fanned him for five minutes or more. No practiced eye observing the peculiar bluish pallor of his complexion, and the marked difficulty with which he drew his breath, could have failed to perceive that the great organ of life was in this man, what the housekeeper had stated it to be, too weak for the function which it was called on to perform. The heart labored over its work as if it had been the heart of a worn-out old man.

"Are you relieved, sir?" asked Mrs. Lecount. "Can you think a little? Can you exercise your better judgment?"

She rose and put her hand over his heart with as much mechanical attention and as little genuine interest as if she had been feeling the plates at dinner to ascertain if they had been properly warmed. "Yes," she went on, seating herself again, and resuming the exercise of the fan; "you are getting better already, Mr. Noel.—Don't ask me about this anonymous letter until you have thought for yourself, and have given your own opinion first." She went on with the fanning, and looked him hard in the face all the time. "Think," she said; "think, sir, without troubling yourself to express your thoughts. Trust to my intimate sympathy with you to read them. Yes, Mr. Noel, this letter is a paltry attempt to frighten you. What does it say? It says you are the object of a conspiracy directed by Miss Vanstone. We know that already—the lady of the inflamed eyes has told us. We snap our fingers at the conspiracy. What does the letter say next? It says the writer has valuable information to give you if you will pay for it. What did you call this person yourself just now, sir?"

"I called him a scoundrel," said Noel Vanstone, recovering his self-importance, and raising himself gradually in his chair.

"I agree with you in that, sir, as I agree in everything else," proceeded Mrs. Lecount. "He is a scoundrel who really has this information and who means what he says, or he is a mouthpiece of Miss Vanstone's, and she has caused this letter to be written for the purpose of puzzling us by another form of disguise. Whether the letter is true, or whether the letter is false—am I not reading your own wiser thoughts now, Mr. Noel?—you know better than to put your enemies on their guard by employing the police in this matter too soon. I quite agree with you—no police just yet. You will allow this anonymous man, or anonymous woman, to suppose you are easily frightened; you will lay a trap for the information in return for the trap laid for your money; you will answer the letter, and see what comes of the answer; and you will only pay the expense of employing the police when you know the expense is necessary. I agree with you again—no expense, if we can help it. In every particular, Mr. Noel, my mind and your mind in this matter are one."

"It strikes you in that light, Lecount—does it?" said Noel Vanstone. "I think so myself; I certainly think so. I won't pay the police a farthing if I can possibly help it." He took up the letter again, and became fretfully perplexed over a second reading of it. "But the man wants money!" he broke out, impatiently. "You seem to forget, Lecount, that the man wants money."

"Money which you offer him, sir," rejoined Mrs. Lecount; "but—as your thoughts have already anticipated—money which you don't give him. No! no! you say to this man: 'Hold out your hand, sir;' and when he has held it, you give him a smack for his pains, and put your own hand back in your pocket.—I am so glad to see you laughing, Mr. Noel! so glad to see you getting back your good spirits. We will answer the letter by advertisement, as the writer directs—advertisement is so cheap! Your poor hand is trembling a little—shall I hold the pen for you? I am not fit to do more; but I can always promise to hold the pen."

Without waiting for his reply she went into the back parlor, and returned with pen, ink, and paper. Arranging a blotting-book on her knees, and looking a model of cheerful submission, she placed herself once more in front of her master's chair.

"Shall I write from your dictation, sir?" she inquired. "Or shall I make a little sketch, and will you correct it afterward? I will make a little sketch. Let me see the letter. We are to advertise in the Times, and we are to address 'An Unknown Friend.' What shall I say, Mr. Noel? Stay; I will write it, and then you can see for yourself: 'An Unknown Friend is requested to mention (by advertisement) an address at which a letter can reach him. The receipt of the information which he offers will be acknowledged by a reward of—' What sum of money do you wish me to set down, sir?"

"Set down nothing," said Noel Vanstone, with a sudden outbreak of impatience. "Money matters are my business—I say money matters are my business, Lecount. Leave it to me."

"Certainly, sir," replied Mrs. Lecount, handing her master the blotting-book. "You will not forget to be liberal in offering money when you know beforehand you don't mean to part with it?"

"Don't dictate, Lecount! I won't submit to dictation!" said Noel Vanstone, asserting his own independence more and more impatiently. "I mean to conduct this business for myself. I am master, Lecount!"

"You are master, sir."

"My father was master before me. And I am my father's son. I tell you, Lecount, I am my father's son!"

Mrs. Lecount bowed submissively.

"I mean to set down any sum of money I think right," pursued Noel Vanstone, nodding his little flaxen head vehemently. "I mean to send this advertisement myself. The servant shall take it to the stationer's to be put into the Times. When I ring the bell twice, send the servant. You understand, Lecount? Send the servant."

Mrs. Lecount bowed again and walked slowly to the door. She knew to a nicety when to lead her master and when to let him go alone. Experience had taught her to govern him in all essential points by giving way to him afterward on all points of minor detail. It was a characteristic of his weak nature—as it is of all weak natures—to assert itself obstinately on trifles. The filling in of the blank in the advertisement was the trifle in this case; and Mrs. Lecount quieted her master's suspicions that she was leading him by instantly conceding it. "My mule has kicked," she thought to herself, in her own language, as she opened the door. "I can do no more with him to-day."

"Lecount!" cried her master, as she stepped into the passage. "Come back."

Mrs. Lecount came back.

"You're not offended with me, are you?" asked Noel Vanstone, uneasily.

"Certainly not, sir," replied Mrs. Lecount. "As you said just now—you are master."

"Good creature! Give me your hand." He kissed her hand, and smiled in high approval of his own affectionate proceeding. "Lecount, you are a worthy creature!"

"Thank you, sir," said Mrs. Lecount. She courtesied and went out. "If he had any brains in that monkey head of his," she said to herself in the passage, "what a rascal he would be!"

Left by himself, Noel Vanstone became absorbed in anxious reflection over the blank space in the advertisement. Mrs. Lecount's apparently superfluous hint to him to be liberal in offering money when he knew he had no intention of parting with it, had been founded on an intimate knowledge of his character. He had inherited his father's sordid love of money, without inheriting his father's hard-headed capacity for seeing the uses to which money can be put. His one idea in connection with his wealth was the idea of keeping it. He was such an inborn miser that the bare prospect of being liberal in theory only daunted him. He took up the pen; laid it down again; and read the anonymous letter for the third time, shaking his head over it suspiciously. "If I offer this man a large sum of money," he thought, on a sudden, "how do I know he may not find a means of actually making me pay it? Women are always in a hurry. Lecount is always in a hurry. I have got the afternoon before me—I'll take the afternoon to consider it."

He fretfully put away the blotting-book and the sketch of the advertisement on the chair which Mrs. Lecount had just left. As he returned to his own seat, he shook his little head solemnly, and arranged his white dressing-gown over his knees with the air of a man absorbed in anxious thought. Minute after minute passed away; the quarters and the half-hours succeeded each other on the dial of Mrs. Lecount's watch, and still Noel Vanstone remained lost in doubt; still no summons for the servants disturbed the tranquillity of the parlor bell.

Meanwhile, after parting with Mrs. Lecount, Magdalen had cautiously abstained from crossing the road to her lodgings, and had only ventured to return after making a circuit in the neighborhood. When she found herself once more in Vauxhall Walk, the first object which attracted her attention was a cab drawn up before the door of the lodgings. A few steps more in advance showed her the landlady's daughter standing at the cab door engaged in a dispute with the driver on the subject of his fare. Noticing that the girl's back was turned toward her, Magdalen instantly profited by that circumstance and slipped unobserved into the house.

She glided along the passage, ascended the stairs, and found herself, on the first landing, face to face with her traveling companion! There stood Mrs. Wragge, with a pile of small parcels hugged up in her arms, anxiously waiting the issue of the dispute with the cabman in the street. To return was impossible—the sound of the angry voices below was advancing into the passage. To hesitate was worse than useless. But one choice was left—the choice of going on—and Magdalen desperately took it. She pushed by Mrs. Wragge without a word, ran into her own room, tore off her cloak, bonnet and wig, and threw them down out of sight in the blank space between the sofa-bedstead and the wall.

For the first few moments, astonishment bereft Mrs. Wragge of the power of speech, and rooted her to the spot where she stood. Two out of the collection of parcels in her arms fell from them on the stairs. The sight of that catastrophe roused her. "Thieves!" cried Mrs. Wragge, suddenly struck by an idea. "Thieves!"

Magdalen heard her through the room door, which she had not had time to close completely. "Is that you, Mrs. Wragge?" she called out in her own voice. "What is the matter?" She snatched up a towel while she spoke, dipped it in water, and passed it rapidly over the lower part of her face. At the sound of the familiar voice Mrs. Wragge turned round—dropped a third parcel—and, forgetting it in her astonishment, ascended the second flight of stairs. Magdalen stepped out on the first-floor landing, with the towel held over her forehead as if she was suffering from headache. Her false eyebrows required time for their removal, and a headache assumed for the occasion suggested the most convenient pretext she could devise for hiding them as they were hidden now.

"What are you disturbing the house for?" she asked. "Pray be quiet; I am half blind with the headache."

"Anything wrong, ma'am?" inquired the landlady from the passage.

"Nothing whatever," replied Magdalen. "My friend is timid; and the dispute with the cabman has frightened her. Pay the man what he wants, and let him go."

"Where is She?" asked Mrs. Wragge, in a tremulous whisper. "Where's the woman who scuttled by me into your room?"

"Pooh!" said Magdalen. "No woman scuttled by you—as you call it. Look in and see for yourself."

She threw open the door. Mrs. Wragge walked into the room—looked all over it—saw nobody—and indicated her astonishment at the result by dropping a fourth parcel, and trembling helplessly from head to foot.

"I saw her go in here," said Mrs. Wragge, in awestruck accents. "A woman in a gray cloak and a poke bonnet. A rude woman. She scuttled by me on the stairs—she did. Here's the room, and no woman in it. Give us a Prayer-book!" cried Mrs. Wragge, turning deadly pale, and letting her whole remaining collection of parcels fall about her in a little cascade of commodities. "I want to read something Good. I want to think of my latter end. I've seen a Ghost!"

"Nonsense!" said Magdalen. "You're dreaming; the shopping has been too much for you. Go into your own room and take your bonnet off."

"I've heard tell of ghosts in night-gowns, ghosts in sheets, and ghosts in chains," proceeded Mrs. Wragge, standing petrified in her own magic circle of linen-drapers' parcels. "Here's a worse ghost than any of 'em—a ghost in a gray cloak and a poke bonnet. I know what it is," continued Mrs. Wragge, melting into penitent tears. "It's a judgment on me for being so happy away from the captain. It's a judgment on me for having been down at heel in half the shops in London, first with one shoe and then with the other, all the time I've been out. I'm a sinful creature. Don't let go of me—whatever you do, my dear, don't let go of me!" She caught Magdalen fast by the arm and fell into another trembling fit at the bare idea of being left by herself.

The one remaining chance in such an emergency as this was to submit to circumstances. Magdalen took Mrs. Wragge to a chair; having first placed it in such a position as might enable her to turn her back on her traveling-companion, while she removed the false eyebrows by the help of a little water. "Wait a minute there," she said, "and try if you can compose yourself while I bathe my head."

"Compose myself?" repeated Mrs. Wragge. "How am I to compose myself when my head feels off my shoulders? The worst Buzzing I ever had with the Cookery-book was nothing to the Buzzing I've got now with the Ghost. Here's a miserable end to a holiday! You may take me back again, my dear, whenever you like—I've had enough of it already!"

Having at last succeeded in removing the eyebrows, Magdalen was free to combat the unfortunate impression produced on her companion's mind by every weapon of persuasion which her ingenuity could employ.

The attempt proved useless. Mrs. Wragge persisted—on evidence which, it may be remarked in parenthesis, would have satisfied many wiser ghost-seers than herself—in believing that she had been supernaturally favored by a visitor from the world of spirits. All that Magdalen could do was to ascertain, by cautious investigation, that Mrs. Wragge had not been quick enough to identify the supposed ghost with the character of the old North-country lady in the Entertainment. Having satisfied herself on this point, she had no resource but to leave the rest to the natural incapability of retaining impressions—unless those impressions were perpetually renewed—which was one of the characteristic infirmities of her companion's weak mind. After fortifying Mrs. Wragge by reiterated assurances that one appearance (according to all the laws and regulations of ghosts) meant nothing unless it was immediately followed by two more—after patiently leading back her attention to the parcels dropped on the floor and on the stairs—and after promising to keep the door of communication ajar between the two rooms if Mrs. Wragge would engage on her side to retire to her own chamber, and to say no more on the terrible subject of the ghost—Magdalen at last secured the privilege of reflecting uninterruptedly on the events of that memorable day.

Two serious consequences had followed her first step forward. Mrs. Lecount had entrapped her into speaking in her own voice, and accident had confronted her with Mrs. Wragge in disguise.

What advantage had she gained to set against these disasters? The advantage of knowing more of Noel Vanstone and of Mrs. Lecount than she might have discovered in months if she had trusted to inquiries made for her by others. One uncertainty which had hitherto perplexed her was set at rest already. The scheme she had privately devised against Michael Vanstone—which Captain Wragge's sharp insight had partially penetrated when she first warned him that their partnership must be dissolved—was a scheme which she could now plainly see must be abandoned as hopeless, in the case of Michael Vanstone's son. The father's habits of speculation had been the pivot on which the whole machinery of her meditated conspiracy had been constructed to turn. No such vantage-ground was discoverable in the doubly sordid character of the son. Noel Vanstone was invulnerable on the very point which had presented itself in his father as open to attack.

Having reached this conclusion, how was she to shape her future course? What new means could she discover which would lead her secretly to her end, in defiance of Mrs. Lecount's malicious vigilance and Noel Vanstone's miserly distrust?

She was seated before the looking-glass, mechanically combing out her hair, while that all-important consideration occupied her mind. The agitation of the moment had raised a feverish color in her cheeks, and had brightened the light in her large gray eyes. She was conscious of looking her best; conscious how her beauty gained by contrast, after the removal of the disguise. Her lovely light brown hair looked thicker and softer than ever, now that it had escaped from its imprisonment under the gray wig. She twisted it this way and that, with quick, dexterous fingers; she laid it in masses on her shoulders; she threw it back from them in a heap and turned sidewise to see how it fell—to see her back and shoulders freed from the artificial deformities of the padded cloak. After a moment she faced the looking-glass once more; plunged both hands deep in her hair; and, resting her elbows on the table, looked closer and closer at the reflection of herself, until her breath began to dim the glass. "I can twist any man alive round my finger," she thought, with a smile of superb triumph, "as long as I keep my looks! If that contemptible wretch saw me now—" She shrank from following that thought to its end, with a sudden horror of herself: she drew back from the glass, shuddering, and put her hands over her face. "Oh, Frank!" she murmured, "but for you, what a wretch I might be!" Her eager fingers snatched the little white silk bag from its hiding-place in her bosom; her lips devoured it with silent kisses. "My darling! my angel! Oh, Frank, how I love you!" The tears gushed into her eyes. She passionately dried them, restored the bag to its place, and turned her back on the looking-glass. "No more of myself," she thought; "no more of my mad, miserable self for to-day!"

Shrinking from all further contemplation of her next step in advance—shrinking from the fast-darkening future, with which Noel Vanstone was now associated in her inmost thoughts—she looked impatiently about the room for some homely occupation which might take her out of herself. The disguise which she had flung down between the wall and the bed recurred to her memory. It was impossible to leave it there. Mrs. Wragge (now occupied in sorting her parcels) might weary of her employment, might come in again at a moment's notice, might pass near the bed, and see the gray cloak. What was to be done?

Her first thought was to put the disguise back in her trunk. But after what had happened, there was danger in trusting it so near to herself while she and Mrs. Wragge were together under the same roof. She resolved to be rid of it that evening, and boldly determined on sending it back to Birmingham. Her bonnet-box fitted into her trunk. She took the box out, thrust in the wig and cloak, and remorselessly flattened down the bonnet at the top. The gown (which she had not yet taken off) was her own; Mrs. Wragge had been accustomed to see her in it—there was no need to send the gown back. Before closing the box, she hastily traced these lines on a sheet of paper: "I took the inclosed things away by mistake. Please keep them for me, with the rest of my luggage in your possession, until you hear from me again." Putting the paper on the top of the bonnet, she directed the box to Captain Wragge at Birmingham, took it downstairs immediately, and sent the landlady's daughter away with it to the nearest Receiving-house. "That difficulty is disposed of," she thought, as she went back to her own room again.

Mrs. Wragge was still occupied in sorting her parcels on her narrow little bed. She turned round with a faint scream when Magdalen looked in at her. "I thought it was the ghost again," said Mrs. Wragge. "I'm trying to take warning, my dear, by what's happened to me. I've put all my parcels straight, just as the captain would like to see 'em. I'm up at heel with both shoes. If I close my eyes to-night—which I don't think I shall—I'll go to sleep as straight as my legs will let me. And I'll never have another holiday as long as I live. I hope I shall be forgiven," said Mrs. Wragge, mournfully shaking her head. "I humbly hope I shall be forgiven."

"Forgiven!" repeated Magdalen. "If other women wanted as little forgiving as you do—Well! well! Suppose you open some of these parcels. Come! I want to see what you have been buying to-day."

Mrs. Wragge hesitated, sighed penitently, considered a little, stretched out her hand timidly toward one of the parcels, thought of the supernatural warning, and shrank back from her own purchases with a desperate exertion of self-control.

"Open this one." said Magdalen, to encourage her: "what is it?"

Mrs. Wragge's faded blue eyes began to brighten dimly, in spite of her remorse; but she self-denyingly shook her head. The master-passion of shopping might claim his own again—but the ghost was not laid yet.

"Did you get it at a bargain?" asked Magdalen, confidentially.

"Dirt cheap!" cried poor Mrs. Wragge, falling headlong into the snare, and darting at the parcel as eagerly as if nothing had happened.

Magdalen kept her gossiping over her purchases for an hour or more, and then wisely determined to distract her attention from all ghostly recollections in another way by taking her out for a walk.

As they left the lodgings, the door of Noel Vanstone's house opened, and the woman-servant appeared, bent on another errand. She was apparently charged with a letter on this occasion which she carried carefully in her hand. Conscious of having formed no plan yet either for attack or defense, Magdalen wondered, with a momentary dread, whether Mrs. Lecount had decided already on opening fresh communications, and whether the letter was directed to "Miss Garth."

The letter bore no such address. Noel Vanstone had solved his pecuniary problem at last. The blank space in the advertisement was filled up, and Mrs. Lecount's acknowledgment of the captain's anonymous warning was now on its way to insertion in the Times.

THE END OF THE THIRD SCENE.

BETWEEN THE SCENES.

PROGRESS OF THE STORY THROUGH THE POST.

I.

Extract from the Advertising Columns of "The Times."

"AN UNKNOWN FRIEND is requested to mention (by advertisement) an address at which a letter can reach him. The receipt of the information which he offers will be acknowledged by a reward of Five Pounds."

II.

From Captain Wragge to Magdalen.

"Birmingham, July 2d, 1847.

"MY DEAR GIRL—The box containing the articles of costumes which you took away by mistake has come safely to hand. Consider it under my special protection until I hear from you again.

"I embrace this opportunity to assure you once more of my unalterable fidelity to your interests. Without attempting to intrude myself into your confidence, may I inquire whether Mr. Noel Vanstone has consented to do you justice? I greatly fear he has declined—in which case I can lay my hand on my heart, and solemnly declare that his meanness revolts me. Why do I feel a foreboding that you have appealed to him in vain? Why do I find myself viewing this fellow in the light of a noxious insect? We are total strangers to each other; I have no sort of knowledge of him, except the knowledge I picked up in making your inquiries. Has my intense sympathy with your interests made my perceptions prophetic? or, to put it fancifully, is there really such a thing as a former state of existence? and has Mr. Noel Vanstone mortally insulted me—say, in some other planet?

"I write, my dear Magdalen, as you see, with my customary dash of humor. But I am serious in placing my services at your disposal. Don't let the question of terms cause you an instant's hesitation. I accept beforehand any terms you like to mention. If your present plans point that way, I am ready to squeeze Mr. Noel Vanstone, in your interests, till the gold oozes out of him at every pore. Pardon the coarseness of this metaphor. My anxiety to be of service to you rushes into words; lays my meaning, in the rough, at your feet; and leaves your taste to polish it with the choicest ornaments of the English language.

"How is my unfortunate wife? I am afraid you find it quite impossible to keep her up at heel, or to mold her personal appearance into harmony with the eternal laws of symmetry and order. Does she attempt to be too familiar with you? I have always been accustomed to check her, in this respect. She has never been permitted to call me anything but Captain; and on the rare occasions since our union, when circumstances may have obliged her to address me by letter, her opening form of salutation has been rigidly restricted to 'Dear Sir.' Accept these trifling domestic particulars as suggesting hints which may be useful to you in managing Mrs. Wragge; and believe me, in anxious expectation of hearing from you again,

"Devotedly yours,

"HORATIO WRAGGE."

III.

From Norah to Magdalen.

[Forwarded, with the Two Letters that follow it, from the Post-office, Birmingham.]

"Westmoreland House, Kensington, July 1st.

"MY DEAREST MAGDALEN—When you write next (and pray write soon!) address your letter to me at Miss Garth's. I have left my situation; and some little time may elapse before I find another.

"Now it is all over I may acknowledge to you, my darling, that I was not happy. I tried hard to win the affection of the two little girls I had to teach; but they seemed, I am sure I can't tell why, to dislike me from the first. Their mother I have no reason to complain of. But their grandmother, who was really the ruling power in the house, made my life very hard to me. My inexperience in teaching was a constant subject of remark with her; and my difficulties with the children were always visited on me as if they had been entirely of my own making. I tell you this, so that you may not suppose I regret having left my situation. Far from it, my love—I am glad to be out of the house.

"I have saved a little money, Magdalen; and I should so like to spend it in staying a few days with you. My heart aches for a sight of my sister; my ears are weary for the sound of her voice. A word from you telling me where we can meet, is all I want. Think of it—pray think of it.

"Don't suppose I am discouraged by this first check. There are many kind people in the world; and some of them may employ me next time. The way to happiness is often very hard to find; harder, I almost think, for women than for men. But if we only try patiently, and try long enough, we reach it at last—in heaven, if not on earth. I think my way now is the way which leads to seeing you again. Don't forget that, my love, the next time you think of

"NORAH."

IV.

From Miss Garth to Magdalen.

"Westmoreland House, July 1st.

"MY DEAR MAGDALEN—You have no useless remonstrances to apprehend at the sight of my handwriting. My only object in this letter is to tell you something which I know your sister will not tell you of her own accord. She is entirely ignorant that I am writing to you. Keep her in ignorance, if you wish to spare her unnecessary anxiety, and me unnecessary distress.

"Norah's letter, no doubt, tells you that she has left her situation. I feel it my painful duty to add that she has left it on your account.

"The matter occurred in this manner. Messrs. Wyatt, Pendril, and Gwilt are the solicitors of the gentleman in whose family Norah was employed. The life which you have chosen for yourself was known as long ago as December last to all the partners. You were discovered performing in public at Derby by the person who had been employed to trace you at York;

and that discovery was communicated by Mr. Wyatt to Norah's employer a few days since, in reply to direct inquiries about you on that gentleman's part. His wife and his mother (who lives with him) had expressly desired that he would make those inquiries; their doubts having been aroused by Norah's evasive answers when they questioned her about her sister. You know Norah too well to blame her for this. Evasion was the only escape your present life had left her, from telling a downright falsehood.

"That same day, the two ladies of the family, the elder and the younger, sent for your sister, and told her they had discovered that you were a public performer, roaming from place to place in the country under an assumed name. They were just enough not to blame Norah for this; they were just enough to acknowledge that her conduct had been as irreproachable as I had guaranteed it should be when I got her the situation. But, at the same time, they made it a positive condition of her continuing in their employment that she should never permit you to visit her at their house, or to meet her and walk out with her when she was in attendance on the children. Your sister—who has patiently borne all hardships that fell on herself—instantly resented the slur cast on you. She gave her employers warning on the spot. High words followed, and she left the house that evening.

"I have no wish to distress you by representing the loss of this situation in the light of a disaster. Norah was not so happy in it as I had hoped and believed she would be. It was impossible for me to know beforehand that the children were sullen and intractable, or that the husband's mother was accustomed to make her domineering disposition felt by every one in the house. I will readily admit that Norah is well out of this situation. But the harm does not stop here. For all you and I know to the contrary, the harm may go on. What has happened in this situation may happen in another. Your way of life, however pure your conduct may be—and I will do you the justice to believe it pure—is a suspicious way of life to all respectable people. I have lived long enough in this world to know that the sense of Propriety, in nine Englishwomen out of ten, makes no allowances and feels no pity. Norah's next employers may discover you; and Norah may throw up a situation next time which we may never be able to find for her again.

"I leave you to consider this. My child, don't think I am hard on you. I am jealous for your sister's tranquillity. If you will forget the past, Magdalen, and come back, trust to your old governess to forget it too, and to give you the home which your father and mother once gave her. Your friend, my dear, always,

"HARRIET GARTH."

V.

From Francis Clare, Jun., to Magdalen.

"Shanghai, China, April 23d, 1847.

"MY DEAR MAGDALEN—I have deferred answering your letter, in consequence of the distracted state of my mind, which made me unfit to write to you. I am still unfit, but I feel I ought to delay no longer. My sense of honor fortifies me, and I undergo the pain of writing this letter.

"My prospects in China are all at an end. The Firm to which I was brutally consigned, as if I was a bale of merchandise, has worn out my patience by a series of petty insults; and I have felt compelled, from motives of self-respect, to withdraw my services, which were undervalued from the first. My returning to England under these circumstances is out of the question. I have been too cruelly used in my own country to wish to go back to it, even if I could. I propose embarking on board a private trading-vessel in these seas in a mercantile capacity, to make my way, if I can, for myself. How it will end, or what will happen to me next, is more than I can say. It matters little what becomes of me. I am a wanderer and an exile, entirely through the fault of others. The unfeeling desire at home to get rid of me has accomplished its object. I am got rid of for good.

"There is only one more sacrifice left for me to make—the sacrifice of my heart's dearest feelings. With no prospects before me, with no chance of coming home, what hope can I feel of performing my engagement to yourself? None! A more selfish man than I am might hold you to that engagement; a less considerate man than I am might keep you waiting for years—and to no purpose after all. Cruelly as they have been trampled on, my feelings are too sensitive to allow me to do this. I write it with the tears in my eyes—you shall not link your fate to an outcast. Accept these heart-broken lines as releasing you from your promise. Our engagement is at an end.

"The one consolation which supports me in bidding you farewell is, that neither of us is to blame. You may have acted weakly, under my father's influence, but I am sure you acted for the best. Nobody knew what the fatal consequences of driving me out of England would be but myself—and I was not listened to. I yielded to my father, I yielded to you; and this is the end of it!

"I am suffering too acutely to write more. May you never know what my withdrawal from our engagement has cost me! I beg you will not blame yourself. It is not your fault that I have had all my energies misdirected by others—it is not your fault that I have never had a fair chance of getting on in life. Forget the deserted wretch who breathes his heartfelt prayers for your happiness, and who will ever remain your friend and well-wisher.

"FRANCIS CLARE, Jun."

VI.

From Francis Clare, Sen., to Magdalen.

[Inclosing the preceding Letter.]

"I always told your poor father my son was a Fool, but I never knew he was a Scoundrel until the mail came in from China. I have every reason to believe that he has left his employers under the most disgraceful circumstances. Forget him from this time forth, as I do. When you and I last set eyes on each other, you behaved well to me in this business. All I can now say in return, I do say. My girl, I am sorry for you,

"F. C."

VII.

From Mrs. Wragge to her Husband.

"Dear sir for mercy's sake come here and help us She had a dreadful letter I don't know what yesterday but she read it in bed and when I went in with her breakfast I found her dead and if the doctor had not been two doors off nobody else could have brought her to life again and she sits and looks dreadful and won't speak a word her eyes frighten me so I shake from head to foot oh please do come I keep things as tidy as I can and I do like her so and she used to be so kind to me and the landlord says he's afraid she'll destroy herself I wish I could write straight but I do shake so your dutiful wife matilda wragge excuse faults and beg you on my knees come and help us the Doctor good man will put some of his own writing into this for fear you can't make out mine and remain once more your dutiful wife matilda wragge."

Added by the Doctor.

"SIR—I beg to inform you that I was yesterday called into a neighbor's in Vauxhall Walk to attend a young lady who had been suddenly taken ill. I recovered her with great difficulty from one of the most obstinate fainting-fits I ever remember to have met with. Since that time she has had no relapse, but there is apparently some heavy distress weighing on her mind which it has hitherto been found impossible to remove. She sits, as I am informed, perfectly silent, and perfectly unconscious of what goes on about her, for hours together, with a letter in her hand which she will allow nobody to take from her. If this state of depression continues, very distressing mental consequences may follow; and I only do my duty in suggesting that some relative or friend should interfere who has influence enough to rouse her. Your obedient servant,

"RICHARD JARVIS, M.R.C.S."

VIII.

From Norah to Magdalen.

"July 5th.

"For God's sake, write me one line to say if you are still at Birmingham, and where I can find you there! I have just heard from old Mr. Clare. Oh, Magdalen, if you have no pity on yourself, have some pity on me! The thought of you alone among strangers, the thought of you heart-broken under this dreadful blow, never leaves me for an instant. No words can tell how I feel for you! My own love, remember the better days at home before that cowardly villain stole his way into your heart; remember the happy time at Combe-Raven when we were always together. Oh, don't, don't treat me like a stranger! We are alone in the world now—let me come and comfort you, let me be more than a sister to you, if I can. One line—only one line to tell me where I can find you!"

IX.

From Magdalen to Norah.

"July 7th.

"MY DEAREST NORAH—All that your love for me can wish your letter has done. You, and you alone, have found your way to my heart. I could think again, I could feel again, after reading what you have written to me. Let this assurance quiet your anxieties. My mind lives and breathes once more—it was dead until I got your letter.

"The shock I have suffered has left a strange quietness in me. I feel as if I had parted from my former self—as if the hopes once so dear to me had all gone back to some past time from which I am now far removed. I can look at the wreck of my life more calmly, Norah, than you could look at it if we were both together again. I can trust myself already to write to Frank.

"My darling, I think no woman ever knows how utterly she has given herself up to the man she loves—until that man has ill-treated her. Can you pity my weakness if I confess to having felt a pang at my heart when I read that part of your letter which calls Frank a coward and a villain? Nobody can despise me for this as I despise myself. I am like a dog who crawls back and licks the master's hand that has beaten him. But it is so—I would confess it to nobody but you—indeed, indeed it is so. He has deceived and deserted me; he has written me a cruel farewell —but don't call him a villain! If he repented and came back to me, I would die rather than marry him now—but it grates on me to see that word coward written against him in your hand! If he is weak of purpose, who tried his weakness beyond what it could bear? Do you think this would have happened if Michael Vanstone had not robbed us of our own, and forced Frank away from me to China? In a week from to-day the year of waiting would have come to an end, and I should have been Frank's wife, if my marriage portion had not been taken from me.

"You will say, after what has happened, it is well that I have escaped. My love! there is something perverse in my heart which answers, No! Better have been Frank's wretched wife than the free woman I am now.

"I have not written to him. He sends me no address at which I could write, even if I would. But I have not the wish. I will wait before I send him my farewell. If a day ever comes when I have the fortune which my father once promised I should bring to him, do you know what I would do with it? I would send it all to Frank, as my revenge on him for his letter; as the last farewell word on my side to the man who has deserted me. Let me live for that day! Let me live, Norah, in the hope of better times for you, which is all the hope I have left. When I think of your hard life, I can almost feel the tears once more in my weary eyes. I can almost think I have come back again to my former self.

"You will not think me hard-hearted and ungrateful if I say that we must wait a little yet before we meet. I want to be more fit to see you than I am now. I want to put Frank further away from me, and to bring you nearer still. Are these good reasons? I don't know—don't ask me for reasons. Take the kiss I have put for you here, where the little circle is drawn on the paper; and let that bring us together for the present till I write again. Good-by, my love. My heart is true to you, Norah, but I dare not see you yet.

"MAGDALEN."

X.

From Magdalen to Miss Garth.

"MY DEAR MISS GARTH—I have been long in answering your letter; but you know what has happened, and you will forgive me.

"All that I have to say may be said in a few words. You may depend on my never making the general Sense of Propriety my enemy again: I am getting knowledge enough of the world to make it my accomplice next time. Norah will never leave another situation on my account—my life as a public performer is at an end. It was harmless enough, God knows—I may live, and so may you, to mourn the day when I parted from it—but I shall never return to it again. It has left me, as Frank has left me, as all my better thoughts have left me except my thoughts of Norah.

"Enough of myself! Shall I tell you some news to brighten this dull letter? Mr. Michael

Vanstone is dead, and Mr. Noel Vanstone has succeeded to the possession of my fortune and Norah's. He is quite worthy of his inheritance. In his father's place, he would have ruined us as his father did.

"I have no more to say that you would care to know. Don't be distressed about me. I am trying to recover my spirits—I am trying to forget the poor deluded girl who was foolish enough to be fond of Frank in the old days at Combe-Raven. Sometimes a pang comes which tells me the girl won't be forgotten—but not often.

"It was very kind of you, when you wrote to such a lost creature as I am, to sign yourself—always my friend. 'Always' is a bold word, my dear old governess! I wonder whether you will ever want to recall it? It will make no difference if you do, in the gratitude I shall always feel for the trouble you took with me when I was a little girl. I have ill repaid that trouble—ill repaid your kindness to me in after life. I ask your pardon and your pity. The best thing you can do for both of us is to forget me. Affectionately yours,

"MAGDALEN."

"P.S.—I open the envelope to add one line. For God's sake, don't show this letter to Norah!"

XI.

From Magdalen to Captain Wragge.

"Vauxhall Walk, July 17th.

"If I am not mistaken, it was arranged that I should write to you at Birmingham as soon as I felt myself composed enough to think of the future. My mind is settled at last, and I am now able to accept the services which you have so unreservedly offered to me.

"I beg you will forgive the manner in which I received you on your arrival in this house, after hearing the news of my sudden illness. I was quite incapable of controlling myself—I was suffering an agony of mind which for the time deprived me of my senses. It is only your due that I should now thank you for treating me with great forbearance at a time when forbearance was mercy.

"I will mention what I wish you to do as plainly and briefly as I can.

"In the first place, I request you to dispose (as privately as possible) of every article of costume used in the dramatic Entertainment. I have done with our performances forever; and I wish to be set free from everything which might accidentally connect me with them in the future. The key of my box is inclosed in this letter.

"The other box, which contains my own dresses, you will be kind enough to forward to this house. I do not ask you to bring it yourself, because I have a far more important commission to intrust to you.

"Referring to the note which you left for me at your departure, I conclude that you have by this time traced Mr. Noel Vanstone from Vauxhall Walk to the residence which he is now occupying. If you have made the discovery—and if you are quite sure of not having drawn the attention either of Mrs. Lecount or her master to yourself—I wish you to arrange immediately for my residing (with you and Mrs. Wragge) in the same town or village in which Mr. Noel Vanstone has taken up his abode. I write this, it is hardly necessary to say, under the impression that, wherever he may now be living, he is settled in the place for some little time.

"If you can find a small furnished house for me on these conditions which is to be let by the month, take it for a month certain to begin with. Say that it is for your wife, your niece, and yourself, and use any assumed name you please, as long as it is a name that can be trusted to defeat the most suspicious inquiries. I leave this to your experience in such matters. The secret of who we really are must be kept as strictly as if it was a secret on which our lives depend.

"Any expenses to which you may be put in carrying out my wishes I will immediately repay. If you easily find the sort of house I want, there is no need for your returning to London to fetch us. We can join you as soon as we know where to go. The house must be perfectly respectable, and must be reasonably near to Mr. Noel Vanstone's present residence, wherever that is.

"You must allow me to be silent in this letter as to the object which I have now in view. I am unwilling to risk an explanation in writing. When all our preparations are made, you shall hear what I propose to do from my own lips; and I shall expect you to tell me plainly, in return, whether you will or will not give me the help I want on the best terms which I am able to offer you.

"One word more before I seal up this letter.

"If any opportunity falls in your way after you have taken the house, and before we join you, of exchanging a few civil words either with Mr. Noel Vanstone or Mrs. Lecount, take advantage of it. It is very important to my present object that we should become acquainted with each other—as the purely accidental result of our being near neighbors. I want you to smooth the way toward this end if you can, before Mrs. Wragge and I come to you. Pray throw away no chance of observing Mrs. Lecount, in particular, very carefully. Whatever help you can give me at the outset in blindfolding that woman's sharp eyes will be the most precious help I have ever received at your hands.

"There is no need to answer this letter immediately—unless I have written it under a mistaken impression of what you have accomplished since leaving London. I have taken our lodgings on for another week; and I can wait to hear from you until you are able to send me such news as I wish to receive. You may be quite sure of my patience for the future, under all possible circumstances. My caprices are at an end, and my violent temper has tried your forbearance for the last time.

"MAGDALEN."

XII.

From Captain Wragge to Magdalen.

"North Shingles Villa, Aldborough, Suffolk, July 22d.

"MY DEAR GIRL—Your letter has charmed and touched me. Your excuses have gone straight to my heart; and your confidence in my humble abilities has followed in the same direction. The pulse of the old militia-man throbs with pride as he thinks of the trust you have placed in him, and vows to deserve it. Don't be surprised at this genial outburst. All enthusiastic natures must explode occasionally; and my form of explosion is—Words.

"Everything you wanted me to do is done. The house is taken; the name is found; and

I am personally acquainted with Mrs. Lecount. After reading this general statement, you will naturally be interested in possessing your mind next of the accompanying details. Here they are, at your service:

"The day after leaving you in London, I traced Mr. Noel Vanstone to this curious little seaside snuggery. One of his father's innumerable bargains was a house at Aldborough—a rising watering-place, or Mr. Michael Vanstone would not have invested a farthing in it. In this house the despicable little miser, who lived rent free in London, now lives, rent free again, on the coast of Suffolk. He is settled in his present abode for the summer and autumn; and you and Mrs. Wragge have only to join me here, to be established five doors away from him in this elegant villa. I have got the whole house for three guineas a week, with the option of remaining through the autumn at the same price. In a fashionable watering-place, such a residence would have been cheap at double the money.

"Our new name has been chosen with a wary eye to your suggestions. My books—I hope you have not forgotten my Books?—contain, under the heading of Skins To Jump Into, a list of individuals retired from this mortal scene, with whose names, families, and circumstances I am well acquainted. Into some of those Skins I have been compelled to Jump, in the exercise of my profession, at former periods of my career. Others are still in the condition of new dresses and remain to be tried on. The Skin which will exactly fit us originally clothed the bodies of a family named Bygrave. I am in Mr. Bygrave's skin at this moment-and it fits without a wrinkle. If you will oblige me by slipping into Miss Bygrave (Christian name, Susan); and if you will afterward push Mrs. Wragge—anyhow; head foremost if you like—into Mrs. Bygrave (Christian name, Julia), the transformation will be complete. Permit me to inform you that I am your paternal uncle. My worthy brother was established twenty years ago in the mahogany and logwood trade at Belize, Honduras. He died in that place; and is buried on the south-west side of the local cemetery, with a neat monument of native wood carved by a self-taught negro artist. Nineteen months afterward his widow died of apoplexy at a boarding-house in Cheltenham. She was supposed to be the most corpulent woman in England, and was accommodated on the ground-floor of the house in consequence of the difficulty of getting her up and down stairs. You are her only child; you have been under my care since the sad event at Cheltenham; you are twenty-one years old on the second of August next; and, corpulence excepted, you are the living image of your mother. I trouble you with these specimens of my intimate knowledge of our new family Skin, to quiet your mind on the subject of future inquiries. Trust to me and my books to satisfy any amount of inquiry. In the meantime write down our new name and address, and see how they strike you: 'Mr. Bygrave, Mrs. Bygrave, Miss Bygrave; North Shingles Villa, Aldborough.' Upon my life, it reads remarkably well!

"The last detail I have to communicate refers to my acquaintance with Mrs. Lecount.

"We met yesterday, in the grocer's shop here. Keeping my ears open, I found that Mrs. Lecount wanted a particular kind of tea which the man had not got, and which he believed could not be procured any nearer than Ipswich. I instantly saw my way to beginning an acquaintance, at the trifling expense of a journey to that flourishing city. 'I have business to-day in Ipswich,' I said, 'and I propose returning to Aldborough (if I can get back in time) this evening. Pray allow me to take your order for the tea, and to bring it back with my own parcels.' Mrs. Lecount politely declined giving me the trouble—I politely insisted on taking it. We fell into conversation. There is no need to trouble you with our talk. The result of it on my mind is—that Mrs. Lecount's one weak point, if she has such a thing at all, is a taste for science, implanted by her deceased husband, the professor. I think I see a chance here of working my way into her good graces, and casting a little needful dust into those handsome black eyes of hers. Acting on this idea when I purchased the lady's tea at Ipswich, I also bought on my own account that far-famed pocket-manual of knowledge, 'Joyce's Scientific Dialogues.' Possessing, as I do, a quick memory and boundless confidence in myself, I propose privately inflating my new skin with as much ready-made science as it will hold, and presenting Mr. Bygrave to Mrs. Lecount's notice in the character of the most highly informed man she has met with since the professor's death. The necessity of blindfolding that woman (to use your own admirable expression) is as clear to me as to you. If it is to be done in the way I propose, make your mind easy—Wragge, inflated by Joyce, is the man to do it.

"You now have my whole budget of news. Am I, or am I not, worthy of your confidence in me? I say nothing of my devouring anxiety to know what your objects really are—that anxiety will be satisfied when we meet. Never yet, my dear girl, did I long to administer a productive pecuniary Squeeze to any human creature, as I long to administer it to Mr. Noel Vanstone. I say no more. Verbum sap. Pardon the pedantry of a Latin quotation, and believe me,

"Entirely yours,

"HORATIO WRAGGE.

"P.S.—I await my instructions, as you requested. You have only to say whether I shall return to London for the purpose of escorting you to this place, or whether I shall wait here to receive you. The house is in perfect order, the weather is charming, and the sea is as smooth as Mrs. Lecount's apron. She has just passed the window, and we have exchanged bows. A sharp woman, my dear Magdalen; but Joyce and I together may prove a trifle too much for her."

XIII.

Extract from the "East Suffolk Argus."

"ALDBOROUGH.—We notice with pleasure the arrival of visitors to this healthful and far-famed watering-place earlier in the season than usual during the present year. Esto Perpetua is all we have to say.

"VISITORS' LIST.—Arrivals since our last. North Shingles Villa—Mrs. Bygrave; Miss Bygrave."

THE FOURTH SCENE.

ALDBOROUGH, SUFFOLK.

CHAPTER I.

THE most striking spectacle presented to a stranger by the shores of Suffolk is the extraordinary defenselessness of the land against the encroachments of the sea.

At Aldborough, as elsewhere on this coast, local traditions are, for the most part, traditions which have been literally drowned. The site of the old town, once a populous and thriving port, has almost entirely disappeared in the sea. The German Ocean has swallowed up streets, market-places, jetties, and public walks; and the merciless waters, consummating their work of devastation, closed, no longer than eighty years since, over the salt-master's cottage at Aldborough, now famous in memory only as the birthplace of the poet CRABBE.

Thrust back year after year by the advancing waves, the inhabitants have receded, in the present century, to the last morsel of land which is firm enough to be built on—a strip of ground hemmed in between a marsh on one side and the sea on the other. Here, trusting for their future security to certain sand-hills which the capricious waves have thrown up to encourage them, the people of Aldborough have boldly established their quaint little watering-place. The first fragment of their earthly possessions is a low natural dike of shingle, surmounted by a public path which runs parallel with the sea. Bordering this path, in a broken, uneven line, are the villa residences of modern Aldborough—fanciful little houses, standing mostly in their own gardens, and possessing here and there, as horticultural ornaments, staring figure-heads of ships doing duty for statues among the flowers. Viewed from the low level on which these villas stand, the sea, in certain conditions of the atmosphere, appears to be higher than the land: coasting-vessels gliding by assume gigantic proportions, and look alarmingly near the windows. Intermixed with the houses of the better sort are buildings of other forms and periods. In one direction the tiny Gothic town-hall of old Aldborough—once the center of the vanished port and borough—now stands, fronting the modern villas close on the margin of the sea. At another point, a wooden tower of observation, crowned by the figure-head of a wrecked Russian vessel, rises high above the neighboring houses, and discloses through its scuttle-window grave men in dark clothing seated on the topmost story, perpetually on the watch—the pilots of Aldborough looking out from their tower for ships in want of help. Behind the row of buildings thus curiously intermingled runs the one straggling street of the town, with its sturdy pilots' cottages, its mouldering marine store-houses, and its composite shops. Toward the northern end this street is bounded by the one eminence visible over all the marshy flat—a low wooded hill, on which the church is built. At its opposite extremity the street leads to a deserted martello tower, and to the forlorn outlying suburb of Slaughden, between the river Alde and the sea. Such are the main characteristics of this curious little outpost on the shores of England as it appears at the present time.

On a hot and cloudy July afternoon, and on the second day which had elapsed since he had written to Magdalen, Captain Wragge sauntered through the gate of North Shingles Villa to meet the arrival of the coach, which then connected Aldborough with the Eastern Counties Railway. He reached the principal inn as the coach drove up, and was ready at the door to receive Magdalen and Mrs. Wragge, on their leaving the vehicle.

The captain's reception of his wife was not characterized by an instant's unnecessary waste of time. He looked distrustfully at her shoes—raised himself on tiptoe—set her bonnet straight for her with a sharp tug—-said, in a loud whisper, "hold your tongue"—and left her, for the time being, without further notice. His welcome to Magdalen, beginning with the usual flow of words, stopped suddenly in the middle of the first sentence. Captain Wragge's eye was a sharp one, and it instantly showed him something in the look and manner of his old pupil which denoted a serious change.

There was a settled composure on her face which, except when she spoke, made it look as still and cold as marble. Her voice was softer and more equable, her eyes were steadier, her step was slower than of old. When she smiled, the smile came and went suddenly, and showed a little nervous contraction on one side of her mouth never visible there before. She was perfectly patient with Mrs. Wragge; she treated the captain with a courtesy and consideration entirely new in his experience of her—but she was interested in nothing. The curious little shops in the back street; the high impending sea; the old town-hall on the beach; the pilots, the fishermen, the passing ships—she noticed all these objects as indifferently as if Aldborough had been familiar to her from her infancy. Even when the captain drew up at the garden-gate of North Shingles, and introduced her triumphantly to the new house, she hardly looked at it. The first question she asked related not to her own residence, but to Noel Vanstone's.

"How near to us does he live?" she inquired, with the only betrayal of emotion which had escaped her yet.

Captain Wragge answered by pointing to the fifth villa from North Shingles, on the Slaughden side of Aldborough. Magdalen suddenly drew back from the garden-gate as he indicated the situation, and walked away by herself to obtain a nearer view of the house. Captain Wragge looked after her, and shook his head, discontentedly.

"May I speak now?" inquired a meek voice behind him, articulating respectfully ten inches above the top of his straw hat.

The captain turned round, and confronted his wife. The more than ordinary bewilderment visible in her face at once suggested to him that Magdalen had failed to carry out the directions in his letter; and that Mrs. Wragge had arrived at Aldborough without being properly aware of the total transformation to be accomplished in her identity and her name. The necessity of setting this doubt at rest was too serious to be trifled with; and Captain Wragge instituted the necessary inquiries without a moment's delay.

"Stand straight, and listen to me," he began. "I have a question to ask you. Do you know whose Skin you are in at this moment? Do you know that you are dead and buried in London; and that you have risen like a phoenix from the ashes of Mrs. Wragge? No! you evidently don't know it. This is perfectly disgraceful. What is your name?"

"Matilda," answered Mrs. Wragge, in a state of the densest bewilderment.

"Nothing of the sort!" cried the captain, fiercely. "How dare you tell me your name's Matilda? Your name is Julia. Who am I?—Hold that basket of sandwiches straight, or I'll pitch it into the sea!—Who am I?"

"I don't know," said Mrs. Wragge, meekly taking refuge in the negative side of the question this time.

"Sit down!" said her husband, pointing to the low garden wall of North Shingles Villa. "More to the right! More still! That will do. You don't know?" repeated the captain, sternly confronting his wife as soon as he had contrived, by seating her, to place her face on a level with his own. "Don't let me hear you say that a second time. Don't let me have a woman who doesn't know who I am to operate on my beard to-morrow morning. Look at me! More to the left—more still—that will do. Who am I? I'm Mr. Bygrave—Christian name, Thomas. Who are you? You're Mrs. Bygrave—Christian name, Julia. Who is that young lady who traveled with you from London? That young lady is Miss Bygrave—Christian name, Susan. I'm her clever uncle Tom; and you're her addle-headed aunt Julia. Say it all over to me instantly, like the Catechism! What is your name?"

"Spare my poor head!" pleaded Mrs. Wragge. "Oh, please spare my poor head till I've got the stage-coach out of it!"

"Don't distress her," said Magdalen, joining them at that moment. "She will learn it in time. Come into the house."

Captain Wragge shook his wary head once more. "We are beginning badly," he said, with less politeness than usual. "My wife's stupidity stands in our way already."

They went into the house. Magdalen was perfectly satisfied with all the captain's arrangements; she accepted the room which he had set apart for her; approved of the woman servant whom he had engaged; presented herself at tea-time the moment she was summoned but still showed no interest whatever in the new scene around her. Soon after the table was cleared, although the daylight had not yet faded out, Mrs. Wragge's customary drowsiness after fatigue of any kind overcame her, and she received her husband's orders to leave the room (taking care that she left it "up at heel"), and to betake herself (strictly in the character of Mrs. Bygrave) to bed. As soon as they were left alone, the captain looked hard at Magdalen, and waited to be spoken to. She said nothing. He ventured next on opening the conversation by a polite inquiry after the state of her health. "You look fatigued," he remarked, in his most insinuating manner. "I am afraid the journey has been too much for you."

"No," she said, looking out listlessly through the window; "I am not more tired than usual. I am always weary now; weary at going to bed, weary at getting up. If you would like to hear what I have to say to you to-night, I am willing and ready to say it. Can't we go out? It is very hot here; and the droning of those men's voices is beyond all endurance." She pointed through the window to a group of boatmen idling, as only nautical men can idle, against the garden wall. "Is there no quiet walk in this wretched place?" she asked, impatiently. "Can't we breathe a little fresh air, and escape being annoyed by strangers?"

"There is perfect solitude within half an hour's walk of the house," replied the ready captain.

"Very well. Come out, then."

With a weary sigh she took up her straw bonnet and her light muslin scarf from the side-table upon which she had thrown them on coming in, and carelessly led the way to the door.

Captain Wragge followed her to the garden gate, then stopped, struck by a new idea.

"Excuse me," he whispered, confidentially. "In my wife's existing state of ignorance as to who she is, we had better not trust her alone in the house with a new servant. I'll privately turn the key on her, in case she wakes before we come back. Safe bind, safe find—you know the proverb!—I will be with you again in a moment."

He hastened back to the house, and Magdalen seated herself on the garden wall to await his return.

She had hardly settled herself in that position when two gentlemen walking together, whose approach along the public path she had not previously noticed, passed close by her.

The dress of one of the two strangers showed him to be a clergyman. His companion's station in life was less easily discernible to ordinary observation. Practiced eyes would probably have seen enough in his look, his manner, and his walk to show that he was a sailor. He was a man in the prime of life; tall, spare, and muscular; his face sun-burned to a deep brown; his black hair just turning gray; his eyes dark, deep and firm—the eyes of a man with an iron resolution and a habit of command. He was the nearest of the two to Magdalen, as he and his friend passed the place where she was sitting; and he looked at her with a sudden surprise at her beauty, with an open, hearty, undisguised admiration, which was too evidently sincere, too evidently beyond his own control, to be justly resented as insolent; and yet, in her humor at that moment, Magdalen did resent it. She felt the man's resolute black eyes strike through her with an electric suddenness; and frowning at him impatiently, she turned away her head and looked back at the house.

The next moment she glanced round again to see if he had gone on. He had advanced a few yards—had then evidently stopped—and was now in the very act of turning to look at her once more. His companion, the clergyman, noticing that Magdalen appeared to be annoyed, took him familiarly by the arm, and, half in jest, half in earnest, forced him to walk on. The two disappeared round the corner of the next house. As they turned it, the sun-burned sailor twice stopped his companion again, and twice looked back.

"A friend of yours?" inquired Captain Wragge, joining Magdalen at that moment.

"Certainly not," she replied; "a perfect stranger. He stared at me in the most impertinent manner. Does he belong to this place?"

"I'll find out in a moment," said the compliant captain, joining the group of boatmen, and putting his questions right and left, with the easy familiarity which distinguished him. He returned in a few minutes with a complete budget of information. The clergyman was well known as the rector of a place situated some few miles inland. The dark man with him was his wife's brother, commander of a ship in the merchant-service. He was supposed to be staying with his relatives, as their guest for a short time only, preparatory to sailing on another voyage. The clergyman's name was Strickland, and the merchant-captain's name was Kirke; and that was all the boatmen knew about either of them.

"It is of no consequence who they are," said Magdalen, carelessly. "The man's rudeness merely annoyed me for the moment. Let us have done with him. I have something else to think of, and so have you. Where is the solitary walk you mentioned just now? Which way do we go?"

The captain pointed southward toward Slaughden, and offered his arm.

Magdalen hesitated before she took it. Her eyes wandered away inquiringly to Noel Vanstone's house. He was out in the garden, pacing backward and forward over the little lawn, with his head high in the air, and with Mrs. Lecount demurely in attendance on him, carrying her master's green fan. Seeing this, Magdalen at once took Captain Wragge's right arm, so as to place herself nearest to the garden when they passed it on their walk.

"The eyes of our neighbors are on us; and the least your niece can do is to take your arm," she said, with a bitter laugh. "Come! let us go on."

"They are looking this way," whispered the captain. "Shall I introduce you to Mrs. Lecount?"

"Not to-night," she answered. "Wait, and hear what I have to say to you first."

They passed the garden wall. Captain Wragge took off his hat with a smart flourish, and received a gracious bow from Mrs. Lecount in return. Magdalen saw the housekeeper survey her face, her figure, and her dress, with that reluctant interest, that distrustful curiosity, which women feel in observing each other. As she walked on beyond the house, the sharp voice of Noel Vanstone reached her through the evening stillness. "A fine girl, Lecount," she heard him say. "You know I am a judge of that sort of thing—a fine girl!"

As those words were spoken, Captain Wragge looked round at his companion in sudden surprise. Her hand was trembling violently on his arm, and her lips were fast closed with an expression of speechless pain.

Slowly and in silence the two walked on until they reached the southern limit of the houses, and entered on a little wilderness of shingle and withered grass—the desolate end of Aldborough, the lonely beginning of Slaughden.

It was a dull, airless evening. Eastward, was the gray majesty of the sea, hushed in breathless calm; the horizon line invisibly melting into the monotonous, misty sky; the idle ships shadowy and still on the idle water. Southward, the high ridge of the sea dike, and the grim, massive circle of a martello tower reared high on its mound of grass, closed the view darkly on all that lay beyond. Westward, a lurid streak of sunset glowed red in the dreary heaven, blackened the fringing trees on the far borders of the great inland marsh, and turned its little gleaming water-pools to pools of blood. Nearer to the eye, the sullen flow of the tidal river Alde ebbed noiselessly from the muddy banks; and nearer still, lonely and unprosperous by the bleak water-side, lay the lost little port of Slaughden, with its forlorn wharfs and warehouses of decaying wood, and its few scattered coasting-vessels deserted on the oozy river-shore. No fall of waves was heard on the beach, no trickling of waters bubbled audibly from the idle stream. Now and then the cry of a sea-bird rose from the region of the marsh; and at intervals, from farmhouses far in the inland waste, the faint winding of horns to call the cattle home traveled mournfully through the evening calm.

Magdalen drew her hand from the captain's arm, and led the way to the mound of the martello tower. "I am weary of walking," she said. "Let us stop and rest here."

She seated herself on the slope, and resting on her elbow, mechanically pulled up and scattered from her into the air the tufts of grass growing under her hand. After silently occupying herself in this way for some minutes, she turned suddenly on Captain Wragge. "Do

I surprise you?" she asked, with a startling abruptness. "Do you find me changed?"

The captain's ready tact warned him that the time had come to be plain with her, and to reserve his flowers of speech for a more appropriate occasion.

"If you ask the question, I must answer it," he replied. "Yes, I do find you changed."

She pulled up another tuft of grass. "I suppose you can guess the reason?" she said.

The captain was wisely silent. He only answered by a bow.

"I have lost all care for myself," she went on, tearing faster and faster at the tufts of grass. "Saying that is not saying much, perhaps, but it may help you to understand me. There are things I would have died sooner than do at one time—things it would have turned me cold to think of. I don't care now whether I do them or not. I am nothing to myself; I am no more interested in myself than I am in these handfuls of grass. I suppose I have lost something. What is it? Heart? Conscience? I don't know. Do you? What nonsense I am talking! Who cares what I have lost? It has gone; and there's an end of it. I suppose my outside is the best side of me—and that's left, at any rate. I have not lost my good looks, have I? There! there! never mind answering; don't trouble yourself to pay me compliments. I have been admired enough to-day. First the sailor, and then Mr. Noel Vanstone—enough for any woman's vanity, surely! Have I any right to call myself a woman? Perhaps not: I am only a girl in my teens. Oh, me, I feel as if I was forty!" She scattered the last fragments of grass to the winds; and turning her back on the captain, let her head droop till her cheek touched the turf bank. "It feels soft and friendly," she said, nestling to it with a hopeless tenderness horrible to see. "It doesn't cast me off. Mother Earth! The only mother I have left!"

Captain Wragge looked at her in silent surprise. Such experience of humanity as he possessed was powerless to sound to its depths the terrible self-abandonment which had burst its way to the surface in her reckless words—which was now fast hurrying her to actions more reckless still. "Devilish odd!" he thought to himself, uneasily. "Has the loss of her lover turned her brain?" He considered for a minute longer and then spoke to her. "Leave it till to-morrow," suggested the captain confidentially. "You are a little tired to-night. No hurry, my dear girl—no hurry."

She raised her head instantly, and looked round at him with the same angry resolution, with the same desperate defiance of herself, which he had seen in her face on the memorable day at York when she had acted before him for the first time. "I came here to tell you what is in my mind," she said; "and I will tell it!" She seated herself upright on the slope; and clasping her hands round her knees, looked out steadily, straight before her, at the slowly darkening view. In that strange position, she waited until she had composed herself, and then addressed the captain, without turning her head to look round at him, in these words:

"When you and I first met," she began, abruptly, "I tried hard to keep my thoughts to myself. I know enough by this time to know that I failed. When I first told you at York that Michael Vanstone had ruined us, I believe you guessed for yourself that I, for one, was determined not to submit to it. Whether you guessed or not, it is so. I left my friends with that determination in my mind; and I feel it in me now stronger, ten times stronger, than ever."

"Ten times stronger than ever," echoed the captain. "Exactly so—the natural result of firmness of character."

"No—the natural result of having nothing else to think of. I had something else to think of before you found me ill in Vauxhall Walk. I have nothing else to think of now. Remember that, if you find me for the future always harping on the same string. One question first. Did you guess what I meant to do on that morning when you showed me the newspaper, and when I read the account of Michael Vanstone's death?"

"Generally," replied Captain Wragge—"I guessed, generally, that you proposed dipping your hand into his purse and taking from it (most properly) what was your own. I felt deeply hurt at the time by your not permitting me to assist you. Why is she so reserved with me? (I remarked to myself)—why is she so unreasonably reserved?"

"You shall have no reserve to complain of now," pursued Magdalen. "I tell you plainly, if events had not happened as they did, you would have assisted me. If Michael Vanstone had not died, I should have gone to Brighton, and have found my way safely to his acquaintance under an assumed name. I had money enough with me to live on respectably for many months together. I would have employed that time—I would have waited a whole year, if necessary, to destroy Mrs. Lecount's influence over him—and I would have ended by getting that influence, on my own terms, into my own hands. I had the advantage of years, the advantage of novelty, the advantage of downright desperation, all on my side, and I should have succeeded. Before the year was out—before half the year was out—you should have seen Mrs. Lecount dismissed by her master, and you should have seen me taken into the house in her place, as Michael Vanstone's adopted daughter—as the faithful friend—who had saved him from an adventuress in his old age. Girls no older than I am have tried deceptions as hopeless in appearance as mine, and have carried them through to the end. I had my story ready; I had my plans all considered; I had the weak point in that old man to attack in my way, which Mrs. Lecount had found out before me to attack in hers, and I tell you again I should have succeeded."

"I think you would," said the captain. "And what next?"

"Mr. Michael Vanstone would have changed his man of business next. You would have succeeded to the place; and those clever speculations on which he was so fond of venturing would have cost him the fortunes of which he had robbed my sister and myself. To the last farthing, Captain Wragge, as certainly as you sit there, to the last farthing! A bold conspiracy, a shocking deception—wasn't it? I don't care! Any conspiracy, any deception, is justified to my conscience by the vile law which has left us helpless. You talked of my reserve just now. Have I dropped it at last? Have I spoken out at the eleventh hour?"

The captain laid his hand solemnly on his heart, and launched himself once more on his broadest flow of language.

"You fill me with unavailing regret," he said. "If that old man had lived, what a crop I might have reaped from him! What enormous transactions in moral agriculture it might have been my privilege to carry on! Ars longa," said Captain Wragge, pathetically drifting into Latin—"vita brevis! Let us drop a tear on the lost opportunities of the past, and try what the present can do to console us. One conclusion is clear to my mind—the experiment you proposed to try with Mr. Michael Vanstone is totally hopeless, my dear girl, in the case of his son. His son is impervious to all common forms of pecuniary temptation. You may trust my solemn assurance," continued the captain, speaking with an indignant recollection of the answer to his advertisement in the Times, "when I inform you that Mr. Noel Vanstone is emphatically the meanest of mankind."

"I can trust my own experience as well," said Magdalen. "I have seen him, and spoken to him—I know him better than you do. Another disclosure, Captain Wragge, for your private ear! I sent you back certain articles of costume when they had served the purpose for which I took them to London. That purpose was to find my way to Noel Vanstone in disguise, and to judge for myself of Mrs. Lecount and her master. I gained my object; and I tell you again, I know the two people in that house yonder whom we have now to deal with better than you do."

Captain Wragge expressed the profound astonishment, and asked the innocent questions appropriate to the mental condition of a person taken completely by surprise.

"Well," he resumed, when Magdalen had briefly answered him, "and what is the result on your own mind? There must be a result, or we should not be here. You see your way? Of course, my dear girl, you see your way?"

"Yes," she said, quickly. "I see my way."

The captain drew a little nearer to her, with eager curiosity expressed in every line of his vagabond face.

"Go on," he said, in an anxious whisper; "pray go on."

She looked out thoughtfully into the gathering darkness, without answering, without appearing to have heard him. Her lips closed, and her clasped hands tightened mechanically round her knees.

"There is no disguising the fact," said Captain Wragge, warily rousing her into speaking to him. "The son is harder to deal with than the father—"

"Not in my way," she interposed, suddenly.

"Indeed!" said the captain. "Well! they say there is a short cut to everything, if we only look long enough to find it. You have looked long enough, I suppose, and the natural result has followed—you have found it."

"I have not troubled myself to look; I have found it without looking."

"The deuce you have!" cried Captain Wragge, in great perplexity. "My dear girl, is my view of your present position leading me altogether astray? As I understand it, here is Mr. Noel Vanstone in possession of your fortune and your sister's, as his father was, and determined to keep it, as his father was?"

"Yes."

"And here are you—quite helpless to get it by persuasion—quite helpless to get it by law—just as resolute in his ease as you were in his father's, to take it by stratagem in spite of him?"

"Just as resolute. Not for the sake of the fortune—mind that! For the sake of the right."

"Just so. And the means of coming at that right which were hard with the father—who was not a miser—are easy with the son, who is?"

"Perfectly easy."

"Write me down an Ass for the first time in my life!" cried the captain, at the end of his patience. "Hang me if I know what you mean!"

She looked round at him for the first time—looked him straight and steadily in the face.

"I will tell you what I mean," she said. "I mean to marry him."

Captain Wragge started up on his knees, and stopped on them, petrified by astonishment.

"Remember what I told you," said Magdalen, looking away from him again. "I have lost all care for myself. I have only one end in life now, and the sooner I reach it—and die—the better. If—" She stopped, altered her position a little, and pointed with one hand to the fast-ebbing stream beneath her, gleaming dim in the darkening twilight—"if I had been what I once was, I would have thrown myself into that river sooner than do what I am going to do now. As it is, I trouble myself no longer; I weary my mind with no more schemes. The short way and the vile way lies before me. I take it, Captain Wragge, and marry him."

"Keeping him in total ignorance of who you are?" said the captain, slowly rising to his feet, and slowly moving round, so as to see her face. "Marrying him as my niece, Miss Bygrave?"

"As your niece, Miss Bygrave."

"And after the marriage—?" His voice faltered, as he began the question, and he left it unfinished.

"After the marriage," she said, "I shall stand in no further need of your assistance."

The captain stooped as she gave him that answer, looked close at her, and suddenly drew back, without uttering a word. He walked away some paces, and sat down again doggedly on the grass. If Magdalen could have seen his face in the dying light, his face would have startled her. For the first time, probably, since his boyhood, Captain Wragge had changed color. He was deadly pale.

"Have you nothing to say to me?" she asked. "Perhaps you are waiting to hear what terms I have to offer? These are my terms; I pay all our expenses here; and when we part, on the day of the marriage, you take a farewell gift away with you of two hundred pounds. Do you promise me your assistance on those conditions?"

"What am I expected to do?" he asked, with a furtive glance at her, and a sudden distrust in his voice.

"You are expected to preserve my assumed character and your own," she answered, "and you are to prevent any inquiries of Mrs. Lecount's from discovering who I really am. I ask no more. The rest is my responsibility—not yours."

"I have nothing to do with what happens—at any time, or in any place—after the marriage?"

"Nothing whatever."

"I may leave you at the church door if I please?"

"At the church door, with your fee in your pocket."

"Paid from the money in your own possession?"

"Certainly! How else should I pay it?"

Captain Wragge took off his hat, and passed his handkerchief over his face with an air of relief.

"Give me a minute to consider it," he said.

"As many minutes as you like," she rejoined, reclining on the bank in her former position, and returning to her former occupation of tearing up the tufts of grass and flinging them out into the air.

The captain's reflections were not complicated by any unnecessary divergences from the contemplation of his own position to the contemplation of Magdalen's. Utterly incapable of appreciating the injury done her by Frank's infamous treachery to his engagement—an injury which had severed her, at one cruel blow, from the aspiration which, delusion though it was, had been the saving aspiration of her life—Captain Wragge accepted the simple fact of her despair just as he found it, and then looked straight to the consequences of the proposal which she had made to him.

In the prospect before the marriage he saw nothing more serious involved than the practice of a deception, in no important degree different—except in the end to be attained by it—from the deceptions which his vagabond life had long since accustomed him to contemplate and to carry out. In the prospect after the marriage he dimly discerned, through the ominous darkness of the future, the lurking phantoms of Terror and Crime, and the black gulfs behind them of Ruin and Death. A man of boundless audacity and resource, within his own mean limits; beyond those limits, the captain was as deferentially submissive to the majesty of the law as the most harmless man in existence; as cautious in looking after his own personal safety as the veriest coward that ever walked the earth. But one serious question now filled his mind. Could he, on the terms proposed to him, join the conspiracy against Noel Vanstone up to the point of the marriage, and then withdraw from it, without risk of involving himself in the consequences which his experience told him must certainly ensue?

Strange as it may seem, his decision in this emergency was mainly influenced by no less a person than Noel Vanstone himself. The captain might have resisted the money-offer which Magdalen had made to him—for the profits of the Entertainment had filled his pockets with more than three times two hundred pounds. But the prospect of dealing a blow in the dark at the man who had estimated his information and himself at the value of a five pound note proved too much for his caution and his self-control. On the small neutral ground of self-importance, the best men and the worst meet on the same terms. Captain Wragge's indignation, when he saw the answer to his advertisement, stooped to no retrospective estimate of his own conduct; he was as deeply offended, as sincerely angry as if he had made a perfectly honorable proposal, and had been rewarded for it by a personal insult. He had been too full of his own grievance to keep it out of his first letter to Magdalen. He had more or less forgotten himself on every subsequent occasion when Noel Vanstone's name was mentioned. And in now finally deciding the course he should take, it is not too much to say that the motive of money receded, for the first time in his life, into the second place, and the motive of malice carried the day.

"I accept the terms," said Captain Wragge, getting briskly on his legs again. "Subject, of course, to the conditions agreed on between us. We part on the wedding-day. I don't ask where you go: you don't ask where I go. From that time forth we are strangers to each other."

Magdalen rose slowly from the mound. A hopeless depression, a sullen despair, showed itself in her look and manner. She refused the captain's offered hand; and her tones, when she answered him, were so low that he could hardly hear her.

"We understand each other," she said; "and we can now go back. You may introduce me to Mrs. Lecount to-morrow."

"I must ask a few questions first," said the captain, gravely. "There are more risks to be run in this matter, and more pitfalls in our way, than you seem to suppose. I must know the whole history of your morning call on Mrs. Lecount before I put you and that woman on speaking terms with each other."

"Wait till to-morrow," she broke out impatiently. "Don't madden me by talking about it to-night."

The captain said no more. They turned their faces toward Aldborough, and walked slowly back.

By the time they reached the houses night had overtaken them. Neither moon nor stars were visible. A faint noiseless breeze blowing from the land had come with the darkness. Magdalen paused on the lonely public walk to breathe the air more freely. After a while she turned her face from the breeze and looked out toward the sea. The immeasurable silence of the calm waters, lost in the black void of night, was awful. She stood looking into the darkness, as if its mystery had no secrets for her—she advanced toward it slowly, as if it drew her by some hidden attraction into itself.

"I am going down to the sea," she said to her companion. "Wait here, and I will come back."

He lost sight of her in an instant; it was as if the night had swallowed her up. He listened, and counted her footsteps by the crashing of them on the shingle in the deep stillness. They retreated slowly, further and further away into the night. Suddenly the sound of them ceased. Had she paused on her course or had she reached one of the strips of sand left bare by the ebbing tide?

He waited, and listened anxiously. The time passed, and no sound reached him. He still listened, with a growing distrust of the darkness. Another moment, and there came a sound from the invisible shore. Far and faint from the beach below, a long cry moaned through the silence. Then all was still once more.

In sudden alarm, he stepped forward to descend to the beach, and to call to her. Before he could cross the path, footsteps rapidly advancing caught his ear. He waited an instant, and the figure of a man passed quickly along the walk between him and the sea. It was too dark to discern anything of the stranger's face; it was only possible to see that he was a tall man—as tall as that officer in the merchant-service whose name was Kirke.

The figure passed on northward, and was instantly lost to view. Captain Wragge crossed the path, and, advancing a few steps down the beach, stopped and listened again. The crash of footsteps on the shingle caught his ear once more. Slowly, as the sound had left him, that sound now came back. He called, to guide her to him. She came on till he could just see her—a shadow ascending the shingly slope, and growing out of the blackness of the night.

"You alarmed me," he whispered, nervously. "I was afraid something had happened. I heard you cry out as if you were in pain."

"Did you?" she said, carelessly. "I was in pain. It doesn't matter—it's over now."

Her hand mechanically swung something to and fro as she answered him. It was the little white silk bag which she had always kept hidden in her bosom up to this time. One of the relics which it held—one of the relics which she had not had the heart to part with before—was gone from its keeping forever. Alone, on a strange shore, she had torn from her the fondest of her virgin memories, the dearest of her virgin hopes. Alone, on a strange shore, she had taken the lock of Frank's hair from its once-treasured place, and had cast it away from her to the sea and the night.

CHAPTER II.

THE tall man who had passed Captain Wragge in the dark proceeded rapidly along the public walk, struck off across a little waste patch of ground, and entered the open door of the Aldborough Hotel. The light in the passage, falling full on his face as he passed it, proved the truth of Captain Wragge's surmise, and showed the stranger to be Mr. Kirke, of the merchant service.

Meeting the landlord in the passage, Mr. Kirke nodded to him with the familiarity of an old customer. "Have you got the paper?" he asked; "I want to look at the visitors' list."

"I have got it in my room, sir," said the landlord, leading the way into a parlor at the back of the house. "Are there any friends of yours staying here, do you think?"

Without replying, the seaman turned to the list as soon as the newspaper was placed in his hand, and ran his finger down it, name by name. The finger suddenly stopped at this line: "Sea-view Cottage; Mr. Noel Vanstone." Kirke of the merchant-service repeated the name to himself, and put down the paper thoughtfully.

"Have you found anybody you know, captain?" asked the landlord.

"I have found a name I know—a name my father used often to speak of in his time. Is this Mr. Vanstone a family man? Do you know if there is a young lady in the house?"

"I can't say, captain. My wife will be here directly; she is sure to know. It must have been some time ago, if your father knew this Mr. Vanstone?"

"It was some time ago. My father knew a subaltern officer of that name when he was with his regiment in Canada. It would be curious if the person here turned out to be the same man, and if that young lady was his daughter."

"Excuse me, captain—but the young lady seems to hang a little on your mind," said the landlord, with a pleasant smile.

Mr. Kirke looked as if the form which his host's good-humor had just taken was not quite to his mind. He returned abruptly to the subaltern officer and the regiment in Canada. "That poor fellow's story was as miserable a one as ever I heard," he said, looking back again absently at the visitors' list.

"Would there be any harm in telling it, sir?" asked the landlord. "Miserable or not, a story's a story, when you know it to be true."

Mr. Kirke hesitated. "I hardly think I should be doing right to tell it," he said. "If this man, or any relations of his, are still alive, it is not a story they might like strangers to know. All I can tell you is, that my father was the salvation of that young officer under very dreadful circumstances. They parted in Canada. My father remained with his regiment; the young officer sold out and returned to England, and from that moment they lost sight of each other. It would be curious if this Vanstone here was the same man. It would be curious—"

He suddenly checked himself just as another reference to "the young lady" was on the point of passing his lips. At the same moment the landlord's wife came in, and Mr. Kirke at once transferred his inquiries to the higher authority in the house.

"Do you know anything of this Mr. Vanstone who is down here on the visitors' list?" asked the sailor. "Is he an old man?"

"He's a miserable little creature to look at," replied the landlady; "but he's not old, captain."

"Then he's not the man I mean. Perhaps he is the man's son? Has he got any ladies with him?"

The landlady tossed her head, and pursed up her lips disparagingly.

"He has a housekeeper with him," she said. "A middle-aged person—not one of my sort. I dare say I'm wrong—but I don't like a dressy woman in her station of life."

Mr. Kirke began to look puzzled. "I must have made some mistake about the house," he said. "Surely there's a lawn cut octagon-shape at Sea-view Cottage, and a white flag-staff in the middle of the gravel-walk?"

"That's not Sea-view, sir! It's North Shingles you're talking of. Mr. Bygrave's. His wife and his niece came here by the coach to-day. His wife's tall enough to be put in a show, and the worst-dressed woman I ever set eyes on. But Miss Bygrave is worth looking at, if I may venture to say so. She's the finest girl, to my mind, we've had at Aldborough for many a long day. I wonder who they are! Do you know the name, captain?"

"No," said Mr. Kirke, with a shade of disappointment on his dark, weather-beaten face; "I never heard the name before."

After replying in those words, he rose to take his leave. The landlord vainly invited him to drink a parting glass; the landlady vainly pressed him to stay another ten minutes and try a cup of tea. He only replied that his sister expected him, and that he must return to the parsonage immediately.

On leaving the hotel Mr. Kirke set his face westward, and walked inland along the highroad as fast as the darkness would let him.

"Bygrave?" he thought to himself. "Now I know her name, how much am I the wiser for it! If it had been Vanstone, my father's son might have had a chance of making acquaintance with her." He stopped, and looked back in the direction of Aldborough. "What a fool I am!" he burst out suddenly, striking his stick on the ground. "I was forty last birthday." He turned and went on again faster than ever—his head down; his resolute black eyes searching the darkness on the land as they had searched it many a time on the sea from the deck of his ship.

After more than an hour's walking he reached a village, with a primitive little church and parsonage nestled together in a hollow. He entered the house by the back way, and found his sister, the clergyman's wife, sitting alone over her work in the parlor.

"Where is your husband, Lizzie?" he asked, taking a chair in a corner.

"William has gone out to see a sick person. He had just time enough before he went," she added, with a smile, "to tell me about the young lady; and he declares he will never trust himself at Aldborough with you again until you are a steady, married man." She stopped, and looked at her brother more attentively than she had looked at him yet. "Robert!" she said, laying aside her work, and suddenly crossing the room to him. "You look anxious, you look distressed. William only laughed about your meeting with the young lady. Is it serious? Tell me; what is she like?"

He turned his head away at the question.

She took a stool at his feet, and persisted in looking up at him. "Is it serious, Robert?" she repeated, softly.

Kirke's weather-beaten face was accustomed to no concealments—it answered for him before he spoke a word. "Don't tell your husband till I am gone," he said, with a roughness quite new in his sister's experience of him. "I know I only deserve to be laughed at; but it hurts me, for all that."

"Hurts you?" she repeated, in astonishment.

"You can't think me half such a fool, Lizzie, as I think myself," pursued Kirke, bitterly. "A man at my age ought to know better. I didn't set eyes on her for as much as a minute altogether; and there I have been hanging about the place till after nightfall on the chance of seeing her again—skulking, I should have called it, if I had found one of my men doing what I have been doing myself. I believe I'm bewitched. She's a mere girl, Lizzie—I doubt if she's out of her teens—I'm old enough to be her father. It's all one; she stops in my mind in spite of me. I've had her face looking at me, through the pitch darkness, every step of the way to this house; and it's looking at me now—as plain as I see yours, and plainer."

He rose impatiently, and began to walk backward and forward in the room. His sister looked after him, with surprise as well as sympathy expressed in her face. From his boyhood upward she had always been accustomed to see him master of himself. Years since, in the failing fortunes of the family, he had been their example and their support. She had heard of him in the desperate emergencies of a life at sea, when hundreds of his fellow-creatures had looked to his steady self-possession for rescue from close-threatening death—and had not looked in vain. Never, in all her life before, had his sister seen the balance of that calm and equal mind lost as she saw it lost now.

"How can you talk so unreasonably about your age and yourself?" she said. "There is not a woman alive, Robert, who is good enough for you. What is her name?"

"Bygrave. Do you know it?"

"No. But I might soon make acquaintance with her. If we only had a little time before us; if I could only get to Aldborough and see her—but you are going away to-morrow; your ship sails at the end of the week."

"Thank God for that!" said Kirke, fervently.

"Are you glad to be going away?" she asked, more and more amazed at him.

"Right glad, Lizzie, for my own sake. If I ever get to my senses again, I shall find my way back to them on the deck of my ship. This girl has got between me and my thoughts already: she shan't go a step further, and get between me and my duty. I'm determined on that. Fool as I am, I have sense enough left not to trust myself within easy hail of Aldborough to-morrow morning. I'm good for another twenty miles of walking, and I'll begin my journey back tonight."

His sister started up, and caught him fast by the arm. "Robert!" she exclaimed; "you're not serious? You don't mean to leave us on foot, alone in the dark?"

"It's only saying good-by, my dear, the last thing at night instead of the first thing in the morning," he answered, with a smile. "Try and make allowances for me, Lizzie. My life has been passed at sea; and I'm not used to having my mind upset in this way. Men ashore are used to it; men ashore can take it easy. I can't. If I stopped here I shouldn't rest. If I waited till to-morrow, I should only be going back to have another look at her. I don't want to feel more ashamed of myself than I do already. I want to fight my way back to my duty and myself, without stopping to think twice about it. Darkness is nothing to me—I'm used to darkness. I have got the high-road to walk on, and I can't lose my way. Let me go, Lizzie! The only sweetheart I have any business with at my age is my ship. Let me get back to her!"

His sister still kept her hold of his arm, and still pleaded with him to stay till the morning. He listened to her with perfect patience and kindness, but she never shook his determination for an instant.

"What am I to say to William?" she pleaded. "What will he think when he comes back and finds you gone?"

"Tell him I have taken the advice he gave us in his sermon last Sunday. Say I have turned my back on the world, the flesh, and the devil."

"How can you talk so, Robert! And the boys, too—you promised not to go without bidding the boys good-by."

"That's true. I made my little nephews a promise, and I'll keep it." He kicked off his shoes as he spoke, on the mat outside the door. "Light me upstairs, Lizzie; I'll bid the two boys good-by without waking them."

She saw the uselessness of resisting him any longer; and, taking the candle, went before him upstairs.

The boys—both young children—were sleeping together in the same bed. The youngest was his uncle's favorite, and was called by his uncle's name. He lay peacefully asleep, with a rough little toy ship hugged fast in his arms. Kirke's eyes softened as he stole on tiptoe to the child's side, and kissed him with the gentleness of a woman. "Poor little man!" said the sailor, tenderly. "He is as fond of his ship as I was at his age. I'll cut him out a better one when I come back. Will you give me my nephew one of these days, Lizzie, and will you let me make a sailor of him?"

"Oh, Robert, if you were only married and happy, as I am!"

"The time has gone by, my dear. I must make the best of it as I am, with my little nephew there to help me."

He left the room. His sister's tears fell fast as she followed him into the parlor. "There is something so forlorn and dreadful in your leaving us like this," she said. "Shall I go to Aldborough to-morrow, Robert, and try if I can get acquainted with her for your sake?"

"No!" he replied. "Let her be. If it's ordered that I am to see that girl again, I shall see her. Leave it to the future, and you leave it right." He put on his shoes, and took up his hat and stick. "I won't overwalk myself," he said, cheerfully. "If the coach doesn't overtake me on the road, I can wait for it where I stop to breakfast. Dry your eyes, my dear, and give me a kiss."

She was like her brother in features and complexion, and she had a touch of her brother's spirit; she dashed away the tears, and took her leave of him bravely.

"I shall be back in a year's time," said Kirke, falling into his old sailor-like way at the door. "I'll bring you a China shawl, Lizzie, and a chest of tea for your store-room. Don't let the boys forget me, and don't think I'm doing wrong to leave you in this way. I know I am doing right. God bless you and keep you, my dear—and your husband, and your children! Good-by!"

He stooped and kissed her. She ran to the door to look after him. A puff of air extinguished the candle, and the black night shut him out from her in an instant.

Three days afterward the first-class merchantman Deliverance, Kirke, commander, sailed from London for the China Sea.

CHAPTER III.

THE threatening of storm and change passed away with the night. When morning rose over Aldborough, the sun was master in the blue heaven, and the waves were rippling gayly under the summer breeze.

At an hour when no other visitors to the watering—place were yet astir, the indefatigable Wragge appeared at the door of North Shingles Villa, and directed his steps northward, with a neatly-bound copy of "Joyce's Scientific Dialogues" in his hand. Arriving at the waste ground beyond the houses, he descended to the beach and opened his book. The interview of the past night had sharpened his perception of the difficulties to be encountered in the coming enterprise. He was now doubly determined to try the characteristic experiment at which he had hinted in his letter to Magdalen, and to concentrate on himself—in the character of a remarkably well-informed man—the entire interest and attention of the formidable Mrs. Lecount.

Having taken his dose of ready-made science (to use his own expression) the first thing in the morning on an empty stomach, Captain Wragge joined his small family circle at breakfast-time, inflated with information for the day. He observed that Magdalen's face showed plain signs of a sleepless night. She made no complaint: her manner was composed, and her temper perfectly under control. Mrs. Wragge—refreshed by some thirteen consecutive hours of uninterrupted repose—was in excellent spirits, and up at heel (for a wonder) with both shoes. She brought with her into the room several large sheets of tissue-paper, cut crisply into mysterious and many-varying forms, which immediately provoked from her husband the short and sharp question, "What have you got there?"

"Patterns, captain," said Mrs. Wragge, in timidly conciliating tones. "I went shopping in London, and bought an Oriental Cashmere Robe. It cost a deal of money; and I'm going to try and save, by making it myself. I've got my patterns, and my dress-making directions written out as plain as print. I'll be very tidy, captain; I'll keep in my own corner, if you'll please to give me one; and whether my head Buzzes, or whether it don't, I'll sit straight at my work all the same."

"You will do your work," said the captain, sternly, "when you know who you are, who I am, and who that young lady is—not before. Show me your shoes! Good. Show me you cap! Good. Make the breakfast."

When breakfast was over, Mrs. Wragge received her orders to retire into an adjoining room, and to wait there until her husband came to release her. As soon as her back was turned, Captain Wragge at once resumed the conversation which had been suspended, by Magdalen's own desire, on the preceding night. The questions he now put to her all related to the subject of her visit in disguise to Noel Vanstone's house. They were the questions of a thoroughly clear-headed man—short, searching, and straight to the point. In less than half an hour's time he had made himself acquainted with every incident that had happened in Vauxhall Walk.

The conclusions which the captain drew, after gaining his information, were clear and easily stated.

On the adverse side of the question, he expressed his conviction that Mrs. Lecount had certainly detected her visitor to be disguised; that she had never really left the room, though she might have opened and shut the door; and that on both the occasions, therefore, when Magdalen had been betrayed into speaking in her own voice, Mrs. Lecount had heard her. On the favorable side of the question, he was perfectly satisfied that the painted face and eyelids, the wig, and the padded cloak had so effectually concealed Magdalen's identity, that she might in her own person defy the housekeeper's closest scrutiny, so far as the matter of appearance was concerned. The difficulty of deceiving Mrs. Lecount's ears, as well as her eyes, was, he readily admitted, not so easily to be disposed of. But looking to the fact that Magdalen, on both the occasions when she had forgotten herself, had spoken in the heat of anger, he was of opinion that her voice had every reasonable chance of escaping detection, if she carefully avoided all outbursts of temper for the future, and spoke in those more composed and ordinary tones which Mrs. Lecount had not yet heard. Upon the whole, the captain was inclined to pronounce the prospect hopeful, if one serious obstacle were cleared away at the outset—that obstacle being nothing less than the presence on the scene of action of Mrs. Wragge.

To Magdalen's surprise, when the course of her narrative brought her to the story of the ghost, Captain Wragge listened with the air of a man who was more annoyed than amused by what he heard. When she had done, he plainly told her that her unlucky meeting on the stairs of the lodging-house with Mrs. Wragge was, in his opinion, the most serious of all the accidents that had happened in Vauxhall Walk.

"I can deal with the difficulty of my wife's stupidity," he said, "as I have often dealt with it before. I can hammer her new identity into her head, but I can't hammer the ghost out of it. We have no security that the woman in the gray cloak and poke bonnet may not come back to her recollection at the most critical time, and under the most awkward circumstances. In plain English, my dear girl, Mrs. Wragge is a pitfall under our feet at every step we take."

"If we are aware of the pitfall," said Magdalen, "we can take our measures for avoiding it. What do you propose?"

"I propose," replied the captain, "the temporary removal of Mrs. Wragge. Speaking purely in a pecuniary point of view, I can't afford a total separation from her. You have often read of very poor people being suddenly enriched by legacies reaching them from remote and unexpected quarters? Mrs. Wragge's case, when I married her, was one of these. An elderly female relative shared the favors of fortune on that occasion with my wife; and if I only keep up domestic appearances, I happen to know that Mrs. Wragge will prove a second time profitable to me on that elderly relative's death. But for this circumstance, I should probably long since have transferred my wife to the care of society at large—in the agreeable conviction that if I didn't support her, somebody else would. Although I can't afford to take this course, I see no objection to having her comfortably boarded and lodged out of our way for the time being—say, at a retired farm-house, in the character of a lady in infirm mental health. You would find the expense trifling; I should find the relief unutterable. What do you say? Shall I pack her up at once, and take her away by the next coach?"

"No!" replied Magdalen, firmly. "The poor creature's life is hard enough already; I won't help to make it harder. She was affectionately and truly kind to me when I was ill, and I won't allow her to be shut up among strangers while I can help it. The risk of keeping her here is only one risk more. I will face it, Captain Wragge, if you won't."

"Think twice," said the captain, gravely, "before you decide on keeping Mrs. Wragge."

"Once is enough," rejoined Magdalen. "I won't have her sent away."

"Very good," said the captain, resignedly. "I never interfere with questions of sentiment. But I have a word to say on my own behalf. If my services are to be of any use to you, I can't have my hands tied at starting. This is serious. I won't trust my wife and Mrs. Lecount together. I'm afraid, if you're not, and I make it a condition that, if Mrs. Wragge stops here, she keeps her room. If you think her health requires it, you can take her for a walk early in the morning, or late in the evening; but you must never trust her out with the servant, and never trust her out by herself. I put the matter plainly, it is too important to be trifled with. What do you say—yes or no?"

"I say yes," replied Magdalen, after a moment's consideration. "On the understanding that I am to take her out walking, as you propose."

Captain Wragge bowed, and recovered his suavity of manner. "What are our plans?" he inquired. "Shall we start our enterprise this afternoon? Are you ready for your introduction to Mrs. Lecount and her master?"

"Quite ready."

"Good again. We will meet them on the Parade, at their usual hour for going out—two o'clock. It is not twelve yet. I have two hours before me—just time enough to fit my wife into her new Skin. The process is absolutely necessary, to prevent her compromising us with the servant. Don't be afraid about the results; Mrs. Wragge has had a copious selection of assumed names hammered into her head in the course of her matrimonial career. It is merely a question of hammering hard enough—nothing more. I think we have settled everything now. Is there anything I can do before two o'clock? Have you any employment for the morning?"

"No," said Magdalen. "I shall go back to my own room, and try to rest."

"You had a disturbed night, I am afraid?" said the captain, politely opening the door for her.

"I fell asleep once or twice," she answered, carelessly. "I suppose my nerves are a little shaken. The bold black eyes of that man who stared so rudely at me yesterday evening seemed to be looking at me again in my dreams. If we see him to-day, and if he annoys me any more, I must trouble you to speak to him. We will meet here again at two o'clock. Don't be hard with Mrs. Wragge; teach her what she must learn as tenderly as you can."

With those words she left him, and went upstairs.

She lay down on her bed with a heavy sigh, and tried to sleep. It was useless. The dull weariness of herself which now possessed her was not the weariness which finds its remedy in repose. She rose again and sat by the window, looking out listlessly over the sea.

A weaker nature than hers would not have felt the shock of Frank's desertion as she had felt it—as she was feeling it still. A weaker nature would have found refuge in indignation and comfort in tears. The passionate strength of Magdalen's love clung desperately to the sinking wreck of its own delusion-clung, until she tore herself from it, by plain force of will. All that her native pride, her keen sense of wrong could do, was to shame her from dwelling on the thoughts which still caught their breath of life from the undying devotion of the past; which still perversely ascribed Frank's heartless farewell to any cause but the inborn baseness of the man who had written it. The woman never lived yet who could cast a true-love out of her heart because the object of that love was unworthy of her. All she can do is to struggle against it in secret—to sink in the contest if she is weak; to win her way through it if she is strong, by a process of self-laceration which is, of all moral remedies applied to a woman's nature, the most dangerous and the most desperate; of all moral changes, the change that is surest to mark her for life. Magdalen's strong nature had sustained her through the struggle; and the issue of it had left her what she now was.

After sitting by the window for nearly an hour, her eyes looking mechanically at the view, her mind empty of all impressions, and conscious of no thoughts, she shook off the strange waking stupor that possessed her, and rose to prepare herself for the serious business of the day.

She went to the wardrobe and took down from the pegs two bright, delicate muslin dresses, which had been made for summer wear at Combe-Raven a year since, and which had been of too little value to be worth selling when she parted with her other possessions. After placing these dresses side by side on the bed, she looked into the wardrobe once more. It only contained one other summer dress—the plain alpaca gown which she had worn during her memorable interview with Noel Vanstone and Mrs. Lecount. This she left in its place, resolving not to wear it—less from any dread that the housekeeper might recognize a pattern too quiet to be noticed, and too common to be remembered, than from the conviction that it was neither gay enough nor becoming enough for her purpose. After taking a plain white muslin scarf, a pair of light gray kid gloves, and a garden-hat of Tuscan straw, from the drawers of the wardrobe, she locked it, and put the key carefully in her pocket.

Instead of at once proceeding to dress herself, she sat idly looking at the two muslin gowns; careless which she wore, and yet inconsistently hesitating which to choose. "What does it matter!" she said to herself, with a reckless laugh; "I am equally worthless in my own estimation, whichever I put on." She shuddered, as if the sound of her own laughter had startled her, and abruptly caught up the dress which lay nearest to her hand. Its colors were blue and white—the shade of blue which best suited her fair complexion. She hurriedly put on the gown, without going near her looking-glass. For the first time in her life she shrank from meeting the reflection of herself—except for a moment, when she arranged her hair under her garden-hat, leaving the glass again immediately. She drew her scarf over her shoulders and fitted on her gloves, with her back to the toilet-table. "Shall I paint?" she asked herself, feeling instinctively that she was turning pale. "The rouge is still left in my box. It can't make my face more false than it is already." She looked round toward the glass, and again turned away from it. "No!" she said. "I have Mrs. Lecount to face as well as her master. No paint." After consulting her watch, she left the room and went downstairs again. It wanted ten minutes only of two o'clock.

Captain Wragge was waiting for her in the parlor—respectable, in a frock-coat, a stiff summer cravat, and a high white hat; specklessly and cheerfully rural, in a buff waistcoat, gray trousers, and gaiters to match. His collars were higher than ever, and he carried a brand-new camp-stool in his hand. Any tradesman in England who had seen him at that moment would have trusted him on the spot.

"Charming!" said the captain, paternally surveying Magdalen when she entered the room. "So fresh and cool! A little too pale, my dear, and a great deal too serious. Otherwise perfect. Try if you can smile."

"When the time comes for smiling," said Magdalen, bitterly, "trust my dramatic training for any change of face that may be necessary. Where is Mrs. Wragge?"

"Mrs. Wragge has learned her lesson," replied the captain, "and is rewarded by my permission to sit at work in her own room. I sanction her new fancy for dressmaking, because it is sure to absorb all her attention, and to keep her at home. There is no fear of her finishing the Oriental Robe in a hurry, for there is no mistake in the process of making it which she is not certain to commit. She will sit incubating her gown—pardon the expression—like a hen over an addled egg. I assure you, her new whim relieves me. Nothing could be more convenient, under existing circumstances."

He strutted away to the window, looked out, and beckoned to Magdalen to join him. "There they are!" he said, and pointed to the Parade.

Noel Vanstone slowly walked by, as she looked, dressed in a complete suit of old-fashioned nankeen. It was apparently one of the days when the state of his health was at the worst. He leaned on Mrs. Lecount's arm, and was protected from the sun by a light umbrella which she held over him. The housekeeper—dressed to perfection, as usual, in a quiet, lavender-colored summer gown, a black mantilla, an unassuming straw bonnet, and a crisp blue veil—escorted her invalid master with the tenderest attention; sometimes directing his notice respectfully to the various objects of the sea view; sometimes bending her head in graceful acknowledgment of the courtesy of passing strangers on the Parade, who stepped aside to let the invalid pass by. She produced a visible effect among the idlers on the beach. They looked after her with unanimous interest, and exchanged confidential nods of approval which said, as plainly as words could have expressed it, "A very domestic person! a truly superior woman!"

Captain Wragge's party-colored eyes followed Mrs. Lecount with a steady, distrustful attention. "Tough work for us there," he whispered in Magdalen's ear; "tougher work than you think, before we turn that woman out of her place."

"Wait," said Magdalen, quietly. "Wait and see."

She walked to the door. The captain followed her without making any further remark.

"I'll wait till you're married," he thought to himself—"not a moment longer, offer me what you may."

At the house door Magdalen addressed him again.

"We will go that way," she said, pointing southward, "then turn, and meet them as they come back."

Captain Wragge signified his approval of the arrangement, and followed Magdalen to the garden gate. As she opened it to pass through, her attention was attracted by a lady, with a nursery-maid and two little boys behind her, loitering on the path outside the garden wall. The lady started, looked eagerly, and smiled to herself as Magdalen came out. Curiosity had got the better of Kirke's sister, and she had come to Aldborough for the express purpose of seeing Miss Bygrave.

Something in the shape of the lady's face, something in the expression of her dark eyes, reminded Magdalen of the merchant-captain whose uncontrolled admiration had annoyed her on the previous evening. She instantly returned the stranger's scrutiny by a frowning, ungracious look. The lady colored, paid the look back with interest, and slowly walked on.

"A hard, bold, bad girl," thought Kirke's sister. "What could Robert be thinking of to admire her? I am almost glad he is gone. I hope and trust he will never set eyes on Miss Bygrave again."

"What boors the people are here!" said Magdalen to Captain Wragge. "That woman was even ruder than the man last night. She is like him in the face. I wonder who she is?"

"I'll find out directly," said the captain. "We can't be too cautious about strangers." He at once appealed to his friends, the boatmen. They were close at hand, and Magdalen heard the questions and answers plainly.

"How are you all this morning?" said Captain Wragge, in his easy jocular way. "And how's the wind? Nor'-west and by west, is it? Very good. Who is that lady?"

"That's Mrs. Strickland, sir."

"Ay! ay! The clergyman's wife and the captain's sister. Where's the captain to-day?"

"On his way to London, I should think, sir. His ship sails for China at the end of the week."

China! As that one word passed the man's lips, a pang of the old sorrow struck Magdalen to the heart. Stranger as he was, she began to hate the bare mention of the merchant-captain's name. He had troubled her dreams of the past night; and now, when she was most desperately and recklessly bent on forgetting her old home-existence, he had been indirectly the cause of recalling her mind to Frank.

"Come!" she said, angrily, to her companion. "What do we care about the man or his ship? Come away."

"By all means," said Captain Wragge. "As long as we don't find friends of the Bygraves, what do we care about anybody?"

They walked on southward for ten minutes or more, then turned and walked back again to meet Noel Vanstone and Mrs. Lecount.

CHAPTER IV.

CAPTAIN WRAGGE and Magdalen retraced their steps until they were again within view of North Shingles Villa before any signs appeared of Mrs. Lecount and her master. At that point the housekeeper's lavender-colored dress, the umbrella, and the feeble little figure in nankeen walking under it, became visible in the distance. The captain slackened his pace immediately, and issued his directions to Magdalen for her conduct at the coming interview in these words:

"Don't forget your smile," he said. "In all other respects you will do. The walk has improved your complexion, and the hat becomes you. Look Mrs. Lecount steadily in the face; show no embarrassment when you speak; and if Mr. Noel Vanstone pays you pointed attention, don't take too much notice of him while his housekeeper's eye is on you. Mind one thing! I have been at Joyce's Scientific Dialogues all the morning; and I am quite serious in meaning to give Mrs. Lecount the full benefit of my studies. If I can't contrive to divert her attention from you and her master, I won't give sixpence for our chance of success. Small-talk won't succeed with that woman; compliments won't succeed; jokes won't succeed—ready-made science may recall the deceased professor, and ready-made science may do. We must establish a code of signals to let you know what I am about. Observe this camp-stool. When I shift it from my left hand to my right, I am talking Joyce. When I shift it from my right hand to my left, I am talking Wragge. In the first case, don't interrupt me—I am leading up to my point. In the second case, say anything you like; my remarks are not of the slightest consequence. Would you like a rehearsal? Are you sure you understand? Very good—take my arm, and look happy. Steady! here they are."

The meeting took place nearly midway between Sea-view Cottage and North Shingles. Captain Wragge took off his tall white hat and opened the interview immediately on the friendliest terms.

"Good-morning, Mrs. Lecount," he said, with the frank and cheerful politeness of a naturally sociable man. "Good-morning, Mr. Vanstone; I am sorry to see you suffering to-day. Mrs. Lecount, permit me to introduce my niece—my niece, Miss Bygrave. My dear girl, this is Mr. Noel Vanstone, our neighbor at Sea-view Cottage. We must positively be sociable at Aldborough, Mrs. Lecount. There is only one walk in the place (as my niece remarked to me just now, Mr. Vanstone); and on that walk we must all meet every time we go out. And why not? Are we formal people on either side? Nothing of the sort; we are just the reverse. You possess the Continental facility of manner, Mr. Vanstone—I match you with the blunt cordiality of an old-fashioned Englishman—the ladies mingle together in harmonious variety, like flowers on the same bed—and the result is a mutual interest in making our sojourn at the sea-side agreeable to each other. Pardon my flow of spirits; pardon my feeling so cheerful and so young. The Iodine in the sea-air, Mrs. Lecount—the notorious effect of the Iodine in the sea-air!"

"You arrived yesterday, Miss Bygrave, did you not?" said the housekeeper, as soon as the captain's deluge of language had come to an end.

She addressed those words to Magdalen with a gentle motherly interest in her youth and beauty, chastened by the deferential amiability which became her situation in Noel Vanstone's household. Not the faintest token of suspicion or surprise betrayed itself in her face, her voice, or her manner, while she and Magdalen now looked at each other. It was plain at the outset that the true face and figure which she now saw recalled nothing to her mind of the false face and figure which she had seen in Vauxhall Walk. The disguise had evidently been complete enough even to baffle the penetration of Mrs. Lecount.

"My aunt and I came here yesterday evening," said Magdalen. "We found the latter part of the journey very fatiguing. I dare say you found it so, too?"

She designedly made her answer longer than was necessary for the purpose of discovering, at the earliest opportunity, the effect which the sound of her voice produced on Mrs. Lecount.

The housekeeper's thin lips maintained their motherly smile; the housekeeper's amiable manner lost none of its modest deference, but the expression of her eyes suddenly changed from a look of attention to a look of inquiry. Magdalen quietly said a few words more, and then waited again for results. The change spread gradually all over Mrs. Lecount's face, the motherly smile died away, and the amiable manner betrayed a slight touch of restraint. Still no signs of positive recognition appeared; the housekeeper's expression remained what it had been from the first—an expression of inquiry, and nothing more.

"You complained of fatigue, sir, a few minutes since," she said, dropping all further conversation with Magdalen and addressing her master. "Will you go indoors and rest?"

The proprietor of Sea-view Cottage had hitherto confined himself to bowing, simpering and admiring Magdalen through his half-closed eyelids. There was no mistaking the sudden flutter and agitation in his manner, and the heightened color in his wizen little face. Even the reptile temperament of Noel Vanstone warmed under the influence of the sex: he had an undeniably appreciative eye for a handsome woman, and Magdalen's grace and beauty were not thrown away on him.

"Will you go indoors, sir, and rest?" asked the housekeeper, repeating her question.

"Not yet, Lecount," said her master. "I fancy I feel stronger; I fancy I can go on a little." He turned simpering to Magdalen, and added, in a lower tone: "I have found a new interest in my walk, Miss Bygrave. Don't desert us, or you will take the interest away with you."

He smiled and smirked in the highest approval of the ingenuity of his own compliment—from which Captain Wragge dexterously diverted the housekeeper's attention by ranging himself on her side of the path and speaking to her at the same moment. They all four walked on slowly. Mrs. Lecount said nothing more. She kept fast hold of her master's arm, and looked across him at Magdalen with the dangerous expression of inquiry more marked than ever in her handsome black eyes. That look was not lost on the wary Wragge. He shifted his indicative camp-stool from the left hand to the right, and opened his scientific batteries on the spot.

"A busy scene, Mrs. Lecount," said the captain, politely waving his camp-stool over the sea and the passing ships. "The greatness of England, ma'am—the true greatness of England. Pray observe how heavily some of those vessels are laden! I am often inclined to wonder whether the British sailor is at all aware, when he has got his cargo on board, of the Hydrostatic importance of the operation that he has performed. If I were suddenly transported to the deck of one of those ships (which Heaven forbid, for I suffer at sea); and if I said to a member of the crew: 'Jack! you have done wonders; you have grasped the Theory of Floating Vessels'—how the gallant fellow would stare! And yet on that theory Jack's life depends. If he loads his vessel one-thirtieth part more than he ought, what happens? He sails past Aldborough, I grant you, in safety. He enters the Thames, I grant you again, in safety. He gets on into the fresh water as far, let us say, as Greenwich; and—down he goes! Down, ma'am, to the bottom of the river, as a matter of scientific certainty!"

Here he paused, and left Mrs. Lecount no polite alternative but to request an explanation.

"With infinite pleasure, ma'am," said the captain, drowning in the deepest notes of his voice the feeble treble in which Noel Vanstone paid his compliments to Magdalen. "We will start, if you please, with a first principle. All bodies whatever that float on the surface of the water displace as much fluid as is equal in weight to the weight of the bodies. Good. We have got our first principle. What do we deduce from it? Manifestly this: That, in order to keep a vessel above water, it is necessary to take care that the vessel and its cargo shall be of less weight than the weight of a quantity of water—pray follow me here!—of a quantity of water equal in bulk to that part of the vessel which it will be safe to immerse in the water. Now, ma'am, salt-water is specifically thirty times heavier than fresh or river water, and a vessel in the German Ocean will not sink so deep as a vessel in the Thames. Consequently, when we load our ship with a view to the London market, we have (Hydrostatically speaking) three alternatives. Either we load with one-thirtieth part less than we can carry at sea; or we take one-thirtieth part out at the mouth of the river; or we do neither the one nor the other, and, as I have already had the honor of remarking—down we go! Such," said the captain, shifting the camp-stool back again from his right hand to his left, in token that Joyce was done with for the time being; "such, my dear madam, is the Theory of Floating Vessels. Permit me to add, in conclusion, you are heartily welcome to it."

"Thank you, sir," said Mrs. Lecount. "You have unintentionally saddened me; but the information I have received is not the less precious on that account. It is long, long ago, Mr. Bygrave, since I have heard myself addressed in the language of science. My dear husband made me his companion—my dear husband improved my mind as you have been trying to improve it. Nobody has taken pains with my intellect since. Many thanks, sir. Your kind consideration for me is not thrown away."

She sighed with a plaintive humility, and privately opened her ears to the conversation on the other side of her.

A minute earlier she would have heard her master expressing himself in the most flattering terms on the subject of Miss Bygrave's appearance in her sea-side costume. But Magdalen had seen Captain Wragge's signal with the camp-stool, and had at once diverted Noel Vanstone to the topic of himself and his possessions by a neatly-timed question about his house at Aldborough.

"I don't wish to alarm you, Miss Bygrave," were the first words of Noel Vanstone's which caught Mrs. Lecount's attention, "but there is only one safe house in Aldborough, and that house is mine. The sea may destroy all the other houses—it can't destroy Mine. My father took care of that; my father was a remarkable man. He had My house built on piles. I have reason to believe they are the strongest piles in England. Nothing can possibly knock them down—I don't care what the sea does—nothing can possibly knock them down."

"Then, if the sea invades us," said Magdalen, "we must all run for refuge to you."

Noel Vanstone saw his way to another compliment; and, at the same moment, the wary captain saw his way to another burst of science.

"I could almost wish the invasion might happen," murmured one of the gentlemen, "to give me the happiness of offering the refuge."

"I could almost swear the wind had shifted again!" exclaimed the other. "Where is a man I can ask? Oh, there he is. Boatman! How's the wind now? Nor'west and by west still—hey? And southeast and by south yesterday evening—ha? Is there anything more remarkable, Mrs. Lecount, than the variableness of the wind in this climate?" proceeded the captain, shifting the camp-stool to the scientific side of him. "Is there any natural phenomenon more bewildering to the scientific inquirer? You will tell me that the electric fluid which abounds in the air is the principal cause of this variableness. You will remind me of the experiment of that illustrious philosopher who measured the velocity of a great storm by a flight of small feathers. My dear madam, I grant all your propositions—"

"I beg your pardon, sir," said Mrs. Lecount; "you kindly attribute to me a knowledge that I don't possess. Propositions, I regret to say, are quite beyond me."

"Don't misunderstand me, ma'am," continued the captain, politely unconscious of the interruption. "My remarks apply to the temperate zone only. Place me on the coasts beyond the tropics—place me where the wind blows toward the shore in the day-time, and toward the sea by night—and I instantly advance toward conclusive experiments. For example, I know that the heat of the sun during the day rarefies the air over the land, and so causes the wind. You challenge me to prove it. I escort you down the kitchen stairs (with your kind permission); take my largest pie-dish out of the cook's hands; I fill it with cold water. Good! that dish of cold water represents the ocean. I next provide myself with one of our most precious domestic conveniences, a hot-water plate; I fill it with hot water and I put it in the middle of the pie-dish. Good again! the hot-water plate represents the land rarefying the air over it. Bear that in mind, and give me a lighted candle. I hold my lighted candle over the cold water, and blow it out. The smoke immediately moves from the dish to the plate. Before you have time to express your satisfaction, I light the candle once more, and reverse the whole proceeding. I fill the pie-dish with hot-water, and the plate with cold; I blow the candle out again, and the smoke moves this time from the plate to the dish. The smell is disagreeable—but the experiment is conclusive."

He shifted the camp-stool back again, and looked at Mrs. Lecount with his ingratiating smile. "You don't find me long-winded, ma'am—do you?" he said, in his easy, cheerful way, just as the housekeeper was privately opening her ears once more to the conversation on the other side of her.

"I am amazed, sir, by the range of your information," replied Mrs. Lecount, observing the captain with some perplexity—but thus far with no distrust. She thought him eccentric, even for an Englishman, and possibly a little vain of his knowledge. But he had at least paid her the implied compliment of addressing that knowledge to herself; and she felt it the more sensibly, from having hitherto found her scientific sympathies with her deceased husband treated with no great respect by the people with whom she came in contact. "Have you extended your inquiries, sir," she proceeded, after a momentary hesitation, "to my late husband's branch of science? I merely ask, Mr. Bygrave, because (though I am only a woman) I think I might exchange ideas with you on the subject of the reptile creation."

Captain Wragge was far too sharp to risk his ready-made science on the enemy's ground. The old militia-man shook his wary head.

"Too vast a subject, ma'am," he said, "for a smatterer like me. The life and labors of such a philosopher as your husband, Mrs. Lecount, warn men of my intellectual caliber not to measure themselves with a giant. May I inquire," proceeded the captain, softly smoothing the way for future intercourse with Sea-view Cottage, "whether you possess any scientific memorials of the late Professor?"

"I possess his Tank, sir," said Mrs. Lecount, modestly casting her eyes on the ground, "and one of his Subjects—a little foreign Toad."

"His Tank!" exclaimed the captain, in tones of mournful interest; "and his Toad! Pardon my blunt way of speaking my mind, ma'am. You possess an object of public interest; and, as one of the public, I acknowledge my curiosity to see it."

Mrs. Lecount's smooth cheeks colored with pleasure. The one assailable place in that cold and secret nature was the place occupied by the memory of the Professor. Her pride in his scientific achievements, and her mortification at finding them but little known out of his own country, were genuine feelings. Never had Captain Wragge burned his adulterated incense on the flimsy altar of human vanity to better purpose than he was burning it now.

"You are very good, sir," said Mrs. Lecount. "In honoring my husband's memory, you honor me. But though you kindly treat me on a footing of equality, I must not forget that I fill a domestic situation. I shall feel it a privilege to show you my relics, if you will allow me to ask my master's permission first."

She turned to Noel Vanstone; her perfectly sincere intention of making the proposed request, mingling—in that strange complexity of motives which is found so much oftener in a woman's mind than in a man's—with her jealous distrust of the impression which Magdalen had produced on her master.

"May I make a request, sir?" asked Mrs. Lecount, after waiting a moment to catch any fragments of tenderly-personal talk that might reach her, and after being again neatly baffled by Magdalen—thanks to the camp-stool. "Mr. Bygrave is one of the few persons in England who appreciate my husband's scientific labors. He honors me by wishing to see my little world of reptiles. May I show it to him?"

"By all means, Lecount," said Noel Vanstone, graciously. "You are an excellent creature, and I like to oblige you. Lecount's Tank, Mr. Bygrave, is the only Tank in England—Lecount's Toad is the oldest Toad in the world. Will you come and drink tea at seven o'clock to-night? And will you prevail on Miss Bygrave to accompany you? I want her to see my house. I don't think she has any idea what a strong house it is. Come and survey my premises, Miss Bygrave. You shall have a stick and rap on the walls; you shall go upstairs and stamp on the floors, and then you shall hear what it all cost." His eyes wrinkled up cunningly at the corners, and he slipped another tender speech into Magdalen's ear, under cover of the all-predominating voice in which Captain Wragge thanked him for the invitation. "Come punctually at seven," he whispered, "and pray wear that charming hat!"

Mrs. Lecount's lips closed ominously. She set down the captain's niece as a very serious drawback to the intellectual luxury of the captain's society.

"You are fatiguing yourself, sir," she said to her master. "This is one of your bad days. Let me recommend you to be careful; let me beg you to walk back."

Having carried his point by inviting the new acquaintances to tea, Noel Vanstone proved to be unexpectedly docile. He acknowledged that he was a little fatigued, and turned back at once in obedience to the housekeeper's advice.

"Take my arm, sir—take my arm on the other side," said Captain Wragge, as they turned to retrace their steps. His party-colored eyes looked significantly at Magdalen while he spoke, and warned her not to stretch Mrs. Lecount's endurance too far at starting. She instantly understood him; and, in spite of Noel Vanstone's reiterated assertions that he stood in no need of the captain's arm, placed herself at once by the housekeeper's side. Mrs. Lecount recovered her good-humor, and opened another conversation with Magdalen by making the one inquiry of all others which, under existing circumstances, was the hardest to answer.

"I presume Mrs. Bygrave is too tired, after her journey, to come out to-day?" said Mrs. Lecount. "Shall we have the pleasure of seeing her tomorrow?"

"Probably not," replied Magdalen. "My aunt is in delicate health."

"A complicated case, my dear madam," added the captain; conscious that Mrs. Wragge's personal appearance (if she happened to be seen by accident) would offer the flattest of all possible contradictions to what Magdalen had just said of her. "There is some remote nervous mischief which doesn't express itself externally. You would think my wife the picture of health if you looked at her, and yet, so delusive are appearances, I am obliged to forbid her all excitement. She sees no society—our medical attendant, I regret to say, absolutely prohibits it."

"Very sad," said Mrs. Lecount. "The poor lady must often feel lonely, sir, when you and your niece are away from her?"

"No," replied the captain. "Mrs. Bygrave is a naturally domestic woman. When she is able to employ herself, she finds unlimited resources in her needle and thread." Having reached this stage of the explanation, and having purposely skirted, as it were, round the confines of truth, in the event of the housekeeper's curiosity leading her to make any private inquiries on the subject of Mrs. Wragge, the captain wisely checked his fluent tongue from carrying him into any further details. "I have great hope from the air of this place," he remarked, in conclusion. "The Iodine, as I have already observed, does wonders."

Mrs. Lecount acknowledged the virtues of Iodine, in the briefest possible form of words, and withdrew into the innermost sanctuary of her own thoughts. "Some mystery here," said the housekeeper to herself. "A lady who looks the picture of health; a lady who suffers from a complicated nervous malady; and a lady whose hand is steady enough to use her needle and thread—is a living mass of contradictions I don't quite understand. Do you make a long stay at Aldborough, sir?" she added aloud, her eyes resting for a moment, in steady scrutiny, on the captain's face.

"It all depends, my dear madam, on Mrs. Bygrave. I trust we shall stay through the autumn. You are settled at Sea-view Cottage, I presume, for the season?"

"You must ask my master, sir. It is for him to decide, not for me."

The answer was an unfortunate one. Noel Vanstone had been secretly annoyed by the change in the walking arrangements, which had separated him from Magdalen. He attributed that change to the meddling influence of Mrs. Lecount, and he now took the earliest opportunity of resenting it on the spot.

"I have nothing to do with our stay at Aldborough," he broke out, peevishly. "You know as well as I do, Lecount, it all depends on you. Mrs. Lecount has a brother in Switzerland," he went on, addressing himself to the captain—"a brother who is seriously ill. If he gets worse, she will have to go there to see him. I can't accompany her, and I can't be left in the house by myself. I shall have to break up my establishment at Aldborough, and stay with some friends. It all depends on you, Lecount—or on your brother, which comes to the same thing. If it depended on me," continued Mr. Noel Vanstone, looking pointedly at Magdalen across the housekeeper, "I should stay at Aldborough all through the autumn with the greatest pleasure. With the greatest pleasure," he reiterated, repeating the words with a tender look for Magdalen, and a spiteful accent for Mrs. Lecount.

Thus far Captain Wragge had remained silent; carefully noting in his mind the promising possibilities of a separation between Mrs. Lecount and her master which Noel Vanstone's little fretful outbreak had just disclosed to him. An ominous trembling in the housekeeper's thin lips, as her master openly exposed her family affairs before strangers, and openly set her jealously at defiance, now warned him to interfere. If the misunderstanding were permitted to proceed to extremities, there was a chance that the invitation for that evening to Sea-view Cottage might be put off. Now, as ever, equal to the occasion, Captain Wragge called his useful information once more to the rescue. Under the learned auspices of Joyce, he plunged, for the third time, into the ocean of science, and brought up another pearl. He was still haranguing (on Pneumatics this time), still improving Mrs. Lecount's mind with his politest perseverance and his smoothest flow of language—when the walking party stopped at Noel Vanstone's door.

"Bless my soul, here we are at your house, sir!" said the captain, interrupting himself in the middle of one of his graphic sentences. "I won't keep you standing a moment. Not a word of apology, Mrs. Lecount, I beg and pray! I will put that curious point in Pneumatics more clearly before you on a future occasion. In the meantime I need only repeat that you can perform the experiment I have just mentioned to your own entire satisfaction with a bladder, an exhausted receiver, and a square box. At seven o'clock this evening, sir—at seven o'clock, Mrs. Lecount. We have had a remarkably pleasant walk, and a most instructive interchange of ideas. Now, my dear girl, your aunt is waiting for us."

While Mrs. Lecount stepped aside to open the garden gate, Noel Vanstone seized his opportunity and shot a last tender glance at Magdalen, under shelter of the umbrella, which he had taken into his own hands for that express purpose. "Don't forget," he said, with the sweetest smile; "don't forget, when you come this evening, to wear that charming hat!" Before he could add any last words, Mrs. Lecount glided back to her place, and the sheltering umbrella changed hands again immediately.

"An excellent morning's work!" said Captain Wragge, as he and Magdalen walked on together to North Shingles. "You and I and Joyce have all three done wonders. We have secured a friendly invitation at the first day's fishing for it."

He paused for an answer; and, receiving none, observed Magdalen more attentively than he had observed her yet. Her face had turned deadly pale again; her eyes looked out mechanically straight before her in heedless, reckless despair.

"What is the matter?" he asked, with the greatest surprise. "Are you ill?"

She made no reply; she hardly seemed to hear him.

"Are you getting alarmed about Mrs. Lecount?" he inquired next. "There is not the least reason for alarm. She may fancy she has heard something like your voice before, but your face evidently bewilders her. Keep your temper, and you keep her in the dark. Keep her in the dark, and you will put that two hundred pounds into my hands before the autumn is over."

He waited again for an answer, and again she remained silent. The captain tried for the third time in another direction.

"Did you get any letters this morning?" he went on. "Is there bad news again from home? Any fresh difficulties with your sister?"

"Say nothing about my sister!" she broke out passionately. "Neither you nor I are fit to speak of her."

She said those words at the garden-gate, and hurried into the house by herself. He followed her, and heard the door of her own room violently shut to, violently locked and double-locked. Solacing his indignation by an oath, Captain Wragge sullenly went into one of the parlors on the ground-floor to look after his wife. The room communicated with a smaller and darker room at the back of the house by means of a quaint little door with a window in the upper half of it. Softly approaching this door, the captain lifted the white muslin curtain which hung over the window, and looked into the inner room.

There was Mrs. Wragge, with her cap on one side, and her shoes down at heel; with a row of pins between her teeth; with the Oriental Cashmere Robe slowly slipping off the table; with her scissors suspended uncertain in one hand, and her written directions for dressmaking held doubtfully in the other—so absorbed over the invincible difficulties of her employment as to be perfectly unconscious that she was at that moment the object of her husband's superintending eye. Under other circumstances she would have been soon brought to a sense of her situation by the sound of his voice. But Captain Wragge was too anxious about Magdalen to waste any time on his wife, after satisfying himself that she was safe in her seclusion, and that she might be trusted to remain there.

He left the parlor, and, after a little hesitation in the passage, stole upstairs and listened anxiously outside Magdalen's door. A dull sound of sobbing—a sound stifled in her handkerchief, or stifled in the bed-clothes—was all that caught his ear. He returned at once to the ground-floor, with some faint suspicion of the truth dawning on his mind at last.

"The devil take that sweetheart of hers!" thought the captain. "Mr. Noel Vanstone has raised the ghost of him at starting."

CHAPTER V.

WHEN Magdalen appeared in the parlor shortly before seven o'clock, not a trace of discomposure was visible in her manner. She looked and spoke as quietly and unconcernedly as usual.

The lowering distrust on Captain Wragge's face cleared away at the sight of her. There had been moments during the afternoon when he had seriously doubted whether the pleasure of satisfying the grudge he owed to Noel Vanstone, and the prospect of earning the sum of two hundred pounds, would not be dearly purchased by running the risk of discovery to which Magdalen's uncertain temper might expose him at any hour of the day. The plain proof now before him of her powers of self-control relieved his mind of a serious anxiety. It mattered little to the captain what she suffered in the privacy of her own chamber, as long as she came out of it with a face that would bear inspection, and a voice that betrayed nothing.

On the way to Sea-view Cottage, Captain Wragge expressed his intention of asking the housekeeper a few sympathizing questions on the subject of her invalid brother in Switzerland. He was of opinion that the critical condition of this gentleman's health might exercise an important influence on the future progress of the conspiracy. Any chance of a separation, he remarked, between the housekeeper and her master was, under existing circumstances, a chance which merited the closest investigation. "If we can only get Mrs. Lecount out of the way at the right time," whispered the captain, as he opened his host's garden gate, "our man is caught!"

In a minute more Magdalen was again under Noel Vanstone's roof; this time in the character of his own invited guest.

The proceedings of the evening were for the most part a repetition of the proceedings during the morning walk. Noel Vanstone vibrated between his admiration of Magdalen's beauty and his glorification of his own possessions. Captain Wragge's inexhaustible outbursts of information—relieved by delicately-indirect inquiries relating to Mrs. Lecount's brother—perpetually diverted the housekeeper's jealous vigilance from dwelling on the looks and language of her master. So the evening passed until ten o'clock. By that time the captain's ready-made science was exhausted, and the housekeeper's temper was forcing its way to the surface. Once more Captain Wragge warned Magdalen by a look, and, in spite of Noel Vanstone's hospitable protest, wisely rose to say good-night.

"I have got my information," remarked the captain on the way back. "Mrs. Lecount's brother lives at Zurich. He is a bachelor; he possesses a little money, and his sister is his nearest relation. If he will only be so obliging as to break up altogether, he will save us a world of trouble with Mrs. Lecount."

It was a fine moonlight night. He looked round at Magdalen, as he said those words, to see if her intractable depression of spirits had seized on her again.

No! her variable humor had changed once more. She looked about her with a flaunting, feverish gayety; she scoffed at the bare idea of any serious difficulty with Mrs. Lecount; she mimicked Noel Vanstone's high-pitched voice, and repeated Noel Vanstone's high-flown compliments, with a bitter enjoyment of turning him into ridicule. Instead of running into the house as before, she sauntered carelessly by her companion's side, humming little snatches of song, and kicking the loose pebbles right and left on the garden-walk. Captain Wragge hailed the change in her as the best of good omens. He thought he saw plain signs that the family spirit was at last coming back again.

"Well," he said, as he lit her bedroom candle for her, "when we all meet on the Parade tomorrow, we shall see, as our nautical friends say, how the land lies. One thing I can tell you, my dear girl—I have used my eyes to very little purpose if there is not a storm brewing tonight in Mr. Noel Vanstone's domestic atmosphere."

The captain's habitual penetration had not misled him. As soon as the door of Sea-view

Cottage was closed on the parting guests, Mrs. Lecount made an effort to assert the authority which Magdalen's influence was threatening already.

She employed every artifice of which she was mistress to ascertain Magdalen's true position in Noel Vanstone's estimation. She tried again and again to lure him into an unconscious confession of the pleasure which he felt already in the society of the beautiful Miss Bygrave; she twined herself in and out of every weakness in his character, as the frogs and efts twined themselves in and out of the rock-work of her Aquarium. But she made one serious mistake which very clever people in their intercourse with their intellectual inferiors are almost universally apt to commit—she trusted implicitly to the folly of a fool. She forgot that one of the lowest of human qualities—cunning—is exactly the capacity which is often most largely developed in the lowest of intellectual natures. If she had been honestly angry with her master, she would probably have frightened him. If she had opened her mind plainly to his view, she would have astonished him by presenting a chain of ideas to his limited perceptions which they were not strong enough to grasp; his curiosity would have led him to ask for an explanation; and by practicing on that curiosity, she might have had him at her mercy. As it was, she set her cunning against his, and the fool proved a match for her. Noel Vanstone, to whom all large-minded motives under heaven were inscrutable mysteries, saw the small-minded motive at the bottom of his housekeeper's conduct with as instantaneous a penetration as if he had been a man of the highest ability. Mrs. Lecount left him for the night, foiled, and knowing she was foiled—left him, with the tigerish side of her uppermost, and a low-lived longing in her elegant finger-nails to set them in her master's face.

She was not a woman to be beaten by one defeat or by a hundred. She was positively determined to think, and think again, until she had found a means of checking the growing intimacy with the Bygraves at once and forever. In the solitude of her own room she recovered her composure, and set herself for the first time to review the conclusions which she had gathered from the events of the day.

There was something vaguely familiar to her in the voice of this Miss Bygrave, and, at the same time, in unaccountable contradiction, something strange to her as well. The face and figure of the young lady were entirely new to her. It was a striking face, and a striking figure; and if she had seen either at any former period, she would certainly have remembered it. Miss Bygrave was unquestionably a stranger; and yet—

She had got no further than this during the day; she could get no further now: the chain of thought broke. Her mind took up the fragments, and formed another chain which attached itself to the lady who was kept in seclusion—to the aunt, who looked well, and yet was nervous; who was nervous, and yet able to ply her needle and thread. An incomprehensible resemblance to some unremembered voice in the niece; an unintelligible malady which kept the aunt secluded from public view; an extraordinary range of scientific cultivation in the uncle, associated with a coarseness and audacity of manner which by no means suggested the idea of a man engaged in studious pursuits—were the members of this small family of three what they seemed on the surface of them?

With that question on her mind, she went to bed.

As soon as the candle was out, the darkness seemed to communicate some inexplicable perversity to her thoughts. They wandered back from present things to past, in spite of her.

They brought her old master back to life again; they revived forgotten sayings and doings in the English circle at Zurich; they veered away to the old man's death-bed at Brighton; they moved from Brighton to London; they entered the bare, comfortless room at Vauxhall Walk; they set the Aquarium back in its place on the kitchen table, and put the false Miss Garth in the chair by the side of it, shading her inflamed eyes from the light; they placed the anonymous letter, the letter which glanced darkly at a conspiracy, in her hand again, and brought her with it into her master's presence; they recalled the discussion about filling in the blank space in the advertisement, and the quarrel that followed when she told Noel Vanstone that the sum he had offered was preposterously small; they revived an old doubt which had not troubled her for weeks past—a doubt whether the threatened conspiracy had evaporated in mere words, or whether she and her master were likely to hear of it again. At this point her thoughts broke off once more, and there was a momentary blank. The next instant she started up in bed; her heart beating violently, her head whirling as if she had lost her senses. With electric suddenness her mind pieced together its scattered multitude of thoughts, and put them before her plainly under one intelligible form. In the all-mastering agitation of the moment, she clapped her hands together, and cried out suddenly in the darkness:

"Miss Vanstone again!!!"

She got out of bed and kindled the light once more. Steady as her nerves were, the shock of her own suspicion had shaken them. Her firm hand trembled as she opened her dressing-case and took from it a little bottle of sal-volatile. In spite of her smooth cheeks and her well-preserved hair, she looked every year of her age as she mixed the spirit with water, greedily drank it, and, wrapping her dressing-gown round her, sat down on the bedside to get possession again of her calmer self.

She was quite incapable of tracing the mental process which had led her to discovery. She could not get sufficiently far from herself to see that her half-formed conclusions on the subject of the Bygraves had ended in making that family objects of suspicion to her; that the association of ideas had thereupon carried her mind back to that other object of suspicion which was represented by the conspiracy against her master; and that the two ideas of those two separate subjects of distrust, coming suddenly in contact, had struck the light. She was not able to reason back in this way from the effect to the cause. She could only feel that the suspicion had become more than a suspicion already: conviction itself could not have been more firmly rooted in her mind.

Looking back at Magdalen by the new light now thrown on her, Mrs. Lecount would fain have persuaded herself that she recognized some traces left of the false Miss Garth's face and figure in the graceful and beautiful girl who had sat at her master's table hardly an hour since—that she found resemblances now, which she had never thought of before, between the angry voice she had heard in Vauxhall Walk and the smooth, well-bred tones which still hung on her ears after the evening's experience downstairs. She would fain have persuaded herself that she had reached these results with no undue straining of the truth as she really knew it, but the effort was in vain.

Mrs. Lecount was not a woman to waste time and thought in trying to impose on herself. She accepted the inevitable conclusion that the guesswork of a moment had led her to discovery. And, more than that, she recognized the plain truth—unwelcome as it was—that the conviction now fixed in her own mind was thus far unsupported by a single fragment of producible evidence to justify it to the minds of others.

Under these circumstances, what was the safe course to take with her master?

If she candidly told him, when they met the next morning, what had passed through her mind that night, her knowledge of Noel Vanstone warned her that one of two results would certainly happen. Either he would be angry and disputatious; would ask for proofs; and, finding none forthcoming, would accuse her of alarming him without a cause, to serve her own jealous end of keeping Magdalen out of the house; or he would be seriously startled, would clamor for the protection of the law, and would warn the Bygraves to stand on their defense at the outset. If Magdalen only had been concerned in the plot this latter consequence would have assumed no great importance in the housekeeper's mind. But seeing the deception as she now saw it, she was far too clever a woman to fail in estimating the captain's inexhaustible fertility of resource at its true value. "If I can't meet this impudent villain with plain proofs to help me," thought Mrs. Lecount, "I may open my master's eyes to-morrow morning, and Mr. Bygrave will shut them up again before night. The rascal is playing with all his own cards under the table, and he will win the game to a certainty, if he sees my hand at starting."

This policy of waiting was so manifestly the wise policy—the wily Mr. Bygrave was so sure to have provided himself, in case of emergency, with evidence to prove the identity which he and his niece had assumed for their purpose—that Mrs. Lecount at once decided to keep her own counsel the next morning, and to pause before attacking the conspiracy until she could produce unanswerable facts to help her. Her master's acquaintance with the Bygraves was only an acquaintance of one day's standing. There was no fear of its developing into a dangerous intimacy if she merely allowed it to continue for a few days more, and if she permanently checked it, at the latest, in a week's time.

In that period what measures could she take to remove the obstacles which now stood in her way, and to provide herself with the weapons which she now wanted?

Reflection showed her three different chances in her favor—three different ways of arriving at the necessary discovery.

The first chance was to cultivate friendly terms with Magdalen, and then, taking her unawares, to entrap her into betraying herself in Noel Vanstone's presence. The second chance was to write to the elder Miss Vanstone, and to ask (with some alarming reason for putting the question) for information on the subject of her younger sister's whereabouts, and of any peculiarities in her personal appearance which might enable a stranger to identify her. The third chance was to penetrate the mystery of Mrs. Bygrave's seclusion, and to ascertain at a personal interview whether the invalid lady's real complaint might not possibly be a defective capacity for keeping her husband's secrets. Resolving to try all three chances, in the order in which they are here enumerated, and to set her snares for Magdalen on the day that was now already at hand, Mrs. Lecount at last took off her dressing-gown and allowed her weaker nature to plead with her for a little sleep.

The dawn was breaking over the cold gray sea as she lay down in her bed again. The last idea in her mind before she fell asleep was characteristic of the woman—it was an idea that threatened the captain. "He has trifled with the sacred memory of my husband," thought the Professor's widow. "On my life and honor, I will make him pay for it."

Early the next morning Magdalen began the day, according to her agreement with the captain, by taking Mrs. Wragge out for a little exercise at an hour when there was no fear of her attracting the public attention. She pleaded hard to be left at home; having the Oriental Cashmere Robe still on her mind, and feeling it necessary to read her directions for dressmaking, for the hundredth time at least, before (to use her own expression) she could "screw up her courage to put the scissors into the stuff." But her companion would take no denial, and she was forced to go out. The one guileless purpose of the life which Magdalen now led was the resolution that poor Mrs. Wragge should not be made a prisoner on her account; and to that resolution she mechanically clung, as the last token left her by which she knew her better-self.

They returned later than usual to breakfast. While Mrs. Wragge was upstairs, straightening herself from head to foot to meet the morning inspection of her husband's orderly eye; and while Magdalen and the captain were waiting for her in the parlor, the servant came in with a note from Sea-view Cottage. The messenger was waiting for an answer, and the note was addressed to Captain Wragge.

The captain opened the note and read these lines:

"DEAR SIR—Mr. Noel Vanstone desires me to write and tell you that he proposes enjoying this fine day by taking a long drive to a place on the coast here called Dunwich. He is anxious to know if you will share the expense of a carriage, and give him the pleasure of your company and Miss Bygrave's company on this excursion. I am kindly permitted to be one of the party; and if I may say so without impropriety, I would venture to add that I shall feel as much pleasure as my master if you and your young lady will consent to join us. We propose leaving Aldborough punctually at eleven o'clock. Believe me, dear sir, your humble servant,

"VIRGINIE LECOUNT."

"Who is the letter from?" asked Magdalen, noticing a change in Captain Wragge's face as he read it. "What do they want with us at Sea-view Cottage?"

"Pardon me," said the captain, gravely, "this requires consideration. Let me have a minute or two to think."

He took a few turns up and down the room, then suddenly stepped aside to a table in a corner on which his writing materials were placed. "I was not born yesterday, ma'am!" said the captain, speaking jocosely to himself. He winked his brown eye, took up his pen, and wrote the answer.

"Can you speak now?" inquired Magdalen, when the servant had left the room. "What does that letter say, and how have you answered it?"

The captain placed the letter in her hand. "I have accepted the invitation," he replied, quietly.

Magdalen read the letter. "Hidden enmity yesterday," she said, "and open friendship to-day. What does it mean?"

"It means," said Captain Wragge, "that Mrs. Lecount is even sharper than I thought her. She has found you out."

"Impossible," cried Magdalen. "Quite impossible in the time."

"I can't say how she has found you out," proceeded the captain, with perfect composure.

"She may know more of your voice than we supposed she knew. Or she may have thought us, on reflection, rather a suspicious family; and anything suspicious in which a woman was concerned may have taken her mind back to that morning call of yours in Vauxhall Walk. Whichever way it may be, the meaning of this sudden change is clear enough. She has found you out; and she wants to put her discovery to the proof by slipping in an awkward question or two, under cover of a little friendly talk. My experience of humanity has been a varied one, and Mrs. Lecount is not the first sharp practitioner in petticoats whom I have had to deal with. All the world's a stage, my dear girl, and one of the scenes on our little stage is shut in from this moment."

With those words he took his copy of Joyce's Scientific Dialogues out of his pocket. "You're done with already, my friend!" said the captain, giving his useful information a farewell smack with his hand, and locking it up in the cupboard. "Such is human popularity!" continued the indomitable vagabond, putting the key cheerfully in his pocket. "Yesterday Joyce was my all-in-all. To-day I don't care that for him!" He snapped his fingers and sat down to breakfast.

"I don't understand you," said Magdalen, looking at him angrily. "Are you leaving me to my own resources for the future?"

"My dear girl!" cried Captain Wragge, "can't you accustom yourself to my dash of humor yet? I have done with my ready-made science simply because I am quite sure that Mrs. Lecount has done believing in me. Haven't I accepted the invitation to Dunwich? Make your mind easy. The help I have given you already counts for nothing compared with the help I am going to give you now. My honor is concerned in bowling out Mrs. Lecount. This last move of hers has made it a personal matter between us. The woman actually thinks she can take me in!!!" cried the captain, striking his knife-handle on the table in a transport of virtuous indignation. "By heavens, I never was so insulted before in my life! Draw your chair in to the table, my dear, and give me half a minute's attention to what I have to say next."

Magdalen obeyed him. Captain Wragge cautiously lowered his voice before he went on.

"I have told you all along," he said, "the one thing needful is never to let Mrs. Lecount catch you with your wits wool-gathering. I say the same after what has happened this morning. Let her suspect you! I defy her to find a fragment of foundation for her suspicions, unless we help her. We shall see to-day if she has been foolish enough to betray herself to her master before she has any facts to support her. I doubt it. If she has told him, we will rain down proofs of our identity with the Bygraves on his feeble little head till it absolutely aches with conviction. You have two things to do on this excursion. First, to distrust every word Mrs. Lecount says to you. Secondly, to exert all your fascinations, and make sure of Mr. Noel Vanstone, dating from to-day. I will give you the opportunity when we leave the carriage and take our walk at Dunwich. Wear your hat, wear your smile; do your figure justice, lace tight; put on your neatest boots and brightest gloves; tie the miserable little wretch to your apron-string—tie him fast; and leave the whole management of the matter after that to me. Steady! here is Mrs. Wragge: we must be doubly careful in looking after her now. Show me your cap, Mrs. Wragge! show me your shoes! What do I see on your apron? A spot? I won't have spots! Take it off after breakfast, and put on another. Pull your chair to the middle of the table—more to the left—more still. Make the breakfast."

At a quarter before eleven Mrs. Wragge (with her own entire concurrence) was dismissed to the back room, to bewilder herself over the science of dressmaking for the rest of the day. Punctually as the clock struck the hour, Mrs. Lecount and her master drove up to the gate of North Shingles, and found Magdalen and Captain Wragge waiting for them in the garden.

On the way to Dunwich nothing occurred to disturb the enjoyment of the drive. Noel Vanstone was in excellent health and high good-humor. Lecount had apologized for the little misunderstanding of the previous night; Lecount had petitioned for the excursion as a treat to herself. He thought of these concessions, and looked at Magdalen, and smirked and simpered without intermission. Mrs. Lecount acted her part to perfection. She was motherly with Magdalen and tenderly attentive to Noel Vanstone. She was deeply interested in Captain Wragge's conversation, and meekly disappointed to find it turn on general subjects, to the exclusion of science. Not a word or look escaped her which hinted in the remotest degree at her real purpose. She was dressed with her customary elegance and propriety; and she was the only one of the party on that sultry summer's day who was perfectly cool in the hottest part of the journey.

As they left the carriage on their arrival at Dunwich, the captain seized a moment when Mrs. Lecount's eye was off him and fortified Magdalen by a last warning word.

"'Ware the cat!" he whispered. "She will show her claws on the way back."

They left the village and walked to the ruins of a convent near at hand—the last relic of the once populous city of Dunwich which has survived the destruction of the place, centuries since, by the all-devouring sea. After looking at the ruins, they sought the shade of a little wood between the village and the low sand-hills which overlook the German Ocean. Here Captain Wragge maneuvered so as to let Magdalen and Noel Vanstone advance some distance in front of Mrs. Lecount and himself, took the wrong path, and immediately lost his way with the most consummate dexterity. After a few minutes' wandering (in the wrong direction), he reached an open space near the sea; and politely opening his camp-stool for the housekeeper's accommodation, proposed waiting where they were until the missing members of the party came that way and discovered them.

Mrs. Lecount accepted the proposal. She was perfectly well aware that her escort had lost himself on purpose, but that discovery exercised no disturbing influence on the smooth amiability of her manner. Her day of reckoning with the captain had not come yet—she merely added the new item to her list, and availed herself of the camp-stool. Captain Wragge stretched himself in a romantic attitude at her feet, and the two determined enemies (grouped like two lovers in a picture) fell into as easy and pleasant a conversation as if they had been friends of twenty years' standing.

"I know you, ma'am!" thought the captain, while Mrs. Lecount was talking to him. "You would like to catch me tripping in my ready-made science, and you wouldn't object to drown me in the Professor's Tank!"

"You villain with the brown eye and the green!" thought Mrs. Lecount, as the captain caught the ball of conversation in his turn; "thick as your skin is, I'll sting you through it yet!"

In this frame of mind toward each other they talked fluently on general subjects, on public affairs, on local scenery, on society in England and society in Switzerland, on health, climate, books, marriage and money—talked, without a moment's pause, without a single misunderstanding on either side for nearly an hour, before Magdalen and Noel Vanstone strayed that way and made the party of four complete again.

When they reached the inn at which the carriage was waiting for them, Captain Wragge left Mrs. Lecount in undisturbed possession of her master, and signed to Magdalen to drop back for a moment and speak to him.

"Well?" asked the captain, in a whisper, "is he fast to your apron-string?"

She shuddered from head to foot as she answered.

"He has kissed my hand," she said. "Does that tell you enough? Don't let him sit next me on the way home! I have borne all I can bear—spare me for the rest of the day."

"I'll put you on the front seat of the carriage," replied the captain, "side by side with me."

On the journey back Mrs. Lecount verified Captain Wragge's prediction. She showed her claws.

The time could not have been better chosen; the circumstances could hardly have favored her more. Magdalen's spirits were depressed: she was weary in body and mind; and she sat exactly opposite the housekeeper, who had been compelled, by the new arrangement, to occupy the seat of honor next her master. With every facility for observing the slightest changes that passed over Magdalen's face, Mrs. Lecount tried her first experiment by leading the conversation to the subject of London, and to the relative advantages offered to residents by the various quarters of the metropolis on both sides of the river. The ever-ready Wragge penetrated her intention sooner than she had anticipated, and interposed immediately. "You're coming to Vauxhall Walk, ma'am," thought the captain; "I'll get there before you."

He entered at once into a purely fictitious description of the various quarters of London in which he had himself resided; and, adroitly mentioning Vauxhall Walk as one of them, saved Magdalen from the sudden question relating to that very locality with which Mrs. Lecount had proposed startling her, to begin with. From his residences he passed smoothly to himself, and poured his whole family history (in the character of Mr. Bygrave) into the housekeeper's ears—not forgetting his brother's grave in Honduras, with the monument by the self-taught negro artist, and his brother's hugely corpulent widow, on the ground-floor of the boarding-house at Cheltenham. As a means of giving Magdalen time to compose herself, this outburst of autobiographical information attained its object, but it answered no other purpose. Mrs. Lecount listened, without being imposed on by a single word the captain said to her. He merely confirmed her conviction of the hopelessness of taking Noel Vanstone into her confidence before she had facts to help her against Captain Wragge's otherwise unassailable position in the identity which he had assumed. She quietly waited until he had done, and then returned to the charge.

"It is a coincidence that your uncle should have once resided in Vauxhall Walk," she said, addressing herself to Magdalen. "Mr. Noel has a house in the same place, and we lived there before we came to Aldborough. May I inquire, Miss Bygrave, whether you know anything of a lady named Miss Garth?"

This time she put the question before the captain could interfere. Magdalen ought to have been prepared for it by what had already passed in her presence, but her nerves had been shaken by the earlier events of the day; and she could only answer the question in the negative, after an instant's preliminary pause to control herself. Her hesitation was of too momentary a nature to attract the attention of any unsuspicious person. But it lasted long enough to confirm Mrs. Lecount's private convictions, and to encourage her to advance a little further.

"I only asked," she continued, steadily fixing her eyes on Magdalen, steadily disregarding the efforts which Captain Wragge made to join in the conversation, "because Miss Garth is a stranger to me, and I am curious to find out what I can about her. The day before we left town, Miss Bygrave, a person who presented herself under the name I have mentioned paid us a visit under very extraordinary circumstances."

With a smooth, ingratiating manner, with a refinement of contempt which was little less than devilish in its ingenious assumption of the language of pity, she now boldly described Magdalen's appearance in disguise in Magdalen's own presence. She slightingly referred to the master and mistress of Combe-Raven as persons who had always annoyed the elder and more respectable branch of the family; she mourned over the children as following their parents' example, and attempting to take a mercenary advantage of Mr. Noel Vanstone, under the protection of a respectable person's character and a respectable person's name. Cleverly including her master in the conversation, so as to prevent the captain from effecting a diversion in that quarter; sparing no petty aggravation; striking at every tender place which the tongue of a spiteful woman can wound, she would, beyond all doubt, have carried her point, and tortured Magdalen into openly betraying herself, if Captain Wragge had not checked her in full career by a loud exclamation of alarm, and a sudden clutch at Magdalen's wrist.

"Ten thousand pardons, my dear madam!" cried the captain. "I see in my niece's face, I feel in my niece's pulse, that one of her violent neuralgic attacks has come on again. My dear girl, why hesitate among friends to confess that you are in pain? What mistimed politeness! Her face shows she is suffering—doesn't it Mrs. Lecount? Darting pains, Mr. Vanstone, darting pains on the left side of the head. Pull down your veil, my dear, and lean on me. Our friends will excuse you; our excellent friends will excuse you for the rest of the day."

Before Mrs. Lecount could throw an instant's doubt on the genuineness of the neuralgic attack, her master's fidgety sympathy declared itself exactly as the captain had anticipated, in the most active manifestations. He stopped the carriage, and insisted on an immediate change in the arrangement of the places—the comfortable back seat for Miss Bygrave and her uncle, the front seat for Lecount and himself. Had Lecount got her smelling-bottle? Excellent creature! let her give it directly to Miss Bygrave, and let the coachman drive carefully. If the coachman shook Miss Bygrave he should not have a half-penny for himself. Mesmerism was frequently useful in these cases. Mr. Noel Vanstone's father had been the most powerful mesmerist in Europe, and Mr. Noel Vanstone was his father's son. Might he mesmerize? Might he order that infernal coachman to draw up in a shady place adapted for the purpose? Would medical help be preferred? Could medical help be found any nearer than Aldborough? That ass of a coachman didn't know. Stop every respectable man who passed in a gig, and ask him if he was a doctor! So Mr. Noel Vanstone ran on, with brief intervals for breathing-time, in a continually-ascending scale of sympathy and self-importance, throughout the drive home.

Mrs. Lecount accepted her defeat without uttering a word. From the moment when Captain Wragge interrupted her, her thin lips closed and opened no more for the remainder of the journey. The warmest expressions of her master's anxiety for the suffering young lady provoked from her no outward manifestations of anger. She took as little notice of him as possible. She paid no attention whatever to the captain, whose exasperating consideration for his vanquished enemy made him more polite to her than ever. The nearer and the nearer they got to Aldborough the more and more fixedly Mrs. Lecount's hard black eyes looked at Magdalen reclining on the opposite seat, with her eyes closed and her veil down.

It was only when the carriage stopped at North Shingles, and when Captain Wragge was handing Magdalen out, that the housekeeper at last condescended to notice him. As he smiled and took off his hat at the carriage door, the strong restraint she had laid on herself suddenly gave way, and she flashed one look at him which scorched up the captain's politeness on the spot. He turned at once, with a hasty acknowledgment of Noel Vanstone's last sympathetic inquiries, and took Magdalen into the house. "I told you she would show her claws," he said. "It is not my fault that she scratched you before I could stop her. She hasn't hurt you, has she?"

"She has hurt me, to some purpose," said Magdalen—"she has given me the courage to go on. Say what must be done to-morrow, and trust me to do it." She sighed heavily as she said those words, and went up to her room.

Captain Wragge walked meditatively into the parlor, and sat down to consider. He felt by no means so certain as he could have wished of the next proceeding on the part of the enemy after the defeat of that day. The housekeeper's farewell look had plainly informed him that she was not at the end of her resources yet, and the old militia-man felt the full importance of preparing himself in good time to meet the next step which she took in advance. He lit a cigar, and bent his wary mind on the dangers of the future.

While Captain Wragge was considering in the parlor at North Shingles, Mrs. Lecount was meditating in her bedroom at Sea View. Her exasperation at the failure of her first attempt to expose the conspiracy had not blinded her to the instant necessity of making a second effort before Noel Vanstone's growing infatuation got beyond her control. The snare set for Magdalen having failed, the chance of entrapping Magdalen's sister was the next chance to try. Mrs. Lecount ordered a cup of tea, opened her writing-case, and began the rough draft of a letter to be sent to Miss Vanstone, the elder, by the morrow's post.

So the day's skirmish ended. The heat of the battle was yet to come.

CHAPTER VI.

ALL human penetration has its limits. Accurately as Captain Wragge had seen his way hitherto, even his sharp insight was now at fault. He finished his cigar with the mortifying conviction that he was totally unprepared for Mrs. Lecount's next proceeding. In this emergency, his experience warned him that there was one safe course, and one only, which he could take. He resolved to try the confusing effect on the housekeeper of a complete change of tactics before she had time to press her advantage and attack him in the dark. With this view he sent the servant upstairs to request that Miss Bygrave would come down and speak to him.

"I hope I don't disturb you," said the captain, when Magdalen entered the room. "Allow me to apologize for the smell of tobacco, and to say two words on the subject of our next proceedings. To put it with my customary frankness, Mrs. Lecount puzzles me, and I propose to return the compliment by puzzling her. The course of action which I have to suggest is a very simple one. I have had the honor of giving you a severe neuralgic attack already, and I beg your permission (when Mr. Noel Vanstone sends to inquire to-morrow morning) to take the further liberty of laying you up altogether. Question from Sea-view Cottage: 'How is Miss

Bygrave this morning?' Answer from North Shingles: 'Much worse: Miss Bygrave is confined to her room.' Question repeated every day, say for a fortnight: 'How is Miss Bygrave?' Answer repeated, if necessary, for the same time: 'No better.' Can you bear the imprisonment? I see no objection to your getting a breath of fresh air the first thing in the morning, or the last thing at night. But for the whole of the day, there is no disguising it, you must put yourself in the same category with Mrs. Wragge—you must keep your room."

"What is your object in wishing me to do this?" inquired Magdalen.

"My object is twofold," replied the captain. "I blush for my own stupidity; but the fact is, I can't see my way plainly to Mrs. Lecount's next move. All I feel sure of is, that she means to make another attempt at opening her master's eyes to the truth. Whatever means she may employ to discover your identity, personal communication with you must be necessary to the accomplishment of her object. Very good. If I stop that communication, I put an obstacle in her way at starting—or, as we say at cards, I force her hand. Do you see the point?"

Magdalen saw it plainly. The captain went on.

"My second reason for shutting you up," he said, "refers entirely to Mrs. Lecount's master. The growth of love, my dear girl, is, in one respect, unlike all other growths—it flourishes under adverse circumstances. Our first course of action is to make Mr. Noel Vanstone feel the charm of your society. Our next is to drive him distracted by the loss of it. I should have proposed a few more meetings, with a view to furthering this end, but for our present critical position toward Mrs. Lecount. As it is, we must trust to the effect you produced yesterday, and try the experiment of a sudden separation rather sooner than I could have otherwise wished. I shall see Mr. Noel Vanstone, though you don't; and if there is a raw place established anywhere about the region of that gentleman's heart, trust me to hit him on it! You are now in full possession of my views. Take your time to consider, and give me your answer—Yes or no."

"Any change is for the better," said Magdalen "which keeps me out of the company of Mrs. Lecount and her master! Let it be as you wish."

She had hitherto answered faintly and wearily; but she spoke those last words with a heightened tone and a rising color—signs which warned Captain Wragge not to press her further.

"Very good," said the captain. "As usual, we understand each other. I see you are tired; and I won't detain you any longer."

He rose to open the door, stopped half-way to it, and came back again. "Leave me to arrange matters with the servant downstairs," he continued. "You can't absolutely keep your bed, and we must purchase the girl's discretion when she answers the door, without taking her into our confidence, of course. I will make her understand that she is to say you are ill, just as she might say you are not at home, as a way of keeping unwelcome acquaintances out of the house. Allow me to open the door for you—I beg your pardon, you are going into Mrs. Wragge's work-room instead of going to your own."

"I know I am," said Magdalen. "I wish to remove Mrs. Wragge from the miserable room she is in now, and to take her upstairs with me."

"For the evening?"

"For the whole fortnight."

Captain Wragge followed her into the dining-room, and wisely closed the door before he spoke again.

"Do you seriously mean to inflict my wife's society on yourself for a fortnight?" he asked, in great surprise.

"Your wife is the only innocent creature in this guilty house," she burst out vehemently. "I must and will have her with me!"

"Pray don't agitate yourself," said the captain. "Take Mrs. Wragge, by all means. I don't want her." Having resigned the partner of his existence in those terms, he discreetly returned to the parlor. "The weakness of the sex!" thought the captain, tapping his sagacious head. "Lay a strain on the female intellect, and the female temper gives way directly."

The strain to which the captain alluded was not confined that evening to the female intellect at North Shingles: it extended to the female intellect at Sea View. For nearly two hours Mrs. Lecount sat at her desk writing, correcting, and writing again, before she could produce a letter to Miss Vanstone, the elder, which exactly accomplished the object she wanted to attain. At last the rough draft was completed to her satisfaction; and she made a fair copy of it forthwith, to be posted the next day.

Her letter thus produced was a masterpiece of ingenuity. After the first preliminary sentences, the housekeeper plainly informed Norah of the appearance of the visitor in disguise at Vauxhall Walk; of the conversation which passed at the interview; and of her own suspicion that the person claiming to be Miss Garth was, in all probability, the younger Miss Vanstone herself. Having told the truth thus far, Mrs. Lecount next proceeded to say that her master was in possession of evidence which would justify him in putting the law in force; that he knew the conspiracy with which he was threatened to be then in process of direction against him at Aldborough; and that he only hesitated to protect himself in deference to family considerations, and in the hope that the elder Miss Vanstone might so influence her sister as to render it unnecessary to proceed to extremities.

Under these circumstances (the letter continued) it was plainly necessary that the disguised visitor to Vauxhall Walk should be properly identified; for if Mrs. Lecount's guess proved to be wrong, and if the person turned out to be a stranger, Mr. Noel Vanstone was positively resolved to prosecute in his own defense. Events at Aldborough, on which it was not necessary to dwell, would enable Mrs. Lecount in a few days to gain sight of the suspected person in her own character. But as the housekeeper was entirely unacquainted with the younger Miss Vanstone, it was obviously desirable that some better informed person should, in this particular, take the matter in hand. If the elder Miss Vanstone happened to be at liberty to come to Aldborough herself, would she kindly write and say so? and Mrs. Lecount would write back again to appoint a day. If, on the other hand, Miss Vanstone was prevented from taking the journey, Mrs. Lecount suggested that her reply should contain the fullest description of her sister's personal appearance—should mention any little peculiarities which might exist in the way of marks on her face or her hands—and should state (in case she had written lately) what the address was in her last letter, and failing that, what the post-mark was on the envelope. With this information to help her, Mrs. Lecount would, in the interest of the misguided young lady herself, accept the responsibility of privately identifying her, and would write back immediately to acquaint the elder Miss Vanstone with the result.

The difficulty of sending this letter to the right address gave Mrs. Lecount very little trouble. Remembering the name of the lawyer who had pleaded the cause of the two sisters in Michael Vanstone's time, she directed her letter to "Miss Vanstone, care of——Pendril, Esquire, London." This she inclosed in a second envelope, addressed to Mr. Noel Vanstone's solicitor, with a line inside, requesting that gentleman to send it at once to the office of Mr. Pendril.

"Now," thought Mrs. Lecount, as she locked the letter up in her desk, preparatory to posting it the next day with her own hand, "now I have got her!"

The next morning the servant from Sea View came, with her master's compliments, to make inquiries after Miss Bygrave's health. Captain Wragge's bulletin was duly announced—Miss Bygrave was so ill as to be confined to her room.

On the reception of this intelligence, Noel Vanstone's anxiety led him to call at North Shingles himself when he went out for his afternoon walk. Miss Bygrave was no better. He inquired if he could see Mr. Bygrave. The worthy captain was prepared to meet this emergency. He thought a little irritating suspense would do Noel Vanstone no harm, and he had carefully charged the servant, in case of necessity, with her answer: "Mr. Bygrave begged to be excused; he was not able to see any one."

On the second day inquiries were made as before, by message in the morning, and by Noel Vanstone himself in the afternoon. The morning answer (relating to Magdalen) was, "a shade better." The afternoon answer (relating to Captain Wragge) was, "Mr. Bygrave has just gone out." That evening Noel Vanstone's temper was very uncertain, and Mrs. Lecount's patience and tact were sorely tried in the effort to avoid offending him.

On the third morning the report of the suffering young lady was less favorable—"Miss Bygrave was still very poorly, and not able to leave her bed." The servant returning to Sea View with this message, met the postman, and took into the breakfast-room with her two letters addressed to Mrs. Lecount.

The first letter was in a handwriting familiar to the housekeeper. It was from the medical attendant on her invalid brother at Zurich; and it announced that the patient's malady had latterly altered in so marked a manner for the better that there was every hope now of preserving his life.

The address on the second letter was in a strange handwriting. Mrs. Lecount, concluding that it was the answer from Miss Vanstone, waited to read it until breakfast was over, and she could retire to her own room.

She opened the letter, looked at once for the name at the end, and started a little as she read it. The signature was not "Norah Vanstone," but "Harriet Garth."

Miss Garth announced that the elder Miss Vanstone had, a week since, accepted an engagement as governess, subject to the condition of joining the family of her employer at their temporary residence in the south of France, and of returning with them when they came back to England, probably in a month or six weeks' time. During the interval of this necessary absence Miss Vanstone had requested Miss Garth to open all her letters, her main object in making that arrangement being to provide for the speedy answering of any communication which might arrive for her from her sister. Miss Magdalen Vanstone had not written since the middle of July—on which occasion the postmark on the letter showed that it must have been posted in London, in the district of Lambeth—and her elder sister had left England in a state of the most distressing anxiety on her account.

Having completed this explanation, Miss Garth then mentioned that family circumstances prevented her from traveling personally to Aldborough to assist Mrs. Lecount's object, but that she was provided with a substitute; in every way fitter for the purpose, in the person of Mr. Pendril. That gentleman was well acquainted with Miss Magdalen Vanstone, and his professional experience and discretion would render his assistance doubly valuable. He had kindly consented to travel to Aldborough whenever it might be thought necessary. But as his time was very valuable, Miss Garth specially requested that he might not be sent for until Mrs. Lecount was quite sure of the day on which his services might be required.

While proposing this arrangement, Miss Garth added that she thought it right to furnish her correspondent with a written description of the younger Miss Vanstone as well. An emergency might happen which would allow Mrs. Lecount no time for securing Mr. Pendril's services; and the execution of Mr. Noel Vanstone's intentions toward the unhappy girl who was the object of his forbearance might be fatally delayed by an unforeseen difficulty in establishing her identity. The personal description, transmitted under these circumstances, then followed. It omitted no personal peculiarity by which Magdalen could be recognized, and it included the "two little moles close together on the left side of the neck," which had been formerly mentioned in the printed handbills sent to York.

In conclusion, Miss Garth expressed her fears that Mrs. Lecount's suspicions were only too likely to be proved true. While, however, there was the faintest chance that the conspiracy might turn out to be directed by a stranger, Miss Garth felt bound, in gratitude toward Mr. Noel Vanstone, to assist the legal proceedings which would in that case be instituted. She accordingly appended her own formal denial—which she would personally repeat if necessary—of any identity between herself and the person in disguise who had made use of her name. She was the Miss Garth who had filled the situation of the late Mr. Andrew Vanstone's governess, and she had never in her life been in, or near, the neighborhood of Vauxhall Wall.

With this disclaimer, and with the writer's fervent assurances that she would do all for Magdalen's advantage which her sister might have done if her sister had been in England, the letter concluded. It was signed in full, and was dated with the business-like accuracy in such matters which had always distinguished Miss Garth's character.

This letter placed a formidable weapon in the housekeeper's hands.

It provided a means of establishing Magdalen's identity through the intervention of a lawyer by profession. It contained a personal description minute enough to be used to advantage, if necessary, before Mr. Pendril's appearance. It presented a signed exposure of the false Miss Garth under the hand of the true Miss Garth; and it established the fact that the last letter received by the elder Miss Vanstone from the younger had been posted (and therefore probably written) in the neighborhood of Vauxhall Walk. If any later letter had been received with the Aldborough postmark, the chain of evidence, so far as the question of localities was concerned, might doubtless have been more complete. But as it was, there was testimony enough (aided as that testimony might be by the fragment of the brown alpaca dress still in Mrs. Lecount's possession) to raise the veil which hung over the conspiracy, and to place Mr.

Noel Vanstone face to face with the plain and startling truth.

The one obstacle which now stood in the way of immediate action on the housekeeper's part was the obstacle of Miss Bygrave's present seclusion within the limits of her own room. The question of gaining personal access to her was a question which must be decided before any communication could be opened with Mr. Pendril. Mrs. Lecount put on her bonnet at once, and called at North Shingles to try what discoveries she could make for herself before post-time.

On this occasion Mr. Bygrave was at home, and she was admitted without the least difficulty.

Careful consideration that morning had decided Captain Wragge on advancing matters a little nearer to the crisis. The means by which he proposed achieving this result made it necessary for him to see the housekeeper and her master separately, and to set them at variance by producing two totally opposite impressions relating to himself on their minds. Mrs. Lecount's visit, therefore, instead of causing him any embarrassment, was the most welcome occurrence he could have wished for. He received her in the parlor with a marked restraint of manner for which she was quite unprepared. His ingratiating smile was gone, and an impenetrable solemnity of countenance appeared in its stead.

"I have ventured to intrude on you, sir," said Mrs. Lecount, "to express the regret with which both my master and I have heard of Miss Bygrave's illness. Is there no improvement?"

"No, ma'am," replied the captain, as briefly as possible. "My niece is no better."

"I have had some experience, Mr. Bygrave, in nursing. If I could be of any use—"

"Thank you, Mrs. Lecount. There is no necessity for our taking advantage of your kindness."

This plain answer was followed by a moment's silence. The housekeeper felt some little perplexity. What had become of Mr. Bygrave's elaborate courtesy, and Mr. Bygrave's many words? Did he want to offend her? If he did, Mrs. Lecount then and there determined that he should not gain his object.

"May I inquire the nature of the illness?" she persisted. "It is not connected, I hope, with our excursion to Dunwich?"

"I regret to say, ma'am," replied the captain, "it began with that neuralgic attack in the carriage."

"So! so!" thought Mrs. Lecount. "He doesn't even try to make me think the illness a real one; he throws off the mask at starting.—Is it a nervous illness, sir?" she added, aloud.

The captain answered by a solemn affirmative inclination of the head.

"Then you have two nervous sufferers in the house, Mr. Bygrave?"

"Yes, ma'am—two. My wife and my niece."

"That is rather a strange coincidence of misfortunes."

"It is, ma'am. Very strange."

In spite of Mrs. Lecount's resolution not to be offended, Captain Wragge's exasperating insensibility to every stroke she aimed at him began to ruffle her. She was conscious of some little difficulty in securing her self-possession before she could say anything more.

"Is there no immediate hope," she resumed, "of Miss Bygrave being able to leave her room?"

"None whatever, ma'am."

"You are satisfied, I suppose, with the medical attendance?"

"I have no medical attendance," said the captain, composedly. "I watch the case myself."

The gathering venom in Mrs. Lecount swelled up at that reply, and overflowed at her lips.

"Your smattering of science, sir," she said, with a malicious smile, "includes, I presume, a smattering of medicine as well?"

"It does, ma'am," answered the captain, without the slightest disturbance of face or manner. "I know as much of one as I do of the other."

The tone in which he spoke those words left Mrs. Lecount but one dignified alternative. She rose to terminate the interview. The temptation of the moment proved too much for her, and she could not resist casting the shadow of a threat over Captain Wragge at parting.

"I defer thanking you, sir, for the manner in which you have received me," she said, "until I can pay my debt of obligation to some purpose. In the meantime I am glad to infer, from the absence of a medical attendant in the house, that Miss Bygrave's illness is much less serious than I had supposed it to be when I came here."

"I never contradict a lady, ma'am," rejoined the incorrigible captain. "If it is your pleasure, when we next meet to think my niece quite well, I shall bow resignedly to the expression of your opinion." With those words, he followed the housekeeper into the passage, and politely opened the door for her. "I mark the trick, ma'am!" he said to himself, as he closed it again. "The trump-card in your hand is a sight of my niece, and I'll take care you don't play it!"

He returned to the parlor, and composedly awaited the next event which was likely to happen—a visit from Mrs. Lecount's master. In less than an hour results justified Captain Wragge's anticipations, and Noel Vanstone walked in.

"My dear sir!" cried the captain, cordially seizing his visitor's reluctant hand, "I know what you have come for. Mrs. Lecount has told you of her visit here, and has no doubt declared that my niece's illness is a mere subterfuge. You feel surprised—you feel hurt—you suspect me of trifling with your kind sympathies—in short, you require an explanation. That explanation you shall have. Take a seat. Mr. Vanstone. I am about to throw myself on your sense and judgment as a man of the world. I acknowledge that we are in a false position, sir; and I tell you plainly at the outset—your housekeeper is the cause of it."

For once in his life, Noel Vanstone opened his eyes. "Lecount!" he exclaimed, in the utmost bewilderment.

"The same, sir," replied Captain Wragge. "I am afraid I offended Mrs. Lecount, when she came here this morning, by a want of cordiality in my manner. I am a plain man, and I can't assume what I don't feel. Far be it from me to breathe a word against your housekeeper's character. She is, no doubt, a most excellent and trustworthy woman, but she has one serious failing common to persons at her time of life who occupy her situation—she is jealous of her influence over her master, although you may not have observed it."

"I beg your pardon," interposed Noel Vanstone; "my observation is remarkably quick. Nothing escapes me."

"In that case, sir," resumed the captain, "you cannot fail to have noticed that Mrs. Lecount has allowed her jealousy to affect her conduct toward my niece?"

Noel Vanstone thought of the domestic passage at arms between Mrs. Lecount and himself when his guests of the evening had left Sea View, and failed to see his way to any direct reply. He expressed the utmost surprise and distress—he thought Lecount had done her best to be agreeable on the drive to Dunwich—he hoped and trusted there was some unfortunate mistake.

"Do you mean to say, sir," pursued the captain, severely, "that you have not noticed the circumstance yourself? As a man of honor and a man of observation, you can't tell me that! Your housekeeper's superficial civility has not hidden your housekeeper's real feeling. My niece has seen it, and so have you, and so have I. My niece, Mr. Vanstone, is a sensitive, high-spirited girl; and she has positively declined to cultivate Mrs. Lecount's society for the future. Don't misunderstand me! To my niece as well as to myself, the attraction of your society, Mr. Vanstone, remains the same. Miss Bygrave simply declines to be an apple of discord (if you will permit the classical allusion) cast into your household. I think she is right so far, and I frankly confess that I have exaggerated a nervous indisposition, from which she is really suffering, into a serious illness—purely and entirely to prevent these two ladies for the present from meeting every day on the Parade, and from carrying unpleasant impressions of each other into your domestic establishment and mine."

"I allow nothing unpleasant in my establishment," remarked Noel Vanstone. "I'm master—you must have noticed that already, Mr. Bygrave—I'm master."

"No doubt of it, my dear sir. But to live morning, noon, and night in the perpetual exercise of your authority is more like the life of a governor of a prison than the life of a master of a household. The wear and tear—consider the wear and tear."

"It strikes you in that light, does it?" said Noel Vanstone, soothed by Captain Wragge's ready recognition of his authority. "I don't know that you're not right. But I must take some steps directly. I won't be made ridiculous—I'll send Lecount away altogether, sooner than be made ridiculous." His color rose, and he folded his little arms fiercely. Captain Wragge's artfully irritating explanation had awakened that dormant suspicion of his housekeeper's influence over him which habitually lay hidden in his mind, and which Mrs. Lecount was now not present to charm back to repose as usual. "What must Miss Bygrave think of me!" he exclaimed, with a sudden outburst of vexation. "I'll send Lecount away. Damme, I'll send Lecount away on the spot!"

"No, no, no!" said the captain, whose interest it was to avoid driving Mrs. Lecount to any desperate extremities. "Why take strong measures when mild measures will do? Mrs. Lecount is an old servant; Mrs. Lecount is attached and useful. She has this little drawback of jealousy—jealousy of her domestic position with her bachelor master. She sees you paying courteous attention to a handsome young lady; she sees that young lady properly sensible of your politeness; and, poor soul, she loses her temper! What is the obvious remedy? Humor her—make a manly concession to the weaker sex. If Mrs. Lecount is with you, the next time we meet on the Parade, walk the other way. If Mrs. Lecount is not with you, give us the pleasure of your company by all means. In short, my dear sir, try the suaviter in modo (as we classical men say) before you commit yourself to the fortiter in re!"

There was one excellent reason why Noel Vanstone should take Captain Wragge's conciliatory advice. An open rupture with Mrs. Lecount—even if he could have summoned the courage to face it—would imply the recognition of her claims to a provision, in acknowledgment of the services she had rendered to his father and to himself. His sordid nature quailed within him at the bare prospect of expressing the emotion of gratitude in a pecuniary form; and, after first consulting appearances by a show of hesitation, he consented to adopt the captain's suggestion, and to humor Mrs. Lecount.

"But I must be considered in this matter," proceeded Noel Vanstone. "My concession to Lecount's weakness must not be misunderstood. Miss Bygrave must not be allowed to suppose I am afraid of my housekeeper."

The captain declared that no such idea ever had entered, or ever could enter, Miss Bygrave's mind. Noel Vanstone returned to the subject nevertheless, again and again, with his customary pertinacity. Would it be indiscreet if he asked leave to set himself right personally with Miss Bygrave? Was there any hope that he might have the happiness of seeing her on that day? or, if not, on the next day? or if not, on the day after? Captain Wragge answered cautiously: he felt the importance of not rousing Noel Vanstone's distrust by too great an alacrity in complying with his wishes.

"An interview to-day, my dear sir, is out of the question," he said. "She is not well enough; she wants repose. To-morrow I propose taking her out before the heat of the day begins—not merely to avoid embarrassment, after what has happened with Mrs. Lecount, but because the morning air and the morning quiet are essential in these nervous cases. We are early people here—we shall start at seven o'clock. If you are early, too, and if you would like to join us, I need hardly say that we can feel no objection to your company on our morning walk. The hour, I am aware, is an unusual one—but later in the day my niece may be resting on the sofa, and may not be able to see visitors."

Having made this proposal purely for the purpose of enabling Noel Vanstone to escape to North Shingles at an hour in the morning when his housekeeper would be probably in bed, Captain Wragge left him to take the hint, if he could, as indirectly as it had been given. He proved sharp enough (the case being one in which his own interests were concerned) to close with the proposal on the spot. Politely declaring that he was always an early man when the morning presented any special attraction to him, he accepted the appointment for seven o'clock, and rose soon afterward to take his leave.

"One word at parting," said Captain Wragge. "This conversation is entirely between ourselves. Mrs. Lecount must know nothing of the impression she has produced on my niece. I have only mentioned it to you to account for my apparently churlish conduct and to satisfy your own mind. In confidence, Mr. Vanstone—strictly in confidence. Good-morning!"

With these parting words, the captain bowed his visitor out. Unless some unexpected disaster occurred, he now saw his way safely to the end of the enterprise. He had gained two important steps in advance that morning. He had sown the seeds of variance between the housekeeper and her master, and he had given Noel Vanstone a common interest with Magdalen and himself, in keeping a secret from Mrs. Lecount. "We have caught our man," thought Captain Wragge, cheerfully rubbing his hands—"we have caught our man at last!"

On leaving North Shingles Noel Vanstone walked straight home, fully restored to his place in his own estimation, and sternly determined to carry matters with a high hand if he found himself in collision with Mrs. Lecount.

The housekeeper received her master at the door with her mildest manner and her gentlest smile. She addressed him with downcast eyes; she opposed to his contemplated assertion of independence a barrier of impenetrable respect.

"May I venture to ask, sir," she began, "if your visit to North Shingles has led you to form the same conclusion as mine on the subject of Miss Bygrave's illness?"

"Certainly not, Lecount. I consider your conclusion to have been both hasty and prejudiced."

"I am sorry to hear it, sir. I felt hurt by Mr. Bygrave's rude reception of me, but I was not aware that my judgment was prejudiced by it. Perhaps he received you, sir, with a warmer welcome?"

"He received me like a gentleman—that is all I think it necessary to say, Lecount—he received me like a gentleman."

This answer satisfied Mrs. Lecount on the one doubtful point that had perplexed her. Whatever Mr. Bygrave's sudden coolness toward herself might mean, his polite reception of her master implied that the risk of detection had not daunted him, and that the plot was still in full progress. The housekeeper's eyes brightened; she had expressly calculated on this result. After a moment's thinking, she addressed her master with another question: "You will probably visit Mr. Bygrave again, sir?"

"Of course I shall visit him—if I please."

"And perhaps see Miss Bygrave, if she gets better?"

"Why not? I should be glad to know why not? Is it necessary to ask your leave first, Lecount?"

"By no means, sir. As you have often said (and as I have often agreed with you), you are master. It may surprise you to hear it, Mr. Noel, but I have a private reason for wishing that you should see Miss Bygrave again."

Mr. Noel started a little, and looked at his housekeeper with some curiosity.

"I have a strange fancy of my own, sir, about that young lady," proceeded Mrs. Lecount. "If you will excuse my fancy, and indulge it, you will do me a favor for which I shall be very grateful."

"A fancy?" repeated her master, in growing surprise. "What fancy?"

"Only this, sir," said Mrs. Lecount.

She took from one of the neat little pockets of her apron a morsel of note-paper, carefully folded into the smallest possible compass, and respectfully placed it in Noel Vanstone's hands.

"If you are willing to oblige an old and faithful servant, Mr. Noel," she said, in a very quiet and very impressive manner, "you will kindly put that morsel of paper into your waistcoat pocket; you will open and read it, for the first time, when you are next in Miss Bygrave's company, and you will say nothing of what has now passed between us to any living creature, from this time to that. I promise to explain my strange request, sir, when you have done what I ask, and when your next interview with Miss Bygrave has come to an end."

She courtesied with her best grace, and quietly left the room.

Noel Vanstone looked from the folded paper to the door, and from the door back to the folded paper, in unutterable astonishment. A mystery in his own house! under his own nose! What did it mean?

It meant that Mrs. Lecount had not wasted her time that morning. While the captain was casting the net over his visitor at North Shingles, the housekeeper was steadily mining the ground under his feet. The folded paper contained nothing less than a carefully written extract from the personal description of Magdalen in Miss Garth's letter. With a daring ingenuity which even Captain Wragge might have envied, Mrs. Lecount had found her instrument for exposing the conspiracy in the unsuspecting person of the victim himself!

CHAPTER VII.

LATE that evening, when Magdalen and Mrs. Wragge came back from their walk in the dark, the captain stopped Magdalen on her way upstairs to inform her of the proceedings of the day. He added the expression of his opinion that the time had come for bringing Noel Vanstone, with the least possible delay, to the point of making a proposal. She merely answered that she understood him, and that she would do what was required of her. Captain Wragge requested her in that case to oblige him by joining a walking excursion in Mr. Noel Vanstone's company at seven o'clock the next morning. "I will be ready," she replied. "Is there anything more?" There was nothing more. Magdalen bade him good-night and returned to her own room.

She had shown the same disinclination to remain any longer than was necessary in the captain's company throughout the three days of her seclusion in the house.

During all that time, instead of appearing to weary of Mrs. Wragge's society, she had patiently, almost eagerly, associated herself with her companion's one absorbing pursuit. She who had often chafed and fretted in past days under the monotony of her life in the freedom of Combe-Raven, now accepted without a murmur the monotony of her life at Mrs. Wragge's work-table. She who had hated the sight of her needle and thread in old times—who had never yet worn an article of dress of her own making—now toiled as anxiously over the making of Mrs. Wragge's gown, and bore as patiently with Mrs. Wragge's blunders, as if the sole object of her existence had been the successful completion of that one dress. Anything was welcome to her—the trivial difficulties of fitting a gown: the small, ceaseless chatter of the poor half-witted creature who was so proud of her assistance, and so happy in her company—anything was welcome that shut her out from the coming future, from the destiny to which she stood self-condemned. That sorely-wounded nature was soothed by such a trifle now as the grasp of her companion's rough and friendly hand—that desolate heart was cheered, when night parted them, by Mrs. Wragge's kiss.

The captain's isolated position in the house produced no depressing effect on the captain's easy and equal spirits. Instead of resenting Magdalen's systematic avoidance of his society, he looked to results, and highly approved of it. The more she neglected him for his wife the more directly useful she became in the character of Mrs. Wragge's self-appointed guardian. He had more than once seriously contemplated revoking the concession which had been extorted from him, and removing his wife, at his own sole responsibility, out of harm's way; and he had only abandoned the idea on discovering that Magdalen's resolution to keep Mrs. Wragge in her own company was really serious. While the two were together, his main anxiety was set at rest. They kept their door locked by his own desire while he was out of the house, and, whatever Mrs. Wragge might do, Magdalen was to be trusted not to open it until he came back. That night Captain Wragge enjoyed his cigar with a mind at ease, and sipped his brandy-and-water in happy ignorance of the pitfall which Mrs. Lecount had prepared for him in the morning.

Punctually at seven o'clock Noel Vanstone made his appearance. The moment he entered the room Captain Wragge detected a change in his visitor's look and manner. "Something wrong!" thought the captain. "We have not done with Mrs. Lecount yet."

"How is Miss Bygrave this morning?" asked Noel Vanstone. "Well enough, I hope, for our early walk?" His half-closed eyes, weak and watery with the morning light and the morning air, looked about the room furtively, and he shifted his place in a restless manner from one chair to another, as he made those polite inquiries.

"My niece is better—she is dressing for the walk," replied the captain, steadily observing his restless little friend while he spoke. "Mr. Vanstone!" he added, on a sudden, "I am a plain Englishman—excuse my blunt way of speaking my mind. You don't meet me this morning as cordially as you met me yesterday. There is something unsettled in your face. I distrust that housekeeper of yours, sir! Has she been presuming on your forbearance? Has she been trying to poison your mind against me or my niece?"

If Noel Vanstone had obeyed Mrs. Lecount's injunctions, and had kept her little morsel of note-paper folded in his pocket until the time came to use it, Captain Wragge's designedly blunt appeal might not have found him unprepared with an answer. But curiosity had got the better of him; he had opened the note at night, and again in the morning; it had seriously perplexed and startled him; and it had left his mind far too disturbed to allow him the possession of his ordinary resources. He hesitated; and his answer, when he succeeded in making it, began with a prevarication.

Captain Wragge stopped him before he had got beyond his first sentence.

"Pardon me, sir," said the captain, in his loftiest manner. "If you have secrets to keep, you have only to say so, and I have done. I intrude on no man's secrets. At the same time, Mr. Vanstone, you must allow me to recall to your memory that I met you yesterday without any reserves on my side. I admitted you to my frankest and fullest confidence, sir—and, highly as I prize the advantages of your society, I can't consent to cultivate your friendship on any other than equal terms." He threw open his respectable frock-coat and surveyed his visitor with a manly and virtuous severity.

"I mean no offense!" cried Noel Vanstone, piteously. "Why do you interrupt me, Mr. Bygrave? Why don't you let me explain? I mean no offense."

"No offense is taken, sir," said the captain. "You have a perfect right to the exercise of your own discretion. I am not offended—I only claim for myself the same privilege which I accord to you." He rose with great dignity and rang the bell. "Tell Miss Bygrave," he said to the servant, "that our walk this morning is put off until another opportunity, and that I won't trouble her to come downstairs."

This strong proceeding had the desired effect. Noel Vanstone vehemently pleaded for a moment's private conversation before the message was delivered. Captain Wragge's severity partially relaxed. He sent the servant downstairs again, and, resuming his chair, waited confidently for results. In calculating the facilities for practicing on his visitor's weakness, he had one great superiority over Mrs. Lecount. His judgment was not warped by latent female jealousies, and he avoided the error into which the housekeeper had fallen, self-deluded—the error of underrating the impression on Noel Vanstone that Magdalen had produced. One of the forces in this world which no middle-aged woman is capable of estimating at its full value, when it acts against her, is the force of beauty in a woman younger than herself.

"You are so hasty, Mr. Bygrave—you won't give me time—you won't wait and hear what I have to say!" cried Noel Vanstone, piteously, when the servant had closed the parlor door.

"My family failing, sir—the blood of the Bygraves. Accept my excuses. We are alone, as you wished; pray proceed."

Placed between the alternatives of losing Magdalen's society or betraying Mrs. Lecount, unenlightened by any suspicion of the housekeeper's ultimate object, cowed by the immovable scrutiny of Captain Wragge's inquiring eye, Noel Vanstone was not long in making his choice. He confusedly described his singular interview of the previous evening with Mrs. Lecount, and, taking the folded paper from his pocket, placed it in the captain's hand.

A suspicion of the truth dawned on Captain Wragge's mind the moment he saw the mysterious note. He withdrew to the window before he opened it. The first lines that attracted his attention were these: "Oblige me, Mr. Noel, by comparing the young lady who is now in your company with the personal description which follows these lines, and which has been communicated to me by a friend. You shall know the name of the person described—which I have left a blank—as soon as the evidence of your own eyes has forced you to believe what you would refuse to credit on the unsupported testimony of Virginie Lecount."

That was enough for the captain. Before he had read a word of the description itself, he knew what Mrs. Lecount had done, and felt, with a profound sense of humiliation, that his female enemy had taken him by surprise.

There was no time to think; the whole enterprise was threatened with irrevocable overthrow. The one resource in Captain Wragge's present situation was to act instantly on the first impulse of his own audacity. Line by line he read on, and still the ready inventiveness which had never deserted him yet failed to answer the call made on it now. He came to the closing sentence—to the last words which mentioned the two little moles on Magdalen's neck. At that crowning point of the description, an idea crossed his mind; his party-colored eyes twinkled; his curly lips twisted up at the corners; Wragge was himself again. He wheeled round suddenly from the window, and looked Noel Vanstone straight in the face with a grimly-quiet suggestiveness of something serious to come.

"Pray, sir, do you happen to know anything of Mrs. Lecount's family?" he inquired.

"A respectable family," said Noel Vanstone—"that's all I know. Why do you ask?"

"I am not usually a betting man," pursued Captain Wragge. "But on this occasion I will lay you any wager you like there is madness in your housekeeper's family."

"Madness!" repeated Noel Vanstone, amazedly

"Madness!" reiterated the captain, sternly tapping the note with his forefinger. "I see the cunning of insanity, the suspicion of insanity, the feline treachery of insanity in every line of this deplorable document. There is a far more alarming reason, sir, than I had supposed for Mrs. Lecount's behavior to my niece. It is clear to me that Miss Bygrave resembles some other lady who has seriously offended your housekeeper—who has been formerly connected, perhaps, with an outbreak of insanity in your housekeeper—and who is now evidently confused with my niece in your housekeeper's wandering mind. That is my conviction, Mr. Vanstone. I may be right, or I may be wrong. All I say is this—neither you, nor any man, can assign a sane motive for the production of that incomprehensible document, and for the use which you are requested to make of it."

"I don't think Lecount's mad," said Noel Vanstone, with a very blank look, and a very discomposed manner. "It couldn't have escaped me, with my habits of observation; it couldn't possibly have escaped me if Lecount had been mad."

"Very good, my dear sir. In my opinion, she is the subject of an insane delusion. In your opinion, she is in possession of her senses, and has some mysterious motive which neither you nor I can fathom. Either way, there can be no harm in putting Mrs. Lecount's description to the test, not only as a matter of curiosity, but for our own private satisfaction on both sides. It is of course impossible to tell my niece that she is to be made the subject of such a preposterous experiment as that note of yours suggests. But you can use your own eyes, Mr. Vanstone; you can keep your own counsel; and—mad or not—you can at least tell your housekeeper, on the testimony of your own senses, that she is wrong. Let me look at the description again. The greater part of it is not worth two straws for any purpose of identification; hundreds of young ladies have tall figures, fair complexions, light brown hair, and light gray eyes. You will say, on the other hand, hundreds of young ladies have not got two little moles close together on the left side of the neck. Quite true. The moles supply us with what we scientific men call a Crucial Test. When my niece comes downstairs, sir, you have my full permission to take the liberty of looking at her neck."

Noel Vanstone expressed his high approval of the Crucial Test by smirking and simpering for the first time that morning.

"Of looking at her neck," repeated the captain, returning the note to his visitor, and then making for the door. "I will go upstairs myself, Mr. Vanstone," he continued, "and inspect Miss Bygrave's walking-dress. If she has innocently placed any obstacles in your way, if her hair is a little too low, or her frill is a little too high, I will exert my authority, on the first harmless pretext I can think of, to have those obstacles removed. All I ask is, that you will choose your opportunity discreetly, and that you will not allow my niece to suppose that her neck is the object of a gentleman's inspection."

The moment he was out of the parlor Captain Wragge ascended the stairs at the top of his speed and knocked at Magdalen's door. She opened it to him in her walking-dress, obedient to the signal agreed on between them which summoned her downstairs.

"What have you done with your paints and powders?" asked the captain, without wasting a word in preliminary explanations. "They were not in the box of costumes which I sold for you at Birmingham. Where are they?"

"I have got them here," replied Magdalen. "What can you possibly mean by wanting them now?"

"Bring them instantly into my dressing-room—the whole collection, brushes, palette, and everything. Don't waste time in asking questions; I'll tell you what has happened as we go on. Every moment is precious to us. Follow me instantly!"

His face plainly showed that there was a serious reason for his strange proposal. Magdalen secured her collection of cosmetics and followed him into the dressing-room. He locked the door, placed her on a chair close to the light, and then told her what had happened.

"We are on the brink of detection," proceeded the captain, carefully mixing his colors with liquid glue, and with a strong "drier" added from a bottle in his own possession. "There is only one chance for us (lift up your hair from the left side of your neck)—I have told Mr. Noel Vanstone to take a private opportunity of looking at you; and I am going to give the lie direct to that she-devil Lecount by painting out your moles."

"They can't be painted out," said Magdalen. "No color will stop on them."

"My color will," remarked Captain Wragge. "I have tried a variety of professions in my time—the profession of painting among the rest. Did you ever hear of such a thing as a Black Eye? I lived some months once in the neighborhood of Drury Lane entirely on Black Eyes. My flesh-color stood on bruises of all sorts, shades, and sizes, and it will stand, I promise you, on your moles."

With this assurance, the captain dipped his brush into a little lump of opaque color which he had mixed in a saucer, and which he had graduated as nearly as the materials would permit to the color of Magdalen's skin. After first passing a cambric handkerchief, with some white powder on it, over the part of her neck on which he designed to operate, he placed two layers of color on the moles with the tip of the brush. The process was performed in a few moments, and the moles, as if by magic, disappeared from view. Nothing but the closest inspection could have discovered the artifice by which they had been concealed; at the distance of two or three feet only, it was perfectly invisible.

"Wait here five minutes," said Captain Wragge, "to let the paint dry—and then join us in the parlor. Mrs. Lecount herself would be puzzled if she looked at you now."

"Stop!" said Magdalen. "There is one thing you have not told me yet. How did Mrs. Lecount get the description which you read downstairs? Whatever else she has seen of me, she has not seen the mark on my neck—it is too far back, and too high up; my hair hides it."

"Who knows of the mark?" asked Captain Wragge.

She turned deadly pale under the anguish of a sudden recollection of Frank.

"My sister knows it," she said, faintly.

"Mrs. Lecount may have written to your sister," suggested the captain:

"Do you think my sister would tell a stranger what no stranger has a right to know? Never! never!"

"Is there nobody else who could tell Mrs. Lecount? The mark was mentioned in the handbills at York. Who put it there?"

"Not Norah! Perhaps Mr. Pendril. Perhaps Miss Garth."

"Then Mrs. Lecount has written to Mr. Pendril or Miss Garth—more likely to Miss Garth. The governess would be easier to deal with than the lawyer."

"What can she have said to Miss Garth?"

Captain Wragge considered a little.

"I can't say what Mrs. Lecount may have written," he said, "but I can tell you what I should have written in Mrs. Lecount's place. I should have frightened Miss Garth by false reports about you, to begin with, and then I should have asked for personal particulars, to help a benevolent stranger in restoring you to your friends." The angry glitter flashed up instantly in Magdalen's eyes.

"What you would have done is what Mrs. Lecount has done," she said, indignantly. "Neither lawyer nor governess shall dispute my right to my own will and my own way. If Miss Garth thinks she can control my actions by corresponding with Mrs. Lecount, I will show Miss Garth she is mistaken! It is high time, Captain Wragge, to have done with these wretched risks of discovery. We will take the short way to the end we have in view sooner than Mrs. Lecount or Miss Garth think for. How long can you give me to wring an offer of marriage out of that creature downstairs?"

"I dare not give you long," replied Captain Wragge. "Now your friends know where you are, they may come down on us at a day's notice. Could you manage it in a week?"

"I'll manage it in half the time," she said, with a hard, defiant laugh. "Leave us together this morning as you left us at Dunwich, and take Mrs. Wragge with you, as an excuse for parting company. Is the paint dry yet? Go downstairs and tell him I am coming directly."

So, for the second time, Miss Garth's well-meant efforts defeated their own end. So the fatal force of circumstance turned the hand that would fain have held Magdalen back into the hand that drove her on.

The captain returned to his visitor in the parlor, after first stopping on his way to issue his orders for the walking excursion to Mrs. Wragge.

"I am shocked to have kept you waiting," he said, sitting down again confidentially by Noel Vanstone's side. "My only excuse is, that my niece had accidentally dressed her hair so as to defeat our object. I have been persuading her to alter it, and young ladies are apt to be a little obstinate on questions relating to their toilet. Give her a chair on that side of you when she comes in, and take your look at her neck comfortably before we start for our walk."

Magdalen entered the room as he said those words, and after the first greetings were exchanged, took the chair presented to her with the most unsuspicious readiness. Noel Vanstone applied the Crucial Test on the spot, with the highest appreciation of the fair material which was the subject of experiment. Not the vestige of a mole was visible on any part of the smooth white surface of Miss Bygrave's neck. It mutely answered the blinking inquiry of Noel Vanstone's half-closed eyes by the flattest practical contradiction of Mrs. Lecount. That one central incident in the events of the morning was of all the incidents that had hitherto occurred, the most important in its results. That one discovery shook the housekeeper's hold on her master as nothing had shaken it yet.

In a few minutes Mrs. Wragge made her appearance, and excited as much surprise in Noel Vanstone's mind as he was capable of feeling while absorbed in the enjoyment of Magdalen's society. The walking-party left the house at once, directing their steps northward, so as not to pass the windows of Sea-view Cottage. To Mrs. Wragge's unutterable astonishment, her husband, for the first time in the course of their married life, politely offered her his arm, and led her on in advance of the young people, as if the privilege of walking alone with her presented some special attraction to him! "Step out!" whispered the captain, fiercely. "Leave your niece and Mr. Vanstone alone! If I catch you looking back at them, I'll put the Oriental Cashmere Robe on the top of the kitchen fire! Turn your toes out, and keep step—confound you, keep step!" Mrs. Wragge kept step to the best of her limited ability. Her sturdy knees trembled under her. She firmly believed the captain was intoxicated.

The walk lasted for rather more than an hour. Before nine o'clock they were all back again at North Shingles. The ladies went at once into the house. Noel Vanstone remained with Captain Wragge in the garden. "Well," said the captain, "what do you think now of Mrs. Lecount?"

"Damn Lecount!" replied Noel Vanstone, in great agitation. "I'm half inclined to agree with you. I'm half inclined to think my infernal housekeeper is mad."

He spoke fretfully and unwillingly, as if the merest allusion to Mrs. Lecount was distasteful to him. His color came and went; his manner was absent and undecided; he fidgeted restlessly about the garden walk. It would have been plain to a far less acute observation than Captain Wragge's, that Magdalen had met his advances by an unexpected grace and readiness of encouragement which had entirely overthrown his self-control.

"I never enjoyed a walk so much in my life!" he exclaimed, with a sudden outburst of enthusiasm. "I hope Miss Bygrave feels all the better, for it. Do you go out at the same time to-morrow morning? May I join you again?"

"By all means, Mr. Vanstone," said the Captain, cordially. "Excuse me for returning to the subject—but what do you propose saying to Mrs. Lecount?"

"I don't know. Lecount is a perfect nuisance! What would you do, Mr. Bygrave, if you were in my place?"

"Allow me to ask a question, my dear sir, before I tell you. What is your breakfast-hour?"

"Half-past nine."

"Is Mrs. Lecount an early riser?"

"No. Lecount is lazy in the morning. I hate lazy women! If you were in my place, what should you say to her?"

"I should say nothing," replied Captain Wragge. "I should return at once by the back way; I should let Mrs. Lecount see me in the front garden as if I was taking a turn before breakfast; and I should leave her to suppose that I was only just out of my room. If she asks you whether you mean to come here today, say No. Secure a quiet life until circumstances force you to give her an answer. Then tell the plain truth—say that Mr. Bygrave's niece and Mrs. Lecount's description are at variance with each other in the most important particular, and beg that the subject may not be mentioned again. There is my advice. What do you think of it?"

If Noel Vanstone could have looked into his counselor's mind, he might have thought the captain's advice excellently adapted to serve the captain's interests. As long as Mrs. Lecount could be kept in ignorance of her master's visits to North Shingles, so long she would wait until the opportunity came for trying her experiment, and so long she might be trusted not to endanger the conspiracy by any further proceedings. Necessarily incapable of viewing Captain Wragge's advice under this aspect, Noel Vanstone simply looked at it as offering him a temporary means of escape from an explanation with his housekeeper. He eagerly declared that the course of action suggested to him should be followed to the letter, and returned to Sea View without further delay.

On this occasion Captain Wragge's anticipations were in no respect falsified by Mrs. Lecount's conduct. She had no suspicion of her master's visit to North Shingles: she had made up her mind, if necessary, to wait patiently for his interview with Miss Bygrave until the end of the week; and she did not embarrass him by any unexpected questions when he announced his intention of holding no personal communication with the Bygraves on that day. All she said was, "Don't you feel well enough, Mr. Noel? or don't you feel inclined?" He answered, shortly, "I don't feel well enough"; and there the conversation ended.

The next day the proceedings of the previous morning were exactly repeated. This time Noel Vanstone went home rapturously with a keepsake in his breast-pocket; he had taken tender possession of one of Miss Bygrave's gloves. At intervals during the day, whenever he was alone, he took out the glove and kissed it with a devotion which was almost passionate in its fervor. The miserable little creature luxuriated in his moments of stolen happiness with a speechless and stealthy delight which was a new sensation to him. The few young girls whom he had met with, in his father's narrow circle at Zurich, had felt a mischievous pleasure in treating him like a quaint little plaything; the strongest impression he could make on their hearts was an impression in which their lap-dogs might have rivaled him; the deepest interest he could create in them was the interest they might have felt in a new trinket or a new dress. The only women who had hitherto invited his admiration, and taken his compliments seriously had been women whose charms were on the wane, and whose chances of marriage were fast failing them. For the first time in his life he had now passed hours of happiness in the society of a beautiful girl, who had left him to think of her afterward without a single humiliating remembrance to lower him in his own esteem.

Anxiously as he tried to hide it, the change produced in his look and manner by the new feeling awakened in him was not a change which could be concealed from Mrs. Lecount. On the second day she pointedly asked him whether he had not made an arrangement to call on the Bygraves. He denied it as before. "Perhaps you are going to-morrow, Mr. Noel?" persisted the housekeeper. He was at the end of his resources; he was impatient to be rid of her inquiries; he trusted to his friend at North Shingles to help him; and this time he answered Yes. "If you see the young lady," proceeded Mrs. Lecount, "don't forget that note of mine, sir, which you have in your waistcoat-pocket." No more was said on either side, but by that night's post the housekeeper wrote to Miss Garth. The letter merely acknowledged, with thanks, the receipt of Miss Garth's communication, and informed her that in a few days Mrs. Lecount hoped to be in a position to write again and summon Mr. Pendril to Aldborough.

Late in the evening, when the parlor at North Shingles began to get dark, and when the captain rang the bell for candles as usual, he was surprised by hearing Magdalen's voice in the passage telling the servant to take the lights downstairs again. She knocked at the door immediately afterward, and glided into the obscurity of the room like a ghost.

"I have a question to ask you about your plans for to-morrow," she said. "My eyes are very weak this evening, and I hope you will not object to dispense with the candles for a few minutes."

She spoke in low, stifled tones, and felt her way noiselessly to a chair far removed from the captain in the darkest part of the room. Sitting near the window, he could just discern the dim outline of her dress, he could just hear the faint accents of her voice. For the last two days he had seen nothing of her except during their morning walk. On that afternoon he had found his wife crying in the little backroom down-stairs. She could only tell him that Magdalen had frightened her—that Magdalen was going the way again which she had gone when the letter came from China in the terrible past time at Vauxhall Walk.

"I was sorry to her that you were ill to-day, from Mrs. Wragge," said the captain, unconsciously dropping his voice almost to a whisper as he spoke.

"It doesn't matter," she answered quietly, out of the darkness. "I am strong enough to suffer, and live. Other girls in my place would have been happier—they would have suffered, and died. It doesn't matter; it will be all the same a hundred years hence. Is he coming again tomorrow morning at seven o'clock?"

"He is coming, if you feel no objection to it."

"I have no objection to make; I have done with objecting. But I should like to have the time altered. I don't look my best in the early morning—-I have bad nights, and I rise haggard and worn. Write him a note this evening, and tell him to come at twelve o'clock."

"Twelve is rather late, under the circumstances, for you to be seen out walking."

"I have no intention of walking. Let him be shown into the parlor—"

Her voice died away in silence before she ended the sentence.

"Yes?" said Captain Wragge.

"And leave me alone in the parlor to receive him."

"I understand," said the captain. "An admirable idea. I'll be out of the way in the dining-room while he is here, and you can come and tell me about it when he has gone."

There was another moment of silence.

"Is there no way but telling you?" she asked, suddenly. "I can control myself while he is with me, but I can't answer for what I may say or do afterward. Is there no other way?"

"Plenty of ways," said the captain. "Here is the first that occurs to me. Leave the blind down over the window of your room upstairs before he comes. I will go out on the beach, and wait there within sight of the house. When I see him come out again, I will look at the window. If he has said nothing, leave the blind down. If he has made you an offer, draw the blind up. The signal is simplicity itself; we can't misunderstand each other. Look your best to-morrow! Make sure of him, my dear girl—make sure of him, if you possibly can."

He had spoken loud enough to feel certain that she had heard him, but no answering word came from her. The dead silence was only disturbed by the rustling of her dress, which told him she had risen from her chair. Her shadowy presence crossed the room again; the door shut softly; she was gone. He rang the bell hurriedly for the lights. The servant found him standing close at the window, looking less self-possessed than usual. He told her he felt a little poorly, and sent her to the cupboard for the brandy.

At a few minutes before twelve the next day Captain Wragge withdrew to his post of observation, concealing himself behind a fishing-boat drawn up on the beach. Punctually as the hour struck, he saw Noel Vanstone approach North Shingles and open the garden gate. When the house door had closed on the visitor, Captain Wragge settled himself comfortably against the side of the boat and lit his cigar.

He smoked for half an hour—for ten minutes over the half-hour, by his watch. He finished the cigar down to the last morsel of it that he could hold in his lips. Just as he had thrown away the end, the door opened again and Noel Vanstone came out.

The captain looked up instantly at Magdalen's window. In the absorbing excitement of the moment, he counted the seconds. She might get from the parlor to her own room in less than a minute. He counted to thirty, and nothing happened. He counted to fifty, and nothing happened. He gave up counting, and left the boat impatiently, to return to the house.

As he took his first step forward he saw the signal.

The blind was drawn up.

Cautiously ascending the eminence of the beach, Captain Wragge looked toward Sea-view Cottage before he showed himself on the Parade. Noel Vanstone had reached home again; he was just entering his own door.

"If all your money was offered me to stand in your shoes," said the captain, looking after him—"rich as you are, I wouldn't take it!"

CHAPTER VIII.

ON returning to the house, Captain Wragge received a significant message from the servant. "Mr. Noel Vanstone would call again at two o'clock that afternoon, when he hoped to have the pleasure of finding Mr. Bygrave at home."

The captain's first inquiry after hearing this message referred to Magdalen. "Where was Miss Bygrave?" "In her own room." "Where was Mrs. Bygrave?" "In the back parlor." Captain Wragge turned his steps at once in the latter direction, and found his wife, for the second time, in tears. She had been sent out of Magdalen's room for the whole day, and she was at her wits' end to know what she had done to deserve it. Shortening her lamentations without ceremony, her husband sent her upstairs on the spot, with instructions to knock at the door, and to inquire whether Magdalen could give five minutes' attention to a question of importance which must be settled before two o'clock.

The answer returned was in the negative. Magdalen requested that the subject on which she was asked to decide might be mentioned to her in writing. She engaged to reply in the same way, on the understanding that Mrs. Wragge, and not the servant, should be employed to deliver the note and to take back the answer.

Captain Wragge forthwith opened his paper-case and wrote these lines: "Accept my warmest congratulations on the result of your interview with Mr. N. V. He is coming again at two o'clock—no doubt to make his proposals in due form. The question to decide is, whether I shall press him or not on the subject of settlements. The considerations for your own mind are two in number. First, whether the said pressure (without at all underrating your influence over him) may not squeeze for a long time before it squeezes money out of Mr. N. V. Secondly, whether we are altogether justified—considering our present position toward a certain sharp practitioner in petticoats—in running the risk of delay. Consider these points, and let me have your decision as soon as convenient."

The answer returned to this note was written in crooked, blotted characters, strangely unlike Magdalen's usually firm and clear handwriting. It only contained these words: "Give yourself no trouble about settlements. Leave the use to which he is to put his money for the future in my hands."

"Did you see her?" asked the captain, when his wife had delivered the answer.

"I tried," said Mrs. Wragge, with a fresh burst of tears—"but she only opened the door far enough to put out her hand. I took and gave it a little squeeze—and, oh poor soul, it felt so cold in mine!"

When Mrs. Lecount's master made his appearance at two o'clock, he stood alarmingly in need of an anodyne application from Mrs. Lecount's green fan. The agitation of making his avowal to Magdalen; the terror of finding himself discovered by the housekeeper; the tormenting suspicion of the hard pecuniary conditions which Magdalen's relative and guardian might impose on him—all these emotions, stirring in conflict together, had overpowered his feebly-working heart with a trial that strained it sorely. He gasped for breath as he sat down in the parlor at North Shingles, and that ominous bluish pallor which always overspread his face in moments of agitation now made its warning appearance again. Captain Wragge seized the brandy bottle in genuine alarm, and forced his visitor to drink a wine-glassful of the spirit before a word was said between them on either side.

Restored by the stimulant, and encouraged by the readiness with which the captain anticipated everything that he had to say, Noel Vanstone contrived to state the serious object of his visit in tolerably plain terms. All the conventional preliminaries proper to the occasion were easily disposed of. The suitor's family was respectable; his position in life was undeniably satisfactory; his attachment, though hasty, was evidently disinterested and sincere. All that Captain Wragge had to do was to refer to these various considerations with a happy choice of language in a voice that trembled with manly emotion, and this he did to perfection. For the first half-hour of the interview, no allusion whatever was made to the delicate and dangerous part of the subject. The captain waited until he had composed his visitor, and when that result was achieved came smoothly to the point in these terms:

"There is one little difficulty, Mr. Vanstone, which I think we have both overlooked. Your housekeeper's recent conduct inclines me to fear that she will view the approaching change in your life with anything but a friendly eye. Probably you have not thought it necessary yet to inform her of the new tie which you propose to form?"

Noel Vanstone turned pale at the bare idea of explaining himself to Mrs. Lecount.

"I can't tell what I'm to do," he said, glancing aside nervously at the window, as if he expected to see the housekeeper peeping in. "I hate all awkward positions, and this is the most unpleasant position I ever was placed in. You don't know what a terrible woman Lecount is. I'm not afraid of her; pray don't suppose I'm afraid of her—"

At those words his fears rose in his throat, and gave him the lie direct by stopping his utterance.

"Pray don't trouble yourself to explain," said Captain Wragge, coming to the rescue. "This is the common story, Mr. Vanstone. Here is a woman who has grown old in your service, and in your father's service before you; a woman who has contrived, in all sorts of small, underhand ways, to presume systematically on her position for years and years past; a woman, in short, whom your inconsiderate but perfectly natural kindness has allowed to claim a right of property in you—"

"Property!" cried Noel Vanstone, mistaking the captain, and letting the truth escape him through sheer inability to conceal his fears any longer. "I don't know what amount of property she won't claim. She'll make me pay for my father as well as for myself. Thousands, Mr. Bygrave—thousands of pounds sterling out of my pocket!!!" He clasped his hands in despair at the picture of pecuniary compulsion which his fancy had conjured up—his own golden life-blood spouting from him in great jets of prodigality, under the lancet of Mrs. Lecount.

"Gently, Mr. Vanstone—gently! The woman knows nothing so far, and the money is not gone yet."

"No, no; the money is not gone, as you say. I'm only nervous about it; I can't help being nervous. You were saying something just now; you were going to give me advice. I value your advice; you don't know how highly I value your advice." He said those words with a conciliatory smile which was more than helpless; it was absolutely servile in its dependence on his judicious friend.

"I was only assuring you, my dear sir, that I understood your position," said the captain. "I see your difficulty as plainly as you can see it yourself. Tell a woman like Mrs. Lecount that she must come off her domestic throne, to make way for a young and beautiful successor, armed with the authority of a wife, and an unpleasant scene must be the inevitable result. An unpleasant scene, Mr. Vanstone, if your opinion of your housekeeper's sanity is well founded. Something far more serious, if my opinion that her intellect is unsettled happens to turn out the right one."

"I don't say it isn't my opinion, too," rejoined Noel Vanstone. "Especially after what has happened to-day."

Captain Wragge immediately begged to know what the event alluded to might be.

Noel Vanstone thereupon explained—with an infinite number of parentheses all referring to himself—that Mrs. Lecount had put the dreaded question relating to the little note in her master's pocket barely an hour since. He had answered her inquiry as Mr. Bygrave had advised him. On hearing that the accuracy of the personal description had been fairly put to the test, and had failed in the one important particular of the moles on the neck, Mrs. Lecount had considered a little, and had then asked him whether he had shown her note to Mr. Bygrave before the experiment was tried. He had answered in the negative, as the only safe form of reply that he could think of on the spur of the moment, and the housekeeper had then addressed him in these strange and startling words: "You are keeping the truth from me, Mr. Noel. You are trusting strangers, and doubting your old servant and your old friend. Every time you go to Mr. Bygrave's house, every time you see Miss Bygrave, you are drawing nearer and nearer to your destruction. They have got the bandage over your eyes in spite of me; but I tell them, and tell you, before many days are over I will take it off!" To this extraordinary outbreak—

accompanied as it was by an expression in Mrs. Lecount's face which he had never seen there before—Noel Vanstone had made no reply. Mr. Bygrave's conviction that there was a lurking taint of insanity in the housekeeper's blood had recurred to his memory, and he had left the room at the first opportunity.

Captain Wragge listened with the closest attention to the narrative thus presented to him. But one conclusion could be drawn from it—it was a plain warning to him to hasten the end.

"I am not surprised," he said, gravely, "to hear that you are inclining more favorably to my opinion. After what you have just told me, Mr. Vanstone, no sensible man could do otherwise. This is becoming serious. I hardly know what results may not be expected to follow the communication of your approaching change in life to Mrs. Lecount. My niece may be involved in those results. She is nervous; she is sensitive in the highest degree; she is the innocent object of this woman's unreasoning hatred and distrust. You alarm me, sir! I am not easily thrown off my balance, but I acknowledge you alarm me for the future." He frowned, shook his head, and looked at his visitor despondently.

Noel Vanstone began to feel uneasy. The change in Mr. Bygrave's manner seemed ominous of a reconsideration of his proposals from a new and unfavorable point of view. He took counsel of his inborn cowardice and his inborn cunning, and proposed a solution of the difficulty discovered by himself.

"Why should we tell Lecount at all?" he asked. "What right has Lecount to know? Can't we be married without letting her into the secret? And can't somebody tell her afterward when we are both out of her reach?"

Captain Wragge received this proposal with an expression of surprise which did infinite credit to his power of control over his own countenance. His foremost object throughout the interview had been to conduct it to this point, or, in other words, to make the first idea of keeping the marriage a secret from Mrs. Lecount emanate from Noel Vanstone instead of from himself. No one knew better than the captain that the only responsibilities which a weak man ever accepts are responsibilities which can be perpetually pointed out to him as resting exclusively on his own shoulders.

"I am accustomed to set my face against clandestine proceedings of all kinds," said Captain Wragge. "But there are exceptions to the strictest rules; and I am bound to admit, Mr. Vanstone, that your position in this matter is an exceptional position, if ever there was one yet. The course you have just proposed—however unbecoming I may think it, however distasteful it may be to myself—would not only spare you a very serious embarrassment (to say the least of it), but would also protect you from the personal assertion of those pecuniary claims on the part of your housekeeper to which you have already adverted. These are both desirable results to achieve—to say nothing of the removal, on my side, of all apprehension of annoyance to my niece. On the other hand, however, a marriage solemnized with such privacy as you propose must be a hasty marriage; for, as we are situated, the longer the delay the greater will be the risk that our secret may escape our keeping. I am not against hasty marriages where a mutual flame is fanned by an adequate income. My own was a love-match contracted in a hurry. There are plenty of instances in the experience of every one, of short courtships and speedy marriages, which have turned up trumps—I beg your pardon—which have turned out well after all. But if you and my niece, Mr. Vanstone, are to add one to the number of these eases, the usual preliminaries of marriage among the higher classes must be hastened by some means. You doubtless understand me as now referring to the subject of settlements."

"I'll take another teaspoonful of brandy," said Noel Vanstone, holding out his glass with a trembling hand as the word "settlements" passed Captain Wragge's lips.

"I'll take a teaspoonful with you," said the captain, nimbly dismounting from the pedestal of his respectability, and sipping his brandy with the highest relish. Noel Vanstone, after nervously following his host's example, composed himself to meet the coming ordeal, with reclining head and grasping hands, in the position familiarly associated to all civilized humanity with a seat in a dentist's chair.

The captain put down his empty glass and got up again on his pedestal.

"We were talking of settlements," he resumed. "I have already mentioned, Mr. Vanstone, at an early period of our conversation, that my niece presents the man of her choice with no other dowry than the most inestimable of all gifts—the gift of herself. This circumstance, however (as you are no doubt aware), does not disentitle me to make the customary stipulations with her future husband. According to the usual course in this matter, my lawyer would see yours—consultations would take place—delays would occur—strangers would be in possession of your intentions—and Mrs. Lecount would, sooner or later, arrive at that knowledge of the truth which you are anxious to keep from her. Do you agree with me so far?"

Unutterable apprehension closed Noel Vanstone's lips. He could only reply by an inclination of the head.

"Very good," said the captain. "Now, sir, you may possibly have observed that I am a man of a very original turn of mind. If I have not hitherto struck you in that light, it may then be necessary to mention that there are some subjects on which I persist in thinking for myself. The subject of marriage settlements is one of them. What, let me ask you, does a parent or guardian in my present condition usually do? After having trusted the man whom he has chosen for his son-in-law with the sacred deposit of a woman's happiness, he turns round on that man, and declines to trust him with the infinitely inferior responsibility of providing for her pecuniary future. He fetters his son-in-law with the most binding document the law can produce, and employs with the husband of his own child the same precautions which he would use if he were dealing with a stranger and a rogue. I call such conduct as this inconsistent and unbecoming in the last degree. You will not find it my course of conduct, Mr. Vanstone—you will not find me preaching what I don't practice. If I trust you with my niece, I trust you with every inferior responsibility toward her and toward me. Give me your hand, sir; tell me, on your word of honor, that you will provide for your wife as becomes her position and your means, and the question of settlements is decided between us from this moment at once and forever!" Having carried out Magdalen's instructions in this lofty tone, he threw open his respectable frockcoat, and sat with head erect and hand extended, the model of parental feeling and the picture of human integrity.

For one moment Noel Vanstone remained literally petrified by astonishment. The next, he started from his chair and wrung the hand of his magnanimous friend in a perfect transport of admiration. Never yet, throughout his long and varied career, had Captain Wragge felt such difficulty in keeping his countenance as he felt now. Contempt for the outburst of miserly gratitude of which he was the object; triumph in the sense of successful conspiracy against a man who had rated the offer of his protection at five pounds; regret at the lost opportunity of effecting a fine stroke of moral agriculture, which his dread of involving himself in coming consequences had forced him to let slip—all these varied emotions agitated the captain's mind; all strove together to find their way to the surface through the outlets of his face or his tongue. He allowed Noel Vanstone to keep possession of his hand, and to heap one series of shrill protestations and promises on another, until he had regained his usual mastery over himself. That result achieved, he put the little man back in his chair, and returned forthwith to the subject of Mrs. Lecount.

"Suppose we now revert to the difficulty which we have not conquered yet," said the captain. "Let us say that I do violence to my own habits and feelings; that I allow the considerations I have already mentioned to weigh with me; and that I sanction your wish to be united to my niece without the knowledge of Mrs. Lecount. Allow me to inquire in that case what means you can suggest for the accomplishment of your end?"

"I can't suggest anything," replied Noel Vanstone, helplessly. "Would you object to suggest for me?"

"You are making a bolder request than you think, Mr. Vanstone. I never do things by halves. When I am acting with my customary candor, I am frank (as you know already) to the utmost verge of imprudence. When exceptional circumstances compel me to take an opposite course, there isn't a slyer fox alive than I am. If, at your express request, I take off my honest English coat here and put on a Jesuit's gown—if, purely out of sympathy for your awkward position, I consent to keep your secret for you from Mrs. Lecount—I must have no unseasonable scruples to contend with on your part. If it is neck or nothing on my side, sir, it must be neck or nothing on yours also."

"Neck or nothing, by all means," said Noel Vanstone, briskly—"on the understanding that you go first. I have no scruples about keeping Lecount in the dark. But she is devilish cunning, Mr. Bygrave. How is it to be done?"

"You shall hear directly," replied the captain. "Before I develop my views, I should like to have your opinion on an abstract question of morality. What do you think, my dear sir, of pious frauds in general?"

Noel Vanstone looked a little embarrassed by the question.

"Shall I put it more plainly?" continued Captain Wragge. "What do you say to the universally-accepted maxim that 'all stratagems are fair in love and war'?—Yes or No?"

"Yes!" answered Noel Vanstone, with the utmost readiness.

"One more question and I have done," said the captain. "Do you see any particular objection to practicing a pious fraud on Mrs. Lecount?"

Noel Vanstone's resolution began to falter a little.

"Is Lecount likely to find it out?" he asked cautiously.

"She can't possibly discover it until you are married and out of her reach."

"You are sure of that?"

"Quite sure."

"Play any trick you like on Lecount," said Noel Vanstone, with an air of unutterable relief. "I have had my suspicions lately that she is trying to domineer over me; I am beginning to feel that I have borne with Lecount long enough. I wish I was well rid of her."

"You shall have your wish," said Captain Wragge. "You shall be rid of her in a week or ten days."

Noel Vanstone rose eagerly and approached the captain's chair.

"You don't say so!" he exclaimed. "How do you mean to send her away?"

"I mean to send her on a journey," replied Captain Wragge.

"Where?"

"From your house at Aldborough to her brother's bedside at Zurich."

Noel Vanstone started back at the answer, and returned suddenly to his chair.

"How can you do that?" he inquired, in the greatest perplexity. "Her brother (hang him!) is much better. She had another letter from Zurich to say so, this morning."

"Did you see the letter?"

"Yes. She always worries about her brother—she would show it to me."

"Who was it from? and what did it say?"

"It was from the doctor—he always writes to her. I don't care two straws about her brother, and I don't remember much of the letter, except that it was a short one. The fellow was much better; and if the doctor didn't write again, she might take it for granted that he was getting well. That was the substance of it."

"Did you notice where she put the letter when you gave it her back again?"

"Yes. She put it in the drawer where she keeps her account-books."

"Can you get at that drawer?"

"Of course I can. I have got a duplicate key—I always insist on a duplicate key of the place where she keeps her account books. I never allow the account-books to be locked up from my inspection: it's a rule of the house."

"Be so good as to get that letter to-day, Mr. Vanstone, without your housekeeper's knowledge, and add to the favor by letting me have it here privately for an hour or two."

"What do you want it for?"

"I have some more questions to ask before I tell you. Have you any intimate friend at Zurich whom you could trust to help you in playing a trick on Mrs. Lecount?"

"What sort of help do you mean?" asked Noel Vanstone.

"Suppose," said the captain, "you were to send a letter addressed to Mrs. Lecount at Aldborough, inclosed in another letter addressed to one of your friends abroad? And suppose you were to instruct that friend to help a harmless practical joke by posting Mrs. Lecount's letter at Zurich? Do you know any one who could be trusted to do that?"

"I know two people who could be trusted!" cried Noel Vanstone. "Both ladies—both spinsters—both bitter enemies of Lecount's. But what is your drift, Mr. Bygrave? Though I am not usually wanting in penetration, I don't altogether see your drift."

"You shall see it directly, Mr. Vanstone."

With those words he rose, withdrew to his desk in the corner of the room, and wrote a few lines on a sheet of note-paper. After first reading them carefully to himself, he beckoned to Noel Vanstone to come and read them too.

"A few minutes since," said the captain, pointing complacently to his own composition with the feather end of his pen, "I had the honor of suggesting a pious fraud on Mrs. Lecount. There it is!"

He resigned his chair at the writing-table to his visitor. Noel Vanstone sat down, and read these lines:

"MY DEAR MADAM—Since I last wrote, I deeply regret to inform you that your brother has suffered a relapse. The symptoms are so serious, that it is my painful duty to summon you instantly to his bedside. I am making every effort to resist the renewed progress of the malady, and I have not yet lost all hope of success. But I cannot reconcile it to my conscience to leave you in ignorance of a serious change in my patient for the worse, which may be attended by fatal results. With much sympathy, I remain, etc. etc."

Captain Wragge waited with some anxiety for the effect which this letter might produce. Mean, selfish, and cowardly as he was, even Noel Vanstone might feel some compunction at practicing such a deception as was here suggested on a woman who stood toward him in the position of Mrs. Lecount. She had served him faithfully, however interested her motives might be—she had lived since he was a lad in the full possession of his father's confidence—she was living now under the protection of his own roof. Could be fail to remember this; and, remembering it, could he lend his aid without hesitation to the scheme which was now proposed to him? Captain Wragge unconsciously retained belief enough in human nature to doubt it. To his surprise, and, it must be added, to his relief, also, his apprehensions proved to be groundless. The only emotions aroused in Noel Vanstone's mind by a perusal of the letter were a hearty admiration of his friend's idea, and a vainglorious anxiety to claim the credit to himself of being the person who carried it out. Examples may be found every day of a fool who is no coward; examples may be found occasionally of a fool who is not cunning; but it may reasonably be doubted whether there is a producible instance anywhere of a fool who is not cruel.

"Perfect!" cried Noel Vanstone, clapping his hands. "Mr. Bygrave, you are as good as Figaro in the French comedy. Talking of French, there is one serious mistake in this clever letter of yours—it is written in the wrong language. When the doctor writes to Lecount, he writes in French. Perhaps you meant me to translate it? You can't manage without my help, can you? I write French as fluently as I write English. Just look at me! I'll translate it, while I sit here, in two strokes of the pen."

He completed the translation almost as rapidly as Captain Wragge had produced the original. "Wait a minute!" he cried, in high critical triumph at discovering another defect in the composition of his ingenious friend. "The doctor always dates his letters. Here is no date to yours."

"I leave the date to you," said the captain, with a sardonic smile. "You have discovered the fault, my dear sir—pray correct it!"

Noel Vanstone mentally looked into the great gulf which separates the faculty that can discover a defect, from the faculty that can apply a remedy, and, following the example of many a wiser man, declined to cross over it.

"I couldn't think of taking the liberty," he said, politely. "Perhaps you had a motive for leaving the date out?"

"Perhaps I had," replied Captain Wragge, with his easiest good-humor. "The date must depend on the time a letter takes to get to Zurich. I have had no experience on that point—you must have had plenty of experience in your father's time. Give me the benefit of your information, and we will add the date before you leave the writing-table."

Noel Vanstone's experience was, as Captain Wragge had anticipated, perfectly competent to settle the question of time. The railway resources of the Continent (in the year eighteen hundred and forty-seven) were but scanty; and a letter sent at that period from England to Zurich, and from Zurich back again to England, occupied ten days in making the double journey by post.

"Date the letter in French five days on from to-morrow," said the captain, when he had got his information. "Very good. The next thing is to let me have the doctor's note as soon as you can. I may be obliged to practice some hours before I can copy your translation in an exact imitation of the doctor's handwriting. Have you got any foreign note-paper? Let me have a few sheets, and send, at the same time, an envelope addressed to one of those lady-friends of yours at Zurich, accompanied by the necessary request to post the inclosure. This is all I need trouble you to do, Mr. Vanstone. Don't let me seem inhospitable; but the sooner you can supply me with my materials, the better I shall be pleased. We entirely understand each other, I suppose? Having accepted your proposal for my niece's hand, I sanction a private marriage in consideration of the circumstances on your side. A little harmless stratagem is necessary to forward your views. I invent the stratagem at your request, and you make use of it without the least hesitation. The result is, that in ten days from to-morrow Mrs. Lecount will be on her way to Switzerland; in fifteen days from to-morrow Mrs. Lecount will reach Zurich, and discover the trick we have played her; in twenty days from to-morrow Mrs. Lecount will be back at Aldborough, and will find her master's wedding-cards on the table, and her master himself away on his honey-moon trip. I put it arithmetically, for the sake of putting it plain. God bless you. Good-morning!"

"I suppose I may have the happiness of seeing Miss Bygrave to-morrow?" said Noel Vanstone, turning round at the door.

"We must be careful," replied Captain Wragge. "I don't forbid to-morrow, but I make no promise beyond that. Permit me to remind you that we have got Mrs. Lecount to manage for the next ten days."

"I wish Lecount was at the bottom of the German Ocean!" exclaimed Noel Vanstone, fervently. "It's all very well for you to manage her—you don't live in the house. What am I to do?"

"I'll tell you to-morrow," said the captain. "Go out for your walk alone, and drop in here, as you dropped in to-day, at two o'clock. In the meantime, don't forget those things I want you to send me. Seal them up together in a large envelope. When you have done that, ask Mrs. Lecount to walk out with you as usual; and while she is upstairs putting her bonnet on, send the servant across to me. You understand? Good-morning."

An hour afterward, the sealed envelope, with its inclosures, reached Captain Wragge in perfect safety. The double task of exactly imitating a strange handwriting, and accurately copying words written in a language with which he was but slightly acquainted, presented more difficulties to be overcome than the captain had anticipated. It was eleven o'clock before the employment which he had undertaken was successfully completed, and the letter to Zurich ready for the post.

Before going to bed, he walked out on the deserted Parade to breathe the cool night air. All the lights were extinguished in Sea-view Cottage, when he looked that way, except the light in the housekeeper's window. Captain Wragge shook his head suspiciously. He had gained experience enough by this time to distrust the wakefulness of Mrs. Lecount.

CHAPTER IX.

IF Captain Wragge could have looked into Mrs. Lecount's room while he stood on the Parade watching the light in her window, he would have seen the housekeeper sitting absorbed in meditation over a worthless little morsel of brown stuff which lay on her toilet-table.

However exasperating to herself the conclusion might be, Mrs. Lecount could not fail to see that she had been thus far met and baffled successfully at every point. What was she to do next? If she sent for Mr. Pendril when he came to Aldborough (with only a few hours spared from his business at her disposal), what definite course would there be for him to follow? If she showed Noel Vanstone the original letter from which her note had been copied, he would apply instantly to the writer for an explanation: would expose the fabricated story by which Mrs. Lecount had succeeded in imposing on Miss Garth; and would, in any event, still declare, on the evidence of his own eyes, that the test by the marks on the neck had utterly failed. Miss Vanstone, the elder, whose unexpected presence at Aldborough might have done wonders—whose voice in the hall at North Shingles, even if she had been admitted no further, might have reached her sister's ears and led to instant results—Miss Vanstone, the elder, was out of the country, and was not likely to return for a month at least. Look as anxiously as Mrs. Lecount might along the course which she had hitherto followed, she failed to see her way through the accumulated obstacles which now barred her advance.

Other women in this position might have waited until circumstances altered, and helped them. Mrs. Lecount boldly retraced her steps, and determined to find her way to her end in a new direction. Resigning for the present all further attempt to prove that the false Miss Bygrave was the true Magdalen Vanstone, she resolved to narrow the range of her next efforts; to leave the actual question of Magdalen's identity untouched; and to rest satisfied with convincing her master of this simple fact—that the young lady who was charming him at North Shingles, and the disguised woman who had terrified him in Vauxhall Walk, were one and the same person.

The means of effecting this new object were, to all appearance, far less easy of attainment than the means of effecting the object which Mrs. Lecount had just resigned. Here no help was to be expected from others, no ostensibly benevolent motives could be put forward as a blind—no appeal could be made to Mr. Pendril or to Miss Garth. Here the housekeeper's only chance of success depended, in the first place, on her being able to effect a stolen entrance into Mr. Bygrave's house, and, in the second place, on her ability to discover whether that memorable alpaca dress from which she had secretly cut the fragment of stuff happened to form part of Miss Bygrave's wardrobe.

Taking the difficulties now before her in their order as they occurred, Mrs. Lecount first resolved to devote the next few days to watching the habits of the inmates of North Shingles, from early in the morning to late at night, and to testing the capacity of the one servant in the house to resist the temptation of a bribe. Assuming that results proved successful, and that, either by money or by stratagem, she gained admission to North Shingles (without the knowledge of Mr. Bygrave or his niece), she turned next to the second difficulty of the two—the difficulty of obtaining access to Miss Bygrave's wardrobe.

If the servant proved corruptible, all obstacles in this direction might be considered as removed beforehand. But if the servant proved honest, the new problem was no easy one to solve.

Long and careful consideration of the question led the housekeeper at last to the bold resolution of obtaining an interview—if the servant failed her—with Mrs. Bygrave herself. What was the true cause of this lady's mysterious seclusion? Was she a person of the strictest and the most inconvenient integrity? or a person who could not be depended on to preserve a secret? or a person who was as artful as Mr. Bygrave himself, and who was kept in reserve to forward the object of some new deception which was yet to come? In the first two cases, Mrs. Lecount could trust in her own powers of dissimulation, and in the results which they might achieve. In the last case (if no other end was gained), it might be of vital importance to her to discover an enemy hidden in the dark. In any event, she determined to run the risk. Of the three chances in her favor on which she had reckoned at the outset of the struggle—the chance of entrapping Magdalen by word of mouth, the chance of entrapping her by the help of her friends, and the chance of entrapping her by means of Mrs. Bygrave—two had been tried, and two had failed. The third remained to be tested yet; and the third might succeed.

So, the captain's enemy plotted against him in the privacy of her own chamber, while the captain watched the light in her window from the beach outside.

Before breakfast the next morning, Captain Wragge posted the forged letter to Zurich with his own hand. He went back to North Shingles with his mind not quite decided on the course to take with Mrs. Lecount during the all-important interval of the next ten days.

Greatly to his surprise, his doubts on this point were abruptly decided by Magdalen herself.

He found her waiting for him in the room where the breakfast was laid. She was walking restlessly to and fro, with her head drooping on her bosom and her hair hanging disordered over her shoulders. The moment she looked up on his entrance, the captain felt the fear which Mrs. Wragge had felt before him—the fear that her mind would be struck prostrate again, as it had been struck once already, when Frank's letter reached her in Vauxhall Walk.

"Is he coming again to-day?" she asked, pushing away from her the chair which Captain Wragge offered, with such violence that she threw it on the floor.

"Yes," said the captain, wisely answering her in the fewest words. "He is coming at two o'clock."

"Take me away!" she exclaimed, tossing her hair back wildly from her face. "Take me away before he comes. I can't get over the horror of marrying him while I am in this hateful place; take me somewhere where I can forget it, or I shall go mad! Give me two days' rest—two days out of sight of that horrible sea—two days out of prison in this horrible house—two days anywhere in the wide world away from Aldborough. I'll come back with you! I'll go through with it to the end! Only give me two days' escape from that man and everything belonging to him! Do you hear, you villain?" she cried, seizing his arm and shaking it in a frenzy of passion; "I have been tortured enough—I can bear it no longer!"

There was but one way of quieting her, and the captain instantly took it.

"If you will try to control yourself," he said, "you shall leave Aldborough in an hour's time."

She dropped his arm, and leaned back heavily against the wall behind her.

"I'll try," she answered, struggling for breath, but looking at him less wildly. "You shan't complain of me, if I can help it." She attempted confusedly to take her handkerchief from her apron pocket, and failed to find it. The captain took it out for her. Her eyes softened, and she drew her breath more freely as she received the handkerchief from him. "You are a kinder man than I thought you were," she said; "I am sorry I spoke so passionately to you just now—I am very, very sorry." The tears stole into her eyes, and she offered him her hand with the native grace and gentleness of happier days. "Be friends with me again," she said, pleadingly. "I'm only a girl, Captain Wragge—I'm only a girl!"

He took her hand in silence, patted it for a moment, and then opened the door for her to go back to her own room again. There was genuine regret in his face as he showed her that trifling attention. He was a vagabond and a cheat; he had lived a mean, shuffling, degraded life, but he was human; and she had found her way to the lost sympathies in him which not even the self-profanation of a swindler's existence could wholly destroy. "Damn the breakfast!" he said, when the servant came in for her orders. "Go to the inn directly, and say I want a carriage and pair at the door in an hour's time." He went out into the passage, still chafing under a sense of mental disturbance which was new to him, and shouted to his wife more fiercely than ever—"Pack up what we want for a week's absence, and be ready in half an hour!" Having issued those directions, he returned to the breakfast-room, and looked at the half-spread table with an impatient wonder at his disinclination to do justice to his own meal. "She has rubbed off the edge of my appetite," he said to himself, with a forced laugh. "I'll try a cigar, and a turn in the fresh air."

If he had been twenty years younger, those remedies might have failed him. But where is the man to be found whose internal policy succumbs to revolution when that man is on the wrong side of fifty? Exercise and change of place gave the captain back into the possession of himself. He recovered the lost sense of the flavor of his cigar, and recalled his wandering attention to the question of his approaching absence from Aldborough. A few minutes' consideration satisfied his mind that Magdalen's outbreak had forced him to take the course of all others which, on a fair review of existing emergencies, it was now most desirable to adopt.

Captain Wragge's inquiries on the evening when he and Magdalen had drunk tea at Sea View had certainly informed him that the housekeeper's brother possessed a modest competence;

that his sister was his nearest living relative; and that there were some unscrupulous cousins on the spot who were anxious to usurp the place in his will which properly belonged to Mrs. Lecount. Here were strong motives to take the housekeeper to Zurich when the false report of her brother's relapse reached England. But if any idea of Noel Vanstone's true position dawned on her in the meantime, who could say whether she might not, at the eleventh hour, prefer asserting her large pecuniary interest in her master, to defending her small pecuniary interest at her brother's bedside? While that question remained undecided, the plain necessity of checking the growth of Noel Vanstone's intimacy with the family at North Shingles did not admit of a doubt; and of all means of effecting that object, none could be less open to suspicion than the temporary removal of the household from their residence at Aldborough. Thoroughly satisfied with the soundness of this conclusion, Captain Wragge made straight for Sea-view Cottage, to apologize and explain before the carriage came and the departure took place.

Noel Vanstone was easily accessible to visitors; he was walking in the garden before breakfast. His disappointment and vexation were freely expressed when he heard the news which his friend had to communicate. The captain's fluent tongue, however, soon impressed on him the necessity of resignation to present circumstances. The bare hint that the "pious fraud" might fail after all, if anything happened in the ten days' interval to enlighten Mrs. Lecount, had an instant effect in making Noel Vanstone as patient and as submissive as could be wished.

"I won't tell you where we are going, for two good reasons," said Captain Wragge, when his preliminary explanations were completed. "In the first place, I haven't made up my mind yet; and, in the second place, if you don't know where our destination is, Mrs. Lecount can't worm it out of you. I have not the least doubt she is watching us at this moment from behind her window-curtain. When she asks what I wanted with you this morning, tell her I came to say good-by for a few days, finding my niece not so well again, and wishing to take her on a short visit to some friends to try change of air. If you could produce an impression on Mrs. Lecount's mind (without overdoing it), that you are a little disappointed in me, and that you are rather inclined to doubt my heartiness in cultivating your acquaintance, you will greatly help our present object. You may depend on our return to North Shingles in four or five days at furthest. If anything strikes me in the meanwhile, the post is always at our service, and I won't fail to write to you."

"Won't Miss Bygrave write to me?" inquired Noel Vanstone, piteously. "Did she know you were coming here? Did she send me no message?"

"Unpardonable on my part to have forgotten it!" cried the captain. "She sent you her love."

Noel Vanstone closed his eyes in silent ecstasy.

When he opened them again Captain Wragge had passed through the garden gate and was on his way back to North Shingles. As soon as his own door had closed on him, Mrs. Lecount descended from the post of observation which the captain had rightly suspected her of occupying, and addressed the inquiry to her master which the captain had rightly foreseen would follow his departure. The reply she received produced but one impression on her mind. She at once set it down as a falsehood, and returned to her own window to keep watch over North Shingles more vigilantly than ever.

To her utter astonishment, after a lapse of less than half an hour she saw an empty carriage draw up at Mr. Bygrave's door. Luggage was brought out and packed on the vehicle. Miss Bygrave appeared, and took her seat in it. She was followed into the carriage by a lady of great size and stature, whom the housekeeper conjectured to be Mrs. Bygrave. The servant came next, and stood waiting on the path. The last person to appear was Mr. Bygrave. He locked the house door, and took the key away with him to a cottage near at hand, which was the residence of the landlord of North Shingles. On his return, he nodded to the servant, who walked away by herself toward the humbler quarter of the little town, and joined the ladies in the carriage. The coachman mounted the box, and the vehicle disappeared.

Mrs. Lecount laid down the opera-glass, through which she had been closely investigating these proceedings, with a feeling of helpless perplexity which she was almost ashamed to acknowledge to herself. The secret of Mr. Bygrave's object in suddenly emptying his house at Aldborough of every living creature in it was an impenetrable mystery to her.

Submitting herself to circumstances with a ready resignation which Captain Wragge had not shown, on his side, in a similar situation, Mrs. Lecount wasted neither time nor temper in unprofitable guess-work. She left the mystery to thicken or to clear, as the future might decide, and looked exclusively at the uses to which she might put the morning's event in her own interests. Whatever might have become of the family at North Shingles, the servant was left behind, and the servant was exactly the person whose assistance might now be of vital importance to the housekeeper's projects. Mrs. Lecount put on her bonnet, inspected the collection of loose silver in her purse, and set forth on the spot to make the servant's acquaintance.

She went first to the cottage at which Mr. Bygrave had left the key of North Shingles, to discover the servant's present address from the landlord. So far as this object was concerned, her errand proved successful. The landlord knew that the girl had been allowed to go home for a few days to her friends, and knew in what part of Aldborough her friends lived. But here his sources of information suddenly dried up. He knew nothing of the destination to which Mr. Bygrave and his family had betaken themselves, and he was perfectly ignorant of the number of days over which their absence might be expected to extend. All he could say was, that he had not received a notice to quit from his tenant, and that he had been requested to keep the key of the house in his possession until Mr. Bygrave returned to claim it in his own person.

Baffled, but not discouraged, Mrs. Lecount turned her steps next toward the back street of Aldborough, and astonished the servant's relatives by conferring on them the honor of a morning call.

Easily imposed on at starting by Mrs. Lecount's pretense of calling to engage her, under the impression that she had left Mr. Bygrave's service, the servant did her best to answer the questions put to her. But she knew as little as the landlord of her master's plans. All she could say about them was, that she had not been dismissed, and that she was to await the receipt of a note recalling her when necessary to her situation at North Shingles. Not having expected to find her better informed on this part of the subject, Mrs. Lecount smoothly shifted her ground, and led the woman into talking generally of the advantages and defects of her situation in Mr. Bygrave's family.

Profiting by the knowledge gained, in this indirect manner, of the little secrets of the household, Mrs. Lecount made two discoveries. She found out, in the first place, that the servant (having enough to do in attending to the coarser part of the domestic work) was in no position to disclose the secrets of Miss Bygrave's wardrobe, which were known only to the young lady herself and to her aunt. In the second place, the housekeeper ascertained that the true reason of Mrs. Bygrave's rigid seclusion was to be found in the simple fact that she was little better than an idiot, and that her husband was probably ashamed of allowing her to be seen in public. These apparently trivial discoveries enlightened Mrs. Lecount on a very important point which had been previously involved in doubt. She was now satisfied that the likeliest way to obtaining a private investigation of Magdalen's wardrobe lay through deluding the imbecile lady, and not through bribing the ignorant servant.

Having reached that conclusion—pregnant with coming assaults on the weakly-fortified discretion of poor Mrs. Wragge—the housekeeper cautiously abstained from exhibiting herself any longer under an inquisitive aspect. She changed the conversation to local topics, waited until she was sure of leaving an excellent impression behind her, and then took her leave.

Three days passed; and Mrs. Lecount and her master—each with their widely-different ends in view—watched with equal anxiety for the first signs of returning life in the direction of North Shingles. In that interval, no letter either from the uncle or the niece arrived for Noel Vanstone. His sincere feeling of irritation under this neglectful treatment greatly assisted the effect of those feigned doubts on the subject of his absent friends which the captain had recommended him to express in the housekeeper's presence. He confessed his apprehensions of having been mistaken, not in Mr. Bygrave only, but even in his niece as well, with such a genuine air of annoyance that he actually contributed a new element of confusion to the existing perplexities of Mrs. Lecount.

On the morning of the fourth day Noel Vanstone met the postman in the garden; and, to his great relief, discovered among the letters delivered to him a note from Mr. Bygrave.

The date of the note was "Woodbridge," and it contained a few lines only. Mr. Bygrave mentioned that his niece was better, and that she sent her love as before. He proposed returning to Aldborough on the next day, when he would have some new considerations of a strictly private nature to present to Mr. Noel Vanstone's mind. In the meantime he would beg Mr. Vanstone not to call at North Shingles until he received a special invitation to do so—which invitation should certainly be given on the day when the family returned. The motive of this apparently strange request should be explained to Mr. Vanstone's perfect satisfaction when he was once more united to his friends. Until that period arrived, the strictest caution was enjoined on him in all his communications with Mrs. Lecount; and the instant destruction of Mr. Bygrave's letter, after due perusal of it, was (if the classical phrase might be pardoned) a sine qua non.

The fifth day came. Noel Vanstone (after submitting himself to the sine qua non, and destroying the letter) waited anxiously for results; while Mrs. Lecount, on her side, watched patiently for events. Toward three o'clock in the afternoon the carriage appeared again at the gate of North Shingles. Mr. Bygrave got out and tripped away briskly to the landlord's cottage for the key. He returned with the servant at his heels. Miss Bygrave left the carriage; her giant relative followed her example; the house door was opened; the trunks were taken off; the carriage disappeared, and the Bygraves were at home again!

Four o'clock struck, five o'clock, six o'clock, and nothing happened. In half an hour more, Mr. Bygrave—spruce, speckless, and respectable as ever—appeared on the Parade, sauntering composedly in the direction of Sea View.

Instead of at once entering the house, he passed it; stopped, as if struck by a sudden recollection; and, retracing his steps, asked for Mr. Vanstone at the door. Mr. Vanstone came out hospitably into the passage. Pitching his voice to a tone which could be easily heard by any listening individual through any open door in the bedroom regions, Mr. Bygrave announced the object of his visit on the door-mat in the fewest possible words. He had been staying with a distant relative. The distant relative possessed two pictures—Gems by the Old Masters—which he was willing to dispose of, and which he had intrusted for that purpose to Mr. Bygrave's care. If Mr. Noel Vanstone, as an amateur in such matters, wished to see the Gems, they would be visible in half an hour's time, when Mr. Bygrave would have returned to North Shingles.

Having delivered himself of this incomprehensible announcement, the arch-conspirator laid his significant forefinger along the side of his short Roman nose, said, "Fine weather, isn't it? Good-afternoon!" and sauntered out inscrutably to continue his walk on the Parade.

On the expiration of the half-hour Noel Vanstone presented himself at North Shingles, with the ardor of a lover burning inextinguishably in his bosom, through the superincumbent mental fog of a thoroughly bewildered man. To his inexpressible happiness, he found Magdalen alone in the parlor. Never yet had she looked so beautiful in his eyes. The rest and relief of her four days' absence from Aldborough had not failed to produce their results; she had more than recovered her composure. Vibrating perpetually from one violent extreme to another, she had now passed from the passionate despair of five days since to a feverish exaltation of spirits which defied all remorse and confronted all consequences. Her eyes sparkled; her cheeks were bright with color; she talked incessantly, with a forlorn mockery of the girlish gayety of past days; she laughed with a deplorable persistency in laughing; she imitated Mrs. Lecount's smooth voice, and Mrs. Lecount's insinuating graces of manner with an overcharged resemblance to the original, which was but the coarse reflection of the delicately-accurate mimicry of former times. Noel Vanstone, who had never yet seen her as he saw her now, was enchanted; his weak head whirled with an intoxication of enjoyment; his wizen cheeks flushed as if they had caught the infection from hers. The half-hour during which he was alone with her passed like five minutes to him. When that time had elapsed, and when she suddenly left him—to obey a previously-arranged summons to her aunt's presence—miser as he was, he would have paid at that moment five golden sovereigns out of his pocket for five golden minutes more passed in her society.

The door had hardly closed on Magdalen before it opened again, and the captain walked in. He entered on the explanations which his visitor naturally expected from him with the unceremonious abruptness of a man hard pressed for time, and determined to make the most of every moment at his disposal.

"Since we last saw each other," he began, "I have been reckoning up the chances for and against us as we stand at present. The result on my own mind is this: If you are still at Aldborough when that letter from Zurich reaches Mrs. Lecount, all the pains we have taken will have been pains thrown away. If your housekeeper had fifty brothers all dying together, she would throw the whole fifty over sooner than leave you alone at Sea View while we are your neighbors at North Shingles."

Noel Vanstone's flushed cheek turned pale with dismay. His own knowledge of Mrs. Lecount told him that this view of the case was the right one.

"If we go away again," proceeded the captain, "nothing will be gained, for nothing would persuade your housekeeper, in that case, that we have not left you the means of following us. You must leave Aldborough this time; and, what is more, you must go without leaving a single visible trace behind you for us to follow. If we accomplish this object in the course of the next five days, Mrs. Lecount will take the journey to Zurich. If we fail, she will be a fixture at Sea View, to a dead certainty. Don't ask questions! I have got your instructions ready for you, and I want your closest attention to them. Your marriage with my niece depends on your not forgetting a word of what I am now going to tell you.—One question first. Have you followed my advice? Have you told Mrs. Lecount you are beginning to think yourself mistaken in me?"

"I did worse than that," replied Noel Vanstone penitently. "I committed an outrage on my own feelings. I disgraced myself by saying that I doubted Miss Bygrave!"

"Go on disgracing yourself, my dear sir! Doubt us both with all your might, and I'll help you. One question more. Did I speak loud enough this afternoon? Did Mrs. Lecount hear me?"

"Yes. Lecount opened her door; Lecount heard you. What made you give me that message? I see no pictures here. Is this another pious fraud, Mr. Bygrave?"

"Admirably guessed, Mr. Vanstone! You will see the object of my imaginary picture-dealing in the very next words which I am now about to address to you. When you get back to Sea View, this is what you are to say to Mrs. Lecount. Tell her that my relative's works of Art are two worthless pictures—copies from the Old Masters, which I have tried to sell you as originals at an exorbitant price. Say you suspect me of being little better than a plausible impostor, and pity my unfortunate niece for being associated with such a rascal as I am. There is your text to speak from. Say in many words what I have just said in a few. You can do that, can't you?"

"Of course I can do it," said Noel Vanstone. "But I can tell you one thing—Lecount won't believe me."

"Wait a little, Mr. Vanstone; I have not done with my instructions yet. You understand what I have just told you? Very good. We may get on from to-day to to-morrow. Go out to-morrow with Mrs. Lecount at your usual time. I will meet you on the Parade, and bow to you. Instead of returning my bow, look the other way. In plain English, cut me! That is easy enough to do, isn't it?"

"She won't believe me, Mr. Bygrave—she won't believe me!"

"Wait a little again, Mr. Vanstone. There are more instructions to come. You have got your directions for to-day, and you have got your directions for to-morrow. Now for the day after. The day after is the seventh day since we sent the letter to Zurich. On the seventh day decline to go out walking as before, from dread of the annoyance of meeting me again. Grumble about the smallness of the place; complain of your health; wish you had never come to Aldborough, and never made acquaintances with the Bygraves; and when you have well worried Mrs. Lecount with your discontent, ask her on a sudden if she can't suggest a change for the better. If you put that question to her naturally, do you think she can be depended on to answer it?"

"She won't want to be questioned at all," replied Noel Vanstone, irritably. "I have only got to say I am tired of Aldborough; and, if she believes me—which she won't; I'm quite positive, Mr. Bygrave, she won't!—she will have her suggestion ready before I can ask for it."

"Ay! ay!" said the captain eagerly. "There is some place, then, that Mrs. Lecount wants to go to this autumn?"

"She wants to go there (hang her!) every autumn."

"To go where?"

"To Admiral Bartram's—you don't know him, do you?—at St. Crux-in-the-Marsh."

"Don't lose your patience, Mr. Vanstone! What you are now telling me is of the most vital importance to the object we have in view. Who is Admiral Bartram?"

"An old friend of my father's. My father laid him under obligations—my father lent him money when they were both young men. I am like one of the family at St. Crux; my room is always kept ready for me. Not that there's any family at the admiral's except his nephew, George Bartram. George is my cousin; I'm as intimate with George as my father was with the admiral; and I've been sharper than my father, for I haven't lent my friend any money. Lecount always makes a show of liking George—I believe to annoy me. She likes the admiral, too; he flatters her vanity. He always invites her to come with me to St. Crux. He lets her have one of the best bedrooms, and treats her as if she was a lady. She is as proud as Lucifer—she likes being treated like a lady—and she pesters me every autumn to go to St. Crux. What's the matter? What are you taking out your pocketbook for?"

"I want the admiral's address, Mr. Vanstone, for a purpose which I will explain immediately."

With those words, Captain Wragge opened his pocketbook and wrote down the address from Noel Vanstone's dictation, as follows: "Admiral Bartram, St. Crux-in-the-Marsh, near Ossory, Essex."

"Good!" cried the captain, closing his pocketbook again. "The only difficulty that stood in our way is now cleared out of it. Patience, Mr. Vanstone—patience! Let us take up my instructions again at the point where we dropped them. Give me five minutes' more attention, and you will see your way to your marriage as plainly as I see it. On the day after to-morrow you declare you are tired of Aldborough, and Mrs. Lecount suggests St. Crux. You don't say yes or no on the spot; you take the next day to consider it, and you make up your mind the last thing at night to go to St. Crux the first thing in the morning. Are you in the habit of superintending your own packing up, or do you usually shift all the trouble of it on Mrs. Lecount's shoulders?"

"Lecount has all the trouble, of course; Lecount is paid for it! But I don't really go, do I?"

"You go as fast as horses can take you to the railway without having held any previous communication with this house, either personally or by letter. You leave Mrs. Lecount behind to pack up your curiosities, to settle with the tradespeople, and to follow you to St. Crux the next morning. The next morning is the tenth morning. On the tenth morning she receives the letter from Zurich; and if you only carry out my instructions, Mr. Vanstone, as sure as you sit there, to Zurich she goes."

Noel Vanstone's color began to rise again, as the captain's stratagem dawned on him at last in its true light.

"And what am I to do at St. Crux?" he inquired.

"Wait there till I call for you," replied the captain. "As soon as Mrs. Lecount's back is turned, I will go to the church here and give the necessary notice of the marriage. The same day or the next, I will travel to the address written down in my pocketbook, pick you up at the admiral's, and take you on to London with me to get the license. With that document in our possession, we shall be on our way back to Aldborough while Mrs. Lecount is on her way out to Zurich; and before she starts on her return journey, you and my niece will be man and wife! There are your future prospects for you. What do you think of them?"

"What a head you have got!" cried Noel Vanstone, in a sudden outburst of enthusiasm. "You're the most extraordinary man I ever met with. One would think you had done nothing all your life but take people in."

Captain Wragge received that unconscious tribute to his native genius with the complacency of a man who felt that he thoroughly deserved it.

"I have told you already, my dear sir," he said, modestly, "that I never do things by halves. Pardon me for reminding you that we have no time for exchanging mutual civilities. Are you quite sure about your instructions? I dare not write them down for fear of accidents. Try the system of artificial memory; count your instructions off after me, on your thumb and your four fingers. To-day you tell Mrs. Lecount I have tried to take you in with my relative's works of Art. To-morrow you cut me on the Parade. The day after you refuse to go out, you get tired of Aldborough, and you allow Mrs. Lecount to make her suggestion. The next day you accept the suggestion. And the next day to that you go to St. Crux. Once more, my dear sir! Thumb—works of Art. Forefinger—cut me on the Parade. Middle finger—tired of Aldborough. Third finger—take Lecount's advice. Little finger—off to St. Crux. Nothing can be clearer—nothing can be easier to do. Is there anything you don't understand? Anything that I can explain over again before you go?"

"Only one thing," said Noel Vanstone. "Is it settled that I am not to come here again before I go to St. Crux?"

"Most decidedly!" answered the captain. "The whole success of the enterprise depends on your keeping away. Mrs. Lecount will try the credibility of everything you say to her by one test—the test of your communicating, or not, with this house. She will watch you night and day! Don't call here, don't send messages, don't write letters; don't even go out by yourself. Let her see you start for St. Crux on her suggestion, with the absolute certainty in her own mind that you have followed her advice without communicating it in any form whatever to me or to my niece. Do that, and she must believe you, on the best of all evidence for our interests, and the worst for hers—the evidence of her own senses."

With those last words of caution, he shook the little man warmly by the hand and sent him home on the spot.

CHAPTER X.

ON returning to Sea View, Noel Vanstone executed the instructions which prescribed his line of conduct for the first of the five days with unimpeachable accuracy. A faint smile of contempt hovered about Mrs. Lecount's lips while the story of Mr. Bygrave's attempt to pass off his spurious pictures as originals was in progress, but she did not trouble herself to utter a single word of remark when it had come to an end. "Just what I said!" thought Noel Vanstone, cunningly watching her face; "she doesn't believe a word of it!"

The next day the meeting occurred on the Parade. Mr. Bygrave took off his hat, and Noel Vanstone looked the other way. The captain's start of surprise and scowl of indignation were executed to perfection, but they plainly failed to impose on Mrs. Lecount. "I am afraid, sir, you have offended Mr. Bygrave to-day," she ironically remarked. "Happily for you, he is an excellent Christian! and I venture to predict that he will forgive you to-morrow."

Noel Vanstone wisely refrained from committing himself to an answer. Once more he privately applauded his own penetration; once more he triumphed over his ingenious friend.

Thus far the captain's instructions had been too clear and simple to be mistaken by any one. But they advanced in complication with the advance of time, and on the third day Noel Vanstone fell confusedly into the commission of a slight error. After expressing the necessary weariness of Aldborough, and the consequent anxiety for change of scene, he was met (as he had anticipated) by an immediate suggestion from the housekeeper, recommending a visit to St. Crux. In giving his answer to the advice thus tendered, he made his first mistake. Instead of deferring his decision until the next day, he accepted Mrs. Lecount's suggestion on the day when it was offered to him.

The consequences of this error were of no great importance. The housekeeper merely set herself to watch her master one day earlier than had been calculated on—a result which had been already provided for by the wise precautionary measure of forbidding Noel Vanstone all communication with North Shingles. Doubting, as Captain Wragge had foreseen, the sincerity of her master's desire to break off his connection with the Bygraves by going to St. Crux, Mrs. Lecount tested the truth or falsehood of the impression produced on her own mind by vigilantly watching for signs of secret communication on one side or on the other. The close attention with which she had hitherto observed the out-goings and in-comings at North Shingles was now entirely transferred to her master. For the rest of that third day she never let him out of her sight; she never allowed any third person who came to the house, on any pretense whatever, a minute's chance of private communication with him. At intervals through the night she stole to the door of his room, to listen and assure herself that he was in bed; and before sunrise the next morning, the coast-guardsman going his rounds was surprised to see a lady who had risen as early as himself engaged over her work at one of the upper windows of Sea View.

On the fourth morning Noel Vanstone came down to breakfast conscious of the mistake that he had committed on the previous day. The obvious course to take, for the purpose of gaining time, was to declare that his mind was still undecided. He made the assertion boldly when the housekeeper asked him if he meant to move that day. Again Mrs. Lecount offered no remark, and again the signs and tokens of incredulity showed themselves in her face. Vacillation of purpose was not at all unusual in her experience of her master. But on this occasion she believed that his caprice of conduct was assumed for the purpose of gaining time to communicate with North Shingles, and she accordingly set her watch on him once more with doubled and trebled vigilance.

No letters came that morning. Toward noon the weather changed for the worse, and all idea of walking out as usual was abandoned. Hour after hour, while her master sat in one of the parlors, Mrs. Lecount kept watch in the other, with the door into the passage open, and with a full view of North Shingles through the convenient side-window at which she had established herself. Not a sign that was suspicious appeared, not a sound that was suspicious caught her ear. As the evening closed in, her master's hesitation came to an end. He was disgusted with the weather; he hated the place; he foresaw the annoyance of more meetings with Mr. Bygrave, and he was determined to go to St. Crux the first thing the next morning. Lecount could stay behind to pack up the curiosities and settle with the trades-people, and could follow him to the admiral's on the next day. The housekeeper was a little staggered by the tone and manner in which he gave these orders. He had, to her own certain knowledge, effected no communication of any sort with North Shingles, and yet he seemed determined to leave Aldborough at the earliest possible opportunity. For the first time she hesitated in her adherence to her own conclusions. She remembered that her master had complained of the Bygraves before they returned to Aldborough; and she was conscious that her own incredulity had once already misled her when the appearance of the traveling-carriage at the door had proved even Mr. Bygrave himself to be as good as his word.

Still Mrs. Lecount determined to act with unrelenting caution to the last. That night, when the doors were closed, she privately removed the keys from the door in front and the door at the back. She then softly opened her bedroom window and sat down by it, with her bonnet and cloak on, to prevent her taking cold. Noel Vanstone's window was on the same side of the house as her own. If any one came in the dark to speak to him from the garden beneath, they would speak to his housekeeper as well. Prepared at all points to intercept every form of clandestine communication which stratagem could invent, Mrs. Lecount watched through the quiet night. When morning came, she stole downstairs before the servant was up, restored the keys to their places, and re-occupied her position in the parlor until Noel Vanstone made his appearance at the breakfast-table. Had he altered his mind? No. He declined posting to the railway on account of the expense, but he was as firm as ever in his resolution to go to St. Crux. He desired that an inside place might be secured for him in the early coach. Suspicious to the last, Mrs. Lecount sent the baker's man to take the place. He was a public servant, and Mr. Bygrave would not suspect him of performing a private errand.

The coach called at Sea View. Mrs. Lecount saw her master established in his place, and ascertained that the other three inside seats were already occupied by strangers. She inquired of the coachman if the outside places (all of which were not yet filled up) had their full complement of passengers also. The man replied in the affirmative. He had two gentlemen to call for in the town, and the others would take their places at the inn. Mrs. Lecount forthwith turned her steps toward the inn, and took up her position on the Parade opposite from a point of view which would enable her to see the last of the coach on its departure. In ten minutes more it rattled away, full outside and in; and the housekeeper's own eyes assured her that neither Mr. Bygrave himself, nor any one belonging to North Shingles, was among the passengers.

There was only one more precaution to take, and Mrs. Lecount did not neglect it. Mr. Bygrave had doubtless seen the coach call at Sea View. He might hire a carriage and follow it to the railway on pure speculation. Mrs. Lecount remained within view of the inn (the only place at which a carriage could be obtained) for nearly an hour longer, waiting for events. Nothing happened; no carriage made its appearance; no pursuit of Noel Vanstone was now within the range of human possibility. The long strain on Mrs. Lecount's mind relaxed at last. She left her seat on the Parade, and returned in higher spirits than usual, to perform the closing household ceremonies at Sea View.

She sat down alone in the parlor and drew a long breath of relief. Captain Wragge's calculations had not deceived him. The evidence of her own senses had at last conquered the housekeeper's incredulity, and had literally forced her into the opposite extreme of belief.

Estimating the events of the last three days from her own experience of them; knowing (as she certainly knew) that the first idea of going to St. Crux had been started by herself, and that her master had found no opportunity and shown no inclination to inform the family at North Shingles that he had accepted her proposal, Mrs. Lecount was fairly compelled to acknowledge that not a fragment of foundation remained to justify the continued suspicion of treachery in her own mind. Looking at the succession of circumstances under the new light thrown on them by results, she could see nothing unaccountable, nothing contradictory anywhere. The attempt to pass off the forged pictures as originals was in perfect harmony with the character of such a man as Mr. Bygrave. Her master's indignation at the attempt to impose on him; his plainly-expressed suspicion that Miss Bygrave was privy to it; his disappointment in the niece; his contemptuous treatment of the uncle on the Parade; his weariness of the place which had been the scene of his rash intimacy with strangers, and his readiness to quit it that morning, all commended themselves as genuine realities to the housekeeper's mind, for one sufficient reason. Her own eyes had seen Noel Vanstone take his departure from Aldborough without leaving, or attempting to leave, a single trace behind him for the Bygraves to follow.

Thus far the housekeeper's conclusions led her, but no further. She was too shrewd a woman to trust the future to chance and fortune. Her master's variable temper might relent. Accident might at any time give Mr. Bygrave an opportunity of repairing the error that he had committed, and of artfully regaining his lost place in Noel Vanstone's estimation. Admitting that circumstances had at last declared themselves unmistakably in her favor, Mrs. Lecount was not the less convinced that nothing would permanently assure her master's security for the future but the plain exposure of the conspiracy which she had striven to accomplish from the first—which she was resolved to accomplish still.

"I always enjoy myself at St. Crux," thought Mrs. Lecount, opening her account-books, and sorting the tradesmen's bills. "The admiral is a gentleman, the house is noble, the table is excellent. No matter! Here at Sea View I stay by myself till I have seen the inside of Miss Bygrave's wardrobe."

She packed her master's collection of curiosities in their various cases, settled the claims of the trades-people, and superintended the covering of the furniture in the course of the day. Toward nightfall she went out, bent on investigation, and ventured into the garden at North Shingles under cover of the darkness. She saw the light in the parlor window, and the lights in the windows of the rooms upstairs, as usual. After an instant's hesitation she stole to the house door, and noiselessly tried the handle from the outside. It turned the lock as she had expected, from her experience of houses at Aldborough and at other watering-places, but the door resisted her; the door was distrustfully bolted on the inside. After making that discovery, she went round to the back of the house, and ascertained that the door on that side was secured in the same manner. "Bolt your doors, Mr. Bygrave, as fast as you like," said the housekeeper, stealing back again to the Parade. "You can't bolt the entrance to your servant's pocket. The best lock you have may be opened by a golden key."

She went back to bed. The ceaseless watching, the unrelaxing excitement of the last two days, had worn her out.

The next morning she rose at seven o'clock. In half an hour more she saw the punctual Mr. Bygrave—as she had seen him on many previous mornings at the same time—issue from the gate of North Shingles, with his towels under his arm, and make his way to a boat that was waiting for him on the beach. Swimming was one among the many personal accomplishments of which the captain was master. He was rowed out to sea every morning, and took his bath luxuriously in the deep blue water. Mrs. Lecount had already computed the time consumed in this recreation by her watch, and had discovered that a full hour usually elapsed from the moment when he embarked on the beach to the moment when he returned.

During that period she had never seen any other inhabitant of North Shingles leave the house. The servant was no doubt at her work in the kitchen; Mrs. Bygrave was probably still in her bed; and Miss Bygrave (if she was up at that early hour) had perhaps received directions not to venture out in her uncle's absence. The difficulty of meeting the obstacle of Magdalen's presence in the house had been, for some days past, the one difficulty which all Mrs. Lecount's ingenuity had thus far proved unable to overcome.

She sat at the window for a quarter of an hour after the captain's boat had left the beach with her mind hard at work, and her eyes fixed mechanically on North Shingles—she sat considering what written excuse she could send to her master for delaying her departure from Aldborough for some days to come—when the door of the house she was watching suddenly opened, and Magdalen herself appeared in the garden. There was no mistaking her figure and her dress. She took a few steps hastily toward the gate, stopped and pulled down the veil of her garden hat as if she felt the clear morning light too much for her, then hurried out on the Parade and walked away northward, in such haste, or in such pre-occupation of mind, that she went through the garden gate without closing it after her.

Mrs. Lecount started up from her chair with a moment's doubt of the evidence of her own eyes. Had the opportunity which she had been vainly plotting to produce actually offered itself to her of its own accord? Had the chances declared themselves at last in her favor, after steadily acting against her for so long? There was no doubt of it: in the popular phrase, "her luck had turned." She snatched up her bonnet and mantilla, and made for North Shingles without an instant's hesitation. Mr. Bygrave out at sea; Miss Bygrave away for a walk; Mrs. Bygrave and the servant both at home, and both easily dealt with—the opportunity was not to be lost; the risk was well worth running!

This time the house door was easily opened: no one had bolted it again after Magdalen's departure. Mrs. Lecount closed the door softly, listened for a moment in the passage, and heard the servant noisily occupied in the kitchen with her pots and pans. "If my lucky star leads me straight into Miss Bygrave's room," thought the housekeeper, stealing noiselessly up the stairs, "I may find my way to her wardrobe without disturbing anybody."

She tried the door nearest to the front of the house on the right-hand side of the landing. Capricious chance had deserted her already. The lock was turned. She tried the door opposite, on her left hand. The boots ranged symmetrically in a row, and the razors on the dressing-table, told her at once that she had not found the right room yet. She returned to the right-hand side of the landing, walked down a little passage leading to the back of the house, and tried a third door. The door opened, and the two opposite extremes of female humanity, Mrs. Wragge and Mrs. Lecount, stood face to face in an instant!

"I beg ten thousand pardons!" said Mrs. Lecount, with the most consummate self-possession.

"Lord bless us and save us!" cried Mrs. Wragge, with the most helpless amazement.

The two exclamations were uttered in a moment, and in that moment Mrs. Lecount took the measure of her victim. Nothing of the least importance escaped her. She noticed the Oriental Cashmere Robe lying half made, and half unpicked again, on the table; she noticed the imbecile foot of Mrs. Wragge searching blindly in the neighborhood of her chair for a lost shoe; she noticed that there was a second door in the room besides the door by which she had entered, and a second chair within easy reach, on which she might do well to seat herself in a friendly and confidential way. "Pray don't resent my intrusion," pleaded Mrs. Lecount, taking the chair. "Pray allow me to explain myself!"

Speaking in her softest voice, surveying Mrs. Wragge with a sweet smile on her insinuating lips, and a melting interest in her handsome black eyes, the housekeeper told her little introductory series of falsehoods with an artless truthfulness of manner which the Father of Lies himself might have envied. She had heard from Mr. Bygrave that Mrs. Bygrave was a great invalid; she had constantly reproached herself, in her idle half-hours at Sea View (where she filled the situation of Mr. Noel Vanstone's housekeeper), for not having offered her friendly services to Mrs. Bygrave; she had been directed by her master (doubtless well known to Mrs. Bygrave, as one of her husband's friends, and, naturally, one of her charming niece's admirers), to join him that day at the residence to which he had removed from Aldborough; she was obliged to leave early, but she could not reconcile it to her conscience to go without calling to apologize for her apparent want of neighborly consideration; she had found nobody in the house; she had not been able to make the servant hear; she had presumed (not discovering that apartment downstairs) that Mrs. Bygrave's boudoir might be on the upper story; she had thoughtlessly committed an intrusion of which she was sincerely ashamed, and she could now only trust to Mrs. Bygrave's indulgence to excuse and forgive her.

A less elaborate apology might have served Mrs. Lecount's purpose. As soon as Mrs. Wragge's struggling perceptions had grasped the fact that her unexpected visitor was a neighbor well known to her by repute, her whole being became absorbed in admiration of Mrs. Lecount's lady-like manners, and Mrs. Lecount's perfectly-fitting gown! "What a noble way she has of talking!" thought poor Mrs. Wragge, as the housekeeper reached her closing sentence. "And, oh my heart alive, how nicely she's dressed!"

"I see I disturb you," pursued Mrs. Lecount, artfully availing herself of the Oriental Cashmere Robe as a means ready at hand of reaching the end she had in view—"I see I disturb you, ma'am, over an occupation which, I know by experience, requires the closest attention. Dear, dear me, you are un picking the dress again, I see, after it has been made! This is my own experience again, Mrs. Bygrave. Some dresses are so obstinate! Some dresses seem to say to one, in so many words, 'No! you may do what you like with me; I won't fit!'"

Mrs. Wragge was greatly struck by this happy remark. She burst out laughing, and clapped her great hands in hearty approval.

"That's what this gown has been saying to me ever since I first put the scissors into it," she exclaimed, cheerfully. "I know I've got an awful big back, but that's no reason. Why should a gown be weeks on hand, and then not meet behind you after all? It hangs over my Boasom like a sack—it does. Look here, ma'am, at the skirt. It won't come right. It draggles in front, and cocks up behind. It shows my heels—and, Lord knows, I get into scrapes enough about my heels, without showing them into the bargain!"

"May I ask a favor?" inquired Mrs. Lecount, confidentially. "May I try, Mrs. Bygrave, if I can make my experience of any use to you? I think our bosoms, ma'am, are our great difficulty. Now, this bosom of yours?—Shall I say in plain words what I think? This bosom of yours is an Enormous Mistake!"

"Don't say that!" cried Mrs. Wragge, imploringly. "Don't please, there's a good soul! It's an awful big one, I know; but it's modeled, for all that, from one of Magdalen's own."

She was far too deeply interested on the subject of the dress to notice that she had forgotten herself already, and that she had referred to Magdalen by her own name. Mrs. Lecount's sharp ears detected the mistake the instant it was committed. "So! so!" she thought. "One discovery already. If I had ever doubted my own suspicions, here is an estimable lady who would now have set me right.—I beg your pardon," she proceeded, aloud, "did you say this was modeled from one of your niece's dresses?"

"Yes," said Mrs. Wragge. "It's as like as two peas."

"Then," replied Mrs. Lecount, adroitly, "there must be some serious mistake in the making of your niece's dress. Can you show it to me?"

"Bless your heart—yes!" cried Mrs. Wragge. "Step this way, ma'am; and bring the gown along with you, please. It keeps sliding off, out of pure aggravation, if you lay it out on the table. There's lots of room on the bed in here."

She opened the door of communication and led the way eagerly into Magdalen's room. As Mrs. Lecount followed, she stole a look at her watch. Never before had time flown as it flew that morning! In twenty minutes more Mr. Bygrave would be back from his bath.

"There!" said Mrs. Wragge, throwing open the wardrobe, and taking a dress down from one of the pegs. "Look there! There's plaits on her Boasom, and plaits on mine. Six of one and half a dozen of the other; and mine are the biggest—that's all!"

Mrs. Lecount shook her head gravely, and entered forthwith into subtleties of disquisition on the art of dressmaking which had the desired effect of utterly bewildering the proprietor of the Oriental Cashmere Robe in less than three minutes.

"Don't!" cried Mrs. Wragge, imploringly. "Don't go on like that! I'm miles behind you; and my head's Buzzing already. Tell us, like a good soul, what's to be done. You said something about the pattern just now. Perhaps I'm too big for the pattern? I can't help it if I am. Many's the good cry I had, when I was a growing girl, over my own size! There's half too much of me, ma'am—measure me along or measure me across, I don't deny it—there's half too much of me, anyway."

"My dear madam," protested Mrs. Lecount, "you do yourself a wrong! Permit me to assure you that you possess a commanding figure—a figure of Minerva. A majestic simplicity in the form of a woman imperatively demands a majestic simplicity in the form of that woman's dress. The laws of costume are classical; the laws of costume must not be trifled with! Plaits for Venus, puffs for Juno, folds for Minerva. I venture to suggest a total change of pattern. Your niece has other dresses in her collection. Why may we not find a Minerva pattern among them?"

As she said those words, she led the way back to the wardrobe.

Mrs. Wragge followed, and took the dresses out one by one, shaking her head despondently. Silk dresses appeared, muslin dresses appeared. The one dress which remained invisible was the dress of which Mrs. Lecount was in search.

"There's the lot of 'em," said Mrs. Wragge. "They may do for Venus and the two other Ones (I've seen 'em in picters without a morsel of decent linen among the three), but they won't do for Me."

"Surely there is another dress left?" said Mrs. Lecount, pointing to the wardrobe, but touching nothing in it. "Surely I see something hanging in the corner behind that dark shawl?"

Mrs. Wragge removed the shawl; Mrs. Lecount opened the door of the wardrobe a little wider. There—hitched carelessly on the innermost peg—there, with its white spots, and its double flounce, was the brown Alpaca dress!

The suddenness and completeness of the discovery threw the housekeeper, practiced dissembler as she was, completely off her guard. She started at the sight of the dress. The instant afterward her eyes turned uneasily toward Mrs. Wragge. Had the start been observed? It had passed entirely unnoticed. Mrs. Wragge's whole attention was fixed on the Alpaca dress: she was staring at it incomprehensibly, with an expression of the utmost dismay.

"You seem alarmed, ma'am," said Mrs. Lecount. "What is there in the wardrobe to frighten you?"

"I'd have given a crown piece out of my pocket," said Mrs. Wragge, "not to have set my eyes on that gown. It had gone clean out of my head, and now it's come back again. Cover it up!" cried Mrs. Wragge, throwing the shawl over the dress in a sudden fit of desperation. "If I look at it much longer, I shall think I'm back again in Vauxhall Walk!"

Vauxhall Walk! Those two words told Mrs. Lecount she was on the brink of another discovery. She stole a second look at her watch. There was barely ten minutes to spare before the time when Mr. Bygrave might return; there was not one of those ten minutes which might not bring his niece back to the house. Caution counseled Mrs. Lecount to go, without running any more risks. Curiosity rooted her to the spot, and gave the courage to stay at all hazards until the time was up. Her amiable smile began to harden a little as she probed her way tenderly into Mrs. Wragge's feeble mind.

"You have some unpleasant remembrances of Vauxhall Walk?" she said, with the gentlest possible tone of inquiry in her voice. "Or perhaps I should say, unpleasant remembrances of that dress belonging to your niece?"

"The last time I saw her with that gown on," said Mrs. Wragge, dropping into a chair and beginning to tremble, "was the time when I came back from shopping and saw the Ghost."

"The Ghost?" repeated Mrs. Lecount, clasping her hands in graceful astonishment. "Dear madam, pardon me! Is there such a thing in the world? Where did you see it? In Vauxhall

Walk? Tell me—you are the first lady I ever met with who has seen a ghost—pray tell me!"

Flattered by the position of importance which she had suddenly assumed in the housekeeper's eyes, Mrs. Wragge entered at full length into the narrative of her supernatural adventure. The breathless eagerness with which Mrs. Lecount listened to her description of the specter's costume, the specter's hurry on the stairs, and the specter's disappearance in the bedroom; the extraordinary interest which Mrs. Lecount displayed on hearing that the dress in the wardrobe was the very dress in which Magdalen happened to be attired at the awful moment when the ghost vanished, encouraged Mrs. Wragge to wade deeper and deeper into details, and to involve herself in a confusion of collateral circumstances out of which there seemed to be no prospect of her emerging for hours to come. Faster and faster the inexorable minutes flew by; nearer and nearer came the fatal moment of Mr. Bygrave's return. Mrs. Lecount looked at her watch for the third time, without an attempt on this occasion to conceal the action from her companion's notice. There were literally two minutes left for her to get clear of North Shingles. Two minutes would be enough, if no accident happened. She had discovered the Alpaca dress; she had heard the whole story of the adventure in Vauxhall Walk; and, more than that, she had even informed herself of the number of the house—which Mrs. Wragge happened to remember, because it answered to the number of years in her own age. All that was necessary to her master's complete enlightenment she had now accomplished. Even if there had been time to stay longer, there was nothing worth staying for. "I'll strike this worthy idiot dumb with a coup d'etat," thought the housekeeper, "and vanish before she recovers herself."

"Horrible!" cried Mrs. Lecount, interrupting the ghostly narrative by a shrill little scream and making for the door, to Mrs. Wragge's unutterable astonishment, without the least ceremony. "You freeze the very marrow of my bones. Good-morning!" She coolly tossed the Oriental Cashmere Robe into Mrs. Wragge's expansive lap and left the room in an instant.

As she swiftly descended the stairs, she heard the door of the bedroom open.

"Where are your manners?" cried a voice from above, hailing her feebly over the banisters. "What do you mean by pitching my gown at me in that way? You ought to be ashamed of yourself!" pursued Mrs. Wragge, turning from a lamb to a lioness, as she gradually realized the indignity offered to the Cashmere Robe. "You nasty foreigner, you ought to be ashamed of yourself!"

Pursued by this valedictory address, Mrs. Lecount reached the house door, and opened it without interruption. She glided rapidly along the garden path, passed through the gate, and finding herself safe on the Parade, stopped, and looked toward the sea.

The first object which her eyes encountered was the figure of Mr. Bygrave standing motionless on the beach—a petrified bather, with his towels in his hand! One glance at him was enough to show that he had seen the housekeeper passing out through his garden gate.

Rightly conjecturing that Mr. Bygrave's first impulse would lead him to make instant inquiries in his own house, Mrs. Lecount pursued her way back to Sea View as composedly as if nothing had happened. When she entered the parlor where her solitary breakfast was waiting for her, she was surprised to see a letter lying on the table. She approached to take it up with an expression of impatience, thinking it might be some tradesman's bill which she had forgotten.

It was the forged letter from Zurich.

CHAPTER XI.

THE postmark and the handwriting on the address (admirably imitated from the original) warned Mrs. Lecount of the contents of the letter before she opened it.

After waiting a moment to compose herself, she read the announcement of her brother's relapse.

There was nothing in the handwriting, there was no expression in any part of the letter which could suggest to her mind the faintest suspicion of foul play. Not the shadow of a doubt occurred to her that the summons to her brother's bedside was genuine. The hand that held the letter dropped heavily into her lap; she became pale, and old, and haggard in a moment. Thoughts, far removed from her present aims and interests; remembrances that carried her back to other lands than England, to other times than the time of her life in service, prolonged their inner shadows to the surface, and showed the traces of their mysterious passage darkly on her face. The minutes followed each other, and still the servant below stairs waited vainly for the parlor bell. The minutes followed each other, and still she sat, tearless and quiet, dead to the present and the future, living in the past.

The entrance of the servant, uncalled, roused her. With a heavy sigh, the cold and secret woman folded the letter up again and addressed herself to the interests and the duties of the passing time.

She decided the question of going or not going to Zurich, after a very brief consideration of it. Before she had drawn her chair to the breakfast-table she had resolved to go.

Admirably as Captain Wragge's stratagem had worked, it might have failed—unassisted by the occurrence of the morning—to achieve this result. The very accident against which it had been the captain's chief anxiety to guard—the accident which had just taken place in spite of him—was, of all the events that could have happened, the one event which falsified every previous calculation, by directly forwarding the main purpose of the conspiracy! If Mrs. Lecount had not obtained the information of which she was in search before the receipt of the letter from Zurich, the letter might have addressed her in vain. She would have hesitated before deciding to leave England, and that hesitation might have proved fatal to the captain's scheme.

As it was, with the plain proofs in her possession, with the gown discovered in Magdalen's wardrobe, with the piece cut out of it in her own pocketbook, and with the knowledge, obtained from Mrs. Wragge, of the very house in which the disguise had been put on, Mrs. Lecount had now at her command the means of warning Noel Vanstone as she had never been able to warn him yet, or, in other words, the means of guarding against any dangerous tendencies toward reconciliation with the Bygraves which might otherwise have entered his mind during her absence at Zurich. The only difficulty which now perplexed her was the difficulty of deciding whether she should communicate with her master personally or by writing, before her departure from England.

She looked again at the doctor's letter. The word "instantly," in the sentence which summoned her to her dying brother, was twice underlined. Admiral Bartram's house was at some distance from the railway; the time consumed in driving to St. Crux, and driving back again, might be time fatally lost on the journey to Zurich. Although she would infinitely have preferred a personal interview with Noel Vanstone, there was no choice on a matter of life and death but to save the precious hours by writing to him.

After sending to secure a place at once in the early coach, she sat down to write to her master.

Her first thought was to tell him all that had happened at North Shingles that morning. On reflection, however, she rejected the idea. Once already (in copying the personal description from Miss Garth's letter) she had trusted her weapons in her master's hands, and Mr. Bygrave had contrived to turn them against her. She resolved this time to keep them strictly in her own possession. The secret of the missing fragment of the Alpaca dress was known to no living creature but herself; and, until her return to England, she determined to keep it to herself. The necessary impression might be produced on Noel Vanstone's mind without venturing into details. She knew by experience the form of letter which might be trusted to produce an effect on him, and she now wrote it in these words:

"DEAR MR. NOEL—Sad news has reached me from Switzerland. My beloved brother is dying and his medical attendant summons me instantly to Zurich. The serious necessity of availing myself of the earliest means of conveyance to the Continent leaves me but one alternative. I must profit by the permission to leave England, if necessary, which you kindly granted to me at the beginning of my brother's illness, and I must avoid all delay by going straight to London, instead of turning aside, as I should have liked, to see you first at St. Crux.

"Painfully as I am affected by the family calamity which has fallen on me, I cannot let this opportunity pass without adverting to another subject which seriously concerns your welfare, and in which (on that account) your old housekeeper feels the deepest interest.

"I am going to surprise and shock you, Mr. Noel. Pray don't be agitated! pray compose yourself!

"The impudent attempt to cheat you, which has happily opened your eyes to the true character of our neighbors at North Shingles, was not the only object which Mr. Bygrave had in forcing himself on your acquaintance. The infamous conspiracy with which you were threatened in London has been in full progress against you under Mr. Bygrave's direction, at Aldborough. Accident—I will tell you what accident when we meet—has put me in possession of information precious to your future security. I have discovered, to an absolute certainty, that the person calling herself Miss Bygrave is no other than the woman who visited us in disguise at Vauxhall Walk.

"I suspected this from the first, but I had no evidence to support my suspicions; I had no means of combating the false impression produced on you. My hands, I thank Heaven, are tied no longer. I possess absolute proof of the assertion that I have just made—proof that your own eyes can see—proof that would satisfy you, if you were judge in a Court of Justice.

"Perhaps even yet, Mr. Noel, you will refuse to believe me? Be it so. Believe me or not, I have one last favor to ask, which your English sense of fair play will not deny me.

"This melancholy journey of mine will keep me away from England for a fortnight, or, at most, for three weeks. You will oblige me—and you will certainly not sacrifice your own convenience and pleasure—by staying through that interval with your friends at St. Crux. If, before my return, some unexpected circumstance throws you once more into the company of the Bygraves, and if your natural kindness of heart inclines you to receive the excuses which they will, in that case, certainly address to you, place one trifling restraint on yourself, for your own sake, if not for mine. Suspend your flirtation with the young lady (I beg pardon of all other young ladies for calling her so!) until my return. If, when I come back, I fail to prove to you that Miss Bygrave is the woman who wore that disguise, and used those threatening words, in Vauxhall Wall, I will engage to leave your service at a day's notice; and I will atone for the sin of bearing false witness against my neighbor by resigning every claim I have to your grateful remembrance, on your father's account as well as on your own. I make this engagement without reserves of any kind; and I promise to abide by it—if my proofs fail—on the faith of a good Catholic, and the word of an honest woman. Your faithful servant,

"VIRGINIE LECOUNT."

The closing sentences of this letter—as the housekeeper well knew when she wrote them—embodied the one appeal to Noel Vanstone which could be certainly trusted to produce a deep and lasting effect. She might have staked her oath, her life, or her reputation, on proving the assertion which she had made, and have failed to leave a permanent impression on his mind. But when she staked not only her position in his service, but her pecuniary claims on him as well, she at once absorbed the ruling passion of his life in expectation of the result. There was not a doubt of it, in the strongest of all his interests—the interest of saving his money—he would wait.

"Checkmate for Mr. Bygrave!" thought Mrs. Lecount, as she sealed and directed the letter. "The battle is over—the game is played out."

While Mrs. Lecount was providing for her master's future security at Sea View, events were in full progress at North Shingles.

As soon as Captain Wragge recovered his astonishment at the housekeeper's appearance on his own premises, he hurried into the house, and, guided by his own forebodings of the disaster that had happened, made straight for his wife's room.

Never, in all her former experience, had poor Mrs. Wragge felt the full weight of the captain's indignation as she felt it now. All the little intelligence she naturally possessed vanished at once in the whirlwind of her husband's rage. The only plain facts which he could extract from her were two in number. In the first place, Magdalen's rash desertion of her post proved to have no better reason to excuse it than Magdalen's incorrigible impatience: she had passed a sleepless night; she had risen feverish and wretched; and she had gone out, reckless of all consequences, to cool her burning head in the fresh air. In the second place, Mrs. Wragge had, on her own confession, seen Mrs. Lecount, had talked with Mrs. Lecount, and had ended by telling Mrs. Lecount the story of the ghost. Having made these discoveries, Captain Wragge wasted no time in contending with his wife's terror and confusion. He withdrew at once to a window which commanded an uninterrupted prospect of Noel Vanstone's house, and there established himself on the watch for events at Sea View, precisely as Mrs. Lecount had established herself on the watch for events at North Shingles.

Not a word of comment on the disaster of the morning escaped him when Magdalen returned and found him at his post. His flow of language seemed at last to have run dry. "I told you what Mrs. Wragge would do," he said, "and Mrs. Wragge has done it." He sat unflinchingly at the window with a patience which Mrs. Lecount herself could not have surpassed. The one active proceeding in which he seemed to think it necessary to engage was performed by deputy.

He sent the servant to the inn to hire a chaise and a fast horse, and to say that he would call himself before noon that day and tell the hostler when the vehicle would be wanted. Not a sign of impatience escaped him until the time drew near for the departure of the early coach. Then the captain's curly lips began to twitch with anxiety, and the captain's restless fingers beat the devil's tattoo unremittingly on the window-pane.

The coach appeared at last, and drew up at Sea View. In a minute more, Captain Wragge's own observation informed him that one among the passengers who left Aldborough that morning was—Mrs. Lecount.

The main uncertainty disposed of, a serious question—suggested by the events of the morning—still remained to be solved. Which was the destined end of Mrs. Lecount's journey—Zurich or St. Crux? That she would certainly inform her master of Mrs. Wragge's ghost story, and of every other disclosure in relation to names and places which might have escaped Mrs. Wragge's lips, was beyond all doubt. But of the two ways at her disposal of doing the mischief—either personally or by letter—it was vitally important to the captain to know which she had chosen. If she had gone to the admiral's, no choice would be left him but to follow the coach, to catch the train by which she traveled, and to outstrip her afterward on the drive from the station in Essex to St. Crux. If, on the contrary, she had been contented with writing to her master, it would only be necessary to devise measures for intercepting the letter. The captain decided on going to the post-office, in the first place. Assuming that the housekeeper had written, she would not have left the letter at the mercy of the servant—she would have seen it safely in the letter-box before leaving Aldborough.

"Good-morning," said the captain, cheerfully addressing the postmaster. "I am Mr. Bygrave of North Shingles. I think you have a letter in the box, addressed to Mr.—?"

The postmaster was a short man, and consequently a man with a proper idea of his own importance. He solemnly checked Captain Wragge in full career.

"When a letter is once posted, sir," he said, "nobody out of the office has any business with it until it reaches its address."

The captain was not a man to be daunted, even by a postmaster. A bright idea struck him. He took out his pocketbook, in which Admiral Bartram's address was written, and returned to the charge.

"Suppose a letter has been wrongly directed by mistake?" he began. "And suppose the writer wants to correct the error after the letter is put into the box?"

"When a letter is once posted, sir," reiterated the impenetrable local authority, "nobody out of the office touches it on any pretense whatever."

"Granted, with all my heart," persisted the captain. "I don't want to touch it—I only want to explain myself. A lady has posted a letter here, addressed to 'Noel Vanstone, Esq., Admiral Bartram's, St. Crux-in-the-Marsh, Essex.' She wrote in a great hurry, and she is not quite certain whether she added the name of the post-town, 'Ossory.' It is of the last importance that the delivery of the letter should not be delayed. What is to hinder your facilitating the post-office work, and obliging a lady, by adding the name of the post-town (if it happens to be left out), with your own hand? I put it to you as a zealous officer, what possible objection can there be to granting my request?"

The postmaster was compelled to acknowledge that there could be no objection, provided nothing but a necessary line was added to the address, provided nobody touched the letter but himself, and provided the precious time of the post-office was not suffered to run to waste. As there happened to be nothing particular to do at that moment, he would readily oblige the lady at Mr. Bygrave's request.

Captain Wragge watched the postmaster's hands, as they sorted the letters in the box, with breathless eagerness. Was the letter there? Would the hands of the zealous public servant suddenly stop? Yes! They stopped, and picked out a letter from the rest.

"'Noel Vanstone, Esquire,' did you say?" asked the postmaster, keeping the letter in his own hand.

"'Noel Vanstone, Esquire,'" replied the captain, "'Admiral Bartram's, St. Crux-in-the-Marsh.'"

"Ossory, Essex," chimed in the postmaster, throwing the letter back into the box. "The lady has made no mistake, sir. The address is quite right."

Nothing but a timely consideration of the heavy debt he owed to appearances prevented Captain Wragge from throwing his tall white hat up in the air as soon as he found the street once more. All further doubt was now at an end. Mrs. Lecount had written to her master—therefore Mrs. Lecount was on her way to Zurich!

With his head higher than ever, with the tails of his respectable frock-coat floating behind him in the breeze, with his bosom's native impudence sitting lightly on its throne, the captain strutted to the inn and called for the railway time-table. After making certain calculations (in black and white, as a matter of course), he ordered his chaise to be ready in an hour—so as to reach the railway in time for the second train running to London—with which there happened to be no communication from Aldborough by coach.

His next proceeding was of a far more serious kind; his next proceeding implied a terrible certainty of success. The day of the week was Thursday. From the inn he went to the church, saw the clerk, and gave the necessary notice for a marriage by license on the following Monday.

Bold as he was, his nerves were a little shaken by this last achievement; his hand trembled as it lifted the latch of the garden gate. He doctored his nerves with brandy and water before he sent for Magdalen to inform her of the proceedings of the morning. Another outbreak might reasonably be expected when she heard that the last irrevocable step had been taken, and that notice had been given of the wedding-day.

The captain's watch warned him to lose no time in emptying his glass. In a few minutes he sent the necessary message upstairs. While waiting for Magdalen's appearance, he provided himself with certain materials which were now necessary to carry the enterprise to its crowning point. In the first place, he wrote his assumed name (by no means in so fine a hand as usual) on a blank visiting-card, and added underneath these words: "Not a moment is to be lost. I am waiting for you at the door—come down to me directly." His next proceeding was to take some half-dozen envelopes out of the case, and to direct them all alike to the following address: "Thomas Bygrave, Esq., Mussared's Hotel, Salisbury Street, Strand, London." After carefully placing the envelopes and the card in his breast-pocket, he shut up the desk. As he rose from the writing-table, Magdalen came into the room.

The captain took a moment to decide on the best method of opening the interview, and determined, in his own phrase, to dash at it. In two words he told Magdalen what had happened, and informed her that Monday was to be her wedding-day.

He was prepared to quiet her, if she burst into a frenzy of passion; to reason with her, if she begged for time; to sympathize with her, if she melted into tears. To his inexpressible surprise, results falsified all his calculations. She heard him without uttering a word, without shedding a tear. When he had done, she dropped into a chair. Her large gray eyes stared at him vacantly. In one mysterious instant all her beauty left her; her face stiffened awfully, like the face of a corpse. For the first time in the captain's experience of her, fear—all-mastering fear—had taken possession of her, body and soul.

"You are not flinching," he said, trying to rouse her. "Surely you are not flinching at the last moment?"

No light of intelligence came into her eyes, no change passed over her face. But she heard him—for she moved a little in the chair, and slowly shook her head.

"You planned this marriage of your own freewill," pursued the captain, with the furtive look and the faltering voice of a man ill at ease. "It was your own idea—not mine. I won't have the responsibility laid on my shoulders—no! not for twice two hundred pounds. If your resolution fails you; if you think better of it—?"

He stopped. Her face was changing; her lips were moving at last. She slowly raised her left hand, with the fingers outspread; she looked at it as if it was a hand that was strange to her; she counted the days on it, the days before the marriage.

"Friday, one," she whispered to herself; "Saturday, two; Sunday, three; Monday—" Her hands dropped into her lap, her face stiffened again; the deadly fear fastened its paralyzing hold on her once more, and the next words died away on her lips.

Captain Wragge took out his handkerchief and wiped his forehead.

"Damn the two hundred pounds!" he said. "Two thousand wouldn't pay me for this!"

He put the handkerchief back, took the envelopes which he had addressed to himself out of his pocket, and, approaching her closely for the first time, laid his hand on her arm.

"Rouse yourself," he said, "I have a last word to say to you. Can you listen?"

She struggled, and roused herself—a faint tinge of color stole over her white cheeks—she bowed her head.

"Look at these," pursued Captain Wragge, holding up the envelopes. "If I turn these to the use for which they have been written, Mrs. Lecount's master will never receive Mrs. Lecount's letter. If I tear them up, he will know by to-morrow's post that you are the woman who visited him in Vauxhall Walk. Say the word! Shall I tear the envelopes up, or shall I put them back in my pocket?"

There was a pause of dead silence. The murmur of the summer waves on the shingle of the beach and the voices of the summer idlers on the Parade floated through the open window, and filled the empty stillness of the room.

She raised her head; she lifted her hand and pointed steadily to the envelopes.

"Put them back," she said.

"Do you mean it?" he asked.

"I mean it."

As she gave that answer, there was a sound of wheels on the road outside.

"You hear those wheels?" said Captain Wragge.

"I hear them."

"You see the chaise?" said the captain, pointing through the window as the chaise which had been ordered from the inn made its appearance at the garden gate.

"I see it."

"And, of your own free-will, you tell me to go?"

"Yes. Go!"

Without another word he left her. The servant was waiting at the door with his traveling bag. "Miss Bygrave is not well," he said. "Tell your mistress to go to her in the parlor."

He stepped into the chaise, and started on the first stage of the journey to St. Crux.

CHAPTER XII.

TOWARD three o'clock in the afternoon Captain Wragge stopped at the nearest station to Ossory which the railway passed in its course through Essex. Inquiries made on the spot informed him that he might drive to St. Crux, remain there for a quarter of an hour, and return to the station in time for an evening train to London. In ten minutes more the captain was on the road again, driving rapidly in the direction of the coast.

After proceeding some miles on the highway, the carriage turned off, and the coachman involved himself in an intricate network of cross-roads.

"Are we far from St. Crux?" asked the captain, growing impatient, after mile on mile had been passed without a sign of reaching the journey's end.

"You'll see the house, sir, at the next turn in the road," said the man.

The next turn in the road brought them within view of the open country again. Ahead of the carriage, Captain Wragge saw a long dark line against the sky—the line of the sea-wall which protects the low coast of Essex from inundation. The flat intermediate country was intersected by a labyrinth of tidal streams, winding up from the invisible sea in strange fantastic curves—rivers at high water, and channels of mud at low. On his right hand was a quaint little village, mostly composed of wooden houses, straggling down to the brink of one of the tidal streams. On his left hand, further away, rose the gloomy ruins of an abbey, with a desolate pile of buildings, which covered two sides of a square attached to it. One of the streams from the sea (called, in Essex, "backwaters") curled almost entirely round the house. Another, from an opposite quarter, appeared to run straight through the grounds, and to separate one side of the shapeless mass of buildings, which was in moderate repair, from another, which was little better than a ruin. Bridges of wood and bridges of brick crossed the stream, and gave access to the house from all points of the compass. No human creature appeared in the neighborhood, and no sound was heard but the hoarse barking of a house-dog from an invisible courtyard.

"Which door shall I drive to, sir?" asked the coachman. "The front or the back?"

"The back," said Captain Wragge, feeling that the less notice he attracted in his present position, the safer that position might be.

The carriage twice crossed the stream before the coachman made his way through the grounds into a dreary inclosure of stone. At an open door on the inhabited side of the place sat a weather-beaten old man, busily at work on a half-finished model of a ship. He rose and came to the carriage door, lifting up his spectacles on his forehead, and looking disconcerted at the appearance of a stranger.

"Is Mr. Noel Vanstone staying here?" asked Captain Wragge.

"Yes, sir," replied the old man. "Mr. Noel came yesterday."

"Take that card to Mr. Vanstone, if you please," said the captain, "and say I am waiting here to see him."

In a few minutes Noel Vanstone made his appearance, breathless and eager—absorbed in anxiety for news from Aldborough. Captain Wragge opened the carriage door, seized his outstretched hand, and pulled him in without ceremony.

"Your housekeeper has gone," whispered the captain, "and you are to be married on Monday. Don't agitate yourself, and don't express your feelings—there isn't time for it. Get the first active servant you can find in the house to pack your bag in ten minutes, take leave of the admiral, and come back at once with me to the London train."

Noel Vanstone faintly attempted to ask a question. The captain declined to hear it.

"As much talk as you like on the road," he said. "Time is too precious for talking here. How do we know Lecount may not think better of it? How do we know she may not turn back before she gets to Zurich?"

That startling consideration terrified Noel Vanstone into instant submission.

"What shall I say to the admiral?" he asked, helplessly.

"Tell him you are going to be married, to be sure! What does it matter, now Lecount's back is turned? If he wonders you didn't tell him before, say it's a runaway match, and the bride is waiting for you. Stop! Any letters addressed to you in your absence will be sent to this place, of course? Give the admiral these envelopes, and tell him to forward your letters under cover to me. I am an old customer at the hotel we are going to; and if we find the place full, the landlord may be depended on to take care of any letters with my name on them. A safe address in London for your correspondence may be of the greatest importance. How do we know Lecount may not write to you on her way to Zurich?"

"What a head you have got!" cried Noel Vanstone, eagerly taking the envelopes. "You think of everything."

He left the carriage in high excitement, and ran back into the house. In ten minutes more Captain Wragge had him in safe custody, and the horses started on their return journey.

The travelers reached London in good time that evening, and found accommodation at the hotel.

Knowing the restless, inquisitive nature of the man he had to deal with, Captain Wragge had anticipated some little difficulty and embarrassment in meeting the questions which Noel Vanstone might put to him on the way to London. To his great relief, a startling domestic discovery absorbed his traveling companion's whole attention at the outset of the journey. By some extraordinary oversight, Miss Bygrave had been left, on the eve of her marriage, unprovided with a maid. Noel Vanstone declared that he would take the whole responsibility of correcting this deficiency in the arrangements, on his own shoulders; he would not trouble Mr. Bygrave to give him any assistance; he would confer, when they got to their journey's end, with the landlady of the hotel, and would examine the candidates for the vacant office himself. All the way to London, he returned again and again to the same subject; all the evening, at the hotel, he was in and out of the landlady's sitting-room, until he fairly obliged her to lock the door. In every other proceeding which related to his marriage, he had been kept in the background; he had been compelled to follow in the footsteps of his ingenious friend. In the matter of the lady's maid he claimed his fitting position at last—he followed nobody; he took the lead!

The forenoon of the next day was devoted to obtaining the license—the personal distinction of making the declaration on oath being eagerly accepted by Noel Vanstone, who swore, in perfect good faith (on information previously obtained from the captain) that the lady was of age. The document procured, the bridegroom returned to examine the characters and qualifications of the women-servants out of the place whom the landlady had engaged to summon to the hotel, while Captain Wragge turned his steps, "on business personal to himself," toward the residence of a friend in a distant quarter of London.

The captain's friend was connected with the law, and the captain's business was of a twofold nature. His first object was to inform himself of the legal bearings of the approaching marriage on the future of the husband and the wife. His second object was to provide beforehand for destroying all traces of the destination to which he might betake himself when he left Aldborough on the wedding-day. Having reached his end successfully in both these cases, he returned to the hotel, and found Noel Vanstone nursing his offended dignity in the landlady's sitting-room. Three ladies' maids had appeared to pass their examination, and had all, on coming to the question of wages, impudently declined accepting the place. A fourth candidate was expected to present herself on the next day; and, until she made her appearance, Noel Vanstone positively declined removing from the metropolis. Captain Wragge showed his annoyance openly at the unnecessary delay thus occasioned in the return to Aldborough, but without producing any effect. Noel Vanstone shook his obstinate little head, and solemnly refused to trifle with his responsibilities.

The first event which occurred on Saturday morning was the arrival of Mrs. Lecount's letter to her master, inclosed in one of the envelopes which the captain had addressed to himself. He received it (by previous arrangement with the waiter) in his bedroom—read it with the closest attention—and put it away carefully in his pocketbook. The letter was ominous of serious events to come when the housekeeper returned to England; and it was due to Magdalen—who was the person threatened—to place the warning of danger in her own possession.

Later in the day the fourth candidate appeared for the maid's situation—a young woman of small expectations and subdued manners, who looked (as the landlady remarked) like a person overtaken by misfortune. She passed the ordeal of examination successfully, and accepted the wages offered with out a murmur. The engagement having been ratified on both sides, fresh delays ensued, of which Noel Vanstone was once more the cause. He had not yet made up his mind whether he would, or would not, give more than a guinea for the wedding-ring; and he wasted the rest of the day to such disastrous purpose in one jeweler's shop after another, that he and the captain, and the new lady's maid (who traveled with them), were barely in time to catch the last train from London that evening. It was late at night when they left the railway at the nearest station to Aldborough. Captain Wragge had been strangely silent all through the journey. His mind was ill at ease. He had left Magdalen, under very critical circumstances, with no fit person to control her, and he was wholly ignorant of the progress of events in his absence at North Shingles.

CHAPTER XIII.

WHAT had happened at Aldborough in Captain Wragge's absence? Events had occurred which the captain's utmost dexterity might have found it hard to remedy.

As soon as the chaise had left North Shingles, Mrs. Wragge received the message which her husband had charged the servant to deliver. She hastened into the parlor, bewildered by her stormy interview with the captain, and penitently conscious that she had done wrong, without knowing what the wrong was. If Magdalen's mind had been unoccupied by the one idea of the marriage which now filled it—if she had possessed composure enough to listen to Mrs. Wragge's rambling narrative of what had happened during her interview with the housekeeper—Mrs. Lecount's visit to the wardrobe must, sooner or later, have formed part of the disclosure; and Magdalen, although she might never have guessed the truth, must at least have been warned that there was some element of danger lurking treacherously in the Alpaca dress. As it was, no such consequence as this followed Mrs. Wragge's appearance in the parlor; for no such consequence was now possible.

Events which had happened earlier in the morning, events which had happened for days and weeks past, had vanished as completely from Magdalen's mind as if they had never taken place. The horror of the coming Monday—the merciless certainty implied in the appointment of the day and hour—petrified all feeling in her, and annihilated all thought. Mrs. Wragge made three separate attempts to enter on the subject of the housekeeper's visit. The first time she might as well have addressed herself to the wind, or to the sea. The second attempt seemed likely to be more successful. Magdalen sighed, listened for a moment indifferently, and then dismissed the subject. "It doesn't matter," she said. "The end has come all the same. I'm not angry with you. Say no more." Later in the day, from not knowing what else to talk about, Mrs. Wragge tried again. This time Magdalen turned on her impatiently. "For God's sake, don't worry me about trifles! I can't bear it." Mrs. Wragge closed her lips on the spot, and returned to the subject no more. Magdalen, who had been kind to her at all other times, had angrily forbidden it. The captain—utterly ignorant of Mrs. Lecount's interest in the secrets of the wardrobe—had never so much as approached it. All the information that he had extracted from his wife's mental confusion, he had extracted by putting direct questions, derived purely from the resources of his own knowledge. He had insisted on plain answers, without excuses of any kind; he had carried his point as usual; and his departure the same morning had left him no chance of re-opening the question, even if his irritation against his wife had permitted him to do so. There the Alpaca dress hung, neglected in the dark—the unnoticed, unsuspected center of dangers that were still to come.

Toward the afternoon Mrs. Wragge took courage to start a suggestion of her own—she pleaded for a little turn in the fresh air.

Magdalen passively put on her hat; passively accompanied her companion along the public walk, until they reached its northward extremity. Here the beach was left solitary, and here they sat down, side by side, on the shingle. It was a bright, exhilarating day; pleasure-boats were sailing on the calm blue water; Aldborough was idling happily afloat and ashore. Mrs. Wragge recovered her spirits in the gayety of the prospect—she amused herself like a child, by tossing pebbles into the sea. From time to time she stole a questioning glance at Magdalen, and saw no encouragement in her manner, no change to cordiality in her face. She sat silent on the slope of the shingle, with her elbow on her knee, and her head resting on her hand, looking out over the sea—looking with rapt attention, and yet with eyes that seemed to notice nothing. Mrs. Wragge wearied of the pebbles, and lost her interest in looking at the pleasure-boats. Her great head began to nod heavily, and she dozed in the warm, drowsy air. When she woke, the pleasure-boats were far off; their sails were white specks in the distance. The idlers on the beach were thinned in number; the sun was low in the heaven; the blue sea was darker, and rippled by a breeze. Changes on sky and earth and ocean told of the waning day; change was everywhere—except close at her side. There Magdalen sat, in the same position, with weary eyes that still looked over the sea, and still saw nothing.

"Oh, do speak to me!" said Mrs. Wragge.

Magdalen started, and looked about her vacantly.

"It's late," she said, shivering under the first sensation that reached her of the rising breeze. "Come home; you want your tea." They walked home in silence.

"Don't be angry with me for asking," said Mrs. Wragge, as they sat together at the tea-table. "Are you troubled, my dear, in your mind?"

"Yes," replied Magdalen. "Don't notice me. My trouble will soon be over."

She waited patiently until Mrs. Wragge had made an end of the meal, and then went upstairs to her own room.

"Monday!" she said, as she sat down at her toilet-table. "Something may happen before Monday comes!"

Her fingers wandered mechanically among the brushes and combs, the tiny bottles and cases placed on the table. She set them in order, now in one way, and now in another—then on a sudden pushed them away from her in a heap. For a minute or two her hands remained idle. That interval passed, they grew restless again, and pulled the two little drawers backward and forward in their grooves. Among the objects laid in one of them was a Prayer-book which had belonged to her at Combe-Raven, and which she had saved with her other relics of the past, when she and her sister had taken their farewell of home. She opened the Prayer-book, after a long hesitation, at the Marriage Service, shut it again before she had read a line, and put it back hurriedly in one of the drawers. After turning the key in the locks, she rose and walked to the window. "The horrible sea!" she said, turning from it with a shudder of disgust—"the lonely, dreary, horrible sea!"

She went back to the drawer, and took the Prayer-book out for the second time, half opened it again at the Marriage Service, and impatiently threw it back into the drawer. This time, after turning the lock, she took the key away, walked with it in her hand to the open window, and threw it violently from her into the garden. It fell on a bed thickly planted with flowers. It was invisible; it was lost. The sense of its loss seemed to relieve her.

"Something may happen on Friday; something may happen on Saturday; something may happen on Sunday. Three days still!"

She closed the green shutters outside the window and drew the curtains to darken the room still more. Her head felt heavy; her eyes were burning hot. She threw herself on her bed, with a sullen impulse to sleep away the time. The quiet of the house helped her; the darkness of the room helped her; the stupor of mind into which she had fallen had its effect on her senses; she dropped into a broken sleep. Her restless hands moved incessantly, her head tossed from side to side of the pillow, but still she slept. Ere long words fell by ones and twos from her lips; words whispered in her sleep, growing more and more continuous, more and more articulate, the longer the sleep lasted—words which seemed to calm her restlessness and to hush her into deeper repose. She smiled; she was in the happy land of dreams; Frank's name escaped her. "Do you love me, Frank?" she whispered. "Oh, my darling, say it again! say it again!"

The time passed, the room grew darker; and still she slumbered and dreamed. Toward sunset—without any noise inside the house or out to account for it—she started up on the bed, awake again in an instant. The drowsy obscurity of the room struck her with terror. She ran to the window, pushed open the shutters, and leaned far out into the evening air and the evening light. Her eyes devoured the trivial sights on the beach; her ears drank in the welcome murmur of the sea. Anything to deliver her from the waking impression which her dreams had left! No more darkness, no more repose. Sleep that came mercifully to others came treacherously to her. Sleep had only closed her eyes on the future, to open them on the past.

She went down again into the parlor, eager to talk—no matter how idly, no matter on what trifles. The room was empty. Perhaps Mrs. Wragge had gone to her work—perhaps she was too tired to talk. Magdalen took her hat from the table and went out. The sea that she had shrunk from, a few hours since, looked friendly now. How lovely it was in its cool evening blue! What a god-like joy in the happy multitude of waves leaping up to the light of heaven!

She stayed out until the night fell and the stars appeared. The night steadied her.

By slow degrees her mind recovered its balance and she looked her position unflinchingly in the face. The vain hope that accident might defeat the very end for which, of her own free-will, she had ceaselessly plotted and toiled, vanished and left her; self-dissipated in its own weakness. She knew the true alternative, and faced it. On one side was the revolting ordeal of the marriage; on the other, the abandonment of her purpose. Was it too late to choose between the sacrifice of the purpose and the sacrifice of herself? Yes! too late. The backward path had closed behind her. Time that no wish could change, Time that no prayers could recall, had made her purpose a part of herself: once she had governed it; now it governed her. The more she shrank, the harder she struggled, the more mercilessly it drove her on. No other feeling in her was strong enough to master it—not even the horror that was maddening her—the horror of her marriage.

Toward nine o'clock she went back to the house.

"Walking again!" said Mrs. Wragge, meeting her at the door. "Come in and sit down, my dear. How tired you must be!"

Magdalen smiled, and patted Mrs. Wragge kindly on the shoulder.

"You forget how strong I am," she said. "Nothing hurts me."

She lit her candle and went upstairs again into her room. As she returned to the old place by her toilet-table, the vain hope in the three days of delay, the vain hope of deliverance by accident, came back to her—this time in a form more tangible than the form which it had hitherto worn.

"Friday, Saturday, Sunday. Something may happen to him; something may happen to me. Something serious; something fatal. One of us may die."

A sudden change came over her face. She shivered, though there was no cold in the air. She started, though there was no noise to alarm her.

"One of us may die. I may be the one."

She fell into deep thought, roused herself after a while, and, opening the door, called to Mrs. Wragge to come and speak to her.

"You were right in thinking I should fatigue myself," she said. "My walk has been a little too much for me. I feel tired, and I am going to bed. Good-night." She kissed Mrs. Wragge and softly closed the door again.

After a few turns backward and forward in the room, she abruptly opened her writing-case and began a letter to her sister. The letter grew and grew under her hands; she filled sheet after sheet of note-paper. Her heart was full of her subject: it was her own story addressed to Norah. She shed no tears; she was composed to a quiet sadness. Her pen ran smoothly on. After writing for more than two hours, she left off while the letter was still unfinished. There was no signature attached to it—there was a blank space reserved, to be filled up at some other time. After putting away the case, with the sheets of writing secured inside it, she walked to the window for air, and stood there looking out.

The moon was waning over the sea. The breeze of the earlier hours had died out. On earth and ocean, the spirit of the Night brooded in a deep and awful calm.

Her head drooped low on her bosom, and all the view waned before her eyes with the waning moon. She saw no sea, no sky. Death, the Tempter, was busy at her heart. Death, the Tempter, pointed homeward, to the grave of her dead parents in Combe-Raven churchyard.

"Nineteen last birthday," she thought. "Only nineteen!" She moved away from the window, hesitated, and then looked out again at the view. "The beautiful night!" she said, gratefully. "Oh, the beautiful night!"

She left the window and lay down on her bed. Sleep, that had come treacherously before, came mercifully now; came deep and dreamless, the image of her last waking thought—the image of Death.

Early the next morning Mrs. Wragge went into Magdalen's room, and found that she had risen betimes. She was sitting before the glass, drawing the comb slowly through and through her hair—thoughtful and quiet.

"How do you feel this morning, my dear?" asked Mrs. Wragge. "Quite well again?"

"Yes."

After replying in the affirmative, she stopped, considered for a moment, and suddenly contradicted herself.

"No," she said, "not quite well. I am suffering a little from toothache."

As she altered her first answer in those words she gave a twist to her hair with the comb, so that it fell forward and hid her face.

At breakfast she was very silent, and she took nothing but a cup of tea.

"Let me go to the chemist's and get something," said Mrs. Wragge.

"No, thank you."

"Do let me!"

"No!"

She refused for the second time, sharply and angrily. As usual, Mrs. Wragge submitted, and let her have her own way. When breakfast was over, she rose, without a word of explanation, and went out. Mrs. Wragge watched her from the window and saw that she took the direction of the chemist's shop.

On reaching the chemist's door she stopped—paused before entering the shop, and looked in at the window—hesitated, and walked away a little—hesitated again, and took the first turning which led back to the beach.

Without looking about her, without caring what place she chose, she seated herself on the shingle. The only persons who were near to her, in the position she now occupied, were a nursemaid and two little boys. The youngest of the two had a tiny toy-ship in his hand. After looking at Magdalen for a little while with the quaintest gravity and attention, the boy suddenly approached her, and opened the way to an acquaintance by putting his toy composedly on her lap.

"Look at my ship," said the child, crossing his hands on Magdalen's knee.

She was not usually patient with children. In happier days she would not have met the boy's advance toward her as she met it now. The hard despair in her eyes left them suddenly; her fast-closed lips parted and trembled. She put the ship back into the child's hands and lifted him on her lap.

"Will you give me a kiss?" she said, faintly. The boy looked at his ship as if he would rather have kissed the ship.

She repeated the question—repeated it almost humbly. The child put his hand up to her neck and kissed her.

"If I was your sister, would you love me?" All the misery of her friendless position, all the wasted tenderness of her heart, poured from her in those words.

"Would you love me?" she repeated, hiding her face on the bosom of the child's frock.

"Yes," said the boy. "Look at my ship."

She looked at the ship through her gathering tears.

"What do you call it?" she asked, trying hard to find her way even to the interest of a child.

"I call it Uncle Kirke's ship," said the boy. "Uncle Kirke has gone away."

The name recalled nothing to her memory. No remembrances but old remembrances lived in her now. "Gone?" she repeated absently, thinking what she should say to her little friend next.

"Yes," said the boy. "Gone to China."

Even from the lips of a child that word struck her to the heart. She put Kirke's little nephew off her lap, and instantly left the beach.

As she turned back to the house, the struggle of the past night renewed itself in her mind. But the sense of relief which the child had brought to her, the reviving tenderness which she had felt while he sat on her knee, influenced her still. She was conscious of a dawning hope, opening freshly on her thoughts, as the boy's innocent eyes had opened on her face when he came to her on the beach. Was it too late to turn back? Once more she asked herself that question, and now, for the first time, she asked it in doubt.

She ran up to her own room with a lurking distrust in her changed self which warned her to act, and not to think. Without waiting to remove her shawl or to take off her hat, she opened her writing-case and addressed these lines to Captain Wragge as fast as her pen could trace them:

"You will find the money I promised you inclosed in this. My resolution has failed me. The horror of marrying him is more than I can face. I have left Aldborough. Pity my weakness, and forget me. Let us never meet again."

With throbbing heart, with eager, trembling fingers, she drew her little white silk bag from her bosom and took out the banknotes to inclose them in the letter. Her hand searched impetuously; her hand had lost its discrimination of touch. She grasped the whole contents of the bag in one handful of papers, and drew them out violently, tearing some and disarranging the folds of others. As she threw them down before her on the table, the first object that met her eye was her own handwriting, faded already with time. She looked closer, and saw the words she had copied from her dead father's letter—saw the lawyer's brief and terrible commentary on them confronting her at the bottom of the page:

Mr. Vanstone's daughters are Nobody's Children, and the law leaves them helpless at their uncle's mercy.

Her throbbing heart stopped; her trembling hands grew icily quiet. All the Past rose before her in mute, overwhelming reproach. She took up the lines which her own hand had written hardly a minute since, and looked at the ink, still wet on the letters, with a vacant incredulity.

The color that had risen on her cheeks faded from them once more. The hard despair looked out again, cold and glittering, in her tearless eyes. She folded the banknotes carefully, and put them back in her bag. She pressed the copy of her father's letter to her lips, and returned it to its place with the banknotes. When the bag was in her bosom again, she waited a little, with her face hidden in her hands, then deliberately tore up the lines addressed to Captain Wragge. Before the ink was dry, the letter lay in fragments on the floor.

"No!" she said, as the last morsel of the torn paper dropped from her hand. "On the way I go there is no turning back."

She rose composedly and left the room. While descending the stairs, she met Mrs. Wragge coming up. "Going out again, my dear?" asked Mrs. Wragge. "May I go with you?"

Magdalen's attention wandered. Instead of answering the question, she absently answered her own thoughts.

"Thousands of women marry for money," she said. "Why shouldn't I?"

The helpless perplexity of Mrs. Wragge's face as she spoke those words roused her to a sense of present things. "My poor dear!" she said; "I puzzle you, don't I? Never mind what I say—all girls talk nonsense, and I'm no better than the rest of them. Come! I'll give you a treat. You shall enjoy yourself while the captain is away. We will have a long drive by ourselves. Put on your smart bonnet, and come with me to the hotel. I'll tell the landlady to put a nice cold dinner into a basket. You shall have all the things you like, and I'll wait on you. When you are an old, old woman, you will remember me kindly, won't you? You will say: 'She wasn't a bad girl; hundreds worse than she was live and prosper, and nobody blames them.' There! there! go and put your bonnet on. Oh, my God, what is my heart made of! How it lives and lives, when other girls' hearts would have died in them long ago!"

In half an hour more she and Mrs. Wragge were seated together in the carriage. One of the horses was restive at starting. "Flog him," she cried angrily to the driver. "What are you frightened about? Flog him! Suppose the carriage was upset," she said, turning suddenly to her companion; "and suppose I was thrown out and killed on the spot? Nonsense! don't look at me in that way. I'm like your husband; I have a dash of humor, and I'm only joking."

They were out the whole day. When they reached home again, it was after dark. The long succession of hours passed in the fresh air left them both with the same sense of fatigue. Again that night Magdalen slept the deep dreamless sleep of the night before. And so the Friday closed.

Her last thought at night had been the thought which had sustained her throughout the day. She had laid her head on the pillow with the same reckless resolution to submit to the coming trial which had already expressed itself in words when she and Mrs. Wragge met by accident on the stairs. When she woke on the morning of Saturday, the resolution was gone. The Friday's thoughts—the Friday's events even—were blotted out of her mind. Once again, creeping chill through the flow of her young blood, she felt the slow and deadly prompting of despair which had come to her in the waning moonlight, which had whispered to her in the awful calm.

"I saw the end as the end must be," she said to herself, "on Thursday night. I have been wrong ever since."

When she and her companion met that morning, she reiterated her complaint of suffering from the toothache; she repeated her refusal to allow Mrs. Wragge to procure a remedy; she left the house after breakfast, in the direction of the chemist's shop, exactly as she had left it on the morning before.

This time she entered the shop without an instant's hesitation.

"I have got an attack of toothache," she said, abruptly, to an elderly man who stood behind the counter.

"May I look at the tooth, miss?"

"There is no necessity to look. It is a hollow tooth. I think I have caught cold in it."

The chemist recommended various remedies which were in vogue fifteen years since. She declined purchasing any of them.

"I have always found Laudanum relieve the pain better than anything else," she said, trifling with the bottles on the counter, and looking at them while she spoke, instead of looking at the chemist. "Let me have some Laudanum."

"Certainly, miss. Excuse my asking the question—it is only a matter of form. You are staying at Aldborough, I think?"

"Yes. I am Miss Bygrave, of North Shingles."

The chemist bowed; and, turning to his shelves, filled an ordinary half-ounce bottle with laudanum immediately. In ascertaining his customer's name and address beforehand, the owner of the shop had taken a precaution which was natural to a careful man, but which was by no means universal, under similar circumstances, in the state of the law at that time.

"Shall I put you up a little cotton wool with the laudanum?" he asked, after he had placed a label on the bottle, and had written a word on it in large letters.

"If you please. What have you just written on the bottle?" She put the question sharply, with something of distrust as well as curiosity in her manner.

The chemist answered the question by turning the label toward her. She saw written on it, in large letters—POISON.

"I like to be on the safe side, miss," said the old man, smiling. "Very worthy people in other respects are often sadly careless where poisons are concerned."

She began trifling again with the bottles on the counter, and put another question, with an ill-concealed anxiety to hear the answer.

"Is there danger," she asked, "in such a little drop of Laudanum as that?"

"There is Death in it, miss," replied the chemist, quietly.

"Death to a child, or to a person in delicate health?"

"Death to the strongest man in England, let him be who he may."

With that answer, the chemist sealed up the bottle in its wrapping of white paper and handed the laudanum to Magdalen across the counter. She laughed as she took it from him, and paid for it.

"There will be no fear of accidents at North Shingles," she said. "I shall keep the bottle locked up in my dressing-case. If it doesn't relieve the pain, I must come to you again, and try some other remedy. Good-morning."

"Good-morning, miss."

She went straight back to the house without once looking up, without noticing any one who passed her. She brushed by Mrs. Wragge in the passage as she might have brushed by a piece of furniture. She ascended the stairs, and caught her foot twice in her dress, from sheer inattention to the common precaution of holding it up. The trivial daily interests of life had lost their hold on her already.

In the privacy of her own room, she took the bottle from its wrapping, and threw the paper and the cotton wool into the fire-place. At the moment when she did this there was a knock at the door. She hid the little bottle, and looked up impatiently. Mrs. Wragge came into the room.

"Have you got something for your toothache, my dear?"

"Yes."

"Can I do anything to help you?"

"No."

Mrs. Wragge still lingered uneasily near the door. Her manner showed plainly that she had something more to say.

"What is it?" asked Magdalen, sharply.

"Don't be angry," said Mrs. Wragge. "I'm not settled in my mind about the captain. He's a great writer, and he hasn't written. He's as quick as lightning, and he hasn't come back. Here's Saturday, and no signs of him. Has he run away, do you think? Has anything happened to him?"

"I should think not. Go downstairs; I'll come and speak to you about it directly."

As soon as she was alone again, Magdalen rose from her chair, advanced toward a cupboard in the room which locked, and paused for a moment, with her hand on the key, in doubt. Mrs. Wragge's appearance had disturbed the whole current of her thoughts. Mrs. Wragge's last question, trifling as it was, had checked her on the verge of the precipice—had roused the old vain hope in her once more of release by accident.

"Why not?" she said. "Why may something not have happened to one of them?"

She placed the laudanum in the cupboard, locked it, and put the key in her packet. "Time enough still," she thought, "before Monday. I'll wait till the captain comes back."

After some consultation downstairs, it was agreed that the servant should sit up that night, in expectation of her master's return. The day passed quietly, without events of any kind. Magdalen dreamed away the hours over a book. A weary patience of expectation was all she felt now—the poignant torment of thought was dulled and blunted at last. She passed the day and the evening in the parlor, vaguely conscious of a strange feeling of aversion to going back to her own room. As the night advanced, as the noises ceased indoors and out, her restlessness began to return. She endeavored to quiet herself by reading. Books failed to fix her attention. The newspaper was lying in a corner of the room: she tried the newspaper next.

She looked mechanically at the headings of the articles; she listlessly turned over page after page, until her wandering attention was arrested by the narrative of an Execution in a distant part of England. There was nothing to strike her in the story of the crime, and yet she read it. It was a common, horribly common, act of bloodshed—the murder of a woman in farm-service by a man in the same employment who was jealous of her. He had been convicted on no extraordinary evidence, he had been hanged under no unusual circumstances. He had made his confession, when he knew there was no hope for him, like other criminals of his class, and the newspaper had printed it at the end of the article, in these terms:

"I kept company with the deceased for a year or thereabouts. I said I would marry her when I had money enough. She said I had money enough now. We had a quarrel. She refused to walk out with me any more; she wouldn't draw me my beer; she took up with my fellow-servant, David Crouch. I went to her on the Saturday, and said I would marry her as soon as we could be asked in church if she would give up Crouch. She laughed at me. She turned me out of the wash-house, and the rest of them saw her turn me out. I was not easy in my mind. I went and sat on the gate—the gate in the meadow they call Pettit's Piece. I thought I would shoot her. I went and fetched my gun and loaded it. I went out into Pettit's Piece again. I was hard put to it to make up my mind. I thought I would try my luck—I mean try whether to kill her or not—-by throwing up the Spud of the plow into the air. I said to myself, if it falls flat, I'll spare her; if it falls point in the earth, I'll kill her. I took a good swing with it, and shied it up. It fell point in the earth. I went and shot her. It was a bad job, but I did it. I did it, as they said I did it at the trial. I hope the Lord will have mercy on me. I wish my mother to have my old clothes. I have no more to say."

In the happier days of her life, Magdalen would have passed over the narrative of the execution, and the printed confession which accompanied it unread; the subject would have failed to attract her. She read the horrible story now—read it with an interest unintelligible to herself. Her attention, which had wandered over higher and better things, followed every sentence of the murderer's hideously direct confession from beginning to end. If the man or the woman had been known to her, if the place had been familiar to her memory, she could hardly have followed the narrative more closely, or have felt a more distinct impression of it left on her mind. She laid down the paper, wondering at herself; she took it up once more, and tried to read some other portion of the contents. The effort was useless; her attention wandered again. She threw the paper away, and went out into the garden. The night was dark; the stars were few and faint. She could just see the gravel-walk—she could just pace backward and forward between the house door and the gate.

The confession in the newspaper had taken a fearful hold on her mind. As she paced the walk, the black night opened over the sea, and showed her the murderer in the field hurling the Spud of the plow into the air. She ran, shuddering, back to the house. The murderer followed her into the parlor. She seized the candle and went up into her room. The vision of her own distempered fancy followed her to the place where the laudanum was hidden, and vanished there.

It was midnight, and there was no sign yet of the captain's return.

She took from the writing-case the long letter which she had written to Norah, and slowly read it through. The letter quieted her. When she reached the blank space left at the end, she hurriedly turned back and began it over again.

One o'clock struck from the church clock, and still the captain never appeared.

She read the letter for the second time; she turned back obstinately, despairingly, and began it for the third time. As she once more reached the last page, she looked at her watch. It was a quarter to two. She had just put the watch back in the belt of her dress, when there came to her—far off in the stillness of the morning—a sound of wheels.

She dropped the letter and clasped her cold hands in her lap and listened. The sound came on, faster and faster, nearer and nearer—the trivial sound to all other ears; the sound of Doom to hers. It passed the side of the house; it traveled a little further on; it stopped. She heard a loud knocking—then the opening of a window—then voices—then a long silence—than the wheels again coming back—then the opening of the door below, and the sound of the captain's voice in the passage.

She could endure it no longer. She opened her door a little way and called to him.

He ran upstairs instantly, astonished that she was not in bed. She spoke to him through the narrow opening of the door, keeping herself hidden behind it, for she was afraid to let him see her face.

"Has anything gone wrong?" she asked.

"Make your mind easy," he answered. "Nothing has gone wrong."

"Is no accident likely to happen between this and Monday?"

"None whatever. The marriage is a certainty."

"A certainty?"

"Yes."

"Good-night."

She put her hand out through the door. He took it with some little surprise; it was not often in his experience that she gave him her hand of her own accord.

"You have sat up too long," he said, as he felt the clasp of her cold fingers. "I am afraid you will have a bad night—I'm afraid you will not sleep."

She softly closed the door.

"I shall sleep," she said, "sounder than you think for."

It was past two o'clock when she shut herself up alone in her room. Her chair stood in its customary place by the toilet-table. She sat down for a few minutes thoughtfully, then opened her letter to Norah, and turned to the end where the blank space was left. The last lines written above the space ran thus: "... I have laid my whole heart bare to you; I have hidden nothing. It has come to this. The end I have toiled for, at such terrible cost to myself, is an end which I must reach or die. It is wickedness, madness, what you will—but it is so. There are now two journeys before me to choose between. If I can marry him—the journey to the church. If the profanation of myself is more than I can bear—the journey to the grave!"

Under that last sentence, she wrote these lines:

"My choice is made. If the cruel law will let you, lay me with my father and mother in the churchyard at home. Farewell, my love! Be always innocent; be always happy. If Frank ever asks about me, say I died forgiving him. Don't grieve long for me, Norah—I am not worth it."

She sealed the letter, and addressed it to her sister. The tears gathered in her eyes as she laid it on the table. She waited until her sight was clear again, and then took the banknotes once more from the little bag in her bosom. After wrapping them in a sheet of note paper, she wrote Captain Wragge's name on the inclosure, and added these words below it: "Lock the door of my room, and leave me till my sister comes. The money I promised you is in this. You are not to blame; it is my fault, and mine only. If you have any friendly remembrance of me, be kind to your wife for my sake."

After placing the inclosure by the letter to Norah, she rose and looked round the room. Some few little things in it were not in their places. She set them in order, and drew the curtains on either side at the head of her bed. Her own dress was the next object of her scrutiny. It was all as neat, as pure, as prettily arranged as ever. Nothing about her was disordered but her hair. Some tresses had fallen loose on one side of her head; she carefully put them back in their places with the help of her glass. "How pale I look!" she thought, with a faint smile. "Shall I be paler still when they find me in the morning?"

She went straight to the place where the laudanum was hidden, and took it out. The bottle was so small that it lay easily in the palm of her hand. She let it remain there for a little while, and stood looking at it.

"DEATH!" she said. "In this drop of brown drink—DEATH!"

As the words passed her lips, an agony of unutterable horror seized on her in an instant. She crossed the room unsteadily, with a maddening confusion in her head, with a suffocating anguish at her heart. She caught at the table to support herself. The faint clink of the bottle, as it fell harmlessly from her loosened grasp and rolled against some porcelain object on the table, struck through her brain like the stroke of a knife. The sound of her own voice, sunk to a whisper—her voice only uttering that one word, Death—rushed in her ears like the rushing of a wind. She dragged herself to the bedside, and rested her head against it, sitting on the floor. "Oh, my life! my life!" she thought; "what is my life worth, that I cling to it like this?"

An interval passed, and she felt her strength returning. She raised herself on her knees and hid her face on the bed. She tried to pray—to pray to be forgiven for seeking the refuge of death. Frantic words burst from her lips—words which would have risen to cries, if she had not stifled them in the bed-clothes. She started to her feet; despair strengthened her with a headlong fury against herself. In one moment she was back at the table; in another, the poison was once more in her hand.

She removed the cork and lifted the bottle to her mouth.

At the first cold touch of the glass on her lips, her strong young life leaped up in her leaping blood, and fought with the whole frenzy of its loathing against the close terror of Death. Every active power in the exuberant vital force that was in her rose in revolt against the destruction which her own will would fain have wreaked on her own life. She paused: for the second time, she paused in spite of herself. There, in the glorious perfection of her youth and health—there, trembling on the verge of human existence, she stood; with the kiss of the Destroyer close at her lips, and Nature, faithful to its sacred trust, fighting for the salvation of her to the last.

No word passed her lips. Her cheeks flushed deep; her breath came thick and fast. With the poison still in her hand, with the sense that she might faint in another moment, she made for the window, and threw back the curtain that covered it.

The new day had risen. The broad gray dawn flowed in on her, over the quiet eastern sea.

She saw the waters heaving, large and silent, in the misty calm; she felt the fresh breath of the morning flutter cool on her face. Her strength returned; her mind cleared a little. At the sight of the sea, her memory recalled the walk in the garden overnight, and the picture which her distempered fancy had painted on the black void. In thought, she saw the picture again—the murderer hurling the Spud of the plow into the air, and setting the life or death of the woman who had deserted him on the hazard of the falling point. The infection of that terrible superstition seized on her mind as suddenly as the new day had burst on her view. The premise of release which she saw in it from the horror of her own hesitation roused the last energies of her despair. She resolved to end the struggle by setting her life or death on the hazard of a chance.

On what chance?

The sea showed it to her. Dimly distinguishable through the mist, she saw a little fleet of coasting-vessels slowly drifting toward the house, all following the same direction with the favoring set of the tide. In half an hour—perhaps in less—the fleet would have passed her window. The hands of her watch pointed to four o'clock. She seated herself close at the side of the window, with her back toward the quarter from which the vessels were drifting down on her—with the poison placed on the window-sill and the watch on her lap. For one half-hour to come she determined to wait there and count the vessels as they went by. If in that time an even number passed her, the sign given should be a sign to live. If the uneven number prevailed, the end should be Death.

With that final resolution, she rested her head against the window and waited for the ships to pass.

The first came, high, dark and near in the mist, gliding silently over the silent sea. An interval—and the second followed, with the third close after it. Another interval, longer and longer drawn out—and nothing passed. She looked at her watch. Twelve minutes, and three ships. Three.

The fourth came, slower than the rest, larger than the rest, further off in the mist than the rest. The interval followed; a long interval once more. Then the next vessel passed, darkest and nearest of all. Five. The next uneven number—

Five.

She looked at her watch again. Nineteen minutes, and five ships. Twenty minutes. Twenty-one, two, three—and no sixth vessel. Twenty-four, and the sixth came by. Twenty-five, twenty-six, twenty-seven, twenty-eight, and the next uneven number—the fatal Seven—glided into view. Two minutes to the end of the half-hour. And seven ships.

Twenty-nine, and nothing followed in the wake of the seventh ship. The minute-hand of the watch moved on half-way to thirty, and still the white heaving sea was a misty blank. Without moving her head from the window, she took the poison in one hand, and raised the watch in the other. As the quick seconds counted each other out, her eyes, as quick as they, looked from the watch to the sea, from the sea to the watch—looked for the last time at the sea—and saw the EIGHTH ship.

She never moved, she never spoke. The death of thought, the death of feeling, seemed to have come to her already. She put back the poison mechanically on the ledge of the window and watched, as in a dream, the ship gliding smoothly on its silent way—gliding till it melted dimly into shadow—gliding till it was lost in the mist.

The strain on her mind relaxed when the Messenger of Life had passed from her sight.

"Providence?" she whispered faintly to herself. "Or chance?"

Her eyes closed, and her head fell back. When the sense of life returned to her, the morning sun was warm on her face—the blue heaven looked down on her—and the sea was a sea of gold.

She fell on her knees at the window and burst into tears.

Toward noon that day, the captain, waiting below stairs, and hearing no movement in Magdalen's room, felt uneasy at the long silence. He desired the new maid to follow him upstairs, and, pointing to the door, told her to go in softly and see whether her mistress was awake.

The maid entered the room, remained there a moment, and came out again, closing the door gently.

"She looks beautiful, sir," said the girl; "and she's sleeping as quietly as a new-born child."

CHAPTER XIV.

THE morning of her husband's return to North Shingles was a morning memorable forever in the domestic calendar of Mrs. Wragge. She dated from that occasion the first announcement which reached her of Magdalen's marriage.

It had been Mrs. Wragge's earthly lot to pass her life in a state of perpetual surprise. Never yet, however, had she wandered in such a maze of astonishment as the maze in which she lost herself when the captain coolly told her the truth. She had been sharp enough to suspect Mr. Noel Vanstone of coming to the house in the character of a sweetheart on approval; and she had dimly interpreted certain expressions of impatience which had fallen from Magdalen's lips as boding ill for the success of his suit, but her utmost penetration had never reached as far as a suspicion of the impending marriage. She rose from one climax of amazement to another, as her husband proceeded with his disclosure. A wedding in the family at a day's notice! and that wedding Magdalen's! and not a single new dress ordered for anybody, the bride included! and the Oriental Cashmere Robe totally unavailable on the occasion when she might have worn it to the greatest advantage! Mrs. Wragge dropped crookedly into a chair, and beat her disorderly hands on her unsymmetrical knees, in utter forgetfulness of the captain's presence and the captain's terrible eye. It would not have surprised her to hear that the world had come to an end, and that the only mortal whom Destiny had overlooked, in winding up the affairs of this earthly planet, was herself!

Leaving his wife to recover her composure by her own unaided efforts, Captain Wragge withdrew to wait for Magdalen's appearance in the lower regions of the house. It was close on one o'clock before the sound of footsteps in the room above warned him that she was awake and stirring. He called at once for the maid (whose name he had ascertained to be Louisa), and sent her upstairs to her mistress for the second time.

Magdalen was standing by her dressing-table when a faint tap at the door suddenly roused her. The tap was followed by the sound of a meek voice, which announced itself as the voice of "her maid," and inquired if Miss Bygrave needed any assistance that morning.

"Not at present," said Magdalen, as soon as she had recovered the surprise of finding herself unexpectedly provided with an attendant. "I will ring when I want you."

After dismissing the woman with that answer, she accidentally looked from the door to the window. Any speculations on the subject of the new servant in which she might otherwise have engaged were instantly suspended by the sight of the bottle of laudanum, still standing on the ledge of the window, where she had left it at sunrise. She took it once more in her hand, with a strange confusion of feeling—with a vague doubt even yet, whether the sight of it reminded her of a terrible reality or a terrible dream. Her first impulse was to rid herself of it on the spot. She raised the bottle to throw the contents out of the window, and paused, in sudden distrust of the impulse that had come to her. "I have accepted my new life," she thought. "How do I know what that life may have in store for me?" She turned from the window and went back to the table. "I may be forced to drink it yet," she said, and put the laudanum into her dressing-case.

Her mind was not at ease when she had done this: there seemed to be some indefinable ingratitude in the act. Still she made no attempt to remove the bottle from its hiding-place. She hurried on her toilet; she hastened the time when she could ring for the maid, and forget herself and her waking thoughts in a new subject. After touching the bell, she took from the table her letter to Norah and her letter to the captain, put them both into her dressing-case with the laudanum, and locked it securely with the key which she kept attached to her watch-chain.

Magdalen's first impression of her attendant was not an agreeable one. She could not investigate the girl with the experienced eye of the landlady at the London hotel, who had characterized the stranger as a young person overtaken by misfortune, and who had showed plainly, by her look and manner, of what nature she suspected that misfortune to be. But with this drawback, Magdalen was perfectly competent to detect the tokens of sickness and sorrow lurking under the surface of the new maid's activity and politeness. She suspected the girl was ill-tempered; she disliked her name; and she was indisposed to welcome any servant who had been engaged by Noel Vanstone. But after the first few minutes, "Louisa" grew on her liking. She answered all the questions put to her with perfect directness; she appeared to understand her duties thoroughly; and she never spoke until she was spoken to first. After making all the inquiries that occurred to her at the time, and after determining to give the maid a fair trial, Magdalen rose to leave the room. The very air in it was still heavy to her with the oppression of the past night.

"Have you anything more to say to me?" she asked, turning to the servant, with her hand on the door.

"I beg your pardon, miss," said Louisa, very respectfully and very quietly. "I think my master told me that the marriage was to be to-morrow?"

Magdalen repressed the shudder that stole over her at that reference to the marriage on the lips of a stranger, and answered in the affirmative.

"It's a very short time, miss, to prepare in. If you would be so kind as to give me my orders about the packing before you go downstairs—?"

"There are no such preparations to make as you suppose," said Magdalen, hastily. "The few things I have here can be all packed at once, if you like. I shall wear the same dress to-morrow which I have on to-day. Leave out the straw bonnet and the light shawl, and put everything else into my boxes. I have no new dresses to pack; I have nothing ordered for the occasion of any sort." She tried to add some commonplace phrases of explanation, accounting as probably as might be for the absence of the usual wedding outfit and wedding-dress. But no further reference to the marriage would pass her lips, and without an other word she abruptly left the room.

The meek and melancholy Louisa stood lost in astonishment. "Something wrong here," she thought. "I'm half afraid of my new place already." She sighed resignedly, shook her head, and went to the wardrobe. She first examined the drawers underneath, took out the various articles of linen laid inside, and placed them on chairs. Opening the upper part of the wardrobe next, she ranged the dresses in it side by side on the bed. Her last proceeding was to push the empty boxes into the middle of the room, and to compare the space at her disposal with the articles of dress which she had to pack. She completed her preliminary calculations with the ready self-reliance of a woman who thoroughly understood her business, and began the packing forthwith. Just as she had placed the first article of linen in the smaller box, the door of the room opened, and the house-servant, eager for gossip, came in.

"What do you want?" asked Louisa, quietly.

"Did you ever hear of anything like this!" said the house-servant, entering on her subject immediately.

"Like what?"

"Like this marriage, to be sure. You're London bred, they tell me. Did you ever hear of a young lady being married without a single new thing to her back? No wedding veil, and no wedding breakfast, and no wedding favors for the servants. It's flying in the face of Providence—that's what I say. I'm only a poor servant, I know. But it's wicked, downright wicked—and I don't care who hears me!"

Louisa went on with the packing.

"Look at her dresses!" persisted the house-servant, waving her hand indignantly at the bed. "I'm only a poor girl, but I wouldn't marry the best man alive without a new gown to my back. Look here! look at this dowdy brown thing here. Alpaca! You're not going to pack this Alpaca thing, are you? Why, it's hardly fit for a servant! I don't know that I'd take a gift of it if it was offered me. It would do for me if I took it up in the skirt, and let it out in the waist—and it wouldn't look so bad with a bit of bright trimming, would it?"

"Let that dress alone, if you please," said Louisa, as quietly as ever.

"What did you say?" inquired the other, doubting whether her ears had not deceived her.

"I said, let that dress alone. It belongs to my mistress, and I have my mistress's orders to pack up everything in the room. You are not helping me by coming here—you are very much in my way."

"Well!" said the house-servant, "you may be London bred, as they say. But if these are your London manners, give me Suffolk!" She opened the door with an angry snatch at the handle, shut it violently, opened it again, and looked in. "Give me Suffolk!" said the house-servant, with a parting nod of her head to point the edge of her sarcasm.

Louisa proceeded impenetrably with her packing up.

Having neatly disposed of the linen in the smaller box, she turned her attention to the dresses next. After passing them carefully in review, to ascertain which was the least valuable of the collection, and to place that one at the bottom of the trunk for the rest to lie on, she made her choice with very little difficulty. The first gown which she put into the box was—the brown Alpaca dress.

Meanwhile Magdalen had joined the captain downstairs. Although he could not fail to notice the languor in her face and the listlessness of all her movements, he was relieved to find that she met him with perfect composure. She was even self-possessed enough to ask him for news of his journey, with no other signs of agitation than a passing change of color and a little trembling of the lips.

"So much for the past," said Captain Wragge, when his narrative of the expedition to London by way of St. Crux had come to an end. "Now for the present. The bridegroom—"

"If it makes no difference," she interposed, "call him Mr. Noel Vanstone."

"With all my heart. Mr. Noel Vanstone is coming here this afternoon to dine and spend the evening. He will be tiresome in the last degree; but, like all tiresome people, he is not to be got rid of on any terms. Before he comes, I have a last word or two of caution for your private ear. By this time to-morrow we shall have parted—without any certain knowledge, on either side, of our ever meeting again. I am anxious to serve your interests faithfully to the last; I am anxious you should feel that I have done all I could for your future security when we say good-by."

Magdalen looked at him in surprise. He spoke in altered tones. He was agitated; he was strangely in earnest. Something in his look and manner took her memory back to the first night at Aldborough, when she had opened her mind to him in the darkening solitude—when they two had sat together alone on the slope of the martello tower. "I have no reason to think otherwise than kindly of you," she said.

Captain Wragge suddenly left his chair, and took a turn backward and forward in the room. Magdalen's last words seemed to have produced some extraordinary disturbance in him.

"Damn it!" he broke out; "I can't let you say that. You have reason to think ill of me. I have cheated you. You never got your fair share of profit from the Entertainment, from first to last. There! now the murder's out!"

Magdalen smiled, and signed to him to come back to his chair.

"I know you cheated me," she said, quietly. "You were in the exercise of your profession, Captain Wragge. I expected it when I joined you. I made no complaint at the time, and I make none now. If the money you took is any recompense for all the trouble I have given you, you are heartily welcome to it."

"Will you shake hands on that?" asked the captain, with an awkwardness and hesitation strongly at variance with his customary ease of manner.

Magdalen gave him her hand. He wrung it hard. "You are a strange girl," he said, trying to speak lightly. "You have laid a hold on me that I don't quite understand. I'm half uncomfortable at taking the money from you now; and yet you don't want it, do you?" He hesitated. "I almost wish," he said, "I had never met you on the Walls of York."

"It is too late to wish that, Captain Wragge. Say no more. You only distress me—say no more. We have other subjects to talk about. What were those words of caution which you had for my private ear?"

The captain took another turn in the room, and struggled back again into his every-day character. He produced from his pocketbook Mrs. Lecount's letter to her master, and handed it to Magdalen.

"There is the letter that might have ruined us if it had ever reached its address," he said. "Read it carefully. I have a question to ask you when you have done."

Magdalen read the letter. "What is this proof," she inquired, "which Mrs. Lecount relies on so confidently!"

"The very question I was going to ask you," said Captain Wragge. "Consult your memory of what happened when you tried that experiment in Vauxhall Walk. Did Mrs. Lecount get no other chance against you than the chances you have told me of already?"

"She discovered that my face was disguised, and she heard me speak in my own voice."

"And nothing more?"

"Nothing more."

"Very good. Then my interpretation of the letter is clearly the right one. The proof Mrs. Lecount relies on is my wife's infernal ghost story—which is, in plain English, the story of Miss Bygrave having been seen in Miss Vanstone's disguise; the witness being the very person who is afterward presented at Aldborough in the character of Miss Bygrave's aunt. An excellent chance for Mrs. Lecount, if she can only lay her hand at the right time on Mrs. Wragge, and no chance at all, if she can't. Make your mind easy on that point. Mrs. Lecount and my wife have seen the last of each other. In the meantime, don't neglect the warning I give you, in giving you this letter. Tear it up, for fear of accidents, but don't forget it."

"Trust me to remember it," replied Magdalen, destroying the letter while she spoke. "Have you anything more to tell me?"

"I have some information to give you," said Captain Wragge, "which may be useful, because it relates to your future security. Mind, I want to know nothing about your proceedings when to-morrow is over; we settled that when we first discussed this matter. I ask no questions, and I make no guesses. All I want to do now is to warn you of your legal position after your marriage, and to leave you to make what use you please of your knowledge, at your own sole discretion. I took a lawyer's opinion on the point when I was in London, thinking it might be useful to you."

"It is sure to be useful. What did the lawyer say?"

"To put it plainly, this is what he said. If Mr. Noel Vanstone ever discovers that you have knowingly married him under a false name, he can apply to the Ecclesiastical Court to have his marriage declared null and void. The issue of the application would rest with the judges. But if he could prove that he had been intentionally deceived, the legal opinion is that his case would be a strong one."

"Suppose I chose to apply on my side?" said Magdalen, eagerly. "What then?"

"You might make the application," replied the captain. "But remember one thing—you would come into Court with the acknowledgment of your own deception. I leave you to imagine what the judges would think of that."

"Did the lawyer tell you anything else?"

"One thing besides," said Captain Wragge. "Whatever the law might do with the marriage in the lifetime of both the parties to it—on the death of either one of them, no application made by the survivor would avail; and, as to the case of that survivor, the marriage would remain valid. You understand? If he dies, or if you die—and if no application has been made to the Court—he the survivor, or you the survivor, would have no power of disputing the marriage. But in the lifetime of both of you, if he claimed to have the marriage dissolved, the chances are all in favor of his carrying his point."

He looked at Magdalen with a furtive curiosity as he said those words. She turned her head aside, absently tying her watch-chain into a loop and untying it again, evidently thinking with the closest attention over what he had last said to her. Captain Wragge walked uneasily to the window and looked out. The first object that caught his eye was Mr. Noel Vanstone approaching from Sea View. He returned instantly to his former place in the room, and addressed himself to Magdalen once more.

"Here is Mr. Noel Vanstone," he said. "One last caution before he comes in. Be on your guard with him about your age. He put the question to me before he got the License. I took the shortest way out of the difficulty, and told him you were twenty-one, and he made the declaration accordingly. Never mind about me; after to-morrow I am invisible. But, in your own interests, don't forget, if the subject turns up, that you were of age when you were married. There is nothing more. You are provided with every necessary warning that I can give you. Whatever happens in the future, remember I have done my best."

He hurried to the door without waiting for an answer, and went out into the garden to receive his guest.

Noel Vanstone made his appearance at the gate, solemnly carrying his bridal offering to North Shingles with both hands. The object in question was an ancient casket (one of his father's bargains); inside the casket reposed an old-fashioned carbuncle brooch, set in silver (another of his father's bargains)—bridal presents both, possessing the inestimable merit of leaving his money undisturbed in his pocket. He shook his head portentously when the captain inquired after his health and spirits. He had passed a wakeful night; ungovernable apprehensions of Lecount's sudden re-appearance had beset him as soon as he found himself alone at Sea View. Sea View was redolent of Lecount: Sea View (though built on piles, and the strongest house in England) was henceforth odious to him. He had felt this all night; he had also felt his responsibilities. There was the lady's maid, to begin with. Now he had hired her, he began to think she wouldn't do. She might fall sick on his hands; she might have deceived him by a false character; she and the landlady of the hotel might have been in league together. Horrible! Really horrible to think of. Then there was the other responsibility—perhaps the heavier of the two—the responsibility of deciding where he was to go and spend his honeymoon to-morrow. He would have preferred one of his father's empty houses: But except at Vauxhall Walk (which he supposed would be objected to), and at Aldborough (which was of course out of the question) all the houses were let. He would put himself in Mr. Bygrave's hands. Where had Mr. Bygrave spent his own honeymoon? Given the British Islands to choose from, where would Mr. Bygrave pitch his tent, on a careful review of all the circumstances?

At this point the bridegroom's questions suddenly came to an end, and the bridegroom's face exhibited an expression of ungovernable astonishment. His judicious friend, whose advice had been at his disposal in every other emergency, suddenly turned round on him, in the emergency of the honeymoon, and flatly declined discussing the subject.

"No!" said the captain, as Noel Vanstone opened his lips to plead for a hearing, "you must really excuse me. My point of view in this matter is, as usual, a peculiar one. For some time past I have been living in an atmosphere of deception, to suit your convenience. That atmosphere, my good sir, is getting close; my Moral Being requires ventilation. Settle the choice of a locality with my niece, and leave me, at my particular request, in total ignorance of the subject. Mrs. Lecount is certain to come here on her return from Zurich, and is certain to ask me where you are gone. You may think it strange, Mr. Vanstone; but when I tell her I don't know, I wish to enjoy the unaccustomed luxury of feeling, for once in a way, that I am speaking the truth!"

With those words, he opened the sitting-room door, introduced Noel Vanstone to Magdalen's presence, bowed himself out of the room again, and set forth alone to while away the rest of the afternoon by taking a walk. His face showed plain tokens of anxiety, and his party-colored eyes looked hither and thither distrustfully, as he sauntered along the shore. "The time hangs heavy on our hands," thought the captain. "I wish to-morrow was come and gone."

The day passed and nothing happened; the evening and the night followed, placidly and uneventfully. Monday came, a cloudless, lovely day; Monday confirmed the captain's assertion that the marriage was a certainty. Toward ten o'clock, the clerk, ascending the church steps quoted the old proverb to the pew-opener, meeting him under the porch: "Happy the bride on whom the sun shines!"

In a quarter of an hour more the wedding-party was in the vestry, and the clergyman led the way to the altar. Carefully as the secret of the marriage had been kept, the opening of the church in the morning had been enough to betray it. A small congregation, almost entirely composed of women, were scattered here and there among the pews. Kirke's sister and her children were staying with a friend at Aldborough, and Kirke's sister was one of the congregation.

As the wedding-party entered the church, the haunting terror of Mrs. Lecount spread from Noel Vanstone to the captain. For the first few minutes, the eyes of both of them looked among the women in the pews with the same searching scrutiny, and looked away again with the same sense of relief. The clergyman noticed that look, and investigated the License more closely than usual. The clerk began to doubt privately whether the old proverb about the bride was a proverb to be always depended on. The female members of the congregation murmured among themselves at the inexcusable disregard of appearances implied in the bride's dress. Kirke's sister whispered venomously in her friend's ear, "Thank God for to-day for Robert's sake." Mrs. Wragge cried silently, with the dread of some threatening calamity she knew not what. The one person present who remained outwardly undisturbed was Magdalen herself. She stood, with tearless resignation, in her place before the altar—stood, as if all the sources of human emotion were frozen up within her.

The clergyman opened the Book.

It was done. The awful words which speak from earth to Heaven were pronounced. The children of the two dead brothers—inheritors of the implacable enmity which had parted their parents—were Man and Wife.

From that moment events hurried with a headlong rapidity to the parting scene. They were back at the house while the words of the Marriage Service seemed still ringing in their ears. Before they had been five minutes indoors the carriage drew up at the garden gate. In a minute more the opportunity came for which Magdalen and the captain had been on the watch—the opportunity of speaking together in private for the last time. She still preserved her icy resignation; she seemed beyond all reach now of the fear that had once mastered her, of the remorse that had once tortured her soul. With a firm hand she gave him the promised money. With a firm face she looked her last at him. "I'm not to blame," he whispered, eagerly; "I have only done what you asked me." She bowed her head; she bent it toward him kindly and let him touch her fore-head with his lips. "Take care!" he said. "My last words are—for God's sake take care when I'm gone!" She turned from him with a smile, and spoke her farewell words to his wife. Mrs. Wragge tried hard to face her loss bravely—the loss of the friend whose presence had fallen like light from Heaven over the dim pathway of her life. "You have been very good to me, my dear; I thank you kindly; I thank you with all my heart." She could say no more; she clung to Magdalen in a passion of tears, as her mother might have clung to her, if her mother had lived to see that horrible day. "I'm frightened for you!" cried the poor creature, in a wild, wailing voice. "Oh, my darling, I'm frightened for you!" Magdalen desperately drew herself free—kissed her—and hurried out to the door. The expression of that artless gratitude, the cry of that guileless love, shook her as nothing else had shaken her that day. It was a refuge to get to the carriage—a refuge, though the man she had married stood there waiting for her at the door.

Mrs. Wragge tried to follow her into the garden. But the captain had seen Magdalen's face as she ran out, and he steadily held his wife back in the passage. From that distance the last farewells were exchanged. As long as the carriage was in sight, Magdalen looked back at them; she waved her handkerchief as she turned the corner. In a moment more the last thread which bound her to them was broken; the familiar companionship of many months was a thing of the past already!

Captain Wragge closed the house door on the idlers who were looking in from the Parade. He led his wife back into the sitting-room, and spoke to her with a forbearance which she had never yet experienced from him.

"She has gone her way," he said, "and in another hour we shall have gone ours. Cry your cry out—I don't deny she's worth crying for."

Even then—even when the dread of Magdalen's future was at its darkest in his mind—the ruling habit of the man's life clung to him. Mechanically he unlocked his dispatch-box. Mechanically he opened his Book of Accounts, and made the closing entry—the entry of his last transaction with Magdalen—in black and white. "By Rec'd from Miss Vanstone," wrote the captain, with a gloomy brow, "Two hundred pounds."

"You won't be angry with me?" said Mrs. Wragge, looking timidly at her husband through her tears. "I want a word of comfort, captain. Oh, do tell me, when shall I see her again?"

The captain closed the book, and answered in one inexorable word: "Never!"

Between eleven and twelve o'clock that night Mrs. Lecount drove into Zurich.

Her brother's house, when she stopped before it, was shut up. With some difficulty and delay the servant was aroused. She held up her hands in speechless amazement when she opened the door and saw who the visitor was.

"Is my brother alive?" asked Mrs. Lecount, entering the house.

"Alive!" echoed the servant. "He has gone holiday-making into the country, to finish his recovery in the fine fresh air."

The housekeeper staggered back against the wall of the passage. The coachman and the servant put her into a chair. Her face was livid, and her teeth chattered in her head.

"Send for my brother's doctor," she said, as soon as she could speak.

The doctor came. She handed him a letter before he could say a word.

"Did you write that letter?"

He looked it over rapidly, and answered her without hesitation,

"Certainly not!"

"It is your handwriting."

"It is a forgery of my handwriting."

She rose from the chair with a new strength in her.

"When does the return mail start for Paris?" she asked.

"In half an hour."

"Send instantly and take me a place in it!"

The servant hesitated, the doctor protested. She turned a deaf ear to them both.

"Send!" she reiterated, "or I will go myself."

They obeyed. The servant went to take the place: the doctor remained and held a conversation with Mrs. Lecount. When the half-hour had passed, he helped her into her place in the mail, and charged the conductor privately to take care of his passenger.

"She has traveled from England without stopping," said the doctor; "and she is traveling back again without rest. Be careful of her, or she will break down under the double journey."

The mail started. Before the first hour of the new day was at an end Mrs. Lecount was on her way back to England.

THE END OF THE FOURTH SCENE.

BETWEEN THE SCENES.

PROGRESS OF THE STORY THROUGH THE POST.

I.

From George Bartram to Noel Vanstone.

"St. Crux, September 4th, 1847.

"MY DEAR NOEL—Here are two plain questions at starting. In the name of all that is mysterious, what are you hiding for? And why is everything relating to your marriage kept an impenetrable secret from your oldest friends?

"I have been to Aldborough to try if I could trace you from that place, and have come back as wise as I went. I have applied to your lawyer in London, and have been told, in reply, that you have forbidden him to disclose the place of your retreat to any one without first receiving your permission to do so. All I could prevail on him to say was, that he would forward any letter which might be sent to his care. I write accordingly, and mind this, I expect an answer.

"You may ask, in your ill-tempered way, what business I have to meddle with affairs of yours which it is your pleasure to keep private. My dear Noel, there is a serious reason for our opening communications with you from this house. You don't know what events have taken place at St. Crux since you ran away to get married; and though I detest writing letters, I must lose an hour's shooting to-day in trying to enlighten you.

"On the twenty-third of last month, the admiral and I were disturbed over our wine after dinner by the announcement that a visitor had unexpectedly arrived at St. Crux. Who do you think the visitor was? Mrs. Lecount!

"My uncle, with that old-fashioned bachelor gallantry of his which pays equal respect to all wearers of petticoats, left the table directly to welcome Mrs. Lecount. While I was debating whether I should follow him or not, my meditations were suddenly brought to an end by a loud call from the admiral. I ran into the morning-room, and there was your unfortunate housekeeper on the sofa, with all the women servants about her, more dead than alive. She had traveled from England to Zurich, and from Zurich back again to England, without stopping; and she looked, seriously and literally, at death's door. I immediately agreed with my uncle that the first thing to be done was to send for medical help. We dispatched a groom on the spot, and, at Mrs. Lecount's own request, sent all the servants in a body out of the room.

"As soon as we were alone, Mrs. Lecount surprised us by a singular question. She asked if you had received a letter which she had addressed to you before leaving England at this house. When we told her that the letter had been forwarded, under cover to your friend Mr. Bygrave, by your own particular request, she turned as pale as ashes; and when we added that you had left us in company with this same Mr. Bygrave, she clasped her hands and stared at us as if she had taken leave of her senses. Her next question was, 'Where is Mr. Noel now?' We could only give her one reply—Mr. Noel had not informed us. She looked perfectly thunderstruck at that answer. 'He has gone to his ruin!' she said. 'He has gone away in company with the greatest villain in England. I must find him! I tell you I must find Mr. Noel! If I don't find him at once, it will be too late. He will be married!' she burst out quite frantically. 'On my honor and my oath, he will be married!' The admiral, incautiously perhaps, but with the best intentions, told her you were married already. She gave a scream that made the windows ring again and dropped back on the sofa in a fainting-fit. The doctor came in the nick of time, and soon brought her to. But she was taken ill the same night; she has grown worse and worse ever since; and the last medical report is, that the fever from which she has been suffering is in a fair way to settle on her brain.

"Now, my dear Noel, neither my uncle nor I have any wish to intrude ourselves on your confidence. We are naturally astonished at the extraordinary mystery which hangs over you and your marriage, and we cannot be blind to the fact that your housekeeper has, apparently, some strong reason of her own for viewing Mrs. Noel Vanstone with an enmity and distrust which we are quite ready to believe that lady has done nothing to deserve. Whatever strange misunderstanding there may have been in your household, is your business (if you choose to keep it to yourself), and not ours. All we have any right to do is to tell you what the doctor says. His patient has been delirious; he declines to answer for her life if she goes on as she is going on now; and he thinks—finding that she is perpetually talking of her master—that your presence would be useful in quieting her, if you could come here at once, and exert your influence before it is too late.

"What do you say? Will you emerge from the darkness that surrounds you and come to St. Crux? If this was the case of an ordinary servant, I could understand your hesitating to leave the delights of your honeymoon for any such object as is here proposed to you. But, my dear fellow, Mrs. Lecount is not an ordinary servant. You are under obligations to her fidelity and attachment in your father's time, as well as in your own; and if you can quiet the anxieties which seem to be driving this unfortunate woman mad, I really think you ought to come here and do so. Your leaving Mrs. Noel Vanstone is of course out of the question. There is no necessity for any such hard-hearted proceeding. The admiral desires me to remind you that he is your oldest friend living, and that his house is at your wife's disposal, as it has always been at yours. In this great rambling-place she need dread no near association with the sick-room; and, with all my uncle's oddities, I am sure she will not think the offer of his friendship an offer to be despised.

"Have I told you already that I went to Aldborough to try and find a clew to your whereabouts? I can't be at the trouble of looking back to see; so, if I have told you, I tell you again. The truth is, I made an acquaintance at Aldborough of whom you know something—at least by report.

"After applying vainly at Sea View, I went to the hotel to inquire about you. The landlady could give me no information; but the moment I mentioned your name, she asked if I was related to you; and when I told her I was your cousin, she said there was a young lady then at the hotel whose name was Vanstone also, who was in great distress about a missing relative, and who might prove of some use to me—or I to her—if we knew of each other's errand at Aldborough. I had not the least idea who she was, but I sent in my card at a venture; and in five minutes afterward I found myself in the presence of one of the most charming women these eyes ever looked on.

"Our first words of explanation informed me that my family name was known to her by repute. Who do you think she was? The eldest daughter of my uncle and yours—Andrew Vanstone. I had often heard my poor mother in past years speak of her brother Andrew, and I knew of that sad story at Combe-Raven. But our families, as you are aware, had always been estranged, and I had never seen my charming cousin before. She has the dark eyes and hair, and the gentle, retiring manners that I always admire in a woman. I don't want to renew our old disagreement about your father's conduct to those two sisters, or to deny that his brother Andrew may have behaved badly to him; I am willing to admit that the high moral position he took in the matter is quite unassailable by such a miserable sinner as I am; and I will not dispute that my own spendthrift habits incapacitate me from offering any opinion on the conduct of other people's pecuniary affairs. But, with all these allowances and drawbacks, I can tell you one thing, Noel. If you ever see the elder Miss Vanstone, I venture to prophesy that, for the first time in your life, you will doubt the propriety of following your father's example.

"She told me her little story, poor thing, most simply and unaffectedly. She is now occupying her second situation as a governess—and, as usual, I, who know everybody, know the family. They are friends of my uncle's, whom he has lost sight of latterly—the Tyrrels of Portland Place—and they treat Miss Vanstone with as much kindness and consideration as if she was a member of the family. One of their old servants accompanied her to Aldborough, her object in traveling to that place being what the landlady of the hotel had stated it to be. The family reverses have, it seems, had a serious effect on Miss Vanstone's younger sister, who has left her friends and who has been missing from home for some time. She had been last heard of at Aldborough; and her elder sister, on her return from the Continent with the Tyrrels, had instantly set out to make inquiries at that place.

"This was all Miss Vanstone told me. She asked whether you had seen anything of her sister, or whether Mrs. Lecount knew anything of her sister—I suppose because she was aware you had been at Aldborough. Of course I could tell her nothing. She entered into no details on the subject, and I could not presume to ask her for any. All I did was to set to work with might and main to assist her inquiries. The attempt was an utter failure; nobody could give us any information. We tried personal description of course; and strange to say, the only young lady formerly staying at Aldborough who answered the description was, of all the people in the world, the lady you have married! If she had not had an uncle and aunt (both of whom have left the place), I should have begun to suspect that you had married your cousin without knowing it! Is this the clew to the mystery? Don't be angry; I must have my little joke, and I can't help writing as carelessly as I talk. The end of it was, our inquiries were all baffled, and I traveled back with Miss Vanstone and her attendant as far as our station here. I think I shall call on the Tyrrels when I am next in London. I have certainly treated that family with the most inexcusable neglect.

"Here I am at the end of my third sheet of note-paper! I don't often take the pen in hand; but when I do, you will agree with me that I am in no hurry to lay it aside again. Treat the rest of my letter as you like, but consider what I have told you about Mrs. Lecount, and remember that time is of consequence.

"Ever yours,

"GEORGE BARTRAM."

II.

From Norah Vanstone to Miss Garth.

"Portland Place.

"MY DEAR MISS GARTH—More sorrow, more disappointment! I have just returned from Aldborough, without making any discovery. Magdalen is still lost to us.

"I cannot attribute this new overthrow of my hopes to any want of perseverance or penetration in making the necessary inquiries. My inexperience in such matters was most kindly and unexpectedly assisted by Mr. George Bartram. By a strange coincidence, he happened to be at Aldborough, inquiring after Mr. Noel Vanstone, at the very time when I was there inquiring after Magdalen. He sent in his card, and knowing, when I looked at the name, that he was my cousin—if I may call him so—I thought there would be no impropriety in my seeing him and asking his advice. I abstained from entering into particulars for Magdalen's sake, and I made no allusion to that letter of Mrs. Lecount's which you answered for me. I only told him Magdalen was missing, and had been last heard of at Aldborough. The kindness which he showed in devoting himself to my assistance exceeds all description. He treated me, in my forlorn situation, with a delicacy and respect which I shall remember gratefully long after he has himself perhaps forgotten our meeting altogether. He is quite young—not more than thirty, I should think. In face and figure, he reminded me a little of the portrait of my father at Combe-Raven—I mean the portrait in the dining-room, of my father when he was a young man.

"Useless as our inquiries were, there is one result of them which has left a very strange and shocking impression on my mind.

"It appears that Mr. Noel Vanstone has lately married, under mysterious circumstances, a young lady whom he met with at Aldborough, named Bygrave. He has gone away with his wife, telling nobody but his lawyer where he has gone to. This I heard from Mr. George Bartram, who was endeavoring to trace him, for the purpose of communicating the news of his housekeeper's serious illness—the housekeeper being the same Mrs. Lecount whose letter you answered. So far, you may say, there is nothing which need particularly interest either of us. But I think you will be as much surprised as I was when I tell you that the description given by the people at Aldborough of Miss Bygrave's appearance is most startlingly and unaccountably like the description of Magdalen's appearance. This discovery, taken in connection with all the circumstances we know of, has had an effect on my mind which I cannot describe to you—which I dare not realize to myself. Pray come and see me! I have never felt so wretched about Magdalen as I feel now. Suspense must have weakened my nerves in some strange way. I feel superstitious about the slightest things. This accidental resemblance of a total stranger to Magdalen fills me every now and then with the most horrible misgivings—merely because Mr. Noel Vanstone's name happens to be mixed up with it. Once more, pray come to me; I have so much to say to you that I cannot, and dare not, say in writing.

"Gratefully and affectionately yours,

"NORAH."

III.

From Mr. John Loscombe (Solicitor) to George Bartram, Esq.

"Lincoln's Inn, London, September 6th, 1847.

"SIR—I beg to acknowledge the receipt of your note, inclosing a letter addressed to my client, Mr. Noel Vanstone, and requesting that I will forward the same to Mr. Vanstone's present address.

"Since I last had the pleasure of communicating with you on this subject, my position toward my client is entirely altered. Three days ago I received a letter from him, which stated his intention of changing his place of residence on the next day then ensuing, but which left me entirely in ignorance on the subject of the locality to which it was his intention to remove. I have not heard from him since; and, as he had previously drawn on me for a larger sum of money than usual, there would be no present necessity for his writing to me again—assuming that it is his wish to keep his place of residence concealed from every one, myself included.

"Under these circumstances, I think it right to return you your letter, with the assurance that I will let you know, if I happen to be again placed in a position to forward it to its destination.

"Your obedient servant,

"JOHN LOSCOMBE."

IV.

From Norah Vanstone to Miss Garth.

"Portland Place.

"MY DEAR MISS GARTH—Forget the letter I wrote to you yesterday, and all the gloomy forebodings that it contains. This morning's post has brought new life to me. I have just received a letter, addressed to me at your house, and forwarded here, in your absence from home yesterday, by your sister. Can you guess who the writer is?—Magdalen!

"The letter is very short; it seems to have been written in a hurry. She says she has been dreaming of me for some nights past, and the dreams have made her fear that her long silence has caused me more distress on her account than she is worth. She writes, therefore, to assure me that she is safe and well—that she hopes to see me before long—and that she has something to tell me, when we meet, which will try my sisterly love for her as nothing has tried it yet. The letter is not dated; but the postmark is 'Allonby,' which I have found, on referring to the Gazetteer, to be a little sea-side place in Cumberland. There is no hope of my being able to write back, for Magdalen expressly says that she is on the eve of departure from her present residence, and that she is not at liberty to say where she is going to next, or to leave instructions for forwarding any letters after her.

"In happier times I should have thought this letter very far from being a satisfactory one, and I should have been seriously alarmed by that allusion to a future confidence on her part which will try my love for her as nothing has tried it yet. But after all the suspense I have suffered, the happiness of seeing her handwriting again seems to fill my heart and to keep all other feelings out of it. I don't send you her letter, because I know you are coming to me soon, and I want to have the pleasure of seeing you read it.

"Ever affectionately yours,

"NORAH.

"P.S.—Mr. George Bartram called on Mrs. Tyrrel to-day. He insisted on being introduced to the children. When he was gone, Mrs. Tyrrel laughed in her good-humored way, and said that his anxiety to see the children looked, to her mind, very much like an anxiety to see me. You may imagine how my spirits are improved when I can occupy my pen in writing such nonsense as this!"

V.

From Mrs. Lecount to Mr. de Bleriot, General Agent, London.

"St. Crux, October 23d, 1847.

"DEAR SIR—I have been long in thanking you for the kind letter which promises me your assistance, in friendly remembrance of the commercial relations formerly existing between my brother and yourself. The truth is, I have over-taxed my strength on my recovery from a long and dangerous illness; and for the last ten days I have been suffering under a relapse. I am now better again, and able to enter on the business which you so kindly offer to undertake for me.

"The person whose present place of abode it is of the utmost importance to me to discover is Mr. Noel Vanstone. I have lived, for many years past, in this gentleman's service as house-keeper; and not having received my formal dismissal, I consider myself in his service still. During my absence on the Continent he was privately married at Aldborough, in Suffolk, on the eighteenth of August last. He left Aldborough the same day, taking his wife with him to some place of retreat which was kept a secret from everybody except his lawyer, Mr. Loscombe, of Lincoln's Inn. After a short time he again removed, on the 4th of September, without informing Mr. Loscombe, on this occasion, of his new place of abode. From that date to this the lawyer has remained (or has pretended to remain) in total ignorance of where he now is. Application has been made to Mr. Loscombe, under the circumstances, to mention what that former place of residence was, of which Mr. Vanstone is known to have informed him. Mr. Loscombe has declined acceding to this request, for want of formal permission to disclose his client's proceedings after leaving Aldborough. I have all these latter particulars from Mr. Loscombe's correspondent—the nephew of the gentleman who owns this house, and whose charity has given me an asylum, during the heavy affliction of my sickness, under his own roof.

"I believe the reasons which have induced Mr. Noel Vanstone to keep himself and his wife in hiding are reasons which relate entirely to myself. In the first place, he is aware that the circumstances under which he has married are such as to give me the right of regarding him with a just indignation. In the second place, he knows that my faithful services, rendered through a period of twenty years, to his father and to himself, forbid him, in common decency, to cast me out helpless on the world without a provision for the end of my life. He is the meanest of living men, and his wife is the vilest of living women. As long as he can avoid fulfilling his obligations to me, he will; and his wife's encouragement may be trusted to fortify him in his ingratitude.

"My object in determining to find him out is briefly this. His marriage has exposed him to consequences which a man of ten times his courage could not face without shrinking. Of those consequences he knows nothing. His wife knows, and keeps him in ignorance. I know, and can enlighten him. His security from the danger that threatens him is in my hands alone; and he shall pay the price of his rescue to the last farthing of the debt that justice claims for me as my due—no more, and no less.

"I have now laid my mind before you, as you told me, without reserve. You know why I want to find this man, and what I mean to do when I find him. I leave it to your sympathy for me to answer the serious question that remains: How is the discovery to be made? If a first trace of them can be found, after their departure from Aldborough, I believe careful inquiry will suffice for the rest. The personal appearance of the wife, and the extraordinary contrast between her husband and herself, are certain to be remarked, and remembered, by every stranger who sees them.

"When you favor me with your answer, please address it to 'Care of Admiral Bartram, St. Crux-in the-Marsh, near Ossory, Essex'. Your much obliged

"VIRGINIE LECOUNT."

VI.

From Mr. de Bleriot to Mrs. Lecount.

"Dark's Buildings, Kingsland,

"October 25th, 1847.

"Private and Confidential.

"DEAR MADAM—I hasten to reply to your favor of Saturday's date. Circumstances have enabled me to forward your interests, by consulting a friend of mine possessing great experience in the management of private inquiries of all sorts. I have placed your case before him (without mentioning names); and I am happy to inform you that my views and his views of the proper course to take agree in every particular.

"Both myself and friend, then, are of opinion that little or nothing can be done toward tracing the parties you mention, until the place of their temporary residence after they left Aldborough has been discovered first. If this can be done, the sooner it is done the better. Judging from your letter, some weeks must have passed since the lawyer received his information that they had shifted their quarters. As they are both remarkable-looking people, the strangers who may have assisted them on their travels have probably not forgotten them yet. Nevertheless, expedition is desirable.

"The question for you to consider is, whether they may not possibly have communicated the address of which we stand in need to some other person besides the lawyer. The husband may have written to members of his family, or the wife may have written to members of her family. Both myself and friend are of opinion that the latter chance is the likelier of the two. If you have any means of access in the direction of the wife's family, we strongly recommend you to make use of them. If not, please supply us with the names of any of her near relations or intimate female friends whom you know, and we will endeavor to get access for you.

"In any case, we request you will at once favor us with the most exact personal description that can be written of both the parties. We may require your assistance, in this important particular, at five minutes' notice. Favor us, therefore, with the description by return of post. In the meantime, we will endeavor to ascertain on our side whether any information is to be privately obtained at Mr. Loscombe's office. The lawyer himself is probably altogether beyond our reach. But if any one of his clerks can be advantageously treated with on such terms as may not overtax your pecuniary resources, accept my assurance that the opportunity shall be made the most of by, dear madam, your faithful servant,

"ALFRED DE BLERIOT."

VII.

From Mr. Pendril to Norah Vanstone.

"Serle Street, October 27th. 1847.

"MY DEAR MISS VANSTONE—A lady named Lecount (formerly attached to Mr. Noel Vanstone's service in the capacity of housekeeper) has called at my office this morning, and has asked me to furnish her with your address. I have begged her to excuse my immediate compliance with her request, and to favor me with a call to-morrow morning, when I shall be prepared to meet her with a definite answer.

"My hesitation in this matter does not proceed from any distrust of Mrs. Lecount personally, for I know nothing whatever to her prejudice. But in making her request to me, she stated that the object of the desired interview was to speak to you privately on the subject of your sister. Forgive me for acknowledging that I determined to withhold the address as soon as I heard this. You will make allowances for your old friend, and your sincere well-wisher? You will not take it amiss if I express my strong disapproval of your allowing yourself, on any pretense whatever, to be mixed up for the future with your sister's proceedings.

"I will not distress you by saying more than this. But I feel too deep an interest in your welfare, and too sincere an admiration of the patience with which you have borne all your trials, to say less.

"If I cannot prevail on you to follow my advice, you have only to say so, and Mrs. Lecount shall have your address to-morrow. In this case (which I cannot contemplate without the greatest unwillingness), let me at least recommend you to stipulate that Miss Garth shall be present at the interview. In any matter with which your sister is concerned, you may want an old friend's advice, and an old friend's protection against your own generous impulses. If I could have helped you in this way, I would; but Mrs. Lecount gave me indirectly to understand that the subject to be discussed was of too delicate a nature to permit of my presence. Whatever this objection may be really worth, it cannot apply to Miss Garth, who has brought you both up from childhood. I say, again, therefore, if you see Mrs. Lecount, see her in Miss Garth's company.

"Always most truly yours,

"WILLIAM PENDRIL."

VIII.

From Norah Vanstone to Mr. Pendril.

"Portland Place, Wednesday.

"DEAR MR. PENDRIL—Pray don't think I am ungrateful for your kindness. Indeed, indeed I am not! But I must see Mrs. Lecount. You were not aware when you wrote to me that I had received a few lines from Magdalen—not telling me where she is, but holding out the hope of our meeting before long. Perhaps Mrs. Lecount may have something to say to me on this very subject. Even if it should not be so, my sister—do what she may—is still my sister.

I can't desert her; I can't turn my back on any one who comes to me in her name. You know, dear Mr. Pendril, I have always been obstinate on this subject, and you have always borne with me. Let me owe another obligation to you which I can never return, and bear with me still!

"Need I say that I willingly accept that part of your advice which refers to Miss Garth? I have already written to beg that she will come here at four to-morrow afternoon. When you see Mrs. Lecount, please inform her that Miss Garth will be with me, and that she will find us both ready to receive her here to-morrow at four o'clock. Gratefully yours,

"NORAH VANSTONE."

IX.

From Mr. de Bleriot to Mrs. Lecount.

"Private.

"Dark's Buildings, October 28th.

"DEAR MADAM—One of Mr. Loscombe's clerks has proved amenable to a small pecuniary consideration, and has mentioned a circumstance which it may be of some importance to you to know.

"Nearly a month since, accident gave the clerk in question an opportunity of looking into one of the documents on his master's table, which had attracted his attention from a slight peculiarity in the form and color of the paper. He had only time, during Mr. Loscombe's momentary absence, to satisfy his curiosity by looking at the beginning of the document and at the end. At the beginning he saw the customary form used in making a will; at the end he discovered the signature of Mr. Noel Vanstone, with the names of two attesting witnesses, and the date (of which he is quite certain)—the thirtieth of September last.

"Before the clerk had time to make any further investigations, his master returned, sorted the papers on the table, and carefully locked up the will in the strong box devoted to the custody of Mr. Noel Vanstone's documents. It has been ascertained that, at the close of September, Mr. Loscombe was absent from the office. If he was then employed in superintending the execution of his client's will—which is quite possible—it follows clearly that he was in the secret of Mr. Vanstone's address after the removal of the 4th of September; and if you can do nothing on your side, it may be desirable to have the lawyer watched on ours. In any case, it is certainly ascertained that Mr. Noel Vanstone has made his will since his marriage. I leave you to draw your own conclusions from that fact, and remain, in the hope of hearing from you shortly,

"Your faithful servant,

"ALFRED DE BLERIOT."

X.

From Miss Garth to Mr. Pendril.

"Portland Place, October 28th.

"MY DEAR SIR—Mrs. Lecount has just left us. If it was not too late to wish, I should wish, from the bottom of my heart, that Norah had taken your advice, and had refused to see her.

"I write in such distress of mind that I cannot hope to give you a clear and complete account of the interview. I can only tell you briefly what Mrs. Lecount has done, and what our situation now is. The rest must be left until I am more composed, and until I can speak to you personally.

"You will remember my informing you of the letter which Mrs. Lecount addressed to Norah from Aldborough, and which I answered for her in her absence. When Mrs. Lecount made her appearance to-day, her first words announced to us that she had come to renew the subject. As well as I can remember it, this is what she said, addressing herself to Norah:

"'I wrote to you on the subject of your sister, Miss Vanstone, some little time since, and Miss Garth was so good as to answer the letter. What I feared at that time has come true. Your sister has defied all my efforts to check her; she has disappeared in company with my master, Mr. Noel Vanstone; and she is now in a position of danger which may lead to her disgrace and ruin at a moment's notice. It is my interest to recover my master, it is your interest to save your sister. Tell me—for time is precious—have you any news of her?'

"Norah answered, as well as her terror and distress would allow her, 'I have had a letter, but there was no address on it.'

"Mrs. Lecount asked, 'Was there no postmark on the envelope?'

"Norah said, 'Yes; Allonby.'

"'Allonby is better than nothing,' said Mrs. Lecount. 'Allonby may help you to trace her. Where is Allonby?'

"Norah told her. It all passed in a minute. I had been too much confused and startled to interfere before, but I composed myself sufficiently to interfere now.

"'You have entered into no particulars,' I said. 'You have only frightened us—you have told us nothing.'

"'You shall hear the particulars, ma'am,' said Mrs. Lecount; 'and you and Miss Vanstone shall judge for yourselves if I have frightened you without a cause.'

"Upon this, she entered at once upon a long narrative, which I cannot—I might almost say, which I dare not—repeat. You will understand the horror we both felt when I tell you the end. If Mrs. Lecount's statement is to be relied on, Magdalen has carried her mad resolution of recovering her father's fortune to the last and most desperate extremity—she has married Michael Vanstone's son under a false name. Her husband is at this moment still persuaded that her maiden name was Bygrave, and that she is really the niece of a scoundrel who assisted her imposture, and whom I recognize, by the description of him, to have been Captain Wragge.

"I spare you Mrs. Lecount's cool avowal, when she rose to leave us, of her own mercenary motives in wishing to discover her master and to enlighten him. I spare you the hints she dropped of Magdalen's purpose in contracting this infamous marriage. The one aim and object of my letter is to implore you to assist me in quieting Norah's anguish of mind. The shock she has received at hearing this news of her sister is not the worst result of what has happened. She has persuaded herself that the answers she innocently gave, in her distress, to Mrs. Lecount's questions on the subject of her letter—the answers wrung from her under the sudden pressure of confusion and alarm—may be used to Magdalen's prejudice by the woman who purposely startled her into giving the information. I can only prevent her from taking some desperate step on her side—some step by which she may forfeit the friendship and protection of the excellent people with whom she is now living—by reminding her that if Mrs. Lecount traces her master by means of the postmark on the letter, we may trace Magdalen at the same time, and by the same means. Whatever objection you may personally feel to renewing the efforts for the rescue of this miserable girl which failed so lamentably at York, I entreat you, for Norah's sake, to take the same steps now which we took then. Send me the only assurance which will quiet her—the assurance, under your own hand, that the search on our side has begun. If you will do this, you may trust me, when the time comes, to stand between these two sisters, and to defend Norah's peace, character, and future prosperity at any price.

"Most sincerely yours,

"HARRIET GARTH."

XI.

From Mrs. Lecount to Mr. de Bleriot.

"October 28th.

"DEAR SIR—I have found the trace you wanted. Mrs. Noel Vanstone has written to her sister. The letter contains no address, but the postmark is Allonby, in Cumberland. From Allonby, therefore, the inquiries must begin. You have already in your possession the personal description of both husband and wife. I urgently recommend you not to lose one unnecessary moment. If it is possible to send to Cumberland immediately on receipt of this letter, I beg you will do so.

"I have another word to say before I close my note—a word about the discovery in Mr. Loscombe's office.

"It is no surprise to me to hear that Mr. Noel Vanstone has made his will since his marriage, and I am at no loss to guess in whose favor the will is made. If I succeed in finding my master, let that person get the money if that person can. A course to follow in this matter has presented itself to my mind since I received your letter, but my ignorance of details of business and intricacies of law leaves me still uncertain whether my idea is capable of ready and certain execution. I know no professional person whom I can trust in this delicate and dangerous business. Is your large experience in other matters large enough to help me in this? I will call at your office to-morrow at two o'clock, for the purpose of consulting you on the subject. It is of the greatest importance, when I next see Mr. Noel Vanstone, that he should find me thoroughly prepared beforehand in this matter of the will. Your much obliged servant,

"VIRGINIE LECOUNT."

XII.

From Mr. Pendril to Miss Garth.

"Serle Street, October 29th.

"DEAR MISS GARTH—I have only a moment to assure you of the sorrow with which I have read your letter. The circumstances under which you urge your request, and the reasons you give for making it, are sufficient to silence any objection I might otherwise feel to the course you propose. A trustworthy person, whom I have myself instructed, will start for Allonby to-day, and as soon as I receive any news from him, you shall hear of it by special messenger. Tell Miss Vanstone this, and pray add the sincere expression of my sympathy and regard.

"Faithfully yours,

"WILLIAM PENDRIL."

XIII.

From Mr. de Bleriot to Mrs. Lecount.

"Dark's Buildings. November 1st.

"DEAR MADAM—I have the pleasure of informing you that the discovery has been made with far less trouble than I had anticipated.

"Mr. and Mrs. Noel Vanstone have been traced across the Solway Firth to Dumfries, and thence to a cottage a few miles from the town, on the banks of the Nith. The exact address is Baliol Cottage, near Dumfries.

"This information, though easily hunted up, has nevertheless been obtained under rather singular circumstances.

"Before leaving Allonby, the persons in my employ discovered, to their surprise, that a stranger was in the place pursuing the same inquiry as themselves. In the absence of any instructions preparing them for such an occurrence as this, they took their own view of the circumstance. Considering the man as an intruder on their business, whose success might deprive them of the credit and reward of making the discovery, they took advantage of their superiority in numbers, and of their being first in the field, and carefully misled the stranger before they ventured any further with their own investigations. I am in possession of the details of their proceedings, with which I need not trouble you. The end is, that this person, whoever he may be, was cleverly turned back southward on a false scent before the men in my employment crossed the Firth.

"I mention the circumstance, as you may be better able than I am to find a clew to it, and as it may possibly be of a nature to induce you to hasten your journey.

"Your faithful servant,

"ALFRED DE BLERIOT."

XIV.

From Mrs. Lecount to Mr. de Bleriot.

"November 1st.

"DEAR SIR—One line to say that your letter has just reached me at my lodging in London. I think I know who sent the strange man to inquire at Allonby. It matters little. Before he finds out his mistake, I shall be at Dumfries. My luggage is packed, and I start for the North by the next train.

"Your deeply obliged

"VIRGINIE LECOUNT."

THE FIFTH SCENE

BALIOL COTTAGE, DUMFRIES.

CHAPTER I.

TOWARD eleven o'clock, on the morning of the third of November, the breakfast-table at Baliol Cottage presented that essentially comfortless appearance which is caused by a meal in a state of transition—that is to say, by a meal prepared for two persons, which has been already eaten by one, and which has not yet been approached by the other. It must be a hardy appetite which can contemplate without a momentary discouragement the battered egg-shell, the fish half stripped to a skeleton, the crumbs in the plate, and the dregs in the cup. There is surely a wise submission to those weaknesses in human nature which must be respected and not reproved, in the sympathizing rapidity with which servants in places of public refreshment clear away all signs of the customer in the past, from the eyes of the customer in the present. Although his predecessor may have been the wife of his bosom or the child of his loins, no man can find himself confronted at table by the traces of a vanished eater, without a passing sense of injury in connection with the idea of his own meal.

Some such impression as this found its way into the mind of Mr. Noel Vanstone when he entered the lonely breakfast-parlor at Baliol Cottage shortly after eleven o'clock. He looked at the table with a frown, and rang the bell with an expression of disgust.

"Clear away this mess," he said, when the servant appeared. "Has your mistress gone?"

"Yes, sir—nearly an hour ago."

"Is Louisa downstairs?"

"Yes, sir."

"When you have put the table right, send Louisa up to me."

He walked away to the window. The momentary irritation passed away from his face; but it left an expression there which remained—an expression of pining discontent. Personally, his marriage had altered him for the worse. His wizen little cheeks were beginning to shrink into hollows, his frail little figure had already contracted a slight stoop. The former delicacy of his complexion had gone—the sickly paleness of it was all that remained. His thin flaxen mustaches were no longer pragmatically waxed and twisted into a curl: their weak feathery ends hung meekly pendent over the querulous corners of his mouth. If the ten or twelve weeks since his marriage had been counted by his locks, they might have reckoned as ten or twelve years. He stood at the window mechanically picking leaves from a pot of heath placed in front of it, and drearily humming the forlorn fragment of a tune.

The prospect from the window overlooked the course of the Nith at a bend of the river a few miles above Dumfries. Here and there, through wintry gaps in the wooded bank, broad tracts of the level cultivated valley met the eye. Boats passed on the river, and carts plodded along the high-road on their way to Dumfries. The sky was clear; the November sun shone as pleasantly as if the year had been younger by two good months; and the view, noted in Scotland for its bright and peaceful charm, was presented at the best which its wintry aspect could assume. If it had been hidden in mist or drenched with rain, Mr. Noel Vanstone would, to all appearance, have found it as attractive as he found it now. He waited at the window until he heard Louisa's knock at the door, then turned back sullenly to the breakfast-table and told her to come in.

"Make the tea," he said. "I know nothing about it. I'm left here neglected. Nobody helps me."

The discreet Louisa silently and submissively obeyed.

"Did your mistress leave any message for me," he asked, "before she went away?"

"No message in particular, sir. My mistress only said she should be too late if she waited breakfast any longer."

"Did she say nothing else?"

"She told me at the carriage door, sir, that she would most likely be back in a week."

"Was she in good spirits at the carriage door?"

"No, sir. I thought my mistress seemed very anxious and uneasy. Is there anything more I can do, sir?"

"I don't know. Wait a minute."

He proceeded discontentedly with his breakfast. Louisa waited resignedly at the door.

"I think your mistress has been in bad spirits lately," he resumed, with a sudden outbreak of petulance.

"My mistress has not been very cheerful, sir."

"What do you mean by not very cheerful? Do you mean to prevaricate? Am I nobody in the house? Am I to be kept in the dark about everything? Is your mistress to go away on her own affairs, and leave me at home like a child—and am I not even to ask a question about her? Am I to be prevaricated with by a servant? I won't be prevaricated with! Not very cheerful? What do you mean by not very cheerful?"

"I only meant that my mistress was not in good spirits, sir."

"Why couldn't you say it, then? Don't you know the value of words? The most dreadful consequences sometimes happen from not knowing the value of words. Did your mistress tell you she was going to London?"

"Yes, sir."

"What did you think when your mistress told you she was going to London? Did you think it odd she was going without me?"

"I did not presume to think it odd, sir.—Is there anything more I can do for you, if you please, sir?"

"What sort of a morning is it out? Is it warm? Is the sun on the garden?"

"Yes, sir."

"Have you seen the sun yourself on the garden?"

"Yes, sir."

"Get me my great-coat; I'll take a little turn. Has the man brushed it? Did you see the man brush it yourself? What do you mean by saying he has brushed it, when you didn't see him? Let me look at the tails. If there's a speck of dust on the tails, I'll turn the man off!—Help me on with it."

Louisa helped him on with his coat, and gave him his hat. He went out irritably. The coat was a large one (it had belonged to his father); the hat was a large one (it was a misfit purchased as a bargain by himself). He was submerged in his hat and coat; he looked singularly small, and frail, and miserable, as he slowly wended his way, in the wintry sunlight, down the garden walk. The path sloped gently from the back of the house to the water side, from which it was parted by a low wooden fence. After pacing backward and forward slowly for some little time, he stopped at the lower extremity of the garden, and, leaning on the fence, looked down listlessly at the smooth flow of the river.

His thoughts still ran on the subject of his first fretful question to Louisa—he was still brooding over the circumstances under which his wife had left the cottage that morning, and over the want of consideration toward himself implied in the manner of her departure. The longer he thought of his grievance, the more acutely he resented it. He was capable of great tenderness of feeling where any injury to his sense of his own importance was concerned. His head drooped little by little on his arms, as they rested on the fence, and, in the deep sincerity of his mortification, he sighed bitterly.

The sigh was answered by a voice close at his side.

"You were happier with me, sir," said the voice, in accents of tender regret.

He looked up with a scream—literally, with a scream—and confronted Mrs. Lecount.

Was it the specter of the woman, or the woman herself? Her hair was white; her face had fallen away; her eyes looked out large, bright, and haggard over her hollow cheeks. She was withered and old. Her dress hung loose round her wasted figure; not a trace of its buxom autumnal beauty remained. The quietly impenetrable resolution, the smoothly insinuating voice—these were the only relics of the past which sickness and suffering had left in Mrs. Lecount.

"Compose yourself, Mr. Noel," she said, gently. "You have no cause to be alarmed at seeing me. Your servant, when I inquired, said you were in the garden, and I came here to find you. I have traced you out, sir, with no resentment against yourself, with no wish to distress you by so much as the shadow of a reproach. I come here on what has been, and is still, the business of my life—your service."

He recovered himself a little, but he was still incapable of speech. He held fast by the fence, and stared at her.

"Try to possess your mind, sir, of what I say," proceeded Mrs. Lecount. "I have come here not as your enemy, but as your friend. I have been tried by sickness, I have been tried by distress. Nothing remains of me but my heart. My heart forgives you; my heart, in your sore need—need which you have yet to feel-places me at your service. Take my arm, Mr. Noel. A little turn in the sun will help you to recover yourself."

She put his hand through her arm and marched him slowly up the garden walk. Before she had been five minutes in his company, she had resumed full possession of him in her own right.

"Now down again, Mr. Noel," she said. "Gently down again, in this fine sunlight. I have much to say to you, sir, which you never expected to hear from me. Let me ask a little domestic question first. They told me at the house door Mrs. Noel Vanstone was gone away on a journey. Has she gone for long?"

Her master's hand trembled on her arm as she put that question. Instead of answering it, he tried faintly to plead for himself. The first words that escaped him were prompted by his first returning sense—the sense that his housekeeper had taken him into custody. He tried to make his peace with Mrs. Lecount.

"I always meant to do something for you," he said, coaxingly. "You would have heard from me before long. Upon my word and honor, Lecount, you would have heard from me before long!"

"I don't doubt it, sir," replied Mrs. Lecount. "But for the present, never mind about Me. You and your interests first."

"How did you come here?" he asked, looking at her in astonishment. "How came you to find me out?"

"It is a long story, sir; I will tell it you some other time. Let it be enough to say now that I have found you. Will Mrs. Noel be back again at the house to-day? A little louder, sir; I can hardly hear you. So! so! Not back again for a week! And where has she gone? To London, did you say? And what for?—I am not inquisitive, Mr. Noel; I am asking serious questions, under serious necessity. Why has your wife left you here, and gone to London by herself?"

They were down at the fence again as she made that last inquiry, and they waited, leaning against it, while Noel Vanstone answered. Her reiterated assurances that she bore him no malice were producing their effect; he was beginning to recover himself. The old helpless habit of addressing all his complaints to his housekeeper was returning already with the re-appearance of Mrs. Lecount—returning insidiously, in company with that besetting anxiety to talk about his grievances, which had got the better of him at the breakfast-table, and which had shown the wound inflicted on his vanity to his wife's maid.

"I can't answer for Mrs. Noel Vanstone," he said, spitefully. "Mrs. Noel Vanstone has not treated me with the consideration which is my due. She has taken my permission for granted, and she has only thought proper to tell me that the object of her journey is to see her friends in London. She went away this morning without bidding me good-by. She takes her own way as if I was nobody; she treats me like a child. You may not believe it, Lecount, but I don't even know who her friends are. I am left quite in the dark; I am left to guess for myself that her friends in London are her uncle and aunt."

Mrs. Lecount privately considered the question by the help of her own knowledge obtained in London. She soon reached the obvious conclusion. After writing to her sister in the first instance, Magdalen had now, in all probability, followed the letter in person. There was little doubt that the friends she had gone to visit in London were her sister and Miss Garth.

"Not her uncle and aunt, sir," resumed Mrs. Lecount, composedly. "A secret for your private ear! She has no uncle and aunt. Another little turn before I explain myself—another little turn to compose your spirits."

She took him into custody once more, and marched him back toward the house.

"Mr. Noel!" she said, suddenly stopping in the middle of the walk. "Do you know what was the worst mischief you ever did yourself in your life? I will tell you. That worst mischief was sending me to Zurich."

His hand began to tremble on her arm once more.

"I didn't do it!" he cried piteously. "It was all Mr. Bygrave."

"You acknowledge, sir, that Mr. Bygrave deceived me?" proceeded Mrs. Lecount. "I am glad to hear that. You will be all the readier to make the next discovery which is waiting for you—the discovery that Mr. Bygrave has deceived you. He is not here to slip through my fingers now, and I am not the helpless woman in this place that I was at Aldborough. Thank God!"

She uttered that devout exclamation through her set teeth. All her hatred of Captain Wragge hissed out of her lips in those two words.

"Oblige me, sir, by holding one side of my traveling-bag," she resumed, "while I open it and take something out."

The interior of the bag disclosed a series of neatly-folded papers, all laid together in order, and numbered outside. Mrs. Lecount took out one of the papers, and shut up the bag again with a loud snap of the spring that closed it.

"At Aldborough, Mr. Noel, I had only my own opinion to support me," she remarked. "My own opinion was nothing against Miss Bygrave's youth and beauty, and Mr. Bygrave's ready wit. I could only hope to attack your infatuation with proofs, and at that time I had not got them. I have got them now! I am armed at all points with proofs; I bristle from head to foot with proofs; I break my forced silence, and speak with the emphasis of my proofs. Do you know this writing, sir?"

He shrank back from the paper which she offered to him.

"I don't understand this," he said, nervously. "I don't know what you want, or what you mean."

Mrs. Lecount forced the paper into his hand. "You shall know what I mean, sir, if you will give me a moment's attention," she said. "On the day after you went away to St. Crux, I obtained admission to Mr. Bygrave's house, and I had some talk in private with Mr. Bygrave's wife. That talk supplied me with the means to convince you which I had wanted to find for weeks and weeks past. I wrote you a letter to say so—I wrote to tell you that I would forfeit my place in your service, and my expectations from your generosity, if I did not prove to you when I came back from Switzerland that my own private suspicion of Miss Bygrave was the truth. I directed that letter to you at St. Crux, and I posted it myself. Now, Mr. Noel, read the paper which I have forced into your hand. It is Admiral Bartram's written affirmation that my letter came to St. Crux, and that he inclosed it to you, under cover to Mr. Bygrave, at your own request. Did Mr. Bygrave ever give you that letter? Don't agitate yourself, sir! One word of reply will do—Yes or No."

He read the paper, and looked up at her with growing bewilderment and fear. She obstinately waited until he spoke. "No," he said, faintly; "I never got the letter."

"First proof!" said Mrs. Lecount, taking the paper from him, and putting it back in the bag. "One more, with your kind permission, before we come to things more serious still. I gave you a written description, sir, at Aldborough, of a person not named, and I asked you to compare it with Miss Bygrave the next time you were in her company. After having first shown the description to Mr. Bygrave—it is useless to deny it now, Mr. Noel; your friend at North Shingles is not here to help you!—after having first shown my note to Mr. Bygrave, you made the comparison, and you found it fail in the most important particular. There were two little moles placed close together on the left side of the neck, in my description of the unknown lady, and there were no little moles at all when you looked at Miss Bygrave's neck. I am old enough to be your mother, Mr. Noel. If the question is not indelicate, may I ask what the present state of your knowledge is on the subject of your wife's neck?"

She looked at him with a merciless steadiness. He drew back a few steps, cowering under her eye. "I can't say," he stammered. "I don't know. What do you mean by these questions? I never thought about the moles afterward; I never looked. She wears her hair low—"

"She has excellent reasons to wear it low, sir," remarked Mrs. Lecount. "We will try and lift that hair before we have done with the subject. When I came out here to find you in the garden, I saw a neat young person through the kitchen window, with her work in her hand, who looked to my eyes like a lady's maid. Is this young person your wife's maid? I beg your pardon, sir, did you say yes? In that case, another question, if you please. Did you engage her, or did your wife?"

"I engaged her—"

"While I was away? While I was in total ignorance that you meant to have a wife, or a wife's maid?"

"Yes."

"Under those circumstances, Mr. Noel, you cannot possibly suspect me of conspiring to deceive you, with the maid for my instrument. Go into the house, sir, while I wait here. Ask the woman who dresses Mrs. Noel Vanstone's hair morning and night whether her mistress has a mark on the left side of her neck, and (if so) what that mark is?"

He walked a few steps toward the house without uttering a word, then stopped, and looked back at Mrs. Lecount. His blinking eyes were steady, and his wizen face had become suddenly composed. Mrs. Lecount advanced a little and joined him. She saw the change; but, with all her experience of him, she failed to interpret the true meaning of it.

"Are you in want of a pretense, sir?" she asked. "Are you at a loss to account to your wife's maid for such a question as I wish you to put to her? Pretenses are easily found which will do for persons in her station of life. Say I have come here with news of a legacy for Mrs. Noel Vanstone, and that there is a question of her identity to settle before she can receive the money."

She pointed to the house. He paid no attention to the sign. His face grew paler and paler. Without moving or speaking he stood and looked at her.

"Are you afraid?" asked Mrs. Lecount.

Those words roused him; those words lit a spark of the fire of manhood in him at last.

He turned on her like a sheep on a dog.

"I won't be questioned and ordered!" he broke out, trembling violently under the new sensation of his own courage. "I won't be threatened and mystified any longer! How did you find me out at this place? What do you mean by coming here with your hints and your mysteries? What have you got to say against my wife?"

Mrs. Lecount composedly opened the traveling-bag and took out her smelling bottle, in case of emergency.

"You have spoken to me in plain words," she said. "In plain words, sir, you shall have your answer. Are you too angry to listen?"

Her looks and tones alarmed him, in spite of himself. His courage began to sink again; and, desperately as he tried to steady it, his voice trembled when he answered her.

"Give me my answer," he said, "and give it at once."

"Your commands shall be obeyed, sir, to the letter," replied Mrs. Lecount. "I have come here with two objects. To open your eyes to your own situation, and to save your fortune—perhaps your life. Your situation is this. Miss Bygrave has married you under a false character and a false name. Can you rouse your memory? Can you call to mind the disguised woman who threatened you in Vauxhall Walk? That woman—as certainly as I stand here—is now your wife."

He looked at her in breathless silence, his lips falling apart, his eyes fixed in vacant inquiry. The suddenness of the disclosure had overreached its own end. It had stupefied him.

"My wife?" he repeated, and burst into an imbecile laugh.

"Your wife," reiterated Mrs. Lecount.

At the repetition of those two words the strain on his faculties relaxed. A thought dawned on him for the first time. His eyes fixed on her with a furtive alarm, and he drew back hastily. "Mad!" he said to himself, with a sudden remembrance of what his friend Mr. Bygrave had told him at Aldborough, sharpened by his own sense of the haggard change that he saw in her face.

He spoke in a whisper, but Mrs. Lecount heard him. She was close at his side again in an instant. For the first time, her self-possession failed her, and she caught him angrily by the arm.

"Will you put my madness to the proof, sir?" she asked.

He shook off her hold; he began to gather courage again, in the intense sincerity of his disbelief, courage to face the assertion which she persisted in forcing on him.

"Yes," he answered. "What must I do?"

"Do what I told you," said Mrs. Lecount. "Ask the maid that question about her mistress on the spot. And if she tells you the mark is there, do one thing more. Take me up into your wife's room, and open her wardrobe in my presence with your own hands."

"What do you want with her wardrobe?" he asked.

"You shall know when you open it."

"Very strange!" he said to himself, vacantly. "It's like a scene in a novel—it's like nothing in real life." He went slowly into the house, and Mrs. Lecount waited for him in the garden.

After an absence of a few minutes only he appeared again, on the top of the flight of steps which led into the garden from the house. He held by the iron rail with one hand, while with the other he beckoned to Mrs. Lecount to join him on the steps.

"What does the maid say?" she asked, as she approached him. "Is the mark there?"

He answered in a whisper, "Yes." What he had heard from the maid had produced a marked change in him. The horror of the coming discovery had laid its paralyzing hold on his mind. He moved mechanically; he looked and spoke like a man in a dream.

"Will you take my arm, sir?"

He shook his head, and, preceding her along the passage and up the stairs, led the way into his wife's room. When she joined him and locked the door, he stood passively waiting for his directions, without making any remark, without showing any external appearance of surprise. He had not removed either his hat or coat. Mrs. Lecount took them off for him. "Thank you," he said, with the docility of a well-trained child. "It's like a scene in a novel—it's like nothing in real life."

The bed-chamber was not very large, and the furniture was heavy and old-fashioned. But evidences of Magdalen's natural taste and refinement were visible everywhere, in the little embellishments that graced and enlivened the aspect of the room. The perfume of dried rose-leaves hung fragrant on the cool air. Mrs. Lecount sniffed the perfume with a disparaging frown and threw the window up to its full height. "Pah!" she said, with a shudder of virtuous disgust, "the atmosphere of deceit!"

She seated herself near the window. The wardrobe stood against the wall opposite, and the bed was at the side of the room on her right hand. "Open the wardrobe, Mr. Noel," she said. "I don't go near it. I touch nothing in it myself. Take out the dresses with your own hand and put them on the bed. Take them out one by one until I tell you to stop."

He obeyed her. "I'll do it as well as I can," he said. "My hands are cold, and my head feels half asleep."

The dresses to be removed were not many, for Magdalen had taken some of them away with her. After he had put two dresses on the bed, he was obliged to search in the inner recesses of the wardrobe before he could find a third. When he produced it, Mrs. Lecount made a sign to him to stop. The end was reached already; he had found the brown Alpaca dress.

"Lay it out on the bed, sir," said Mrs. Lecount. "You will see a double flounce running round the bottom of it. Lift up the outer flounce, and pass the inner one through your fingers, inch by inch. If you come to a place where there is a morsel of the stuff missing, stop and look up at me."

He passed the flounce slowly through his fingers for a minute or more, then stopped and looked up. Mrs. Lecount produced her pocket-book and opened it.

"Every word I now speak, sir, is of serious consequence to you and to me," she said. "Listen with your closest attention. When the woman calling herself Miss Garth came to see us in Vauxhall Walk, I knelt down behind the chair in which she was sitting and I cut a morsel of stuff from the dress she wore, which might help me to know that dress if I ever saw it again. I did this while the woman's whole attention was absorbed in talking to you. The morsel of stuff has been kept in my pocketbook from that time to this. See for yourself, Mr. Noel, if it fits the gap in that dress which your own hands have just taken from your wife's wardrobe."

She rose and handed him the fragment of stuff across the bed. He put it into the vacant space in the flounce as well as his trembling fingers would let him.

"Does it fit, sir?" asked Mrs. Lecount.

The dress dropped from his hands, and the deadly bluish pallor—which every doctor who attended him had warned his housekeeper to dread—overspread his face slowly. Mrs. Lecount had not reckoned on such an answer to her question as she now saw in his cheeks. She hurried round to him, with the smelling-bottle in her hand. He dropped to his knees and caught at her dress with the grasp of a drowning man. "Save me!" he gasped, in a hoarse, breathless whisper. "Oh, Lecount, save me!"

"I promise to save you," said Mrs. Lecount; "I am here with the means and the resolution to save you. Come away from this place—come nearer to the air." She raised him as she spoke, and led him across the room to the window. "Do you feel the chill pain again on your left side?" she asked, with the first signs of alarm that she had shown yet. "Has your wife got any eau-de-cologne, any sal-volatile in her room? Don't exhaust yourself by speaking—point to the place!"

He pointed to a little triangular cupboard of old worm-eaten walnut-wood fixed high in a corner of the room. Mrs. Lecount tried the door: it was locked.

As she made that discovery, she saw his head sink back gradually on the easy-chair in which she had placed him. The warning of the doctors in past years—"If you ever let him faint, you let him die"—recurred to her memory as if it had been spoken the day before. She looked at the cupboard again. In a recess under it lay some ends of cord, placed there apparently for purposes of packing. Without an instant's hesitation, she snatched up a morsel of cord, tied one end fast round the knob of the cupboard door, and seizing the other end in both hands, pulled it suddenly with the exertion of her whole strength. The rotten wood gave way, the cupboard doors flew open, and a heap of little trifles poured out noisily on the floor. Without stopping to notice the broken china and glass at her feet, she looked into the dark recesses of the cupboard and saw the gleam of two glass bottles. One was put away at the extreme back of the shelf, the other was a little in advance, almost hiding it. She snatched them both out at once, and took them, one in each hand, to the window, where she could read their labels in the clearer light.

The bottle in her right hand was the first bottle she looked at. It was marked—Sal-volatile.

She instantly laid the other bottle aside on the table without looking at it. The other bottle lay there, waiting its turn. It held a dark liquid, and it was labeled—POISON.

CHAPTER II.

MRS. LECOUNT mixed the sal-volatile with water, and administered it immediately. The stimulant had its effect. In a few minutes Noel Vanstone was able to raise himself in the chair without assistance; his color changed again for the better, and his breath came and went more freely.

"How do you feel now, sir?" asked Mrs. Lecount. "Are you warm again on your left side?"

He paid no attention to that inquiry; his eyes, wandering about the room, turned by chance toward the table. To Mrs. Lecount's surprise, instead of answering her, he bent forward in his chair, and looked with staring eyes and pointing hand at the second bottle which she had taken from the cupboard, and which she had hastily laid aside without paying attention to it. Seeing that some new alarm possessed him, she advanced to the table, and looked where he looked. The labeled side of the bottle was full in view; and there, in the plain handwriting of the chemist at Aldborough, was the one startling word confronting them both—"Poison."

Even Mrs. Lecount's self-possession was shaken by that discovery. She was not prepared to see her own darkest forebodings—the unacknowledged offspring of her hatred for Magdalen—realized as she saw them realized now. The suicide-despair in which the poison had been procured; the suicide-purpose for which, in distrust of the future, the poison had been kept, had brought with them their own retribution. There the bottle lay, in Magdalen's absence, a false witness of treason which had never entered her mind—treason against her husband's life!

With his hand still mechanically pointing at the table Noel Vanstone raised his head and looked up at Mrs. Lecount.

"I took it from the cupboard," she said, answering the look. "I took both bottles out together, not knowing which might be the bottle I wanted. I am as much shocked, as much frightened, as you are."

"Poison!" he said to himself, slowly. "Poison locked up by my wife in the cupboard in her own room." He stopped, and looked at Mrs. Lecount once more. "For me?" he asked, in a vacant, inquiring tone.

"We will not talk of it, sir, until your mind is more at ease," said Mrs. Lecount. "In the meantime, the danger that lies waiting in this bottle shall be instantly destroyed in your presence." She took out the cork, and threw the laudanum out of window, and the empty bottle after it. "Let us try to forget this dreadful discovery for the present," she resumed; "let us go downstairs at once. All that I have now to say to you can be said in another room."

She helped him to rise from the chair, and took his arm in her own. "It is well for him; it is well for me," she thought, as they went downstairs together, "that I came when I did."

On crossing the passage, she stepped to the front door, where the carriage was waiting which had brought her from Dumfries, and instructed the coachman to put up his horses at the nearest inn, and to call again for her in two hours' time. This done, she accompanied Noel Vanstone into the sitting-room, stirred up the fire, and placed him before it comfortably in an easy-chair. He sat for a few minutes, warming his hands feebly like an old man, and staring straight into the flame. Then he spoke.

"When the woman came and threatened me in Vauxhall Walk," he began, still staring into the fire, "you came back to the parlor after she was gone, and you told me—?" He stopped, shivered a little, and lost the thread of his recollections at that point.

"I told you, sir," said Mrs. Lecount, "that the woman was, in my opinion, Miss Vanstone herself. Don't start, Mr. Noel! Your wife is away, and I am here to take care of you. Say to yourself, if you feel frightened, 'Lecount is here; Lecount will take care of me.' The truth must be told, sir, however hard to bear the truth may be. Miss Magdalen Vanstone was the woman who came to you in disguise; and the woman who came to you in disguise is the woman you have married. The conspiracy which she threatened you with in London is the conspiracy which has made her your wife. That is the plain truth. You have seen the dress upstairs. If that dress had been no longer in existence, I should still have had my proofs to convince you. Thanks to my interview with Mrs. Bygrave I have discovered the house your wife lodged at in London; it was opposite our house in Vauxhall Walk. I have laid my hand on one of the landlady's daughters, who watched your wife from an inner room, and saw her put on the disguise; who can speak to her identity, and to the identity of her companion, Mrs. Bygrave; and who has furnished me, at my own request, with a written statement of facts, which she is ready to affirm on oath if any person ventures to contradict her. You shall read the statement, Mr. Noel, if you like, when you are fitter to understand it. You shall also read a letter in the handwriting of Miss Garth—who will repeat to you personally every word she has written to me—a letter formally denying that she was ever in Vauxhall Walk, and formally asserting that those moles on your wife's neck are marks peculiar to Miss Magdalen Vanstone, whom she has known from childhood. I say it with a just pride—you will find no weak place anywhere in the evidence which I bring you. If Mr. Bygrave had not stolen my letter, you would have had your warning before I was cruelly deceived into going to Zurich; and the proofs which I now bring you, after your marriage, I should then have offered to you before it. Don't hold me responsible, sir, for what has happened since I left England. Blame your uncle's bastard daughter, and blame that villain with the brown eye and the green!"

She spoke her last venomous words as slowly and distinctly as she had spoken all the rest. Noel Vanstone made no answer—he still sat cowering over the fire. She looked round into his face. He was crying silently. "I was so fond of her!" said the miserable little creature; "and I thought she was so fond of Me!"

Mrs. Lecount turned her back on him in disdainful silence. "Fond of her!" As she repeated those words to herself, her haggard face became almost handsome again in the magnificent intensity of its contempt.

She walked to a book-case at the lower end of the room, and began examining the volumes in it. Before she had been long engaged in this way, she was startled by the sound of his voice, affrightedly calling her back. The tears were gone from his face; it was blank again with terror when he now turned it toward her.

"Lecount!" he said, holding to her with both hands. "Can an egg be poisoned? I had an egg for breakfast this morning, and a little toast."

"Make your mind easy, sir," said Mrs. Lecount. "The poison of your wife's deceit is the only poison you have taken yet. If she had resolved already on making you pay the price of your folly with your life, she would not be absent from the house while you were left living in it. Dismiss the thought from your mind. It is the middle of the day; you want refreshment. I have more to say to you in the interests of your own safety—I have something for you to do, which must be done at once. Recruit your strength, and you will do it. I will set you the example of eating, if you still distrust the food in this house. Are you composed enough to give the servant her orders, if I ring the bell? It is necessary to the object I have in view for you, that nobody should think you ill in body or troubled in mind. Try first with me before the servant comes in. Let us see how you look and speak when you say, 'Bring up the lunch.'"

After two rehearsals, Mrs. Lecount considered him fit to give the order, without betraying himself.

The bell was answered by Louisa—Louisa looked hard at Mrs. Lecount. The luncheon was brought up by the house-maid—the house-maid looked hard at Mrs. Lecount. When luncheon was over, the table was cleared by the cook—the cook looked hard at Mrs. Lecount. The three servants were plainly suspicious that something extraordinary was going on in the house. It was hardly possible to doubt that they had arranged to share among themselves the three opportunities which the service of the table afforded them of entering the room.

The curiosity of which she was the object did not escape the penetration of Mrs. Lecount. "I did well," she thought, "to arm myself in good time with the means of reaching my end. If I let the grass grow under my feet, one or the other of those women might get in my way." Roused by this consideration, she produced her traveling-bag from a corner, as soon as the last of the servants had entered the room; and seating herself at the end of the table opposite Noel Vanstone, looked at him for a moment, with a steady, investigating attention. She had carefully regulated the quantity of wine which he had taken at luncheon—she had let him drink exactly enough to fortify, without confusing him; and she now examined his face critically, like an artist examining his picture at the end of the day's work. The result appeared to satisfy her, and she opened the serious business of the interview on the spot.

"Will you look at the written evidence I have mentioned to you, Mr. Noel, before I say any more?" she inquired. "Or are you sufficiently persuaded of the truth to proceed at once to the suggestion which I have now to make to you?"

"Let me hear your suggestion," he said, sullenly resting his elbows on the table, and leaning his head on his hands.

Mrs. Lecount took from her traveling-bag the written evidence to which she had just alluded, and carefully placed the papers on one side of him, within easy reach, if he wished to refer to them. Far from being daunted, she was visibly encouraged by the ungraciousness of his manner. Her experience of him informed her that the sign was a promising one. On those rare occasions when the little resolution that he possessed was roused in him, it invariably asserted itself—like the resolution of most other weak men—aggressively. At such times, in proportion as he was outwardly sullen and discourteous to those about him, his resolution rose; and in proportion as he was considerate and polite, it fell. The tone of the answer he had just given, and the attitude he assumed at the table, convinced Mrs. Lecount that Spanish wine and Scotch mutton had done their duty, and had rallied his sinking courage.

"I will put the question to you for form's sake, sir, if you wish it," she proceeded. "But I am already certain, without any question at all, that you have made your will?"

He nodded his head without looking at her.

"You have made it in your wife's favor?"

He nodded again.

"You have left her everything you possess?"

"No."

Mrs. Lecount looked surprised.

"Did you exercise a reserve toward her, Mr. Noel, of your own accord?" she inquired; "or is it possible that your wife put her own limits to her interest in your will?"

He was uneasily silent—he was plainly ashamed to answer the question. Mrs. Lecount repeated it in a less direct form.

"How much have you left your widow, Mr. Noel, in the event of your death?"

"Eighty thousand pounds."

That reply answered the question. Eighty thousand pounds was exactly the fortune which Michael Vanstone had taken from his brother's orphan children at his brother's death—exactly the fortune of which Michael Vanstone's son had kept possession, in his turn, as pitilessly as his father before him. Noel Vanstone's silence was eloquent of the confession which he was ashamed to make. His doting weakness had, beyond all doubt, placed his whole property at the feet of his wife. And this girl, whose vindictive daring had defied all restraints—this girl, who had not shrunk from her desperate determination even at the church door—had, in the very hour of her triumph, taken part only from the man who would willingly have given all!—had rigorously exacted her father's fortune from him to the last farthing; and had then turned her back on the hand that was tempting her with tens of thousands more! For the moment, Mrs. Lecount was fairly silenced by her own surprise; Magdalen had forced the astonishment from her which is akin to admiration, the astonishment which her enmity would fain have refused. She hated Magdalen with a tenfold hatred from that time.

"I have no doubt, sir," she resumed, after a momentary silence, "that Mrs. Noel gave you excellent reasons why the provision for her at your death should be no more, and no less, than eighty thousand pounds. And, on the other hand, I am equally sure that you, in your innocence of all suspicion, found those reasons conclusive at the time. That time has now gone by. Your eyes are opened, sir; and you will not fail to remark (as I remark) that the Combe-Raven property happens to reach the same sum exactly, as the legacy which your wife's own instructions directed you to leave her. If you are still in any doubt of the motive for which she married you, look in your own will—and there the motive is!"

He raised his head from his hands, and became closely attentive to what she was saying to him, for the first time since they had faced each other at the table. The Combe-Raven property had never been classed by itself in his estimation. It had come to him merged in his father's other possessions, at his father's death. The discovery which had now opened before him was one to which his ordinary habits of thought, as well as his innocence of suspicion, had hitherto closed his eyes. He said nothing; but he looked less sullenly at Mrs. Lecount. His manner was more ingratiating; the high tide of his courage was already on the ebb.

"Your position, sir, must be as plain by this time to you as it is to me," said Mrs. Lecount. "There is only one obstacle now left between this woman and the attainment of her end. That obstacle is your life. After the discovery we have made upstairs, I leave you to consider for yourself what your life is worth."

At those terrible words, the ebbing resolution in him ran out to the last drop. "Don't frighten me!" he pleaded; "I have been frightened enough already." He rose, and dragged his chair after him, round the table to Mrs. Lecount's side. He sat down and caressingly kissed her hand. "You good creature!" he said, in a sinking voice. "You excellent Lecount! Tell me what to do. I'm full of resolution—I'll do anything to save my life!"

"Have you got writing materials in the room, sir?" asked Mrs. Lecount. "Will you put them on the table, if you please?"

While the writing materials were in process of collection, Mrs. Lecount made a new demand on the resources of her traveling-bag. She took two papers from it, each indorsed in the same neat commercial handwriting. One was described as "Draft for proposed Will," and the other as "Draft for proposed Letter." When she placed them before her on the table, her hand shook a little; and she applied the smelling-salts, which she had brought with her in Noel Vanstone's interests, to her own nostrils.

"I had hoped, when I came here, Mr. Noel," she proceeded, "to have given you more time for consideration than it seems safe to give you now. When you first told me of your wife's absence in London, I thought it probable that the object of her journey was to see her sister and Miss Garth. Since the horrible discovery we have made upstairs, I am inclined to alter that opinion. Your wife's determination not to tell you who the friends are whom she has gone to see, fills me with alarm. She may have accomplices in London—accomplices, for anything we know to the contrary, in this house. All three of your servants, sir, have taken the opportunity, in turn, of coming into the room and looking at me. I don't like their looks! Neither you nor I know what may happen from day to day, or even from hour to hour. If you take my advice, you will get the start at once of all possible accidents; and, when the carriage comes back, you will leave this house with me!"

"Yes, yes!" he said, eagerly; "I'll leave the house with you. I wouldn't stop here by myself for any sum of money that could be offered me. What do we want the pen and ink for? Are you to write, or am I?"

"You are to write, sir," said Mrs. Lecount. "The means taken for promoting your own safety are to be means set in motion, from beginning to end, by yourself. I suggest, Mr. Noel—and you decide. Recognize your own position, sir. What is your first and foremost necessity? It is plainly this. You must destroy your wife's interest in your death by making another will."

He vehemently nodded his approval; his color rose, and his blinking eyes brightened in malicious triumph. "She shan't have a farthing," he said to himself, in a whisper—"she shan't have a farthing!"

"When your will is made, sir," proceeded Mrs. Lecount, "you must place it in the hands of a trustworthy person—not my hands, Mr. Noel; I am only your servant! Then, when the will is safe, and when you are safe, write to your wife at this house. Tell her her infamous imposture is discovered; tell her you have made a new will, which leaves her penniless at your death; tell her, in your righteous indignation, that she enters your doors no more. Place yourself in that strong position, and it is no longer you who are at your wife's mercy, but your wife who is at yours. Assert your own power, sir, with the law to help you, and crush this woman into submission to any terms for the future that you please to impose."

He eagerly took up the pen. "Yes," he said, with a vindictive self-importance, "any terms I please to impose." He suddenly checked himself and his face became dejected and perplexed. "How can I do it now?" he asked, throwing down the pen as quickly as he had taken it up.

"Do what, sir?" inquired Mrs. Lecount.

"How can I make my will, with Mr. Loscombe away in London, and no lawyer here to help me?"

Mrs. Lecount gently tapped the papers before her on the table with her forefinger.

"All the help you need, sir, is waiting for you here," she said. "I considered this matter carefully before I came to you; and I provided myself with the confidential assistance of a friend to guide me through those difficulties which I could not penetrate for myself. The friend to whom I refer is a gentleman of Swiss extraction, but born and bred in England. He is not a lawyer by profession—but he has had his own sufficient experience of the law, nevertheless; and he has supplied me, not only with a model by which you may make your will, but with the written sketch of a letter which it is as important for us to have, as the model of the will itself. There is another necessity waiting for you, Mr. Noel, which I have not mentioned yet, but which is no less urgent in its way than the necessity of the will."

"What is it?" he asked, with roused curiosity.

"We will take it in its turn, sir," answered Mrs. Lecount. "Its turn has not come yet. The will, if you please, first. I will dictate from the model in my possession and you will write."

Noel Vanstone looked at the draft for the Will and the draft for the Letter with suspicious curiosity.

"I think I ought to see the papers myself, before you dictate," he said. "It would be more satisfactory to my own mind, Lecount."

"By all means, sir," rejoined Mrs. Lecount, handing him the papers immediately.

He read the draft for the Will first, pausing and knitting his brows distrustfully, wherever he found blank spaces left in the manuscript to be filled in with the names of persons and the enumeration of sums bequeathed to them. Two or three minutes of reading brought him to the end of the paper. He gave it back to Mrs. Lecount without making any objection to it.

The draft for the Letter was a much longer document. He obstinately read it through to the end, with an expression of perplexity and discontent which showed that it was utterly unintelligible to him. "I must have this explained," he said, with a touch of his old self-importance, "before I take any steps in the matter."

"It shall be explained, sir, as we go on," said Mrs. Lecount.

"Every word of it?"

"Every word of it, Mr. Noel, when its turn comes. You have no objection to the will? To the will, then, as I said before, let us devote ourselves first. You have seen for yourself that it is short enough and simple enough for a child to understand it. But if any doubts remain on your mind, by all means compose those doubts by showing your will to a lawyer by profession. In the meantime, let me not be considered intrusive if I remind you that we are all mortal, and that the lost opportunity can never be recalled. While your time is your own, sir, and while your enemies are unsuspicious of you, make your will!"

She opened a sheet of note-paper and smoothed it out before him; she dipped the pen in ink, and placed it in his hands. He took it from her without speaking—he was, to all appearance, suffering under some temporary uneasiness of mind. But the main point was gained. There he sat, with the paper before him, and the pen in his hand; ready at last, in right earnest, to make his will.

"The first question for you to decide, sir," said Mrs. Lecount, after a preliminary glance at her Draft, "is your choice of an executor. I have no desire to influence your decision; but I may, without impropriety, remind you that a wise choice means, in other words, the choice of an old and tried friend whom you know that you can trust."

"It means the admiral, I suppose?" said Noel Vanstone.

Mrs. Lecount bowed.

"Very well," he continued. "The admiral let it be."

There was plainly some oppression still weighing on his mind. Even under the trying circumstances in which he was placed it was not in his nature to take Mrs. Lecount's perfectly sensible and disinterested advice without a word of cavil, as he had taken it now.

"Are you ready, sir?"

"Yes."

Mrs. Lecount dictated the first paragraph from the Draft, as follows:

"This is the last Will and Testament of me, Noel Vanstone, now living at Baliol Cottage, near Dumfries. I revoke, absolutely and in every particular, my former will executed on the thirtieth of September, eighteen hundred and forty-seven; and I hereby appoint Rear-Admiral Arthur Everard Bartram, of St. Crux-in-the-Marsh, Essex, sole executor of this my will."

"Have you written those words, sir?"

"Yes."

Mrs. Lecount laid down the Draft; Noel Vanstone laid down the pen. They neither of them looked at each other. There was a long silence.

"I am waiting, Mr. Noel," said Mrs. Lecount, at last, "to hear what your wishes are in respect to the disposal of your fortune. Your large fortune," she added, with merciless emphasis.

He took up the pen again, and began picking the feathers from the quill in dead silence.

"Perhaps your existing will may help you to instruct me, sir," pursued Mrs. Lecount. "May I inquire to whom you left all your surplus money, after leaving the eighty thousand pounds to your wife?"

If he had answered that question plainly, he must have said: "I have left the whole surplus to my cousin, George Bartram"—and the implied acknowledgment that Mrs. Lecount's name was not mentioned in the will must then have followed in Mrs. Lecount's presence. A much bolder man, in his situation, might have felt the same oppression and the same embarrassment which he was feeling now. He picked the last morsel of feather from the quill; and, desperately leaping the pitfall under his feet, advanced to meet Mrs. Lecount's claims on him of his own accord.

"I would rather not talk of any will but the will I am making now," he said uneasily. "The first thing, Lecount—" He hesitated—put the bare end of the quill into his mouth—gnawed at it thoughtfully—and said no more.

"Yes, sir?" persisted Mrs. Lecount.

"The first thing is—"

"Yes, sir?"

"The first thing is, to—to make some provision for You?"

He spoke the last words in a tone of plaintive interrogation—as if all hope of being met by a magnanimous refusal had not deserted him even yet. Mrs. Lecount enlightened his mind on this point, without a moment's loss of time.

"Thank you, Mr. Noel," she said, with the tone and manner of a woman who was not acknowledging a favor, but receiving a right.

He took another bite at the quill. The perspiration began to appear on his face.

"The difficulty is," he remarked, "to say how much."

"Your lamented father, sir," rejoined Mrs. Lecount, "met that difficulty (if you remember) at the time of his last illness?"

"I don't remember," said Noel Vanstone, doggedly.

"You were on one side of his bed, sir, and I was on the other. We were vainly trying to persuade him to make his will. After telling us he would wait and make his will when he was well again, he looked round at me, and said some kind and feeling words which my memory will treasure to my dying day. Have you forgotten those words, Mr. Noel?"

"Yes," said Mr. Noel, without hesitation.

"In my present situation, sir," retorted Mrs. Lecount, "delicacy forbids me to improve your memory."

She looked at her watch, and relapsed into silence. He clinched his hands, and writhed from side to side of his chair in an agony of indecision. Mrs. Lecount passively refused to take the slightest notice of him.

"What should you say—?" he began, and suddenly stopped again.

"Yes, sir?"

"What should you say to—a thousand pounds?"

Mrs. Lecount rose from her chair, and looked him full in the face, with the majestic indignation of an outraged woman.

"After the service I have rendered you to-day, Mr. Noel," she said, "I have at least earned a claim on your respect, if I have earned nothing more. I wish you good-morning."

"Two thousand!" cried Noel Vanstone, with the courage of despair.

Mrs. Lecount folded up her papers and hung her traveling-bag over her arm in contemptuous silence.

"Three thousand!"

Mrs. Lecount moved with impenetrable dignity from the table to the door.

"Four thousand!"

Mrs. Lecount gathered her shawl round her with a shudder, and opened the door.

"Five thousand!"

He clasped his hands, and wrung them at her in a frenzy of rage and suspense. "Five thousand" was the death-cry of his pecuniary suicide.

Mrs. Lecount softly shut the door again, and came back a step.

"Free of legacy duty, sir?" she inquired.

"No."

Mrs. Lecount turned on her heel and opened the door again.

"Yes."

Mrs. Lecount came back, and resumed her place at the table as if nothing had happened.

"Five thousand pounds, free of legacy duty, was the sum, sir, which your father's grateful regard promised me in his will," she said, quietly. "If you choose to exert your memory, as you have not chosen to exert it yet, your memory will tell you that I speak the truth. I accept your filial performance of your father's promise, Mr. Noel—and there I stop. I scorn to take a mean advantage of my position toward you; I scorn to grasp anything from your fears. You are protected by my respect for myself, and for the Illustrious Name I bear. You are welcome to all that I have done, and to all that I have suffered in your service. The widow of Professor Lecompte, sir, takes what is justly hers—and takes no more!"

As she spoke those words, the traces of sickness seemed, for the moment, to disappear from her face; her eyes shone with a steady inner light; all the woman warmed and brightened in the radiance of her own triumph—the triumph, trebly won, of carrying her point, of vindicating her integrity, and of matching Magdalen's incorruptible self-denial on Magdalen's own ground.

"When you are yourself again, sir, we will proceed. Let us wait a little first."

She gave him time to compose himself; and then, after first looking at her Draft, dictated the second paragraph of the will, in these terms:

"I give and bequeath to Madame Virginie Lecompte (widow of Professor Lecompt e, late of Zurich) the sum of Five Thousand Pounds, free of Legacy Duty. And, in making this bequest, I wish to place it on record that I am not only expressing my own sense of Madame Lecompte's attachment and fidelity in the capacity of my housekeeper, but that I also believe myself to be executing the intentions of my deceased father, who, but for the circumstance of his dying intestate, would have left Madame Lecompte, in his will, the same token of grateful regard for her services which I now leave her in mine."

"Have you written the last words, sir?"

"Yes."

Mrs. Lecount leaned across the table and offered Noel Vanstone her hand.

"Thank you, Mr. Noel," she said. "The five thousand pounds is the acknowledgment on your father's side of what I have done for him. The words in the will are the acknowledgment on yours."

A faint smile flickered over his face for the first time. It comforted him, on reflection, to think that matters might have been worse. There was balm for his wounded spirit in paying the debt of gratitude by a sentence not negotiable at his banker's. Whatever his father might have done, he had got Lecount a bargain, after all!

"A little more writing, sir," resumed Mrs. Lecount, "and your painful but necessary duty will be performed. The trifling matter of my legacy being settled, we may come to the important question that is left. The future direction of a large fortune is now waiting your word of command. To whom is it to go?"

He began to writhe again in his chair. Even under the all-powerful fascination of his wife the parting with his money on paper had not been accomplished without a pang. He had endured the pang; he had resigned himself to the sacrifice. And now here was the dreaded ordeal again, awaiting him mercilessly for the second time!

"Perhaps it may assist your decision, sir, if I repeat a question which I have put to you already," observed Mrs. Lecount. "In the will that you made under your wife's influence, to whom did you leave the surplus money which remained at your own disposal?"

There was no harm in answering the question now. He acknowledged that he had left the money to his cousin George.

"You could have done nothing better, Mr. Noel; and you can do nothing better now," said Mrs. Lecount. "Mr. George and his two sisters are your only relations left. One of those sisters is an incurable invalid, with more than money enough already for all the wants which her affliction allows her to feel. The other is the wife of a man even richer than yourself. To leave the money to these sisters is to waste it. To leave the money to their brother George is to give your cousin exactly the assistance which he will want when he one day inherits his uncle's dilapidated house and his uncle's impoverished estate. A will which names the admiral your executor and Mr. George your heir is the right will for you to make. It does honor to the claims of friendship, and it does justice to the claims of blood."

She spoke warmly; for she spoke with a grateful remembrance of all that she herself owed to the hospitality of St. Crux. Noel Vanstone took up another pen and began to strip the second quill of its feathers as he had stripped the first.

"Yes," he said, reluctantly, "I suppose George must have it—I suppose George has the principal claim on me." He hesitated: he looked at the door, he looked at the window, as if he longed to make his escape by one way or the other. "Oh, Lecount," he cried, piteously, "it's such a large fortune! Let me wait a little before I leave it to anybody."

To his surprise; Mrs. Lecount at once complied with this characteristic request.

"I wish you to wait, sir," she replied. "I have something important to say, before you add another line to your will. A little while since, I told you there was a second necessity connected with your present situation, which had not been provided for yet, but which must be provided for, when the time came. The time has come now. You have a serious difficulty to meet and conquer before you can leave your fortune to your cousin George."

"What difficulty?" he asked.

Mrs. Lecount rose from her chair without answering, stole to the door, and suddenly threw it open. No one was listening outside; the passage was a solitude, from one end to the other.

"I distrust all servants," she said, returning to her place—"your servants particularly. Sit closer, Mr. Noel. What I have now to say to you must be heard by no living creature but ourselves."

CHAPTER III.

THERE was a pause of a few minutes while Mrs. Lecount opened the second of the two papers which lay before her on the table, and refreshed her memory by looking it rapidly through. This done, she once more addressed herself to Noel Vanstone, carefully lowering her voice, so as to render it inaudible to any one who might be listening in the passage outside.

"I must beg your permission, sir," she began, "to return to the subject of your wife. I do so most unwillingly; and I promise you that what I have now to say about her shall be said, for your sake and for mine, in the fewest words. What do we know of this woman, Mr. Noel—judging her by her own confession when she came to us in the character of Miss Garth, and by her own acts afterward at Aldborough? We know that, if death had not snatched your father out of her reach, she was ready with her plot to rob him of the Combe-Raven money. We know that, when you inherited the money in your turn, she was ready with her plot to rob you. We know how she carried that plot through to the end; and we know that nothing but your death is wanted, at this moment, to crown her rapacity and her deception with success. We are sure of these things. We are sure that she is young, bold, and clever—that she has neither doubts, scruples, nor pity—and that she possesses the personal qualities which men in general (quite incomprehensibly to me!) are weak enough to admire. These are not fancies, Mr. Noel, but facts; you know them as well as I do."

He made a sign in the affirmative, and Mrs. Lecount went on:

"Keep in your mind what I have said of the past, sir, and now look with me to the future. I hope and trust you have a long life still before you; but let us, for the moment only, suppose the case of your death—your death leaving this will behind you, which gives your fortune to your cousin George. I am told there is an office in London in which copies of all wills must be kept. Any curious stranger who chooses to pay a shilling for the privilege may enter that office, and may read any will in the place at his or her discretion. Do you see what I am coming to, Mr. Noel? Your disinherited widow pays her shilling, and reads your will. Your disinherited widow sees that the Combe-Raven money, which has gone from your father to you, goes next from you to Mr. George Bartram. What is the certain end of that discovery? The end is, that you leave to your cousin and your friend the legacy of this woman's vengeance and this woman's deceit-vengeance made more resolute, deceit made more devilish than ever, by her exasperation at her own failure. What is your cousin George? He is a generous, unsuspicious man; incapable of deceit himself, and fearing no deception in others. Leave him at the mercy of your wife's unscrupulous fascinations and your wife's unfathomable deceit, and I see the end as certainly as I see you sitting there! She will blind his eyes, as she blinded yours; and, in spite of you, in spite of me, she will have the money!"

She stopped, and left her last words time to gain their hold on his mind. The circumstances had been stated so clearly, the conclusion from them had been so plainly drawn, that he seized her meaning without an effort, and seized it at once.

"I see!" he said, vindictively clinching his hands. "I understand, Lecount! She shan't have a farthing. What shall I do? Shall I leave the money to the admiral?" He paused, and considered a little. "No," he resumed; "there's the same danger in leaving it to the admiral that there is in leaving it to George."

"There is no danger, Mr. Noel, if you take my advice."

"What is your advice?"

"Follow your own idea, sir. Take the pen in hand again, and leave the money to Admiral Bartram."

He mechanically dipped the pen in the ink, and then hesitated.

"You shall know where I am leading you, sir," said Mrs. Lecount, "before you sign your will. In the meantime, let us gain every inch of ground we can, as we go on. I want the will to be all written out before we advance a single step beyond it. Begin your third paragraph, Mr. Noel, under the lines which leave me my legacy of five thousand pounds."

She dictated the last momentous sentence of the will (from the rough draft in her own possession) in these words:

"The whole residue of my estate, after payment of my burial expenses and my lawful debts, I give and bequeath to Rear-Admiral Arthur Everard Bartram, my Executor aforesaid; to be by him applied to such uses as he may think fit.

"Signed, sealed, and delivered, this third day of November, eighteen hundred and forty-seven, by Noel Vanstone, the within-named testator, as and for his last Will and Testament, in the presence of us—"

"Is that all?" asked Noel Vanstone, in astonishment.

"That is enough, sir, to bequeath your fortune to the admiral; and therefore that is all. Now let us go back to the case which we have supposed already. Your widow pays her shilling, and sees this will. There is the Combe-Raven money left to Admiral Bartram, with a declaration in plain words that it is his, to use as he likes. When she sees this, what does she do? She sets her trap for the admiral. He is a bachelor, and he is an old man. Who is to protect him against the arts of this desperate woman? Protect him yourself, sir, with a few more strokes of that pen which has done such wonders already. You have left him this legacy in your will—which your wife sees. Take the legacy away again, in a letter—which is a dead secret between the admiral and you. Put the will and the letter under one cover, and place them in the admiral's possession, with your written directions to him to break the seal on the day of your death. Let the will say what it says now; and let the letter (which is your secret and his) tell him the truth. Say that, in leaving him your fortune, you leave it with the request that he will take his legacy with one hand from you, and give it with the other to his nephew George. Tell him that your trust in this matter rests solely on your confidence in his honor, and on your belief in his affectionate remembrance of your father and yourself. You have known the admiral since you were a boy. He has his little whims and oddities; but he is a gentleman from the crown of his head to the sole of his foot; and he is utterly incapable of proving false to a trust in his honor, reposed by his dead friend. Meet the difficulty boldly, by such a stratagem as this; and you save these two helpless men from your wife's snare, one by means of the other. Here, on one side, is your will, which gives the fortune to the admiral, and sets her plotting accordingly. And there, on the other side, is your letter, which privately puts the money into the nephew's hands!"

The malicious dexterity of this combination was exactly the dexterity which Noel Vanstone was most fit to appreciate. He tried to express his approval and admiration in words. Mrs. Lecount held up her hand warningly and closed his lips.

"Wait, sir, before you express your opinion," she went on. "Half the difficulty is all that we have conquered yet. Let us say, the admiral has made the use of your legacy which you have privately requested him to make of it. Sooner or later, however well the secret may be kept, your wife will discover the truth. What follows that discovery! She lays siege to Mr. George. All you have done is to leave him the money by a roundabout way. There he is, after an interval of time, as much at her mercy as if you had openly mentioned him in your will. What is the remedy for this? The remedy is to mislead her, if we can, for the second time—to set up an obstacle between her and the money, for the protection of your cousin George. Can you guess for yourself, Mr. Noel, what is the most promising obstacle we can put in her way?"

He shook his head. Mrs. Lecount smiled, and startled him into close attention by laying her hand on his arm.

"Put a Woman in her way, sir!" she whispered in her wiliest tones. "We don't believe in that fascinating beauty of hers—whatever you may do. Our lips don't burn to kiss those smooth cheeks. Our arms don't long to be round that supple waist. We see through her smiles and her graces, and her stays and her padding—she can't fascinate us! Put a woman in her way, Mr. Noel! Not a woman in my helpless situation, who is only a servant, but a woman with the authority and the jealousy of a Wife. Make it a condition, in your letter to the admiral, that if Mr. George is a bachelor at the time of your death, he shall marry within a certain time afterward, or he shall not have the legacy. Suppose he remains single in spite of your condition, who is to have the money then? Put a woman in your wife's way, sir, once more—and leave the fortune, in that case, to the married sister of your cousin George."

She paused. Noel Vanstone again attempted to express his opinion, and again Mrs. Lecount's hand extinguished him in silence.

"If you approve, Mr. Noel," she said, "I will take your approval for granted. If you object, I will meet your objection before it is out of your mouth. You may say: Suppose this condition is sufficient to answer the purpose, why hide it in a private letter to the admiral? Why not openly write it down, with my cousin's name, in the will? Only for one reason, sir. Only because the secret way is the sure way, with such a woman as your wife. The more secret you can keep your intentions, the more time you force her to waste in finding them out for herself. That time which she loses is time gained from her treachery by the admiral—time gained by Mr. George (if he is still a bachelor) for his undisturbed choice of a lady—time gained, for her own security, by the object of his choice, who might otherwise be the first object of your wife's suspicion and your wife's hostility. Remember the bottle we have discovered upstairs; and keep this desperate woman ignorant, and therefore harmless, as long as you can. There is my advice, Mr. Noel, in the fewest and plainest words. What do you say, sir? Am I almost as clever in my way as your friend Mr. Bygrave? Can I, too, conspire a little, when the object of my conspiracy is to assist your wishes and to protect your friends?"

Permitted the use of his tongue at last, Noel Vanstone's admiration of Mrs. Lecount expressed itself in terms precisely similar to those which he had used on a former occasion, in paying his compliments to Captain Wragge. "What a head you have got!" were the grateful words which he had once spoken to Mrs. Lecount's bitterest enemy. "What a head you have got!" were the grateful words which he now spoke again to Mrs. Lecount herself. So do extremes meet; and such is sometimes the all-embracing capacity of the approval of a fool!

"Allow my head, sir, to deserve the compliment which you have paid to it," said Mrs.

Lecount. "The letter to the admiral is not written yet. Your will there is a body without a soul—an Adam without an Eve—until the letter is completed and laid by its side. A little more dictation on my part, a little more writing on yours, and our work is done. Pardon me. The letter will be longer than the will; we must have larger paper than the note-paper this time."

The writing-case was searched, and some letter paper was found in it of the size required. Mrs. Lecount resumed her dictation; and Noel Vanstone resumed his pen.

"Baliol Cottage, Dumfries,

"November 3d, 1847.

"Private.

"DEAR ADMIRAL BARTRAM—When you open my Will (in which you are named my sole executor), you will find that I have bequeathed the whole residue of my estate—after payment of one legacy of five thousand pounds—to yourself. It is the purpose of my letter to tell you privately what the object is for which I have left you the fortune which is now placed in your hands.

"I beg you to consider this large legacy as intended, under certain conditions, to be given by you to your nephew George. If your nephew is married at the time of my death, and if his wife is living, I request you to put him at once in possession of your legacy; accompanying it by the expression of my desire (which I am sure he will consider a sacred and binding obligation on him) that he will settle the money on his wife—and on his children, if he has any. If, on the other hand, he is unmarried at the time of my death, or if he is a widower—in either of those cases, I make it a condition of his receiving the legacy, that he shall be married within the period of—"

Mrs. Lecount laid down the Draft letter from which she had been dictating thus far, and informed Noel Vanstone by a sign that his pen might rest.

"We have come to the question of time, sir," she observed. "How long will you give your cousin to marry, if he is single, or a widower, at the time of your death?"

"Shall I give him a year?" inquired Noel Vanstone.

"If we had nothing to consider but the interests of Propriety," said Mrs. Lecount, "I should say a year too, sir—especially if Mr. George should happen to be a widower. But we have your wife to consider, as well as the interests of Propriety. A year of delay, between your death and your cousin's marriage, is a dangerously long time to leave the disposal of your fortune in suspense. Give a determined woman a year to plot and contrive in, and there is no saying what she may not do."

"Six months?" suggested Noel Vanstone.

"Six months, sir," rejoined Mrs. Lecount, "is the preferable time of the two. A six months' interval from the day of your death is enough for Mr. George. You look discomposed, sir; what is the matter?"

"I wish you wouldn't talk so much about my death," he broke out, petulantly. "I don't like it! I hate the very sound of the word!"

Mrs. Lecount smiled resignedly, and referred to her Draft.

"I see the word 'decease' written here," she remarked. "Perhaps, Mr. Noel, you would prefer it?"

"Yes," he said; "I prefer 'Decease.' It doesn't sound so dreadful as 'Death.'"

"Let us go on with the letter, sir."

She resumed her dictation, as follows:

"...in either of those cases, I make it a condition of his receiving the legacy that he shall be married within the period of Six calendar months from the day of my decease; that the woman he marries shall not be a widow; and that his marriage shall be a marriage by Banns, publicly celebrated in the parish church of Ossory—where he has been known from his childhood, and where the family and circumstances of his future wife are likely to be the subject of public interest and inquiry."

"This," said Mrs. Lecount, quietly looking up from the Draft, "is to protect Mr. George, sir, in case the same trap is set for him which was successfully set for you. She will not find her false character and her false name fit quite so easily next time—no, not even with Mr. Bygrave to help her! Another dip of ink, Mr. Noel; let us write the next paragraph. Are you ready?"

"Yes."

Mrs. Lecount went on.

"If your nephew fails to comply with these conditions—that is to say, if being either a bachelor or a widower at the time of my decease, he fails to marry in all respects as I have here instructed him to marry, within Six calendar months from that time—it is my desire that he shall not receive the legacy, or any part of it. I request you, in the case here supposed, to pass him over altogether; and to give the fortune left you in my will to his married sister, Mrs. Girdlestone.

"Having now put you in possession of my motives and intentions, I come to the next question which it is necessary to consider. If, when you open this letter, your nephew is an unmarried man, it is clearly indispensable that he should know of the conditions here imposed on him, as soon, if possible, as you know of them yourself. Are you, under these circumstances, freely to communicate to him what I have here written to you? Or are you to leave him under the impression that no such private expression of my wishes as this is in existence; and are you to state all the conditions relating to his marriage, as if they emanated entirely from yourself?

"If you will adopt this latter alternative, you will add one more to the many obligations under which your friendship has placed me.

"I have serious reason to believe that the possession of my money, and the discovery of any peculiar arrangements relating to the disposal of it, will be objects (after my decease) of the fraud and conspiracy of an unscrupulous person. I am therefore anxious—for your sake, in the first place—that no suspicion of the existence of this letter should be conveyed to the mind of the person to whom I allude. And I am equally desirous—for Mrs. Girdlestone's sake, in the second place—that this same person should be entirely ignorant that the legacy will pass into Mrs. Girdlestone's possession, if your nephew is not married in the given time. I know George's easy, pliable disposition; I dread the attempts that will be made to practice on it; and I feel sure that the prudent course will be, to abstain from trusting him with secrets, the rash revelation of which might be followed by serious, and even dangerous results.

"State the conditions, therefore, to your nephew, as if they were your own. Let him think they have been suggested to your mind by the new responsibilities imposed on you as a man of property, by your position in my will, and by your consequent anxiety to provide for the perpetuation of the family name. If these reasons are not sufficient to satisfy him, there can be no objection to your referring him, for any further explanations which he may desire, to his wedding-day.

"I have done. My last wishes are now confided to you, in implicit reliance on your honor, and on your tender regard for the memory of your friend. Of the miserable circumstances which compel me to write as I have written here, I say nothing. You will hear of them, if my life is spared, from my own lips—for you will be the first friend whom I shall consult in my difficulty and distress. Keep this letter strictly secret, and strictly in your own possession, until my requests are complied with. Let no human being but yourself know where it is, on any pretense whatever.

"Believe me, dear Admiral Bartram, affectionately yours,

"NOEL VANSTONE."

"Have you signed, sir?" asked Mrs. Lecount. "Let me look the letter over, if you please, before we seal it up."

She read the letter carefully. In Noel Vanstone's close, cramped handwriting, it filled two pages of letter-paper, and ended at the top of the third page. Instead of using an envelope, Mrs. Lecount folded it, neatly and securely, in the old-fashioned way. She lit the taper in the ink-stand, and returned the letter to the writer.

"Seal it, Mr. Noel," she said, "with your own hand, and your own seal." She extinguished the taper, and handed him the pen again. "Address the letter, sir," she proceeded, "to Admiral Bartram, St. Crux-in-the-Marsh, Essex. Now, add these words, and sign them, above the address: To be kept in your own possession, and to be opened by yourself only, on the day of my death—or 'Decease,' if you prefer it—Noel Vanstone. Have you done? Let me look at it again. Quite right in every particular. Accept my congratulations, sir. If your wife has not plotted her last plot for the Combe-Raven money, it is not your fault, Mr. Noel—and not mine!"

Finding his attention released by the completion of the letter, Noel Vanstone reverted at once to purely personal considerations. "There is my packing-up to be thought of now," he said. "I can't go away without my warm things."

"Excuse me, sir," rejoined Mrs. Lecount, "there is the Will to be signed first; and there must be two persons found to witness your signature." She looked out of the front window, and saw the carriage waiting at the door. "The coachman will do for one of the witnesses," she said. "He is in respectable service at Dumfries, and he can be found if he happens to be wanted. We must have one of your own servants, I suppose, for the other witness. They are all detestable women; but the cook is the least ill-looking of the three. Send for the cook, sir; while I go out and call the coachman. When we have got our witnesses here, you have only to speak to them in these words: 'I have a document here to sign, and I wish you to write your names on it, as witnesses of my signature.' Nothing more, Mr. Noel! Say those few words in your usual manner—and, when the signing is over, I will see myself to your packing-up, and your warm things."

She went to the front door, and summoned the coachman to the parlor. On her return, she found the cook already in the room. The cook looked mysteriously offended, and stared without intermission at Mrs. Lecount. In a minute more the coachman—an elderly man—came in. He was preceded by a relishing odor of whisky; but his head was Scotch; and nothing but his odor betrayed him.

"I have a document here to sign," said Noel Vanstone, repeating his lesson; "and I wish you to write your names on it, as witnesses of my signature."

The coachman looked at the will. The cook never removed her eyes from Mrs. Lecount.

"Ye'll no object, sir," said the coachman, with the national caution showing itself in every wrinkle on his face—"ye'll no object, sir, to tell me, first, what the Doecument may be?"

Mrs. Lecount interposed before Noel Vanstone's indignation could express itself in words.

"You must tell the man, sir, that this is your Will," she said. "When he witnesses your signature, he can see as much for himself if he looks at the top of the page."

"Ay, ay," said the coachman, looking at the top of the page immediately. "His last Will and Testament. Hech, sirs! there's a sair confronting of Death in a Doecument like yon! A' flesh is grass," continued the coachman, exhaling an additional puff of whisky, and looking up devoutly at the ceiling. "Tak' those words in connection with that other Screepture: Many are ca'ad, but few are chosen. Tak' that again, in connection with Rev'lations, Chapter the First, verses One to Fefteen. Lay the whole to heart; and what's your Walth, then? Dross, sirs! And your body? (Screepture again.) Clay for the potter! And your life? (Screepture once more.) The Breeth o' your Nostrils!"

The cook listened as if the cook was at church: but she never removed her eyes from Mrs. Lecount.

"You had better sign, sir. This is apparently some custom prevalent in Dumfries during the transaction of business," said Mrs. Lecount, resignedly. "The man means well, I dare say."

She added those last words in a soothing tone, for she saw that Noel Vanstone's indignation was fast merging into alarm. The coachman's outburst of exhortation seemed to have inspired him with fear, as well as disgust.

He dipped the pen in the ink, and signed the Will without uttering a word. The coachman (descending instantly from Theology to Business) watched the signature with the most scrupulous attention; and signed his own name as witness, with an implied commentary on the proceeding, in the form of another puff of whisky, exhaled through the medium of a heavy sigh. The cook looked away from Mrs. Lecount with an effort—signed her name in a violent hurry—and looked back again with a start, as if she expected to see a loaded pistol (produced in the interval) in the housekeeper's hands. "Thank you," said Mrs. Lecount, in her friendliest manner. The cook shut up her lips aggressively and looked at her master. "You may go!" said her master. The cook coughed contemptuously, and went.

"We shan't keep you long," said Mrs. Lecount, dismissing the coachman. "In half an hour, or less, we shall be ready for the journey back."

The coachman's austere countenance relaxed for the first time. He smiled mysteriously, and approached Mrs. Lecount on tiptoe.

"Ye'll no forget one thing, my leddy," he said, with the most ingratiating politeness. "Ye'll no forget the witnessing as weel as the driving, when ye pay me for my day's wark!" He laughed with guttural gravity; and, leaving his atmosphere behind him, stalked out of the room.

"Lecount," said Noel Vanstone, as soon as the coachman closed the door, "did I hear you tell that man we should be ready in half an hour?"

"Yes, sir."

"Are you blind?"

He asked the question with an angry stamp of his foot. Mrs. Lecount looked at him in astonishment.

"Can't you see the brute is drunk?" he went on, more and more irritably. "Is my life nothing? Am I to be left at the mercy of a drunken coachman? I won't trust that man to drive me, for any consideration under heaven! I'm surprised you could think of it, Lecount."

"The man has been drinking, sir," said Mrs. Lecount. "It is easy to see and to smell that. But he is evidently used to drinking. If he is sober enough to walk quite straight—which he certainly does—and to sign his name in an excellent handwriting—which you may see for yourself on the Will—I venture to think he is sober enough to drive us to Dumfries."

"Nothing of the sort! You're a foreigner, Lecount; you don't understand these people. They drink whisky from morning to night. Whisky is the strongest spirit that's made; whisky is notorious for its effect on the brain. I tell you, I won't run the risk. I never was driven, and I never will be driven, by anybody but a sober man."

"Must I go back to Dumfries by myself, sir?"

"And leave me here? Leave me alone in this house after what has happened? How do I know my wife may not come back to-night? How do I know her journey is not a blind to mislead me? Have you no feeling, Lecount? Can you leave me in my miserable situation—?" He sank into a chair and burst out crying over his own idea, before he had completed the expression of it in words. "Too bad!" he said, with his handkerchief over his face—"too bad!"

It was impossible not to pity him. If ever mortal was pitiable, he was the man. He had broken down at last, under the conflict of violent emotions which had been roused in him since the morning. The effort to follow Mrs. Lecount along the mazes of intricate combination through which she had steadily led the way, had upheld him while that effort lasted: the moment it was at an end, he dropped. The coachman had hastened a result—of which the coachman was far from being the cause.

"You surprise me—you distress me, sir," said Mrs. Lecount. "I entreat you to compose yourself. I will stay here, if you wish it, with pleasure—I will stay here to-night, for your sake. You want rest and quiet after this dreadful day. The coachman shall be instantly sent away, Mr. Noel. I will give him a note to the landlord of the hotel, and the carriage shall come back for us to-morrow morning, with another man to drive it."

The prospect which those words presented cheered him. He wiped his eyes, and kissed Mrs. Lecount's hand. "Yes!" he said, faintly; "send the coachman away—and you stop here. You good creature! You excellent Lecount! Send the drunken brute away, and come back directly. We will be comfortable by the fire, Lecount—and have a nice little dinner—and try to make it like old times." His weak voice faltered; he returned to the fire side, and melted into tears again under the pathetic influence of his own idea.

Mrs. Lecount left him for a minute to dismiss the coachman. When she returned to the parlor she found him with his hand on the bell.

"What do you want, sir?" she asked.

"I want to tell the servants to get your room ready," he answered. "I wish to show you every attention, Lecount."

"You are all kindness, Mr. Noel; but wait one moment. It may be well to have these papers put out of the way before the servant comes in again. If you will place the Will and the Sealed Letter together in one envelope—and if you will direct it to the admiral—I will take care that the inclosure so addressed is safely placed in his own hands. Will you come to the table, Mr. Noel, only for one minute more?"

No! He was obstinate; he refused to move from the fire; he was sick and tired of writing: he wished he had never been born, and he loathed the sight of pen and ink. All Mrs. Lecount's patience and all Mrs. Lecount's persuasion were required to induce him to write the admiral's address for the second time. She only succeeded by bringing the blank envelope to him upon the paper-case, and putting it coaxingly on his lap. He grumbled, he even swore, but he directed the envelope at last, in these terms: "To Admiral Bartram, St. Crux-in-the-Marsh. Favored by Mrs. Lecount." With that final act of compliance his docility came to an end. He refused, in the fiercest terms, to seal the envelope. There was no need to press this proceeding on him. His seal lay ready on the table, and it mattered nothing whether he used it, or whether a person in his confidence used it for him. Mrs. Lecount sealed the envelope, with its two important inclosures placed safely inside.

She opened her traveling-bag for the last time, and pausing for a moment before she put the sealed packet away, looked at it with a triumph too deep for words. She smiled as she dropped it into the bag. Not the shadow of a suspicion that the Will might contain superfluous phrases and expressions which no practical lawyer would have used; not the vestige of a doubt whether the Letter was quite as complete a document as a practical lawyer might have made it, troubled her mind. In blind reliance—born of her hatred for Magdalen and her hunger for revenge—in blind reliance on her own abilities and on her friend's law, she trusted the future implicitly to the promise of the morning's work.

As she locked her traveling-bag Noel Vanstone rang the bell. On this occasion, the summons was answered by Louisa.

"Get the spare room ready," said her master; "this lady will sleep here to-night. And air my warm things; this lady and I are going away to-morrow morning."

The civil and submissive Louisa received her orders in sullen silence—darted an angry look at her master's impenetrable guest—and left the room. The servants were evidently all attached to their mistress's interests, and were all of one opinion on the subject of Mrs. Lecount.

"That's done!" said Noel Vanstone, with a sigh of infinite relief. "Come and sit down, Lecount. Let's be comfortable—let's gossip over the fire."

Mrs. Lecount accepted the invitation and drew an easy-chair to his side. He took her hand with a confidential tenderness, and held it in his while the talk went on. A stranger, looking in through the window, would have taken them for mother and son, and would have thought to himself: "What a happy home!"

The gossip, led by Noel Vanstone, consisted as usual of an endless string of questions, and was devoted entirely to the subject of himself and his future prospects. Where would Lecount take him to when they went away the next morning? Why to London? Why should he be left in London, while Lecount went on to St. Crux to give the admiral the Letter and the Will? Because his wife might follow him, if he went to the admiral's? Well, there was something in that. And because he ought to be safely concealed from her, in some comfortable lodging, near Mr. Loscombe? Why near Mr. Loscombe? Ah, yes, to be sure—to know what the law would do to help him. Would the law set him free from the Wretch who had deceived him? How tiresome of Lecount not to know! Would the law say he had gone and married himself a second time, because he had been living with the Wretch, like husband and wife, in Scotland? Anything that publicly assumed to be a marriage was a marriage (he had heard) in Scotland. How excessively tiresome of Lecount to sit there and say she knew nothing about it! Was he to stay long in London by himself, with nobody but Mr. Loscombe to speak to? Would Lecount come back to him as soon as she had put those important papers in the admiral's own hands? Would Lecount consider herself still in his service? The good Lecount! the excellent Lecount! And after all the law-business was over—what then? Why not leave this horrid England and go abroad again? Why not go to France, to some cheap place near Paris? Say Versailles? say St. Germain? In a nice little French house—cheap? With a nice French bonne to cook—who wouldn't waste his substance in the grease-pot? With a nice little garden—where he could work himself, and get health, and save the expense of keeping a gardener? It wasn't a bad idea. And it seemed to promise well for the future—didn't it, Lecount?

So he ran on—the poor weak creature! the abject, miserable little man!

As the darkness gathered at the close of the short November day he began to grow drowsy—his ceaseless questions came to an end at last—he fell asleep. The wind outside sang its mournful winter-song; the tramp of passing footsteps, the roll of passing wheels on the road ceased in dreary silence. He slept on quietly. The firelight rose and fell on his wizen little face and his nervous, drooping hands. Mrs. Lecount had not pitied him yet. She began to pity him now. Her point was gained; her interest in his will was secured; he had put his future life, of his own accord, under her fostering care—the fire was comfortable; the circumstances were favorable to the growth of Christian feeling. "Poor wretch!" said Mrs. Lecount, looking at him with a grave compassion—"poor wretch!"

The dinner-hour roused him. He was cheerful at dinner; he reverted to the idea of the cheap little house in France; he smirked and simpered; and talked French to Mrs. Lecount, while the house-maid and Louisa waited, turn and turn about, under protest. When dinner was over, he returned to his comfortable chair before the fire, and Mrs. Lecount followed him. He resumed the conversation—which meant, in his case, repeating his questions. But he was not so quick and ready with them as he had been earlier in the day. They began to flag—they continued, at longer and longer intervals—they ceased altogether. Toward nine o'clock he fell asleep again.

It was not a quiet sleep this time. He muttered, and ground his teeth, and rolled his head from side to side of the chair. Mrs. Lecount purposely made noise enough to rouse him. He woke, with a vacant eye and a flushed cheek. He walked about the room restlessly, with a new idea in his mind—the idea of writing a terrible letter; a letter of eternal farewell to his wife. How was it to be written? In what language should he express his feelings? The powers of Shakespeare himself would be unequal to the emergency! He had been the victim of an outrage entirely without parallel. A wretch had crept into his bosom! A viper had hidden herself at his fireside! Where could words be found to brand her with the infamy she deserved? He stopped, with a suffocating sense in him of his own impotent rage—he stopped, and shook his fist tremulously in the empty air.

Mrs. Lecount interfered with an energy and a resolution inspired by serious alarm. After the heavy strain that had been laid on his weakness already, such an outbreak of passionate agitation as was now bursting from him might be the destruction of his rest that night and of his strength to travel the next day. With infinite difficulty, with endless promises to return to the subject, and to advise him about it in the morning, she prevailed on him, at last, to go upstairs and compose himself for the night. She gave him her arm to assist him. On the way upstairs his attention, to her great relief, became suddenly absorbed by a new fancy. He remembered a certain warm and comfortable mixture of wine, eggs, sugar, and spices, which she had often been accustomed to make for him in former times, and which he thought he should relish exceedingly before he went to bed. Mrs. Lecount helped him on with his dressing-gown—then went down-stairs again to make his warm drink for him at the parlor fire.

She rang the bell and ordered the necessary ingredients for the mixture, in Noel Vanstone's name. The servants, with the small ingenious malice of their race, brought up the materials one by one, and kept her waiting for each of them as long as possible. She had got the saucepan, and the spoon, and the tumbler, and the nutmeg-grater, and the wine—but not the egg, the sugar, or the spices—when she heard him above, walking backward and forward noisily in his room; exciting himself on the old subject again, beyond all doubt.

She went upstairs once more; but he was too quick for her—he heard her outside the door; and when she opened it, she found him in his chair, with his back cunningly turned toward her. Knowing him too well to attempt any remonstrance, she merely announced the speedy arrival of the warm drink and turned to leave the room. On her way out, she noticed a table in a corner, with an inkstand and a paper-case on it, and tried, without attracting his attention, to take the writing materials away. He was too quick for her again. He asked, angrily, if she doubted his promise. She put the writing materials back on the table, for fear of offending him, and left the room.

In half an hour more the mixture was ready. She carried it up to him, foaming and fragrant, in a large tumbler. "He will sleep after this," she thought to herself, as she opened the door; "I have made it stronger than usual on purpose."

He had changed his place. He was sitting at the table in the corner—still with his back to her, writing. This time his quick ears had not served him; this time she caught him in the fact.

"Oh, Mr. Noel! Mr. Noel!" she said, reproachfully, "what is your promise worth?"

He made no answer. He was sitting with his left elbow on the table, and with his head resting on his left hand. His right hand lay back on the paper, with the pen lying loose in it. "Your drink, Mr. Noel," she said, in a kinder tone, feeling unwilling to offend him. He took no notice of her. She went to the table to rouse him. Was he deep in thought?

He was dead!

THE END OF THE FIFTH SCENE.

BETWEEN THE SCENES.

PROGRESS OF THE STORY THROUGH THE POST.

I.

From Mrs. Noel Vanstone to Mr. Loscombe.

"Park Terrace, St. John's Wood, November 5th.

"DEAR SIR—I came to London yesterday for the purpose of seeing a relative, leaving Mr. Vanstone at Baliol Cottage, and proposing to return to him in the course of the week. I reached London late last night, and drove to these lodgings, having written to secure accommodation beforehand.

"This morning's post has brought me a letter from my own maid, whom I left at Baliol Cottage, with instructions to write to me if anything extraordinary took place in my absence. You will find the girl's letter inclosed in this. I have had some experience of her; and I believe she is to be strictly depended on to tell the truth.

"I purposely abstain from troubling you by any useless allusions to myself. When you have read my maid's letter, you will understand the shock which the news contained in it has caused me. I can only repeat that I place implicit belief in her statement. I am firmly persuaded that my husband's former housekeeper has found him out, has practiced on his weakness in my absence, and has prevailed on him to make another Will. From what I know of this woman, I feel no doubt that she has used her influence over Mr. Vanstone to deprive me, if possible, of all future interests in my husband's fortune.

"Under such circumstances as these, it is in the last degree important—for more reasons than I need mention here—that I should see Mr. Vanstone, and come to an explanation with him, at the earliest possible opportunity. You will find that my maid thoughtfully kept her letter open until the last moment before post-time—without, however, having any later news to give me than that Mrs. Lecount was to sleep at the cottage last night and that she and Mr. Vanstone were to leave together this morning. But for that last piece of intelligence, I should have been on my way back to Scotland before now. As it is, I cannot decide for myself what I ought to do next. My going back to Dumfries, after Mr. Vanstone has left it, seems like taking a journey for nothing —and my staying in London appears to be almost equally useless.

"Will you kindly advise me in this difficulty? I will come to you at Lincoln's Inn at any time this afternoon or to-morrow which you may appoint. My next few hours are engaged. As soon as this letter is dispatched, I am going to Kensington, with the object of ascertaining whether certain doubts I feel about the means by which Mrs. Lecount may have accomplished her discovery are well founded or not. If you will let me have your answer by return of post, I will not fail to get back to St. John's Wood in time to receive it. Believe me, dear sir, yours sincerely,

"MAGDALEN VANSTONE."

II.

From Mr. Loscombe to Mrs. Noel Vanstone.

"Lincoln's Inn, November 5th.

"DEAR MADAM—Your letter and its inclosure have caused me great concern and surprise. Pressure of business allows me no hope of being able to see you either to-day or to-morrow morning. But if three o'clock to-morrow afternoon will suit you, at that hour you will find me at your service.

"I cannot pretend to offer a positive opinion until I know more of the particulars connected with this extraordinary business than I find communicated either in your letter or in your maid's. But with this reserve, I venture to suggest that your remaining in London until to-morrow may possibly lead to other results besides your consultation at my chambers. There is at least a chance that you or I may hear something further in this strange matter by the morning's post. I remain, dear madam, faithfully yours,

"JOHN LOSCOMBE."

III.

From Mrs. Noel Vanstone to Miss Garth.

"November 5th, Two o'Clock.

"I have just returned from Westmoreland House—after purposely leaving it in secret, and purposely avoiding you under your own roof. You shall know why I came, and why I went away. It is due to my remembrance of old times not to treat you like a stranger, although I can never again treat you like a friend.

"I set forth on the third from the North to London. My only object in taking this long journey was to see Norah. I had been suffering for many weary weeks past such remorse as only miserable women like me can feel. Perhaps the suffering weakened me; perhaps it roused some old forgotten tenderness—God knows!—I can't explain it; I can only tell you that I began to think of Norah by day, and to dream of Norah by night, till I was almost heartbroken. I have no better reason than this to give for running all the risks which I ran, and coming to London to see her. I don't wish to claim more for myself than I deserve; I don't wish to tell you I was the reformed and repenting creature whom you might have approved. I had only one feeling in me that I know of. I wanted to put my arms round Norah's neck, and cry my heart out on Norah's bosom. Childish enough, I dare say. Something might have come of it; nothing might have come of it—who knows?

"I had no means of finding Norah without your assistance. However you might disapprove of what I had done, I thought you would not refuse to help me to find my sister. When I lay down last night in my strange bed, I said to myself, 'I will ask Miss Garth, for my father's sake and my mother's sake, to tell me.' You don't know what a comfort I felt in that thought. How should you? What do good women like you know of miserable sinners like me? All you know is that you pray for us at church.

"Well, I fell asleep happily that night—for the first time since my marriage. When the morning came, I paid the penalty of daring to be happy only for one night. When the morning came, a letter came with it, which told me that my bitterest enemy on earth (you have meddled sufficiently with my affairs to know what enemy I mean) had revenged herself on me in my absence. In following the impulse which led me to my sister, I had gone to my ruin.

"The mischief was beyond all present remedy, when I received the news of it. Whatever had happened, whatever might happen, I made up my mind to persist in my resolution of seeing Norah before I did anything else. I suspected you of being concerned in the disaster which had overtaken me—because I felt positively certain at Aldborough that you and Mrs. Lecount had written to each other. But I never suspected Norah. If I lay on my death-bed at this moment I could say with a safe conscience I never suspected Norah.

"So I went this morning to Westmoreland House to ask you for my sister's address, and to acknowledge plainly that I suspected you of being again in correspondence with Mrs. Lecount.

"When I inquired for you at the door, they told me you had gone out, but that you were expected back before long. They asked me if I would see your sister, who was then in the school-room. I desired that your sister should on no account be disturbed: my business was not with her, but with you. I begged to be allowed to wait in a room by myself until you returned.

"They showed me into the double room on the ground-floor, divided by curtains—as it was when I last remember it. There was a fire in the outer division of the room, but none in the inner; and for that reason, I suppose, the curtains were drawn. The servant was very civil and attentive to me. I have learned to be thankful for civility and attention, and I spoke to her as cheerfully as I could. I said to her, 'I shall see Miss Garth here, as she comes up to the door, and I can beckon her in through the long window.' The servant said I could do so, if you came that way, but that you let yourself in sometimes with your own key by the back-garden gate; and if you did this, she would take care to let you know of my visit. I mention these trifles, to show you that there was no pre-meditated deceit in my mind when I came to the house.

"I waited a weary time, and you never came: I don't know whether my impatience made me think so, or whether the large fire burning made the room really as hot as I felt it to be—I only know that, after a while, I passed through the curtains into the inner room, to try the cooler atmosphere.

"I walked to the long window which leads into the back garden, to look out, and almost at the same time I heard the door opened—the door of the room I had just left, and your voice and the voice of some other woman, a stranger to me, talking. The stranger was one of the parlor-boarders, I dare say. I gathered from the first words you exchanged together, that you had met in the passage—she on her way downstairs, and you on your way in from the back garden. Her next question and your next answer informed me that this person was a friend of my sister's, who felt a strong interest in her, and who knew that you had just returned from a visit to Norah. So far, I only hesitated to show myself, because I shrank, in my painful situation, from facing a stranger. But when I heard my own name immediately afterward on your lips and on hers, then I purposely came nearer to the curtain between us, and purposely listened.

"A mean action, you will say? Call it mean, if you like. What better can you expect from such a woman as I am?

"You were always famous for your memory. There is no necessity for my repeating the words you spoke to your friend, and the words your friend spoke to you, hardly an hour since. When you read these lines, you will know, as well as I know, what those words told me. I ask for no particulars; I will take all your reasons and all your excuses for granted. It is enough for me to know that you and Mr. Pendril have been searching for me again, and that Norah is in the conspiracy this time, to reclaim me in spite of myself. It is enough for me to know that my letter to my sister has been turned into a trap to catch me, and that Mrs. Lecount's revenge has accomplished its object by means of information received from Norah's lips.

"Shall I tell you what I suffered when I heard these things? No; it would only be a waste of time to tell you. Whatever I suffer, I deserve it—don't I?

"I waited in that inner room—knowing my own violent temper, and not trusting myself to see you, after what I had heard—I waited in that inner room, trembling lest the servant should tell you of my visit before I could find an opportunity of leaving the house. No such misfortune happened. The servant, no doubt, heard the voices upstairs, and supposed that we had met each other in the passage. I don't know how long or how short a time it was before you left the room to go and take off your bonnet—you went, and your friend went with you. I raised the long window softly, and stepped into the back garden. The way by which you returned to the house was the way by which I left it. No blame attaches to the servant. As usual, where I am concerned, nobody is to blame but me.

"Time enough has passed now to quiet my mind a little. You know how strong I am? You remember how I used to fight against all my illnesses when I was a child? Now I am a woman, I fight against my miseries in the same way. Don't pity me, Miss Garth! Don't pity me!

"I have no harsh feeling against Norah. The hope I had of seeing her is a hope taken from me; the consolation I had in writing to her is a consolation denied me for the future. I am cut to the heart; but I have no angry feeling toward my sister. She means well, poor soul—I dare say she means well. It would distress her, if she knew what has happened. Don't tell her. Conceal my visit, and burn my letter.

"A last word to yourself and I have done:

"If I rightly understand my present situation, your spies are still searching for me to just as little purpose as they searched at York. Dismiss them—you are wasting your money to no purpose. If you discovered me to-morrow, what could you do? My position has altered. I am no longer the poor outcast girl, the vagabond public performer, whom you once hunted after. I have done what I told you I would do—I have made the general sense of propriety my accomplice this time. Do you know who I am? I am a respectable married woman, accountable for my actions to nobody under heaven but my husband. I have got a place in the world, and a name in the world, at last. Even the law, which is the friend of all you respectable people, has recognized my existence, and has become my friend too! The Archbishop of Canterbury gave me his license to be married, and the vicar of Aldborough performed the service. If I found your spies following me in the street, and if I chose to claim protection from them, the law would acknowledge my claim. You forget what wonders my wickedness has done for me. It has made Nobody's Child Somebody's Wife.

"If you will give these considerations their due weight; if you will exert your excellent common sense, I have no fear of being obliged to appeal to my newly-found friend and protector—the law. You will feel, by this time, that you have meddled with me at last to some purpose. I am estranged from Norah—I am discovered by my husband—I am defeated by Mrs. Lecount. You have driven me to the last extremity; you have strengthened me to fight the battle of my life with the resolution which only a lost and friendless woman can feel. Badly as your schemes have prospered, they have not proved totally useless after all!

"I have no more to say. If you ever speak about me to Norah, tell her that a day may come when she will see me again—the day when we two sisters have recovered our natural rights; the day when I put Norah's fortune into Norah's hand.

"Those are my last words. Remember them the next time you feel tempted to meddle with me again.

"MAGDALEN VANSTONE."

IV.

From Mr. Loscombe to Mrs. Noel Vanstone.

"Lincoln's Inn, November 6th.

"DEAR MADAM—This morning's post has doubtless brought you the same shocking news which it has brought to me. You must know by this time that a terrible affliction has befallen you—the affliction of your husband's sudden death.

"I am on the point of starting for the North, to make all needful inquiries, and to perform whatever duties I may with propriety undertake, as solicitor to the deceased gentleman. Let me earnestly recommend you not to follow me to Baliol Cottage, until I have had time to write to you first, and to give you such advice as I cannot, through ignorance of all the circumstances, pretend to offer now. You may rely on my writing, after my arrival in Scotland, by the first post. I remain, dear madam, faithfully yours,

"JOHN LOSCOMBE."

V.

From Mr. Pendril to Miss Garth.

"Serle Street, November 6th.

"DEAR MISS GARTH—I return you Mrs. Noel Vanstone's letter. I can understand your mortification at the tone in which it is written, and your distress at the manner in which this unhappy woman has interpreted the conversation that she overheard at your house. I cannot honestly add that I lament what has happened. My opinion has never altered since the Combe-Raven time. I believe Mrs. Noel Vanstone to be one of the most reckless, desperate, and perverted women living; and any circumstances that estrange her from her sister are circumstances which I welcome, for her sister's sake.

"There cannot be a moment's doubt on the course you ought to follow in this matter. Even Mrs. Noel Vanstone herself acknowledges the propriety of sparing her sister additional and unnecessary distress. By all means, keep Miss Vanstone in ignorance of the visit to Kensington, and of the letter which has followed it. It would be not only unwise, but absolutely cruel, to enlighten her. If we had any remedy to apply, or even any hope to offer, we might feel some hesitation in keeping our secret. But there is no remedy, and no hope. Mrs. Noel Vanstone is perfectly justified in the view she takes of her own position. Neither you nor I can assert the smallest right to control her.

"I have already taken the necessary measures for putting an end to our useless inquiries. In a few days I will write to Miss Vanstone, and will do my best to tranquilize her mind on the subject of her sister. If I can find no sufficient excuse to satisfy her, it will be better she should think we have discovered nothing than that she should know the truth. Believe me most truly yours,

"WILLIAM PENDRIL."

VI.

From Mr. Loscombe to Mrs. Noel Vanstone.

"Lincoln's Inn, November 15th.

"DEAR MADAM—In compliance with your request, I now proceed to communicate to you in writing what (but for the calamity which has so recently befallen you) I should have preferred communicating by word of mouth. Be pleased to consider this letter as strictly confidential between yourself and me.

"I inclose, as you desire, a copy of the Will executed by your late husband on the third of this month. There can be no question of the genuineness of the original document. I protested, as a matter of form, against Admiral Bartram's solicitor assuming a position of authority at Baliol Cottage. But he took the position, nevertheless; acting as legal representative of the sole Executor under the second Will. I am bound to say I should have done the same myself in his place.

"The serious question follows, What can we do for the best in your interests? The Will executed under my professional superintendence, on the thirtieth of September last, is at present superseded and revoked by the second and later Will, executed on the third of November. Can we dispute this document?

"I doubt the possibility of disputing the new Will on the face of it. It is no doubt irregularly expressed; but it is dated, signed, and witnessed as the law directs; and the perfectly simple and straightforward provisions that it contains are in no respect, that I can see, technically open to attack.

"This being the case, can we dispute the Will on the ground that it has been executed when the Testator was not in a fit state to dispose of his own property? or when the Testator was subjected to undue and improper influence?

"In the first of these cases, the medical evidence would put an obstacle in our way. We cannot assert that previous illness had weakened the Testator's mind. It is clear that he died suddenly, as the doctors had all along declared he would die, of disease of the heart. He was out walking in his garden, as usual, on the day of his death; he ate a hearty dinner; none of the persons in his service noticed any change in him; he was a little more irritable with them than usual, but that was all. It is impossible to attack the state of his faculties: there is no case to go into court with, so far.

"Can we declare that he acted under undue influence; or, in plainer terms, under the influence of Mrs. Lecount?

"There are serious difficulties, again, in the way of taking this course. We cannot assert, for example, that Mrs. Lecount has assumed a place in the will which she has no fair claim to occupy. She has cunningly limited her own legacy, not only to what is fairly due her, but to what the late Mr. Michael Vanstone himself had the intention of leaving her. If I were examined on the subject, I should be compelled to acknowledge that I had heard him express this intention myself. It is only the truth to say that I have heard him express it more than once. There is no point of attack in Mrs. Lecount's legacy, and there is no point of attack in your late husband's choice of an executor. He has made the wise choice, and the natural choice, of the oldest and trustiest friend he had in the world.

"One more consideration remains—the most important which I have yet approached, and therefore the consideration which I have reserved to the last. On the thirtieth of September, the Testator executes a will, leaving his widow sole executrix, with a legacy of eighty thousand pounds. On the third of November following, he expressly revokes this will, and leaves another in its stead, in which his widow is never once mentioned, and in which the whole residue of his estate, after payment of one comparatively trifling legacy, is left to a friend.

"It rests entirely with you to say whether any valid reason can or can not be produced to explain such an extraordinary proceeding as this. If no reason can be assigned—and I know of none myself—I think we have a point here which deserves our careful consideration; for it may be a point which is open to attack. Pray understand that I am now appealing to you solely as a lawyer, who is obliged to look all possible eventualities in the face. I have no wish to intrude on your private affairs; I have no wish to write a word which could be construed into any indirect reflection on yourself.

"If you tell me that, so far as you know, your husband capriciously struck you out of his will, without assignable reason or motive for doing so, and without other obvious explanation of his conduct than that he acted in this matter entirely under the influence of Mrs. Lecount, I will immediately take Counsel's opinion touching the propriety of disputing the will on this ground. If, on the other hand, you tell me that there are reasons (known to yourself, though unknown to me) for not taking the course I propose, I will accept that intimation without troubling you, unless you wish it, to explain yourself further. In this latter event, I will write to you again; for I shall then have something more to say, which may greatly surprise you, on the subject of the Will.

"Faithfully yours,

"JOHN LOSCOMBE."

VII.

From Mrs. Noel Vanstone to Mr. Loscombe.

"November 16th.

"DEAR SIR—Accept my best thanks for the kindness and consideration with which you have treated me; and let the anxieties under which I am now suffering plead my excuse, if I reply to your letter without ceremony, in the fewest possible words.

"I have my own reasons for not hesitating to answer your question in the negative. It is impossible for us to go to law, as you propose, on the subject of the Will.

"Believe me, dear sir, yours gratefully,

"MAGDALEN VANSTONE."

VIII.

From Mr. Loscombe to Mrs. Noel Vanstone.

"Lincoln's Inn. November 17th.

"DEAR MADAM—I beg to acknowledge the receipt of your letter, answering my proposal in the negative, for reasons of your own. Under these circumstances—on which I offer no comment—I beg to perform my promise of again communicating with you on the subject of your late husband's Will.

"Be so kind as to look at your copy of the document. You will find that the clause which devises the whole residue of your husband's estate to Admiral Bartram ends in these terms: to be by him applied to such uses as he may think fit.

"Simple as they may seem to you, these are very remarkable words. In the first place, no practical lawyer would have used them in drawing your husband's will. In the second place, they are utterly useless to serve any plain straightforward purpose. The legacy is left unconditionally to the admiral; and in the same breath he is told that he may do what he likes with it! The phrase points clearly to one of two conclusions. It has either dropped from the writer's pen in pure ignorance, or it has been carefully set where it appears to serve the purpose of a snare. I am firmly persuaded that the latter explanation is the right one. The words are expressly intended to mislead some person—yourself in all probability—and the cunning which has put them to that use is a cunning which (as constantly happens when uninstructed persons meddle with law) has overreached itself. My thirty years' experience reads those words in a sense exactly opposite to the sense which they are intended to convey. I say that Admiral Bartram is not free to apply his legacy to such purposes as he may think fit; I believe he is privately controlled by a supplementary document in the shape of a Secret Trust.

"I can easily explain to you what I mean by a Secret Trust. It is usually contained in the form of a letter from a Testator to his Executors, privately informing them of testamentary intentions on his part which he has not thought proper openly to acknowledge in his will. I leave you a hundred pounds; and I write a private letter enjoining you, on taking the legacy, not to devote it to your own purposes, but to give it to some third person, whose name I have my own reasons for not mentioning in my will. That is a Secret Trust.

"If I am right in my own persuasion that such a document as I here describe is at this moment in Admiral Bartram's possession—a persuasion based, in the first instance, on the extraordinary words that I have quoted to you; and, in the second instance, on purely legal considerations with which it is needless to incumber my letter—if I am right in this opinion, the discovery of the Secret Trust would be, in all probability, a most important discovery to your interests. I will not trouble you with technical reasons, or with references to my experience in these matters, which only a professional man could understand. I will merely say that I don't give up your cause as utterly lost, until the conviction now impressed on my own mind is proved to be wrong.

"I can add no more, while this important question still remains involved in doubt; neither can I suggest any means of solving that doubt. If the existence of the Trust was proved, and if the nature of the stipulations contained in it was made known to me, I could then say positively what the legal chances were of your being able to set up a Case on the strength of it: and I could also tell you whether I should or should not feel justified in personally undertaking that Case under a private arrangement with yourself.

"As things are, I can make no arrangement, and offer no advice. I can only put you confidentially in possession of my private opinion, leaving you entirely free to draw your own inferences from it, and regretting that I cannot write more confidently and more definitely than I have written here. All that I could conscientiously say on this very difficult and delicate subject, I have said.

"Believe me, dear madam, faithfully yours,

"JOHN LOSCOMBE.

"P.S.—I omitted one consideration in my last letter, which I may mention here, in order to show you that no point in connection with the case has escaped me. If it had been possible to show that Mr. Vanstone was domiciled in Scotland at the time of his death, we might have asserted your interests by means of the Scotch law, which does not allow a husband the power of absolutely disinheriting his wife. But it is impossible to assert that Mr. Vanstone was legally domiciled in Scotland. He came there as a visitor only; he occupied a furnished house for the season; and he never expressed, either by word or deed, the slightest intention of settling permanently in the North."

IX.

From Mrs. Noel Vanstone to Mr. Loscombe.

"DEAR SIR—I have read your letter more than once, with the deepest interest and attention; and the oftener I read it, the more firmly I believe that there is really such a Letter as you mention in Admiral Bartram's hands.

"It is my interest that the discovery should be made, and I at once acknowledge to you that I am determined to find the means of secretly and certainly making it. My resolution rests on other motives than the motives which you might naturally suppose would influence me. I only tell you this, in case you feel inclined to remonstrate. There is good reason for what I say, when I assure you that remonstrance will be useless.

"I ask for no assistance in this matter; I will trouble nobody for advice. You shall not be involved in any rash proceedings on my part. Whatever danger there may be, I will risk it. Whatever delays may happen, I will bear them patiently. I am lonely and friendless, and surely troubled in mind, but I am strong enough to win my way through worse trials than these. My spirits will rise again, and my time will come. If that Secret Trust is in Admiral Bartram's possession—when you next see me, you shall see me with it in my own hands. Yours gratefully,

"MAGDALEN VANSTONE."

THE SIXTH SCENE.

ST. JOHN'S WOOD.

CHAPTER I.

IT wanted little more than a fortnight to Christmas; but the weather showed no signs yet of the frost and snow, conventionally associated with the coming season. The atmosphere was unnaturally warm, and the old year was dying feebly in sapping rain and enervating mist.

Toward the close of the December afternoon, Magdalen sat alone in the lodging which she had occupied since her arrival in London. The fire burned sluggishly in the narrow little grate; the view of the wet houses and soaking gardens opposite was darkening fast; and the bell of the suburban muffin-boy tinkled in the distance drearily. Sitting close over the fire, with a little money lying loose in her lap, Magdalen absently shifted the coins to and fro on the smooth surface of her dress, incessantly altering their positions toward each other, as if they were pieces of a "child's puzzle" which she was trying to put together. The dim fire-light flaming up on her faintly from time to time showed changes which would have told their own tale sadly to friends of former days. Her dress had become loose through the wasting of her figure; but she had not cared to alter it. The old restlessness in her movements, the old mobility in her expression, appeared no more. Her face passively maintained its haggard composure, its changeless unnatural calm. Mr. Pendril might have softened his hard sentence on her, if he had seen her now; and Mrs. Lecount, in the plenitude of her triumph, might have pitied her fallen enemy at last.

Hardly four months had passed since the wedding-day at Aldborough, and the penalty for that day was paid already—paid in unavailing remorse, in hopeless isolation, in irremediable defeat! Let this be said for her; let the truth which has been told of the fault be told of the expiation as well. Let it be recorded of her that she enjoyed no secret triumph on the day of her success. The horror of herself with which her own act had inspired her, had risen to its climax when the design of her marriage was achieved. She had never suffered in secret as she suffered when the Combe-Raven money was left to her in her husband's will. She had never felt the means taken to accomplish her end so unutterably degrading to herself, as she felt them on the day when the end was reached. Out of that feeling had grown the remorse which had hurried her to seek pardon and consolation in her sister's love. Never since it had first entered her heart, never since she had first felt it sacred to her at her father's grave, had the Purpose to which she had vowed herself, so nearly lost its hold on her as at this time. Never might Norah's influence have achieved such good as on the day when that influence was lost—the day when the fatal words were overheard at Miss Garth's—the day when the fatal letter from Scotland told of Mrs. Lecount's revenge.

The harm was done; the chance was gone. Time and Hope alike had both passed her by.

Faintly and more faintly the inner voices now pleaded with her to pause on the downward way. The discovery which had poisoned her heart with its first distrust of her sister; the tidings which had followed it of her husband's death; the sting of Mrs. Lecount's triumph, felt through all, had done their work. The remorse which had embittered her married life was deadened now to a dull despair. It was too late to make the atonement of confession—too late to lay bare to the miserable husband the deeper secrets that had once lurked in the heart of the miserable wife. Innocent of all thought of the hideous treachery which Mrs. Lecount had imputed to her—she was guilty of knowing how his health was broken when she married him; guilty of knowing, when he left her the Combe-Raven money, that the accident of a moment, harmless to other men, might place his life in jeopardy, and effect her release. His death had told her this—had told her plainly what she had shrunk, in his lifetime, from openly acknowledging to herself. From the dull torment of that reproach; from the dreary wretchedness of doubting everybody, even to Norah herself; from the bitter sense of her defeated schemes; from the blank solitude of her friendless life—what refuge was left? But one refuge now. She turned to the relentless Purpose which was hurrying her to her ruin, and cried to it with the daring of her despair—Drive me on!

For days and days together she had bent her mind on the one object which occupied it since she had received the lawyer's letter. For days and days together she had toiled to meet the first necessity of her position—to find a means of discovering the Secret Trust. There was no hope, this time, of assistance from Captain Wragge. Long practice had made the old militia-man an adept in the art of vanishing. The plow of the moral agriculturist left no furrows—not a trace of him was to be found! Mr. Loscombe was too cautious to commit himself to an active course of any kind; he passively maintained his opinions and left the rest to his client—-he desired to know nothing until the Trust was placed in his hands. Magdalen's interests were now in Magdalen's own sole care. Risk or no risk, what she did next she must do by herself.

The prospect had not daunted her. Alone she had calculated the chances that might be tried. Alone she was now determined to make the attempt.

"The time has come," she said to herself, as she sat over the fire. "I must sound Louisa first."

She collected the scattered coins in her lap, and placed them in a little heap on the table, then rose and rang the bell. The landlady answered it.

"Is my servant downstairs?" inquired Magdalen.

"Yes, ma'am. She is having her tea."

"When she has done, say I want her up here. Wait a moment. You will find your money on the table—the money I owe you for last week. Can you find it? or would you like to have a candle?"

"It's rather dark, ma'am."

Magdalen lit a candle. "What notice must I give you," she asked, as she put the candle on the table, "before I leave?"

"A week is the usual notice, ma'am. I hope you have no objection to make to the house?"

"None whatever. I only ask the question, because I may be obliged to leave these lodgings rather sooner than I anticipated. Is the money right?"

"Quite right, ma'am. Here is your receipt."

"Thank you. Don't forget to send Louisa to me as soon as she has done her tea."

The landlady withdrew. As soon as she was alone again, Magdalen extinguished the candle, and drew an empty chair close to her own chair on the hearth. This done, she resumed her former place, and waited until Louisa appeared. There was doubt in her face as she sat looking mechanically into the fire. "A poor chance," she thought to herself; "but, poor as it is, a chance that I must try."

In ten minutes more, Louisa's meek knock was softly audible outside. She was surprised, on entering the room, to find no other light in it than the light of the fire.

"Will you have the candles, ma'am?" she inquired, respectfully.

"We will have candles if you wish for them yourself," replied Magdalen; "not otherwise. I have something to say to you. When I have said it, you shall decide whether we sit together in the dark or in the light."

Louisa waited near the door, and listened to those strange words in silent astonishment.

"Come here," said Magdalen, pointing to the empty chair; "come here and sit down."

Louisa advanced, and timidly removed the chair from its position at her mistress's side. Magdalen instantly drew it back again. "No!" she said. "Come closer—come close by me." After a moment's hesitation, Louisa obeyed.

"I ask you to sit near me," pursued Magdalen, "because I wish to speak to you on equal terms. Whatever distinctions there might once have been between us are now at an end. I am a lonely woman thrown helpless on my own resources, without rank or place in the world. I may or may not keep you as my friend. As mistress and maid the connection between us must come to an end."

"Oh, ma'am, don't, don't say that!" pleaded Louisa, faintly.

Magdalen sorrowfully and steadily went on.

"When you first came to me," she resumed, "I thought I should not like you. I have learned to like you—I have learned to be grateful to you. From first to last you have been faithful and good to me. The least I can do in return is not to stand in the way of your future prospects."

"Don't send me away, ma'am!" said Louisa, imploringly. "If you can only help me with a little money now and then, I'll wait for my wages—I will, indeed."

Magdalen took her hand and went on, as sorrowfully and as steadily as before.

"My future life is all darkness, all uncertainty," she said. "The next step I may take may lead me to my prosperity or may lead me to my ruin. Can I ask you to share such a prospect as this? If your future was as uncertain as mine is—if you, too, were a friendless woman thrown on the world—my conscience might be easy in letting you cast your lot with mine. I might accept your attachment, for I might feel I was not wronging you. How can I feel this in your case? You have a future to look to. You are an excellent servant; you can get another place—a far better place than mine. You can refer to me; and if the character I give is not considered sufficient, you can refer to the mistress you served before me—"

At the instant when that reference to the girl's last employer escaped Magdalen's lips, Louisa snatched her hand away and started up affrightedly from her chair. There was a moment's silence. Both mistress and maid were equally taken by surprise.

Magdalen was the first to recover herself.

"Is it getting too dark?" she asked, significantly. "Are you going to light the candles, after all?"

Louisa drew back into the dimmest corner of the room.

"You suspect me, ma'am!" she answered out of the darkness, in a breathless whisper. "Who has told you? How did you find out—?" She stopped, and burst into tears. "I deserve your suspicion," she said, struggling to compose herself. "I can't deny it to you. You have treated me so kindly; you have made me so fond of you! Forgive me, Mrs. Vanstone—I am a wretch; I have deceived you."

"Come here and sit down by me again," said Magdalen. "Come—or I will get up myself and bring you back."

Louisa slowly returned to her place. Dim as the fire-light was, she seemed to fear it. She held her handkerchief over her face, and shrank from her mistress as she seated herself again in the chair.

"You are wrong in thinking that any one has betrayed you to me," said Magdalen. "All that I know of you is, what your own looks and ways have told me. You have had some secret trouble weighing on your mind ever since you have been in my service. I confess I have spoken with the wish to find out more of you and your past life than I have found out yet—not because I am curious, but because I have my secret troubles too. Are you an unhappy woman, like me? If you are, I will take you into my confidence. If you have nothing to tell me—if you choose to keep your secret—I don't blame you; I only say, Let us part. I won't ask how you have deceived me. I will only remember that you have been an honest and faithful and competent servant while I have employed you; and I will say as much in your favor to any new mistress you like to send to me."

She waited for the reply. For a moment, and only for a moment, Louisa hesitated. The girl's nature was weak, but not depraved. She was honestly attached to her mistress; and she spoke with a courage which Magdalen had not expected from her.

"If you send me away, ma'am," she said, "I won't take my character from you till I have told you the truth; I won't return your kindness by deceiving you a second time. Did my master ever tell you how he engaged me?"

"No. I never asked him, and he never told me."

"He engaged me, ma'am, with a written character—"

"Yes?"

"The character was a false one."

Magdalen drew back in amazement. The confession she heard was not the confession she had anticipated.

"Did your mistress refuse to give you a character?" she asked. "Why?"

Louisa dropped on her knees and hid her face in her mistress's lap. "Don't ask me!" she said. "I'm a miserable, degraded creature; I'm not fit to be in the same room with you!"

Magdalen bent over her, and whispered a question in her ear. Louisa whispered back the one sad word of reply.

"Has he deserted you?" asked Magdalen, after waiting a moment, and thinking first.

"No."

"Do you love him?"

"Dearly."

The remembrance of her own loveless marriage stung Magdalen to the quick.

"For God's sake, don't kneel to me!" she cried, passionately. "If there is a degraded woman in this room, I am the woman—not you!"

She raised the girl by main force from her knees, and put her back in the chair. They both waited a little in silence. Keeping her hand on Louisa's shoulder, Magdalen seated herself again, and looked with unutterable bitterness of sorrow into the dying fire. "Oh," she thought, "what happy women there are in the world! Wives who love their husbands! Mothers who are not ashamed to own their children! Are you quieter?" she asked, gently addressing Louisa once more. "Can you answer me, if I ask you something else? Where is the child?"

"The child is out at nurse."

"Does the father help to support it?"

"He does all he can, ma'am."

"What is he? Is he in service? Is he in a trade?"

"His father is a master-carpenter—he works in his father's yard."

"If he has got work, why has he not married you?"

"It is his father's fault, ma'am—not his. His father has no pity on us. He would be turned out of house and home if he married me."

"Can he get no work elsewhere?"

"It's hard to get good work in London, ma'am. There are so many in London—they take the bread out of each other's mouths. If we had only had the money to emigrate, he would have married me long since."

"Would he marry you if you had the money now?"

"I am sure he would, ma'am. He could get plenty of work in Australia, and double and treble the wages he gets here. He is trying hard, and I am trying hard, to save a little toward it—I put by all I can spare from my child. But it is so little! If we live for years to come, there seems no hope for us. I know I have done wrong every way—I know I don't deserve to be happy. But how could I let my child suffer?—I was obliged to go to service. My mistress was hard on me, and my health broke down in trying to live by my needle. I would never have deceived anybody by a false character, if there had been another chance for me. I was alone and helpless, ma'am; and I can only ask you to forgive me."

"Ask better women than I am," said Magdalen, sadly. "I am only fit to feel for you, and I do feel for you with all my heart. In your place I should have gone into service with a false character, too. Say no more of the past—you don't know how you hurt me in speaking of it.

Talk of the future. I think I can help you, and do you no harm. I think you can help me, and do me the greatest of all services in return. Wait, and you shall hear what I mean. Suppose you were married—how much would it cost for you and your husband to emigrate?"

Louisa mentioned the cost of a steerage passage to Australia for a man and his wife. She spoke in low, hopeless tones. Moderate as the sum was, it looked like unattainable wealth in her eyes.

Magdalen started in her chair, and took the girl's hand once more.

"Louisa!" she said, earnestly; "if I gave you the money, what would you do for me in return?"

The proposal seemed to strike Louisa speechless with astonishment. She trembled violently, and said nothing. Magdalen repeated her words.

"Oh, ma'am, do you mean it?" said the girl. "Do you really mean it?"

"Yes," replied Magdalen; "I really mean it. What would you do for me in return?"

"Do?" repeated Louisa. "Oh what is there I would not do!" She tried to kiss her mistress's hand; but Magdalen would not permit it. She resolutely, almost roughly, drew her hand away.

"I am laying you under no obligation," she said. "We are serving each other—that is all. Sit quiet, and let me think."

For the next ten minutes there was silence in the room. At the end of that time Magdalen took out her watch and held it close to the grate. There was just firelight enough to show her the hour. It was close on six o'clock.

"Are you composed enough to go downstairs and deliver a message?" she asked, rising from her chair as she spoke to Louisa again. "It is a very simple message—it is only to tell the boy that I want a cab as soon as he can get me one. I must go out immediately. You shall know why later in the evening. I have much more to say to you; but there is no time to say it now. When I am gone, bring your work up here, and wait for my return. I shall be back before bed-time."

Without another word of explanation, she hurriedly lit a candle and withdrew into the bedroom to put on her bonnet and shawl.

CHAPTER II.

BETWEEN nine and ten o'clock the same evening, Louisa, waiting anxiously, heard the long-expected knock at the house door. She ran downstairs at once and let her mistress in.

Magdalen's face was flushed. She showed far more agitation on returning to the house than she had shown on leaving it. "Keep your place at the table," she said to Louisa, impatiently; "but lay aside your work. I want you to attend carefully to what I am going to say."

Louisa obeyed. Magdalen seated herself at the opposite side of the table, and moved the candles, so as to obtain a clear and uninterrupted view of her servant's face.

"Have you noticed a respectable elderly woman," she began, abruptly, "who has been here once or twice in the last fortnight to pay me a visit?"

"Yes, ma'am; I think I let her in the second time she came. An elderly person named

Mrs. Attwood?"

"That is the person I mean. Mrs. Attwood is Mr. Loscombe's housekeeper; not the housekeeper at his private residence, but the housekeeper at his offices in Lincoln's Inn. I promised to go and drink tea with her some evening this week, and I have been to-night. It is strange of me, is it not, to be on these familiar terms with a woman in Mrs. Attwood's situation?"

Louisa made no answer in words. Her face spoke for her: she could hardly avoid thinking it strange.

"I had a motive for making friends with Mrs. Attwood," Magdalen went on. "She is a widow, with a large family of daughters. Her daughters are all in service. One of them is an under-housemaid in the service of Admiral Bartram, at St. Crux-in-the-Marsh. I found that out from Mrs. Attwood's master; and as soon as I arrived at the discovery, I privately determined to make Mrs. Attwood's acquaintance. Stranger still, is it not?"

Louisa began to look a little uneasy. Her mistress's manner was at variance with her mistress's words—it was plainly suggestive of something startling to come.

"What attraction Mrs. Attwood finds in my society," Magdalen continued, "I cannot presume to say. I can only tell you she has seen better days; she is an educated person; and she may like my society on that account. At any rate, she has readily met my advances toward her. What attraction I find in this good woman, on my side, is soon told. I have a great curiosity—an unaccountable curiosity, you will think—about the present course of household affairs at St. Crux-in-the-Marsh. Mrs. Attwood's daughter is a good girl, and constantly writes to her mother. Her mother is proud of the letters and proud of the girl, and is ready enough to talk about her daughter and her daughter's place. That is Mrs. Attwood's attraction to me. You understand, so far?"

Yes—Louisa understood. Magdalen went on. "Thanks to Mrs. Attwood and Mrs. Attwood's daughter," she said, "I know some curious particulars already of the household at St. Crux. Servants' tongues and servants' letters—as I need not tell you—are oftener occupied with their masters and mistresses than their masters and mistresses suppose. The only mistress at St. Crux is the housekeeper. But there is a master—Admiral Bartram. He appears to be a strange old man, whose whims and fancies amuse his servants as well as his friends. One of his fancies (the only one we need trouble ourselves to notice) is, that he had men enough about him when he was living at sea, and that now he is living on shore, he will be waited on by women-servants alone. The one man in the house is an old sailor, who has been all his life with his master—he is a kind of pensioner at St. Crux, and has little or nothing to do with the housework. The other servants, indoors, are all women; and instead of a footman to wait on him at dinner, the admiral has a parlor-maid. The parlor-maid now at St. Crux is engaged to be married, and as soon as her master can suit himself she is going away. These discoveries I made some days since. But when I saw Mrs. Attwood to-night, she had received another letter from her daughter in the interval, and that letter has helped me to find out something more. The housekeeper is at her wits' end to find a new servant. Her master insists on youth and good looks—he leaves everything else to the housekeeper—but he will have that. All the inquiries made in the neighborhood have failed to produce the sort of parlor-maid whom the admiral wants. If nothing can be done in the next fortnight or three weeks, the housekeeper will advertise in the Times, and will come to London herself to see the applicants, and to make strict personal inquiry into their characters."

Louisa looked at her mistress more attentively than ever. The expression of perplexity left her face, and a shade of disappointment appeared there in its stead. "Bear in mind what I have said," pursued Magdalen; "and wait a minute more, while I ask you some questions. Don't think you understand me yet—I can assure you, you don't understand me. Have you always lived in service as lady's maid?"

"No, ma'am."

"Have you ever lived as parlor-maid?"

"Only in one place, ma'am, and not for long there."

"I suppose you lived long enough to learn your duties?"

"Yes, ma'am."

"What were your duties besides waiting at table?"

"I had to show visitors in."

"Yes; and what else?"

"I had the plate and the glass to look after; and the table-linen was all under my care. I had to answer all the bells, except in the bedrooms. There were other little odds and ends sometimes to do—"

"But your regular duties were the duties you have just mentioned?"

"Yes, ma'am."

"How long ago is it since you lived in service as a parlor-maid?"

"A little better than two years, ma'am."

"I suppose you have not forgotten how to wait at table, and clean plate, and the rest of it, in that time?"

At this question Louisa's attention, which had been wandering more and more during the progress of Magdalen's inquiries, wandered away altogether. Her gathering anxieties got the better of her discretion, and even of her timidity. Instead of answering her mistress, she suddenly and confusedly ventured on a question of her own.

"I beg your pardon, ma'am," she said. "Did you mean me to offer for the parlor-maid's place at St. Crux?"

"You?" replied Magdalen. "Certainly not! Have you forgotten what I said to you in this room before I went out? I mean you to be married, and go to Australia with your husband and your child. You have not waited as I told you, to hear me explain myself. You have drawn your own conclusions, and you have drawn them wrong. I asked a question just now, which you have not answered—I asked if you had forgotten your parlor-maid's duties?"

"Oh, no, ma'am!" Louisa had replied rather unwillingly thus far. She answered readily and confidently now.

"Could you teach the duties to another servant?" asked Magdalen.

"Yes, ma'am—easily, if she was quick and attentive."

"Could you teach the duties to Me?"

Louisa started, and changed color. "You, ma'am!" she exclaimed, half in incredulity, half in alarm.

"Yes," said Magdalen. "Could you qualify me to take the parlor-maid's place at St. Crux?"

Plain as those words were, the bewilderment which they produced in Louisa's mind seemed to render her incapable of comprehending her mistress's proposal. "You, ma'am!" she repeated, vacantly.

"I shall perhaps help you to understand this extraordinary project of mine," said Magdalen, "if I tell you plainly what the object of it is. Do you remember what I said to you about Mr. Vanstone's will when you came here from Scotland to join me?"

"Yes, ma'am. You told me you had been left out of the will altogether. I'm sure my fellow-servant would never have been one of the witnesses if she had known—"

"Never mind that now. I don't blame your fellow-servant—I blame nobody but Mrs. Lecount. Let me go on with what I was saying. It is not at all certain that Mrs. Lecount can do me the mischief which Mrs. Lecount intended. There is a chance that my lawyer, Mr. Loscombe, may be able to gain me what is fairly my due, in spite of the will. The chance turns on my discovering a letter which Mr. Loscombe believes, and which I believe, to be kept privately in Admiral Bartram's possession. I have not the least hope of getting at that letter if I make the attempt in my own person. Mrs. Lecount has poisoned the admiral's mind against me, and Mr. Vanstone has given him a secret to keep from me. If I wrote to him, he would not answer my letter. If I went to his house, the door would be closed in my face. I must find my way into St. Crux as a stranger—I must be in a position to look about the house, unsuspected—I must be there with plenty of time on my hands. All the circumstances are in my favor, if I am received into the house as a servant; and as a servant I mean to go."

"But you are a lady, ma'am," objected Louisa, in the greatest perplexity. "The servants at St. Crux would find you out."

"I am not at all afraid of their finding me out," said Magdalen. "I know how to disguise myself in other people's characters more cleverly than you suppose. Leave me to face the chances of discovery—that is my risk. Let us talk of nothing now but what concerns you. Don't decide yet whether you will, or will not, give me the help I want. Wait, and hear first what the help is. You are quick and clever at your needle. Can you make me the sort of gown which it is proper for a servant to wear—and can you alter one of my best silk dresses so as to make it fit yourself —in a week's time?"

"I think I could get them done in a week, ma'am. But why am I to wear—"

"Wait a little, and you will see. I shall give the landlady her week's notice to-morrow. In the interval, while you are making the dresses, I can be learning the parlor-maid's duties. When the house-servant here has brought up the dinner, and when you and I are alone in the room—instead of your waiting on me, as usual, I will wait on you. (I am quite serious; don't interrupt me!) Whatever I can learn besides, without hindering you, I will practice carefully at every opportunity. When the week is over, and the dresses are done, we will leave this place, and go into other lodgings—you as the mistress and I as the maid."

"I should be found out, ma'am," interposed Louisa, trembling at the prospect before her.

"I am not a lady."

"And I am," said Magdalen, bitterly. "Shall I tell you what a lady is? A lady is a woman who wears a silk gown, and has a sense of her own importance. I shall put the gown on your back, and the sense in your head. You speak good English; you are naturally quiet and self-restrained; if you can only conquer your timidity, I have not the least fear of you. There will be time enough in the new lodging for you to practice your character, and for me to practice mine. There will be time enough to make some more dresses—another gown for me, and your wedding-dress (which I mean to give you) for yourself. I shall have the newspaper sent every day. When the advertisement appears, I shall answer it—in any name I can take on the spur of the moment; in your name, if you like to lend it to me; and when the housekeeper asks me for my character, I shall refer her to you. She will see you in the position of mistress, and me in the position of maid—no suspicion can possibly enter her mind, unless you put it there. If you only have the courage to follow my instructions, and to say what I shall tell you to say, the interview will be over in ten minutes."

"You frighten me, ma'am," said Louisa, still trembling. "You take my breath away with surprise. Courage! Where shall I find courage?"

"Where I keep it for you," said Magdalen—"in the passage-money to Australia. Look at the new prospect which gives you a husband, and restores you to your child—and you will find your courage there."

Louisa's sad face brightened; Louisa's faint heart beat quick. A spark of her mistress's spirit flew up into her eyes as she thought of the golden future.

"If you accept my proposal," pursued Magdalen, "you can be asked in church at once, if you like. I promise you the money on the day when the advertisement appears in the newspaper. The risk of the housekeeper's rejecting me is my risk—not yours. My good looks are sadly gone off, I know. But I think I can still hold my place against the other servants—I think I can still look the parlor-maid whom Admiral Bartram wants. There is nothing for you to fear in this matter; I should not have mentioned it if there had been. The only danger is the danger of my being discovered at St. Crux, and that falls entirely on me. By the time I am in the admiral's house you will be married, and the ship will be taking you to your new life."

Louisa's face, now brightening with hope, now clouding again with fear, showed plain signs of the struggle which it cost her to decide. She tried to gain time; she attempted confusedly to speak a few words of gratitude; but her mistress silenced her.

"You owe me no thanks," said Magdalen. "I tell you again, we are only helping each other. I have very little money, but it is enough for your purpose, and I give it you freely. I have led a wretched life; I have made others wretched about me. I can't even make you happy, except by tempting you to a new deceit. There! there! it's not your fault. Worse women than you are will help me, if you refuse. Decide as you like, but don't be afraid of taking the money. If I succeed, I shall not want it. If I fail—"

She stopped, rose abruptly from her chair, and hid her face from Louisa by walking away to the fire-place.

"If I fail," she resumed, warming her foot carelessly at the fender, "all the money in the world will be of no use to me. Never mind why—never mind Me—think of yourself. I won't take advantage of the confession you have made to me; I won't influence you against your will. Do as you yourself think best. But remember one thing—my mind is made up; nothing you can say or do will change it."

Her sudden removal from the table, the altered tones of her voice as she spoke the last words, appeared to renew Louisa's hesitation. She clasped her hands together in her lap, and wrung them hard. "This has come on me very suddenly, ma'am," said the girl. "I am sorely tempted to say Yes; and yet I am almost afraid—"

"Take the night to consider it," interposed Magdalen, keeping her face persistently turned toward the fire; "and tell me what you have decided to do, when you come into my room to-morrow morning. I shall want no help to-night—I can undress myself. You are not so strong as I am; you are tired, I dare say. Don't sit up on my account. Good-night, Louisa, and pleasant dreams!"

Her voice sank lower and lower as she spoke those kind words. She sighed heavily, and, leaning her arm on the mantel-piece, laid her head on it with a reckless weariness miserable to see. Louisa had not left the room, as she supposed—Louisa came softly to her side, and kissed her hand. Magdalen started; but she made no attempt, this time, to draw her hand away. The sense of her own horrible isolation subdued her, at the touch of the servant's lips. Her proud heart melted; her eyes filled with burning tears. "Don't distress me!" she said, faintly. "The time for kindness has gone by; it only overpowers me now. Good-night!"

When the morning came, the affirmative answer which Magdalen had anticipated was the answer given.

On that day the landlady received her week's notice to quit, and Louisa's needle flew fast through the stitches of the parlor-maid's dress.

THE END OF THE SIXTH SCENE.

BETWEEN THE SCENES.

PROGRESS OF THE STORY THROUGH THE POST.

I.

From Miss Garth to Mr. Pendril.

"Westmoreland House, January 3d, 1848.

"DEAR MR. PENDRIL—I write, as you kindly requested, to report how Norah is going on, and to tell you what changes I see for the better in the state of her mind on the subject of her sister.

"I cannot say that she is becoming resigned to Magdalen's continued silence—I know her faithful nature too well to say it. I can only tell you that she is beginning to find relief from the heavy pressure of sorrow and suspense in new thoughts and new hopes. I doubt if she has yet realized this in her own mind; but I see the result, although she is not conscious of it herself. I see her heart opening to the consolation of another interest and another love. She has not said a word to me on the subject, nor have I said a word to her. But as certainly as I know that Mr. George Bartram's visits have lately grown more and more frequent to the family at Portland Place—so certainly I can assure you that Norah is finding a relief under her suspense, which is not of my bringing, and a hope in the future, which I have not taught her to feel.

"It is needless for me to say that I tell you this in the strictest confidence. God knows whether the happy prospect which seems to me to be just dawning will grow brighter or not as time goes on. The oftener I see Mr. George Bartram—and he has called on me more than once—the stronger my liking for him grows. To my poor judgment he seems to be a gentleman in the highest and truest sense of the word. If I could live to see Norah his wife, I should almost feel that I had lived long enough. But who can discern the future? We have suffered so much that I am afraid to hope.

"Have you heard anything of Magdalen? I don't know why or how it is; but since I have known of her husband's death, my old tenderness for her seems to cling to me more obstinately than ever. Always yours truly,

"HARRIET GARTH."

II

From Mr. Pendril to Miss Garth.

"Serle Street, January 4th, 1848.

"DEAR MISS GARTH—Of Mrs. Noel Vanstone herself I have heard nothing. But I have learned, since I saw you, that the report of the position in which she is left by the death of her husband may be depended upon as the truth. No legacy of any kind is bequeathed to her. Her name is not once mentioned in her husband's will.

"Knowing what we know, it is not to be concealed that this circumstance threatens us with more embarrassment, and perhaps with more distress. Mrs. Noel Vanstone is not the woman to submit, without a desperate resistance, to the total overthrow of all her schemes and all her hopes. The mere fact that nothing whatever has been heard of her since her husband's death is suggestive to my mind of serious mischief to come. In her situation, and with her temper, the quieter she is now, the more inveterately I, for one, distrust her in the future. It is impossible to say to what violent measures her present extremity may not drive her. It is impossible to feel sure that she may not be the cause of some public scandal this time, which may affect her innocent sister as well as herself.

"I know you will not misinterpret the motive which has led me to write these lines; I know you will not think that I am inconsiderate enough to cause you unnecessary alarm. My sincere anxiety to see that happy prospect realized to which your letter alludes has caused me to write far less reservedly than I might otherwise have written. I strongly urge you to use your influence, on every occasion when you can fairly exert it, to strengthen that growing attachment, and to place it beyond the reach of any coming disasters, while you have the opportunity of doing so. When I tell you that the fortune of which Mrs. Noel Vanstone has been deprived is entirely bequeathed to Admiral Bartram; and when I add that Mr. George Bartram is generally understood to be his uncle's heir—you will, I think, acknowledge that I am not warning you without a cause. Yours most truly,

"WILLIAM PENDRIL."

III.

From Admiral Bartram to Mrs. Drake (housekeeper at St. Crux).

"St. Crux, January 10th, 1848.

"MRS. DRAKE—I have received your letter from London, stating that you have found me a new parlor-maid at last, and that the girl is ready to return with you to St. Crux when your other errands in town allow you to come back.

"This arrangement must be altered immediately, for a reason which I am heartily sorry to have to write.

"The illness of my niece, Mrs. Girdlestone—which appeared to be so slight as to alarm none of us, doctors included—has ended fatally. I received this morning the shocking news of her death. Her husband is said to be quite frantic with grief. Mr. George has already gone to his brother-in-law's, to superintend the last melancholy duties and I must follow him before the funeral takes place. We propose to take Mr. Girdlestone away afterward, and to try the effect on him of change of place and new scenes. Under these sad circumstances, I may be absent from St. Crux a month or six weeks at least; the house will be shut up, and the new servant will not be wanted until my return.

"You will therefore tell the girl, on receiving this letter, that a death in the family has caused a temporary change in our arrangements. If she is willing to wait, you may safely engage her to come here in six weeks' time; I shall be back then, if Mr. George is not. If she refuses, pay her what compensation is right, and so have done with her. Yours,

"ARTHUR BARTRAM."

IV.

From Mrs. Drake to Admiral Bartram.

"January 11th.

"HONORED SIR—I hope to get my errands done, and to return to St. Crux to-morrow, but write to save you anxiety, in case of delay.

"The young woman whom I have engaged (Louisa by name) is willing to wait your time; and her present mistress, taking an interest in her welfare, will provide for her during the interval. She understands that she is to enter on her new service in six weeks from the present date—namely, on the twenty-fifth of February next.

"Begging you will accept my respectful sympathy under the sad bereavement which has befallen the family,

"I remain, honored sir, your humble servant,

"SOPHIA DRAKE."

THE SEVENTH SCENE.

ST. CRUX-IN-THE-MARSH.

CHAPTER I.

"THIS is where you are to sleep. Put yourself tidy, and then come down again to my room. The admiral has returned, and you will have to begin by waiting on him at dinner to-day."

With those words, Mrs. Drake, the housekeeper, closed the door; and the new parlor-maid was left alone in her bed-chamber at St. Crux.

That day was the eventful twenty-fifth of February. In barely four months from the time when Mrs. Lecount had placed her master's private Instructions in his Executor's hands, the one combination of circumstances against which it had been her first and foremost object to provide was exactly the combination which had now taken place. Mr. Noel Vanstone's widow and Admiral Bartram's Secret Trust were together in the same house.

Thus far, events had declared themselves without an exception in Magdalen's favor. Thus far, the path which had led her to St. Crux had been a path without an obstacle: Louisa, whose name she had now taken, had sailed three days since for Australia, with her husband and her child; she was the only living creature whom Magdalen had trusted with her secret, and she was by this time out of sight of the English land. The girl had been careful, reliable and faithfully devoted to her mistress's interests to the last. She had passed the ordeal of her interview with the housekeeper, and had forgotten none of the instructions by which she had been prepared to meet it. She had herself proposed to turn the six weeks' delay, caused by the death in the admiral's family, to good account, by continuing the all-important practice of those domestic lessons, on the perfect acquirement of which her mistress's daring stratagem depended for its success. Thanks to the time thus gained, when Louisa's marriage was over, and the day of parting had come, Magdalen had learned and mastered, in the nicest detail, everything that her former servant could teach her. On the day when she passed the doors of St. Crux she entered on her desperate venture, strong in the ready presence of mind under emergencies which her later life had taught her, stronger still in the trained capacity that she possessed for the assumption of a character not her own, strongest of all in her two months' daily familiarity with the practical duties of the position which she had undertaken to fill.

As soon as Mrs. Drake's departure had left her alone, she unpacked her box, and dressed herself for the evening.

She put on a lavender-colored stuff-gown—half-mourning for Mrs. Girdlestone; ordered for all the servants, under the admiral's instructions—a white muslin apron, and a neat white cap and collar, with ribbons to match the gown. In this servant's costume—in the plain gown fastening high round her neck, in the neat little white cap at the back of her head—in this simple dress, to the eyes of all men, not linen-drapers, at once the most modest and the most alluring that a woman can wear, the sad changes which mental suffering had wrought in her beauty almost disappeared from view. In the evening costume of a lady, with her bosom uncovered, with her figure armed, rather than dressed, in unpliable silk, the admiral might have passed her by without notice in his own drawing-room. In the evening costume of a servant, no admirer of beauty could have looked at her once and not have turned again to look at her for the second time.

Descending the stairs, on her way to the house-keeper's room, she passed by the entrances to two long stone corridors, with rows of doors opening on them; one corridor situated on the second, and one on the first floor of the house. "Many rooms!" she thought, as she looked at the doors. "Weary work searching here for what I have come to find!"

On reaching the ground-floor she was met by a weather-beaten old man, who stopped and stared at her with an appearance of great interest. He was the same old man whom Captain Wragge had seen in the backyard at St. Crux, at work on the model of a ship. All round the neighborhood he was known, far and wide, as "the admiral's coxswain." His name was Mazey. Sixty years had written their story of hard work at sea, and hard drinking on shore, on the veteran's grim and wrinkled face. Sixty years had proved his fidelity, and had brought his battered old carcass, at the end of the voyage, into port in his master's house.

Seeing no one else of whom she could inquire, Magdalen requested the old man to show her the way that led to the housekeeper's room.

"I'll show you, my dear," said old Mazey, speaking in the high and hollow voice peculiar to the deaf. "You're the new maid—eh? And a fine-grown girl, too! His honor, the admiral, likes a parlor-maid with a clean run fore and aft. You'll do, my dear—you'll do."

"You must not mind what Mr. Mazey says to you," remarked the housekeeper, opening her door as the old sailor expressed his approval of Magdalen in these terms. "He is privileged to talk as he pleases; and he is very tiresome and slovenly in his habits; but he means no harm."

With that apology for the veteran, Mrs. Drake led Magdalen first to the pantry, and next to the linen-room, installing her, with all due formality, in her own domestic dominions. This ceremony completed, the new parlor-maid was taken upstairs, and was shown the dining-room, which opened out of the corridor on the first floor. Here she was directed to lay the cloth, and to prepare the table for one person only—Mr. George Bartram not having returned with his uncle to St. Crux. Mrs. Drake's sharp eyes watched Magdalen attentively as she performed this introductory duty; and Mrs. Drake's private convictions, when the table was spread, forced her to acknowledge, so far, that the new servant thoroughly understood her work.

An hour later the soup-tureen was placed on the table; and Magdalen stood alone behind the admiral's empty chair, waiting her master's first inspection of her when he entered the dining-room.

A large bell rang in the lower regions—quick, shambling footsteps pattered on the stone corridor outside—the door opened suddenly—and a tall lean yellow old man, sharp as to his eyes, shrewd as to his lips, fussily restless as to all his movements, entered the room, with two huge Labrador dogs at his heels, and took his seat in a violent hurry. The dogs followed him, and placed themselves, with the utmost gravity and composure, one on each side of his chair. This was Admiral Bartram, and these were the companions of his solitary meal.

"Ay! ay! ay! here's the new parlor-maid, to be sure!" he began, looking sharply, but not at all unkindly, at Magdalen. "What's your name, my good girl? Louisa, is it? I shall call you Lucy, if you don't mind. Take off the cover, my dear—I'm a minute or two late to-day. Don't be unpunctual to-morrow on that account; I am as regular as clock-work generally. How are you after your journey? Did my spring-cart bump you about much in bringing you from the station? Capital soup this—hot as fire—reminds me of the soup we used to have in the West Indies in the year Three. Have you got your half-mourning on? Stand there, and let me see. Ah, yes, very neat, and nice, and tidy. Poor Mrs. Girdlestone! Oh dear, dear, dear, poor Mrs. Girdlestone! You're not afraid of dogs, are you, Lucy? Eh? What? You like dogs? That's right! Always be kind to dumb animals. These two dogs dine with me every day, except when there's company. The dog with the black nose is Brutus, and the dog with the white nose is Cassius. Did you ever hear who Brutus and Cassius were? Ancient Romans? That's right—-good girl. Mind your book and your needle, and we'll get you a good husband one of these days. Take away the soup, my dear, take away the soup!"

This was the man whose secret it was now the one interest of Magdalen's life to surprise! This was the man whose name had supplanted hers in Noel Vanstone's will!

The fish and the roast meat followed; and the admiral's talk rambled on—now in soliloquy, now addressed to the parlor-maid, and now directed to the dogs—as familiarly and as discontentedly as ever. Magdalen observed with some surprise that the companions of the admiral's dinner had, thus far, received no scraps from their master's plate. The two magnificent brutes sat squatted on their haunches, with their great heads over the table, watching the progress of the meal, with the profoundest attention, but apparently expecting no share in it. The roast meat was removed, the admiral's plate was changed, and Magdalen took the silver covers off the two made-dishes on either side of the table. As she handed the first of the savory dishes to her master, the dogs suddenly exhibited a breathless personal interest in the proceedings. Brutus gluttonously watered at the mouth; and the tongue of Cassius, protruding in unutterable expectation, smoked again between his enormous jaws.

The admiral helped himself liberally from the dish; sent Magdalen to the side-table to get him some bread; and, when he thought her eye was off him, furtively tumbled the whole contents of his plate into Brutus's mouth. Cassius whined faintly as his fortunate comrade swallowed the savory mess at a gulp. "Hush! you fool," whispered the admiral. "Your turn next!"

Magdalen presented the second dish. Once more the old gentleman helped himself largely—once more he sent her away to the side-table—once more he tumbled the entire contents of the plate down the dog's throat, selecting Cassius this time, as became a considerate master and an impartial man. When the next course followed—consisting of a plain pudding and an unwholesome "cream"—Magdalen's suspicion of the function of the dogs at the dinner-table was confirmed. While the master took the simple pudding, the dogs swallowed the elaborate cream. The admiral was plainly afraid of offending his cook on the one hand, and of offending his digestion on the other—and Brutus and Cassius were the two trained accomplices who regularly helped him every day off the horns of his dilemma. "Very good! very good!" said the old gentleman, with the most transparent duplicity. "Tell the cook, my dear, a capital cream!"

Having placed the wine and dessert on the table, Magdalen was about to withdraw. Before she could leave the room, her master called her back.

"Stop, stop!" said the admiral; "you don't know the ways of the house yet, Lucy. Put another wine-glass here, at my right hand—the largest you can find, my dear. I've got a third dog, who comes in at dessert—a drunken old sea-dog who has followed my fortunes, afloat and ashore, for fifty years and more. Yes, yes, that's the sort of glass we want. You're a good girl—you're a neat, handy girl. Steady, my dear! there's nothing to be frightened at!"

A sudden thump on the outside of the door, followed by one mighty bark from each of the dogs, had made Magdalen start. "Come in!" shouted the admiral. The door opened; the tails of Brutus and Cassius cheerfully thumped the floor; and old Mazey marched straight up to the right-hand side of his master's chair. The veteran stood there, with his legs wide apart and his balance carefully adjusted, as if the dining-room had been a cabin, and the house a ship pitching in a sea-way.

The admiral filled the large glass with port, filled his own glass with claret, and raised it to his lips.

"God bless the Queen, Mazey," said the admiral.

"God bless the Queen, your honor," said old Mazey, swallowing his port, as the dogs swallowed the made-dishes, at a gulp.

"How's the wind, Mazey?"

"West and by Noathe, your honor."

"Any report to-night, Mazey!"

"No report, your honor."

"Good-evening, Mazey."

"Good-evening, your honor."

The after-dinner ceremony thus completed, old Mazey made his bow, and walked out of the room again. Brutus and Cassius stretched themselves on the rug to digest mushrooms and made gravies in the lubricating heat of the fire. "For what we have received, the Lord make us truly thankful," said the admiral. "Go downstairs, my good girl, and get your supper. A light meal, Lucy, if you take my advice—a light meal, or you will have the nightmare. Early to bed, my dear, and early to rise, makes a parlor-maid healthy and wealthy and wise. That's the wisdom of your ancestors—you mustn't laugh at it. Good-night." In those words Magdalen was dismissed; and so her first day's experience of Admiral Bartram came to an end.

After breakfast the next morning, the admiral's directions to the new parlor-maid included among them one particular order which, in Magdalen's situation, it was especially her interest to receive. In the old gentleman's absence from home that day, on local business which took him to Ossory, she was directed to make herself acquainted with the whole inhabited quarter of the house, and to learn the positions of the various rooms, so as to know where the bells called her when the bells rang. Mrs. Drake was charged with the duty of superintending the voyage of domestic discovery, unless she happened to be otherwise engaged—in which case any one of the inferior servants would be equally competent to act as Magdalen's guide.

At noon the admiral left for Ossory, and Magdalen presented herself in Mrs. Drake's room, to be shown over the house. Mrs. Drake happened to be otherwise engaged, and referred her to the head house-maid. The head house-maid happened on that particular morning to be in the same condition as Mrs. Drake, and referred her to the under-house-maids. The under-house-maids declared they were all behindhand and had not a minute to spare—they suggested, not too civilly, that old Mazey had nothing on earth to do, and that he knew the house as well, or better, than he knew his A B C. Magdalen took the hint, with a secret indignation and contempt which it cost her a hard struggle to conceal. She had suspected, on the previous night, and she was certain now, that the women-servants all incomprehensibly resented her presence among them with the same sullen unanimity of distrust. Mrs. Drake, as she had seen for herself, was really engaged that morning over her accounts. But of all the servants under her who had made their excuses not one had even affected to be more occupied than usual. Their looks said plainly, "We don't like you; and we won't show you over the house."

She found her way to old Mazey, not by the scanty directions given her, but by the sound of the veteran's cracked and quavering voice, singing in some distant seclusion a verse of the immortal sea-song—"Tom Bowling." Just as she stopped among the rambling stone passages on the basement story of the house, uncertain which way to turn next, she heard the tuneless old voice in the distance, singing these lines:

"His form was of the manliest beau-u-u-uty,

His heart was ki-i-ind and soft;

Faithful below Tom did his duty,

But now he's gone alo-o-o-o-oft

—But now he's go-o-o-one aloft!"

Magdalen followed in the direction of the quavering voice, and found herself in a little room looking out on the back yard. There sat old Mazey, with his spectacles low on his nose, and his knotty old hands blundering over the rigging of his model ship. There were Brutus and Cassius digesting before the fire again, and snoring as if they thoroughly enjoyed it. There was Lord Nelson on one wall, in flaming watercolors; and there, on the other, was a portrait of Admiral Bartram's last flagship, in full sail on a sea of slate, with a salmon-colored sky to complete the illusion.

"What, they won't show you over the house—won't they?" said old Mazey. "I will, then! That head house-maid's a sour one, my dear—if ever there was a sour one yet. You're too young and good-looking to please 'em—that's what you are." He rose, took off his spectacles, and feebly mended the fire. "She's as straight as a poplar," said old Mazey, considering Magdalen's figure in drowsy soliloquy. "I say she's as straight as a poplar, and his honor the admiral says so too! Come along, my dear," he proceeded, addressing himself to Magdalen again. "I'll teach you your Pints of the Compass first. When you know your Pints, blow high, blow low, you'll find it plain sailing all over the house."

He led the way to the door—stopped, and suddenly bethinking himself of his miniature ship, went back to put his model away in an empty cupboard—led the way to the door again—stopped once more—remembered that some of the rooms were chilly—and pottered about, swearing and grumbling, and looking for his hat. Magdalen sat down patiently to wait for him. She gratefully contrasted his treatment of her with the treatment she had received from the women. Resist it as firmly, despise it as proudly as we may, all studied unkindness—no matter how contemptible it may be—has a stinging power in it which reaches to the quick. Magdalen only knew how she had felt the small malice of the female servants, by the effect which the rough kindness of the old sailor produced on her afterward. The dumb welcome of the dogs, when the movements in the room had roused them from their sleep, touched her more acutely still. Brutus pushed his mighty muzzle companionably into her hand; and Cassius laid his friendly fore-paw on her lap. Her heart yearned over the two creatures as she patted and caressed them. It seemed only yesterday since she and the dogs at Combe-Raven had roamed the garden together, and had idled away the summer mornings luxuriously on the shady lawn.

Old Mazey found his hat at last, and they started on their exploring expedition, with the dogs after them.

Leaving the basement story of the house, which was entirely devoted to the servants' offices, they ascended to the first floor, and entered the long corridor, with which Magdalen's last night's experience had already made her acquainted. "Put your back ag'in this wall," said old Mazey, pointing to the long wall—pierced at irregular intervals with windows looking out over a courtyard and fish-pond—which formed the right-hand side of the corridor, as Magdalen now stood. "Put your back here," said the veteran, "and look straight afore you. What do you see?"—"The opposite wall of the passage," said Magdalen.—"Ay! ay! what else?"—"The doors leading into the rooms."—"What else?"—"I see nothing else." Old Mazey chuckled, winked, and shook his knotty forefinger at Magdalen, impressively. "You see one of the Pints of the Compass, my dear. When you've got your back ag'in this wall, and when you look straight afore you, you look Noathe. If you ever get lost hereaway, put your back ag'in the wall, look out straight afore you, and say to yourself: 'I look Noathe!' You do that like a good girl, and you won't lose your bearings."

After administering this preliminary dose of instruction, old Mazey opened the first of the doors on the left-hand side of the passage. It led into the dining-room, with which Magdalen was already familiar. The second room was fitted up as a library; and the third, as a morning-room. The fourth and fifth doors—both belonging to dismantled and uninhabited rooms, and both locked-brought them to the end of the north wing of the house, and to the opening of a second and shorter passage, placed at a right angle to the first. Here old Mazey, who had divided his time pretty equally during the investigation of the rooms, in talking of "his honor the Admiral," and whistling to the dogs, returned with all possible expedition to the points of the compass, and gravely directed Magdalen to repeat the ceremony of putting her back against the wall. She attempted to shorten the proceedings, by declaring (quite correctly) that in her present position she knew she was looking east. "Don't you talk about the east, my dear," said old Mazey, proceeding unmoved with his own system of instruction, "till you know the east first. Put your back ag'in this wall, and look straight afore you. What do you see?" The remainder of the catechism proceeded as before. When the end was reached, Magdalen's instructor was satisfied. He chuckled and winked at her once more. "Now you may talk about the east, my dear," said the veteran, "for now you know it."

The east passage, after leading them on for a few yards only, terminated in a vestibule, with a high door in it which faced them as they advanced. The door admitted them to a large and lofty drawing-room, decorated, like all the other apartments, with valuable old-fashioned furniture. Leading the way across this room, Magdalen's conductor pushed back a heavy sliding-door, opposite the door of entrance. "Put your apron over your head," said old Mazey. "We are coming to the Banqueting-Hall now. The floor's mortal cold, and the damp sticks to the place like cockroaches to a collier. His honor the admiral calls it the Arctic Passage. I've got my name for it, too—I call it, Freeze-your-Bones."

Magdalen passed through the doorway, and found herself in the ancient Banqueting-Hall of St. Crux.

On her left hand she saw a row of lofty windows, set deep in embrasures, and extending over a frontage of more than a hundred feet in length. On her right hand, ranged in one long row from end to end of the opposite wall, hung a dismal collection of black, begrimed old pictures, rotting from their frames, and representing battle-scenes by sea and land. Below the pictures, midway down the length of the wall, yawned a huge cavern of a fireplace, surmounted by a towering mantel-piece of black marble. The one object of furniture (if furniture it might be called) visible far or near in the vast emptiness of the place, was a gaunt ancient tripod of curiously chased metal, standing lonely in the middle of the hall, and supporting a wide circular pan, filled deep with ashes from an extinct charcoal fire. The high ceiling, once finely carved and gilt, was foul with dirt and cobwebs; the naked walls at either end of the room were stained with damp; and the cold of the marble floor struck through the narrow strip of matting laid down, parallel with the windows, as a foot-path for passengers across the wilderness of the room. No better name for it could have been devised than the name which old Mazey had found. "Freeze-your-Bones" accurately described, in three words, the Banqueting-Hall at St. Crux.

"Do you never light a fire in this dismal place?" asked Magdalen.

"It all depends on which side of Freeze-your-Bones his honor the admiral lives," said old Mazey. "His honor likes to shift his quarters, sometimes to one side of the house, sometimes to the other. If he lives Noathe of Freeze-your-Bones—which is where you've just come from—we don't waste our coals here. If he lives South of Freeze-your-Bones—which is where we are going to next—we light the fire in the grate and the charcoal in the pan. Every night, when we do that, the damp gets the better of us: every morning, we turn to again, and get the better of the damp."

With this remarkable explanation, old Mazey led the way to the lower end of the Hall, opened more doors, and showed Magdalen through another suite of rooms, four in number, all of moderate size, and all furnished in much the same manner as the rooms in the northern wing. She looked out of the windows, and saw the neglected gardens of St. Crux, overgrown with brambles and weeds. Here and there, at no great distance in the grounds, the smoothly curving line of one of the tidal streams peculiar to the locality wound its way, gleaming in the sunlight, through gaps in the brambles and trees. The more distant view ranged over the flat eastward country beyond, speckled with its scattered little villages; crossed and recrossed by its network of "back-waters"; and terminated abruptly by the long straight line of sea-wall which protects the defenseless coast of Essex from invasion by the sea.

"Have we more rooms still to see?" asked Magdalen, turning from the view of the garden, and looking about her for another door.

"No more, my dear—we've run aground here, and we may as well wear round and put back again," said old Mazey. "There's another side of the house—due south of you as you stand now—which is all tumbling about our ears. You must go out into the garden if you want to see it; it's built off from us by a brick bulkhead, t'other side of this wall here. The monks lived due south of us, my dear, hundreds of years afore his honor the admiral was born or thought of, and a fine time of it they had, as I've heard. They sang in the church all the morning, and drank grog in the orchard all the afternoon. They slept off their grog on the best of feather-beds, and they fattened on the neighborhood all the year round. Lucky beggars! lucky beggars!"

Apostrophizing the monks in these terms, and evidently regretting that he had not lived himself in those good old times, the veteran led the way back through the rooms. On the return passage across "Freeze-your-Bones," Magdalen preceded him. "She's as straight as a poplar," mumbled old Mazey to himself, hobbling along after his youthful companion, and wagging his venerable head in cordial approval. "I never was particular what nation they belonged to; but I always did like 'em straight and fine grown, and I always shall like 'em straight and fine grown, to my dying day."

"Are there more rooms to see upstairs, on the second floor?" asked Magdalen, when they had returned to the point from which they had started.

The naturally clear, distinct tones of her voice had hitherto reached the old sailor's imperfect sense of hearing easily enough. Rather to her surprise, he became stone deaf on a sudden, to her last question.

"Are you sure of your Pints of the Compass?" he inquired. "If you're not sure, put your back ag'in the wall, and we'll go all over 'em again, my dear, beginning with the Noathe."

Magdalen assured him that she felt quite familiar, by this time, with all the points, the "Noathe" included; and then repeated her question in louder tones. The veteran obstinately matched her by becoming deafer than ever.

"Yes, my dear," he said, "you're right; it is chilly in these passages; and unless I go back to my fire, my fire'll go out—won't it? If you don't feel sure of your Pints of the Compass, come in to me and I'll put you right again." He winked benevolently, whistled to the dogs, and hobbled off. Magdalen heard him chuckle over his own success in balking her curiosity on the subject of the second floor. "I know how to deal with 'em!" said old Mazey to himself, in high triumph. "Tall and short, native and foreign, sweethearts and wives—I know how to deal with 'em!"

Left by herself, Magdalen exemplified the excellence of the old sailor's method of treatment, in her particular case, by ascending the stairs immediately, to make her own observations on the second floor. The stone passage here was exactly similar, except that more doors opened out of it, to the passage on the first floor. She opened the two nearest doors, one after another, at a venture, and discovered that both rooms were bed-chambers. The fear of being discovered by one of the woman-servants in a part of the house with which she had no concern, warned her not to push her investigations on the bedroom floor too far at starting. She hurriedly walked down the passage to see where it ended, discovered that it came to its termination in a lumber-room, answering to the position of the vestibule downstairs, and retraced her steps immediately.

On her way back she noticed an object which had previously escaped her attention. It was a low truckle-bed, placed parallel with the wall, and close to one of the doors on the bedroom side. In spite of its strange and comfortless situation, the bed was apparently occupied at night by a sleeper; the sheets were on it, and the end of a thick red fisherman's cap peeped out from under the pillow. She ventured on opening the door near which the bed was placed, and found herself, as she conjectured from certain signs and tokens, in the admiral's sleeping chamber. A moment's observation of the room was all she dared risk, and, softly closing the door again, she returned to the kitchen regions.

The truckle-bed, and the strange position in which it was placed, dwelt on her mind all through the afternoon. Who could possibly sleep in it? The remembrance of the red fisherman's cap, and the knowledge she had already gained of Mazey's dog-like fidelity to his master, helped her to guess that the old sailor might be the occupant of the truckle-bed. But why, with bedrooms enough and to spare, should he occupy that cold and comfortless situation at night? Why should he sleep on guard outside his master's door? Was there some nocturnal danger in the house of which the admiral was afraid? The question seemed absurd, and yet the position of the bed forced it irresistibly on her mind.

Stimulated by her own ungovernable curiosity on this subject, Magdalen ventured to question the housekeeper. She acknowledged having walked from end to end of the passage on the second floor, to see if it was as long as the passage on the first; and she mentioned having noticed with astonishment the position of the truckle-bed. Mrs. Drake answered her implied inquiry shortly and sharply. "I don't blame a young girl like you," said the old lady, "for being a little curious when she first comes into such a strange house as this. But remember, for the future, that your business does not lie on the bedroom story. Mr. Mazey sleeps on that bed you noticed. It is his habit at night to sleep outside his master's door." With that meager explanation Mrs. Drake's lips closed, and opened no more.

Later in the day Magdalen found an opportunity of applying to old Mazey himself. She discovered the veteran in high good humor, smoking his pipe, and warming a tin mug of ale at his own snug fire:

"Mr. Mazey," she asked, boldly, "why do you put your bed in that cold passage?"

"What! you have been upstairs, you young jade, have you?" said old Mazey, looking up from his mug with a leer.

Magdalen smiled and nodded. "Come! come! tell me," she said, coaxingly. "Why do you sleep outside the admiral's door?"

"Why do you part your hair in the middle, my dear?" asked old Mazey, with another leer.

"I suppose, because I am accustomed to do it," answered Magdalen.

"Ay! ay!" said the veteran. "That's why, is it? Well, my dear, the reason why you part your hair in the middle is the reason why I sleep outside the admiral's door. I know how to deal with 'em!" chuckled old Mazey, lapsing into soliloquy, and stirring up his ale in high triumph. "Tall and short, native and foreign, sweethearts and wives—I know how to deal with 'em!"

Magdalen's third and last attempt at solving the mystery of the truckle-bed was made while she was waiting on the admiral at dinner. The old gentleman's questions gave her an opportunity of referring to the subject, without any appearance of presumption or disrespect; but he proved to be quite as impenetrable, in his way, as old Mazey and Mrs. Drake had been in theirs. "It doesn't concern you, my dear," said the admiral, bluntly. "Don't be curious. Look in your Old Testament when you go downstairs, and see what happened in the Garden of Eden through curiosity. Be a good girl, and don't imitate your mother Eve."

Late at night, as Magdalen passed the end of the second-floor passage, proceeding alone on her way up to her own room, she stopped and listened. A screen was placed at the entrance of the corridor, so as to hide it from the view of persons passing on the stairs. The snoring she heard on the other side of the screen encouraged her to slip round it, and to advance a few steps. Shading the light of her candle with her hand, she ventured close to the admiral's door, and saw, to her surprise, that the bed had been moved since she had seen it in the day-time, so as to stand exactly across the door, and to bar the way entirely to any one who might attempt to enter the admiral's room. After this discovery, old Mazey himself, snoring lustily, with the red fisherman's cap pulled down to his eyebrows, and the blankets drawn up to his nose, became an object of secondary importance only, by comparison with his bed. That the veteran did actually sleep on guard before his master's door, and that he and the admiral and the housekeeper were in the secret of this unaccountable proceeding, was now beyond all doubt.

"A strange end," thought Magdalen, pondering over her discovery as she stole upstairs to her own sleeping-room—"a strange end to a strange day!"

CHAPTER II.

THE first week passed, the second week passed, and Magdalen was, to all appearance, no nearer to the discovery of the Secret Trust than on the day when she first entered on her service at St. Crux.

But the fortnight, uneventful as it was, had not been a fortnight lost. Experience had already satisfied her on one important point—experience had shown that she could set the rooted distrust of the other servants safely at defiance. Time had accustomed the women to her presence in the house, without shaking the vague conviction which possessed them all alike, that the newcomer was not one of themselves. All that Magdalen could do in her own defense was to keep the instinctive female suspicion of her confined within those purely negative limits which it had occupied from the first, and this she accomplished.

Day after day the women watched her with the untiring vigilance of malice and distrust, and day after day not the vestige of a discovery rewarded them for their pains. Silently, intelligently, and industriously—with an ever-present remembrance of herself and her place—the new parlor-maid did her work. Her only intervals of rest and relaxation were the intervals passed occasionally in the day with old Mazey and the dogs, and the precious interval of the night during which she was secure from observation in the solitude of her room. Thanks to the superfluity of bed-chambers at St. Crux, each one of the servants had the choice, if she pleased, of sleeping in a room of her own. Alone in the night, Magdalen might dare to be herself again—might dream of the past, and wake from the dream, encountering no curious eyes to notice that she was in tears—might ponder over the future, and be roused by no whisperings in corners, which tainted her with the suspicion of "having something on her mind."

Satisfied, thus far, of the perfect security of her position in the house, she profited next by a second chance in her favor, which—before the fortnight was at an end—relieved her mind of all doubt on the formidable subject of Mrs. Lecount.

Partly from the accidental gossip of the women at the table in the servants' hall; partly from a marked paragraph in a Swiss newspaper, which she had found one morning lying open on the admiral's easy-chair—she gained the welcome assurance that no danger was to be dreaded, this time, from the housekeeper's presence on the scene. Mrs. Lecount had, as it appeared, passed a week or more at St. Crux after the date of her master's death, and had then left England, to live on the interest of her legacy, in honorable and prosperous retirement, in her native place. The paragraph in the Swiss newspaper described the fulfillment of this laudable project. Mrs. Lecount had not only established herself at Zurich, but (wisely mindful of the uncertainty of life) had also settled the charitable uses to which her fortune was to be applied after her death. One half of it was to go to the founding of a "Lecompte Scholarship" for poor students in the University of Geneva. The other half was to be employed by the municipal authorities of Zurich in the maintenance and education of a certain number of orphan girls, natives of the city, who were to be trained for domestic service in later life. The Swiss journalist adverted to these philanthropic bequests in terms of extravagant eulogy. Zurich was congratulated on the possession of a Paragon of public virtue; and William Tell, in the character of benefactor to Switzerland, was compared disadvantageously with Mrs. Lecount.

The third week began, and Magdalen was now at liberty to take her first step forward on the way to the discovery of the Secret Trust.

She ascertained from old Mazey that it was his master's custom, during the winter and spring months, to occupy the rooms in the north wing; and during the summer and autumn to cross the Arctic passage of "Freeze-your-Bones," and live in the eastward apartments which looked out on the garden. While the Banqueting-Hall remained—owing to the admiral's inadequate pecuniary resources—in its damp and dismantled state, and while the interior of St. Crux was thus comfortlessly divided into two separate residences, no more convenient arrangement than this could well have been devised. Now and then (as Magdalen understood from her informant) there were days, both in winter and summer, when the admiral became anxious about the condition of the rooms which he was not occupying at the time, and when he insisted on investigating the state of the furniture, the pictures, and the books with his own eyes. On these occasions, in summer as in winter, a blazing fire was kindled for some days previously in the large grate, and the charcoal was lighted in the tripod-pan, to keep the Banqueting-Hall as warm as circumstances would admit. As soon as the old gentleman's anxieties were set at rest the rooms were shut up again, and "Freeze-your-Bones" was once more abandoned for weeks and weeks together to damp, desolation, and decay. The last of these temporary migrations had taken place only a few days since; the admiral had satisfied himself that the rooms in the east wing were none the worse for the absence of their master, and he might now be safely reckoned on as settled in the north wing for weeks, and perhaps, if the season was cold, for months to come.

Trifling as they might be in themselves, these particulars were of serious importance to Magdalen, for they helped her to fix the limits of the field of search. Assuming that the admiral was likely to keep all his important documents within easy reach of his own hand, she might now feel certain that the Secret Trust was secured in one or other of the rooms in the north wing.

In which room? That question was not easy to answer.

Of the four inhabitable rooms which were all at the admiral's disposal during the day—that is to say, of the dining-room, the library, the morning-room, and the drawing-room opening out of the vestibule—the library appeared to be the apartment in which, if he had a preference, he passed the greater part of his time. There was a table in this room, with drawers that locked; there was a magnificent Italian cabinet, with doors that locked; there were five cupboards under the book-cases, every one of which locked. There were receptacles similarly secured in the other rooms; and in all or any of these papers might be kept.

She had answered the bell, and had seen him locking and unlocking, now in one room, now in another, but oftenest in the library. She had noticed occasionally that his expression was fretful and impatient when he looked round at her from an open cabinet or cupboard and gave his orders; and she inferred that something in connection with his papers and possessions—it might or might not be the Secret Trust—irritated and annoyed him from time to time. She had heard him more than once lock something up in one of the rooms, come out and go into another room, wait there a few minutes, then return to the first room with his keys in his hand, and sharply turn the locks and turn them again. This fidgety anxiety about his keys and his cupboards might be the result of the inbred restlessness of his disposition, aggravated in a naturally active man by the aimless indolence of a life in retirement—a life drifting backward and forward among trifles, with no regular employment to steady it at any given hour of the day. On the other hand, it was just as probable that these comings and goings, these lockings and unlockings, might be attributable to the existence of some private responsibility which had unexpectedly intruded itself into the old man's easy existence, and which tormented him with a sense of oppression new to the experience of his later years. Either one of these interpretations might explain his conduct as reasonably and as probably as the other. Which was the right interpretation of the two, it was, in Magdalen's position, impossible to say.

The one certain discovery at which she arrived was made in her first day's observation of him. The admiral was a rigidly careful man with his keys.

All the smaller keys he kept on a ring in the breast-pocket of his coat. The larger he locked up together; generally, but not always, in one of the drawers of the library table. Sometimes he left them secured in this way at night; sometimes he took them up to the bedroom with him in a little basket. He had no regular times for leaving them or for taking them away with him; he had no discoverable reason for now securing them in the library-table drawer, and now again locking them up in some other place. The inveterate willfulness and caprice of his proceedings in these particulars defied every effort to reduce them to a system, and baffled all attempts at calculating on them beforehand.

The hope of gaining positive information to act on, by laying artful snares for him which he might fall into in his talk, proved, from the outset, to be utterly futile.

In Magdalen's situation all experiments of this sort would have been in the last degree difficult and dangerous with any man. With the admiral they were simply impossible. His tendency to veer about from one subject to another; his habit of keeping his tongue perpetually going, so long as there was anybody, no matter whom, within reach of the sound of his voice; his comical want of all dignity and reserve with his servants, promised, in appearance, much, and performed in reality nothing. No matter how diffidently or how respectfully Magdalen might presume on her master's example, and on her master's evident liking for her, the old man instantly discovered the advance she was making from her proper position, and instantly put her back in it again, with a quaint good humor which inflicted no pain, but with a blunt straightforwardness of purpose which permitted no escape. Contradictory as it may sound, Admiral Bartram was too familiar to be approached; he kept the distance between himself and his servant more effectually than if he had been the proudest man in England. The systematic reserve of a superior toward an inferior may be occasionally overcome—the systematic familiarity never.

Slowly the time dragged on. The fourth week came; and Magdalen had made no new discoveries. The prospect was depressing in the last degree. Even in the apparently hopeless event of her devising a means of getting at the admiral's keys, she could not count on retaining possession of them unsuspected more than a few hours—hours which might be utterly wasted through her not knowing in what direction to begin the search. The Trust might be locked up in any one of some twenty receptacles for papers, situated in four different rooms; and which room was the likeliest to look in, which receptacle was the most promising to begin with, which position among other heaps of papers the one paper needful might be expected to occupy, was more than she could say. Hemmed in by immeasurable uncertainties on every side; condemned, as it were, to wander blindfold on the very brink of success, she waited for the chance that never came, for the event that never happened, with a patience which was sinking already into the patience of despair.

Night after night she looked back over the vanished days, and not an event rose on her memory to distinguish them one from the other. The only interruptions to the weary uniformity of the life at St. Crux were caused by the characteristic delinquencies of old Mazey and the dogs.

At certain intervals, the original wildness broke out in the natures of Brutus and Cassius. The modest comforts of home, the savory charms of made dishes, the decorous joy of digestions accomplished on hearth-rugs, lost all their attractions, and the dogs ungratefully left the house to seek dissipation and adventure in the outer world. On these occasions the established after-dinner formula of question and answer between old Mazey and his master varied a little in one particular. "God bless the Queen, Mazey," and "How's the wind, Mazey?" were followed by a new inquiry: "Where are the dogs, Mazey?" "Out on the loose, your honor, and be damned to 'em," was the veteran's unvarying answer. The admiral always sighed and shook his head gravely at the news, as if Brutus and Cassius had been sons of his own, who treated him with a want of proper filial respect. In two or three days' time the dogs always returned, lean, dirty, and heartily ashamed of themselves. For the whole of the next day they were invariably tied up in disgrace. On the day after they were scrubbed clean, and were formally re-admitted to the dining-room. There, Civilization, acting through the subtle medium of the Saucepan, recovered its hold on them; and the admiral's two prodigal sons, when they saw the covers removed, watered at the mouth as copiously as ever.

Old Mazey, in his way, proved to be just as disreputably inclined on certain occasions as the dogs. At intervals, the original wildness in his nature broke out; he, too, lost all relish for the comforts of home, and ungratefully left the house. He usually disappeared in the afternoon, and returned at night as drunk as liquor could make him. He was by many degrees too seasoned a vessel to meet with any disasters on these occasions. His wicked old legs might take roundabout methods of progression, but they never failed him; his wicked old eyes might see double, but they always showed him the way home. Try as hard as they might, the servants could never succeed in persuading him that he was drunk; he always scorned the imputation. He even declined to admit the idea privately into his mind, until he had first tested his condition by an infallible criterion of his own.

It was his habit, in these cases of Bacchanalian emergency, to stagger obstinately into his room on the ground-floor, to take the model-ship out of the cupboard, and to try if he could proceed with the never-to-be-completed employment of setting up the rigging. When he had smashed the tiny spars, and snapped asunder the delicate ropes—then, and not till then, the veteran admitted facts as they were, on the authority of practical evidence. "Ay! ay!" he used to say confidentially to himself, "the women are right. Drunk again, Mazey—drunk again!" Having reached this discovery, it was his habit to wait cunningly in the lower regions until the admiral was safe in his room, and then to ascend in discreet list slippers to his post. Too wary to attempt getting into the truckle-bed (which would have been only inviting the catastrophe of a fall against his master's door), he always walked himself sober up and down the passage. More than once Magdalen had peeped round the screen, and had seen the old sailor unsteadily keeping his watch, and fancying himself once more at his duty on board ship. "This is an uncommonly lively vessel in a sea-way," he used to mutter under his breath, when his legs took him down the passage in zigzag directions, or left him for the moment studying the "Pints of the Compass" on his own system, with his back against the wall. "A nasty night, mind you," he would maunder on, taking another turn. "As dark as your pocket, and the wind heading us again from the old quarter." On the next day old Mazey, like the dogs, was kept downstairs in disgrace. On the day after, like the dogs again, he was reinstated in his privileges; and another change was introduced in the after-dinner formula. On entering the room, the old sailor stopped short and made his excuses in this brief yet comprehensive form of words, with his back against the door: "Please your honor, I'm ashamed of myself." So the apology began and ended. "This mustn't happen again, Mazey," the admiral used to answer. "It shan't happen again, your honor." "Very good. Come here, and drink your glass of wine. God bless the Queen, Mazey." The veteran tossed off his port, and the dialogue ended as usual.

So the days passed, with no incidents more important than these to relieve their monotony, until the end of the fourth week was at hand.

On the last day, an event happened; on the last day, the long deferred promise of the future unexpectedly began to dawn. While Magdalen was spreading the cloth in the dining-room, as usual, Mrs. Drake looked in, and instructed her on this occasion, for the first time, to lay the table for two persons. The admiral had received a letter from his nephew. Early that evening Mr. George Bartram was expected to return to St. Crux.

CHAPTER III.

AFTER placing the second cover, Magdalen awaited the ringing of the dinner-bell, with an interest and impatience which she found it no easy task to conceal. The return of Mr. Bartram would, in all probability, produce a change in the life of the house; and from change of any kind, no matter how trifling, something might be hoped. The nephew might be accessible to influences which had failed to reach the uncle. In any case, the two would talk of their affairs over their dinner; and through that talk—proceeding day after day in her presence—the way to discovery, now absolutely invisible, might, sooner or later, show itself.

At last the bell rang, the door opened, and the two gentlemen entered the room together.

Magdalen was struck, as her sister had been struck, by George Bartram's resemblance to her father—judging by the portrait at Combe-Raven, which presented the likeness of Andrew Vanstone in his younger days. The light hair and florid complexion, the bright blue eyes and hardy upright figure, familiar to her in the picture, were all recalled to her memory, as the nephew followed the uncle across the room and took his place at table. She was not prepared for this sudden revival of the lost associations of home. Her attention wandered as she tried to conceal its effect on her; and she made a blunder in waiting at table, for the first time since she had entered the house.

A quaint reprimand from the admiral, half in jest, half in earnest, gave her time to recover herself. She ventured another look at George Bartram. The impression which he produced on her this time roused her curiosity immediately. His face and manner plainly expressed anxiety and preoccupation of mind. He looked oftener at his plate than at his uncle, and at Magdalen herself (except one passing inspection of the new parlor-maid, when the admiral spoke to her) he never looked at all. Some uncertainty was evidently troubling his thoughts; some oppression was weighing on his natural freedom of manner. What uncertainty? what oppression? Would any personal revelations come out, little by little, in the course of conversation at the dinner-table?

No. One set of dishes followed another set of dishes, and nothing in the shape of a personal revelation took place. The conversation halted on irregularly, between public affairs on one side and trifling private topics on the other. Politics, home and foreign, took their turn with the small household history of St. Crux; the leaders of the revolution which expelled Louis Philippe from the throne of France marched side by side, in the dinner-table review, with old Mazey and the dogs. The dessert was put on the table, the old sailor came in, drank his loyal toast, paid his respects to "Master George," and went out again. Magdalen followed him, on her way back to the servants' offices, having heard nothing in the conversation of the slightest importance to the furtherance of her own design, from the first word of it to the last. She struggled hard not to lose heart and hope on the first day. They could hardly talk again to-morrow, they could hardly talk again the next day, of the French Revolution and the dogs. Time might do wonders yet; and time was all her own.

Left together over their wine, the uncle and nephew drew their easy-chairs on either side of the fire; and, in Magdalen's absence, began the very conversation which it was Magdalen's interest to hear.

"Claret, George?" said the admiral, pushing the bottle across the table. "You look out of spirits."

"I am a little anxious, sir," replied George, leaving his glass empty, and looking straight into the fire.

"I am glad to hear it," rejoined the admiral. "I am more than a little anxious myself, I can tell you. Here we are at the last days of March—and nothing done! Your time comes to an end on the third of May; and there you sit, as if you had years still before you, to turn round in."

George smiled, and resignedly helped himself to some wine.

"Am I really to understand, sir," he asked, "that you are serious in what you said to me last November? Are you actually resolved to bind me to that incomprehensible condition?"

"I don't call it incomprehensible," said the admiral, irritably.

"Don't you, sir? I am to inherit your estate, unconditionally—as you have generously settled it from the first. But I am not to touch a farthing of the fortune poor Noel left you unless I am married within a certain time. The house and lands are to be mine (thanks to your kindness) under any circumstances. But the money with which I might improve them both is to be arbitrarily taken away from me, if I am not a married man on the third of May. I am sadly wanting in intelligence, I dare say, but a more incomprehensible proceeding I never heard of!"

"No snapping and snarling, George! Say your say out. We don't understand sneering in Her Majesty's Navy!"

"I mean no offense, sir. But I think it's a little hard to astonish me by a change of proceeding on your part, entirely foreign to my experience of your character—and then, when I naturally ask for an explanation, to turn round coolly and leave me in the dark. If you and Noel came to some private arrangement together before he made his will, why not tell me? Why set up a mystery between us, where no mystery need be?"

"I won't have it, George!" cried the admiral, angrily drumming on the table with the nutcrackers. "You are trying to draw me like a badger, but I won't be drawn! I'll make any conditions I please; and I'll be accountable to nobody for them unless I like. It's quite bad enough to have worries and responsibilities laid on my unlucky shoulders that I never bargained for—never mind what worries: they're not yours, they're mine—without being questioned and cross-questioned as if I was a witness in a box. Here's a pretty fellow!" continued the admiral, apostrophizing his nephew in red-hot irritation, and addressing himself to the dogs on the hearth-rug for want of a better audience. "Here's a pretty fellow? He is asked to help himself to two uncommonly comfortable things in their way—a fortune and a wife; he is allowed six months to get the wife in (we should have got her, in the Navy, bag and baggage, in six days); he has a round dozen of nice girls, to my certain knowledge, in one part of the country and another, all at his disposal to choose from, and what does he do? He sits month after month, with his lazy legs crossed before him; he leaves the girls to pine on the stem, and he bothers his uncle to know the reason why! I pity the poor unfortunate women. Men were made of flesh and blood, and plenty of it, too, in my time. They're made of machinery now."

"I can only repeat, sir, I am sorry to have offended you," said George.

"Pooh! pooh! you needn't look at me in that languishing way if you are," retorted the admiral. "Stick to your wine, and I'll forgive you. Your good health, George. I'm glad to see you again at St. Crux. Look at that plateful of sponge-cakes! The cook has sent them up in honor of your return. We can't hurt her feelings, and we can't spoil our wine. Here!"—The admiral tossed four sponge-cakes in quick succession down the accommodating throats of the dogs. "I am sorry, George," the old gentleman gravely proceeded; "I am really sorry you haven't got your eye on one of those nice girls. You don't know what a loss you're inflicting on yourself; you don't know what trouble and mortification you're causing me by this shilly-shally conduct of yours."

"If you would only allow me to explain myself, sir, you would view my conduct in a totally different light. I am ready to marry to-morrow, if the lady will have me."

"The devil you are! So you have got a lady in your eye, after all? Why in Heaven's name couldn't you tell me so before? Never mind, I'll forgive you everything, now I know you have laid your hand on a wife. Fill your glass again. Here's her health in a bumper. By-the-by, who is she?"

"I'll tell you directly, admiral. When we began this conversation, I mentioned that I was a little anxious—"

"She's not one of my round dozen of nice girls—aha, Master George, I see that in your face already! Why are you anxious?"

"I am afraid you will disapprove of my choice, sir."

"Don't beat about the bush! How the deuce can I say whether I disapprove or not, if you won't tell me who she is?"

"She is the eldest daughter of Andrew Vanstone, of Combe-Raven."

"Who!!!"

"Miss Vanstone, sir."

The admiral put down his glass of wine untasted.

"You're right, George," he said. "I do disapprove of your choice —strongly disapprove of it."

"Is it the misfortune of her birth, sir, that you object to?"

"God forbid! the misfortune of her birth is not her fault, poor thing. You know as well as I do, George, what I object to."

"You object to her sister?"

"Certainly! The most liberal man alive might object to her sister, I think."

"It's hard, sir, to make Miss Vanstone suffer for her sister's faults."

"Faults, do you call them? You have a mighty convenient memory, George, when your own interests are concerned."

"Call them crimes if you like, sir—I say again, it's hard on Miss Vanstone. Miss Vanstone's life is pure of all reproach. From first to last she has borne her hard lot with such patience, and sweetness, and courage as not one woman in a thousand would have shown in her place. Ask Miss Garth, who has known her from childhood. Ask Mrs. Tyrrel, who blesses the day when she came into the house—"

"Ask a fiddlestick's end! I beg your pardon, George, but you are enough to try the patience of a saint. My good fellow, I don't deny Miss Vanstone's virtues. I'll admit, if you like, she's the best woman that ever put on a petticoat. That is not the question—"

"Excuse me, admiral—it is the question, if she is to be my wife."

"Hear me out, George; look at it from my point of view, as well as your own. What did your cousin Noel do? Your cousin Noel fell a victim, poor fellow, to one of the vilest conspiracies I ever heard of, and the prime mover of that conspiracy was Miss Vanstone's damnable sister. She deceived him in the most infamous manner; and as soon as she was down for a handsome legacy in his will, she had the poison ready to take his life. This is the truth; we know it from Mrs. Lecount, who found the bottle locked up in her own room. If you marry Miss Vanstone, you make this wretch your sister-in-law. She becomes a member of our family. All the disgrace of what she has done; all the disgrace of what she may do—and the Devil, who possesses her, only knows what lengths she may go to next—becomes our disgrace. Good heavens, George, consider what a position that is! Consider what pitch you touch, if you make this woman your sister-in-law."

"You have put your side of the question, admiral," said George resolutely; "now let me put mine. A certain impression is produced on me by a young lady whom I meet with under very interesting circumstances. I don't act headlong on that impression, as I might have done if I had been some years younger; I wait, and put it to the trial. Every time I see this young lady the impression strengthens; her beauty grows on me, her character grows on me; when I am away from her, I am restless and dissatisfied; when I am with her, I am the happiest man alive. All I hear of her conduct from those who know her best more than confirms the high opinion I have formed of her. The one drawback I can discover is caused by a misfortune for which she is not responsible—the misfortune of having a sister who is utterly unworthy of her. Does this discovery—an unpleasant discovery, I grant you—destroy all those good qualities in Miss Vanstone for which I love and admire her? Nothing of the sort—it only makes her good qualities all the more precious to me by contrast. If I am to have a drawback to contend with—and who expects anything else in this world?—I would infinitely rather have the drawback attached to my wife's sister than to my wife. My wife's sister is not essential to my happiness, but my wife is. In my opinion, sir, Mrs. Noel Vanstone has done mischief enough already. I don't see the necessity of letting her do more mischief, by depriving me of a good wife. Right or wrong, that is my point of view. I don't wish to trouble you with any questions of sentiment. All I wish to say is that I am old enough by this time to know my own mind, and that my mind is made up. If my marriage is essential to the execution of your intentions on my behalf, there is only one woman in the world whom I can marry, and that woman is Miss Vanstone."

There was no resisting this plain declaration. Admiral Bartram rose from his chair without making any reply, and walked perturbedly up and down the room.

The situation was emphatically a serious one. Mrs. Girdlestone's death had already produced the failure of one of the two objects contemplated by the Secret Trust. If the third of May arrived and found George a single man, the second (and last) of the objects would then have failed in its turn. In little more than a fortnight, at the very latest, the Banns must be published in Ossory church, or the time would fail for compliance with one of the stipulations insisted on in the Trust. Obstinate as the admiral was by nature, strongly as he felt the objections which attached to his nephew's contemplated alliance, he recoiled in spite of himself, as he paced the room and saw the facts on either side immovably staring him in the face.

"Are you engaged to Miss Vanstone?" he asked, suddenly.

"No, sir," replied George. "I thought it due to your uniform kindness to me to speak to you on the subject first."

"Much obliged, I'm sure. And you have put off speaking to me to the last moment, just as you put off everything else. Do you think Miss Vanstone will say yes when you ask her?"

George hesitated.

"The devil take your modesty!" shouted the admiral. "This is not a time for modesty; this is a time for speaking out. Will she or won't she?"

"I think she will, sir."

The admiral laughed sardonically, and took another turn in the room. He suddenly stopped, put his hands in his pockets, and stood still in a corner, deep in thought. After an interval of a few minutes, his face cleared a little; it brightened with the dawning of a new idea. He walked round briskly to George's side of the fire, and laid his hand kindly on his nephew's shoulder.

"You're wrong, George," he said; "but it is too late now to set you right. On the sixteenth of next month the Banns must be put up in Ossory church, or you will lose the money. Have you told Miss Vanstone the position you stand in? Or have you put that off to the eleventh hour, like everything else?"

"The position is so extraordinary, sir, and it might lead to so much misapprehension of my motives, that I have felt unwilling to allude to it. I hardly know how I can tell her of it at all."

"Try the experiment of telling her friends. Let them know it's a question of money, and they will overcome her scruples, if you can't. But that is not what I had to say to you. How long do you propose stopping here this time?"

"I thought of staying a few days, and then—"

"And then of going back to London and making your offer, I suppose? Will a week give you time enough to pick your opportunity with Miss Vanstone—a week out of the fortnight or so that you have to spare?"

"I will stay here a week, admiral, with pleasure, if you wish it."

"I don't wish it. I want you to pack up your traps and be off to-morrow."

George looked at his uncle in silent astonishment.

"You found some letters waiting for you when you got here," proceeded the admiral. "Was one of those letters from my old friend, Sir Franklin Brock?"

"Yes, sir."

"Was it an invitation to you to go and stay at the Grange?"

"Yes, sir."

"To go at once?"

"At once, if I could manage it."

"Very good. I want you to manage it; I want you to start for the Grange to-morrow."

George looked back at the fire, and sighed impatiently.

"I understand you now, admiral," he said. "You are entirely mistaken in me. My attachment to Miss Vanstone is not to be shaken in that manner."

Admiral Bartram took his quarter-deck walk again, up and down the room.

"One good turn deserves another, George," said the old gentleman. "If I am willing to make concessions on my side, the least you can do is to meet me half-way, and make concessions on yours."

"I don't deny it, sir."

"Very well. Now listen to my proposal. Give me a fair hearing, George—a fair hearing is every man's privilege. I will be perfectly just to begin with. I won't attempt to deny that you honestly believe Miss Vanstone is the only woman in the world who can make you happy. I don't question that. What I do question is, whether you really know your own mind in this matter quite so well as you think you know it yourself. You can't deny, George, that you have been in love with a good many women in your time? Among the rest of them, you have been in love with Miss Brock. No longer ago than this time last year there was a sneaking kindness between you and that young lady, to say the least of it. And quite right, too! Miss Brock is one of that round dozen of darlings I mentioned over our first glass of wine."

"You are confusing an idle flirtation, sir, with a serious attachment," said George. "You are altogether mistaken—you are, indeed."

"Likely enough; I don't pretend to be infallible—I leave that to my juniors. But I happen to have known you, George, since you were the height of my old telescope; and I want to have this serious attachment of yours put to the test. If you can satisfy me that your whole heart and soul are as strongly set on Miss Vanstone as you suppose them to be, I must knock under to necessity, and keep my objections to myself. But I must be satisfied first. Go to the Grange to-morrow, and stay there a week in Miss Brock's society. Give that charming girl a fair chance of lighting up the old flame again if she can, and then come back to St. Crux, and let me hear the result. If you tell me, as an honest man, that your attachment to Miss Vanstone still remains unshaken, you will have heard the last of my objections from that moment. Whatever misgivings I may feel in my own mind, I will say nothing, and do nothing, adverse to your wishes. There is my proposal. I dare say it looks like an old man's folly, in your eyes. But the old man won't trouble you much longer, George; and it may be a pleasant reflection, when you have got sons of your own, to remember that you humored him in his last days."

He came back to the fire-place as he said those words, and laid his hand once more on his nephew's shoulder. George took the hand and pressed it affectionately. In the tenderest and best sense of the word, his uncle had been a father to him.

"I will do what you ask me, sir," he replied, "if you seriously wish it. But it is only right to tell you that the experiment will be perfectly useless. However, if you prefer my passing a week at the Grange to my passing it here, to the Grange I will go."

"Thank you, George," said the admiral, bluntly. "I expected as much from you, and you have not disappointed me.—If Miss Brock doesn't get us out of this mess," thought the wily old gentleman, as he resumed his place at the table, "my nephew's weather-cock of a head has turned steady with a vengeance!—We'll consider the question settled for to-night, George," he continued, aloud, "and call another subject. These family anxieties don't improve the flavor of my old claret. The bottle stands with you. What are they doing at the theaters in London? We always patronized the theaters, in my time, in the Navy. We used to like a good tragedy to begin with, and a hornpipe to cheer us up at the end of the entertainment."

For the rest of the evening, the talk flowed in the ordinary channels. Admiral Bartram only returned to the forbidden subject when he and his nephew parted for the night.

"You won't forget to-morrow, George?"

"Certainly not, sir. I'll take the dog-cart, and drive myself over after breakfast."

Before noon the next day Mr. George Bartram had left the house, and the last chance in Magdalen's favor had left it with him.

CHAPTER IV.

WHEN the servants' dinner-bell at St. Crux rang as usual on the day of George Bartram's departure, it was remarked that the new parlor-maid's place at table remained empty. One of the inferior servants was sent to her room to make inquiries, and returned with the information that "Louisa" felt a little faint, and begged that her attendance at table might be excused for that day. Upon this, the superior authority of the housekeeper was invoked, and Mrs. Drake went upstairs immediately to ascertain the truth for herself. Her first look of inquiry satisfied her that the parlor-maid's indisposition, whatever the cause of it might be, was certainly not assumed to serve any idle or sullen purpose of her own. She respectfully declined taking any of the remedies which the housekeeper offered, and merely requested permission to try the efficacy of a walk in the fresh air.

"I have been accustomed to more exercise, ma'am, than I take here," she said. "Might I go into the garden, and try what the air will do for me?"

"Certainly. Can you walk by yourself, or shall I send some one with you?"

"I will go by myself, if you please, ma'am."

"Very well. Put on your bonnet and shawl, and, when you get out, keep in the east garden. The admiral sometimes walks in the north garden, and he might feel surprised at seeing you there. Come to my room, when you have had air and exercise enough, and let me see how you are."

In a few minutes more Magdalen was out in the east garden. The sky was clear and sunny; but the cold shadow of the house rested on the garden walk and chilled the midday air. She walked toward the ruins of the old monastery, situated on the south side of the more modern range of buildings. Here there were lonely open spaces to breathe in freely; here the pale March sunshine stole through the gaps of desolation and decay, and met her invitingly with the genial promise of spring.

She ascended three or four riven stone steps, and seated herself on some ruined fragments beyond them, full in the sunshine. The place she had chosen had once been the entrance to the church. In centuries long gone by, the stream of human sin and human suffering had flowed, day after day, to the confessional, over the place where she now sat. Of all the miserable women who had trodden those old stones in the bygone time, no more miserable creature had touched them than the woman whose feet rested on them now.

Her hands trembled as she placed them on either side of her, to support herself on the stone seat. She laid them on her lap; they trembled there. She held them out, and looked at them wonderingly; they trembled as she looked. "Like an old woman!" she said, faintly, and let them drop again at her side.

For the first time, that morning, the cruel discovery had forced itself on her mind—the discovery that her strength was failing her, at the time when she had most confidently trusted to it, at the time when she wanted it most. She had felt the surprise of Mr. Bartram's unexpected departure, as if it had been the shock of the severest calamity that could have befallen her. That one check to her hopes—a check which at other times would only have roused the resisting power in her to new efforts—had struck her with as suffocating a terror, had prostrated her with as all-mastering a despair, as if she had been overwhelmed by the crowning disaster of expulsion from St. Crux. But one warning could be read in such a change as this. Into the space of little more than a year she had crowded the wearing and wasting emotions of a life. The bountiful gifts of health and strength, so prodigally heaped on her by Nature, so long abused with impunity, were failing her at last.

She looked up at the far faint blue of the sky. She heard the joyous singing of birds among the ivy that clothed the ruins. Oh the cold distance of the heavens! Oh the pitiless happiness of the birds! Oh the lonely horror of sitting there, and feeling old and weak and worn, in the heyday of her youth! She rose with a last effort of resolution, and tried to keep back the hysterical passion swelling at her heart by moving and looking about her. Rapidly and more rapidly she walked to and fro in the sunshine. The exercise helped her, through the very fatigue that she felt from it. She forced the rising tears desperately back to their sources; she fought with the clinging pain, and wrenched it from its hold. Little by little her mind began to clear again: the despairing fear of herself grew less vividly present to her thoughts. There were reserves of youth and strength in her still to be wasted; there was a spirit sorely wounded, but not yet subdued.

She gradually extended the limits of her walk; she gradually recovered the exercise of her observation.

At the western extremity the remains of the monastery were in a less ruinous condition than at the eastern. In certain places, where the stout old walls still stood, repairs had been made at some former time. Roofs of red tile had been laid roughly over four of the ancient cells; wooden doors had been added; and the old monastic chambers had been used as sheds to hold the multifarious lumber of St. Crux. No padlocks guarded any of the doors. Magdalen had only to push them to let the daylight in on the litter inside. She resolved to investigate the sheds one after the other—not from curiosity, not with the idea of making discoveries of any sort. Her only object was to fill up the vacant time, and to keep the thoughts that unnerved her from returning to her mind.

The first shed she opened contained the gardener's utensils, large and small. The second was littered with fragments of broken furniture, empty picture-frames of worm-eaten wood, shattered vases, boxes without covers, and books torn from their bindings. As Magdalen turned to leave the shed, after one careless glance round her at the lumber that it contained, her foot struck something on the ground which tinkled against a fragment of china lying near it. She stooped, and discovered that the tinkling substance was a rusty key.

She picked up the key and looked at it. She walked out into the air, and considered a little. More old forgotten keys were probably lying about among the lumber in the sheds. What if she collected all she could find, and tried them, one after another, in the locks of the cabinets and cupboards now closed against her? Was there chance enough that any one of them might fit to justify her in venturing on the experiment? If the locks at St. Crux were as old-fashioned as the furniture—if there were no protective niceties of modern invention to contend against—there was chance enough beyond all question. Who could say whether the very key in her hand might not be the lost duplicate of one of the keys on the admiral's bunch? In the dearth of all other means of finding the way to her end, the risk was worth running. A flash of the old spirit sparkled in her weary eyes as she turned and re-entered the shed.

Half an hour more brought her to the limits of the time which she could venture to allow herself in the open air. In that interval she had searched the sheds from first to last, and had found five more keys. "Five more chances!" she thought to herself, as she hid the keys, and hastily returned to the house.

After first reporting herself in the housekeeper's room, she went upstairs to remove her bonnet and shawl; taking that opportunity to hide the keys in her bed-chamber until night came. They were crusted thick with rust and dirt; but she dared not attempt to clean them until bed-time secluded her from the prying eyes of the servants in the solitude of her room.

When the dinner hour brought her, as usual, into personal contact with the admiral, she was at once struck by a change in him. For the first time in her experience the old gentleman was silent and depressed. He ate less than usual, and he hardly said five words to her from the beginning of the meal to the end. Some unwelcome subject of reflection had evidently fixed itself on his mind, and remained there persistently, in spite of his efforts to shake it off. At intervals through the evening, she wondered with an ever-growing perplexity what the subject could be.

At last the lagging hours reached their end, and bed-time came. Before she slept that night Magdalen had cleaned the keys from all impurities, and had oiled the wards, to help them smoothly into the locks. The last difficulty that remained was the difficulty of choosing the time when the experiment might be tried with the least risk of interruption and discovery. After carefully considering the question overnight, Magdalen could only resolve to wait and be guided by the events of the next day.

The morning came, and for the first time at St. Crux events justified the trust she had placed in them. The morning came, and the one remaining difficulty that perplexed her was unexpectedly smoothed away by no less a person than the admiral himself! To the surprise of every one in the house, he announced at breakfast that he had arranged to start for London in an hour; that he should pass the night in town; and that he might be expected to return to St. Crux in time for dinner on the next day. He volunteered no further explanations to the housekeeper or to any one else, but it was easy to see that his errand to London was of no ordinary importance in his own estimation. He swallowed his breakfast in a violent hurry, and he was impatiently ready for the carriage before it came to the door.

Experience had taught Magdalen to be cautious. She waited a little, after Admiral Bartram's departure, before she ventured on trying her experiment with the keys. It was well she did so. Mrs. Drake took advantage of the admiral's absence to review the condition of the apartments on the first floor. The results of the investigation by no means satisfied her; brooms and dusters were set to work; and the house-maids were in and out of the rooms perpetually, as long as the daylight lasted.

The evening passed, and still the safe opportunity for which Magdalen was on the watch never presented itself. Bed-time came again, and found her placed between the two alternatives of trusting to the doubtful chances of the next morning, or of trying the keys boldly in the dead of night. In former times she would have made her choice without hesitation. She hesitated now; but the wreck of her old courage still sustained her, and she determined to make the venture at night.

They kept early hours at St. Crux. If she waited in her room until half-past eleven, she would wait long enough. At that time she stole out on to the staircase, with the keys in her pocket, and the candle in her hand.

On passing the entrance to the corridor on the bedroom floor, she stopped and listened. No sound of snoring, no shuffling of infirm footsteps was to be heard on the other side of the screen. She looked round it distrustfully. The stone passage was a solitude, and the truckle-bed was empty. Her own eyes had shown her old Mazey on his way to the upper regions, more than an hour since, with a candle in his hand. Had he taken advantage of his master's absence to enjoy the unaccustomed luxury of sleeping in a room? As the thought occurred to her, a sound from the further end of the corridor just caught her ear. She softly advanced toward it, and heard through the door of the last and remotest of the spare bed-chambers the veteran's lusty snoring in the room inside. The discovery was startling, in more senses than one. It deepened the impenetrable mystery of the truckle-bed; for it showed plainly that old Mazey had no barbarous preference of his own for passing his nights in the corridor; he occupied that strange and comfortless sleeping-place purely and entirely on his master's account.

It was no time for dwelling on the reflections which this conclusion might suggest. Magdalen retraced her steps along the passage, and descended to the first floor. Passing the doors nearest to her, she tried the library first. On the staircase and in the corridors she had felt her heart throbbing fast with an unutterable fear; but a sense of security returned to her when she found herself within the four walls of the room, and when she had closed the door on the ghostly quiet outside.

The first lock she tried was the lock of the table-drawer. None of the keys fitted it. Her next experiment was made on the cabinet. Would the second attempt fail, like the first?

No! One of the keys fitted; one of the keys, with a little patient management, turned the lock. She looked in eagerly. There were open shelves above, and one long drawer under them. The shelves were devoted to specimens of curious minerals, neatly labeled and arranged. The drawer was divided into compartments. Two of the compartments contained papers. In the first, she discovered nothing but a collection of receipted bills. In the second, she found a heap of business documents; but the writing, yellow with age, was enough of itself to warn her that the Trust was not there. She shut the doors of the cabinet, and, after locking them again with some little difficulty, proceeded to try the keys in the bookcase cupboards next, before she continued her investigations in the other rooms.

The bookcase cupboards were unassailable, the drawers and cupboards in all the other rooms were unassailable. One after another she tried them patiently in regular succession. It was useless. The chance which the cabinet in the library had offered in her favor was the first chance and the last.

She went back to her room, seeing nothing but her own gliding shadow, hearing nothing but her own stealthy footfall in the midnight stillness of the house. After mechanically putting the keys away in their former hiding-place, she looked toward her bed, and turned away from it, shuddering. The warning remembrance of what she had suffered that morning in the garden was vividly present to her mind. "Another chance tried," she thought to herself, "and another chance lost! I shall break down again if I think of it; and I shall think of it if I lie awake in the dark." She had brought a work-box with her to St. Crux, as one of the many little things which in her character of a servant it was desirable to possess; and she now opened the box and applied herself resolutely to work. Her want of dexterity with her needle assisted the object she had in view; it obliged her to pay the closest attention to her employment; it forced her thoughts away from the two subjects of all others which she now dreaded most—herself and the future.

The next day, as he had arranged, the admiral returned. His visit to London had not improved his spirits. The shadow of some unconquerable doubt still clouded his face; his restless tongue was strangely quiet, while Magdalen waited on him at his solitary meal. That night the snoring resounded once more on the inner side of the screen, and old Mazey was back again in the comfortless truckle-bed.

Three more days passed—April came. On the second of the month —returning as unexpectedly as he had departed a week before—Mr. George Bartram re-appeared at St. Crux.

He came back early in the afternoon, and had an interview with his uncle in the library. The interview over, he left the house again, and was driven to the railway by the groom in time to catch the last train to London that night. The groom noticed, on the road, that "Mr. George seemed to be rather pleased than otherwise at leaving St. Crux." He also remarked, on his return, that the admiral swore at him for overdriving the horses—an indication of ill-temper, on the part of his master, which he described as being entirely without precedent in all his former experience. Magdalen, in her department of service, had suffered in like manner under the old man's irritable humor: he had been dissatisfied with everything she did in the dining-room; and he had found fault with all the dishes, one after another, from the mutton-broth to the toasted cheese.

The next two days passed as usual. On the third day an event happened. In appearance, it was nothing more important than a ring at the drawing-room bell. In reality, it was the forerunner of approaching catastrophe—the formidable herald of the end.

It was Magdalen's business to answer the bell. On reaching the drawing-room door, she knocked as usual. There was no reply. After again knocking, and again receiving no answer, she ventured into the room, and was instantly met by a current of cold air flowing full on her face. The heavy sliding door in the opposite wall was pushed back, and the Arctic atmosphere of Freeze-your-Bones was pouring unhindered into the empty room.

She waited near the door, doubtful what to do next; it was certainly the drawing-room bell that had rung, and no other. She waited, looking through the open doorway opposite, down the wilderness of the dismantled Hall.

A little consideration satisfied her that it would be best to go downstairs again, and wait there for a second summons from the bell. On turning to leave the room, she happened to look back once more, and exactly at that moment she saw the door open at the opposite extremity of the Banqueting-Hall—the door leading into the first of the apartments in the east wing. A tall man came out, wearing his great coat and his hat, and rapidly approached the drawing-room. His gait betrayed him, while he was still too far off for his features to be seen. Before he was quite half-way across the Hall, Magdalen had recognized—the admiral.

He looked, not irritated only, but surprised as well, at finding his parlor-maid waiting for him in the drawing-room, and inquired, sharply and suspiciously, what she wanted there? Magdalen replied that she had come there to answer the bell. His face cleared a little when he heard the explanation. "Yes, yes; to be sure," he said. "I did ring, and then I forgot it." He pulled the sliding door back into its place as he spoke. "Coals," he resumed, impatiently, pointing to the empty scuttle. "I rang for coals."

Magdalen went back to the kitchen regions. After communicating the admiral's order to the servant whose special duty it was to attend to the fires, she returned to the pantry, and, gently closing the door, sat down alone to think.

It had been her impression in the drawing-room—and it was her impression still—that she had accidentally surprised Admiral Bartram on a visit to the east rooms, which, for some urgent reason of his own, he wished to keep a secret. Haunted day and night by the one dominant idea that now possessed her, she leaped all logical difficulties at a bound, and at once associated the suspicion of a secret proceeding on the admiral's part with the kindred suspicion which pointed to him as the depositary of the Secret Trust. Up to this time it had been her settled belief that he kept all his important documents in one or other of the suite of rooms which he happened to be occupying for the time being. Why—she now asked herself, with a sudden distrust of the conclusion which had hitherto satisfied her mind—why might he not lock some of them up in the other rooms as well? The remembrance of the keys still concealed in their hiding-place in her room sharpened her sense of the reasonableness of this new view. With one unimportant exception, those keys had all failed when she tried them in the rooms on the north side of the house. Might they not succeed with the cabinets and cupboards in the east rooms, on which she had never tried them, or thought of trying them, yet? If there was a chance, however small, of turning them to better account than she had turned them thus far, it was a chance to be tried. If there was a possibility, however remote, that the Trust might be hidden in any one of the locked repositories in the east wing, it was a possibility to be put to the test. When? Her own experience answered the question. At the time when no prying eyes were open, and no accidents were to be feared—when the house was quiet—in the dead of night.

She knew enough of her changed self to dread the enervating influence of delay. She determined to run the risk headlong that night.

More blunders escaped her when dinner-time came; the admiral's criticisms on her waiting at table were sharper than ever. His hardest words inflicted no pain on her; she scarcely heard him—her mind was dull to every sense but the sense of the coming trial. The evening which had passed slowly to her on the night of her first experiment with the keys passed quickly now. When bed-time came, bed-time took her by surprise.

She waited longer on this occasion than she had waited before. The admiral was at home; he might alter his mind and go downstairs again, after he had gone up to his room; he might have forgotten something in the library and might return to fetch it. Midnight struck from the clock in the servants' hall before she ventured out of her room, with the keys again in her pocket, with the candle again in her hand.

At the first of the stairs on which she set her foot to descend, an all-mastering hesitation, an unintelligible shrinking from some peril unknown, seized her on a sudden. She waited, and reasoned with herself. She had recoiled from no sacrifices, she had yielded to no fears, in carrying out the stratagem by which she had gained admission to St. Crux; and now, when the long array of difficulties at the outset had been patiently conquered, now, when by sheer force of resolution the starting-point was gained, she hesitated to advance. "I shrank from nothing to get here," she said to herself. "What madness possesses me that I shrink now?"

Every pulse in her quickened at the thought, with an animating shame that nerved her to go on. She descended the stairs, from the third floor to the second, from the second to the first, without trusting herself to pause again within easy reach of her own room. In another minute, she had reached the end of the corridor, had crossed the vestibule, and had entered the drawing-room. It was only when her grasp was on the heavy brass handle of the sliding door—it was only at the moment before she pushed the door back—that she waited to take breath. The Banqueting-Hall was close on the other side of the wooden partition against which she stood; her excited imagination felt the death-like chill of it flowing over her already.

She pushed back the sliding door a few inches—and stopped in momentary alarm. When the admiral had closed it in her presence that day, she had heard no noise. When old Mazey had opened it to show her the rooms in the east wing, she had heard no noise. Now, in the night silence, she noticed for the first time that the door made a sound—a dull, rushing sound, like the wind.

She roused herself, and pushed it further back—pushed it halfway into the hollow chamber in the wall constructed to receive it. She advanced boldly into the gap, and met the night view of the Banqueting-Hall face to face.

The moon was rounding the southern side of the house. Her paling beams streamed through the nearer windows, and lay in long strips of slanting light on the marble pavement of the Hall. The black shadows of the pediments between each window, alternating with the strips of light, heightened the wan glare of the moonshine on the floor. Toward its lower end, the Hall melted mysteriously into darkness. The ceiling was lost to view; the yawning fire-place, the overhanging mantel-piece, the long row of battle pictures above, were all swallowed up in night. But one visible object was discernible, besides the gleaming windows and the moon-striped floor. Midway in the last and furthest of the strips of light, the tripod rose erect on its gaunt black legs, like a monster called to life by the moon—a monster rising through the light, and melting invisibly into the upper shadows of the Hall. Far and near, all sound lay dead, drowned in the stagnant cold. The soothing hush of night was awful here. The deep abysses of darkness hid abysses of silence more immeasurable still.

She stood motionless in the door-way, with straining eyes, with straining ears. She looked for some moving thing, she listened for some rising sound, and looked and listened in vain. A quick ceaseless shivering ran through her from head to foot. The shivering of fear, or the shivering of cold? The bare doubt roused her resolute will. "Now," she thought, advancing a step through the door-way, "or never! I'll count the strips of moonlight three times over, and cross the Hall."

"One, two, three, four, five. One, two, three, four, five. One, two, three, four, five."

As the final number passed her lips at the third time of counting, she crossed the Hall. Looking for nothing, listening for nothing, one hand holding the candle, the other mechanically grasping the folds of her dress, she sped, ghost-like, down the length of the ghostly place. She reached the door of the first of the eastern rooms, opened it, and ran in. The sudden relief of attaining a refuge, the sudden entrance into a new atmosphere, overpowered her for the moment. She had just time to put the candle safely on a table before she dropped giddy and breathless into the nearest chair.

Little by little she felt the rest quieting her. In a few minutes she became conscious of the triumph of having won her way to the east rooms. In a few minutes she was strong enough to rise from the chair, to take the keys from her pocket, and to look round her.

The first objects of furniture in the room which attracted her attention were an old bureau of carved oak, and a heavy buhl table with a cabinet attached. She tried the bureau first; it looked the likeliest receptacle for papers of the two. Three of the keys proved to be of a size to enter the lock, but none of them would turn it. The bureau was unassailable. She left it, and paused to trim the wick of the candle before she tried the buhl cabinet next.

At the moment when she raised her hand to the candle, she heard the stillness of the Banqueting-Hall shudder with the terror of a sound—a sound faint and momentary, like the distant rushing of the wind.

The sliding door in the drawing-room had moved.

Which way had it moved? Had an unknown hand pushed it back in its socket further than she had pushed it, or pulled it to again, and closed it? The horror of being shut out all night, by some undiscoverable agency, from the life of the house, was stronger in her than the horror of looking across the Banqueting-Hall. She made desperately for the door of the room.

It had fallen to silently after her when she had come in, but it was not closed. She pulled it open, and looked.

The sight that met her eyes rooted her, panic-stricken, to the spot.

Close to the first of the row of windows, counting from the drawing-room, and full in the gleam of it, she saw a solitary figure. It stood motionless, rising out of the furthest strip of moonlight on the floor. As she looked, it suddenly disappeared. In another instant she saw it again, in the second strip of moonlight—lost it again—saw it in the third strip—lost it once more—and saw it in the fourth. Moment by moment it advanced, now mysteriously lost in the shadow, now suddenly visible again in the light, until it reached the fifth and nearest strip of moonlight. There it paused, and strayed aside slowly to the middle of the Hall. It stopped at the tripod, and stood, shivering audibly in the silence, with its hands raised over the dead ashes, in the action of warming them at a fire. It turned back again, moving down the path of the moonlight, stopped at the fifth window, turned once more, and came on softly through the shadow straight to the place where Magdalen stood.

Her voice was dumb, her will was helpless. Every sense in her but the seeing sense was paralyzed. The seeing sense—held fast in the fetters of its own terror—looked unchangeably straightforward, as it had looked from the first. There she stood in the door-way, full in the path of the figure advancing on her through the shadow, nearer and nearer, step by step.

It came close.

The bonds of horror that held her burst asunder when it was within arm's-length. She started back. The light of the candle on the table fell full on its face, and showed her—Admiral Bartram.

A long, gray dressing-gown was wrapped round him. His head was uncovered; his feet were bare. In his left hand he carried his little basket of keys. He passed Magdalen slowly, his lips whispering without intermission, his open eyes staring straight before him with the glassy stare of death. His eyes revealed to her the terrifying truth. He was walking in his sleep.

The terror of seeing him as she saw him now was not the terror she had felt when her eyes first lighted on him—an apparition in the moon-light, a specter in the ghostly Hall. This time she could struggle against the shock; she could feel the depth of her own fear.

He passed her, and stopped in the middle of the room. Magdalen ventured near enough to him to be within reach of his voice as he muttered to himself. She ventured nearer still, and heard the name of her dead husband fall distinctly from the sleep-walker's lips.

"Noel!" he said, in the low monotonous tones of a dreamer talking in his sleep, "my good fellow, Noel, take it back again! It worries me day and night. I don't know where it's safe; I don't know where to put it. Take it back, Noel—take it back!"

As those words escaped him, he walked to the buhl cabinet. He sat down in the chair placed before it, and searched in the basket among his keys. Magdalen softly followed him, and stood behind his chair, waiting with the candle in her hand. He found the key, and unlocked the cabinet. Without an instant's hesitation, he drew out a drawer, the second of a row. The one thing in the drawer was a folded letter. He removed it, and put it down before him on the table. "Take it back, Noel!" he repeated, mechanically; "take it back!"

Magdalen looked over his shoulder and read these lines, traced in her husband's handwriting, at the top of the letter: To be kept in your own possession, and to be opened by yourself only on the day of my decease. Noel Vanstone. She saw the words plainly, with the admiral's name and the admiral's address written under them.

The Trust within reach of her hand! The Trust traced to its hiding-place at last!

She took one step forward, to steal round his chair and to snatch the letter from the table. At the instant when she moved, he took it up once more, locked the cabinet, and, rising, turned and faced her.

In the impulse of the moment, she stretched out her hand toward the hand in which he held the letter. The yellow candle-light fell full on him. The awful death-in-life of his face—the mystery of the sleeping body, moving in unconscious obedience to the dreaming mind—daunted her. Her hand trembled, and dropped again at her side.

He put the key of the cabinet back in the basket, and crossed the room to the bureau, with the basket in one hand and the letter in the other. Magdalen set the candle on the table again, and watched him. As he had opened the cabinet, so he now opened the bureau. Once more Magdalen stretched out her hand, and once more she recoiled before the mystery and the terror of his sleep. He put the letter in a drawer at the back of the bureau, and closed the heavy oaken lid again. "Yes," he said. "Safer there, as you say, Noel—safer there." So he spoke. So, time after time, the words that betrayed him revealed the dead man living and speaking again in the dream.

Had he locked the bureau? Magdalen had not heard the lock turn. As he slowly moved away, walking back once more toward the middle of the room, she tried the lid. It was locked. That discovery made, she looked to see what he was doing next. He was leaving the room again, with the basket of keys in his hand. When her first glance overtook him, he was crossing the threshold of the door.

Some inscrutable fascination possessed her, some mysterious attraction drew her after him, in spite of herself. She took up the candle and followed him mechanically, as if she too were walking in her sleep. One behind the other, in slow and noiseless progress, they crossed the Banqueting-Hall. One behind the other, they passed through the drawing-room, and along the corridor, and up the stairs. She followed him to his own door. He went in, and shut it behind him softly. She stopped, and looked toward the truckle-bed. It was pushed aside at the foot, some little distance away from the bedroom door. Who had moved it? She held the candle close and looked toward the pillow, with a sudden curiosity and a sudden doubt.

The truckle-bed was empty.

The discovery startled her for the moment, and for the moment only. Plain as the inferences were to be drawn from it, she never drew them. Her mind, slowly recovering the exercise of its faculties, was still under the influence of the earlier and the deeper impressions produced on it. Her mind followed the admiral into his room, as her body had followed him across the Banqueting-Hall.

Had he lain down again in his bed? Was he still asleep? She listened at the door. Not a sound was audible in the room. She tried the door, and, finding it not locked, softly opened it a few inches and listened again. The rise and fall of his low, regular breathing instantly caught her ear. He was still asleep.

She went into the room, and, shading the candle-light with her hand, approached the bedside to look at him. The dream was past; the old man's sleep was deep and peaceful; his lips were still; his quiet hand was laid over the coverlet in motionless repose. He lay with his face turned toward the right-hand side of the bed. A little table stood there within reach of his hand. Four objects were placed on it; his candle, his matches, his customary night drink of lemonade, and his basket of keys.

The idea of possessing herself of his keys that night (if an opportunity offered when the basket was not in his hand) had first crossed her mind when she saw him go into his room. She had lost it again for the moment, in the surprise of discovering the empty truckle-bed. She now recovered it the instant the table attracted her attention. It was useless to waste time in trying to choose the one key wanted from the rest—the one key was not well enough known to her to be readily identified. She took all the keys from the table, in the basket as they lay, and noiselessly closed the door behind her on leaving the room.

The truckle-bed, as she passed it, obtruded itself again on her attention, and forced her to think of it. After a moment's consideration, she moved the foot of the bed back to its customary position across the door. Whether he was in the house or out of it, the veteran might return to his deserted post at any moment. If he saw the bed moved from its usual place, he might suspect something wrong, he might rouse his master, and the loss of the keys might be discovered.

Nothing happened as she descended the stairs, nothing happened as she passed along the corridor; the house was as silent and as solitary as ever. She crossed the Banqueting-Hall this time without hesitation; the events of the night had hardened her mind against all imaginary terrors. "Now, I have got it!" she whispered to herself, in an irrepressible outburst of exaltation, as she entered the first of the east rooms and put her candle on the top of the old bureau.

Even yet there was a trial in store for her patience. Some minutes elapsed—minutes that seemed hours—before she found the right key and raised the lid of the bureau. At last she drew out the inner drawer! At last she had the letter in her hand!

It had been sealed, but the seal was broken. She opened it on the spot, to make sure that she had actually possessed herself of the Trust before leaving the room. The end of the letter was the first part of it she turned to. It came to its conclusion high on the third page, and it was signed by Noel Vanstone. Below the name these lines were added in the admiral's handwriting:

"This letter was received by me at the same time with the will of my friend, Noel Vanstone. In the event of my death, without leaving any other directions respecting it, I beg my nephew and my executors to understand that I consider the requests made in this document as absolutely binding on me.

"ARTHUR EVERARD BARTRAM."

She left those lines unread. She just noticed that they were not in Noel Vanstone's handwriting; and, passing over them instantly, as immaterial to the object in view, turned the leaves of the letter, and transferred her attention to the opening sentences on the first page. She read these words:

"DEAR ADMIRAL BARTRAM—When you open my Will (in which you are named my sole executor), you will find that I have bequeathed the whole residue of my estate—after payment of one legacy of five thousand pounds—to yourself. It is the purpose of my letter to tell you privately what the object is for which I have left you the fortune which is now placed in your hands.

"I beg you to consider this large legacy as intended—"

She had proceeded thus far with breathless curiosity and interest, when her attention suddenly failed her. Something—she was too deeply absorbed to know what—had got between her and the letter. Was it a sound in the Banqueting-Hall again? She looked over her shoulder at the door behind her, and listened. Nothing was to be heard, nothing was to be seen. She returned to the letter.

The writing was cramped and close. In her impatient curiosity to read more, she failed to find the lost place again. Her eyes, attracted by a blot, lighted on a sentence lower in the page than the sentence at which she had left off. The first three words she saw riveted her attention anew—they were the first words she had met with in the letter which directly referred to George Bartram. In the sudden excitement of that discovery, she read the rest of the sentence eagerly, before she made any second attempt to return to the lost place:

"If your nephew fails to comply with these conditions—that is to say, if, being either a bachelor or a widower at the time of my decease, he fails to marry in all respects as I have here instructed him to marry, within six calendar months from that time—it is my desire that he shall not receive—"

She had read to that point, to that last word and no further, when a hand passed suddenly from behind her between the letter and her eye, and gripped her fast by the wrist in an instant.

She turned with a shriek of terror, and found herself face to face with old Mazey.

The veteran's eyes were bloodshot; his hand was heavy; his list slippers were twisted crookedly on his feet; and his body swayed to and fro on his widely parted legs. If he had tested his condition that night by the unfailing criterion of the model ship, he must have inevitably pronounced sentence on himself in the usual form: "Drunk again, Mazey; drunk again."

"You young Jezebel!" said the old sailor, with a leer on one side of his face, and a frown on the other. "The next time you take to night-walking in the neighborhood of Freeze-your-Bones, use those sharp eyes of yours first, and make sure there's nobody else night walking in the garden outside. Drop it, Jezebel! drop it!"

Keeping fast hold of Magdalen's arm with one hand, he took the letter from her with the other, put it back into the open drawer, and locked the bureau. She never struggled with him, she never spoke. Her energy was gone; her powers of resistance were crushed. The terrors of that horrible night, following one close on the other in reiterated shocks, had struck her down at last. She yielded as submissively, she trembled as helplessly, as the weakest woman living.

Old Mazey dropped her arm, and pointed with drunken solemnity to a chair in an inner corner of the room. She sat down, still without uttering a word. The veteran (breathing very hard over it) steadied himself on both elbows against the slanting top of the bureau, and from that commanding position addressed Magdalen once more.

"Come and be locked up!" said old Mazey, wagging his venerable head with judicial severity. "There'll be a court of inquiry to-morrow morning, and I'm witness—worse luck!—I'm witness. You young jade, you've committed burglary—that's what you've done. His honor the admiral's keys stolen; his honor the admiral's desk ransacked; and his honor the admiral's private letters broke open. Burglary! Burglary! Come and be locked up!" He slowly recovered an upright position, with the assistance of his hands, backed by the solid resisting power of the bureau; and lapsed into lachrymose soliloquy. "Who'd have thought it?" said old Mazey, paternally watering at the eyes. "Take the outside of her, and she's as straight as a poplar; take the inside of her, and she's as crooked as Sin. Such a fine-grown girl, too. What a pity! what a pity!"

"Don't hurt me!" said Magdalen, faintly, as old Mazey staggered up to the chair, and took her by the wrist again. "I'm frightened, Mr. Mazey—I'm dreadfully frightened."

"Hurt you?" repeated the veteran. "I'm a deal too fond of you—and more shame for me at my age!—to hurt you. If I let go of your wrist, will you walk straight before me, where I can see you all the way? Will you be a good girl, and walk straight up to your own door?"

Magdalen gave the promise required of her—gave it with an eager longing to reach the refuge of her room. She rose, and tried to take the candle from the bureau, but old Mazey's cunning hand was too quick for her. "Let the candle be," said the veteran, winking in momentary forgetfulness of his responsible position. "You're a trifle quicker on your legs than I am, my dear, and you might leave me in the lurch, if I don't carry the light."

They returned to the inhabited side of the house. Staggering after Magdalen, with the basket of keys in one hand and the candle in the other, old Mazey sorrowfully compared her figure with the straightness of the poplar, and her disposition with the crookedness of Sin, all the way across "Freeze-your-Bones," and all the way upstairs to her own door. Arrived at that destination, he peremptorily refused to give her the candle until he had first seen her safely inside the room. The conditions being complied with, he resigned the light with one hand, and made a dash with the other at the key, drew it from the inside of the lock, and instantly closed the door. Magdalen heard him outside chuckling over his own dexterity, and fitting the key into the lock again with infinite difficulty. At last he secured the door, with a deep grunt of relief. "There she is safe!" Magdalen heard him say, in regretful soliloquy. "As fine a girl as ever I sat eyes on. What a pity! what a pity!"

The last sounds of his voice died out in the distance; and she was left alone in her room.

Holding fast by the banister, old Mazey made his way down to the corridor on the second floor, in which a night light was always burning. He advanced to the truckle-bed, and, steadying himself against the opposite wall, looked at it attentively. Prolonged contemplation of his own resting-place for the night apparently failed to satisfy him. He shook his head ominously, and, taking from the side-pocket of his great-coat a pair of old patched slippers, surveyed them with an aspect of illimitable doubt. "I'm all abroad to-night," he mumbled to himself. "Troubled in my mind—that's what it is—troubled in my mind."

The old patched slippers and the veteran's existing perplexities happened to be intimately associated one with the other, in the relation of cause and effect. The slippers belonged to the admiral, who had taken one of his unreasonable fancies to this particular pair, and who still persisted in wearing them long after they were unfit for his service. Early that afternoon old Mazey had taken the slippers to the village cobbler to get them repaired on the spot, before his master called for them the next morning; he sat superintending the progress and completion of the work until evening came, when he and the cobbler betook themselves to the village inn to drink each other's healths at parting. They had prolonged this social ceremony till far into the night, and they had parted, as a necessary consequence, in a finished and perfect state of intoxication on either side.

If the drinking-bout had led to no other result than those night wanderings in the grounds of St. Crux, which had shown old Mazey the light in the east windows, his memory would unquestionably have presented it to him the next morning in the aspect of one of the praiseworthy achievements of his life. But another consequence had sprung from it, which the old sailor now saw dimly, through the interposing bewilderment left in his brain by the drink. He had committed a breach of discipline, and a breach of trust. In plainer words, he had deserted his post.

The one safeguard against Admiral Bartram's constitutional tendency to somnambulism was the watch and ward which his faithful old servant kept outside his door. No entreaties had ever prevailed on him to submit to the usual precaution taken in such cases. He peremptorily declined to be locked into his room; he even ignored his own liability, whenever a dream disturbed him, to walk in his sleep. Over and over again, old Mazey had been roused by the admiral's attempts to push past the truckle-bed, or to step over it, in his sleep; and over and over again, when the veteran had reported the fact the next morning, his master had declined to believe him. As the old sailor now stood, staring in vacant inquiry at the bed-chamber door, these incidents of the past rose confusedly on his memory, and forced on him the serious question whether the admiral had left his room during the earlier hours of the night. If by any mischance the sleep-walking fit had seized him, the slippers in old Mazey's hand pointed straight to the conclusion that followed—his master must have passed barefoot in the cold night over the stone stairs and passages of St. Crux. "Lord send he's been quiet!" muttered old Mazey, daunted, bold as he was and drunk as he was, by the bare contemplation of that prospect. "If his honor's been walking to-night, it will be the death of him!"

He roused himself for the moment by main force—strong in his dog-like fidelity to the admiral, though strong in nothing else—and fought off the stupor of the drink. He looked at the bed with steadier eyes and a clearer mind. Magdalen's precaution in returning it to its customary position presented it to him necessarily in the aspect of a bed which had never been moved from its place. He next examined the counterpane carefully. Not the faintest vestige appeared of the indentation which must have been left by footsteps passing over it. There was the plain evidence before him—the evidence recognizable at last by his own bewildered eyes—that the admiral had never moved from his room.

"I'll take the Pledge to-morrow!" mumbled old Mazey, in an outburst of grateful relief. The next moment the fumes of the liquor floated back insidiously over his brain; and the veteran, returning to his customary remedy, paced the passage in zigzag as usual, and kept watch on the deck of an imaginary ship.

Soon after sunrise, Magdalen suddenly heard the grating of the key from outside in the lock of the door. The door opened, and old Mazey re-appeared on the threshold. The first fever of his intoxication had cooled, with time, into a mild, penitential glow. He breathed harder than ever, in a succession of low growls, and wagged his venerable head at his own delinquencies without intermission.

"How are you now, you young land-shark in petticoats?" inquired the old sailor. "Has your conscience been quiet enough to let you go to sleep?"

"I have not slept," said Magdalen, drawing back from him in doubt of what he might do next. "I have no remembrance of what happened after you locked the door—I think I must have fainted. Don't frighten me again, Mr. Mazey! I feel miserably weak and ill. What do you want?"

"I want to say something serious," replied old Mazey, with impenetrable solemnity. "It's been on my mind to come here and make a clean breast of it, for the last hour or more. Mark my words, young woman. I'm going to disgrace myself."

Magdalen drew further and further back, and looked at him in rising alarm.

"I know my duty to his honor the admiral," proceeded old Mazey, waving his hand drearily in the direction of his master's door. "But, try as hard as I may, I can't find it in my heart, you young jade, to be witness against you. I liked the make of you (especially about the waist) when you first came into the house, and I can't help liking the make of you still—though you have committed burglary, and though you are as crooked as Sin. I've cast the eyes of indulgence on fine-grown girls all my life, and it's too late in the day to cast the eyes of severity on 'em now. I'm seventy-seven, or seventy-eight, I don't rightly know which. I'm a battered old hulk, with my seams opening, and my pumps choked, and the waters of Death powering in on me as fast as they can. I'm as miserable a sinner as you'll meet with anywhere in these parts—Thomas Nagle, the cobbler, only excepted; and he's worse than I am, for he's the younger of the two, and he ought to know better. But the long and short or it is, I shall go down to my grave with an eye of indulgence for a fine-grown girl. More shame for me, you young Jezebel—more shame for me!"

The veteran's unmanageable eyes began to leer again in spite of him, as he concluded his harangue in these terms: the last reserves of austerity left in his face entrenched themselves dismally round the corners of his mouth. Magdalen approached him again, and tried to speak. He solemnly motioned her back with another dreary wave of his hand.

"No carneying!" said old Mazey; "I'm bad enough already, without that. It's my duty to make my report to his honor the admiral, and I will make it. But if you like to give the house the slip before the burglary's reported, and the court of inquiry begins, I'll disgrace myself by letting you go. It's market morning at Ossory, and Dawkes will be driving the light cart over in a quarter of an hour's time. Dawkes will take you if I ask him. I know my duty—my duty is to turn the key on you, and see Dawkes damned first. But I can't find it in my heart to be hard on a fine girl like you. It's bred in the bone, and it wunt come out of the flesh. More shame for me, I tell you again—more shame for me!"

The proposal thus strangely and suddenly presented to her took Magdalen completely by surprise. She had been far too seriously shaken by the events of the night to be capable of deciding on any subject at a moment's notice. "You are very good to me, Mr. Mazey," she said. "May I have a minute by myself to think?"

"Yes, you may," replied the veteran, facing about forthwith and leaving the room. "They're all alike," proceeded old Mazey, with his head still running on the sex. "Whatever you offer 'em, they always want something more. Tall and short, native and foreign, sweethearts and wives, they're all alike!"

Left by herself, Magdalen reached her decision with far less difficulty than she had anticipated.

If she remained in the house, there were only two courses before her—to charge old Mazey with speaking under the influence of a drunken delusion, or to submit to circumstances. Though she owed to the old sailor her defeat in the very hour of success, his consideration for her at that moment forbade the idea of defending herself at his expense—even supposing, what was in the last degree improbable, that the defense would be credited. In the second of the two cases (the case of submission to circumstances), but one result could be expected—instant dismissal, and perhaps discovery as well. What object was to be gained by braving that degradation—by leaving the house publicly disgraced in the eyes of the servants who had hated and distrusted her from the first? The accident which had literally snatched the Trust from her possession when she had it in her hand was irreparable. The one apparent compensation under the disaster—in other words, the discovery that the Trust actually existed, and that George Bartram's marriage within a given time was one of the objects contained in it—was a compensation which could only be estimated at its true value by placing it under the light of Mr. Loscombe's experience. Every motive of which she was conscious was a motive which urged her to leave the house secretly while the chance was at her disposal. She looked out into the passage, and called softly to old Mazey to come back.

"I accept your offer thankfully, Mr. Mazey," she said. "You don't know what hard measure you dealt out to me when you took that letter from my hand. But you did your duty, and I can be grateful to you for sparing me this morning, hard as you were upon me last night. I am not such a bad girl as you think me—I am not, indeed."

Old Mazey dismissed the subject with another dreary wave of his hand.

"Let it be," said the veteran; "let it be! It makes no difference, my girl, to such an old rascal as I am. If you were fifty times worse than you are, I should let you go all the same. Put on your bonnet and shawl, and come along. I'm a disgrace to myself and a warning to others—that's what I am. No luggage, mind! Leave all your rattle-traps behind you: to be overhauled, if necessary, at his honor the admiral's discretion. I can be hard enough on your boxes, you young Jezebel, if I can't be hard on you."

With these words, old Mazey led the way out of the room. "The less I see of her the better—especially about the waist," he said to himself, as he hobbled downstairs with the help of the banisters.

The cart was standing in the back yard when they reached the lower regions of the house, and Dawkes (otherwise the farm-bailiff's man) was fastening the last buckle of the horse's harness. The hoar-frost of the morning was still white in the shade. The sparkling points of it glistened brightly on the shaggy coats of Brutus and Cassius, as they idled about the yard, waiting, with steaming mouths and slowly wagging tails, to see the cart drive off. Old Mazey went out alone and used his influence with Dawkes, who, staring in stolid amazement, put a leather cushion on the cart-seat for his fellow-traveler. Shivering in the sharp morning air, Magdalen waited, while the preliminaries of departure were in progress, conscious of nothing but a giddy bewilderment of thought, and a helpless suspension of feeling. The events of the night confused themselves hideously with the trivial circumstances passing before her eyes in the courtyard. She started with the sudden terror of the night when old Mazey re-appeared to summon her out to the cart. She trembled with the helpless confusion of the night when the veteran cast the eyes of indulgence on her for the last time, and gave her a kiss on the cheek at parting. The next minute she felt him help her into the cart, and pat her on the back. The next, she heard him tell her in a confidential whisper that, sitting or standing, she was as straight as a poplar either way. Then there was a pause, in which nothing was said, and nothing done; and then the driver took the reins in hand and mounted to his place.

She roused herself at the parting moment and looked back. The last sight she saw at St. Crux was old Mazey wagging his head in the courtyard, with his fellow-profligates, the dogs, keeping time to him with their tails. The last words she heard were the words in which the veteran paid his farewell tribute to her charms:

"Burglary or no burglary," said old Mazey, "she's a fine-grown girl, if ever there was a fine one yet. What a pity! what a pity!"

THE END OF THE SEVENTH SCENE.

BETWEEN THE SCENES.

PROGRESS OF THE STORY THROUGH THE POST.

I.

From George Bartram to Admiral Bartram.

"London, April 3d, 1848.

"MY DEAR UNCLE—One hasty line, to inform you of a temporary obstacle, which we neither of us anticipated when we took leave of each other at St. Crux. While I was wasting the last days of the week at the Grange, the Tyrrels must have been making their arrangements for leaving London. I have just come from Portland Place. The house is shut up, and the family (Miss Vanstone, of course, included) left England yesterday, to pass the season in Paris.

"Pray don't let yourself be annoyed by this little check at starting. It is of no serious importance whatever. I have got the address at which the Tyrrels are living, and I mean to cross the Channel after them by the mail to-night. I shall find my opportunity in Paris just as soon as I could have found it in London. The grass shall not grow under my feet, I promise you. For once in my life, I will take Time as fiercely by the forelock as if I was the most impetuous man in England; and, rely on it, the moment I know the result, you shall know the result, too. Affectionately yours,

"GEORGE BARTRAM."

II.

From George Bartram to Miss Garth.

"Paris, April 13th.

"DEAR MISS GARTH—I have just written, with a heavy heart, to my uncle, and I think I owe it to your kind interest in me not to omit writing next to you.

"You will feel for my disappointment, I am sure, when I tell you, in the fewest and plainest words, that Miss Vanstone has refused me.

"My vanity may have grievously misled me, but I confess I expected a very different result. My vanity may be misleading me still; for I must acknowledge to you privately that I think Miss Vanstone was sorry to refuse me. The reason she gave for her decision—no doubt a sufficient reason in her estimation—did not at the time, and does not now, seem sufficient to me. She spoke in the sweetest and kindest manner, but she firmly declared that 'her family misfortunes' left her no honorable alternative—but to think of my own interests as I had not thought of them myself—and gratefully to decline accepting my offer.

"She was so painfully agitated that I could not venture to plead my own cause as I might otherwise have pleaded it. At the first attempt I made to touch the personal question, she entreated me to spare her, and abruptly left the room. I am still ignorant whether I am to interpret the 'family misfortunes' which have set up this barrier between us, as meaning the misfortune for which her parents alone are to blame, or the misfortune of her having such a woman as Mrs. Noel Vanstone for her sister. In whichever of these circumstances the obstacle lies, it is no obstacle in my estimation. Can nothing remove it? Is there no hope? Forgive me for asking these questions. I cannot bear up against my bitter disappointment. Neither she, nor you, nor any one but myself, can know how I love her.

"Ever most truly yours,

"GEORGE BARTRAM.

"P. S.—I shall leave for England in a day or two, passing through London on my way to St. Crux. There are family reasons, connected with the hateful subject of money, which make me look forward with anything but pleasure to my next interview with my uncle. If you address your letter to Long's Hotel, it will be sure to reach me."

III.

From Miss Garth to George Bartram.

"Westmoreland House, April 16th.

"DEAR MR. BARTRAM—You only did me justice in supposing that your letter would distress me. If you had supposed that it would make me excessively angry as well, you would not have been far wrong. I have no patience with the pride and perversity of the young women of the present day.

"I have heard from Norah. It is a long letter, stating the particulars in full detail. I am now going to put all the confidence in your honor and your discretion which I really feel. For your sake, and for Norah's, I am going to let you know what the scruple really is which has misled her into the pride and folly of refusing you. I am old enough to speak out; and I can tell you, if she had only been wise enough to let her own wishes guide her, she would have said Yes—and gladly, too.

"The original cause of all the mischief is no less a person than your worthy uncle—Admiral Bartram.

"It seems that the admiral took it into his head (I suppose during your absence) to go to London by himself and to satisfy some curiosity of his own about Norah by calling in Portland Place, under pretense of renewing his old friendship with the Tyrrels. He came at luncheon-time, and saw Norah; and, from all I can hear, was apparently better pleased with her than he expected or wished to be when he came into the house.

"So far, this is mere guess-work; but it is unluckily certain that he and Mrs. Tyrrel had some talk together alone when luncheon was over. Your name was not mentioned; but when their conversation fell on Norah, you were in both their minds, of course. The admiral (doing her full justice personally) declared himself smitten with pity for her hard lot in life. The scandalous conduct of her sister must always stand (he feared) in the way of her future advantage. Who could marry her, without first making it a condition that she and her sister were to be absolute strangers to each other? And even then, the objection would remain—the serious objection to the husband's family—of being connected by marriage with such a woman as Mrs. Noel Vanstone. It was very sad; it was not the poor girl's fault, but it was none the less true that her sister was her rock ahead in life. So he ran on, with no real ill-feeling toward Norah, but with an obstinate belief in his own prejudices which bore the aspect of ill-feeling, and which people with more temper than judgment would be but too readily disposed to resent accordingly.

"Unfortunately, Mrs. Tyrrel is one of those people. She is an excellent, warm-hearted woman, with a quick temper and very little judgment; strongly attached to Norah, and heartily interested in Norah's welfare. From all I can learn, she first resented the expression of the admiral's opinion, in his presence, as worldly and selfish in the last degree; and then interpreted it, behind his back, as a hint to discourage his nephew's visits, which was a downright insult offered to a lady in her own house. This was foolish enough so far; but worse folly was to come.

"As soon as your uncle was gone, Mrs. Tyrrel, most unwisely and improperly, sent for Norah, and, repeating the conversation that had taken place, warned her of the reception she might expect from the man who stood toward you in the position of a father, if she accepted an offer of marriage on your part. When I tell you that Norah's faithful attachment to her sister still remains unshaken, and that there lies hidden under her noble submission to the unhappy circumstances of her life a proud susceptibility to slights of all kinds, which is deeply seated in her nature—you will understand the true motive of the refusal which has so naturally and so justly disappointed you. They are all three equally to blame in this matter. Your uncle was wrong to state his objections so roundly and inconsiderately as he did. Mrs. Tyrrel was wrong to let her temper get the better of her, and to suppose herself insulted where no insult was intended. And Norah was wrong to place a scruple of pride, and a hopeless belief in her sister which no strangers can be expected to share, above the higher claims of an attachment which might have secured the happiness and the prosperity of her future life.

"But the mischief has been done. The next question is, can the harm be remedied?

"I hope and believe it can. My advice is this: Don't take No for an answer. Give her time enough to reflect on what she has done, and to regret it (as I believe she will regret it) in secret; trust to my influence over her to plead your cause for you at every opportunity I can find; wait patiently for the right moment, and ask her again. Men, being accustomed to act on reflection themselves, are a great deal too apt to believe that women act on reflection, too. Women do nothing of the sort. They act on impulse; and, in nine cases out of ten, they are heartily sorry for it afterward.

"In the meanwhile, you must help your own interests by inducing your uncle to alter his opinion, or at least to make the concession of keeping his opinion to himself. Mrs. Tyrrel has rushed to the conclusion that the harm he has done he did intentionally—which is as much as to say, in so many words, that he had a prophetic conviction, when he came into the house, of what she would do when he left it. My explanation of the matter is a much simpler one. I believe that the knowledge of your attachment naturally aroused his curiosity to see the object of it, and that Mrs. Tyrrel's injudicious praises of Norah irritated his objections into openly declaring themselves. Anyway, your course lies equally plain before you. Use your influence over your uncle to persuade him into setting matters right again; trust my settled resolution to see Norah your wife before six months more are over our heads; and believe me, your friend and well-wisher,

"HARRIET GARTH."

IV.

From Mrs. Drake to George Bartram.

"St. Crux, April 17th.

"SIR—I direct these lines to the hotel you usually stay at in London, hoping that you may return soon enough from foreign parts to receive my letter without delay.

"I am sorry to say that some unpleasant events have taken place at St. Crux since you left it, and that my honored master, the admiral, is far from enjoying his usual good health. On both these accounts, I venture to write to you on my own responsibility, for I think your presence is needed in the house.

"Early in the month a most regrettable circumstance took place. Our new parlor-maid was discovered by Mr. Mazey, at a late hour of the night (with her master's basket of keys in her possession), prying into the private documents kept in the east library. The girl removed herself from the house the next morning before we were any of us astir, and she has not been heard of since. This event has annoyed and alarmed my master very seriously; and to make matters worse, on the day when the girl's treacherous conduct was discovered, the admiral was seized with the first symptoms of a severe inflammatory cold. He was not himself aware, nor was any one else, how he had caught the chill. The doctor was sent for, and kept the inflammation down until the day before yesterday, when it broke out again, under circumstances which I am sure you will be sorry to hear, as I am truly sorry to write of them.

"On the date I have just mentioned—I mean the fifteenth of the month—my master himself informed me that he had been dreadfully disappointed by a letter received from you, which had come in the morning from foreign parts, and had brought him bad news. He did not tell me what the news was—but I have never, in all the years I have passed in the admiral's service, seen him so distressingly upset, and so unlike himself, as he was on that day. At night his uneasiness seemed to increase. He was in such a state of irritation that he could not bear the sound of Mr. Mazey's hard breathing outside his door, and he laid his positive orders on the old man to go into one of the bedrooms for that night. Mr. Mazey, to his own great regret, was of course obliged to obey.

"Our only means of preventing the admiral from leaving his room in his sleep, if the fit unfortunately took him, being now removed, Mr. Mazey and I agreed to keep watch by turns through the night, sitting, with the door ajar, in one of the empty rooms near our master's bed-chamber. We could think of nothing better to do than this, knowing he would not allow us to lock him in, and not having the door key in our possession, even if we could have ventured to secure him in his room without his permission. I kept watch for the first two hours, and then Mr. Mazey took my place. After having been some little time in my own room, it occurred to me that the old man was hard of hearing, and that if his eyes grew at all heavy in the night, his ears were not to be trusted to warn him if anything happened. I slipped on my clothes again, and went back to Mr. Mazey. He was neither asleep nor awake—he was between the two. My mind misgave me, and I went on to the admiral's room. The door was open, and the bed was empty.

"Mr. Mazey and I went downstairs instantly. We looked in all the north rooms, one after another, and found no traces of him. I thought of the drawing-room next, and, being the more active of the two, went first to examine it. The moment I turned the sharp corner of the passage, I saw my master coming toward me through the open drawing-room door, asleep and dreaming, with his keys in his hands. The sliding door behind him was open also; and the fear came to me then, and has remained with me ever since, that his dream had led him through the Banqueting-Hall into the east rooms. We abstained from waking him, and followed his steps until he returned of his own accord to his bed-chamber. The next morning, I grieve to say, all the bad symptoms came back; and none of the remedies employed have succeeded in getting the better of them yet. By the doctor's advice, we refrained from telling the admiral what had happened. He is still under the impression that he passed the night as usual in his own room.

"I have been careful to enter into all the particulars of this unfortunate accident, because neither Mr. Mazey nor myself desire to screen ourselves from blame, if blame we have deserved. We both acted for the best, and we both beg and pray you will consider our responsible situation, and come as soon as possible to St. Crux. Our honored master is very hard to manage; and the doctor thinks, as we do, that your presence is wanted in the house.

"I remain, sir, with Mr. Mazey's respects and my own, your humble servant,

"SOPHIA DRAKE."

V.

From George Bartram to Miss Garth.

"St. Crux, April 22d.

"DEAR MISS GARTH—Pray excuse my not thanking you sooner for your kind and consoling letter. We are in sad trouble at St. Crux. Any little irritation I might have felt at my poor uncle's unlucky interference in Portland Place is all forgotten in the misfortune of his serious illness. He is suffering from internal inflammation, produced by cold; and symptoms have shown themselves which are dangerous at his age. A physician from London is now in the house. You shall hear more in a few days. Meantime, believe me, with sincere gratitude,

"Yours most truly,

"GEORGE BARTRAM."

VI.

From Mr. Loscombe to Mrs. Noel Vanstone.

"Lincoln's Inn Fields, May 6th.

"DEAR MADAM—I have unexpectedly received some information which is of the most vital importance to your interests. The news of Admiral Bartram's death has reached me this morning. He expired at his own house, on the fourth of the present month.

"This event at once disposes of the considerations which I had previously endeavored to impress on you, in relation to your discovery at St. Crux. The wisest course we can now follow is to open communications at once with the executors of the deceased gentleman; addressing them through the medium of the admiral's legal adviser, in the first instance.

"I have dispatched a letter this day to the solicitor in question. It simply warns him that we have lately become aware of the existence of a private Document, controlling the deceased gentleman in his use of the legacy devised to him by Mr. Noel Vanstone's will. My letter assumes that the document will be easily found among the admiral's papers; and it mentions that I am the solicitor appointed by Mrs. Noel Vanstone to receive communications on her behalf. My object in taking this step is to cause a search to be instituted for the Trust—in the very probable event of the executors not having met with it yet—before the usual measures are adopted for the administration of the admiral's estate. We will threaten legal proceedings, if we find that the object does not succeed. But I anticipate no such necessity. Admiral Bartram's executors must be men of high standing and position; and they will do justice to you and to themselves in this matter by looking for the Trust.

"Under these circumstances, you will naturally ask, 'What are our prospects when the document is found?' Our prospects have a bright side and a dark side. Let us take the bright side to begin with.

"What do we actually know?

"We know, first, that the Trust does really exist. Secondly, that there is a provision in it relating to the marriage of Mr. George Bartram in a given time. Thirdly, that the time (six months from the date of your husband's death) expired on the third of this month. Fourthly, that Mr. George Bartram (as I have found out by inquiry, in the absence of any positive information on the subject possessed by yourself) is, at the present moment, a single man. The conclusion naturally follows, that the object contemplated by the Trust, in this case, is an object that has failed.

"If no other provisions have been inserted in the document—or if, being inserted, those other provisions should be discovered to have failed also—I believe it to be impossible (especially if evidence can be found that the admiral himself considered the Trust binding on him) for the executors to deal with your husband's fortune as legally forming part of Admiral Bartram's estate. The legacy is expressly declared to have been left to him, on the understanding that he applies it to certain stated objects—and those objects have failed. What is to be done with the money? It was not left to the admiral himself, on the testator's own showing; and the purposes for which it was left have not been, and cannot be, carried out. I believe (if the case here supposed really happens) that the money must revert to the testator's estate. In that event the Law, dealing with it as a matter of necessity, divides it into two equal portions. One half goes to Mr. Noel Vanstone's childless widow, and the other half is divided among Mr. Noel Vanstone's next of kin.

"You will no doubt discover the obvious objection to the case in our favor, as I have here put it. You will see that it depends for its practical realization not on one contingency, but on a series of contingencies, which must all happen exactly as we wish them to happen. I admit the force of the objection; but I can tell you, at the same time, that these said contingencies are by no means so improbable as they may look on the face of them.

"We have every reason to believe that the Trust, like the Will, was not drawn by a lawyer. That is one circumstance in our favor that is enough of itself to cast a doubt on the soundness of all, or any, of the remaining provisions which we may not be acquainted with. Another chance which we may count on is to be found, as I think, in that strange handwriting, placed under the signature on the third page of the Letter, which you saw, but which you, unhappily, omitted to read. All the probabilities point to those lines as written by Admiral Bartram: and the position which they occupy is certainly consistent with the theory that they touch the important subject of his own sense of obligation under the Trust.

"I wish to raise no false hopes in your mind. I only desire to satisfy you that we have a case worth trying.

"As for the dark side of the prospect, I need not enlarge on it. After what I have already written, you will understand that the existence of a sound provision, unknown to us, in the Trust, which has been properly carried out by the admiral—or which can be properly carried out by his representatives—would be necessarily fatal to our hopes. The legacy would be, in this case, devoted to the purpose or purposes contemplated by your husband—and, from that moment, you would have no claim.

"I have only to add, that as soon as I hear from the late admiral's man of business, you shall know the result.

"Believe me, dear madam, faithfully yours,

"JOHN LOSCOMBE."

VII.

From George Bartram to Miss Garth.

"St. Crux, May 15th.

"DEAR MISS GARTH—I trouble you with another letter: partly to thank you for your kind expression of sympathy with me, under the loss that I have sustained; and partly to tell you of an extraordinary application made to my uncle's executors, in which you and Miss Vanstone may both feel interested, as Mrs. Noel Vanstone is directly concerned in it.

"Knowing my own ignorance of legal technicalities, I inclose a copy of the application, instead of trying to describe it. You will notice as suspicious, that no explanation is given of the manner in which the alleged discovery of one of my uncle's secrets was made, by persons who are total strangers to him.

"On being made acquainted with the circumstances, the executors at once applied to me. I could give them no positive information—for my uncle never consulted me on matters of business. But I felt in honor bound to tell them, that during the last six months of his life, the admiral had occasionally let fall expressions of impatience in my hearing, which led to the conclusion that he was annoyed by a private responsibility of some kind. I also mentioned that he had imposed a very strange condition on me—a condition which, in spite of his own assurances to the contrary, I was persuaded could not have emanated from himself—of marrying within a given time (which time has now expired), or of not receiving from him a certain sum of money, which I believed to be the same in amount as the sum bequeathed to him in my cousin's will. The executors agreed with me that these circumstances gave a color of probability to an otherwise incredible story; and they decided that a search should be instituted for the Secret Trust, nothing in the slightest degree resembling this same Trust having been discovered, up to that time, among the admiral's papers.

"The search (no trifle in such a house as this) has now been in full progress for a week. It is superintended by both the executors, and by my uncle's lawyer, who is personally, as well as professionally, known to Mr. Loscombe (Mrs. Noel Vanstone's solicitor), and who has been included in the proceedings at the express request of Mr. Loscombe himself. Up to this time, nothing whatever has been found. Thousands and thousands of letters have been examined, and not one of them bears the remotest resemblance to the letter we are looking for.

"Another week will bring the search to an end. It is only at my express request that it will be persevered with so long. But as the admiral's generosity has made me sole heir to everything he possessed, I feel bound to do the fullest justice to the interests of others, however hostile to myself those interests may be.

"With this view, I have not hesitated to reveal to the lawyer a constitutional peculiarity of my poor uncle's, which was always kept a secret among us at his own request—I mean his tendency to somnambulism. I mentioned that he had been discovered (by the housekeeper and his old servant) walking in his sleep, about three weeks before his death, and that the part of the house in which he had been seen, and the basket of keys which he was carrying in his hand, suggested the inference that he had come from one of the rooms in the east wing, and that he might have opened some of the pieces of furniture in one of them. I surprised the lawyer (who seemed to be quite ignorant of the extraordinary actions constantly performed by somnambulists), by informing him that my uncle could find his way about the house, lock and unlock doors, and remove objects of all kinds from one place to another, as easily in his sleep as in his waking hours. And I declared that, while I felt the faintest doubt in my own mind whether he might not have been dreaming of the Trust on the night in question, and putting the dream in action in his sleep, I should not feel satisfied unless the rooms in the east wing were searched again.

"It is only right to add that there is not the least foundation in fact for this idea of mine. During the latter part of his fatal illness, my poor uncle was quite incapable of speaking on any subject whatever. From the time of my arrival at St. Crux, in the middle of last month, to the time of his death, not a word dropped from him which referred in the remotest way to the Secret Trust.

"Here then, for the present, the matter rests. If you think it right to communicate the contents of this letter to Miss Vanstone, pray tell her that it will not be my fault if her sister's assertion (however preposterous it may seem to my uncle's executors) is not fairly put to the proof.

"Believe me, dear Miss Garth, always truly yours,

"GEORGE BARTRAM.

"P. S.—As soon as all business matters are settled, I am going abroad for some months, to try the relief of change of scene. The house will be shut up, and left under the charge of Mrs. Drake. I have not forgotten your once telling me that you should like to see St. Crux, if you ever found yourself in this neighborhood. If you are at all likely to be in Essex during the time when I am abroad, I have provided against the chance of your being disappointed, by leaving instructions with Mrs. Drake to give you, and any friends of yours, the freest admission to the house and grounds."

VIII.

From Mr. Loscombe to Mrs. Noel Vanstone.

"Lincoln's Inn Fields, May 24th.

"DEAR MADAM—After a whole fortnight's search—conducted, I am bound to admit, with the most conscientious and unrelaxing care—no such document as the Secret Trust has been found among the papers left at St. Crux by the late Admiral Bartram.

"Under these circumstances, the executors have decided on acting under the only recognizable authority which they have to guide them—the admiral's own will. This document (executed some years since) bequeaths the whole of his estate, both real and personal (that is to say, all the lands he possesses, and all the money he possesses, at the time of his death), to his nephew. The will is plain, and the result is inevitable. Your husband's fortune is lost to you from this moment. Mr. George Bartram legally inherits it, as he legally inherits the house and estate of St. Crux.

"I make no comment upon this extraordinary close to the proceedings. The Trust may have been destroyed, or the Trust may be hidden in some place of concealment inaccessible to discovery. Either way, it is, in my opinion, impossible to found any valid legal declaration on a knowledge of the document so fragmentary and so incomplete as the knowledge which you possess. If other lawyers differ from me on this point, by all means consult them. I have devoted money enough and time enough to the unfortunate attempt to assert your interests; and my connection with the matter must, from this moment, be considered at an end.

"Your obedient servant,

"JOHN LOSCOMBE."

IX.

From Mrs. Ruddock (Lodging-house Keeper) to Mr. Loscombe.

"Park Terrace, St. John's Wood, June 2d.

"SIR—Having, by Mrs. Noel Vanstone's directions, taken letters for her to the post, addressed to you—and knowing no one else to apply to—I beg to inquire whether you are acquainted with any of her friends; for I think it right that they should be stirred up to take some steps about her.

"Mrs. Vanstone first came to me in November last, when she and her maid occupied my apartments. On that occasion, and again on this, she has given me no cause to complain of her. She has behaved like a lady, and paid me my due. I am writing, as a mother of a family, under a sense of responsibility—I am not writing with an interested motive.

"After proper warning given, Mrs. Vanstone (who is now quite alone) leaves me to-morrow. She has not concealed from me that her circumstances are fallen very low, and that she cannot afford to remain in my house. This is all she has told me—I know nothing of where she is going, or what she means to do next. But I have every reason to believe she desires to destroy all traces by which she might be found, after leaving this place—for I discovered her in tears yesterday, burning letters which were doubtless letters from her friends. In looks and conduct she has altered most shockingly in the last week. I believe there is some dreadful trouble on her mind; and I am afraid, from what I see of her, that she is on the eve of a serious illness. It is very sad to see such a young woman so utterly deserted and friendless as she is now.

"Excuse my troubling you with this letter; it is on my conscience to write it. If you know any of her relations, please warn them that time is not to be wasted. If they lose to-morrow, they may lose the last chance of finding her.

"Your humble servant,

"CATHERINE RUDDOCK."

X.

From Mr. Loscombe to Mrs. Ruddock.

"Lincoln's Inn Fields, June 2d.

"MADAM—MY only connection with Mrs. Noel Vanstone was a professional one, and that connection is now at an end. I am not acquainted with any of her friends; and I cannot undertake to interfere personally, either with her present or future proceedings.

"Regretting my inability to afford you any assistance, I remain, your obedient servant,

"JOHN LOSCOMBE."

THE LAST SCENE.

AARON'S BUILDINGS

CHAPTER I.

ON the seventh of June, the owners of the merchantman Deliverance received news that the ship had touched at Plymouth to land passengers, and had then continued her homeward voyage to the Port of London. Five days later, the vessel was in the river, and was towed into the East India Docks.

Having transacted the business on shore for which he was personally responsible, Captain Kirke made the necessary arrangements, by letter, for visiting his brother-in-law's parsonage in Suffolk, on the seventeenth of the month. As usual in such cases, he received a list of commissions to execute for his sister on the day before he left London. One of these commissions took him into the neighborhood of Camden Town. He drove to his destination from the Docks; and then, dismissing the vehicle, set forth to walk back southward, toward the New Road.

He was not well acquainted with the district; and his attention wandered further and further away from the scene around him as he went on. His thoughts, roused by the prospect of seeing his sister again, had led his memory back to the night when he had parted from her, leaving the house on foot. The spell so strangely laid on him, in that past time, had kept its hold through all after-events. The face that had haunted him on the lonely road had haunted him again on the lonely sea. The woman who had followed him, as in a dream, to his sister's door, had followed him—thought of his thought, and spirit of his spirit—to the deck of his ship. Through storm and calm on the voyage out, through storm and calm on the voyage home, she had been with him. In the ceaseless turmoil of the London streets, she was with him now. He knew what the first question on his lips would be, when he had seen his sister and her boys. "I shall try to talk of something else," he thought; "but when Lizzie and I am alone, it will come out in spite of me."

The necessity of waiting to let a string of carts pass at a turning before he crossed awakened him to present things. He looked about in a momentary confusion. The street was strangc to him; hc had lost his way.

The first foot passenger of whom he inquired appeared to have no time to waste in giving information. Hurriedly directing him to cross to the other side of the road, to turn down the first street he came to on his right hand, and then to ask again, the stranger unceremoniously hastened on without waiting to be thanked.

Kirke followed his directions and took the turning on his right. The street was short and narrow, and the houses on either side were of the poorer order. He looked up as he passed the corner to see what the name of the place might be. It was called "Aaron's Buildings."

Low down on the side of the "Buildings" along which he was walking, a little crowd of idlers was assembled round two cabs, both drawn up before the door of the same house. Kirke advanced to the crowd, to ask his way of any civil stranger among them who might not be in a hurry this time. On approaching the cabs, he found a woman disputing with the drivers; and heard enough to inform him that two vehicles had been sent for by mistake, where only one was wanted.

The house door was open; and when he turned that way next, he looked easily into the passage, over the heads of the people in front of him.

The sight that met his eyes should have been shielded in pity from the observation of the street. He saw a slatternly girl, with a frightened face, standing by an old chair placed in the middle of the passage, and holding a woman on the chair, too weak and helpless to support herself—a woman apparently in the last stage of illness, who was about to be removed, when the dispute outside was ended, in one of the cabs. Her head was drooping when he first saw her, and an old shawl which covered it had fallen forward so as to hide the upper part of her face.

Before he could look away again, the girl in charge of her raised her head and restored the shawl to its place. The action disclosed her face to view, for an instant only, before her head drooped once more on her bosom. In that instant he saw the woman whose beauty was the haunting remembrance of his life—whose image had been vivid in his mind not five minutes since.

The shock of the double recognition—the recognition, at the same moment, of the face, and of the dreadful change in it—struck him speechless and helpless. The steady presence of mind in all emergencies which had become a habit of his life, failed him for the first time. The poverty-stricken street, the squalid mob round the door, swam before his eyes. He staggered back and caught at the iron railings of the house behind him.

"Where are they taking her to?" he heard a woman ask, close at his side.

"To the hospital, if they will have her," was the reply. "And to the work-house, if they won't."

That horrible answer roused him. He pushed his way through the crowd and entered the house.

The misunderstanding on the pavement had been set right, and one of the cabs had driven off.

As he crossed the threshold of the door he confronted the people of the house at the moment when they were moving her. The cabman who had remained was on one side of the chair, and the woman who had been disputing with the two drivers was on the other. They were just lifting her, when Kirke's tall figure darkened the door.

"What are you doing with that lady?" he asked.

The cabman looked up with the insolence of his reply visible in his eyes, before his lips could utter it. But the woman, quicker than he, saw the suppressed agitation in Kirke's face, and dropped her hold of the chair in an instant.

"Do you know her, sir?" asked the woman, eagerly. "Are you one of her friends?"

"Yes," said Kirke, without hesitation.

"It's not my fault, sir," pleaded the woman, shirking under the look he fixed on her. "I would have waited patiently till her friends found her—I would, indeed!"

Kirke made no reply. He turned, and spoke to the cabman.

"Go out," he said, "and close the door after you. I'll send you down your money directly. What room in the house did you take her from, when you brought her here?" he resumed, addressing himself to the woman again.

"The first floor back, sir."

"Show me the way to it."

He stooped, and lifted Magdalen in his arms. Her head rested gently on the sailor's breast; her eyes looked up wonderingly into the sailor's face. She smiled, and whispered to him vacantly. Her mind had wandered back to old days at home; and her few broken words showed that she fancied herself a child again in her father's arms. "Poor papa!" she said, softly. "Why do you look so sorry? Poor papa!"

The woman led the way into the back room on the first floor. It was very small; it was miserably furnished. But the little bed was clean, and the few things in the room were neatly kept. Kirke laid her tenderly on the bed. She caught one of his hands in her burning fingers. "Don't distress mamma about me," she said. "Send for Norah." Kirke tried gently to release his hand; but she only clasped it the more eagerly. He sat down by the bedside to wait until it pleased her to release him. The woman stood looking at them and crying, in a corner of the room. Kirke observed her attentively. "Speak," he said, after an interval, in low, quiet tones. "Speak in her presence; and tell me the truth."

With many words, with many tears, the woman spoke.

She had let her first floor to the lady a fortnight since. The lady had paid a week's rent, and had given the name of Gray. She had been out from morning till night, for the first three days, and had come home again, on every occasion, with a wretchedly weary, disappointed look. The woman of the house had suspected that she was in hiding from her friends, under a false name; and that she had been vainly trying to raise money, or to get some employment, on the three days when she was out for so long, and when she looked so disappointed on coming home. However that might be, on the fourth day she had fallen ill, with shivering fits and hot fits, turn and turn about. On the fifth day she was worse; and on the sixth, she was too sleepy at one time, and too light-headed at another, to be spoken to. The chemist (who did the doctoring in those parts) had come and looked at her, and had said he thought it was a bad fever. He had left a "saline draught," which the woman of the house had paid for out of her own pocket, and had administered without effect. She had ventured on searching the only box which the lady had brought with her; and had found nothing in it but a few necessary articles of linen—no dresses, no ornaments, not so much as the fragment of a letter which might help in discovering her friends. Between the risk of keeping her under these circumstances, and the barbarity of turning a sick woman into the street, the landlady herself had not hesitated. She would willingly have kept her tenant, on the chance of the lady's recovery, and on the chance of her friends turning up. But not half an hour since, her husband—who never came near the house, except to take her money—had come to rob her of her little earnings, as usual. She had been obliged to tell him that no rent was in hand for the first floor, and that none was likely to be in hand until the lady recovered, or her friends found her. On hearing this, he had mercilessly insisted—well or ill—that the lady should go. There was the hospital to take her to;

and if the hospital shut its doors, there was the workhouse to try next. If she was not out of the place in an hour's time, he threatened to come back and take her out himself. His wife knew but too well that he was brute enough to be as good as his word; and no other choice had been left her but to do as she had done, for the sake of the lady herself.

The woman told her shocking story, with every appearance of being honestly ashamed of it. Toward the end, Kirke felt the clasp of the burning fingers slackening round his hand. He looked back at the bed again. Her weary eyes were closing; and, with her face still turned toward the sailor, she was sinking into sleep.

"Is there any one in the front room?" said Kirke, in a whisper. "Come in there; I have something to say to you."

The woman followed him through the door of communication between the rooms.

"How much does she owe you?" he asked.

The landlady mentioned the sum. Kirke put it down before her on the table.

"Where is your husband?" was his next question.

"Waiting at the public-house, sir, till the hour is up."

"You can take him the money or not, as you think right," said Kirke, quietly. "I have only one thing to tell you, as far as your husband is concerned. If you want to see every bone in his skin broken, let him come to the house while I am in it. Stop! I have something more to say. Do you know of any doctor in the neighborhood who can be depended on?"

"Not in our neighborhood, sir. But I know of one within half an hour's walk of us."

"Take the cab at the door; and, if you find him at home, bring him back in it. Say I am waiting here for his opinion on a very serious case. He shall be well paid, and you shall be well paid. Make haste!"

The woman left the room.

Kirke sat down alone, to wait for her return. He hid his face in his hands, and tried to realize the strange and touching situation in which the accident of a moment had placed him.

Hidden in the squalid by-ways of London under a false name; cast, friendless and helpless, on the mercy of strangers, by illness which had struck her prostrate, mind and body alike—so he met her again, the woman who had opened a new world of beauty to his mind; the woman who had called Love to life in him by a look! What horrible misfortune had struck her so cruelly, and struck her so low? What mysterious destiny had guided him to the last refuge of her poverty and despair, in the hour of her sorest need? "If it is ordered that I am to see her again, I shall see her." Those words came back to him now—the memorable words that he had spoken to his sister at parting. With that thought in his heart, he had gone where his duty called him. Months and months had passed; thousands and thousands of miles, protracting their desolate length on the unresting waters had rolled between them. And through the lapse of time, and over the waste of oceans—day after day, and night after night, as the winds of heaven blew, and the good ship toiled on before them—he had advanced nearer and nearer to the end that was waiting for him; he had journeyed blindfold to the meeting on the threshold of that miserable door. "What has brought me here?" he said to himself in a whisper. "The mercy of chance? No. The mercy of God."

He waited, unregardful of the place, unconscious of the time, until the sound of footsteps on the stairs came suddenly between him and his thoughts. The door opened, and the doctor was shown into the room.

"Dr. Merrick," said the landlady, placing a chair for him.

"Mr. Merrick," said the visitor, smiling quietly as he took the chair. "I am not a physician—I am a surgeon in general practice."

Physician or surgeon, there was something in his face and manner which told Kirke at a glance that he was a man to be relied on.

After a few preliminary words on either side, Mr. Merrick sent the landlady into the bedroom to see if his patient was awake or asleep. The woman returned, and said she was "betwixt the two, light in the head again, and burning hot." The doctor went at once into the bedroom, telling the landlady to follow him, and to close the door behind her.

A weary time passed before he came back into the front room. When he re-appeared, his face spoke for him, before any question could be asked.

"Is it a serious illness?" said Kirke his voice sinking low, his eyes anxiously fixed on the doctor's face.

"It is a dangerous illness," said Mr. Merrick, with an emphasis on the word.

He drew his chair nearer to Kirke and looked at him attentively.

"May I ask you some questions which are not strictly medical?" he inquired.

Kirke bowed.

"Can you tell me what her life has been before she came into this house, and before she fell ill?"

"I have no means of knowing. I have just returned to England after a long absence."

"Did you know of her coming here?"

"I only discovered it by accident."

"Has she no female relations? No mother? no sister? no one to take care of her but yourself?"

"No one—unless I can succeed in tracing her relations. No one but myself."

Mr. Merrick was silent. He looked at Kirke more attentively than ever. "Strange!" thought the doctor. "He is here, in sole charge of her—and is this all he knows?"

Kirke saw the doubt in his face; and addressed himself straight to that doubt, before another word passed between them,

"I see my position here surprises you," he said, simply. "Will you consider it the position of a relation—the position of her brother or her father—until her friends can be found?" His voice faltered, and he laid his hand earnestly on the doctor's arm. "I have taken this trust on myself," he said; "and as God shall judge me, I will not be unworthy of it!"

The poor weary head lay on his breast again, the poor fevered fingers clasped his hand once more, as he spoke those words.

"I believe you," said the doctor, warmly. "I believe you are an honest man.—Pardon me if I have seemed to intrude myself on your confidence. I respect your reserve—from this moment it is sacred to me. In justice to both of us, let me say that the questions I have asked were not prompted by mere curiosity. No common cause will account for the illness which has laid my patient on that bed. She has suffered some long-continued mental trial, some wearing and terrible suspense—and she has broken down under it. It might have helped me if I could have known what the nature of the trial was, and how long or how short a time elapsed before she sank under it. In that hope I spoke."

"When you told me she was dangerously ill," said Kirke, "did you mean danger to her reason or to her life?"

"To both," replied Mr. Merrick. "Her whole nervous system has given way; all the ordinary functions of her brain are in a state of collapse. I can give you no plainer explanation than that of the nature of the malady. The fever which frightens the people of the house is merely the effect. The cause is what I have told you. She may lie on that bed for weeks to come; passing alternately, without a gleam of consciousness, from a state of delirium to a state of repose. You must not be alarmed if you find her sleep lasting far beyond the natural time. That sleep is a better remedy than any I can give, and nothing must disturb it. All our art can accomplish is to watch her, to help her with stimulants from time to time, and to wait for what Nature will do."

"Must she remain here? Is there no hope of our being able to remove her to a better place?"

"No hope whatever, for the present. She has already been disturbed, as I understand, and she is seriously the worse for it. Even if she gets better, even if she comes to herself again, it would still be a dangerous experiment to move her too soon—the least excitement or alarm would be fatal to her. You must make the best of this place as it is. The landlady has my directions; and I will send a good nurse to help her. There is nothing more to be done. So far as her life can be said to be in any human hands, it is as much in your hands now as in mine. Everything depends on the care that is taken of her, under your direction, in this house." With those farewell words he rose and quitted the room.

Left by himself, Kirke walked to the door of communication, and, knocking at it softly, told the landlady he wished to speak with her.

He was far more composed, far more like his own resolute self, after his interview with the doctor, than he had been before it. A man living in the artificial social atmosphere which this man had never breathed would have felt painfully the worldly side of the situation—its novelty and strangeness; the serious present difficulty in which it placed him; the numberless misinterpretations in the future to which it might lead. Kirke never gave the situation a thought. He saw nothing but the duty it claimed from him—a duty which the doctor's farewell words had put plainly before his mind. Everything depended on the care taken of her, under his direction, in that house. There was his responsibility, and he unconsciously acted under it, exactly as he would have acted in a case of emergency with women and children on board his own ship. He questioned the landlady in short, sharp sentences; the only change in him was in the lowered tone of his voice, and in the anxious looks which he cast, from time to time, at the room where she lay.

"Do you understand what the doctor has told you?"

"Yes, sir."

"The house must be kept quiet. Who lives in the house?"

"Only me and my daughter, sir; we live in the parlors. Times have gone badly with us since Lady Day. Both the rooms above this are to let."

"I will take them both, and the two rooms down here as well. Do you know of any active trustworthy man who can run on errands for me?"

"Yes, sir. Shall I go—?"

"No; let your daughter go. You must not leave the house until the nurse comes. Don't send the messenger up here. Men of that sort tread heavily. I'll go down, and speak to him at the door."

He went down when the messenger came, and sent him first to purchase pen, ink, and paper. The man's next errand dispatched him to make inquiries for a person who could provide for deadening the sound of passing wheels in the street by laying down tan before the house in the usual way. This object accomplished, the messenger received two letters to post. The first was addressed to Kirke's brother-in-law. It told him, in few and plain words, what had happened; and left him to break the news to his wife as he thought best. The second letter was directed to the landlord of the Aldborough Hotel. Magdalen's assumed name at North Shingles was the only name by which Kirke knew her; and the one chance of tracing her relatives that he could discern was the chance of discovering her reputed uncle and aunt by means of inquiries starting from Aldborough.

Toward the close of the afternoon a decent middle-aged woman came to the house, with a letter from Mr. Merrick. She was well known to the doctor as a trustworthy and careful person, who had nursed his own wife; and she would be assisted, from time to time, by a lady who was a member of a religious Sisterhood in the district, and whose compassionate interest had been warmly aroused in the case. Toward eight o'clock that evening the doctor himself would call and see that his patient wanted for nothing.

The arrival of the nurse, and the relief of knowing that she was to be trusted, left Kirke free to think of himself. His luggage was ready packed for his contemplated journey to Suffolk the next day. It was merely necessary to transport it from the hotel to the house in Aaron's Buildings.

He stopped once only on his way to the hotel to look at a toyshop in one of the great thoroughfares. The miniature ships in the window reminded him of his nephew. "My little name-sake will be sadly disappointed at not seeing me to-morrow," he thought. "I must make it up to the boy by sending him something from his uncle." He went into the shop and bought one of the ships. It was secured in a box, and packed and directed in his presence. He put a card on the deck of the miniature vessel before the cover of the box was nailed on, bearing this inscription: "A ship for the little sailor, with the big sailor's love."—"Children like to be written to, ma'am," he said, apologetically, to the woman behind the counter. "Send the box as soon as you can—I am anxious the boy should get it to-morrow."

Toward the dusk of the evening he returned with his luggage to Aaron's Buildings. He took off his boots in the passage and carried his trunk upstairs himself; stopping, as he passed the first floor, to make his inquiries. Mr. Merrick was present to answer them.

"She was awake and wandering," said the doctor, "a few minutes since. But we have succeeded in composing her, and she is sleeping now."

"Have no words escaped her, sir, which might help us to find her friends?"

Mr. Merrick shook his head.

"Weeks and weeks may pass yet," he said, "and that poor girl's story may still be a sealed secret to all of us. We can only wait."

So the day ended—the first of many days that were to come.

CHAPTER II.

THE warm sunlight of July shining softly through a green blind; an open window with fresh flowers set on the sill; a strange bed, in a strange room; a giant figure of the female sex (like a dream of Mrs. Wragge) towering aloft on one side of the bed, and trying to clap its hands; another woman (quickly) stopping the hands before they could make any noise; a mild expostulating voice (like a dream of Mrs. Wragge again) breaking the silence in these words, "She knows me, ma'am, she knows me; if I mustn't be happy, it will be the death of me!"—such were the first sights, such were the first sounds, to which, after six weeks of oblivion, Magdalen suddenly and strangely awoke.

After a little, the sights grew dim again, and the sounds sank into silence. Sleep, the merciful, took her once more, and hushed her back to repose.

Another day—and the sights were clearer, the sounds were louder. Another—and she heard a man's voice, through the door, asking for news from the sick-room. The voice was strange to her; it was always cautiously lowered to the same quiet tone. It inquired after her, in the morning, when she woke—at noon, when she took her refreshment—in the evening, before she dropped asleep again. "Who is so anxious about me?" That was the first thought her mind was strong enough to form—"Who is so anxious about me?"

More days—and she could speak to the nurse at her bedside; she could answer the questions of an elderly man, who knew far more about her than she knew about herself, and who told her he was Mr. Merrick, the doctor; she could sit up in bed, supported by pillows, wondering what had happened to her, and where she was; she could feel a growing curiosity about that quiet voice, which still asked after her, morning, noon, and night, on the other side of the door.

Another day's delay—and Mr. Merrick asked her if she was strong enough to see an old friend. A meek voice, behind him, articulating high in the air, said, "It's only me." The voice was followed by the prodigious bodily apparition of Mrs. Wragge, with her cap all awry, and one of her shoes in the next room. "Oh, look at her! look at her!" cried Mrs. Wragge, in an ecstasy, dropping on her knees at Magdalen's bedside, with a thump that shook the house. "Bless her heart, she's well enough to laugh at me already. 'Cheer, boys, cheer—!' I beg your pardon, doctor, my conduct isn't ladylike, I know. It's my head, sir; it isn't me. I must give vent somehow, or my head will burst!" No coherent sentence, in answer to any sort of question put to her, could be extracted that morning from Mrs. Wragge. She rose from one climax of verbal confusion to another—and finished her visit under the bed, groping inscrutably for the second shoe.

The morrow came—and Mr. Merrick promised that she should see another old friend on the next day. In the evening, when the inquiring voice asked after her, as usual, and when the door was opened a few inches to give the reply, she answered faintly for herself: "I am better, thank you." There was a moment of silence—and then, just as the door was shut again, the voice sank to a whisper, and said, fervently, "Thank God!" Who was he? She had asked them all, and no one would tell her. Who was he?

The next day came; and she heard her door opened softly. Brisk footsteps tripped into the room; a lithe little figure advanced to the bed-side. Was it a dream again? No! There he was in his own evergreen reality, with the copious flow of language pouring smoothly from his lips; with the lambent dash of humor twinkling in his party-colored eyes—there he was, more audacious, more persuasive, more respectable than ever, in a suit of glossy black, with a speckless white cravat, and a rampant shirt frill—the unblushing, the invincible, unchangeable Wragge!

"Not a word, my dear girl!" said the captain, seating himself comfortably at the bedside, in his old confidential way. "I am to do all the talking; and, I think you will own, a more competent man for the purpose could not possibly have been found. I am really delighted—honestly delighted, if I may use such an apparently inappropriate word—to see you again, and to see you getting well. I have often thought of you; I have often missed you; I have often said to myself—never mind what! Clear the stage, and drop the curtain on the past. Dum vivimus, vivamus! Pardon the pedantry of a Latin quotation, my dear, and tell me how I look. Am I, or am I not, the picture of a prosperous man?"

Magdalen attempted to answer him. The captain's deluge of words flowed over her again in a moment.

"Don't exert yourself," he said. "I'll put all your questions for you. What have I been about? Why do I look so remarkably well off? And how in the world did I find my way to this house? My dear girl, I have been occupied, since we last saw each other, in slightly modifying my old professional habits. I have shifted from Moral Agriculture to Medical Agriculture. Formerly I preyed on the public sympathy, now I prey on the public stomach. Stomach and sympathy, sympathy and stomach—look them both fairly in the face when you reach the wrong side of fifty, and you will agree with me that they come to much the same thing. However that may be, here I am—incredible as it may appear—a man with an income, at last. The founders of my fortune are three in number. Their names are Aloes, Scammony, and Gamboge. In plainer words, I am now living—on a Pill. I made a little money (if you remember) by my friendly connection with you. I made a little more by the happy decease (Requiescat in Pace!) of that female relative of Mrs. Wragge's from whom, as I told you, my wife had expectations. Very good. What do you think I did? I invested the whole of my capital, at one fell swoop, in advertisements, and purchased my drugs and my pill-boxes on credit. The result is now before you. Here I am, a Grand Financial Fact. Here I am, with my clothes positively paid for; with a balance at my banker's; with my servant in livery, and my gig at the door; solvent, flourishing, popular—and all on a Pill."

Magdalen smiled. The captain's face assumed an expression of mock gravity; he looked as if there was a serious side to the question, and as if he meant to put it next.

"It's no laughing matter to the public, my dear," he said. "They can't get rid of me and my Pill; they must take us. There is not a single form of appeal in the whole range of human advertisement which I am not making to the unfortunate public at this moment. Hire the last new novel, there I am, inside the boards of the book. Send for the last new Song—the instant you open the leaves, I drop out of it. Take a cab—I fly in at the window in red. Buy a box of tooth-powder at the chemist's—I wrap it up for you in blue. Show yourself at the theater—I flutter down on you in yellow. The mere titles of my advertisements are quite irresistible. Let me quote a few from last week's issue. Proverbial Title: 'A Pill in time saves Nine.' Familiar Title: 'Excuse me, how is your Stomach?' Patriotic Title: 'What are the three characteristics of a true-born Englishman? His Hearth, his Home, and his Pill.' Title in the form of a nursery dialogue: 'Mamma, I am not well.' 'What is the matter, my pet?' 'I want a little Pill.' Title in the form of a Historical Anecdote: 'New Discovery in the Mine of English History. When the Princes were smothered in the Tower, their faithful attendant collected all their little possessions left behind them. Among the touching trifles dear to the poor boys, he found a tiny Box. It contained the Pill of the Period. Is it necessary to say how inferior that Pill was to its Successor, which prince and peasant alike may now obtain?'—Et cetera, et cetera. The place in which my Pill is made is an advertisement in itself. I have got one of the largest shops in London. Behind one counter (visible to the public through the lucid medium of plate-glass) are four-and-twenty young men, in white aprons, making the Pill. Behind another counter are four-and-twenty young men, in white cravats, making the boxes. At the bottom of the shop are three elderly accountants, posting the vast financial transactions accruing from the Pill in three enormous ledgers. Over the door are my name, portrait, and autograph, expanded to colossal proportions, and surrounded in flowing letters, by the motto of the establishment, 'Down with the Doctors!' Even Mrs. Wragge contributes her quota to this prodigious enterprise. She is the celebrated woman whom I have cured of indescribable agonies from every complaint under the sun. Her portrait is engraved on all the wrappers, with the following inscription beneath it: 'Before she took the Pill you might have blown this patient away with a feather. Look at her now!!!' Last, not least, my dear girl, the Pill is the cause of my finding my way to this house. My department in the prodigious Enterprise already mentioned is to scour the United Kingdom in a gig, establishing Agencies everywhere. While founding one of those Agencies, I heard of a certain friend of mine, who had lately landed in England, after a long sea-voyage. I got his address in London—he was a lodger in this house. I called on him forthwith, and was stunned by the news of your illness. Such, in brief, is the history of my existing connection with British Medicine; and so it happens that you see me at the present moment sitting in the present chair, now as ever, yours truly, Horatio Wragge." In these terms the captain brought his personal statement to a close. He looked more and more attentively at Magdalen, the nearer he got to the conclusion. Was there some latent importance attaching to his last words which did not appear on the face of them? There was. His visit to the sick-room had a serious object, and that object he had now approached.

In describing the circumstances under which he had become acquainted with Magdalen's present position, Captain Wragge had skirted, with his customary dexterity, round the remote boundaries of truth. Emboldened by the absence of any public scandal in connection with Noel Vanstone's marriage, or with the event of his death as announced in the newspaper obituary, the captain, roaming the eastern circuit, had ventured back to Aldborough a fortnight since, to establish an agency there for the sale of his wonderful Pill. No one had recognized him but the landlady of the hotel, who at once insisted on his entering the house and reading Kirke's letter to her husband. The same night Captain Wragge was in London, and was closeted with the sailor in the second-floor room at Aaron's Buildings.

The serious nature of the situation, the indisputable certainty that Kirke must fail in tracing Magdalen's friends unless he first knew who she really was, had decided the captain on disclosing part, at least, of the truth. Declining to enter into any particulars—for family reasons, which Magdalen might explain on her recovery, if she pleased—he astounded Kirke by telling him that the friendless woman whom he had rescued, and whom he had only known up to that moment as Miss Bygrave—was no other than the youngest daughter of Andrew Vanstone. The disclosure, on Kirke's side, of his father's connection with the young officer in Canada, had followed naturally on the revelation of Magdalen's real name. Captain Wragge had expressed his surprise, but had made no further remark at the time. A fortnight later, however, when the patient's recovery forced the serious difficulty on the doctor of meeting the questions which Magdalen was sure to ask, the captain's ingenuity had come, as usual, to the rescue.

"You can't tell her the truth," he said, "without awakening painful recollections of her stay at Aldborough, into which I am not at liberty to enter. Don't acknowledge just yet that Mr. Kirke only knew her as Miss Bygrave of North Shingles when he found her in this house. Tell her boldly that he knew who she was, and that he felt (what she must feel) that he had a hereditary right to help and protect her as his father's son. I am, as I have already told you," continued the captain, sticking fast to his old assertion, "a distant relative of the Combe-Raven family; and, if there is nobody else at hand to help you through this difficulty, my services are freely at your disposal."

No one else was at hand, and the emergency was a serious one. Strangers undertaking the responsibility might ignorantly jar on past recollections, which it would, perhaps, be the death of her to revive too soon. Near relatives might, by their premature appearance at the bedside, produce the same deplorable result. The alternative lay between irritating and alarming her by leaving her inquiries unanswered, or trusting Captain Wragge. In the doctor's opinion, the second risk was the least serious risk of the two—and the captain was now seated at Magdalen's bedside in discharge of the trust confided to him.

Would she ask the question which it had been the private object of all Captain Wragge's preliminary talk lightly and pleasantly to provoke? Yes; as soon as his silence gave her the opportunity, she asked it: "Who was that friend of his living in the house?"

"You ought by rights to know him as well as I do," said the captain. "He is the son of one of your father's old military friends, when your father was quartered with his regiment in Canada. Your cheeks mustn't flush up! If they do, I shall go away."

She was astonished, but not agitated. Captain Wragge had begun by interesting her in the remote past, which she only knew by hearsay, before he ventured on the delicate ground of her own experience.

In a moment more she advanced to her next question: "What was his name?"

"Kirke," proceeded the captain. "Did you never hear of his father, Major Kirke, commanding officer of the regiment in Canada? Did you never hear that the major helped your father through a great difficulty, like the best of good fellows and good friends?"

Yes; she faintly fancied she had heard something about her father and an officer who had once been very good to him when he was a young man. But she could not look back so long. "Was Mr. Kirke poor?" Even Captain Wragge's penetration was puzzled by that question. He gave the true answer at hazard. "No," he said, "not poor."

Her next inquiry showed what she had been thinking of. "If Mr. Kirke was not poor, why did he come to live in that house?"

"She has caught me!" thought the captain. "There is only one way out of it—I must administer another dose of truth. Mr. Kirke discovered you here by chance," he proceeded, aloud, "very ill, and not nicely attended to. Somebody was wanted to take care of you while you were not able to take care of yourself. Why not Mr. Kirke? He was the son of your father's old friend—which is the next thing to being your old friend. Who had a better claim to send for the right doctor, and get the right nurse, when I was not here to cure you with my wonderful Pill? Gently! gently! you mustn't take hold of my superfine black coat-sleeve in that unceremonious manner."

He put her hand back on the bed, but she was not to be checked in that way. She persisted in asking another question.—How came Mr. Kirke to know her? She had never seen him; she had never heard of him in her life.

"Very likely," said Captain Wragge. "But your never having seen him is no reason why he should not have seen you."

"When did he see me?"

The captain corked up his doses of truth on the spot without a moment's hesitation. "Some time ago, my dear. I can't exactly say when."

"Only once?"

Captain Wragge suddenly saw his way to the administration of another dose. "Yes," he said, "only once."

She reflected a little. The next question involved the simultaneous expression of two ideas, and the next question cost her an effort.

"He only saw me once," she said, "and he only saw me some time ago. How came he to remember me when he found me here?"

"Aha!" said the captain. "Now you have hit the right nail on the head at last. You can't possibly be more surprised at his remembering you than I am. A word of advice, my dear. When you are well enough to get up and see Mr. Kirke, try how that sharp question of yours sounds in his ears, and insist on his answering it himself." Slipping out of the dilemma in that characteristically adroit manner, Captain Wragge got briskly on his legs again and took up his hat.

"Wait!" she pleaded. "I want to ask you—"

"Not another word," said the captain. "I have given you quite enough to think of for one day. My time is up, and my gig is waiting for me. I am off, to scour the country as usual. I am off, to cultivate the field of public indigestion with the triple plowshare of aloes, scammony and gamboge." He stopped and turned round at the door. "By-the-by, a message from my unfortunate wife. If you will allow her to come and see you again, Mrs. Wragge solemnly promises not to lose her shoe next time. I don't believe her. What do you say? May she come?"

"Yes; whenever she likes," said Magdalen. "If I ever get well again, may poor Mrs. Wragge come and stay with me?"

"Certainly, my dear. If you have no objection, I will provide her beforehand with a few thousand impressions in red, blue, and yellow of her own portrait ('You might have blown this patient away with a feather before she took the Pill. Look at her now!'). She is sure to drop herself about perpetually wherever she goes, and the most gratifying results, in an advertising point of view, must inevitably follow. Don't think me mercenary—I merely understand the age I live in." He stopped on his way out, for the second time, and turned round once more at the door. "You have been a remarkably good girl," he said, "and you deserve to be rewarded for it. I'll give you a last piece of information before I go. Have you heard anybody inquiring after you, for the last day or two, outside your door? Ah! I see you have. A word in your ear, my dear. That's Mr. Kirke." He tripped away from the bedside as briskly as ever. Magdalen heard him advertising himself to the nurse before he closed the door. "If you are ever asked about it," he said, in a confidential whisper, "the name is Wragge, and the Pill is to be had in neat boxes, price thirteen pence half-penny, government stamp included. Take a few copies of the portrait of a female patient, whom you might have blown away with a feather before she took the Pill, and whom you are simply requested to contemplate now. Many thanks. Good-morning."

The door closed and Magdalen was alone again. She felt no sense of solitude; Captain Wragge had left her with something new to think of. Hour after hour her mind dwelt wonderingly on Mr. Kirke, until the evening came, and she heard his voice again through the half-opened door.

"I am very grateful," she said to him, before the nurse could answer his inquiries—"very, very grateful for all your goodness to me."

"Try to get well," he replied, kindly. "You will more than reward me, if you try to get well."

The next morning Mr. Merrick found her impatient to leave her bed, and be moved to the sofa in the front room. The doctor said he supposed she wanted a change. "Yes," she replied; "I want to see Mr. Kirke." The doctor consented to move her on the next day, but he positively forbade the additional excitement of seeing anybody until the day after. She attempted a remonstrance—Mr. Merrick was impenetrable. She tried, when he was gone, to win the nurse by persuasion—the nurse was impenetrable, too.

On the next day they wrapped her in shawls, and carried her in to the sofa, and made her a little bed on it. On the table near at hand were some flowers and a number of an illustrated paper. She immediately asked who had put them there. The nurse (failing to notice a warning look from the doctor) said Mr. Kirke had thought that she might like the flowers, and that the pictures in the paper might amuse her. After that reply, her anxiety to see Mr. Kirke became too ungovernable to be trifled with. The doctor left the room at once to fetch him.

She looked eagerly at the opening door. Her first glance at him as he came in raised a doubt in her mind whether she now saw that tall figure and that open sun-burned face for the first time. But she was too weak and too agitated to follow her recollections as far back as Aldborough. She resigned the attempt, and only looked at him. He stopped at the foot of the sofa and said a few cheering words. She beckoned to him to come nearer, and offered him her wasted hand. He tenderly took it in his, and sat down by her. They were both silent. His face told her of the sorrow and the sympathy which his silence would fain have concealed. She still held his hand—consciously now—as persistently as she had held it on the day when he found her. Her eyes closed, after a vain effort to speak to him, and the tears rolled slowly over her wan white cheeks.

The doctor signed to Kirke to wait and give her time. She recovered a little and looked at him. "How kind you have been to me!" she murmured. "And how little I have deserved it!"

"Hush! hush!" he said. "You don't know what a happiness it was to me to help you."

The sound of his voice seemed to strengthen her, and to give her courage. She lay looking at him with an eager interest, with a gratitude which artlessly ignored all the conventional restraints that interpose between a woman and a man. "Where did you see me," she said, suddenly, "before you found me here?"

Kirke hesitated. Mr. Merrick came to his assistance.

"I forbid you to say a word about the past to Mr. Kirke," interposed the doctor; "and I forbid Mr. Kirke to say a word about it to you. You are beginning a new life to-day, and the only recollections I sanction are recollections five minutes old."

She looked at the doctor and smiled. "I must ask him one question," she said, and turned back again to Kirke. "Is it true that you had only seen me once before you came to this house?"

"Quite true!" He made the reply with a sudden change of color which she instantly detected. Her brightening eyes looked at him more earnestly than ever, as she put her next question.

"How came you to remember me after only seeing me once?"

His hand unconsciously closed on hers, and pressed it for the first time. He attempted to answer, and hesitated at the first word. "I have a good memory," he said at last; and suddenly looked away from her with a confusion so strangely unlike his customary self-possession of manner that the doctor and the nurse both noticed it.

Every nerve in her body felt that momentary pressure of his hand, with the exquisite susceptibility which accompanies the first faltering advance on the way to health. She looked at his changing color, she listened to his hesitating words, with every sensitive perception of her sex and age quickened to seize intuitively on the truth. In the moment when he looked away from her, she gently took her hand from him, and turned her head aside on the pillow. "Can it be?" she thought, with a flutter of delicious fear at her heart, with a glow of delicious confusion burning on her cheeks. "Can it be?"

The doctor made another sign to Kirke. He understood it, and rose immediately. The momentary discomposure in his face and manner had both disappeared. He was satisfied in his own mind that he had successfully kept his secret, and in the relief of feeling that conviction he had become himself again.

"Good-by till to-morrow," he said, as he left the room.

"Good-by," she answered, softly, without looking at him.

Mr. Merrick took the chair which Kirke had resigned, and laid his hand on her pulse. "Just what I feared," remarked the doctor; "too quick by half."

She petulantly snatched away her wrist. "Don't!" she said, shrinking from him. "Pray don't touch me!"

Mr. Merrick good-humoredly gave up his place to the nurse. "I'll return in half an hour," he whispered, "and carry her back to bed. Don't let her talk. Show her the pictures in the newspaper, and keep her quiet in that way."

When the doctor returned, the nurse reported that the newspaper had not been wanted. The patient's conduct had been exemplary. She had not been at all restless, and she had never spoken a word.

The days passed, and the time grew longer and longer which the doctor allowed her to spend in the front room. She was soon able to dispense with the bed on the sofa—she could be dressed, and could sit up, supported by pillows, in an arm-chair. Her hours of emancipation from the bedroom represented the great daily event of her life. They were the hours she passed in Kirke's society.

She had a double interest in him now—her interest in the man whose protecting care had saved her reason and her life; her interest in the man whose heart's deepest secret she had surprised. Little by little they grew as easy and familiar with each other as old friends; little by little she presumed on all her privileges, and wound her way unsuspected into the most intimate knowledge of his nature.

Her questions were endless. Everything that he could tell her of himself and his life she drew from him delicately and insensibly: he, the least self-conscious of mankind, became an egotist in her dexterous hands. She found out his pride in his ship, and practiced on it without remorse. She drew him into talking of the fine qualities of the vessel, of the great things the vessel had done in emergencies, as he had never in his life talked yet to any living creature on shore. She found him out in private seafaring anxieties and unutterable seafaring exultations which he had kept a secret from his own mate. She watched his kindling face with a delicious sense of triumph in adding fuel to the fire; she trapped him into forgetting all considerations of time and place, and striking as hearty a stroke on the rickety little lodging-house table, in the fervor of his talk, as if his hand had descended on the solid bulwark of his ship. His confusion at the discovery of his own forgetfulness secretly delighted her; she could have cried with pleasure when he penitently wondered what he could possibly have been thinking of.

At other times she drew him from dwelling on the pleasures of his life, and led him into talking of its perils—the perils of that jealous mistress the sea, which had absorbed so much of his existence, which had kept him so strangely innocent and ignorant of the world on shore. Twice he had been shipwrecked. Times innumerable he and all with him had been threatened with death, and had escaped their doom by the narrowness of a hair-breadth. He was always unwilling at the outset to speak of this dark and dreadful side of his life: it was only by adroitly tempting him, by laying little snares for him in his talk, that she lured him into telling her of the terrors of the great deep. She sat listening to him with a breathless interest, looking at him with a breathless wonder, as those fearful stories—made doubly vivid by the simple language in which he told them—fell, one by one, from his lips. His noble unconsciousness of his own heroism—the artless modesty with which he described his own acts of dauntless endurance and devoted courage, without an idea that they were anything more than plain acts of duty to which he was bound by the vocation that he followed—raised him to a place in her estimation so hopelessly high above her that she became uneasy and impatient until she had pulled down the idol again which she herself had set up. It was on these occasions that she most rigidly exacted from him all those little familiar attentions so precious to women in their intercourse with men. "This hand," she thought, with an exquisite delight in secretly following the idea while he was close to her—"this hand that has rescued the drowning from death is shifting my pillows so tenderly that I hardly know when they are moved. This hand that has seized men mad with mutiny, and driven them back to their duty by main force, is mixing my lemonade and peeling my fruit more delicately and more neatly than I could do it for myself. Oh, if I could be a man, how I should like to be such a man as this!"

She never allowed her thoughts, while she was in his presence, to lead her beyond that point. It was only when the night had separated them that she ventured to let her mind dwell on the self-sacrificing devotion which had so mercifully rescued her. Kirke little knew how she thought of him, in the secrecy of her own chamber, during the quiet hours that elapsed before she sank to sleep. No suspicion crossed his mind of the influence which he was exerting over her—of the new spirit which he was breathing into that new life, so sensitively open to impression in the first freshness of its recovered sense. "She has nobody else to amuse her, poor thing," he used to think, sadly, sitting alone in his small second-floor room. "If a rough fellow like me can beguile the weary hours till her friends come here, she is heartily welcome to all that I can tell her."

He was out of spirits and restless now whenever he was by himself. Little by little he fell into a habit of taking long, lonely walks at night, when Magdalen thought he was sleeping upstairs. Once he went away abruptly in the day-time—on business, as he said. Something had passed between Magdalen and himself the evening before which had led her into telling him her age. "Twenty last birthday," he thought. "Take twenty from forty-one. An easy sum in subtraction—as easy a sum as my little nephew could wish for." He walked to the Docks, and looked bitterly at the shipping. "I mustn't forget how a ship is made," he said. "It won't be long before I am back at the old work again." On leaving the Docks he paid a visit to a brother sailor—a married man. In the course of conversation he asked how much older his friend might be than his friend's wife. There was six years' difference between them. "I suppose that's difference enough?" said Kirke. "Yes," said his friend; "quite enough. Are you looking out for a wife at last? Try a seasoned woman of thirty-five—that's your mark, Kirke, as near as I can calculate."

The time passed smoothly and quickly—the present time, in which she was recovering so happily—the present time, which he was beginning to distrust already.

Early one morning Mr. Merrick surprised Kirke by a visit in his little room on the second floor.

"I came to the conclusion yesterday," said the doctor, entering abruptly on his business, "that our patient was strong enough to justify us at last in running all risks, and communicating with her friends; and I have accordingly followed the clew which that queer fellow, Captain Wragge, put into our hands. You remember he advised us to apply to Mr. Pendril, the lawyer? I saw Mr. Pendril two days ago, and was referred by him—not overwillingly, as I thought—to a lady named Miss Garth. I heard enough from her to satisfy me that we have exercised a wise caution in acting as we have done. It is a very, very sad story; and I am bound to say that I, for one, make great allowances for the poor girl downstairs. Her only relation in the world is her elder sister. I have suggested that the sister shall write to her in the first instance, and then, if the letter does her no harm, follow it personally in a day or two. I have not given the address, by way of preventing any visits from being paid here without my permission. All I have done is to undertake to forward the letter, and I shall probably find it at my house when I get back. Can you stop at home until I send my man with it? There is not the least hope of my being able to bring it myself. All you need do is to watch for an opportunity when she is not in the front room, and to put the letter where she can see it when she comes in. The handwriting on the address will break the news before she opens the letter. Say nothing to her about it—take care that the landlady is within call—and leave her to herself. I know I can trust you to follow my directions, and that is why I ask you to do us this service. You look out of spirits this morning. Natural enough. You're used to plenty of fresh air, captain, and you're beginning to pine in this close place."

"May I ask a question, doctor? Is she pining in this close place, too? When her sister comes, will her sister take her away?"

"Decidedly, if my advice is followed. She will be well enough to be moved in a week or less. Good-day. You are certainly out of spirits, and your hand feels feverish. Pining for the blue water, captain—pining for the blue water!" With that expression of opinion, the doctor cheerfully went out.

In an hour the letter arrived. Kirke took it from the landlady reluctantly, and almost roughly, without looking at it. Having ascertained that Magdalen was still engaged at her toilet, and having explained to the landlady the necessity of remaining within call, he went downstairs immediately, and put the letter on the table in the front room. Magdalen heard the sound of the familiar step on the floor. "I shall soon be ready," she called to him, through the door.

He made no reply; he took his hat and went out. After a momentary hesitation, he turned his face eastward, and called on the ship-owners who employed him, at their office in Cornhill.

CHAPTER III.

MAGDALEN'S first glance round the empty room showed her the letter on the table. The address, as the doctor had predicted, broke the news the moment she looked at it.

Not a word escaped her. She sat down by the table, pale and silent, with the letter in her lap. Twice she attempted to open it, and twice she put it back again. The bygone time was not alone in her mind as she looked at her sister's handwriting: the fear of Kirke was there with it. "My past life!" she thought. "What will he think of me when he knows my past life?"

She made another effort, and broke the seal. A second letter dropped out of the inclosure, addressed to her in a handwriting with which she was not familiar. She put the second letter aside and read the lines which Norah had written:

"Ventnor, Isle of Wight, August 24th.

"MY DEAREST MAGDALEN—When you read this letter, try to think we have only been parted since yesterday; and dismiss from your mind (as I have dismissed from mine) the past and all that belongs to it.

"I am strictly forbidden to agitate you, or to weary you by writing a long letter. Is it wrong to tell you that I am the happiest woman living? I hope not, for I can't keep the secret to myself.

"My darling, prepare yourself for the greatest surprise I have ever caused you. I am married. It is only a week to-day since I parted with my old name—it is only a week since I have been the happy wife of George Bartram, of St. Crux.

"There were difficulties at first in the way of our marriage, some of them, I am afraid, of my making. Happily for me, my husband knew from the beginning that I really loved him: he gave me a second chance of telling him so, after I had lost the first, and, as you see, I was wise enough to take it. You ought to be especially interested, my love, in this marriage, for you are the cause of it. If I had not gone to Aldborough to search for the lost trace of you—if George had not been brought there at the same time by circumstances in which you were concerned, my husband and I might never have met. When we look back to our first impressions of each other, we look back to you.

"I must keep my promise not to weary you; I must bring this letter (sorely against my will) to an end. Patience! patience! I shall see you soon. George and I are both coming to London to take you back with us to Ventnor. This is my husband's invitation, mind, as well as mine. Don't suppose I married him, Magdalen, until I had taught him to think of you as I think—to wish with my wishes, and to hope with my hopes. I could say so much more about this, so much more about George, if I might only give my thoughts and my pen their own way; but I must leave Miss Garth (at her own special request) a blank space to fill up on the last page of this letter; and I must only add one word more before I say good-by—a word to warn you that I have another surprise in store, which I am keeping in reserve until we meet. Don't attempt to guess what it is. You might guess for ages, and be no nearer than you are now to the discovery of the truth. Your affectionate sister,

"NORAH BARTRAM."

(Added by Miss Garth.)

"MY DEAR CHILD—If I had ever lost my old loving recollection of you, I should feel it in my heart again now, when I know that it has pleased God to restore you to us from the brink of the grave. I add these lines to your sister's letter because I am not sure that you are quite so fit yet, as she thinks you, to accept her proposal. She has not said a word of her husband or herself which is not true. But Mr. Bartram is a stranger to you; and if you think you can recover more easily and more pleasantly to yourself under the wing of your old governess than under the protection of your new brother-in-law, come to me first, and trust to my reconciling Norah to the change of plans. I have secured the refusal of a little cottage at Shanklin, near enough to your sister to allow of your seeing each other whenever you like, and far enough away, at the same time, to secure you the privilege, when you wish it, of being alone. Send me one line before we meet to say Yes or No, and I will write to Shanklin by the next post.

"Always yours affectionately,

"HARRIET GARTH"

The letter dropped from Magdalen's hand. Thoughts which had never risen in her mind yet rose in it now.

Norah, whose courage under undeserved calamity had been the courage of resignation—

Norah, who had patiently accepted her hard lot; who from first to last had meditated no vengeance and stooped to no deceit—Norah had reached the end which all her sister's ingenuity, all her sister's resolution, and all her sister's daring had failed to achieve. Openly and honorably, with love on one side and love on the other, Norah had married the man who possessed the Combe-Raven money—and Magdalen's own scheme to recover it had opened the way to the event which had brought husband and wife together.

As the light of that overwhelming discovery broke on her mind, the old strife was renewed; and Good and Evil struggled once more which should win her—but with added forces this time; with the new spirit that had been breathed into her new life; with the nobler sense that had grown with the growth of her gratitude to the man who had saved her, fighting on the better side. All the higher impulses of her nature, which had never, from first to last, let her err with impunity—which had tortured her, before her marriage and after it, with the remorse that no woman inherently heartless and inherently wicked can feel—all the nobler elements in her character, gathered their forces for the crowning struggle and strengthened her to meet, with no unworthy shrinking, the revelation that had opened on her view. Clearer and clearer, in the light of its own immortal life, the truth rose before her from the ashes of her dead passions, from the grave of her buried hopes. When she looked at the letter again—when she read the words once more which told her that the recovery of the lost fortune was her sister's triumph, not hers, she had victoriously trampled down all little jealousies and all mean regrets; she could say in her hearts of hearts, "Norah has deserved it!"

The day wore on. She sat absorbed in her own thoughts, and heedless of the second letter which she had not opened yet, until Kirke's return.

He stopped on the landing outside, and, opening the door a little way only, asked, without entering the room, if she wanted anything that he could send her. She begged him to come in. His face was worn and weary; he looked older than she had seen him look yet. "Did you put my letter on the table for me?" she asked.

"Yes. I put it there at the doctor's request."

"I suppose the doctor told you it was from my sister? She is coming to see me, and Miss Garth is coming to see me. They will thank you for all your goodness to me better than I can."

"I have no claim on their thanks," he answered, sternly. "What I have done was not done for them, but for you." He waited a little, and looked at her. His face would have betrayed him in that look, his voice would have betrayed him in the next words he spoke, if she had not guessed the truth already. "When your friends come here," he resumed, "they will take you away, I suppose, to some better place than this."

"They can take me to no place," she said, gently, "which I shall think of as I think of the place where you found me. They can take me to no dearer friend than the friend who saved my life."

There was a moment's silence between them.

"We have been very happy here," he went on, in lower and lower tones. "You won't forget me when we have said good-by?"

She turned pale as the words passed his lips, and, leaving her chair, knelt down at the table, so as to look up into his face, and to force him to look into hers.

"Why do you talk of it?" she asked. "We are not going to say good-by, at least not yet."

"I thought—" he began.

"Yes?"

"I thought your friends were coming here—"

She eagerly interrupted him. "Do you think I would go away with anybody," she said, "even with the dearest relation I have in the world, and leave you here, not knowing and not caring whether I ever saw you again? Oh, you don't think that of me!" she exclaimed, with the passionate tears springing into her eyes—"I'm sure you don't think that of me!"

"No," he said; "I never have thought, I never can think, unjustly or unworthily of you."

Before he could add another word she left the table as suddenly as she had approached it, and returned to her chair. He had unconsciously replied in terms that reminded her of the hard necessity which still remained unfulfilled—the necessity of telling him the story of the past. Not an idea of concealing that story from his knowledge crossed her mind. "Will he love me, when he knows the truth, as he loves me now?" That was her only thought as she tried to approach the subject in his presence without shrinking from it.

"Let us put my own feelings out of the question," she said. "There is a reason for my not going away, unless I first have the assurance of seeing you again. You have a claim—the strongest claim of any one—to know how I came here, unknown to my friends, and how it was that you found me fallen so low."

"I make no claim," he said, hastily. "I wish to know nothing which distresses you to tell me."

"You have always done your duty," she rejoined, with a faint smile. "Let me take example from you, if I can, and try to do mine."

"I am old enough to be your father," he said, bitterly. "Duty is more easily done at my age than it is at yours."

His age was so constantly in his mind now that he fancied it must be in her mind too. She had never given it a thought. The reference he had just made to it did not divert her for a moment from the subject on which she was speaking to him.

"You don't know how I value your good opinion of me," she said, struggling resolutely to sustain her sinking courage. "How can I deserve your kindness, how can I feel that I am worthy of your regard, until I have opened my heart to you? Oh, don't encourage me in my own miserable weakness! Help me to tell the truth—force me to tell it, for my own sake if not for yours!"

He was deeply moved by the fervent sincerity of that appeal.

"You shall tell it," he said. "You are right—and I was wrong." He waited a little, and considered. "Would it be easier to you," he asked, with delicate consideration for her, "to write it than to tell it?"

She caught gratefully at the suggestion. "Far easier," she replied. "I can be sure of myself—I can be sure of hiding nothing from you, if I write it. Don't write to me on your side!" she added, suddenly, seeing with a woman's instinctive quickness of penetration the danger of totally renouncing her personal influence over him. "Wait till we meet, and tell me with your own lips what you think."

"Where shall I tell it?"

"Here!" she said eagerly. "Here, where you found me helpless—here, where you have brought me back to life, and where I have first learned to know you. I can bear the hardest words you say to me if you will only say them in this room. It is impossible I can be away longer than a month; a month will be enough and more than enough. If I come back—" She stopped confusedly. "I am thinking of myself," she said, "when I ought to be thinking of you. You have your own occupations and your own friends. Will you decide for us? Will you say how it shall be?"

"It shall be as you wish. If you come back in a month, you will find me here."

"Will it cause you no sacrifice of your own comfort and your own plans?"

"It will cause me nothing," he replied, "but a journey back to the City." He rose and took his hat. "I must go there at once," he added, "or I shall not be in time."

"It is a promise between us?" she said, and held out her hand.

"Yes," he answered, a little sadly; "it is a promise."

Slight as it was, the shade of melancholy in his manner pained her. Forgetting all other anxieties in the anxiety to cheer him, she gently pressed the hand he gave her. "If that won't tell him the truth," she thought, "nothing will."

It failed to tell him the truth; but it forced a question on his mind which he had not ventured to ask himself before. "Is it her gratitude, or her love; that is speaking to me?" he wondered. "If I was only a younger man, I might almost hope it was her love." That terrible sum in subtraction which had first presented itself on the day when she told him her age began to trouble him again as he left the house. He took twenty from forty-one, at intervals, all the way back to the ship-owners' office in Cornhill.

Left by herself, Magdalen approached the table to write the line of answer which Miss Garth requested, and gratefully to accept the proposal that had been made to her.

The second letter which she had laid aside and forgotten was the first object that caught her eye on changing her place. She opened it immediately, and, not recognizing the handwriting, looked at the signature. To her unutterable astonishment, her correspondent proved to be no less a person than—old Mr. Clare!

The philosopher's letter dispensed with all the ordinary forms of address, and entered on the subject without prefatory phrases of any kind, in these uncompromising terms:

"I have more news for you of that contemptible cur, my son. Here it is in the fewest possible words.

"I always told you, if you remember, that Frank was a Sneak. The very first trace recovered of him, after his running away from his employers in China, presents him in that character. Where do you think he turns up next? He turns up, hidden behind a couple of flour barrels, on board an English vessel bound homeward from Hong-Kong to London.

"The name of the ship was the Deliverance, and the commander was one Captain Kirke. Instead of acting like a sensible man, and throwing Frank overboard, Captain Kirke was fool enough to listen to his story. He made the most of his misfortunes, you may be sure. He was half starved; he was an Englishman lost in a strange country, without a friend to help him; his only chance of getting home was to sneak into the hold of an English vessel—and he had sneaked in, accordingly, at Hong-Kong, two days since. That was his story. Any other lout in Frank's situation would have been rope's ended by any other captain. Deserving no pity from anybody, Frank was, as a matter of course, coddled and compassionated on the spot. The captain took him by the hand, the crew pitied him, and the passengers patted him on the back. He was fed, clothed, and presented with his passage home. Luck enough so far, you will say. Nothing of the sort; nothing like luck enough for my despicable son.

"The ship touched at the Cape of Good Hope. Among his other acts of folly Captain Kirke took a woman passenger on board at that place—not a young woman by any means—the elderly widow of a rich colonist. Is it necessary to say that she forthwith became deeply interested in Frank and his misfortunes? Is it necessary to tell you what followed? Look back at my son's career, and you will see that what followed was all of a piece with what went before. He didn't deserve your poor father's interest in him—and he got it. He didn't deserve your attachment—and he got it. He didn't deserve the best place in one of the best offices in London; he didn't deserve an equally good chance in one of the best mercantile houses in China; he didn't deserve food, clothing, pity, and a free passage home—and he got them all. Last, not least, he didn't even deserve to marry a woman old enough to be his grandmother—and he has done it! Not five minutes since I sent his wedding-cards out to the dust-hole, and tossed the letter that came with them into the fire. The last piece of information which that letter contains is that he and his wife are looking out for a house and estate to suit them. Mark my words! Frank will get one of the best estates in England; a seat in the House of Commons will follow as a matter of course; and one of the legislators of this Ass-ridden country will be—MY LOUT!

"If you are the sensible girl I have always taken you for, you have long since learned to rate Frank at his true value, and the news I send you will only confirm your contempt for him. I wish your poor father could but have lived to see this day! Often as I have missed my old gossip, I don't know that I ever felt the loss of him so keenly as I felt it when Frank's wedding-cards and Frank's letter came to this house. Your friend, if you ever want one,

"FRANCIS CLARE, Sen."

With one momentary disturbance of her composure, produced by the appearance of Kirke's name in Mr. Clare's singular narrative, Magdalen read the letter steadily through from beginning to end. The time when it could have distressed her was gone by; the scales had long since fallen from her eyes. Mr. Clare himself would have been satisfied if he had seen the quiet contempt on her face as she laid aside his letter. The only serious thought it cost her was a thought in which Kirke was concerned. The careless manner in which he had referred in her presence to the passengers on board his ship, without mentioning any of them by their names, showed her that Frank must have kept silence on the subject of the engagement once existing between them. The confession of that vanished delusion was left for her to make, as part of the story of the past which she had pledged herself unreservedly to reveal.

She wrote to Miss Garth, and sent the letter to the post immediately.

The next morning brought a line of rejoinder. Miss Garth had written to secure the cottage at Shanklin, and Mr. Merrick had consented to Magdalen's removal on the following day. Norah would be the first to arrive at the house; and Miss Garth would follow, with a comfortable carriage to take the invalid to the railway. Every needful arrangement had been made for her; the effort of moving was the one effort she would have to make.

Magdalen read the letter thankfully, but her thoughts wandered from it, and followed Kirke on his return to the City. What was the business which had once already taken him there in the morning? And why had the promise exchanged between them obliged him to go to the City again, for the second time in one day?

Was it by any chance business relating to the sea? Were his employers tempting him to go back to his ship?

CHAPTER IV.

THE first agitation of the meeting between the sisters was over; the first vivid impressions, half pleasurable, half painful, had softened a little, and Norah and Magdalen sat together hand in hand, each rapt in the silent fullness of her own joy. Magdalen was the first to speak.

"You have something to tell me, Norah?"

"I have a thousand things to tell you, my love; and you have ten thousand things to tell me.—Do you mean that second surprise which I told you of in my letter?"

"Yes. I suppose it must concern me very nearly, or you would hardly have thought of mentioning it in your first letter?"

"It does concern you very nearly. You have heard of George's house in Essex? You must be familiar, at least, with the name of St. Crux?—What is there to start at, my dear? I am afraid you are hardly strong enough for any more surprises just yet?"

"Quite strong enough, Norah. I have something to say to you about St. Crux—I have a surprise, on my side, for you."

"Will you tell it me now?"

"Not now. You shall know it when we are at the seaside; you shall know it before I accept the kindness which has invited me to your husband's house."

"What can it be? Why not tell me at once?"

"You used often to set me the example of patience, Norah, in old times; will you set me the example now?"

"With all my heart. Shall I return to my own story as well? Yes? Then we will go back to it at once. I was telling you that St. Crux is George's house, in Essex, the house he inherited from his uncle. Knowing that Miss Garth had a curiosity to see the place, he left word (when he went abroad after the admiral's death) that she and any friends who came with her were to be admitted, if she happened to find herself in the neighborhood during his absence. Miss Garth and I, and a large party of Mr. Tyrrel's friends, found ourselves in the neighborhood not long after George's departure. We had all been invited to see the launch of Mr. Tyrrel's new yacht from the builder's yard at Wivenhoe, in Essex. When the launch was over, the rest of the company returned to Colchester to dine. Miss Garth and I contrived to get into the same carriage together, with nobody but my two little pupils for our companions. We gave the coachman his orders, and drove round by St. Crux. The moment Miss Garth mentioned her name we were let in, and shown all over the house. I don't know how to describe it to you. It is the most bewildering place I ever saw in my life—"

"Don't attempt to describe it, Norah. Go on with your story instead."

"Very well. My story takes me straight into one of the rooms at St. Crux—a room about as long as your street here—so dreary, so dirty, and so dreadfully cold that I shiver at the bare recollection of it. Miss Garth was for getting out of it again as speedily as possible, and so was I. But the housekeeper declined to let us off without first looking at a singular piece of furniture, the only piece of furniture in the comfortless place. She called it a tripod, I think. (There is nothing to be alarmed at, Magdalen; I assure you there is nothing to be alarmed at!) At any rate, it was a strange, three-legged thing, which supported a great panful of charcoal ashes at the top. It was considered by all good judges (the housekeeper told us) a wonderful piece of chasing in metal; and she especially pointed out the beauty of some scroll-work running round the inside of the pan, with Latin mottoes on it, signifying—I forget what. I felt not the slightest interest in the thing myself, but I looked close at the scroll-work to satisfy the housekeeper. To confess the truth, she was rather tiresome with her mechanically learned lecture on fine metal work; and, while she was talking, I found myself idly stirring the soft feathery white ashes backward and forward with my hand, pretending to listen, with my mind a hundred miles away from her. I don't know how long or how short a time I had been playing with the ashes, when my fingers suddenly encountered a piece of crumpled paper hidden deep among them. When I brought it to the surface, it proved to be a letter—a long letter full of cramped, close writing.—You have anticipated my story, Magdalen, before I can end it! You know as well as I do that the letter which my idle fingers found was the Secret Trust. Hold out your hand, my dear. I have got George's permission to show it to you, and there it is!"

She put the Trust into her sister's hand. Magdalen took it from her mechanically. "You!" she said, looking at her sister with the remembrance of all that she had vainly ventured, of all that she had vainly suffered, at St. Crux—"you have found it!"

"Yes," said Norah, gayly; "the Trust has proved no exception to the general perversity of all lost things. Look for them, and they remain invisible. Leave them alone, and they reveal themselves! You and your lawyer, Magdalen, were both justified in supposing that your interest in this discovery was an interest of no common kind. I spare you all our consultations after I had produced the crumpled paper from the ashes. It ended in George's lawyer being written to, and in George himself being recalled from the Continent. Miss Garth and I both saw him immediately on his return. He did what neither of us could do—he solved the mystery of the Trust being hidden in the charcoal ashes. Admiral Bartram, you must know, was all his life subject to fits of somnambulism. He had been found walking in his sleep not long before his death—just at the time, too, when he was sadly troubled in his mind on the subject of that very letter in your hand. George's idea is that he must have fancied he was doing in his sleep what he would have died rather than do in his waking moments—destroying the Trust. The fire had been lighted in the pan not long before, and he no doubt saw it still burning in his dream. This was George's explanation of the strange position of the letter when I discovered it. The question of what was to be done with the letter itself came next, and was no easy question for a woman to understand. But I determined to master it, and I did master it, because it related to you."

"Let me try to master it, in my turn," said Magdalen. "I have a particular reason for wishing to know as much about this letter as you know yourself. What has it done for others, and what is it to do for me?"

"My dear Magdalen, how strangely you look at it! how strangely you talk of it! Worthless as it may appear, that morsel of paper gives you a fortune."

"Is my only claim to the fortune the claim which this letter gives me?"

"Yes; the letter is your only claim. Shall I try if I can explain it in two words? Taken by itself, the letter might, in the lawyer's opinion, have been made a matter for dispute, though I am sure George would have sanctioned no proceeding of that sort. Taken, however, with the postscript which Admiral Bartram attached to it (you will see the lines if you look under the signature on the third page), it becomes legally binding, as well as morally binding, on the admiral's representatives. I have exhausted my small stock of legal words, and must go on in my own language instead of in the lawyer's. The end of the thing was simply this. All the money went back to Mr. Noel Vanstone's estate (another legal word! my vocabulary is richer than I thought), for one plain reason—that it had not been employed as Mr. Noel Vanstone directed. If Mrs. Girdlestone had lived, or if George had married me a few months earlier, results would have been just the other way. As it is, half the money has been already divided between Mr. Noel Vanstone's next of kin; which means, translated into plain English, my husband, and his poor bedridden sister—who took the money formally, one day, to satisfy the lawyer, and who gave it back again generously, the next, to satisfy herself. So much for one half of this legacy. The other half, my dear, is all yours. How strangely events happen, Magdalen! It is only two years since you and I were left disinherited orphans—and we are sharing our poor father's fortune between us, after all!"

"Wait a little, Norah. Our shares come to us in very different ways."

"Do they? Mine comes to me by my husband. Yours comes to you—" She stopped confusedly, and changed color. "Forgive me, my own love!" she said, putting Magdalen's hand to her lips. "I have forgotten what I ought to have remembered. I have thoughtlessly distressed you!"

"No!" said Magdalen; "you have encouraged me."

"Encouraged you?"

"You shall see."

With those words, she rose quietly from the sofa, and walked to the open window. Before Norah could follow her, she had torn the Trust to pieces, and had cast the fragments into the street.

She came back to the sofa and laid her head, with a deep sigh of relief, on Norah's bosom. "I will owe nothing to my past life," she said. "I have parted with it as I have parted with those torn morsels of paper. All the thoughts and all the hopes belonging to it are put away from me forever!"

"Magdalen, my husband will never allow you! I will never allow you myself—"

"Hush! hush! What your husband thinks right, Norah, you and I will think right too. I will take from you what I would never have taken if that letter had given it to me. The end I dreamed of has come. Nothing is changed but the position I once thought we might hold toward each other. Better as it is, my love—far, far better as it is!"

So she made the last sacrifice of the old perversity and the old pride. So she entered on the new and nobler life.

* * * * * *

A month had passed. The autumn sunshine was bright even in the murky streets, and the clocks in the neighborhood were just striking two, as Magdalen returned alone to the house in Aaron's Buildings.

"Is he waiting for me?" she asked, anxiously, when the landlady let her in.

He was waiting in the front room. Magdalen stole up the stairs and knocked at the door. He called to her carelessly and absently to come in, plainly thinking that it was only the servant who applied for permission to enter the room.

"You hardly expected me so soon?" she said speaking on the threshold, and pausing there to enjoy his surprise as he started to his feet and looked at her.

The only traces of illness still visible in her face left a delicacy in its outline which added refinement to her beauty. She was simply dressed in muslin. Her plain straw bonnet had no other ornament than the white ribbon with which it was sparingly trimmed. She had never looked lovelier in her best days than she looked now, as she advanced to the table at which he had been sitting, with a little basket of flowers that she had brought with her from the country, and offered him her hand.

He looked anxious and careworn when she saw him closer. She interrupted his first inquiries and congratulations to ask if he had remained in London since they had parted—if he had not even gone away, for a few days only, to see his friends in Suffolk? No; he had been in London ever since. He never told her that the pretty parsonage house in Suffolk wanted all those associations with herself in which the poor four walls at Aaron's Buildings were so rich. He only said he had been in London ever since.

"I wonder," she asked, looking him attentively in the face, "if you are as happy to see me again as I am to see you?"

"Perhaps I am even happier, in my different way," he answered, with a smile.

She took off her bonnet and scarf, and seated herself once more in her own arm-chair. "I suppose this street is very ugly," she said; "and I am sure nobody can deny that the house is very small. And yet—and yet it feels like coming home again. Sit there where you used to sit; tell me about yourself. I want to know all that you have done, all that you have thought even, while I have been away." She tried to resume the endless succession of questions by means of which she was accustomed to lure him into speaking of himself. But she put them far less spontaneously, far less adroitly, than usual. Her one all-absorbing anxiety in entering that room was not an anxiety to be trifled with. After a quarter of an hour wasted in constrained inquiries on one side, in reluctant replies on the other, she ventured near the dangerous subject at last.

"Have you received the letters I wrote to you from the seaside?" she asked, suddenly looking away from him for the first time.

"Yes," he said; "all."

"Have you read them?"

"Every one of them—many times over."

Her heart beat as if it would suffocate her. She had kept her promise bravely. The whole story of her life, from the time of the home-wreck at Combe-Raven to the time when she had destroyed the Secret Trust in her sister's presence, had been all laid before him. Nothing that she had done, nothing even that she had thought, had been concealed from his knowledge. As he would have kept a pledged engagement with her, so she had kept her pledged engagement with him. She had not faltered in the resolution to do this; and now she faltered over the one decisive question which she had come there to ask. Strong as the desire in her was to know if she had lost or won him, the fear of knowing was at that moment stronger still. She waited and trembled; she waited, and said no more.

"May I speak to you about your letters?" he asked. "May I tell you—?"

If she had looked at him as he said those few words, she would have seen what he thought of her in his face. She would have seen, innocent as he was in this world's knowledge, that he knew the priceless value, the all-ennobling virtue, of a woman who speaks the truth. But she had no courage to look at him—no courage to raise her eyes from her lap.

"Not just yet," she said, faintly. "Not quite so soon after we have met again."

She rose hurriedly from her chair, and walked to the window, turned back again into the room, and approached the table, close to where he was sitting. The writing materials scattered near him offered her a pretext for changing the subject, and she seized on it directly. "Were you writing a letter," she asked, "when I came in?"

"I was thinking about it," he replied. "It was not a letter to be written without thinking first." He rose as he answered her to gather the writing materials together and put them away.

"Why should I interrupt you?" she said. "Why not let me try whether I can't help you instead? Is it a secret?"

"No, not a secret."

He hesitated as he answered her. She instantly guessed the truth.

"Is it about your ship?"

He little knew how she had been thinking in her absence from him of the business which he believed that he had concealed from her. He little knew that she had learned already to be jealous of his ship. "Do they want you to return to your old life?" she went on. "Do they want you to go back to the sea? Must you say Yes or No at once?"

"At once."

"If I had not come in when I did would you have said Yes?"

She unconsciously laid her hand on his arm, forgetting all inferior considerations in her breathless anxiety to hear his next words. The confession of his love was within a hair-breadth of escaping him; but he checked the utterance of it even yet. "I don't care for myself," he thought; "but how can I be certain of not distressing her?"

"Would you have said Yes?" she repeated.

"I was doubting," he answered—"I was doubting between Yes and No."

Her hand tightened on his arm; a sudden trembling seized her in every limb, she could bear it no longer. All her heart went out to him in her next words:

"Were you doubting for my sake?"

"Yes," he said. "Take my confession in return for yours—I was doubting for your sake."

She said no more; she only looked at him. In that look the truth reached him at last. The next instant she was folded in his arms, and was shedding delicious tears of joy, with her face hidden on his bosom.

"Do I deserve my happiness?" she murmured, asking the one question at last. "Oh, I know how the poor narrow people who have never felt and never suffered would answer me if I asked them what I ask you. If they knew my story, they would forget all the provocation, and only remember the offense; they would fasten on my sin, and pass all my suffering by. But you are not one of them! Tell me if you have any shadow of a misgiving! Tell me if you doubt that the one dear object of all my life to come is to live worthy of you! I asked you to wait and see me; I asked you, if there was any hard truth to be told, to tell it me here with your own lips. Tell it, my love, my husband!—tell it me now!"

She looked up, still clinging to him as she clung to the hope of her better life to come.

"Tell me the truth!" she repeated.

"With my own lips?"

"Yes!" she answered, eagerly. "Say what you think of me with your own lips."

He stooped and kissed her.

MAN AND WIFE

PROLOGUE.—THE IRISH MARRIAGE.

Part the First.

THE VILLA AT HAMPSTEAD. I.

ON a summer's morning, between thirty and forty years ago, two girls were crying bitterly in the cabin of an East Indian passenger ship, bound outward, from Gravesend to Bombay.

They were both of the same age—eighteen. They had both, from childhood upward, been close and dear friends at the same school. They were now parting for the first time—and parting, it might be, for life.

The name of one was Blanche. The name of the other was Anne.

Both were the children of poor parents, both had been pupil-teachers at the school; and both were destined to earn their own bread. Personally speaking, and socially speaking, these were the only points of resemblance between them.

Blanche was passably attractive and passably intelligent, and no more. Anne was rarely beautiful and rarely endowed. Blanche's parents were worthy people, whose first consideration was to secure, at any sacrifice, the future well-being of their child. Anne's parents were heartless and depraved. Their one idea, in connection with their daughter, was to speculate on her beauty, and to turn her abilities to profitable account.

The girls were starting in life under widely different conditions. Blanche was going to India, to be governess in the household of a Judge, under care of the Judge's wife. Anne was to wait at home until the first opportunity offered of sending her cheaply to Milan. There, among strangers, she was to be perfected in the actress's and the singer's art; then to return to England, and make the fortune of her family on the lyric stage.

Such were the prospects of the two as they sat together in the cabin of the Indiaman locked fast in each other's arms, and crying bitterly. The whispered farewell talk exchanged between them—exaggerated and impulsive as girls' talk is apt to be—came honestly, in each case, straight from the heart.

"Blanche! you may be married in India. Make your husband bring you back to England."

"Anne! you may take a dislike to the stage. Come out to India if you do."

"In England or out of England, married or not married, we will meet, darling—if it's years hence—with all the old love between us; friends who help each other, sisters who trust each other, for life! Vow it, Blanche!"

"I vow it, Anne!"

"With all your heart and soul?"

"With all my heart and soul!"

The sails were spread to the wind, and the ship began to move in the water. It was necessary to appeal to the captain's authority before the girls could be parted. The captain interfered gently and firmly. "Come, my dear," he said, putting his arm round Anne; "you won't mind me! I have got a daughter of my own." Anne's head fell on the sailor's shoulder. He put her, with his own hands, into the shore-boat alongside. In five minutes more the ship had gathered way; the boat was at the landing-stage—and the girls had seen the last of each other for many a long year to come.

This was in the summer of eighteen hundred and thirty-one.

II.

Twenty-four years later—in the summer of eighteen hundred and fifty-five—there was a villa at Hampstead to be let, furnished.

The house was still occupied by the persons who desired to let it. On the evening on which this scene opens a lady and two gentlemen were seated at the dinner-table. The lady had reached the mature age of forty-two. She was still a rarely beautiful woman. Her husband, some years younger than herself, faced her at the table, sitting silent and constrained, and never, even by accident, looking at his wife. The third person was a guest. The husband's name was Vanborough. The guest's name was Kendrew.

It was the end of the dinner. The fruit and the wine were on the table. Mr. Vanborough pushed the bottles in silence to Mr. Kendrew. The lady of the house looked round at the servant who was waiting, and said, "Tell the children to come in."

The door opened, and a girl twelve years old entered, lending by the hand a younger girl of five. They were both prettily dressed in white, with sashes of the same shade of light blue. But there was no family resemblance between them. The elder girl was frail and delicate, with a pale, sensitive face. The younger was light and florid, with round red cheeks and bright, saucy eyes—a charming little picture of happiness and health.

Mr. Kendrew looked inquiringly at the youngest of the two girls.

"Here is a young lady," he said, "who is a total stranger to me."

"If you had not been a total stranger yourself for a whole year past," answered Mrs. Vanborough, "you would never have made that confession. This is little Blanche—the only child of the dearest friend I have. When Blanche's mother and I last saw each other we were two poor school-girls beginning the world. My friend went to India, and married there late in life. You may have heard of her husband—the famous Indian officer, Sir Thomas Lundie? Yes: 'the rich Sir Thomas,' as you call him. Lady Lundie is now on her way back to England, for the first time since she left it—I am afraid to say how many years since. I expected her yesterday; I expect her to-day—she may come at any moment. We exchanged promises to meet, in the ship that took her to India—'vows' we called them in the dear old times. Imagine how changed we shall find each other when we do meet again at last!"

"In the mean time," said Mr. Kendrew, "your friend appears to have sent you her little daughter to represent her? It's a long journey for so young a traveler."

"A journey ordered by the doctors in India a year since," rejoined Mrs. Vanborough. "They said Blanche's health required English air. Sir Thomas was ill at the time, and his wife couldn't leave him. She had to send the child to England, and who should she send her to but me? Look at her now, and say if the English air hasn't agreed with her! We two mothers, Mr. Kendrew, seem literally to live again in our children. I have an only child. My friend has an only child. My daughter is little Anne—as I was. My friend's daughter is little Blanche—as she was. And, to crown it all, those two girls have taken the same fancy to each other which we took to each other in the by-gone days at school. One has often heard of hereditary hatred. Is there such a thing as hereditary love as well?"

Before the guest could answer, his attention was claimed by the master of the house.

"Kendrew," said Mr. Vanborough, "when you have had enough of domestic sentiment, suppose you take a glass of wine?"

The words were spoken with undisguised contempt of tone and manner. Mrs. Vanborough's color rose. She waited, and controlled the momentary irritation. When she spoke to her husband it was evidently with a wish to soothe and conciliate him.

"I am afraid, my dear, you are not well this evening?"

"I shall be better when those children have done clattering with their knives and forks."

The girls were peeling fruit. The younger one went on. The elder stopped, and looked at her mother. Mrs. Vanborough beckoned to Blanche to come to her, and pointed toward the French window opening to the floor.

"Would you like to eat your fruit in the garden, Blanche?"

"Yes," said Blanche, "if Anne will go with me."

Anne rose at once, and the two girls went away together into the garden, hand in hand. On their departure Mr. Kendrew wisely started a new subject. He referred to the letting of the house.

"The loss of the garden will be a sad loss to those two young ladies," he said. "It really seems to be a pity that you should be giving up this pretty place."

"Leaving the house is not the worst of the sacrifice," answered Mrs. Vanborough. "If John finds Hampstead too far for him from London, of course we must move. The only hardship that I complain of is the hardship of having the house to let."

Mr. Vanborough looked across the table, as ungraciously as possible, at his wife.

"What have you to do with it?" he asked.

Mrs. Vanborough tried to clear the conjugal horizon by a smile.

"My dear John," she said, gently, "you forget that, while you are at business, I am here all day. I can't help seeing the people who come to look at the house. Such people!" she continued, turning to Mr. Kendrew. "They distrust every thing, from the scraper at the door to the chimneys on the roof. They force their way in at all hours. They ask all sorts of impudent questions—and they show you plainly that they don't mean to believe your answers, before you have time to make them. Some wretch of a woman says, 'Do you think the drains are right?'—and sniffs suspiciously, before I can say Yes. Some brute of a man asks, 'Are you quite sure this house is solidly built, ma'am?'—and jumps on the floor at the full stretch of his legs, without waiting for me to reply. Nobody believes in our gravel soil and our south aspect. Nobody wants any of our improvements. The moment they hear of John's Artesian well, they look as if they never drank water. And, if they happen to pass my poultry-yard, they instantly lose all appreciation of the merits of a fresh egg!"

Mr. Kendrew laughed. "I have been through it all in my time," he said. "The people who want to take a house are the born enemies of the people who want to let a house. Odd—isn't it, Vanborough?"

Mr. Vanborough's sullen humor resisted his friend as obstinately as it had resisted his wife.

"I dare say," he answered. "I wasn't listening."

This time the tone was almost brutal. Mrs. Vanborough looked at her husband with unconcealed surprise and distress.

"John!" she said. "What can be the matter with you? Are you in pain?"

"A man may be anxious and worried, I suppose, without being actually in pain."

"I am sorry to hear you are worried. Is it business?"

"Yes—business."

"Consult Mr. Kendrew."

"I am waiting to consult him."

Mrs. Vanborough rose immediately. "Ring, dear," she said, "when you want coffee." As she passed her husband she stopped and laid her hand tenderly on his forehead. "I wish I could smooth out that frown!" she whispered. Mr. Vanborough impatiently shook his head. Mrs. Vanborough sighed as she turned to the door. Her husband called to her before she could leave the room.

"Mind we are not interrupted!"

"I will do my best, John." She looked at Mr. Kendrew, holding the door open for her; and resumed, with an effort, her former lightness of tone. "But don't forget our 'born enemies!' Somebody may come, even at this hour of the evening, who wants to see the house."

The two gentlemen were left alone over their wine. There was a strong personal contrast between them. Mr. Vanborough was tall and dark—a dashing, handsome man; with an energy in his face which all the world saw; with an inbred falseness under it which only a special observer could detect. Mr. Kendrew was short and light—slow and awkward in manner, except when something happened to rouse him. Looking in his face, the world saw an ugly and undemonstrative little man. The special observer, penetrating under the surface, found a fine nature beneath, resting on a steady foundation of honor and truth.

Mr. Vanborough opened the conversation.

"If you ever marry," he said, "don't be such a fool, Kendrew, as I have been. Don't take a wife from the stage."

"If I could get such a wife as yours," replied the other, "I would take her from the stage to-morrow. A beautiful woman, a clever woman, a woman of unblemished character, and a woman who truly loves you. Man alive! what do you want more?"

"I want a great deal more. I want a woman highly connected and highly bred—a woman who can receive the best society in England, and open her husband's way to a position in the world."

"A position in the world!" cried Mr. Kendrew. "Here is a man whose father has left him half a million of money—with the one condition annexed to it of taking his father's place at the head of one of the greatest mercantile houses in England. And he talks about a position, as if he was a junior clerk in his own office! What on earth does your ambition see, beyond what your ambition has already got?"

Mr. Vanborough finished his glass of wine, and looked his friend steadily in the face.

"My ambition," he said, "sees a Parliamentary career, with a Peerage at the end of it—and with no obstacle in the way but my estimable wife."

Mr. Kendrew lifted his hand warningly. "Don't talk in that way," he said. "If you're joking—it's a joke I don't see. If you're in earnest—you force a suspicion on me which I would rather not feel. Let us change the subject."

"No! Let us have it out at once. What do you suspect?"

"I suspect you are getting tired of your wife."

"She is forty-two, and I am thirty-five; and I have been married to her for thirteen years. You know all that—and you only suspect I am tired of her. Bless your innocence! Have you any thing more to say?"

"If you force me to it, I take the freedom of an old friend, and I say you are not treating her fairly. It's nearly two years since you broke up your establishment abroad, and came to England on your father's death. With the exception of myself, and one or two other friends of former days, you have presented your wife to nobody. Your new position has smoothed the way for you into the best society. You never take your wife with you. You go out as if you were a single man. I have reason to know that you are actually believed to be a single man, among these new acquaintances of yours, in more than one quarter. Forgive me for speaking my mind bluntly—I say what I think. It's unworthy of you to keep your wife buried here, as if you were ashamed of her."

"I am ashamed of her."

"Vanborough!"

"Wait a little! you are not to have it all your own way, my good fellow. What are the facts? Thirteen years ago I fell in love with a handsome public singer, and married her. My father was angry with me; and I had to go and live with her abroad. It didn't matter, abroad. My father forgave me on his death-bed, and I had to bring her home again. It does matter, at home. I find myself, with a great career opening before me, tied to a woman whose relations are (as you well know) the lowest of the low. A woman without the slightest distinction of manner, or the slightest aspiration beyond her nursery and her kitchen, her piano and her books. Is that a wife who can help me to make my place in society?—who can smooth my way through social obstacles and political obstacles, to the House of Lords? By Jupiter! if ever there was a woman to be 'buried' (as you call it), that woman is my wife. And, what's more, if you want the truth, it's because I can't bury her here that I'm going to leave this house. She has got a cursed knack of making acquaintances wherever she goes. She'll have a circle of friends about her if I leave her in this neighborhood much longer. Friends who remember her as the famous opera-singer. Friends who will see her swindling scoundrel of a father (when my back is turned) coming drunk to the door to borrow money of her! I tell you, my marriage has wrecked my prospects. It's no use talking to me of my wife's virtues. She is a millstone round my neck, with all her virtues. If I had not been a born idiot I should have waited, and married a woman who would have been of some use to me; a woman with high connections—"

Mr. Kendrew touched his host's arm, and suddenly interrupted him.

"To come to the point," he said—"a woman like Lady Jane Parnell."

Mr. Vanborough started. His eyes fell, for the first time, before the eyes of his friend.

"What do you know about Lady Jane?" he asked.

"Nothing. I don't move in Lady Jane's world—but I do go sometimes to the opera. I saw you with her last night in her box; and I heard what was said in the stalls near me. You were openly spoken of as the favored man who was singled out from the rest by Lady Jane. Imagine what would happen if your wife heard that! You are wrong, Vanborough—you are in every way wrong. You alarm, you distress, you disappoint me. I never sought this explanation—but now it has come, I won't shrink from it. Reconsider your conduct; reconsider what you have said to me—or you count me no longer among your friends. No! I want no farther talk about it now. We are both getting hot—we may end in saying what had better have been left unsaid. Once more, let us change the subject. You wrote me word that you wanted me here to-day, because you needed my advice on a matter of some importance. What is it?"

Silence followed that question. Mr. Vanborough's face betrayed signs of embarrassment. He poured himself out another glass of wine, and drank it at a draught before he replied.

"It's not so easy to tell you what I want," he said, "after the tone you have taken with me about my wife."

Mr. Kendrew looked surprised.

"Is Mrs. Vanborough concerned in the matter?" he asked.

"Yes."

"Does she know about it?"

"No."

"Have you kept the thing a secret out of regard for her?"

"Yes."

"Have I any right to advise on it?"

"You have the right of an old friend."

"Then, why not tell me frankly what it is?"

There was another moment of embarrassment on Mr. Vanborough's part.

"It will come better," he answered, "from a third person, whom I expect here every minute. He is in possession of all the facts—and he is better able to state them than I am."

"Who is the person?"

"My friend, Delamayn."

"Your lawyer?"

"Yes—the junior partner in the firm of Delamayn, Hawke, and Delamayn. Do you know him?"

"I am acquainted with him. His wife's family were friends of mine before he married. I don't like him."

"You're rather hard to please to-day! Delamayn is a rising man, if ever there was one yet. A man with a career before him, and with courage enough to pursue it. He is going to leave the Firm, and try his luck at the Bar. Every body says he will do great things. What's your objection to him?"

"I have no objection whatever. We meet with people occasionally whom we dislike without knowing why. Without knowing why, I dislike Mr. Delamayn."

"Whatever you do you must put up with him this evening. He will be here directly."

He was there at that moment. The servant opened the door, and announced—"Mr. Delamayn."

III.

Externally speaking, the rising solicitor, who was going to try his luck at the Bar, looked like a man who was going to succeed. His hard, hairless face, his watchful gray eyes, his thin, resolute lips, said plainly, in so many words, "I mean to get on in the world; and, if you are in my way, I mean to get on at your expense." Mr. Delamayn was habitually polite to every body—but he had never been known to say one unnecessary word to his dearest friend. A man of rare ability; a man of unblemished honor (as the code of the world goes); but not a man to be taken familiarly by the hand. You would never have borrowed money of him—but you would have trusted him with untold gold. Involved in private and personal troubles, you would have hesitated at asking him to help you. Involved in public and producible troubles, you would have said, Here is my man. Sure to push his way—nobody could look at him and doubt it—sure to push his way.

"Kendrew is an old friend of mine," said Mr. Vanborough, addressing himself to the lawyer. "Whatever you have to say to me you may say before him. Will you have some wine?"

"No—thank you."

"Have you brought any news?"

"Yes."

"Have you got the written opinions of the two barristers?"

"No."

"Why not?"

"'Because nothing of the sort is necessary. If the facts of the case are correctly stated there is not the slightest doubt about the law."

With that reply Mr. Delamayn took a written paper from his pocket, and spread it out on the table before him.

"What is that?" asked Mr. Vanborough.

"The case relating to your marriage."

Mr. Kendrew started, and showed the first tokens of interest in the proceedings which had escaped him yet. Mr. Delamayn looked at him for a moment, and went on.

"The case," he resumed, "as originally stated by you, and taken down in writing by our head-clerk."

Mr. Vanborough's temper began to show itself again.

"What have we got to do with that now?" he asked. "You have made your inquiries to prove the correctness of my statement—haven't you?"

"Yes."

"And you have found out that I am right?"

"I have found out that you are right—if the case is right. I wish to be sure that no mistake has occurred between you and the clerk. This is a very important matter. I am going to take the responsibility of giving an opinion which may be followed by serious consequences; and I mean to assure myself that the opinion is given on a sound basis, first. I have some questions to ask you. Don't be impatient, if you please. They won't take long."

He referred to the manuscript, and put the first question.

"You were married at Inchmallock, in Ireland, Mr. Vanborough, thirteen years since?"

"Yes."

"Your wife—then Miss Anne Silvester—was a Roman Catholic?"

"Yes."

"Her father and mother were Roman Catholics?"

"They were."

"Your father and mother were Protestants? and you were baptized and brought up in the Church of England?"

"All right!"

"Miss Anne Silvester felt, and expressed, a strong repugnance to marrying you, because you and she belonged to different religious communities?"

"She did."

"You got over her objection by consenting to become a Roman Catholic, like herself?"

"It was the shortest way with her and it didn't matter to me."

"You were formally received into the Roman Catholic Church?"

"I went through the whole ceremony."

"Abroad or at home?"

"Abroad."

"How long was it before the date of your marriage?"

"Six weeks before I was married."

Referring perpetually to the paper in his hand, Mr. Delamayn was especially careful in comparing that last answer with the answer given to the head-clerk.

"Quite right," he said, and went on with his questions.

"The priest who married you was one Ambrose Redman—a young man recently appointed to his clerical duties?"

"Yes."

"Did he ask if you were both Roman Catholics?"

"Yes."

"Did he ask any thing more?"

"No."

"Are you sure he never inquired whether you had both been Catholics for more than one year before you came to him to be married?"

"I am certain of it."

"He must have forgotten that part of his duty—or being only a beginner, he may well have been ignorant of it altogether. Did neither you nor the lady think of informing him on the point?"

"Neither I nor the lady knew there was any necessity for informing him."

Mr. Delamayn folded up the manuscript, and put it back in his pocket.

"Right," he said, "in every particular."

Mr. Vanborough's swarthy complexion slowly turned pale. He cast one furtive glance at Mr. Kendrew, and turned away again.

"Well," he said to the lawyer, "now for your opinion! What is the law?"

"The law," answered Mr. Delamayn, "is beyond all doubt or dispute. Your marriage with Miss Anne Silvester is no marriage at all."

Mr. Kendrew started to his feet.

"What do you mean?" he asked, sternly.

The rising solicitor lifted his eyebrows in polite surprise. If Mr. Kendrew wanted information, why should Mr. Kendrew ask for it in that way? "Do you wish me to go into the law of the case?" he inquired.

"I do."

Mr. Delamayn stated the law, as that law still stands—to the disgrace of the English Legislature and the English Nation.

"By the Irish Statute of George the Second," he said, "every marriage celebrated by a Popish priest between two Protestants, or between a Papist and any person who has been a Protestant within twelve months before the marriage, is declared null and void. And by two other Acts of the same reign such a celebration of marriage is made a felony on the part of the priest. The clergy in Ireland of other religious denominations have been relieved from this law. But it still remains in force so far as the Roman Catholic priesthood is concerned."

"Is such a state of things possible in the age we live in!" exclaimed Mr. Kendrew.

Mr. Delamayn smiled. He had outgrown the customary illusions as to the age we live in.

"There are other instances in which the Irish marriage-law presents some curious anomalies of its own," he went on. "It is felony, as I have just told you, for a Roman Catholic priest to celebrate a marriage which may be lawfully celebrated by a parochial clergyman, a Presbyterian minister, and a Non-conformist minister. It is also felony (by another law) on the part of a parochial clergyman to celebrate a marriage that may be lawfully celebrated by a Roman Catholic priest. And it is again felony (by yet another law) for a Presbyterian minister and a Non-conformist minister to celebrate a marriage which may be lawfully celebrated by a clergyman of the Established Church. An odd state of things. Foreigners might possibly think it a scandalous state of things. In this country we don't appear to mind it. Returning to the present case, the results stand thus: Mr. Vanborough is a single man; Mrs. Vanborough is a single woman; their child is illegitimate, and the priest, Ambrose Redman, is liable to be tried, and punished, as a felon, for marrying them."

"An infamous law!" said Mr. Kendrew.

"It is the law," returned Mr. Delamayn, as a sufficient answer to him.

Thus far not a word had escaped the master of the house. He sat with his lips fast closed and his eyes riveted on the table, thinking.

Mr. Kendrew turned to him, and broke the silence.

"Am I to understand," he asked, "that the advice you wanted from me related to this?"

"Yes."

"You mean to tell me that, foreseeing the present interview and the result to which it might lead, you felt any doubt as to the course you were bound to take? Am I really to understand that you hesitate to set this dreadful mistake right, and to make the woman who is your wife in the sight of Heaven your wife in the sight of the law?"

"If you choose to put it in that light," said Mr. Vanborough; "if you won't consider—"

"I want a plain answer to my question—'yes, or no.'"

"Let me speak, will you! A man has a right to explain himself, I suppose?"

Mr. Kendrew stopped him by a gesture of disgust.

"I won't trouble you to explain yourself," he said. "I prefer to leave the house. You have given me a lesson, Sir, which I shall not forget. I find that one man may have known another from the days when they were both boys, and may have seen nothing but the false surface of him in all that time. I am ashamed of having ever been your friend. You are a stranger to me from this moment."

With those words he left the room.

"That is a curiously hot-headed man," remarked Mr. Delamayn. "If you will allow me, I think I'll change my mind. I'll have a glass of wine."

Mr. Vanborough rose to his feet without replying, and took a turn in the room impatiently. Scoundrel as he was—in intention, if not yet in act—the loss of the oldest friend he had in the world staggered him for the moment.

"This is an awkward business, Delamayn," he said. "What would you advise me to do?"

Mr. Delamayn shook his head, and sipped his claret.

"I decline to advise you," he answered. "I take no responsibility, beyond the responsibility of stating the law as it stands, in your case."

Mr. Vanborough sat down again at the table, to consider the alternative of asserting or not asserting his freedom from the marriage tie. He had not had much time thus far for turning the matter over in his mind. But for his residence on the Continent the question of the flaw in his marriage might no doubt have been raised long since. As things were, the question had only taken its rise in a chance conversation with Mr. Delamayn in the summer of that year.

For some minutes the lawyer sat silent, sipping his wine, and the husband sat silent, thinking his own thoughts. The first change that came over the scene was produced by the appearance of a servant in the dining-room.

Mr. Vanborough looked up at the man with a sudden outbreak of anger.

"What do you want here?"

The man was a well-bred English servant. In other words, a human machine, doing its duty impenetrably when it was once wound up. He had his words to speak, and he spoke them.

"There is a lady at the door, Sir, who wishes to see the house."

"The house is not to be seen at this time of the evening."

The machine had a message to deliver, and delivered it.

"The lady desired me to present her apologies, Sir. I was to tell you she was much pressed for time. This was the last house on the house agent's list, and her coachman is stupid about finding his way in strange places."

"Hold your tongue, and tell the lady to go to the devil!"

Mr. Delamayn interfered—partly in the interests of his client, partly in the interests of propriety.

"You attach some importance, I think, to letting this house as soon as possible?" he said.

"Of course I do!"

"Is it wise—on account of a momentary annoyance—to lose an opportunity of laying your hand on a tenant?"

"Wise or not, it's an infernal nuisance to be disturbed by a stranger."

"Just as you please. I don't wish to interfere. I only wish to say—in case you are thinking of my convenience as your guest—that it will be no nuisance to me."

The servant impenetrably waited. Mr. Vanborough impatiently gave way.

"Very well. Let her in. Mind, if she comes here, she's only to look into the room, and go out again. If she wants to ask questions, she must go to the agent."

Mr. Delamayn interfered once more, in the interests, this time, of the lady of the house.

"Might it not be desirable," he suggested, "to consult Mrs. Vanborough before you quite decide?"

"Where's your mistress?"

"In the garden, or the paddock, Sir—I am not sure which."

"We can't send all over the grounds in search of her. Tell the house-maid, and show the lady in."

The servant withdrew. Mr. Delamayn helped himself to a second glass of wine.

"Excellent claret," he said. "Do you get it direct from Bordeaux?"

There was no answer. Mr. Vanborough had returned to the contemplation of the alternative between freeing himself or not freeing himself from the marriage tie. One of his elbows was on the table, he bit fiercely at his finger-nails. He muttered between his teeth, "What am I to do?"

A sound of rustling silk made itself gently audible in the passage outside. The door opened, and the lady who had come to see the house appeared in the dining-room.

IV.

She was tall and elegant; beautifully dressed, in the happiest combination of simplicity and splendor. A light summer veil hung over her face. She lifted it, and made her apologies for disturbing the gentlemen over their wine, with the unaffected ease and grace of a highly-bred woman.

"Pray accept my excuses for this intrusion. I am ashamed to disturb you. One look at the room will be quite enough."

Thus far she had addressed Mr. Delamayn, who happened to be nearest to her. Looking round the room her eye fell on Mr. Vanborough. She started, with a loud exclamation of astonishment. "You!" she said. "Good Heavens! who would have thought of meeting you here?"

Mr. Vanborough, on his side, stood petrified.

"Lady Jane!" he exclaimed. "Is it possible?"

He barely looked at her while she spoke. His eyes wandered guiltily toward the window which led into the garden. The situation was a terrible one—equally terrible if his wife discovered Lady Jane, or if Lady Jane discovered his wife. For the moment nobody was visible on the lawn. There was time, if the chance only offered—there was time for him to get the visitor out of the house. The visitor, innocent of all knowledge of the truth, gayly offered him her hand.

"I believe in mesmerism for the first time," she said. "This is an instance of magnetic sympathy, Mr. Vanborough. An invalid friend of mine wants a furnished house at Hampstead. I undertake to find one for her, and the day I select to make the discovery is the day you select for dining with a friend. A last house at Hampstead is left on my list—and in that house I meet you. Astonishing!" She turned to Mr. Delamayn. "I presume I am addressing the owner of the house?" Before a word could be said by either of the gentlemen she noticed the garden. "What pretty grounds! Do I see a lady in the garden? I hope I have not driven her away." She looked round, and appealed to Mr. Vanborough. "Your friend's wife?" she asked, and, on this occasion, waited for a reply.

In Mr. Vanborough's situation what reply was possible?

Mrs. Vanborough was not only visible—but audible—in the garden; giving her orders to one of the out-of-door servants with the tone and manner which proclaimed the mistress of the house. Suppose he said, "She is not my friend's wife?" Female curiosity would inevitably put the next question, "Who is she?" Suppose he invented an explanation? The explanation would take time, and time would give his wife an opportunity of discovering Lady Jane. Seeing all these considerations in one breathless moment, Mr. Vanborough took the shortest and the boldest way out of the difficulty. He answered silently by an affirmative inclination of the head, which dextrously turned Mrs. Vanborough into to Mrs. Delamayn without allowing Mr. Delamayn the opportunity of hearing it.

But the lawyer's eye was habitually watchful, and the lawyer saw him.

Mastering in a moment his first natural astonishment at the liberty taken with him, Mr. Delamayn drew the inevitable conclusion that there was something wrong, and that there was an attempt (not to be permitted for a moment) to mix him up in it. He advanced, resolute to contradict his client, to his client's own face.

The voluble Lady Jane interrupted him before he could open his lips.

"Might I ask one question? Is the aspect south? Of course it is! I ought to see by the sun that the aspect is south. These and the other two are, I suppose, the only rooms on the ground-floor? And is it quiet? Of course it's quiet! A charming house. Far more likely to suit my friend than any I have seen yet. Will you give me the refusal of it till to-morrow?" There she stopped for breath, and gave Mr. Delamayn his first opportunity of speaking to her.

"I beg your ladyship's pardon," he began. "I really can't—"

Mr. Vanborough—passing close behind him and whispering as he passed—stopped the lawyer before he could say a word more.

"For God's sake, don't contradict me! My wife is coming this way!"

At the same moment (still supposing that Mr. Delamayn was the master of the house) Lady Jane returned to the charge.

"You appear to feel some hesitation," she said. "Do you want a reference?" She smiled satirically, and summoned her friend to her aid. "Mr. Vanborough!"

Mr. Vanborough, stealing step by step nearer to the window—intent, come what might of it, on keeping his wife out of the room—neither heeded nor heard her. Lady Jane followed him, and tapped him briskly on the shoulder with her parasol.

At that moment Mrs. Vanborough appeared on the garden side of the window.

"Am I in the way?" she asked, addressing her husband, after one steady look at Lady Jane. "This lady appears to be an old friend of yours." There was a tone of sarcasm in that allusion to the parasol, which might develop into a tone of jealousy at a moment's notice.

Lady Jane was not in the least disconcerted. She had her double privilege of familiarity with the men whom she liked—her privilege as a woman of high rank, and her privilege as a young widow. She bowed to Mrs. Vanborough, with all the highly-finished politeness of the order to which she belonged.

"The lady of the house, I presume?" she said, with a gracious smile.

Mrs. Vanborough returned the bow coldly—entered the room first—and then answered, "Yes."

Lady Jane turned to Mr. Vanborough.

"Present me!" she said, submitting resignedly to the formalities of the middle classes.

Mr. Vanborough obeyed, without looking at his wife, and without mentioning his wife's name.

"Lady Jane Parnell," he said, passing over the introduction as rapidly as possible. "Let me see you to your carriage," he added, offering his arm. "I will take care that you have the refusal of the house. You may trust it all to me."

No! Lady Jane was accustomed to leave a favorable impression behind her wherever she went. It was a habit with her to be charming (in widely different ways) to both sexes. The social experience of the upper classes is, in England, an experience of universal welcome. Lady Jane declined to leave until she had thawed the icy reception of the lady of the house.

"I must repeat my apologies," she said to Mrs. Vanborough, "for coming at this inconvenient time. My intrusion appears to have sadly disturbed the two gentlemen. Mr. Vanborough looks as if he wished me a hundred miles away. And as for your husband—" She stopped and glanced toward Mr. Delamayn. "Pardon me for speaking in that familiar way. I have not the pleasure of knowing your husband's name."

In speechless amazement Mrs. Vanborough's eyes followed the direction of Lady Jane's eyes—and rested on the lawyer, personally a total stranger to her.

Mr. Delamayn, resolutely waiting his opportunity to speak, seized it once more—and held it this time.

"I beg your pardon," he said. "There is some misapprehension here, for which I am in no way responsible. I am not that lady's husband."

It was Lady Jane's turn to be astonished. She looked at the lawyer. Useless! Mr. Delamayn had set himself right—Mr. Delamayn declined to interfere further. He silently took a chair at the other end of the room. Lady Jane addressed Mr. Vanborough.

"Whatever the mistake may be," she said, "you are responsible for it. You certainly told me this lady was your friend's wife."

"What!!!" cried Mrs. Vanborough—loudly, sternly, incredulously.

The inbred pride of the great lady began to appear behind the thin outer veil of politeness that covered it.

"I will speak louder if you wish it," she said. "Mr. Vanborough told me you were that gentleman's wife."

Mr. Vanborough whispered fiercely to his wife through his clenched teeth.

"The whole thing is a mistake. Go into the garden again!"

Mrs. Vanborough's indignation was suspended for the moment in dread, as she saw the passion and the terror struggling in her husband's face.

"How you look at me!" she said. "How you speak to me!"

He only repeated, "Go into the garden!"

Lady Jane began to perceive, what the lawyer had discovered some minutes previously—

that there was something wrong in the villa at Hampstead. The lady of the house was a lady in an anomalous position of some kind. And as the house, to all appearance, belonged to Mr. Vanborough's friend, Mr. Vanborough's friend must (in spite of his recent disclaimer) be in some way responsible for it. Arriving, naturally enough, at this erroneous conclusion, Lady Jane's eyes rested for an instant on Mrs. Vanborough with a finely contemptuous expression of inquiry which would have roused the spirit of the tamest woman in existence. The implied insult stung the wife's sensitive nature to the quick. She turned once more to her husband—this time without flinching.

"Who is that woman?" she asked.

Lady Jane was equal to the emergency. The manner in which she wrapped herself up in her own virtue, without the slightest pretension on the one hand, and without the slightest compromise on the other, was a sight to see.

"Mr. Vanborough," she said, "you offered to take me to my carriage just now. I begin to understand that I had better have accepted the offer at once. Give me your arm."

"Stop!" said Mrs. Vanborough, "your ladyship's looks are looks of contempt; your ladyship's words can bear but one interpretation. I am innocently involved in some vile deception which I don't understand. But this I do know—I won't submit to be insulted in my own house. After what you have just said I forbid my husband to give you his arm."

Her husband!

Lady Jane looked at Mr. Vanborough—at Mr. Vanborough, whom she loved; whom she had honestly believed to be a single man; whom she had suspected, up to that moment, of nothing worse than of trying to screen the frailties of his friend. She dropped her highly-bred tone; she lost her highly-bred manners. The sense of her injury (if this was true), the pang of her jealousy (if that woman was his wife), stripped the human nature in her bare of all disguises, raised the angry color in her cheeks, and struck the angry fire out of her eyes.

"If you can tell the truth, Sir," she said, haughtily, "be so good as to tell it now. Have you been falsely presenting yourself to the world—falsely presenting yourself to me—in the character and with the aspirations of a single man? Is that lady your wife?"

"Do you hear her? do you see her?" cried Mrs. Vanborough, appealing to her husband, in her turn. She suddenly drew back from him, shuddering from head to foot. "He hesitates!" she said to herself, faintly. "Good God! he hesitates!"

Lady Jane sternly repeated her question.

"Is that lady your wife?"

He roused his scoundrel-courage, and said the fatal word:

"No!"

Mrs. Vanborough staggered back. She caught at the white curtains of the window to save herself from falling, and tore them. She looked at her husband, with the torn curtain clenched fast in her hand. She asked herself, "Am I mad? or is he?"

Lady Jane drew a deep breath of relief. He was not married! He was only a profligate single man. A profligate single man is shocking—but reclaimable. It is possible to blame him severely, and to insist on his reformation in the most uncompromising terms. It is also possible to forgive him, and marry him. Lady Jane took the necessary position under the circumstances with perfect tact. She inflicted reproof in the present without excluding hope in the future.

"I have made a very painful discovery," she said, gravely, to Mr. Vanborough. "It rests with you to persuade me to forget it! Good-evening!"

She accompanied the last words by a farewell look which aroused Mrs. Vanborough to frenzy. She sprang forward and prevented Lady Jane from leaving the room.

"No!" she said. "You don't go yet!"

Mr. Vanborough came forward to interfere. His wife eyed him with a terrible look, and turned from him with a terrible contempt. "That man has lied!" she said. "In justice to myself, I insist on proving it!" She struck a bell on a table near her. The servant came in. "Fetch my writing-desk out of the next room." She waited—with her back turned on her husband, with her eyes fixed on Lady Jane. Defenseless and alone she stood on the wreck of her married life, superior to the husband's treachery, the lawyer's indifference, and her rival's contempt. At that dreadful moment her beauty shone out again with a gleam of its old glory. The grand woman, who in the old stage days had held thousands breathless over the mimic woes of the scene, stood there grander than ever, in her own woe, and held the three people who looked at her breathless till she spoke again.

The servant came in with the desk. She took out a paper and handed it to Lady Jane.

"I was a singer on the stage," she said, "when I was a single woman. The slander to which such women are exposed doubted my marriage. I provided myself with the paper in your hand. It speaks for itself. Even the highest society, madam, respects that!"

Lady Jane examined the paper. It was a marriage-certificate. She turned deadly pale, and beckoned to Mr. Vanborough. "Are you deceiving me?" she asked.

Mr. Vanborough looked back into the far corner of the room, in which the lawyer sat, impenetrably waiting for events. "Oblige me by coming here for a moment," he said.

Mr. Delamayn rose and complied with the request. Mr. Vanborough addressed himself to Lady Jane.

"I beg to refer you to my man of business. He is not interested in deceiving you."

"Am I required simply to speak to the fact?" asked Mr. Delamayn. "I decline to do more."

"You are not wanted to do more."

Listening intently to that interchange of question and answer, Mrs. Vanborough advanced a step in silence. The high courage that had sustained her against outrage which had openly declared itself shrank under the sense of something coming which she had not foreseen. A nameless dread throbbed at her heart and crept among the roots of her hair.

Lady Jane handed the certificate to the lawyer.

"In two words, Sir," she said, impatiently, "what is this?"

"In two words, madam," answered Mr. Delamayn; "waste paper."

"He is not married?"

"He is not married."

After a moment's hesitation Lady Jane looked round at Mrs. Vanborough, standing silent at her side—looked, and started back in terror. "Take me away!" she cried, shrinking from the ghastly face that confronted her with the fixed stare of agony in the great, glittering eyes. "Take me away! That woman will murder me!"

Mr. Vanborough gave her his arm and led her to the door. There was dead silence in the room as he did it. Step by step the wife's eyes followed them with the same dreadful stare, till the door closed and shut them out. The lawyer, left alone with the disowned and deserted woman, put the useless certificate silently on the table. She looked from him to the paper, and dropped, without a cry to warn him, without an effort to save herself, senseless at his feet.

He lifted her from the floor and placed her on the sofa, and waited to see if Mr. Vanborough would come back. Looking at the beautiful face—still beautiful, even in the swoon—he owned it was hard on her. Yes! in his own impenetrable way, the rising lawyer owned it was hard on her.

But the law justified it. There was no doubt in this case. The law justified it.

The trampling of horses and the grating of wheels sounded outside. Lady Jane's carriage was driving away. Would the husband come back? (See what a thing habit is! Even Mr. Delamayn still mechanically thought of him as the husband—in the face of the law! in the face of the facts!)

No. Then minutes passed. And no sign of the husband coming back.

It was not wise to make a scandal in the house. It was not desirable (on his own sole responsibility) to let the servants see what had happened. Still, there she lay senseless. The cool evening air came in through the open window and lifted the light ribbons in her lace cap, lifted the little lock of hair that had broken loose and drooped over her neck. Still, there she lay—the wife who had loved him, the mother of his child—there she lay.

He stretched out his hand to ring the bell and summon help.

At the same moment the quiet of the summer evening was once more disturbed. He held his hand suspended over the bell. The noise outside came nearer. It was again the trampling of horses and the grating of wheels. Advancing—rapidly advancing—stopping at the house.

Was Lady Jane coming back?

Was the husband coming back?

There was a loud ring at the bell—a quick opening of the house-door—a rustling of a woman's dress in the passage. The door of the room opened, and the woman appeared—alone. Not Lady Jane. A stranger—older, years older, than Lady Jane. A plain woman, perhaps, at other times. A woman almost beautiful now, with the eager happiness that beamed in her face.

She saw the figure on the sofa. She ran to it with a cry—a cry of recognition and a cry of terror in one. She dropped on her knees—and laid that helpless head on her bosom, and kissed, with a sister's kisses, that cold, white cheek.

"Oh, my darling!" she said. "Is it thus we meet again?"

Yes! After all the years that had passed since the parting in the cabin of the ship, it was thus the two school-friends met again.

Part the Second.

THE MARCH OF TIME. V.

ADVANCING from time past to time present, the Prologue leaves the date last attained (the summer of eighteen hundred and fifty-five), and travels on through an interval of twelve years—tells who lived, who died, who prospered, and who failed among the persons concerned in the tragedy at the Hampstead villa—and, this done, leaves the reader at the opening of THE STORY in the spring of eighteen hundred and sixty-eight.

The record begins with a marriage—the marriage of Mr. Vanborough and Lady Jane Parnell.

In three months from the memorable day when his solicitor had informed him that he was a free man, Mr. Vanborough possessed the wife he desired, to grace the head of his table and to push his fortunes in the world—the Legislature of Great Britain being the humble servant of his treachery, and the respectable accomplice of his crime.

He entered Parliament. He gave (thanks to his wife) six of the grandest dinners, and two of the most crowded balls of the season. He made a successful first speech in the House of Commons. He endowed a church in a poor neighborhood. He wrote an article which attracted attention in a quarterly review. He discovered, denounced, and remedied a crying abuse in the administration of a public charity. He received (thanks once more to his wife) a member of the Royal family among the visitors at his country house in the autumn recess. These were his triumphs, and this his rate of progress on the way to the peerage, during the first year of his life as the husband of Lady Jane.

There was but one more favor that Fortune could confer on her spoiled child—and Fortune bestowed it. There was a spot on Mr. Vanborough's past life as long as the woman lived whom he had disowned and deserted. At the end of the first year Death took her—and the spot was rubbed out.

She had met the merciless injury inflicted on her with a rare patience, with an admirable courage. It is due to Mr. Vanborough to admit that he broke her heart, with the strictest attention to propriety. He offered (through his lawyer) a handsome provision for her and for her child. It was rejected, without an instant's hesitation. She repudiated his money—she repudiated his name. By the name which she had borne in her maiden days—the name which she had made illustrious in her Art—the mother and daughter were known to all who cared to inquire after them when they had sunk in the world.

There was no false pride in the resolute attitude which she thus assumed after her husband had forsaken her. Mrs. Silvester (as she was now called) gratefully accepted for herself, and for Miss Silvester, the assistance of the dear old friend who had found her again in her affliction, and who remained faithful to her to the end. They lived with Lady Lundie until the mother was strong enough to carry out the plan of life which she had arranged for the future, and to earn her bread as a teacher of singing. To all appearance she rallied, and became herself again, in a few months' time. She was making her way; she was winning sympathy, confidence, and respect every where—when she sank suddenly at the opening of her new life. Nobody could account for it. The doctors themselves were divided in opinion. Scientifically speaking, there was no reason why she should die. It was a mere figure of speech—in no degree satisfactory to any reasonable mind—to say, as Lady Lundie said, that she had got her death-blow on the day when her husband deserted her. The one thing certain was the fact—account for it as you might. In spite of science (which meant little), in spite of her own courage (which meant much), the woman dropped at her post and died.

In the latter part of her illness her mind gave way. The friend of her old school-days, sitting at the bedside, heard her talking as if she thought herself back again in the cabin of the ship. The poor soul found the tone, almost the look, that had been lost for so many years—the tone of the past time when the two girls had gone their different ways in the world. She said, "we will meet, darling, with all the old love between us," just as she had said almost a lifetime since. Before the end her mind rallied. She surprised the doctor and the nurse by begging them gently to leave the room. When they had gone she looked at Lady Lundie, and woke, as it seemed, to consciousness from a dream.

"Blanche," she said, "you will take care of my child?"

"She shall be my child, Anne, when you are gone."

The dying woman paused, and thought for a little. A sudden trembling seized her.

"Keep it a secret!" she said. "I am afraid for my child."

"Afraid? After what I have promised you?"

She solemnly repeated the words, "I am afraid for my child."

"Why?"

"My Anne is my second self—isn't she?"

"Yes."

"She is as fond of your child as I was of you?"

"Yes."

"She is not called by her father's name—she is called by mine. She is Anne Silvester as I was. Blanche! Will she end like Me?"

The question was put with the laboring breath, with the heavy accents which tell that death is near. It chilled the living woman who heard it to the marrow of her bones.

"Don't think that!" she cried, horror-struck. "For God's sake, don't think that!"

The wildness began to appear again in Anne Silvester's eyes. She made feebly impatient signs with her hands. Lady Lundie bent over her, and heard her whisper, "Lift me up."

She lay in her friend's arms; she looked up in her friend's face; she went back wildly to her fear for her child.

"Don't bring her up like Me! She must be a governess—she must get her bread. Don't let her act! don't let her sing! don't let her go on the stage!" She stopped—her voice suddenly recovered its sweetness of tone—she smiled faintly—she said the old girlish words once more, in the old girlish way, "Vow it, Blanche!" Lady Lundie kissed her, and answered, as she had answered when they parted in the ship, "I vow it, Anne!"

The head sank, never to be lifted more. The last look of life flickered in the filmy eyes and went out. For a moment afterward her lips moved. Lady Lundie put her ear close to them, and heard the dreadful question reiterated, in the same dreadful words: "She is Anne Silvester—as I was. Will she end like Me?"

VI.

Five years passed—and the lives of the three men who had sat at the dinner-table in the Hampstead villa began, in their altered aspects, to reveal the progress of time and change.

Mr. Kendrew; Mr. Delamayn; Mr. Vanborough. Let the order in which they are here named be the order in which their lives are reviewed, as seen once more after a lapse of five years.

How the husband's friend marked his sense of the husband's treachery has been told already. How he felt the death of the deserted wife is still left to tell. Report, which sees the inmost hearts of men, and delights in turning them outward to the public view, had always declared that Mr. Kendrew's life had its secret, and that the secret was a hopeless passion for the beautiful woman who had married his friend. Not a hint ever dropped to any living soul, not a word ever spoken to the woman herself, could be produced in proof of the assertion while the woman lived. When she died Report started up again more confidently than ever, and appealed to the man's own conduct as proof against the man himself.

He attended the funeral—though he was no relation. He took a few blades of grass from the turf with which they covered her grave—when he thought that nobody was looking at him. He disappeared from his club. He traveled. He came back. He admitted that he was weary of England. He applied for, and obtained, an appointment in one of the colonies. To what conclusion did all this point? Was it not plain that his usual course of life had lost its attraction for him, when the object of his infatuation had ceased to exist? It might have been so—guesses less likely have been made at the truth, and have hit the mark. It is, at any rate, certain that he left England, never to return again. Another man lost, Report said. Add to that, a man in ten thousand—and, for once, Report might claim to be right.

Mr. Delamayn comes next.

The rising solicitor was struck off the roll, at his own request—and entered himself as a student at one of the Inns of Court. For three years nothing was known of him but that he was reading hard and keeping his terms. He was called to the Bar. His late partners in the firm knew they could trust him, and put business into his hands. In two years he made himself a position in Court. At the end of the two years he made himself a position out of Court. He appeared as "Junior" in "a famous case," in which the honor of a great family, and the title to a great estate were concerned. His "Senior" fell ill on the eve of the trial. He conducted the case for the defendant and won it. The defendant said, "What can I do for you?" Mr. Delamayn answered, "Put me into Parliament." Being a landed gentleman, the defendant had only to issue the necessary orders—and behold, Mr. Delamayn was in Parliament!

In the House of Commons the new member and Mr. Vanborough met again.

They sat on the same bench, and sided with the same party. Mr. Delamayn noticed that Mr. Vanborough was looking old and worn and gray. He put a few questions to a well-informed person. The well-informed person shook his head. Mr. Vanborough was rich; Mr. Vanborough was well-connected (through his wife); Mr. Van borough was a sound man in every sense of the word; but—nobody liked him. He had done very well the first year, and there it had ended. He was undeniably clever, but he produced a disagreeable impression in the House. He gave splendid entertainments, but he wasn't popular in society. His party respected him, but when they had any thing to give they passed him over. He had a temper of his own, if the truth must be told; and with nothing against him—on the contrary, with every thing in his favor—he didn't make friends. A soured man. At home and abroad, a soured man.

VII.

Five years more passed, dating from the day when the deserted wife was laid in her grave. It was now the year eighteen hundred and sixty six.

On a certain day in that year two special items of news appeared in the papers—the news of an elevation to the peerage, and the news of a suicide.

Getting on well at the Bar, Mr. Delamayn got on better still in Parliament. He became one of the prominent men in the House. Spoke clearly, sensibly, and modestly, and was never too long. Held the House, where men of higher abilities "bored" it. The chiefs of his party said openly, "We must do something for Delamayn," The opportunity offered, and the chiefs kept their word. Their Solicitor-General was advanced a step, and they put Delamayn in his place. There was an outcry on the part of the older members of the Bar. The Ministry answered, "We want a man who is listened to in the House, and we have got him." The papers supported the new nomination. A great debate came off, and the new Solicitor-General justified the Ministry and the papers. His enemies said, derisively, "He will be Lord Chancellor in a year or two!" His friends made genial jokes in his domestic circle, which pointed to the same conclusion. They warned his two sons, Julius and Geoffrey (then at college), to be careful what acquaintances they made, as they might find themselves the sons of a lord at a moment's notice. It really began to look like something of the sort. Always rising, Mr. Delamayn rose next to be Attorney-General. About the same time—so true it is that "nothing succeeds like success"—a childless relative died and left him a fortune. In the summer of 'sixty-six a Chief Judgeship fell vacant. The Ministry had made a previous appointment which had been universally unpopular. They saw their way to supplying the place of their Attorney-General, and they offered the judicial appointment to Mr. Delamayn. He preferred remaining in the House of Commons, and refused to accept it. The Ministry declined to take No for an answer. They whispered confidentially, "Will you take it with a peerage?" Mr. Delamayn consulted his wife, and took it with a peerage. The London Gazette announced him to the world as Baron Holchester of Holchester. And the friends of the family rubbed their hands and said, "What did we tell you? Here are our two young friends, Julius and Geoffrey, the sons of a lord!"

And where was Mr. Vanborough all this time? Exactly where we left him five years since.

He was as rich, or richer, than ever. He was as well-connected as ever. He was as ambitious as ever. But there it ended. He stood still in the House; he stood still in society; nobody liked him; he made no friends. It was all the old story over again, with this difference, that the soured man was sourer; the gray head, grayer; and the irritable temper more unendurable than ever. His wife had her rooms in the house and he had his, and the confidential servants took care that they never met on the stairs. They had no children. They only saw each other at their grand dinners and balls. People ate at their table, and danced on their floor, and compared notes afterward, and said how dull it was. Step by step the man who had once been Mr. Vanborough's lawyer rose, till the peerage received him, and he could rise no longer; while Mr.

Vanborough, on the lower round of the ladder, looked up, and noted it, with no more chance (rich as he was and well-connected as he was) of climbing to the House of Lords than your chance or mine.

The man's career was ended; and on the day when the nomination of the new peer was announced, the man ended with it.

He laid the newspaper aside without making any remark, and went out. His carriage set him down, where the green fields still remain, on the northwest of London, near the foot-path which leads to Hampstead. He walked alone to the villa where he had once lived with the woman whom he had so cruelly wronged. New houses had risen round it, part of the old garden had been sold and built on. After a moment's hesitation he went to the gate and rang the bell. He gave the servant his card. The servant's master knew the name as the name of a man of great wealth, and of a Member of Parliament. He asked politely to what fortunate circumstance he owed the honor of that visit. Mr. Vanborough answered, briefly and simply, "I once lived here; I have associations with the place with which it is not necessary for me to trouble you. Will you excuse what must seem to you a very strange request? I should like to see the dining-room again, if there is no objection, and if I am disturbing nobody."

The "strange requests" of rich men are of the nature of "privileged communications," for this excellent reason, that they are sure not to be requests for money. Mr. Vanborough was shown into the dining-room. The master of the house, secretly wondering, watched him.

He walked straight to a certain spot on the carpet, not far from the window that led into the garden, and nearly opposite the door. On that spot he stood silently, with his head on his breast—thinking. Was it there he had seen her for the last time, on the day when he left the room forever? Yes; it was there. After a minute or so he roused himself, but in a dreamy, absent manner. He said it was a pretty place, and expressed his thanks, and looked back before the door closed, and then went his way again. His carriage picked him up where it had set him down. He drove to the residence of the new Lord Holchester, and left a card for him. Then he went home. Arrived at his house, his secretary reminded him that he had an appointment in ten minutes' time. He thanked the secretary in the same dreamy, absent manner in which he had thanked the owner of the villa, and went into his dressing-room. The person with whom he had made the appointment came, and the secretary sent the valet up stairs to knock at the door. There was no answer. On trying the lock it proved to be turned inside. They broke open the door, and saw him lying on the sofa. They went close to look—and found him dead by his own hand.

VIII.

Drawing fast to its close, the Prologue reverts to the two girls—and tells, in a few words, how the years passed with Anne and Blanche.

Lady Lundie more than redeemed the solemn pledge that she had given to her friend. Preserved from every temptation which might lure her into a longing to follow her mother's career; trained for a teacher's life, with all the arts and all the advantages that money could procure, Anne's first and only essays as a governess were made, under Lady Lundie's own roof, on Lady Lundie's own child. The difference in the ages of the girls—seven years—the love between them, which seemed, as time went on, to grow with their growth, favored the trial of the experiment. In the double relation of teacher and friend to little Blanche, the girlhood of Anne Silvester the younger passed safely, happily, uneventfully, in the modest sanctuary of home. Who could imagine a contrast more complete than the contrast between her early life and her mother's? Who could see any thing but a death-bed delusion in the terrible question which had tortured the mother's last moments: "Will she end like Me?"

But two events of importance occurred in the quiet family circle during the lapse of years which is now under review. In eighteen hundred and fifty-eight the household was enlivened by the arrival of Sir Thomas Lundie. In eighteen hundred and sixty-five the household was broken up by the return of Sir Thomas to India, accompanied by his wife.

Lady Lundie's health had been failing for some time previously. The medical men, consulted on the case, agreed that a sea-voyage was the one change needful to restore their patient's wasted strength—exactly at the time, as it happened, when Sir Thomas was due again in India. For his wife's sake, he agreed to defer his return, by taking the sea-voyage with her. The one difficulty to get over was the difficulty of leaving Blanche and Anne behind in England.

Appealed to on this point, the doctors had declared that at Blanche's critical time of life they could not sanction her going to India with her mother. At the same time, near and dear relatives came forward, who were ready and anxious to give Blanche and her governess a home—Sir Thomas, on his side, engaging to bring his wife back in a year and a half, or, at most, in two years' time. Assailed in all directions, Lady Lundie's natural unwillingness to leave the girls was overruled. She consented to the parting—with a mind secretly depressed, and secretly doubtful of the future.

At the last moment she drew Anne Silvester on one side, out of hearing of the rest. Anne was then a young woman of twenty-two, and Blanche a girl of fifteen.

"My dear," she said, simply, "I must tell you what I can not tell Sir Thomas, and what I am afraid to tell Blanche. I am going away, with a mind that misgives me. I am persuaded I shall not live to return to England; and, when I am dead, I believe my husband will marry again. Years ago your mother was uneasy, on her death-bed, about your future. I am uneasy, now, about Blanche's future. I promised my dear dead friend that you should be like my own child to me—and it quieted her mind. Quiet my mind, Anne, before I go. Whatever happens in years to come—promise me to be always, what you are now, a sister to Blanche."

She held out her hand for the last time. With a full heart Anne Silvester kissed it, and gave the promise.

IX.

In two months from that time one of the forebodings which had weighed on Lady Lundie's mind was fulfilled. She died on the voyage, and was buried at sea.

In a year more the second misgiving was confirmed. Sir Thomas Lundie married again. He brought his second wife to England toward the close of eighteen hundred and sixty six.

Time, in the new household, promised to pass as quietly as in the old. Sir Thomas remembered and respected the trust which his first wife had placed in Anne. The second Lady Lundie, wisely guiding her conduct in this matter by the conduct of her husband, left things as she found them in the new house. At the opening of eighteen hundred and sixty-seven the relations between Anne and Blanche were relations of sisterly sympathy and sisterly love. The prospect in the future was as fair as a prospect could be.

At this date, of the persons concerned in the tragedy of twelve years since at the Hampstead villa, three were dead; and one was self-exiled in a foreign land. There now remained living Anne and Blanche, who had been children at the time; and the rising solicitor who had discovered the flaw in the Irish marriage—once Mr. Delamayn: now Lord Holchester.

THE STORY.

FIRST SCENE.—THE SUMMER-HOUSE.

CHAPTER THE FIRST.

THE OWLS.

IN the spring of the year eighteen hundred and sixty-eight there lived, in a certain county of North Britain, two venerable White Owls.

The Owls inhabited a decayed and deserted summer-house. The summer-house stood in grounds attached to a country seat in Perthshire, known by the name of Windygates.

The situation of Windygates had been skillfully chosen in that part of the county where the fertile lowlands first begin to merge into the mountain region beyond. The mansion-house was intelligently laid out, and luxuriously furnished. The stables offered a model for ventilation and space; and the gardens and grounds were fit for a prince.

Possessed of these advantages, at starting, Windygates, nevertheless, went the road to ruin in due course of time. The curse of litigation fell on house and lands. For more than ten years an interminable lawsuit coiled itself closer and closer round the place, sequestering it from human habitation, and even from human approach. The mansion was closed. The garden became a wilderness of weeds. The summer-house was choked up by creeping plants; and the appearance of the creepers was followed by the appearance of the birds of night.

For years the Owls lived undisturbed on the property which they had acquired by the oldest of all existing rights—the right of taking. Throughout the day they sat peaceful and solemn, with closed eyes, in the cool darkness shed round them by the ivy. With the twilight they roused themselves softly to the business of life. In sage and silent companionship of two, they went flying, noiseless, along the quiet lanes in search of a meal. At one time they would beat a field like a setter dog, and drop down in an instant on a mouse unaware of them. At another time—moving spectral over the black surface of the water—they would try the lake for a change, and catch a perch as they had caught the mouse. Their catholic digestions were equally tolerant of a rat or an insect. And there were moments, proud moments, in their lives, when they were clever enough to snatch a small bird at roost off his perch. On those occasions the sense of superiority which the large bird feels every where over the small, warmed their cool blood, and set them screeching cheerfully in the stillness of the night.

So, for years, the Owls slept their happy sleep by day, and found their comfortable meal when darkness fell. They had come, with the creepers, into possession of the summer-house. Consequently, the creepers were a part of the constitution of the summer-house. And consequently the Owls were the guardians of the Constitution. There are some human owls who reason as they did, and who are, in this respect—as also in respect of snatching smaller birds off their roosts—wonderfully like them.

The constitution of the summer-house had lasted until the spring of the year eighteen hundred and sixty-eight, when the unhallowed footsteps of innovation passed that way; and the venerable privileges of the Owls were assailed, for the first time, from the world outside.

Two featherless beings appeared, uninvited, at the door of the summer-house, surveyed the constitutional creepers, and said, "These must come down"—looked around at the horrid light of noonday, and said, "That must come in"—went away, thereupon, and were heard, in the distance, agreeing together, "To-morrow it shall be done."

And the Owls said, "Have we honored the summer-house by occupying it all these years—and is the horrid light of noonday to be let in on us at last? My lords and gentlemen, the Constitution is destroyed!"

They passed a resolution to that effect, as is the manner of their kind. And then they shut their eyes again, and felt that they had done their duty.

The same night, on their way to the fields, they observed with dismay a light in one of the windows of the house. What did the light mean?

It meant, in the first place, that the lawsuit was over at last. It meant, in the second place that the owner of Windygates, wanting money, had decided on letting the property. It meant, in the third place, that the property had found a tenant, and was to be renovated immediately out of doors and in. The Owls shrieked as they flapped along the lanes in the darkness, And that night they struck at a mouse—and missed him.

The next morning, the Owls—fast asleep in charge of the Constitution—were roused by voices of featherless beings all round them. They opened their eyes, under protest, and saw instruments of destruction attacking the creepers. Now in one direction, and now in another, those instruments let in on the summer-house the horrid light of day. But the Owls were equal to the occasion. They ruffled their feathers, and cried, "No surrender!" The featherless beings plied their work cheerfully, and answered, "Reform!" The creepers were torn down this way and that. The horrid daylight poured in brighter and brighter. The Owls had barely time to pass a new resolution, namely, "That we do stand by the Constitution," when a ray of the outer sunlight flashed into their eyes, and sent them flying headlong to the nearest shade. There they sat winking, while the summer-house was cleared of the rank growth that had choked it up, while the rotten wood-work was renewed, while all the murky place was purified with air and light. And when the world saw it, and said, "Now we shall do!" the Owls shut their eyes in pious remembrance of the darkness, and answered, "My lords and gentlemen, the Constitution is destroyed!"

CHAPTER THE SECOND.

THE GUESTS.

Who was responsible for the reform of the summer-house? The new tenant at Windygates was responsible.

And who was the new tenant?

Come, and see.

In the spring of eighteen hundred and sixty-eight the summer-house had been the dismal dwelling-place of a pair of owls. In the autumn of the same year the summer-house was the lively gathering-place of a crowd of ladies and gentlemen, assembled at a lawn party—the guests of the tenant who had taken Windygates.

The scene—at the opening of the party—was as pleasant to look at as light and beauty and movement could make it.

Inside the summer-house the butterfly-brightness of the women in their summer dresses shone radiant out of the gloom shed round it by the dreary modern clothing of the men. Outside the summer-house, seen through three arched openings, the cool green prospect of a lawn led away, in the distance, to flower-beds and shrubberies, and, farther still, disclosed, through a break in the trees, a grand stone house which closed the view, with a fountain in front of it playing in the sun.

They were half of them laughing, they were all of them talking—the comfortable hum of their voices was at its loudest; the cheery pealing of the laughter was soaring to its highest notes—when one dominant voice, rising clear and shrill above all the rest, called imperatively for silence. The moment after, a young lady stepped into the vacant space in front of the summer-house, and surveyed the throng of guests as a general in command surveys a regiment under review.

She was young, she was pretty, she was plump, she was fair. She was not the least embarrassed by her prominent position. She was dressed in the height of the fashion. A hat, like a cheese-plate, was tilted over her forehead. A balloon of light brown hair soared, fully inflated, from the crown of her head. A cataract of beads poured over her bosom. A pair of cock-chafers in enamel (frightfully like the living originals) hung at her ears. Her scanty skirts shone splendid with the blue of heaven. Her ankles twinkled in striped stockings. Her shoes were of the sort called "Watteau." And her heels were of the height at which men shudder, and ask themselves (in contemplating an otherwise lovable woman), "Can this charming person straighten her knees?"

The young lady thus presenting herself to the general view was Miss Blanche Lundie—once the little rosy Blanche whom the Prologue has introduced to the reader. Age, at the present time, eighteen. Position, excellent. Money, certain. Temper, quick. Disposition, variable. In a word, a child of the modern time—with the merits of the age we live in, and the failings of the age we live in—and a substance of sincerity and truth and feeling underlying it all.

"Now then, good people," cried Miss Blanche, "silence, if you please! We are going to choose sides at croquet. Business, business, business!"

Upon this, a second lady among the company assumed a position of prominence, and answered the young person who had just spoken with a look of mild reproof, and in a tone of benevolent protest.

The second lady was tall, and solid, and five-and-thirty. She presented to the general observation a cruel aquiline nose, an obstinate straight chin, magnificent dark hair and eyes, a serene splendor of fawn-colored apparel, and a lazy grace of movement which was attractive at first sight, but inexpressibly monotonous and wearisome on a longer acquaintance. This was Lady Lundie the Second, now the widow (after four months only of married life) of Sir Thomas Lundie, deceased. In other words, the step-mother of Blanche, and the enviable person who had taken the house and lands of Windygates.

"My dear," said Lady Lundie, "words have their meanings—even on a young lady's lips. Do you call Croquet, 'business?'"

"You don't call it pleasure, surely?" said a gravely ironical voice in the back-ground of the summer-house.

The ranks of the visitors parted before the last speaker, and disclosed to view, in the midst of that modern assembly, a gentleman of the bygone time.

The manner of this gentleman was distinguished by a pliant grace and courtesy unknown to the present generation. The attire of this gentleman was composed of a many-folded white cravat, a close-buttoned blue dress-coat, and nankeen trousers with gaiters to match, ridiculous to the present generation. The talk of this gentleman ran in an easy flow—revealing an independent habit of mind, and exhibiting a carefully-polished capacity for satirical retort—dreaded and disliked by the present generation. Personally, he was little and wiry and slim—with a bright white head, and sparkling black eyes, and a wry twist of humor curling sharply at the corners of his lips. At his lower extremities, he exhibited the deformity which is popularly known as "a club-foot." But he carried his lameness, as he carried his years, gayly. He was socially celebrated for his ivory cane, with a snuff-box artfully let into the knob at the top—and he was socially dreaded for a hatred of modern institutions, which expressed itself in season and out of season, and which always showed the same, fatal knack of hitting smartly on the weakest place. Such was Sir Patrick Lundie; brother of the late baronet, Sir Thomas; and inheritor, at Sir Thomas's death, of the title and estates.

Miss Blanche—taking no notice of her step-mother's reproof, or of her uncle's commentary on it—pointed to a table on which croquet mallets and balls were laid ready, and recalled the attention of the company to the matter in hand.

"I head one side, ladies and gentlemen," she resumed. "And Lady Lundie heads the other. We choose our players turn and turn about. Mamma has the advantage of me in years. So mamma chooses first."

With a look at her step-daughter—which, being interpreted, meant, "I would send you back to the nursery, miss, if I could!"—Lady Lundie turned and ran her eye over her guests. She had evidently made up her mind, beforehand, what player to pick out first.

"I choose Miss Silvester," she said—with a special emphasis laid on the name.

At that there was another parting among the crowd. To us (who know her), it was Anne who now appeared. Strangers, who saw her for the first time, saw a lady in the prime of her life—a lady plainly dressed in unornamented white—who advanced slowly, and confronted the mistress of the house.

A certain proportion—and not a small one—of the men at the lawn-party had been brought there by friends who were privileged to introduce them. The moment she appeared every one of those men suddenly became interested in the lady who had been chosen first.

"That's a very charming woman," whispered one of the strangers at the house to one of the friends of the house. "Who is she?"

The friend whispered back.

"Miss Lundie's governess—that's all."

The moment during which the question was put and answered was also the moment which brought Lady Lundie and Miss Silvester face to face in the presence of the company.

The stranger at the house looked at the two women, and whispered again.

"Something wrong between the lady and the governess," he said.

The friend looked also, and answered, in one emphatic word:

"Evidently!"

There are certain women whose influence over men is an unfathomable mystery to observers of their own sex. The governess was one of those women. She had inherited the charm, but not the beauty, of her unhappy mother. Judge her by the standard set up in the illustrated gift-books and the print-shop windows—and the sentence must have inevitably followed. "She has not a single good feature in her face."

There was nothing individually remarkable about Miss Silvester, seen in a state of repose. She was of the average height. She was as well made as most women. In hair and complexion she was neither light nor dark, but provokingly neutral just between the two. Worse even than this, there were positive defects in her face, which it was impossible to deny. A nervous contraction at one corner of her mouth drew up the lips out of the symmetrically right line, when, they moved. A nervous uncertainty in the eye on the same side narrowly escaped presenting the deformity of a "cast." And yet, with these indisputable drawbacks, here was one of those women—the formidable few—who have the hearts of men and the peace of families at their mercy. She moved—and there was some subtle charm, Sir, in the movement, that made you look back, and suspend your conversation with your friend, and watch her silently while she walked. She sat by you and talked to you—and behold, a sensitive something passed into that little twist at the corner of the mouth, and into that nervous uncertainty in the soft gray eye, which turned defect into beauty—which enchained your senses—which made your nerves thrill if she touched you by accident, and set your heart beating if you looked at the same book with her, and felt her breath on your face. All this, let it be well understood, only happened if you were a man.

If you saw her with the eyes of a woman, the results were of quite another kind. In that case you merely turned to your nearest female friend, and said, with unaffected pity for the other sex, "What can the men see in her!"

The eyes of the lady of the house and the eyes of the governess met, with marked distrust on either side. Few people could have failed to see what the stranger and the friend had noticed alike—that there was something smoldering under the surface here. Miss Silvester spoke first.

"Thank you, Lady Lundie," she said. "I would rather not play."

Lady Lundie assumed an extreme surprise which passed the limits of good-breeding.

"Oh, indeed?" she rejoined, sharply. "Considering that we are all here for the purpose of playing, that seems rather remarkable. Is any thing wrong, Miss Silvester?"

A flush appeared on the delicate paleness of Miss Silvester's face. But she did her duty as a woman and a governess. She submitted, and so preserved appearances, for that time.

"Nothing is the matter," she answered. "I am not very well this morning. But I will play if you wish it."

"I do wish it," answered Lady Lundie.

Miss Silvester turned aside toward one of the entrances into the summer-house. She waited for events, looking out over the lawn, with a visible inner disturbance, marked over the bosom by the rise and fall of her white dress.

It was Blanche's turn to select the next player.

In some preliminary uncertainty as to her choice she looked about among the guests, and caught the eye of a gentleman in the front ranks. He stood side by side with Sir Patrick—a striking representative of the school that is among us—as Sir Patrick was a striking representative of the school that has passed away.

The modern gentleman was young and florid, tall and strong. The parting of his curly Saxon locks began in the center of his forehead, traveled over the top of his head, and ended, rigidly-central, at the ruddy nape of his neck. His features were as perfectly regular and as perfectly unintelligent as human features can be. His expression preserved an immovable composure wonderful to behold. The muscles of his brawny arms showed through the sleeves of his light summer coat. He was deep in the chest, thin in the flanks, firm on the legs—in two words a magnificent human animal, wrought up to the highest pitch of physical development, from head to foot. This was Mr. Geoffrey Delamayn—commonly called "the honorable;" and meriting that distinction in more ways than one. He was honorable, in the first place, as being the son (second son) of that once-rising solicitor, who was now Lord Holchester. He was honorable, in the second place, as having won the highest popular distinction which the educational system of modern England can bestow—he had pulled the stroke-oar in a University boat-race. Add to this, that nobody had ever seen him read any thing but a newspaper, and that nobody had ever known him to be backward in settling a bet—and the picture of this distinguished young Englishman will be, for the present, complete.

Blanche's eye naturally rested on him. Blanche's voice naturally picked him out as the first player on her side.

"I choose Mr. Delamayn," she said.

As the name passed her lips the flush on Miss Silvester's face died away, and a deadly paleness took its place. She made a movement to leave the summer-house—checked herself abruptly—and laid one hand on the back of a rustic seat at her side. A gentleman behind her, looking at the hand, saw it clench itself so suddenly and so fiercely that the glove on it split. The gentleman made a mental memorandum, and registered Miss Silvester in his private books as "the devil's own temper."

Meanwhile Mr. Delamayn, by a strange coincidence, took exactly the same course which Miss Silvester had taken before him. He, too, attempted to withdraw from the coming game.

"Thanks very much," he said. "Could you additionally honor me by choosing somebody else? It's not in my line."

Fifty years ago such an answer as this, addressed to a lady, would have been considered inexcusably impertinent. The social code of the present time hailed it as something frankly amusing. The company laughed. Blanche lost her temper.

"Can't we interest you in any thing but severe muscular exertion, Mr. Delamayn?" she asked, sharply. "Must you always be pulling in a boat-race, or flying over a high jump? If you had a mind, you would want to relax it. You have got muscles instead. Why not relax them?"

The shafts of Miss Lundie's bitter wit glided off Mr. Geoffrey Delamayn like water off a duck's back.

"Just as you please," he said, with stolid good-humor. "Don't be offended. I came here with ladies—and they wouldn't let me smoke. I miss my smoke. I thought I'd slip away a bit and have it. All right! I'll play."

"Oh! smoke by all means!" retorted Blanche. "I shall choose somebody else. I won't have you!"

The honorable young gentleman looked unaffectedly relieved. The petulant young lady turned her back on him, and surveyed the guests at the other extremity of the summer-house.

"Who shall I choose?" she said to herself.

A dark young man—with a face burned gipsy-brown by the sun; with something in his look and manner suggestive of a roving life, and perhaps of a familiar acquaintance with the sea—advanced shyly, and said, in a whisper:

"Choose me!"

Blanche's face broke prettily into a charming smile. Judging from appearances, the dark young man had a place in her estimation peculiarly his own.

"You!" she said, coquettishly. "You are going to leave us in an hour's time!"

He ventured a step nearer. "I am coming back," he pleaded, "the day after to-morrow."

"You play very badly!"

"I might improve—if you would teach me."

"Might you? Then I will teach you!" She turned, bright and rosy, to her step-mother. "I choose Mr. Arnold Brinkworth," she said.

Here, again, there appeared to be something in a name unknown to celebrity, which nevertheless produced its effect—not, this time, on Miss Silvester, but on Sir Patrick. He looked at Mr. Brinkworth with a sudden interest and curiosity. If the lady of the house had not claimed his attention at the moment he would evidently have spoken to the dark young man.

But it was Lady Lundie's turn to choose a second player on her side. Her brother-in-law was a person of some importance; and she had her own motives for ingratiating herself with the head of the family. She surprised the whole company by choosing Sir Patrick.

"Mamma!" cried Blanche. "What can you be thinking of? Sir Patrick won't play. Croquet wasn't discovered in his time."

Sir Patrick never allowed "his time" to be made the subject of disparaging remarks by the younger generation without paying the younger generation back in its own coin.

"In my time, my dear," he said to his niece, "people were expected to bring some agreeable quality with them to social meetings of this sort. In your time you have dispensed with all that. Here," remarked the old gentleman, taking up a croquet mallet from the table near him, "is one of the qualifications for success in modern society. And here," he added, taking up a ball, "is another. Very good. Live and learn. I'll play! I'll play!"

Lady Lundie (born impervious to all sense of irony) smiled graciously.

"I knew Sir Patrick would play," she said, "to please me."

Sir Patrick bowed with satirical politeness.

"Lady Lundie," he answered, "you read me like a book." To the astonishment of all persons present under forty he emphasized those words by laying his hand on his heart, and quoting poetry. "I may say with Dryden," added the gallant old gentleman:

"'Old as I am, for ladies' love unfit,

The power of beauty I remember yet.'"

Lady Lundie looked unaffectedly shocked. Mr. Delamayn went a step farther. He interfered on the spot—with the air of a man who feels himself imperatively called upon to perform a public duty.

"Dryden never said that," he remarked, "I'll answer for it."

Sir Patrick wheeled round with the help of his ivory cane, and looked Mr. Delamayn hard in the face.

"Do you know Dryden, Sir, better than I do?" he asked.

The Honorable Geoffrey answered, modestly, "I should say I did. I have rowed three races with him, and we trained together."

Sir Patrick looked round him with a sour smile of triumph.

"Then let me tell you, Sir," he said, "that you trained with a man who died nearly two hundred years ago."

Mr. Delamayn appealed, in genuine bewilderment, to the company generally:

"What does this old gentleman mean?" he asked. "I am speaking of Tom Dryden, of Corpus. Every body in the University knows him."

"I am speaking," echoed Sir Patrick, "of John Dryden the Poet. Apparently, every body in the University does not know him!"

Mr. Delamayn answered, with a cordial earnestness very pleasant to see:

"Give you my word of honor, I never heard of him before in my life! Don't be angry, Sir. I'm not offended with you." He smiled, and took out his brier-wood pipe. "Got a light?" he asked, in the friendliest possible manner.

Sir Patrick answered, with a total absence of cordiality:

"I don't smoke, Sir."

Mr. Delamayn looked at him, without taking the slightest offense:

"You don't smoke!" he repeated. "I wonder how you get through your spare time?"

Sir Patrick closed the conversation:

"Sir," he said, with a low bow, "you may wonder."

While this little skirmish was proceeding Lady Lundie and her step-daughter had organized the game; and the company, players and spectators, were beginning to move toward the lawn. Sir Patrick stopped his niece on her way out, with the dark young man in close attendance on her.

"Leave Mr. Brinkworth with me," he said. "I want to speak to him."

Blanche issued her orders immediately. Mr. Brinkworth was sentenced to stay with Sir Patrick until she wanted him for the game. Mr. Brinkworth wondered, and obeyed.

During the exercise of this act of authority a circumstance occurred at the other end of the summer-house. Taking advantage of the confusion caused by the general movement to the lawn, Miss Silvester suddenly placed herself close to Mr. Delamayn.

"In ten minutes," she whispered, "the summer-house will be empty. Meet me here."

The Honorable Geoffrey started, and looked furtively at the visitors about him.

"Do you think it's safe?" he whispered back.

The governess's sensitive lips trembled, with fear or with anger, it was hard to say which.

"I insist on it!" she answered, and left him.

Mr. Delamayn knitted his handsome eyebrows as he looked after her, and then left the summer-house in his turn. The rose-garden at the back of the building was solitary for the moment. He took out his pipe and hid himself among the roses. The smoke came from his mouth in hot and hasty puffs. He was usually the gentlest of masters—to his pipe. When he hurried that confidential servant, it was a sure sign of disturbance in the inner man.

CHAPTER THE THIRD.

THE DISCOVERIES.

BUT two persons were now left in the summer-house—Arnold Brinkworth and Sir Patrick Lundie.

"Mr. Brinkworth," said the old gentleman, "I have had no opportunity of speaking to you before this; and (as I hear that you are to leave us, to-day) I may find no opportunity at a later time. I want to introduce myself. Your father was one of my dearest friends—let me make a friend of your father's son."

He held out his hands, and mentioned his name.

Arnold recognized it directly. "Oh, Sir Patrick!" he said, warmly, "if my poor father had only taken your advice—"

"He would have thought twice before he gambled away his fortune on the turf; and he might have been alive here among us, instead of dying an exile in a foreign land," said Sir Patrick, finishing the sentence which the other had begun. "No more of that! Let's talk of something else. Lady Lundie wrote to me about you the other day. She told me your aunt was dead, and had left you heir to her property in Scotland. Is that true?—It is?—I congratulate you with all my heart. Why are you visiting here, instead of looking after your house and lands? Oh! it's only three-and-twenty miles from this; and you're going to look after it to-day, by the next train? Quite right. And—what? what?—coming back again the day after to-morrow? Why should you come back? Some special attraction here, I suppose? I hope it's the right sort of attraction. You're very young—you're exposed to all sorts of temptations. Have you got a solid foundation of good sense at the bottom of you? It is not inherited from your poor father, if you have. You must have been a mere boy when he ruined his children's prospects. How have you lived from that time to this? What were you doing when your aunt's will made an idle man of you for life?"

The question was a searching one. Arnold answered it, without the slightest hesitation; speaking with an unaffected modesty and simplicity which at once won Sir Patrick's heart.

"I was a boy at Eton, Sir," he said, "when my father's losses ruined him. I had to leave school, and get my own living; and I have got it, in a roughish way, from that time to this. In plain English, I have followed the sea—in the merchant-service."

"In plainer English still, you met adversity like a brave lad, and you have fairly earned the good luck that has fallen to you," rejoined Sir Patrick. "Give me your hand—I have taken a liking to you. You're not like the other young fellows of the present time. I shall call you 'Arnold.' You mus'n't return the compliment and call me 'Patrick,' mind—I'm too old to be treated in that way. Well, and how do you get on here? What sort of a woman is my sister-in-law? and what sort of a house is this?"

Arnold burst out laughing.

"Those are extraordinary questions for you to put to me," he said. "You talk, Sir, as if you were a stranger here!"

Sir Patrick touched a spring in the knob of his ivory cane. A little gold lid flew up, and disclosed the snuff-box hidden inside. He took a pinch, and chuckled satirically over some passing thought, which he did not think it necessary to communicate to his young friend.

"I talk as if I was a stranger here, do I?" he resumed. "That's exactly what I am. Lady Lundie and I correspond on excellent terms; but we run in different grooves, and we see each other as seldom as possible. My story," continued the pleasant old man, with a charming frankness which leveled all differences of age and rank between Arnold and himself, "is not entirely unlike yours; though I am old enough to be your grandfather. I was getting my living, in my way (as a crusty old Scotch lawyer), when my brother married again. His death, without leaving a son by either of his wives, gave me a lift in the world, like you. Here I am (to my own sincere regret) the present baronet. Yes, to my sincere regret! All sorts of responsibilities which I never bargained for are thrust on my shoulders. I am the head of the family; I am my niece's guardian; I am compelled to appear at this lawn-party—and (between ourselves) I am as completely out of my element as a man can be. Not a single familiar face meets me among all these fine people. Do you know any body here?"

"I have one friend at Windygates," said Arnold. "He came here this morning, like you. Geoffrey Delamayn."

As he made the reply, Miss Silvester appeared at the entrance to the summer-house. A shadow of annoyance passed over her face when she saw that the place was occupied. She vanished, unnoticed, and glided back to the game.

Sir Patrick looked at the son of his old friend, with every appearance of being disappointed in the young man for the first time.

"Your choice of a friend rather surprises me," he said.

Arnold artlessly accepted the words as an appeal to him for information.

"I beg your pardon, Sir—there's nothing surprising in it," he returned. "We were school-fellows at Eton, in the old times. And I have met Geoffrey since, when he was yachting, and when I was with my ship. Geoffrey saved my life, Sir Patrick," he added, his voice rising, and his eyes brightening with honest admiration of his friend. "But for him, I should have been drowned in a boat-accident. Isn't that a good reason for his being a friend of mine?"

"It depends entirely on the value you set on your life," said Sir Patrick.

"The value I set on my life?" repeated Arnold. "I set a high value on it, of course!"

"In that case, Mr. Delamayn has laid you under an obligation."

"Which I can never repay!"

"Which you will repay one of these days, with interest—if I know any thing of human nature," answered Sir Patrick.

He said the words with the emphasis of strong conviction. They were barely spoken when Mr. Delamayn appeared (exactly as Miss Silvester had appeared) at the entrance to the summer-house. He, too, vanished, unnoticed—like Miss Silvester again. But there the parallel stopped. The Honorable Geoffrey's expression, on discovering the place to be occupied, was, unmistakably an expression of relief.

Arnold drew the right inference, this time, from Sir Patrick's language and Sir Patrick's tones. He eagerly took up the defense of his friend.

"You said that rather bitterly, Sir," he remarked. "What has Geoffrey done to offend you?"

"He presumes to exist—that's what he has done," retorted Sir Patrick. "Don't stare! I am speaking generally. Your friend is the model young Briton of the present time. I don't like the model young Briton. I don't see the sense of crowing over him as a superb national production, because he is big and strong, and drinks beer with impunity, and takes a cold shower bath all the year round. There is far too much glorification in England, just now, of the mere physical qualities which an Englishman shares with the savage and the brute. And the ill results are beginning to show themselves already! We are readier than we ever were to practice all that is rough in our national customs, and to excuse all that is violent and brutish in our national acts. Read the popular books—attend the popular amusements; and you will find at the bottom of them all a lessening regard for the gentler graces of civilized life, and a growing admiration for the virtues of the aboriginal Britons!"

Arnold listened in blank amazement. He had been the innocent means of relieving Sir Patrick's mind of an accumulation of social protest, unprovided with an issue for some time past. "How hot you are over it, Sir!" he exclaimed, in irrepressible astonishment.

Sir Patrick instantly recovered himself. The genuine wonder expressed in the young man's face was irresistible.

"Almost as hot," he said, "as if I was cheering at a boat-race, or wrangling over a betting-book—eh? Ah, we were so easily heated when I was a young man! Let's change the subject. I know nothing to the prejudice of your friend, Mr. Delamayn. It's the cant of the day," cried Sir Patrick, relapsing again, "to take these physically-wholesome men for granted as being morally-wholesome men into the bargain. Time will show whether the cant of the day is right.—So you are actually coming back to Lady Lundie's after a mere flying visit to your own property? I repeat, that is a most extraordinary proceeding on the part of a landed gentleman like you. What's the attraction here—eh?"

Before Arnold could reply Blanche called to him from the lawn. His color rose, and he turned eagerly to go out. Sir Patrick nodded his head with the air of a man who had been answered to his own entire satisfaction. "Oh!" he said, "that's the attraction, is it?"

Arnold's life at sea had left him singularly ignorant of the ways of the world on shore. Instead of taking the joke, he looked confused. A deeper tinge of color reddened his dark cheeks. "I didn't say so," he answered, a little irritably.

Sir Patrick lifted two of his white, wrinkled old fingers, and good-humoredly patted the young sailor on the cheek.

"Yes you did," he said. "In red letters."

The little gold lid in the knob of the ivory cane flew up, and the old gentleman rewarded himself for that neat retort with a pinch of snuff. At the same moment Blanche made her appearance on the scene.

"Mr. Brinkworth," she said, "I shall want you directly. Uncle, it's your turn to play."

"Bless my soul!" cried Sir Patrick, "I forgot the game." He looked about him, and saw his mallet and ball left waiting on the table. "Where are the modern substitutes for conversation? Oh, here they are!" He bowled the ball out before him on to the lawn, and tucked the mallet, as if it was an umbrella, under his arm. "Who was the first mistaken person," he said to himself, as he briskly hobbled out, "who discovered that human life was a serious thing? Here am I, with one foot in the grave; and the most serious question before me at the present moment is, Shall I get through the Hoops?"

Arnold and Blanche were left together.

Among the personal privileges which Nature has accorded to women, there are surely none more enviable than their privilege of always looking their best when they look at the man they love. When Blanche's eyes turned on Arnold after her uncle had gone out, not even the hideous fashionable disfigurements of the inflated "chignon" and the tilted hat could destroy the triple charm of youth, beauty, and tenderness beaming in her face. Arnold looked at her—and remembered, as he had never remembered yet, that he was going by the next train, and that he was leaving her in the society of more than one admiring man of his own age. The experience of a whole fortnight passed under the same roof with her had proved Blanche to be the most charming girl in existence. It was possible that she might not be mortally offended with him if he told her so. He determined that he would tell her so at that auspicious moment.

But who shall presume to measure the abyss that lies between the Intention and the Execution? Arnold's resolution to speak was as firmly settled as a resolution could be. And what came of it? Alas for human infirmity! Nothing came of it but silence.

"You don't look quite at your ease, Mr. Brinkworth," said Blanche. "What has Sir Patrick been saying to you? My uncle sharpens his wit on every body. He has been sharpening it on you?"

Arnold began to see his way. At an immeasurable distance—but still he saw it.

"Sir Patrick is a terrible old man," he answered. "Just before you came in he discovered one of my secrets by only looking in my face." He paused, rallied his courage, pushed on at all hazards, and came headlong to the point. "I wonder," he asked, bluntly, "whether you take after your uncle?"

Blanche instantly understood him. With time at her disposal, she would have taken him lightly in hand, and led him, by fine gradations, to the object in view. But in two minutes or less it would be Arnold's turn to play. "He is going to make me an offer," thought Blanche; "and he has about a minute to do it in. He shall do it!"

"What!" she exclaimed, "do you think the gift of discovery runs in the family?"

Arnold made a plunge.

"I wish it did!" he said.

Blanche looked the picture of astonishment.

"Why?" she asked.

"If you could see in my face what Sir Patrick saw—"

He had only to finish the sentence, and the thing was done. But the tender passion perversely delights in raising obstacles to itself. A sudden timidity seized on Arnold exactly at the wrong moment. He stopped short, in the most awkward manner possible.

Blanche heard from the lawn the blow of the mallet on the ball, and the laughter of the company at some blunder of Sir Patrick's. The precious seconds were slipping away. She could have boxed Arnold on both ears for being so unreasonably afraid of her.

"Well," she said, impatiently, "if I did look in your face, what should I see?"

Arnold made another plunge. He answered: "You would see that I want a little encouragement."

"From me?"

"Yes—if you please."

Blanche looked back over her shoulder. The summer-house stood on an eminence, approached by steps. The players on the lawn beneath were audible, but not visible. Any one of them might appear, unexpectedly, at a moment's notice. Blanche listened. There was no sound of approaching footsteps—there was a general hush, and then another bang of the mallet on the ball and then a clapping of hands. Sir Patrick was a privileged person. He had been allowed, in all probability, to try again; and he was succeeding at the second effort. This implied a reprieve of some seconds. Blanche looked back again at Arnold.

"Consider yourself encouraged," she whispered; and instantly added, with the ineradicable female instinct of self-defense, "within limits!"

Arnold made a last plunge—straight to the bottom, this time.

"Consider yourself loved," he burst out, "without any limits at all."

It was all over—the words were spoken—he had got her by the hand. Again the perversity of the tender passion showed itself more strongly than ever. The confession which Blanche had been longing to hear, had barely escaped her lover's lips before Blanche protested against it! She struggled to release her hand. She formally appealed to Arnold to let her go.

Arnold only held her the tighter.

"Do try to like me a little!" he pleaded. "I am so fond of you!"

Who was to resist such wooing as this?—when you were privately fond of him yourself, remember, and when you were certain to be interrupted in another moment! Blanche left off struggling, and looked up at her young sailor with a smile.

"Did you learn this method of making love in the merchant-service?" she inquired, saucily.

Arnold persisted in contemplating his prospects from the serious point of view.

"I'll go back to the merchant-service," he said, "if I have made you angry with me."

Blanche administered another dose of encouragement.

"Anger, Mr. Brinkworth, is one of the bad passions," she answered, demurely. "A young lady who has been properly brought up has no bad passions."

There was a sudden cry from the players on the lawn—a cry for "Mr. Brinkworth." Blanche tried to push him out. Arnold was immovable.

"Say something to encourage me before I go," he pleaded. "One word will do. Say, Yes."

Blanche shook her head. Now she had got him, the temptation to tease him was irresistible.

"Quite impossible!" she rejoined. "If you want any more encouragement, you must speak to my uncle."

"I'll speak to him," returned Arnold, "before I leave the house."

There was another cry for "Mr. Brinkworth." Blanche made another effort to push him out.

"Go!" she said. "And mind you get through the hoop!"

She had both hands on his shoulders—her face was close to his—she was simply irresistible. Arnold caught her round the waist and kissed her. Needless to tell him to get through the hoop. He had surely got through it already! Blanche was speechless. Arnold's last effort in the art of courtship had taken away her breath. Before she could recover herself a sound of approaching footsteps became plainly audible. Arnold gave her a last squeeze, and ran out.

She sank on the nearest chair, and closed her eyes in a flutter of delicious confusion.

The footsteps ascending to the summer-house came nearer. Blanche opened her eyes, and saw Anne Silvester, standing alone, looking at her. She sprang to her feet, and threw her arms impulsively round Anne's neck.

"You don't know what has happened," she whispered. "Wish me joy, darling. He has said the words. He is mine for life!"

All the sisterly love and sisterly confidence of many years was expressed in that embrace, and in the tone in which the words were spoken. The hearts of the mothers, in the past time, could hardly have been closer to each other—as it seemed—than the hearts of the daughters were now. And yet, if Blanche had looked up in Anne's face at that moment, she must have seen that Anne's mind was far away from her little love-story.

"You know who it is?" she went on, after waiting for a reply.

"Mr. Brinkworth?"

"Of course! Who else should it be?"

"And you are really happy, my love?"

"Happy?" repeated Blanche "Mind! this is strictly between ourselves. I am ready to jump out of my skin for joy. I love him! I love him! I love him!" she cried, with a childish pleasure in repeating the words. They were echoed by a heavy sigh. Blanche instantly looked up into Anne's face. "What's the matter?" she asked, with a sudden change of voice and manner.

"Nothing."

Blanche's observation saw too plainly to be blinded in that way.

"There is something the matter," she said. "Is it money?" she added, after a moment's consideration. "Bills to pay? I have got plenty of money, Anne. I'll lend you what you like."

"No, no, my dear!"

Blanche drew back, a little hurt. Anne was keeping her at a distance for the first time in Blanche's experience of her.

"I tell you all my secrets," she said. "Why are you keeping a secret from me? Do you know that you have been looking anxious and out of spirits for some time past? Perhaps you don't like Mr. Brinkworth? No? you do like him? Is it my marrying, then? I believe it is! You fancy we shall be parted, you goose? As if I could do without you! Of course, when I am married to Arnold, you will come and live with us. That's quite understood between us—isn't it?"

Anne drew herself suddenly, almost roughly, away from Blanche, and pointed out to the steps.

"There is somebody coming," she said. "Look!"

The person coming was Arnold. It was Blanche's turn to play, and he had volunteered to fetch her.

Blanche's attention—easily enough distracted on other occasions—remained steadily fixed on Anne.

"You are not yourself," she said, "and I must know the reason of it. I will wait till to-night; and then you will tell me, when you come into my room. Don't look like that! You shall tell me. And there's a kiss for you in the mean time!"

She joined Arnold, and recovered her gayety the moment she looked at him.

"Well? Have you got through the hoops?"

"Never mind the hoops. I have broken the ice with Sir Patrick."

"What! before all the company!"

"Of course not! I have made an appointment to speak to him here."

They went laughing down the steps, and joined the game.

Left alone, Anne Silvester walked slowly to the inner and darker part of the summer-house. A glass, in a carved wooden frame, was fixed against one of the side walls. She stopped and looked into it—looked, shuddering, at the reflection of herself.

"Is the time coming," she said, "when even Blanche will see what I am in my face?"

She turned aside from the glass. With a sudden cry of despair she flung up her arms and laid them heavily against the wall, and rested her head on them with her back to the light. At the same moment a man's figure appeared—standing dark in the flood of sunshine at the entrance to the summer-house. The man was Geoffrey Delamayn.

CHAPTER THE FOURTH.

THE TWO.

He advanced a few steps, and stopped. Absorbed in herself, Anne failed to hear him. She never moved.

"I have come, as you made a point of it," he said, sullenly. "But, mind you, it isn't safe."

At the sound of his voice, Anne turned toward him. A change of expression appeared in her face, as she slowly advanced from the back of the summer-house, which revealed a likeness to her mother, not perceivable at other times. As the mother had looked, in by-gone days, at the man who had disowned her, so the daughter looked at Geoffrey Delamayn—with the same terrible composure, and the same terrible contempt.

"Well?" he asked. "What have you got to say to me?"

"Mr. Delamayn," she answered, "you are one of the fortunate people of this world. You are a nobleman's son. You are a handsome man. You are popular at your college. You are free of the best houses in England. Are you something besides all this? Are you a coward and a scoundrel as well?"

He started—opened his lips to speak—checked himself—and made an uneasy attempt to laugh it off. "Come!" he said, "keep your temper."

The suppressed passion in her began to force its way to the surface.

"Keep my temper?" she repeated. "Do you of all men expect me to control myself? What a memory yours must be! Have you forgotten the time when I was fool enough to think you were fond of me? and mad enough to believe you could keep a promise?"

He persisted in trying to laugh it off. "Mad is a strongish word to use, Miss Silvester!"

"Mad is the right word! I look back at my own infatuation—and I can't account for it; I can't understand myself. What was there in you," she asked, with an outbreak of contemptuous surprise, "to attract such a woman as I am?"

His inexhaustible good-nature was proof even against this. He put his hands in his pockets, and said, "I'm sure I don't know."

She turned away from him. The frank brutality of the answer had not offended her. It forced her, cruelly forced her, to remember that she had nobody but herself to blame for the position in which she stood at that moment. She was unwilling to let him see how the remembrance hurt her—that was all. A sad, sad story; but it must be told. In her mother's time she had been the sweetest, the most lovable of children. In later days, under the care of her mother's friend, her girlhood had passed so harmlessly and so happily—it seemed as if the sleeping passions might sleep forever! She had lived on to the prime of her womanhood—and then, when the treasure of her life was at its richest, in one fatal moment she had flung it away on the man in whose presence she now stood.

Was she without excuse? No: not utterly without excuse.

She had seen him under other aspects than the aspect which he presented now. She had seen him, the hero of the river-race, the first and foremost man in a trial of strength and skill which had roused the enthusiasm of all England. She had seen him, the central object of the interest of a nation; the idol of the popular worship and the popular applause. His were the arms whose muscle was celebrated in the newspapers. He was first among the heroes hailed by ten thousand roaring throats as the pride and flower of England. A woman, in an atmosphere of red-hot enthusiasm, witnesses the apotheosis of Physical Strength. Is it reasonable—is it just—to expect her to ask herself, in cold blood, What (morally and intellectually) is all this worth?—and that, when the man who is the object of the apotheosis, notices her, is presented to her, finds her to his taste, and singles her out from the rest? No. While humanity is humanity, the woman is not utterly without excuse.

Has she escaped, without suffering for it?

Look at her as she stands there, tortured by the knowledge of her own secret—the hideous secret which she is hiding from the innocent girl, whom she loves with a sister's love. Look at her, bowed down under a humiliation which is unutterable in words. She has seen him below the surface—now, when it is too late. She rates him at his true value—now, when her reputation is at his mercy. Ask her the question: What was there to love in a man who can speak to you as that man has spoken, who can treat you as that man is treating you now? you so clever, so cultivated, so refined—what, in Heaven's name, could you see in him? Ask her that, and she will have no answer to give. She will not even remind you that he was once your model of manly beauty, too—that you waved your handkerchief till you could wave it no longer, when he took his seat, with the others, in the boat—that your heart was like to jump out of your bosom, on that later occasion when he leaped the last hurdle at the foot-race, and won it by a head. In the bitterness of her remorse, she will not even seek for that excuse for herself. Is there no atoning suffering to be seen here? Do your sympathies shrink from such a character as this? Follow her, good friends of virtue, on the pilgrimage that leads, by steep and thorny ways, to the purer atmosphere and the nobler life. Your fellow-creature, who has sinned and has repented—you have the authority of the Divine Teacher for it—is your fellow-creature, purified and ennobled. A joy among the angels of heaven—oh, my brothers and sisters of the earth, have I not laid my hand on a fit companion for You?

There was a moment of silence in the summer-house. The cheerful tumult of the lawn-party was pleasantly audible from the distance. Outside, the hum of voices, the laughter of girls, the thump of the croquet-mallet against the ball. Inside, nothing but a woman forcing back the bitter tears of sorrow and shame—and a man who was tired of her.

She roused herself. She was her mother's daughter; and she had a spark of her mother's spirit. Her life depended on the issue of that interview. It was useless—without father or brother to take her part—to lose the last chance of appealing to him. She dashed away the tears—time enough to cry, is time easily found in a woman's existence—she dashed away the tears, and spoke to him again, more gently than she had spoken yet.

"You have been three weeks, Geoffrey, at your brother Julius's place, not ten miles from here; and you have never once ridden over to see me. You would not have come to-day, if I had not written to you to insist on it. Is that the treatment I have deserved?"

She paused. There was no answer.

"Do you hear me?" she asked, advancing and speaking in louder tones.

He was still silent. It was not in human endurance to bear his contempt. The warning of a coming outbreak began to show itself in her face. He met it, beforehand, with an impenetrable front. Feeling nervous about the interview, while he was waiting in the rose-garden—now that he stood committed to it, he was in full possession of himself. He was composed enough to remember that he had not put his pipe in its case—composed enough to set that little matter right before other matters went any farther. He took the case out of one pocket, and the pipe out of another.

"Go on," he said, quietly. "I hear you."

She struck the pipe out of his hand at a blow. If she had had the strength she would have struck him down with it on the floor of the summer-house.

"How dare you use me in this way?" she burst out, vehemently. "Your conduct is infamous. Defend it if you can!"

He made no attempt to defend it. He looked, with an expression of genuine anxiety, at the fallen pipe. It was beautifully colored—it had cost him ten shillings. "I'll pick up my pipe first," he said. His face brightened pleasantly—he looked handsomer than ever—as he examined the precious object, and put it back in the case. "All right," he said to himself. "She hasn't broken it." His attitude as he looked at her again, was the perfection of easy grace—the grace that attends on cultivated strength in a state of repose. "I put it to your own common-sense," he said, in the most reasonable manner, "what's the good of bullying me? You don't want them to hear you, out on the lawn there—do you? You women are all alike. There's no beating a little prudence into your heads, try how one may."

There he waited, expecting her to speak. She waited, on her side, and forced him to go on.

"Look here," he said, "there's no need to quarrel, you know. I don't want to break my promise; but what can I do? I'm not the eldest son. I'm dependent on my father for every farthing I have; and I'm on bad terms with him already. Can't you see it yourself? You're a lady, and all that, I know. But you're only a governess. It's your interest as well as mine to wait till my father has provided for me. Here it is in a nut-shell: if I marry you now, I'm a ruined man."

The answer came, this time.

"You villain if you don't marry me, I am a ruined woman!"

"What do you mean?"

"You know what I mean. Don't look at me in that way."

"How do you expect me to look at a woman who calls me a villain to my face?"

She suddenly changed her tone. The savage element in humanity—let the modern optimists who doubt its existence look at any uncultivated man (no matter how muscular), woman (no matter how beautiful), or child (no matter how young)—began to show itself furtively in his eyes, to utter itself furtively in his voice. Was he to blame for the manner in which he looked at her and spoke to her? Not he! What had there been in the training of his life (at school or at college) to soften and subdue the savage element in him? About as much as there had been in the training of his ancestors (without the school or the college) five hundred years since.

It was plain that one of them must give way. The woman had the most at stake—and the woman set the example of submission.

"Don't be hard on me," she pleaded. "I don't mean to be hard on you. My temper gets the better of me. You know my temper. I am sorry I forgot myself. Geoffrey, my whole future is in your hands. Will you do me justice?"

She came nearer, and laid her hand persuasively on his arm.

"Haven't you a word to say to me? No answer? Not even a look?" She waited a moment more. A marked change came over her. She turned slowly to leave the summer-house. "I am sorry to have troubled you, Mr. Delamayn. I won't detain you any longer."

He looked at her. There was a tone in her voice that he had never heard before. There was a light in her eyes that he had never seen in them before. Suddenly and fiercely he reached out his hand, and stopped her.

"Where are you going?" he asked.

She answered, looking him straight in the face, "Where many a miserable woman has gone before me. Out of the world."

He drew her nearer to him, and eyed her closely. Even his intelligence discovered that he had brought her to bay, and that she really meant it!

"Do you mean you will destroy yourself?" he said.

"Yes. I mean I will destroy myself."

He dropped her arm. "By Jupiter, she does mean it!"

With that conviction in him, he pushed one of the chairs in the summer-house to her with his foot, and signed to her to take it. "Sit down!" he said, roughly. She had frightened him—and fear comes seldom to men of his type. They feel it, when it does come, with an angry distrust; they grow loud and brutal, in instinctive protest against it. "Sit down!" he repeated. She obeyed him. "Haven't you got a word to say to me?" he asked, with an oath. No! there she sat, immovable, reckless how it ended—as only women can be, when women's minds are made up. He took a turn in the summer-house and came back, and struck his hand angrily on the rail of her chair. "What do you want?"

"You know what I want."

He took another turn. There was nothing for it but to give way on his side, or run the risk of something happening which might cause an awkward scandal, and come to his father's ears.

"Look here, Anne," he began, abruptly. "I have got something to propose."

She looked up at him.

"What do you say to a private marriage?"

Without asking a single question, without making objections, she answered him, speaking as bluntly as he had spoken himself:

"I consent to a private marriage."

He began to temporize directly.

"I own I don't see how it's to be managed—"

She stopped him there.

"I do!"

"What!" he cried out, suspiciously. "You have thought of it yourself, have you?"

"Yes."

"And planned for it?"

"And planned for it!"

"Why didn't you tell me so before?"

She answered haughtily; insisting on the respect which is due to women—the respect which was doubly due from him, in her position.

"Because you owed it to me, Sir, to speak first."

"Very well. I've spoken first. Will you wait a little?"

"Not a day!"

The tone was positive. There was no mistaking it. Her mind was made up.

"Where's the hurry?"

"Have you eyes?" she asked, vehemently. "Have you ears? Do you see how Lady Lundie looks at me? Do you hear how Lady Lundie speaks to me? I am suspected by that woman. My shameful dismissal from this house may be a question of a few hours." Her head sunk on her bosom; she wrung her clasped hands as they rested on her lap. "And, oh, Blanche!" she moaned to herself, the tears gathering again, and falling, this time, unchecked. "Blanche, who looks up to me! Blanche, who loves me! Blanche, who told me, in this very place, that I was to live with her when she was married!" She started up from the chair; the tears dried suddenly; the hard despair settled again, wan and white, on her face. "Let me go! What is death, compared to such a life as is waiting for me?" She looked him over, in one disdainful glance from head to foot; her voice rose to its loudest and firmest tones. "Why, even you; would have the courage to die if you were in my place!"

Geoffrey glanced round toward the lawn.

"Hush!" he said. "They will hear you!"

"Let them hear me! When I am past hearing them, what does it matter?"

He put her back by main force on the chair. In another moment they must have heard her, through all the noise and laughter of the game.

"Say what you want," he resumed, "and I'll do it. Only be reasonable. I can't marry you to-day."

"You can!"

"What nonsense you talk! The house and grounds are swarming with company. It can't be!"

"It can! I have been thinking about it ever since we came to this house. I have got something to propose to you. Will you hear it, or not?"

"Speak lower!"

"Will you hear it, or not?"

"There's somebody coming!"

"Will you hear it, or not?"

"The devil take your obstinacy! Yes!"

The answer had been wrung from him. Still, it was the answer she wanted—it opened the door to hope. The instant he had consented to hear her her mind awakened to the serious necessity of averting discovery by any third person who might stray idly into the summer-house. She held up her hand for silence, and listened to what was going forward on the lawn.

The dull thump of the croquet-mallet against the ball was no longer to be heard. The game had stopped.

In a moment more she heard her own name called. An interval of another instant passed, and a familiar voice said, "I know where she is. I'll fetch her."

She turned to Geoffrey, and pointed to the back of the summer-house.

"It's my turn to play," she said. "And Blanche is coming here to look for me. Wait there, and I'll stop her on the steps."

She went out at once. It was a critical moment. Discovery, which meant moral-ruin to the woman, meant money-ruin to the man. Geoffrey had not exaggerated his position with his father. Lord Holchester had twice paid his debts, and had declined to see him since. One more outrage on his father's rigid sense of propriety, and he would be left out of the will as well as kept out of the house. He looked for a means of retreat, in case there was no escaping unperceived by the front entrance. A door—intended for the use of servants, when picnics and gipsy tea-parties were given in the summer-house—had been made in the back wall. It opened outward, and it was locked. With his strength it was easy to remove that obstacle. He put his shoulder to the door. At the moment when he burst it open he felt a hand on his arm. Anne was behind him, alone.

"You may want it before long," she said, observing the open door, without expressing any surprise, "You don't want it now. Another person will play for me—I have told Blanche I am not well. Sit down. I have secured a respite of five minutes, and I must make the most of it. In that time, or less, Lady Lundie's suspicions will bring her here—to see how I am. For the present, shut the door."

She seated herself, and pointed to a second chair. He took it—with his eye on the closed door.

"Come to the point!" he said, impatiently. "What is it?"

"You can marry me privately to-day," she answered. "Listen—and I will tell you how!"

CHAPTER THE FIFTH.

THE PLAN.

SHE took his hand, and began with all the art of persuasion that she possessed.

"One question, Geoffrey, before I say what I want to say. Lady Lundie has invited you to stay at Windygates. Do you accept her invitation? or do you go back to your brother's in the evening?"

"I can't go back in the evening—they've put a visitor into my room. I'm obliged to stay here. My brother has done it on purpose. Julius helps me when I'm hard up—and bullies me afterward. He has sent me here, on duty for the family. Somebody must be civil to Lady Lundie—and I'm the sacrifice."

She took him up at his last word. "Don't make the sacrifice," she said. "Apologize to Lady Lundie, and say you are obliged to go back."

"Why?"

"Because we must both leave this place to-day."

There was a double objection to that. If he left Lady Lundie's, he would fail to establish a future pecuniary claim on his brother's indulgence. And if he left with Anne, the eyes of the world would see them, and the whispers of the world might come to his father's ears.

"If we go away together," he said, "good-by to my prospects, and yours too."

"I don't mean that we shall leave together," she explained. "We will leave separately—and I will go first."

"There will be a hue and cry after you, when you are missed."

"There will be a dance when the croquet is over. I don't dance—and I shall not be missed. There will be time, and opportunity to get to my own room. I shall leave a letter there for Lady Lundie, and a letter"—her voice trembled for a moment—"and a letter for Blanche. Don't interrupt me! I have thought of this, as I have thought of every thing else. The confession I shall make will be the truth in a few hours, if it's not the truth now. My letters will say I am privately married, and called away unexpectedly to join my husband. There will be a scandal in the house, I know. But there will be no excuse for sending after me, when I am under my husband's protection. So far as you are personally concerned there are no discoveries to fear—and nothing which it is not perfectly safe and perfectly easy to do. Wait here an hour after I have gone to save appearances; and then follow me."

"Follow you?" interposed Geoffrey. "Where?" She drew her chair nearer to him, and whispered the next words in his ear.

"To a lonely little mountain inn—four miles from this."

"An inn!"

"Why not?"

"An inn is a public place."

A movement of natural impatience escaped her—but she controlled herself, and went on as quietly as before:

"The place I mean is the loneliest place in the neighborhood. You have no prying eyes to dread there. I have picked it out expressly for that reason. It's away from the railway; it's away from the high-road: it's kept by a decent, respectable Scotchwoman—"

"Decent, respectable Scotchwomen who keep inns," interposed Geoffrey, "don't cotton to young ladies who are traveling alone. The landlady won't receive you."

It was a well-aimed objection—but it missed the mark. A woman bent on her marriage is a woman who can meet the objections of the whole world, single-handed, and refute them all.

"I have provided for every thing," she said, "and I have provided for that. I shall tell the landlady I am on my wedding-trip. I shall say my husband is sight-seeing, on foot, among the mountains in the neighborhood—"

"She is sure to believe that!" said Geoffrey.

"She is sure to disbelieve it, if you like. Let her! You have only to appear, and to ask for your wife—and there is my story proved to be true! She may be the most suspicious woman living, as long as I am alone with her. The moment you join me, you set her suspicions at rest. Leave me to do my part. My part is the hard one. Will you do yours?"

It was impossible to say No: she had fairly cut the ground from under his feet. He shifted his ground. Any thing rather than say Yes!

"I suppose you know how we are to be married?" he asked. "All I can say is—I don't."

"You do!" she retorted. "You know that we are in Scotland. You know that there are neither forms, ceremonies, nor delays in marriage, here. The plan I have proposed to you secures my being received at the inn, and makes it easy and natural for you to join me there afterward. The rest is in our own hands. A man and a woman who wish to be married (in Scotland) have only to secure the necessary witnesses and the thing is done. If the landlady chooses to resent the deception practiced on her, after that, the landlady may do as she pleases. We shall have gained our object in spite of her—and, what is more, we shall have gained it without risk to you."

"Don't lay it all on my shoulders," Geoffrey rejoined. "You women go headlong at every thing. Say we are married. We must separate afterward—or how are we to keep it a secret?"

"Certainly. You will go back, of course, to your brother's house, as if nothing had happened."

"And what is to become of you?"

"I shall go to London."

"What are you to do in London?"

"Haven't I already told you that I have thought of every thing? When I get to London I shall apply to some of my mother's old friends—friends of hers in the time when she was a musician. Every body tells me I have a voice—if I had only cultivated it. I will cultivate it! I can live, and live respectably, as a concert singer. I have saved money enough to support me, while I am learning—and my mother's friends will help me, for her sake."

So, in the new life that she was marking out, was she now unconsciously reflecting in herself the life of her mother before her. Here was the mother's career as a public singer, chosen (in spite of all efforts to prevent it) by the child! Here (though with other motives, and under other circumstances) was the mother's irregular marriage in Ireland, on the point of being followed by the daughter's irregular marriage in Scotland! And here, stranger still, was the man who was answerable for it—the son of the man who had found the flaw in the Irish marriage, and had shown the way by which her mother was thrown on the world! "My Anne is my second self. She is not called by her father's name; she is called by mine. She is Anne Silvester as I was. Will she end like Me?"—The answer to those words—the last words that had trembled on the dying mother's lips—was coming fast. Through the chances and changes of many years, the future was pressing near—and Anne Silvester stood on the brink of it.

"Well?" she resumed. "Are you at the end of your objections? Can you give me a plain answer at last?"

No! He had another objection ready as the words passed her lips.

"Suppose the witnesses at the inn happen to know me?" he said. "Suppose it comes to my father's ears in that way?"

"Suppose you drive me to my death?" she retorted, starting to her feet. "Your father shall know the truth, in that case—I swear it!"

He rose, on his side, and drew back from her. She followed him up. There was a clapping of hands, at the same moment, on the lawn. Somebody had evidently made a brilliant stroke which promised to decide the game. There was no security now that Blanche might not return again. There was every prospect, the game being over, that Lady Lundie would be free. Anne brought the interview to its crisis, without wasting a moment more.

"Mr. Geoffrey Delamayn," she said. "You have bargained for a private marriage, and I have consented. Are you, or are you not, ready to marry me on your own terms?"

"Give me a minute to think!"

"Not an instant. Once for all, is it Yes, or No?"

He couldn't say "Yes," even then. But he said what was equivalent to it. He asked, savagely, "Where is the inn?"

She put her arm in his, and whispered, rapidly, "Pass the road on the right that leads to the railway. Follow the path over the moor, and the sheep-track up the hill. The first house you come to after that is the inn. You understand!"

He nodded his head, with a sullen frown, and took his pipe out of his pocket again.

"Let it alone this time," he said, meeting her eye. "My mind's upset. When a man's mind's upset, a man can't smoke. What's the name of the place?"

"Craig Fernie."

"Who am I to ask for at the door?"

"For your wife."

"Suppose they want you to give your name when you get there?"

"If I must give a name, I shall call myself Mrs., instead of Miss, Silvester. But I shall do my best to avoid giving any name. And you will do your best to avoid making a mistake, by only asking for me as your wife. Is there any thing else you want to know?"

"Yes."

"Be quick about it! What is it?"

"How am I to know you have got away from here?"

"If you don't hear from me in half an hour from the time when I have left you, you may be sure I have got away. Hush!"

Two voices, in conversation, were audible at the bottom of the steps—Lady Lundie's voice and Sir Patrick's. Anne pointed to the door in the back wall of the summer-house. She had just pulled it to again, after Geoffrey had passed through it, when Lady Lundie and Sir Patrick appeared at the top of the steps.

CHAPTER THE SIXTH.

THE SUITOR.

LADY LUNDIE pointed significantly to the door, and addressed herself to Sir Patrick's private ear.

"Observe!" she said. "Miss Silvester has just got rid of somebody."

Sir Patrick deliberately looked in the wrong direction, and (in the politest possible manner) observed—nothing.

Lady Lundie advanced into the summer-house. Suspicious hatred of the governess was written legibly in every line of her face. Suspicious distrust of the governess's illness spoke plainly in every tone of her voice.

"May I inquire, Miss Silvester, if your sufferings are relieved?"

"I am no better, Lady Lundie."

"I beg your pardon?"

"I said I was no better."

"You appear to be able to stand up. When I am ill, I am not so fortunate. I am obliged to lie down."'

"I will follow your example, Lady Lundie. If you will be so good as to excuse me, I will leave you, and lie down in my own room."

She could say no more. The interview with Geoffrey had worn her out; there was no spirit left in her to resist the petty malice of the woman, after bearing, as she had borne it, the brutish indifference of the man. In another moment the hysterical suffering which she was keeping down would have forced its way outward in tears. Without waiting to know whether she was excused or not, without stopping to hear a word more, she left the summer-house.

Lady Lundie's magnificent black eyes opened to their utmost width, and blazed with their most dazzling brightness. She appealed to Sir Patrick, poised easily on his ivory cane, and looking out at the lawn-party, the picture of venerable innocence.

"After what I have already told you, Sir Patrick, of Miss Silvester's conduct, may I ask whether you consider that proceeding at all extraordinary?"

The old gentleman touched the spring in the knob of his cane, and answered, in the courtly manner of the old school:

"I consider no proceeding extraordinary Lady Lundie, which emanates from your enchanting sex."

He bowed, and took his pinch. With a little jaunty flourish of the hand, he dusted the stray grains of snuff off his finger and thumb, and looked back again at the lawn-party, and became more absorbed in the diversions of his young friends than ever.

Lady Lundie stood her ground, plainly determined to force a serious expression of opinion from her brother-in-law. Before she could speak again, Arnold and Blanche appeared together at the bottom of the steps. "And when does the dancing begin?" inquired Sir Patrick, advancing to meet them, and looking as if he felt the deepest interest in a speedy settlement of the question.

"The very thing I was going to ask mamma," returned Blanche. "Is she in there with Anne? Is Anne better?"

Lady Lundie forthwith appeared, and took the answer to that inquiry on herself.

"Miss Silvester has retired to her room. Miss Silvester persists in being ill. Have you noticed, Sir Patrick, that these half-bred sort of people are almost invariably rude when they are ill?"

Blanche's bright face flushed up. "If you think Anne a half-bred person, Lady Lundie, you stand alone in your opinion. My uncle doesn't agree with you, I'm sure."

Sir Patrick's interest in the first quadrille became almost painful to see. "Do tell me, my dear, when is the dancing going to begin?"

"The sooner the better," interposed Lady Lundie; "before Blanche picks another quarrel with me on the subject of Miss Silvester."

Blanche looked at her uncle. "Begin! begin! Don't lose time!" cried the ardent Sir Patrick, pointing toward the house with his cane. "Certainly, uncle! Any thing that you wish!" With that parting shot at her step-mother, Blanche withdrew. Arnold, who had thus far waited in silence at the foot of the steps, looked appealingly at Sir Patrick. The train which was to take him to his newly inherited property would start in less than an hour; and he had not presented himself to Blanche's guardian in the character of Blanche's suitor yet! Sir Patrick's indifference to all domestic claims on him—claims of persons who loved, and claims of persons who hated, it didn't matter which—remained perfectly unassailable. There he stood, poised on his cane, humming an old Scotch air. And there was Lady Lundie, resolute not to leave him till he had seen the governess with her eyes and judged the governess with her mind. She returned to the charge—in spite of Sir Patrick, humming at the top of the steps, and of Arnold, waiting at the bottom. (Her enemies said, "No wonder poor Sir Thomas died in a few months after his marriage!" And, oh dear me, our enemies are sometimes right!)

"I must once more remind you, Sir Patrick, that I have serious reason to doubt whether Miss Silvester is a fit companion for Blanche. My governess has something on her mind. She has fits of crying in private. She is up and walking about her room when she ought to be asleep. She posts her own letters—and, she has lately been excessively insolent to Me. There is something wrong. I must take some steps in the matter—and it is only proper that I should do so with your sanction, as head of the family."

"Consider me as abdicating my position, Lady Lundie, in your favor."

"Sir Patrick, I beg you to observe that I am speaking seriously, and that I expect a serious reply."

"My good lady, ask me for any thing else and it is at your service. I have not made a serious reply since I gave up practice at the Scottish Bar. At my age," added Sir Patrick, cunningly drifting into generalities, "nothing is serious—except Indigestion. I say, with the philosopher, 'Life is a comedy to those who think, and tragedy to those who feel.'" He took his sister-in-law's hand, and kissed it. "Dear Lady Lundie, why feel?"

Lady Lundie, who had never "felt" in her life, appeared perversely determined to feel, on this occasion. She was offended—and she showed it plainly.

"When you are next called on, Sir Patrick, to judge of Miss Silvester's conduct," she said, "unless I am entirely mistaken, you will find yourself compelled to consider it as something beyond a joke." With those words, she walked out of the summer-house—and so forwarded Arnold's interests by leaving Blanche's guardian alone at last.

It was an excellent opportunity. The guests were safe in the house—there was no interruption to be feared, Arnold showed himself. Sir Patrick (perfectly undisturbed by Lady Lundie's parting speech) sat down in the summer-house, without noticing his young friend, and asked himself a question founded on profound observation of the female sex. "Were there ever two women yet with a quarrel between them," thought the old gentleman, "who didn't want to drag a man into it? Let them drag me in, if they can!"

Arnold advanced a step, and modestly announced himself. "I hope I am not in the way, Sir Patrick?"

"In the way? of course not! Bless my soul, how serious the boy looks! Are you going to appeal to me as the head of the family next?"

It was exactly what Arnold was about to do. But it was plain that if he admitted it just then Sir Patrick (for some unintelligible reason) would decline to listen to him. He answered cautiously, "I asked leave to consult you in private, Sir; and you kindly said you would give me the opportunity before I left Windygates?"

"Ay! ay! to be sure. I remember. We were both engaged in the serious business of croquet at the time—and it was doubtful which of us did that business most clumsily. Well, here is the opportunity; and here am I, with all my worldly experience, at your service. I have only one caution to give you. Don't appeal to me as 'the head of the family.' My resignation is in Lady Lundie's hands."

He was, as usual, half in jest, half in earnest. The wry twist of humor showed itself at the corners of his lips. Arnold was at a loss how to approach Sir Patrick on the subject of his niece without reminding him of his domestic responsibilities on the one hand, and without setting himself up as a target for the shafts of Sir Patrick's wit on the other. In this difficulty, he committed a mistake at the outset. He hesitated.

"Don't hurry yourself," said Sir Patrick. "Collect your ideas. I can wait! I can wait!"

Arnold collected his ideas—and committed a second mistake. He determined on feeling his way cautiously at first. Under the circumstances (and with such a man as he had now to deal with), it was perhaps the rashest resolution at which he could possibly have arrived—it was the mouse attempting to outmanoeuvre the cat.

"You have been very kind, Sir, in offering me the benefit of your experience," he began.

"I want a word of advice."

"Suppose you take it sitting?" suggested Sir Patrick. "Get a chair." His sharp eyes followed Arnold with an expression of malicious enjoyment. "Wants my advice?" he thought. "The young humbug wants nothing of the sort—he wants my niece."

Arnold sat down under Sir Patrick's eye, with a well-founded suspicion that he was destined to suffer, before he got up again, under Sir Patrick's tongue.

"I am only a young man," he went on, moving uneasily in his chair, "and I am beginning a new life—"

"Any thing wrong with the chair?" asked Sir Patrick. "Begin your new life comfortably, and get another."

"There's nothing wrong with the chair, Sir. Would you—"

"Would I keep the chair, in that case? Certainly."

"I mean, would you advise me—"

"My good fellow, I'm waiting to advise you. (I'm sure there's something wrong with that chair. Why be obstinate about it? Why not get another?)"

"Please don't notice the chair, Sir Patrick—you put me out. I want—in short—perhaps it's a curious question—"

"I can't say till I have heard it," remarked Sir Patrick. "However, we will admit it, for form's sake, if you like. Say it's a curious question. Or let us express it more strongly, if that will help you. Say it's the most extraordinary question that ever was put, since the beginning of the world, from one human being to another."

"It's this!" Arnold burst out, desperately. "I want to be married!"

"That isn't a question," objected Sir Patrick. "It's an assertion. You say, I want to be married. And I say, Just so! And there's an end of it."

Arnold's head began to whirl. "Would you advise me to get married, Sir?" he said, piteously. "That's what I meant."

"Oh! That's the object of the present interview, is it? Would I advise you to marry, eh?"

(Having caught the mouse by this time, the cat lifted his paw and let the luckless little creature breathe again. Sir Patrick's manner suddenly freed itself from any slight signs of impatience which it might have hitherto shown, and became as pleasantly easy and confidential as a manner could be. He touched the knob of his cane, and helped himself, with infinite zest and enjoyment, to a pinch of snuff.)

"Would I advise you to marry?" repeated Sir Patrick. "Two courses are open to us, Mr. Arnold, in treating that question. We may put it briefly, or we may put it at great length. I am for putting it briefly. What do you say?"

"What you say, Sir Patrick."

"Very good. May I begin by making an inquiry relating to your past life?"

"Certainly!"

"Very good again. When you were in the merchant service, did you ever have any experience in buying provisions ashore?"

Arnold stared. If any relation existed between that question and the subject in hand it was an impenetrable relation to him. He answered, in unconcealed bewilderment, "Plenty of experience, Sir."

"I'm coming to the point," pursued Sir Patrick. "Don't be astonished. I'm coming to the point. What did you think of your moist sugar when you bought it at the grocer's?"

"Think?" repeated Arnold. "Why, I thought it was moist sugar, to be sure!"

"Marry, by all means!" cried Sir Patrick. "You are one of the few men who can try that experiment with a fair chance of success."

The suddenness of the answer fairly took away Arnold's breath. There was something perfectly electric in the brevity of his venerable friend. He stared harder than ever.

"Don't you understand me?" asked Sir Patrick.

"I don't understand what the moist sugar has got to do with it, Sir."

"You don't see that?"

"Not a bit!"

"Then I'll show you," said Sir Patrick, crossing his legs, and setting in comfortably for a good talk "You go to the tea-shop, and get your moist sugar. You take it on the understanding that it is moist sugar. But it isn't any thing of the sort. It's a compound of adulterations made up to look like sugar. You shut your eyes to that awkward fact, and swallow your adulterated mess in various articles of food; and you and your sugar get on together in that way as well as you can. Do you follow me, so far?"

Yes. Arnold (quite in the dark) followed, so far.

"Very good," pursued Sir Patrick. "You go to the marriage-shop, and get a wife. You take her on the understanding—let us say—that she has lovely yellow hair, that she has an exquisite complexion, that her figure is the perfection of plumpness, and that she is just tall enough to carry the plumpness off. You bring her home, and you discover that it's the old story of the sugar over again. Your wife is an adulterated article. Her lovely yellow hair is—dye. Her exquisite skin is—pearl powder. Her plumpness is—padding. And three inches of her height are—in the boot-maker's heels. Shut your eyes, and swallow your adulterated wife as you swallow your adulterated sugar—and, I tell you again, you are one of the few men who can try the marriage experiment with a fair chance of success."

With that he uncrossed his legs again, and looked hard at Arnold. Arnold read the lesson, at last, in the right way. He gave up the hopeless attempt to circumvent Sir Patrick, and—come what might of it—dashed at a direct allusion to Sir Patrick's niece.

"That may be all very true, Sir, of some young ladies," he said. "There is one I know of, who is nearly related to you, and who doesn't deserve what you have said of the rest of them."

This was coming to the point. Sir Patrick showed his approval of Arnold's frankness by coming to the point himself, as readily as his own whimsical humor would let him.

"Is this female phenomenon my niece?" he inquired.

"Yes, Sir Patrick."

"May I ask how you know that my niece is not an adulterated article, like the rest of them?"

Arnold's indignation loosened the last restraints that tied Arnold's tongue. He exploded in the three words which mean three volumes in every circulating library in the kingdom.

"I love her."

Sir Patrick sat back in his chair, and stretched out his legs luxuriously.

"That's the most convincing answer I ever heard in my life," he said.

"I'm in earnest!" cried Arnold, reckless by this time of every consideration but one. "Put me to the test, Sir! put me to the test!"

"Oh, very well. The test is easily put." He looked at Arnold, with the irrepressible humor twinkling merrily in his eyes, and twitching sharply at the corners of his lips. "My niece has a beautiful complexion. Do you believe in her complexion?"

"There's a beautiful sky above our heads," returned Arnold. "I believe in the sky."

"Do you?" retorted Sir Patrick. "You were evidently never caught in a shower. My niece has an immense quantity of hair. Are you convinced that it all grows on her head?"

"I defy any other woman's head to produce the like of it!"

"My dear Arnold, you greatly underrate the existing resources of the trade in hair! Look into the shop-windows. When you next go to London pray look into the show-windows. In the mean time, what do you think of my niece's figure?"

"Oh, come! there can't be any doubt about that! Any man, with eyes in his head, can see it's the loveliest figure in the world."

Sir Patrick laughed softly, and crossed his legs again.

"My good fellow, of course it is! The loveliest figure in the world is the commonest thing in the world. At a rough guess, there are forty ladies at this lawn-party. Every one of them possesses a beautiful figure. It varies in price; and when it's particularly seductive you may swear it comes from Paris. Why, how you stare! When I asked you what you thought of my niece's figure, I meant—how much of it comes from Nature, and how much of it comes from the Shop? I don't know, mind! Do you?"

"I'll take my oath to every inch of it!"

"Shop?"

"Nature!"

Sir Patrick rose to his feet; his satirical humor was silenced at last.

"If ever I have a son," he thought to himself, "that son shall go to sea!" He took Arnold's arm, as a preliminary to putting an end to Arnold's suspense. "If I can be serious about any thing," he resumed, "it's time to be serious with you. I am convinced of the sincerity of your attachment. All I know of you is in your favor, and your birth and position are beyond dispute. If you have Blanche's consent, you have mine." Arnold attempted to express his gratitude. Sir Patrick, declining to hear him, went on. "And remember this, in the future. When you next want any thing that I can give you, ask for it plainly. Don't attempt to mystify me on the next occasion, and I will promise, on my side, not to mystify you. There, that's understood.

Now about this journey of yours to see your estate. Property has its duties, Master Arnold, as well as its rights. The time is fast coming when its rights will be disputed, if its duties are not performed. I have got a new interest in you, and I mean to see that you do your duty. It's settled you are to leave Windygates to-day. Is it arranged how you are to go?"

"Yes, Sir Patrick. Lady Lundie has kindly ordered the gig to take me to the station, in time for the next train."

"When are you to be ready?"

Arnold looked at his watch. "In a quarter of an hour."

"Very good. Mind you are ready. Stop a minute! you will have plenty of time to speak to Blanche when I have done with you. You don't appear to me to be sufficiently anxious about seeing your own property."

"I am not very anxious to leave Blanche, Sir—that's the truth of it."

"Never mind Blanche. Blanche is not business. They both begin with a B—and that's the only connection between them. I hear you have got one of the finest houses in this part of Scotland. How long are you going to stay in Scotland? How long are you going to stay in it?"

"I have arranged (as I have already told you, Sir) to return to Windygates the day after to-morrow."

"What! Here is a man with a palace waiting to receive him—and he is only going to stop one clear day in it!"

"I am not going to stop in it at all, Sir Patrick—I am going to stay with the steward. I'm only wanted to be present to-morrow at a dinner to my tenants—and, when that's over, there's nothing in the world to prevent my coming back here. The steward himself told me so in his last letter."

"Oh, if the steward told you so, of course there is nothing more to be said!"

"Don't object to my coming back! pray don't, Sir Patrick! I'll promise to live in my new house when I have got Blanche to live in it with me. If you won't mind, I'll go and tell her at once that it all belongs to her as well as to me."

"Gently! gently! you talk as if you were married to her already!"

"It's as good as done, Sir! Where's the difficulty in the way now?"

As he asked the question the shadow of some third person, advancing from the side of the summer-house, was thrown forward on the open sunlit space at the top of the steps. In a moment more the shadow was followed by the substance—in the shape of a groom in his riding livery. The man was plainly a stranger to the place. He started, and touched his hat, when he saw the two gentlemen in the summer-house.

"What do you want?" asked Sir Patrick

"I beg your pardon, Sir; I was sent by my master—"

"Who is your master?"

"The Honorable Mr. Delamayn, Sir."

"Do you mean Mr. Geoffrey Delamayn?" asked Arnold.

"No, Sir. Mr. Geoffrey's brother—Mr. Julius. I have ridden over from the house, Sir, with a message from my master to Mr. Geoffrey."

"Can't you find him?"

"They told me I should find him hereabouts, Sir. But I'm a stranger, and don't rightly know where to look." He stopped, and took a card out of his pocket. "My master said it was very important I should deliver this immediately. Would you be pleased to tell me, gentlemen, if you happen to know where Mr. Geoffrey is?"

Arnold turned to Sir Patrick. "I haven't seen him. Have you?"

"I have smelt him," answered Sir Patrick, "ever since I have been in the summer-house. There is a detestable taint of tobacco in the air—suggestive (disagreeably suggestive to my mind) of your friend, Mr. Delamayn."

Arnold laughed, and stepped outside the summer-house.

"If you are right, Sir Patrick, we will find him at once." He looked around, and shouted, "Geoffrey!"

A voice from the rose-garden shouted back, "Hullo!"

"You're wanted. Come here!"

Geoffrey appeared, sauntering doggedly, with his pipe in his mouth, and his hands in his pockets.

"Who wants me?"

"A groom—from your brother."

That answer appeared to electrify the lounging and lazy athlete. Geoffrey hurried, with eager steps, to the summer-house. He addressed the groom before the man had time to speak With horror and dismay in his face, he exclaimed:

"By Jupiter! Ratcatcher has relapsed!"

Sir Patrick and Arnold looked at each other in blank amazement.

"The best horse in my brother's stables!" cried Geoffrey, explaining, and appealing to them, in a breath. "I left written directions with the coachman, I measured out his physic for three days; I bled him," said Geoffrey, in a voice broken by emotion—"I bled him myself, last night."

"I beg your pardon, Sir—" began the groom.

"What's the use of begging my pardon? You're a pack of infernal fools! Where's your horse? I'll ride back, and break every bone in the coachman's skin! Where's your horse?"

"If you please, Sir, it isn't Ratcatcher. Ratcatcher's all right."

"Ratcatcher's all right? Then what the devil is it?"

"It's a message, Sir."

"About what?"

"About my lord."

"Oh! About my father?" He took out his handkerchief, and passed it over his forehead, with a deep gasp of relief. "I thought it was Ratcatcher," he said, looking at Arnold, with a smile. He put his pipe into his mouth, and rekindled the dying ashes of the tobacco. "Well?" he went on, when the pipe was in working order, and his voice was composed again: "What's up with my father?"

"A telegram from London, Sir. Bad news of my lord."

The man produced his master's card.

Geoffrey read on it (written in his brother's handwriting) these words:

"I have only a moment to scribble a line on my card. Our father is dangerously ill—his lawyer has been sent for. Come with me to London by the first train. Meet at the junction."

Without a word to any one of the three persons present, all silently looking at him, Geoffrey consulted his watch. Anne had told him to wait half an hour, and to assume that she had gone if he failed to hear from her in that time. The interval had passed—and no communication of any sort had reached him. The flight from the house had been safely accomplished. Anne Silvester was, at that moment, on her way to the mountain inn.

CHAPTER THE SEVENTH.

THE DEBT.

ARNOLD was the first who broke the silence. "Is your father seriously ill?" he asked.

Geoffrey answered by handing him the card.

Sir Patrick, who had stood apart (while the question of Ratcatcher's relapse was under discussion) sardonically studying the manners and customs of modern English youth, now came forward, and took his part in the proceedings. Lady Lundie herself must have acknowledged that he spoke and acted as became the head of the family, on t his occasion.

"Am I right in supposing that Mr. Delamayn's father is dangerously ill?" he asked, addressing himself to Arnold.

"Dangerously ill, in London," Arnold answered. "Geoffrey must leave Windygates with me. The train I am traveling by meets the train his brother is traveling by, at the junction. I shall leave him at the second station from here."

"Didn't you tell me that Lady Lundie was going to send you to the railway in a gig?"

"Yes."

"If the servant drives, there will be three of you—and there will be no room."

"We had better ask for some other vehicle," suggested Arnold.

Sir Patrick looked at his watch. There was no time to change the carriage. He turned to Geoffrey. "Can you drive, Mr. Delamayn?"

Still impenetrably silent, Geoffrey replied by a nod of the head.

Without noticing the unceremonious manner in which he had been answered, Sir Patrick went on:

"In that case, you can leave the gig in charge of the station-master. I'll tell the servant that he will not be wanted to drive."

"Let me save you the trouble, Sir Patrick," said Arnold.

Sir Patrick declined, by a gesture. He turned again, with undiminished courtesy, to Geoffrey. "It is one of the duties of hospitality, Mr. Delamayn, to hasten your departure, under these sad circumstances. Lady Lundie is engaged with her guests. I will see myself that there is no unnecessary delay in sending you to the station." He bowed—and left the summer-house.

Arnold said a word of sympathy to his friend, when they were alone.

"I am sorry for this, Geoffrey. I hope and trust you will get to London in time."

He stopped. There was something in Geoffrey's face—a strange mixture of doubt and bewilderment, of annoyance and hesitation—which was not to be accounted for as the natural result of the news that he had received. His color shifted and changed; he picked fretfully at his finger-nails; he looked at Arnold as if he was going to speak—and then looked away again, in silence.

"Is there something amiss, Geoffrey, besides this bad news about your father?" asked Arnold.

"I'm in the devil's own mess," was the answer.

"Can I do any thing to help you?"

Instead of making a direct reply, Geoffrey lifted his mighty hand, and gave Arnold a friendly slap on the shoulder which shook him from head to foot. Arnold steadied himself, and waited—wondering what was coming next.

"I say, old fellow!" said Geoffrey.

"Yes."

"Do you remember when the boat turned keel upward in Lisbon Harbor?"

Arnold started. If he could have called to mind his first interview in the summer-house with his father's old friend he might have remembered Sir Patrick's prediction that he would sooner or later pay, with interest, the debt he owed to the man who had saved his life. As it was his memory reverted at a bound to the time of the boat-accident. In the ardor of his gratitude and the innocence of his heart, he almost resented his friend's question as a reproach which he had not deserved.

"Do you think I can ever forget," he cried, warmly, "that you swam ashore with me and saved my life?"

Geoffrey ventured a step nearer to the object that he had in view.

"One good turn deserves another," he said, "don't it?"

Arnold took his hand. "Only tell me!" he eagerly rejoined—"only tell me what I can do!"

"You are going to-day to see your new place, ain't you?"

"Yes."

"Can you put off going till to-morrow?"

"If it's any thing serious—of course I can!"

Geoffrey looked round at the entrance to the summer-house, to make sure that they were alone.

"You know the governess here, don't you?" he said, in a whisper.

"Miss Silvester?"

"Yes. I've got into a little difficulty with Miss Silvester. And there isn't a living soul I can ask to help me but you."

"You know I will help you. What is it?"

"It isn't so easy to say. Never mind—you're no saint either, are you? You'll keep it a secret, of course? Look here! I've acted like an infernal fool. I've gone and got the girl into a scrape—"

Arnold drew back, suddenly understanding him.

"Good heavens, Geoffrey! You don't mean—"

"I do! Wait a bit—that's not the worst of it. She has left the house."

"Left the house?"

"Left, for good and all. She can't come back again."

"Why not?"

"Because she's written to her missus. Women (hang 'em!) never do these things by halves. She's left a letter to say she's privately married, and gone off to her husband. Her husband is—Me. Not that I'm married to her yet, you understand. I have only promised to marry her. She has gone on first (on the sly) to a place four miles from this. And we settled I was to follow, and marry her privately this afternoon. That's out of the question now. While she's expecting me at the inn I shall be bowling along to London. Somebody must tell her what has happened—or she'll play the devil, and the whole business will burst up. I can't trust any of the people here. I'm done for, old chap, unless you help me."

Arnold lifted his hands in dismay. "It's the most dreadful situation, Geoffrey, I ever heard of in my life!"

Geoffrey thoroughly agreed with him. "Enough to knock a man over," he said, "isn't it? I'd give something for a drink of beer." He produced his everlasting pipe, from sheer force of habit. "Got a match?" he asked.

Arnold's mind was too preoccupied to notice the question.

"I hope you won't think I'm making light of your father's illness," he said, earnestly. "But it seems to me—I must say it—it seems to me that the poor girl has the first claim on you."

Geoffrey looked at him in surly amazement.

"The first claim on me? Do you think I'm going to risk being cut out of my father's will? Not for the best woman that ever put on a petticoat!"

Arnold's admiration of his friend was the solidly-founded admiration of many years; admiration for a man who could row, box, wrestle, jump—above all, who could swim—as few other men could perform those exercises in contemporary England. But that answer shook his faith. Only for the moment—unhappily for Arnold, only for the moment.

"You know best," he returned, a little coldly. "What can I do?"

Geoffrey took his arm—roughly as he took every thing; but in a companionable and confidential way.

"Go, like a good fellow, and tell her what has happened. We'll start from here as if we were both going to the railway; and I'll drop you at the foot-path, in the gig. You can get on to your own place afterward by the evening train. It puts you to no inconvenience, and it's doing the kind thing by an old friend. There's no risk of being found out. I'm to drive, remember! There's no servant with us, old boy, to notice, and tell tales."

Even Arnold began to see dimly by this time that he was likely to pay his debt of obligation with interest—as Sir Patrick had foretold.

"What am I to say to her?" he asked. "I'm bound to do all I can do to help you, and I will. But what am I to say?"

It was a natural question to put. It was not an easy question to answer. What a man, under given muscular circumstances, could do, no person living knew better than Geoffrey Delamayn. Of what a man, under given social circumstances, could say, no person living knew less.

"Say?" he repeated. "Look here! say I'm half distracted, and all that. And—wait a bit—tell her to stop where she is till I write to her."

Arnold hesitated. Absolutely ignorant of that low and limited form of knowledge which is called "knowledge of the world," his inbred delicacy of mind revealed to him the serious difficulty of the position which his friend was asking him to occupy as plainly as if he was looking at it through the warily-gathered experience of society of a man of twice his age.

"Can't you write to her now, Geoffrey?" he asked.

"What's the good of that?"

"Consider for a minute, and you will see. You have trusted me with a very awkward secret. I may be wrong—I never was mixed up in such a matter before—but to present myself to this lady as your messenger seems exposing her to a dreadful humiliation. Am I to go and tell her to her face: 'I know what you are hiding from the knowledge of all the world;' and is she to be expected to endure it?"

"Bosh!" said Geoffrey. "They can endure a deal more than you think. I wish you had heard how she bullied me, in this very place. My good fellow, you don't understand women. The grand secret, in dealing with a woman, is to take her as you take a cat, by the scruff of the neck—"

"I can't face her—unless you will help me by breaking the thing to her first. I'll stick at no sacrifice to serve you; but—hang it!—make allowances, Geoffrey, for the difficulty you are putting me in. I am almost a stranger; I don't know how Miss Silvester may receive me, before I can open my lips."

Those last words touched the question on its practical side. The matter-of-fact view of the difficulty was a view which Geoffrey instantly recognized and understood.

"She has the devil's own temper," he said. "There's no denying that. Perhaps I'd better write. Have we time to go into the house?"

"No. The house is full of people, and we haven't a minute to spare. Write at once, and write here. I have got a pencil."

"What am I to write on?"

"Any thing—your brother's card."

Geoffrey took the pencil which Arnold offered to him, and looked at the card. The lines his brother had written covered it. There was no room left. He felt in his pocket, and produced a letter—the letter which Anne had referred to at the interview between them—the letter which she had written to insist on his attending the lawn-party at Windygates.

"This will do," he said. "It's one of Anne's own letters to me. There's room on the fourth page. If I write," he added, turning suddenly on Arnold, "you promise to take it to her? Your hand on the bargain!"

He held out the hand which had saved Arnold's life in Lisbon Harbor, and received Arnold's promise, in remembrance of that time.

"All right, old fellow. I can tell you how to find the place as we go along in the gig. By-the-by, there's one thing that's rather important. I'd better mention it while I think of it."

"What is that?"

"You mustn't present yourself at the inn in your own name; and you mustn't ask for her by her name."

"Who am I to ask for?"

"It's a little awkward. She has gone there as a married woman, in case they're particular about taking her in—"

"I understand. Go on."

"And she has planned to tell them (by way of making it all right and straight for both of us, you know) that she expects her husband to join her. If I had been able to go I should have asked at the door for 'my wife.' You are going in my place—"

"And I must ask at the door for 'my wife,' or I shall expose Miss Silvester to unpleasant consequences?"

"You don't object?"

"Not I! I don't care what I say to the people of the inn. It's the meeting with Miss Silvester that I'm afraid of."

"I'll put that right for you—never fear!"

He went at once to the table and rapidly scribbled a few lines—then stopped and considered. "Will that do?" he asked himself. "No; I'd better say something spooney to quiet her." He considered again, added a line, and brought his hand down on the table with a cheery smack. "That will do the business! Read it yourself, Arnold—it's not so badly written."

Arnold read the note without appearing to share his friend's favorable opinion of it.

"This is rather short," he said.

"Have I time to make it longer?"

"Perhaps not. But let Miss Silvester see for herself that you have no time to make it longer. The train starts in less than half an hour. Put the time."

"Oh, all right! and the date too, if you like."

He had just added the desired words and figures, and had given the revised letter to Arnold, when Sir Patrick returned to announce that the gig was waiting.

"Come!" he said. "You haven't a moment to lose!"

Geoffrey started to his feet. Arnold hesitated.

"I must see Blanche!" he pleaded. "I can't leave Blanche without saying good-by. Where is she?"

Sir Patrick pointed to the steps, with a smile. Blanche had followed him from the house. Arnold ran out to her instantly.

"Going?" she said, a little sadly.

"I shall be back in two days," Arnold whispered. "It's all right! Sir Patrick consents."

She held him fast by the arm. The hurried parting before other people seemed to be not a parting to Blanche's taste.

"You will lose the train!" cried Sir Patrick.

Geoffrey seized Arnold by the arm which Blanche was holding, and tore him—literally tore him—away. The two were out of sight, in the shrubbery, before Blanche's indignation found words, and addressed itself to her uncle.

"Why is that brute going away with Mr. Brinkworth?" she asked.

"Mr. Delamayn is called to London by his father's illness," replied Sir Patrick. "You don't like him?"

"I hate him!"

Sir Patrick reflected a little.

"She is a young girl of eighteen," he thought to himself. "And I am an old man of seventy. Curious, that we should agree about any thing. More than curious that we should agree in disliking Mr. Delamayn."

He roused himself, and looked again at Blanche. She was seated at the table, with her head on her hand; absent, and out of spirits—thinking of Arnold, and set, with the future all smooth before them, not thinking happily.

"Why, Blanche! Blanche!" cried Sir Patrick, "one would think he had gone for a voyage round the world. You silly child! he will be back again the day after to-morrow."

"I wish he hadn't gone with that man!" said Blanche. "I wish he hadn't got that man for a friend!"

"There! there! the man was rude enough I own. Never mind! he will leave the man at the second station. Come back to the ball-room with me. Dance it off, my dear—dance it off!"

"No," returned Blanche. "I'm in no humor for dancing. I shall go up stairs, and talk about it to Anne."

"You will do nothing of the sort!" said a third voice, suddenly joining in the conversation.

Both uncle and niece looked up, and found Lady Lundie at the top of the summer-house steps.

"I forbid you to mention that woman's name again in my hearing," pursued her ladyship. "Sir Patrick! I warned you (if you remember?) that the matter of the governess was not a matter to be trifled with. My worst anticipations are realized. Miss Silvester has left the house!"

CHAPTER THE EIGHTH.

THE SCANDAL.

IT was still early in the afternoon when the guests at Lady Lundie's lawn-party began to compare notes together in corners, and to agree in arriving at a general conviction that "some thing was wrong."

Blanche had mysteriously disappeared from her partners in the dance. Lady Lundie had mysteriously abandoned her guests. Blanche had not come back. Lady Lundie had returned with an artificial smile, and a preoccupied manner. She acknowledged that she was "not very well." The same excuse had been given to account for Blanche's absence—and, again (some time previously), to explain Miss Silvester's withdrawal from the croquet! A wit among the gentlemen declared it reminded him of declining a verb. "I am not very well; thou art not very well; she is not very well"—and so on. Sir Patrick too! Only think of the sociable Sir Patrick being in a state of seclusion—pacing up and down by himself in the loneliest part of the garden. And the servants again! it had even spread to the servants! They were presuming to whisper in corners, like their betters. The house-maids appeared, spasmodically, where house maids had no business to be. Doors banged and petticoats whisked in the upper regions. Something wrong—depend upon it, something wrong! "We had much better go away. My dear, order the carriage"—"Louisa, love, no more dancing; your papa is going."—"Good-afternoon, Lady Lundie!"—"Haw! thanks very much!"—"So sorry for dear Blanche!"—"Oh, it's been too charming!" So Society jabbered its poor, nonsensical little jargon, and got itself politely out of the way before the storm came.

This was exactly the consummation of events for which Sir Patrick had been waiting in the seclusion of the garden.

There was no evading the responsibility which was now thrust upon him. Lady Lundie had announced it as a settled resolution, on her part, to trace Anne to the place in which she had taken refuge, and discover (purely in the interests of virtue) whether she actually was married or not. Blanche (already overwrought by the excitement of the day) had broken into an hysterical passion of tears on hearing the news, and had then, on recovering, taken a view of her own of Anne's flight from the house. Anne would never have kept her marriage a secret from Blanche; Anne would never have written such a formal farewell letter as she had written to Blanche—if things were going as smoothly with her as she was trying to make them believe at Windygates. Some dreadful trouble had fallen on Anne and Blanche was determined (as Lady Lundie was determined) to find out where she had gone, and to follow, and help her.

It was plain to Sir Patrick (to whom both ladies had opened their hearts, at separate interviews) that his sister-in-law, in one way, and his niece in another, were equally likely—if not duly restrained—to plunge headlong into acts of indiscretion which might lead to very undesirable results. A man in authority was sorely needed at Windygates that afternoon—and Sir Patrick was fain to acknowledge that he was the man.

"Much is to be said for, and much is to be said against a single life," thought the old gentleman, walking up and down the sequestered garden-path to which he had retired, and applying himself at shorter intervals than usual to the knob of his ivory cane. "This, however, is, I take it, certain. A man's married friends can't prevent him from leading the life of a bachelor, if he pleases. But they can, and do, take devilish good care that he sha'n't enjoy it!"

Sir Patrick's meditations were interrupted by the appearance of a servant, previously instructed to keep him informed of the progress of events at the house.

"They're all gone, Sir Patrick," said the man.

"That's a comfort, Simpson. We have no visitors to deal with now, except the visitors who are staying in the house?"

"None, Sir Patrick."

"They're all gentlemen, are they not?"

"Yes, Sir Patrick."

"That's another comfort, Simpson. Very good. I'll see Lady Lundie first."

Does any other form of human resolution approach the firmness of a woman who is bent on discovering the frailties of another woman whom she hates? You may move rocks, under a given set of circumstances. But here is a delicate being in petticoats, who shrieks if a spider drops on her neck, and shudders if you approach her after having eaten an onion. Can you move her, under a given set of circumstances, as set forth above? Not you!

Sir Patrick found her ladyship instituting her inquiries on the same admirably exhaustive system which is pursued, in cases of disappearance, by the police. Who was the last witness who had seen the missing person? Who was the last servant who had seen Anne Silvester? Begin with the men-servants, from the butler at the top to the stable boy at the bottom. Go on with the women-servants, from the cook in all her glory to the small female child who weeds the garden. Lady Lundie had cross-examined her way downward as far as the page, when Sir Patrick joined her.

"My dear lady! pardon me for reminding you again, that this is a free country, and that you have no claim whatever to investigate Miss Silvester's proceedings after she has left your house."

Lady Lundie raised her eyes, devotionally, to the ceiling. She looked like a martyr to duty. If you had seen her ladyship at that moment, you would have said yourself, "A martyr to duty."

"No, Sir Patrick! As a Christian woman, that is not my way of looking at it. This unhappy person has lived under my roof. This unhappy person has been the companion of Blanche. I am responsible—I am, in a manner, morally responsible. I would give the world to be able to dismiss it as you do. But no! I must be satisfied that she is married. In the interests of propriety. For the quieting of my own conscience. Before I lay my head on my pillow to-night, Sir Patrick—before I lay my head on my pillow to-night!"

"One word, Lady Lundie—"

"No!" repeated her ladyship, with the most pathetic gentleness. "You are right, I dare say, from the worldly point of view. I can't take the worldly point of view. The worldly point of view hurts me." She turned, with impressive gravity, to the page. "You know where you will go, Jonathan, if you tell lies!"

Jonathan was lazy, Jonathan was pimply, Jonathan was fat—but Jonathan was orthodox. He answered that he did know; and, what is more, he mentioned the place.

Sir Patrick saw that further opposition on his part, at that moment, would be worse than useless. He wisely determined to wait, before he interfered again, until Lady Lundie had thoroughly exhausted herself and her inquiries. At the same time—as it was impossible, in the present state of her ladyship's temper, to provide against what might happen if the inquiries after Anne unluckily proved successful—he decided on taking measures to clear the house of the guests (in the interests of all parties) for the next four-and-twenty hours.

"I only want to ask you a question, Lady Lundie," he resumed. "The position of the gentlemen who are staying here is not a very pleasant one while all this is going on. If you had been content to let the matter pass without notice, we should have done very well. As things are, don't you think it will be more convenient to every body if I relieve you of the responsibility of entertaining your guests?"

"As head of the family?" stipulated Lady Lundie.

"As head of the family!" answered Sir Patrick.

"I gratefully accept the proposal," said Lady Lundie.

"I beg you won't mention it," rejoined Sir Patrick.

He quitted the room, leaving Jonathan under examination. He and his brother (the late Sir Thomas) had chosen widely different paths in life, and had seen but little of each other since the time when they had been boys. Sir Patrick's recollections (on leaving Lady Lundie) appeared to have taken him back to that time, and to have inspired him with a certain tenderness for his brother's memory. He shook his head, and sighed a sad little sigh. "Poor Tom!" he said to himself, softly, after he had shut the door on his brother's widow. "Poor Tom!"

On crossing the hall, he stopped the first servant he met, to inquire after Blanche. Miss Blanche was quiet, up stairs, closeted with her maid in her own room. "Quiet?" thought Sir Patrick. "That's a bad sign. I shall hear more of my niece."

Pending that event, the next thing to do was to find the guests. Unerring instinct led Sir Patrick to the billiard-room. There he found them, in solemn conclave assembled, wondering what they had better do. Sir Patrick put them all at their ease in two minutes.

"What do you say to a day's shooting to-morrow?" he asked.

Every man present—sportsman or not—said yes.

"You can start from this house," pursued Sir Patrick; "or you can start from a shooting-cottage which is on the Windygates property—among the woods, on the other side of the moor. The weather looks pretty well settled (for Scotland), and there are plenty of horses in the stables. It is useless to conceal from you, gentlemen, that events have taken a certain unexpected turn in my sister-in-law's family circle. You will be equally Lady Lundie's guests, whether you choose the cottage or the house. For the next twenty-four hours (let us say)—which shall it be?"

Every body—with or without rheumatism—answered "the cottage."

"Very good," pursued Sir Patrick, "It is arranged to ride over to the shooting-cottage this evening, and to try the moor, on that side, the first thing in the morning. If events here will allow me, I shall be delighted to accompany you, and do the honors as well as I can. If not, I am sure you will accept my apologies for to-night, and permit Lady Lundie's steward to see to your comfort in my place."

Adopted unanimously. Sir Patrick left the guests to their billiards, and went out to give the necessary orders at the stables.

In the mean time Blanche remained portentously quiet in the upper regions of the house; while Lady Lundie steadily pursued her inquiries down stairs. She got on from Jonathan (last of the males, indoors) to the coachman (first of the males, out-of-doors), and dug down, man by man, through that new stratum, until she struck the stable-boy at the bottom. Not an atom of information having been extracted in the house or out of the house, from man or boy, her ladyship fell back on the women next. She pulled the bell, and summoned the cook—Hester Dethridge.

A very remarkable-looking person entered the room.

Elderly and quiet; scrupulously clean; eminently respectable; her gray hair neat and smooth under her modest white cap; her eyes, set deep in their orbits, looking straight at any person who spoke to her—here, at a first view, was a steady, trust-worthy woman. Here also on closer inspection, was a woman with the seal of some terrible past suffering set on her for the rest of her life. You felt it, rather than saw it, in the look of immovable endurance which underlain her expression—in the deathlike tranquillity which never disappeared from her manner. Her story was a sad one—so far as it was known. She had entered Lady Lundie's service at the period of Lady Lundie's marriage to Sir Thomas. Her character (given by the clergyman of her parish) described her as having been married to an inveterate drunkard, and as having suffered unutterably during her husband's lifetime. There were drawbacks to engaging her, now that she was a widow. On one of the many occasions on which her husband had personally ill-treated her, he had struck her a blow which had produced very remarkable nervous results. She had lain insensible many days together, and had recovered with the total loss of her speech. In addition to this objection, she was odd, at times, in her manner; and she made it a condition of accepting any situation, that she should be privileged to sleep in a room by herself As a set-off against all this, it was to be said, on the other side of the question, that she was sober; rigidly honest in all her dealings; and one of the best cooks in England. In consideration of this last merit, the late Sir Thomas had decided on giving her a trial, and had discovered that he had never dined in his life as he dined when Hester Dethridge was at the head of his kitchen. She remained after his death in his widow's service. Lady Lundie was far from liking her. An unpleasant suspicion attached to the cook, which Sir Thomas had over-looked, but which persons less sensible of the immense importance of dining well could not fail to regard as a serious objection to her. Medical men, consulted about her case discovered certain physiological anomalies in it which led them to suspect the woman of feigning dumbness, for some reason best known to herself. She obstinately declined to learn the deaf and dumb alphabet—on the ground that dumbness was not associated with deafness in her case. Stratagems were invented (seeing that she really did possess the use of her ears) to entrap her into also using her speech, and failed. Efforts were made to induce her to answer questions relating to her past life in her husband's time. She flatly declined to reply to them, one and all. At certain intervals, strange impulses to get a holiday away from the house appeared to seize her. If she was resisted, she passively declined to do her work. If she was threatened with dismissal, she impenetrably bowed her head, as much as to say, "Give me the word, and I go." Over and over again, Lady Lundie had decided, naturally enough, on no longer keeping such a servant as this; but she had never yet carried the decision to execution. A cook who is a perfect mistress of her art, who asks for no perquisites, who allows no waste, who never quarrels with the other servants, who drinks nothing stronger than tea, who is to be trusted with untold gold—is not a cook easily replaced. In this mortal life we put up with many persons and things, as Lady Lundie put up with her cook. The woman lived, as it were, on the brink of dismissal—but thus far the woman kept her place—getting her holidays when she asked for them (which, to do her justice, was not often) and sleeping always (go where she might with the family) with a locked door, in a room by herself.

Hester Dethridge advanced slowly to the table at which Lady Lundie was sitting. A slate and pencil hung at her side, which she used for making such replies as were not to be expressed by a gesture or by a motion of the head. She took up the slate and pencil, and waited with stony submission for her mistress to begin.

Lady Lundie opened the proceedings with the regular formula of inquiry which she had used with all the other servants,

"Do you know that Miss Silvester has left the house?"

The cook nodded her head affirmatively.

"Do you know at what time she left it?"

Another affirmative reply. The first which Lady Lundie had received to that question yet. She eagerly went on to the next inquiry.

"Have you seen her since she left the house?"

A third affirmative reply.

"Where?"

Hester Dethridge wrote slowly on the slate, in singularly firm upright characters for a woman in her position of life, these words:

"On the road that leads to the railway. Nigh to Mistress Chew's Farm."

"What did you want at Chew's Farm?"

Hester Dethridge wrote: "I wanted eggs for the kitchen, and a breath of fresh air for myself."

"Did Miss Silvester see you?"

A negative shake of the head.

"Did she take the turning that leads to the railway?"

Another negative shake of the head.

"She went on, toward the moor?"

An affirmative reply.

"What did she do when she got to the moor?"

Hester Dethridge wrote: "She took the footpath which leads to Craig Fernie."

Lady Lundie rose excitedly to her feet. There was but one place that a stranger could go to at Craig Fernie. "The inn!" exclaimed her ladyship. "She has gone to the inn!"

Hester Dethridge waited immovably. Lady Lundie put a last precautionary question, in these words:

"Have you reported what you have seen to any body else?"

An affirmative reply. Lady Lundie had not bargained for that. Hester Dethridge (she thought) must surely have misunderstood her.

"Do you mean that you have told somebody else what you have just told me?"

Another affirmative reply.

"A person who questioned you, as I have done?"

A third affirmative reply.

"Who was it?"

Hester Dethridge wrote on her slate: "Miss Blanche."

Lady Lundie stepped back, staggered by the discovery that Blanche's resolution to trace Anne Silvester was, to all appearance, as firmly settled as her own. Her step-daughter was keeping her own counsel, and acting on her own responsibility—her step-daughter might be an awkward obstacle in the way. The manner in which Anne had left the house had mortally offended Lady Lundie. An inveterately vindictive woman, she had resolved to discover whatever compromising elements might exist in the governess's secret, and to make them public property (from a paramount sense of duty, of course) among her own circle of friends. But to do this—with Blanche acting (as might certainly be anticipated) in direct opposition to her, and openly espousing Miss Silvester's interests—was manifestly impossible.

The first thing to be done—and that instantly—was to inform Blanche that she was discovered, and to forbid her to stir in the matter.

Lady Lundie rang the bell twice—thus intimating, according to the laws of the household, that she required the attendance of her own maid. She then turned to the cook—still waiting her pleasure, with stony composure, slate in hand.

"You have done wrong," said her ladyship, severely. "I am your mistress. You are bound to answer your mistress—"

Hester Dethridge bowed her head, in icy acknowledgment of the principle laid down—so far.

The bow was an interruption. Lady Lundie resented it.

"But Miss Blanche is not your mistress," she went on, sternly. "You are very much to blame for answering Miss Blanche's inquiries about Miss Silvester."

Hester Dethridge, perfectly unmoved, wrote her justification on her slate, in two stiff sentences: "I had no orders not to answer. I keep nobody's secrets but my own."

That reply settled the question of the cook's dismissal—the question which had been pending for months past.

"You are an insolent woman! I have borne with you long enough—I will bear with you no longer. When your month is up, you go!"

In those words Lady Lundie dismissed Hester Dethridge from her service.

Not the slightest change passed over the sinister tranquillity of the cook. She bowed her head again, in acknowledgment of the sentence pronounced on her—dropped her slate at her side—turned about—and left the room. The woman was alive in the world, and working in the world; and yet (so far as all human interests were concerned) she was as completely out of the world as if she had been screwed down in her coffin, and laid in her grave.

Lady Lundie's maid came into the room as Hester left it.

"Go up stairs to Miss Blanche," said her mistress, "and say I want her here. Wait a minute!" She paused, and considered. Blanche might decline to submit to her step-mother's interference with her. It might be necessary to appeal to the higher authority of her guardian. "Do you know where Sir Patrick is?" asked Lady Lundie.

"I heard Simpson say, my lady, that Sir Patrick was at the stables."

"Send Simpson with a message. My compliments to Sir Patrick—and I wish to see him immediately."

The preparations for the departure to the shooting-cottage were just completed; and the one question that remained to be settled was, whether Sir Patrick could accompany the party—when the man-servant appeared with the message from his mistress.

"Will you give me a quarter of an hour, gentlemen?" asked Sir Patrick. "In that time I shall know for certain whether I can go with you or not."

As a matter of course, the guests decided to wait. The younger men among them (being Englishmen) naturally occupied their leisure time in betting. Would Sir Patrick get the better of the domestic crisis? or would the domestic crisis get the better of Sir Patrick? The domestic crisis was backed, at two to one, to win.

Punctually at the expiration of the quarter of an hour, Sir Patrick reappeared. The domestic crisis had betrayed the blind confidence which youth and inexperience had placed in it. Sir Patrick had won the day.

"Things are settled and quiet, gentlemen; and I am able to accompany you," he said. "There are two ways to the shooting-cottage. One—the longest—passes by the inn at Craig Fernie. I am compelled to ask you to go with me by that way. While you push on to the cottage, I must drop behind, and say a word to a person who is staying at the inn."

He had quieted Lady Lundie—he had even quieted Blanche. But it was evidently on the condition that he was to go to Craig Fernie in their places, and to see Anne Silvester himself. Without a word more of explanation he mounted his horse, and led the way out. The shooting-party left Windygates.

SECOND SCENE.—THE INN.

CHAPTER THE NINTH.

ANNE.

"YE'LL just permit me to remind ye again, young leddy, that the hottle's full—exceptin' only this settin'-room, and the bedchamber yonder belonging to it."

So spoke "Mistress Inchbare," landlady of the Craig Fernie Inn, to Anne Silvester, standing in the parlor, purse in hand, and offering the price of the two rooms before she claimed permission to occupy them.

The time of the afternoon was about the time when Geoffrey Delamayn had started in the train, on his journey to London. About the time also, when Arnold Brinkworth had crossed the moor, and was mounting the first rising ground which led to the inn.

Mistress Inchbare was tall and thin, and decent and dry. Mistress Inchbare's unlovable hair clung fast round her head in wiry little yellow curls. Mistress Inchbare's hard bones showed themselves, like Mistress Inchbare's hard Presbyterianism, without any concealment or compromise. In short, a savagely-respectable woman who plumed herself on presiding over a savagely-respectable inn.

There was no competition to interfere with Mistress Inchbare. She regulated her own prices, and made her own rules. If you objected to her prices, and revolted from her rules, you were free to go. In other words, you were free to cast yourself, in the capacity of houseless wanderer, on the scanty mercy of a Scotch wilderness. The village of Craig Fernie was a collection of hovels. The country about Craig Fernie, mountain on one side and moor on the other, held no second house of public entertainment, for miles and miles round, at any point of the compass. No rambling individual but the helpless British Tourist wanted food and shelter from strangers in that part of Scotland; and nobody but Mistress Inchbare had food and shelter to sell. A more thoroughly independent person than this was not to be found on the face of the hotel-keeping earth. The most universal of all civilized terrors—the terror of appearing unfavorably in the newspapers—was a sensation absolutely unknown to the Empress of the Inn. You lost your temper, and threatened to send her bill for exhibition in the public journals. Mistress Inchbare raised no objection to your taking any course you pleased with it. "Eh, man! send the bill whar' ye like, as long as ye pay it first. There's nae such thing as a newspaper ever darkens my doors. Ye've got the Auld and New Testaments in your bedchambers, and the natural history o' Pairthshire on the coffee-room table—and if that's no' reading eneugh for ye, ye may een gae back South again, and get the rest of it there."

This was the inn at which Anne Silvester had appeared alone, with nothing but a little bag in her hand. This was the woman whose reluctance to receive her she innocently expected to overcome by showing her purse.

"Mention your charge for the rooms," she said. "I am willing to pay for them beforehand."

Her majesty, Mrs. Inchbare, never even looked at her subject's poor little purse.

"It just comes to this, mistress," she answered. "I'm no' free to tak' your money, if I'm no' free to let ye the last rooms left in the hoose. The Craig Fernie hottle is a faimily hottle—and has its ain gude name to keep up. Ye're ower-well-looking, my young leddy, to be traveling alone."

The time had been when Anne would have answered sharply enough. The hard necessities of her position made her patient now.

"I have already told you," she said, "my husband is coming here to join me." She sighed wearily as she repeated her ready-made story—and dropped into the nearest chair, from sheer inability to stand any longer.

Mistress Inchbare looked at her, with the exact measure of compassionate interest which she might have shown if she had been looking at a stray dog who had fallen footsore at the door of the inn.

"Weel! weel! sae let it be. Bide awhile, and rest ye. We'll no' chairge ye for that—and we'll see if your husband comes. I'll just let the rooms, mistress, to him,, instead o' lettin' them to you. And, sae, good-morrow t' ye." With that final announcement of her royal will and pleasure, the Empress of the Inn withdrew.

Anne made no reply. She watched the landlady out of the room—and then struggled to control herself no longer. In her position, suspicion was doubly insult. The hot tears of shame gathered in her eyes; and the heart-ache wrung her, poor soul—wrung her without mercy.

A trifling noise in the room startled her. She looked up, and detected a man in a corner, dusting the furniture, and apparently acting in the capacity of attendant at the inn. He had shown her into the parlor on her arrival; but he had remained so quietly in the room that she had never noticed him since, until that moment.

He was an ancient man—with one eye filmy and blind, and one eye moist and merry. His head was bald; his feet were gouty; his nose was justly celebrated as the largest nose and the reddest nose in that part of Scotland. The mild wisdom of years was expressed mysteriously in his mellow smile. In contact with this wicked world, his manner revealed that happy mixture of two extremes—the servility which just touches independence, and the independence which just touches servility—attained by no men in existence but Scotchmen. Enormous native impudence, which amused but never offended; immeasurable cunning, masquerading habitually under the double disguise of quaint prejudice and dry humor, were the solid moral foundations on which the character of this elderly person was built. No amount of whisky ever made him drunk; and no violence of bell-ringing ever hurried his movements. Such was the headwaiter at the Craig Fernie Inn; known, far and wide, to local fame, as "Maister Bishopriggs, Mistress Inchbare's right-hand man."

"What are you doing there?" Anne asked, sharply.

Mr. Bishopriggs turned himself about on his gouty feet; waved his duster gently in the air; and looked at Anne, with a mild, paternal smile.

"Eh! Am just doostin' the things; and setin' the room in decent order for ye."

"For me? Did you hear what the landlady said?"

Mr. Bishopriggs advanced confidentially, and pointed with a very unsteady forefinger to the purse which Anne still held in her hand.

"Never fash yoursel' aboot the landleddy!" said the sage chief of the Craig Fernie waiters. "Your purse speaks for you, my lassie. Pet it up!" cried Mr. Bishopriggs, waving temptation away from him with the duster. "In wi' it into yer pocket! Sae long as the warld's the warld, I'll uphaud it any where—while there's siller in the purse, there's gude in the woman!"

Anne's patience, which had resisted harder trials, gave way at this.

"What do you mean by speaking to me in that familiar manner?" she asked, rising angrily to her feet again.

Mr. Bishopriggs tucked his duster under his arm, and proceeded to satisfy Anne that he shared the landlady's view of her position, without sharing the severity of the landlady's principles. "There's nae man livin'," said Mr. Bishopriggs, "looks with mair indulgence at human frailty than my ain sel'. Am I no' to be familiar wi' ye—when I'm auld eneugh to be a fether to ye, and ready to be a fether to ye till further notice? Hech! hech! Order your bit dinner lassie. Husband or no husband, ye've got a stomach, and ye must een eat. There's fesh and there's fowl—or, maybe, ye'll be for the sheep's head singit, when they've done with it at the tabble dot?"

There was but one way of getting rid of him: "Order what you like," Anne said, "and leave the room." Mr. Bishopriggs highly approved of the first half of the sentence, and totally overlooked the second.

"Ay, ay—just pet a' yer little interests in my hands; it's the wisest thing ye can do. Ask for Maister Bishopriggs (that's me) when ye want a decent 'sponsible man to gi' ye a word of advice. Set ye doon again—set ye doon. And don't tak' the arm-chair. Hech! hech! yer husband will be coming, ye know, and he's sure to want it!" With that seasonable pleasantry the venerable Bishopriggs winked, and went out.

Anne looked at her watch. By her calculation it was not far from the hour when Geoffrey might be expected to arrive at the inn, assuming Geoffrey to have left Windygates at the time agreed on. A little more patience, and the landlady's scruples would be satisfied, and the ordeal would be at an end.

Could she have met him nowhere else than at this barbarous house, and among these barbarous people?

No. Outside the doors of Windygates she had not a friend to help her in all Scotland. There was no place at her disposal but the inn; and she had only to be thankful that it occupied a sequestered situation, and was not likely to be visited by any of Lady Lundie's friends. Whatever the risk might be, the end in view justified her in confronting it. Her whole future depended on Geoffrey's making an honest woman of her. Not her future with him—that way there was no hope; that way her life was wasted. Her future with Blanche—she looked forward to nothing now but her future with Blanche.

Her spirits sank lower and lower. The tears rose again. It would only irritate him if he came and found her crying. She tried to divert her mind by looking about the room.

There was very little to see. Except that it was solidly built of good sound stone, the Craig

Fernie hotel differed in no other important respect from the average of second-rate English inns. There was the usual slippery black sofa—constructed to let you slide when you wanted to rest. There was the usual highly-varnished arm-chair, expressly manufactured to test the endurance of the human spine. There was the usual paper on the walls, of the pattern designed to make your eyes ache and your head giddy. There were the usual engravings, which humanity never tires of contemplating. The Royal Portrait, in the first place of honor. The next greatest of all human beings—the Duke of Wellington—in the second place of honor. The third greatest of all human beings—the local member of parliament—in the third place of honor; and a hunting scene, in the dark. A door opposite the door of admission from the passage opened into the bedroom; and a window at the side looked out on the open space in front of the hotel, and commanded a view of the vast expanse of the Craig Fernie moor, stretching away below the rising ground on which the house was built.

Anne turned in despair from the view in the room to the view from the window. Within the last half hour it had changed for the worse. The clouds had gathered; the sun was hidden; the light on the landscape was gray and dull. Anne turned from the window, as she had turned from the room. She was just making the hopeless attempt to rest her weary limbs on the sofa, when the sound of voices and footsteps in the passage caught her ear.

Was Geoffrey's voice among them? No.

Were the strangers coming in?

The landlady had declined to let her have the rooms: it was quite possible that the strangers might be coming to look at them. There was no knowing who they might be. In the impulse of the moment she flew to the bedchamber and locked herself in.

The door from the passage opened, and Arnold Brinkworth—shown in by Mr. Bishopriggs—entered the sitting-room.

"Nobody here!" exclaimed Arnold, looking round. "Where is she?"

Mr. Bishopriggs pointed to the bedroom door. "Eh! yer good leddy's joost in the bedchamber, nae doot!"

Arnold started. He had felt no difficulty (when he and Geoffrey had discussed the question at Windygates) about presenting himself at the inn in the assumed character of Anne's husband. But the result of putting the deception in practice was, to say the least of it, a little embarrassing at first. Here was the waiter describing Miss Silvester as his "good lady;" and leaving it (most naturally and properly) to the "good lady's" husband to knock at her bedroom door, and tell her that he was there. In despair of knowing what else to do at the moment, Arnold asked for the landlady, whom he had not seen on arriving at the inn.

"The landleddy's just tottin' up the ledgers o' the hottle in her ain room," answered Mr. Bishopriggs. "She'll be here anon—the wearyful woman!—speerin' who ye are and what ye are, and takin' a' the business o' the hoose on her ain pair o' shouthers." He dropped the subject of the landlady, and put in a plea for himself. "I ha' lookit after a' the leddy's little comforts, Sir," he whispered. "Trust in me! trust in me!"

Arnold's attention was absorbed in the very serious difficulty of announcing his arrival to Anne. "How am I to get her out?" he said to himself, with a look of perplexity directed at the bedroom door.

He had spoken loud enough for the waiter to hear him. Arnold's look of perplexity was instantly reflected on the face of Mr. Bishopriggs. The head-waiter at Craig Fernie possessed an immense experience of the manners and customs of newly-married people on their honeymoon trip. He had been a second father (with excellent pecuniary results) to innumerable brides and bridegrooms. He knew young married couples in all their varieties:—The couples who try to behave as if they had been married for many years; the couples who attempt no concealment, and take advice from competent authorities about them. The couples who are bashfully talkative before third persons; the couples who are bashfully silent under similar circumstances. The couples who don't know what to do, the couples who wish it was over; the couples who must never be intruded upon without careful preliminary knocking at the door; the couples who can eat and drink in the intervals of "bliss," and the other couples who can't. But the bridegroom who stood helpless on one side of the door, and the bride who remained locked in on the other, were new varieties of the nuptial species, even in the vast experience of Mr. Bishopriggs himself.

"Hoo are ye to get her oot?" he repeated. "I'll show ye hoo!" He advanced as rapidly as his gouty feet would let him, and knocked at the bedroom door. "Eh, my leddy! here he is in flesh and bluid. Mercy preserve us! do ye lock the door of the nuptial chamber in your husband's face?"

At that unanswerable appeal the lock was heard turning in the door. Mr. Bishopriggs winked at Arnold with his one available eye, and laid his forefinger knowingly along his enormous nose. "I'm away before she falls into your arms! Rely on it I'll no come in again without knocking first!"

He left Arnold alone in the room. The bedroom door opened slowly by a few inches at a time. Anne's voice was just audible speaking cautiously behind it.

"Is that you, Geoffrey?"

Arnold's heart began to beat fast, in anticipation of the disclosure which was now close at hand. He knew neither what to say or do—he remained silent.

Anne repeated the question in louder tones:

"Is that you?"

There was the certain prospect of alarming her, if some reply was not given. There was no help for it. Come what come might, Arnold answered, in a whisper:

"Yes."

The door was flung wide open. Anne Silvester appeared on the threshold, confronting him.

"Mr. Brinkworth!!!" she exclaimed, standing petrified with astonishment.

For a moment more neither of them spoke. Anne advanced one step into the sitting-room, and put the next inevitable question, with an instantaneous change from surprise to suspicion.

"What do you want here?"

Geoffrey's letter represented the only possible excuse for Arnold's appearance in that place, and at that time.

"I have got a letter for you," he said—and offered it to her.

She was instantly on her guard. They were little better than strangers to each other, as Arnold had said. A sickening presentiment of some treachery on Geoffrey's part struck cold to her heart. She refused to take the letter.

"I expect no letter," she said. "Who told you I was here?" She put the question, not only with a tone of suspicion, but with a look of contempt. The look was not an easy one for a man to bear. It required a momentary exertion of self-control on Arnold's part, before he could trust himself to answer with due consideration for her. "Is there a watch set on my actions?" she went on, with rising anger. "And are you the spy?"

"You haven't known me very long, Miss Silvester," Arnold answered, quietly. "But you ought to know me better than to say that. I am the bearer of a letter from Geoffrey."

She was an the point of following his example, and of speaking of Geoffrey by his Christian name, on her side. But she checked herself, before the word had passed her lips.

"Do you mean Mr. Delamayn?" she asked, coldly.

"Yes."

"What occasion have I for a letter from Mr. Delamayn?"

She was determined to acknowledge nothing—she kept him obstinately at arm's-length. Arnold did, as a matter of instinct, what a man of larger experience would have done, as a matter of calculation—he closed with her boldly, then and there.

"Miss Silvester! it's no use beating about the bush. If you won't take the letter, you force me to speak out. I am here on a very unpleasant errand. I begin to wish, from the bottom of my heart, I had never undertaken it."

A quick spasm of pain passed across her face. She was beginning, dimly beginning, to understand him. He hesitated. His generous nature shrank from hurting her.

"Go on," she said, with an effort.

"Try not to be angry with me, Miss Silvester. Geoffrey and I are old friends. Geoffrey knows he can trust me—"

"Trust you?" she interposed. "Stop!"

Arnold waited. She went on, speaking to herself, not to him.

"When I was in the other room I asked if Geoffrey was there. And this man answered for him." She sprang forward with a cry of horror.

"Has he told you—"

"For God's sake, read his letter!"

She violently pushed back the hand with which Arnold once more offered the letter. "You don't look at me! He has told you!"

"Read his letter," persisted Arnold. "In justice to him, if you won't in justice to me."

The situation was too painful to be endured. Arnold looked at her, this time, with a man's resolution in his eyes—spoke to her, this time, with a man's resolution in his voice. She took the letter.

"I beg your pardon, Sir," she said, with a sudden humiliation of tone and manner, inexpressibly shocking, inexpressibly pitiable to see. "I understand my position at last. I am a woman doubly betrayed. Please to excuse what I said to you just now, when I supposed myself to have some claim on your respect. Perhaps you will grant me your pity? I can ask for nothing more."

Arnold was silent. Words were useless in the face of such utter self-abandonment as this. Any man living—even Geoffrey himself—must have felt for her at that moment.

She looked for the first time at the letter. She opened it on the wrong side. "My own letter!" she said to herself. "In the hands of another man!"

"Look at the last page," said Arnold.

She turned to the last page, and read the hurried penciled lines. "Villain! villain! villain!" At the third repetition of the word, she crushed the letter in the palm of her hand, and flung it from her to the other end of the room. The instant after, the fire that had flamed up in her died out. Feebly and slowly she reached out her hand to the nearest chair, and sat down in it with her back to Arnold. "He has deserted me!" was all she said. The words fell low and quiet on the silence: they were the utterance of an immeasurable despair.

"You are wrong!" exclaimed Arnold. "Indeed, indeed you are wrong! It's no excuse—it's the truth. I was present when the message came about his father."

She never heeded him, and never moved. She only repeated the words

"He has deserted me!"

"Don't take it in that way!" pleaded Arnold—"pray don't! It's dreadful to hear you; it is indeed. I am sure he has not deserted you." There was no answer; no sign that she heard him; she sat there, struck to stone. It was impossible to call the landlady in at such a moment as this. In despair of knowing how else to rouse her, Arnold drew a chair to her side, and patted her timidly on the shoulder. "Come!" he said, in his single-hearted, boyish way. "Cheer up a little!"

She slowly turned her head, and looked at him with a dull surprise.

"Didn't you say he had told you every thing?" she asked.

"Yes."

"Don't you despise a woman like me?"

Arnold's heart went back, at that dreadful question, to the one woman who was eternally sacred to him—to the woman from whose bosom he had drawn the breath of life.

"Does the man live," he said, "who can think of his mother—and despise women?"

That answer set the prisoned misery in her free. She gave him her hand—she faintly thanked him. The merciful tears came to her at last.

Arnold rose, and turned away to the window in despair. "I mean well," he said. "And yet I only distress her!"

She heard him, and straggled to compose herself "No," she answered, "you comfort me. Don't mind my crying—I'm the better for it." She looked round at him gratefully. "I won't distress you, Mr. Brinkworth. I ought to thank you—and I do. Come back or I shall think you are angry with me." Arnold went back to her. She gave him her hand once more. "One doesn't understand people all at once," she said, simply. "I thought you were like other men—I didn't know till to-day how kind you could be. Did you walk here?" she added, suddenly, with an effort to change the subject. "Are you tired? I have not been kindly received at this place—but I'm sure I may offer you whatever the inn affords."

It was impossible not to feel for her—it was impossible not to be interested in her. Arnold's honest longing to help her expressed itself a little too openly when he spoke next. "All I want, Miss Silvester, is to be of some service to you, if I can," he said. "Is there any thing I can do to make your position here more comfortable? You will stay at this place, won't you? Geoffrey wishes it."

She shuddered, and looked away. "Yes! yes!" she answered, hurriedly.

"You will hear from Geoffrey," Arnold went on, "to-morrow or next day. I know he means to write."

"For Heaven's sake, don't speak of him any more!" she cried out. "How do you think I can look you in the face—" Her cheeks flushed deep, and her eyes rested on him with a momentary firmness. "Mind this! I am his wife, if promises can make me his wife! He has pledged his word to me by all that is sacred!" She checked herself impatiently. "What am I saying? What interest can you have in this miserable state of things? Don't let us talk of it! I have something else to say to you. Let us go back to my troubles here. Did you see the landlady when you came in?"

"No. I only saw the waiter."

"The landlady has made some absurd difficulty about letting me have these rooms because I came here alone."

"She won't make any difficulty now," said Arnold. "I have settled that."

"You!"

Arnold smiled. After what had passed, it was an indescribable relief to him to see the humorous side of his own position at the inn.

"Certainly," he answered. "When I asked for the lady who had arrived here alone this afternoon—"

"Yes."

"I was told, in your interests, to ask for her as my wife."

Anne looked at him—in alarm as well as in surprise.

"You asked for me as your wife?" she repeated.

"Yes. I haven't done wrong—have I? As I understood it, there was no alternative. Geoffrey told me you had settled with him to present yourself here as a married lady, whose husband was coming to join her."

"I thought of him when I said that. I never thought of you."

"Natural enough. Still, it comes to the same thing (doesn't it?) with the people of this house."

"I don't understand you."

"I will try and explain myself a little better. Geoffrey said your position here depended on my asking for you at the door (as he would have asked for you if he had come) in the character of your husband."

"He had no right to say that."

"No right? After what you have told me of the landlady, just think what might have happened if he had not said it! I haven't had much experience myself of these things. But—allow me to ask—wouldn't it have been a little awkward (at my age) if I had come here and inquired for you as a friend? Don't you think, in that case, the landlady might have made some additional difficulty about letting you have the rooms?"

It was beyond dispute that the landlady would have refused to let the rooms at all. It was equally plain that the deception which Arnold had practiced on the people of the inn was a deception which Anne had herself rendered necessary, in her own interests. She was not to blame; it was clearly impossible for her to have foreseen such an event as Geoffrey's departure for London. Still, she felt an uneasy sense of responsibility—a vague dread of what might happen next. She sat nervously twisting her handkerchief in her lap, and made no answer.

"Don't suppose I object to this little stratagem," Arnold went on. "I am serving my old friend, and I am helping the lady who is soon to be his wife."

Anne rose abruptly to her feet, and amazed him by a very unexpected question.

"Mr. Brinkworth," she said, "forgive me the rudeness of something I am about to say to you. When are you going away?"

Arnold burst out laughing.

"When I am quite sure I can do nothing more to assist you," he answered.

"Pray don't think of me any longer."

"In your situation! who else am I to think of?"

Anne laid her hand earnestly on his arm, and answered:

"Blanche!"

"Blanche?" repeated Arnold, utterly at a loss to understand her.

"Yes—Blanche. She found time to tell me what had passed between you this morning before I left Windygates. I know you have made her an offer: I know you are engaged to be married to her."

Arnold was delighted to hear it. He had been merely unwilling to leave her thus far. He was absolutely determined to stay with her now.

"Don't expect me to go after that!" he said. "Come and sit down again, and let's talk about Blanche."

Anne declined impatiently, by a gesture. Arnold was too deeply interested in the new topic to take any notice of it.

"You know all about her habits and her tastes," he went on, "and what she likes, and what she dislikes. It's most important that I should talk to you about her. When we are husband and wife, Blanche is to have all her own way in every thing. That's my idea of the Whole Duty of Man—when Man is married. You are still standing? Let me give you a chair."

It was cruel—under other circumstances it would have been impossible—to disappoint him. But the vague fear of consequences which had taken possession of Anne was not to be trifled with. She had no clear conception of the risk (and it is to be added, in justice to Geoffrey, that he had no clear conception of the risk) on which Arnold had unconsciously ventured, in undertaking his errand to the inn. Neither of them had any adequate idea (few people have) of the infamous absence of all needful warning, of all decent precaution and restraint, which makes the marriage law of Scotland a trap to catch unmarried men and women, to this day. But, while Geoffrey's mind was incapable of looking beyond the present emergency, Anne's finer intelligence told her that a country which offered such facilities for private marriage as the facilities of which she had proposed to take advantage in her own case, was not a country in which a man could act as Arnold had acted, without danger of some serious embarrassment following as the possible result. With this motive to animate her, she resolutely declined to take the offered chair, or to enter into the proposed conversation.

"Whatever we have to say about Blanche, Mr. Brinkworth, must be said at some fitter time. I beg you will leave me."

"Leave you!"

"Yes. Leave me to the solitude that is best for me, and to the sorrow that I have deserved. Thank you—and good-by."

Arnold made no attempt to disguise his disappointment and surprise.

"If I must go, I must," he said, "But why are you in such a hurry?"

"I don't want you to call me your wife again before the people of this inn."

"Is that all? What on earth are you afraid of?"

She was unable fully to realize her own apprehensions. She was doubly unable to express them in words. In her anxiety to produce some reason which might prevail on him to go, she drifted back into that very conversation about Blanche into which she had declined to enter but the moment before.

"I have reasons for being afraid," she said. "One that I can't give; and one that I can. Suppose Blanche heard of what you have done? The longer you stay here—the more people you see—the more chance there is that she might hear of it."

"And what if she did?" asked Arnold, in his own straightforward way. "Do you think she would be angry with me for making myself useful to you?"

"Yes," rejoined Anne, sharply, "if she was jealous of me."

Arnold's unlimited belief in Blanche expressed itself, without the slightest compromise, in two words:

"That's impossible!"

Anxious as she was, miserable as she was, a faint smile flitted over Anne's face.

"Sir Patrick would tell you, Mr. Brinkworth, that nothing is impossible where women are concerned." She dropped her momentary lightness of tone, and went on as earnestly as ever. "You can't put yourself in Blanche's place—I can. Once more, I beg you to go. I don't like your coming here, in this way! I don't like it at all!"

She held out her hand to take leave. At the same moment there was a loud knock at the door of the room.

Anne sank into the chair at her side, and uttered a faint cry of alarm. Arnold, perfectly impenetrable to all sense of his position, asked what there was to frighten her—and answered the knock in the two customary words:

"Come in!"

CHAPTER THE TENTH.

MR. BISHOPRIGGS.

THE knock at the door was repeated—a louder knock than before.

"Are you deaf?" shouted Arnold.

The door opened, little by little, an inch at a time. Mr. Bishopriggs appeared mysteriously, with the cloth for dinner over his arm, and with his second in command behind him, bearing "the furnishing of the table" (as it was called at Craig Fernie) on a tray.

"What the deuce were you waiting for?" asked Arnold. "I told you to come in."

"And I tauld you," answered Mr. Bishopriggs, "that I wadna come in without knocking first. Eh, man!" he went on, dismissing his second in command, and laying the cloth with his own venerable hands, "d'ye think I've lived in this hottle in blinded eegnorance of hoo young married couples pass the time when they're left to themselves? Twa knocks at the door—and an unco trouble in opening it, after that—is joost the least ye can do for them! Whar' do ye think, noo, I'll set the places for you and your leddy there?"

Anne walked away to the window, in undisguised disgust. Arnold found Mr. Bishopriggs to be quite irresistible. He answered, humoring the joke,

"One at the top and one at the bottom of the table, I suppose?"

"One at tap and one at bottom?" repeated Mr. Bishopriggs, in high disdain. "De'il a bit of it! Baith yer chairs as close together as chairs can be. Hech! hech!—haven't I caught 'em, after goodness knows hoo many preleeminary knocks at the door, dining on their husbands' knees, and steemulating a man's appetite by feeding him at the fork's end like a child? Eh!" sighed the sage of Craig Fernie, "it's a short life wi' that nuptial business, and a merry one! A mouth for yer billin' and cooin'; and a' the rest o' yer days for wondering ye were ever such a fule, and wishing it was a' to be done ower again.—Ye'll be for a bottle o' sherry wine, nae doot? and a drap toddy afterwards, to do yer digestin' on?"

Arnold nodded—and then, in obedience to a signal from Anne, joined her at the window. Mr. Bishopriggs looked after them attentively—observed that they were talking in whispers—and approved of that proceeding, as representing another of the established customs of young married couples at inns, in the presence of third persons appointed to wait on them.

"Ay! ay!" he said, looking over his shoulder at Arnold, "gae to your deerie! gae to your deerie! and leave a' the solid business o' life to Me. Ye've Screepture warrant for it. A man maun leave fether and mother (I'm yer fether), and cleave to his wife. My certie! 'cleave' is a strong word—there's nae sort o' doot aboot it, when it comes to 'cleaving!'" He wagged his head thoughtfully, and walked to the side-table in a corner, to cut the bread.

As he took up the knife, his one wary eye detected a morsel of crumpled paper, lying lost between the table and the wall. It was the letter from Geoffrey, which Anne had flung from her, in the first indignation of reading it—and which neither she nor Arnold had thought of since.

"What's that I see yonder?" muttered Mr. Bishopriggs, under his breath. "Mair litter in the room, after I've doosted and tidied it wi' my ain hands!"

He picked up the crumpled paper, and partly opened it. "Eh! what's here? Writing on it in ink? and writing on it in pencil? Who may this belong to?" He looked round cautiously toward Arnold and Anne. They were both still talking in whispers, and both standing with their backs to him, looking out of the window. "Here it is, clean forgotten and dune with!" thought Mr. Bishopriggs. "Noo what would a fule do, if he fund this? A fule wad light his pipe wi' it, and then wonder whether he wadna ha' dune better to read it first. And what wad a wise man do, in a seemilar position?" He practically answered that question by putting the letter into his pocket. It might be worth keeping, or it might not; five minutes' private examination of it would decide the alternative, at the first convenient opportunity. "Am gaun' to breeng the dinner in!" he called out to Arnold. "And, mind ye, there's nae knocking at the door possible, when I've got the tray in baith my hands, and mairs the pity, the gout in baith my feet." With that friendly warning, Mr. Bishopriggs went his way to the regions of the kitchen.

Arnold continued his conversation with Anne in terms which showed that the question of his leaving the inn had been the question once more discussed between them while they were standing at the window.

"You see we can't help it," he said. "The waiter has gone to bring the dinner in. What will they think in the house, if I go away already, and leave 'my wife' to dine alone?"

It was so plainly necessary to keep up appearances for the present, that there was nothing more to be said. Arnold was committing a serious imprudence—and yet, on this occasion, Arnold was right. Anne's annoyance at feeling that conclusion forced on her produced the first betrayal of impatience which she had shown yet. She left Arnold at the window, and flung herself on the sofa. "A curse seems to follow me!" she thought, bitterly. "This will end ill—and I shall be answerable for it!"

In the mean time Mr. Bishopriggs had found the dinner in the kitchen, ready, and waiting for him. Instead of at once taking the tray on which it was placed into the sitting-room, he conveyed it privately into his own pantry, and shut the door.

"Lie ye there, my freend, till the spare moment comes—and I'll look at ye again," he said, putting the letter away carefully in the dresser-drawer. "Noo aboot the dinner o' they twa turtle-doves in the parlor?" he continued, directing his attention to the dinner tray. "I maun joost see that the cook's 's dune her duty—the creatures are no' capable o' decidin' that knotty point for their ain selves." He took off one of the covers, and picked bits, here and there, out of the dish with the fork, "Eh! eh! the collops are no' that bad!" He took off another cover, and shook his head in solemn doubt. "Here's the green meat. I doot green meat's windy diet for a man at my time o' life!" He put the cover on again, and tried the next dish. "The fesh? What the de'il does the woman fry the trout for? Boil it next time, ye betch, wi' a pinch o' saut and a spunefu' o' vinegar." He drew the cork from a bottle of sherry, and decanted the wine. "The sherry wine?" he said, in tones of deep feeling, holding the decanter up to the light. "Hoo do I know but what it may be corkit? I maun taste and try. It's on my conscience, as an honest man, to taste and try." He forthwith relieved his conscience—copiously. There was a vacant space, of no inconsiderable dimensions, left in the decanter. Mr. Bishopriggs gravely filled it up from the water-bottle. "Eh! it's joost addin' ten years to the age o' the wine. The turtle-doves will be nane the waur—and I mysel' am a glass o' sherry the better. Praise Providence for a' its maircies!" Having relieved himself of that devout aspiration, he took up the tray again, and decided on letting the turtle-doves have their dinner.

The conversation in the parlor (dropped for the moment) had been renewed, in the absence of Mr. Bishopriggs. Too restless to remain long in one place, Anne had risen again from the sofa, and had rejoined Arnold at the window.

"Where do your friends at Lady Lundie's believe you to be now?" she asked, abruptly.

"I am believed," replied Arnold, "to be meeting my tenants, and taking possession of my estate."

"How are you to get to your estate to-night?"

"By railway, I suppose. By-the-by, what excuse am I to make for going away after dinner? We are sure to have the landlady in here before long. What will she say to my going off by myself to the train, and leaving 'my wife' behind me?"

"Mr. Brinkworth! that joke—if it is a joke—is worn out!"

"I beg your pardon," said Arnold.

"You may leave your excuse to me," pursued Anne. "Do you go by the up train, or the down?"

"By the up train."

The door opened suddenly; and Mr. Bishopriggs appeared with the dinner. Anne nervously separated herself from Arnold. The one available eye of Mr. Bishopriggs followed her reproachfully, as he put the dishes on the table.

"I warned ye baith, it was a clean impossibility to knock at the door this time. Don't blame me, young madam—don't blame me!"

"Where will you sit?" asked Arnold, by way of diverting Anne's attention from the familiarities of Father Bishopriggs.

"Any where!" she answered, impatiently; snatching up a chair, and placing it at the bottom of the table.

Mr. Bishopriggs politely, but firmly, put the chair back again in its place.

"Lord's sake! what are ye doin'? It's clean contrary to a' the laws and customs o' the honey-mune, to sit as far away from your husband as that!"

He waved his persuasive napkin to one of the two chairs placed close together at the table.

Arnold interfered once more, and prevented another outbreak of impatience from Anne.

"What does it matter?" he said. "Let the man have his way."

"Get it over as soon as you can," she returned. "I can't, and won't, bear it much longer."

They took their places at the table, with Father Bishopriggs behind them, in the mixed character of major domo and guardian angel.

"Here's the trout!" he cried, taking the cover off with a flourish. "Half an hour since, he was loupin' in the water. There he lies noo, fried in the dish. An emblem o' human life for ye! When ye can spare any leisure time from yer twa selves, meditate on that."

Arnold took up the spoon, to give Anne one of the trout. Mr. Bishopriggs clapped the cover on the dish again, with a countenance expressive of devout horror.

"Is there naebody gaun' to say grace?" he asked.

"Come! come!" said Arnold. "The fish is getting cold."

Mr. Bishopriggs piously closed his available eye, and held the cover firmly on the dish. "For what ye're gaun' to receive, may ye baith be truly thankful!" He opened his available eye, and whipped the cover off again. "My conscience is easy noo. Fall to! Fall to!"

"Send him away!" said Anne. "His familiarity is beyond all endurance."

"You needn't wait," said Arnold.

"Eh! but I'm here to wait," objected Mr. Bishopriggs. "What's the use o' my gaun' away, when ye'll want me anon to change the plates for ye?" He considered for a moment (privately consulting his experience) and arrived at a satisfactory conclusion as to Arnold's motive for wanting to get rid of him. "Tak' her on yer knee," he whispered in Arnold's ear, "as soon as ye like! Feed him at the fork's end," he added to Anne, "whenever ye please! I'll think of something else, and look out at the proaspect." He winked—and went to the window.

"Come! come!" said Arnold to Anne. "There's a comic side to all this. Try and see it as I do."

Mr. Bishopriggs returned from the window, and announced the appearance of a new element of embarrassment in the situation at the inn.

"My certie!" he said, "it's weel ye cam' when ye did. It's ill getting to this hottle in a storm."

Anne started and looked round at him. "A storm coming!" she exclaimed.

"Eh! ye're well hoosed here—ye needn't mind it. There's the cloud down the valley," he added, pointing out of the window, "coming up one way, when the wind's blawing the other. The storm's brewing, my leddy, when ye see that!"

There was another knock at the door. As Arnold had predicted, the landlady made her appearance on the scene.

"I ha' just lookit in, Sir," said Mrs. Inchbare, addressing herself exclusively to Arnold, "to see ye've got what ye want."

"Oh! you are the landlady? Very nice, ma'am—very nice."

Mistress Inchbare had her own private motive for entering the room, and came to it without further preface.

"Ye'll excuse me, Sir," she proceeded. "I wasna in the way when ye cam' here, or I suld ha' made bauld to ask ye the question which I maun e'en ask noo. Am I to understand that ye hire these rooms for yersel', and this leddy here—yer wife?"

Anne raised her head to speak. Arnold pressed her hand warningly, under the table, and silenced her.

"Certainly," he said. "I take the rooms for myself, and this lady here—my wife!"

Anne made a second attempt to speak.

"This gentleman—" she began.

Arnold stopped her for the second time.

"This gentleman?" repeated Mrs. Inchbare, with a broad stare of surprise. "I'm only a puir woman, my leddy—d'ye mean yer husband here?"

Arnold's warning hand touched Anne's, for the third time. Mistress Inchbare's eyes remained fixed on her in merciless inquiry. To have given utterance to the contradiction which trembled on her lips would have been to involve Arnold (after all that he had sacrificed for her) in the scandal which would inevitably follow—a scandal which would be talked of in the neighborhood, and which might find its way to Blanche's ears. White and cold, her eyes never moving from the table, she accepted the landlady's implied correction, and faintly repeated the words: "My husband."

Mistress Inchbare drew a breath of virtuous relief, and waited for what Anne had to say next. Arnold came considerately to the rescue, and got her out of the room.

"Never mind," he said to Anne; "I know what it is, and I'll see about it. She's always like this, ma'am, when a storm's coming," he went on, turning to the landlady. "No, thank you—I know how to manage her. Well send to you, if we want your assistance."

"At yer ain pleasure, Sir," answered Mistress Inchbare. She turned, and apologized to Anne (under protest), with a stiff courtesy. "No offense, my leddy! Ye'll remember that ye cam' here alane, and that the hottle has its ain gude name to keep up." Having once more vindicated "the hottle," she made the long-desired move to the door, and left the room.

"I'm faint!" Anne whispered. "Give me some water."

There was no water on the table. Arnold ordered it of Mr. Bishopriggs—who had remained passive in the back-ground (a model of discreet attention) as long as the mistress was in the room.

"Mr. Brinkworth!" said Anne, when they were alone, "you are acting with inexcusable rashness. That woman's question was an impertinence. Why did you answer it? Why did you force me—?"

She stopped, unable to finish the sentence. Arnold insisted on her drinking a glass of wine—and then defended himself with the patient consideration for her which he had shown from the first.

"Why didn't I have the inn door shut in your face"—he asked, good humoredly—"with a storm coming on, and without a place in which you can take refuge? No, no, Miss Silvester! I don't presume to blame you for any scruples you may feel—but scruples are sadly out of place with such a woman as that landlady. I am responsible for your safety to Geoffrey; and Geoffrey expects to find you here. Let's change the subject. The water is a long time coming. Try another glass of wine. No? Well—here is Blanche's health" (he took some of the wine himself), "in the weakest sherry I ever drank in my life." As he set down his glass, Mr. Bishopriggs came in with the water. Arnold hailed him satirically. "Well? have you got the water? or have you used it all for the sherry?"

Mr. Bishopriggs stopped in the middle of the room, thunder-struck at the aspersion cast on the wine.

"Is that the way ye talk of the auldest bottle o' sherry wine in Scotland?" he asked, gravely. "What's the warld coming to? The new generation's a foot beyond my fathoming. The maircies o' Providence, as shown to man in the choicest veentages o' Spain, are clean thrown away on 'em."

"Have you brought the water?"

"I ha' brought the water—and mair than the water. I ha' brought ye news from ootside. There's a company o' gentlemen on horseback, joost cantering by to what they ca' the shootin' cottage, a mile from this."

"Well—and what have we got to do with it?"

"Bide a wee! There's ane o' them has drawn bridle at the hottle, and he's speerin' after the leddy that cam' here alane. The leddy's your leddy, as sure as saxpence. I doot," said Mr. Bishopriggs, walking away to the window, "that's what ye've got to do with it."

Arnold looked at Anne.

"Do you expect any body?"

"Is it Geoffrey?"

"Impossible. Geoffrey is on his way to London."

"There he is, any way," resumed Mr. Bishopriggs, at the window. "He's loupin' down from his horse. He's turning this way. Lord save us!" he exclaimed, with a start of consternation, "what do I see? That incarnate deevil, Sir Paitrick himself!"

Arnold sprang to his feet.

"Do you mean Sir Patrick Lundie?"

Anne ran to the window.

"It is Sir Patrick!" she said. "Hide yourself before he comes in!"

"Hide myself?"

"What will he think if he sees you with me?"

He was Blanche's guardian, and he believed Arnold to be at that moment visiting his new property. What he would think was not difficult to foresee. Arnold turned for help to Mr. Bishopriggs.

"Where can I go?"

Mr. Bishopriggs pointed to the bedroom door.

"Whar' can ye go? There's the nuptial chamber!"

"Impossible!"

Mr. Bishopriggs expressed the utmost extremity of human amazement by a long whistle, on one note.

"Whew! Is that the way ye talk o' the nuptial chamber already?"

"Find me some other place—I'll make it worth your while."

"Eh! there's my paintry! I trow that's some other place; and the door's at the end o' the passage."

Arnold hurried out. Mr. Bishopriggs—evidently under the impression that the case before him was a case of elopement, with Sir Patrick mixed up in it in the capacity of guardian—addressed himself, in friendly confidence, to Anne.

"My certie, mistress! it's ill wark deceivin' Sir Paitrick, if that's what ye've dune. Ye must know, I was ance a bit clerk body in his chambers at Embro—"

The voice of Mistress Inchbare, calling for the head-waiter, rose shrill and imperative from the regions of the bar. Mr. Bishopriggs disappeared. Anne remained, standing helpless by the window. It was plain by this time that the place of her retreat had been discovered at Windygates. The one doubt to decide, now, was whether it would be wise or not to receive Sir Patrick, for the purpose of discovering whether he came as friend or enemy to the inn.

CHAPTER THE ELEVENTH.

SIR PATRICK.

THE doubt was practically decided before Anne had determined what to do. She was still at the window when the sitting-room door was thrown open, and Sir Patrick appeared, obsequiously shown in by Mr. Bishopriggs.

"Ye're kindly welcome, Sir Paitrick. Hech, Sirs! the sight of you is gude for sair eyne."

Sir Patrick turned and looked at Mr. Bishopriggs—as he might have looked at some troublesome insect which he had driven out of the window, and which had returned on him again.

"What, you scoundrel! have you drifted into an honest employment at last?"

Mr. Bishopriggs rubbed his hands cheerfully, and took his tone from his superior, with supple readiness,

"Ye're always in the right of it, Sir Paitrick! Wut, raal wut in that aboot the honest employment, and me drifting into it. Lord's sake, Sir, hoo well ye wear!"

Dismissing Mr. Bishopriggs by a sign, Sir Patrick advanced to Anne.

"I am committing an intrusion, madam which must, I am afraid, appear unpardonable in your eyes," he said. "May I hope you will excuse me when I have made you acquainted with my motive?"

He spoke with scrupulous politeness. His knowledge of Anne was of the slightest possible kind. Like other men, he had felt the attraction of her unaffected grace and gentleness on the few occasions when he had been in her company—and that was all. If he had belonged to the present generation he would, under the circumstances, have fallen into one of the besetting sins of England in these days—the tendency (to borrow an illustration from the stage) to "strike an attitude" in the presence of a social emergency. A man of the present period, in Sir Patrick's position, would have struck an attitude of (what is called) chivalrous respect; and would have addressed Anne in a tone of ready-made sympathy, which it was simply impossible for a stranger really to feel. Sir Patrick affected nothing of the sort. One of the besetting sins of his time was the habitual concealment of our better selves—upon the whole, a far less dangerous national error than the habitual advertisement of our better selves, which has become the practice, public and privately, of society in this age. Sir Patrick assumed, if anything, less sympathy on this occasion than he really felt. Courteous to all women, he was as courteous as usual to Anne—and no more.

"I am quite at a loss, Sir, to know what brings you to this place. The servant here informs me that you are one of a party of gentlemen who have just passed by the inn, and who have all gone on except yourself." In those guarded terms Anne opened the interview with the unwelcome visitor, on her side.

Sir Patrick admitted the fact, without betraying the slightest embarrassment.

"The servant is quite right," he said. "I am one of the party. And I have purposely allowed them to go on to the keeper's cottage without me. Having admitted this, may I count on receiving your permission to explain the motive of my visit?"

Necessarily suspicious of him, as coming from Windygates, Anne answered in few and formal words, as coldly as before.

"Explain it, Sir Patrick, if you please, as briefly as possible."

Sir Patrick bowed. He was not in the least offended; he was even (if the confession may be made without degrading him in the public estimation) privately amused. Conscious of having honestly presented himself at the inn in Anne's interests, as well as in the interests of the ladies at Windygates, it appealed to his sense of humor to find himself kept at arm's-length by the very woman whom he had come to benefit. The temptation was strong on him to treat his errand from his own whimsical point of view. He gravely took out his watch, and noted the time to a second, before he spoke again.

"I have an event to relate in which you are interested," he said. "And I have two messages to deliver, which I hope you will not object to receive. The event I undertake to describe in one minute. The messages I promise to dispose of in two minutes more. Total duration of this intrusion on your time—three minutes."

He placed a chair for Anne, and waited until she had permitted him, by a sign, to take a second chair for himself.

"We will begin with the event," he resumed. "Your arrival at this place is no secret at Windygates. You were seen on the foot-road to Craig Fernie by one of the female servants. And the inference naturally drawn is, that you were on your way to the inn. It may be important for you to know this; and I have taken the liberty of mentioning it accordingly." He consulted his watch. "Event related. Time, one minute."

He had excited her curiosity, to begin with. "Which of the women saw me?" she asked, impulsively.

Sir Patrick (watch in hand) declined to prolong the interview by answering any incidental inquiries which might arise in the course of it.

"Pardon me," he rejoined; "I am pledged to occupy three minutes only. I have no room for the woman. With your kind permission, I will get on to the messages next."

Anne remained silent. Sir Patrick went on.

"First message: 'Lady Lundie's compliments to her step-daughter's late governess—with whose married name she is not acquainted. Lady Lundie regrets to say that Sir Patrick, as head of the family, has threatened to return to Edinburgh, unless she consents to be guided by his advice in the course she pursues with the late governess. Lady Lundie, accordingly, foregoes her intention of calling at the Craig Fernie inn, to express her sentiments and make her inquiries in person, and commits to Sir Patrick the duty of expressing her sentiments; reserving to herself the right of making her inquiries at the next convenient opportunity. Through the medium of her brother-in-law, she begs to inform the late governess that all intercourse is at an end between them, and that she declines to act as reference in case of future emergency.'—Message textually correct. Expressive of Lady Lundie's view of your sudden departure from the house. Time, two minutes."

Anne's color rose. Anne's pride was up in arms on the spot.

"The impertinence of Lady Lundie's message is no more than I should have expected from her," she said. "I am only surprised at Sir Patrick's delivering it."

"Sir Patrick's motives will appear presently," rejoined the incorrigible old gentleman. "Second message: 'Blanche's fondest love. Is dying to be acquainted with Anne's husband, and to be informed of Anne's married name. Feels indescribable anxiety and apprehension on Anne's account. Insists on hearing from Anne immediately. Longs, as she never longed for any thing yet, to order her pony-chaise and drive full gallop to the inn. Yields, under irresistible pressure, to the exertion of her guardian's authority, and commits the expression of her feelings to Sir Patrick, who is a born tyrant, and doesn't in the least mind breaking other people's hearts.' Sir Patrick, speaking for himself, places his sister-in-law's view and his niece's view, side by side, before the lady whom he has now the honor of addressing, and on whose confidence he is especially careful not to intrude. Reminds the lady that his influence at Windygates, however strenuously he may exert it, is not likely to last forever. Requests her to consider whether his sister-in-law's view and his niece's view in collision, may not lead to very undesirable domestic results; and leaves her to take the course which seems best to herself under those circumstances.—Second message delivered textually. Time, three minutes. A storm coming on. A quarter of an hour's ride from here to the shooting-cottage. Madam, I wish you good-evening."

He bowed lower than ever—and, without a word more, quietly left the room.

Anne's first impulse was (excusably enough, poor soul) an impulse of resentment.

"Thank you, Sir Patrick!" she said, with a bitter look at the closing door. "The sympathy of society with a friendless woman could hardly have been expressed in a more amusing way!"

The little irritation of the moment passed off with the moment. Anne's own intelligence and good sense showed her the position in its truer light.

She recognized in Sir Patrick's abrupt departure Sir Patrick's considerate resolution to spare her from entering into any details on the subject of her position at the inn. He had given her a friendly warning; and he had delicately left her to decide for herself as to the assistance which she might render him in maintaining tranquillity at Windygates. She went at once to a side-table in the room, on which writing materials were placed, and sat down to write to Blanche.

"I can do nothing with Lady Lundie," she thought. "But I have more influence than any body else over Blanche and I can prevent the collision between them which Sir Patrick dreads."

She began the letter. "My dearest Blanche, I have seen Sir Patrick, and he has given me your message. I will set your mind at ease about me as soon as I can. But, before I say any thing else, let me entreat you, as the greatest favor you can do to your sister and your friend, not to enter into any disputes about me with Lady Lundie, and not to commit the imprudence—the useless imprudence, my love—of coming here." She stopped—the paper swam before her eyes. "My own darling!" she thought, "who could have foreseen that I should ever shrink from the thought of seeing you?" She sighed, and dipped the pen in the ink, and went on with the letter.

The sky darkened rapidly as the evening fell. The wind swept in fainter and fainter gusts across the dreary moor. Far and wide over the face of Nature the stillness was fast falling which tells of a coming storm.

CHAPTER THE TWELFTH.

ARNOLD.

MEANWHILE Arnold remained shut up in the head-waiter's pantry—chafing secretly at the position forced upon him.

He was, for the first time in his life, in hiding from another person, and that person a man. Twice—stung to it by the inevitable loss of self-respect which his situation occasioned—he had gone to the door, determined to face Sir Patrick boldly; and twice he had abandoned the idea, in mercy to Anne. It would have been impossible for him to set himself right with Blanche's guardian without betraying the unhappy woman whose secret he was bound in honor to keep. "I wish to Heaven I had never come here!" was the useless aspiration that escaped him, as he doggedly seated himself on the dresser to wait till Sir Patrick's departure set him free.

After an interval—not by any means the long interval which he had anticipated—his solitude was enlivened by the appearance of Father Bishopriggs.

"Well?" cried Arnold, jumping off the dresser, "is the coast clear?"

There were occasions when Mr. Bishopriggs became, on a sudden, unexpectedly hard of hearing, This was one of them.

"Hoo do ye find the paintry?" he asked, without paying the slightest attention to Arnold's question. "Snug and private? A Patmos in the weelderness, as ye may say!"

His one available eye, which had begun by looking at Arnold's face, dropped slowly downward, and fixed itself, in mute but eloquent expectation, on Arnold's waistcoat pocket.

"I understand!" said Arnold. "I promised to pay you for the Patmos—eh? There you are!"

Mr. Bishopriggs pocketed the money with a dreary smile and a sympathetic shake of the head. Other waiters would have returned thanks. The sage of Craig Fernie returned a few brief remarks instead. Admirable in many things, Father Bishopriggs was especially great at drawing a moral. He drew a moral on this occasion from his own gratuity.

"There I am—as ye say. Mercy presairve us! ye need the siller at every turn, when there's a woman at yer heels. It's an awfu' reflection—ye canna hae any thing to do wi' the sex they ca' the opposite sex without its being an expense to ye. There's this young leddy o' yours, I doot she'll ha' been an expense to ye from the first. When you were coortin' her, ye did it, I'll go bail, wi' the open hand. Presents and keep-sakes, flowers and jewelery, and little dogues. Sair expenses all of them!"

"Hang your reflections! Has Sir Patrick left the inn?"

The reflections of Mr. Bishopriggs declined to be disposed of in any thing approaching to a summary way. On they flowed from their parent source, as slowly and as smoothly as ever!

"Noo ye're married to her, there's her bonnets and goons and under-clothin'—her ribbons, laces, furbelows, and fallals. A sair expense again!"

"What is the expense of cutting your reflections short, Mr. Bishopriggs?"

"Thirdly, and lastly, if ye canna agree wi' her as time gaes on—if there's incompaitibeelity of temper betwixt ye—in short, if ye want a wee bit separation, hech, Sirs! ye pet yer hand in yer poaket, and come to an aimicable understandin' wi' her in that way. Or, maybe she takes ye into Court, and pets her hand in your poaket, and comes to a hoastile understandin' wi' ye there. Show me a woman—and I'll show ye a man not far off wha' has mair expenses on his back than he ever bairgained for." Arnold's patience would last no longer—he turned to the door. Mr. Bishopriggs, with equal alacrity on his side, turned to the matter in hand. "Yes, Sir! The room is e'en clear o' Sir Paitrick, and the leddy's alane, and waitin' for ye."

In a moment more Arnold was back in the sitting-room.

"Well?" he asked, anxiously. "What is it? Bad news from Lady Lundie's?"

Anne closed and directed the letter to Blanche, which she had just completed. "No," she replied. "Nothing to interest you."

"What did Sir Patrick want?"

"Only to warn me. They have found out at Windygates that I am here."

"That's awkward, isn't it?"

"Not in the least. I can manage perfectly; I have nothing to fear. Don't think of me—think of yourself."

"I am not suspected, am I?"

"Thank heaven—no. But there is no knowing what may happen if you stay here. Ring the bell at once, and ask the waiter about the trains."

Struck by the unusual obscurity of the sky at that hour of the evening, Arnold went to the window. The rain had come—and was falling heavily. The view on the moor was fast disappearing in mist and darkness.

"Pleasant weather to travel in!" he said.

"The railway!" Anne exclaimed, impatiently. "It's getting late. See about the railway!"

Arnold walked to the fire-place to ring the bell. The railway time-table hanging over it met his eye.

"Here's the information I want," he said to Anne; "if I only knew how to get at it. 'Down'—'Up'—'A. M.'—P. M.' What a cursed confusion! I believe they do it on purpose."

Anne joined him at the fire-place.

"I understand it—I'll help you. Did you say it was the up train you wanted?"

"What is the name of the station you stop at?"

Arnold told her. She followed the intricate net-work of lines and figures with her finger—suddenly stopped—looked again to make sure—and turned from the time-table with a face of blank despair. The last train for the day had gone an hour since.

In the silence which followed that discovery, a first flash of lightning passed across the window and the low roll of thunder sounded the outbreak of the storm.

"What's to be done now?" asked Arnold.

In the face of the storm, Anne answered without hesitation, "You must take a carriage, and drive."

"Drive? They told me it was three-and-twenty miles, by railway, from the station to my place—let alone the distance from this inn to the station."

"What does the distance matter? Mr. Brinkworth, you can't possibly stay here!"

A second flash of lightning crossed the window; the roll of the thunder came nearer. Even Arnold's good temper began to be a little ruffled by Anne's determination to get rid of him. He sat down with the air of a man who had made up his mind not to leave the house.

"Do you hear that?" he asked, as the sound of the thunder died away grandly, and the hard pattering of the rain on the window became audible once more. "If I ordered horses, do you think they would let me have them, in such weather as this? And, if they did, do you suppose the horses could face it on the moor? No, no, Miss Silvester—I am sorry to be in the way, but the train has gone, and the night and the storm have come. I have no choice but to stay here!"

Anne still maintained her own view, but less resolutely than before. "After what you have told the landlady," she said, "think of the embarrassment, the cruel embarrassment of our position, if you stop at the inn till to-morrow morning!"

"Is that all?" returned Arnold.

Anne looked up at him, quickly and angrily. No! he was quite unconscious of having said any thing that could offend her. His rough masculine sense broke its way unconsciously through all the little feminine subtleties and delicacies of his companion, and looked the position practically in the face for what it was worth, and no more. "Where's the embarrassment?" he asked, pointing to the bedroom door. "There's your room, all ready for you. And here's the sofa, in this room, all ready for me. If you had seen the places I have slept in at sea—!"

She interrupted him, without ceremony. The places he had slept in, at sea, were of no earthly importance. The one question to consider, was the place he was to sleep in that night.

"If you must stay," she rejoined, "can't you get a room in some other part of the house?"

But one last mistake in dealing with her, in her present nervous condition, was left to make—and the innocent Arnold made it. "In some other part of the house?" he repeated, jestingly. "The landlady would be scandalized. Mr. Bishopriggs would never allow it!"

She rose, and stamped her foot impatiently on the floor. "Don't joke!" she exclaimed. "This is no laughing matter." She paced the room excitedly. "I don't like it! I don't like it!"

Arnold looked after her, with a stare of boyish wonder.

"What puts you out so?" he asked. "Is it the storm?"

She threw herself on the sofa again. "Yes," she said, shortly. "It's the storm."

Arnold's inexhaustible good-nature was at once roused to activity again.

"Shall we have the candles," he suggested, "and shut the weather out?" She turned irritably on the sofa, without replying. "I'll promise to go away the first thing in the morning!" he went on. "Do try and take it easy—and don't be angry with me. Come! come! you wouldn't turn a dog out, Miss Silvester, on such a night as this!"

He was irresistible. The most sensitive woman breathing could not have accused him of failing toward her in any single essential of consideration and respect. He wanted tact, poor fellow—but who could expect him to have learned that always superficial (and sometimes dangerous) accomplishment, in the life he had led at sea? At the sight of his honest, pleading face, Anne recovered possession of her gentler and sweeter self. She made her excuses for her irritability with a grace that enchanted him. "We'll have a pleasant evening of it yet!" cried Arnold, in his hearty way—and rang the bell.

The bell was hung outside the door of that Patmos in the wilderness—otherwise known as the head-waiter's pantry. Mr. Bishopriggs (employing his brief leisure in the seclusion of his own apartment) had just mixed a glass of the hot and comforting liquor called "toddy" in the language of North Britain, and was just lifting it to his lips, when the summons from Arnold invited him to leave his grog.

"Haud yer screechin' tongue!" cried Mr. Bishopriggs, addressing the bell through the door. "Ye're waur than a woman when ye aince begin!"

The bell—like the woman—went on again. Mr. Bishopriggs, equally pertinacious, went on with his toddy.

"Ay! ay! ye may e'en ring yer heart out—but ye won't part a Scotchman from his glass. It's maybe the end of their dinner they'll be wantin'. Sir Paitrick cam' in at the fair beginning of it, and spoilt the collops, like the dour deevil he is!" The bell rang for the third time. "Ay! ay! ring awa'! I doot yon young gentleman's little better than a belly-god—there's a scandalous haste to comfort the carnal part o' him in a' this ringin'! He knows naething o' wine," added Mr. Bishopriggs, on whose mind Arnold's discovery of the watered sherry still dwelt unpleasantly.

The lightning quickened, and lit the sitting-room horribly with its lurid glare; the thunder rolled nearer and nearer over the black gulf of the moor. Arnold had just raised his hand to ring for the fourth time, when the inevitable knock was heard at the door. It was useless to say "come in." The immutable laws of Bishopriggs had decided that a second knock was necessary. Storm or no storm, the second knock came—and then, and not till then, the sage appeared, with the dish of untasted "collops" in his hand.

"Candles!" said Arnold.

Mr. Bishopriggs set the "collops" (in the language of England, minced meat) upon the table, lit the candles on the mantle-piece, faced about with the fire of recent toddy flaming in his nose, and waited for further orders, before he went back to his second glass. Anne declined to return to the dinner. Arnold ordered Mr. Bishopriggs to close the shutters, and sat down to dine by himself.

"It looks greasy, and smells greasy," he said to Anne, turning over the collops with a spoon. "I won't be ten minutes dining. Will you have some tea?"

Anne declined again.

Arnold tried her once more. "What shall we do to get through the evening?"

"Do what you like," she answered, resignedly.

Arnold's mind was suddenly illuminated by an idea.

"I have got it!" he exclaimed. "We'll kill the time as our cabin-passengers used to kill it at sea." He looked over his shoulder at Mr. Bishopriggs. "Waiter! bring a pack of cards."

"What's that ye're wantin'?" asked Mr. Bishopriggs, doubting the evidence of his own senses.

"A pack of cards," repeated Arnold.

"Cairds?" echoed Mr. Bishopriggs. "A pack o' cairds? The deevil's allegories in the deevil's own colors—red and black! I wunna execute yer order. For yer ain saul's sake, I wunna do it. Ha' ye lived to your time o' life, and are ye no' awakened yet to the awfu' seenfulness o' gamblin' wi' the cairds?"

"Just as you please," returned Arnold. "You will find me awakened—when I go away—to the awful folly of feeing a waiter."

"Does that mean that ye're bent on the cairds?" asked Mr. Bishopriggs, suddenly betraying signs of worldly anxiety in his look and manner.

"Yes—that means I am bent on the cards."

"I tak' up my testimony against 'em—but I'm no' telling ye that I canna lay my hand on 'em if I like. What do they say in my country? 'Him that will to Coupar, maun to Coupar.' And what do they say in your country? 'Needs must when the deevil drives.'" With that excellent reason for turning his back on his own principles, Mr. Bishopriggs shuffled out of the room to fetch the cards.

The dresser-drawer in the pantry contained a choice selection of miscellaneous objects—a pack of cards being among them. In searching for the cards, the wary hand of the head-waiter came in contact with a morsel of crumpled-up paper. He drew it out, and recognized the letter which he had picked up in the sitting-room some hours since.

"Ay! ay! I'll do weel, I trow, to look at this while my mind's runnin' on it," said Mr. Bishopriggs. "The cairds may e'en find their way to the parlor by other hands than mine."

He forthwith sent the cards to Arnold by his second in command, closed the pantry door, and carefully smoothed out the crumpled sheet of paper on which the two letters were written. This done, he trimmed his candle, and began with the letter in ink, which occupied the first three pages of the sheet of note-paper.

It ran thus:

"WINDYGATES HOUSE, August 12, 1868.

"GEOFFREY DELAMAYN,—I have waited in the hope that you would ride over from your brother's place, and see me—and I have waited in vain. Your conduct to me is cruelty itself; I will bear it no longer. Consider! in your own interests, consider—before you drive the miserable woman who has trusted you to despair. You have promised me marriage by all that is sacred. I claim your promise. I insist on nothing less than to be what you vowed I should be—what I have waited all this weary time to be—what I am, in the sight of Heaven, your wedded wife. Lady Lundie gives a lawn-party here on the 14th. I know you have been asked. I expect you to accept her invitation. If I don't see you, I won't answer for what may happen. My mind is made up to endure this suspense no longer. Oh, Geoffrey, remember the past! Be faithful—be just—to your loving wife,

"ANNE SILVESTER."

Mr. Bishopriggs paused. His commentary on the correspondence, so far, was simple enough. "Hot words (in ink) from the leddy to the gentleman!" He ran his eye over the second letter, on the fourth page of the paper, and added, cynically, "A trifle caulder (in pencil) from the gentleman to the leddy! The way o' the warld, Sirs! From the time o' Adam downwards, the way o' the warld!"

The second letter ran thus:

"DEAR ANNE,—Just called to London to my father. They have telegraphed him in a bad way. Stop where you are, and I will write you. Trust the bearer. Upon my soul, I'll keep my promise. Your loving husband that is to be,

"GEOFFREY DELAMAYN."

WINDYGATES HOUSE, Augt. 14, 4 P. M.

"In a mortal hurry. Train starts at 4.30."

There it ended!

"Who are the pairties in the parlor? Is ane o' them 'Silvester?' and t'other 'Delamayn?'" pondered Mr. Bishopriggs, slowly folding the letter up again in its original form. "Hech, Sirs! what, being intairpreted, may a' this mean?"

He mixed himself a second glass of toddy, as an aid to reflection, and sat sipping the liquor, and twisting and turning the letter in his gouty fingers. It was not easy to see his way to the true connection between the lady and gentleman in the parlor and the two letters now in his own possession. They might be themselves the writers of the letters, or they might be only friends of the writers. Who was to decide?

In the first case, the lady's object would appear to have been as good as gained; for the two had certainly asserted themselves to be man and wife, in his own presence, and in the presence of the landlady. In the second case, the correspondence so carelessly thrown aside might, for all a stranger knew to the contrary, prove to be of some importance in the future. Acting on this latter view, Mr. Bishopriggs—whose past experience as "a bit clerk body," in Sir Patrick's chambers, had made a man of business of him—produced his pen and ink, and indorsed the letter with a brief dated statement of the circumstances under which he had found it. "I'll do weel to keep the Doecument," he thought to himself. "Wha knows but there'll be a reward offered for it ane o' these days? Eh! eh! there may be the warth o' a fi' pun' note in this, to a puir lad like me!"

With that comforting reflection, he drew out a battered tin cash-box from the inner recesses of the drawer, and locked up the stolen correspondence to bide its time.

The storm rose higher and higher as the evening advanced.

In the sitting-room, the state of affairs, perpetually changing, now presented itself under another new aspect.

Arnold had finished his dinner, and had sent it away. He had next drawn a side-table up to the sofa on which Anne lay—had shuffled the pack of cards—and was now using all his powers of persuasion to induce her to try one game at Ecarte with him, by way of diverting her attention from the tumult of the storm. In sheer weariness, she gave up contesting the matter; and, raising herself languidly on the sofa, said she would try to play. "Nothing can make matters worse than they are," she thought, despairingly, as Arnold dealt the cards for her. "Nothing can justify my inflicting my own wretchedness on this kind-hearted boy!"

Two worse players never probably sat down to a game. Anne's attention perpetually wandered; and Anne's companion was, in all human probability, the most incapable card-player in Europe.

Anne turned up the trump—the nine of Diamonds. Arnold looked at his hand—and "proposed." Anne declined to change the cards. Arnold announced, with undiminished good-humor, that he saw his way clearly, now, to losing the game, and then played his first card—the Queen of Trumps!

Anne took it with the King, and forgot to declare the King. She played the ten of Trumps.

Arnold unexpectedly discovered the eight of Trumps in his hand. "What a pity!" he said, as he played it. "Hullo! you haven't marked the King! I'll do it for you. That's two—no, three—to you. I said I should lose the game. Couldn't be expected to do any thing (could I?) with such a hand as mine. I've lost every thing now I've lost my trumps. You to play."

Anne looked at her hand. At the same moment the lightning flashed into the room through the ill-closed shutters; the roar of the thunder burst over the house, and shook it to its foundation. The screaming of some hysterical female tourist, and the barking of a dog, rose shrill from the upper floor of the inn. Anne's nerves could support it no longer. She flung her cards on the table, and sprang to her feet.

"I can play no more," she said. "Forgive me—I am quite unequal to it. My head burns! my heart stifles me!"

She began to pace the room again. Aggravated by the effect of the storm on her nerves, her first vague distrust of the false position into which she and Arnold had allowed themselves to drift had strengthened, by this time, into a downright horror of their situation which was not to be endured. Nothing could justify such a risk as the risk they were now running! They had dined together like married people—and there they were, at that moment, shut in together, and passing the evening like man and wife!

"Oh, Mr. Brinkworth!" she pleaded. "Think—for Blanche's sake, think—is there no way out of this?"

Arnold was quietly collecting the scattered cards.

"Blanche, again?" he said, with the most exasperating composure. "I wonder how she feels, in this storm?"

In Anne's excited state, the reply almost maddened her. She turned from Arnold, and hurried to the door.

"I don't care!" she cried, wildly. "I won't let this deception go on. I'll do what I ought to have done before. Come what may of it, I'll tell the landlady the truth!"

She had opened the door, and was on the point of stepping into the passage—when she stopped, and started violently. Was it possible, in that dreadful weather, that she had actually heard the sound of carriage wheels on the strip of paved road outside the inn?

Yes! others had heard the sound too. The hobbling figure of Mr. Bishopriggs passed her in the passage, making for the house door. The hard voice of the landlady rang through the inn, ejaculating astonishment in broad Scotch. Anne closed the sitting-room door again, and turned to Arnold—who had risen, in surprise, to his feet.

"Travelers!" she exclaimed. "At this time!"

"And in this weather!" added Arnold.

"Can it be Geoffrey?" she asked—going back to the old vain delusion that he might yet feel for her, and return.

Arnold shook his head. "Not Geoffrey. Whoever else it may be—not Geoffrey!"

Mrs. Inchbare suddenly entered the room—with her cap-ribbons flying, her eyes staring, and her bones looking harder than ever.

"Eh, mistress!" she said to Anne. "Wha do ye think has driven here to see ye, from Windygates Hoose, and been owertaken in the storm?"

Anne was speechless. Arnold put the question: "Who is it?"

"Wha is't?" repeated Mrs. Inchbare. "It's joost the bonny young leddy—Miss Blanche hersel'."

An irrepressible cry of horror burst from Anne. The landlady set it down to the lightning, which flashed into the room again at the same moment.

"Eh, mistress! ye'll find Miss Blanche a bit baulder than to skirl at a flash o' lightning, that gait! Here she is, the bonny birdie!" exclaimed Mrs. Inchbare, deferentially backing out into the passage again.

Blanche's voice reached them, calling for Anne.

Anne caught Arnold by the hand and wrung it hard. "Go!" she whispered. The next instant she was at the mantle-piece, and had blown out both the candles.

Another flash of lightning came through the darkness, and showed Blanche's figure standing at the door.

CHAPTER THE THIRTEENTH.

BLANCHE.

MRS. INCHBARE was the first person who acted in the emergency. She called for lights; and sternly rebuked the house-maid, who brought them, for not having closed the house door. "Ye feckless ne'er-do-weel!" cried the landlady; "the wind's blawn the candles oot."

The woman declared (with perfect truth) that the door had been closed. An awkward dispute might have ensued if Blanche had not diverted Mrs. Inchbare's attention to herself. The appearance of the lights disclosed her, wet through with her arms round Anne's neck. Mrs.

Inchbare digressed at once to the pressing question of changing the young lady's clothes, and gave Anne the opportunity of looking round her, unobserved. Arnold had made his escape before the candles had been brought in.

In the mean time Blanche's attention was absorbed in her own dripping skirts.

"Good gracious! I'm absolutely distilling rain from every part of me. And I'm making you, Anne, as wet as I am! Lend me some dry things. You can't? Mrs. Inchbare, what does your experience suggest? Which had I better do? Go to bed while my clothes are being dried? or borrow from your wardrobe—though you are a head and shoulders taller than I am?"

Mrs. Inchbare instantly bustled out to fetch the choicest garments that her wardrobe could produce. The moment the door had closed on her Blanche looked round the room in her turn.

The rights of affection having been already asserted, the claims of curiosity naturally pressed for satisfaction next.

"Somebody passed me in the dark," she whispered. "Was it your husband? I'm dying to be introduced to him. And, oh my dear! what is your married name?"

Anne answered, coldly, "Wait a little. I can't speak about it yet."

"Are you ill?" asked Blanche.

"I am a little nervous."

"Has any thing unpleasant happened between you and my uncle? You have seen him, haven't you?"

"Yes."

"Did he give you my message?"

"He gave me your message.—Blanche! you promised him to stay at Windygates. Why, in the name of heaven, did you come here to-night?"

"If you were half as fond of me as I am of you," returned Blanche, "you wouldn't ask that. I tried hard to keep my promise, but I couldn't do it. It was all very well, while my uncle was laying down the law—with Lady Lundie in a rage, and the dogs barking, and the doors banging, and all that. The excitement kept me up. But when my uncle had gone, and the dreadful gray, quiet, rainy evening came, and it had all calmed down again, there was no bearing it. The house—without you—was like a tomb. If I had had Arnold with me I might have done very well. But I was all by myself. Think of that! Not a soul to speak to! There wasn't a horrible thing that could possibly happen to you that I didn't fancy was going to happen. I went into your empty room and looked at your things. That settled it, my darling! I rushed down stairs—carried away, positively carried away, by an Impulse beyond human resistance. How could I help it? I ask any reasonable person how could I help it? I ran to the stables and found Jacob. Impulse—all impulse! I said, 'Get the pony-chaise—I must have a drive—I don't care if it rains—you come with me.' All in a breath, and all impulse! Jacob behaved like an angel. He said, 'All right, miss.' I am perfectly certain Jacob would die for me if I asked him. He is drinking hot grog at this moment, to prevent him from catching cold, by my express orders. He had the pony-chaise out in two minutes; and off we went. Lady Lundie, my dear, prostrate in her own room—too much sal volatile. I hate her. The rain got worse. I didn't mind it. Jacob didn't mind it. The pony didn't mind it. They had both caught my impulse—especially the pony. It didn't come on to thunder till some time afterward; and then we were nearer Craig Fernie than Windygates—to say nothing of your being at one place and not at the other. The lightning was quite awful on the moor. If I had had one of the horses, he would have been frightened. The pony shook his darling little head, and dashed through it. He is to have beer. A mash with beer in it—by my express orders. When he has done we'll borrow a lantern, and go into the stable, and kiss him. In the mean time, my dear, here I am—wet through in a thunderstorm, which doesn't in the least matter—and determined to satisfy my own mind about you, which matters a great deal, and must and shall be done before I rest to-night!"

She turned Anne, by main force, as she spoke, toward the light of the candles.

Her tone changed the moment she looked at Anne's face.

"I knew it!" she said. "You would never have kept the most interesting event in your life a secret from me—you would never have written me such a cold formal letter as the letter you left in your room—if there had not been something wrong. I said so at the time. I know it now! Why has your husband forced you to leave Windygates at a moment's notice? Why does he slip out of the room in the dark, as if he was afraid of being seen? Anne! Anne! what has come to you? Why do you receive me in this way?"

At that critical moment Mrs. Inchbare reappeared, with the choicest selection of wearing apparel which her wardrobe could furnish. Anne hailed the welcome interruption. She took the candles, and led the way into the bedroom immediately.

"Change your wet clothes first," she said. "We can talk after that."

The bedroom door had hardly been closed a minute before there was a tap at it. Signing to Mrs. Inchbare not to interrupt the services she was rendering to Blanche, Anne passed quickly into the sitting-room, and closed the door behind her. To her infinite relief, she only found herself face to face with the discreet Mr. Bishopriggs.

"What do you want?" she asked.

The eye of Mr. Bishopriggs announced, by a wink, that his mission was of a confidential nature. The hand of Mr. Bishopriggs wavered; the breath of Mr. Bishopriggs exhaled a spirituous fume. He slowly produced a slip of paper, with some lines of writing on it.

"From ye ken who," he explained, jocosely. "A bit love-letter, I trow, from him that's dear to ye. Eh! he's an awfu' reprobate is him that's dear to ye. Miss, in the bedchamber there, will nae doot be the one he's jilted for you? I see it all—ye can't blind Me—I ha' been a frail person my ain self, in my time. Hech! he's safe and sound, is the reprobate. I ha' lookit after a' his little creature-comforts—I'm joost a fether to him, as well as a fether to you. Trust Bishopriggs—when puir human nature wants a bit pat on the back, trust Bishopriggs."

While the sage was speaking these comfortable words, Anne was reading the lines traced on the paper. They were signed by Arnold; and they ran thus:

"I am in the smoking-room of the inn. It rests with you to say whether I must stop there. I don't believe Blanche would be jealous. If I knew how to explain my being at the inn without betraying the confidence which you and Geoffrey have placed in me, I wouldn't be away from her another moment. It does grate on me so! At the same time, I don't want to make your position harder than it is. Think of yourself first. I leave it in your hands. You have only to say,

Wait, by the bearer—and I shall understand that I am to stay where I am till I hear from you again."

Anne looked up from the message.

"Ask him to wait," she said; "and I will send word to him again."

"Wi' mony loves and kisses," suggested Mr. Bishopriggs, as a necessary supplement to the message. "Eh! it comes as easy as A. B. C. to a man o' my experience. Ye can ha' nae better gae-between than yer puir servant to command, Sawmuel Bishopriggs. I understand ye baith pairfeckly." He laid his forefinger along his flaming nose, and withdrew.

Without allowing herself to hesitate for an instant, Anne opened the bedroom door—with the resolution of relieving Arnold from the new sacrifice imposed on him by owning the truth.

"Is that you?" asked Blanche.

At the sound of her voice, Anne started back guiltily. "I'll be with you in a moment," she answered, and closed the door again between them.

No! it was not to be done. Something in Blanche's trivial question—or something, perhaps, in the sight of Blanche's face—roused the warning instinct in Anne, which silenced her on the very brink of the disclosure. At the last moment the iron chain of circumstances made itself felt, binding her without mercy to the hateful, the degrading deceit. Could she own the truth, about Geoffrey and herself, to Blanche? and, without owning it, could she explain and justify Arnold's conduct in joining her privately at Craig Fernie? A shameful confession made to an innocent girl; a risk of fatally shaking Arnold's place in Blanche's estimation; a scandal at the inn, in the disgrace of which the others would be involved with herself—this was the price at which she must speak, if she followed her first impulse, and said, in so many words, "Arnold is here."

It was not to be thought of. Cost what it might in present wretchedness—end how it might, if the deception was discovered in the future—Blanche must be kept in ignorance of the truth, Arnold must be kept in hiding until she had gone.

Anne opened the door for the second time, and went in.

The business of the toilet was standing still. Blanche was in confidential communication with Mrs. Inchbare. At the moment when Anne entered the room she was eagerly questioning the landlady about her friend's "invisible husband"—she was just saying, "Do tell me! what is he like?"

The capacity for accurate observation is a capacity so uncommon, and is so seldom associated, even where it does exist, with the equally rare gift of accurately describing the thing or the person observed, that Anne's dread of the consequences if Mrs. Inchbare was allowed time to comply with Blanches request, was, in all probability, a dread misplaced. Right or wrong, however, the alarm that she felt hurried her into taking measures for dismissing the landlady on the spot. "We mustn't keep you from your occupations any longer," she said to Mrs. Inchbare. "I will give Miss Lundie all the help she needs."

Barred from advancing in one direction, Blanche's curiosity turned back, and tried in another. She boldly addressed herself to Anne.

"I must know something about him," she said. "Is he shy before strangers? I heard you whispering with him on the other side of the door. Are you jealous, Anne? Are you afraid I shall fascinate him in this dress?"

Blanche, in Mrs. Inchbare's best gown—an ancient and high-waisted silk garment, of the hue called "bottle-green," pinned up in front, and trailing far behind her—with a short, orange-colored shawl over her shoulders, and a towel tied turban fashion round her head, to dry her wet hair, looked at once the strangest and the prettiest human anomaly that ever was seen. "For heaven's sake," she said, gayly, "don't tell your husband I am in Mrs. Inchbare's clothes! I want to appear suddenly, without a word to warn him of what a figure I am! I should have nothing left to wish for in this world," she added, "if Arnold could only see me now!"

Looking in the glass, she noticed Anne's face reflected behind her, and started at the sight of it.

"What is the matter?" she asked. "Your face frightens me."

It was useless to prolong the pain of the inevitable misunderstanding between them. The one course to take was to silence all further inquiries then and there. Strongly as she felt this, Anne's inbred loyalty to Blanche still shrank from deceiving her to her face. "I might write it," she thought. "I can't say it, with Arnold Brinkworth in the same house with her!" Write it? As she reconsidered the word, a sudden idea struck her. She opened the bedroom door, and led the way back into the sitting-room.

"Gone again!" exclaimed Blanche, looking uneasily round the empty room. "Anne! there's something so strange in all this, that I neither can, nor will, put up with your silence any longer. It's not just, it's not kind, to shut me out of your confidence, after we have lived together like sisters all our lives!"

Anne sighed bitterly, and kissed her on the forehead. "You shall know all I can tell you—all I dare tell you," she said, gently. "Don't reproach me. It hurts me more than you think."

She turned away to the side table, and came back with a letter in her hand. "Read that," she said, and handed it to Blanche.

Blanche saw her own name, on the address, in the handwriting of Anne.

"What does this mean?" she asked.

"I wrote to you, after Sir Patrick had left me," Anne replied. "I meant you to have received my letter to-morrow, in time to prevent any little imprudence into which your anxiety might hurry you. All that I can say to you is said there. Spare me the distress of speaking. Read it, Blanche."

Blanche still held the letter, unopened.

"A letter from you to me! when we are both together, and both alone in the same room! It's worse than formal, Anne! It's as if there was a quarrel between us. Why should it distress you to speak to me?"

Anne's eyes dropped to the ground. She pointed to the letter for the second time.

Blanche broke the seal.

She passed rapidly over the opening sentences, and devoted all her attention to the second paragraph.

"And now, my love, you will expect me to atone for the surprise and distress that I have caused you, by explaining what my situation really is, and by telling you all my plans for the future. Dearest Blanche! don't think me untrue to the affection we bear toward each other—don't think there is any change in my heart toward you—believe only that I am a very unhappy woman, and that I am in a position which forces me, against my own will, to be silent about myself. Silent even to you, the sister of my love—the one person in the world who is dearest to me! A time may come when I shall be able to open my heart to you. Oh, what good it will do me! what a relief it will be! For the present, I must be silent. For the present, we must be parted. God knows what it costs me to write this. I think of the dear old days that are gone; I remember how I promised your mother to be a sister to you, when her kind eyes looked at me, for the last time—your mother, who was an angel from heaven to mine! All this comes back on me now, and breaks my heart. But it must be! my own Blanche, for the present, it must be! I will write often—I will think of you, my darling, night and day, till a happier future unites us again. God bless you, my dear one! And God help me!"

Blanche silently crossed the room to the sofa on which Anne was sitting, and stood there for a moment, looking at her. She sat down, and laid her head on Anne's shoulder. Sorrowfully and quietly, she put the letter into her bosom—and took Anne's hand, and kissed it.

"All my questions are answered, dear. I will wait your time."

It was simply, sweetly, generously said.

Anne burst into tears.

The rain still fell, but the storm was dying away.

Blanche left the sofa, and, going to the window, opened the shutters to look out at the night. She suddenly came back to Anne.

"I see lights," she said—"the lights of a carriage coming up out of the darkness of the moor. They are sending after me, from Windygates. Go into the bedroom. It's just possible Lady Lundie may have come for me herself."

The ordinary relations of the two toward each other were completely reversed. Anne was like a child in Blanche's hands. She rose, and withdrew.

Left alone, Blanche took the letter out of her bosom, and read it again, in the interval of waiting for the carriage.

The second reading confirmed her in a resolution which she had privately taken, while she had been sitting by Anne on the sofa—a resolution destined to lead to far more serious results in the future than any previsions of hers could anticipate. Sir Patrick was the one person she knew on whose discretion and experience she could implicitly rely. She determined, in Anne's own interests, to take her uncle into her confidence, and to tell him all that had happened at the inn "I'll first make him forgive me," thought Blanche. "And then I'll see if he thinks as I do, when I tell him about Anne."

The carriage drew up at the door; and Mrs. Inchbare showed in—not Lady Lundie, but Lady Lundie's maid.

The woman's account of what had happened at Windygates was simple enough. Lady Lundie had, as a matter of course, placed the right interpretation on Blanche's abrupt departure in the pony-chaise, and had ordered the carriage, with the firm determination of following her step-daughter herself. But the agitations and anxieties of the day had proved too much for her. She had been seized by one of the attacks of giddiness to which she was always subject after excessive mental irritation; and, eager as she was (on more accounts than one) to go to the inn herself, she had been compelled, in Sir Patrick's absence, to commit the pursuit of Blanche to her own maid, in whose age and good sense she could place every confidence. The woman seeing the state of the weather—had thoughtfully brought a box with her, containing a change of wearing apparel. In offering it to Blanche, she added, with all due respect, that she had full powers from her mistress to go on, if necessary, to the shooting-cottage, and to place the matter in Sir Patrick's hands. This said, she left it to her young lady to decide for herself, whether she would return to Windygates, under present circumstances, or not.

Blanche took the box from the woman's hands, and joined Anne in the bedroom, to dress herself for the drive home.

"I am going back to a good scolding," she said. "But a scolding is no novelty in my experience of Lady Lundie. I'm not uneasy about that, Anne—I'm uneasy about you. Can I be sure of one thing—do you stay here for the present?"

The worst that could happen at the inn had happened. Nothing was to be gained now—and every thing might be lost—by leaving the place at which Geoffrey had promised to write to her. Anne answered that she proposed remaining at the inn for the present.

"You promise to write to me?"

"Yes."

"If there is any thing I can do for you—?"

"There is nothing, my love."

"There may be. If you want to see me, we can meet at Windygates without being discovered. Come at luncheon-time—go around by the shrubbery—and step in at the library window. You know as well as I do there is nobody in the library at that hour. Don't say it's impossible—you don't know what may happen. I shall wait ten minutes every day on the chance of seeing you. That's settled—and it's settled that you write. Before I go, darling, is there any thing else we can think of for the future?"

At those words Anne suddenly shook off the depression that weighed on her. She caught Blanche in her arms, she held Blanche to her bosom with a fierce energy. "Will you always be to me, in the future, what you are now?" she asked, abruptly. "Or is the time coming when you will hate me?" She prevented any reply by a kiss—and pushed Blanche toward the door. "We have had a happy time together in the years that are gone," she said, with a farewell wave of her hand. "Thank God for that! And never mind the rest."

She threw open the bedroom door, and called to the maid, in the sitting-room. "Miss Lundie is waiting for you." Blanche pressed her hand, and left her.

Anne waited a while in the bedroom, listening to the sound made by the departure of the carriage from the inn door. Little by little, the tramp of the horses and the noise of the rolling wheels lessened and lessened. When the last faint sounds were lost in silence she stood for a moment thinking—then, rousing on a sudden, hurried into the sitting-room, and rang the bell.

"I shall go mad," she said to herself, "if I stay here alone."

Even Mr. Bishopriggs felt the necessity of being silent when he stood face to face with her on answering the bell.

"I want to speak to him. Send him here instantly."

Mr. Bishopriggs understood her, and withdrew.

Arnold came in.

"Has she gone?" were the first words he said.

"She has gone. She won't suspect you when you see her again. I have told her nothing. Don't ask me for my reasons!"

"I have no wish to ask you."

"Be angry with me, if you like!"

"I have no wish to be angry with you."

He spoke and looked like an altered man. Quietly seating himself at the table, he rested his head on his hand—and so remained silent. Anne was taken completely by surprise. She drew near, and looked at him curiously. Let a woman's mood be what it may, it is certain to feel the influence of any change for which she is unprepared in the manner of a man—when that man interests her. The cause of this is not to be found in the variableness of her humor. It is far more probably to be traced to the noble abnegation of Self, which is one of the grandest—and to the credit of woman be it said—one of the commonest virtues of the sex. Little by little, the sweet feminine charm of Anne's face came softly and sadly back. The inbred nobility of the woman's nature answered the call which the man had unconsciously made on it. She touched Arnold on the shoulder.

"This has been hard on you," she said. "And I am to blame for it. Try and forgive me, Mr. Brinkworth. I am sincerely sorry. I wish with all my heart I could comfort you!"

"Thank you, Miss Silvester. It was not a very pleasant feeling, to be hiding from Blanche as if I was afraid of her—and it's set me thinking, I suppose, for the first time in my life. Never mind. It's all over now. Can I do any thing for you?"

"What do you propose doing to-night?"

"What I have proposed doing all along—my duty by Geoffrey. I have promised him to see you through your difficulties here, and to provide for your safety till he comes back. I can only make sure of doing that by keeping up appearances, and staying in the sitting-room to-night. When we next meet it will be under pleasanter circumstances, I hope. I shall always be glad to think that I was of some service to you. In the mean time I shall be most likely away to-morrow morning before you are up."

Anne held out her hand to take leave. Nothing could undo what had been done. The time for warning and remonstrance had passed away.

"You have not befriended an ungrateful woman," she said. "The day may yet come, Mr. Brinkworth, when I shall prove it."

"I hope not, Miss Silvester. Good-by, and good luck!"

She withdrew into her own room. Arnold locked the sitting-room door, and stretched himself on the sofa for the night.

The morning was bright, the air was delicious after the storm.

Arnold had gone, as he had promised, before Anne was out of her room. It was understood at the inn that important business had unexpectedly called him south. Mr. Bishopriggs had been presented with a handsome gratuity; and Mrs. Inchbare had been informed that the rooms were taken for a week certain.

In every quarter but one the march of events had now, to all appearance, fallen back into a quiet course. Arnold was on his way to his estate; Blanche was safe at Windygates; Anne's residence at the inn was assured for a week to come. The one present doubt was the doubt which hung over Geoffrey's movements. The one event still involved in darkness turned on the question of life or death waiting for solution in London—otherwise, the question of Lord Holchester's health. Taken by itself, the alternative, either way, was plain enough. If my lord lived—Geoffrey would be free to come back, and marry her privately in Scotland. If my lord died—Geoffrey would be free to send for her, and marry her publicly in London. But could Geoffrey be relied on?

Anne went out on to the terrace-ground in front of the inn. The cool morning breeze blew steadily. Towering white clouds sailed in grand procession over the heavens, now obscuring, and now revealing the sun. Yellow light and purple shadow chased each other over the broad brown surface of the moor—even as hope and fear chased each other over Anne's mind, brooding on what might come to her with the coming time.

She turned away, weary of questioning the impenetrable future, and went back to the inn.

Crossing the hall she looked at the clock. It was past the hour when the train from Perthshire was due in London. Geoffrey and his brother were, at that moment, on their way to Lord Holchester's house.

THIRD SCENE.—LONDON.

CHAPTER THE FOURTEENTH.

GEOFFREY AS A LETTER-WRITER.

LORD HOLCHESTER'S servants—with the butler at their head—were on the look-out for Mr. Julius Delamayn's arrival from Scotland. The appearance of the two brothers together took the whole domestic establishment by surprise. Inquiries were addressed to the butler by Julius; Geoffrey standing by, and taking no other than a listener's part in the proceedings.

"Is my father alive?"

"His lordship, I am rejoiced to say, has astonished the doctors, Sir. He rallied last night in the most wonderful way. If things go on for the next eight-and-forty hours as they are going now, my lord's recovery is considered certain."

"What was the illness?"

"A paralytic stroke, Sir. When her ladyship telegraphed to you in Scotland the doctors had given his lordship up."

"Is my mother at home?"

"Her ladyship is at home to you, Sir."'

The butler laid a special emphasis on the personal pronoun. Julius turned to his brother. The change for the better in the state of Lord Holchester's health made Geoffrey's position, at that moment, an embarrassing one. He had been positively forbidden to enter the house. His one excuse for setting that prohibitory sentence at defiance rested on the assumption that his father was actually dying. As matters now stood, Lord Holchester's order remained in full force. The under-servants in the hall (charged to obey that order as they valued their places) looked from "Mr. Geoffrey" to the butler, The butler looked from "Mr. Geoffrey" to "Mr. Julius." Julius looked at his brother. There was an awkward pause. The position of the second son was the position of a wild beast in the house—a creature to be got rid of, without risk to yourself, if you only knew how.

Geoffrey spoke, and solved the problem

"Open the door, one of you fellows," he said to the footmen. "I'm off."

"Wait a minute," interposed his brother. "It will be a sad disappointment to my mother to know that you have been here, and gone away again without seeing her. These are no ordinary circumstances, Geoffrey. Come up stairs with me—I'll take it on myself."

"I'm blessed if I take it on myself!" returned Geoffrey. "Open the door!"

"Wait here, at any rate," pleaded Julius, "till I can send you down a message."

"Send your message to Nagle's Hotel. I'm at home at Nagle's—I'm not at home here."

At that point the discussion was interrupted by the appearance of a little terrier in the hall. Seeing strangers, the dog began to bark. Perfect tranquillity in the house had been absolutely insisted on by the doctors; and the servants, all trying together to catch the animal and quiet him, simply aggravated the noise he was making. Geoffrey solved this problem also in his own decisive way. He swung round as the dog was passing him, and kicked it with his heavy boot. The little creature fell on the spot, whining piteously. "My lady's pet dog!" exclaimed the butler. "You've broken its ribs, Sir." "I've broken it of barking, you mean," retorted Geoffrey. "Ribs be hanged!" He turned to his brother. "That settles it," he said, jocosely. "I'd better defer the pleasure of calling on dear mamma till the next opportunity. Ta-ta, Julius. You know where to find me. Come, and dine. We'll give you a steak at Nagle's that will make a man of you."

He went out. The tall footmen eyed his lordship's second son with unaffected respect. They had seen him, in public, at the annual festival of the Christian-Pugilistic-Association, with "the gloves" on. He could have beaten the biggest man in the hall within an inch of his life in three minutes. The porter bowed as he threw open the door. The whole interest and attention of the domestic establishment then present was concentrated on Geoffrey. Julius went up stairs to his mother without attracting the slightest notice.

The month was August. The streets were empty. The vilest breeze that blows—a hot east wind in London—was the breeze abroad on that day. Even Geoffrey appeared to feel the influence of the weather as the cab carried him from his father's door to the hotel. He took off his hat, and unbuttoned his waistcoat, and lit his everlasting pipe, and growled and grumbled between his teeth in the intervals of smoking. Was it only the hot wind that wrung from him these demonstrations of discomfort? Or was there some secret anxiety in his mind which assisted the depressing influences of the day? There was a secret anxiety in his mind. And the name of it was—Anne.

As things actually were at that moment, what course was he to take with the unhappy woman who was waiting to hear from him at the Scotch inn?

To write? or not to write? That was the question with Geoffrey.

The preliminary difficulty, relating to addressing a letter to Anne at the inn, had been already provided for. She had decided—if it proved necessary to give her name, before Geoffrey joined her—to call herself Mrs., instead of Miss, Silvester. A letter addressed to "Mrs. Silvester" might be trusted to find its way to her without causing any embarrassment. The doubt was not here. The doubt lay, as usual, between two alternatives. Which course would it be wisest to take?—to inform Anne, by that day's post, that an interval of forty-eight hours must elapse before his father's recovery could be considered certain? Or to wait till the interval was over, and be guided by the result? Considering the alternatives in the cab, he decided that the wise course was to temporize with Anne, by reporting matters as they then stood.

Arrived at the hotel, he sat down to write the letter—doubted—and tore it up—doubted again—and began again—doubted once more—and tore up the second letter—rose to his feet—and owned to himself (in unprintable language) that he couldn't for the life of him decide which was safest—to write or to wait.

In this difficulty, his healthy physical instincts sent him to healthy physical remedies for relief. "My mind's in a muddle," said Geoffrey. "I'll try a bath."

It was an elaborate bath, proceeding through many rooms, and combining many postures and applications. He steamed. He plunged. He simmered. He stood under a pipe, and received a cataract of cold water on his head. He was laid on his back; he was laid on his stomach; he was respectfully pounded and kneaded, from head to foot, by the knuckles of accomplished practitioners. He came out of it all, sleek, clear rosy, beautiful. He returned to the hotel, and took up the writing materials—and behold the intolerable indecision seized him again, declining to be washed out! This time he laid it all to Anne. "That infernal woman will be the ruin of me," said Geoffrey, taking up his hat. "I must try the dumb-bells."

The pursuit of the new remedy for stimulating a sluggish brain took him to a public house, kept by the professional pedestrian who had the honor of training him when he contended at Athletic Sports.

"A private room and the dumb-bells!" cried Geoffrey. "The heaviest you have got."

He stripped himself of his upper clothing, and set to work, with the heavy weights in each hand, waving them up and down, and backward and forward, in every attainable variety of movement, till his magnificent muscles seemed on the point of starting through his sleek skin. Little by little his animal spirits roused themselves. The strong exertion intoxicated the strong man. In sheer excitement he swore cheerfully—invoking thunder and lightning, explosion and blood, in return for the compliments profusely paid to him by the pedestrian and the pedestrian's son. "Pen, ink, and paper!" he roared, when he could use the dumb-bells no longer. "My mind's made up; I'll write, and have done with it!" He sat down to his writing on the spot; actually finished the letter; another minute would have dispatched it to the post—and, in that minute, the maddening indecision took possession of him once more. He opened the letter again, read it over again, and tore it up again. "I'm out of my mind!" cried Geoffrey, fixing his big bewildered blue eyes fiercely on the professor who trained him. "Thunder and lightning! Explosion and blood! Send for Crouch."

Crouch (known and respected wherever English manhood is known and respected) was a retired prize-fighter. He appeared with the third and last remedy for clearing the mind known to the Honorable Geoffrey Delamayn—namely, two pair of boxing-gloves in a carpet-bag.

The gentleman and the prize-fighter put on the gloves, and faced each other in the classically correct posture of pugilistic defense. "None of your play, mind!" growled Geoffrey. "Fight, you beggar, as if you were in the Ring again with orders to win." No man knew better than the great and terrible Crouch what real fighting meant, and what heavy blows might be given even with such apparently harmless weapons as stuffed and padded gloves. He pretended, and only pretended, to comply with his patron's request. Geoffrey rewarded him for his polite forbearance by knocking him down. The great and terrible rose with unruffled composure. "Well hit, Sir!" he said. "Try it with the other hand now." Geoffrey's temper was not under similar control. Invoking everlasting destruction on the frequently-blackened eyes of Crouch, he threatened instant withdrawal of his patronage and support unless the polite pugilist hit, then and there, as hard as he could. The hero of a hundred fights quailed at the dreadful prospect. "I've got a family to support," remarked Crouch. "If you will have it, Sir—there it is!" The fall of Geoffrey followed, and shook the house. He was on his legs again in an instant—not satisfied even yet. "None of your body-hitting!" he roared. "Stick to my head. Thunder and lightning! explosion and blood! Knock it out of me! Stick to the head!" Obedient Crouch stuck to the head. The two gave and took blows which would have stunned—possibly have killed—any civilized member of the community. Now on one side of his patron's iron skull, and now on the other, the hammering of the prize-fighter's gloves fell, thump upon thump, horrible to hear—until even Geoffrey himself had had enough of it. "Thank you, Crouch," he said, speaking civilly to the man for the first time. "That will do. I feel nice and clear again." He shook his head two or three times, he was rubbed down like a horse by the professional runner; he drank a mighty draught of malt liquor; he recovered his good-humor as if by magic. "Want the pen and ink, Sir?" inquired his pedestrian host. "Not I!" answered Geoffrey. "The muddle's out of me now. Pen and ink be hanged! I shall look up some of our fellows, and go to the play." He left the public house in the happiest condition of mental calm. Inspired by the stimulant application of Crouch's gloves, his torpid cunning had been shaken up into excellent working order at last. Write to Anne? Who but a fool would write to such a woman as that until he was forced to it? Wait and see what the chances of the next eight-and-forty hours might bring forth, and then write to her, or desert her, as the event might decide. It lay in a nut-shell, if you could only see it. Thanks to Crouch, he did see it—and so away in a pleasant temper for a dinner with "our fellows" and an evening at the play!

CHAPTER THE FIFTEENTH.

GEOFFREY IN THE MARRIAGE MARKET.

THE interval of eight-and-forty hours passed—without the occurrence of any personal communication between the two brothers in that time.

Julius, remaining at his father's house, sent brief written bulletins of Lord Holchester's health to his brother at the hotel. The first bulletin said, "Going on well. Doctors satisfied." The second was firmer in tone. "Going on excellently. Doctors very sanguine." The third was the most explicit of all. "I am to see my father in an hour from this. The doctors answer for his recovery. Depend on my putting in a good word for you, if I can; and wait to hear from me further at the hotel."

Geoffrey's face darkened as he read the third bulletin. He called once more for the hated writing materials. There could be no doubt now as to the necessity of communicating with Anne. Lord Holchester's recovery had put him back again in the same critical position which he had occupied at Windygates. To keep Anne from committing some final act of despair, which would connect him with a public scandal, and ruin him so far as his expectations from his father were concerned, was, once more, the only safe policy that Geoffrey could pursue. His letter began and ended in twenty words:

"DEAR ANNE,—Have only just heard that my father is turning the corner. Stay where you are. Will write again."

Having dispatched this Spartan composition by the post, Geoffrey lit his pipe, and waited the event of the interview between Lord Holchester and his eldest son.

Julius found his father alarmingly altered in personal appearance, but in full possession of his faculties nevertheless. Unable to return the pressure of his son's hand—unable even to turn in the bed without help—the hard eye of the old lawyer was as keen, the hard mind of the old lawyer was as clear, as ever. His grand ambition was to see Julius in Parliament. Julius was offering himself for election in Perthshire, by his father's express desire, at that moment. Lord Holchester entered eagerly into politics before his eldest son had been two minutes by his bedside.

"Much obliged, Julius, for your congratulations. Men of my sort are not easily killed. (Look at Brougham and Lyndhurst!) You won't be called to the Upper House yet. You will begin in the House of Commons—precisely as I wished. What are your prospects with the constituency? Tell me exactly how you stand, and where I can be of use to you."

"Surely, Sir, you are hardly recovered enough to enter on matters of business yet?"

"I am quite recovered enough. I want some present interest to occupy me. My thoughts are beginning to drift back to past times, and to things which are better forgotten." A sudden contraction crossed his livid face. He looked hard at his son, and entered abruptly on a new question. "Julius!" he resumed, "have you ever heard of a young woman named Anne Silvester?"

Julius answered in the negative. He and his wife had exchanged cards with Lady Lundie, and had excused themselves from accepting her invitation to the lawn-party. With the exception of Blanche, they were both quite ignorant of the persons who composed the family circle at Windygates.

"Make a memorandum of the name," Lord Holchester went on. "Anne Silvester. Her father and mother are dead. I knew her father in former times. Her mother was ill-used. It was a bad business. I have been thinking of it again, for the first time for many years. If the girl is alive and about the world she may remember our family name. Help her, Julius, if she ever wants help, and applies to you." The painful contraction passed across his face once more. Were his thoughts taking him back to the memorable summer evening at the Hampstead villa? Did he see the deserted woman swooning at his feet again? "About your election?" he asked, impatiently. "My mind is not used to be idle. Give it something to do."

Julius stated his position as plainly and as briefly as he could. The father found nothing to object to in the report—except the son's absence from the field of action. He blamed Lady Holchester for summoning Julius to London. He was annoyed at his son's being there, at the bedside, when he ought to have been addressing the electors. "It's inconvenient, Julius," he said, petulantly. "Don't you see it yourself?"

Having previously arranged with his mother to take the first opportunity that offered of risking a reference to Geoffrey, Julius decided to "see it" in a light for which his father was not prepared. The opportunity was before him. He took it on the spot.

"It is no inconvenience to me, Sir," he replied, "and it is no inconvenience to my brother either. Geoffrey was anxious about you too. Geoffrey has come to London with me."

Lord Holchester looked at his eldest son with a grimly-satirical expression of surprise.

"Have I not already told you," he rejoined, "that my mind is not affected by my illness? Geoffrey anxious about me! Anxiety is one of the civilized emotions. Man in his savage state is incapable of feeling it."

"My brother is not a savage, Sir."

"His stomach is generally full, and his skin is covered with linen and cloth, instead of red ochre and oil. So far, certainly, your brother is civilized. In all other respects your brother is a savage."

"I know what you mean, Sir. But there is something to be said for Geoffrey's way of life. He cultivates his courage and his strength. Courage and strength are fine qualities, surely, in their way?"

"Excellent qualities, as far as they go. If you want to know how far that is, challenge Geoffrey to write a sentence of decent English, and see if his courage doesn't fail him there. Give him his books to read for his degree, and, strong as he is, he will be taken ill at the sight of them. You wish me to see your brother. Nothing will induce me to see him, until his way of life (as you call it) is altered altogether. I have but one hope of its ever being altered now. It is barely possible that the influence of a sensible woman—possessed of such advantages of birth and fortune as may compel respect, even from a savage—might produce its effect on Geoffrey. If he wishes to find his way back into this house, let him find his way back into good society first, and bring me a daughter-in-law to plead his cause for him—whom his mother and I can respect and receive. When that happens, I shall begin to have some belief in Geoffrey. Until it does happen, don't introduce your brother into any future conversations which you may have with Me. To return to your election. I have some advice to give you before you go back. You will do well to go back to-night. Lift me up on the pillow. I shall speak more easily with my head high."

His son lifted him on the pillows, and once more entreated him to spare himself.

It was useless. No remonstrances shook the iron resolution of the man who had hewed his way through the rank and file of political humanity to his own high place apart from the rest. Helpless, ghastly, snatched out of the very jaws of death, there he lay, steadily distilling the clear common-sense which had won him all his worldly rewards into the mind of his son. Not a hint was missed, not a caution was forgotten, that could guide Julius safely through the miry political ways which he had trodden so safely and so dextrously himself. An hour more had passed before the impenetrable old man closed his weary eyes, and consented to take his nourishment and compose himself to rest. His last words, rendered barely articulate by exhaustion, still sang the praises of party manoeuvres and political strife. "It's a grand career! I miss the House of Commons, Julius, as I miss nothing else!"

Left free to pursue his own thoughts, and to guide his own movements, Julius went straight from Lord Holchester's bedside to Lady Holchester's boudoir.

"Has your father said any thing about Geoffrey?" was his mother's first question as soon as he entered the room.

"My father gives Geoffrey a last chance, if Geoffrey will only take it."

Lady Holchester's face clouded. "I know," she said, with a look of disappointment. "His last chance is to read for his degree. Hopeless, my dear. Quite hopeless! If it had only been something easier than that; something that rested with me—"

"It does rest with you," interposed Julius. "My dear mother!—can you believe it?—Geoffrey's last chance is (in one word) Marriage!"

"Oh, Julius! it's too good to be true!"

Julius repeated his father's own words. Lady Holchester looked twenty years younger as she listened. When he had done she rang the bell.

"No matter who calls," she said to the servant, "I am not at home." She turned to Julius, kissed him, and made a place for him on the sofa by her side. "Geoffrey shall take that chance," she said, gayly—"I will answer for it! I have three women in my mind, any one of whom would suit him. Sit down, my dear, and let us consider carefully which of the three will be most likely to attract Geoffrey, and to come up to your father's standard of what his daughter-in-law ought to be. When we have decided, don't trust to writing. Go yourself and see Geoffrey at his hotel."

Mother and son entered on their consultation—and innocently sowed the seeds of a terrible harvest to come.

CHAPTER THE SIXTEENTH.

GEOFFREY AS A PUBLIC CHARACTER.

TIME had advanced to after noon before the selection of Geoffrey's future wife was accomplished, and before the instructions of Geoffrey's brother were complete enough to justify the opening of the matrimonial negotiation at Nagle's Hotel.

"Don't leave him till you have got his promise," were Lady Holchester's last words when her son started on his mission.

"If Geoffrey doesn't jump at what I am going to offer him," was the son's reply, "I shall agree with my father that the case is hopeless; and I shall end, like my father, in giving Geoffrey up."

This was strong language for Julius to use. It was not easy to rouse the disciplined and equable temperament of Lord Holchester's eldest son. No two men were ever more thoroughly unlike each other than these two brothers. It is melancholy to acknowledge it of the blood relation of a "stroke oar," but it must be owned, in the interests of truth, that Julius cultivated his intelligence. This degenerate Briton could digest books—and couldn't digest beer. Could learn languages—and couldn't learn to row. Practiced the foreign vice of perfecting himself in the art of playing on a musical instrument and couldn't learn the English virtue of knowing a good horse when he saw him. Got through life. (Heaven only knows how!) without either a biceps or a betting-book. Had openly acknowledged, in English society, that he didn't think the barking of a pack of hounds the finest music in the world. Could go to foreign parts, and see a mountain which nobody had ever got to the top of yet—and didn't instantly feel his honor as an Englishman involved in getting to the top of it himself. Such people may, and do, exist among the inferior races of the Continent. Let us thank Heaven, Sir, that England never has been, and never will be, the right place for them!

Arrived at Nagle's Hotel, and finding nobody to inquire of in the hall, Julius applied to the young lady who sat behind the window of "the bar." The young lady was reading something so deeply interesting in the evening newspaper that she never even heard him. Julius went into the coffee-room.

The waiter, in his corner, was absorbed over a second newspaper. Three gentlemen, at three different tables, were absorbed in a third, fourth, and fifth newspaper. They all alike went on with their reading without noticing the entrance of the stranger. Julius ventured on disturbing the waiter by asking for Mr. Geoffrey Delamayn. At the sound of that illustrious name the waiter looked up with a start. "Are you Mr. Delamayn's brother, Sir?"

"Yes."

The three gentlemen at the tables looked up with a start. The light of Geoffrey's celebrity fell, reflected, on Geoffrey's brother, and made a public character of him.

"You'll find Mr. Geoffrey, Sir," said the waiter, in a flurried, excited manner, "at the Cock and Bottle, Putney."

"I expected to find him here. I had an appointment with him at this hotel."

The waiter opened his eyes on Julius with an expression of blank astonishment. "Haven't you heard the news, Sir?"

"No!"

"God bless my soul!" exclaimed the waiter—and offered the newspaper.

"God bless my soul!" exclaimed the three gentlemen—and offered the three newspapers.

"What is it?" asked Julius.

"What is it?" repeated the waiter, in a hollow voice. "The most dreadful thing that's happened in my time. It's all up, Sir, with the great Foot-Race at Fulham. Tinkler has gone stale."

The three gentlemen dropped solemnly back into their three chairs, and repeated the dreadful intelligence, in chorus—"Tinkler has gone stale."

A man who stands face to face with a great national disaster, and who doesn't understand it, is a man who will do wisely to hold his tongue and enlighten his mind without asking other people to help him. Julius accepted the waiter's newspaper, and sat down to make (if possible) two discoveries: First, as to whether "Tinkler" did, or did not, mean a man. Second, as to what particular form of human affliction you implied when you described that man as "gone stale."

There was no difficulty in finding the news. It was printed in the largest type, and was followed by a personal statement of the facts, taken one way—which was followed, in its turn, by another personal statement of the facts, taken in another way. More particulars, and further personal statements, were promised in later editions. The royal salute of British journalism thundered the announcement of Tinkler's staleness before a people prostrate on the national betting book.

Divested of exaggeration, the facts were few enough and simple enough. A famous Athletic Association of the North had challenged a famous Athletic Association of the South. The usual "Sports" were to take place—such as running, jumping, "putting" the hammer, throwing cricket-balls, and the like—and the whole was to wind up with a Foot-Race of unexampled length and difficulty in the annals of human achievement between the two best men on either side. "Tinkler" was the best man on the side of the South. "Tinkler" was backed in innumerable betting-books to win. And Tinkler's lungs had suddenly given way under stress of training! A prospect of witnessing a prodigious achievement in foot-racing, and (more important still) a prospect of winning and losing large sums of money, was suddenly withdrawn from the eyes of the British people. The "South" could produce no second opponent worthy of the North out of its own associated resources. Surveying the athletic world in general, but one man existed who might possibly replace "Tinkler"—and it was doubtful, in the last degree, whether he would consent to come forward under the circumstances. The name of that man—Julius read it with horror—was Geoffrey Delamayn.

Profound silence reigned in the coffee-room. Julius laid down the newspaper, and looked about him. The waiter was busy, in his corner, with a pencil and a betting-book. The three gentlemen were busy, at the three tables, with pencils and betting-books.

"Try and persuade him!" said the waiter, piteously, as Delamayn's brother rose to leave the room.

"Try and persuade him!" echoed the three gentlemen, as Delamayn's brother opened the door and went out.

Julius called a cab and told the driver (busy with a pencil and a betting-book) to go to the Cock and Bottle, Putney. The man brightened into a new being at the prospect. No need to hurry him; he drove, unasked, at the top of his horse's speed.

As the cab drew near to its destination the signs of a great national excitement appeared, and multiplied. The lips of a people pronounced, with a grand unanimity, the name of "Tinkler." The heart of a people hung suspended (mostly in the public houses) on the chances for and against the possibility of replacing "Tinkler" by another man. The scene in front of the inn was impressive in the highest degree. Even the London blackguard stood awed and quiet in the presence of the national calamity. Even the irrepressible man with the apron, who always turns up to sell nuts and sweetmeats in a crowd, plied his trade in silence, and found few indeed (to the credit of the nation be it spoken) who had the heart to crack a nut at such a time as this. The police were on the spot, in large numbers, and in mute sympathy with the people, touching to see. Julius, on being stopped at the door, mentioned his name—and received an ovation. His brother! oh, heavens, his brother! The people closed round him, the people shook hands with him, the people invoked blessings on his head. Julius was half suffocated, when the police rescued him, and landed him safe in the privileged haven on the inner side of the public house door. A deafening tumult broke out, as he entered, from the regions above stairs. A distant voice screamed, "Mind yourselves!" A hatless shouting man tore down through the people congregated on the stairs. "Hooray! Hooray! He's promised to do it! He's entered for the race!" Hundreds on hundreds of voices took up the cry. A roar of cheering burst from the people outside. Reporters for the newspapers raced, in frantic procession, out of the inn, and rushed into cabs to put the news in print. The hand of the landlord, leading Julius carefully up stairs by the arm, trembled with excitement. "His brother, gentlemen! his brother!" At those magic words a lane was made through the throng. At those magic words the closed door of the council-chamber flew open; and Julius found himself among the Athletes of his native country, in full parliament assembled. Is any description of them needed? The description of Geoffrey applies to them all. The manhood and muscle of England resemble the wool and mutton of England, in this respect, that there is about as much variety in a flock of athletes as in a flock of sheep. Julius looked about him, and saw the same man in the same dress, with the same health, strength, tone, tastes, habits, conversation, and pursuits, repeated infinitely in every part of the room. The din was deafening; the enthusiasm (to an uninitiated stranger) something at once hideous and terrifying to behold. Geoffrey had been lifted bodily on to the table, in his chair, so as to be visible to the whole room. They sang round him, they danced round him, they cheered round him, they swore round him. He was hailed, in maudlin terms of endearment, by grateful giants with tears in their eyes. "Dear old man!" "Glorious, noble, splendid, beautiful fellow!" They hugged him. They patted him on the back. They wrung his hands. They prodded and punched his muscles. They embraced the noble legs that were going to run the unexampled race. At the opposite end of the room, where it was physically impossible to get near the hero, the enthusiasm vented itself in feats of strength and acts of destruction. Hercules I. cleared a space with his elbows, and laid down—and Hercules II. took him up in his teeth. Hercules III. seized the poker from the fireplace, and broke it on his arm. Hercules IV. followed with the tongs, and shattered them on his neck. The smashing of the furniture and the pulling down of the house seemed likely to succeed—when Geoffrey's eye lighted by accident on Julius, and Geoffrey's voice, calling fiercely for his brother, hushed the wild assembly into sudden attention, and turned the fiery enthusiasm into a new course. Hooray for his brother! One, two, three—and up with his brother on our shoulders! Four five, six—and on with his brother, over our heads, to the other end of the room! See, boys—see! the hero has got him by the collar! the hero has lifted him on the table! The hero heated red-hot with his own triumph, welcomes the poor little snob cheerfully, with a volley of oaths. "Thunder and lightning! Explosion and blood! What's up now, Julius? What's up now?"

Julius recovered his breath, and arranged his coat. The quiet little man, who had just muscle enough to lift a dictionary from the shelf, and just training enough to play the fiddle, so far from being daunted by the rough reception accorded to him, appeared to feel no other sentiment in relation to it than a sentiment of unmitigated contempt.

"You're not frightened, are you?" said Geoffrey. "Our fellows are a roughish lot, but they mean well."

"I am not frightened," answered Julius. "I am only wondering—when the Schools and Universities of England turn out such a set of ruffians as these—how long the Schools and Universities of England will last."

"Mind what you are about, Julius! They'll cart you out of window if they hear you."

"They will only confirm my opinion of them, Geoffrey, if they do."

Here the assembly, seeing but not hearing the colloquy between the two brothers, became uneasy on the subject of the coming race. A roar of voices summoned Geoffrey to announce it, if there was any thing wrong. Having pacified the meeting, Geoffrey turned again to his brother, and asked him, in no amiable mood, what the devil he wanted there?

"I want to tell you something, before I go back to Scotland," answered Julius. "My father is willing to give you a last chance. If you don't take it, my doors are closed against you as well as his."

Nothing is more remarkable, in its way, than the sound common-sense and admirable self-restraint exhibited by the youth of the present time when confronted by an emergency in which their own interests are concerned. Instead of resenting the tone which his brother had taken with him, Geoffrey instantly descended from the pedestal of glory on which he stood, and placed himself without a struggle in the hands which vicariously held his destiny—otherwise, the hands which vicariously held the purse. In five minutes more the meeting had been dismissed, with all needful assurances relating to Geoffrey's share in the coming Sports—and the two brothers were closeted together in one of the private rooms of the inn.

"Out with it!" said Geoffrey. "And don't be long about it."

"I won't be five minutes," replied Julius. "I go back to-night by the mail-train; and I have a great deal to do in the mean time. Here it is, in plain words: My father consents to see you again, if you choose to settle in life—with his approval. And my mother has discovered where you may find a wife. Birth, beauty, and money are all offered to you. Take them—and you recover your position as Lord Holchester's son. Refuse them—and you go to ruin your own way."

Geoffrey's reception of the news from home was not of the most reassuring kind. Instead of answering he struck his fist furiously on the table, and cursed with all his heart some absent woman unnamed.

"I have nothing to do with any degrading connection which you may have formed," Julius went on. "I have only to put the matter before you exactly as it stands, and to leave you to decide for yourself. The lady in question was formerly Miss Newenden—a descendant of one of the oldest families in England. She is now Mrs. Glenarm—the young widow (and the childless widow) of the great iron-master of that name. Birth and fortune—she unites both. Her income is a clear ten thousand a year. My father can and will, make it fifteen thousand, if you are lucky enough to persuade her to marry you. My mother answers for her personal qualities. And my wife has met her at our house in London. She is now, as I hear, staying with some friends in Scotland; and when I get back I will take care that an invitation is sent to her to pay her next visit at my house. It remains, of course, to be seen whether you are fortunate enough to produce a favorable impression on her. In the mean time you will be doing every thing that my father can ask of you, if you make the attempt."

Geoffrey impatiently dismissed that part of the question from all consideration.

"If she don't cotton to a man who's going to run in the Great Race at Fulham," he said, "there are plenty as good as she is who will! That's not the difficulty. Bother that!"

"I tell you again, I have nothing to do with your difficulties," Julius resumed. "Take the rest of the day to consider what I have said to you. If you decide to accept the proposal, I shall expect you to prove you are in earnest by meeting me at the station to-night. We will travel back to Scotland together. You will complete your interrupted visit at Lady Lundie's (it is important, in my interests, that you should treat a person of her position in the county with all due respect); and my wife will make the necessary arrangements with Mrs. Glenarm, in anticipation of your return to our house. There is nothing more to be said, and no further necessity of my staying here. If you join me at the station to-night, your sister-in-law and I will do all we can to help you. If I travel back to Scotland alone, don't trouble yourself to follow—I have done with you." He shook hands with his brother, and went out.

Left alone, Geoffrey lit his pipe and sent for the landlord.

"Get me a boat. I shall scull myself up the river for an hour or two. And put in some towels. I may take a swim."

The landlord received the order—with a caution addressed to his illustrious guest.

"Don't show yourself in front of the house, Sir! If you let the people see you, they're in such a state of excitement, the police won't answer for keeping them in order."

"All right. I'll go out by the back way."

He took a turn up and down the room. What were the difficulties to be overcome before he could profit by the golden prospect which his brother had offered to him? The Sports? No! The committee had promised to defer the day, if he wished it—and a month's training, in his physical condition, would be amply enough for him. Had he any personal objection to trying his luck with Mrs. Glenarm? Not he! Any woman would do—provided his father was satisfied, and the money was all right. The obstacle which was really in his way was the obstacle of the woman whom he had ruined. Anne! The one insuperable difficulty was the difficulty of dealing with Anne.

"We'll see how it looks," he said to himself, "after a pull up the river!"

The landlord and the police inspector smuggled him out by the back way unknown to the expectant populace in front The two men stood on the river-bank admiring him, as he pulled away from them, with his long, powerful, easy, beautiful stroke.

"That's what I call the pride and flower of England!" said the inspector. "Has the betting on him begun?"

"Six to four," said the landlord, "and no takers."

Julius went early to the station that night. His mother was very anxious. "Don't let Geoffrey find an excuse in your example," she said, "if he is late."

The first person whom Julius saw on getting out of the carriage was Geoffrey—with his ticket taken, and his portmanteau in charge of the guard.

FOURTH SCENE.—WINDYGATES.

CHAPTER THE SEVENTEENTH

NEAR IT.

THE Library at Windygates was the largest and the handsomest room in the house. The two grand divisions under which Literature is usually arranged in these days occupied the customary places in it. On the shelves which ran round the walls were the books which humanity in general respects—and does not read. On the tables distributed over the floor were the books which humanity in general reads—and does not respect. In the first class, the works of the wise ancients; and the Histories, Biographies, and Essays of writers of more modern times—otherwise the Solid Literature, which is universally respected, and occasionally read. In the second class, the Novels of our own day—otherwise the Light Literature, which is universally read, and occasionally respected. At Windygates, as elsewhere, we believed History to be high literature, because it assumed to be true to Authorities (of which we knew little)—and Fiction to be low literature, because it attempted to be true to Nature (of which we knew less). At Windygates as elsewhere, we were always more or less satisfied with ourselves, if we were publicly discovered consulting our History—and more or less ashamed of ourselves, if we were publicly discovered devouring our Fiction. An architectural peculiarity in the original arrangement of the library favored the development of this common and curious form of human stupidity. While a row of luxurious arm-chairs, in the main thoroughfare of the room, invited the reader of solid literature to reveal himself in the act of cultivating a virtue, a row of snug little curtained recesses, opening at intervals out of one of the walls, enabled the reader of light literature to conceal himself in the act of indulging a vice. For the rest, all the minor accessories of this spacious and tranquil place were as plentiful and as well chosen as the heart could desire. And solid literature and light literature, and great writers and small, were all bounteously illuminated alike by a fine broad flow of the light of heaven, pouring into the room through windows that opened to the floor.

It was the fourth day from the day of Lady Lundie's garden-party, and it wanted an hour or more of the time at which the luncheon-bell usually rang.

The guests at Windygates were most of them in the garden, enjoying the morning sunshine, after a prevalent mist and rain for some days past. Two gentlemen (exceptions to the general rule) were alone in the library. They were the two last gentlemen in the world who could possibly be supposed to have any legitimate motive for meeting each other in a place of literary seclusion. One was Arnold Brinkworth, and the other was Geoffrey Delamayn.

They had arrived together at Windygates that morning. Geoffrey had traveled from London with his brother by the train of the previous night. Arnold, delayed in getting away at his own time, from his own property, by ceremonies incidental to his position which were not to be abridged without giving offense to many worthy people—had caught the passing train early that morning at the station nearest to him, and had returned to Lady Lundie's, as he had left Lady Lundie's, in company with his friend.

After a short preliminary interview with Blanche, Arnold had rejoined Geoffrey in the safe retirement of the library, to say what was still left to be said between them on the subject of Anne. Having completed his report of events at Craig Fernie, he was now naturally waiting to hear what Geoffrey had to say on his side. To Arnold's astonishment, Geoffrey coolly turned away to leave the library without uttering a word.

Arnold stopped him without ceremony.

"Not quite so fast, Geoffrey," he said. "I have an interest in Miss Silvester's welfare as well as in yours. Now you are back again in Scotland, what are you going to do?"

If Geoffrey had told the truth, he must have stated his position much as follows:

He had necessarily decided on deserting Anne when he had decided on joining his brother on the journey back. But he had advanced no farther than this. How he was to abandon the woman who had trusted him, without seeing his own dastardly conduct dragged into the light of day, was more than he yet knew. A vague idea of at once pacifying and deluding Anne, by a marriage which should be no marriage at all, had crossed his mind on the journey. He had asked himself whether a trap of that sort might not be easily set in a country notorious for the looseness of its marriage laws—if a man only knew how? And he had thought it likely that his well-informed brother, who lived in Scotland, might be tricked into innocently telling him what he wanted to know. He had turned the conversation to the subject of Scotch marriages in general by way of trying the experiment. Julius had not studied the question; Julius knew nothing about it; and there the experiment had come to an end. As the necessary result of the check thus encountered, he was now in Scotland with absolutely nothing to trust to as a means of effecting his release but the chapter of accidents, aided by his own resolution to marry Mrs. Glenarm. Such was his position, and such should have been the substance of his reply when he was confronted by Arnold's question, and plainly asked what he meant to do.

"The right thing," he answered, unblushingly. "And no mistake about it."

"I'm glad to hear you see your way so plainly," returned Arnold. "In your place, I should have been all abroad. I was wondering, only the other day, whether you would end, as I should have ended, in consulting Sir Patrick."

Geoffrey eyed him sharply.

"Consult Sir Patrick?" he repeated. "Why would you have done that?"

"I shouldn't have known how to set about marrying her," replied Arnold. "And—being in Scotland—I should have applied to Sir Patrick (without mentioning names, of course), because he would be sure to know all about it."

"Suppose I don't see my way quite so plainly as you think," said Geoffrey. "Would you advise me—"

"To consult Sir Patrick? Certainly! He has passed his life in the practice of the Scotch law. Didn't you know that?"

"No."

"Then take my advice—and consult him. You needn't mention names. You can say it's the case of a friend."

The idea was a new one and a good one. Geoffrey looked longingly toward the door. Eager to make Sir Patrick his innocent accomplice on the spot, he made a second attempt to leave the library; and made it for the second time in vain. Arnold had more unwelcome inquiries to make, and more advice to give unasked.

"How have you arranged about meeting Miss Silvester?" he went on. "You can't go to the hotel in the character of her husband. I have prevented that. Where else are you to meet her? She is all alone; she must be weary of waiting, poor thing. Can you manage matters so as to see her to-day?"

After staring hard at Arnold while he was speaking, Geoffrey burst out laughing when he had done. A disinterested anxiety for the welfare of another person was one of those refinements of feeling which a muscular education had not fitted him to understand.

"I say, old boy," he burst out, "you seem to take an extraordinary interest in Miss Silvester! You haven't fallen in love with her yourself—have you?"

"Come! come!" said Arnold, seriously. "Neither she nor I deserve to be sneered at, in that way. I have made a sacrifice to your interests, Geoffrey—and so has she."

Geoffrey's face became serious again. His secret was in Arnold's hands; and his estimate of Arnold's character was founded, unconsciously, on his experience of himself. "All right," he said, by way of timely apology and concession. "I was only joking."

"As much joking as you please, when you have married her," replied Arnold. "It seems serious enough, to my mind, till then." He stopped—considered—and laid his hand very earnestly on Geoffrey's arm. "Mind!" he resumed. "You are not to breathe a word to any living soul, of my having been near the inn!"

"I've promised to hold my tongue, once already. What do you want more?"

"I am anxious, Geoffrey. I was at Craig Fernie, remember, when Blanche came there! She has been telling me all that happened, poor darling, in the firm persuasion that I was miles off at the time. I swear I couldn't look her in the face! What would she think of me, if she knew the truth? Pray be careful! pray be careful!"

Geoffrey's patience began to fail him.

"We had all this out," he said, "on the way here from the station. What's the good of going over the ground again?"

"You're quite right," said Arnold, good-humoredly. "The fact is—I'm out of sorts, this morning. My mind misgives me—I don't know why."

"Mind?" repeated Geoffrey, in high contempt. "It's flesh—that's what's the matter with you. You're nigh on a stone over your right weight. Mind he hanged! A man in healthy training don't know that he has got a mind. Take a turn with the dumb-bells, and a run up hill with a great-coat on. Sweat it off, Arnold! Sweat it off!"

With that excellent advice, he turned to leave the room for the third time. Fate appeared to have determined to keep him imprisoned in the library, that morning. On this occasion, it was a servant who got in the way—a servant, with a letter and a message. "The man waits for answer."

Geoffrey looked at the letter. It was in his brother's handwriting. He had left Julius at the junction about three hours since. What could Julius possibly have to say to him now?

He opened the letter. Julius had to announce that Fortune was favoring them already. He had heard news of Mrs. Glenarm, as soon as he reached home. She had called on his wife, during his absence in London—she had been invited to the house—and she had promised to accept the invitation early in the week. "Early in the week," Julius wrote, "may mean to-morrow. Make your apologies to Lady Lundie; and take care not to offend her. Say that family reasons, which you hope soon to have the pleasure of confiding to her, oblige you to appeal once more to her indulgence—and come to-morrow, and help us to receive Mrs. Glenarm."

Even Geoffrey was startled, when he found himself met by a sudden necessity for acting on his own decision. Anne knew where his brother lived. Suppose Anne (not knowing where else to find him) appeared at his brother's house, and claimed him in the presence of Mrs. Glenarm? He gave orders to have the messenger kept waiting, and said he would send back a written reply.

"From Craig Fernie?" asked Arnold, pointing to the letter in his friend's hand.

Geoffrey looked up with a frown. He had just opened his lips to answer that ill-timed reference to Anne, in no very friendly terms, when a voice, calling to Arnold from the lawn outside, announced the appearance of a third person in the library, and warned the two gentlemen that their private interview was at an end.

CHAPTER THE EIGHTEENTH.

NEARER STILL.

BLANCHE stepped lightly into the room, through one of the open French windows.

"What are you doing here?" she said to Arnold.

"Nothing. I was just going to look for you in the garden."

"The garden is insufferable, this morning." Saying those words, she fanned herself with her handkerchief, and noticed Geoffrey's presence in the room with a look of very thinly-concealed annoyance at the discovery. "Wait till I am married!" she thought. "Mr. Delamayn will be cleverer than I take him to be, if he gets much of his friend's company then!"

"A trifle too hot—eh?" said Geoffrey, seeing her eyes fixed on him, and supposing that he was expected to say something.

Having performed that duty he walked away without waiting for a reply; and seated himself with his letter, at one of the writing-tables in the library.

"Sir Patrick is quite right about the young men of the present day," said Blanche, turning to Arnold. "Here is this one asks me a question, and doesn't wait for an answer. There are three more of them, out in the garden, who have been talking of nothing, for the last hour, but the pedigrees of horses and the muscles of men. When we are married, Arnold, don't present any of your male friends to me, unless they have turned fifty. What shall we do till luncheon-time? It's cool and quiet in here among the books. I want a mild excitement—and I have got absolutely nothing to do. Suppose you read me some poetry?"

"While he is here?" asked Arnold, pointing to the personified antithesis of poetry—

otherwise to Geoffrey, seated with his back to them at the farther end of the library.

"Pooh!" said Blanche. "There's only an animal in the room. We needn't mind him!"

"I say!" exclaimed Arnold. "You're as bitter, this morning, as Sir Patrick himself. What will you say to Me when we are married if you talk in that way of my friend?"

Blanche stole her hand into Arnold's hand and gave it a little significant squeeze. "I shall always be nice to you," she whispered—with a look that contained a host of pretty promises in itself. Arnold returned the look (Geoffrey was unquestionably in the way!). Their eyes met tenderly (why couldn't the great awkward brute write his letters somewhere else?). With a faint little sigh, Blanche dropped resignedly into one of the comfortable arm-chairs—and asked once more for "some poetry," in a voice that faltered softly, and with a color that was brighter than usual.

"Whose poetry am I to read?" inquired Arnold.

"Any body's," said Blanche. "This is another of my impulses. I am dying for some poetry. I don't know whose poetry. And I don't know why."

Arnold went straight to the nearest book-shelf, and took down the first volume that his hand lighted on—a solid quarto, bound in sober brown.

"Well?" asked Blanche. "What have you found?"

Arnold opened the volume, and conscientiously read the title exactly as it stood:

"Paradise Lost. A Poem. By John Milton."

"I have never read Milton," said Blanche. "Have you?"

"No."

"Another instance of sympathy between us. No educated person ought to be ignorant of Milton. Let us be educated persons. Please begin."

"At the beginning?"

"Of course! Stop! You musn't sit all that way off—you must sit where I can look at you. My attention wanders if I don't look at people while they read."

Arnold took a stool at Blanche's feet, and opened the "First Book" of Paradise Lost. His "system" as a reader of blank verse was simplicity itself. In poetry we are some of us (as many living poets can testify) all for sound; and some of us (as few living poets can testify) all for sense. Arnold was for sound. He ended every line inexorably with a full stop; and he got on to his full stop as fast as the inevitable impediment of the words would let him. He began:

"Of Man's first disobedience and the fruit.

Of that forbidden tree whose mortal taste.

Brought death into the world and all our woe.

With loss of Eden till one greater Man.

Restore us and regain the blissful seat.

Sing heavenly Muse—"

"Beautiful!" said Blanche. "What a shame it seems to have had Milton all this time in the library and never to have read him yet! We will have Mornings with Milton, Arnold. He seems long; but we are both young, and we may live to get to the end of him. Do you know dear, now I look at you again, you don't seem to have come back to Windygates in good spirits."

"Don't I? I can't account for it."

"I can. It's sympathy with Me. I am out of spirits too."

"You!"

"Yes. After what I saw at Craig Fernie, I grow more and more uneasy about Anne. You will understand that, I am sure, after what I told you this morning?"

Arnold looked back, in a violent hurry, from Blanche to Milton. That renewed reference to events at Craig Fernie was a renewed reproach to him for his conduct at the inn. He attempted to silence her by pointing to Geoffrey.

"Don't forget," he whispered, "that there is somebody in the room besides ourselves."

Blanche shrugged her shoulders contemptuously.

"What does he matter?" she asked. "What does he know or care about Anne?"

There was only one other chance of diverting her from the delicate subject. Arnold went on reading headlong, two lines in advance of the place at which he had left off, with more sound and less sense than ever:

"In the beginning how the heavens and earth.

Rose out of Chaos or if Sion hill—"

At "Sion hill," Blanche interrupted him again.

"Do wait a little, Arnold. I can't have Milton crammed down my throat in that way. Besides I had something to say. Did I tell you that I consulted my uncle about Anne? I don't think I did. I caught him alone in this very room. I told him all I have told you. I showed him Anne's letter. And I said, 'What do you think?' He took a little time (and a great deal of snuff) before he would say what he thought. When he did speak, he told me I might quite possibly be right in suspecting Anne's husband to be a very abominable person. His keeping himself out of my way was (just as I thought) a suspicious circumstance, to begin with. And then there was the sudden extinguishing of the candles, when I first went in. I thought (and Mrs. Inchbare thought) it was done by the wind. Sir Patrick suspects it was done by the horrid man himself, to prevent me from seeing him when I entered the room. I am firmly persuaded Sir Patrick is right. What do you think?"

"I think we had better go on," said Arnold, with his head down over his book. "We seem to be forgetting Milton."

"How you do worry about Milton! That last bit wasn't as interesting as the other. Is there any love in Paradise Lost?"

"Perhaps we may find some if we go on."

"Very well, then. Go on. And be quick about it."

Arnold was so quick about it that he lost his place. Instead of going on he went back. He read once more:

"In the beginning how the heavens and earth.

Rose out of Chaos or if Sion hill—"

"You read that before," said Blanche.

"I think not."

"I'm sure you did. When you said 'Sion hill' I recollect I thought of the Methodists directly. I couldn't have thought of the Methodists, if you hadn't said 'Sion hill.' It stands to reason."

"I'll try the next page," said Arnold. "I can't have read that before—for I haven't turned over yet."

Blanche threw herself back in her chair, and flung her handkerchief resignedly over her face. "The flies," she explained. "I'm not going to sleep. Try the next page. Oh, dear me, try the next page!"

Arnold proceeded:

"Say first for heaven hides nothing from thy view.

Nor the deep tract of hell say first what cause.

Moved our grand parents in that happy state—"

Blanche suddenly threw the handkerchief off again, and sat bolt upright in her chair. "Shut it up," she cried. "I can't bear any more. Leave off, Arnold—leave off!"

"What's, the matter now?"

"'That happy state,'" said Blanche. "What does 'that happy state' mean? Marriage, of course! And marriage reminds me of Anne. I won't have any more. Paradise Lost is painful. Shut it up. Well, my next question to Sir Patrick was, of course, to know what he thought Anne's husband had done. The wretch had behaved infamously to her in some way. In what way? Was it any thing to do with her marriage? My uncle considered again. He thought it quite possible. Private marriages were dangerous things (he said)—especially in Scotland. He asked me if they had been married in Scotland. I couldn't tell him—I only said, 'Suppose they were? What then?' 'It's barely possible, in that case,' says Sir Patrick, 'that Miss Silvester may be feeling uneasy about her marriage. She may even have reason—or may think she has reason—to doubt whether it is a marriage at all.'"

Arnold started, and looked round at Geoffrey still sitting at the writing-table with his back turned on them. Utterly as Blanche and Sir Patrick were mistaken in their estimate of Anne's position at Craig Fernie, they had drifted, nevertheless, into discussing the very question in which Geoffrey and Miss Silvester were interested—the question of marriage in Scotland. It was impossible in Blanche's presence to tell Geoffrey that he might do well to listen to Sir Patrick's opinion, even at second-hand. Perhaps the words had found their way to him? perhaps he was listening already, of his own accord?

(He was listening. Blanche's last words had found their way to him, while he was pondering over his half-finished letter to his brother. He waited to hear more—without moving, and with the pen suspended in his hand.)

Blanche proceeded, absently winding her fingers in and out of Arnold's hair as he sat at her feet:

"It flashed on me instantly that Sir Patrick had discovered the truth. Of course I told him so. He laughed, and said I mustn't jump at conclusions We were guessing quite in the dark; and all the distressing things I had noticed at the inn might admit of some totally different explanation. He would have gone on splitting straws in that provoking way the whole morning if I hadn't stopped him. I was strictly logical. I said I had seen Anne, and he hadn't—and that made all the difference. I said, 'Every thing that puzzled and frightened me in the poor darling is accounted for now. The law must, and shall, reach that man, uncle—and I'll pay for it!' I was so much in earnest that I believe I cried a little. What do you think the dear old man did? He took me on his knee and gave me a kiss; and he said, in the nicest way, that he would adopt my view, for the present, if I would promise not to cry any more; and—wait! the cream of it is to come!—that he would put the view in quite a new light to me as soon as I was composed again. You may imagine how soon I dried my eyes, and what a picture of composure I presented in the course of half a minute. 'Let us take it for granted,' says Sir Patrick, 'that this man unknown has really tried to deceive Miss Silvester, as you and I suppose. I can tell you one thing: it's as likely as not that, in trying to overreach her, he may (without in the least suspecting it) have ended in overreaching himself.'"

(Geoffrey held his breath. The pen dropped unheeded from his fingers. It was coming. The light that his brother couldn't throw on the subject was dawning on it at last!)

Blanche resumed:

"I was so interested, and it made such a tremendous impression on me, that I haven't forgotten a word. 'I mustn't make that poor little head of yours ache with Scotch law,' my uncle said; 'I must put it plainly. There are marriages allowed in Scotland, Blanche, which are called Irregular Marriages—and very abominable things they are. But they have this accidental merit in the present case. It is extremely difficult for a man to pretend to marry in Scotland, and not really to do it. And it is, on the other hand, extremely easy for a man to drift into marrying in Scotland without feeling the slightest suspicion of having done it himself.' That was exactly what he said, Arnold. When we are married, it sha'n't be in Scotland!"

(Geoffrey's ruddy color paled. If this was true he might be caught himself in the trap which he had schemed to set for Anne! Blanche went on with her narrative. He waited and listened.)

"My uncle asked me if I understood him so far. It was as plain as the sun at noonday, of course I understood him! 'Very well, then—now for the application!' says Sir Patrick. 'Once more supposing our guess to be the right one, Miss Silvester may be making herself very unhappy without any real cause. If this invisible man at Craig Fernie has actually meddled, I won't say with marrying her, but only with pretending to make her his wife, and if he has attempted it in Scotland, the chances are nine to one (though he may not believe it, and though she may not believe it) that he has really married her, after all.' My uncle's own words again! Quite needless to say that, half an hour after they were out of his lips, I had sent them to Craig Fernie in a letter to Anne!"

(Geoffrey's stolidly-staring eyes suddenly brightened. A light of the devil's own striking illuminated him. An idea of the devil's own bringing entered his mind. He looked stealthily round at the man whose life he had saved—at the man who had devotedly served him in return. A hideous cunning leered at his mouth and peeped out of his eyes. "Arnold Brinkworth pretended to be married to her at the inn. By the lord Harry! that's a way out of it that never struck me before!" With that thought in his heart he turned back again to his half-finished letter to Julius. For once in his life he was strongly, fiercely agitated. For once in his life he was daunted—and that by his Own Thought! He had written to Julius under a strong sense of the necessity of gaining time to delude Anne into leaving Scotland before he ventured on paying his addresses to Mrs. Glenarm. His letter contained a string of clumsy excuses, intended to delay his return to his brother's house. "No," he said to himself, as he read it again. "Whatever else may do—this won't!" He looked round once more at Arnold, and slowly tore the letter into fragments as he looked.)

In the mean time Blanche had not done yet. "No," she said, when Arnold proposed an adjournment to the garden; "I have something more to say, and you are interested in it, this time." Arnold resigned himself to listen, and worse still to answer, if there was no help for it, in the character of an innocent stranger who had never been near the Craig Fernie inn.

"Well," Blanche resumed, "and what do you think has come of my letter to Anne?"

"I'm sure I don't know."

"Nothing has come of it!"

"Indeed?"

"Absolutely nothing! I know she received the letter yesterday morning. I ought to have had the answer to-day at breakfast."

"Perhaps she thought it didn't require an answer."

"She couldn't have thought that, for reasons that I know of. Besides, in my letter yesterday I implored her to tell me (if it was one line only) whether, in guessing at what her trouble was, Sir Patrick and I had not guessed right. And here is the day getting on, and no answer! What am I to conclude?"

"I really can't say!"

"Is it possible, Arnold, that we have not guessed right, after all? Is the wickedness of that man who blew the candles out wickedness beyond our discovering? The doubt is so dreadful that I have made up my mind not to bear it after to-day. I count on your sympathy and assistance when to-morrow comes!"

Arnold's heart sank. Some new complication was evidently gathering round him. He waited in silence to hear the worst. Blanche bent forward, and whispered to him.

"This is a secret," she said. "If that creature at the writing-table has ears for any thing but rowing and racing, he mustn't hear this! Anne may come to me privately to-day while you are all at luncheon. If she doesn't come and if I don't hear from her, then the mystery of her silence must be cleared up; and You must do it!"

"I!"

"Don't make difficulties! If you can't find your way to Craig Fernie, I can help you. As for Anne, you know what a charming person she is, and you know she will receive you perfectly, for my sake. I must and will have some news of her. I can't break the laws of the household a second time. Sir Patrick sympathizes, but he won't stir. Lady Lundie is a bitter enemy. The servants are threatened with the loss of their places if any one of them goes near Anne. There is nobody but you. And to Anne you go to-morrow, if I don't see her or hear from her to-day!"

This to the man who had passed as Anne's husband at the inn, and who had been forced into the most intimate knowledge of Anne's miserable secret! Arnold rose to put Milton away, with the composure of sheer despair. Any other secret he might, in the last resort, have confided to the discretion of a third person. But a woman's secret—with a woman's reputation depending on his keeping it—was not to be confided to any body, under any stress of circumstances whatever. "If Geoffrey doesn't get me out of this,," he thought, "I shall have no choice but to leave Windygates to-morrow."

As he replaced the book on the shelf, Lady Lundie entered the library from the garden.

"What are you doing here?" she said to her step-daughter.

"Improving my mind," replied Blanche. "Mr. Brinkworth and I have been reading Milton."

"Can you condescend so far, after reading Milton all the morning, as to help me with the invitations for the dinner next week?"

"If you can condescend, Lady Lundie, after feeding the poultry all the morning, I must be humility itself after only reading Milton!"

With that little interchange of the acid amenities of feminine intercourse, step-mother and step-daughter withdrew to a writing-table, to put the virtue of hospitality in practice together.

Arnold joined his friend at the other end of the library.

Geoffrey was sitting with his elbows on the desk, and his clenched fists dug into his cheeks. Great drops of perspiration stood on his forehead, and the fragments of a torn letter lay scattered all round him. He exhibited symptoms of nervous sensibility for the first time in his life—he started when Arnold spoke to him.

"What's the matter, Geoffrey?"

"A letter to answer. And I don't know how."

"From Miss Silvester?" asked Arnold, dropping his voice so as to prevent the ladies at the other end of the room from hearing him.

"No," answered Geoffrey, in a lower voice still.

"Have you heard what Blanche has been saying to me about Miss Silvester?"

"Some of it."

"Did you hear Blanche say that she meant to send me to Craig Fernie to-morrow, if she failed to get news from Miss Silvester to-day?"

"No."

"Then you know it now. That is what Blanche has just said to me."

"Well?"

"Well—there's a limit to what a man can expect even from his best friend. I hope you won't ask me to be Blanche's messenger to-morrow. I can't, and won't, go back to the inn as things are now."

"You have had enough of it—eh?"

"I have had enough of distressing Miss Silvester, and more than enough of deceiving Blanche."

"What do you mean by 'distressing Miss Silvester?'"

"She doesn't take the same easy view that you and I do, Geoffrey, of my passing her off on the people of the inn as my wife."

Geoffrey absently took up a paper-knife. Still with his head down, he began shaving off the topmost layer of paper from the blotting-pad under his hand. Still with his head down, he abruptly broke the silence in a whisper.

"I say!"

"Yes?"

"How did you manage to pass her off as your wife?"

"I told you how, as we were driving from the station here."

"I was thinking of something else. Tell me again."

Arnold told him once more what had happened at the inn. Geoffrey listened, without making any remark. He balanced the paper-knife vacantly on one of his fingers. He was strangely sluggish and strangely silent.

"All that is done and ended," said Arnold shaking him by the shoulder. "It rests with you now to get me out of the difficulty I'm placed in with Blanche. Things must be settled with Miss Silvester to-day."

"Things shall be settled."

"Shall be? What are you waiting for?"

"I'm waiting to do what you told me."

"What I told you?"

"Didn't you tell me to consult Sir Patrick before I married her?"

"To be sure! so I did."

"Well—I am waiting for a chance with Sir Patrick."

"And then?"

"And then—" He looked at Arnold for the first time. "Then," he said, "you may consider it settled."

"The marriage?"

He suddenly looked down again at the blotting-pad. "Yes—the marriage."

Arnold offered his hand in congratulation. Geoffrey never noticed it. His eyes were off the blotting-pad again. He was looking out of the window near him.

"Don't I hear voices outside?" he asked.

"I believe our friends are in the garden," said Arnold. "Sir Patrick may be among them. I'll go and see."

The instant his back was turned Geoffrey snatched up a sheet of note-paper. "Before I forget it!" he said to himself. He wrote the word "Memorandum" at the top of the page, and added these lines beneath it:

"He asked for her by the name of his wife at the door. He said, at dinner, before the landlady and the waiter, 'I take these rooms for my wife.' He made her say he was her husband at the same time. After that he stopped all night. What do the lawyers call this in Scotland?—(Query: a marriage?)"

After folding up the paper he hesitated for a moment. "No!" he thought, "It won't do to trust to what Miss Lundie said about it. I can't be certain till I have consulted Sir Patrick himself."

He put the paper away in his pocket, and wiped the heavy perspiration from his forehead. He was pale—for him, strikingly pale—when Arnold came back.

"Any thing wrong, Geoffrey?—you're as white as ashes."

"It's the heat. Where's Sir Patrick?"

"You may see for yourself."

Arnold pointed to the window. Sir Patrick was crossing the lawn, on his way to the library with a newspaper in his hand; and the guests at Windygates were accompanying him. Sir Patrick was smiling, and saying nothing. The guests were talking excitedly at the tops of their voices. There had apparently been a collision of some kind between the old school and the new. Arnold directed Geoffrey's attention to the state of affairs on the lawn.

"How are you to consult Sir Patrick with all those people about him?"

"I'll consult Sir Patrick, if I take him by the scruff of the neck and carry him into the next county!" He rose to his feet as he spoke those words, and emphasized them under his breath with an oath.

Sir Patrick entered the library, with the guests at his heels.

CHAPTER THE NINETEENTH.

CLOSE ON IT.

THE object of the invasion of the library by the party in the garden appeared to be twofold.

Sir Patrick had entered the room to restore the newspaper to the place from which he had taken it. The guests, to the number of five, had followed him, to appeal in a body to Geoffrey Delamayn. Between these two apparently dissimilar motives there was a connection, not visible on the surface, which was now to assert itself.

Of the five guests, two were middle-aged gentlemen belonging to that large, but indistinct, division of the human family whom the hand of Nature has painted in unobtrusive neutral tint. They had absorbed the ideas of their time with such receptive capacity as they possessed; and they occupied much the same place in society which the chorus in an opera occupies on the stage. They echoed the prevalent sentiment of the moment; and they gave the solo-talker time to fetch his breath.

The three remaining guests were on the right side of thirty. All profoundly versed in horse-racing, in athletic sports, in pipes, beer, billiards, and betting. All profoundly ignorant of every thing else under the sun. All gentlemen by birth, and all marked as such by the stamp of "a University education." They may be personally described as faint reflections of Geoffrey; and they may be numerically distinguished (in the absence of all other distinction) as One, Two, and Three.

Sir Patrick laid the newspaper on the table and placed himself in one of the comfortable arm-chairs. He was instantly assailed, in his domestic capacity, by his irrepressible sister-in-law. Lady Lundie dispatched Blanche to him with the list of her guests at the dinner. "For your uncle's approval, my dear, as head of the family."

While Sir Patrick was looking over the list, and while Arnold was making his way to Blanche, at the back of her uncle's chair, One, Two, and Three—with the Chorus in attendance on them—descended in a body on Geoffrey, at the other end of the room, and appealed in rapid succession to his superior authority, as follows:

"I say, Delamayn. We want You. Here is Sir Patrick running a regular Muck at us. Calls us aboriginal Britons. Tells us we ain't educated. Doubts if we could read, write, and cipher, if he tried us. Swears he's sick of fellows showing their arms and legs, and seeing which fellow's hardest, and who's got three belts of muscle across his wind, and who hasn't, and the like of that. Says a most infernal thing of a chap. Says—because a chap likes a healthy out-of-door life, and trains for rowing and running, and the rest of it, and don't see his way to stewing over his books—therefore he's safe to commit all the crimes in the calendar, murder included. Saw your name down in the newspaper for the Foot-Race; and said, when we asked him if he'd taken the odds, he'd lay any odds we liked against you in the other Race at the University—meaning, old boy, your Degree. Nasty, that about the Degree—in the opinion of Number One. Bad taste in Sir Patrick to rake up what we never mention among ourselves—in the opinion of Number Two. Un-English to sneer at a man in that way behind his back—in the opinion of Number Three. Bring him to book, Delamayn. Your name's in the papers; he can't ride roughshod over You."

The two choral gentlemen agreed (in the minor key) with the general opinion. "Sir Patrick's views are certainly extreme, Smith?" "I think, Jones, it's desirable to hear Mr. Delamayn on the other side."

Geoffrey looked from one to the other of his admirers with an expression on his face which was quite new to them, and with something in his manner which puzzled them all.

"You can't argue with Sir Patrick yourselves," he said, "and you want me to do it?"

One, Two, Three, and the Chorus all answered, "Yes."

"I won't do it."

One, Two, Three, and the Chorus all asked, "Why?"

"Because," answered Geoffrey, "you're all wrong. And Sir Patrick's right."

Not astonishment only, but downright stupefaction, struck the deputation from the garden speechless.

Without saying a word more to any of the persons standing near him, Geoffrey walked straight up to Sir Patrick's arm-chair, and personally addressed him. The satellites followed, and listened (as well they might) in wonder.

"You will lay any odds, Sir," said Geoffrey "against me taking my Degree? You're quite right. I sha'n't take my Degree. You doubt whether I, or any of those fellows behind me, could read, write, and cipher correctly if you tried us. You're right again—we couldn't. You say you don't know why men like Me, and men like Them, may not begin with rowing and running and the like of that, and end in committing all the crimes in the calendar: murder included. Well! you may be right again there. Who's to know what may happen to him? or what he may not end in doing before he dies? It may be Another, or it may be Me. How do I know? and how do you?" He suddenly turned on the deputation, standing thunder-struck behind him. "If you want to know what I think, there it is for you, in plain words."

There was something, not only in the shamelessness of the declaration itself, but in the fierce pleasure that the speaker seemed to feel in making it, which struck the circle of listeners, Sir Patrick included, with a momentary chill.

In the midst of the silence a sixth guest appeared on the lawn, and stepped into the library—a silent, resolute, unassuming, elderly man who had arrived the day before on a visit to Windygates, and who was well known, in and out of London, as one of the first consulting surgeons of his time.

"A discussion going on?" he asked. "Am I in the way?"

"There's no discussion—we are all agreed," cried Geoffrey, answering boisterously for the rest. "The more the merrier, Sir!"

After a glance at Geoffrey, the surgeon suddenly checked himself on the point of advancing to the inner part of the room, and remained standing at the window.

"I beg your pardon," said Sir Patrick, addressing himself to Geoffrey, with a grave dignity which was quite new in Arnold's experience of him. "We are not all agreed. I decline, Mr. Delamayn, to allow you to connect me with such an expression of feeling on your part as we have just heard. The language you have used leaves me no alternative but to meet your statement of what you suppose me to have said by my statement of what I really did say. It is not my fault if the discussion in the garden is revived before another audience in this room—it is yours."

He looked as he spoke to Arnold and Blanche, and from them to the surgeon standing at the window.

The surgeon had found an occupation for himself which completely isolated him among the rest of the guests. Keeping his own face in shadow, he was studying Geoffrey's face, in the full flood of light that fell on it, with a steady attention which must have been generally remarked, if all eyes had not been turned toward Sir Patrick at the time.

It was not an easy face to investigate at that moment.

While Sir Patrick had been speaking Geoffrey had seated himself near the window, doggedly impenetrable to the reproof of which he was the object. In his impatience to consult the one authority competent to decide the question of Arnold's position toward Anne, he had sided with Sir Patrick, as a means of ridding himself of the unwelcome presence of his friends—and he had defeated his own purpose, thanks to his own brutish incapability of bridling himself in the pursuit of it. Whether he was now discouraged under these circumstances, or whether he was simply resigned to bide his time till his time came, it was impossible, judging by outward appearances, to say. With a heavy dropping at the corners of his mouth, with a stolid indifference staring dull in his eyes, there he sat, a man forearmed, in his own obstinate neutrality, against all temptation to engage in the conflict of opinions that was to come.

Sir Patrick took up the newspaper which he had brought in from the garden, and looked once more to see if the surgeon was attending to him.

No! The surgeon's attention was absorbed in his own subject. There he was in the same position, with his mind still hard at work on something in Geoffrey which at once interested and puzzled it! "That man," he was thinking to himself, "has come here this morning after traveling from London all night. Does any ordinary fatigue explain what I see in his face? No!"

"Our little discussion in the garden," resumed Sir Patrick, answering Blanche's inquiring look as she bent over him, "began, my dear, in a paragraph here announcing Mr. Delamayn's forthcoming appearance in a foot-race in the neighborhood of London. I hold very unpopular opinions as to the athletic displays which are so much in vogue in England just now. And it is possible that I may have expressed those opinions a little too strongly, in the heat of discussion, with gentlemen who are opposed to me—I don't doubt, conscientiously opposed—on this question."

A low groan of protest rose from One, Two, and Three, in return for the little compliment which Sir Patrick had paid to them. "How about rowing and running ending in the Old Bailey and the gallows? You said that, Sir—you know you did!"

The two choral gentlemen looked at each other, and agreed with the prevalent sentiment. "It came to that, I think, Smith." "Yes, Jones, it certainly came to that."

The only two men who still cared nothing about it were Geoffrey and the surgeon. There sat the first, stolidly neutral—indifferent alike to the attack and the defense. There stood the second, pursuing his investigation—with the growing interest in it of a man who was beginning to see his way to the end.

"Hear my defense, gentlemen," continued Sir Patrick, as courteously as ever. "You belong, remember, to a nation which especially claims to practice the rules of fair play. I must beg to remind you of what I said in the garden. I started with a concession. I admitted—as every person of the smallest sense must admit—that a man will, in the great majority of cases, be all the fitter for mental exercise if he wisely combines physical exercise along with it. The whole question between the two is a question of proportion and degree, and my complaint of the present time is that the present time doesn't see it. Popular opinion in England seems to me to be, not only getting to consider the cultivation of the muscles as of equal importance with the cultivation of the mind, but to be actually extending—in practice, if not in theory—to the absurd and dangerous length of putting bodily training in the first place of importance, and mental training in the second. To take a case in point: I can discover no enthusiasm in the nation any thing like so genuine and any thing like so general as the enthusiasm excited by your University boat-race. Again: I see this Athletic Education of yours made a matter of public celebration in schools and colleges; and I ask any unprejudiced witness to tell me which excites most popular enthusiasm, and which gets the most prominent place in the public journals—the exhibition, indoors (on Prize-day), of what the boys can do with their minds? or the exhibition, out of doors (on Sports-day), of what the boys can do with their bodies? You know perfectly well which performance excites the loudest cheers, which occupies the prominent place in the newspapers, and which, as a necessary consequence, confers the highest social honors on the hero of the day."

Another murmur from One, Two, and Three. "We have nothing to say to that, Sir; have it all your own way, so far."

Another ratification of agreement with the prevalent opinion between Smith and Jones.

"Very good," pursued Sir Patrick. "We are all of one mind as to which way the public feeling sets. If it is a feeling to be respected and encouraged, show me the national advantage which has resulted from it. Where is the influence of this modern outburst of manly enthusiasm on the serious concerns of life? and how has it improved the character of the people at large? Are we any of us individually readier than we ever were to sacrifice our own little private interests to the public good? Are we dealing with the serious social questions of our time in a conspicuously determined, downright, and definite way? Are we becoming a visibly and indisputably purer people in our code of commercial morals? Is there a healthier and higher tone in those public amusements which faithfully reflect in all countries the public taste? Produce me affirmative answers to these questions, which rest on solid proof, and I'll accept the present mania for athletic sports as something better than an outbreak of our insular boastfulness and our insular barbarity in a new form."

"Question! question!" in a general cry, from One, Two, and Three.

"Question! question!" in meek reverberation, from Smith and Jones.

"That is the question," rejoined Sir Patrick. "You admit the existence of the public feeling and I ask, what good does it do?"

"What harm does it do?" from One, Two, and Three.

"Hear! hear!" from Smith and Jones.

"That's a fair challenge," replied Sir Patrick. "I am bound to meet you on that new ground. I won't point, gentlemen, by way of answer, to the coarseness which I can see growing on our national manners, or to the deterioration which appears to me to be spreading more and more widely in our national tastes. You may tell me with perfect truth that I am too old a man to be a fair judge of manners and tastes which have got beyond my standards. We will try the issue, as it now stands between us, on its abstract merits only. I assert that a state of public feeling which does practically place physical training, in its estimation, above moral and mental training, is a positively bad and dangerous state of feeling in this, that it encourages the inbred reluctance in humanity to submit to the demands which moral and mental cultivation must inevitably make on it. Which am I, as a boy, naturally most ready to do—to try how high I can jump? or to try how much I can learn? Which training comes easiest to me as a young man? The training which teaches me to handle an oar? or the training which teaches me to return good for evil, and to love my neighbor as myself? Of those two experiments, of those two trainings, which ought society in England to meet with the warmest encouragement? And which does society in England practically encourage, as a matter of fact?"

"What did you say yourself just now?" from One, Two, and Three.

"Remarkably well put!" from Smith and Jones.

"I said," admitted Sir Patrick, "that a man will go all the better to his books for his healthy physical exercise. And I say that again—provided the physical exercise be restrained within fit limits. But when public feeling enters into the question, and directly exalts the bodily exercises above the books—then I say public feeling is in a dangerous extreme. The bodily exercises, in that case, will be uppermost in the youth's thoughts, will have the strongest hold on his interest, will take the lion's share of his time, and will, by those means—barring the few purely exceptional instances—slowly and surely end in leaving him, to all good moral and mental purpose, certainly an uncultivated, and, possibly, a dangerous man."

A cry from the camp of the adversaries: "He's got to it at last! A man who leads an out-of-door life, and uses the strength that God has given to him, is a dangerous man. Did any body ever hear the like of that?"

Cry reverberated, with variations, by the two human echoes: "No! Nobody ever heard the like of that!"

"Clear your minds of cant, gentlemen," answered Sir Patrick. "The agricultural laborer leads an out-of-door life, and uses the strength that God has given to him. The sailor in the merchant service does the name. Both are an uncultivated, a shamefully uncultivated, class—and see the result! Look at the Map of Crime, and you will find the most hideous offenses in the calendar, committed—not in the towns, where the average man doesn't lead an out-of-door life, doesn't as a rule, use his strength, but is, as a rule, comparatively cultivated—not in the towns, but in the agricultural districts. As for the English sailor—except when the Royal Navy catches and cultivates him—ask Mr. Brinkworth, who has served in the merchant navy, what sort of specimen of the moral influence of out-of-door life and muscular cultivation he is."

"In nine cases out of ten," said Arnold, "he is as idle and vicious as ruffian as walks the earth."

Another cry from the Opposition: "Are we agricultural laborers? Are we sailors in the merchant service?"

A smart reverberation from the human echoes: "Smith! am I a laborer?" "Jones! am I a sailor?"

"Pray let us not be personal, gentlemen," said Sir Patrick. "I am speaking generally, and I can only meet extreme objections by pushing my argument to extreme limits. The laborer and the sailor have served my purpose. If the laborer and the sailor offend you, by all means let them walk off the stage! I hold to the position which I advanced just now. A man may be well born, well off, well dressed, well fed—but if he is an uncultivated man, he is (in spite of all those advantages) a man with special capacities for evil in him, on that very account. Don't mistake me! I am far from saving that the present rage for exclusively muscular accomplishments must lead inevitably downward to the lowest deep of depravity. Fortunately for society, all special depravity is more or less certainly the result, in the first instance, of special temptation. The ordinary mass of us, thank God, pass through life without being exposed to other than ordinary temptations. Thousands of the young gentlemen, devoted to the favorite pursuits of the present time, will get through existence with no worse consequences to themselves than a coarse tone of mind and manners, and a lamentable incapability of feeling any of those higher and gentler influences which sweeten and purify the lives of more cultivated men. But take the other case (which may occur to any body), the case of a special temptation trying a modern young man of your prosperous class and of mine. And let me beg Mr. Delamayn to honor with his attention what I have now to say, because it refers to the opinion which I did really express—as distinguished from the opinion which he affects to agree with, and which I never advanced."

Geoffrey's indifference showed no signs of giving way. "Go on!" he said—and still sat looking straight before him, with heavy eyes, which noticed nothing, and expressed nothing.

"Take the example which we have now in view," pursued Sir Patrick—"the example of an average young gentleman of our time, blest with every advantage that physical cultivation can bestow on him. Let this man be tried by a temptation which insidiously calls into action, in his own interests, the savage instincts latent in humanity—the instincts of self-seeking and cruelty which are at the bottom of all crime. Let this man be placed toward some other person, guiltless of injuring him, in a position which demands one of two sacrifices: the sacrifice of the other person, or the sacrifice of his own interests and his own desires. His neighbor's happiness, or his neighbor's life, stands, let us say, between him and the attainment of something that he wants. He can wreck the happiness, or strike down the life, without, to his knowledge, any fear of suffering for it himself. What is to prevent him, being the man he is, from going straight to his end, on those conditions? Will the skill in rowing, the swiftness in running, the admirable capacity and endurance in other physical exercises, which he has attained, by a strenuous cultivation in this kind that has excluded any similarly strenuous cultivation in other kinds—will these physical attainments help him to win a purely moral victory over his own selfishness and his own cruelty? They won't even help him to see that it is selfishness, and that it is cruelty. The essential principle of his rowing and racing (a harmless principle enough, if you can be sure of applying it to rowing and racing only) has taught him to take every advantage of another man that his superior strength and superior cunning can suggest. There has been nothing in his training to soften the barbarous hardness in his heart, and to enlighten the barbarous darkness in his mind. Temptation finds this man defenseless, when temptation passes his way. I don't care who he is, or how high he stands accidentally in the social scale—he is, to all moral intents and purposes, an Animal, and nothing more. If my happiness stands in his way—and if he can do it with impunity to himself—he will trample down my happiness. If my life happens to be the next obstacle he encounters—and if he can do it with impunity to himself—he will trample down my life. Not, Mr. Delamayn, in the character of a victim to irresistible fatality, or to blind chance; but in the character of a man who has sown the seed, and reaps the harvest. That, Sir, is the case which I put as an extreme case only, when this discussion began. As an extreme case only—but as a perfectly possible case, at the same time—I restate it now."

Before the advocates of the other side of the question could open their lips to reply, Geoffrey suddenly flung off his indifference, and started to his feet.

"Stop!" he cried, threatening the others, in his fierce impatience to answer for himself, with his clenched fist.

There was a general silence.

Geoffrey turned and looked at Sir Patrick, as if Sir Patrick had personally insulted him.

"Who is this anonymous man, who finds his way to his own ends, and pities nobody and sticks at nothing?" he asked. "Give him a name!"

"I am quoting an example," said Sir Patrick. "I am not attacking a man."

"What right have you," cried Geoffrey—utterly forgetful, in the strange exasperation that had seized on him, of the interest that he had in controlling himself before Sir Patrick—"what right have you to pick out an example of a rowing man who is an infernal scoundrel—when it's quite as likely that a rowing man may be a good fellow: ay! and a better fellow, if you come to that, than ever stood in your shoes!"

"If the one case is quite as likely to occur as the other (which I readily admit)," answered Sir Patrick, "I have surely a right to choose which case I please for illustration. (Wait, Mr. Delamayn! These are the last words I have to say and I mean to say them.) I have taken the example—not of a specially depraved man, as you erroneously suppose—but of an average man, with his average share of the mean, cruel, and dangerous qualities, which are part and parcel of unreformed human nature—as your religion tells you, and as you may see for yourself, if you choose to look at your untaught fellow-creatures any where. I suppose that man to be tried by a temptation to wickedness, out of the common; and I show, to the best of my ability, how completely the moral and mental neglect of himself, which the present material tone of public feeling in England has tacitly encouraged, leaves him at the mercy of all the worst instincts in his nature; and how surely, under those conditions, he must go down (gentleman as he is) step by step—as the lowest vagabond in the streets goes down under his special temptation—from the beginning in ignorance to the end in crime. If you deny my right to take such an example as that, in illustration of the views I advocate, you must either deny that a special temptation to wickedness can assail a man in the position of a gentleman, or you must assert that gentlemen who are naturally superior to all temptation are the only gentlemen who devote themselves to athletic pursuits. There is my defense. In stating my case, I have spoken out of my own sincere respect for the interests of virtue and of learning; out of my own sincere admiration for those young men among us who are resisting the contagion of barbarism about them. In their future is the future hope of England. I have done."

Angrily ready with a violent personal reply, Geoffrey found himself checked, in his turn by another person with something to say, and with a resolution to say it at that particular moment.

For some little time past the surgeon had discontinued his steady investigation of Geoffrey's face, and had given all his attention to the discussion, with the air of a man whose self-imposed task had come to an end. As the last sentence fell from the last speaker's lips, he interposed so quickly and so skillfully between Geoffrey and Sir Patrick, that Geoffrey himself was taken by surprise,

"There is something still wanting to make Sir Patrick's statement of the case complete," he said. "I think I can supply it, from the result of my own professional experience. Before I say what I have to say, Mr. Delamayn will perhaps excuse me, if I venture on giving him a caution to control himself."

"Are you going to make a dead set at me, too?" inquired Geoffrey.

"I am recommending you to keep your temper—nothing more. There are plenty of men who can fly into a passion without doing themselves any particular harm. You are not one of them."

"What do you mean?"

"I don't think the state of your health, Mr. Delamayn, is quite so satisfactory as you may be disposed to consider it yourself."

Geoffrey turned to his admirers and adherents with a roar of derisive laughter. The admirers and adherents all echoed him together. Arnold and Blanche smiled at each other. Even Sir Patrick looked as if he could hardly credit the evidence of his own ears. There stood the modern Hercules, self-vindicated as a Hercules, before all eyes that looked at him. And there, opposite, stood a man whom he could have killed with one blow of his fist, telling him, in serious earnest, that he was not in perfect health!

"You are a rare fellow!" said Geoffrey, half in jest and half in anger. "What's the matter with me?"

"I have undertaken to give you, what I believe to be, a necessary caution," answered the surgeon. "I have not undertaken to tell you what I think is the matter with you. That may be a question for consideration some little time hence. In the meanwhile, I should like to put my impression about you to the test. Have you any objection to answer a question on a matter of no particular importance relating to yourself?"

"Let's hear the question first."

"I have noticed something in your behavior while Sir Patrick was speaking. You are as much interested in opposing his views as any of those gentlemen about you. I don't understand your sitting in silence, and leaving it entirely to the others to put the case on your side—until Sir Patrick said something which happened to irritate you. Had you, all the time before that, no answer ready in your own mind?"

"I had as good answers in my mind as any that have been made here to-day."

"And yet you didn't give them?"

"No; I didn't give them."

"Perhaps you felt—though you knew your objections to be good ones—that it was hardly worth while to take the trouble of putting them into words? In short, you let your friends answer for you, rather than make the effort of answering for yourself?"

Geoffrey looked at his medical adviser with a sudden curiosity and a sudden distrust.

"I say," he asked, "how do you come to know what's going on in my mind—without my telling you of it?"

"It is my business to find out what is going on in people's bodies—and to do that it is sometimes necessary for me to find out (if I can) what is going on in their minds. If I have rightly interpreted what was going on in your mind, there is no need for me to press my question. You have answered it already."

He turned to Sir Patrick next

"There is a side to this subject," he said, "which you have not touched on yet. There is a Physical objection to the present rage for muscular exercises of all sorts, which is quite as strong, in its way, as the Moral objection. You have stated the consequences as they may affect the mind. I can state the consequences as they do affect the body."

"From your own experience?"

"From my own experience. I can tell you, as a medical man, that a proportion, and not by any means a small one, of the young men who are now putting themselves to violent athletic tests of their strength and endurance, are taking that course to the serious and permanent injury of their own health. The public who attend rowing-matches, foot-races, and other exhibitions of that sort, see nothing but the successful results of muscular training. Fathers and mothers at home see the failures. There are households in England—miserable households, to be counted, Sir Patrick, by more than ones and twos—in which there are young men who have to thank the strain laid on their constitutions by the popular physical displays of the present time, for being broken men, and invalided men, for the rest of their lives."

"Do you hear that?" said Sir Patrick, looking at Geoffrey.

Geoffrey carelessly nodded his head. His irritation had had time to subside; the stolid indifference had got possession of him again. He had resumed his chair—he sat, with outstretched legs, staring stupidly at the pattern on the carpet. "What does it matter to Me?" was the sentiment expressed all over him, from head to foot.

The surgeon went on.

"I can see no remedy for this sad state of things," he said, "as long as the public feeling remains what the public feeling is now. A fine healthy-looking young man, with a superb muscular development, longs (naturally enough) to distinguish himself like others. The training-authorities at his college, or elsewhere, take him in hand (naturally enough again) on the strength of outward appearances. And whether they have been right or wrong in choosing him is more than they can say, until the experiment has been tried, and the mischief has been, in many cases, irretrievably done. How many of them are aware of the important physiological truth, that the muscular power of a man is no fair guarantee of his vital power? How many of them know that we all have (as a great French writer puts it) two lives in us—the surface life of the muscles, and the inner life of the heart, lungs, and brain? Even if they did know this—even with medical men to help them—it would be in the last degree doubtful, in most cases, whether any previous examination would result in any reliable discovery of the vital fitness of the man to undergo the stress of muscular exertion laid on him. Apply to any of my brethren; and they will tell you, as the result of their own professional observation, that I am, in no sense, overstating this serious evil, or exaggerating the deplorable and dangerous consequences to which it leads. I have a patient at this moment, who is a young man of twenty, and who possesses one of the finest muscular developments I ever saw in my life. If that young man had consulted me, before he followed the example of the other young men about him, I can not honestly say that I could have foreseen the results. As things are, after going through a certain amount of muscular training, after performing a certain number of muscular feats, he suddenly fainted one day, to the astonishment of his family and friends. I was called in and I have watched the case since. He will probably live, but he will never recover. I am obliged to take precautions with this youth of twenty which I should take with an old man of eighty. He is big enough and muscular enough to sit to a painter as a model for Samson—and only last week I saw him swoon away like a young girl, in his mother's arms."

"Name!" cried Geoffrey's admirers, still fighting the battle on their side, in the absence of any encouragement from Geoffrey himself.

"I am not in the habit of mentioning my patients' names," replied the surgeon. "But if you insist on my producing an example of a man broken by athletic exercises, I can do it."

"Do it! Who is he?"

"You all know him perfectly well."

"Is he in the doctor's hands?"

"Not yet."

"Where is he?"

"There!"

In a pause of breathless silence—with the eyes of every person in the room eagerly fastened on him—the surgeon lifted his hand and pointed to Geoffrey Delamayn.

CHAPTER THE TWENTIETH.

TOUCHING IT.

As soon as the general stupefaction was allayed, the general incredulity asserted itself as a matter of course.

The man who first declared that "seeing" was "believing" laid his finger (whether he knew it himself or not) on one of the fundamental follies of humanity. The easiest of all evidence to receive is the evidence that requires no other judgment to decide on it than the judgment of the eye—and it will be, on that account, the evidence which humanity is most ready to credit, as long as humanity lasts. The eyes of every body looked at Geoffrey; and the judgment of every body decided, on the evidence there visible, that the surgeon must be wrong. Lady Lundie herself (disturbed over her dinner invitations) led the general protest. "Mr. Delamayn in broken health!" she exclaimed, appealing to the better sense of her eminent medical guest. "Really, now, you can't expect us to believe that!"

Stung into action for the second time by the startling assertion of which he had been made the subject, Geoffrey rose, and looked the surgeon, steadily and insolently, straight in the face.

"Do you mean what you say?" he asked.

"Yes."

"You point me out before all these people—"

"One moment, Mr. Delamayn. I admit that I may have been wrong in directing the general attention to you. You have a right to complain of my having answered too publicly the public challenge offered to me by your friends. I apologize for having done that. But I don't retract a single word of what I have said on the subject of your health."

"You stick to it that I'm a broken-down man?"

"I do."

"I wish you were twenty years younger, Sir!"

"Why?"

"I'd ask you to step out on the lawn there and I'd show you whether I'm a broken-down man or not."

Lady Lundie looked at her brother-in-law. Sir Patrick instantly interfered.

"Mr. Delamayn," he said, "you were invited here in the character of a gentleman, and you are a guest in a lady's house."

"No! no!" said the surgeon, good humoredly. "Mr. Delamayn is using a strong argument, Sir Patrick—and that is all. If I were twenty years younger," he went on, addressing himself to Geoffrey, "and if I did step out on the lawn with you, the result wouldn't affect the question between us in the least. I don't say that the violent bodily exercises in which you are famous have damaged your muscular power. I assert that they have damaged your vital power. In what particular way they have affected it I don't consider myself bound to tell you. I simply give you a warning, as a matter of common humanity. You will do well to be content with the success you have already achieved in the field of athletic pursuits, and to alter your mode of life for the future. Accept my excuses, once more, for having said this publicly instead of privately—and don't forget my warning."

He turned to move away to another part of the room. Geoffrey fairly forced him to return to the subject.

"Wait a bit," he said. "You have had your innings. My turn now. I can't give it words as you do; but I can come to the point. And, by the Lord, I'll fix you to it! In ten days or a fortnight from this I'm going into training for the Foot-Race at Fulham. Do you say I shall break down?"

"You will probably get through your training."

"Shall I get through the race?"

"You may possibly get through the race. But if you do—"

"If I do?"

"You will never run another."

"And never row in another match?"

"Never."

"I have been asked to row in the Race, next spring; and I have said I will. Do you tell me, in so many words, that I sha'n't be able to do it?"

"Yes—in so many words."

"Positively?"

"Positively."

"Back your opinion!" cried Geoffrey, tearing his betting-book out of his pocket. "I lay you an even hundred I'm in fit condition to row in the University Match next spring."

"I don't bet, Mr. Delamayn."

With that final reply the surgeon walked away to the other end of the library. Lady Lundie (taking Blanche in custody) withdrew, at the same time, to return to the serious business of her invitations for the dinner. Geoffrey turned defiantly, book in hand, to his college friends about him. The British blood was up; and the British resolution to bet, which successfully defies common decency and common-law from one end of the country to the other, was not to be trifled with.

"Come on!" cried Geoffrey. "Back the doctor, one of you!"

Sir Patrick rose in undisguised disgust, and followed the surgeon. One, Two, and Three, invited to business by their illustrious friend, shook their thick heads at him knowingly, and answered with one accord, in one eloquent word—"Gammon!"

"One of you back him!" persisted Geoffrey, appealing to the two choral gentlemen in the back-ground, with his temper fast rising to fever heat. The two choral gentlemen compared notes, as usual. "We weren't born yesterday, Smith?" "Not if we know it, Jones."

"Smith!" said Geoffrey, with a sudden assumption of politeness ominous of something unpleasant to come.

Smith said "Yes?"—with a smile.

"Jones!"

Jones said "Yes?"—with a reflection of Smith.

"You're a couple of infernal cads—and you haven't got a hundred pound between you!"

"Come! come!" said Arnold, interfering for the first time. "This is shameful, Geoffrey!"

"Why the"—(never mind what!)—"won't they any of them take the bet?"

"If you must be a fool," returned Arnold, a little irritably on his side, "and if nothing else will keep you quiet, I'll take the bet."

"An even hundred on the doctor!" cried Geoffrey. "Done with you!"

His highest aspirations were satisfied; his temper was in perfect order again. He entered the bet in his book; and made his excuses to Smith and Jones in the heartiest way. "No offense, old chaps! Shake hands!" The two choral gentlemen were enchanted with him. "The English aristocracy—eh, Smith?" "Blood and breeding—ah, Jones!"

As soon as he had spoken, Arnold's conscience reproached him: not for betting (who is ashamed of that form of gambling in England?) but for "backing the doctor." With the best intention toward his friend, he was speculating on the failure of his friend's health. He anxiously assured Geoffrey that no man in the room could be more heartily persuaded that the surgeon was wrong than himself. "I don't cry off from the bet," he said. "But, my dear fellow, pray understand that I only take it to please you."

"Bother all that!" answered Geoffrey, with the steady eye to business, which was one of the choicest virtues in his character. "A bet's a bet—and hang your sentiment!" He drew Arnold by the arm out of ear-shot of the others. "I say!" he asked, anxiously. "Do you think I've set the old fogy's back up?"

"Do you mean Sir Patrick?"

Geoffrey nodded, and went on.

"I haven't put that little matter to him yet—about marrying in Scotland, you know. Suppose he cuts up rough with me if I try him now?" His eye wandered cunningly, as he put the question, to the farther end of the room. The surgeon was looking over a port-folio of prints. The ladies were still at work on their notes of invitation. Sir Patrick was alone at the book-shelves immersed in a volume which he had just taken down.

"Make an apology," suggested Arnold. "Sir Patrick may be a little irritable and bitter; but he's a just man and a kind man. Say you were not guilty of any intentional disrespect toward him—and you will say enough."

"All right!"

Sir Patrick, deep in an old Venetian edition of The Decameron, found himself suddenly recalled from medieval Italy to modern England, by no less a person than Geoffrey Delamayn.

"What do you want?" he asked, coldly.

"I want to make an apology," said Geoffrey. "Let by-gones be by-gones—and that sort of thing. I wasn't guilty of any intentional disrespect toward you. Forgive and forget. Not half a bad motto, Sir—eh?"

It was clumsily expressed—but still it was an apology. Not even Geoffrey could appeal to Sir Patrick's courtesy and Sir Patrick's consideration in vain.

"Not a word more, Mr. Delamayn!" said the polite old man. "Accept my excuses for any thing which I may have said too sharply, on my side; and let us by all means forget the rest."

Having met the advance made to him, in those terms, he paused, expecting Geoffrey to leave him free to return to the Decameron. To his unutterable astonishment, Geoffrey suddenly stooped over him, and whispered in his ear, "I want a word in private with you."

Sir Patrick started back, as if Geoffrey had tried to bite him.

"I beg your pardon, Mr. Delamayn—what did you say?"

"Could you give me a word in private?"

Sir Patrick put back the Decameron; and bowed in freezing silence. The confidence of the Honorable Geoffrey Delamayn was the last confidence in the world into which he desired to be drawn. "This is the secret of the apology!" he thought. "What can he possibly want with Me?"

"It's about a friend of mine," pursued Geoffrey; leading the way toward one of the windows. "He's in a scrape, my friend is. And I want to ask your advice. It's strictly private, you know." There he came to a full stop—and looked to see what impression he had produced, so far.

Sir Patrick declined, either by word or gesture, to exhibit the slightest anxiety to hear a word more.

"Would you mind taking a turn in the garden?" asked Geoffrey.

Sir Patrick pointed to his lame foot. "I have had my allowance of walking this morning," he said. "Let my infirmity excuse me."

Geoffrey looked about him for a substitute for the garden, and led the way back again toward one of the convenient curtained recesses opening out of the inner wall of the library. "We shall be private enough here," he said.

Sir Patrick made a final effort to escape the proposed conference—an undisguised effort, this time.

"Pray forgive me, Mr. Delamayn. Are you quite sure that you apply to the right person, in applying to me?"

"You're a Scotch lawyer, ain't you?"

"Certainly."

"And you understand about Scotch marriages—eh?"

Sir Patrick's manner suddenly altered.

"Is that the subject you wish to consult me on?" he asked.

"It's not me. It's my friend."

"Your friend, then?"

"Yes. It's a scrape with a woman. Here in Scotland. My friend don't know whether he's married to her or not."

"I am at your service, Mr. Delamayn."

To Geoffrey's relief—by no means unmixed with surprise—Sir Patrick not only showed no further reluctance to be consulted by him, but actually advanced to meet his wishes, by leading the way to the recess that was nearest to them. The quick brain of the old lawyer had put Geoffrey's application to him for assistance, and Blanche's application to him for assistance, together; and had built its own theory on the basis thus obtained. "Do I see a connection between the present position of Blanche's governess, and the present position of Mr. Delamayn's 'friend?'" thought Sir Patrick. "Stranger extremes than that have met me in my experience. Something may come out of this."

The two strangely-assorted companions seated themselves, one on each side of a little table in the recess. Arnold and the other guests had idled out again on to the lawn. The surgeon with his prints, and the ladies with their invitations, were safely absorbed in a distant part of the library. The conference between the two men, so trifling in appearance, so terrible in its destined influence, not over Anne's future only, but over the future of Arnold and Blanche, was, to all practical purposes, a conference with closed doors.

"Now," said Sir Patrick, "what is the question?"

"The question," said Geoffrey, "is whether my friend is married to her or not?"

"Did he mean to marry her?"

"No."

"He being a single man, and she being a single woman, at the time? And both in Scotland?"

"Yes."

"Very well. Now tell me the circumstances."

Geoffrey hesitated. The art of stating circumstances implies the cultivation of a very rare gift—the gift of arranging ideas. No one was better acquainted with this truth than Sir Patrick. He was purposely puzzling Geoffrey at starting, under the firm conviction that his client had something to conceal from him. The one process that could be depended on for extracting the truth, under those circumstances, was the process of interrogation. If Geoffrey was submitted to it, at the outset, his cunning might take the alarm. Sir Patrick's object was to make the man himself invite interrogation. Geoffrey invited it forthwith, by attempting to state the circumstances, and by involving them in the usual confusion. Sir Patrick waited until he had thoroughly lost the thread of his narrative—and then played for the winning trick.

"Would it be easier to you if I asked a few questions?" he inquired, innocently.

"Much easier."

"I am quite at your service. Suppose we clear the ground to begin with? Are you at liberty to mention names?"

"No."

"Places?"

"No."

"Dates?"

"Do you want me to be particular?"

"Be as particular as you can."

"Will it do, if I say the present year?"

"Yes. Were your friend and the lady—at some time in the present year—traveling together in Scotland?"

"No."

"Living together in Scotland?"

"No."

"What were they doing together in Scotland?"

"Well—they were meeting each other at an inn."

"Oh? They were meeting each other at an inn. Which was first at the rendezvous?"

"The woman was first. Stop a bit! We are getting to it now." He produced from his pocket the written memorandum of Arnold's proceedings at Craig Fernie, which he had taken down from Arnold's own lips. "I've got a bit of note here," he went on. "Perhaps you'd like to have a look at it?"

Sir Patrick took the note—read it rapidly through to himself—then re-read it, sentence by sentence, to Geoffrey; using it as a text to speak from, in making further inquiries.

"'He asked for her by the name of his wife, at the door,'" read Sir Patrick. "Meaning, I presume, the door of the inn? Had the lady previously given herself out as a married woman to the people of the inn?"

"Yes."

"How long had she been at the inn before the gentleman joined her?"

"Only an hour or so."

"Did she give a name?"

"I can't be quite sure—I should say not."

"Did the gentleman give a name?"

"No. I'm certain he didn't."

Sir Patrick returned to the memorandum.

"'He said at dinner, before the landlady and the waiter, I take these rooms for my wife. He made her say he was her husband, at the same time.' Was that done jocosely, Mr. Delamayn—either by the lady or the gentleman?"

"No. It was done in downright earnest."

"You mean it was done to look like earnest, and so to deceive the landlady and the waiter?"

"Yes."

Sir Patrick returned to the memorandum.

"'After that, he stopped all night.' Stopped in the rooms he had taken for himself and his wife?"

"Yes."

"And what happened the next day?"

"He went away. Wait a bit! Said he had business for an excuse."

"That is to say, he kept up the deception with the people of the inn? and left the lady behind him, in the character of his wife?"

"That's it."

"Did he go back to the inn?"

"No."

"How long did the lady stay there, after he had gone?"

"She staid—well, she staid a few days."

"And your friend has not seen her since?"

"No."

"Are your friend and the lady English or Scotch?"

"Both English."

"At the time when they met at the inn, had they either of them arrived in Scotland, from the place in which they were previously living, within a period of less than twenty-one days?"

Geoffrey hesitated. There could be no difficulty in answering for Anne. Lady Lundie and her domestic circle had occupied Windygates for a much longer period than three weeks before the date of the lawn-party. The question, as it affected Arnold, was the only question that required reflection. After searching his memory for details of the conversation which had taken place between them, when he and Arnold had met at the lawn-party, Geoffrey recalled a certain reference on the part of his friend to a performance at the Edinburgh theatre, which at once decided the question of time. Arnold had been necessarily detained in Edinburgh, before his arrival at Windygates, by legal business connected with his inheritance; and he, like Anne, had certainly been in Scotland, before they met at Craig Fernie, for a longer period than a period of three weeks He accordingly informed Sir Patrick that the lady and gentleman had been in Scotland for more than twenty-one days—and then added a question on his own behalf: "Don't let me hurry you, Sir—but, shall you soon have done?"

"I shall have done, after two more questions," answered Sir Patrick. "Am I to understand that the lady claims, on the strength of the circumstances which you have mentioned to me, to be your friend's wife?"

Geoffrey made an affirmative reply. The readiest means of obtaining Sir Patrick's opinion was, in this case, to answer, Yes. In other words, to represent Anne (in the character of "the lady") as claiming to be married to Arnold (in the character of "his friend").

Having made this concession to circumstances, he was, at the same time, quite cunning enough to see that it was of vital importance to the purpose which he had in view, to confine himself strictly to this one perversion of the truth. There could be plainly no depending on the lawyer's opinion, unless that opinion was given on the facts exactly as they had occurred at the inn. To the facts he had, thus far, carefully adhered; and to the facts (with the one inevitable departure from them which had been just forced on him) he determined to adhere to the end.

"Did no letters pass between the lady and gentleman?" pursued Sir Patrick.

"None that I know of," answered Geoffrey, steadily returning to the truth.

"I have done, Mr. Delamayn."

"Well? and what's your opinion?"

"Before I give my opinion I am bound to preface it by a personal statement which you are not to take, if you please, as a statement of the law. You ask me to decide—on the facts with which you have supplied me—whether your friend is, according to the law of Scotland, married or not?"

Geoffrey nodded. "That's it!" he said, eagerly.

"My experience, Mr. Delamayn, is that any single man, in Scotland, may marry any single woman, at any time, and under any circumstances. In short, after thirty years' practice as a lawyer, I don't know what is not a marriage in Scotland."

"In plain English," said Geoffrey, "you mean she's his wife?"

In spite of his cunning; in spite of his self-command, his eyes brightened as he said those words. And the tone in which he spoke—though too carefully guarded to be a tone of triumph—was, to a fine ear, unmistakably a tone of relief.

Neither the look nor the tone was lost on Sir Patrick.

His first suspicion, when he sat down to the conference, had been the obvious suspicion that, in speaking of "his friend," Geoffrey was speaking of himself. But, like all lawyers, he habitually distrusted first impressions, his own included. His object, thus far, had been to solve the problem of Geoffrey's true position and Geoffrey's real motive. He had set the snare accordingly, and had caught his bird.

It was now plain to his mind—first, that this man who was consulting him, was, in all probability, really speaking of the case of another person: secondly, that he had an interest (of what nature it was impossible yet to say) in satisfying his own mind that "his friend" was, by the law of Scotland, indisputably a married man. Having penetrated to that extent the secret which Geoffrey was concealing from him, he abandoned the hope of making any further advance at that present sitting. The next question to clear up in the investigation, was the question of who the anonymous "lady" might be. And the next discovery to make was, whether "the lady" could, or could not, be identified with Anne Silvester. Pending the inevitable delay in reaching that result, the straight course was (in Sir Patrick's present state of uncertainty) the only course to follow in laying down the law. He at once took the question of the marriage in hand—with no concealment whatever, as to the legal bearings of it, from the client who was consulting him.

"Don't rush to conclusions, Mr. Delamayn," he said. "I have only told you what my general experience is thus far. My professional opinion on the special case of your friend has not been given yet."

Geoffrey's face clouded again. Sir Patrick carefully noted the new change in it.

"The law of Scotland," he went on, "so far as it relates to Irregular Marriages, is an outrage on common decency and common-sense. If you think my language in thus describing it too strong—I can refer you to the language of a judicial authority. Lord Deas delivered a recent judgment of marriage in Scotland, from the bench, in these words: 'Consent makes marriage. No form or ceremony, civil or religious; no notice before, or publication after; no cohabitation, no writing, no witnesses even, are essential to the constitution of this, the most important contract which two persons can enter into.'—There is a Scotch judge's own statement of the law that he administers! Observe, at the same time, if you please, that we make full legal provision in Scotland for contracts affecting the sale of houses and lands, horses and dogs. The only contract which we leave without safeguards or precautions of any sort is the contract that unites a man and a woman for life. As for the authority of parents, and the innocence of children, our law recognizes no claim on it either in the one case or in the other. A girl of twelve and a boy of fourteen have nothing to do but to cross the Border, and to be married—without the interposition of the slightest delay or restraint, and without the slightest attempt to inform their parents on the part of the Scotch law. As to the marriages of men and women, even the mere interchange of consent which, as you have just heard, makes them man and wife, is not required to be directly proved: it may be proved by inference. And, more even than that, whatever the law for its consistency may presume, men and women are, in point of fact, held to be married in Scotland where consent has never been interchanged, and where the parties do not even know that they are legally held to be married persons. Are you sufficiently confused about the law of Irregular Marriages in Scotland by this time, Mr. Delamayn? And have I said enough to justify the strong language I used when I undertook to describe it to you?"

"Who's that 'authority' you talked of just now?" inquired Geoffrey. "Couldn't I ask him?"

"You might find him flatly contradicted, if you did ask him by another authority equally learned and equally eminent," answered Sir Patrick. "I am not joking—I am only stating facts. Have you heard of the Queen's Commission?"

"No."

"Then listen to this. In March, 'sixty-five, the Queen appointed a Commission to inquire into the Marriage-Laws of the United Kingdom. The Report of that Commission is published in London; and is accessible to any body who chooses to pay the price of two or three shillings for it. One of the results of the inquiry was, the discovery that high authorities were of entirely contrary opinions on one of the vital questions of Scottish marriage-law. And the Commissioners, in announcing that fact, add that the question of which opinion is right is still disputed, and has never been made the subject of legal decision. Authorities are every where at variance throughout the Report. A haze of doubt and uncertainty hangs in Scotland over the most important contract of civilized life. If no other reason existed for reforming the Scotch marriage-law, there would be reason enough afforded by that one fact. An uncertain marriage-law is a national calamity."

"You can tell me what you think yourself about my friend's case—can't you?" said Geoffrey, still holding obstinately to the end that he had in view.

"Certainly. Now that I have given you due warning of the danger of implicitly relying on any individual opinion, I may give my opinion with a clear conscience. I say that there has not been a positive marriage in this case. There has been evidence in favor of possibly establishing a marriage—nothing more."

The distinction here was far too fine to be appreciated by Geoffrey's mind. He frowned heavily, in bewilderment and disgust.

"Not married!" he exclaimed, "when they said they were man and wife, before witnesses?"

"That is a common popular error," said Sir Patrick. "As I have already told you, witnesses are not legally necessary to make a marriage in Scotland. They are only valuable—as in this case—to help, at some future time, in proving a marriage that is in dispute."

Geoffrey caught at the last words.

"The landlady and the waiter might make it out to be a marriage, then?" he said.

"Yes. And, remember, if you choose to apply to one of my professional colleagues, he might possibly tell you they were married already. A state of the law which allows the interchange of matrimonial consent to be proved by inference leaves a wide door open to conjecture. Your friend refers to a certain lady, in so many words, as his wife. The lady refers to your friend, in so many words, as her husband. In the rooms which they have taken, as man and wife, they remain, as man and wife, till the next morning. Your friend goes away, without undeceiving any body. The lady stays at the inn, for some days after, in the character of his wife. And all these circumstances take place in the presence of competent witnesses. Logically—if not legally—there is apparently an inference of the interchange of matrimonial consent here. I stick to my own opinion, nevertheless. Evidence in proof of a marriage (I say)—nothing more."

While Sir Patrick had been speaking, Geoffrey had been considering with himself. By dint of hard thinking he had found his way to a decisive question on his side.

"Look here!" he said, dropping his heavy hand down on the table. "I want to bring you to book, Sir! Suppose my friend had another lady in his eye?"

"Yes?"

"As things are now—would you advise him to marry her?"

"As things are now—certainly not!"

Geoffrey got briskly on his legs, and closed the interview.

"That will do," he said, "for him and for me."

With those words he walked back, without ceremony, into the main thoroughfare of the room.

"I don't know who your friend is," thought Sir Patrick, looking after him. "But if your interest in the question of his marriage is an honest and a harmless interest, I know no more of human nature than the babe unborn!"

Immediately on leaving Sir Patrick, Geoffrey was encountered by one of the servants in search of him.

"I beg your pardon, Sir," began the man. "The groom from the Honorable Mr. Delamayn's—"

"Yes? The fellow who brought me a note from my brother this morning?"

"He's expected back, Sir—he's afraid he mustn't wait any longer."

"Come here, and I'll give you the answer for him."

He led the way to the writing-table, and referred to Julius's letter again. He ran his eye carelessly over it, until he reached the final lines: "Come to-morrow, and help us to receive Mrs. Glenarm." For a while he paused, with his eye fixed on that sentence; and with the happiness of three people—of Anne, who had loved him; of Arnold, who had served him; of Blanche, guiltless of injuring him—resting on the decision that guided his movements for the next day. After what had passed that morning between Arnold and Blanche, if he remained at Lady Lundie's, he had no alternative but to perform his promise to Anne. If he returned to his brother's house, he had no alternative but to desert Anne, on the infamous pretext that she was Arnold's wife.

He suddenly tossed the letter away from him on the table, and snatched a sheet of note-paper out of the writing-case. "Here goes for Mrs. Glenarm!" he said to himself; and wrote back to his brother, in one line: "Dear Julius, Expect me to-morrow. G. D." The impassible man-servant stood by while he wrote, looking at his magnificent breadth of chest, and thinking what a glorious "staying-power" was there for the last terrible mile of the coming race.

"There you are!" he said, and handed his note to the man.

"All right, Geoffrey?" asked a friendly voice behind him.

He turned—and saw Arnold, anxious for news of the consultation with Sir Patrick.

"Yes," he said. "All right."

————— *NOTE.—There are certain readers who feel a disposition to doubt Facts, when they meet with them in a work of fiction. Persons of this way of thinking may be profitably referred to the book which first suggested to me the idea of writing the present Novel. The book is the Report of the Royal Commissioners on The Laws of Marriage. Published by the Queen's Printers For her Majesty's Stationery Office. (London, 1868.) What Sir Patrick says professionally of Scotch Marriages in this chapter is taken from this high authority. What the lawyer (in the Prologue) says professionally of Irish Marriages is also derived from the same source. It is needless to encumber these pages with quotations. But as a means of satisfying my readers that they may depend on me, I subjoin an extract from my list of references to the Report of the Marriage Commission, which any persons who may be so inclined can verify for themselves.*

Irish Marriages (In the Prologue).—See Report, pages XII., XIII., XXIV.

Irregular Marriages in Scotland.—Statement of the law by Lord Deas. Report, page XVI.—Marriages of children of tender years. Examination of Mr. Muirhead by Lord Chelmsford (Question 689).—Interchange of consent, established by inference. Examination of Mr. Muirhead by the Lord Justice Clerk (Question 654)—Marriage where consent has never been interchanged. Observations of Lord Deas. Report, page XIX.—Contradiction of opinions between authorities. Report, pages XIX., XX.—Legal provision for the sale of horses and dogs. No legal provision for the marriage of men and women. Mr. Seeton's Remarks. Report, page XXX.—Conclusion of the Commissioners. In spite of the arguments advanced before them in favor of not interfering with Irregular Marriages in Scotland, the Commissioners declare their opinion that "Such marriages ought not to continue." (Report, page XXXIV.)

In reference to the arguments (alluded to above) in favor of allowing the present disgraceful state of things to continue, I find them resting mainly on these grounds: That Scotland doesn't like being interfered with by England (!). That Irregular Marriages cost nothing (!!). That they are diminishing in number, and may therefore be trusted, in course of time, to exhaust themselves (!!!). That they act, on certain occasions, in the capacity of a moral trap to catch a profligate man (!!!!). Such is the elevated point of view from which the Institution of Marriage is regarded by some of the most pious and learned men in Scotland. A legal enactment providing for the sale of your wife, when you have done with her, or of your husband; when you "really can't put up with him any longer," appears to be all that is wanting to render this North British estimate of the "Estate of Matrimony" practically complete. It is only fair to add that, of the witnesses giving evidence—oral and written—before the Commissioners, fully one-half regard the Irregular Marriages of Scotland from the Christian and the civilized point of view, and entirely agree with the authoritative conclusion already cited—that such marriages ought to be abolished.

W. C.

CHAPTER THE TWENTY-FIRST.

DONE!

ARNOLD was a little surprised by the curt manner in which Geoffrey answered him.

"Has Sir Patrick said any thing unpleasant?" he asked.

"Sir Patrick has said just what I wanted him to say."

"No difficulty about the marriage?"

"None."

"No fear of Blanche—"

"She won't ask you to go to Craig Fernie—I'll answer for that!" He said the words with a strong emphasis on them, took his brother's letter from the table, snatched up his hat, and went out.

His friends, idling on the lawn, hailed him. He passed by them quickly without answering, without so much as a glance at them over his shoulder. Arriving at the rose-garden, he stopped and took out his pipe; then suddenly changed his mind, and turned back again by another path. There was no certainty, at that hour of the day, of his being left alone in the rose-garden. He had a fierce and hungry longing to be by himself; he felt as if he could have been the death of any body who came and spoke to him at that moment. With his head down and his brows knit heavily, he followed the path to see what it ended in. It ended in a wicket-gate which led into a kitchen-garden. Here he was well out of the way of interruption: there was nothing to attract visitors in the kitchen-garden. He went on to a walnut-tree planted in the middle of the inclosure, with a wooden bench and a broad strip of turf running round it. After first looking about him, he seated himself and lit his pipe.

"I wish it was done!" he said.

He sat, with his elbows on his knees, smoking and thinking. Before long the restlessness that had got possession of him forced him to his feet again. He rose, and paced round and round the strip of greensward under the walnut-tree, like a wild beast in a cage.

What was the meaning of this disturbance in the inner man? Now that he had committed himself to the betrayal of the friend who had trusted and served him, was he torn by remorse?

He was no more torn by remorse than you are while your eye is passing over this sentence. He was simply in a raging fever of impatience to see himself safely landed at the end which he had in view.

Why should he feel remorse? All remorse springs, more or less directly, from the action of two sentiments, which are neither of them inbred in the natural man. The first of these sentiments is the product of the respect which we learn to feel for ourselves. The second is the product of the respect which we learn to feel for others. In their highest manifestations, these two feelings exalt themselves, until the first he comes the love of God, and the second the love of Man. I have injured you, and I repent of it when it is done. Why should I repent of it if I have gained something by it for my own self and if you can't make me feel it by injuring Me? I repent of it because there has been a sense put into me which tells me that I have sinned against Myself, and sinned against You. No such sense as that exists among the instincts of the natural man. And no such feelings as these troubled Geoffrey Delamayn; for Geoffrey Delamayn was the natural man.

When the idea of his scheme had sprung to life in his mind, the novelty of it had startled him—the enormous daring of it, suddenly self-revealed, had daunted him. The signs of emotion which he had betrayed at the writing-table in the library were the signs of mere mental perturbation, and of nothing more.

That first vivid impression past, the idea had made itself familiar to him. He had become composed enough to see such difficulties as it involved, and such consequences as it implied. These had fretted him with a passing trouble; for these he plainly discerned. As for the cruelty and the treachery of the thing he meditated doing—that consideration never crossed the limits of his mental view. His position toward the man whose life he had preserved was the position of a dog. The "noble animal" who has saved you or me from drowning will fly at your throat or mine, under certain conditions, ten minutes afterward. Add to the dog's unreasoning instinct the calculating cunning of a man; suppose yourself to be in a position to say of some trifling thing, "Curious! at such and such a time I happened to pick up such and such an object; and now it turns out to be of some use to me!"—and there you have an index to the state of Geoffrey's feeling toward his friend when he recalled the past or when he contemplated the future. When Arnold had spoken to him at the critical moment, Arnold had violently irritated him; and that was all.

The same impenetrable insensibility, the same primitively natural condition of the moral being, prevented him from being troubled by the slightest sense of pity for Anne. "She's out of my way!" was his first thought. "She's provided for, without any trouble to Me!" was his second. He was not in the least uneasy about her. Not the slightest doubt crossed his mind that, when once she had realized her own situation, when once she saw herself placed between the two alternatives of facing her own ruin or of claiming Arnold as a last resource, she would claim Arnold. She would do it as a matter of course; because he would have done it in her place.

But he wanted it over. He was wild, as he paced round and round the walnut-tree, to hurry on the crisis and be done with it. Give me my freedom to go to the other woman, and to train for the foot-race—that's what I want. They injured? Confusion to them both! It's I who am injured by them. They are the worst enemies I have! They stand in my way.

How to be rid of them? There was the difficulty. He had made up his mind to be rid of them that day. How was he to begin?

There was no picking a quarrel with Arnold, and so beginning with him. This course of proceeding, in Arnold's position toward Blanche, would lead to a scandal at the outset—a scandal which would stand in the way of his making the right impression on Mrs. Glenarm. The woman—lonely and friendless, with her sex and her position both against her if she tried to make a scandal of it—the woman was the one to begin with. Settle it at once and forever with Anne; and leave Arnold to hear of it and deal with it, sooner or later, no matter which.

How was he to break it to her before the day was out?

By going to the inn and openly addressing her to her face as Mrs. Arnold Brinkworth? No! He had had enough, at Windygates, of meeting her face to face. The easy way was to write to her, and send the letter, by the first messenger he could find, to the inn. She might appear afterward at Windygates; she might follow him to his brother's; she might appeal to his father. It didn't matter; he had got the whip-hand of her now. "You are a married woman." There was the one sufficient answer, which was strong enough to back him in denying any thing!

He made out the letter in his own mind. "Something like this would do," he thought, as he went round and round the walnut-tree: "You may be surprised not to have seen me. You have only yourself to thank for it. I know what took place between you and him at the inn. I have had a lawyer's advice. You are Arnold Brinkworth's wife. I wish you joy, and good-by forever." Address those lines: "To Mrs. Arnold Brinkworth;" instruct the messenger to leave the letter late that night, without waiting for an answer; start the first thing the next morning for his brother's house; and behold, it was done!

But even here there was an obstacle—one last exasperating obstacle—still in the way.

If she was known at the inn by any name at all, it was by the name of Mrs. Silvester. A letter addressed to "Mrs. Arnold Brinkworth" would probably not be taken in at the door; or if it was admitted and if it was actually offered to her, she might decline to receive it, as a letter not addressed to herself. A man of readier mental resources would have seen that the name on the outside of the letter mattered little or nothing, so long as the contents were read by the person to whom they were addressed. But Geoffrey's was the order of mind which expresses disturbance by attaching importance to trifles. He attached an absurd importance to preserving absolute consistency in his letter, outside and in. If he declared her to be Arnold Brinkworth's wife, he must direct to her as Arnold Brinkworth's wife; or who could tell what the law might say, or what scrape he might not get himself into by a mere scratch of the pen! The more he thought of it, the more persuaded he felt of his own cleverness here, and the hotter and the angrier he grew.

There is a way out of every thing. And there was surely a way out of this, if he could only see it.

He failed to see it. After dealing with all the great difficulties, the small difficulty proved too much for him. It struck him that he might have been thinking too long about it—considering that he was not accustomed to thinking long about any thing. Besides, his head was getting giddy, with going mechanically round and round the tree. He irritably turned his back on the tree and struck into another path: resolved to think of something else, and then to return to his difficulty, and see it with a new eye.

Leaving his thoughts free to wander where they liked, his thoughts naturally busied themselves with the next subject that was uppermost in his mind, the subject of the Foot-Race. In a week's time his arrangements ought to be made. Now, as to the training, first.

He decided on employing two trainers this time. One to travel to Scotland, and begin with him at his brother's house. The other to take him up, with a fresh eye to him, on his return to London. He turned over in his mind the performances of the formidable rival against whom he was to be matched. That other man was the swiftest runner of the two. The betting in Geoffrey's favor was betting which calculated on the unparalleled length of the race, and on Geoffrey's prodigious powers of endurance. How long he should "wait on" the man? Whereabouts it would be safe to "pick the man up?" How near the end to calculate the man's exhaustion to a nicety, and "put on the spurt," and pass him? These were nice points to decide. The deliberations of a pedestrian-privy-council would be required to help him under this heavy responsibility. What men could he trust? He could trust A. and B.—both of them authorities: both of them stanch. Query about C.? As an authority, unexceptionable; as a man, doubtful. The problem relating to C. brought him to a standstill—and declined to be solved, even then. Never mind! he could always take the advice of A. and B. In the mean time devote C. to the infernal regions; and, thus dismissing him, try and think of something else. What else? Mrs. Glenarm? Oh, bother the women! one of them is the same as another. They all waddle when they run; and they all fill their stomachs before dinner with sloppy tea. That's the only difference between women and men—the rest is nothing but a weak imitation of Us. Devote the women to the infernal regions; and, so dismissing them, try and think of something else. Of what? Of something worth thinking of, this time—of filling another pipe.

He took out his tobacco-pouch; and suddenly suspended operations at the moment of opening it.

What was the object he saw, on the other side of a row of dwarf pear-trees, away to the right? A woman—evidently a servant by her dress—stooping down with her back to him, gathering something: herbs they looked like, as well as he could make them out at the distance.

What was that thing hanging by a string at the woman's side? A slate? Yes. What the deuce did she want with a slate at her side? He was in search of something to divert his mind—and here it was found. "Any thing will do for me," he thought. "Suppose I 'chaff' her a little about her slate?"

He called to the woman across the pear-trees. "Hullo!"

The woman raised herself, and advanced toward him slowly—looking at him, as she came on, with the sunken eyes, the sorrow-stricken face, the stony tranquillity of Hester Dethridge.

Geoffrey was staggered. He had not bargained for exchanging the dullest producible vulgarities of human speech (called in the language of slang, "Chaff") with such a woman as this.

"What's that slate for?" he asked, not knowing what else to say, to begin with.

The woman lifted her hand to her lips—touched them—and shook her head.

"Dumb?"

The woman bowed her head.

"Who are you?"

The woman wrote on her slate, and handed it to him over the pear-trees. He read:—"I am the cook."

"Well, cook, were you born dumb?"

The woman shook her head.

"What struck you dumb?"

The woman wrote on her slate:—"A blow."

"Who gave you the blow?"

She shook her head.

"Won't you tell me?"

She shook her head again.

Her eyes had rested on his face while he was questioning her; staring at him, cold, dull, and changeless as the eyes of a corpse. Firm as his nerves were—dense as he was, on all ordinary occasions, to any thing in the shape of an imaginative impression—the eyes of the dumb cook slowly penetrated him with a stealthy inner chill. Something crept at the marrow of his back, and shuddered under the roots of his hair. He felt a sudden impulse to get away from her. It was simple enough; he had only to say good-morning, and go on. He did say good-morning—but he never moved. He put his hand into his pocket, and offered her some money, as a way of making her go. She stretched out her hand across the pear-trees to take it—and stopped abruptly, with her arm suspended in the air. A sinister change passed over the deathlike tranquillity of her face. Her closed lips slowly dropped apart. Her dull eyes slowly dilated; looked away, sideways, from his eyes; stopped again; and stared, rigid and glittering, over his shoulder—stared as if they saw a sight of horror behind him. "What the devil are you looking at?" he asked—and turned round quickly, with a start. There was neither person nor thing to be seen behind him. He turned back again to the woman. The woman had left him, under the influence of some sudden panic. She was hurrying away from him—running, old as she was—flying the sight of him, as if the sight of him was the pestilence.

"Mad!" he thought—and turned his back on the sight of her.

He found himself (hardly knowing how he had got there) under the walnut-tree once more. In a few minutes his hardy nerves had recovered themselves—he could laugh over the remembrance of the strange impression that had been produced on him. "Frightened for the first time in my life," he thought—"and that by an old woman! It's time I went into training again, when things have come to this!"

He looked at his watch. It was close on the luncheon hour up at the house; and he had not decided yet what to do about his letter to Anne. He resolved to decide, then and there.

The woman—the dumb woman, with the stony face and the horrid eyes—reappeared in his thoughts, and got in the way of his decision. Pooh! some crazed old servant, who might once have been cook; who was kept out of charity now. Nothing more important than that. No more of her! no more of her!

He laid himself down on the grass, and gave his mind to the serious question. How to address Anne as "Mrs. Arnold Brinkworth?" and how to make sure of her receiving the letter?

The dumb old woman got in his way again.

He closed his eyes impatiently, and tried to shut her out in a darkness of his own making.

The woman showed herself through the darkness. He saw her, as if he had just asked her a question, writing on her slate. What she wrote he failed to make out. It was all over in an instant. He started up, with a feeling of astonishment at himself—and, at the same moment his brain cleared with the suddenness of a flash of light. He saw his way, without a conscious effort on his own part, through the difficulty that had troubled him. Two envelopes, of course: an inner one, unsealed, and addressed to "Mrs. Arnold Brinkworth;" an outer one, sealed, and addressed to "Mrs. Silvester:" and there was the problem solved! Surely the simplest problem that had ever puzzled a stupid head.

Why had he not seen it before? Impossible to say.

How came he to have seen it now?

The dumb old woman reappeared in his thoughts—as if the answer to the question lay in something connected with her.

He became alarmed about himself, for the first time in his life. Had this persistent impression, produced by nothing but a crazy old woman, any thing to do with the broken health which the surgeon had talked about? Was his head on the turn? Or had he smoked too much on an empty stomach, and gone too long (after traveling all night) without his customary drink of ale?

He left the garden to put that latter theory to the test forthwith. The betting would have gone dead against him if the public had seen him at that moment. He looked haggard and anxious—and with good reason too. His nervous system had suddenly forced itself on his notice, without the slightest previous introduction, and was saying (in an unknown tongue), Here I am!

Returning to the purely ornamental part of the grounds, Geoffrey encountered one of the footmen giving a message to one of the gardeners. He at once asked for the butler—as the only safe authority to consult in the present emergency.

Conducted to the butler's pantry, Geoffrey requested that functionary to produce a jug of his oldest ale, with appropriate solid nourishment in the shape of "a hunk of bread and cheese."

The butler stared. As a form of condescension among the upper classes this was quite new to him.

"Luncheon will be ready directly, Sir."

"What is there for lunch?"

The butler ran over an appetizing list of good dishes and rare wines.

"The devil take your kickshaws!" said Geoffrey. "Give me my old ale, and my hunk of bread and cheese."

"Where will you take them, Sir?"

"Here, to be sure! And the sooner the better."

The butler issued the necessary orders with all needful alacrity. He spread the simple refreshment demanded, before his distinguished guest, in a state of blank bewilderment. Here was a nobleman's son, and a public celebrity into the bargain, filling himself with bread and cheese and ale, in at once the most voracious and the most unpretending manner, at his table! The butler ventured on a little complimentary familiarity. He smiled, and touched the betting-book in his breast-pocket. "I've put six pound on you, Sir, for the Race." "All right, old boy! you shall win your money!" With those noble words the honorable gentleman clapped him on the back, and held out his tumbler for some more ale. The butler felt trebly an Englishman as he filled the foaming glass. Ah! foreign nations may have their revolutions! foreign aristocracies may tumble down! The British aristocracy lives in the hearts of the people, and lives forever!

"Another!" said Geoffrey, presenting his empty glass. "Here's luck!" He tossed off his liquor at a draught, and nodded to the butler, and went out.

Had the experiment succeeded? Had he proved his own theory about himself to be right? Not a doubt of it! An empty stomach, and a determination of tobacco to the head—these were the true causes of that strange state of mind into which he had fallen in the kitchen-garden. The dumb woman with the stony face vanished as if in a mist. He felt nothing now but a comfortable buzzing in his head, a genial warmth all over him, and an unlimited capacity for carrying any responsibility that could rest on mortal shoulders. Geoffrey was himself again.

He went round toward the library, to write his letter to Anne—and so have done with that, to begin with. The company had collected in the library waiting for the luncheon-bell. All were idly talking; and some would be certain, if he showed himself, to fasten on him. He turned back again, without showing himself. The only way of writing in peace and quietness would be to wait until they were all at luncheon, and then return to the library. The same opportunity would serve also for finding a messenger to take the letter, without exciting attention, and for going away afterward, unseen, on a long walk by himself. An absence of two or three hours would cast the necessary dust in Arnold's eyes; for it would be certainly interpreted by him as meaning absence at an interview with Anne.

He strolled idly through the grounds, farther and farther away from the house.

The talk in the library—aimless and empty enough, for the most part—was talk to the purpose, in one corner of the room, in which Sir Patrick and Blanche were sitting together.

"Uncle! I have been watching you for the last minute or two."

"At my age, Blanche? that is paying me a very pretty compliment."

"Do you know what I have seen?"

"You have seen an old gentleman in want of his lunch."

"I have seen an old gentleman with something on his mind. What is it?"

"Suppressed gout, my dear."

"That won't do! I am not to be put off in that way. Uncle! I want to know—"

"Stop there, Blanche! A young lady who says she 'wants to know,' expresses very dangerous sentiments. Eve 'wanted to know'—and see what it led to. Faust 'wanted to know'—and got into bad company, as the necessary result."

"You are feeling anxious about something," persisted Blanche. "And, what is more, Sir Patrick, you behaved in a most unaccountable manner a little while since."

"When?"

"When you went and hid yourself with Mr. Delamayn in that snug corner there. I saw you lead the way in, while I was at work on Lady Lundie's odious dinner-invitations."

"Oh! you call that being at work, do you? I wonder whether there was ever a woman yet who could give the whole of her mind to any earthly thing that she had to do?"

"Never mind the women! What subject in common could you and Mr. Delamayn possibly have to talk about? And why do I see a wrinkle between your eyebrows, now you have done with him?—a wrinkle which certainly wasn't there before you had that private conference together?"

Before answering, Sir Patrick considered whether he should take Blanche into his confidence or not. The attempt to identify Geoffrey's unnamed "lady," which he was determined to make, would lead him to Craig Fernie, and would no doubt end in obliging him to address himself to Anne. Blanche's intimate knowledge of her friend might unquestionably be made useful to him under these circumstances; and Blanche's discretion was to be trusted in any matter in which Miss Silvester's interests were concerned. On the other hand, caution was imperatively necessary, in the present imperfect state of his information—and caution, in Sir Patrick's mind, carried the day. He decided to wait and see what came first of his investigation at the inn.

"Mr. Delamayn consulted me on a dry point of law, in which a friend of his was interested," said Sir Patrick. "You have wasted your curiosity, my dear, on a subject totally unworthy of a lady's notice."

Blanche's penetration was not to be deceived on such easy terms as these. "Why not say at once that you won't tell me?" she rejoined. "You shutting yourself up with Mr. Delamayn to talk law! You looking absent and anxious about it afterward! I am a very unhappy girl!" said Blanche, with a little, bitter sigh. "There is something in me that seems to repel the people I love. Not a word in confidence can I get from Anne. And not a word in confidence can I get from you. And I do so long to sympathize! It's very hard. I think I shall go to Arnold."

Sir Patrick took his niece's hand.

"Stop a minute, Blanche. About Miss Silvester? Have you heard from her to-day?"

"No. I am more unhappy about her than words can say."

"Suppose somebody went to Craig Fernie and tried to find out the cause of Miss Silvester's silence? Would you believe that somebody sympathized with you then?"

Blanche's face flushed brightly with pleasure and surprise. She raised Sir Patrick's hand gratefully to her lips.

"Oh!" she exclaimed. "You don't mean that you would do that?"

"I am certainly the last person who ought to do it—seeing that you went to the inn in flat rebellion against my orders, and that I only forgave you, on your own promise of amendment, the other day. It is a miserably weak proceeding on the part of 'the head of the family' to be turning his back on his own principles, because his niece happens to be anxious and unhappy. Still (if you could lend me your little carriage), I might take a surly drive toward Craig Fernie, all by myself, and I might stumble against Miss Silvester—in case you have any thing to say."

"Any thing to say?" repeated Blanche. She put her arm round her uncle's neck, and whispered in his ear one of the most interminable messages that ever was sent from one human being to another. Sir Patrick listened, with a growing interest in the inquiry on which he was secretly bent. "The woman must have some noble qualities," he thought, "who can inspire such devotion as this."

While Blanche was whispering to her uncle, a second private conference—of the purely domestic sort—was taking place between Lady Lundie and the butler, in the hall outside the library door.

"I am sorry to say, my lady, Hester Dethridge has broken out again."

"What do you mean?"

"She was all right, my lady, when she went into the kitchen-garden, some time since. She's taken strange again, now she has come back. Wants the rest of the day to herself, your ladyship. Says she's overworked, with all the company in the house—and, I must say, does look like a person troubled and worn out in body and mind."

"Don't talk nonsense, Roberts! The woman is obstinate and idle and insolent. She is now in the house, as you know, under a month's notice to leave. If she doesn't choose to do her duty for that month I shall refuse to give her a character. Who is to cook the dinner to-day if I give Hester Dethridge leave to go out?"

"Any way, my lady, I am afraid the kitchen-maid will have to do her best to-day. Hester is very obstinate, when the fit takes her—as your ladyship says."

"If Hester Dethridge leaves the kitchen-maid to cook the dinner, Roberts, Hester Dethridge leaves my service to-day. I want no more words about it. If she persists in setting my orders at defiance, let her bring her account-book into the library, while we are at lunch, and lay it out my desk. I shall be back in the library after luncheon—and if I see the account-book I shall know what it means. In that case, you will receive my directions to settle with her and send her away. Ring the luncheon-bell."

The luncheon-bell rang. The guests all took the direction of the dining -room; Sir Patrick following, from the far end of the library, with Blanche on his arm. Arrived at the dining-room door, Blanche stopped, and asked her uncle to excuse her if she left him to go in by himself.

"I will be back directly," she said. "I have forgotten something up stairs."

Sir Patrick went in. The dining-room door closed; and Blanche returned alone to the library. Now on one pretense, and now on another, she had, for three days past, faithfully fulfilled the engagement she had made at Craig Fernie to wait ten minutes after luncheon-time in the library, on the chance of seeing Anne. On this, the fourth occasion, the faithful girl sat down alone in the great room, and waited with her eyes fixed on the lawn outside.

Five minutes passed, and nothing living appeared but the birds hopping about the grass.

In less than a minute more Blanche's quick ear caught the faint sound of a woman's dress brushing over the lawn. She ran to the nearest window, looked out, and clapped her hands with a cry of delight. There was the well-known figure, rapidly approaching her! Anne was true to their friendship—Anne had kept her engagement at last!

Blanche hurried out, and drew her into the library in triumph. "This makes amends, love for every thing! You answer my letter in the best of all ways—you bring me your own dear self."

She placed Anne in a chair, and, lifting her veil, saw her plainly in the brilliant mid-day light.

The change in the whole woman was nothing less than dreadful to the loving eyes that rested on her. She looked years older than her real age. There was a dull calm in her face, a stagnant, stupefied submission to any thing, pitiable to see. Three days and nights of solitude and grief, three days and nights of unresting and unpartaken suspense, had crushed that sensitive nature, had frozen that warm heart. The animating spirit was gone—the mere shell of the woman lived and moved, a mockery of her former self.

"Oh, Anne! Anne! What can have happened to you? Are you frightened? There's not the least fear of any body disturbing us. They are all at luncheon, and the servants are at dinner. We have the room entirely to ourselves. My darling! you look so faint and strange! Let me get you something."

Anne drew Blanche's head down and kissed her. It was done in a dull, slow way—without a word, without a tear, without a sigh.

"You're tired—I'm sure you're tired. Have you walked here? You sha'n't go back on foot; I'll take care of that!"

Anne roused herself at those words. She spoke for the first time. The tone was lower than was natural to her; sadder than was natural to her—but the charm of her voice, the native gentleness and beauty of it, seemed to have survived the wreck of all besides.

"I don't go back, Blanche. I have left the inn."

"Left the inn? With your husband?"

She answered the first question—not the second.

"I can't go back," she said. "The inn is no place for me. A curse seems to follow me, Blanche, wherever I go. I am the cause of quarreling and wretchedness, without meaning it, God knows. The old man who is head-waiter at the inn has been kind to me, my dear, in his way, and he and the landlady had hard words together about it. A quarrel, a shocking, violent quarrel. He has lost his place in consequence. The woman, his mistress, lays all the blame of it to my door. She is a hard woman; and she has been harder than ever since Bishopriggs went away. I have missed a letter at the inn—I must have thrown it aside, I suppose, and forgotten it. I only know that I remembered about it, and couldn't find it last night. I told the landlady, and she fastened a quarrel on me almost before the words were out of my mouth. Asked me if I charged her with stealing my letter. Said things to me—I can't repeat them. I am not very well, and not able to deal with people of that sort. I thought it best to leave Craig Fernie this morning. I hope and pray I shall never see Craig Fernie again."

She told her little story with a total absence of emotion of any sort, and laid her head back wearily on the chair when it was done.

Blanche's eyes filled with tears at the sight of her.

"I won't tease you with questions, Anne," she said, gently. "Come up stairs and rest in my room. You're not fit to travel, love. I'll take care that nobody comes near us."

The stable-clock at Windygates struck the quarter to two. Anne raised herself in the chair with a start.

"What time was that?" she asked.

Blanche told her.

"I can't stay," she said. "I have come here to find something out if I can. You won't ask me questions? Don't, Blanche, don't! for the sake of old times."

Blanche turned aside, heart-sick. "I will do nothing, dear, to annoy you," she said, and took Anne's hand, and hid the tears that were beginning to fall over her cheeks.

"I want to know something, Blanche. Will you tell me?"

"Yes. What is it?"

"Who are the gentlemen staying in the house?"

Blanche looked round at her again, in sudden astonishment and alarm. A vague fear seized her that Anne's mind had given way under the heavy weight of trouble laid on it. Anne persisted in pressing her strange request.

"Run over their names, Blanche. I have a reason for wishing to know who the gentlemen are who are staying in the house."

Blanche repeated the names of Lady Lundie's guests, leaving to the last the guests who had arrived last.

"Two more came back this morning," she went on. "Arnold Brinkworth and that hateful friend of his, Mr. Delamayn."

Anne's head sank back once more on the chair. She had found her way without exciting suspicion of the truth, to the one discovery which she had come to Windygates to make. He was in Scotland again, and he had only arrived from London that morning. There was barely time for him to have communicated with Craig Fernie before she left the inn—he, too, who hated letter-writing! The circumstances were all in his favor: there was no reason, there was really and truly no reason, so far, to believe that he had deserted her. The heart of the unhappy woman bounded in her bosom, under the first ray of hope that had warmed it for four days past. Under that sudden revulsion of feeling, her weakened frame shook from head to foot. Her face flushed deep for a moment—then turned deadly pale again. Blanche, anxiously watching her, saw the serious necessity for giving some restorative to her instantly.

"I am going to get you some wine—you will faint, Anne, if you don't take something. I shall be back in a moment; and I can manage it without any body being the wiser."

She pushed Anne's chair close to the nearest open window—a window at the upper end of the library—and ran out.

Blanche had barely left the room, by the door that led into the hall, when Geoffrey entered it by one of the lower windows opening from the lawn.

With his mind absorbed in the letter that he was about to write, he slowly advanced up the room toward the nearest table. Anne, hearing the sound of footsteps, started, and looked round. Her failing strength rallied in an instant, under the sudden relief of seeing him again. She rose and advanced eagerly, with a faint tinge of color in her cheeks. He looked up. The two stood face to face together—alone.

"Geoffrey!"

He looked at her without answering—without advancing a step, on his side. There was an evil light in his eyes; his silence was the brute silence that threatens dumbly. He had made up his mind never to see her again, and she had entrapped him into an interview. He had made up his mind to write, and there she stood forcing him to speak. The sum of her offenses against him was now complete. If there had ever been the faintest hope of her raising even a passing pity in his heart, that hope would have been annihilated now.

She failed to understand the full meaning of his silence. She made her excuses, poor soul, for venturing back to Windygates—her excuses to the man whose purpose at that moment was to throw her helpless on the world.

"Pray forgive me for coming here," she said. "I have done nothing to compromise you, Geoffrey. Nobody but Blanche knows I am at Windygates. And I have contrived to make my inquiries about you without allowing her to suspect our secret." She stopped, and began to tremble. She saw something more in his face than she had read in it at first. "I got your letter," she went on, rallying her sinking courage. "I don't complain of its being so short: you don't like letter-writing, I know. But you promised I should hear from you again. And I have never heard. And oh, Geoffrey, it was so lonely at the inn!"

She stopped again, and supported herself by resting her hand on the table. The faintness was stealing back on her. She tried to go on again. It was useless—she could only look at him now.

"What do you want?" he asked, in the tone of a man who was putting an unimportant question to a total stranger.

A last gleam of her old energy flickered up in her face, like a dying flame.

"I am broken by what I have gone through," she said. "Don't insult me by making me remind you of your promise."

"What promise?"'

"For shame, Geoffrey! for shame! Your promise to marry me."

"You claim my promise after what you have done at the inn?"

She steadied herself against the table with one hand, and put the other hand to her head. Her brain was giddy. The effort to think was too much for her. She said to herself, vacantly, "The inn? What did I do at the inn?"

"I have had a lawyer's advice, mind! I know what I am talking about."

She appeared not to have heard him. She repeated the words, "What did I do at the inn?" and gave it up in despair. Holding by the table, she came close to him and laid her hand on his arm.

"Do you refuse to marry me?" she asked.

He saw the vile opportunity, and said the vile words.

"You're married already to Arnold Brinkworth."

Without a cry to warn him, without an effort to save herself, she dropped senseless at his feet; as her mother had dropped at his father's feet in the by-gone time.

He disentangled himself from the folds of her dress. "Done!" he said, looking down at her as she lay on the floor.

As the word fell from his lips he was startled by a sound in the inner part of the house. One of the library doors had not been completely closed. Light footsteps were audible, advancing rapidly across the hall.

He turned and fled, leaving the library, as he had entered it, by the open window at the lower end of the room.

CHAPTER THE TWENTY-SECOND.

GONE.

BLANCHE came in, with a glass of wine in her hand, and saw the swooning woman on the floor.

She was alarmed, but not surprised, as she knelt by Anne, and raised her head. Her own previous observation of her friend necessarily prevented her from being at any loss to account for the fainting fit. The inevitable delay in getting the wine was—naturally to her mind—alone to blame for the result which now met her view.

If she had been less ready in thus tracing the effect to the cause, she might have gone to the window to see if any thing had happened, out-of-doors, to frighten Anne—might have seen Geoffrey before he had time to turn the corner of the house—and, making that one discovery, might have altered the whole course of events, not in her coming life only, but in the coming lives of others. So do we shape our own destinies, blindfold. So do we hold our poor little tenure of happiness at the capricious mercy of Chance. It is surely a blessed delusion which persuades us that we are the highest product of the great scheme of creation, and sets us doubting whether other planets are inhabited, because other planets are not surrounded by an atmosphere which we can breathe!

After trying such simple remedies as were within her reach, and trying them without success, Blanche became seriously alarmed. Anne lay, to all outward appearance, dead in her arms. She was on the point of calling for help—come what might of the discovery which would ensue—when the door from the hall opened once more, and Hester Dethridge entered the room.

The cook had accepted the alternative which her mistress's message had placed before her, if she insisted on having her own time at her own sole disposal for the rest of that day. Exactly as Lady Lundie had desired, she intimated her resolution to carry her point by placing her account-book on the desk in the library. It was only when this had been done that Blanche received any answer to her entreaties for help. Slowly and deliberately Hester Dethridge walked up to the spot where the young girl knelt with Anne's head on her bosom, and looked at the two without a trace of human emotion in her stern and stony face.

"Don't you see what's happened?" cried Blanche. "Are you alive or dead? Oh, Hester, I can't bring her to! Look at her! look at her!"

Hester Dethridge looked at her, and shook her head. Looked again, thought for a while and wrote on her slate. Held out the slate over Anne's body, and showed what she had written:

"Who has done it?"

"You stupid creature!" said Blanche. "Nobody has done it."

The eyes of Hester Dethridge steadily read the worn white face, telling its own tale of sorrow mutely on Blanche's breast. The mind of Hester Dethridge steadily looked back at her own knowledge of her own miserable married life. She again returned to writing on her slate—again showed the written words to Blanche.

"Brought to it by a man. Let her be—and God will take her."

"You horrid unfeeling woman! how dare you write such an abominable thing!" With this natural outburst of indignation, Blanche looked back at Anne; and, daunted by the death-like persistency of the swoon, appealed again to the mercy of the immovable woman who was looking down at her. "Oh, Hester! for Heaven's sake help me!"

The cook dropped her slate at her side and bent her head gravely in sign that she submitted. She motioned to Blanche to loosen Anne's dress, and then—kneeling on one knee—took Anne to support her while it was being done.

The instant Hester Dethridge touched her, the swooning woman gave signs of life.

A faint shudder ran through her from head to foot—her eyelids trembled—half opened for a moment—and closed again. As they closed, a low sigh fluttered feebly from her lips.

Hester Dethridge put her back in Blanche's arms—considered a little with herself—returned to writing on her slate—and held out the written words once more:

"Shivered when I touched her. That means I have been walking over her grave."

Blanche turned from the sight of the slate, and from the sight of the woman, in horror. "You frighten me!" she said. "You will frighten her if she sees you. I don't mean to offend you; but—leave us, please leave us."

Hester Dethridge accepted her dismissal, as she accepted every thing else. She bowed her head in sign that she understood—looked for the last time at Anne—dropped a stiff courtesy to her young mistress—and left the room.

An hour later the butler had paid her, and she had left the house.

Blanche breathed more freely when she found herself alone. She could feel the relief now of seeing Anne revive.

"Can you hear me, darling?" she whispered. "Can you let me leave you for a moment?"

Anne's eyes slowly opened and looked round her—in that torment and terror of reviving life which marks the awful protest of humanity against its recall to existence when mortal mercy has dared to wake it in the arms of Death.

Blanche rested Anne's head against the nearest chair, and ran to the table upon which she had placed the wine on entering the room.

After swallowing the first few drops Anne begun to feel the effect of the stimulant. Blanche persisted in making her empty the glass, and refrained from asking or answering questions until her recovery under the influence of the wine was complete.

"You have overexerted yourself this morning," she said, as soon as it seemed safe to speak. "Nobody has seen you, darling—nothing has happened. Do you feel like yourself again?"

Anne made an attempt to rise and leave the library; Blanche placed her gently in the chair, and went on:

"There is not the least need to stir. We have another quarter of an hour to ourselves before any body is at all likely to disturb us. I have something to say, Anne—a little proposal to make. Will you listen to me?"

Anne took Blanche's hand, and pressed it gratefully to her lips. She made no other reply. Blanche proceeded:

"I won't ask any questions, my dear—I won't attempt to keep you here against your will—I won't even remind you of my letter yesterday. But I can't let you go, Anne, without having my mind made easy about you in some way. You will relieve all my anxiety, if you will do one thing—one easy thing for my sake."

"What is it, Blanche?"

She put that question with her mind far away from the subject before her. Blanche was too eager in pursuit of her object to notice the absent tone, the purely mechanical manner, in which Anne had spoken to her.

"I want you to consult my uncle," she answered. "Sir Patrick is interested in you; Sir Patrick proposed to me this very day to go and see you at the inn. He is the wisest, the kindest, the dearest old man living—and you can trust him as you could trust nobody else. Will you take my uncle into your confidence, and be guided by his advice?"

With her mind still far away from the subject, Anne looked out absently at the lawn, and made no answer.

"Come!" said Blanche. "One word isn't much to say. Is it Yes or No?"

Still looking out on the lawn—still thinking of something else—Anne yielded, and said "Yes."

Blanche was enchanted. "How well I must have managed it!" she thought. "This is what my uncle means, when my uncle talks of 'putting it strongly.'"

She bent down over Anne, and gayly patted her on the shoulder.

"That's the wisest 'Yes,' darling, you ever said in your life. Wait here—and I'll go in to luncheon, or they will be sending to know what has become of me. Sir Patrick has kept my place for me, next to himself. I shall contrive to tell him what I want; and he will contrive (oh, the blessing of having to do with a clever man; these are so few of them!)—he will contrive to leave the table before the rest, without exciting any body's suspicions. Go away with him at once to the summer-house (we have been at the summer-house all the morning; nobody will go back to it now), and I will follow you as soon as I have satisfied Lady Lundie by eating some lunch. Nobody will be any the wiser but our three selves. In five minutes or less you may expect Sir Patrick. Let me go! We haven't a moment to lose!"

Anne held her back. Anne's attention was concentrated on her now.

"What is it?" she asked.

"Are you going on happily with Arnold, Blanche?"

"Arnold is nicer than ever, my dear."

"Is the day fixed for your marriage?"

"The day will be ages hence. Not till we are back in town, at the end of the autumn. Let me go, Anne!"

"Give me a kiss, Blanche."

Blanche kissed her, and tried to release her hand. Anne held it as if she was drowning, as if her life depended on not letting it go.

"Will you always love me, Blanche, as you love me now?"

"How can you ask me!"

"I said Yes just now. You say Yes too."

Blanche said it. Anne's eyes fastened on her face, with one long, yearning look, and then Anne's hand suddenly dropped hers.

She ran out of the room, more agitated, more uneasy, than she liked to confess to herself. Never had she felt so certain of the urgent necessity of appealing to Sir Patrick's advice as she felt at that moment.

The guests were still safe at the luncheon-table when Blanche entered the dining-room.

Lady Lundie expressed the necessary surprise, in the properly graduated tone of reproof, at her step-daughter's want of punctuality. Blanche made her apologies with the most exemplary humility. She glided into her chair by her uncle's side, and took the first thing that was offered to her. Sir Patrick looked at his niece, and found himself in the company of a model young English Miss—and marveled inwardly what it might mean.

The talk, interrupted for the moment (topics, Politics and Sport—and then, when a change was wanted, Sport and Politics), was resumed again all round the table. Under cover of the conversation, and in the intervals of receiving the attentions of the gentlemen, Blanche whispered to Sir Patrick, "Don't start, uncle. Anne is in the library." (Polite Mr. Smith offered some ham. Gratefully declined.) "Pray, pray, pray go to her; she is waiting to see you—she is in dreadful trouble." (Gallant Mr. Jones proposed fruit tart and cream. Accepted with thanks.) "Take her to the summer-house: I'll follow you when I get the chance. And manage it at once, uncle, if you love me, or you will be too late."

Before Sir Patrick could whisper back a word in reply, Lady Lundie, cutting a cake of the richest Scottish composition, at the other end of the table, publicly proclaimed it to be her "own cake," and, as such, offered her brother-in-law a slice. The slice exhibited an eruption of plums and sweetmeats, overlaid by a perspiration of butter. It has been said that Sir Patrick had reached the age of seventy—it is, therefore, needless to add that he politely declined to commit an unprovoked outrage on his own stomach.

"MY cake!" persisted Lady Lundie, elevating the horrible composition on a fork. "Won't that tempt you?"

Sir Patrick saw his way to slipping out of the room under cover of a compliment to his sister-in-law. He summoned his courtly smile, and laid his hand on his heart.

"A fallible mortal," he said, "is met by a temptation which he can not possibly resist. If he is a wise mortal, also, what does he do?"

"He eats some of My cake," said the prosaic Lady Lundie.

"No!" said Sir Patrick, with a look of unutterable devotion directed at his sister-in-law.

"He flies temptation, dear lady—as I do now." He bowed, and escaped, unsuspected, from the room.

Lady Lundie cast down her eyes, with an expression of virtuous indulgence for human frailty, and divided Sir Patrick's compliment modestly between herself and her cake.

Well aware that his own departure from the table would be followed in a few minutes by the rising of the lady of the house, Sir Patrick hurried to the library as fast as his lame foot would let him. Now that he was alone, his manner became anxious, and his face looked grave.

He entered the room.

Not a sign of Anne Silvester was to be seen any where. The library was a perfect solitude.

"Gone!" said Sir Patrick. "This looks bad."

After a moment's reflection he went back into the hall to get his hat. It was possible that she might have been afraid of discovery if she staid in the library, and that she might have gone on to the summer-house by herself.

If she was not to be found in the summer-house, the quieting of Blanche's mind and the clearing up of her uncle's suspicions alike depended on discovering the place in which Miss Silvester had taken refuge. In this case time would be of importance, and the capacity of making the most of it would be a precious capacity at starting. Arriving rapidly at these conclusions, Sir Patrick rang the bell in the hall which communicated with the servants' offices, and summoned his own valet—a person of tried discretion and fidelity, nearly as old as himself.

"Get your hat, Duncan," he said, when the valet appeared, "and come out with me."

Master and servant set forth together silently on their way through the grounds. Arrived within sight of the summer-house, Sir Patrick ordered Duncan to wait, and went on by himself.

There was not the least need for the precaution that he had taken. The summer-house was as empty as the library. He stepped out again and looked about him. Not a living creature was visible. Sir Patrick summoned his servant to join him.

"Go back to the stables, Duncan," he said, "and say that Miss Lundie lends me her pony-carriage to-day. Let it be got ready at once and kept in the stable-yard. I want to attract as little notice as possible. You are to go with me, and nobody else. Provide yourself with a railway time-table. Have you got any money?"

"Yes, Sir Patrick."

"Did you happen to see the governess (Miss Silvester) on the day when we came here—the day of the lawn-party?"

"I did, Sir Patrick."

"Should you know her again?"

"I thought her a very distinguished-looking person, Sir Patrick. I should certainly know her again."

"Have you any reason to think she noticed you?"

"She never even looked at me, Sir Patrick."

"Very good. Put a change of linen into your bag, Duncan—I may possibly want you to take a journey by railway. Wait for me in the stable-yard. This is a matter in which every thing is trusted to my discretion, and to yours."

"Thank you, Sir Patrick."

With that acknowledgment of the compliment which had been just paid to him, Duncan gravely went his way to the stables; and Duncan's master returned to the summer-house, to wait there until he was joined by Blanche.

Sir Patrick showed signs of failing patience during the interval of expectation through which he was now condemned to pass. He applied perpetually to the snuff-box in the knob of his cane. He fidgeted incessantly in and out of the summer-house. Anne's disappearance had placed a serious obstacle in the way of further discovery; and there was no attacking that obstacle, until precious time had been wasted in waiting to see Blanche.

At last she appeared in view, from the steps of the summer-house; breathless and eager, hasting to the place of meeting as fast as her feet would take her to it.

Sir Patrick considerately advanced, to spare her the shock of making the inevitable discovery. "Blanche," he said. "Try to prepare yourself, my dear, for a disappointment. I am alone."

"You don't mean that you have let her go?"

"My poor child! I have never seen her at all."

Blanche pushed by him, and ran into the summer-house. Sir Patrick followed her. She came out again to meet him, with a look of blank despair. "Oh, uncle! I did so truly pity her! And see how little pity she has for me!"

Sir Patrick put his arm round his niece, and softly patted the fair young head that dropped on his shoulder.

"Don't let us judge her harshly, my dear: we don't know what serious necessity may not plead her excuse. It is plain that she can trust nobody—and that she only consented to see me to get you out of the room and spare you the pain of parting. Compose yourself, Blanche. I don't despair of discovering where she has gone, if you will help me."

Blanche lifted her head, and dried her tears bravely.

"My father himself wasn't kinder to me than you are," she said. "Only tell me, uncle, what I can do!"

"I want to hear exactly what happened in the library," said Sir Patrick. "Forget nothing, my dear child, no matter how trifling it may be. Trifles are precious to us, and minutes are precious to us, now."

Blanche followed her instructions to the letter, her uncle listening with the closest attention. When she had completed her narrative, Sir Patrick suggested leaving the summer-house. "I have ordered your chaise," he said; "and I can tell you what I propose doing on our way to the stable-yard."

"Let me drive you, uncle!"

"Forgive me, my dear, for saying No to that. Your step-mother's suspicions are very easily excited—and you had better not be seen with me if my inquiries take me to the Craig Fernie inn. I promise, if you will remain here, to tell you every thing when I come back. Join the others in any plan they have for the afternoon—and you will prevent my absence from exciting any thing more than a passing remark. You will do as I tell you? That's a good girl! Now you shall hear how I propose to search for this poor lady, and how your little story has helped me."

He paused, considering with himself whether he should begin by telling Blanche of his consultation with Geoffrey. Once more, he decided that question in the negative. Better to still defer taking her into his confidence until he had performed the errand of investigation on which he was now setting forth.

"What you have told me, Blanche, divides itself, in my mind, into two heads," began Sir Patrick. "There is what happened in the library before your own eyes; and there is what Miss Silvester told you had happened at the inn. As to the event in the library (in the first place), it is too late now to inquire whether that fainting-fit was the result, as you say, of mere exhaustion—or whether it was the result of something that occurred while you were out of the room."

"What could have happened while I was out of the room?"

"I know no more than you do, my dear. It is simply one of the possibilities in the case, and, as such, I notice it. To get on to what practically concerns us; if Miss Silvester is in delicate health it is impossible that she could get, unassisted, to any great distance from Windygates. She may have taken refuge in one of the cottages in our immediate neighborhood. Or she may have met with some passing vehicle from one of the farms on its way to the station, and may have asked the person driving to give her a seat in it. Or she may have walked as far as she can, and may have stopped to rest in some sheltered place, among the lanes to the south of this house."

"I'll inquire at the cottages, uncle, while you are gone."

"My dear child, there must be a dozen cottages, at least, within a circle of one mile from Windygates! Your inquiries would probably occupy you for the whole afternoon. I won't ask what Lady Lundie would think of your being away all that time by yourself. I will only remind you of two things. You would be making a public matter of an investigation which it is essential to pursue as privately as possible; and, even if you happened to hit on the right cottage your inquiries would be completely baffled, and you would discover nothing."

"Why not?"

"I know the Scottish peasant better than you do, Blanche. In his intelligence and his sense of self-respect he is a very different being from the English peasant. He would receive you civilly, because you are a young lady; but he would let you see, at the same time, that he considered you had taken advantage of the difference between your position and his position to commit an intrusion. And if Miss Silvester had appealed, in confidence, to his hospitality, and if he had granted it, no power on earth would induce him to tell any person living that she was under his roof—without her express permission."

"But, uncle, if it's of no use making inquiries of any body, how are we to find her?"

"I don't say that nobody will answer our inquiries, my dear—I only say the peasantry won't answer them, if your friend has trusted herself to their protection. The way to find her is to look on, beyond what Miss Silvester may be doing at the present moment, to what Miss Silvester contemplates doing—let us say, before the day is out. We may assume, I think (after what has happened), that, as soon as she can leave this neighborhood, she assuredly will leave it. Do you agree, so far?"

"Yes! yes! Go on."

"Very well. She is a woman, and she is (to say the least of it) not strong. She can only leave this neighborhood either by hiring a vehicle or by traveling on the railway. I propose going first to the station. At the rate at which your pony gets over the ground, there is a fair chance, in spite of the time we have lost, of my being there as soon as she is—assuming that she leaves by the first train, up or down, that passes."

"There is a train in half an hour, uncle. She can never get there in time for that."

"She may be less exhausted than we think; or she may get a lift; or she may not be alone. How do we know but somebody may have been waiting in the lane—her husband, if there is such a person—to help her? No! I shall assume she is now on her way to the station; and I shall get there as fast as possible—"

"And stop her, if you find her there?"

"What I do, Blanche, must be left to my discretion. If I find her there, I must act for the best. If I don't find her there, I shall leave Duncan (who goes with me) on the watch for the remaining trains, until the last to-night. He knows Miss Silvester by sight, and he is sure that she has never noticed him. Whether she goes north or south, early or late, Duncan will have my orders to follow her. He is thoroughly to be relied on. If she takes the railway, I answer for it we shall know where she goes."

"How clever of you to think of Duncan!"

"Not in the least, my dear. Duncan is my factotum; and the course I am taking is the obvious course which would have occurred to any body. Let us get to the really difficult part of it now. Suppose she hires a carriage?"

"There are none to be had, except at the station."

"There are farmers about here—and farmers have light carts, or chaises, or something of the sort. It is in the last degree unlikely that they would consent to let her have them. Still, women break through difficulties which stop men. And this is a clever woman, Blanche—a woman, you may depend on it, who is bent on preventing you from tracing her. I confess I wish we had somebody we could trust lounging about where those two roads branch off from the road that leads to the railway. I must go in another direction; I can't do it."

"Arnold can do it!"

Sir Patrick looked a little doubtful. "Arnold is an excellent fellow," he said. "But can we trust to his discretion?"

"He is, next to you, the most perfectly discreet person I know," rejoined Blanche, in a very positive manner; "and, what is more, I have told him every thing about Anne, except what has happened to-day. I am afraid I shall tell him that, when I feel lonely and miserable, after you have gone. There is something in Arnold—I don't know what it is—that comforts me. Besides, do you think he would betray a secret that I gave him to keep? You don't know how devoted he is to me!"

"My dear Blanche, I am not the cherished object of his devotion; of course I don't know! You are the only authority on that point. I stand corrected. Let us have Arnold, by all means. Caution him to be careful; and send him out by himself, where the roads meet. We have now only one other place left in which there is a chance of finding a trace of her. I undertake to make the necessary investigation at the Craig Fernie inn."

"The Craig Fernie inn? Uncle! you have forgotten what I told you."

"Wait a little, my dear. Miss Silvester herself has left the inn, I grant you. But (if we should unhappily fail in finding her by any other means) Miss Silvester has left a trace to guide us at Craig Fernie. That trace must be picked up at once, in case of accidents. You don't seem to follow me? I am getting over the ground as fast as the pony gets over it. I have arrived at the second of those two heads into which your story divides itself in my mind. What did Miss Silvester tell you had happened at the inn?"

"She lost a letter at the inn."

"Exactly. She lost a letter at the inn; that is one event. And Bishopriggs, the waiter, has quarreled with Mrs. Inchbare, and has left his situation; that is another event. As to the letter first. It is either really lost, or it has been stolen. In either case, if we can lay our hands on it, there is at least a chance of its helping us to discover something. As to Bishopriggs, next—"

"You're not going to talk about the waiter, surely?"

"I am! Bishopriggs possesses two important merits. He is a link in my chain of reasoning; and he is an old friend of mine."

"A friend of yours?"

"We live in days, my dear, when one workman talks of another workman as 'that gentleman.'—I march with the age, and feel bound to mention my clerk as my friend. A few years since Bishopriggs was employed in the clerks' room at my chambers. He is one of the most intelligent and most unscrupulous old vagabonds in Scotland; perfectly honest as to all average matters involving pounds, shillings, and pence; perfectly unprincipled in the pursuit of his own interests, where the violation of a trust lies on the boundary-line which marks the limit of the law. I made two unpleasant discoveries when I had him in my employment. I found that he had contrived to supply himself with a duplicate of my seal; and I had the strongest reason to suspect him of tampering with some papers belonging to two of my clients. He had done no actual mischief, so far; and I had no time to waste in making out the necessary case against him. He was dismissed from my service, as a man who was not to be trusted to respect any letters or papers that happened to pass through his hands."

"I see, uncle! I see!"

"Plain enough now—isn't it? If that missing letter of Miss Silvester's is a letter of no importance, I am inclined to believe that it is merely lost, and may be found again. If, on the other hand, there is any thing in it that could promise the most remote advantage to any person in possession of it, then, in the execrable slang of the day, I will lay any odds, Blanche, that Bishopriggs has got the letter!"

"And he has left the inn! How unfortunate!"

"Unfortunate as causing delay—nothing worse than that. Unless I am very much mistaken, Bishopriggs will come back to the inn. The old rascal (there is no denying it) is a most amusing person. He left a terrible blank when he left my clerks' room. Old customers at Craig Fernie (especially the English), in missing Bishopriggs, will, you may rely on it, miss one of the attractions of the inn. Mrs. Inchbare is not a woman to let her dignity stand in the way of her business. She and Bishopriggs will come together again, sooner or later, and make it up. When I have put certain questions to her, which may possibly lead to very important results, I shall leave a letter for Bishopriggs in Mrs. Inchbare's hands. The letter will tell him I have something for him to do, and will contain an address at which he can write to me. I shall hear of him, Blanche and, if the letter is in his possession, I shall get it."

"Won't he be afraid—if he has stolen the letter—to tell you he has got it?"

"Very well put, my child. He might hesitate with other people. But I have my own way of dealing with him—and I know how to make him tell Me.—Enough of Bishopriggs till his time comes. There is one other point, in regard to Miss Silvester. I may have to describe her. How was she dressed when she came here? Remember, I am a man—and (if an Englishwoman's dress can be described in an Englishwoman's language) tell me, in English, what she had on."

"She wore a straw hat, with corn-flowers in it, and a white veil. Corn-flowers at one side uncle, which is less common than cornflowers in front. And she had on a light gray shawl. And a Pique;—"

"There you go with your French! Not a word more! A straw hat, with a white veil, and with corn-flowers at one side of the hat. And a light gray shawl. That's as much as the ordinary male mind can take in; and that will do. I have got my instructions, and saved precious time. So far so good. Here we are at the end of our conference—in other words, at the gate of the stable-yard. You understand what you have to do while I am away?"

"I have to send Arnold to the cross-roads. And I have to behave (if I can) as if nothing had happened."

"Good child! Well put again! you have got what I call grasp of mind, Blanche. An invaluable faculty! You will govern the future domestic kingdom. Arnold will be nothing but a constitutional husband. Those are the only husbands who are thoroughly happy. You shall hear every thing, my love, when I come lack. Got your bag, Duncan? Good. And the time-table? Good. You take the reins—I won't drive. I want to think. Driving is incompatible with intellectual exertion. A man puts his mind into his horse, and sinks to the level of that useful animal—as a necessary condition of getting to his destination without being upset. God bless you, Blanche! To the station, Duncan! to the station!"

CHAPTER THE TWENTY-THIRD.

TRACED.

THE chaise rattled our through the gates. The dogs barked furiously. Sir Patrick looked round, and waved his hand as he turned the corner of the road. Blanche was left alone in the yard.

She lingered a little, absently patting the dogs. They had especial claims on her sympathy at that moment; they, too, evidently thought it hard to be left behind at the house. After a while she roused herself. Sir Patrick had left the responsibility of superintending the crossroads on her shoulders. There was something to be done yet before the arrangements for tracing Anne were complete. Blanche left the yard to do it.

On her way back to the house she met Arnold, dispatched by Lady Lundie in search of her.

The plan of occupation for the afternoon had been settled during Blanche's absence. Some demon had whispered to Lady Lundie to cultivate a taste for feudal antiquities, and to insist on spreading that taste among her guests. She had proposed an excursion to an old baronial castle among the hills—far to the westward (fortunately for Sir Patrick's chance of escaping discovery) of the hills at Craig Fernie. Some of the guests were to ride, and some to accompany their hostess in the open carriage. Looking right and left for proselytes, Lady Lundie had necessarily remarked the disappearance of certain members of her circle. Mr. Delamayn had vanished, nobody knew where. Sir Patrick and Blanche had followed his example. Her ladyship had observed, upon this, with some asperity, that if they were all to treat each other in that unceremonious manner, the sooner Windygates was turned into a Penitentiary, on the silent system, the fitter the house would be for the people who inhabited it. Under these circumstances, Arnold suggested that Blanche would do well to make her excuses as soon as possible at head-quarters, and accept the seat in the carriage which her step-mother wished her to take. "We are in for the feudal antiquities, Blanche; and we must help each other through as well as we can. If you will go in the carriage, I'll go too."

Blanche shook her head.

"There are serious reasons for my keeping up appearances," she said. "I shall go in the carriage. You mustn't go at all."

Arnold naturally looked a little surprised, and asked to be favored with an explanation.

Blanche took his arm and hugged it close. Now that Anne was lost, Arnold was more precious to her than ever. She literally hungered to hear at that moment, from his own lips, how fond he was of her. It mattered nothing that she was already perfectly satisfied on this point. It was so nice (after he had said it five hundred times already) to make him say it once more!

"Suppose I had no explanation to give?" she said. "Would you stay behind by yourself to please me?"

"I would do any thing to please you!"

"Do you really love me as much as that?"

They were still in the yard; and the only witnesses present were the dogs. Arnold answered in the language without words—which is nevertheless the most expressive language in use, between men and women, all over the world.

"This is not doing my duty," said Blanche, penitently. "But, oh Arnold, I am so anxious and so miserable! And it is such a consolation to know that you won't turn your back on me too!"

With that preface she told him what had happened in the library. Even Blanche's estimate of her lover's capacity for sympathizing with her was more than realized by the effect which her narrative produced on Arnold. He was not merely surprised and sorry for her. His face showed plainly that he felt genuine concern and distress. He had never stood higher in Blanche's opinion than he stood at that moment.

"What is to be done?" he asked. "How does Sir Patrick propose to find her?"

Blanche repeated Sir Patrick's instructions relating to the crossroads, and also to the serious necessity of pursuing the investigation in the strictest privacy. Arnold (relieved from all fear of being sent back to Craig Fernie) undertook to do every thing that was asked of him, and promised to keep the secret from every body.

They went back to the house, and met with an icy welcome from Lady Lundie. Her ladyship repeated her remark on the subject of turning Windygates into a Penitentiary for

Blanche's benefit. She received Arnold's petition to be excused from going to see the castle with the barest civility. "Oh, take your walk by all means! You may meet your friend, Mr. Delamayn—who appears to have such a passion for walking that he can't even wait till luncheon is over. As for Sir Patrick—Oh! Sir Patrick has borrowed the pony-carriage? and gone out driving by himself?—I'm sure I never meant to offend my brother-in-law when I offered him a slice of my poor little cake. Don't let me offend any body else. Dispose of your afternoon, Blanche, without the slightest reference to me. Nobody seems inclined to visit the ruins—the most interesting relic of feudal times in Perthshire, Mr. Brinkworth. It doesn't matter—oh, dear me, it doesn't matter! I can't force my guests to feel an intelligent curiosity on the subject of Scottish Antiquities. No! no! my dear Blanche!—it won't be the first time, or the last, that I have driven out alone. I don't at all object to being alone. 'My mind to me a kingdom is,' as the poet says." So Lady Lundie's outraged self-importance asserted its violated claims on human respect, until her distinguished medical guest came to the rescue and smoothed his hostess's ruffled plumes. The surgeon (he privately detested ruins) begged to go. Blanche begged to go. Smith and Jones (profoundly interested in feudal antiquities) said they would sit behind, in the "rumble"—rather than miss this unexpected treat. One, Two, and Three caught the infection, and volunteered to be the escort on horseback. Lady Lundie's celebrated "smile" (warranted to remain unaltered on her face for hours together) made its appearance once more. She issued her orders with the most charming amiability. "We'll take the guidebook," said her ladyship, with the eye to mean economy, which is only to be met with in very rich people, "and save a shilling to the man who shows the ruins." With that she went up stairs to array herself for the drive, and looked in the glass; and saw a perfectly virtuous, fascinating, and accomplished woman, facing her irresistibly in a new French bonnet!

At a private signal from Blanche, Arnold slipped out and repaired to his post, where the roads crossed the road that led to the railway.

There was a space of open heath on one side of him, and the stonewall and gates of a farmhouse inclosure on the other. Arnold sat down on the soft heather—and lit a cigar—and tried to see his way through the double mystery of Anne's appearance and Anne's flight.

He had interpreted his friend's absence exactly as his friend had anticipated: he could only assume that Geoffrey had gone to keep a private appointment with Anne. Miss Silvester's appearance at Windygates alone, and Miss Silvester's anxiety to hear the names of the gentlemen who were staying in the house, seemed, under these circumstances, to point to the plain conclusion that the two had, in some way, unfortunately missed each other. But what could be the motive of her flight? Whether she knew of some other place in which she might meet Geoffrey? or whether she had gone back to the inn? or whether she had acted under some sudden impulse of despair?—were questions which Arnold was necessarily quite incompetent to solve. There was no choice but to wait until an opportunity offered of reporting what had happened to Geoffrey himself.

After the lapse of half an hour, the sound of some approaching vehicle—the first sound of the sort that he had heard—attracted Arnold's attention. He started up, and saw the pony-chaise approaching him along the road from the station. Sir Patrick, this time, was compelled to drive himself—Duncan was not with him. On discovering Arnold, he stopped the pony.

"So! so!" said the old gentleman. "You have heard all about it, I see? You understand that this is to be a secret from every body, till further notice? Very good, Has any thing happened since you have been here?"

"Nothing. Have you made any discoveries, Sir Patrick?"

"None. I got to the station before the train. No signs of Miss Silvester any where. I have left Duncan on the watch—with orders not to stir till the last train has passed to-night."

"I don't think she will turn up at the station," said Arnold. "I fancy she has gone back to Craig Fernie."

"Quite possible. I am now on my way to Craig Fernie, to make inquiries about her. I don't know how long I may be detained, or what it may lead to. If you see Blanche before I do tell her I have instructed the station-master to let me know (if Miss Silvester does take the railway) what place she books for. Thanks to that arrangement, we sha'n't have to wait for news till Duncan can telegraph that he has seen her to her journey's end. In the mean time, you understand what you are wanted to do here?"

"Blanche has explained every thing to me."

"Stick to your post, and make good use of your eyes. You were accustomed to that, you know, when you were at sea. It's no great hardship to pass a few hours in this delicious summer air. I see you have contracted the vile modern habit of smoking—that will be occupation enough to amuse you, no doubt! Keep the roads in view; and, if she does come your way, don't attempt to stop her—you can't do that. Speak to her (quite innocently, mind!), by way of getting time enough to notice the face of the man who is driving her, and the name (if there is one) on his cart. Do that, and you will do enough. Pah! how that cigar poisons the air! What will have become of your stomach when you get to my age?"

"I sha'n't complain, Sir Patrick, if I can eat as good a dinner as you do."

"That reminds me! I met somebody I knew at the station. Hester Dethridge has left her place, and gone to London by the train. We may feed at Windygates—we have done with dining now. It has been a final quarrel this time between the mistress and the cook. I have given Hester my address in London, and told her to let me know before she decides on another place. A woman who can't talk, and a woman who can cook, is simply a woman who has arrived at absolute perfection. Such a treasure shall not go out of the family, if I can help it. Did you notice the Bechamel sauce at lunch? Pooh! a young man who smokes cigars doesn't know the difference between Bechamel sauce and melted butter. Good afternoon! good afternoon!"

He slackened the reins, and away he went to Craig Fernie. Counting by years, the pony was twenty, and the pony's driver was seventy. Counting by vivacity and spirit, two of the most youthful characters in Scotland had got together that afternoon in the same chaise.

An hour more wore itself slowly out; and nothing had passed Arnold on the cross-roads but a few stray foot-passengers, a heavy wagon, and a gig with an old woman in it. He rose again from the heather, weary of inaction, and resolved to walk backward and forward, within view of his post, for a change. At the second turn, when his face happened to be set toward the open heath, he noticed another foot-passenger—apparently a man—far away in the empty distance. Was the person coming toward him?

He advanced a little. The stranger was doubtless advancing too, so rapidly did his figure now reveal itself, beyond all doubt, as the figure of a man. A few minutes more and Arnold fancied he recognized it. Yet a little longer, and he was quite sure. There was no mistaking the lithe strength and grace of that man, and the smooth easy swiftness with which he covered his ground. It was the hero of the coming foot-race. It was Geoffrey on his way back to Windygates House.

Arnold hurried forward to meet him. Geoffrey stood still, poising himself on his stick, and let the other come up.

"Have you heard what has happened at the house?" asked Arnold.

He instinctively checked the next question as it rose to his lips. There was a settled defiance in the expression of Geoffrey's face, which Arnold was quite at a loss to understand. He looked like a man who had made up his mind to confront any thing that could happen, and to contradict any body who spoke to him.

"Something seems to have annoyed you?" said Arnold.

"What's up at the house?" returned Geoffrey, with his loudest voice and his hardest look.

"Miss Silvester has been at the house."

"Who saw her?"

"Nobody but Blanche."

"Well?"

"Well, she was miserably weak and ill, so ill that she fainted, poor thing, in the library. Blanche brought her to."

"And what then?"

"We were all at lunch at the time. Blanche left the library, to speak privately to her uncle. When she went back Miss Silvester was gone, and nothing has been seen of her since."

"A row at the house?"

"Nobody knows of it at the house, except Blanche—"

"And you? And how many besides?"

"And Sir Patrick. Nobody else."

"Nobody else? Any thing more?"

Arnold remembered his promise to keep the investigation then on foot a secret from every body. Geoffrey's manner made him—unconsciously to himself—readier than he might otherwise have been to consider Geoffrey as included in the general prohibition.

"Nothing more," he answered.

Geoffrey dug the point of his stick deep into the soft, sandy ground. He looked at the stick, then suddenly pulled it out of the ground and looked at Arnold. "Good-afternoon!" he said, and went on his way again by himself.

Arnold followed, and stopped him. For a moment the two men looked at each other without a word passing on either side. Arnold spoke first.

"You're out of humor, Geoffrey. What has upset you in this way? Have you and Miss Silvester missed each other?"

Geoffrey was silent.

"Have you seen her since she left Windygates?"

No reply.

"Do you know where Miss Silvester is now?"

Still no reply. Still the same mutely-insolent defiance of look and manner. Arnold's dark color began to deepen.

"Why don't you answer me?" he said.

"Because I have had enough of it."

"Enough of what?"

"Enough of being worried about Miss Silvester. Miss Silvester's my business—not yours."

"Gently, Geoffrey! Don't forget that I have been mixed up in that business—without seeking it myself."

"There's no fear of my forgetting. You have cast it in my teeth often enough."

"Cast it in your teeth?"

"Yes! Am I never to hear the last of my obligation to you? The devil take the obligation! I'm sick of the sound of it."

There was a spirit in Arnold—not easily brought to the surface, through the overlying simplicity and good-humor of his ordinary character—which, once roused, was a spirit not readily quelled. Geoffrey had roused it at last.

"When you come to your senses," he said, "I'll remember old times—and receive your apology. Till you do come to your senses, go your way by yourself. I have no more to say to you."

Geoffrey set his teeth, and came one step nearer. Arnold's eyes met his, with a look which steadily and firmly challenged him—though he was the stronger man of the two—to force the quarrel a step further, if he dared. The one human virtue which Geoffrey respected and understood was the virtue of courage. And there it was before him—the undeniable courage of the weaker man. The callous scoundrel was touched on the one tender place in his whole being. He turned, and went on his way in silence.

Left by himself, Arnold's head dropped on his breast. The friend who had saved his life—the one friend he possessed, who was associated with his earliest and happiest remembrances of old days—had grossly insulted him: and had left him deliberately, without the slightest expression of regret. Arnold's affectionate nature—simple, loyal, clinging where it once fastened—was wounded to the quick. Geoffrey's fast-retreating figure, in the open view before him, became blurred and indistinct. He put his hand over his eyes, and hid, with a boyish shame, the hot tears that told of the heartache, and that honored the man who shed them.

He was still struggling with the emotion which had overpowered him, when something happened at the place where the roads met.

The four roads pointed as nearly as might be toward the four points of the compass. Arnold was now on the road to the eastward, having advanced in that direction to meet Geoffrey, between two and three hundred yards from the farm-house inclosure before which he had kept his watch. The road to the westward, curving away behind the farm, led to the nearest market-town. The road to the south was the way to the station. And the road to the north led back to Windygates House.

While Geoffrey was still fifty yards from the turning which would take him back to Windygates—while the tears were still standing thickly in Arnold's eyes—the gate of the farm inclosure opened. A light four-wheel chaise came out with a man driving, and a woman sitting by his side. The woman was Anne Silvester, and the man was the owner of the farm.

Instead of taking the way which led to the station, the chaise pursued the westward road to the market-town. Proceeding in this direction, the backs of the persons in the vehicle were necessarily turned on Geoffrey, advancing behind them from the eastward. He just carelessly noticed the shabby little chaise, and then turned off north on his way to Windygates.

By the time Arnold was composed enough to look round him, the chaise had taken the curve in the road which wound behind the farmhouse. He returned—faithful to the engagement which he had undertaken—to his post before the inclosure. The chaise was then a speck in the distance. In a minute more it was a speck out of sight.

So (to use Sir Patrick's phrase) had the woman broken through difficulties which would have stopped a man. So, in her sore need, had Anne Silvester won the sympathy which had given her a place, by the farmer's side, in the vehicle that took him on his own business to the market-town. And so, by a hair's-breadth, did she escape the treble risk of discovery which threatened her—from Geoffrey, on his way back; from Arnold, at his post; and from the valet, on the watch for her appearance at the station.

The afternoon wore on. The servants at Windygates, airing themselves in the grounds—in the absence of their mistress and her guests—were disturbed, for the moment, by the unexpected return of one of "the gentlefolks." Mr. Geoffrey Delamayn reappeared at the house alone; went straight to the smoking-room; and calling for another supply of the old ale, settled himself in an arm-chair with the newspaper, and began to smoke.

He soon tired of reading, and fell into thinking of what had happened during the latter part of his walk.

The prospect before him had more than realized the most sanguine anticipations that he could have formed of it. He had braced himself—after what had happened in the library—to face the outbreak of a serious scandal, on his return to the house. And here—when he came back—was nothing to face! Here were three people (Sir Patrick, Arnold, and Blanche) who must at least know that Anne was in some serious trouble keeping the secret as carefully as if they felt that his interests were at stake! And, more wonderful still, here was Anne herself—so far from raising a hue and cry after him—actually taking flight without saying a word that could compromise him with any living soul!

What in the name of wonder did it mean? He did his best to find his way to an explanation of some sort; and he actually contrived to account for the silence of Blanche and her uncle, and Arnold. It was pretty clear that they must have all three combined to keep Lady Lundie in ignorance of her runaway governess's return to the house.

But the secret of Anne's silence completely baffled him.

He was simply incapable of conceiving that the horror of seeing herself set up as an obstacle to Blanche's marriage might have been vivid enough to overpower all sense of her own wrongs, and to hurry her away, resolute, in her ignorance of what else to do, never to return again, and never to let living eyes rest on her in the character of Arnold's wife. "It's clean beyond my making out," was the final conclusion at which Geoffrey arrived. "If it's her interest to hold her tongue, it's my interest to hold mine, and there's an end of it for the present!"

He put up his feet on a chair, and rested his magnificent muscles after his walk, and filled another pipe, in thorough contentment with himself. No interference to dread from Anne, no more awkward questions (on the terms they were on now) to come from Arnold. He looked back at the quarrel on the heath with a certain complacency—he did his friend justice; though they had disagreed. "Who would have thought the fellow had so much pluck in him!" he said to himself as he struck the match and lit his second pipe.

An hour more wore on; and Sir Patrick was the next person who returned.

He was thoughtful, but in no sense depressed. Judging by appearances, his errand to Craig Fernie had certainly not ended in disappointment. The old gentleman hummed his favorite little Scotch air—rather absently, perhaps—and took his pinch of snuff from the knob of his ivory cane much as usual. He went to the library bell and summoned a servant.

"Any body been here for me?"—"No, Sir Patrick."—"No letters?"—"No, Sir Patrick."—"Very well. Come up stairs to my room, and help me on with my dressing-gown." The man helped him to his dressing-gown and slippers "Is Miss Lundie at home?"—"No, Sir Patrick. They're all away with my lady on an excursion."—"Very good. Get me a cup of coffee; and wake me half an hour before dinner, in case I take a nap." The servant went out. Sir Patrick stretched himself on the sofa. "Ay! ay! a little aching in the back, and a certain stiffness in the legs. I dare say the pony feels just as I do. Age, I suppose, in both cases? Well! well! well! let's try and be young at heart. 'The rest' (as Pope says) 'is leather and prunella.'" He returned resignedly to his little Scotch air. The servant came in with the coffee. And then the room was quiet, except for the low humming of insects and the gentle rustling of the creepers at the window. For five minutes or so Sir Patrick sipped his coffee, and meditated—by no means in the character of a man who was depressed by any recent disappointment. In five minutes more he was asleep.

A little later, and the party returned from the ruins.

With the one exception of their lady-leader, the whole expedition was depressed—Smith and Jones, in particular, being quite speechless. Lady Lundie alone still met feudal antiquities with a cheerful front. She had cheated the man who showed the ruins of his shilling, and she was thoroughly well satisfied with herself. Her voice was flute-like in its melody, and the celebrated "smile" had never been in better order. "Deeply interesting!" said her ladyship, descending from the carriage with ponderous grace, and addressing herself to Geoffrey, lounging under the portico of the house. "You have had a loss, Mr. Delamayn. The next time you go out for a walk, give your hostess a word of warning, and you won't repent it." Blanche (looking very weary and anxious) questioned the servant, the moment she got in, about Arnold and her uncle. Sir Patrick was invisible up stairs. Mr. Brinkworth had not come back. It wanted only twenty minutes of dinner-time; and full evening-dress was insisted on at Windygates. Blanche, nevertheless, still lingered in the hall in the hope of seeing Arnold before she went up stairs. The hope was realized. As the clock struck the quarter he came in. And he, too, was out of spirits like the rest!

"Have you seen her?" asked Blanche.

"No," said Arnold, in the most perfect good faith. "The way she has escaped by is not the way by the cross-roads—I answer for that."

They separated to dress. When the party assembled again, in the library, before dinner, Blanche found her way, the moment he entered the room, to Sir Patrick's side.

"News, uncle! I'm dying for news."

"Good news, my dear—so far."

"You have found Anne?"

"Not exactly that."

"You have heard of her at Craig Fernie?"

"I have made some important discoveries at Craig Fernie, Blanche. Hush! here's your step-mother. Wait till after dinner, and you may hear more than I can tell you now. There may be news from the station between this and then."

The dinner was a wearisome ordeal to at least two other persons present besides Blanche. Arnold, sitting opposite to Geoffrey, without exchanging a word with him, felt the altered relations between his former friend and himself very painfully. Sir Patrick, missing the skilled hand of Hester Dethridge in every dish that was offered to him, marked the dinner among the wasted opportunities of his life, and resented his sister-in-law's flow of spirits as something simply inhuman under present circumstances. Blanche followed Lady Lundie into the drawing-room in a state of burning impatience for the rising of the gentlemen from their wine. Her step-mother—mapping out a new antiquarian excursion for the next day, and finding Blanche's ears closed to her occasional remarks on baronial Scotland five hundred years since—lamented, with satirical emphasis, the absence of an intelligent companion of her own sex; and stretched her majestic figure on the sofa to wait until an audience worthy of her flowed in from the dining-room. Before very long—so soothing is the influence of an after-dinner view of feudal antiquities, taken through the medium of an approving conscience—Lady Lundie's eyes closed; and from Lady Lundie's nose there poured, at intervals, a sound, deep like her ladyship's learning; regular, like her ladyship's habits—a sound associated with nightcaps and bedrooms, evoked alike by Nature, the leveler, from high and low—the sound (oh, Truth what enormities find publicity in thy name!)—the sound of a Snore.

Free to do as she pleased, Blanche left the echoes of the drawing-room in undisturbed enjoyment of Lady Lundie's audible repose.

She went into the library, and turned over the novels. Went out again, and looked across the hall at the dining-room door. Would the men never have done talking their politics and drinking their wine? She went up to her own room, and changed her ear-rings, and scolded her maid. Descended once more—and made an alarming discovery in a dark corner of the hall.

Two men were standing there, hat in hand whispering to the butler. The butler, leaving them, went into the dining-room—came out again with Sir Patrick—and said to the two men, "Step this way, please." The two men came out into the light. Murdoch, the station-master; and Duncan, the valet! News of Anne!

"Oh, uncle, let me stay!" pleaded Blanche.

Sir Patrick hesitated. It was impossible to say—as matters stood at that moment—what distressing intelligence the two men might not have brought of the missing woman. Duncan's return, accompanied by the station-master, looked serious. Blanche instantly penetrated the secret of her uncle's hesitation. She turned pale, and caught him by the arm. "Don't send me away," she whispered. "I can bear any thing but suspense."

"Out with it!" said Sir Patrick, holding his niece's hand. "Is she found or not?"

"She's gone by the up-train," said the station-master. "And we know where."

Sir Patrick breathed freely; Blanche's color came back. In different ways, the relief to both of them was equally great.

"You had my orders to follow her," said Sir Patrick to Duncan. "Why have you come back?"

"Your man is not to blame, Sir," interposed the station-master. "The lady took the train at Kirkandrew."

Sir Patrick started and looked at the station-master. "Ay? ay? The next station—the market-town. Inexcusably stupid of me. I never thought of that."

"I took the liberty of telegraphing your description of the lady to Kirkandrew, Sir Patrick, in case of accidents."

"I stand corrected, Mr. Murdoch. Your head, in this matter, has been the sharper head of the two. Well?"

"There's the answer, Sir."

Sir Patrick and Blanche read the telegram together.

"Kirkandrew. Up train. 7.40 P.M. Lady as described. No luggage. Bag in her hand. Traveling alone. Ticket—second-class. Place—Edinburgh."

"Edinburgh!" repeated Blanche. "Oh, uncle! we shall lose her in a great place like that!"

"We shall find her, my dear; and you shall see how. Duncan, get me pen, ink, and paper. Mr. Murdoch, you are going back to the station, I suppose?"

"Yes, Sir Patrick."

"I will give you a telegram, to be sent at once to Edinburgh."

He wrote a carefully-worded telegraphic message, and addressed it to The Sheriff of Mid-Lothian.

"The Sheriff is an old friend of mine," he explained to his niece. "And he is now in Edinburgh. Long before the train gets to the terminus he will receive this personal description of Miss Silvester, with my request to have all her movements carefully watched till further notice. The police are entirely at his disposal; and the best men will be selected for the purpose. I have asked for an answer by telegraph. Keep a special messenger ready for it at the station, Mr. Murdoch. Thank you; good-evening. Duncan, get your supper, and make yourself comfortable. Blanche, my dear, go back to the drawing-room, and expect us in to tea immediately. You will know where your friend is before you go to bed to-night."

With those comforting words he returned to the gentlemen. In ten minutes more they all appeared in the drawing-room; and Lady Lundie (firmly persuaded that she had never closed her eyes) was back again in baronial Scotland five hundred years since.

Blanche, watching her opportunity, caught her uncle alone.

"Now for your promise," she said. "You have made some important discoveries at Craig Fernie. What are they?"

Sir Patrick's eye turned toward Geoffrey, dozing in an arm-chair in a corner of the room. He showed a certain disposition to trifle with the curiosity of his niece.

"After the discovery we have already made," he said, "can't you wait, my dear, till we get the telegram from Edinburgh?"

"That is just what it's impossible for me to do! The telegram won't come for hours yet. I want something to go on with in the mean time."

She seated herself on a sofa in the corner opposite Geoffrey, and pointed to the vacant place by her side.

Sir Patrick had promised—Sir Patrick had no choice but to keep his word. After another look at Geoffrey, he took the vacant place by his niece.

CHAPTER THE TWENTY-FOURTH.

BACKWARD.

"WELL?" whispered Blanche, taking her uncle confidentially by the arm.

"Well," said Sir Patrick, with a spark of his satirical humor flashing out at his niece, "I am going to do a very rash thing. I am going to place a serious trust in the hands of a girl of eighteen."

"The girl's hands will keep it, uncle—though she is only eighteen."

"I must run the risk, my dear; your intimate knowledge of Miss Silvester may be of the greatest assistance to me in the next step I take. You shall know all that I can tell you, but I must warn you first. I can only admit you into my confidence by startling you with a great surprise. Do you follow me, so far?"

"Yes! yes!"

"If you fail to control yourself, you place an obstacle in the way of my being of some future use to Miss Silvester. Remember that, and now prepare for the surprise. What did I tell you before dinner?"

"You said you had made discoveries at Craig Fernie. What have you found out?"

"I have found out that there is a certain person who is in full possession of the information which Miss Silvester has concealed from you and from me. The person is within our reach. The person is in this neighborhood. The person is in this room!"

He caught up Blanche's hand, resting on his arm, and pressed it significantly. She looked at him with the cry of surprise suspended on her lips—waited a little with her eyes fixed on Fir Patrick's face—struggled resolutely, and composed herself.

"Point the person out." She said the words with a self-possession which won her uncle's hearty approval. Blanche had done wonders for a girl in her teens.

"Look!" said Sir Patrick; "and tell me what you see."

"I see Lady Lundie, at the other end of the room, with the map of Perthshire and the Baronial Antiquities of Scotland on the table. And I see every body but you and me obliged to listen to her."

"Every body?"

Blanche looked carefully round the room, and noticed Geoffrey in the opposite corner; fast asleep by this time in his arm-chair.

"Uncle! you don't mean—?"

"There is the man."

"Mr. Delamayn—!"

"Mr. Delamayn knows every thing."

Blanche held mechanically by her uncle's arm, and looked at the sleeping man as if her eyes could never see enough of him.

"You saw me in the library in private consultation with Mr. Delamayn," resumed Sir Patrick. "I have to acknowledge, my dear, that you were quite right in thinking this a suspicious circumstance, And I am now to justify myself for having purposely kept you in the dark up to the present time."

With those introductory words, he briefly reverted to the earlier occurrences of the day, and then added, by way of commentary, a statement of the conclusions which events had suggested to his own mind.

The events, it may be remembered, were three in number. First, Geoffrey's private conference with Sir Patrick on the subject of Irregular Marriages in Scotland. Secondly, Anne Silvester's appearance at Windygates. Thirdly, Anne's flight.

The conclusions which had thereupon suggested themselves to Sir Patrick's mind were six in number.

First, that a connection of some sort might possibly exist between Geoffrey's acknowledged difficulty about his friend, and Miss Silvester's presumed difficulty about herself. Secondly, that Geoffrey had really put to Sir Patrick—not his own case—but the case of a friend. Thirdly, that Geoffrey had some interest (of no harmless kind) in establishing the fact of his friend's marriage. Fourthly, that Anne's anxiety (as described by Blanche) to hear the names of the gentlemen who were staying at Windygates, pointed, in all probability, to Geoffrey. Fifthly, that this last inference disturbed the second conclusion, and reopened the doubt whether Geoffrey had not been stating his own case, after all, under pretense of stating the case of a friend. Sixthly, that the one way of obtaining any enlightenment on this point, and on all the other points involved in mystery, was to go to Craig Fernie, and consult Mrs. Inchbare's experience during the period of Anne's residence at the inn. Sir Patrick's apology for keeping all this a secret from his niece followed. He had shrunk from agitating her on the subject until he could be sure of proving his conclusions to be true. The proof had been obtained; and he was now, therefore, ready to open his mind to Blanche without reserve.

"So much, my dear," proceeded Sir Patrick, "for those necessary explanations which are also the necessary nuisances of human intercourse. You now know as much as I did when I arrived at Craig Fernie—and you are, therefore, in a position to appreciate the value of my discoveries at the inn. Do you understand every thing, so far?"

"Perfectly!"

"Very good. I drove up to the inn; and—behold me closeted with Mrs. Inchbare in her own private parlor! (My reputation may or may not suffer, but Mrs. Inchbare's bones are above suspicion!) It was a long business, Blanche. A more sour-tempered, cunning, and distrustful witness I never examined in all my experience at the Bar. She would have upset the temper of any mortal man but a lawyer. We have such wonderful tempers in our profession; and we can be so aggravating when we like! In short, my dear, Mrs. Inchbare was a she-cat, and I was a he-cat—and I clawed the truth out of her at last. The result was well worth arriving at, as you shall see. Mr. Delamayn had described to me certain remarkable circumstances as taking place between a lady and a gentleman at an inn: the object of the parties being to pass themselves off at the time as man and wife. Every one of those circumstances, Blanche, occurred at Craig Fernie, between a lady and a gentleman, on the day when Miss Silvester disappeared from this house And—wait!—being pressed for her name, after the gentleman had left her behind him at the inn, the name the lady gave was, 'Mrs. Silvester.' What do you think of that?"

"Think! I'm bewildered—I can't realize it."

"It's a startling discovery, my dear child—there is no denying that. Shall I wait a little, and let you recover yourself?"

"No! no! Go on! The gentleman, uncle? The gentleman who was with Anne? Who is he? Not Mr. Delamayn?"

"Not Mr. Delamayn," said Sir Patrick. "If I have proved nothing else, I have proved that."

"What need was there to prove it? Mr. Delamayn went to London on the day of the lawn-party. And Arnold—"

"And Arnold went with him as far as the second station from this. Quite true! But how was I to know what Mr. Delamayn might have done after Arnold had left him? I could only make sure that he had not gone back privately to the inn, by getting the proof from Mrs. Inchbare."

"How did you get it?"

"I asked her to describe the gentleman who was with Miss Silvester. Mrs. Inchbare's description (vague as you will presently find it to be) completely exonerates that man," said Sir Patrick, pointing to Geoffrey still asleep in his chair. "He is not the person who passed Miss Silvester off as his wife at Craig Fernie. He spoke the truth when he described the case to me as the case of a friend."

"But who is the friend?" persisted Blanche. "That's what I want to know."

"That's what I want to know, too."

"Tell me exactly, uncle, what Mrs. Inchbare said. I have lived with Anne all my life. I must have seen the man somewhere."

"If you can identify him by Mrs. Inchbare's description," returned Sir Patrick, "you will be a great deal cleverer than I am. Here is the picture of the man, as painted by the landlady: Young; middle-sized; dark hair, eyes, and complexion; nice temper, pleasant way of speaking. Leave out 'young,' and the rest is the exact contrary of Mr. Delamayn. So far, Mrs. Inchbare guides us plainly enough. But how are we to apply her description to the right person? There must be, at the lowest computation, five hundred thousand men in England who are young, middle-sized, dark, nice-tempered, and pleasant spoken. One of the footmen here answers that description in every particular."

"And Arnold answers it," said Blanche—as a still stronger instance of the provoking vagueness of the description.

"And Arnold answers it," repeated Sir Patrick, quite agreeing with her.

They had barely said those words when Arnold himself appeared, approaching Sir Patrick with a pack of cards in his hand.

There—at the very moment when they had both guessed the truth, without feeling the slightest suspicion of it in their own minds—there stood Discovery, presenting itself unconsciously to eyes incapable of seeing it, in the person of the man who had passed Anne Silvester off as his wife at the Craig Fernie inn! The terrible caprice of Chance, the merciless irony of Circumstance, could go no further than this. The three had their feet on the brink of the precipice at that moment. And two of them were smiling at an odd coincidence; and one of them was shuffling a pack of cards!

"We have done with the Antiquities at last!" said Arnold; "and we are going to play at Whist. Sir Patrick, will you choose a card?"

"Too soon after dinner, my good fellow, for me. Play the first rubber, and then give me another chance. By-the-way," he added "Miss Silvester has been traced to Kirkandrew. How is it that you never saw her go by?"

"She can't have gone my way, Sir Patrick, or I must have seen her."

Having justified himself in those terms, he was recalled to the other end of the room by the whist-party, impatient for the cards which he had in his hand.

"What were we talking of when he interrupted us?" said Sir Patrick to Blanche.

"Of the man, uncle, who was with Miss Silvester at the inn."

"It's useless to pursue that inquiry, my dear, with nothing better than Mrs. Inchbare's description to help us."

Blanche looked round at the sleeping Geoffrey.

"And he knows!" she said. "It's maddening, uncle, to look at the brute snoring in his chair!"

Sir Patrick held up a warning hand. Before a word more could be said between them they were silenced again by another interruption.

The whist-party comprised Lady Lundie and the surgeon, playing as partners against Smith and Jones. Arnold sat behind the surgeon, taking a lesson in the game. One, Two, and Three, thus left to their own devices, naturally thought of the billiard-table; and, detecting Geoffrey asleep in his corner, advanced to disturb his slumbers, under the all-sufficing apology of "Pool." Geoffrey roused himself, and rubbed his eyes, and said, drowsily, "All right." As he rose, he looked at the opposite corner in which Sir Patrick and his niece were sitting. Blanche's self-possession, resolutely as she struggled to preserve it, was not strong enough to keep her eyes from turning toward Geoffrey with an expression which betrayed the reluctant interest that she now felt in him. He stopped, noticing something entirely new in the look with which the young lady was regarding him.

"Beg your pardon," said Geoffrey. "Do you wish to speak to me?"

Blanche's face flushed all over. Her uncle came to the rescue.

"Miss Lundie and I hope you have slept well Mr. Delamayn," said Sir Patrick, jocosely. "That's all."

"Oh? That's all?" said Geoffrey still looking at Blanche. "Beg your pardon again. Deuced long walk, and deuced heavy dinner. Natural consequence—a nap."

Sir Patrick eyed him closely. It was plain that he had been honestly puzzled at finding himself an object of special attention on Blanche's part. "See you in the billiard-room?" he said, carelessly, and followed his companions out of the room—as usual, without waiting for an answer.

"Mind what you are about," said Sir Patrick to his niece. "That man is quicker than he looks. We commit a serious mistake if we put him on his guard at starting."

"It sha'n't happen again, uncle," said Blanche. "But think of his being in Anne's confidence, and of my being shut out of it!"

"In his friend's confidence, you mean, my dear; and (if we only avoid awakening his suspicion) there is no knowing how soon he may say or do something which may show us who his friend is."

"But he is going back to his brother's to-morrow—he said so at dinner-time."

"So much the better. He will be out of the way of seeing strange things in a certain young lady's face. His brother's house is within easy reach of this; and I am his legal adviser. My experience tells me that he has not done consulting me yet—and that he will let out something more next time. So much for our chance of seeing the light through Mr. Delamayn—if we can't see it in any other way. And that is not our only chance, remember. I have something to tell you about Bishopriggs and the lost letter."

"Is it found?"

"No. I satisfied myself about that—I had it searched for, under my own eye. The letter is stolen, Blanche; and Bishopriggs has got it. I have left a line for him, in Mrs. Inchbare's care. The old rascal is missed already by the visitors at the inn, just as I told you he would be. His mistress is feeling the penalty of having been fool enough to vent her ill temper on her head-waiter. She lays the whole blame of the quarrel on Miss Silvester, of course. Bishopriggs neglected every body at the inn to wait on Miss Silvester. Bishopriggs was insolent on being remonstrated with, and Miss Silvester encouraged him—and so on. The result will be—now Miss Silvester has gone—that Bishopriggs will return to Craig Fernie before the autumn is over. We are sailing with wind and tide, my dear. Come, and learn to play whist."

He rose to join the card-players. Blanche detained him.

"You haven't told me one thing yet," she said. "Whoever the man may be, is Anne married to him?"

"Whoever the man may be," returned Sir Patrick, "he had better not attempt to marry any body else."

So the niece unconsciously put the question, and so the uncle unconsciously gave the answer on which depended the whole happiness of Blanche's life to come, The "man!" How lightly they both talked of the "man!" Would nothing happen to rouse the faintest suspicion—in their minds or in Arnold's mind—that Arnold was the "man" himself?

"You mean that she is married?" said Blanche.

"I don't go as far as that."

"You mean that she is not married?"

"I don't go so far as that."

"Oh! the law!"

"Provoking, isn't it, my dear? I can tell you, professionally, that (in my opinion) she has grounds to go on if she claims to be the man's wife. That is what I meant by my answer; and, until we know more, that is all I can say."

"When shall we know more? When shall we get the telegram?"

"Not for some hours yet. Come, and learn to play whist."

"I think I would rather talk to Arnold, uncle, if you don't mind."

"By all means! But don't talk to him about what I have been telling you to-night. He and Mr. Delamayn are old associates, remember; and he might blunder into telling his friend what his friend had better not know. Sad (isn't it?) for me to be instilling these lessons of duplicity into the youthful mind. A wise person once said, 'The older a man gets the worse he gets.' That wise person, my dear, had me in his eye, and was perfectly right."

He mitigated the pain of that confession with a pinch of snuff, and went to the whist table to wait until the end of the rubber gave him a place at the game.

CHAPTER THE TWENTY-FIFTH.

FORWARD.

BLANCHE found her lover as attentive as usual to her slightest wish, but not in his customary good spirits. He pleaded fatigue, after his long watch at the cross-roads, as an excuse for his depression. As long as there was any hope of a reconciliation with Geoffrey, he was unwilling to tell Blanche what had happened that afternoon. The hope grew fainter and fainter as the evening advanced. Arnold purposely suggested a visit to the billiard-room, and joined the game, with Blanche, to give Geoffrey an opportunity of saying the few gracious words which would have made them friends again. Geoffrey never spoke the words; he obstinately ignored Arnold's presence in the room.

At the card-table the whist went on interminably. Lady Lundie, Sir Patrick, and the surgeon, were all inveterate players, evenly matched. Smith and Jones (joining the game alternately) were aids to whist, exactly as they were aids to conversation. The same safe and modest mediocrity of style distinguished the proceedings of these two gentlemen in all the affairs of life.

The time wore on to midnight. They went to bed late and they rose late at Windygates House. Under that hospitable roof, no intrusive hints, in the shape of flat candlesticks exhibiting themselves with ostentatious virtue on side-tables, hurried the guest to his room; no vile bell rang him ruthlessly out of bed the next morning, and insisted on his breakfasting at a given hour. Life has surely hardships enough that are inevitable without gratuitously adding the hardship of absolute government, administered by a clock?

It was a quarter past twelve when Lady Lundie rose blandly from the whist-table, and said that she supposed somebody must set the example of going to bed. Sir Patrick and Smith, the surgeon and Jones, agreed on a last rubber. Blanche vanished while her stepmother's eye was on her; and appeared again in the drawing-room, when Lady Lundie was safe in the hands of her maid. Nobody followed the example of the mistress of the house but Arnold. He left the billiard-room with the certainty that it was all over now between Geoffrey and himself. Not even the attraction of Blanche proved strong enough to detain him that night. He went his way to bed.

It was past one o'clock. The final rubber was at an end, the accounts were settled at the card-table; the surgeon had strolled into the billiard-room, and Smith and Jones had followed him, when Duncan came in, at last, with the telegram in his hand.

Blanche turned from the broad, calm autumn moonlight which had drawn her to the window, and looked over her uncle's shoulder while he opened the telegram.

She read the first line—and that was enough. The whole scaffolding of hope built round that morsel of paper fell to the ground in an instant. The train from Kirkandrew had reached Edinburgh at the usual time. Every passenger in it had passed under the eyes of the police, and nothing had been seen of any person who answered the description given of Anne!

Sir Patrick pointed to the two last sentences in the telegram: "Inquiries telegraphed to Falkirk. If with any result, you shall know."

"We must hope for the best, Blanche. They evidently suspect her of having got out at the junction of the two railways for the purpose of giving the telegraph the slip. There is no help for it. Go to bed, child—go to bed."

Blanche kissed her uncle in silence and went away. The bright young face was sad with the first hopeless sorrow which the old man had yet seen in it. His niece's parting look dwelt painfully on his mind when he was up in his room, with the faithful Duncan getting him ready for his bed.

"This is a bad business, Duncan. I don't like to say so to Miss Lundie; but I greatly fear the governess has baffled us."

"It seems likely, Sir Patrick. The poor young lady looks quite heart-broken about it."

"You noticed that too, did you? She has lived all her life, you see, with Miss Silvester; and there is a very strong attachment between them. I am uneasy about my niece, Duncan. I am afraid this disappointment will have a serious effect on her."

"She's young, Sir Patrick."

"Yes, my friend, she's young; but the young (when they are good for any thing) have warm hearts. Winter hasn't stolen on them, Duncan! And they feel keenly."

"I think there's reason to hope, Sir, that Miss Lundie may get over it more easily than you suppose."

"What reason, pray?"

"A person in my position can hardly venture to speak freely, Sir, on a delicate matter of this kind."

Sir Patrick's temper flashed out, half-seriously, half-whimsically, as usual.

"Is that a snap at Me, you old dog? If I am not your friend, as well as your master, who is? Am I in the habit of keeping any of my harmless fellow-creatures at a distance? I despise the cant of modern Liberalism; but it's not the less true that I have, all my life, protested against the inhuman separation of classes in England. We are, in that respect, brag as we may of our national virtue, the most unchristian people in the civilized world."

"I beg your pardon, Sir Patrick—"

"God help me! I'm talking polities at this time of night! It's your fault, Duncan. What do you mean by casting my station in my teeth, because I can't put my night-cap on comfortably till you have brushed my hair? I have a good mind to get up and brush yours. There! there! I'm uneasy about my niece—nervous irritability, my good fellow, that's all. Let's hear what you have to say about Miss Lundie. And go on with my hair. And don't be a humbug."

"I was about to remind you, Sir Patrick, that Miss Lundie has another interest in her life to turn to. If this matter of Miss Silvester ends badly—and I own it begins to look as if it would—I should hurry my niece's marriage, Sir, and see if that wouldn't console her."

Sir Patrick started under the gentle discipline of the hair-brush in Duncan's hand.

"That's very sensibly put," said the old gentleman. "Duncan! you are, what I call, a clear-minded man. Well worth thinking of, old Truepenny! If the worst comes to the worst, well worth thinking of!"

It was not the first time that Duncan's steady good sense had struck light, under the form of a new thought, in his master's mind. But never yet had he wrought such mischief as the mischief which he had innocently done now. He had sent Sir Patrick to bed with the fatal idea of hastening the marriage of Arnold and Blanche.

The situation of affairs at Windygates—now that Anne had apparently obliterated all trace of herself—was becoming serious. The one chance on which the discovery of Arnold's position depended, was the chance that accident might reveal the truth in the lapse of time. In this posture of circumstances, Sir Patrick now resolved—if nothing happened to relieve Blanche's anxiety in the course of the week—to advance the celebration of the marriage from the end of the autumn (as originally contemplated) to the first fortnight of the ensuing month. As dates then stood, the change led (so far as free scope for the development of accident was concerned) to this serious result. It abridged a lapse of three months into an interval of three weeks.

The next morning came; and Blanche marked it as a memorable morning, by committing an act of imprudence, which struck away one more of the chances of discovery that had existed, before the arrival of the Edinburgh telegram on the previous day.

She had passed a sleepless night; fevered in mind and body; thinking, hour after hour, of nothing but Anne. At sunrise she could endure it no longer. Her power to control herself was completely exhausted; her own impulses led her as they pleased. She got up, determined not to let Geoffrey leave the house without risking an effort to make him reveal what he knew about Anne. It was nothing less than downright treason to Sir Patrick to act on her own responsibility in this way. She knew it was wrong; she was heartily ashamed of herself for doing it. But the demon that possesses women with a recklessness all their own, at the critical moments of their lives, had got her—and she did it.

Geoffrey had arranged overnight, to breakfast early, by himself, and to walk the ten miles to his brother's house; sending a servant to fetch his luggage later in the day.

He had got on his hat; he was standing in the hall, searching his pocket for his second self, the pipe—when Blanche suddenly appeared from the morning-room, and placed herself between him and the house door.

"Up early—eh?" said Geoffrey. "I'm off to my brother's."

She made no reply. He looked at her closer. The girl's eyes were trying to read his face, with an utter carelessness of concealment, which forbade (even to his mind) all unworthy interpretation of her motive for stopping him on his way out.

"Any commands for me?" he inquired

This time she answered him. "I have something to ask you," she said.

He smiled graciously, and opened his tobacco-pouch. He was fresh and strong after his night's sleep—healthy and handsome and good-humored. The house-maids had had a peep at him that morning, and had wished—like Desdemona, with a difference—that "Heaven had made all three of them such a man."

"Well," he said, "what is it?"

She put her question, without a single word of preface—purposely to surprise him.

"Mr. Delamayn," she said, "do you know where Anne Silvester is this morning?"

He was filling his pipe as she spoke, and he dropped some of the tobacco on the floor. Instead of answering before he picked up the tobacco he answered after—in surly self-possession, and in one word—"No."

"Do you know nothing about her?"

He devoted himself doggedly to the filling of his pipe. "Nothing."

"On your word of honor, as a gentleman?"

"On my word of honor, as a gentleman."

He put back his tobacco-pouch in his pocket. His handsome face was as hard as stone. His clear blue eyes defied all the girls in England put together to see into his mind. "Have you done, Miss Lundie?" he asked, suddenly changing to a bantering politeness of tone and manner.

Blanche saw that it was hopeless—saw that she had compromised her own interests by her own headlong act. Sir Patrick's warning words came back reproachfully to her now when it was too late. "We commit a serious mistake if we put him on his guard at starting."

There was but one course to take now. "Yes," she said. "I have done."

"My turn now," rejoined Geoffrey. "You want to know where Miss Silvester is. Why do you ask Me?"

Blanche did all that could be done toward repairing the error that she had committed. She kept Geoffrey as far away as Geoffrey had kept her from the truth.

"I happen to know," she replied "that Miss Silvester left the place at which she had been staying about the time when you went out walking yesterday. And I thought you might have seen her."

"Oh? That's the reason—is it?" said Geoffrey, with a smile.

The smile stung Blanche's sensitive temper to the quick. She made a final effort to control herself, before her indignation got the better of her.

"I have no more to say, Mr. Delamayn." With that reply she turned her back on him, and closed the door of the morning-room between them.

Geoffrey descended the house steps and lit his pipe. He was not at the slightest loss, on this occasion, to account for what had happened. He assumed at once that Arnold had taken a mean revenge on him after his conduct of the day before, and had told the whole secret of his errand at Craig Fernie to Blanche. The thing would get next, no doubt, to Sir Patrick's ears; and Sir Patrick would thereupon be probably the first person who revealed to Arnold the position in which he had placed himself with Anne. All right! Sir Patrick would be an excellent witness to appeal to, when the scandal broke out, and when the time came for repudiating Anne's claim on him as the barefaced imposture of a woman who was married already to another man. He puffed away unconcernedly at his pipe, and started, at his swinging, steady pace, for his brother's house.

Blanche remained alone in the morning-room. The prospect of getting at the truth, by means of what Geoffrey might say on the next occasion when he consulted Sir Patrick, was a prospect that she herself had closed from that moment. She sat down in despair by the window. It commanded a view of the little side-terrace which had been Anne's favorite walk at Windygates. With weary eyes and aching heart the poor child looked at the familiar place; and asked herself, with the bitter repentance that comes too late, if she had destroyed the last chance of finding Anne!

She sat passively at the window, while the hours of the morning wore on, until the postman came. Before the servant could take the letter bag she was in the hall to receive it. Was it possible to hope that the bag had brought tidings of Anne? She sorted the letters; and lighted suddenly on a letter to herself. It bore the Kirkandrew postmark, and It was addressed to her in Anne's handwriting.

She tore the letter open, and read these lines:

"I have left you forever, Blanche. God bless and reward you! God make you a happy woman in all your life to come! Cruel as you will think me, love, I have never been so truly your sister as I am now. I can only tell you this—I can never tell you more. Forgive me, and forget me, our lives are parted lives from this day."

Going down to breakfast about his usual hour, Sir Patrick missed Blanche, whom he was accustomed to see waiting for him at the table at that time. The room was empty; the other members of the household having all finished their morning meal. Sir Patrick disliked breakfasting alone. He sent Duncan with a message, to be given to Blanche's maid.

The maid appeared in due time Miss Lundie was unable to leave her room. She sent a letter to her uncle, with her love—and begged he would read it.

Sir Patrick opened the letter and saw what Anne had written to Blanche.

He waited a little, reflecting, with evident pain and anxiety, on what he had read—then opened his own letters, and hurriedly looked at the signatures. There was nothing for him from his friend, the sheriff, at Edinburgh, and no communication from the railway, in the shape of a telegram. He had decided, overnight, on waiting till the end of the week before he interfered in the matter of Blanche's marriage. The events of the morning determined him on not waiting another day. Duncan returned to the breakfast-room to pour out his master's coffee. Sir Patrick sent him away again with a second message,

"Do you know where Lady Lundie is, Duncan?"

"Yes, Sir Patrick."

"My compliments to her ladyship. If she is not otherwise engaged, I shall be glad to speak to her privately in an hour's time."

CHAPTER THE TWENTY-SIXTH.

DROPPED.

SIR PATRICK made a bad breakfast. Blanche's absence fretted him, and Anne Silvester's letter puzzled him.

He read it, short as it was, a second time, and a third. If it meant any thing, it meant that the motive at the bottom of Anne's flight was to accomplish the sacrifice of herself to the happiness of Blanche. She had parted for life from his niece for his niece's sake! What did this mean? And how was it to be reconciled with Anne's position—as described to him by Mrs. Inchbare during his visit to Craig Fernie?

All Sir Patrick's ingenuity, and all Sir Patrick's experience, failed to find so much as the shadow of an answer to that question.

While he was still pondering over the letter, Arnold and the surgeon entered the breakfast-room together.

"Have you heard about Blanche?" asked Arnold, excitedly. "She is in no danger, Sir Patrick—the worst of it is over now."

The surgeon interposed before Sir Patrick could appeal to him.

"Mr. Brinkworth's interest in the young lady a little exaggerates the state of the case," he said. "I have seen her, at Lady Lundie's request; and I can assure you that there is not the slightest reason for any present alarm. Miss Lundie has had a nervous attack, which has yielded to the simplest domestic remedies. The only anxiety you need feel is connected with the management of her in the future. She is suffering from some mental distress, which it is not for me, but for her friends, to alleviate and remove. If you can turn her thoughts from the painful subject—whatever it may be—on which they are dwelling now, you will do all that needs to be done." He took up a newspaper from the table, and strolled out into the garden, leaving Sir Patrick and Arnold together.

"You heard that?" said Sir Patrick.

"Is he right, do you think?" asked Arnold.

"Right? Do you suppose a man gets his reputation by making mistakes? You're one of the new generation, Master Arnold. You can all of you stare at a famous man; but you haven't an atom of respect for his fame. If Shakspeare came to life again, and talked of playwriting, the first pretentious nobody who sat opposite at dinner would differ with him as composedly as he might differ with you and me. Veneration is dead among us; the present age has buried it, without a stone to mark the place. So much for that! Let's get back to Blanche. I suppose you can guess what the painful subject is that's dwelling on her mind? Miss Silvester has baffled me, and baffled the Edinburgh police. Blanche discovered that we had failed last night and Blanche received that letter this morning."

He pushed Anne's letter across the breakfast-table.

Arnold read it, and handed it back without a word. Viewed by the new light in which he saw Geoffrey's character after the quarrel on the heath, the letter conveyed but one conclusion to his mind. Geoffrey had deserted her.

"Well?" said Sir Patrick. "Do you understand what it means?"

"I understand Blanche's wretchedness when she read it."

He said no more than that. It was plain that no information which he could afford—even if he had considered himself at liberty to give it—would be of the slightest use in assisting Sir Patrick to trace Miss Silvester, under present circumstances, There was—unhappily—no temptation to induce him to break the honorable silence which he had maintained thus far. And—more unfortunately still—assuming the temptation to present itself, Arnold's capacity to resist it had never been so strong a capacity as it was now.

To the two powerful motives which had hitherto tied his tongue—respect for Anne's reputation, and reluctance to reveal to Blanche the deception which he had been compelled to practice on her at the inn—to these two motives there was now added a third. The meanness of betraying the confidence which Geoffrey had reposed in him would be doubled meanness if he proved false to his trust after Geoffrey had personally insulted him. The paltry revenge which that false friend had unhesitatingly suspected him of taking was a revenge of which Arnold's nature was simply incapable. Never had his lips been more effectually sealed than at this moment—when his whole future depended on Sir Patrick's discovering the part that he had played in past events at Craig Fernie.

"Yes! yes!" resumed Sir Patrick, impatiently. "Blanche's distress is intelligible enough. But here is my niece apparently answerable for this unhappy woman's disappearance. Can you explain what my niece has got to do with it?"

"I! Blanche herself is completely mystified. How should I know?"

Answering in those terms, he spoke with perfect sincerity. Anne's vague distrust of the position in which they had innocently placed themselves at the inn had produced no corresponding effect on Arnold at the time. He had not regarded it; he had not even understood it. As a necessary result, not the faintest suspicion of the motive under which Anne was acting existed in his mind now.

Sir Patrick put the letter into his pocket-book, and abandoned all further attempt at interpreting the meaning of it in despair.

"Enough, and more than enough, of groping in the dark," he said. "One point is clear to me after what has happened up stairs this morning. We must accept the position in which Miss Silvester has placed us. I shall give up all further effort to trace her from this moment."

"Surely that will be a dreadful disappointment to Blanche, Sir Patrick?"

"I don't deny it. We must face that result."

"If you are sure there is nothing else to be done, I suppose we must."

"I am not sure of anything of the sort, Master Arnold! There are two chances still left of throwing light on this matter, which are both of them independent of any thing that Miss Silvester can do to keep it in the dark."

"Then why not try them, Sir? It seems hard to drop Miss Silvester when she is in trouble."

"We can't help her against her own will," rejoined Sir Patrick. "And we can't run the risk, after that nervous attack this morning, of subjecting Blanche to any further suspense. I have thought of my niece's interests throughout this business; and if I now change my mind, and decline to agitate her by more experiments, ending (quite possibly) in more failures, it is because I am thinking of her interests still. I have no other motive. However numerous my weaknesses may be, ambition to distinguish myself as a detective policeman is not one of them. The case, from the police point of view, is by no means a lost case. I drop it, nevertheless, for Blanche's sake. Instead of encouraging her thoughts to dwell on this melancholy business, we must apply the remedy suggested by our medical friend."

"How is that to be done?" asked Arnold.

The sly twist of humor began to show itself in Sir Patrick's face.

"Has she nothing to think of in the future, which is a pleasanter subject of reflection than the loss of her friend?" he asked. "You are interested, my young gentleman, in the remedy that is to cure Blanche. You are one of the drugs in the moral prescription. Can you guess what it is?"

Arnold started to his feet, and brightened into a new being.

"Perhaps you object to be hurried?" said Sir Patrick.

"Object! If Blanche will only consent, I'll take her to church as soon as she comes down stairs!"

"Thank you!" said Sir Patrick, dryly. "Mr. Arnold Brinkworth, may you always be as ready to take Time by the forelock as you are now! Sit down again; and don't talk nonsense. It is just possible—if Blanche consents (as you say), and if we can hurry the lawyers—that you may be married in three weeks' or a month's time."

"What have the lawyers got to do with it?"

"My good fellow, this is not a marriage in a novel! This is the most unromantic affair of the sort that ever happened. Here are a young gentleman and a young lady, both rich people; both well matched in birth and character; one of age, and the other marrying with the full consent and approval of her guardian. What is the consequence of this purely prosaic state of things? Lawyers and settlements, of course!"

"Come into the library, Sir Patrick; and I'll soon settle the settlements! A bit of paper, and a dip of ink. 'I hereby give every blessed farthing I have got in the world to my dear Blanche.' Sign that; stick a wafer on at the side; clap your finger on the wafer; 'I deliver this as my act and deed;' and there it is—done!"

"Is it, really? You are a born legislator. You create and codify your own system all in a breath. Moses-Justinian-Mahomet, give me your arm! There is one atom of sense in what you have just said. 'Come into the library'—is a suggestion worth attending to. Do you happen, among your other superfluities, to have such a thing as a lawyer about you?"

"I have got two. One in London, and one in Edinburgh."

"We will take the nearest of the two, because we are in a hurry. Who is the Edinburgh lawyer? Pringle of Pitt Street? Couldn't be a better man. Come and write to him. You have given me your abstract of a marriage settlement with the brevity of an ancient Roman. I scorn to be outdone by an amateur lawyer. Here is my abstract: You are just and generous to Blanche; Blanche is just and generous to you; and you both combine to be just and generous together to your children. There is a model settlement! and there are your instructions to Pringle of Pitt Street! Can you do it by yourself? No; of course you can't. Now don't be slovenly-minded! See the points in their order as they come. You are going to be married; you state to whom, you add that I am the lady's guardian; you give the name and address of my lawyer in Edinburgh; you write your instructions plainly in the fewest words, and leave details to your legal adviser; you refer the lawyers to each other; you request that the draft settlements be prepared as speedily as possible, and you give your address at this house. There are the heads. Can't you do it now? Oh, the rising generation! Oh, the progress we are making in these enlightened modern times! There! there! you can marry Blanche, and make her happy, and increase the population—and all without knowing how to write the English language. One can only say with the learned Bevorskius, looking out of his window at the illimitable loves of the sparrows, 'How merciful is Heaven to its creatures!' Take up the pen. I'll dictate! I'll dictate!"

Sir Patrick read the letter over, approved of it, and saw it safe in the box for the post. This done, he peremptorily forbade Arnold to speak to his niece on the subject of the marriage without his express permission. "There's somebody else's consent to be got," he said, "besides Blanche's consent and mine."

"Lady Lundie?"

"Lady Lundie. Strictly speaking, I am the only authority. But my sister-in-law is Blanche's step-mother, and she is appointed guardian in the event of my death. She has a right to be consulted—in courtesy, if not in law. Would you like to do it?"

Arnold's face fell. He looked at Sir Patrick in silent dismay.

"What! you can't even speak to such a perfectly pliable person as Lady Lundie? You may have been a very useful fellow at sea. A more helpless young man I never met with on shore. Get out with you into the garden among the other sparrows! Somebody must confront her ladyship. And if you won't—I must."

He pushed Arnold out of the library, and applied meditatively to the knob of his cane. His gayety disappeared, now that he was alone. His experience of Lady Lundie's character told him that, in attempting to win her approval to any scheme for hurrying Blanche's marriage, he was undertaking no easy task. "I suppose," mused Sir Patrick, thinking of his late brother—"I suppose poor Tom had some way of managing her. How did he do it, I wonder? If she had been the wife of a bricklayer, she is the sort of woman who would have been kept in perfect order by a vigorous and regular application of her husband's fist. But Tom wasn't a bricklayer. I wonder how Tom did it?" After a little hard thinking on this point Sir Patrick gave up the problem as beyond human solution. "It must be done," he concluded. "And my own mother-wit must help me to do it."

In that resigned frame of mind he knocked at the door of Lady Lundie's boudoir.

CHAPTER THE TWENTY-SEVENTH.

OUTWITTED.

SIR PATRICK found his sister-in-law immersed in domestic business. Her ladyship's correspondence and visiting list, her ladyship's household bills and ledgers; her ladyship's Diary and Memorandum-book (bound in scarlet morocco); her ladyship's desk, envelope-case, match-box, and taper candlestick (all in ebony and silver); her ladyship herself, presiding over her responsibilities, and wielding her materials, equal to any calls of emergency, beautifully dressed in correct morning costume, blessed with perfect health both of the secretions and the principles; absolutely void of vice, and formidably full of virtue, presented, to every properly-constituted mind, the most imposing spectacle known to humanity—the British Matron on her throne, asking the world in general, When will you produce the like of Me?

"I am afraid I disturb you," said Sir Patrick. "I am a perfectly idle person. Shall I look in a little later?"

Lady Lundie put her hand to her head, and smiled faintly.

"A little pressure here, Sir Patrick. Pray sit down. Duty finds me earnest; Duty finds me cheerful; Duty finds me accessible. From a poor, weak woman, Duty must expect no more. Now what is it?" (Her ladyship consulted her scarlet memorandum-book.) "I have got it here, under its proper head, distinguished by initial letters. P.—the poor. No. H.M.—heathen missions. No. V.T.A.—Visitors to arrive. No. P. I. P.—Here it is: private interview with Patrick. Will you forgive me the little harmless familiarity of omitting your title? Thank you! You are always so good. I am quite at your service when you like to begin. If it's any thing painful, pray don't hesitate. I am quite prepared."

With that intimation her ladyship threw herself back in her chair, with her elbows on the arms, and her fingers joined at the tips, as if she was receiving a deputation. "Yes?" she said, interrogatively. Sir Patrick paid a private tribute of pity to his late brother's memory, and entered on his business.

"We won't call it a painful matter," he began. "Let us say it's a matter of domestic anxiety. Blanche—"

Lady Lundie emitted a faint scream, and put her hand over her eyes.

"Must you?" cried her ladyship, in a tone of touching remonstrance. "Oh, Sir Patrick, must you?"

"Yes. I must."

Lady Lundie's magnificent eyes looked up at that hidden court of human appeal which is lodged in the ceiling. The hidden court looked down at Lady Lundie, and saw—Duty advertising itself in the largest capital letters.

"Go on, Sir Patrick. The motto of woman is Self-sacrifice. You sha'n't see how you distress me. Go on."

Sir Patrick went on impenetrably—without betraying the slightest expression of sympathy or surprise.

"I was about to refer to the nervous attack from which Blanche has suffered this morning," he said. "May I ask whether you have been informed of the cause to which the attack is attributable?"

"There!" exclaimed Lady Lundie with a sudden bound in her chair, and a sudden development of vocal power to correspond. "The one thing I shrank from speaking of! the cruel, cruel, cruel behavior I was prepared to pass over! And Sir Patrick hints on it! Innocently—don't let me do an injustice—innocently hints on it!"

"Hints on what, my dear Madam?"

"Blanche's conduct to me this morning. Blanche's heartless secrecy. Blanche's undutiful silence. I repeat the words: Heartless secrecy. Undutiful silence."

"Allow me for one moment, Lady Lundie—"

"Allow me, Sir Patrick! Heaven knows how unwilling I am to speak of it. Heaven knows that not a word of reference to it escaped my lips. But you leave me no choice now. As mistress of the household, as a Christian woman, as the widow of your dear brother, as a mother to this misguided girl, I must state the facts. I know you mean well; I know you wish to spare me. Quite useless! I must state the facts."

Sir Patrick bowed, and submitted. (If he had only been a bricklayer! and if Lady Lundie had not been, what her ladyship unquestionably was, the strongest person of the two!)

"Permit me to draw a veil, for your sake," said Lady Lundie, "over the horrors—I can not, with the best wish to spare you, conscientiously call them by any other name—the horrors that took place up stairs. The moment I heard that Blanche was ill I was at my post. Duty will always find me ready, Sir Patrick, to my dying day. Shocking as the whole thing was, I presided calmly over the screams and sobs of my step-daughter. I closed my ears to the profane violence of her language. I set the necessary example, as an English gentlewoman at the head of her household. It was only when I distinctly heard the name of a person, never to be mentioned again in my family circle, issue (if I may use the expression) from Blanche's lips that I began to be really alarmed. I said to my maid: 'Hopkins, this is not Hysteria. This is a possession of the devil. Fetch the chloroform.'"

Chloroform, applied in the capacity of an exorcism, was entirely new to Sir Patrick. He preserved his gravity with considerable difficulty. Lady Lundie went on:

"Hopkins is an excellent person—but Hopkins has a tongue. She met our distinguished medical guest in the corridor, and told him. He was so good as to come to the door. I was shocked to trouble him to act in his professional capacity while he was a visitor, an honored visitor, in my house. Besides, I considered it more a case for a clergyman than for a medical man. However, there was no help for it after Hopkins's tongue. I requested our eminent friend to favor us with—I think the exact scientific term is—a Prognosis. He took the purely material view which was only to be expected from a person in his profession. He prognosed—am I right? Did he prognose? or did he diagnose? A habit of speaking correctly is so important, Sir Patrick! and I should be so grieved to mislead you!"

"Never mind, Lady Lundie! I have heard the medical report. Don't trouble yourself to repeat it."

"Don't trouble myself to repeat it?" echoed Lady Lundie—with her dignity up in arms at the bare prospect of finding her remarks abridged. "Ah, Sir Patrick! that little constitutional impatience of yours!—Oh, dear me! how often you must have given way to it, and how often you must have regretted it, in your time!"

"My dear lady! if you wish to repeat the report, why not say so, in plain words? Don't let me hurry you. Let us have the prognosis, by all means."

Lady Lundie shook her head compassionately, and smiled with angelic sadness. "Our little besetting sins!" she said. "What slaves we are to our little besetting sins! Take a turn in the room—do!"

Any ordinary man would have lost his temper. But the law (as Sir Patrick had told his niece) has a special temper of its own. Without exhibiting the smallest irritation, Sir Patrick dextrously applied his sister-in-law's blister to his sister-in-law herself.

"What an eye you have!" he said. "I was impatient. I am impatient. I am dying to know what Blanche said to you when she got better?"

The British Matron froze up into a matron of stone on the spot.

"Nothing!" answered her ladyship, with a vicious snap of her teeth, as if she had tried to bite the word before it escaped her.

"Nothing!" exclaimed Sir Patrick.

"Nothing," repeated Lady Lundie, with her most formidable emphasis of look and tone. "I applied all the remedies with my own hands; I cut her laces with my own scissors, I completely wetted her head through with cold water; I remained with her until she was quite exhausted—I took her in my arms, and folded her to my bosom; I sent every body out of the room; I said, 'Dear child, confide in me.' And how were my advances—my motherly advances—met? I have already told you. By heartless secrecy. By undutiful silence."

Sir Patrick pressed the blister a little closer to the skin. "She was probably afraid to speak," he said.

"Afraid? Oh!" cried Lady Lundie, distrusting the evidence of her own senses. "You can't have said that? I have evidently misapprehended you. You didn't really say, afraid?"

"I said she was probably afraid—"

"Stop! I can't be told to my face that I have failed to do my duty by Blanche. No, Sir Patrick! I can bear a great deal; but I can't bear that. After having been more than a mother to your dear brother's child; after having been an elder sister to Blanche; after having toiled—I say toiled, Sir Patrick!—to cultivate her intelligence (with the sweet lines of the poet ever present to my memory: 'Delightful task to rear the tender mind, and teach the young idea how to shoot!'); after having done all I have done—a place in the carriage only yesterday, and a visit to the most interesting relic of feudal times in Perthshire—after having sacrificed all I have sacrificed, to be told that I have behaved in such a manner to Blanche as to frighten her when I ask her to confide in me, is a little too cruel. I have a sensitive—an unduly sensitive nature, dear Sir Patrick. Forgive me for wincing when I am wounded. Forgive me for feeling it when the wound is dealt me by a person whom I revere."

Her ladyship put her handkerchief to her eyes. Any other man would have taken off the blister. Sir Patrick pressed it harder than ever.

"You quite mistake me," he replied. "I meant that Blanche was afraid to tell you the true cause of her illness. The true cause is anxiety about Miss Silvester."

Lady Lundie emitted another scream—a loud scream this time—and closed her eyes in horror.

"I can run out of the house," cried her ladyship, wildly. "I can fly to the uttermost corners of the earth; but I can not hear that person's name mentioned! No, Sir Patrick! not in my presence! not in my room! not while I am mistress at Windygates House!"

"I am sorry to say any thing that is disagreeable to you, Lady Lundie. But the nature of my errand here obliges me to touch—as lightly as possible—on something which has happened in your house without your knowledge."

Lady Lundie suddenly opened her eyes, and became the picture of attention. A casual observer might have supposed her ladyship to be not wholly inaccessible to the vulgar emotion of curiosity.

"A visitor came to Windygates yesterday, while we were all at lunch," proceeded Sir Patrick. "She—"

Lady Lundie seized the scarlet memorandum-book, and stopped her brother-in-law, before he could get any further. Her ladyship's next words escaped her lips spasmodically, like words let at intervals out of a trap.

"I undertake—as a woman accustomed to self-restraint, Sir Patrick—I undertake to control myself, on one condition. I won't have the name mentioned. I won't have the sex mentioned. Say, 'The Person,' if you please. 'The Person,'" continued Lady Lundie, opening her memorandum-book and taking up her pen, "committed an audacious invasion of my premises yesterday?"

Sir Patrick bowed. Her ladyship made a note—a fiercely-penned note that scratched the paper viciously—and then proceeded to examine her brother-in-law, in the capacity of witness.

"What part of my house did 'The Person' invade? Be very careful, Sir Patrick! I propose to place myself under the protection of a justice of the peace; and this is a memorandum of my statement. The library—did I understand you to say? Just so—the library."

"Add," said Sir Patrick, with another pressure on the blister, "that The Person had an interview with Blanche in the library."

Lady Lundie's pen suddenly stuck in the paper, and scattered a little shower of ink-drops all round it. "The library," repeated her ladyship, in a voice suggestive of approaching suffocation. "I undertake to control myself, Sir Patrick! Any thing missing from the library?"

"Nothing missing, Lady Lundie, but The Person herself. She—"

"No, Sir Patrick! I won't have it! In the name of my own sex, I won't have it!"

"Pray pardon me—I forgot that 'she' was a prohibited pronoun on the present occasion. The Person has written a farewell letter to Blanche, and has gone nobody knows where. The distress produced by these events is alone answerable for what has happened to Blanche this morning. If you bear that in mind—and if you remember what your own opinion is of Miss Silvester—you will understand why Blanche hesitated to admit you into her confidence."

There he waited for a reply. Lady Lundie was too deeply absorbed in completing her memorandum to be conscious of his presence in the room.

"'Carriage to be at the door at two-thirty,'" said Lady Lundie, repeating the final words of the memorandum while she wrote them. "'Inquire for the nearest justice of the peace, and place the privacy of Windygates under the protection of the law.'—I beg your pardon!" exclaimed her ladyship, becoming conscious again of Sir Patrick's presence. "Have I missed any thing particularly painful? Pray mention it if I have!"

"You have missed nothing of the slightest importance," returned Sir Patrick. "I have placed you in possession of facts which you had a right to know; and we have now only to return to our medical friend's report on Blanche's health. You were about to favor me, I think, with the Prognosis?"

"Diagnosis!" said her ladyship, spitefully. "I had forgotten at the time—I remember now. Prognosis is entirely wrong."

"I sit corrected, Lady Lundie. Diagnosis."

"You have informed me, Sir Patrick, that you were already acquainted with the Diagnosis. It is quite needless for me to repeat it now."

"I was anxious to correct my own impression, my dear lady, by comparing it with yours."

"You are very good. You are a learned man. I am only a poor ignorant woman. Your impression can not possibly require correcting by mine."

"My impression, Lady Lundie, was that our so friend recommended moral, rather than medical, treatment for Blanche. If we can turn her thoughts from the painful subject on which they are now dwelling, we shall do all that is needful. Those were his own words, as I remember them. Do you confirm me?"

"Can I presume to dispute with you, Sir Patrick? You are a master of refined irony, I know. I am afraid it's all thrown away on poor me."

(The law kept its wonderful temper! The law met the most exasperating of living women with a counter-power of defensive aggravation all its own!)

"I take that as confirming me, Lady Lundie. Thank you. Now, as to the method of carrying out our friend's advice. The method seems plain. All we can do to divert Blanche's mind is to turn Blanche's attention to some other subject of reflection less painful than the subject which occupies her now. Do you agree, so far?"

"Why place the whole responsibility on my shoulders?" inquired Lady Lundie.

"Out of profound deference for your opinion," answered Sir Patrick. "Strictly speaking, no doubt, any serious responsibility rests with me. I am Blanche's guardian—"

"Thank God!" cried Lady Lundie, with a perfect explosion of pious fervor.

"I hear an outburst of devout thankfulness," remarked Sir Patrick. "Am I to take it as expressing—let me say—some little doubt, on your part, as to the prospect of managing Blanche successfully, under present circumstances?"

Lady Lundie's temper began to give way again—exactly as her brother-in-law had anticipated.

"You are to take it," she said, "as expressing my conviction that I saddled myself with the charge of an incorrigibly heartless, obstinate and perverse girl, when I undertook the care of Blanche."

"Did you say 'incorrigibly?'"

"I said 'incorrigibly.'"

"If the case is as hopeless as that, my dear Madam—as Blanche's guardian, I ought to find means to relieve you of the charge of Blanche."

"Nobody shall relieve me of a duty that I have once undertaken!" retorted Lady Lundie. "Not if I die at my post!"

"Suppose it was consistent with your duty," pleaded Sir Patrick, "to be relieved at your post? Suppose it was in harmony with that 'self-sacrifice' which is 'the motto of women?'"

"I don't understand you, Sir Patrick. Be so good as to explain yourself."

Sir Patrick assumed a new character—the character of a hesitating man. He cast a look of respectful inquiry at his sister-in-law, sighed, and shook his head.

"No!" he said. "It would be asking too much. Even with your high standard of duty, it would be asking too much."

"Nothing which you can ask me in the name of duty is too much."

"No! no! Let me remind you. Human nature has its limits."

"A Christian gentlewoman's sense of duty knows no limits."

"Oh, surely yes!"

"Sir Patrick! after what I have just said your perseverance in doubting me amounts to something like an insult!"

"Don't say that! Let me put a case. Let's suppose the future interests of another person depend on your saying, Yes—when all your own most cherished ideas and opinions urge you to say, No. Do you really mean to tell me that you could trample your own convictions under foot, if it could be shown that the purely abstract consideration of duty was involved in the sacrifice?"

"Yes!" cried Lady Lundie, mounting the pedestal of her virtue on the spot. "Yes—without a moment's hesitation!"

"I sit corrected, Lady Lundie. You embolden me to proceed. Allow me to ask (after what I just heard)—whether it is not your duty to act on advice given for Blanche's benefit, by one the highest medical authorities in England?" Her ladyship admitted that it was her duty; pending a more favorable opportunity for contradicting her brother-in-law.

"Very good," pursued Sir Patrick. "Assuming that Blanche is like most other human beings, and has some prospect of happiness to contemplate, if she could only be made to see it—are we not bound to make her see it, by our moral obligation to act on the medical advice?" He cast a courteously-persuasive look at her ladyship, and paused in the most innocent manner for a reply.

If Lady Lundie had not been bent—thanks to the irritation fomented by her brother-in-law—on disputing the ground with him, inch by inch, she must have seen signs, by this time, of the snare that was being set for her. As it was, she saw nothing but the opportunity of disparaging Blanche and contradicting Sir Patrick.

"If my step-daughter had any such prospect as you describe," she answered, "I should of course say, Yes. But Blanche's is an ill-regulated mind. An ill-regulated mind has no prospect of happiness."

"Pardon me," said Sir Patrick. "Blanche has a prospect of happiness. In other words, Blanche has a prospect of being married. And what is more, Arnold Brinkworth is ready to marry her as soon as the settlements can be prepared."

Lady Lundie started in her chair—turned crimson with rage—and opened her lips to speak. Sir Patrick rose to his feet, and went on before she could utter a word.

"I beg to relieve you, Lady Lundie—by means which you have just acknowledged it to be your duty to accept—of all further charge of an incorrigible girl. As Blanche's guardian, I have the honor of proposing that her marriage be advanced to a day to be hereafter named in the first fortnight of the ensuing month."

In those words he closed the trap which he had set for his sister-in-law, and waited to see what came of it.

A thoroughly spiteful woman, thoroughly roused, is capable of subordinating every other consideration to the one imperative necessity of gratifying her spite. There was but one way now of turning the tables on Sir Patrick—and Lady Lundie took it. She hated him, at that moment, so intensely, that not even the assertion of her own obstinate will promised her more than a tame satisfaction, by comparison with the priceless enjoyment of beating her brother-in-law with his own weapons.

"My dear Sir Patrick!" she said, with a little silvery laugh, "you have wasted much precious time and many eloquent words in trying to entrap me into giving my consent, when you might have had it for the asking. I think the idea of hastening Blanche's marriage an excellent one. I am charmed to transfer the charge of such a person as my step-daughter to the unfortunate young man who is willing to take her off my hands. The less he sees of Blanche's character the more satisfied I shall feel of his performing his engagement to marry her. Pray hurry the lawyers, Sir Patrick, and let it be a week sooner rather than a week later, if you wish to please Me."

Her ladyship rose in her grandest proportions, and made a courtesy which was nothing less than a triumph of polite satire in dumb show. Sir Patrick answered by a profound bow and a smile which said, eloquently, "I believe every word of that charming answer. Admirable woman—adieu!"

So the one person in the family circle, whose opposition might have forced Sir Patrick to submit to a timely delay, was silenced by adroit management of the vices of her own character. So, in despite of herself, Lady Lundie was won over to the project for hurrying the marriage of Arnold and Blanche.

CHAPTER THE TWENTY-EIGHTH.

STIFLED.

IT is the nature of Truth to struggle to the light. In more than one direction, the truth strove to pierce the overlying darkness, and to reveal itself to view, during the interval between the date of Sir Patrick's victory and the date of the wedding-day.

Signs of perturbation under the surface, suggestive of some hidden influence at work, were not wanting, as the time passed on. The one thing missing was the prophetic faculty that could read those signs aright at Windygates House.

On the very day when Sir Patrick's dextrous treatment of his sister-in-law had smoothed the way to the hastening of the marriage, an obstacle was raised to the new arrangement by no less a person than Blanche herself. She had sufficiently recovered, toward noon, to be able to receive Arnold in her own little sitting-room. It proved to be a very brief interview. A quarter of an hour later, Arnold appeared before Sir Patrick—while the old gentleman was sunning himself in the garden—with a face of blank despair. Blanche had indignantly declined even to think of such a thing as her marriage, at a time when she was heart-broken by the discovery that Anne had left her forever.

"You gave me leave to mention it, Sir Patrick—didn't you?" said Arnold.

Sir Patrick shifted round a little, so as to get the sun on his back, and admitted that he had given leave.

"If I had only known, I would rather have cut my tongue out than have said a word about it. What do you think she did? She burst out crying, and ordered me to leave the room."

It was a lovely morning—a cool breeze tempered the heat of the sun; the birds were singing; the garden wore its brightest look. Sir Patrick was supremely comfortable. The little wearisome vexations of this mortal life had retired to a respectful distance from him. He positively declined to invite them to come any nearer.

"Here is a world," said the old gentleman, getting the sun a little more broadly on his back, "which a merciful Creator has filled with lovely sights, harmonious sounds, delicious scents; and here are creatures with faculties expressly made for enjoyment of those sights, sounds, and scents—to say nothing of Love, Dinner, and Sleep, all thrown into the bargain. And these same creatures hate, starve, toss sleepless on their pillows, see nothing pleasant, hear nothing pleasant, smell nothing pleasant—cry bitter tears, say hard words, contract painful illnesses; wither, sink, age, die! What does it mean, Arnold? And how much longer is it all to go on?"

The fine connecting link between the blindness of Blanche to the advantage of being married, and the blindness of humanity to the advantage of being in existence, though sufficiently perceptible no doubt to venerable Philosophy ripening in the sun, was absolutely invisible to Arnold. He deliberately dropped the vast question opened by Sir Patrick; and, reverting to Blanche, asked what was to be done.

"What do you do with a fire, when you can't extinguish it?" said Sir Patrick. "You let it blaze till it goes out. What do you do with a woman when you can't pacify her? Let her blaze till she goes out."

Arnold failed to see the wisdom embodied in that excellent advice. "I thought you would have helped me to put things right with Blanche," he said.

"I am helping you. Let Blanche alone. Don't speak of the marriage again, the next time you see her. If she mentions it, beg her pardon, and tell her you won't press the question any more. I shall see her in an hour or two, and I shall take exactly the same tone myself. You have put the idea into her mind—leave it there to ripen. Give her distress about Miss Silvester nothing to feed on. Don't stimulate it by contradiction; don't rouse it to defend itself by disparagement of her lost friend. Leave Time to edge her gently nearer and nearer to the husband who is waiting for her—and take my word for it, Time will have her ready when the settlements are ready."

Toward the luncheon hour Sir Patrick saw Blanche, and put in practice the principle which he had laid down. She was perfectly tranquil before her uncle left her. A little later, Arnold was forgiven. A little later still, the old gentleman's sharp observation noted that his niece was unusually thoughtful, and that she looked at Arnold, from time to time, with an interest of a new kind—an interest which shyly hid itself from Arnold's view. Sir Patrick went up to dress for dinner, with a comfortable inner conviction that the difficulties which had beset him were settled at last. Sir Patrick had never been more mistaken in his life.

The business of the toilet was far advanced. Duncan had just placed the glass in a good light; and Duncan's master was at that turning point in his daily life which consisted in attaining, or not attaining, absolute perfection in the tying of his white cravat—when some outer barbarian, ignorant of the first principles of dressing a gentleman's throat, presumed to knock at the bedroom door. Neither master nor servant moved or breathed until the integrity of the cravat was placed beyond the reach of accident. Then Sir Patrick cast the look of final criticism in the glass, and breathed again when he saw that it was done.

"A little labored in style, Duncan. But not bad, considering the interruption?"

"By no means, Sir Patrick."

"See who it is."

Duncan went to the door; and returned, to his master, with an excuse for the interruption, in the shape of a telegram!

Sir Patrick started at the sight of that unwelcome message. "Sign the receipt, Duncan," he said—and opened the envelope. Yes! Exactly as he had anticipated! News of Miss Silvester, on the very day when he had decided to abandon all further attempt at discovering her. The telegram ran thus:

"Message received from Falkirk this morning. Lady, as described, left the train at Falkirk last night. Went on, by the first train this morning, to Glasgow. Wait further instructions."

"Is the messenger to take any thing back, Sir Patrick?"

"No. I must consider what I am to do. If I find it necessary I will send to the station. Here is news of Miss Silvester, Duncan," continued Sir Patrick, when the messenger had gone.

"She has been traced to Glasgow."

"Glasgow is a large place, Sir Patrick."

"Yes. Even if they have telegraphed on and had her watched (which doesn't appear), she may escape us again at Glasgow. I am the last man in the world, I hope, to shrink from accepting my fair share of any responsibility. But I own I would have given something to have kept this telegram out of the house. It raises the most awkward question I have had to decide on for many a long day past. Help me on with my coat. I must think of it! I must think of it!"

Sir Patrick went down to dinner in no agreeable frame of mind. The unexpected recovery of the lost trace of Miss Silvester—there is no disguising it—seriously annoyed him.

The dinner-party that day, assembling punctually at the stroke of the bell, had to wait a quarter of an hour before the hostess came down stairs.

Lady Lundie's apology, when she entered the library, informed her guests that she had been detained by some neighbors who had called at an unusually late hour. Mr. and Mrs. Julius Delamayn, finding themselves near Windygates, had favored her with a visit, on their way home, and had left cards of invitation for a garden-party at their house.

Lady Lundie was charmed with her new acquaintances. They had included every body who was staying at Windygates in their invitation. They had been as pleasant and easy as old friends. Mrs. Delamayn had brought the kindest message from one of her guests—Mrs. Glenarm—to say that she remembered meeting Lady Lundie in London, in the time of the late Sir Thomas, and was anxious to improve the acquaintance. Mr. Julius Delamayn had given a most amusing account of his brother. Geoffrey had sent to London for a trainer; and the whole household was on the tip-toe of expectation to witness the magnificent spectacle of an athlete preparing himself for a foot-race. The ladies, with Mrs. Glenarm at their head, were hard at work, studying the profound and complicated question of human running—the muscles employed in it, the preparation required for it, the heroes eminent in it. The men had been all occupied that morning in assisting Geoffrey to measure a mile, for his exercising-ground, in a remote part of the park—where there was an empty cottage, which was to be fitted with all the necessary appliances for the reception of Geoffrey and his trainer. "You will see the last of my brother," Julius had said, "at the garden-party. After that he retires into athletic privacy, and has but one interest in life—the interest of watching the disappearance of his own superfluous flesh." Throughout the dinner Lady Lundie was in oppressively good spirits, singing the praises of her new friends. Sir Patrick, on the other hand, had never been so silent within the memory of mortal man. He talked with an effort; and he listened with a greater effort still. To answer or not to answer the telegram in his pocket? To persist or not to persist in his resolution to leave Miss Silvester to go her own way? Those were the questions which insisted on coming round to him as regularly as the dishes themselves came round in the orderly progression of the dinner.

Blanche—-who had not felt equal to taking her place at the table—appeared in the drawing-room afterward.

Sir Patrick came in to tea, with the gentlemen, still uncertain as to the right course to take in the matter of the telegram. One look at Blanche's sad face and Blanche's altered manner decided him. What would be the result if he roused new hopes by resuming the effort to trace Miss Silvester, and if he lost the trace a second time? He had only to look at his niece and to see. Could any consideration justify him in turning her mind back on the memory of the friend who had left her at the moment when it was just beginning to look forward for relief to the prospect of her marriage? Nothing could justify him; and nothing should induce him to do it.

Reasoning—soundly enough, from his own point of view—on that basis, Sir Patrick determined on sending no further instructions to his friend at Edinburgh. That night he warned Duncan to preserve the strictest silence as to the arrival of the telegram. He burned it, in case of accidents, with his own hand, in his own room.

Rising the next day and looking out of his window, Sir Patrick saw the two young people taking their morning walk at a moment when they happened to cross the open grassy space which separated the two shrubberies at Windygates. Arnold's arm was round Blanche's waist, and they were talking confidentially with their heads close together. "She is coming round already!" thought the old gentleman, as the two disappeared again in the second shrubbery from view. "Thank Heaven! things are running smoothly at last!"

Among the ornaments of Sir Patrick's bed room there was a view (taken from above) of one of the Highland waterfalls. If he had looked at the picture when he turned away from his window, he might have remarked that a river which is running with its utmost smoothness at one moment may be a river which plunges into its most violent agitation at another; and he might have remembered, with certain misgivings, that the progress of a stream of water has been long since likened, with the universal consent of humanity, to the progress of the stream of life.

FIFTH SCENE.—GLASGOW.

CHAPTER THE TWENTY-NINTH.

ANNE AMONG THE LAWYERS.

ON the day when Sir Patrick received the second of the two telegrams sent to him from Edinburgh, four respectable inhabitants of the City of Glasgow were startled by the appearance of an object of interest on the monotonous horizon of their daily lives.

The persons receiving this wholesome shock were—Mr. and Mrs. Karnegie of the Sheep's Head Hotel—and Mr. Camp, and Mr. Crum, attached as "Writers" to the honorable profession of the Law.

It was still early in the day when a lady arrived, in a cab from the railway, at the Sheep's Head Hotel. Her luggage consisted of a black box, and of a well-worn leather bag which she carried in her hand. The name on the box (recently written on a new luggage label, as the color of the ink and paper showed) was a very good name in its way, common to a very great number of ladies, both in Scotland and England. It was "Mrs. Graham."

Encountering the landlord at the entrance to the hotel, "Mrs. Graham" asked to be accommodated with a bedroom, and was transferred in due course to the chamber-maid on duty at the time. Returning to the little room behind the bar, in which the accounts were kept, Mr. Karnegie surprised his wife by moving more briskly, and looking much brighter than usual. Being questioned, Mr. Karnegie (who had cast the eye of a landlord on the black box in the passage) announced that one "Mrs. Graham" had just arrived, and was then and there to be booked as inhabiting Room Number Seventeen. Being informed (with considerable asperity of tone and manner) that this answer failed to account for the interest which appeared to have been inspired in him by a total stranger, Mr. Karnegie came to the point, and confessed that "Mrs. Graham" was one of the sweetest-looking women he had seen for many a long day, and that he feared she was very seriously out of health.

Upon that reply the eyes of Mrs. Karnegie developed in size, and the color of Mrs. Karnegie deepened in tint. She got up from her chair and said that it might be just as well if she personally superintended the installation of "Mrs. Graham" in her room, and personally satisfied herself that "Mrs. Graham" was a fit inmate to be received at the Sheep's Head Hotel. Mr. Karnegie thereupon did what he always did—he agreed with his wife.

Mrs. Karnegie was absent for some little time. On her return her eyes had a certain tigerish cast in them when they rested on Mr. Karnegie. She ordered tea and some light refreshment to be taken to Number Seventeen. This done—without any visible provocation to account for the remark—she turned upon her husband, and said, "Mr. Karnegie you are a fool." Mr. Karnegie asked, "Why, my dear?" Mrs. Karnegie snapped her fingers, and said, "That for her good looks! You don't know a good-looking woman when you see her." Mr. Karnegie agreed with his wife.

Nothing more was said until the waiter appeared at the bar with his tray. Mrs. Karnegie, having first waived the tray off, without instituting her customary investigation, sat down suddenly with a thump, and said to her husband (who had not uttered a word in the interval), "Don't talk to Me about her being out of health! That for her health! It's trouble on her mind." Mr. Karnegie said, "Is it now?" Mrs. Karnegie replied, "When I have said, It is, I consider myself insulted if another person says, Is it?" Mr. Karnegie agreed with his wife.

There was another interval. Mrs. Karnegie added up a bill, with a face of disgust. Mr. Karnegie looked at her with a face of wonder. Mrs. Karnegie suddenly asked him why he wasted his looks on her, when he would have "Mrs. Graham" to look at before long. Mr. Karnegie, upon that, attempted to compromise the matter by looking, in the interim, at his own boots. Mrs. Karnegie wished to know whether after twenty years of married life, she was considered to be not worth answering by her own husband. Treated with bare civility (she expected no more), she might have gone on to explain that "Mrs. Graham" was going out. She might also have been prevailed on to mention that "Mrs. Graham" had asked her a very remarkable question of a business nature, at the interview between them up stairs. As it was, Mrs. Karnegie's lips were sealed, and let Mr. Karnegie deny if he dared, that he richly deserved it. Mr. Karnegie agreed with his wife.

In half an hour more, "Mrs. Graham" came down stairs; and a cab was sent for. Mr. Karnegie, in fear of the consequences if he did otherwise, kept in a corner. Mrs. Karnegie followed him into the corner, and asked him how he dared act in that way? Did he presume to think, after twenty years of married life, that his wife was jealous? "Go, you brute, and hand Mrs. Graham into the cab!"

Mr. Karnegie obeyed. He asked, at the cab window, to what part of Glasgow he should tell the driver to go. The reply informed him that the driver was to take "Mrs. Graham" to the office of Mr. Camp, the lawyer. Assuming "Mrs. Graham" to be a stranger in Glasgow, and remembering that Mr. Camp was Mr. Karnegie's lawyer, the inference appeared to be, that "Mrs. Graham's" remarkable question, addressed to the landlady, had related to legal business, and to the discovery of a trust-worthy person capable of transacting it for her.

Returning to the bar, Mr. Karnegie found his eldest daughter in charge of the books, the bills, and the waiters. Mrs. Karnegie had retired to her own room, justly indignant with her husband for his infamous conduct in handing "Mrs. Graham" into the cab before her own eyes. "It's the old story, Pa," remarked Miss Karnegie, with the most perfect composure. "Ma told you to do it, of course; and then Ma says you've insulted her before all the servants. I wonder how you bear it?" Mr. Karnegie looked at his boots, and answered, "I wonder, too, my dear." Miss Karnegie said, "You're not going to Ma, are you?" Mr. Karnegie looked up from his boots, and answered, "I must, my dear."

Mr. Camp sat in his private room, absorbed over his papers. Multitudinous as those documents were, they appeared to be not sufficiently numerous to satisfy Mr. Camp. He rang his bell, and ordered more.

The clerk appearing with a new pile of papers, appeared also with a message. A lady, recommended by Mrs. Karnegie, of the Sheep's Head, wished to consult Mr. Camp professionally. Mr. Camp looked at his watch, counting out precious time before him, in a little stand on the table, and said, "Show the lady in, in ten minutes."

In ten minutes the lady appeared. She took the client's chair and lifted her veil. The same effect which had been produced on Mr. Karnegie was once more produced on Mr. Camp. For the first time, for many a long year past, he felt personally interested in a total stranger. It might have been something in her eyes, or it might have been something in her manner. Whatever it was, it took softly hold of him, and made him, to his own exceeding surprise, unmistakably anxious to hear what she had to say!

The lady announced—in a low sweet voice touched with a quiet sadness—that her business related to a question of marriage (as marriage is understood by Scottish law), and that her own peace of mind, and the happiness of a person very dear to her, were concerned alike in the opinion which Mr. Camp might give when he had been placed in possession of the facts.

She then proceeded to state the facts, without mentioning names: relating in every particular precisely the same succession of events which Geoffrey Delamayn had already related to Sir Patrick Lundie—with this one difference, that she acknowledged herself to be the woman who was personally concerned in knowing whether, by Scottish law, she was now held to be a married woman or not.

Mr. Camp's opinion given upon this, after certain questions had been asked and answered, differed from Sir Patrick's opinion, as given at Windygates. He too quoted the language used by the eminent judge—Lord Deas—but he drew an inference of his own from it. "In Scotland, consent makes marriage," he said; "and consent may be proved by inference. I see a plain inference of matrimonial consent in the circumstances which you have related to me and I say you are a married woman."

The effect produced on the lady, when sentence was pronounced on her in those terms, was so distressing that Mr. Camp sent a message up stairs to his wife; and Mrs. Camp appeared in her husband's private room, in business hours, for the first time in her life. When Mrs. Camp's services had in some degree restored the lady to herself, Mr. Camp followed with a word of professional comfort. He, like Sir Patrick, acknowledged the scandalous divergence of opinions produced by the confusion and uncertainty of the marriage-law of Scotland. He, like Sir Patrick, declared it to be quite possible that another lawyer might arrive at another conclusion. "Go," he said, giving her his card, with a line of writing on it, "to my colleague, Mr. Crum; and say I sent you."

The lady gratefully thanked Mr. Camp and his wife, and went next to the office of Mr. Crum.

Mr. Crum was the older lawyer of the two, and the harder lawyer of the two; but he, too, felt the influence which the charm that there was in this woman exercised, more or less, over every man who came in contact with her. He listened with a patience which was rare with him: he put his questions with a gentleness which was rarer still; and when he was in possession of the circumstances—-behold, his opinion flatly contradicted the opinion of Mr. Camp!

"No marriage, ma'am," he said, positively. "Evidence in favor of perhaps establishing a marriage, if you propose to claim the man. But that, as I understand it, is exactly what you don't wish to do."

The relief to the lady, on hearing this, almost overpowered her. For some minutes she was unable to speak. Mr. Crum did, what he had never done yet in all his experience as a lawyer. He patted a client on the shoulder, and, more extraordinary still, he gave a client permission to waste his time. "Wait, and compose yourself," said Mr. Crum—administering the law of humanity. The lady composed herself. "I must ask you some questions, ma'am," said Mr. Crum—administering the law of the land. The lady bowed, and waited for him to begin.

"I know, thus far, that you decline to claim the gentleman," said Mr. Cram. "I want to know now whether the gentleman is likely to claim you."

The answer to this was given in the most positive terms. The gentleman was not even aware of the position in which he stood. And, more yet, he was engaged to be married to the dearest friend whom the lady had in the world.

Mr. Crum opened his eyes—considered—and put another question as delicately as he could. "Would it be painful to you to tell me how the gentleman came to occupy the awkward position in which he stands now?"

The lady acknowledged that it would be indescribably painful to her to answer that question.

Mr. Crum offered a suggestion under the form of an inquiry:

"Would it be painful to you to reveal the circumstances—in the interests of the gentleman's future prospects—to some discreet person (a legal person would be best) who is not, what I am, a stranger to you both?"

The lady declared herself willing to make any sacrifice, on those conditions—no matter how painful it might be—for her friend's sake.

Mr. Crum considered a little longer, and then delivered his word of advice:

"At the present stage of the affair," he said, "I need only tell you what is the first step that you ought to take under the circumstances. Inform the gentleman at once—either by word of mouth or by writing—of the position in which he stands: and authorize him to place the case in the hands of a person known to you both, who is competent to decide on what you are to do next. Do I understand that you know of such a person so qualified?"

The lady answered that she knew of such a person.

Mr. Crum asked if a day had been fixed for the gentleman's marriage.

The lady answered that she had made this inquiry herself on the last occasion when she had seen the gentleman's betrothed wife. The marriage was to take place, on a day to be hereafter chosen, at the end of the autumn.

"That," said Mr. Crum, "is a fortunate circumstance. You have time before you. Time is, here, of very great importance. Be careful not to waste it."

The lady said she would return to her hotel and write by that night's post, to warn the gentleman of the position in which he stood, and to authorize him to refer the matter to a competent and trust-worthy friend known to them both.

On rising to leave the room she was seized with giddiness, and with some sudden pang of pain, which turned her deadly pale and forced her to drop back into her chair. Mr. Crum had no wife; but he possessed a housekeeper—and he offered to send for her. The lady made a sign in the negative. She drank a little water, and conquered the pain. "I am sorry to have alarmed you," she said. "It's nothing—I am better now." Mr. Crum gave her his arm, and put her into the cab. She looked so pale and faint that he proposed sending his housekeeper with her. No: it was only five minutes' drive to the hotel. The lady thanked him—and went her way back by herself.

"The letter!" she said, when she was alone. "If I can only live long enough to write the letter!"

CHAPTER THE THIRTIETH.

ANNE IN THE NEWSPAPERS.

MRS. KARNEGIE was a woman of feeble intelligence and violent temper; prompt to take offense, and not, for the most part, easy to appease. But Mrs. Karnegie being—as we all are in our various degrees—a compound of many opposite qualities, possessed a character with more than one side to it, and had her human merits as well as her human faults. Seeds of sound good feeling were scattered away in the remoter corners of her nature, and only waited for the fertilizing occasion that was to help them to spring up. The occasion exerted that benign influence when the cab brought Mr. Crum's client back to the hotel. The face of the weary, heart-sick woman, as she slowly crossed the hall, roused all that was heartiest and best in Mrs. Karnegie's nature, and said to her, as if in words, "Jealous of this broken creature? Oh, wife and mother is there no appeal to your common womanhood here?"

"I am afraid you have overtired yourself, ma'am. Let me send you something up stairs?"

"Send me pen, ink, and paper," was the answer. "I must write a letter. I must do it at once."

It was useless to remonstrate with her. She was ready to accept any thing proposed, provided the writing materials were supplied first. Mrs. Karnegie sent them up, and then compounded a certain mixture of eggs and hot wine for which The Sheep's Head was famous, with her own hands. In five minutes or so it was ready—and Miss Karnegie was dispatched by her mother (who had other business on hand at the time) to take it up stairs.

After the lapse of a few moments a cry of alarm was heard from the upper landing. Mrs. Karnegie recognized her daughter's voice, and hastened to the bedroom floor.

"Oh, mamma! Look at her! look at her!"

The letter was on the table with the first lines written. The woman was on the sofa with her handkerchief twisted between her set teeth, and her tortured face terrible to look at. Mrs. Karnegie raised her a little, examined her closely—then suddenly changed color, and sent her daughter out of the room with directions to dispatch a messenger instantly for medical help.

Left alone with the sufferer, Mrs. Karnegie carried her to her bed. As she was laid down her left hand fell helpless over the side of the bed. Mrs. Karnegie suddenly checked the word of sympathy as it rose to her lips—suddenly lifted the hand, and looked, with a momentary sternness of scrutiny, at the third finger. There was a ring on it. Mrs. Karnegie's face softened on the instant: the word of pity that had been suspended the moment before passed her lips freely now. "Poor soul!" said the respectable landlady, taking appearances for granted. "Where's your husband, dear? Try and tell me."

The doctor made his appearance, and went up to the patient.

Time passed, and Mr. Karnegie and his daughter, carrying on the business of the hotel, received a message from up stairs which was ominous of something out of the common. The message gave the name and address of an experienced nurse—with the doctor's compliments, and would Mr. Karnegie have the kindness to send for her immediately.

The nurse was found and sent up stairs.

Time went on, and the business of the hotel went on, and it was getting to be late in the evening, when Mrs. Karnegie appeared at last in the parlor behind the bar. The landlady's face was grave, the landlady's manner was subdued. "Very, very ill," was the only reply she made to her daughter's inquiries. When she and her husband were together, a little later, she told the news from up stairs in greater detail. "A child born dead," said Mrs. Karnegie, in gentler tones than were customary with her. "And the mother dying, poor thing, so far as I can see."

A little later the doctor came down. Dead? No.—Likely to live? Impossible to say. The doctor returned twice in the course of the night. Both times he had but one answer. "Wait till to-morrow."

The next day came. She rallied a little. Toward the afternoon she began to speak. She expressed no surprise at seeing strangers by her bedside: her mind wandered. She passed again into insensibility. Then back to delirium once more. The doctor said, "This may last for weeks. Or it may end suddenly in death. It's time you did something toward finding her friends."

(Her friends! She had left the one friend she had forever!)

Mr. Camp was summoned to give his advice. The first thing he asked for was the unfinished letter.

It was blotted, it was illegible in more places than one. With pains and care they made out the address at the beginning, and here and there some fragments of the lines that followed. It began: "Dear Mr. Brinkworth." Then the writing got, little by little, worse and worse. To the eyes of the strangers who looked at it, it ran thus: "I should ill requite * * * Blanche's interests * * * For God's sake! * * * don't think of me * * *" There was a little more, but not so much as one word, in those last lines, was legible.

The names mentioned in the letter were reported by the doctor and the nurse to be also the names on her lips when she spoke in her wanderings. "Mr. Brinkworth" and "Blanche"—her mind ran incessantly on those two persons. The one intelligible thing that she mentioned in connection with them was the letter. She was perpetually trying, trying, trying to take that unfinished letter to the post; and she could never get there. Sometimes the post was across the sea. Sometimes it was at the top of an inaccessible mountain. Sometimes it was built in by prodigious walls all round it. Sometimes a man stopped her cruelly at the moment when she was close at the post, and forced her back thousands of miles away from it. She once or twice mentioned this visionary man by his name. They made it out to be "Geoffrey."

Finding no clew to her identity either in the letter that she had tried to write or in the wild words that escaped her from time to time, it was decided to search her luggage, and to look at the clothes which she had worn when she arrived at the hotel.

Her black box sufficiently proclaimed itself as recently purchased. On opening it the address of a Glasgow trunk-maker was discovered inside. The linen was also new, and unmarked. The receipted shop-bill was found with it. The tradesmen, sent for in each case and questioned, referred to their books. It was proved that the box and the linen had both been purchased on the day when she appeared at the hotel.

Her black bag was opened next. A sum of between eighty and ninety pounds in Bank of England notes; a few simple articles belonging to the toilet; materials for needle-work; and a photographic portrait of a young lady, inscribed, "To Anne, from Blanche," were found in the bag—but no letters, and nothing whatever that could afford the slightest clew by which the owner could be traced. The pocket in her dress was searched next. It contained a purse, an empty card-case, and a new handkerchief unmarked.

Mr. Camp shook his head.

"A woman's luggage without any letters in it," he said, "suggests to my mind a woman who has a motive of her own for keeping her movements a secret. I suspect she has destroyed her letters, and emptied her card-case, with that view." Mrs. Karnegie's report, after examining the linen which the so-called "Mrs. Graham" had worn when she arrived at the inn, proved the soundness of the lawyer's opinion. In every case the marks had been cut out. Mrs. Karnegie began to doubt whether the ring which she had seen on the third finger of the lady's left hand had been placed there with the sanction of the law.

There was but one chance left of discovering—or rather of attempting to discover—her friends. Mr. Camp drew out an advertisement to be inserted in the Glasgow newspapers. If those newspapers happened to be seen by any member of her family, she would, in all probability, be claimed. In the contrary event there would be nothing for it but to wait for her recovery or her death—with the money belonging to her sealed up, and deposited in the landlord's strongbox.

The advertisement appeared. They waited for three days afterward, and nothing came of it. No change of importance occurred, during the same period, in the condition of the suffering woman. Mr. Camp looked in, toward evening, and said, "We have done our best. There is no help for it but to wait."

Far away in Perthshire that third evening was marked as a joyful occasion at Windygates House. Blanche had consented at last to listen to Arnold's entreaties, and had sanctioned the writing of a letter to London to order her wedding-dress.

SIXTH SCENE.—SWANHAVEN LODGE.

CHAPTER THE THIRTY-FIRST

SEEDS OF THE FUTURE (FIRST SOWING).

"NOT SO large as Windygates. But—shall we say snug, Jones?"

"And comfortable, Smith. I quite agree with you."

Such was the judgment pronounced by the two choral gentlemen on Julius Delamayn's house in Scotland. It was, as usual with Smith and Jones, a sound judgment—as far as it went. Swanhaven Lodge was not half the size of Windygates; but it had been inhabited for two centuries when the foundations of Windygates were first laid—and it possessed the advantages, without inheriting the drawbacks, of its age. There is in an old house a friendly adaptation to the human character, as there is in an old hat a friendly adaptation to the human head. The visitor who left Swanhaven quitted it with something like a sense of leaving home. Among the few houses not our own which take a strong hold on our sympathies this was one. The ornamental grounds were far inferior in size and splendor to the grounds at Windygates. But the park was beautiful—less carefully laid out, but also less monotonous than an English park. The lake on the northern boundary of the estate, famous for its breed of swans, was one of the curiosities of the neighborhood; and the house had a history, associating it with more than one celebrated Scottish name, which had been written and illustrated by Julius Delamayn. Visitors to Swanhaven Lodge were invariably presented with a copy of the volume (privately printed). One in twenty read it. The rest were "charmed," and looked at the pictures.

The day was the last day of August, and the occasion was the garden-party given by Mr. and Mrs. Delamayn.

Smith and Jones—following, with the other guests at Windygates, in Lady Lundie's train—exchanged their opinions on the merits of the house, standing on a terrace at the back, near a flight of steps which led down into the garden. They formed the van-guard of the visitors, appearing by twos and threes from the reception rooms, and all bent on going to see the swans before the amusements of the day began. Julius Delamayn came out with the first detachment, recruited Smith and Jones, and other wandering bachelors, by the way, and set forth for the lake. An interval of a minute or two passed—and the terrace remained empty. Then two ladies—at the head of a second detachment of visitors—appeared under the old stone porch which sheltered the entrance on that side of the house. One of the ladies was a modest, pleasant little person, very simply dressed. The other was of the tall and formidable type of "fine women," clad in dazzling array. The first was Mrs. Julius Delamayn. The second was Lady Lundie.

"Exquisite!" cried her ladyship, surveying the old mullioned windows of the house, with their framing of creepers, and the grand stone buttresses projecting at intervals from the wall, each with its bright little circle of flowers blooming round the base. "I am really grieved that Sir Patrick should have missed this."

"I think you said, Lady Lundie, that Sir Patrick had been called to Edinburgh by family business?"

"Business, Mrs. Delamayn, which is any thing but agreeable to me, as one member of the family. It has altered all my arrangements for the autumn. My step-daughter is to be married next week."

"Is it so near as that? May I ask who the gentleman is?"

"Mr. Arnold Brinkworth."

"Surely I have some association with that name?"

"You have probably heard of him, Mrs. Delamayn, as the heir to Miss Brinkworth's Scotch property?"

"Exactly! Have you brought Mr. Brinkworth here to-day?"

"I bring his apologies, as well as Sir Patrick's. They went to Edinburgh together the day before yesterday. The lawyers engage to have the settlements ready in three or four days more, if a personal consultation can be managed. Some formal question, I believe, connected with title-deeds. Sir Patrick thought the safest way and the speediest way would be to take Mr. Brinkworth with him to Edinburgh—to get the business over to-day—and to wait until we join them, on our way south, to-morrow."

"You leave Windygates, in this lovely weather?"

"Most unwillingly! The truth is, Mrs. Delamayn, I am at my step-daughter's mercy. Her uncle has the authority, as her guardian—and the use he makes of it is to give her her own way in every thing. It was only on Friday last that she consented to let the day be fixed—and even then she made it a positive condition that the marriage was not to take place in Scotland. Pure willfulness! But what can I do? Sir Patrick submits; and Mr. Brinkworth submits. If I am to be present at the marriage I must follow their example. I feel it my duty to be present—and, as a matter of course, I sacrifice myself. We start for London to-morrow."

"Is Miss Lundie to be married in London at this time of year?"

"No. We only pass through, on our way to Sir Patrick's place in Kent—the place that came to him with the title; the place associated with the last days of my beloved husband. Another trial for me! The marriage is to be solemnized on the scene of my bereavement. My old wound is to be reopened on Monday next—simply because my step-daughter has taken a dislike to Windygates."

"This day week, then, is the day of the marriage?"

"Yes. This day week. There have been reasons for hurrying it which I need not trouble you with. No words can say how I wish it was over.—But, my dear Mrs. Delamayn, how thoughtless of me to assail you with my family worries! You are so sympathetic. That is my only excuse. Don't let me keep you from your guests. I could linger in this sweet place forever! Where is Mrs. Glenarm?"

"I really don't know. I missed her when we came out on the terrace. She will very likely join us at the lake. Do you care about seeing the lake, Lady Lundie?"

"I adore the beauties of Nature, Mrs. Delamayn—especially lakes!"

"We have something to show you besides; we have a breed of swans on the lake, peculiar to the place. My husband has gone on with some of our friends; and I believe we are expected to follow, as soon as the rest of the party—in charge of my sister—have seen the house."

"And what a house, Mrs. Delamayn! Historical associations in every corner of it! It is such a relief to my mind to take refuge in the past. When I am far away from this sweet place I shall people Swanhaven with its departed inmates, and share the joys and sorrows of centuries since."

As Lady Lundie announced, in these terms, her intention of adding to the population of the past, the last of the guests who had been roaming over the old house appeared under the porch. Among the members forming this final addition to the garden-party were Blanche, and a friend of her own age whom she had met at Swanhaven. The two girls lagged behind the rest, talking confidentially, arm in arm—the subject (it is surely needless to add) being the coming marriage.

"But, dearest Blanche, why are you not to be married at Windygates?"

"I detest Windygates, Janet. I have the most miserable associations with the place. Don't ask me what they are! The effort of my life is not to think of them now. I long to see the last of Windygates. As for being married there, I have made it a condition that I am not to be married in Scotland at all."

"What has poor Scotland done to forfeit your good opinion, my dear?"

"Poor Scotland, Janet, is a place where people don't know whether they are married or not. I have heard all about it from my uncle. And I know somebody who has been a victim—an innocent victim—to a Scotch marriage."

"Absurd, Blanche! You are thinking of runaway matches, and making Scotland responsible for the difficulties of people who daren't own the truth!"

"I am not at all absurd. I am thinking of the dearest friend I have. If you only knew—"

"My dear! I am Scotch, remember! You can be married just as well—I really must insist on that—in Scotland as in England."

"I hate Scotland!"

"Blanche!"

"I never was so unhappy in my life as I have been in Scotland. I never want to see it again. I am determined to be married in England—from the dear old house where I used to live when I was a little girl. My uncle is quite willing. He understands me and feels for me."

"Is that as much as to say that I don't understand you and feel for you? Perhaps I had better relieve you of my company, Blanche?"

"If you are going to speak to me in that way, perhaps you had!"

"Am I to hear my native country run down and not to say a word in defense of it?"

"Oh! you Scotch people make such a fuss about your native country!"

"We Scotch people! you are of Scotch extraction yourself, and you ought to be ashamed to talk in that way. I wish you good-morning!"

"I wish you a better temper!"

A minute since the two young ladies had been like twin roses on one stalk. Now they parted with red cheeks and hostile sentiments and cutting words. How ardent is the warmth of youth! how unspeakably delicate the fragility of female friendship!

The flock of visitors followed Mrs. Delamayn to the shores of the lake. For a few minutes after the terrace was left a solitude. Then there appeared under the porch a single gentleman, lounging out with a flower in his mouth and his hands in his pockets. This was the strongest man at Swanhaven—otherwise, Geoffrey Delamayn.

After a moment a lady appeared behind him, walking softly, so as not to be heard. She was superbly dressed after the newest and the most costly Parisian design. The brooch on her bosom was a single diamond of resplendent water and great size. The fan in her hand was a master-piece of the finest Indian workmanship. She looked what she was, a person possessed of plenty of superfluous money, but not additionally blest with plenty of superfluous intelligence to correspond. This was the childless young widow of the great ironmaster—otherwise, Mrs. Glenarm.

The rich woman tapped the strong man coquettishly on the shoulder with her fan. "Ah! you bad boy!" she said, with a slightly-labored archness of look and manner. "Have I found you at last?"

Geoffrey sauntered on to the terrace—keeping the lady behind him with a thoroughly savage superiority to all civilized submission to the sex—and looked at his watch.

"I said I'd come here when I'd got half an hour to myself," he mumbled, turning the flower carelessly between his teeth. "I've got half an hour, and here I am."

"Did you come for the sake of seeing the visitors, or did you come for the sake of seeing Me?"

Geoffrey smiled graciously, and gave the flower another turn in his teeth. "You. Of course."

The iron-master's widow took his arm, and looked up at him—as only a young woman would have dared to look up—with the searching summer light streaming in its full brilliancy on her face.

Reduced to the plain expression of what it is really worth, the average English idea of beauty in women may be summed up in three words—youth, health, plumpness. The more spiritual charm of intelligence and vivacity, the subtler attraction of delicacy of line and fitness of detail, are little looked for and seldom appreciated by the mass of men in this island. It is impossible otherwise to account for the extraordinary blindness of perception which (to give one instance only) makes nine Englishmen out of ten who visit France come back declaring that they have not seen a single pretty Frenchwoman, in or out of Paris, in the whole country. Our popular type of beauty proclaims itself, in its fullest material development, at every shop in which an illustrated periodical is sold. The same fleshy-faced girl, with the same inane smile, and with no other expression whatever, appears under every form of illustration, week after week, and month after month, all the year round. Those who wish to know what Mrs. Glenarm was like, have only to go out and stop at any bookseller's or news-vendor's shop, and there they will see her in the first illustration, with a young woman in it, which they discover in the window. The one noticeable peculiarity in Mrs. Glenarm's purely commonplace and purely material beauty, which would have struck an observant and a cultivated man, was the curious girlishness of her look and manner. No stranger speaking to this woman—who had been a wife at twenty, and who was now a widow at twenty-four—would ever have thought of addressing her otherwise than as "Miss."

"Is that the use you make of a flower when I give it to you?" she said to Geoffrey. "Mumbling it in your teeth, you wretch, as if you were a horse!"

"If you come to that," returned Geoffrey, "I'm more a horse than a man. I'm going to run in a race, and the public are betting on me. Haw! haw! Five to four."

"Five to four! I believe he thinks of nothing but betting. You great heavy creature, I can't move you. Don't you see I want to go like the rest of them to the lake? No! you're not to let go of my arm! You're to take me."

"Can't do it. Must be back with Perry in half an hour."

(Perry was the trainer from London. He had arrived sooner than he had been expected, and had entered on his functions three days since.)

"Don't talk to me about Perry! A little vulgar wretch. Put him off. You won't? Do you mean to say you are such a brute that you would rather be with Perry than be with me?"

"The betting's at five to four, my dear. And the race comes off in a month from this."

"Oh! go away to your beloved Perry! I hate you. I hope you'll lose the race. Stop in your cottage. Pray don't come back to the house. And—mind this!—don't presume to say 'my dear' to me again."

"It ain't presuming half far enough, is it? Wait a bit. Give me till the race is run—and then I'll presume to marry you."

"You! You will be as old as Methuselah, if you wait till I am your wife. I dare say Perry has got a sister. Suppose you ask him? She would be just the right person for you."

Geoffrey gave the flower another turn in his teeth, and looked as if he thought the idea worth considering.

"All right," he said. "Any thing to be agreeable to you. I'll ask Perry."

He turned away, as if he was going to do it at once. Mrs. Glenarm put out a little hand, ravishingly clothed in a blush-colored glove, and laid it on the athlete's mighty arm. She pinched those iron muscles (the pride and glory of England) gently. "What a man you are!" she said. "I never met with any body like you before!"

The whole secret of the power that Geoffrey had acquired over her was in those words.

They had been together at Swanhaven for little more than ten days; and in that time he had made the conquest of Mrs. Glenarm. On the day before the garden-party—in one of the leisure intervals allowed him by Perry—he had caught her alone, had taken her by the arm, and had asked her, in so many words, if she would marry him. Instances on record of women who have been wooed and won in ten days are—to speak it with all possible respect—not wanting. But an instance of a woman willing to have it known still remains to be discovered. The iron-master's widow exacted a promise of secrecy before the committed herself When Geoffrey had pledged his word to hold his tongue in public until she gave him leave to speak, Mrs. Glenarm, without further hesitation, said Yes—having, be it observed, said No, in the course of the last two years, to at least half a dozen men who were Geoffrey's superiors in every conceivable respect, except personal comeliness and personal strength.

There is a reason for every thing; and there was a reason for this.

However persistently the epicene theorists of modern times may deny it, it is nevertheless a truth plainly visible in the whole past history of the sexes that the natural condition of a woman is to find her master in a man. Look in the face of any woman who is in no direct way dependent on a man: and, as certainly as you see the sun in a cloudless sky, you see a woman who is not happy. The want of a master is their great unknown want; the possession of a master is—unconsciously to themselves—the only possible completion of their lives. In ninety-nine cases out of a hundred this one primitive instinct is at the bottom of the otherwise inexplicable sacrifice, when we see a woman, of her own free will, throw herself away on a man who is unworthy of her. This one primitive instinct was at the bottom of the otherwise inexplicable facility of self-surrender exhibited by Mrs. Glenarm.

Up to the time of her meeting with Geoffrey, the young widow had gathered but one experience in her intercourse with the world—the experience of a chartered tyrant. In the brief six months of her married life with the man whose grand-daughter she might have been—and ought to have been—she had only to lift her finger to be obeyed. The doting old husband was the willing slave of the petulant young wife's slightest caprice. At a later period, when society offered its triple welcome to her birth, her beauty, and her wealth—go where she might, she found herself the object of the same prostrate admiration among the suitors who vied with each other in the rivalry for her hand. For the first time in her life she encountered a man with a will of his own when she met Geoffrey Delamayn at Swanhaven Lodge.

Geoffrey's occupation of the moment especially favored the conflict between the woman's assertion of her influence and the man's assertion of his will.

During the days that had intervened between his return to his brother's house and the arrival of the trainer, Geoffrey had submitted himself to all needful preliminaries of the physical discipline which was to prepare him for the race. He knew, by previous experience, what exercise he ought to take, what hours he ought to keep, what temptations at the table he was bound to resist. Over and over again Mrs. Glenarm tried to lure him into committing infractions of his own discipline—and over and over again the influence with men which had never failed her before failed her now. Nothing she could say, nothing she could do, would move this man. Perry arrived; and Geoffrey's defiance of every attempted exercise of the charming feminine tyranny, to which every one else had bowed, grew more outrageous and more immovable than ever. Mrs. Glenarm became as jealous of Perry as if Perry had been a woman. She flew into passions; she burst into tears; she flirted with other men; she threatened to leave the house. All quite useless! Geoffrey never once missed an appointment with Perry; never once touched any thing to eat or drink that she could offer him, if Perry had forbidden it. No other human pursuit is so hostile to the influence of the sex as the pursuit of athletic sports. No men are so entirely beyond the reach of women as the men whose lives are passed in the cultivation of their own physical strength. Geoffrey resisted Mrs. Glenarm without the slightest effort. He casually extorted her admiration, and undesignedly forced her respect. She clung to him, as a hero; she recoiled from him, as a brute; she struggled with him, submitted to him, despised him, adored him, in a breath. And the clew to it all, confused and contradictory as it seemed, lay in one simple fact—Mrs. Glenarm had found her master.

"Take me to the lake, Geoffrey!" she said, with a little pleading pressure of the blush-colored hand.

Geoffrey looked at his watch. "Perry expects me in twenty minutes," he said.

"Perry again!"

"Yes."

Mrs. Glenarm raised her fan, in a sudden outburst of fury, and broke it with one smart blow on Geoffrey's face.

"There!" she cried, with a stamp of her foot. "My poor fan broken! You monster, all through you!"

Geoffrey coolly took the broken fan and put it in his pocket. "I'll write to London," he said, "and get you another. Come along! Kiss, and make it up."

He looked over each shoulder, to make sure that they were alone then lifted her off the ground (she was no light weight), held her up in the air like a baby, and gave her a rough loud-sounding kiss on each cheek. "With kind compliments from yours truly!" he said—and burst out laughing, and put her down again.

"How dare you do that?" cried Mrs. Glenarm. "I shall claim Mrs. Delamayn's protection if I am to be insulted in this way! I will never forgive you, Sir!" As she said those indignant words she shot a look at him which flatly contradicted them. The next moment she was leaning on his arm, and was looking at him wonderingly, for the thousandth time, as an entire novelty in her experience of male human kind. "How rough you are, Geoffrey!" she said, softly. He smiled in recognition of that artless homage to the manly virtue of his character. She saw the smile, and instantly made another effort to dispute the hateful supremacy of Perry. "Put him off!" whispered the daughter of Eve, determined to lure Adam into taking a bite of the apple. "Come, Geoffrey, dear, never mind Perry, this once. Take me to the lake!"

Geoffrey looked at his watch. "Perry expects me in a quarter of an hour," he said.

Mrs. Glenarm's indignation assumed a new form. She burst out crying. Geoffrey surveyed her for a moment with a broad stare of surprise—and then took her by both arms, and shook her!

"Look here!" he said, impatiently. "Can you coach me through my training?"

"I would if I could!"

"That's nothing to do with it! Can you turn me out, fit, on the day of the race? Yes? or No?"

"No."

"Then dry your eyes and let Perry do it."

Mrs. Glenarm dried her eyes, and made another effort.

"I'm not fit to be seen," she said. "I'm so agitated, I don't know what to do. Come indoors, Geoffrey—and have a cup of tea."

Geoffrey shook his head. "Perry forbids tea," he said, "in the middle of the day."

"You brute!" cried Mrs. Glenarm.

"Do you want me to lose the race?" retorted Geoffrey.

"Yes!"

With that answer she left him at last, and ran back into the house.

Geoffrey took a turn on the terrace—considered a little—stopped—and looked at the porch under which the irate widow had disappeared from his view. "Ten thousand a year," he said, thinking of the matrimonial prospect which he was placing in peril. "And devilish well earned," he added, going into the house, under protest, to appease Mrs. Glenarm.

The offended lady was on a sofa, in the solitary drawing-room. Geoffrey sat down by her. She declined to look at him. "Don't be a fool!" said Geoffrey, in his most persuasive manner. Mrs. Glenarm put her handkerchief to her eyes. Geoffrey took it away again without ceremony. Mrs. Glenarm rose to leave the room. Geoffrey stopped her by main force. Mrs. Glenarm threatened to summon the servants. Geoffrey said, "All right! I don't care if the whole house knows I'm fond of you!" Mrs. Glenarm looked at the door, and whispered "Hush! for Heaven's sake!" Geoffrey put her arm in his, and said, "Come along with me: I've got something to say to you." Mrs. Glenarm drew back, and shook her head. Geoffrey put his arm round her waist, and walked her out of the room, and out of the house—taking the direction, not of the terrace, but of a fir plantation on the opposite side of the grounds. Arrived among the trees, he stopped and held up a warning forefinger before the offended lady's face. "You're just the sort of woman I like," he said; "and there ain't a man living who's half as sweet on you as I am. You leave off bullying me about Perry, and I'll tell you what I'll do—I'll let you see me take a Sprint."

He drew back a step, and fixed his big blue eyes on her, with a look which said, "You are a highly-favored woman, if ever there was one yet!" Curiosity instantly took the leading place among the emotions of Mrs. Glenarm. "What's a Sprint, Geoffrey?" she asked.

"A short run, to try me at the top of my speed. There ain't another living soul in all England that I'd let see it but you. Now am I a brute?"

Mrs. Glenarm was conquered again, for the hundredth time at least. She said, softly, "Oh, Geoffrey, if you could only be always like this!" Her eyes lifted themselves admiringly to his. She took his arm again of her own accord, and pressed it with a loving clasp. Geoffrey prophetically felt the ten thousand a year in his pocket. "Do you really love me?" whispered Mrs. Glenarm. "Don't I!" answered the hero. The peace was made, and the two walked on again.

They passed through the plantation, and came out on some open ground, rising and falling prettily, in little hillocks and hollows. The last of the hillocks sloped down into a smooth level plain, with a fringe of sheltering trees on its farther side—with a snug little stone cottage among the trees—and with a smart little man, walking up and down before the cottage, holding his hands behind him. The level plain was the hero's exercising ground; the cottage was the hero's retreat; and the smart little man was the hero's trainer.

If Mrs. Glenarm hated Perry, Perry (judging by appearances) was in no danger of loving Mrs. Glenarm. As Geoffrey approached with his companion, the trainer came to a stand-still, and stared silently at the lady. The lady, on her side, declined to observe that any such person as the trainer was then in existence, and present in bodily form on the scene.

"How about time?" said Geoffrey.

Perry consulted an elaborate watch, constructed to mark time to the fifth of a second, and answered Geoffrey, with his eye all the while on Mrs. Glenarm.

"You've got five minutes to spare."

"Show me where you run, I'm dying to see it!" said the eager widow, taking possession of Geoffrey's arm with both hands.

Geoffrey led her back to a place (marked by a sapling with a little flag attached to it) at some short distance from the cottage. She glided along by his side, with subtle undulations of movement which appeared to complete the exasperation of Perry. He waited until she was out of hearing—and then he invoked (let us say) the blasts of heaven on the fashionably-dressed head of Mrs. Glenarm.

"You take your place there," said Geoffrey, posting her by the sapling. "When I pass you—" He stopped, and surveyed her with a good-humored masculine pity. "How the devil am I to make you understand it?" he went on. "Look here! when I pass you, it will be at what you would call (if I was a horse) full gallop. Hold your tongue—I haven't done yet. You're to look on after me as I leave you, to where the edge of the cottage wall cuts the trees. When you have lost sight of me behind the wall, you'll have seen me run my three hundred yards from this flag. You're in luck's way! Perry tries me at the long Sprint to-day. You understand you're to stop here? Very well then—let me go and get my toggery on."

"Sha'n't I see you again, Geoffrey?"

"Haven't I just told you that you'll see me run?"

"Yes—but after that?"

"After that, I'm sponged and rubbed down—and rest in the cottage."

"You'll come to us this evening?"

He nodded, and left her. The face of Perry looked unutterable things when he and Geoffrey met at the door of the cottage.

"I've got a question to ask you, Mr. Delamayn," said the trainer. "Do you want me? or don't you?"

"Of course I want you."

"What did I say when I first come here?" proceeded Perry, sternly. "I said, 'I won't have nobody a looking on at a man I'm training. These here ladies and gentlemen may all have made up their minds to see you. I've made up my mind not to have no lookers-on. I won't have you timed at your work by nobody but me. I won't have every blessed yard of ground you cover put in the noospapers. I won't have a living soul in the secret of what you can do, and what you can't, except our two selves.'—Did I say that, Mr. Delamayn? or didn't I?"

"All right!"

"Did I say it? or didn't I?"

"Of course you did!"

"Then don't you bring no more women here. It's clean against rules. And I won't have it."

Any other living creature adopting this tone of remonstrance would probably have had reason to repent it. But Geoffrey himself was afraid to show his temper in the presence of Perry. In view of the coming race, the first and foremost of British trainers was not to be trifled with, even by the first and foremost of British athletes.

"She won't come again," said Geoffrey. "She's going away from Swanhaven in two days' time."

"I've put every shilling I'm worth in the world on you," pursued Perry, relapsing into tenderness. "And I tell you I felt it! It cut me to the heart when I see you coming along with a woman at your heels. It's a fraud on his backers, I says to myself—that's what it is, a fraud on his backers!"

"Shut up!" said Geoffrey. "And come and help me to win your money." He kicked open the door of the cottage—and athlete and trainer disappeared from view.

After waiting a few minutes by the little flag, Mrs. Glenarm saw the two men approaching her from the cottage. Dressed in a close-fitting costume, light and elastic, adapting itself to every movement, and made to answer every purpose required by the exercise in which he was about to engage, Geoffrey's physical advantages showed themselves in their best and bravest aspect. His head sat proud and easy on his firm, white throat, bared to the air. The rising of his mighty chest, as he drew in deep draughts of the fragrant summer breeze; the play of his lithe and supple loins; the easy, elastic stride of his straight and shapely legs, presented a triumph of physical manhood in its highest type. Mrs. Glenarm's eyes devoured him in silent admiration. He looked like a young god of mythology—like a statue animated with color and life. "Oh, Geoffrey!" she exclaimed, softly, as he went by. He neither answered, nor looked: he had other business on hand than listening to soft nonsense. He was gathering himself up for the effort; his lips were set; his fists were lightly clenched. Perry posted himself at his place, grim and silent, with the watch in his hand. Geoffrey walked on beyond the flag, so as to give himself start enough to reach his full speed as he passed it. "Now then!" said Perry. In an instant more, he flew by (to Mrs. Glenarm's excited imagination) like an arrow from a bow. His action was perfect. His speed, at its utmost rate of exertion, preserved its rare underlying elements of strength and steadiness. Less and less and less he grew to the eyes that followed his course; still lightly flying over the ground, still firmly keeping the straight line. A moment more, and the runner vanished behind the wall of the cottage, and the stop-watch of the trainer returned to its place in his pocket.

In her eagerness to know the result, Mrs. Glenarm forget her jealousy of Perry.

"How long has he been?" she asked.

"There's a good many besides you would be glad to know that," said Perry.

"Mr. Delamayn will tell me, you rude man!"

"That depends, ma'am, on whether I tell him."

With this reply, Perry hurried back to the cottage.

Not a word passed while the trainer was attending to his man, and while the man was recovering his breath. When Geoffrey had been carefully rubbed down, and clothed again in his ordinary garments, Perry pulled a comfortable easy-chair out of a corner. Geoffrey fell into the chair, rather than sat down in it. Perry started, and looked at him attentively.

"Well?" said Geoffrey. "How about the time? Long? short? or middling?"

"Very good time," said Perry.

"How long?"

"When did you say the lady was going, Mr. Delamayn?"

"In two days."

"Very well, Sir. I'll tell you 'how long' when the lady's gone."

Geoffrey made no attempt to insist on an immediate reply. He smiled faintly. After an interval of less than ten minutes he stretched out his legs and closed his eyes.

"Going to sleep?" said Perry.

Geoffrey opened his eyes with an effort. "No," he said. The word had hardly passed his lips before his eyes closed again.

"Hullo!" said Perry, watching him. "I don't like that."

He went closer to the chair. There was no doubt about it. The man was asleep.

Perry emitted a long whistle under his breath. He stooped and laid two of his fingers softly on Geoffrey's pulse. The beat was slow, heavy, and labored. It was unmistakably the pulse of an exhausted man.

The trainer changed color, and took a turn in the room. He opened a cupboard, and produced from it his diary of the preceding year. The entries relating to the last occasion on which he had prepared Geoffrey for a foot-race included the fullest details. He turned to the report of the first trial, at three hundred yards, full speed. The time was, by one or two seconds, not so good as the time on this occasion. But the result, afterward, was utterly different. There it was, in Perry's own words: "Pulse good. Man in high spirits. Ready, if I would have let him, to run it over again."

Perry looked round at the same man, a year afterward—utterly worn out, and fast asleep in the chair.

He fetched pen, ink, and paper out of the cupboard, and wrote two letters—both marked "Private." The first was to a medical man, a great authority among trainers. The second was to Perry's own agent in London, whom he knew he could trust. The letter pledged the agent to the strictest secrecy, and directed him to back Geoffrey's opponent in the Foot-Race for a sum equal to the sum which Perry had betted on Geoffrey himself. "If you have got any money of your own on him," the letter concluded, "do as I do. 'Hedge'—and hold your tongue."

"Another of 'em gone stale!" said the trainer, looking round again at the sleeping man. "He'll lose the race."

CHAPTER THE THIRTY-SECOND.

SEEDS OF THE FUTURE (SECOND SOWING).

AND what did the visitors say of the Swans?

They said, "Oh, what a number of them!"—which was all that was to be said by persons ignorant of the natural history of aquatic birds.

And what did the visitors say of the lake?

Some of them said, "How solemn!" Some of them said, "How romantic!" Some of them said nothing—but privately thought it a dismal scene.

Here again the popular sentiment struck the right note at starting. The lake was hidden in the centre of a fir wood. Except in the middle, where the sunlight reached them, the waters lay black under the sombre shadow of the trees. The one break in the plantation was at the farther end of the lake. The one sign of movement and life to be seen was the ghostly gliding of the swans on the dead-still surface of the water. It was solemn—as they said; it was romantic—as they said. It was dismal—as they thought. Pages of description could express no more. Let pages of description be absent, therefore, in this place.

Having satiated itself with the swans, having exhausted the lake, the general curiosity reverted to the break in the trees at the farther end—remarked a startlingly artificial object, intruding itself on the scene, in the shape of a large red curtain, which hung between two of the tallest firs, and closed the prospect beyond from view—requested an explanation of the curtain from Julius Delamayn—and received for answer that the mystery should be revealed on the arrival of his wife with the tardy remainder of the guests who had loitered about the house.

On the appearance of Mrs. Delamayn and the stragglers, the united party coasted the shore of the lake, and stood assembled in front of the curtain. Pointing to the silken cords hanging at either side of it, Julius Delamayn picked out two little girls (children of his wife's sister), and sent them to the cords, with instructions to pull, and see what happened. The nieces of Julius pulled with the eager hands of children in the presence of a mystery—the curtains parted in the middle, and a cry of universal astonishment and delight saluted the scene revealed to view.

At the end of a broad avenue of firs a cool green glade spread its grassy carpet in the midst of the surrounding plantation. The ground at the farther end of the glade rose; and here, on the lower slopes, a bright little spring of water bubbled out between gray old granite rocks.

Along the right-hand edge of the turf ran a row of tables, arrayed in spotless white, and covered with refreshments waiting for the guests. On the opposite side was a band of music, which burst into harmony at the moment when the curtains were drawn. Looking back through the avenue, the eye caught a distant glimpse of the lake, where the sunlight played on the water, and the plumage of the gliding swans flashed softly in brilliant white. Such was the charming surprise which Julius Delamayn had arranged for his friends. It was only at moments like these—or when he and his wife were playing Sonatas in the modest little music-room at Swanhaven—that Lord Holchester's eldest son was really happy. He secretly groaned over the duties which his position as a landed gentleman imposed upon him; and he suffered under some of the highest privileges of his rank and station as under social martyrdom in its cruelest form.

"We'll dine first," said Julius, "and dance afterward. There is the programme!"

He led the way to the tables, with the two ladies nearest to him—utterly careless whether they were or were not among the ladies of the highest rank then present. To Lady Lundie's astonishment he took the first seat he came to, without appearing to care what place he occupied at his own feast. The guests, following his example, sat where they pleased, reckless of precedents and dignities. Mrs. Delamayn, feeling a special interest in a young lady who was shortly to be a bride, took Blanche's arm. Lady Lundie attached herself resolutely to her hostess on the other side. The three sat together. Mrs. Delamayn did her best to encourage Blanche to talk, and Blanche did her best to meet the advances made to her. The experiment succeeded but poorly on either side. Mrs. Delamayn gave it up in despair, and turned to Lady Lundie, with a strong suspicion that some unpleasant subject of reflection was preying privately on the bride's mind. The conclusion was soundly drawn. Blanche's little outbreak of temper with her friend on the terrace, and Blanche's present deficiency of gayety and spirit, were attributable to the same cause. She hid it from her uncle, she hid it from Arnold—but she was as anxious as ever, and as wretched as ever, about Anne; and she was still on the watch (no matter what Sir Patrick might say or do) to seize the first opportunity of renewing the search for her lost friend.

Meanwhile the eating, the drinking, and the talking went merrily on. The band played its liveliest melodies; the servants kept the glasses constantly filled: round all the tables gayety and freedom reigned supreme. The one conversation in progress, in which the talkers were not in social harmony with each other, was the conversation at Blanche's side, between her step-mother and Mrs. Delamayn.

Among Lady Lundie's other accomplishments the power of making disagreeable discoveries ranked high. At the dinner in the glade she had not failed to notice—what every body else had passed over—the absence at the festival of the hostess's brother-in-law; and more remarkable still, the disappearance of a lady who was actually one of the guests staying in the house: in plainer words, the disappearance of Mrs. Glenarm.

"Am I mistaken?" said her ladyship, lifting her eye-glass, and looking round the tables. "Surely there is a member of our party missing? I don't see Mr. Geoffrey Delamayn."

"Geoffrey promised to be here. But he is not particularly attentive, as you may have noticed, to keeping engagements of this sort. Every thing is sacrificed to his training. We only see him at rare intervals now."

With that reply Mrs. Delamayn attempted to change the subject. Lady Lundie lifted her eye-glass, and looked round the tables for the second time.

"Pardon me," persisted her ladyship—"but is it possible that I have discovered another absentee? I don't see Mrs. Glenarm. Yet surely she must be here! Mrs. Glenarm is not training for a foot-race. Do you see her? I don't."

"I missed her when we went out on the terrace, and I have not seen her since."

"Isn't it very odd, dear Mrs. Delamayn?"

"Our guests at Swanhaven, Lady Lundie, have perfect liberty to do as they please."

In those words Mrs. Delamayn (as she fondly imagined) dismissed the subject. But Lady Lundie's robust curiosity proved unassailable by even the broadest hint. Carried away, in all probability, by the infection of merriment about her, her ladyship displayed unexpected reserves of vivacity. The mind declines to realize it; but it is not the less true that this majestic woman actually simpered!

"Shall we put two and two together?" said Lady Lundie, with a ponderous playfulness wonderful to see. "Here, on the one hand, is Mr. Geoffrey Delamayn—a young single man. And here, on the other, is Mrs. Glenarm—a young widow. Rank on the side of the young single man; riches on the side of the young widow. And both mysteriously absent at the same time, from the same pleasant party. Ha, Mrs. Delamayn! should I guess wrong, if I guessed that you will have a marriage in the family, too, before long?"

Mrs. Delamayn looked a little annoyed. She had entered, with all her heart, into the conspiracy for making a match between Geoffrey and Mrs. Glenarm. But she was not prepared to own that the lady's facility had (in spite of all attempts to conceal it from discovery) made the conspiracy obviously successful in ten days' time.

"I am not in the secrets of the lady and gentleman whom you mention," she replied, dryly.

A heavy body is slow to acquire movement—and slow to abandon movement, when once acquired. The playfulness of Lady Lundie, being essentially heavy, followed the same rule. She still persisted in being as lively as ever.

"Oh, what a diplomatic answer!" exclaimed her ladyship. "I think I can interpret it, though, for all that. A little bird tells me that I shall see a Mrs. Geoffrey Delamayn in London, next season. And I, for one, shall not be surprised to find myself congratulating Mrs. Glenarm."

"If you persist in letting your imagination run away with you, Lady Lundie, I can't possibly help it. I can only request permission to keep the bridle on mine."

This time, even Lady Lundie understood that it would be wise to say no more. She smiled and nodded, in high private approval of her own extraordinary cleverness. If she had been asked at that moment who was the most brilliant Englishwoman living, she would have looked inward on herself—and would have seen, as in a glass brightly, Lady Lundie, of Windygates.

From the moment when the talk at her side entered on the subject of Geoffrey Delamayn and Mrs. Glenarm—and throughout the brief period during which it remained occupied with that topic—Blanche became conscious of a strong smell of some spirituous liquor wafted down on her, as she fancied, from behind and from above. Finding the odor grow stronger and stronger, she looked round to see whether any special manufacture of grog was proceeding inexplicably at the back of her chair. The moment she moved her head, her attention was claimed by a pair of tremulous gouty old hands, offering her a grouse pie, profusely sprinkled with truffles.

"Eh, my bonny Miss!" whispered a persuasive voice at her ear, "ye're joost stairving in a land o' plenty. Tak' my advice, and ye'll tak' the best thing at tebble—groose-poy, and trufflers."

Blanche looked up.

There he was—the man of the canny eye, the fatherly manner, and the mighty nose—Bishopriggs—preserved in spirits and ministering at the festival at Swanhaven Lodge!

Blanche had only seen him for a moment on the memorable night of the storm, when she had surprised Anne at the inn. But instants passed in the society of Bishopriggs were as good as hours spent in the company of inferior men. Blanche instantly recognized him; instantly called to mind Sir Patrick's conviction that he was in possession of Anne's lost letter; instantly rushed to the conclusion that, in discovering Bishopriggs, she had discovered a chance of tracing Anne. Her first impulse was to claim acquaintance with him on the spot. But the eyes of her neighbors were on her, warning her to wait. She took a little of the pie, and looked hard at Bishopriggs. That discreet man, showing no sign of recognition on his side, bowed respectfully, and went on round the table.

"I wonder whether he has got the letter about him?" thought Blanche.

He had not only got the letter about him—but, more than that, he was actually then on the look-out for the means of turning the letter to profitable pecuniary account.

The domestic establishment of Swanhaven Lodge included no formidable array of servants. When Mrs. Delamayn gave a large party, she depended for such additional assistance as was needed partly on the contributions of her friends, partly on the resources of the principal inn at Kirkandrew. Mr. Bishopriggs, serving at the time (in the absence of any better employment) as a supernumerary at the inn, made one among the waiters who could be spared to assist at the garden-party. The name of the gentleman by whom he was to be employed for the day had struck him, when he first heard it, as having a familiar sound. He had made his inquiries; and had then betaken himself for additional information, to the letter which he had picked up from the parlor floor at Craig Fernie.

The sheet of note-paper, lost by Anne, contained, it may be remembered, two letters—one signed by herself; the other signed by Geoffrey—and both suggestive, to a stranger's eye, of relations between the writers which they were interested in concealing from the public view.

Thinking it just possible—if he kept his eyes and ears well open at Swanhaven—that he might improve his prospect of making a marketable commodity of the stolen correspondence, Mr. Bishopriggs had put the letter in his pocket when he left Kirkandrew. He had recognized Blanche, as a friend of the lady at the inn—and as a person who might perhaps be turned to account, in that capacity. And he had, moreover, heard every word of the conversation between Lady Lundie and Mrs. Delamayn on the subject of Geoffrey and Mrs. Glenarm. There were hours to be passed before the guests would retire, and before the waiters would be dismissed. The conviction was strong in the mind of Mr. Bishopriggs that he might find good reason yet for congratulating himself on the chance which had associated him with the festivities at Swanhaven Lodge.

It was still early in the afternoon when the gayety at the dinner-table began, in certain quarters, to show signs of wearing out.

The younger members of the party—especially the ladies—grew restless with the appearance of the dessert. One after another they looked longingly at the smooth level of elastic turf in the middle of the glade. One after another they beat time absently with their fingers to the waltz which the musicians happened to be playing at the moment. Noticing these symptoms, Mrs. Delamayn set the example of rising; and her husband sent a message to the band. In ten minutes more the first quadrille was in progress on the grass; the spectators were picturesquely grouped round, looking on; and the servants and waiters, no longer wanted, had retired out of sight, to a picnic of their own.

The last person to leave the deserted tables was the venerable Bishopriggs. He alone, of the men in attendance, had contrived to combine a sufficient appearance of waiting on the company with a clandestine attention to his own personal need of refreshment. Instead of hurrying away to the servants' dinner with the rest, he made the round of the tables, apparently clearing away the crumbs—actually, emptying the wine-glasses. Immersed in this occupation, he was startled by a lady's voice behind him, and, turning as quickly as he could, found himself face to face with Miss Lundie.

"I want some cold water," said Blanche. "Be so good as to get me some from the spring."

She pointed to the bubbling rivulet at the farther end of the glade.

Bishopriggs looked unaffectedly shocked.

"Lord's sake, miss," he exclaimed "d'ye relly mean to offend yer stomach wi' cauld water—when there's wine to be had for the asking!"

Blanche gave him a look. Slowness of perception was not on the list of the failings of Bishopriggs. He took up a tumbler, winked with his one available eye, and led the way to the rivulet. There was nothing remarkable in the spectacle of a young lady who wanted a glass of spring-water, or of a waiter who was getting it for her. Nobody was surprised; and (with the band playing) nobody could by any chance overhear what might be said at the spring-side.

"Do you remember me at the inn on the night of the storm?" asked Blanche.

Mr. Bishopriggs had his reasons (carefully inclosed in his pocketbook) for not being too ready to commit himself with Blanche at starting.

"I'm no' saying I canna remember ye, miss. Whar's the man would mak' sic an answer as that to a bonny young leddy like you?"

By way of assisting his memory Blanche took out her purse. Bishopriggs became absorbed in the scenery. He looked at the running water with the eye of a man who thoroughly distrusted it, viewed as a beverage.

"There ye go," he said, addressing himself to the rivulet, "bubblin' to yer ain annihilation in the loch yonder! It's little I know that's gude aboot ye, in yer unconvairted state. Ye're a type o' human life, they say. I tak' up my testimony against that. Ye're a type o' naething at all till ye're heated wi' fire, and sweetened wi' sugar, and strengthened wi' whusky; and then ye're a type o' toddy—and human life (I grant it) has got something to say to ye in that capacity!"

"I have heard more about you, since I was at the inn," proceeded Blanche, "than you may suppose." (She opened her purse: Mr. Bishopriggs became the picture of attention.) "You were very, very kind to a lady who was staying at Craig Fernie," she went on, earnestly. "I know that you have lost your place at the inn, because you gave all your attention to that lady. She is my dearest friend, Mr. Bishopriggs. I want to thank you. I do thank you. Please accept what I have got here?"

All the girl's heart was in her eyes and in her voice as she emptied her purse into the gouty (and greedy) old hand of Bishopriggs.

A young lady with a well-filled purse (no matter how rich the young lady may be) is a combination not often witnessed in any country on the civilized earth. Either the money is always spent, or the money has been forgotten on the toilet-table at home. Blanche's purse contained a sovereign and some six or seven shillings in silver. As pocket-money for an heiress it was contemptible. But as a gratuity to Bishopriggs it was magnificent. The old rascal put the money into his pocket with one hand, and dashed away the tears of sensibility, which he had not shed, with the other.

"Cast yer bread on the waters," cried Mr. Bishopriggs, with his one eye raised devotionally to the sky, "and ye sall find it again after monny days! Heeh! hech! didna I say when I first set eyes on that puir leddy, 'I feel like a fether to ye?' It's seemply mairvelous to see hoo a man's ain gude deeds find him oot in this lower warld o' ours. If ever I heard the voice o' naitural affection speaking in my ain breast," pursued Mr. Bishopriggs, with his eye fixed in uneasy expectation on Blanche, "it joost spak' trumpet-tongued when that winsome creature first lookit at me. Will it be she now that told ye of the wee bit sairvice I rendered to her in the time when I was in bondage at the hottle?"

"Yes—she told me herself."

"Might I mak' sae bauld as to ask whar' she may be at the present time?"

"I don't know, Mr. Bishopriggs. I am more miserable about it than I can say. She has gone away—and I don't know where."

"Ow! ow! that's bad. And the bit husband-creature danglin' at her petticoat's tail one day, and awa' wi' the sunrise next mornin'—have they baith taken leg-bail together?"

"I know nothing of him; I never saw him. You saw him. Tell me—what was he like?"

"Eh! he was joost a puir weak creature. Didn't know a glass o' good sherry-wine when he'd got it. Free wi' the siller—that's a' ye can say for him—free wi' the siller!"

Finding it impossible to extract from Mr. Bishopriggs any clearer description of the man who had been with Anne at the inn than this, Blanche approached the main object of the interview. Too anxious to waste time in circumlocution, she turned the conversation at once to the delicate and doubtful subject of the lost letter.

"There is something else that I want to say to you," she resumed. "My friend had a loss while she was staying at the inn."

The clouds of doubt rolled off the mind of Mr. Bishopriggs. The lady's friend knew of the lost letter. And, better still, the lady's friend looked as if she wanted it!

"Ay! ay!" he said, with all due appearance of carelessness. "Like eneugh. From the mistress downward, they're a' kittle cattle at the inn since I've left 'em. What may it ha' been that she lost?"

"She lost a letter."

The look of uneasy expectation reappeared in the eye of Mr. Bishopriggs. It was a question—and a serious question, from his point of view—whether any suspicion of theft was attached to the disappearance of the letter.

"When ye say 'lost,'" he asked, "d'ye mean stolen?"

Blanche was quite quick enough to see the necessity of quieting his mind on this point.

"Oh no!" she answered. "Not stolen. Only lost. Did you hear about it?"

"Wherefore suld I ha' heard aboot it?" He looked hard at Blanche—and detected a momentary hesitation in her face. "Tell me this, my young leddy," he went on, advancing warily near to the point. "When ye're speering for news o' your friend's lost letter—what sets ye on comin' to me?"

Those words were decisive. It is hardly too much to say that Blanche's future depended on Blanche's answer to that question.

If she could have produced the money; and if she had said, boldly, "You have got the letter, Mr. Bishopriggs: I pledge my word that no questions shall be asked, and I offer you ten pounds for it"—in all probability the bargain would have been struck; and the whole course of coming events would, in that case, have been altered. But she had no money left; and there were no friends, in the circle at Swanhaven, to whom she could apply, without being misinterpreted, for a loan of ten pounds, to be privately intrusted to her on the spot.

Under stress of sheer necessity Blanche abandoned all hope of making any present appeal of a pecuniary nature to the confidence of Bishopriggs.

The one other way of attaining her object that she could see was to arm herself with the influence of Sir Patrick's name. A man, placed in her position, would have thought it mere madness to venture on such a risk as this. But Blanche—with one act of rashness already on her conscience—rushed, woman-like, straight to the commission of another. The same headlong eagerness to reach her end, which had hurried her into questioning Geoffrey before he left Windygates, now drove her, just as recklessly, into taking the management of Bishopriggs out of Sir Patrick's skilled and practiced hands. The starving sisterly love in her hungered for a trace of Anne. Her heart whispered, Risk it! And Blanche risked it on the spot.

"Sir Patrick set me on coming to you," she said.

The opening hand of Mr. Bishopriggs—ready to deliver the letter, and receive the reward—closed again instantly as she spoke those words.

"Sir Paitrick?" he repeated "Ow! ow! ye've een tauld Sir Paitrick aboot it, have ye? There's a chiel wi' a lang head on his shouthers, if ever there was ane yet! What might Sir Paitrick ha' said?"

Blanche noticed a change in his tone. Blanche was rigidly careful (when it was too late) to answer him in guarded terms.

"Sir Patrick thought you might have found the letter," she said, "and might not have remembered about it again until after you had left the inn."

Bishopriggs looked back into his own personal experience of his old master—and drew the correct conclusion that Sir Patrick's view of his connection with the disappearance of the letter was not the purely unsuspicious view reported by Blanche. "The dour auld deevil," he thought to himself, "knows me better than that!"

"Well?" asked Blanche, impatiently. "Is Sir Patrick right?"

"Richt?" rejoined Bishopriggs, briskly. "He's as far awa' from the truth as John o' Groat's House is from Jericho."

"You know nothing of the letter?"

"Deil a bit I know o' the letter. The first I ha' heard o' it is what I hear noo."

Blanche's heart sank within her. Had she defeated her own object, and cut the ground from under Sir Patrick's feet, for the second time? Surely not! There was unquestionably a chance, on this occasion, that the man might be prevailed upon to place the trust in her uncle which he was too cautious to confide to a stranger like herself. The one wise thing to do now was to pave the way for the exertion of Sir Patrick's superior influence, and Sir Patrick's superior skill. She resumed the conversation with that object in view.

"I am sorry to hear that Sir Patrick has guessed wrong," she resumed. "My friend was anxious to recover the letter when I last saw her; and I hoped to hear news of it from you. However, right or wrong, Sir Patrick has some reasons for wishing to see you—and I take the opportunity of telling you so. He has left a letter to wait for you at the Craig Fernie inn."

"I'm thinking the letter will ha' lang eneugh to wait, if it waits till I gae back for it to the hottle," remarked Bishopriggs.

"In that case," said Blanche, promptly, "you had better give me an address at which Sir Patrick can write to you. You wouldn't, I suppose, wish me to say that I had seen you here, and that you refused to communicate with him?"

"Never think it!" cried Bishopriggs, fervently. "If there's ain thing mair than anither that I'm carefu' to presairve intact, it's joost the respectful attention that I owe to Sir Paitrick. I'll make sae bauld, miss, au to chairge ye wi' that bit caird. I'm no' settled in ony place yet (mair's the pity at my time o' life!), but Sir Paitrick may hear o' me, when Sir Paitrick has need o' me, there." He handed a dirty little card to Blanche containing the name and address of a butcher in Edinburgh. "Sawmuel Bishopriggs," he went on, glibly. "Care o' Davie Dow, flesher; Cowgate; Embro. My Patmos in the weelderness, miss, for the time being."

Blanche received the address with a sense of unspeakable relief. If she had once more ventured on taking Sir Patrick's place, and once more failed in justifying her rashness by the results, she had at least gained some atoning advantage, this time, by opening a means of communication between her uncle and Bishopriggs. "You will hear from Sir Patrick," she said, and nodded kindly, and returned to her place among the guests.

"I'll hear from Sir Paitrick, wull I?" repeated Bishopriggs when he was left by himself. "Sir Paitrick will wark naething less than a meeracle if he finds Sawmuel Bishopriggs at the Cowgate, Embro!"

He laughed softly over his own cleverness; and withdrew to a lonely place in the plantation, in which he could consult the stolen correspondence without fear of being observed by any living creature. Once more the truth had tried to struggle into light, before the day of the marriage, and once more Blanche had innocently helped the darkness to keep it from view.

CHAPTER THE THIRTY-THIRD.

SEEDS OF THE FUTURE (THIRD SOWING).

AFTER a new and attentive reading of Anne's letter to Geoffrey, and of Geoffrey's letter to Anne, Bishopriggs laid down comfortably under a tree, and set himself the task of seeing his position plainly as it was at that moment.

The profitable disposal of the correspondence to Blanche was no longer among the possibilities involved in the case. As for treating with Sir Patrick, Bishopriggs determined to keep equally dear of the Cowgate, Edinburgh, and of Mrs. Inchbare's inn, so long as there was the faintest chance of his pushing his own interests in any other quarter. No person living would be capable of so certainly extracting the correspondence from him, on such ruinously cheap terms as his old master. "I'll no' put myself under Sir Paitrick's thumb," thought Bishopriggs, "till I've gane my ain rounds among the lave o' them first."

Rendered into intelligible English, this resolution pledged him to hold no communication with Sir Patrick—until he had first tested his success in negotiating with other persons, who might be equally interested in getting possession of the correspondence, and more liberal in giving hush-money to the thief who had stolen it.

Who were the "other persons" at his disposal, under these circumstances?

He had only to recall the conversation which he had overheard between Lady Lundie and Mrs. Delamayn to arrive at the discovery of one person, to begin with, who was directly interested in getting possession of his own letter. Mr. Geoffrey Delamayn was in a fair way of being married to a lady named Mrs. Glenarm. And here was this same Mr. Geoffrey Delamayn in matrimonial correspondence, little more than a fortnight since, with another lady—who signed herself "Anne Silvester."

Whatever his position between the two women might be, his interest in possessing himself of the correspondence was plain beyond all doubt. It was equally clear that the first thing to be done by Bishopriggs was to find the means of obtaining a personal interview with him. If the interview led to nothing else, it would decide one important question which still remained to be solved. The lady whom Bishopriggs had waited on at Craig Fernie might well be "Anne Silvester." Was Mr. Geoffrey Delamayn, in that case, the gentleman who had passed as her husband at the inn?

Bishopriggs rose to his gouty feet with all possible alacrity, and hobbled away to make the necessary inquiries, addressing himself, not to the men-servants at the dinner-table, who would be sure to insist on his joining them, but to the women-servants left in charge of the empty house.

He easily obtained the necessary directions for finding the cottage. But he was warned that Mr. Geoffrey Delamayn's trainer allowed nobody to see his patron at exercise, and that he would certainly be ordered off again the moment he appeared on the scene.

Bearing this caution in mind, Bishopriggs made a circuit, on reaching the open ground, so as to approach the cottage at the back, under shelter of the trees behind it. One look at Mr. Geoffrey Delamayn was all that he wanted in the first instance. They were welcome to order him off again, as long as he obtained that.

He was still hesitating at the outer line of the trees, when he heard a loud, imperative voice, calling from the front of the cottage, "Now, Mr. Geoffrey! Time's up!" Another voice answered, "All right!" and, after an interval, Geoffrey Delamayn appeared on the open ground, proceeding to the point from which he was accustomed to walk his measured mile.

Advancing a few steps to look at his man more closely, Bishopriggs was instantly detected by the quick eye of the trainer. "Hullo!" cried Perry, "what do you want here?" Bishopriggs opened his lips to make an excuse. "Who the devil are you?" roared Geoffrey. The trainer answered the question out of the resources of his own experience. "A spy, Sir—sent to time you at your work." Geoffrey lifted his mighty fist, and sprang forward a step. Perry held his patron back. "You can't do that, Sir," he said; "the man's too old. No fear of his turning up again—you've scared him out of his wits." The statement was strictly true. The terror of Bishopriggs at the sight of Geoffrey's fist restored to him the activity of his youth. He ran for the first time for twenty years; and only stopped to remember his infirmities, and to catch his breath, when he was out of sight of the cottage, among the trees.

He sat down to rest and recover himself, with the comforting inner conviction that, in one respect at least, he had gained his point. The furious savage, with the eyes that darted fire and the fist that threatened destruction, was a total stranger to him. In other words, not the man who had passed as the lady's husband at the inn.

At the same time it was equally certain that he was the man involved in the compromising correspondence which Bishopriggs possessed. To appeal, however, to his interest in obtaining the letter was entirely incompatible (after the recent exhibition of his fist) with the strong regard which Bishopriggs felt for his own personal security. There was no alternative now but to open negotiations with the one other person concerned in the matter (fortunately, on this occasion, a person of the gentler sex), who was actually within reach. Mrs. Glenarm was at Swanhaven. She had a direct interest in clearing up the question of a prior claim to Mr. Geoffrey Delamayn on the part of another woman. And she could only do that by getting the correspondence into her own hands.

"Praise Providence for a' its mercies!" said Bishopriggs, getting on his feet again. "I've got twa strings, as they say, to my boo. I trow the woman's the canny string o' the twa—and we'll een try the twanging of her."

He set forth on his road back again, to search among the company at the lake for Mrs. Glenarm.

The dance had reached its climax of animation when Bishopriggs reappeared on the scene of his duties; and the ranks of the company had been recruited, in his absence, by the very person whom it was now his foremost object to approach.

Receiving, with supple submission, a reprimand for his prolonged absence from the chief of the servants, Bishopriggs—keeping his one observant eye carefully on the look-out—busied himself in promoting the circulation of ices and cool drinks.

While he was thus occupied, his attention was attracted by two persons who, in very different ways, stood out prominently as marked characters among the rank and file of the guests.

The first person was a vivacious, irascible old gentleman, who persisted in treating the undeniable fact of his age on the footing of a scandalous false report set afloat by Time. He was superbly strapped and padded. His hair, his teeth, and his complexion were triumphs of artificial youth. When he was not occupied among the youngest women present—which was very seldom—he attached himself exclusively to the youngest men. He insisted on joining every dance. Twice he measured his length upon the grass, but nothing daunted him. He was waltzing again, with another young woman, at the next dance, as if nothing had happened. Inquiring who this effervescent old gentleman might be, Bishopriggs discovered that he was a retired officer in the navy; commonly known (among his inferiors) as "The Tartar;" more formally described in society as Captain Newenden, the last male representative of one of the oldest families in England.

The second person, who appeared to occupy a position of distinction at the dance in the glade, was a lady.

To the eye of Bishopriggs, she was a miracle of beauty, with a small fortune for a poor man carried about her in silk, lace, and jewelry. No woman present was the object of such special attention among the men as this fascinating and priceless creature. She sat fanning herself with a matchless work of art (supposed to be a handkerchief) representing an island of cambric in the midst of an ocean of lace. She was surrounded by a little court of admirers, who fetched and carried at her slightest nod, like well-trained dogs. Sometimes they brought refreshments, which she had asked for, only to decline taking them when they came. Sometimes they brought information of what was going on among the dancers, which the lady had been eager to receive when they went away, and in which she had ceased to feel the smallest interest when they came back. Every body burst into ejaculations of distress when she was asked to account for her absence from the dinner, and answered, "My poor nerves." Every body said, "What should we have done without you!"—when she doubted if she had done wisely in joining the party at all. Inquiring who this favored lady might be, Bishopriggs discovered that she was the niece of the indomitable old gentleman who would dance—or, more plainly still, no less a person than his contemplated customer, Mrs. Glenarm.

With all his enormous assurance Bishopriggs was daunted when he found himself facing the question of what he was to do next.

To open negotiations with Mrs. Glenarm, under present circumstances, was, for a man in his position, simply impossible. But, apart from this, the prospect of profitably addressing himself to that lady in the future was, to say the least of it, beset with difficulties of no common kind.

Supposing the means of disclosing Geoffrey's position to her to be found—what would she do, when she received her warning? She would in all probability apply to one of two formidable men, both of whom were interested in the matter. If she went straight to the man accused of attempting to marry her, at a time when he was already engaged to another woman—Bishopriggs would find himself confronted with the owner of that terrible fist, which had justly terrified him even on a distant and cursory view. If, on the other hand she placed her interests in the care of her uncle—Bishopriggs had only to look at the captain, and to calculate his chance of imposing terms on a man who owed Life a bill of more than sixty years' date, and who openly defied time to recover the debt.

With these serious obstacles standing in the way, what was to be done? The only alternative left was to approach Mrs. Glenarm under shelter of the dark.

Reaching this conclusion, Bishopriggs decided to ascertain from the servants what the lady's future movements might be; and, thus informed, to startle her by anonymous warnings, conveyed through the post, and claiming their answer through the advertising channel of a newspaper. Here was the certainty of alarming her, coupled with the certainty of safety to himself! Little did Mrs. Glenarm dream, when she capriciously stopped a servant going by with some glasses of lemonade, that the wretched old creature who offered the tray contemplated corresponding with her before the week was out, in the double character of her "Well-Wisher" and her "True Friend."

The evening advanced. The shadows lengthened. The waters of the lake grew pitchy black. The gliding of the ghostly swans became rare and more rare. The elders of the party thought of the drive home. The juniors (excepting Captain Newenden) began to flag at the dance. Little by little the comfortable attractions of the house—tea, coffee, and candle-light in snug rooms—resumed their influence. The guests abandoned the glade; and the fingers and lungs of the musicians rested at last.

Lady Lundie and her party were the first to send for the carriage and say farewell; the break-up of the household at Windygates on the next day, and the journey south, being sufficient apologies for setting the example of retreat. In an hour more the only visitors left were the guests staying at Swanhaven Lodge.

The company gone, the hired waiters from Kirkandrew were paid and dismissed.

On the journey back the silence of Bishopriggs created some surprise among his comrades.

"I've got my ain concerns to think of," was the only answer he vouchsafed to the remonstrances addressed to him. The "concerns" alluded to, comprehended, among other changes of plan, his departure from Kirkandrew the next day—with a reference, in case of inquiries, to his convenient friend at the Cowgate, Edinburgh. His actual destination—to be kept a secret from every body—was Perth. The neighborhood of this town—as stated on the authority of her own maid—was the part of Scotland to which the rich widow contemplated removing when she left Swanhaven in two days' time. At Perth, Bishopriggs knew of more than one place in which he could get temporary employment—and at Perth he determined to make his first anonymous advances to Mrs. Glenarm.

The remainder of the evening passed quietly enough at the Lodge.

The guests were sleepy and dull after the excitement of the day. Mrs. Glenarm retired early. At eleven o'clock Julius Delamayn was the only person left up in the house. He was understood to be in his study, preparing an address to the electors, based on instructions sent from London by his father. He was actually occupied in the music-room—now that there was nobody to discover him—playing exercises softly on his beloved violin.

At the trainer's cottage a trifling incident occured, that night, which afforded materials for a note in Perry's professional diary.

Geoffrey had sustained the later trial of walking for a given time and distance, at his full speed, without showing any of those symptoms of exhaustion which had followed the more serious experiment of running, to which he had been subjected earlier in the day. Perry, honestly bent—though he had privately hedged his own bets—on doing his best to bring his man in good order to the post on the day of the race, had forbidden Geoffrey to pay his evening visit to the house, and had sent him to bed earlier than usual. The trainer was alone, looking over his own written rules, and considering what modifications he should introduce into the diet and exercises of the next day, when he was startled by a sound of groaning from the bedroom in which his patron lay asleep.

He went in, and found Geoffrey rolling to and fro on the pillow, with his face contorted, with his hands clenched, and with the perspiration standing thick on his forehead—suffering evidently under the nervous oppression produced by the phantom-terrors of a dream.

Perry spoke to him, and pulled him up in the bed. He woke with a scream. He stared at his trainer in vacant terror, and spoke to his trainer in wild words. "What are your horrid eyes looking at over my shoulder?" he cried out. "Go to the devil—and take your infernal slate with you!" Perry spoke to him once more. "You've been dreaming of somebody, Mr. Delamayn. What's to do about a slate?" Geoffrey looked eagerly round the room, and heaved a heavy breath of relief. "I could have sworn she was staring at me over the dwarf pear-trees," he said. "All right, I know where I am now." Perry (attributing the dream to nothing more important than a passing indigestion) administered some brandy and water, and left him to drop off again to sleep. He fretfully forbade the extinguishing of the light. "Afraid of the dark?" said Perry, with a laugh. No. He was afraid of dreaming again of the dumb cook at Windygates House.

SEVENTH SCENE.—HAM FARM.

CHAPTER THE THIRTY-FOURTH.

THE NIGHT BEFORE.

THE time was the night before the marriage. The place was Sir Patrick's house in Kent.

The lawyers had kept their word. The settlements had been forwarded, and had been signed two days since.

With the exception of the surgeon and one of the three young gentlemen from the University, who had engagements elsewhere, the visitors at Windygates had emigrated southward to be present at the marriage. Besides these gentlemen, there were some ladies among the guests invited by Sir Patrick—all of them family connections, and three of them appointed to the position of Blanche's bridesmaids. Add one or two neighbors to be invited to the breakfast—and the wedding-party would be complete.

There was nothing architecturally remarkable about Sir Patrick's house. Ham Farm possessed neither the splendor of Windygates nor the picturesque antiquarian attraction of Swanhaven. It was a perfectly commonplace English country seat, surrounded by perfectly commonplace English scenery. Snug monotony welcomed you when you went in, and snug monotony met you again when you turned to the window and looked out.

The animation and variety wanting at Ham Farm were far from being supplied by the company in the house. It was remembered, at an after-period, that a duller wedding-party had never been assembled together.

Sir Patrick, having no early associations with the place, openly admitted that his residence in Kent preyed on his spirits, and that he would have infinitely preferred a room at the inn in the village. The effort to sustain his customary vivacity was not encouraged by persons and circumstances about him. Lady Lundie's fidelity to the memory of the late Sir Thomas, on the scene of his last illness and death, persisted in asserting itself, under an ostentation of concealment which tried even the trained temper of Sir Patrick himself. Blanche, still depressed by her private anxieties about Anne, was in no condition of mind to look gayly at the last memorable days of her maiden life. Arnold, sacrificed—by express stipulation on the part of Lady Lundie—to the prurient delicacy which forbids the bridegroom, before marriage, to sleep in the same house with the bride, found himself ruthlessly shut out from Sir Patrick's hospitality, and exiled every night to a bedroom at the inn. He accepted his solitary doom with a resignation which extended its sobering influence to his customary flow of spirits. As for the ladies, the elder among them existed in a state of chronic protest against Lady Lundie, and the younger were absorbed in the essentially serious occupation of considering and comparing their wedding-dresses. The two young gentlemen from the University performed prodigies of yawning, in the intervals of prodigies of billiard playing. Smith said, in despair, "There's no making things pleasant in this house, Jones." And Jones sighed, and mildly agreed with him.

On the Sunday evening—which was the evening before the marriage—the dullness, as a matter of course, reached its climax.

But two of the occupations in which people may indulge on week days are regarded as harmless on Sunday by the obstinately anti-Christian tone of feeling which prevails in this matter among the Anglo-Saxon race. It is not sinful to wrangle in religious controversy; and it is not sinful to slumber over a religious book. The ladies at Ham Farm practiced the pious observance of the evening on this plan. The seniors of the sex wrangled in Sunday controversy; and the juniors of the sex slumbered over Sunday books. As for the men, it is unnecessary to say that the young ones smoked when they were not yawning, and yawned when they were not smoking. Sir Patrick staid in the library, sorting old letters and examining old accounts. Every person in the house felt the oppression of the senseless social prohibitions which they had imposed on themselves. And yet every person in the house would have been scandalized if the plain question had been put: You know this is a tyranny of your own making, you know you don't really believe in it, you know you don't really like it—why do you submit? The freest people on the civilized earth are the only people on the civilized earth who dare not face that question.

The evening dragged its slow length on; the welcome time drew nearer and nearer for oblivion in bed. Arnold was silently contemplating, for the last time, his customary prospects of banishment to the inn, when he became aware that Sir Patrick was making signs to him. He rose and followed his host into the empty dining-room. Sir Patrick carefully closed the door. What did it mean?

It meant—so far as Arnold was concerned—that a private conversation was about to diversify the monotony of the long Sunday evening at Ham Farm.

"I have a word to say to you, Arnold," the old gentleman began, "before you become a married man. Do you remember the conversation at dinner yesterday, about the dancing-party at Swanhaven Lodge?"

"Yes."

"Do you remember what Lady Lundie said while the topic was on the table?"

"She told me, what I can't believe, that Geoffrey Delamayn was going to be married to Mrs. Glenarm."

"Exactly! I observed that you appeared to be startled by what my sister-in-law had said; and when you declared that appearances must certainly have misled her, you looked and spoke (to my mind) like a man animated by a strong feeling of indignation. Was I wrong in drawing that conclusion?"

"No, Sir Patrick. You were right."

"Have you any objection to tell me why you felt indignant?"

Arnold hesitated.

"You are probably at a loss to know what interest I can feel in the matter?"

Arnold admitted it with his customary frankness.

"In that case," rejoined Sir Patrick, "I had better go on at once with the matter in hand—

leaving you to see for yourself the connection between what I am about to say, and the question that I have just put. When I have done, you shall then reply to me or not, exactly as you think right. My dear boy, the subject on which I want to speak to you is—Miss Silvester."

Arnold started. Sir Patrick looked at him with a moment's attention, and went on:

"My niece has her faults of temper and her failings of judgment," he said. "But she has one atoning quality (among many others) which ought to make—and which I believe will make—the happiness of your married life. In the popular phrase, Blanche is as true as steel. Once her friend, always her friend. Do you see what I am coming to? She has said nothing about it, Arnold; but she has not yielded one inch in her resolution to reunite herself to Miss Silvester. One of the first questions you will have to determine, after to-morrow, will be the question of whether you do, or not, sanction your wife in attempting to communicate with her lost friend."

Arnold answered without the slightest reserve

"I am heartily sorry for Blanche's lost friend, Sir Patrick. My wife will have my full approval if she tries to bring Miss Silvester back—and my best help too, if I can give it."

Those words were earnestly spoken. It was plain that they came from his heart.

"I think you are wrong," said Sir Patrick. "I, too, am sorry for Miss Silvester. But I am convinced that she has not left Blanche without a serious reason for it. And I believe you will be encouraging your wife in a hopeless effort, if you encourage her to persist in the search for her lost friend. However, it is your affair, and not mine. Do you wish me to offer you any facilities for tracing Miss Silvester which I may happen to possess?"

"If you can help us over any obstacles at starting, Sir Patrick, it will be a kindness to Blanche, and a kindness to me."

"Very good. I suppose you remember what I said to you, one morning, when we were talking of Miss Silvester at Windygates?"

"You said you had determined to let her go her own way."

"Quite right! On the evening of the day when I said that I received information that Miss Silvester had been traced to Glasgow. You won't require me to explain why I never mentioned this to you or to Blanche. In mentioning it now, I communicate to you the only positive information, on the subject of the missing woman, which I possess. There are two other chances of finding her (of a more speculative kind) which can only be tested by inducing two men (both equally difficult to deal with) to confess what they know. One of those two men is—a person named Bishopriggs, formerly waiter at the Craig Fernie inn."

Arnold started, and changed color. Sir Patrick (silently noticing him) stated the circumstances relating to Anne's lost letter, and to the conclusion in his own mind which pointed to Bishopriggs as the person in possession of it.

"I have to add," he proceeded, "that Blanche, unfortunately, found an opportunity of speaking to Bishopriggs at Swanhaven. When she and Lady Lundie joined us at Edinburgh she showed me privately a card which had been given to her by Bishopriggs. He had described it as the address at which he might be heard of—and Blanche entreated me, before we started for London, to put the reference to the test. I told her that she had committed a serious mistake in attempting to deal with Bishopriggs on her own responsibility; and I warned her of the result in which I was firmly persuaded the inquiry would end. She declined to believe that Bishopriggs had deceived her. I saw that she would take the matter into her own hands again unless I interfered; and I went to the place. Exactly as I had anticipated, the person to whom the card referred me had not heard of Bishopriggs for years, and knew nothing whatever about his present movements. Blanche had simply put him on his guard, and shown him the propriety of keeping out of the way. If you should ever meet with him in the future—say nothing to your wife, and communicate with me. I decline to assist you in searching for Miss Silvester; but I have no objection to assist in recovering a stolen letter from a thief. So much for Bishopriggs.—Now as to the other man."

"Who is he?"

"Your friend, Mr. Geoffrey Delamayn."

Arnold sprang to his feet in ungovernable surprise.

"I appear to astonish you," remarked Sir Patrick.

Arnold sat down again, and waited, in speechless suspense, to hear what was coming next.

"I have reason to know," said Sir Patrick, "that Mr. Delamayn is thoroughly well acquainted with the nature of Miss Silvester's present troubles. What his actual connection is with them, and how he came into possession of his information, I have not found out. My discovery begins and ends with the simple fact that he has the information."

"May I ask one question, Sir Patrick?"

"What is it?"

"How did you find out about Geoffrey Delamayn?"

"It would occupy a long time," answered Sir Patrick, "to tell you how—and it is not at all necessary to our purpose that you should know. My present obligation merely binds me to tell you—in strict confidence, mind!—that Miss Silvester's secrets are no secrets to Mr. Delamayn. I leave to your discretion the use you may make of that information. You are now entirely on a par with me in relation to your knowledge of the case of Miss Silvester. Let us return to the question which I asked you when we first came into the room. Do you see the connection, now, between that question, and what I have said since?"

Arnold was slow to see the connection. His mind was running on Sir Patrick's discovery. Little dreaming that he was indebted to Mrs. Inchb are's incomplete description of him for his own escape from detection, he was wondering how it had happened that he had remained unsuspected, while Geoffrey's position had been (in part at least) revealed to view.

"I asked you," resumed Sir Patrick, attempting to help him, "why the mere report that your friend was likely to marry Mrs. Glenarm roused your indignation, and you hesitated at giving an answer. Do you hesitate still?"

"It's not easy to give an answer, Sir Patrick."

"Let us put it in another way. I assume that your view of the report takes its rise in some knowledge, on your part, of Mr. Delamayn's private affairs, which the rest of us don't possess.—Is that conclusion correct?"

"Quite correct."

"Is what you know about Mr. Delamayn connected with any thing that you know about Miss Silvester?"

If Arnold had felt himself at liberty to answer that question, Sir Patrick's suspicions would have been aroused, and Sir Patrick's resolution would have forced a full disclosure from him before he left the house.

It was getting on to midnight. The first hour of the wedding-day was at hand, as the Truth made its final effort to struggle into light. The dark Phantoms of Trouble and Terror to come were waiting near them both at that moment. Arnold hesitated again—hesitated painfully. Sir Patrick paused for his answer. The clock in the hall struck the quarter to twelve.

"I can't tell you!" said Arnold.

"Is it a secret?"

"Yes."

"Committed to your honor?"

"Doubly committed to my honor."

"What do you mean?"

"I mean that Geoffrey and I have quarreled since he took me into his confidence. I am doubly bound to respect his confidence after that."

"Is the cause of your quarrel a secret also?"

"Yes."

Sir Patrick looked Arnold steadily in the face.

"I have felt an inveterate distrust of Mr. Delamayn from the first," he said. "Answer me this. Have you any reason to think—since we first talked about your friend in the summer-house at Windygates—that my opinion of him might have been the right one after all?"

"He has bitterly disappointed me," answered Arnold. "I can say no more."

"You have had very little experience of the world," proceeded Sir Patrick. "And you have just acknowledged that you have had reason to distrust your experience of your friend. Are you quite sure that you are acting wisely in keeping his secret from me? Are you quite sure that you will not repent the course you are taking to-night?" He laid a marked emphasis on those last words. "Think, Arnold," he added, kindly. "Think before you answer."

"I feel bound in honor to keep his secret," said Arnold. "No thinking can alter that."

Sir Patrick rose, and brought the interview to an end.

"There is nothing more to be said." With those words he gave Arnold his hand, and, pressing it cordially, wished him good-night.

Going out into the hall, Arnold found Blanche alone, looking at the barometer.

"The glass is at Set Fair, my darling," he whispered. "Good-night for the last time!"

He took her in his arms, and kissed her. At the moment when he released her Blanche slipped a little note into his hand.

"Read it," she whispered, "when you are alone at the inn."

So they parted on the eve of their wedding day.

CHAPTER THE THIRTY-FIFTH.

THE DAY.

THE promise of the weather-glass was fulfilled. The sun shone on Blanche's marriage.

At nine in the morning the first of the proceedings of the day began. It was essentially of a clandestine nature. The bride and bridegroom evaded the restraints of lawful authority, and presumed to meet together privately, before they were married, in the conservatory at Ham Farm.

"You have read my letter, Arnold?"

"I have come here to answer it, Blanche. But why not have told me? Why write?"

"Because I put off telling you so long; and because I didn't know how you might take it; and for fifty other reasons. Never mind! I've made my confession. I haven't a single secret now which is not your secret too. There's time to say No, Arnold, if you think I ought to have no room in my heart for any body but you. My uncle tells me I am obstinate and wrong in refusing to give Anne up. If you agree with him, say the word, dear, before you make me your wife."

"Shall I tell you what I said to Sir Patrick last night?"

"About this?"

"Yes. The confession (as you call it) which you make in your pretty note, is the very thing that Sir Patrick spoke to me about in the dining-room before I went away. He told me your heart was set on finding Miss Silvester. And he asked me what I meant to do about it when we were married."

"And you said—?"

Arnold repeated his answer to Sir Patrick, with fervid embellishments of the original language, suitable to the emergency. Blanche's delight expressed itself in the form of two unblushing outrages on propriety, committed in close succession. She threw her arms round Arnold's neck; and she actually kissed him three hours before the consent of State and Church sanctioned her in taking that proceeding. Let us shudder—but let us not blame her. These are the consequences of free institutions.

"Now," said Arnold, "it's my turn to take to pen and ink. I have a letter to write before we are married as well as you. Only there's this difference between us—I want you to help me."

"Who are you going to write to?"

"To my lawyer in Edinburgh. There will be no time unless I do it now. We start for Switzerland this afternoon—don't we?'

"Yes."

"Very well. I want to relieve your mind, my darling before we go. Wouldn't you like to know—while we are away—that the right people are on the look-out for Miss Silvester? Sir Patrick has told me of the last place that she has been traced to—and my lawyer will set the right people at work. Come and help me to put it in the proper language, and the whole thing will be in train."

"Oh, Arnold! can I ever love you enough to reward you for this!"

"We shall see, Blanche—in Switzerland."

They audaciously penetrated, arm in arm, into Sir Patrick's own study—entirely at their disposal, as they well knew, at that hour of the morning. With Sir Patrick's pens and Sir Patrick's paper they produced a letter of instructions, deliberately reopening the investigation which Sir Patrick's superior wisdom had closed. Neither pains nor money were to be spared by the lawyer in at once taking measures (beginning at Glasgow) to find Anne. The report of the result was to be addressed to Arnold, under cover to Sir Patrick at Ham Farm. By the time the letter was completed the morning had advanced to ten o'clock. Blanche left Arnold to array herself in her bridal splendor—after another outrage on propriety, and more consequences of free institutions.

The next proceedings were of a public and avowable nature, and strictly followed the customary precedents on such occasions.

Village nymphs strewed flowers on the path to the church door (and sent in the bill the same day). Village swains rang the joy-bells (and got drunk on their money the same evening). There was the proper and awful pause while the bridegroom was kept waiting at the church. There was the proper and pitiless staring of all the female spectators when the bride was led to the altar. There was the clergyman's preliminary look at the license—which meant official caution. And there was the clerk's preliminary look at the bridegroom—which meant official fees. All the women appeared to be in their natural element; and all the men appeared to be out of it.

Then the service began—rightly-considered, the most terrible, surely, of all mortal ceremonies—the service which binds two human beings, who know next to nothing of each other's natures, to risk the tremendous experiment of living together till death parts them—the service which says, in effect if not in words, Take your leap in the dark: we sanctify, but we don't insure, it!

The ceremony went on, without the slightest obstacle to mar its effect. There were no unforeseen interruptions. There were no ominous mistakes.

The last words were spoken, and the book was closed. They signed their names on the register; the husband was congratulated; the wife was embraced. They went back aga in to the house, with more flowers strewn at their feet. The wedding-breakfast was hurried; the wedding-speeches were curtailed: there was no time to be wasted, if the young couple were to catch the tidal train.

In an hour more the carriage had whirled them away to the station, and the guests had given them the farewell cheer from the steps of the house. Young, happy, fondly attached to each other, raised securely above all the sordid cares of life, what a golden future was theirs! Married with the sanction of the Family and the blessing of the Church—who could suppose that the time was coming, nevertheless, when the blighting question would fall on them, in the spring-time of their love: Are you Man and Wife?

CHAPTER THE THIRTY-SIXTH.

THE TRUTH AT LAST.

Two days after the marriage—on Wednesday, the ninth of September a packet of letters, received at Windygates, was forwarded by Lady Lundie's steward to Ham Farm.

With one exception, the letters were all addressed either to Sir Patrick or to his sister-in-law. The one exception was directed to "Arnold Brinkworth, Esq., care of Lady Lundie, Windygates House, Perthshire"—and the envelope was specially protected by a seal.

Noticing that the post-mark was "Glasgow," Sir Patrick (to whom the letter had been delivered) looked with a certain distrust at the handwriting on the address. It was not known to him—but it was obviously the handwriting of a woman. Lady Lundie was sitting opposite to him at the table. He said, carelessly, "A letter for Arnold"—and pushed it across to her. Her ladyship took up the letter, and dropped it, the instant she looked at the handwriting, as if it had burned her fingers.

"The Person again!" exclaimed Lady Lundie. "The Person, presuming to address Arnold Brinkworth, at My house!"

"Miss Silvester?" asked Sir Patrick.

"No," said her ladyship, shutting her teeth with a snap. "The Person may insult me by addressing a letter to my care. But the Person's name shall not pollute my lips. Not even in your house, Sir Patrick. Not even to please you."

Sir Patrick was sufficiently answered. After all that had happened—after her farewell letter to Blanche—here was Miss Silvester writing to Blanche's husband, of her own accord! It was unaccountable, to say the least of it. He took the letter back, and looked at it again. Lady Lundie's steward was a methodical man. He had indorsed each letter received at Windygates with the date of its delivery. The letter addressed to Arnold had been delivered on Monday, the seventh of September—on Arnold's wedding day.

What did it mean?

It was pure waste of time to inquire. Sir Patrick rose to lock the letter up in one of the drawers of the writing-table behind him. Lady Lundie interfered (in the interest of morality).

"Sir Patrick!"

"Yes?"

"Don't you consider it your duty to open that letter?"

"My dear lady! what can you possibly be thinking of?"

The most virtuous of living women had her answer ready on the spot.

"I am thinking," said Lady Lundie, "of Arnold's moral welfare."

Sir Patrick smiled. On the long list of those respectable disguises under which we assert our own importance, or gratify our own love of meddling in our neighbor's affairs, a moral regard for the welfare of others figures in the foremost place, and stands deservedly as number one.

"We shall probably hear from Arnold in a day or two," said Sir Patrick, locking the letter up in the drawer. "He shall have it as soon as I know where to send it to him."

The next morning brought news of the bride and bridegroom.

They reported themselves to be too supremely happy to care where they lived, so long as they lived together. Every question but the question of Love was left in the competent hands of their courier. This sensible and trust-worthy man had decided that Paris was not to be thought of as a place of residence by any sane human being in the month of September. He had arranged that they were to leave for Baden—on their way to Switzerland—on the tenth. Letters were accordingly to be addressed to that place, until further notice. If the courier liked Baden, they would probably stay there for some time. If the courier took a fancy for the mountains, they would in that case go on to Switzerland. In the mean while nothing mattered to Arnold but Blanche—and nothing mattered to Blanche but Arnold.

Sir Patrick re-directed Anne Silvester's letter to Arnold, at the Poste Restante, Baden. A second letter, which had arrived that morning (addressed to Arnold in a legal handwriting, and bearing the post-mark of Edinburgh), was forwarded in the same way, and at the same time.

Two days later Ham Farm was deserted by the guests. Lady Lundie had gone back to Windygates. The rest had separated in their different directions. Sir Patrick, who also contemplated returning to Scotland, remained behind for a week—a solitary prisoner in his own country house. Accumulated arrears of business, with which it was impossible for his steward to deal single-handed, obliged him to remain at his estates in Kent for that time. To a man without a taste for partridge-shooting the ordeal was a trying one. Sir Patrick got through the day with the help of his business and his books. In the evening the rector of a neighboring parish drove over to dinner, and engaged his host at the noble but obsolete game of Piquet. They arranged to meet at each other's houses on alternate days. The rector was an admirable player; and Sir Patrick, though a born Presbyterian, blessed the Church of England from the bottom of his heart.

Three more days passed. Business at Ham Farm began to draw to an end. The time for Sir Patrick's journey to Scotland came nearer. The two partners at Piquet agreed to meet for a final game, on the next night, at the rector's house. But (let us take comfort in remembering it) our superiors in Church and State are as completely at the mercy of circumstances as the humblest and the poorest of us. That last game of Piquet between the baronet and the parson was never to be played.

On the afternoon of the fourth day Sir Patrick came in from a drive, and found a letter from Arnold waiting for him, which had been delivered by the second post.

Judged by externals only, it was a letter of an unusually perplexing—possibly also of an unusually interesting—kind. Arnold was one of the last persons in the world whom any of his friends would have suspected of being a lengthy correspondent. Here, nevertheless, was a letter from him, of three times the customary bulk and weight—and, apparently, of more than common importance, in the matter of news, besides. At the top the envelope was marked "Immediate.." And at one side (also underlined) was the ominous word, "Private.."

"Nothing wrong, I hope?" thought Sir Patrick.

He opened the envelope.

Two inclosures fell out on the table. He looked at them for a moment. They were the two letters which he had forwarded to Baden. The third letter remaining in his hand and occupying a double sheet, was from Arnold himself. Sir Patrick read Arnold's letter first. It was dated "Baden," and it began as follows:

"My Dear Sir Patrick,—Don't be alarmed, if you can possibly help it. I am in a terrible mess."

Sir Patrick looked up for a moment from the letter. Given a young man who dates from "Baden," and declares himself to be in "a terrible mess," as representing the circumstances of the case—what is the interpretation to be placed on them? Sir Patrick drew the inevitable conclusion. Arnold had been gambling.

He shook his head, and went on with the letter.

"I must say, dreadful as it is, that I am not to blame—nor she either, poor thing."

Sir Patrick paused again. "She?" Blanche had apparently been gambling too? Nothing was wanting to complete the picture but an announcement in the next sentence, presenting the courier as carried away, in his turn, by the insatiate passion for play. Sir Patrick resumed:

"You can not, I am sure, expect me to have known the law. And as for poor Miss Silvester—"

"Miss Silvester?" What had Miss Silvester to do with it? And what could be the meaning of the reference to "the law?"

Sir Patrick had read the letter, thus far, standing up. A vague distrust stole over him at the appearance of Miss Silvester's name in connection with the lines which had preceded it. He felt nothing approaching to a clear prevision of what was to come. Some indescribable influence was at work in him, which shook his nerves, and made him feel the infirmities of his age (as it seemed) on a sudden. It went no further than that. He was obliged to sit down: he was obliged to wait a moment before he went on.

The letter proceeded, in these words:

"And, as for poor Miss Silvester, though she felt, as she reminds me, some misgivings—still, she never could have foreseen, being no lawyer either, how it was to end. I hardly know the best way to break it to you. I can't, and won't, believe it myself. But even if it should be true, I am quite sure you will find a way out of it for us. I will stick at nothing, and Miss Silvester (as you will see by her letter) will stick at nothing either, to set things right. Of course, I have not said one word to my darling Blanche, who is quite happy, and suspects nothing. All this, dear Sir Patrick, is very badly written, I am afraid, but it is meant to prepare you, and to put the best side on matters at starting. However, the truth must be told—and shame on the Scotch law is what I say. This it is, in short: Geoffrey Delamayn is even a greater scoundrel than you think him; and I bitterly repent (as things have turned out) having held my tongue that night when you and I had our private talk at Ham Farm. You will think I am mixing two things up together. But I am not. Please to keep this about Geoffrey in your mind, and piece it together with what I have next to say. The worst is still to come. Miss Silvester's letter (inclosed) tells me this terrible thing. You must know that I went to her privately, as Geoffrey's messenger, on the day of the lawn-party at Windygates. Well—how it could have happened, Heaven only knows—but there is reason to fear that I married her, without being aware of it myself, in August last, at the Craig Fernie inn."

The letter dropped from Sir Patrick's hand. He sank back in the chair, stunned for the moment, under the shock that had fallen on him.

He rallied, and rose bewildered to his feet. He took a turn in the room. He stopped, and summoned his will, and steadied himself by main force. He picked up the letter, and read the last sentence again. His face flushed. He was on the point of yielding himself to a useless out burst of anger against Arnold, when his better sense checked him at the last moment. "One fool in the family is, enough," he said. "My business in this dreadful emergency is to keep my head clear for Blanche's sake."

He waited once more, to make sure of his own composure—and turned again to the letter, to see what the writer had to say for himself, in the way of explanation and excuse.

Arnold had plenty to say—with the drawback of not knowing how to say it. It was hard to decide which quality in his letter was most marked—the total absence of arrangement, or the total absence of reserve. Without beginning, middle, or end, he told the story of his fatal connection with the troubles of Anne Silvester, from the memorable day when Geoffrey Delamayn sent him to Craig Fernie, to the equally memorable night when Sir Patrick had tried vainly to make him open his lips at Ham Farm.

"I own I have behaved like a fool," the letter concluded, "in keeping Geoffrey Delamayn's secret for him—as things have turned out. But how could I tell upon him without compromising Miss Silvester? Read her letter, and you will see what she says, and how generously she releases me. It's no use saying I am sorry I wasn't more cautious. The mischief is done. I'll stick at nothing—as I have said before—to undo it. Only tell me what is the first step I am to take; and, as long as it don't part me from Blanche, rely on my taking it. Waiting to hear from you, I remain, dear Sir Patrick, yours in great perplexity, Arnold Brinkworth."

Sir Patrick folded the letter, and looked at the two inclosures lying on the table. His eye was hard, his brow was frowning, as he put his hand to take up Anne's letter. The letter from Arnold's agent in Edinburgh lay nearer to him. As it happened, he took that first.

It was short enough, and clearly enough written, to invite a reading before he put it down again. The lawyer reported that he had made the necessary inquiries at Glasgow, with this result. Anne had been traced to The Sheep's Head Hotel. She had lain there utterly helpless, from illness, until the beginning of September. She had been advertised, without result, in the Glasgow newspapers. On the 5th of September she had sufficiently recovered to be able to leave the hotel. She had been seen at the railway station on the same day—but from that point all trace of her had been lost once more. The lawyer had accordingly stopped the proceedings, and now waited further instructions from his client.

This letter was not without its effect in encouraging Sir Patrick to suspend the harsh and hasty judgment of Anne, which any man, placed in his present situation, must have been inclined to form. Her illness claimed its small share of sympathy. Her friendless position—so plainly and so sadly revealed by the advertising in the newspapers—pleaded for merciful construction of faults committed, if faults there were. Gravely, but not angrily, Sir Patrick opened her letter—the letter that cast a doubt on his niece's marriage.

Thus Anne Silvester wrote:

"GLASGOW, September 5.

"DEAR MR. BRINKWORTH,—Nearly three weeks since I attempted to write to you from this place. I was seized by sudden illness while I was engaged over my letter; and from that time to this I have laid helpless in bed—very near, as they tell me, to death. I was strong enough to be dressed, and to sit up for a little while yesterday and the day before. To-day, I have made a better advance toward recovery. I can hold my pen and control my thoughts. The first use to which I put this improvement is to write these lines.

"I am going (so far as I know) to surprise—possibly to alarm—you. There is no escaping from it, for you or for me; it must be done.

"Thinking of how best to introduce what I am now obliged to say, I can find no better way than this. I must ask you to take your memory back to a day which we have both bitter reason to regret—the day when Geoffrey Delamayn sent you to see me at the inn at Craig Fernie.

"You may possibly not remember—it unhappily produced no impression on you at the time—that I felt, and expressed, more than once on that occasion, a very great dislike to your passing me off on the people of the inn as your wife. It was necessary to my being permitted to remain at Craig Fernie that you should do so. I knew this; but still I shrank from it. It was impossible for me to contradict you, without involving you in the painful consequences, and running the risk of making a scandal which might find its way to Blanche's ears. I knew this also; but still my conscience reproached me. It was a vague feeling. I was quite unaware of the actual danger in which you were placing yourself, or I would have spoken out, no matter what came of it. I had what is called a presentiment that you were not acting discreetly—nothing more. As I love and honor my mother's memory—as I trust in the mercy of God—this is the truth.

"You left the inn the next morning, and we have not met since.

"A few days after you went away my anxieties grew more than I could bear alone. I went secretly to Windygates, and had an interview with Blanche.

"She was absent for a few minutes from the room in which we had met. In that interval I saw Geoffrey Delamayn for the first time since I had left him at Lady Lundie's lawn-party. He treated me as if I was a stranger. He told me that he had found out all that had passed between us at the inn. He said he had taken a lawyer's opinion. Oh, Mr. Brinkworth! how can I break it to you? how can I write the words which repeat what he said to me next? It must be done. Cruel as it is, it must be done. He refused to my face to marry me. He said I was married already. He said I was your wife.

"Now you know why I have referred you to what I felt (and confessed to feeling) when we were together at Craig Fernie. If you think hard thoughts, and say hard words of me, I can claim no right to blame you. I am innocent—and yet it is my fault.

"My head swims, and the foolish tears are rising in spite of me. I must leave off, and rest a little.

"I have been sitting at the window, and watching the people in the street as they go by. They are all strangers. But, somehow, the sight of them seems to rest my mind. The hum of the great city gives me heart, and helps me to go on.

"I can not trust myself to write of the man who has betrayed us both. Disgraced and broken as I am, there is something still left in me which lifts me above him. If he came repentant, at this moment, and offered me all that rank and wealth and worldly consideration can give, I would rather be what I am now than be his wife.

"Let me speak of you; and (for Blanche's sake) let me speak of myself.

"I ought, no doubt, to have waited to see you at Windygates, and to have told you at once of what had happened. But I was weak and ill and the shock of hearing what I heard fell so heavily on me that I fainted. After I came to myself I was so horrified, when I thought of you and Blanche that a sort of madness possessed me. I had but one idea—the idea of running away and hiding myself.

"My mind got clearer and quieter on the way to this place; and, arrived here, I did what I hope and believe was the best thing I could do. I consulted two lawyers. They differed in opinion as to whether we were married or not—according to the law which decides on such things in Scotland. The first said Yes. The second said No—but advised me to write immediately and tell you the position in which you stood. I attempted to write the same day, and fell ill as you know.

"Thank God, the delay that has happened is of no consequence. I asked Blanche, at Windygates, when you were to be married—and she told me not until the end of the autumn. It is only the fifth of September now. You have plenty of time before you. For all our sakes, make good use of it.

"What are you to do?

"Go at once to Sir Patrick Lundie, and show him this letter. Follow his advice—no matter how it may affect me. I should ill requite your kindness, I should be false indeed to the love I bear to Blanche, if I hesitated to brave any exposure that may now be necessary in your interests and in hers. You have been all that is generous, all that is delicate, all that is kind in this matter. You have kept my disgraceful secret—I am quite sure of it—with the fidelity of an honorable man who has had a woman's reputation placed in his charge. I release you, with my whole heart, dear Mr. Brinkworth, from your pledge. I entreat you, on my knees, to consider yourself free to reveal the truth. I will make any acknowledgment, on my side, that is needful under the circumstances—no matter how public it may be. Release yourself at any price; and then, and not till then, give back your regard to the miserable woman who has laden you with the burden of her sorrow, and darkened your life for a moment with the shadow of her shame.

"Pray don't think there is any painful sacrifice involved in this. The quieting of my own mind is involved in it—and that is all.

"What has life left for me? Nothing but the barren necessity of living. When I think of the future now, my mind passes over the years that may be left to me in this world. Sometimes I dare to hope that the Divine Mercy of Christ—which once pleaded on earth for a woman like me—may plead, when death has taken me, for my spirit in Heaven. Sometimes I dare to hope that I may see my mother, and Blanche's mother, in the better world. Their hearts were bound together as the hearts of sisters while they were here; and they left to their children the legacy of their love. Oh, help me to say, if we meet again, that not in vain I promised to be a sister to Blanche! The debt I owe to her is the hereditary debt of my mother's gratitude. And what am I now? An obstacle in the way of the happiness of her life. Sacrifice me to that happiness, for God's sake! It is the one thing I have left to live for. Again and again I say it—I care nothing for myself. I have no right to be considered; I have no wish to be considered. Tell the whole truth about me, and call me to bear witness to it as publicly as you please!

"I have waited a little, once more, trying to think, before I close my letter, what there may be still left to write.

"I can not think of any thing left but the duty of informing you how you may find me if you wish to write—or if it is thought necessary that we should meet again.

"One word before I tell you this.

"It is impossible for me to guess what you will do, or what you will be advised to do by others, when you get my letter. I don't even know that you may not already have heard of what your position is from Geoffrey Delamayn himself. In this event, or in the event of your thinking it desirable to take Blanche into your confidence, I venture to suggest that you should appoint some person whom you can trust to see me on your behalf—or, if you can not do this that you should see me in the presence of a third person. The man who has not hesitated to betray us both, will not hesitate to misrepresent us in the vilest way, if he can do it in the future. For your own sake, let us be careful to give lying tongues no opportunity of assailing your place in Blanche's estimation. Don't act so as to risk putting yourself in a false position again! Don't let it be possible that a feeling unworthy of her should be roused in the loving and generous nature of your future wife!

"This written, I may now tell you how to communicate with me after I have left this place.

"You will find on the slip of paper inclosed the name and address of the second of the two lawyers whom I consulted in Glasgow. It is arranged between us that I am to inform him, by letter, of the next place to which I remove, and that he is to communicate the information either to you or to Sir Patrick Lundie, on your applying for it personally or by writing. I don't yet know myself where I may find refuge. Nothing is certain but that I can not, in my present state of weakness, travel far.

"If you wonder why I move at all until I am stronger, I can only give a reason which may appear fanciful and overstrained.

"I have been informed that I was advertised in the Glasgow newspapers during the time when I lay at this hotel, a stranger at the point of death. Trouble has perhaps made me morbidly suspicious. I am afraid of what may happen if I stay here, after my place of residence has been made publicly known. So, as soon as I can move, I go away in secret. It will be enough for me, if I can find rest and peace in some quiet place, in the country round Glasgow. You need feel no anxiety about my means of living. I have money enough for all that I need—and, if I get well again, I know how to earn my bread.

"I send no message to Blanche—I dare not till this is over. Wait till she is your happy wife; and then give her a kiss, and say it comes from Anne.

"Try and forgive me, dear Mr. Brinkworth. I have said all. Yours gratefully,

"ANNE SILVESTER."

Sir Patrick put the letter down with unfeigned respect for the woman who had written it.

Something of the personal influence which Anne exercised more or less over all the men with whom she came in contact seemed to communicate itself to the old lawyer through the medium of her letter. His thoughts perversely wandered away from the serious and pressing question of his niece's position into a region of purely speculative inquiry relating to Anne. What infatuation (he asked himself) had placed that noble creature at the mercy of such a man as Geoffrey Delamayn?

We have all, at one time or another in our lives, been perplexed as Sir Patrick was perplexed now.

If we know any thing by experience, we know that women cast themselves away impulsively on unworthy men, and that men ruin themselves headlong for unworthy w omen. We have the institution of Divorce actually among us, existing mainly because the two sexes are perpetually placing themselves in these anomalous relations toward each other. And yet, at every fresh instance which comes before us, we persist in being astonished to find that the man and the woman have not chosen each other on rational and producible grounds! We expect human passion to act on logical principles; and human fallibility—with love for its guide—to be above all danger of making a mistake! Ask the wisest among Anne Silvester's sex what they saw to rationally justify them in choosing the men to whom they have given their hearts and their lives, and you will be putting a question to those wise women which they never once thought of putting to themselves. Nay, more still. Look into your own experience, and say frankly, Could you justify your own excellent choice at the time when you irrevocably made it? Could you have put your reasons on paper when you first owned to yourself that you loved him? And would the reasons have borne critical inspection if you had?

Sir Patrick gave it up in despair. The interests of his niece were at stake. He wisely determined to rouse his mind by occupying himself with the practical necessities of the moment. It was essential to send an apology to the rector, in the first place, so as to leave the evening at his disposal for considering what preliminary course of conduct he should advise Arnold to pursue.

After writing a few lines of apology to his partner at Piquet—assigning family business as the excuse for breaking his engagement—Sir Patrick rang the bell. The faithful Duncan appeared, and saw at once in his master s face that something had happened.

"Send a man with this to the Rectory," said Sir Patrick. "I can't dine out to-day. I must have a chop at home."

"I am afraid, Sir Patrick—if I may be excused for remarking it—you have had some bad news?"

"The worst possible news, Duncan. I can't tell you about it now. Wait within hearing of the bell. In the mean time let nobody interrupt me. If the steward himself comes I can't see him."

After thinking it over carefully, Sir Patrick decided that there was no alternative but to send a message to Arnold and Blanche, summoning them back to England in the first place. The necessity of questioning Arnold, in the minutest detail, as to every thing that had happened between Anne Silvester and himself at the Craig Fernie inn, was the first and foremost necessity of the case.

At the same time it appeared to be desirable, for Blanche's sake, to keep her in ignorance, for the present at least, of what had happened. Sir Patrick met this difficulty with characteristic ingenuity and readiness of resource.

He wrote a telegram to Arnold, expressed in the following terms:

"Your letter and inclosures received. Return to Ham Farm as soon as you conveniently can. Keep the thing still a secret from Blanche. Tell her, as the reason for coming back, that the lost trace of Anne Silvester has been recovered, and that there may be reasons for her returning to England before any thing further can be done."

Duncan having been dispatched to the station with this message, Duncan's master proceeded to calculate the question of time.

Arnold would in all probability receive the telegram at Baden, on the next day, September the seventeenth. In three days more he and Blanche might be expected to reach Ham Farm. During the interval thus placed at his disposal Sir Patrick would have ample time in which to recover himself, and to see his way to acting for the best in the alarming emergency that now confronted him.

On the nineteenth Sir Patrick received a telegram informing him that he might expect to see the young couple late in the evening on the twentieth.

Late in the evening the sound of carriage-wheels was audible on the drive; and Sir Patrick, opening the door of his room, heard the familiar voices in the hall.

"Well!" cried Blanche, catching sight of him at the door, "is Anne found?"

"Not just yet, my dear."

"Is there news of her?"

"Yes."

"Am I in time to be of use?"

"In excellent time. You shall hear all about it to-morrow. Go and take off your traveling-things, and come down again to supper as soon as you can."

Blanche kissed him, and went on up stairs. She had, as her uncle thought in the glimpse he had caught of her, been improved by her marriage. It had quieted and steadied her. There were graces in her look and manner which Sir Patrick had not noticed before. Arnold, on his side, appeared to less advantage. He was restless and anxious; his position with Miss Silvester seemed to be preying on his mind. As soon as his young wife's back was turned, he appealed to Sir Patrick in an eager whisper.

"I hardly dare ask you what I have got it on my mind to say," he began. "I must bear it if you are angry with me, Sir Patrick. But—only tell me one thing. Is there a way out of it for us? Have you thought of that?"

"I can not trust myself to speak of it clearly and composedly to-night," said Sir Patrick. "Be satisfied if I tell you that I have thought it all out—and wait for the rest till to-morrow."

Other persons concerned in the coming drama had had past difficulties to think out, and future movements to consider, during the interval occupied by Arnold and Blanche on their return journey to England. Between the seventeenth and the twentieth of September Geoffrey Delamayn had left Swanhaven, on the way to his new training quarters in the neighborhood in which the Foot-Race at Fulham was to be run. Between the same dates, also, Captain Newenden had taken the opportunity, while passing through London on his way south, to consult his solicitors. The object of the conference was to find means of discovering an anonymous letter-writer in Scotland, who had presumed to cause serious annoyance to Mrs. Glenarm.

Thus, by ones and twos, converging from widely distant quarters, they were now beginning to draw together, in the near neighborhood of the great city which was soon destined to assemble them all, for the first and the last time in this world, face to face.

CHAPTER THE THIRTY-SEVENTH.

THE WAY OUT.

BREAKFAST was just over. Blanche, seeing a pleasantly-idle morning before her, proposed to Arnold to take a stroll in the grounds.

The garden was blight with sunshine, and the bride was bright with good-humor. She caught her uncle's eye, looking at her admiringly, and paid him a little compliment in return. "You have no idea," she said, "how nice it is to be back at Ham Farm!"

"I am to understand then," rejoined Sir Patrick, "that I am forgiven for interrupting the honey-moon?"

"You are more than forgiven for interrupting it," said Blanche—"you are thanked. As a married woman," she proceeded, with the air of a matron of at least twenty years' standing, "I have been thinking the subject over; and I have arrived at the conclusion that a honey-moon which takes the form of a tour on the Continent, is one of our national abuses which stands in need of reform. When you are in love with each other (consider a marriage without love to be no marriage at all), what do you want with the excitement of seeing strange places? Isn't it excitement enough, and isn't it strange enough, to a newly-married woman to see such a total novelty as a husband? What is the most interesting object on the face of creation to a man in Arnold's position? The Alps? Certainly not! The most interesting object is the wife. And the proper time for a bridal tour is the time—say ten or a dozen years later—when you are beginning (not to get tired of each other, that's out of the question) but to get a little too well used to each other. Then take your tour to Switzerland—and you give the Alps a chance. A succession of honey-moon trips, in the autumn of married life—there is my proposal for an improvement on the present state of things! Come into the garden, Arnold; and let us calculate how long it will be before we get weary of each other, and want the beauties of nature to keep us company."

Arnold looked appealingly to Sir Patrick. Not a word had passed between them, as yet, on the serious subject of Anne Silvester's letter. Sir Patrick undertook the responsibility of making the necessary excuses to Blanche.

"Forgive me," he said, "if I ask leave to interfere with your monopoly of Arnold for a little while. I have something to say to him about his property in Scotland. Will you leave him with me, if I promise to release him as soon as possible?"

Blanche smiled graciously. "You shall have him as long as you like, uncle. There's your hat," she added, tossing it to her husband, gayly. "I brought it in for you when I got my own. You will find me on the lawn."

She nodded, and went out.

"Let me hear the worst at once, Sir Patrick," Arnold began. "Is it serious? Do you think I am to blame?"

"I will answer your last question first," said Sir Patrick. "Do I think you are to blame? Yes—in this way. You committed an act of unpardonable rashness when you consented to go, as Geoffrey Delamayn's messenger, to Miss Silvester at the inn. Having once placed yourself in that false position, you could hardly have acted, afterward, otherwise than you did. You could not be expected to know the Scotch law. And, as an honorable man, you were bound to keep a secret confided to you, in which the reputation of a woman was concerned. Your first and last error in this matter, was the fatal error of involving yourself in responsibilities which belonged exclusively to another man."

"The man had saved my life." pleaded Arnold—"and I believed I was giving service for service to my dearest friend."

"As to your other question," proceeded Sir Patrick. "Do I consider your position to be a serious one? Most assuredly, I do! So long as we are not absolutely certain that Blanche is your lawful wife, the position is more than serious: it is unendurable. I maintain the opinion, mind, out of which (thanks to your honorable silence) that scoundrel Delamayn contrived to cheat me. I told him, what I now tell you—that your sayings and doings at Craig Fernie, do not constitute a marriage, according to Scottish law. But," pursued Sir Patrick, holding up a warning forefinger at Arnold, "you have read it in Miss Silvester's letter, and you may now take it also as a result of my experience, that no individual opinion, in a matter of this kind, is to be relied on. Of two lawyers, consulted by Miss Silvester at Glasgow, one draws a directly opposite conclusion to mine, and decides that you and she are married. I believe him to be wrong, but in our situation, we have no other choice than to boldly encounter the view of the case which he represents. In plain English, we must begin by looking the worst in the face."

Arnold twisted the traveling hat which Blanche had thrown to him, nervously, in both hands. "Supposing the worst comes to the worst," he asked, "what will happen?"

Sir Patrick shook his head.

"It is not easy to tell you," he said, "without entering into the legal aspect of the case. I shall only puzzle you if I do that. Suppose we look at the matter in its social bearings—I mean, as it may possibly affect you and Blanche, and your unborn children?"

Arnold gave the hat a tighter twist than ever. "I never thought of the children," he said, with a look of consternation.

"The children may present themselves," returned Sir Patrick, dryly, "for all that. Now listen. It may have occurred to your mind that the plain way out of our present dilemma is for you and Miss Silvester, respectively, to affirm what we know to be the truth—namely, that you never had the slightest intention of marrying each other. Beware of founding any hopes on any such remedy as that! If you reckon on it, you reckon without Geoffrey Delamayn. He is interested, remember, in proving you and Miss Silvester to be man and wife. Circumstances may arise—I won't waste time in guessing at what they may be—which will enable a third person to produce the landlady and the waiter at Craig Fernie in evidence against you—and to assert that your declaration and Miss Silvester's declaration are the result of collusion between you two. Don't start! Such things have happened before now. Miss Silvester is poor; and Blanche is rich. You may be made to stand in the awkward position of a man who is denying his marriage with a poor woman, in order to establish his marriage with an heiress: Miss Silvester presumably aiding the fraud, with two strong interests of her own as inducements—the interest of asserting the claim to be the wife of a man of rank, and the interest of earning her reward in money for resigning you to Blanche. There is a case which a scoundrel might set up—and with some appearance of truth too—in a court of justice!"

"Surely, the law wouldn't allow him to do that?"

"The law will argue any thing, with any body who will pay the law for the use of its brains and its time. Let that view of the matter alone now. Delamayn can set the case going, if he likes, without applying to any lawyer to help him. He has only to cause a report to reach Blanche's ears which publicly asserts that she is not your lawful wife. With her temper, do you suppose she would leave us a minute's peace till the matter was cleared up? Or take it the other way. Comfort yourself, if you will, with the idea that this affair will trouble nobody in the present. How are we to know it may not turn up in the future under circumstances which may place the legitimacy of your children in doubt? We have a man to deal with who sticks at nothing. We have a state of the law which can only be described as one scandalous uncertainty from beginning to end. And we have two people (Bishopriggs and Mrs. Inchbare) who can, and will, speak to what took place between you and Anne Silvester at the inn. For Blanche's sake, and for the sake of your unborn children, we must face this matter on the spot—and settle it at once and forever. The question before us now is this. Shall we open the proceedings by communicating with Miss Silvester or not?"

At that important point in the conversation they were interrupted by the reappearance of Blanche. Had she, by any accident, heard what they had been saying?

No; it was the old story of most interruptions. Idleness that considers nothing, had come to look at Industry that bears every thing. It is a law of nature, apparently, that the people in this world who have nothing to do can not support the sight of an uninterrupted occupation in the hands of their neighbors. Blanche produced a new specimen from Arnold's collection of hats. "I have been thinking about it in the garden," she said, quite seriously. "Here is the brown one with the high crown. You look better in this than in the white one with the low crown. I have come to change them, that's all." She changed the hats with Arnold, and went on, without the faintest suspicion that she was in the way. "Wear the brown one when you come out—and come soon, dear. I won't stay an instant longer, uncle—I wouldn't interrupt you for the world." She kissed her hand to Sir Patrick, and smiled at her husband, and went out.

"What were we saying?" asked Arnold. "It's awkward to be interrupted in this way, isn't it?"

"If I know any thing of female human nature," returned Sir Patrick, composedly, "your wife will be in and out of the room, in that way, the whole morning. I give her ten minutes, Arnold, before she changes her mind again on the serious and weighty subject of the white hat and the brown. These little interruptions—otherwise quite charming—raised a doubt in my mind. Wouldn't it be wise (I ask myself), if we made a virtue of necessity, and took Blanche into the conversation? What do you say to calling her back and telling her the truth?"

Arnold started, and changed color.

"There are difficulties in the way," he said.

"My good fellow! at every step of this business there are difficulties in the way. Sooner or later, your wife must know what has happened. The time for telling her is, no doubt, a matter for your decision, not mine. All I say is this. Consider whether the disclosure won't come from you with a better grace, if you make it before you are fairly driven to the wall, and obliged to open your lips."

Arnold rose to his feet—took a turn in the room—sat down again—and looked at Sir Patrick, with the expression of a thoroughly bewildered and thoroughly helpless man.

"I don't know what to do," he said. "It beats me altogether. The truth is, Sir Patrick, I was fairly forced, at Craig Fernie, into deceiving Blanche—in what might seem to her a very unfeeling, and a very unpardonable way."

"That sounds awkward! What do you mean?"

"I'll try and tell you. You remember when you went to the inn to see Miss Silvester? Well, being there privately at the time, of course I was obliged to keep out of your way."

"I see! And, when Blanche came afterward, you were obliged to hide from Blanche, exactly as you had hidden from me?"

"Worse even than that! A day or two later, Blanche took me into her confidence. She spoke to me of her visit to the inn, as if I was a perfect stranger to the circumstances. She told me to my face, Sir Patrick, of the invisible man who had kept so strangely out of her way—without the faintest suspicion that I was the man. And I never opened my lips to set her right! I was obliged to be silent, or I must have betrayed Miss Silvester. What will Blanche think of me, if I tell her now? That's the question!"

Blanche's name had barely passed her husband's lips before Blanche herself verified Sir Patrick's prediction, by reappearing at the open French window, with the superseded white hat in her hand.

"Haven't you done yet!" she exclaimed. "I am shocked, uncle, to interrupt you again—but these horrid hats of Arnold's are beginning to weigh upon my mind. On reconsideration, I think the white hat with the low crown is the most becoming of the two. Change again, dear. Yes! the brown hat is hideous. There's a beggar at the gate. Before I go quite distracted, I shall give him the brown hat, and have done with the difficulty in that manner. Am I very much in the way of business? I'm afraid I must appear restless? Indeed, I am restless. I can't imagine what is the matter with me this morning."

"I can tell you," said Sir Patrick, in his gravest and dryest manner. "You are suffering, Blanche, from a malady which is exceedingly common among the young ladies of England. As a disease it is quite incurable—and the name of it is Nothing-to-Do."

Blanche dropped her uncle a smart little courtesy. "You might have told me I was in the way in fewer words than that." She whisked round, kicked the disgraced brown hat out into the veranda before her, and left the two gentlemen alone once more.

"Your position with your wife, Arnold," resumed Sir Patrick, returning gravely to the matter in hand, "is certainly a difficult one." He paused, thinking of the evening when he and Blanche had illustrated the vagueness of Mrs. Inchbare's description of the man at the inn, by citing Arnold himself as being one of the hundreds of innocent people who answered to it! "Perhaps," he added, "the situation is even more difficult than you suppose. It would have been certainly easier for you—and it would have looked more honorable in her estimation—if you had made the inevitable confession before your marriage. I am, in some degree, answerable for your not having done this—as well as for the far more serious dilemma with Miss Silvester in which you now stand. If I had not innocently hastened your marriage with Blanche, Miss Silvester's admirable letter would have reached us in ample time to prevent mischief. It's useless to dwell on that now. Cheer up, Arnold! I am bound to show you the way out of the labyrinth, no matter what the difficulties may be—and, please God, I will do it!"

He pointed to a table at the other end of the room, on which writing materials were placed. "I hate moving the moment I have had my breakfast," he said. "We won't go into the library. Bring me the pen and ink here."

"Are you going to write to Miss Silvester?"

"That is the question before us which we have not settled yet. Before I decide, I want to be in possession of the facts—down to the smallest detail of what took place between you and Miss Silvester at the inn. There is only one way of getting at those facts. I am going to examine you as if I had you before me in the witness-box in court."

With that preface, and with Arnold's letter from Baden in his hand as a brief to speak from, Sir Patrick put his questions in clear and endless succession; and Arnold patiently and faithfully answered them all.

The examination proceeded uninterruptedly until it had reached that point in the progress of events at which Anne had crushed Geoffrey Delamayn's letter in her hand, and had thrown it from her indignantly to the other end of the room. There, for the first time, Sir Patrick dipped his pen in the ink, apparently intending to take a note. "Be very careful here," he said; "I want to know every thing that you can tell me about that letter."

"The letter is lost," said Arnold.

"The letter has been stolen by Bishopriggs," returned Sir Patrick, "and is in the possession of Bishopriggs at this moment."

"Why, you know more about it than I do!" exclaimed Arnold.

"I sincerely hope not. I don't know what was inside the letter. Do you?"

"Yes. Part of it at least."

"Part of it?"

"There were two letters written, on the same sheet of paper," said Arnold. "One of them was written by Geoffrey Delamayn—and that is the one I know about."

Sir Patrick started. His face brightened; he made a hasty note. "Go on," he said, eagerly. "How came the letters to be written on the same sheet? Explain that!"

Arnold explained that Geoffrey, in the absence of any thing else to write his excuses on to Anne, had written to her on the fourth or blank page of a letter which had been addressed to him by Anne herself.

"Did you read that letter?" asked Sir Patrick.

"I might have read it if I had liked."

"And you didn't read it?"

"No."

"Why?"

"Out of delicacy."

Even Sir Patrick's carefully trained temper was not proof against this. "That is the most misplaced act of delicacy I ever heard of in my life!" cried the old gentleman, warmly. "Never mind! it's useless to regret it now. At any rate, you read Delamayn's answer to Miss Silvester's letter?"

"Yes—I did."

"Repeat it—as nearly as you can remember at this distance of time."

"It was so short," said Arnold, "that there is hardly any thing to repeat. As well as I remember, Geoffrey said he was called away to London by his father's illness. He told Miss Silvester to stop where she was; and he referred her to me, as messenger. That's all I recollect of it now."

"Cudgel your brains, my good fellow! this is very important. Did he make no allusion to his engagement to marry Miss Silvester at Craig Fernie? Didn't he try to pacify her by an apology of some sort?"

The question roused Arnold's memory to make another effort.

"Yes," he answered. "Geoffrey said something about being true to his engagement, or keeping his promise or words to that effect."

"You're sure of what you say now?"

"I am certain of it."

Sir Patrick made another note.

"Was the letter signed?" he asked, when he had done.

"Yes."

"And dated?"

"Yes." Arnold's memory made a second effort, after he had given his second affirmative answer. "Wait a little," he said. "I remember something else about the letter. It was not only dated. The time of day at which it was written was put as well."

"How came he to do that?"

"I suggested it. The letter was so short I felt ashamed to deliver it as it stood. I told him to put the time—so as to show her that he was obliged to write in a hurry. He put the time when the train started; and (I think) the time when the letter was written as well."

"And you delivered that letter to Miss Silvester, with your own hand, as soon as you saw her at the inn?"

"I did."

Sir Patrick made a third note, and pushed the paper away from him with an air of supreme satisfaction.

"I always suspected that lost letter to be an important document," he said—"or Bishopriggs would never have stolen it. We must get possession of it, Arnold, at any sacrifice. The first thing to be done (exactly as I anticipated), is to write to the Glasgow lawyer, and find Miss Silvester."

"Wait a little!" cried a voice at the veranda. "Don't forget that I have come back from Baden to help you!"

Sir Patrick and Arnold both looked up. This time Blanche had heard the last words that had passed between them. She sat down at the table by Sir Patrick's side, and laid her hand caressingly on his shoulder.

"You are quite right, uncle," she said. "I am suffering this morning from the malady of having nothing to do. Are you going to write to Anne? Don't. Let me write instead."

Sir Patrick declined to resign the pen.

"The person who knows Miss Silvester's address," he said, "is a lawyer in Glasgow. I am going to write to the lawyer. When he sends us word where she is—then, Blanche, will be the time to employ your good offices in winning back your friend."

He drew the writing materials once more with in his reach, and, suspending the remainder of Arnold's examination for the present, began his letter to Mr. Crum.

Blanche pleaded hard for an occupation of some sort. "Can nobody give me something to do?" she asked. "Glasgow is such a long way off, and waiting is such weary work. Don't sit there staring at me, Arnold! Can't you suggest something?"

Arnold, for once, displayed an unexpected readiness of resource.

"If you want to write," he said, "you owe Lady Lundie a letter. It's three days since you heard from her—and you haven't answered her yet."

Sir Patrick paused, and looked up quickly from his writing-desk.

"Lady Lundie?" he muttered, inquiringly.

"Yes," said Blanche. "It's quite true; I owe her a letter. And of course I ought to tell her we have come back to England. She will be finely provoked when she hears why!"

The prospect of provoking Lady Lundie seemed to rouse Blanche s dormant energies. She took a sheet of her uncle's note-paper, and began writing her answer then and there.

Sir Patrick completed his communication to the lawyer—after a look at Blanche, which expressed any thing rather than approval of her present employment. Having placed his completed note in the postbag, he silently signed to Arnold to follow him into the garden. They went out together, leaving Blanche absorbed over her letter to her step-mother.

"Is my wife doing any thing wrong?" asked Arnold, who had noticed the look which Sir Patrick had cast on Blanche.

"Your wife is making mischief as fast as her fingers can spread it."

Arnold stared. "She must answer Lady Lundie's letter," he said.

"Unquestionably."

"And she must tell Lady Lundie we have come back."

"I don't deny it."

"Then what is the objection to her writing?"

Sir Patrick took a pinch of snuff—and pointed with his ivory cane to the bees humming busily about the flower-beds in the sunshine of the autumn morning.

"I'll show you the objection," he said. "Suppose Blanche told one of those inveterately intrusive insects that the honey in the flowers happens, through an unexpected accident, to have come to an end—do you think he would take the statement for granted? No. He would plunge head-foremost into the nearest flower, and investigate it for himself."

"Well?" said Arnold.

"Well—there is Blanche in the breakfast-room telling Lady Lundie that the bridal tour happens, through an unexpected accident, to have come to an end. Do you think Lady Lundie is the sort of person to take the statement for granted? Nothing of the sort! Lady Lundie, like the bee, will insist on investigating for herself. How it will end, if she discovers the truth—and what new complications she may not introduce into a matter which, Heaven knows, is complicated enough already—I leave you to imagine. My poor powers of prevision are not equal to it."

Before Arnold could answer, Blanche joined them from the breakfast-room.

"I've done it," she said. "It was an awkward letter to write—and it's a comfort to have it over."

"You have done it, my dear," remarked Sir Patrick, quietly. "And it may be a comfort. But it's not over."

"What do you mean?"

"I think, Blanche, we shall hear from your step-mother by return of post."

CHAPTER THE THIRTY-EIGHTH.

THE NEWS FROM GLASGOW.

THE letters to Lady Lundie and to Mr. Crum having been dispatched on Monday, the return of the post might be looked for on Wednesday afternoon at Ham Farm.

Sir Patrick and Arnold held more than one private consultation, during the interval, on the delicate and difficult subject of admitting Blanche to a knowledge of what had happened. The wise elder advised and the inexperienced junior listened. "Think of it," said Sir Patrick; "and do it." And Arnold thought of it—and left it undone.

Let those who feel inclined to blame him remember that he had only been married a fortnight. It is hard, surely, after but two weeks' possession of your wife, to appear before her in the character of an offender on trial—and to find that an angel of retribution has been thrown into the bargain by the liberal destiny which bestowed on you the woman whom you adore!

They were all three at home on the Wednesday afternoon, looking out for the postman.

The correspondence delivered included (exactly as Sir Patrick had foreseen) a letter from Lady Lundie. Further investigation, on the far more interesting subject of the expected news from Glasgow, revealed—nothing. The lawyer had not answered Sir Patrick's inquiry by return of post.

"Is that a bad sign?" asked Blanche.

"It is a sign that something has happened," answered her uncle. "Mr. Crum is possibly expecting to receive some special information, and is waiting on the chance of being able to communicate it. We must hope, my dear, in to-morrow's post."

"Open Lady Lundie's letter in the mean time," said Blanche. "Are you sure it is for you—and not for me?"

There was no doubt about it. Her ladyship's reply was ominously addressed to her ladyship's brother-in-law. "I know what that means." said Blanche, eying her uncle eagerly while he was reading the letter. "If you mention Anne's name you insult my step-mother. I have mentioned it freely. Lady Lundie is mortally offended with me."

Rash judgment of youth! A lady who takes a dignified attitude, in a family emergency, is never mortally offended—she is only deeply grieved. Lady Lundie took a dignified attitude. "I well know," wrote this estimable and Christian woman, "that I have been all along regarded in the light of an intruder by the family connections of my late beloved husband. But I was hardly prepared to find myself entirely shut out from all domestic confidence, at a time when some serious domestic catastrophe has but too evidently taken place. I have no desire, dear Sir Patrick, to intrude. Feeling it, however, to be quite inconsistent with a due regard for my own position—after what has happened—to correspond with Blanche, I address myself to the head of the family, purely in the interests of propriety. Permit me to ask whether—under circumstances which appear to be serious enough to require the recall of my step-daughter and her husband from their wedding tour—you think it DECENT to keep the widow of the late Sir Thomas Lundie entirely in the dark? Pray consider this—not at all out of regard for Me!—but out of regard for your own position with Society. Curiosity is, as you know, foreign to my nature. But when this dreadful scandal (whatever it may be) comes out—which, dear Sir Patrick, it can not fail to do—what will the world think, when it asks for Lady Lundie's, opinion, and hears that Lady Lundie knew nothing about it? Whichever way you may decide I shall take no offense. I may possibly be wounded—but that won't matter. My little round of duties will find me still earnest, still cheerful. And even if you shut me out, my best wishes will find their way, nevertheless, to Ham Farm. May I add—without encountering a sneer—that the prayers of a lonely woman are offered for the welfare of all?"

"Well?" said Blanche.

Sir Patrick folded up the letter, and put it in his pocket.

"You have your step-mother's best wishes, my dear." Having answered in those terms, he bowed to his niece with his best grace, and walked out of the room.

"Do I think it decent," he repeated to himself, as he closed the door, "to leave the widow of the late Sir Thomas Lundie in the dark? When a lady's temper is a little ruffled, I think it more than decent, I think it absolutely desirable, to let that lady have the last word." He went into the library, and dropped his sister-in-law's remonstrance into a box, labeled "Unanswered Letters." Having got rid of it in that way, he hummed his favorite little Scotch air—and put on his hat, and went out to sun himself in the garden.

Meanwhile, Blanche was not quite satisfied with Sir Patrick's reply. She appealed to her husband. "There is something wrong," she said—"and my uncle is hiding it from me."

Arnold could have desired no better opportunity than she had offered to him, in those words, for making the long-deferred disclosure to her of the truth. He lifted his eyes to Blanche's face. By an unhappy fatality she was looking charmingly that morning. How would she look if he told her the story of the hiding at the inn? Arnold was still in love with her—and Arnold said nothing.

The next day's post brought not only the anticipated letter from Mr. Crum, but an unexpected Glasgow newspaper as well.

This time Blanche had no reason to complain that her uncle kept his correspondence a secret from her. After reading the lawyer's letter, with an interest and agitation which showed that the contents had taken him by surprise, he handed it to Arnold and his niece. "Bad news there," he said. "We must share it together."

After acknowledging the receipt of Sir Patrick's letter of inquiry, Mr. Crum began by stating all that he knew of Miss Silvester's movements—dating from the time when she had left the Sheep's Head Hotel. About a fortnight since he had received a letter from her informing him that she had found a suitable place of residence in a village near Glasgow. Feeling a strong interest in Miss Silvester, Mr. Crum had visited her some few days afterward. He had satisfied himself that she was lodging with respectable people, and was as comfortably situated as circumstances would permit. For a week more he had heard nothing from the lady. At the expiration of that time he had received a letter from her, telling him that she had read something in a Glasgow newspaper, of that day's date, which seriously concerned herself, and which would oblige her to travel northward immediately as fast as her strength would permit. At a later period, when she would be more certain of her own movements, she engaged to write again, and let Mr. Crum know where he might communicate with her if necessary. In the mean time, she could only thank him for his kindness, and beg him to take care of any letters or messages which might be left for her. Since the receipt of this communication the lawyer had heard nothing further. He had waited for the morning's post in the hope of being able to report that he had received some further intelligence. The hope had not been realized. He had now stated all that he knew himself thus far—and he had forwarded a copy of the newspaper alluded to by Miss Silvester, on the chance that an examination of it by Sir Patrick might possibly lead to further discoveries. In conclusion, he pledged himself to write again the moment he had any information to send.

Blanche snatched up the newspaper, and opened it. "Let me look!" she said. "I can find what Anne saw here if any body can!"

She ran her eye eagerly over column after column and page after page—and dropped the newspaper on her lap with a gesture of despair.

"Nothing!" she exclaimed. "Nothing any where, that I can see, to interest Anne. Nothing to interest any body—except Lady Lundie," she went on, brushing the newspaper off her lap. "It turns out to be all true, Arnold, at Swanhaven. Geoffrey Delamayn is going to marry Mrs. Glenarm."

"What!" cried Arnold; the idea instantly flashing on him that this was the news which Anne had seen.

Sir Patrick gave him a warning look, and picked up the newspaper from the floor.

"I may as well run through it, Blanche, and make quite sure that you have missed nothing," he said.

The report to which Blanche had referred was among the paragraphs arranged under the heading of "Fashionable News." "A matrimonial alliance" (the Glasgow journal announced) "was in prospect between the Honorable Geoffrey Delamayn and the lovely and accomplished relict of the late Mathew Glenarm, Esq., formerly Miss Newenden." The marriage would, in all probability, "be solemnized in Scotland, before the end of the present autumn;" and the wedding breakfast, it was whispered, "would collect a large and fashionable party at Swanhaven Lodge."

Sir Patrick handed the newspaper silently to Arnold. It was plain to any one who knew Anne Silvester's story that those were the words which had found their fatal way to her in her place of rest. The inference that followed seemed to be hardly less clear. But one intelligible object, in the opinion of Sir Patrick, could be at the end of her journey to the north. The deserted woman had rallied the last relics of her old energy—and had devoted herself to the desperate purpose of stopping the marriage of Mrs. Glenarm.

Blanche was the first to break the silence.

"It seems like a fatality," she said. "Perpetual failure! Perpetual disappointment! Are Anne and I doomed never to meet again?"

She looked at her uncle. Sir Patrick showed none of his customary cheerfulness in the face of disaster.

"She has promised to write to Mr. Crum," he said. "And Mr. Crum has promised to let us know when he hears from her. That is the only prospect before us. We must accept it as resignedly as we can."

Blanche wandered out listlessly among the flowers in the conservatory. Sir Patrick made no secret of the impression produced upon him by Mr. Crum's letter, when he and Arnold were left alone.

"There is no denying," he said, "that matters have taken a very serious turn. My plans and calculations are all thrown out. It is impossible to foresee what new mischief may not come of it, if those two women meet; or what desperate act Delamayn may not commit, if he finds himself driven to the wall. As things are, I own frankly I don't know what to do next. A great light of the Presbyterian Church," he added, with a momentary outbreak of his whimsical humor, "once declared, in my hearing, that the invention of printing was nothing more or less than a proof of the intellectual activity of the Devil. Upon my honor, I feel for the first time in my life inclined to agree with him."

He mechanically took up the Glasgow journal, which Arnold had laid aside, while he spoke.

"What's this!" he exclaimed, as a name caught his eye in the first line of the newspaper at which he happened to look. "Mrs. Glenarm again! Are they turning the iron-master's widow into a public character?"

There the name of the widow was, unquestionably; figuring for the second time in type, in a letter of the gossiping sort, supplied by an "Occasional Correspondent," and distinguished by the title of "Sayings and Doings in the North." After tattling pleasantly of the prospects of the shooting season, of the fashions from Paris, of an accident to a tourist, and of a scandal in the Scottish Kirk, the writer proceeded to the narrative of a case of interest, relating to a marriage in the sphere known (in the language of footmen) as the sphere of "high life."

Considerable sensation (the correspondent announced) had been caused in Perth and its neighborhood, by the exposure of an anonymous attempt at extortion, of which a lady of distinction had lately been made the object. As her name had already been publicly mentioned in an application to the magistrates, there could be no impropriety in stating that the lady in question was Mrs. Glenarm—whose approaching union with the Honorable Geoffrey Delamayn was alluded to in another column of the journal.

Mrs. Glenarm had, it appeared, received an anonymous letter, on the first day of her arrival as guest at the house of a friend, residing in the neighborhood of Perth. The letter warned her that there was an obstacle, of which she was herself probably not aware, in the way of her projected marriage with Mr. Geoffrey Delamayn. That gentleman had seriously compromised himself with another lady; and the lady would oppose his marriage to Mrs. Glenarm, with proof in writing to produce in support of her claim. The proof was contained in two letters exchanged between the parties, and signed by their names; and the correspondence was placed at Mrs. Glenarm's disposal, on two conditions, as follows:

First, that she should offer a sufficiently liberal price to induce the present possessor of the letters to part with them. Secondly, that she should consent to adopt such a method of paying the money as should satisfy the person that he was in no danger of finding himself brought within reach of the law. The answer to these two proposals was directed to be made through the medium of an advertisement in the local newspaper—distinguished by this address, "To a Friend in the Dark."

Certain turns of expression, and one or two mistakes in spelling, pointed to this insolent letter as being, in all probability, the production of a Scotchman, in the lower ranks of life. Mrs. Glenarm had at once shown it to her nearest relative, Captain Newenden. The captain had sought legal advice in Perth. It had been decided, after due consideration, to insert the advertisement demanded, and to take measures to entrap the writer of the letter into revealing himself—without, it is needless to add, allowing the fellow really to profit by his attempted act of extortion.

The cunning of the "Friend in the Dark" (whoever he might be) had, on trying the proposed experiment, proved to be more than a match for the lawyers. He had successfully eluded not only the snare first set for him, but others subsequently laid. A second, and a third, anonymous letter, one more impudent than the other had been received by Mrs. Glenarm, assuring that lady and the friends who were acting for her that they were only wasting time and raising the price which would be asked for the correspondence, by the course they were taking. Captain Newenden had thereupon, in default of knowing what other course to pursue, appealed publicly to the city magistrates, and a reward had been offered, under the sanction of the municipal authorities, for the discovery of the man. This proceeding also having proved quite fruitless, it was understood that the captain had arranged, with the concurrence of his English solicitors, to place the matter in the hands of an experienced officer of the London police.

Here, so far as the newspaper correspondent was aware, the affair rested for the present.

It was only necessary to add, that Mrs. Glenarm had left the neighborhood of Perth, in order to escape further annoyance; and had placed herself under the protection of friends in another part of the county. Mr. Geoffrey Delamayn, whose fair fame had been assailed (it was needless, the correspondent added in parenthesis, to say how groundlessly), was understood to have expressed, not only the indignation natural under the circumstances but also his extreme regret at not finding himself in a position to aid Captain Newenden's efforts to bring the anonymous slanderer to justice. The honorable gentleman was, as the sporting public were well aware, then in course of strict training for his forthcoming appearance at the Fulham Foot-Race. So important was it considered that his mind should not be harassed by annoyances, in his present responsible position, that his trainer and his principal backers had thought it desirable to hasten his removal to the neighborhood of Fulham—where the exercises which were to prepare him for the race were now being continued on the spot.

"The mystery seems to thicken," said Arnold.

"Quite the contrary," returned Sir Patrick, briskly. "The mystery is clearing fast—thanks to the Glasgow newspaper. I shall be spared the trouble of dealing with Bishopriggs for the stolen letter. Miss Silvester has gone to Perth, to recover her correspondence with Geoffrey Delamayn."

"Do you think she would recognize it," said Arnold, pointing to the newspaper, "in the account given of it here?"

"Certainly! And she could hardly fail, in my opinion, to get a step farther than that. Unless I am entirely mistaken, the authorship of the anonymous letters has not mystified her."

"How could she guess at that?"

"In this way, as I think. Whatever she may have previously thought, she must suspect, by this time, that the missing correspondence has been stolen, and not lost. Now, there are only two persons whom she can think of, as probably guilty of the theft—Mrs. Inchbare or Bishopriggs. The newspaper description of the style of the anonymous letters declares it to be the style of a Scotchman in the lower ranks of life—in other words, points plainly to Bishopriggs. You see that? Very well. Now suppose she recovers the stolen property. What is likely to happen then? She will be more or less than woman if she doesn't make her way next, provided with her proofs in writing, to Mrs. Glenarm. She may innocently help, or she may innocently frustrate, the end we have in view—either way, our course is clear before us again. Our interest in communicating with Miss Silvester remains precisely the same interest that it was before we received the Glasgow newspaper. I propose to wait till Sunday, on the chance that Mr. Crum may write again. If we don't hear from him, I shall start for Scotland on Monday morning, and take my chance of finding my way to Miss Silvester, through Mrs. Glenarm."

"Leaving me behind?"

"Leaving you behind. Somebody must stay with Blanche. After having only been a fortnight married, must I remind you of that?"

"Don't you think Mr. Crum will write before Monday?"

"It will be such a fortunate circumstance for us, if he does write, that I don't venture to anticipate it."

"You are down on our luck, Sir."

"I detest slang, Arnold. But slang, I own, expresses my state of mind, in this instance, with an accuracy which almost reconciles me to the use of it—for once in a way."

"Every body's luck turns sooner or later," persisted Arnold. "I can't help thinking our luck is on the turn at last. Would you mind taking a bet, Sir Patrick?"

"Apply at the stables. I leave betting, as I leave cleaning the horses, to my groom."

With that crabbed answer he closed the conversation for the day.

The hours passed, and time brought the post again in due course—and the post decided in Arnold's favor! Sir Patrick's want of confidence in the favoring patronage of Fortune was practically rebuked by the arrival of a second letter from the Glasgow lawyer on the next day.

"I have the pleasure of announcing" (Mr. Crum wrote) "that I have heard from Miss Silvester, by the next postal delivery ensuing, after I had dispatched my letter to Ham Farm. She writes, very briefly, to inform me that she has decided on establishing her next place of residence in London. The reason assigned for taking this step—which she certainly did not contemplate when I last saw her—is that she finds herself approaching the end of her pecuniary resources. Having already decided on adopting, as a means of living, the calling of a concert-singer, she has arranged to place her interests in the hands of an old friend of her late mother (who appears to have belonged also to the musical profession): a dramatic and musical agent long established in the metropolis, and well known to her as a trustworthy and respectable man. She sends me the name and address of this person—a copy of which you will find on the inclosed slip of paper—in the event of my having occasion to write to her, before she is settled in London. This is the whole substance of her letter. I have only to add, that it does not contain the slightest allusion to the nature of the errand on which she left Glasgow."

Sir Patrick happened to be alone when he opened Mr. Crum's letter.

His first proceeding, after reading it, was to consult the railway time-table hanging in the hall. Having done this, he returned to the library—wrote a short note of inquiry, addressed to the musical agent—and rang the bell.

"Miss Silvester is expected in London, Duncan. I want a discreet person to communicate with her. You are the person."

Duncan bowed. Sir Pa trick handed him the note.

"If you start at once you will be in time to catch the train. Go to that address, and inquire for Miss Silvester. If she has arrived, give her my compliments, and say I will have the honor of calling on her (on Mr. Brinkworth's behalf) at the earliest date which she may find it convenient to appoint. Be quick about it—and you will have time to get back before the last train. Have Mr. and Mrs. Brinkworth returned from their drive?"

"No, Sir Patrick."

Pending the return of Arnold and Blanche, Sir Patrick looked at Mr. Crum's letter for the second time.

He was not quite satisfied that the pecuniary motive was really the motive at the bottom of Anne's journey south. Remembering that Geoffrey's trainers had removed him to the neighborhood of London, he was inclined to doubt whether some serious quarrel had not taken place between Anne and Mrs. Glenarm—and whether some direct appeal to Geoffrey himself might not be in contemplation as the result. In that event, Sir Patrick's advice and assistance would be placed, without scruple, at Miss Silvester's disposal. By asserting her claim, in opposition to the claim of Mrs. Glenarm, she was also asserting herself to be an unmarried woman, and was thus serving Blanche's interests as well as her own. "I owe it to Blanche to help her," thought Sir Patrick. "And I owe it to myself to bring Geoffrey Delamayn to a day of reckoning if I can."

The barking of the dogs in the yard announced the return of the carriage. Sir Patrick went out to meet Arnold and Blanche at the gate, and tell them the news.

Punctual to the time at which he was expected, the discreet Duncan reappeared with a note from the musical agent.

Miss Silvester had not yet reached London; but she was expected to arrive not later than Tuesday in the ensuing week. The agent had already been favored with her instructions to pay the strictest attention to any commands received from Sir Patrick Lundie. He would take care that Sir Patrick's message should be given to Miss Silvester as soon as she arrived.

At last, then, there was news to be relied on! At last there was a prospect of seeing her! Blanche was radiant with happiness, Arnold was in high spirits for the first time since his return from Baden.

Sir Patrick tried hard to catch the infection of gayety from his young friends; but, to his own surprise, not less than to theirs, the effort proved fruitless. With the tide of events turning decidedly in his favor—relieved of the necessity of taking a doubtful journey to Scotland; assured of obtaining his interview with Anne in a few days' time—he was out of spirits all through the evening.

"Still down on our luck!" exclaimed Arnold, as he and his host finished their last game of billiards, and parted for the night. "Surely, we couldn't wish for a more promising prospect than our prospect next week?"

Sir Patrick laid his hand on Arnold's shoulder.

"Let us look indulgently together," he said, in his whimsically grave way, "at the humiliating spectacle of an old man's folly. I feel, at this moment, Arnold, as if I would give every thing that I possess in the world to have passed over next week, and to be landed safely in the time beyond it."

"But why?"

"There is the folly! I can't tell why. With every reason to be in better spirits than usual, I am unaccountably, irrationally, invincibly depressed. What are we to conclude from that? Am I the object of a supernatural warning of misfortune to come? Or am I the object of a temporary derangement of the functions of the liver? There is the question. Who is to decide it? How contemptible is humanity, Arnold, rightly understood! Give me my candle, and let's hope it's the liver."

EIGHTH SCENE—THE PANTRY.

CHAPTER THE THIRTY-NINTH.

ANNE WINS A VICTORY.

ON a certain evening in the month of September (at that period of the month when Arnold and Blanche were traveling back from Baden to Ham Farm) an ancient man—with one eye filmy and blind, and one eye moist and merry—sat alone in the pantry of the Harp of Scotland Inn, Perth, pounding the sugar softly in a glass of whisky-punch. He has hitherto been personally distinguished in these pages as the self-appointed father of Anne Silvester and the humble servant of Blanche at the dance at Swanhaven Lodge. He now dawns on the view in amicable relations with a third lady—and assumes the mystic character of Mrs. Glenarm's "Friend in the Dark."

Arriving in Perth the day after the festivities at Swanhaven, Bishopriggs proceeded to the Harp of Scotland—at which establishment for the reception of travelers he possessed the advantage of being known to the landlord as Mrs. Inchbare's right-hand man, and of standing high on the head-waiter's list of old and intimate friends.

Inquiring for the waiter first by the name of Thomas (otherwise Tammy) Pennyquick, Bishopriggs found his friend in sore distress of body and mind. Contending vainly against the disabling advances of rheumatism, Thomas Pennyquick ruefully contemplated the prospect of being laid up at home by a long illness—with a wife and children to support, and with the emoluments attached to his position passing into the pockets of the first stranger who could be found to occupy his place at the inn.

Hearing this doleful story, Bishopriggs cunningly saw his way to serving his own private interests by performing the part of Thomas Pennyquick's generous and devoted friend.

He forthwith offered to fill the place, without taking the emoluments, of the invalided headwaiter—on the understanding, as a matter of course, that the landlord consented to board and lodge him free of expense at the inn. The landlord having readily accepted this condition, Thomas Pennyquick retired to the bosom of his family. And there was Bishopriggs, doubly secured behind a respectable position and a virtuous action against all likelihood of suspicion falling on him as a stranger in Perth—in the event of his correspondence with Mrs. Glenarm being made the object of legal investigation on the part of her friends!

Having opened the campaign in this masterly manner, the same sagacious foresight had distinguished the operations of Bishopriggs throughout.

His correspondence with Mrs. Glenarm was invariably written with the left hand—the writing thus produced defying detection, in all cases, as bearing no resemblance of character whatever to writing produced by persons who habitually use the other hand. A no less far-sighted cunning distinguished his proceedings in answering the advertisements which the lawyers duly inserted in the newspaper. He appointed hours at which he was employed on business-errands for the inn, and places which lay on the way to those errands, for his meetings with Mrs. Glenarm's representatives: a pass-word being determined on, as usual in such cases, by exchanging which the persons concerned could discover each other. However carefully the lawyers might set the snare—whether they had their necessary "witness" disguised as an artist sketching in the neighborhood, or as an old woman selling fruit, or what not—the wary eye of Bishopriggs detected it. He left the pass-word unspoken; he went his way on his errand; he was followed on suspicion; and he was discovered to be only "a respectable person," charged with a message by the landlord of the Harp of Scotland Inn!

To a man intrenched behind such precautions as these, the chance of being detected might well be reckoned among the last of all the chances that could possibly happen.

Discovery was, nevertheless, advancing on Bishopriggs from a quarter which had not been included in his calculations. Anne Silvester was in Perth; forewarned by the newspaper (as Sir Patrick had guessed) that the letters offered to Mrs. Glenarm were the letters between Geoffrey and herself, which she had lost at Craig Fernie, and bent on clearing up the suspicion which pointed to Bishopriggs as the person who was trying to turn the correspondence to pecuniary account. The inquiries made for him, at Anne's request, as soon as she arrived in the town, openly described his name, and his former position as headwaiter at Craig Fernie—and thus led easily to the discovery of him, in his publicly avowed character of Thomas Pennyquick's devoted friend. Toward evening, on the day after she reached Perth, the news came to Anne that Bishopriggs was in service at the inn known as the Harp of Scotland. The landlord of the hotel at which she was staying inquired whether he should send a message for her. She answered, "No, I will take my message myself. All I want is a person to show me the way to the inn."

Secluded in the solitude of the head-waiter's pantry, Bishopriggs sat peacefully melting the sugar in his whisky-punch.

It was the hour of the evening at which a period of tranquillity generally occurred before what was called "the night-business" of the house began. Bishopriggs was accustomed to drink and meditate daily in this interval of repose. He tasted the punch, and smiled contentedly as he set down his glass. The prospect before him looked fairly enough. He had outwitted the lawyers in the preliminary negotiations thus far. All that was needful now was to wait till the terror of a public scandal (sustained by occasional letters from her "Friend in the Dark") had its due effect on Mrs. Glenarm, and hurried her into paying the purchase-money for the correspondence with her own hand. "Let it breed in the brain," he thought, "and the siller will soon come out o' the purse."

His reflections were interrupted by the appearance of a slovenly maid-servant, with a cotton handkerchief tied round her head, and an uncleaned sauce-pan in her hand.

"Eh, Maister Bishopriggs," cried the girl, "here's a braw young leddy speerin' for ye by yer ain name at the door."

"A leddy?" repeated Bishopriggs, with a look of virtuous disgust. "Ye donnert ne'er-do-weel, do you come to a decent, 'sponsible man like me, wi' sic a Cyprian overture as that? What d'ye tak' me for? Mark Antony that lost the world for love (the mair fule he!)? or Don Jovanny that counted his concubines by hundreds, like the blessed Solomon himself? Awa' wi' ye to yer pots and pans; and bid the wandering Venus that sent ye go spin!"

Before the girl could answer she was gently pulled aside from the doorway, and Bishopriggs, thunder-struck, saw Anne Silvester standing in her place.

"You had better tell the servant I am no stranger to you," said Anne, looking toward the kitchen-maid, who stood in the passage staring at her in stolid amazement.

"My ain sister's child!" cried Bishopriggs, lying with his customary readiness. "Go yer ways, Maggie. The bonny lassie's my ain kith and kin. The tongue o' scandal, I trow, has naething to say against that.—Lord save us and guide us!" he added In another tone, as the girl closed the door on them, "what brings ye here?"

"I have something to say to you. I am not very well; I must wait a little first. Give me a chair."

Bishopriggs obeyed in silence. His one available eye rested on Anne, as he produced the chair, with an uneasy and suspicious attention. "I'm wanting to know one thing," he said. "By what meeraiculous means, young madam, do ye happen to ha' fund yer way to this inn?"

Anne told him how her inquiries had been made and what the result had been, plainly and frankly. The clouded face of Bishopriggs began to clear again.

"Hech! hech!" he exclaimed, recovering all his native impudence, "I hae had occasion to remark already, to anither leddy than yersel', that it's seemply mairvelous hoo a man's ain gude deeds find him oot in this lower warld o' ours. I hae dune a gude deed by pure Tammy Pennyquick, and here's a' Pairth ringing wi the report o' it; and Sawmuel Bishopriggs sae weel known that ony stranger has only to ask, and find him. Understand, I beseech ye, that it's no hand o' mine that pets this new feather in my cap. As a gude Calvinist, my saul's clear o' the smallest figment o' belief in Warks. When I look at my ain celeebrity I joost ask, as the Psawmist asked before me, 'Why do the heathen rage, and the people imagine a vain thing?' It seems ye've something to say to me," he added, suddenly reverting to the object of Anne's visit. "Is it humanly possible that ye can ha' come a' the way to Pairth for naething but that?"

The expression of suspicion began to show itself again in his face. Concealing as she best might the disgust that he inspired in her, Anne stated her errand in the most direct manner, and in the fewest possible words.

"I have come here to ask you for something," she said.

"Ay? ay? What may it be ye're wanting of me?"

"I want the letter I lost at Craig Fernie."

Even the solidly-founded self-possession of Bishopriggs himself was shaken by the startling directness of that attack on it. His glib tongue was paralyzed for the moment. "I dinna ken what ye're drivin' at," he said, after an interval, with a sullen consciousness that he had been all but tricked into betraying himself.

The change in his manner convinced Anne that she had found in Bishopriggs the person of whom she was in search.

"You have got my letter," she said, sternly insisting on the truth. "And you are trying to turn it to a disgraceful use. I won't allow you to make a market of my private affairs. You have offered a letter of mine for sale to a stranger. I insist on your restoring it to me before I leave this room!"

Bishopriggs hesitated again. His first suspicion that Anne had been privately instructed by Mrs. Glenarm's lawyers returned to his mind as a suspicion confirmed. He felt the vast importance of making a cautious reply.

"I'll no' waste precious time," he said, after a moment's consideration with himself, "in brushing awa' the fawse breath o' scandal, when it passes my way. It blaws to nae purpose, my young leddy, when it blaws on an honest man like me. Fie for shame on ye for saying what ye've joost said—to me that was a fether to ye at Craig Fernie! Wha' set ye on to it? Will it be man or woman that's misca'ed me behind my back?"

Anne took the Glasgow newspaper from the pocket of her traveling cloak, and placed it before him, open at the paragraph which described the act of extortion attempted on Mrs. Glenarm.

"I have found there," she said, "all that I want to know."

"May a' the tribe o' editors, preenters, paper-makers, news-vendors, and the like, bleeze together in the pit o' Tophet!" With this devout aspiration—internally felt, not openly uttered—Bishopriggs put on his spectacles, and read the passage pointed out to him. "I see naething here touching the name o' Sawmuel Bishopriggs, or the matter o' ony loss ye may or may not ha' had at Craig Fernie," he said, when he had done; still defending his position, with a resolution worthy of a better cause.

Anne's pride recoiled at the prospect of prolonging the discussion with him. She rose to her feet, and said her last words.

"I have learned enough by this time," she answered, "to know that the one argument that prevails with you is the argument of money. If money will spare me the hateful necessity of disputing with you—poor as I am, money you shall have. Be silent, if you please. You are personally interested in what I have to say next."

She opened her purse, and took a five-pound note from it.

"If you choose to own the truth, and produce the letter," she resumed, "I will give you this, as your reward for finding, and restoring to me, something that I had lost. If you persist in your present prevarication, I can, and will, make that sheet of note-paper you have stolen from me nothing but waste paper in your hands. You have threatened Mrs. Glenarm with my interference. Suppose I go to Mrs. Glenarm? Suppose I interfere before the week is out? Suppose I have other letters of Mr. Delamayn's in my possession, and produce them to speak for me? What has Mrs. Glenarm to purchase of you then? Answer me that!"

The color rose on her pale face. Her eyes, dim and weary when she entered the room, looked him brightly through and through in immeasurable contempt. "Answer me that!" she repeated, with a burst of her old energy which revealed the fire and passion of the woman's nature, not quenched even yet!

If Bishopriggs had a merit, it was a rare merit, as men go, of knowing when he was beaten. If he had an accomplishment, it was the accomplishment of retiring defeated, with all the honors of war.

"Mercy presairve us!" he exclaimed, in the most innocent manner. "Is it even You Yersel' that writ the letter to the man ca'ed Jaffray Delamayn, and got the wee bit answer in pencil on the blank page? Hoo, in Heeven's name, was I to know that was the letter ye were after when ye cam' in here? Did ye ever tell me ye were Anne Silvester, at the hottle? Never ance! Was the puir feckless husband-creature ye had wi' ye at the inn, Jaffray Delamayn? Jaffray wad mak' twa o' him, as my ain eyes ha' seen. Gi' ye back yer letter? My certie! noo I know it is yer letter, I'll gi' it back wi' a' the pleasure in life!"

He opened his pocket-book, and took it out, with an alacrity worthy of the honestest man in Christendom—and (more wonderful still) he looked with a perfectly assumed expression of indifference at the five-pound note in Anne's hand.

"Hoot! toot!" he said, "I'm no' that clear in my mind that I'm free to tak' yer money. Eh, weel! weel! I'll een receive it, if ye like, as a bit Memento o' the time when I was o' some sma' sairvice to ye at the hottle. Ye'll no' mind," he added, suddenly returning to business, "writin' me joost a line—in the way o' receipt, ye ken—to clear me o' ony future suspicion in the matter o' the letter?"

Anne threw down the bank-note on the table near which they were standing, and snatched the letter from him.

"You need no receipt," she answered. "There shall be no letter to bear witness against you!"

She lifted her other hand to tear it in pieces. Bishopriggs caught her by both wrists, at the same moment, and held her fast.

"Bide a wee!" he said. "Ye don't get the letter, young madam, without the receipt. It may be a' the same to you, now ye've married the other man, whether Jaffray Delamayn ance promised ye fair in the by-gone time, or no. But, my certie! it's a matter o' some moment to me, that ye've chairged wi' stealin' the letter, and making a market o't, and Lord knows what besides, that I suld hae yer ain acknowledgment for it in black and white. Gi' me my bit receipt—and een do as ye will with yer letter after that!"

Anne's hold of the letter relaxed. She let Bishopriggs repossess himself of it as it dropped on the floor between them, without making an effort to prevent him.

"It may be a' the same to you, now ye've married the other man, whether Jaffray Delamayn ance promised ye fair in the by-gone time, or no." Those words presented Anne's position before her in a light in which she had not seen it yet. She had truly expressed the loathing that Geoffrey now inspired in her, when she had declared, in her letter to Arnold, that, even if he offered her marriage, in atonement for the past, she would rather be what she was than be his wife. It had never occurred to her, until this moment, that others would misinterpret the sensitive pride which had prompted the abandonment of her claim on the man who had ruined her. It had never been brought home to her until now, that if she left him contemptuously to go his own way, and sell himself to the first woman who had money enough to buy him, her conduct would sanction the false conclusion that she was powerless to interfere, because she was married already to another man. The color that had risen in her face vanished, and left it deadly pale again. She began to see that the purpose of her journey to the north was not completed yet.

"I will give you your receipt," she said. "Tell me what to write, and it shall be written."

Bishopriggs dictated the receipt. She wrote and signed it. He put it in his pocket-book with the five-pound note, and handed her the letter in exchange.

"Tear it if ye will," he said. "It matters naething to me."

For a moment she hesitated. A sudden shuddering shook her from head to foot—the forewarning, it might be, of the influence which that letter, saved from destruction by a hair's-breadth, was destined to exercise on her life to come. She recovered herself, and folded her cloak closer to her, as if she had felt a passing chill.

"No," she said; "I will keep the letter."

She folded it and put it in the pocket of her dress. Then turned to go—and stopped at the door.

"One thing more," she added. "Do you know Mrs. Glenarm's present address?"

"Ye're no' reely going to Mistress Glenarm?"

"That is no concern of yours. You can answer my question or not, as you please."

"Eh, my leddy! yer temper's no' what it used to be in the auld times at the hottle. Aweel! aweel! ye ha' gi'en me yer money, and I'll een gi' ye back gude measure for it, on my side. Mistress Glenarm's awa' in private—incog, as they say—to Jaffray Delamayn's brither at Swanhaven Lodge. Ye may rely on the information, and it's no' that easy to come at either. They've keepit it a secret as they think from a' the warld. Hech! hech! Tammy Pennyquick's youngest but twa is page-boy at the hoose where the leddy's been veesitin', on the outskirts o' Pairth. Keep a secret if ye can frae the pawky ears o' yer domestics in the servants' hall!—Eh! she's aff, without a word at parting!" he exclaimed, as Anne left him without ceremony in the middle of his dissertation on secrets and servants' halls. "I trow I ha' gaen out for wool, and come back shorn," he added, reflecting grimly on the disastrous overthrow of the promising speculation on which he had embarked. "My certie! there was naething left for't, when madam's fingers had grippit me, but to slip through them as cannily as I could. What's Jaffray's marrying, or no' marrying, to do wi' her?" he wondered, reverting to the question which Anne had put to him at parting. "And whar's the sense o' her errand, if she's reely bent on finding her way to Mistress Glenarm?"

Whatever the sense of her errand might be, Anne's next proceeding proved that she was really bent on it. After resting two days, she left Perth by the first train in the morning, for Swanhaven Lodge.

NINTH SCENE.—THE MUSIC-ROOM.

CHAPTER THE FORTIETH.

JULIUS MAKES MISCHIEF.

JULIUS DELAMAYN was alone, idly sauntering to and fro, with his violin in his hand, on the terrace at Swanhaven Lodge.

The first mellow light of evening was in the sky. It was the close of the day on which Anne Silvester had left Perth.

Some hours earlier, Julius had sacrificed himself to the duties of his political position—as made for him by his father. He had submitted to the dire necessity of delivering an oration to the electors, at a public meeting in the neighboring town of Kirkandrew. A detestable atmosphere to breathe; a disorderly audience to address; insolent opposition to conciliate; imbecile inquiries to answer; brutish interruptions to endure; greedy petitioners to pacify; and dirty hands to shake: these are the stages by which the aspiring English gentleman is compelled to travel on the journey which leads him from the modest obscurity of private life to the glorious publicity of the House of Commons. Julius paid the preliminary penalties of a political first appearance, as exacted by free institutions, with the necessary patience; and returned to the welcome shelter of home, more indifferent, if possible, to the attractions of Parliamentary distinction than when he set out. The discord of the roaring "people" (still echoing in his ears) had sharpened his customary sensibility to the poetry of sound, as composed by Mozart, and as interpreted by piano and violin. Possessing himself of his beloved instrument, he had gone out on the terrace to cool himself in the evening air, pending the arrival of the servant whom he had summoned by the music-room bell. The man appeared at the glass door which led into the room; and reported, in answer to his master's inquiry, that Mrs. Julius Delamayn was out paying visits, and was not expected to return for another hour at least.

Julius groaned in spirit. The finest music which Mozart has written for the violin associates that instrument with the piano. Without the wife to help him, the husband was mute. After an instant's consideration, Julius hit on an idea which promised, in some degree, to remedy the disaster of Mrs. Delamayn's absence from home.

"Has Mrs. Glenarm gone out, too?" he asked.

"No, Sir."

"My compliments. If Mrs. Glenarm has nothing else to do, will she be so kind as to come to me in the music-room?"

The servant went away with his message. Julius seated himself on one of the terrace-benches, and began to tune his violin.

Mrs. Glenarm—rightly reported by Bishopriggs as having privately taken refuge from her anonymous correspondent at Swanhaven Lodge—was, musically speaking, far from being an efficient substitute for Mrs. Delamayn. Julius possessed, in his wife, one of the few players on the piano-forte under whose subtle touch that shallow and soulless instrument becomes inspired with expression not its own, and produces music instead of noise. The fine organization which can work this miracle had not been bestowed on Mrs. Glenarm. She had been carefully taught; and she was to be trusted to play correctly—and that was all. Julius, hungry for music, and reigned to circumstances, asked for no more.

The servant returned with his answer. Mrs. Glenarm would join Mr. Delamayn in the music-room in ten minutes' time.

Julius rose, relieved, and resumed his sauntering walk; now playing little snatches of music, now stopping to look at the flowers on the terrace, with an eye that enjoyed their beauty, and a hand that fondled them with caressing touch. If Imperial Parliament had seen him at that moment, Imperial Parliament must have given notice of a question to his illustrious father: Is it possible, my lord, that you can have begotten such a Member as this?

After stopping for a moment to tighten one of the strings of his violin, Julius, raising his head from the instrument, was surprised to see a lady approaching him on the terrace. Advancing to meet her, and perceiving that she was a total stranger to him, he assumed that she was, in all probability, a visitor to his wife.

"Have I the honor of speaking to a friend of Mrs. Delamayn's?" he asked. "My wife is not at home, I am sorry to say."

"I am a stranger to Mrs. Delamayn," the lady answered. "The servant informed me that she had gone out; and that I should find Mr. Delamayn here."

Julius bowed—and waited to hear more.

"I must beg you to forgive my intrusion," the stranger went on. "My object is to ask permission to see a lady who is, I have been informed, a guest in your house."

The extraordinary formality of the request rather puzzled Julius.

"Do you mean Mrs. Glenarm?" he asked.

"Yes."

"Pray don't think any permission necessary. A friend of Mrs. Glenarm's may take her welcome for granted in this house."

"I am not a friend of Mrs. Glenarm. I am a total stranger to her."

This made the ceremonious request preferred by the lady a little more intelligible—but it left the lady's object in wishing to speak to Mrs. Glenarm still in the dark. Julius politely waited, until it pleased her to proceed further, and explain herself The explanation did not appear to be an easy one to give. Her eyes dropped to the ground. She hesitated painfully.

"My name—if I mention it," she resumed, without looking up, "may possibly inform you—" She paused. Her color came and went. She hesitated again; struggled with her agitation, and controlled it. "I am Anne Silvester," she said, suddenly raising her pale face, and suddenly steadying her trembling voice.

Julius started, and looked at her in silent surprise.

The name was doubly known to him. Not long since, he had heard it from his father's lips, at his father's bedside. Lord Holchester had charged him, had earnestly charged him, to bear that name in mind, and to help the woman who bore it, if the woman ever applied to him in time to come. Again, he had heard the name, more lately, associated scandalously with the name of his brother. On the receipt of the first of the anonymous letters sent to her, Mrs. Glenarm had not only summoned Geoffrey himself to refute the aspersion cast upon him, but had forwarded a private copy of the letter to his relatives at Swanhaven. Geoffrey's defense had not entirely satisfied Julius that his brother was free from blame. As he now looked at Anne Silvester, the doubt returned upon him strengthened—almost confirmed. Was this woman—so modest, so gentle, so simply and unaffectedly refined—the shameless adventuress denounced by Geoffrey, as claiming him on the strength of a foolish flirtation; knowing herself, at the time, to be privately married to another man? Was this woman—with the voice of a lady, the look of a lady, the manner of a lady—in league (as Geoffrey had declared) with the illiterate vagabond who was attempting to extort money anonymously from Mrs. Glenarm? Impossible! Making every allowance for the proverbial deceitfulness of appearances, impossible!

"Your name has been mentioned to me," said Julius, answering her after a momentary pause. His instincts, as a gentleman, made him shrink from referring to the association of her name with the name of his brother. "My father mentioned you," he added, considerately explaining his knowledge of her in that way, "when I last saw him in London."

"Your father!" She came a step nearer, with a look of distrust as well as a look of astonishment in her face. "Your father is Lord Holchester—is he not?"

"Yes."

"What made him speak of me?"

"He was ill at the time," Julius answered. "And he had been thinking of events in his past life with which I am entirely unacquainted. He said he had known your father and mother. He desired me, if you were ever in want of any assistance, to place my services at your disposal. When he expressed that wish, he spoke very earnestly—he gave me the impression that there was a feeling of regret associated with the recollections on which he had been dwelling."

Slowly, and in silence, Anne drew back to the low wall of the terrace close by. She rested one hand on it to support herself. Julius had said words of terrible import without a suspicion of what he had done. Never until now had Anne Silvester known that the man who had betrayed her was the son of that other man whose discovery of the flaw in the marriage had ended in the betrayal of her mother before her. She felt the shock of the revelation with a chill of superstitious dread. Was the chain of a fatality wound invisibly round her? Turn which way she might was she still going darkly on, in the track of her dead mother, to an appointed and hereditary doom? Present things passed from her view as the awful doubt cast its shadow over her mind. She lived again for a moment in the time when she was a child. She saw the face of her mother once more, with the wan despair on it of the bygone days when the title of wife was denied her, and the social prospect was closed forever.

Julius approached, and roused her.

"Can I get you any thing?" he asked. "You are looking very ill. I hope I have said nothing to distress you?"

The question failed to attract her attention. She put a question herself instead of answering it.

"Did you say you were quite ignorant of what your father was thinking of when he spoke to you about me?"

"Quite ignorant."

"Is your brother likely to know more about it than you do?"

"Certainly not."

She paused, absorbed once more in her own thoughts. Startled, on the memorable day when they had first met, by Geoffrey's family name, she had put the question to him whether there had not been some acquaintance between their parents in the past time. Deceiving her in all else, he had not deceived in this. He had spoken in good faith, when he had declared that he had never heard her father or her mother mentioned at home.

The curiosity of Julius was aroused. He attempted to lead her on into saying more.

"You appear to know what my father was thinking of when he spoke to me," he resumed. "May I ask—"

She interrupted him with a gesture of entreaty.

"Pray don't ask! It's past and over—it can have no interest for you—it has nothing to do with my errand here. I must return," she went on, hurriedly, "to my object in trespassing on your kindness. Have you heard me mentioned, Mr. Delamayn, by another member of your family besides your father?"

Julius had not anticipated that she would approach, of her own accord, the painful subject on which he had himself forborne to touch. He was a little disappointed. He had expected more delicacy of feeling from her than she had shown.

"Is it necessary," he asked, coldly, "to enter on that?"

The blood rose again in Anne's cheeks.

"If it had not been necessary," she answered, "do you think I could have forced myself to mention it to you? Let me remind you that I am here on sufferance. If I don't speak plainly (no matter at what sacrifice to my own feelings), I make my situation more embarrassing than it is already. I have something to tell Mrs. Glenarm relating to the anonymous letters which she has lately received. And I have a word to say to her, next, about her contemplated marriage. Before you allow me to do this, you ought to know who I am. (I have owned it.) You ought to have heard the worst that can be said of my conduct. (Your face tells me you have heard the worst.) After the forbearance you have shown to me, as a perfect stranger, I will not commit the meanness of taking you by surprise. Perhaps, Mr. Delamayn, you understand, now, why I felt myself obliged to refer to your brother. Will you trust me with permission to speak to Mrs. Glenarm?"

It was simply and modestly said—with an unaffected and touching resignation of look and manner. Julius gave her back the respect and the sympathy which, for a moment, he had unjustly withheld from her.

"You have placed a confidence in me," he said "which most persons in your situation would have withheld. I feel bound, in return to place confidence in you. I will take it for granted that your motive in this matter is one which it is my duty to respect. It will be for Mrs. Glenarm to say whether she wishes the interview to take place or not. All that I can do is to leave you free to propose it to her. You are free."

As he spoke the sound of the piano reached them from the music-room. Julius pointed to the glass door which opened on to the terrace.

"You have only to go in by that door," he said, "and you will find Mrs. Glenarm alone."

Anne bowed, and left him. Arrived at the short flight of steps which led up to the door, she paused to collect her thoughts before she went in.

A sudden reluctance to go on and enter the room took possession of her, as she waited with her foot on the lower step. The report of Mrs. Glenarm's contemplated marriage had produced no such effect on her as Sir Patrick had supposed: it had found no love for Geoffrey left to wound, no latent jealousy only waiting to be inflamed. Her object in taking the journey to Perth was completed when her correspondence with Geoffrey was in her own hands again. The change of purpose which had brought her to Swanhaven was due entirely to the new view of her position toward Mrs. Glenarm which the coarse commonsense of Bishopriggs had first suggested to her. If she failed to protest against Mrs. Glenarm's marriage, in the interests of the reparation which Geoffrey owed to her, her conduct would only confirm Geoffrey's audacious assertion that she was a married woman already. For her own sake she might still have hesitated to move in the matter. But Blanche's interests were concerned as well as her own; and, for Blanche's sake, she had resolved on making the journey to Swanhaven Lodge.

At the same time, feeling toward Geoffrey as she felt now—conscious as she was of not really desiring the reparation on which she was about to insist—it was essential to the preservation of her own self-respect that she should have some purpose in view which could justify her to her own conscience in assuming the character of Mrs. Glenarm's rival.

She had only to call to mind the critical situation of Blanche—and to see her purpose before her plainly. Assuming that she could open the coming interview by peaceably proving that her claim on Geoffrey was beyond dispute, she might then, without fear of misconception, take the tone of a friend instead of an enemy, and might, with the best grace, assure Mrs. Glenarm that she had no rivalry to dread, on the one easy condition that she engaged to make Geoffrey repair the evil that he had done. "Marry him without a word against it to dread from me—so long as he unsays the words and undoes the deeds which have thrown a doubt on the marriage of Arnold and Blanche." If she could but bring the interview to this end—there was the way found of extricating Arnold, by her own exertions, from the false position in which she had innocently placed him toward his wife! Such was the object before her, as she now stood on the brink of her interview with Mrs. Glenarm.

Up to this moment, she had firmly believed in her capacity to realize her own visionary project. It was only when she had her foot on the step that a doubt of the success of the coming experiment crossed her mind. For the first time, she saw the weak point in her own reasoning. For the first time, she felt how much she had blindly taken for granted, in assuming that Mrs. Glenarm would have sufficient sense of justice and sufficient command of temper to hear her patiently. All her hopes of success rested on her own favorable estimate of a woman who was a total stranger to her! What if the first words exchanged between them proved the estimate to be wrong?

It was too late to pause and reconsider the position. Julius Delamayn had noticed her hesitation, and was advancing toward her from the end of the terrace. There was no help for it but to master her own irresolution, and to run the risk boldly. "Come what may, I have gone too far to stop here." With that desperate resolution to animate her, she opened the glass door at the top of the steps, and went into the room.

Mrs. Glenarm rose from the piano. The two women—one so richly, the other so plainly dressed; one with her beauty in its full bloom, the other worn and blighted; one with society at her feet, the other an outcast living under the bleak shadow of reproach—the two women stood face to face, and exchanged the cold courtesies of salute between strangers, in silence.

The first to meet the trivial necessities of the situation was Mrs. Glenarm. She good-humoredly put an end to the embarrassment—which the shy visitor appeared to feel acutely—by speaking first.

"I am afraid the servants have not told you?" she said. "Mrs. Delamayn has gone out."

"I beg your pardon—I have not called to see Mrs. Delamayn."

Mrs. Glenarm looked a little surprised. She went on, however, as amiably as before.

"Mr. Delamayn, perhaps?" she suggested. "I expect him here every moment."

Anne explained again. "I have just parted from Mr. Delamayn." Mrs. Glenarm opened her eyes in astonishment. Anne proceeded. "I have come here, if you will excuse the intrusion—"

She hesitated—at a loss how to end the sentence. Mrs. Glenarm, beginning by this time to feel a strong curiosity as to what might be coming next, advanced to the rescue once more.

"Pray don't apologize," she said. "I think I understand that you are so good as to have come to see me. You look tired. Won't you take a chair?"

Anne could stand no longer. She took the offered chair. Mrs. Glenarm resumed her place on the music-stool, and ran her fingers idly over the keys of the piano. "Where did you see Mr. Delamayn?" she went on. "The most irresponsible of men, except when he has got his fiddle in his hand! Is he coming in soon? Are we going to have any music? Have you come to play with us? Mr. Delamayn is a perfect fanatic in music, isn't he? Why isn't he here to introduce us? I suppose you like the classical style, too? Did you know that I was in the music-room? Might I ask your name?"

Frivolous as they were, Mrs. Glenarm's questions were not without their use. They gave Anne time to summon her resolution, and to feel the necessity of explaining herself.

"I am speaking, I believe, to Mrs. Glenarm?" she began.

The good-humored widow smiled and bowed graciously.

"I have come here, Mrs. Glenarm—by Mr. Delamayn's permission—to ask leave to speak to you on a matter in which you are interested."

Mrs. Glenarm's many-ringed fingers paused over the keys of the piano. Mrs. Gle narm's plump face turned on the stranger with a dawning expression of surprise.

"Indeed? I am interested in so many matters. May I ask what this matter is?"

The flippant tone of the speaker jarred on Anne. If Mrs. Glenarm's nature was as shallow as it appeared to be on the surface, there was little hope of any sympathy establishing itself between them.

"I wished to speak to you," she answered, "about something that happened while you were paying a visit in the neighborhood of Perth."

The dawning surprise in Mrs. Glenarm's face became intensified into an expression of distrust. Her hearty manner vanished under a veil of conventional civility, drawn over it suddenly. She looked at Anne. "Never at the best of times a beauty," she thought. "Wretchedly out of health now. Dressed like a servant, and looking like a lady. What does it mean?"

The last doubt was not to be borne in silence by a person of Mrs. Glenarm's temperament. She addressed herself to the solution of it with the most unblushing directness—dextrously excused by the most winning frankness of manner.

"Pardon me," she said. "My memory for faces is a bad one; and I don't think you heard me just now, when I asked for your name. Have we ever met before?"

"Never."

"And yet—if I understand what you are referring to—you wish to speak to me about something which is only interesting to myself and my most intimate friends."

"You understand me quite correctly," said Anne. "I wish to speak to you about some anonymous letters—"

"For the third time, will you permit me to ask for your name?"

"You shall hear it directly—if you will first allow me to finish what I wanted to say. I wish—if I can—to persuade you that I come here as a friend, before I mention my name. You will, I am sure, not be very sorry to hear that you need dread no further annoyance—"

"Pardon me once more," said Mrs. Glenarm, interposing for the second time. "I am at a loss to know to what I am to attribute this kind interest in my affairs on the part of a total stranger."

This time, her tone was more than politely cold—it was politely impertinent. Mrs. Glenarm had lived all her life in good society, and was a perfect mistress of the subtleties of refined insolence in her intercourse with those who incurred her displeasure.

Anne's sensitive nature felt the wound—but Anne's patient courage submitted. She put away from her the insolence which had tried to sting, and went on, gently and firmly, as if nothing had happened.

"The person who wrote to you anonymously," she said, "alluded to a correspondence. He is no longer in possession of it. The correspondence has passed into hands which may be trusted to respect it. It will be put to no base use in the future—I answer for that."

"You answer for that?" repeated Mrs. Glenarm. She suddenly leaned forward over the piano, and fixed her eyes in unconcealed scrutiny on Anne's face. The violent temper, so often found in combination with the weak nature, began to show itself in her rising color, and her lowering brow. "How do you know what the person wrote?" she asked. "How do you know that the correspondence has passed into other hands? Who are you?" Before Anne could answer her, she sprang to her feet, electrified by a new idea. "The man who wrote to me spoke of something else besides a correspondence. He spoke of a woman. I have found you out!" she exclaimed, with a burst of jealous fury. "You are the woman!"

Anne rose on her side, still in firm possession of her self-control.

"Mrs. Glenarm," she said, calmly, "I warn—no, I entreat you—not to take that tone with me. Compose yourself; and I promise to satisfy you that you are more interested than you are willing to believe in what I have still to say. Pray bear with me for a little longer. I admit that you have guessed right. I own that I am the miserable woman who has been ruined and deserted by Geoffrey Delamayn."

"It's false!" cried Mrs. Glenarm. "You wretch! Do you come to me with your trumped-up story? What does Julius Delamayn mean by exposing me to this?" Her indignation at finding herself in the same room with Anne broke its way through, not the restraints only, but the common decencies of politeness. "I'll ring for the servants!" she said. "I'll have you turned out of the house."

She tried to cross the fire-place to ring the bell. Anne, who was standing nearest to it, stepped forward at the same moment. Without saying a word, she motioned with her hand to the other woman to stand back. There was a pause. The two waited, with their eyes steadily fixed on one another—each with her resolution laid bare to the other's view. In a moment more, the finer nature prevailed. Mrs. Glenarm drew back a step in silence.

"Listen to me," said Anne.

"Listen to you?" repeated Mrs. Glenarm. "You have no right to be in this house. You have no right to force yourself in here. Leave the room!"

Anne's patience—so firmly and admirably preserved thus far—began to fail her at last.

"Take care, Mrs. Glenarm!" she said, still struggling with herself. "I am not naturally a patient woman. Trouble has done much to tame my temper—but endurance has its limits. You have reached the limits of mine. I have a claim to be heard—and after what you have said to me, I will be heard!"

"You have no claim! You shameless woman, you are married already. I know the man's name. Arnold Brinkworth."

"Did Geoffrey Delamayn tell you that?"

"I decline to answer a woman who speaks of Mr. Geoffrey Delamayn in that familiar way."

Anne advanced a step nearer.

"Did Geoffrey Delamayn tell you that?" she repeated.

There was a light in her eyes, there was a ring in her voice, which showed that she was roused at last. Mrs. Glenarm answered her, this time.

"He did tell me."

"He lied!"

"He did not! He knew. I believe him. I don't believe you."

"If he told you that I was any thing but a single woman—if he told you that Arnold Brinkworth was married to any body but Miss Lundie of Windygates—I say again he lied!"

"I say again—I believe him, and not you."

"You believe I am Arnold Brinkworth's wife?"

"I am certain of it."

"You tell me that to my face?"

"I tell you to your face—you may have been Geoffrey Delamayn's mistress; you are Arnold Brinkworth's wife."

At those words the long restrained anger leaped up in Anne—all the more hotly for having been hitherto so steadily controlled. In one breathless moment the whirlwind of her indignation swept away, not only all remembrance of the purpose which had brought her to Swanhaven, but all sense even of the unpardonable wrong which she had suffered at Geoffrey's hands. If he had been there, at that moment, and had offered to redeem his pledge, she would have consented to marry him, while Mrs. Glenarm s eye was on her—no matter whether she destroyed herself in her first cool moment afterward or not. The small sting had planted itself at last in the great nature. The noblest woman is only a woman, after all!

"I forbid your marriage to Geoffrey Delamayn! I insist on his performing the promise he gave me, to make me his wife! I have got it here in his own words, in his own writing. On his soul, he swears it to me—he will redeem his pledge. His mistress, did you say? His wife, Mrs. Glenarm, before the week is out!"

In those wild words she cast back the taunt—with the letter held in triumph in her hand.

Daunted for the moment by the doubt now literally forced on her, that Anne might really have the claim on Geoffrey which she advanced, Mrs. Glenarm answered nevertheless with the obstinacy of a woman brought to bay—with a resolution not to be convinced by conviction itself.

"I won't give him up!" she cried. "Your letter is a forgery. You have no proof. I won't, I won't, I won't give him up!" she repeated, with the impotent iteration of an angry child.

Anne pointed disdainfully to the letter that she held. "Here is his pledged and written word," she said. "While I live, you will never be his wife."

"I shall be his wife the day after the race. I am going to him in London—to warn him against You!"

"You will find me in London, before you—with this in my hand. Do you know his writing?"

She held up the letter, open. Mrs. Glenarm's hand flew out with the stealthy rapidity of a cat's paw, to seize and destroy it. Quick as she was, her rival was quicker still. For an instant they faced each other breathless—one with the letter held behind her; one with her hand still stretched out.

At the same moment—before a word more had passed between them—the glass door opened; and Julius Delamayn appeared in the room.

He addressed himself to Anne.

"We decided, on the terrace," he said, quietly, "that you should speak to Mrs. Glenarm, if Mrs. Glenarm wished it. Do you think it desirable that the interview should be continued any longer?"

Anne's head drooped on her breast. The fiery anger in her was quenched in an instant.

"I have been cruelly provoked, Mr. Delamayn," she answered. "But I have no right to plead that." She looked up at him for a moment. The hot tears of shame gathered in her eyes, and fell slowly over her cheeks. She bent her head again, and hid them from him. "The only atonement I can make," she said, "is to ask your pardon, and to leave the house."

In silence, she turned away to the door. In silence, Julius Delamayn paid her the trifling courtesy of opening it for her. She went out.

Mrs. Glenarm's indignation—suspended for the moment—transferred itself to Julius.

"If I have been entrapped into seeing that woman, with your approval," she said, haughtily, "I owe it to myself, Mr. Delamayn, to follow her example, and to leave your house."

"I authorized her to ask you for an interview, Mrs. Glenarm. If she has presumed on the permission that I gave her, I sincerely regret it, and I beg you to accept my apologies. At the same time, I may venture to add, in defense of my conduct, that I thought her—and think her still—a woman to be pitied more than to be blamed."

"To be pitied did you say?" asked Mrs. Glenarm, doubtful whether her ears had not deceived her.

"To be pitied," repeated Julius.

"You may find it convenient, Mr. Delamayn, to forget what your brother has told us about that person. I happen to remember it."

"So do I, Mrs. Glenarm. But, with my experience of Geoffrey—" He hesitated, and ran his fingers nervously over the strings of his violin.

"You don't believe him?" said Mrs. Glenarm.

Julius declined to admit that he doubted his brother's word, to the lady who was about to become his brother's wife.

"I don't quite go that length," he said. "I find it difficult to reconcile what Geoffrey has told us, with Miss Silvester's manner and appearance—"

"Her appearance!" cried Mrs. Glenarm, in a transport of astonishment and disgust. "Her appearance! Oh, the men! I beg your pardon—I ought to have remembered that there is no accounting for tastes. Go on—pray go on!"

"Shall we compose ourselves with a little music?" suggested Julius.

"I particularly request you will go on," answered Mrs. Glenarm, emphatically. "You find it 'impossible to reconcile'—"

"I said 'difficult.'"

"Oh, very well. Difficult to reconcile what Geoffrey told us, with Miss Silvester's manner and appearance. What next? You had something else to say, when I was so rude as to interrupt you. What was it?"

"Only this," said Julius. "I don't find it easy to understand Sir Patrick Lundie's conduct in permitting Mr. Brinkworth to commit bigamy with his niece."

"Wait a minute! The marriage of that horrible woman to Mr. Brinkworth was a private marriage. Of course, Sir Patrick knew nothing about it!"

Julius owned that this might be possible, and made a second attempt to lead the angry lady back to the piano. Useless, once more! Though she shrank from confessing it to herself,

Mrs. Glenarm's belief in the genuineness of her lover's defense had been shaken. The tone taken by Julius—moderate as it was—revived the first startling suspicion of the credibility of Geoffrey's statement which Anne's language and conduct had forced on Mrs. Glenarm. She dropped into the nearest chair, and put her handkerchief to her eyes. "You always hated poor Geoffrey," she said, with a burst of tears. "And now you're defaming him to me!"

Julius managed her admirably. On the point of answering her seriously, he checked himself. "I always hated poor Geoffrey," he repeated, with a smile. "You ought to be the last person to say that, Mrs. Glenarm! I brought him all the way from London expressly to introduce him to you."

"Then I wish you had left him in London!" retorted Mrs. Glenarm, shifting suddenly from tears to temper. "I was a happy woman before I met your brother. I can't give him up!" she burst out, shifting back again from temper to tears. "I don't care if he has deceived me. I won't let another woman have him! I will be his wife!" She threw herself theatrically on her knees before Julius. "Oh, do help me to find out the truth!" she said. "Oh, Julius, pity me! I am so fond of him!"

There was genuine distress in her face, there was true feeling in her voice. Who would have believed that there were reserves of merciless insolence and heartless cruelty in this woman—and that they had been lavishly poured out on a fallen sister not five minutes since?

"I will do all I can," said Julius, raising her. "Let us talk of it when you are more composed. Try a little music," he repeated, "just to quiet your nerves."

"Would you like me to play?" asked Mrs. Glenarm, becoming a model of feminine docility at a moment's notice.

Julius opened the Sonatas of Mozart, and shouldered his violin.

"Let's try the Fifteenth," he said, placing Mrs. Glenarm at the piano. "We will begin with the Adagio. If ever there was divine music written by mortal man, there it is!"

They began. At the third bar Mrs. Glenarm dropped a note—and the bow of Julius paused shuddering on the strings.

"I can't play!" she said. "I am so agitated; I am so anxious. How am I to find out whether that wretch is really married or not? Who can I ask? I can't go to Geoffrey in London—the trainers won't let me see him. I can't appeal to Mr. Brinkworth himself—I am not even acquainted with him. Who else is there? Do think, and tell me!"

There was but one chance of making her return to the Adagio—the chance of hitting on a suggestion which would satisfy and quiet her. Julius laid his violin on the piano, and considered the question before him carefully.

"There are the witnesses," he said. "If Geoffrey's story is to be depended on, the landlady and the waiter at the inn can speak to the facts."

"Low people!" objected Mrs. Glenarm. "People I don't know. People who might take advantage of my situation, and be insolent to me."

Julius considered once more; and made another suggestion. With the fatal ingenuity of innocence, he hit on the idea of referring Mrs. Glenarm to no less a person than Lady Lundie herself!

"There is our good friend at Windygates," he said. "Some whisper of the matter may have reached Lady Lundie's ears. It may be a little awkward to call on her (if she has heard any thing) at the time of a serious family disaster. You are the best judge of that, however. All I can do is to throw out the notion. Windygates isn't very far off—and something might come of it. What do you think?"

Something might come of it! Let it be remembered that Lady Lundie had been left entirely in the dark—that she had written to Sir Patrick in a tone which plainly showed that her self-esteem was wounded and her suspicion roused—and that her first intimation of the serious dilemma in which Arnold Brinkworth stood was now likely, thanks to Julius Delamayn, to reach her from the lips of a mere acquaintance. Let this be remembered; and then let the estimate be formed of what might come of it—not at Windygates only, but also at Ham Farm!

"What do you think?" asked Julius.

Mrs. Glenarm was enchanted. "The very person to go to!" she said. "If I am not let in I can easily write—and explain my object as an apology. Lady Lundie is so right-minded, so sympathetic. If she sees no one else—I have only to confide my anxieties to her, and I am sure she will see me. You will lend me a carriage, won't you? I'll go to Windygates to-morrow."

Julius took his violin off the piano.

"Don't think me very troublesome," he said coaxingly. "Between this and to-morrow we have nothing to do. And it is such music, if you once get into the swing of it! Would you mind trying again?"

Mrs. Glenarm was willing to do any thing to prove her gratitude, after the invaluable hint which she had just received. At the second trial the fair pianist's eye and hand were in perfect harmony. The lovely melody which the Adagio of Mozart's Fifteenth Sonata has given to violin and piano flowed smoothly at last—and Julius Delamayn soared to the seventh heaven of musical delight.

The next day Mrs. Glenarm and Mrs. Delamayn went together to Windygates House.

TENTH SCENE—THE BEDROOM.

CHAPTER THE FORTY-FIRST.

LADY LUNDIE DOES HER DUTY.

THE scene opens on a bedroom—and discloses, in broad daylight, a lady in bed.

Persons with an irritable sense of propriety, whose self-appointed duty it is to be always crying out, are warned to pause before they cry out on this occasion. The lady now presented to view being no less a person than Lady Lundie herself, it follows, as a matter of course, that the utmost demands of propriety are, by the mere assertion of that fact, abundantly and indisputably satisfied. To say that any thing short of direct moral advantage could, by any possibility, accrue to any living creature by the presentation of her ladyship in a horizontal, instead of a perpendicular position, is to assert that Virtue is a question of posture, and that Respectability ceases to assert itself when it ceases to appear in morning or evening dress. Will any body be bold enough to say that? Let nobody cry out, then, on the present occasion.

Lady Lundie was in bed.

Her ladyship had received Blanche's written announcement of the sudden stoppage of the bridal tour; and had penned the answer to Sir Patrick—the receipt of which at Ham Farm has been already described. This done, Lady Lundie felt it due to herself to take a becoming position in her own house, pending the possible arrival of Sir Patrick's reply. What does a right-minded woman do, when she has reason to believe that she is cruelly distrusted by the members of her own family? A right-minded woman feels it so acutely that she falls ill. Lady Lundie fell ill accordingly.

The case being a serious one, a medical practitioner of the highest grade in the profession was required to treat it. A physician from the neighboring town of Kirkandrew was called in.

The physician came in a carriage and pair, with the necessary bald head, and the indispensable white cravat. He felt her ladyship's pulse, and put a few gentle questions. He turned his back solemnly, as only a great doctor can, on his own positive internal conviction that his patient had nothing whatever the matter with her. He said, with every appearance of believing in himself, "Nerves, Lady Lundie. Repose in bed is essentially necessary. I will write a prescription." He prescribed, with perfect gravity: Aromatic Spirits of Ammonia—16 drops. Spirits of Red Lavender—10 drops. Syrup of Orange Peel—2 drams. Camphor Julep—1 ounce. When he had written, Misce fiat Hanstus (instead of Mix a Draught)—when he had added, Ter die Sumendus (instead of To be taken Three times a day)—and when he had certified to his own Latin, by putting his initials at the end, he had only to make his bow; to slip two guineas into his pocket; and to go his way, with an approving professional conscience, in the character of a physician who had done his duty.

Lady Lundie was in bed. The visible part of her ladyship was perfectly attired, with a view to the occasion. A fillet of superb white lace encircled her head. She wore an adorable invalid jacket of white cambric, trimmed with lace and pink ribbons. The rest was—bed-clothes. On a table at her side stood the Red Lavender Draught—in color soothing to the eye; in flavor not unpleasant to the taste. A book of devotional character was near it. The domestic ledgers, and the kitchen report for the day, were ranged modestly behind the devout book. (Not even her ladyship's nerves, observe, were permitted to interfere with her ladyship's duty.) A fan, a smelling-bottle, and a handkerchief lay within reach on the counterpane. The spacious room was partially darkened. One of the lower windows was open, affording her ladyship the necessary cubic supply of air. The late Sir Thomas looked at his widow, in effigy, from the wall opposite the end of the bed. Not a chair was out of its place; not a vestige of wearing apparel dared to show itself outside the sacred limits of the wardrobe and the drawers. The sparkling treasures of the toilet-table glittered in the dim distance, The jugs and basins were of a rare and creamy white; spotless and beautiful to see. Look where you might, you saw a perfect room. Then look at the bed—and you saw a perfect woman, and completed the picture.

It was the day after Anne's appearance at Swanhaven—toward the end of the afternoon.

Lady Lundie's own maid opened the door noiselessly, and stole on tip-toe to the bedside. Her ladyship's eyes were closed. Her ladyship suddenly opened them.

"Not asleep, Hopkins. Suffering. What is it?"

Hopkins laid two cards on the counterpane. "Mrs. Delamayn, my lady—and Mrs. Glenarm."

"They were told I was ill, of course?"

"Yes, my lady. Mrs. Glenarm sent for me. She went into the library, and wrote this note." Hopkins produced the note, neatly folded in three-cornered form.

"Have they gone?"

"No, my lady. Mrs. Glenarm told me Yes or No would do for answer, if you could only have the goodness to read this."

"Thoughtless of Mrs. Glenarm—at a time when the doctor insists on perfect repose," said Lady Lundie. "It doesn't matter. One sacrifice more or less is of very little consequence."

She fortified herself by an application of the smelling-bottle, and opened the note. It ran thus:

"So grieved, dear Lady Lundie, to hear that you are a prisoner in your room! I had taken the opportunity of calling with Mrs. Delamayn, in the hope that I might be able to ask you a question. Will your inexhaustible kindness forgive me if I ask it in writing? Have you had any unexpected news of Mr. Arnold Brinkworth lately? I mean, have you heard any thing about him, which has taken you very much by surprise? I have a serious reason for asking this. I will tell you what it is, the moment you are able to see me. Until then, one word of answer is all I expect. Send word down—Yes, or No. A thousand apologies—and pray get better soon!"

The singular question contained in this note suggested one of two inferences to Lady Lundie's mind. Either Mrs. Glenarm had heard a report of the unexpected return of the married couple to England—or she was in the far more interesting and important position of possessing a clew to the secret of what was going on under the surface at Ham Farm. The phrase used in the note, "I have a serious reason for asking this," appeared to favor the latter of the two interpretations. Impossible as it seemed to be that Mrs. Glenarm could know something about Arnold of which Lady Lundie was in absolute ignorance, her ladyship's curiosity (already powerfully excited by Blanche's mysterious letter) was only to be quieted by obtaining the necessary explanation forthwith, at a personal interview.

"Hopkins," she said, "I must see Mrs. Glenarm."

Hopkins respectfully held up her hands in horror. Company in the bedroom in the present state of her ladyship's health!

"A matter of duty is involved in this, Hopkins. Give me the glass."

Hopkins produced an elegant little hand-mirror. Lady Lundie carefully surveyed herself in it down to the margin of the bedclothes. Above criticism in every respect? Yes—even when the critic was a woman.

"Show Mrs. Glenarm up here."

In a minute or two more the iron-master's widow fluttered into the room—a little over-dressed as usual; and a little profuse in expressions of gratitude for her ladyship's kindness, and of anxiety about her ladyship's health. Lady Lundie endured it as long as she could—then stopped it with a gesture of polite remonstrance, and came to the point.

"Now, my dear—about this question in your note? Is it possible you have heard already that Arnold Brinkworth and his wife have come back from Baden?" Mrs. Glenarm opened her eyes in astonishment. Lady Lundie put it more plainly. "They were to have gone on to Switzerland, you know, for their wedding tour, and they suddenly altered their minds, and came back to England on Sunday last."

"Dear Lady Lundie, it's not that! Have you heard nothing about Mr. Brinkworth except what you have just told me?"

"Nothing."

There was a pause. Mrs. Glenarm toyed hesitatingly with her parasol. Lady Lundie leaned forward in the bed, and looked at her attentively.

"What have you heard about him?" she asked.

Mrs. Glenarm was embarrassed. "It's so difficult to say," she began.

"I can bear any thing but suspense," said Lady Lundie. "Tell me the worst."

Mrs. Glenarm decided to risk it. "Have you never heard," she asked, "that Mr. Brinkworth might possibly have committed himself with another lady before he married Miss Lundie?"

Her ladyship first closed her eyes in horror and then searched blindly on the counterpane for the smelling-bottle. Mrs. Glenarm gave it to her, and waited to see how the invalid bore it before she said any more.

"There are things one must hear," remarked Lady Lundie. "I see an act of duty involved in this. No words can describe how you astonish me. Who told you?"

"Mr. Geoffrey Delamayn told me."

Her ladyship applied for the second time to the smelling-bottle. "Arnold Brinkworth's most intimate friend!" she exclaimed. "He ought to know if any body does. This is dreadful.

Why should Mr. Geoffrey Delamayn tell you?"

"I am going to marry him," answered Mrs. Glenarm. "That is my excuse, dear Lady Lundie, for troubling you in this matter."

Lady Lundie partially opened her eyes in a state of faint bewilderment. "I don't understand," she said. "For Heaven's sake explain yourself!"

"Haven't you heard about the anonymous letters?" asked Mrs. Glenarm.

Yes. Lady Lundie had heard about the letters. But only what the public in general had heard. The name of the lady in the background not mentioned; and Mr. Geoffrey Delamayn assumed to be as innocent as the babe unborn. Any mistake in that assumption? "Give me your hand, my poor dear, and confide it all to me!"

"He is not quite innocent," said Mrs. Glenarm. "He owned to a foolish flirtation—all her doing, no doubt. Of course, I insisted on a distinct explanation. Had she really any claim on him? Not the shadow of a claim. I felt that I only had his word for that—and I told him so. He said he could prove it—he said he knew her to be privately married already. Her husband had disowned and deserted her; she was at the end of her resources; she was desperate enough to attempt any thing. I thought it all very suspicious—until Geoffrey mentioned the man's name. That certainly proved that he had cast off his wife; for I myself knew that he had lately married another person."

Lady Lundie suddenly started up from her pillow—honestly agitated; genuinely alarmed by this time.

"Mr. Delamayn told you the man's name?" she said, breathlessly.

"Yes."

"Do I know it?"

"Don't ask me!"

Lady Lundie fell back on the pillow.

Mrs. Glenarm rose to ring for help. Before she could touch the bell, her ladyship had rallied again.

"Stop!" she cried. "I can confirm it! It's true, Mrs. Glenarm! it's true! Open the silver box on the toilet-table—you will find the key in it. Bring me the top letter. Here! Look at it. I got this from Blanche. Why have they suddenly given up their bridal tour? Why have they gone back to Sir Patrick at Ham Farm? Why have they put me off with an infamous subterfuge to account for it? I felt sure something dreadful had happened. Now I know what it is!" She sank back again, with closed eyes, and repeated the words, in a fierce whisper, to herself. "Now I know what it is!"

Mrs. Glenarm read the letter. The reason given for the suspiciously sudden return of the bride and bridegroom was palpably a subterfuge—and, more remarkable still, the name of Anne Silvester was connected with it. Mrs. Glenarm became strongly agitated on her side.

"This is a confirmation," she said. "Mr. Brinkworth has been found out—the woman is married to him—Geoffrey is free. Oh, my dear friend, what a load of anxiety you have taken off my mind! That vile wretch—"

Lady Lundie suddenly opened her eyes.

"Do you mean," she asked, "the woman who is at the bottom of all the mischief?"

"Yes. I saw her yesterday. She forced herself in at Swanhaven. She called him Geoffrey Delamayn. She declared herself a single woman. She claimed him before my face in the most audacious manner. She shook my faith, Lady Lundie—she shook my faith in Geoffrey!"

"Who is she?"

"Who?" echoed Mrs. Glenarm. "Don't you even know that? Why her name is repeated half a dozen times in this letter!"

Lady Lundie uttered a scream that rang through the room. Mrs. Glenarm started to her feet. The maid appeared at the door in terror. Her ladyship motioned to the woman to withdraw again instantly, and then pointed to Mrs. Glenarm's chair.

"Sit down," she said. "Let me have a minute or two of quiet. I want nothing more."

The silence in the room was unbroken until Lady Lundie spoke again. She asked for Blanche's letter. After reading it carefully, she laid it aside, and fell for a while into deep thought.

"I have done Blanche an injustice!" she exclaimed. "My poor Blanche!"

"You think she knows nothing about it?"

"I am certain of it! You forget, Mrs. Glenarm, that this horrible discovery casts a doubt on my step-daughter's marriage. Do you think, if she knew the truth, she would write of a wretch who has mortally injured her as she writes here? They have put her off with the excuse that she innocently sends to me. I see it as plainly as I see you! Mr. Brinkworth and Sir Patrick are in league to keep us both in the dark. Dear child! I owe her an atonement. If nobody else opens her eyes, I will do it. Sir Patrick shall find that Blanche has a friend in Me!"

A smile—the dangerous smile of an inveterately vindictive woman thoroughly roused—showed itself with a furtive suddenness on her face. Mrs. Glenarm was a little startled. Lady Lundie below the surface—as distinguished from Lady Lundie on the surface—was not a pleasant object to contemplate.

"Pray try to compose yourself," said Mrs. Glenarm. "Dear Lady Lundie, you frighten me!"

The bland surface of her ladyship appeared smoothly once more; drawn back, as it were, over the hidden inner self, which it had left for the moment exposed to view.

"Forgive me for feeling it!" she said, with the patient sweetness which so eminently distinguished her in times of trial. "It falls a little heavily on a poor sick woman—innocent of all suspicion, and insulted by the most heartless neglect. Don't let me distress you. I shall rally, my dear; I shall rally! In this dreadful calamity—this abyss of crime and misery and deceit—I have no one to depend on but myself. For Blanche's sake, the whole thing must be cleared up—probed, my dear, probed to the depths. Blanche must take a position that is worthy of her. Blanche must insist on her rights, under My protection. Never mind what I suffer, or what I sacrifice. There is a work of justice for poor weak Me to do. It shall be done!" said her ladyship, fanning herself with an aspect of illimitable resolution. "It shall be done!"

"But, Lady Lundie what can you do? They are all away in the south. And as for that abominable woman—"

Lady Lundie touched Mrs. Glenarm on the shoulder with her fan.

"I have my surprise in store, dear friend, as well as you. That abominable woman was employed as Blanche's governess in this house. Wait! that is not all. She left us suddenly—ran away—on the pretense of being privately married. I know where she went. I can trace what she did. I can find out who was with her. I can follow Mr. Brinkworth's proceedings, behind Mr. Brinkworth's back. I can search out the truth, without depending on people compromised in this black business, whose interest it is to deceive me. And I will do it to-day!" She closed the fan with a sharp snap of triumph, and settled herself on the pillow in placid enjoyment of her dear friend's surprise.

Mrs. Glenarm drew confidentially closer to the bedside. "How can you manage it?" she asked, eagerly. "Don't think me curious. I have my interest, too, in getting at the truth. Don't leave me out of it, pray!"

"Can you come back to-morrow, at this time?"

"Yes! yes!"

"Come, then—and you shall know."

"Can I be of any use?"

"Not at present."

"Can my uncle be of any use?"

"Do you know where to communicate with Captain Newenden?"

"Yes—he is staying with some friends in Sussex."

"We may possibly want his assistance. I can't tell yet. Don't keep Mrs. Delamayn waiting any longer, my dear. I shall expect you to-morrow."

They exchanged an affectionate embrace. Lady Lundie was left alone.

Her ladyship resigned herself to meditation, with frowning brow and close-shut lips. She looked her full age, and a year or two more, as she lay thinking, with her head on her hand, and her elbow on the pillow. After committing herself to the physician (and to the red lavender draught) the commonest regard for consistency made it necessary that she should keep her bed for that day. And yet it was essential that the proposed inquiries should be instantly set on foot. On the one hand, the problem was not an easy one to solve; on the other, her ladyship was not an easy one to beat. How to send for the landlady at Craig Fernie, without exciting any special suspicion or remark—was the question before her. In less than five minutes she had looked back into her memory of current events at Windygates—and had solved it.

Her first proceeding was to ring the bell for her maid.

"I am afraid I frightened you, Hopkins. The state of my nerves. Mrs. Glenarm was a little sudden with some news that surprised me. I am better now—and able to attend to the household matters. There is a mistake in the butcher's account. Send the cook here."

She took up the domestic ledger and the kitchen report; corrected the butcher; cautioned the cook; and disposed of all arrears of domestic business before Hopkins was summoned again. Having, in this way, dextrously prevented the woman from connecting any thing that her mistress said or did, after Mrs. Glenarm's departure, with any thing that might have passed during Mrs. Glenarm's visit, Lady Lundie felt herself at liberty to pave the way for the investigation on which she was determined to enter before she slept that night.

"So much for the indoor arrangements," she said. "You must be my prime minister, Hopkins, while I lie helpless here. Is there any thing wanted by the people out of doors? The coachman? The gardener?"

"I have just seen the gardener, my lady. He came with last week's accounts. I told him he couldn't see your ladyship to-day."

"Quite right. Had he any report to make?"

"No, my lady."

"Surely, there was something I wanted to say to him—or to somebody else? My memorandum-book, Hopkins. In the basket, on that chair. Why wasn't the basket placed by my bedside?"

Hopkins brought the memorandum-book. Lady Lundie consulted it (without the slightest necessity), with the same masterly gravity exhibited by the doctor when he wrote her prescription (without the slightest necessity also).

"Here it is," she said, recovering the lost remembrance. "Not the gardener, but the gardener's wife. A memorandum to speak to her about Mrs. Inchbare. Observe, Hopkins, the association of ideas. Mrs. Inchbare is associated with the poultry; the poultry are associated with the gardener's wife; the gardener's wife is associated with the gardener—and so the gardener gets into my head. Do you see it? I am always trying to improve your mind. You do see it? Very well. Now about Mrs. Inchbare? Has she been here again?"

"No, my lady."

"I am not at all sure, Hopkins, that I was right in declining to consider the message Mrs. Inchbare sent to me about the poultry. Why shouldn't she offer to take any fowls that I can spare off my hands? She is a respectable woman; and it is important to me to live on good terms with al my neighbors, great and small. Has she got a poultry-yard of her own at Craig Fernie?"

"Yes, my lady. And beautifully kept, I am told."

"I really don't see—on reflection, Hopkins—why I should hesitate to deal with Mrs. Inchbare. (I don't think it beneath me to sell the game killed on my estate to the poulterer.) What was it she wanted to buy? Some of my black Spanish fowls?"

"Yes, my lady. Your ladyship's black Spaniards are famous all round the neighborhood. Nobody has got the breed. And Mrs. Inchbare—"

"Wants to share the distinction of having the breed with me," said Lady Lundie. "I won't appear ungracious. I will see her myself, as soon as I am a little better, and tell her that I have changed my mind. Send one of the men to Craig Fernie with a message. I can't keep a trifling matter of this sort in my memory—send him at once, or I may forget it. He is to say I am willing to see Mrs. Inchbare, about the fowls, the first time she finds it convenient to come this way."

"I am afraid, my lady—Mrs. Inchbare's heart is so set on the black Spaniards—she will find it convenient to come this way at once as fast as her feet can carry her."

"In that case, you must take her to the gardener's wife. Say she is to have some eggs—on condition, of course, of paying the price for them. If she does come, mind I hear of it."

Hopkins withdrew. Hopkins's mistress reclined on her comfortable pillows and fanned herself gently. The vindictive smile reappeared on her face. "I fancy I shall be well enough to see Mrs. Inchbare," she thought to herself. "And it is just possible that the conversation may get beyond the relative merits of her poultry-yard and mine."

A lapse of little more than two hours proved Hopkins's estimate of the latent enthusiasm in Mrs. Inchbare's character to have been correctly formed. The eager landlady appeared at Windygates on the heels of the returning servant. Among the long list of human weaknesses, a passion for poultry seems to have its practical advantages (in the shape of eggs) as compared with the more occult frenzies for collecting snuff-boxes and fiddles, and amassing autographs and old postage-stamps. When the mistress of Craig Fernie was duly announced to the mistress of Windygates, Lady Lundie developed a sense of humor for the first time in her life. Her ladyship was feebly merry (the result, no doubt, of the exhilarating properties of the red lavender draught) on the subject of Mrs. Inchbare and the Spanish fowls.

"Most ridiculous, Hopkins! This poor woman must be suffering from a determination of poultry to the brain. Ill as I am, I should have thought that nothing could amuse me. But, really, this good creature starting up, and rushing here, as you say, as fast as her feet can carry her—it's impossible to resist it! I positively think I must see Mrs. Inchbare. With my active habits, this imprisonment to my room is dreadful. I can neither sleep nor read. Any thing, Hopkins, to divert my mind from myself: It's easy to get rid of her if she is too much for me. Send her up."

Mrs. Inchbare made her appearance, courtesying deferentially; amazed at the condescension which admitted her within the hallowed precincts of Lady Lundie's room.

"Take a chair," said her ladyship, graciously. "I am suffering from illness, as you perceive."

"My certie! sick or well, yer leddyship's a braw sight to see!" returned Mrs. Inchbare profoundly impressed by the elegant costume which illness assumes when illness appears in the regions of high life.

"I am far from being in a fit state to receive any body," proceeded Lady Lundie. "But I had a motive for wishing to speak to you when you next came to my house. I failed to treat a proposal you made to me, a short time since, in a friendly and neighborly way. I beg you to understand that I regret having forgotten the consideration due from a person in my position to a person in yours. I am obliged to say this under very unusual circumstances," added her ladyship, with a glance round her magnificent bedroom, "through your unexpected promptitude in favoring me with a call. You have lost no time, Mrs. Inchbare, in profiting by the message which I had the pleasure of sending to you."

"Eh, my leddy, I wasna' that sure (yer leddyship having ance changed yer mind) but that ye might e'en change again if I failed to strike, as they say, while the iron's het. I crave yer pardon, I'm sure, if I ha' been ower hasty. The pride o' my hairt's in my powltry—and the black Spaniards' (as they ca' them) are a sair temptation to me to break the tenth commandment, sae lang as they're a' in yer leddyship's possession, and nane o' them in mine."

"I am shocked to hear that I have been the innocent cause of your falling into temptation, Mrs. Inchbare! Make your proposal—and I shall be happy to meet it, if I can."

"I must e'en be content wi' what yer leddyship will condescend on. A haitch o' eggs if I can come by naething else."

"There is something else you would prefer to a hatch of eggs?"

"I wad prefer," said Mrs. Inchbare, modestly, "a cock and twa pullets."

"Open the case on the table behind you," said Lady Lundie, "and you will find some writing paper inside. Give me a sheet of it—and the pencil out of the tray."

Eagerly watched by Mrs. Inchbare, she wrote an order to the poultry-woman, and held it out with a gracious smile.

"Take that to the gardener's wife. If you agree with her about the price, you can have the cock and the two pullets."

Mrs. Inchbare opened her lips—no doubt to express the utmost extremity of human gratitude. Before she had said three words, Lady Lundie's impatience to reach the end which she had kept in view from the time when Mrs. Glenarm had left the house burst the bounds which had successfully restrained it thus far. Stopping the landlady without ceremony, she fairly forced the conversation to the subject of Anne Silvester's proceedings at the Craig Fernie inn.

"How are you getting on at the hotel, Mrs. Inchbare? Plenty of tourists, I suppose, at this time of year?"

"Full, my leddy (praise Providence), frae the basement to the ceiling."

"You had a visitor, I think, some time since of whom I know something? A person—" She paused, and put a strong constraint on herself. There was no alternative but to yield to the hard necessity of making her inquiry intelligible. "A lady," she added, "who came to you about the middle of last month."

"Could yer leddyship condescend on her name?"

Lady Lundie put a still stronger constraint on herself. "Silvester," she said, sharply.

"Presairve us a'!" cried Mrs. Inchbare. "It will never be the same that cam' driftin' in by hersel'—wi' a bit bag in her hand, and a husband left daidling an hour or mair on the road behind her?"

"I have no doubt it is the same."

"Will she be a freend o' yer leddyship's?" asked Mrs. Inchbare, feeling her ground cautiously.

"Certainly not!" said Lady Lundie. "I felt a passing curiosity about her—nothing more."

Mrs. Inchbare looked relieved. "To tell ye truth, my leddy, there was nae love lost between us. She had a maisterfu' temper o' her ain—and I was weel pleased when I'd seen the last of her."

"I can quite understand that, Mrs. Inchbare—I know something of her temper myself. Did I understand you to say that she came to your hotel alone, and that her husband joined her shortly afterward?"

"E'en sae, yer leddyship. I was no' free to gi' her house-room in the hottle till her husband daidled in at her heels and answered for her."

"I fancy I must have seen her husband," said Lady Lundie. "What sort of a man was he?"

Mrs. Inchbare replied in much the same words which she had used in answering the similar question put by Sir Patrick.

"Eh! he was ower young for the like o' her. A pratty man, my leddy—betwixt tall and short; wi' bonny brown eyes and cheeks, and fine coal-blaik hair. A nice douce-spoken lad. I hae naething to say against him—except that he cam' late one day, and took leg-bail betimes the next morning, and left madam behind, a load on my hands."

The answer produced precisely the same effect on Lady Lundie which it had produced on Sir Patrick. She, also, felt that it was too vaguely like too many young men of no uncommon humor and complexion to be relied on. But her ladyship possessed one immense advantage over her brother-in-law in attempting to arrive at the truth. She suspected Arnold—and it was possible, in her case, to assist Mrs. Inchbare's memory by hints contributed from her own superior resources of experience and observation.

"Had he any thing about him of the look and way of a sailor?" she asked. "And did you notice, when you spoke to him, that he had a habit of playing with a locket on his watch-chain?"

"There he is, het aff to a T!" cried Mrs. Inchbare. "Yer leddyship's weel acquented wi' him—there's nae doot o' that."

"I thought I had seen him," said Lady Lundie. "A modest, well-behaved young man, Mrs. Inchbare, as you say. Don't let me keep you any longer from the poultry-yard. I am transgressing the doctor's orders in seeing any body. We quite understand each other now, don't we? Very glad to have seen you. Good-evening."

So she dismissed Mrs. Inchbare, when Mrs. Inchbare had served her purpose.

Most women, in her position, would have been content with the information which she had now obtained. But Lady Lundie—having a man like Sir Patrick to deal with—determined to be doubly sure of her facts before she ventured on interfering at Ham Farm. She had learned from Mrs. Inchbare that the so-called husband of Anne Silvester had joined her at Craig Fernie on the day when she arrived at the inn, and had left her again the next morning. Anne had made her escape from Windygates on the occasion of the lawn-party—that is to say, on the fourteenth of August. On the same day Arnold Brinkworth had taken his departure for the purpose of visiting the Scotch property left to him by his aunt. If Mrs. Inchbare was to be depended on, he must have gone to Craig Fernie instead of going to his appointed destination—and must, therefore, have arrived to visit his house and lands one day later than the day which he had originally set apart for that purpose. If this fact could be proved, on the testimony of a disinterested witness, the case against Arnold would be strengthened tenfold; and Lady Lundie might act on her discovery with something like a certainty that her information was to be relied on.

After a little consideration she decided on sending a messenger with a note of inquiry addressed to Arnold's steward. The apology she invented to excuse and account for the strangeness of the proposed question, referred it to a little family discussion as to the exact date of Arnold's arrival at his estate, and to a friendly wager in which the difference of opinion had ended. If the steward could state whether his employer had arrived on the fourteenth or on the fifteenth of August, that was all that would be wanted to decide the question in dispute.

Having written in those terms, Lady Lundie gave the necessary directions for having the note delivered at the earliest possible hour on the next morning; the messenger being ordered to make his way back to Windygates by the first return train on the same day.

This arranged, her ladyship was free to refresh herself with another dose of the red lavender draught, and to sleep the sleep of the just who close their eyes with the composing conviction that they have done their duty.

The events of the next day at Windygates succeeded each other in due course, as follows:

The post arrived, and brought no reply from Sir Patrick. Lady Lundie entered that incident on her mental register of debts owed by her brother-in-law—to be paid, with interest, when the day of reckoning came.

Next in order occurred the return of the messenger with the steward's answer.

He had referred to his Diary; and he had discovered that Mr. Brinkworth had written beforehand to announce his arrival at his estate for the fourteenth of August—but that he had not actually appeared until the fifteenth. The one discovery needed to substantiate Mrs. Inchbare's evidence being now in Lady Lundie's possession, she decided to allow another day to pass—on the chance that Sir Patrick might alter his mind, and write to her. If no letter arrived, and if nothing more was received from Blanche, she resolved to leave Windygates by the next morning's train, and to try the bold experiment of personal interference at Ham Farm.

The third in the succession of events was the appearance of the doctor to pay his professional visit.

A severe shock awaited him. He found his patient cured by the draught! It was contrary to all rule and precedent; it savored of quackery—the red lavender had no business to do what the red lavender had done—but there she was, nevertheless, up and dressed, and contemplating a journey to London on the next day but one. "An act of duty, doctor, is involved in this—whatever the sacrifice, I must go!" No other explanation could be obtained. The patient was plainly determined—nothing remained for the physician but to retreat with unimpaired dignity and a paid fee. He did it. "Our art," he explained to Lady Lundie in confidence, "is nothing, after all, but a choice between alternatives. For instance. I see you—not cured, as you think—but sustained by abnormal excitement. I have to ask which is the least of the two evils—to risk letting you travel, or to irritate you by keeping you at home. With your constitution, we must risk the journey. Be careful to keep the window of the carriage up on the side on which the wind blows. Let the extremities be moderately warm, and the mind easy—and pray don't omit to provide yourself with a second bottle of the Mixture before you start." He made his bow, as before—he slipped two guineas into his pocket, as before—and he went his way, as before, with an approving conscience, in the character of a physician who had done his duty. (What an enviable profession is Medicine! And why don't we all belong to it?)

The last of the events was the arrival of Mrs. Glenarm.

"Well?" she began, eagerly, "what news?"

The narrative of her ladyship's discoveries—recited at full length; and the announcement of her ladyship's resolution—declared in the most uncompromising terms—raised Mrs. Glenarm's excitement to the highest pitch.

"You go to town on Saturday?" she said. "I will go with you. Ever since that woman declared she should be in London before me, I have been dying to hasten my journey—and it is such an opportunity to go with you! I can easily manage it. My uncle and I were to have met in London, early next week, for the foot-race. I have only to write and tell him of my change of plans.—By-the-by, talking of my uncle, I have heard, since I saw you, from the lawyers at Perth."

"More anonymous letters?"

"One more—received by the lawyers this time. My unknown correspondent has written to them to withdraw his proposal, and to announce that he has left Perth. The lawyers recommended me to stop my uncle from spending money uselessly in employing the London police. I have forwarded their letter to the captain; and he will probably be in town to see his solicitors as soon as I get there with you. So much for what I have done in this matter. Dear Lady Lundie—when we are at our journey's end, what do you mean to do?"

"My course is plain," answered her ladyship, calmly. "Sir Patrick will hear from me, on Sunday morning next, at Ham Farm."

"Telling him what you have found out?"

"Certainly not! Telling him that I find myself called to London by business, and that I propose paying him a short visit on Monday next."

"Of course, he must receive you?"

"I think there is no doubt of that. Even his hatred of his brother's widow can hardly go to the length—after leaving my letter unanswered—of closing his doors against me next."

"How will you manage it when you get there?"

"When I get there, my dear, I shall be breathing an atmosphere of treachery and deceit; and, for my poor child's sake (abhorrent as all dissimulation is to me), I must be careful what I do. Not a word will escape my lips until I have first seen Blanche in private. However painful it may be, I shall not shrink from my duty, if my duty compels me to open her eyes to the truth. Sir Patrick and Mr. Brinkworth will have somebody else besides an inexperienced young creature to deal with on Monday next. I shall be there."

With that formidable announcement, Lady Lundie closed the conversation; and Mrs. Glenarm rose to take her leave.

"We meet at the Junction, dear Lady Lundie?"

"At the Junction, on Saturday."

ELEVENTH SCENE.—SIR PATRICK'S HOUSE.

CHAPTER THE FORTY-SECOND.

THE SMOKING-ROOM WINDOW.

"I CAN'T believe it! I won't believe it! You're trying to part me from my husband—you're trying to set me against my dearest friend. It's infamous. It's horrible. What have I done to you? Oh, my head! my head! Are you trying to drive me mad?"

Pale and wild; her hands twisted in her hair; her feet hurrying her aimlessly to and fro in the room—so Blanche answered her step-mother, when the object of Lady Lundie's pilgrimage had been accomplished, and the cruel truth had been plainly told.

Her ladyship sat, superbly composed, looking out through the window at the placid landscape of woods and fields which surrounded Ham Farm.

"I was prepared for this outbreak," she said, sadly. "These wild words relieve your overburdened heart, my poor child. I can wait, Blanche—I can wait!"

Blanche stopped, and confronted Lady Lundie.

"You and I never liked each other," she said. "I wrote you a pert letter from this place. I have always taken Anne's part against you. I have shown you plainly—rudely, I dare say—that I was glad to be married and get away from you. This is not your revenge, is it?"

"Oh, Blanche, Blanche, what thoughts to think! what words to say! I can only pray for you."

"I am mad, Lady Lundie. You bear with mad people. Bear with me. I have been hardly more than a fortnight married. I love him—I love her—with all my heart. Remember what you have told me about them. Remember! remember! remember!"

She reiterated the words with a low cry of pain. Her hands went up to her head again; and she returned restlessly to pacing this way and that in the room.

Lady Lundie tried the effect of a gentle remonstrance. "For your own sake," she said, "don't persist in estranging yourself from me. In this dreadful trial, I am the only friend you have."

Blanche came back to her step-mother's chair; and looked at her steadily, in silence. Lady Lundie submitted to inspection—and bore it perfectly.

"Look into my heart," she said. "Blanche! it bleeds for you!"

Blanche heard, without heeding. Her mind was painfully intent on its own thoughts. "You are a religious woman," she said, abruptly. "Will you swear on your Bible, that what you told me is true?"

"My Bible!" repeated Lady Lundie with sorrowful emphasis. "Oh, my child! have you no part in that precious inheritance? Is it not your Bible, too?"

A momentary triumph showed itself in Blanche's face. "You daren't swear it!" she said. "That's enough for me!"

She turned away scornfully. Lady Lundie caught her by the hand, and drew her sharply back. The suffering saint disappeared, and the woman who was no longer to be trifled with took her place.

"There must be an end to this," she said. "You don't believe what I have told you. Have you courage enough to put it to the test?"

Blanche started, and released her hand. She trembled a little. There was a horrible certainty of conviction expressed in Lady Lundie's sudden change of manner.

"How?" she asked.

"You shall see. Tell me the truth, on your side, first. Where is Sir Patrick? Is he really out, as his servant told me?"

"Yes. He is out with the farm bailiff. You have taken us all by surprise. You wrote that we were to expect you by the next train."

"When does the next train arrive? It is eleven o'clock now."

"Between one and two."

"Sir Patrick will not be back till then?"

"Not till then."

"Where is Mr. Brinkworth?"

"My husband?"

"Your husband—if you like. Is he out, too?"

"He is in the smoking-room."

"Do you mean the long room, built out from the back of the house?"

"Yes."

"Come down stairs at once with me."

Blanche advanced a step—and drew back. "What do you want of me?" she asked, inspired by a sudden distrust.

Lady Lundie turned round, and looked at her impatiently.

"Can't you see yet," she said, sharply, "that your interest and my interest in this matter are one? What have I told you?"

"Don't repeat it!"

"I must repeat it! I have told you that Arnold Brinkworth was privately at Craig Fernie, with Miss Silvester, in the acknowledged character of her husband—when we supposed him to be visiting the estate left him by his aunt. You refuse to believe it—and I am about to put it to the proof. Is it your interest or is it not, to know whether this man deserves the blind belief that you place in him?"

Blanche trembled from head to foot, and made no reply.

"I am going into the garden, to speak to Mr. Brinkworth through the smoking-room window," pursued her ladyship. "Have you the courage to come with me; to wait behind out of sight; and to hear what he says with his own lips? I am not afraid of putting it to that test. Are you?"

The tone in which she asked the question roused Blanche's spirit.

"If I believed him to be guilty," she said, resolutely, "I should not have the courage. I believe him to be innocent. Lead the way, Lady Lundie, as soon as you please."

They left the room—Blanche's own room at Ham Farm—and descended to the hall. Lady Lundie stopped, and consulted the railway time-table hanging near the house-door.

"There is a train to London at a quarter to twelve," she said. "How long does it take to walk to the station?"

"Why do you ask?"

"You will soon know. Answer my question."

"It's a walk of twenty minutes to the station."

Lady Lundie referred to her watch. "There will be just time," she said.

"Time for what?"

"Come into the garden."

With that answer, she led the way out

The smoking-room projected at right angles from the wall of the house, in an oblong form—with a bow-window at the farther end, looking into the garden. Before she turned the corner, and showed herself within the range of view from the window Lady Lundie looked back, and signed to Blanche to wait behind the angle of the wall. Blanche waited.

The next instant she heard the voices in conversation through the open window. Arnold's voice was the first that spoke.

"Lady Lundie! Why, we didn't expect you till luncheon time!"

Lady Lundie was ready with her answer.

"I was able to leave town earlier than I had anticipated. Don't put out your cigar; and don't move. I am not coming in."

The quick interchange of question and answer went on; every word being audible in the perfect stillness of the place. Arnold was the next to speak.

"Have you seen Blanche?"

"Blanche is getting ready to go out with me. We mean to have a walk together. I have many things to say to her. Before we go, I have something to say to you."

"Is it any thing very serious?"

"It is most serious."

"About me?"

"About you. I know where you went on the evening of my lawn-party at Windygates—you went to Craig Fernie."

"Good Heavens! how did you find out—?"

"I know whom you went to meet—Miss Silvester. I know what is said of you and of her—you are man and wife."

"Hush! don't speak so loud. Somebody may hear you!"

"What does it matter if they do? I am the only person whom you have kept out of the secret. You all of you know it here."

"Nothing of the sort! Blanche doesn't know it."

"What! Neither you nor Sir Patrick has told Blanche of the situation you stand in at this moment?"

"Not yet. Sir Patrick leaves it to me. I haven't been able to bring myself to do it. Don't say a word, I entreat you. I don't know how Blanche may interpret it. Her friend is expected in London to-morrow. I want to wait till Sir Patrick can bring them together. Her friend will break it to her better than I can. It's my notion. Sir Patrick thinks it a good one. Stop! you're not going away already?"

"She will be here to look for me if I stay any longer."

"One word! I want to know—"

"You shall know later in the day."

Her ladyship appeared again round the angle of the wall. The next words that passed were words spoken in a whisper.

"Are you satisfied now, Blanche?"

"Have you mercy enough left, Lady Lundie, to take me away from this house?"

"My dear child! Why else did I look at the time-table in the hall?"

CHAPTER THE FORTY-THIRD.

THE EXPLOSION.

ARNOLD'S mind was far from easy when he was left by himself again in the smoking-room.

After wasting some time in vainly trying to guess at the source from which Lady Lundie had derived her information, he put on his hat, and took the direction which led to Blanche's favorite walk at Ham Farm. Without absolutely distrusting her ladyship's discretion, the idea had occurred to him that he would do well to join his wife and her step-mother. By making a third at the interview between them, he might prevent the conversation from assuming a perilously confidential turn.

The search for the ladies proved useless. They had not taken the direction in which he supposed them to have gone.

He returned to the smoking-room, and composed himself to wait for events as patiently as he might. In this passive position—with his thoughts still running on Lady Lundie—his memory reverted to a brief conversation between Sir Patrick and himself, occasioned, on the previous day, by her ladyship's announcement of her proposed visit to Ham Farm. Sir Patrick had at once expressed his conviction that his sister-in-law's journey south had some acknowledged purpose at the bottom of it.

"I am not at all sure, Arnold" (he had said), "that I have done wisely in leaving her letter unanswered. And I am strongly disposed to think that the safest course will be to take her into the secret when she comes to-morrow. We can't help the position in which we are placed. It was impossible (without admitting your wife to our confidence) to prevent Blanche from writing that unlucky letter to her—and, even if we had prevented it, she must have heard in other ways of your return to England. I don't doubt my own discretion, so far; and I don't doubt the convenience of keeping her in the dark, as a means of keeping her from meddling in this business of yours, until I have had time to set it right. But she may, by some unlucky accident, discover the truth for herself—and, in that case, I strongly distrust the influence which she might attempt to exercise on Blanche's mind."

Those were the words—and what had happened on the day after they had been spoken? Lady Lundie had discovered the truth; and she was, at that moment, alone somewhere with Blanche. Arnold took up his hat once more, and set forth on the search for the ladies in another direction.

The second expedition was as fruitless as the first. Nothing was to be seen, and nothing was to be heard, of Lady Lundie and Blanche.

Arnold's watch told him that it was not far from the time when Sir Patrick might be expected to return. In all probability, while he had been looking for them, the ladies had gone back by some other way to the house. He entered the rooms on the ground-floor, one after another. They were all empty. He went up stairs, and knocked at the door of Blanche's room. There was no answer. He opened the door and looked in. The room was empty, like the rooms down stairs. But, close to the entrance, there was a trifling circumstance to attract notice, in the shape of a note lying on the carpet. He picked it up, and saw that it was addressed to him in the handwriting of his wife.

He opened it. The note began, without the usual form of address, in these words:

"I know the abominable secret that you and my uncle have hidden from me. I know your infamy, and her infamy, and the position in which, thanks to you and to her, I now stand. Reproaches would be wasted words, addressed to such a man as you are. I write these lines to tell you that I have placed myself under my step-mother's protection in London. It is useless to attempt to follow me. Others will find out whether the ceremony of marriage which you went through with me is binding on you or not. For myself, I know enough already. I have gone, never to come back, and never to let you see me again.—Blanche."

Hurrying headlong down the stairs with but one clear idea in his mind—the idea of instantly following his wife—Arnold encountered Sir Patrick, standing by a table in the hall, on which cards and notes left by visitors were usually placed, with an open letter in his hand. Seeing in an instant what had happened, he threw one of his arms round Arnold, and stopped him at the house-door.

"You are a man," he said, firmly. "Bear it like a man."

Arnold's head fell on the shoulder of his kind old friend. He burst into tears.

Sir Patrick let the irrepressible outbreak of grief have its way. In those first moments, silence was mercy. He said nothing. The letter which he had been reading (from Lady Lundie, it is needless to say), dropped unheeded at his feet.

Arnold lifted his head, and dashed away the tears.

"I am ashamed of myself," he said. "Let me go."

"Wrong, my poor fellow—doubly wrong!" returned Sir Patrick. "There is no shame in shedding such tears as those. And there is nothing to be done by leaving me."

"I must and will see her!"

"Read that," said Sir Patrick, pointing to the letter on the floor. "See your wife? Your wife is with the woman who has written those lines. Read them."

Arnold read them.

"DEAR SIR PATRICK,—If you had honored me with your confidence, I should have been happy to consult you before I interfered to rescue Blanche from the position in which Mr. Brinkworth has placed her. As it is, your late brother's child is under my protection at my house in London. If you attempt to exercise your authority, it must be by main force—I will submit to nothing less. If Mr. Brinkworth attempts to exercise his authority, he shall establish his right to do so (if he can) in a police-court.

"Very truly yours, JULIA LUNDIE."

Arnold's resolution was not to be shaken even by this. "What do I care," he burst out, hotly, "whether I am dragged through the streets by the police or not! I will see my wife. I will clear myself of the horrible suspicion she has about me. You have shown me your letter. Look at mine!"

Sir Patrick's clear sense saw the wild words that Blanche had written in their true light.

"Do you hold your wife responsible for that letter?" he asked. "I see her step-mother in every line of it. You descend to something unworthy of you, if you seriously defend yourself against this! You can't see it? You persist in holding to your own view? Write, then. You can't get to her—your letter may. No! When you leave this house, you leave it with me. I have conceded something on my side, in allowing you to write. I insist on your conceding something, on your side, in return. Come into the library! I answer for setting things right between you and Blanche, if you will place your interests in my hands. Do you trust me or not?"

Arnold yielded. They went into the library together. Sir Patrick pointed to the writing-table. "Relieve your mind there," he said. "And let me find you a reasonable man again when I come back."

When he returned to the library the letter was written; and Arnold's mind was so far relieved—for the time at least.

"I shall take your letter to Blanche myself," said Sir Patrick, "by the train that leaves for London in half an hour's time."

"You will let me go with you?"

"Not to-day. I shall be back this evening to dinner. You shall hear all that has happened; and you shall accompany me to London to-morrow—if I find it necessary to make any lengthened stay there. Between this and then, after the shock that you have suffered, you will do well to be quiet here. Be satisfied with my assurance that Blanche shall have your letter. I will force my authority on her step-mother to that extent (if her step-mother resists) without scruple. The respect in which I hold the sex only lasts as long as the sex deserves it—and does not extend to Lady Lundie. There is no advantage that a man can take of a woman which I am not fully prepared to take of my sister-in-law."

With that characteristic farewell, he shook hands with Arnold, and departed for the station.

At seven o'clock the dinner was on the table. At seven o'clock Sir Patrick came down stairs to eat it, as perfectly dressed as usual, and as composed as if nothing had happened.

"She has got your letter," he whispered, as he took Arnold's arm, and led him into the dining-room.

"Did she say any thing?"

"Not a word."

"How did she look?"

"As she ought to look—sorry for what she has done."

The dinner began. As a matter of necessity, the subject of Sir Patrick's expedition was dropped while the servants were in the room—to be regularly taken up again by Arnold in the intervals between the courses. He began when the soup was taken away.

"I confess I had hoped to see Blanche come back with you!" he said, sadly enough.

"In other words," returned Sir Patrick, "you forgot the native obstinacy of the sex. Blanche is beginning to feel that she has been wrong. What is the necessary consequence? She naturally persists in being wrong. Let her alone, and leave your letter to have its effect. The serious difficulties in our way don't rest with Blanche. Content yourself with knowing that."

The fish came in, and Arnold was silenced—until his next opportunity came with the next interval in the course of the dinner.

"What are the difficulties?" he asked

"The difficulties are my difficulties and yours," answered Sir Patrick. "My difficulty is, that I can't assert my authority, as guardian, if I assume my niece (as I do) to be a married woman. Your difficulty is, that you can't assert your authority as her husband, until it is distinctly proved that you and Miss Silvester are not man and wife. Lady Lundie was perfectly aware that she would place us in that position, when she removed Blanche from this house. She has cross-examined Mrs. Inchbare; she has written to your steward for the date of your arrival at your estate; she has done every thing, calculated every thing, and foreseen every thing—except my excellent temper. The one mistake she has made, is in thinking she could get the better of that. No, my dear boy! My trump card is my temper. I keep it in my hand, Arnold—I keep it in my hand!"

The next course came in—and there was an end of the subject again. Sir Patrick enjoyed his mutton, and entered on a long and interesting narrative of the history of some rare white Burgundy on the table imported by himself. Arnold resolutely resumed the discussion with the departure of the mutton.

"It seems to be a dead lock," he said.

"No slang!" retorted Sir Patrick.

"For Heaven's sake, Sir, consider my anxiety, and tell me what you propose to do!"

"I propose to take you to London with me to-morrow, on this condition—that you promise me, on your word of honor, not to attempt to see your wife before Saturday next."

"I shall see her then?"

"If you give me your promise."

"I do! I do!"

The next course came in. Sir Patrick entered on the question of the merits of the partridge, viewed as an eatable bird, "By himself, Arnold—plainly roasted, and tested on his own merits—an overrated bird. Being too fond of shooting him in this country, we become too fond of eating him next. Properly understood, he is a vehicle for sauce and truffles—nothing more. Or no—that is hardly doing him justice. I am bound to add that he is honorably associated with the famous French receipt for cooking an olive. Do you know it?"

There was an end of the bird; there was an end of the jelly. Arnold got his next chance—and took it.

"What is to be done in London to-morrow?" he asked.

"To-morrow," answered Sir Patrick, "is a memorable day in our calendar. To-morrow is Tuesday—the day on which I am to see Miss Silvester."

Arnold set down the glass of wine which he was just raising to his lips.

"After what has happened," he said, "I can hardly bear to hear her name mentioned. Miss Silvester has parted me from my wife."

"Miss Silvester may atone for that, Arnold, by uniting you again."

"She has been the ruin of me so far."

"She may be the salvation of you yet."

The cheese came in; and Sir Patrick returned to the Art of Cookery.

"Do you know the receipt for cooking an olive, Arnold?"

"No."

"What does the new generation know? It knows how to row, how to shoot, how to play at cricket, and how to bat. When it has lost its muscle and lost its money—that is to say, when it has grown old—what a generation it will be! It doesn't matter: I sha'n't live to see it. Are you listening, Arnold?"

"Yes, Sir."

"How to cook an olive! Put an olive into a lark, put a lark into a quail; put a quail into a plover; put a plover into a partridge; put a partridge into a pheasant; put a pheasant into a turkey. Good. First, partially roast, then carefully stew—until all is thoroughly done down to the olive. Good again. Next, open the window. Throw out the turkey, the pheasant, the partridge, the plover, the quail, and the lark. Then, eat the olive. The dish is expensive, but (we have it on the highest authority) well worth the sacrifice. The quintessence of the flavor of six birds, concentrated in one olive. Grand idea! Try another glass of the white Burgundy, Arnold."

At last the servants left them—with the wine and dessert on the table.

"I have borne it as long as I can, Sir," said Arnold. "Add to all your kindness to me by telling me at once what happened at Lady Lundie's."

It was a chilly evening. A bright wood fire was burning in the room. Sir Patrick drew his chair to the fire.

"This is exactly what happened," he said. "I found company at Lady Lundie's, to begin with. Two perfect strangers to me. Captain Newenden, and his niece, Mrs. Glenarm. Lady Lundie offered to see me in another room; the two strangers offered to withdraw. I declined both proposals. First check to her ladyship! She has reckoned throughout, Arnold, on our being afraid to face public opinion. I showed her at starting that we were as ready to face it as she was. 'I always accept what the French call accomplished facts,' I said. 'You have brought matters to a crisis, Lady Lundie. So let it be. I have a word to say to my niece (in your presence, if you like); and I have another word to say to you afterward—without presuming to disturb your guests.' The guests sat down again (both naturally devoured by curiosity). Could her ladyship decently refuse me an interview with my own niece, while two witnesses were looking on? Impossible. I saw Blanche (Lady Lundie being present, it is needless to say) in the back drawing-room. I gave her your letter; I said a good word for you; I saw that she was sorry, though she wouldn't own it—and that was enough. We went back into the front drawing-room. I had not spoken five words on our side of the question before it appeared, to my astonishment and delight, that Captain Newenden was in the house on the very question that had brought me into the house—the question of you and Miss Silvester. My business, in the interests of my niece, was to deny your marriage to the lady. His business, in the interests of his niece, was to assert your marriage to the lady. To the unutterable disgust of the two women, we joined issue, in the most friendly manner, on the spot. 'Charmed to have the pleasure of meeting you, Captain Newenden.'—'Delighted to have the honor of making your acquaintance, Sir Patrick.'—'I think we can settle this in two minutes?'—'My own idea perfectly expressed.'—'State your position, Captain.'—'With the greatest pleasure. Here is my niece, Mrs. Glenarm, engaged to marry Mr. Geoffrey Delamayn. All very well, but there happens to be an obstacle—in the shape of a lady. Do I put it plainly?'—'You put it admirably, Captain; but for the loss to the British navy, you ought to have been a lawyer. Pray, go on.'—'You are too good, Sir Patrick. I resume. Mr. Delamayn asserts that this person in the back-ground has no claim on him, and backs his assertion by declaring that she is married already to Mr. Arnold Brinkworth. Lady Lundie and my niece assure me, on evidence which satisfies them, that the assertion is true. The evidence does not satisfy me. 'I hope, Sir Patrick, I don't strike you as being an excessively obstinate man?'—'My dear Sir, you impress me with the highest opinion of your capacity for sifting human testimony! May I ask, next, what course you mean to take?'—'The very thing I was going to mention, Sir Patrick! This is my course. I refuse to sanction my niece's engagement to Mr. Delamayn, until Mr. Delamayn has actually proved his statement by appeal to witnesses of the lady's marriage. He refers me to two witnesses; but declines acting at once in the matter for himself, on the ground that he is in training for a foot-race. I admit that that is an obstacle, and consent to arrange for bringing the two witnesses to London myself. By this post I have written to my lawyers in Perth to look the witnesses up; to offer them the necessary terms (at Mr. Delamayn's expense) for the use of their time; and to produce them by the end of the week. The footrace is on Thursday next. Mr. Delamayn will be able to attend after that, and establish his own assertion by his own witnesses. What do you say, Sir Patrick, to Saturday next (with

Lady Lundie's permission) in this room?'—There is the substance of the captain's statement. He is as old as I am and is dressed to look like thirty; but a very pleasant fellow for all that. I struck my sister-in-law dumb by accepting the proposal without a moment's hesitation. Mrs. Glenarm and Lady Lundie looked at each other in mute amazement. Here was a difference about which two women would have mortally quarreled; and here were two men settling it in the friendliest possible manner. I wish you had seen Lady Lundie's face, when I declared myself deeply indebted to Captain Newenden for rendering any prolonged interview with her ladyship quite unnecessary. 'Thanks to the captain,' I said to her, in the most cordial manner, 'we have absolutely nothing to discuss. I shall catch the next train, and set Arnold Brinkworth's mind quite at ease.' To come back to serious things, I have engaged to produce you, in the presence of every body—your wife included—on Saturday next. I put a bold face on it before the others. But I am bound to tell you that it is by no means easy to say—situated as we are now—what the result of Saturday's inquiry will be. Every thing depends on the issue of my interview with Miss Silvester to-morrow. It is no exaggeration to say, Arnold, that your fate is in her hands."

"I wish to heaven I had never set eyes on her!" said Arnold.

"Lay the saddle on the right horse," returned Sir Patrick. "Wish you had never set eyes on Geoffrey Delamayn."

Arnold hung his head. Sir Patrick's sharp tongue had got the better of him once more.

TWELFTH SCENE.—DRURY LANE.

CHAPTER THE FORTY-FOURTH.

THE LETTER AND THE LAW.

THE many-toned murmur of the current of London life—flowing through the murky channel of Drury Lane—found its muffled way from the front room to the back. Piles of old music lumbered the dusty floor. Stage masks and weapons, and portraits of singers and dancers, hung round the walls. An empty violin case in one corner faced a broken bust of Rossini in another. A frameless print, representing the Trial of Queen Caroline, was pasted over the fireplace. The chairs were genuine specimens of ancient carving in oak. The table was an equally excellent example of dirty modern deal. A small morsel of drugget was on the floor; and a large deposit of soot was on the ceiling. The scene thus presented, revealed itself in the back drawing-room of a house in Drury Lane, devoted to the transaction of musical and theatrical business of the humbler sort. It was late in the afternoon, on Michaelmas-day. Two persons were seated together in the room: they were Anne Silvester and Sir Patrick Lundie.

The opening conversation between them—comprising, on one side, the narrative of what had happened at Perth and at Swanhaven; and, on the other, a statement of the circumstances attending the separation of Arnold and Blanche—had come to an end. It rested with Sir Patrick to lead the way to the next topic. He looked at his companion, and hesitated.

"Do you feel strong enough to go on?" he asked. "If you would prefer to rest a little, pray say so."

"Thank you, Sir Patrick. I am more than ready, I am eager to go on. No words can say how anxious I feel to be of some use to you, if I can. It rests entirely with your experience to show me how."

"I can only do that, Miss Silvester, by asking you without ceremony for all the information that I want. Had you any object in traveling to London, which you have not mentioned to me yet? I mean, of course, any object with which I have a claim (as Arnold Brinkworth's representative) to be acquainted?"

"I had an object, Sir Patrick. And I have failed to accomplish it."

"May I ask what it was?"

"It was to see Geoffrey Delamayn."

Sir Patrick started. "You have attempted to see him! When?"

"This morning."

"Why, you only arrived in London last night!"

"I only arrived," said Anne, "after waiting many days on the journey. I was obliged to rest at Edinburgh, and again at York—and I was afraid I had given Mrs. Glenarm time enough to get to Geoffrey Delamayn before me."

"Afraid?" repeated Sir Patrick. "I understood that you had no serious intention of disputing the scoundrel with Mrs. Glenarm. What motive could possibly have taken you his way?"

"The same motive which took me to Swanhaven."

"What! the idea that it rested with Delamayn to set things right? and that you might bribe him to do it, by consenting to release him, so far as your claims were concerned?"

"Bear with my folly, Sir Patrick, as patiently as you can! I am always alone now; and I get into a habit of brooding over things. I have been brooding over the position in which my misfortunes have placed Mr. Brinkworth. I have been obstinate—unreasonably obstinate—in believing that I could prevail with Geoffrey Delamayn, after I had failed with Mrs. Glenarm. I am obstinate about it still. If he would only have heard me, my madness in going to Fulham might have had its excuse." She sighed bitterly, and said no more.

Sir Patrick took her hand.

"It has its excuse," he said, kindly. "Your motive is beyond reproach. Let me add—to quiet your mind—that, even if Delamayn had been willing to hear you, and had accepted the condition, the result would still have been the same. You are quite wrong in supposing that he has only to speak, and to set this matter right. It has passed entirely beyond his control. The mischief was done when Arnold Brinkworth spent those unlucky hours with you at Craig Fernie."

"Oh, Sir Patrick, if I had only known that, before I went to Fulham this morning!"

She shuddered as she said the words. Something was plainly associated with her visit to Geoffrey, the bare remembrance of which shook her nerves. What was it? Sir Patrick resolved to obtain an answer to that question, before he ventured on proceeding further with the main object of the interview.

"You have told me your reason for going to Fulham," he said. "But I have not heard what happened there yet."

Anne hesitated. "Is it necessary for me to trouble you about that?" she asked—with evident reluctance to enter on the subject.

"It is absolutely necessary," answered Sir Patrick, "because Delamayn is concerned in it."

Anne summoned her resolution, and entered on her narrative in these words:

"The person who carries on the business here discovered the address for me," she began. "I had some difficulty, however, in finding the house. It is little more than a cottage; and it is quite lost in a great garden, surrounded by high walls. I saw a carriage waiting. The coachman was walking his horses up and down—and he showed me the door. It was a high wooden door in the wall, with a grating in it. I rang the bell. A servant-girl opened the grating, and looked at me. She refused to let me in. Her mistress had ordered her to close the door on all strangers—especially strangers who were women. I contrived to pass some money to her through the grating, and asked to speak to her mistress. After waiting some time, I saw another face behind the bars—and it struck me that I recognized it. I suppose I was nervous. It startled me. I said, 'I think we know each other.' There was no answer. The door was suddenly opened—and who do you think stood before me?"

"Was it somebody I know?"

"Yes."

"Man? or woman?"

"It was Hester Dethridge."

"Hester Dethridge!"

"Yes. Dressed just as usual, and looking just as usual—with her slate hanging at her side."

"Astonishing! Where did I last see her? At the Windygates station, to be sure—going to London, after she had left my sister-in-law's service. Has she accepted another place—without letting me know first, as I told her?"

"She is living at Fulham."

"In service?"

"No. As mistress of her own house."

"What! Hester Dethridge in possession of a house of her own? Well! well! why shouldn't she have a rise in the world like other people? Did she let you in?"

"She stood for some time looking at me, in that dull strange way that she has. The servants at Windygates always said she was not in her right mind—and you will say, Sir Patrick, when you hear what happened, that the servants were not mistaken. She must be mad. I said, 'Don't you remember me?' She lifted her slate, and wrote, 'I remember you, in a dead swoon at Windygates House.' I was quite unaware that she had been present when I fainted in the library. The discovery startled me—or that dreadful, dead-cold look that she has in her eyes startled me—I don't know which. I couldn't speak to her just at first. She wrote on her slate again—the strangest question—in these words: 'I said, at the time, brought to it by a man. Did I say true?' If the question had been put in the usual way, by any body else, I should have considered it too insolent to be noticed. Can you understand my answering it, Sir Patrick? I can't understand it myself, now—and yet I did answer. She forced me to it with her stony eyes. I said 'yes.'"

"Did all this take place at the door?"

"At the door."

"When did she let you in?"

"The next thing she did was to let me in. She took me by the arm, in a rough way, and drew me inside the door, and shut it. My nerves are broken; my courage is gone. I crept with cold when she touched me. She dropped my arm. I stood like a child, waiting for what it pleased her to say or do next. She rested her two hands on her sides, and took a long look at me. She made a horrid dumb sound—not as if she was angry; more, if such a thing could be, as if she was satisfied—pleased even, I should have said, if it had been any body but Hester Dethridge. Do you understand it?"

"Not yet. Let me get nearer to understanding it by asking something before you go on. Did she show any attachment to you, when you were both at Windygates?"

"Not the least. She appeared to be incapable of attachment to me, or to any body."

"Did she write any more questions on her slate?"

"Yes. She wrote another question under what she had written just before. Her mind was still running on my fainting fit, and on the 'man' who had 'brought me to it.' She held up the slate; and the words were these: 'Tell me how he served you, did he knock you down?' Most people would have laughed at the question. I was startled by it. I told her, No. She shook her head as if she didn't believe me. She wrote on her slate, 'We are loth to own it when they up with their fists and beat us—ain't we?' I said, 'You are quite wrong.' She went on obstinately with her writing. 'Who is the man?'—was her next question. I had control enough over myself to decline telling her that. She opened the door, and pointed to me to go out. I made a sign entreating her to wait a little. She went back, in her impenetrable way, to the writing on the slate—still about the 'man.' This time, the question was plainer still. She had evidently placed her own interpretation of my appearance at the house. She wrote, 'Is it the man who lodges here?' I saw that she would close the door on me if I didn't answer. My only chance with her was to own that she had guessed right. I said 'Yes. I want to see him.' She took me by the arm, as roughly as before—and led me into the house."

"I begin to understand her," said Sir Patrick. "I remember hearing, in my brother's time, that she had been brutally ill-used by her husband. The association of ideas, even in her confused brain, becomes plain, if you bear that in mind. What is her last remembrance of you? It is the remembrance of a fainting woman at Windygates."

"Yes."

"She makes you acknowledge that she has guessed right, in guessing that a man was, in some way, answerable for the condition in which she found you. A swoon produced by a shock indicted on the mind, is a swoon that she doesn't understand. She looks back into her own experience, and associates it with the exercise of actual physical brutality on the part of the man. And she sees, in you, a reflection of her own sufferings and her own case. It's curious—to a student of human nature. And it explains, what is otherwise unintelligible—her overlooking her own instructions to the servant, and letting you into the house. What happened next?"

"She took me into a room, which I suppose was her own room. She made signs, offering me tea. It was done in the strangest way—without the least appearance of kindness. After what you have just said to me, I think I can in some degree interpret what was going on in her mind. I believe she felt a hard-hearted interest in seeing a woman whom she supposed to be as unfortunate as she had once been herself. I declined taking any tea, and tried to return to the subject of what I wanted in the house. She paid no heed to me. She pointed round the room; and then took me to a window, and pointed round the garden—and then made a sign indicating herself. 'My house; and my garden'—that was what she meant. There were four men in the garden—and Geoffrey Delamayn was one of them. I made another attempt to tell her that I wanted to speak to him. But, no! She had her own idea in her mind. After beckoning to me to leave the window, she led the way to the fire-place, and showed me a sheet of paper with writing on it, framed and placed under a glass, and hung on the wall. She seemed, I thought, to feel some kind of pride in her framed manuscript. At any rate, she insisted on my reading it. It was an extract from a will."

"The will under which she had inherited the house?"

"Yes. Her brother's will. It said, that he regretted, on his death-bed, his estrangement from his only sister, dating from the time when she had married in defiance of his wishes and against his advice. As a proof of his sincere desire to be reconciled with her, before he died, and as some compensation for the sufferings that she had endured at the hands of her deceased husband, he left her an income of two hundred pounds a year, together with the use of his house and garden, for her lifetime. That, as well as I remember, was the substance of what it said."

"Creditable to her brother, and creditable to herself," said Sir Patrick. "Taking her odd character into consideration, I understand her liking it to be seen. What puzzles me, is her letting lodgings with an income of her own to live on."

"That was the very question which I put to her myself. I was obliged to be cautious, and to begin by asking about the lodgers first—the men being still visible out in the garden, to excuse the inquiry. The rooms to let in the house had (as I understood her) been taken by a person acting for Geoffrey Delamayn—his trainer, I presume. He had surprised Hester Dethridge by barely noticing the house, and showing the most extraordinary interest in the garden."

"That is quite intelligible, Miss Silvester. The garden you have described would be just the place he wanted for the exercises of his employer—plenty of space, and well secured from observation by the high walls all round. What next?"

"Next, I got to the question of why she should let her house in lodgings at all. When I asked her that, her face turned harder than ever. She answered me on her slate in these dismal words: 'I have not got a friend in the world. I dare not live alone.' There was her reason! Dreary and dreadful, Sir Patrick, was it not?"

"Dreary indeed! How did it end? Did you get into the garden?"

"Yes—at the second attempt. She seemed suddenly to change her mind; she opened the door for me herself. Passing the window of the room in which I had left her, I looked back. She had taken her place, at a table before the window, apparently watching for what might happen. There was something about her, as her eyes met mine (I can't say what), which made me feel uneasy at the time. Adopting your view, I am almost inclined to think now, horrid as the idea is, that she had the expectation of seeing me treated as she had been treated in former days. It was actually a relief to me—though I knew I was going to run a serious risk—to lose sight of her. As I got nearer to the men in the garden, I heard two of them talking very earnestly to Geoffrey Delamayn. The fourth person, an elderly gentleman, stood apart from the rest at some little distance. I kept as far as I could out of sight, waiting till the talk was over. It was impossible for me to help hearing it. The two men were trying to persuade Geoffrey Delamayn to speak to the elderly gentleman. They pointed to him as a famous medical man. They reiterated over and over again, that his opinion was well worth having—"

Sir Patrick interrupted her. "Did they mention his name?" he asked.

"Yes. They called him Mr. Speedwell."

"The man himself! This is even more interesting, Miss Silvester, than you suppose. I myself heard Mr. Speedwell warn Delamayn that he was in broken health, when we were visiting together at Windygates House last month. Did he do as the other men wished him? Did he speak to the surgeon?"

"No. He sulkily refused—he remembered what you remember. He said, 'See the man who told me I was broken down?—not I!' After confirming it with an oath, he turned away from the others. Unfortunately, he took the direction in which I was standing, and discovered me. The bare sight of me seemed to throw him instantly into a state of frenzy. He—it is impossible for me to repeat the language that he used: it is bad enough to have heard it. I believe, Sir Patrick, but for the two men, who ran up and laid hold of him, that Hester Dethridge would have seen what she expected to see. The change in him was so frightful—even to me, well as I thought I knew him in his fits of passion—I tremble when I think of it. One of the men who had restrained him was almost as brutal, in his way. He declared, in the foulest language, that if Delamayn had a fit, he would lose the race, and that I should be answerable for it. But for Mr. Speedwell, I don't know what I should have done. He came forward directly. 'This is no place either for you, or for me,' he said—and gave me his arm, and led me back to the house. Hester Dethridge met us in the passage, and lifted her hand to stop me. Mr. Speedwell asked her what she wanted. She looked at me, and then looked toward the garden, and made the motion of striking a blow with her clenched fist. For the first time in my experience of her—I hope it was my fancy—I thought I saw her smile. Mr. Speedwell took me out. 'They are well matched in that house,' he said. 'The woman is as complete a savage as the men.' The carriage which I had seen waiting at the door was his. He called it up, and politely offered me a place in it. I said I would only trespass on his kindness as far as to the railway station. While we were talking, Hester Dethridge followed us to the door. She made the same motion again with her clenched hand, and looked back toward the garden—and then looked at me, and nodded her head, as much as to say, 'He will do it yet!' No words can describe how glad I was to see the last of her. I hope and trust I shall never set eyes on her again!"

"Did you hear how Mr. Speedwell came to be at the house? Had he gone of his own accord? or had he been sent for?"

"He had been sent for. I ventured to speak to him about the persons whom I had seen in the garden. Mr. Speedwell explained everything which I was not able of myself to understand, in the kindest manner. One of the two strange men in the garden was the trainer; the other was a doctor, whom the trainer was usually in the habit of consulting. It seems that the real reason for their bringing Geof frey Delamayn away from Scotland when they did, was that the trainer was uneasy, and wanted to be near London for medical advice. The doctor, on being consulted, owned that he was at a loss to understand the symptoms which he was asked to treat. He had himself fetched the great surgeon to Fulham, that morning. Mr. Speedwell abstained from mentioning that he had foreseen what would happen, at Windygates. All he said was, 'I had met Mr. Delamayn in society, and I felt interest enough in the case to pay him a visit—with what result, you have seen yourself.'"

"Did he tell you any thing about Delamayn's health?"

"He said that he had questioned the doctor on the way to Fulham, and that some of the patient's symptoms indicated serious mischief. What the symptoms were I did not hear. Mr. Speedwell only spoke of changes for the worse in him which a woman would be likely to understand. At one time, he would be so dull and heedless that nothing could rouse him. At another, he flew into the most terrible passions without any apparent cause. The trainer had found it almost impossible (in Scotland) to keep him to the right diet; and the doctor had only sanctioned taking the house at Fulham, after being first satisfied, not only of the convenience of the garden, but also that Hester Dethridge could be thoroughly trusted as a cook. With her help, they had placed him on an entirely new diet. But they had found an unexpected difficulty even in doing that. When the trainer took him to the new lodgings, it turned out that he had seen Hester Dethridge at Windygates, and had taken the strongest prejudice against her. On seeing her again at Fulham, he appeared to be absolutely terrified."

"Terrified? Why?"

"Nobody knows why. The trainer and the doctor together could only prevent his leaving the house, by threatening to throw up the responsibility of preparing him for the race, unless he instantly controlled himself, and behaved like a man instead of a child. Since that time, he has become reconciled, little by little, to his new abode—partly through Hester Dethridge's caution in keeping herself always out of his way; and partly through his own appreciation of the change in his diet, which Hester's skill in cookery has enabled the doctor to make. Mr. Speedwell mentioned some things which I have forgotten. I can only repeat, Sir Patrick, the result at which he has arrived in his own mind. Coming from a man of his authority, the opinion seems to me to be startling in the last degree. If Geoffrey Delamayn runs in the race on Thursday next, he will do it at the risk of his life."

"At the risk of dying on the ground?"

"Yes."

Sir Patrick's face became thoughtful. He waited a little before he spoke again.

"We have not wasted our time," he said, "in dwelling on what happened during your visit to Fulham. The possibility of this man's death suggests to my mind serious matter for consideration. It is very desirable, in the interests of my niece and her husband, that I should be able to foresee, if I can, how a fatal result of the race might affect the inquiry which is to be held on Saturday next. I believe you may be able to help me in this."

"You have only to tell me how, Sir Patrick."

"I may count on your being present on Saturday?"

"Certainly."

"You thoroughly understand that, in meeting Blanche, you will meet a person estranged from you, for the present—a friend and sister who has ceased (under Lady Lundie's influence mainly) to feel as a friend and sister toward you now?"

"I was not quite unprepared, Sir Patrick, to hear that Blanche had misjudged me. When I wrote my letter to Mr. Brinkworth, I warned him as delicately as I could, that his wife's jealousy might be very easily roused. You may rely on my self-restraint, no matter how hardly it may be tried. Nothing that Blanche can say or do will alter my grateful remembrance of the past. While I live, I love her. Let that assurance quiet any little anxiety that you may have felt as to my conduct—and tell me how I can serve those interests which I have at heart as well as you."

"You can serve them, Miss Silvester, in this way. You can make me acquainted with the position in which you stood toward Delamayn at the time when you went to the Craig Fernie inn."

"Put any questions to me that you think right, Sir Patrick."

"You mean that?"

"I mean it."

"I will begin by recalling something which you have already told me. Delamayn has promised you marriage—"

"Over and over again!"

"In words?"

"Yes."

"In writing?"

"Yes."

"Do you see what I am coming to?"

"Hardly yet."

"You referred, when we first met in this room, to a letter which you recovered from Bishopriggs, at Perth. I have ascertained from Arnold Brinkworth that the sheet of note-paper stolen from you contained two letters. One was written by you to Delamayn—the other was written by Delamayn to you. The substance of this last Arnold remembered. Your letter he had not read. It is of the utmost importance, Miss Silvester, to let me see that correspondence before we part to-day."

Anne made no answer. She sat with her clasped hands on her lap. Her eyes looked uneasily away from Sir Patrick's face, for the first time.

"Will it not be enough," she asked, after an interval, "if I tell you the substance of my letter, without showing it?"

"It will not be enough," returned Sir Patrick, in the plainest manner. "I hinted—if you remember—at the propriety of my seeing the letter, when you first mentioned it, and I observed that you purposely abstained from understanding me, I am grieved to put you, on this occasion, to a painful test. But if you are to help me at this serious crisis, I have shown you the way."

Anne rose from her chair, and answered by putting the letter into Sir Patrick's hands. "Remember what he has done, since I wrote that," she said. "And try to excuse me, if I own that I am ashamed to show it to you now."

With those words she walked aside to the window. She stood there, with her hand pressed on her breast, looking out absently on the murky London view of house roof and chimney, while Sir Patrick opened the letter.

It is necessary to the right appreciation of events, that other eyes besides Sir Patrick's should follow the brief course of the correspondence in this place.

1. From Anne Silvester to Geoffrey Delamayn.

WINDYGATES HOUSE. August 19, 1868.

"GEOFFREY DELAMAYN,—I have waited in the hope that you would ride over from your brother's place, and see me—and I have waited in vain. Your conduct to me is cruelty itself; I will bear it no longer. Consider! in your own interests, consider—before you drive the miserable woman who has trusted you to despair. You have promised me marriage by all that is sacred. I claim your promise. I insist on nothing less than to be what you vowed I should be—what I have waited all this weary time to be—what I am, in the sight of Heaven, your wedded wife. Lady Lundie gives a lawn-party here on the 14th. I know you have been asked. I expect you to accept her invitation. If I don't see you, I won't answer for what may happen. My mind is made up to endure this suspense no longer. Oh, Geoffrey, remember the past! Be faithful—be just—to your loving wife,

"ANNE SILVESTER."

2. From Geoffrey Delamayn to Anne Silvester.

"DEAR ANNE,—Just called to London to my father. They have telegraphed him in a bad way. Stop where you are, and I will write you. Trust the bearer. Upon my soul, I'll keep my promise. Your loving husband that is to be,

"GEOFFREY DELAMAYN.

"WINDYGATES HOUSE Augt. 14, 4 P. M.

"In a mortal hurry. The train starts 4.30."

Sir Patrick read the correspondence with breathless attention to the end. At the last lines of the last letter he did what he had not done for twenty years past—he sprang to his feet at a bound, and he crossed a room without the help of his ivory cane.

Anne started; and turning round from the window, looked at him in silent surprise. He was under the influence of strong emotion; his face, his voice, his manner, all showed it.

"How long had you been in Scotland, when you wrote this?" He pointed to Anne's letter as he asked the question, put ting it so eagerly that he stammered over the first words. "More than three weeks?" he added, with his bright black eyes fixed in absorbing interest on her face.

"Yes."

"Are you sure of that?"

"I am certain of it."

"You can refer to persons who have seen you?"

"Easily."

He turned the sheet of note-paper, and pointed to Geoffrey's penciled letter on the fourth page.

"How long had he been in Scotland, when he wrote this? More than three weeks, too?"

Anne considered for a moment.

"For God's sake, be careful!" said Sir Patrick. "You don't know what depends on this, If your memory is not clear about it, say so."

"My memory was confused for a moment. It is clear again now. He had been at his brother's in Perthshire three weeks before he wrote that. And before he went to Swanhaven, he spent three or four days in the valley of the Esk."

"Are you sure again?"

"Quite sure!"

"Do you know of any one who saw him in the valley of the Esk?"

"I know of a person who took a note to him, from me."

"A person easily found?"

"Quite easily."

Sir Patrick laid aside the letter, and seized in ungovernable agitation on both her hands.

"Listen to me," he said. "The whole conspiracy against Arnold Brinkworth and you falls to the ground before that correspondence. When you and he met at the inn—"

He paused, and looked at her. Her hands were beginning to tremble in his.

"When you and Arnold Brinkworth met at the inn," he resumed, "the law of Scotland had made you a married woman. On the day, and at the hour, when he wrote those lines at the back of your letter to him, you were Geoffrey Delamayn's wedded wife!"

He stopped, and looked at her again.

Without a word in reply, without the slightest movement in her from head to foot, she looked back at him. The blank stillness of horror was in her face. The deadly cold of horror was in her hands.

In silence, on his side, Sir Patrick drew back a step, with a faint reflection of her dismay in his face. Married—to the villain who had not hesitated to calumniate the woman whom he had ruined, and then to cast her helpless on the world. Married—to the traitor who had not shrunk from betraying Arnold's trust in him, and desolating Arnold's home. Married—to the ruffian who would have struck her that morning, if the hands of his own friends had not held him back. And Sir Patrick had never thought of it! Absorbed in the one idea of Blanche's future, he had never thought of it, till that horror-stricken face looked at him, and said, Think of my future, too!

He came back to her. He took her cold hand once more in his.

"Forgive me," he said, "for thinking first of Blanche."

Blanche's name seemed to rouse her. The life came back to her face; the tender brightness began to shine again in her eyes. He saw that he might venture to speak more plainly still: he went on.

"I see the dreadful sacrifice as you see it. I ask myself, have I any right, has Blanche any right—"

She stopped him by a faint pressure of his hand.

"Yes," she said, softly, "if Blanche's happiness depends on it."

THIRTEENTH SCENE.—FULHAM.

CHAPTER THE FORTY-FIFTH.

THE FOOT-RACE.

A SOLITARY foreigner, drifting about London, drifted toward Fulham on the day of the Foot-Race.

Little by little, he found himself involved in the current of a throng of impetuous English people, all flowing together toward one given point, and all decorated alike with colors of two prevailing hues—pink and yellow. He drifted along with the stream of passengers on the pavement (accompanied by a stream of carriages in the road) until they stopped with one accord at a gate—and paid admission money to a man in office—and poured into a great open space of ground which looked like an uncultivated garden.

Arrived here, the foreign visitor opened his eyes in wonder at the scene revealed to view. He observed thousands of people assembled, composed almost exclusively of the middle and upper classes of society. They were congregated round a vast inclosure; they were elevated on amphitheatrical wooden stands, and they were perched on the roofs of horseless carriages, drawn up in rows. From this congregation there rose such a roar of eager voices as he had never heard yet from any assembled multitude in these islands. Predominating among the cries, he detected one everlasting question. It began with, "Who backs—?" and it ended in the alternate pronouncing of two British names unintelligible to foreign ears. Seeing these extraordinary sights, and hearing these stirring sounds, he applied to a policeman on duty; and said, in his best producible English, "If you please, Sir, what is this?"

The policeman answered, "North against South—Sports."

The foreigner was informed, but not satisfied. He pointed all round the assembly with a circular sweep of his hand; and said, "Why?"

The policeman declined to waste words on a man who could ask such a question as that. He lifted a large purple forefinger, with a broad white nail at the end of it, and pointed gravely to a printed Bill, posted on the wall behind him. The drifting foreigner drifted to the Bill.

After reading it carefully, from top to bottom, he consulted a polite private individual near at hand, who proved to be far more communicative than the policeman. The result on his mind, as a person not thoroughly awakened to the enormous national importance of Athletic Sports, was much as follows:

The color of North is pink. The color of South is yellow. North produces fourteen pink men, and South produces thirteen yellow men. The meeting of pink and yellow is a solemnity. The solemnity takes its rise in an indomitable national passion for hardening the arms and legs, by throwing hammers and cricket-balls with the first, and running and jumping with the second. The object in view is to do this in public rivalry. The ends arrived at are (physically) an excessive development of the muscles, purchased at the expense of an excessive strain on the heart and the lungs—(morally), glory; conferred at the moment by the public applause; confirmed the next day by a report in the newspapers. Any person who presumes to see any physical evil involved in these exercises to the men who practice them, or any moral obstruction in the exhibition itself to those civilizing influences on which the true greatness of all nations depends, is a person without a biceps, who is simply incomprehensible. Muscular England develops itself, and takes no notice of him.

The foreigner mixed with the assembly, and looked more closely at the social spectacle around him.

He had met with these people before. He had seen them (for instance) at the theatre, and observed their manners and customs with considerable curiosity and surprise. When the curtain was down, they were so little interested in what they had come to see, that they had hardly spirit enough to speak to each other between the acts. When the curtain was up, if the play made any appeal to their sympathy with any of the higher and nobler emotions of humanity, they received it as something wearisome, or sneered at it as something absurd. The public feeling of the countrymen of Shakespeare, so far as they represented it, recognized but two duties in the dramatist—the duty of making them laugh, and the duty of getting it over soon. The two great merits of a stage proprietor, in England (judging by the rare applause of his cultivated customers), consisted in spending plenty of money on his scenery, and in hiring plenty of brazen-faced women to exhibit their bosoms and their legs. Not at theatres only; but among other gatherings, in other places, the foreigner had noticed the same stolid languor where any effort was exacted from genteel English brains, and the same stupid contempt where any appeal was made to genteel English hearts. Preserve us from enjoying any thing but jokes and scandal! Preserve us from respecting any thing but rank and money! There were the social aspirations of these insular ladies and gentlemen, as expressed under other circumstances, and as betrayed amidst other scenes. Here, all was changed. Here was the strong feeling, the breathless interest, the hearty enthusiasm, not visible elsewhere. Here were the superb gentlemen who were too weary to speak, when an Art was addressing them, shouting themselves hoarse with burst on burst of genuine applause. Here were the fine ladies who yawned behind their fans, at the bare idea of being called on to think or to feel, waving their handkerchiefs in honest delight, and actually flushing with excitement through their powder and their paint. And all for what? All for running and jumping—all for throwing hammers and balls.

The foreigner looked at it, and tried, as a citizen of a civilized country, to understand it. He was still trying—when there occurred a pause in the performances.

Certain hurdles, which had served to exhibit the present satisfactory state of civilization (in jumping) among the upper classes, were removed. The privileged persons who had duties to perform within the inclosure, looked all round it; and disappeared one after another. A great hush of expectation pervaded the whole assembly. Something of no common interest and importance was evidently about to take place. On a sudden, the silence was broken by a roar of cheering from the mob in the road outside the grounds. People looked at each other excitedly, and said, "One of them has come." The silence prevailed again—and was a second time broken by another roar of applause. People nodded to each other with an air of relief and said, "Both of them have come." Then the great hush fell on the crowd once more, and all eyes looked toward one particular point of the ground, occupied by a little wooden pavilion, with the blinds down over the open windows, and the door closed.

The foreigner was deeply impressed by the silent expectation of the great throng about him. He felt his own sympathies stirred, without knowing why. He believed himself to be on the point of understanding the English people.

Some ceremony of grave importance was evidently in preparation. Was a great orator going to address the assembly? Was a glorious anniversary to be commemorated? Was a religious service to be performed? He looked round him to apply for information once more. Two gentlemen—who contrasted favorably, so far as refinement of manner was concerned, with most of the spectators present—were slowly making their way, at that moment, through the crowd near him. He respectfully asked what national solemnity was now about to take place. They informed him that a pair of strong young men were going to run round the inclosure for a given number of turns, with the object of ascertaining which could run the fastest of the two.

The foreigner lifted his hands and eyes to heaven. Oh, multifarious Providence! who would have suspected that the infinite diversities of thy creation included such beings as these! With that aspiration, he turned his back on the race-course, and left the place.

On his way out of the grounds he had occasion to use his handkerchief, and found that it was gone. He felt next for his purse. His purse was missing too. When he was back again in his own country, intelligent inquiries were addressed to him on the subject of England. He had but one reply to give. "The whole nation is a mystery to me. Of all the English people I only understand the English thieves!"

In the mean time the two gentlemen, making their way through the crowd, reached a wicket-gate in the fence which surrounded the inclosure.

Presenting a written order to the policeman in charge of the gate, they were forthwith admitted within the sacred precincts The closely packed spectators, regarding them with mixed feelings of envy and curiosity, wondered who they might be. Were they referees appointed to act at the coming race? or reporters for the newspapers? or commissioners of police? They were neither the one nor the other. They were only Mr. Speedwell, the surgeon, and Sir Patrick Lundie.

The two gentlemen walked into the centre of the inclosure, and looked round them.

The grass on which they were standing was girdled by a broad smooth path, composed of finely-sifted ashes and sand—and this again was surrounded by the fence and by the spectators ranked behind it. Above the lines thus formed rose on one side the amphitheatres with their tiers of crowded benches, and on the other the long rows of carriages with the sight-seers inside and out. The evening sun was shining brightly, the light and shade lay together in grand masses, the varied colors of objects blended softly one with the other. It was a splendid and an inspiriting scene.

Sir Patrick turned from the rows of eager faces all round him to his friend the surgeon.

"Is there one person to be found in this vast crowd," he asked, "who has come to see the race with the doubt in his mind which has brought us to see it?"

Mr. Speedwell shook his head. "Not one of them knows or cares what the struggle may cost the men who engage in it."

Sir Patrick looked round him again. "I almost wish I had not come to see it," he said. "If this wretched man—"

The surgeon interposed. "Don't dwell needlessly, Sir Patrick, on the gloomy view," he rejoined. "The opinion I have formed has, thus far, no positive grounds to rest on. I am guessing rightly, as I believe, but at the same time I am guessing in the dark. Appearances may have misled me. There may be reserves of vital force in Mr. Delamayn's constitution which I don't suspect. I am here to learn a lesson—not to see a prediction fulfilled. I know his health is broken, and I believe he is going to run this race at his own proper peril. Don't feel too sure beforehand of the event. The event may prove me to be wrong."

For the moment Sir Patrick dropped the subject. He was not in his usual spirits.

Since his interview with Anne had satisfied him that she was Geoffrey's lawful wife, the conviction had inevitably forced itself on his mind that the one possible chance for her in the future, was the chance of Geoffrey's death. Horrible as it was to him, he had been possessed by that one idea—go where he might, do what he might, struggle as he might to force his thoughts in other directions. He looked round the broad ashen path on which the race was to be run, conscious that he had a secret interest in it which it was unutterably repugnant to him to feel. He tried to resume the conversation with his friend, and to lead it to other topics. The effort was useless. In despite of himself, he returned to the one fatal subject of the struggle that was now close at hand.

"How many times must they go round this inclosure," he inquired, "before the race is ended?"

Mr. Speedwell turned toward a gentleman who was approaching them at the moment. "Here is somebody coming who can tell us," he said.

"You know him?"

"He is one of my patients."

"Who is he?"

"After the two runners he is the most important personage on the ground. He is the final authority—the umpire of the race."

The person thus described was a middle-aged man, with a prematurely wrinkled face, with prematurely white hair and with something of a military look about him—brief in speech, and quick in manner.

"The path measures four hundred and forty yards round," he said, when the surgeon had repeated Sir Patrick's question to him. "In plainer words, and not to put you to your arithmetic once round it is a quarter of a mile. Each round is called a 'Lap.' The men must run sixteen Laps to finish the race. Not to put you to your arithmetic again, they must run four miles—the longest race of this kind which it is customary to attempt at Sports like these."

"Professional pedestrians exceed that limit, do they not?"

"Considerably—on certain occasions."

"Are they a long-lived race?"

"Far from it. They are exceptions when they live to be old men."

Mr. Speedwell looked at Sir Patrick. Sir Patrick put a question to the umpire.

"You have just told us," he said, "that the two young men who appear to-day are going to run the longest distance yet attempted in their experience. Is it generally thought, by persons who understand such things, that they are both fit to bear the exertion demanded of them?"

"You can judge for yourself, Sir. Here is one of them."

He pointed toward the pavilion. At the same moment there rose a mighty clapping of hands from the great throng of spectators. Fleetwood, champion of the North, decorated in his pink colors, descended the pavilion steps and walked into the arena.

Young, lithe, and elegant, with supple strength expressed in every movement of his limbs, with a bright smile on his resolute young face, the man of the north won the women's hearts at starting. The murmur of eager talk rose among them on all sides. The men were quieter—especially the men who understood the subject. It was a serious question with these experts whether Fleetwood was not "a little too fine." Superbly trained, it was admitted—but, possibly, a little over-trained for a four-mile race.

The northern hero was followed into the inclosure by his friends and backers, and by his trainer. This last carried a tin can in his hand. "Cold water," the umpire explained. "If he gets exhausted, his trainer will pick him up with a dash of it as he goes by."

A new burst of hand-clapping rattled all round the arena. Delamayn, champion of the South, decorated in his yellow colors, presented himself to the public view.

The immense hum of voices rose louder and louder as he walked into the centre of the great green space. Surprise at the extraordinary contrast between the two men was the prevalent emotion of the moment. Geoffrey was more than a head taller than his antagonist, and broader in full proportion. The women who had been charmed with the easy gait and confident smile of Fleetwood, were all more or less painfully impressed by the sullen strength of the southern man, as he passed before them slowly, with his head down and his brows knit, deaf to the applause showered on him, reckless of the eyes that looked at him; speaking to nobody; concentrated in himself; biding his time. He held the men who understood the subject breathless with interest. There it was! the famous "staying power" that was to endure in the last terrible half-mile of the race, when the nimble and jaunty Fleetwood was run off his legs. Whispers had been spread abroad hinting at something which had gone wrong with Delamayn in his training. And now that all eyes could judge him, his appearance suggested criticism in some quarters. It was exactly the opposite of the criticism passed on his antagonist. The doubt as to Delamayn was whether he had been sufficiently trained. Still the solid strength of the man, the slow, panther-like smoothness of his movements—and, above all, his great reputation in the world of muscle and sport—had their effect. The betting which, with occasional fluctuations, had held steadily in his favor thus far, held, now that he was publicly seen, steadily in his favor still.

"Fleetwood for shorter distances, if you like; but Delamayn for a four-mile race."

"Do you think he sees us?" whispered Sir Patrick to the surgeon.

"He sees nobody."

"Can you judge of the condition he is in, at this distance?"

"He has twice the muscular strength of the other man. His trunk and limbs are magnificent. It is useless to ask me more than that about his condition. We are too far from him to see his face plainly."

The conversation among the audience began to flag again; and the silent expectation set in among them once more. One by one, the different persons officially connected with the race gathered together on the grass. The trainer Perry was among them, with his can of water in his hand, in anxious whispering conversation with his principal—giving him the last words of advice before the start. The trainer's doctor, leaving them together, came up to pay his respects to his illustrious colleague.

"How has he got on since I was at Fulham?" asked Mr. Speedwell.

"First-rate, Sir! It was one of his bad days when you saw him. He has done wonders in the last eight-and-forty hours."

"Is he going to win the race?"

Privately the doctor had done what Perry had done before him—he had backed Geoffrey's antagonist. Publicly he was true to his colors. He cast a disparaging look at Fleetwood—and answered Yes, without the slightest hesitation.

At that point, the conversation was suspended by a sudden movement in the inclosure. The runners were on their way to the starting-place. The moment of the race had come.

Shoulder to shoulder, the two men waited—each with his foot touching the mark. The firing of a pistol gave the signal for the start. At the instant when the report sounded they were off.

Fleetwood at once took the lead, Delamayn following, at from two to three yards behind him. In that order they ran the first round, the second, and the third—both reserving their strength; both watched with breathless interest by every soul in the place. The trainers, with their cans in their hands, ran backward and forward over the grass, meeting their men at certain points, and eying them narrowly, in silence. The official persons stood together in a group; their eyes following the runners round and round with the closest attention. The trainer's doctor, still attached to his illustrious colleague, offered the necessary explanations to Mr. Speedwell and his friend.

"Nothing much to see for the first mile, Sir, except the 'style' of the two men."

"You mean they are not really exerting themselves yet?"

"No. Getting their wind, and feeling their legs. Pretty runner, Fleetwood—if you notice Sir? Gets his legs a trifle better in front, and hardly lifts his heels quite so high as our man. His action's the best of the two; I grant that. But just look, as they come by, which keeps the straightest line. There's where Delamayn has him! It's a steadier, stronger, truer pace; and you'll see it tell when they're half-way through." So, for the first three rounds, the doctor expatiated on the two contrasted "styles"—in terms mercifully adapted to the comprehension of persons unacquainted with the language of the running ring.

At the fourth round—in other words, at the round which completed the first mile, the first change in the relative position of the runners occurred. Delamayn suddenly dashed to the front. Fleetwood smiled as the other passed him. Delamayn held the lead till they were half way through the fifth round—when Fleetwood, at a hint from his trainer, forced the pace. He lightly passed Delamayn in an instant; and led again to the completion of the sixth round.

At the opening of the seventh, Delamayn forced the pace on his side. For a few moments, they ran exactly abreast. Then Delamayn drew away inch by inch; and recovered the lead. The first burst of applause (led by the south) rang out, as the big man beat Fleetwood at his own tactics, and headed him at the critical moment when the race was nearly half run.

"It begins to look as if Delamayn was going to win!" said Sir Patrick.

The trainer's doctor forgot himself. Infected by the rising excitement of every body about him, he let out the truth.

"Wait a bit!" he said. "Fleetwood has got directions to let him pass—Fleetwood is waiting to see what he can do."

"Cunning, you see, Sir Patrick, is one of the elements in a manly sport," said Mr. Speedwell, quietly.

At the end of the seventh round, Fleetwood proved the doctor to be right. He shot past Delamayn like an arrow from a bow. At the end of the eight round, he was leading by two yards. Half the race had then been run. Time, ten minutes and thirty-three seconds.

Toward the end of the ninth round, the pace slackened a little; and Delamayn was in front again. He kept ahead, until the opening of the eleventh round. At that point, Fleetwood flung up one hand in the air with a gesture of triumph; and bounded past Delamayn with a shout of "Hooray for the North!" The shout was echoed by the spectators. In proportion as the exertion began to tell upon the men, so the excitement steadily rose among the people looking at them.

At the twelfth round, Fleetwood was leading by six yards. Cries of triumph rose among the adherents of the north, met by counter-cries of defiance from the south. At the next turn Delamayn resolutely lessened the distance between his antagonist and himself. At the opening of the fourteenth round, they were coming side by side. A few yards more, and Delamayn was in front again, amidst a roar of applause from the whole public voice. Yet a few yards further, and Fleetwood neared him, passed him, dropped behind again, led again, and was passed again at the end of the round. The excitement rose to its highest pitch, as the runners—gasping for breath; with dark flushed faces, and heaving breasts—alternately passed and repassed each other. Oaths were heard now as well as cheers. Women turned pale and men set their teeth, as the last round but one began.

At the opening of it, Delamayn was still in advance. Before six yards more had been covered, Fleetwood betrayed the purpose of his running in the previous round, and electrified the whole assembly, by dashing past his antagonist—for the first time in the race at the top of his speed. Every body present could see, now, that Delamayn had been allowed to lead on sufferance—had been dextrously drawn on to put out his whole power—and had then, and not till then, been seriously deprived of the lead. He made another effort, with a desperate resolution that roused the public enthusiasm to frenzy. While the voices were roaring; while the hats and handkerchiefs were waving round the course; while the actual event of the race was, for one supreme moment, still in doubt—Mr. Speedwell caught Sir Patrick by the arm.

"Prepare yourself!" he whispered. "It's all over."

As the words passed his lips, Delamayn swerved on the path. His trainer dashed water over him. He rallied, and ran another step or two—swerved again—staggered—lifted his arm to his mouth with a hoarse cry of rage—fastened his own teeth in his flesh like a wild beast—and fell senseless on the course.

A Babel of sounds arose. The cries of alarm in some places, mingling with the shouts of triumph from the backers of Fleetwood in others—as their man ran lightly on to win the now uncontested race. Not the inclosure only, but the course itself was invaded by the crowd. In the midst of the tumult the fallen man was drawn on to the grass—with Mr. Speedwell and the trainer's doctor in attendance on him. At the terrible moment when the surgeon laid his hand on the heart, Fleetwood passed the spot—a passage being forced for him through the people by his friends and the police—running the sixteenth and last round of the race.

Had the beaten man fainted under it, or had he died under it? Every body waited, with their eyes riveted on the surgeon's hand.

The surgeon looked up from him, and called for water to throw over his face, for brandy to put into his mouth. He was coming to life again—he had survived the race. The last shout of applause which hailed Fleetwood's victory rang out as they lifted him from the ground to carry him to the pavilion. Sir Patrick (admitted at Mr. Speedwell's request) was the one stranger allowed to pass the door. At the moment when he was ascending the steps, some one touched his arm. It was Captain Newenden.

"Do the doctors answer for his life?" asked the captain. "I can't get my niece to leave the ground till she is satisfied of that."

Mr. Speedwell heard the question and replied to it briefly from the top of the pavilion steps.

"For the present—yes," he said.

The captain thanked him, and disappeared.

They entered the pavilion. The necessary restorative measures were taken under Mr. Speedwell's directions. There the conquered athlete lay: outwardly an inert mass of strength, formidable to look at, even in its fall; inwardly, a weaker creature, in all that constitutes vital force, than the fly that buzzed on the window-pane. By slow degrees the fluttering life came back. The sun was setting; and the evening light was beginning to fail. Mr. Speedwell beckoned to Perry to follow him into an unoccupied corner of the room.

"In half an hour or less he will be well enough to be taken home. Where are his friends? He has a brother—hasn't he?"

"His brother's in Scotland, Sir."

"His father?"

Perry scratched his head. "From all I hear, Sir, he and his father don't agree."

Mr. Speedwell applied to Sir Patrick.

"Do you know any thing of his family affairs?"

"Very little. I believe what the man has told you to be the truth."

"Is his mother living?"

"Yes."

"I will write to her myself. In the mean time, somebody must take him home. He has plenty of friends here. Where are they?"

He looked out of the window as he spoke. A throng of people had gathered round the pavilion, waiting to hear the latest news. Mr. Speedwell directed Perry to go out and search among them for any friends of his employer whom he might know by sight. Perry hesitated, and scratched his head for the second time.

"What are you waiting for?" asked the surgeon, sharply. "You know his friends by sight, don't you?"

"I don't think I shall find them outside," said Perry.

"Why not?"

"They backed him heavily, Sir—and they have all lost."

Deaf to this unanswerable reason for the absence of friends, Mr. Speedwell insisted on sending Perry out to search among the persons who composed the crowd. The trainer returned with his report. "You were right, Sir. There are some of his friends outside. They want to see him."

"Let two or three of them in."

Three came in. They stared at him. They uttered brief expressions of pity in slang. They said to Mr. Speedwell, "We wanted to see him. What is it—eh?"

"It's a break-down in his health."

"Bad training?"

"Athletic Sports."

"Oh! Thank you. Good-evening."

Mr. Speedwell's answer drove them out like a flock of sheep before a dog. There was not even time to put the question to them as to who was to take him home.

"I'll look after him, Sir," said Perry. "You can trust me."

"I'll go too," added the trainer's doctor; "and see him littered down for the night."

(The only two men who had "hedged" their bets, by privately backing his opponent, were also the only two men who volunteered to take him home!)

They went back to the sofa on which he was lying. His bloodshot eyes were rolling heavily and vacantly about him, on the search for something. They rested on the doctor—and looked away again. They turned to Mr. Speedwell—and stopped, riveted on his face. The surgeon bent over him, and said, "What is it?"

He answered with a thick accent and laboring breath—uttering a word at a time: "Shall—I—die?"

"I hope not."

"Sure?"

"No."

He looked round him again. This time his eyes rested on the trainer. Perry came forward.

"What can I do for you, Sir?"

The reply came slowly as before. "My—coat—pocket."

"This one, Sir?"

"No."

"This?"

"Yes. Book."

The trainer felt in the pocket, and produced a betting-book.

"What's to be done with this. Sir?"

"Read."

The trainer held the book before him; open at the last two pages on which entries had been made. He rolled his head impatiently from side to side of the sofa pillow. It was plain that he was not yet sufficiently recovered to be able to read what he had written.

"Shall I read for you, Sir?"

"Yes."

The trainer read three entries, one after another, without result; they had all been honestly settled. At the fourth the prostrate man said, "Stop!" This was the first of the entries which still depended on a future event. It recorded the wager laid at Windygates, when Geoffrey had backed himself (in defiance of the surgeon's opinion) to row in the University boat-race next spring—and had forced Arnold Brinkworth to bet against him.

"Well, Sir? What's to be done about this?"

He collected his strength for the effort; and answered by a word at a time.

"Write—brother—Julius. Pay—Arnold—wins."

His lifted hand, solemnly emphasizing what he said, dropped at his side. He closed his eyes; and fell into a heavy stertorous sleep. Give him his due. Scoundrel as he was, give him his due. The awful moment, when his life was trembling in the balance, found him true to the last living faith left among the men of his tribe and time—the faith of the betting-book.

Sir Patrick and Mr. Speedwell quitted the race-ground together; Geoffrey having been previously removed to his lodgings hard by. They met Arnold Brinkworth at the gate. He had, by his own desire, kept out of view among the crowd; and he decided on walking back by himself. The separation from Blanche had changed him in all his habits. He asked but two favors during the interval which was to elapse before he saw his wife again—to be allowed to bear it in his own way, and to be left alone.

Relieved of the oppression which had kept him silent while the race was in progress, Sir Patrick put a question to the surgeon as they drove home, which had been in his mind from the moment when Geoffrey had lost the day.

"I hardly understand the anxiety you showed about Delamayn," he said, "when you found that he had only fainted under the fatigue. Was it something more than a common fainting fit?"

"It is useless to conceal it now," replied Mr. Speedwell. "He has had a narrow escape from a paralytic stroke."

"Was that what you dreaded when you spoke to him at Windygates?"

"That was what I saw in his face when I gave him the warning. I was right, so far. I was wrong in my estimate of the reserve of vital power left in him. When he dropped on the race-course, I firmly believed we should find him a dead man."

"Is it hereditary paralysis? His father's last illness was of that sort."

Mr. Speedwell smiled. "Hereditary paralysis?" he repeated. "Why the man is (naturally) a phenomenon of health and strength—in the prime of his life. Hereditary paralysis might have found him out thirty years hence. His rowing and his running, for the last four years, are alone answerable for what has happened to-day."

Sir Patrick ventured on a suggestion.

"Surely," he said, "with your name to compel attention to it, you ought to make this public—as a warning to others?"

"It would be quite useless. Delamayn is far from being the first man who has dropped at foot-racing, under the cruel stress laid on the vital organs. The public have a happy knack of forgetting these accidents. They would be quite satisfied when they found the other man (who happens to have got through it) produced as a sufficient answer to me."

Anne Silvester's future was still dwelling on Sir Patrick's mind. His next inquiry related to the serious subject of Geoffrey's prospect of recovery in the time to come.

"He will never recover," said Mr. Speedwell. "Paralysis is hanging over him. How long he may live it is impossible for me to say. Much depends on himself. In his condition, any new imprudence, any violent emotion, may kill him at a moment's notice."

"If no accident happens," said Sir Patrick, "will he be sufficiently himself again to leave his bed and go out?"

"Certainly."

"He has an appointment that I know of for Saturday next. Is it likely that he will be able to keep it?"

"Quite likely."

Sir Patrick said no more. Anne's face was before him again at the memorable moment when he had told her that she was Geoffrey's wife.

FOURTEENTH SCENE.—PORTLAND PLACE.

CHAPTER THE FORTY-SIXTH.

A SCOTCH MARRIAGE.

IT was Saturday, the third of October—the day on which the assertion of Arnold's marriage to Anne Silvester was to be put to the proof.

Toward two o'clock in the afternoon Blanche and her step-mother entered the drawing-room of Lady Lundie's town house in Portland Place.

Since the previous evening the weather had altered for the worse. The rain, which had set in from an early hour that morning, still fell. Viewed from the drawing-room windows, the desolation of Portland Place in the dead season wore its aspect of deepest gloom. The dreary opposite houses were all shut up; the black mud was inches deep in the roadway; the soot, floating in tiny black particles, mixed with the falling rain, and heightened the dirty obscurity of the rising mist. Foot-passengers and vehicles, succeeding each other at rare intervals, left great gaps of silence absolutely uninterrupted by sound. Even the grinders of organs were mute; and the wandering dogs of the street were too wet to bark. Looking back from the view out of Lady Lundie's state windows to the view in Lady Lundie's state room, the melancholy that reigned without was more than matched by the melancholy that reigned within. The house had been shut up for the season: it had not been considered necessary, during its mistress's brief visit, to disturb the existing state of things. Coverings of dim brown hue shrouded the furniture. The chandeliers hung invisible in enormous bags. The silent clocks hibernated under extinguishers dropped over them two months since. The tables, drawn up in corners—loaded with ornaments at other times—had nothing but pen, ink, and paper (suggestive of the coming proceedings) placed on them now. The smell of the house was musty; the voice of the house was still. One melancholy maid haunted the bedrooms up stairs, like a ghost. One melancholy man, appointed to admit the visitors, sat solitary in the lower regions—the last of the flunkies, mouldering in an extinct servants' hall. Not a word passed, in the drawing-room, between Lady Lundie and Blanche. Each waited the appearance of the persons concerned in the coming inquiry, absorbed in her own thoughts. Their situation at the moment was a solemn burlesque of the situation of two ladies who are giving an evening party, and who are waiting to receive their guests. Did neither of them see this? Or, seeing it, did they shrink from acknowledging it? In similar positions, who does not shrink? The occasions are many on which we have excellent reason to laugh when the tears are in our eyes; but only children are bold enough to follow the impulse. So strangely, in human existence, does the mockery of what is serious mingle with the serious reality itself, that nothing but our own self-respect preserves our gravity at some of the most important emergencies in our lives. The two ladies waited the coming ordeal together gravely, as became the occasion. The silent maid flitted noiseless up stairs. The silent man waited motionless in the lower regions. Outside, the street was a desert.

Inside, the house was a tomb.

The church clock struck the hour. Two.

At the same moment the first of the persons concerned in the investigation arrived.

Lady Lundie waited composedly for the opening of the drawing-room door. Blanche started, and trembled. Was it Arnold? Was it Anne?

The door opened—and Blanche drew a breath of relief. The first arrival was only Lady Lundie's solicitor—invited to attend the proceedings on her ladyship's behalf. He was one of that large class of purely mechanical and perfectly mediocre persons connected with the practice of the law who will probably, in a more advanced state of science, be superseded by machinery. He made himself useful in altering the arrangement of the tables and chairs, so as to keep the contending parties effectually separated from each other. He also entreated Lady Lundie to bear in mind that he knew nothing of Scotch law, and that he was there in the capacity of a friend only. This done, he sat down, and looked out with silent interest at the rain—as if it was an operation of Nature which he had never had an opportunity of inspecting before.

The next knock at the door heralded the arrival of a visitor of a totally different order. The melancholy man-servant announced Captain Newenden.

Possibly, in deference to the occasion, possibly, in defiance of the weather, the captain had taken another backward step toward the days of his youth. He was painted and padded, wigged and dressed, to represent the abstract idea of a male human being of five-and twenty in robust health. There might have been a little stiffness in the region of the waist, and a slight want of firmness in the eyelid and the chin. Otherwise there was the fiction of five-and twenty, founded in appearance on the fact of five-and-thirty—with the truth invisible behind it, counting seventy years! Wearing a flower in his buttonhole, and carrying a jaunty little cane in his hand—brisk, rosy, smiling, perfumed—the captain's appearance brightened the dreary room. It was pleasantly suggestive of a morning visit from an idle young man. He appeared to be a little surprised to find Blanche present on the scene of approaching conflict. Lady Lundie thought it due to herself to explain. "My step-daughter is here in direct defiance of my entreaties and my advice. Persons may present themselves whom it is, in my opinion, improper she should see. Revelations will take place which no young woman, in her position, should hear. She insists on it, Captain Newenden—and I am obliged to submit."

The captain shrugged his shoulders, and showed his beautiful teeth.

Blanche was far too deeply interested in the coming ordeal to care to defend herself: she looked as if she had not even heard what her step-mother had said of her. The solicitor remained absorbed in the interesting view of the falling rain. Lady Lundie asked after Mrs. Glenarm. The captain, in reply, described his niece's anxiety as something—something—something, in short, only to be indicated by shaking his ambrosial curls and waving his jaunty cane. Mrs. Delamayn was staying with her until her uncle returned with the news. And where was Julius? Detained in Scotland by election business. And Lord and Lady Holchester? Lord and Lady Holchester knew nothing about it.

There was another knock at the door. Blanche's pale face turned paler still. Was it Arnold? Was it Anne? After a longer delay than usual, the servant announced Mr. Geoffrey Delamayn and Mr. Moy.

Geoffrey, slowly entering first, saluted the two ladies in silence, and noticed no one else. The London solicitor, withdrawing himself for a moment from the absorbing prospect of the rain, pointed to the places reserved for the new-comer and for the legal adviser whom he had brought with him. Geoffrey seated himself, without so much as a glance round the room. Leaning his elbows on his knees, he vacantly traced patterns on the carpet with his clumsy oaken walking-stick. Stolid indifference expressed itself in his lowering brow and his loosely-hanging mouth. The loss of the race, and the circumstances accompanying it, appeared to have made him duller than usual and heavier than usual—and that was all.

Captain Newenden, approaching to speak to him, stopped half-way, hesitated, thought better of it—and addressed himself to Mr. Moy.

Geoffrey's legal adviser—a Scotchman of the ruddy, ready, and convivial type—cordially met the advance. He announced, in reply to the captain's inquiry, that the witnesses (Mrs. Inchbare and Bishopriggs) were waiting below until they were wanted, in the housekeeper's room. Had there been any difficulty in finding them? Not the least. Mrs. Inchbare was, as a matter of course, at her hotel. Inquiries being set on foot for Bishopriggs, it appeared that he and the landlady had come to an understanding, and that he had returned to his old post of headwaiter at the inn. The captain and Mr. Moy kept up the conversation between them, thus begun, with unflagging ease and spirit. Theirs were the only voices heard in the trying interval that elapsed before the next knock was heard at the door.

At last it came. There could be no doubt now as to the persons who might next be expected to enter the room. Lady Lundie took her step-daughter firmly by the hand. She was not sure of what Blanche's first impulse might lead her to do. For the first time in her life, Blanche left her hand willingly in her step-mother's grasp.

The door opened, and they came in.

Sir Patrick Lundie entered first, with Anne Silvester on his arm. Arnold Brinkworth followed them.

Both Sir Patrick and Anne bowed in silence to the persons assembled. Lady Lundie ceremoniously returned her brother-in-law's salute—and pointedly abstained from noticing Anne's presence in the room. Blanche never looked up. Arnold advanced to her, with his hand held out. Lady Lundie rose, and motioned him back. "Not yet, Mr. Brinkworth!" she said, in her most quietly merciless manner. Arnold stood, heedless of her, looking at his wife. His wife lifted her eyes to his; the tears rose in them on the instant. Arnold's dark complexion turned ashy pale under the effort that it cost him to command himself. "I won't distress you," he said, gently—and turned back again to the table at which Sir Patrick and Anne were seated together apart from the rest. Sir Patrick took his hand, and pressed it in silent approval.

The one person who took no part, even as spectator, in the events that followed the appearance of Sir Patrick and his companions in the room—was Geoffrey. The only change visible in him was a change in the handling of his walking-stick. Instead of tracing patterns on the carpet, it beat a tattoo. For the rest, there he sat with his heavy head on his breast and his brawny arms on his knees—weary of it by anticipation before it had begun.

Sir Patrick broke the silence. He addressed himself to his sister-in-law.

"Lady Lundie, are all the persons present whom you expected to see here to-day?"

The gathered venom in Lady Lundie seized the opportunity of planting its first sting.

"All whom I expected are here," she answered. "And more than I expected," she added, with a look at Anne.

The look was not returned—was not even seen. From the moment when she had taken her place by Sir Patrick, Anne's eyes had rested on Blanche. They never moved—they never for an instant lost their tender sadness—when the woman who hated her spoke. All that was beautiful and true in that noble nature seemed to find its one sufficient encouragement in Blanche. As she looked once more at the sister of the unforgotten days of old, its native beauty of expression shone out again in her worn and weary face. Every man in the room (but Geoffrey) looked at her; and every man (but Geoffrey) felt for her.

Sir Patrick addressed a second question to his sister-in-law.

"Is there any one here to represent the interests of Mr. Geoffrey Delamayn?" he asked.

Lady Lundie referred Sir Patrick to Geoffrey himself. Without looking up, Geoffrey motioned with his big brown hand to Mr. Moy, sitting by his side.

Mr. Moy (holding the legal rank in Scotland which corresponds to the rank held by solicitors in England) rose and bowed to Sir Patrick, with the courtesy due to a man eminent in his time at the Scottish Bar.

"I represent Mr. Delamayn," he said. "I congratulate myself, Sir Patrick, on having your ability and experience to appeal to in the conduct of the pending inquiry."

Sir Patrick returned the compliment as well as the bow.

"It is I who should learn from you," he answered. "I have had time, Mr. Moy, to forget what I once knew."

Lady Lundie looked from one to the other with unconcealed impatience as these formal courtesies were exchanged between the lawyers. "Allow me to remind you, gentlemen, of the suspense that we are suffering at this end of the room," she said. "And permit me to ask when you propose to begin?"

Sir Patrick looked invitingly at Mr. Moy. Mr. Moy looked invitingly at Sir Patrick. More formal courtesies! a polite contest this time as to which of the two learned gentlemen should permit the other to speak first! Mr. Moy's modesty proving to be quite immovable, Sir Patrick ended it by opening the proceedings.

"I am here," he said, "to act on behalf of my friend, Mr. Arnold Brinkworth. I beg to present him to you, Mr. Moy as the husband of my niece—to whom he was lawfully married on the seventh of September last, at the Church of Saint Margaret, in the parish of Hawley, Kent. I have a copy of the marriage certificate here—if you wish to look at it."

Mr. Moy's modesty declined to look at it.

"Quite needless, Sir Patrick! I admit that a marriage ceremony took place on the date named, between the persons named; but I contend that it was not a valid marriage. I say, on behalf of my client here present (Mr. Geoffrey Delamayn), that Arnold Brinkworth was married at a date prior to the seventh of September last—namely, on the fourteenth of August in this year, and at a place called Craig Fernie, in Scotland—to a lady named Anne Silvester, now living, and present among us (as I understand) at this moment."

Sir Patrick presented Anne. "This is the lady, Mr. Moy."

Mr. Moy bowed, and made a suggestion. "To save needless formalities, Sir Patrick, shall we take the question of identity as established on both sides?"

Sir Patrick agreed with his learned friend. Lady Lundie opened and shut her fan in undisguised impatience. The London solicitor was deeply interested. Captain Newenden, taking out his handkerchief, and using it as a screen, yawned behind it to his heart's content. Sir Patrick resumed.

"You assert the prior marriage," he said to his colleague. "It rests with you to begin."

Mr. Moy cast a preliminary look round him at the persons assembled.

"The object of our meeting here," he said, "is, if I am not mistaken, of a twofold nature. In the first place, it is thought desirable, by a person who has a special interest in the issue of this inquiry" (he glanced at the captain—the captain suddenly became attentive), "to put my client's assertion, relating to Mr. Brinkworth's marriage, to the proof. In the second place, we are all equally desirous—whatever difference of opinion may otherwise exist—to make this informal inquiry a means, if possible, of avoiding the painful publicity which would result from an appeal to a Court of Law."

At those words the gathered venom in Lady Lundie planted its second sting—under cover of a protest addressed to Mr. Moy.

"I beg to inform you, Sir, on behalf of my step-daughter," she said, "that we have nothing to dread from the widest publicity. We consent to be present at, what you call, 'this informal inquiry,' reserving our right to carry the matter beyond the four walls of this room. I am not referring now to Mr. Brinkworth's chance of clearing himself from an odious suspicion which rests upon him, and upon another Person present. That is an after-matter. The object immediately before us—so far as a woman can pretend to understand it—is to establish my step-daughter's right to call Mr. Brinkworth to account in the character of his wife. If the result, so far, fails to satisfy us in that particular, we shall not hesitate to appeal to a Court of Law." She leaned back in her chair, and opened her fan, and looked round her with the air of a woman who called society to witness that she had done her duty.

An expression of pain crossed Blanche's face while her step-mother was speaking. Lady Lundie took her hand for the second time. Blanche resolutely and pointedly withdrew it—Sir Patrick noticing the action with special interest. Before Mr. Moy could say a word in answer, Arnold centred the general attention on himself by suddenly interfering in the proceedings. Blanche looked at him. A bright flash of color appeared on her face—and left it again. Sir Patrick noted the change of color—and observed her more attentively than ever. Arnold's letter to his wife, with time to help it, had plainly shaken her ladyship's influence over Blanche.

"After what Lady Lundie has said, in my wife's presence," Arnold burst out, in his straightforward, boyish way, "I think I ought to be allowed to say a word on my side. I only want to explain how it was I came to go to Craig Fernie at all—and I challenge Mr. Geoffrey Delamayn to deny it, if he can."

His voice rose at the last words, and his eyes brightened with indignation as he looked at Geoffrey.

Mr. Moy appealed to his learned friend.

"With submission, Sir Patrick, to your better judgment," he said, "this young gentleman's proposal seems to be a little out of place at the present stage of the proceedings."

"Pardon me," answered Sir Patrick. "You have yourself described the proceedings as representing an informal inquiry. An informal proposal—with submission to your better judgment, Mr. Moy—is hardly out of place, under those circumstances, is it?"

Mr. Moy's inexhaustible modesty gave way, without a struggle. The answer which he received had the effect of puzzling him at the outset of the investigation. A man of Sir Patrick's experience must have known that Arnold's mere assertion of his own innocence could be productive of nothing but useless delay in the proceedings. And yet he sanctioned that delay. Was he privately on the watch for any accidental circumstance which might help him to better a case that he knew to be a bad one?

Permitted to speak, Arnold spoke. The unmistakable accent of truth was in every word that he uttered. He gave a fairly coherent account of events, from the time when Geoffrey had claimed his assistance at the lawn-party to the time when he found himself at the door of the inn at Craig Fernie. There Sir Patrick interfered, and closed his lips. He asked leave to appeal to Geoffrey to confirm him. Sir Patrick amazed Mr. Moy by sanctioning this irregularity also. Arnold sternly addressed himself to Geoffrey.

"Do you deny that what I have said is true?" he asked.

Mr. Moy did his duty by his client. "You are not bound to answer," he said, "unless you wish it yourself."

Geoffrey slowly lifted his heavy head, and confronted the man whom he had betrayed.

"I deny every word of it," he answered—with a stolid defiance of tone and manner.

"Have we had enough of assertion and counter-assertion, Sir Patrick, by this time?" asked Mr. Moy, with undiminished politeness.

After first forcing Arnold—with some little difficulty—to control himself, Sir Patrick raised Mr. Moy's astonishment to the culminating point. For reasons of his own, he determined to strengthen the favorable impression which Arnold's statement had plainly produced on his wife before the inquiry proceeded a step farther.

"I must throw myself on your indulgence, Mr. Moy," he said. "I have not had enough of assertion and counter-assertion, even yet."

Mr. Moy leaned back in his chair, with a mixed expression of bewilderment and resignation. Either his colleague's intellect was in a failing state—or his colleague had some purpose in view which had not openly asserted itself yet. He began to suspect that the right reading of the riddle was involved in the latter of those two alternatives. Instead of entering any fresh protest, he wisely waited and watched.

Sir Patrick went on unblushingly from one irregularity to another.

"I request Mr. Moy's permission to revert to the alleged marriage, on the fourteenth of August, at Craig Fernie," he said. "Arnold Brinkworth! answer for yourself, in the presence of the persons here assembled. In all that you said, and all that you did, while you were at the inn, were you not solely influenced by the wish to make Miss Silvester's position as little painful to her as possible, and by anxiety to carry out the instructions given to you by Mr. Geoffrey Delamayn? Is that the whole truth?"

"That is the whole truth, Sir Patrick."

"On the day when you went to Craig Fernie, had you not, a few hours previously, applied for my permission to marry my niece?"

"I applied for your permission, Sir Patrick; and you gave it me."

"From the moment when you entered the inn to the moment when you left it, were you absolutely innocent of the slightest intention to marry Miss Silvester?"

"No such thing as the thought of marrying Miss Silvester ever entered my head."

"And this you say, on your word of honor as a gentleman?"

"On my word of honor as a gentleman."

Sir Patrick turned to Anne.

"Was it a matter of necessity, Miss Silvester, that you should appear in the assumed character of a married woman—on the fourteenth of August last, at the Craig Fernie inn?"

Anne looked away from Blanche for the first time. She replied to Sir Patrick quietly, readily, firmly—Blanche looking at her, and listening to her with eager interest.

"I went to the inn alone, Sir Patrick. The landlady refused, in the plainest terms, to let me stay there, unless she was first satisfied that I was a married woman."

"Which of the two gentlemen did you expect to join you at the inn—Mr. Arnold Brinkworth, or Mr. Geoffrey Delamayn?"

"Mr. Geoffrey Delamayn."

"When Mr. Arnold Brinkworth came in his place and said what was necessary to satisfy the scruples of the landlady, you understood that he was acting in your interests, from motives of kindness only, and under the instructions of Mr. Geoffrey Delamayn?"

"I understood that; and I objected as strongly as I could to Mr. Brinkworth placing himself in a false position on my account."

"Did your objection proceed from any knowledge of the Scottish law of marriage, and of the position in which the peculiarities of that law might place Mr. Brinkworth?"

"I had no knowledge of the Scottish law. I had a vague dislike and dread of the deception which Mr. Brinkworth was practicing on the people of the inn. And I feared that it might lead to some possible misinterpretation of me on the part of a person whom I dearly loved."

"That person being my niece?"

"Yes."

"You appealed to Mr. Brinkworth (knowing of his attachment to my niece), in her name, and for her sake, to leave you to shift for yourself?"

"I did."

"As a gentleman who had given his promise to help and protect a lady, in the absence of the person whom she had depended on to join her, he refused to leave you to shift by yourself?"

"Unhappily, he refused on that account."

"From first to last, you were absolutely innocent of the slightest intention to marry Mr. Brinkworth?"

"I answer, Sir Patrick, as Mr. Brinkworth has answered. No such thing as the thought of marrying him ever entered my head."

"And this you say, on your oath as a Christian woman?"

"On my oath as a Christian woman."

Sir Patrick looked round at Blanche. Her face was hidden in her hands. Her step-mother was vainly appealing to her to compose herself.

In the moment of silence that followed, Mr. Moy interfered in the interests of his client.

"I waive my claim, Sir Patrick, to put any questions on my side. I merely desire to remind you, and to remind the company present, that all that we have just heard is mere assertion—on the part of two persons strongly interested in extricating themselves from a position which fatally compromises them both. The marriage which they deny I am now waiting to prove—not by assertion, on my side, but by appeal to competent witnesses."

After a brief consultation with her own solicitor, Lady Lundie followed Mr. Moy, in stronger language still.

"I wish you to understand, Sir Patrick, before you proceed any farther, that I shall remove my step-daughter from the room if any more attempts are made to harrow her feelings and mislead her judgment. I want words to express my sense of this most cruel and unfair way of conducting the inquiry."

The London lawyer followed, stating his professional approval of his client's view. "As her ladyship's legal adviser," he said, "I support the protest which her ladyship has just made."

Even Captain Newenden agreed in the general disapproval of Sir Patrick's conduct. "Hear, hear!" said the captain, when the lawyer had spoken. "Quite right. I must say, quite right."

Apparently impenetrable to all due sense of his position, Sir Patrick addressed himself to Mr. Moy, as if nothing had happened.

"Do you wish to produce your witnesses at once?" he asked. "I have not the least objection to meet your views—on the understanding that I am permitted to return to the proceedings as interrupted at this point."

Mr. Moy considered. The adversary (there could be no doubt of it by this time) had something in reserve—and the adversary had not yet shown his hand. It was more immediately important to lead him into doing this than to insist on rights and privileges of the purely formal sort. Nothing could shake the strength of the position which Mr. Moy occupied. The longer Sir Patrick's irregularities delayed the proceedings, the more irresistibly the plain facts of the case would assert themselves—with all the force of contrast—out of the mouths of the witnesses who were in attendance down stairs. He determined to wait.

"Reserving my right of objection, Sir Patrick," he answered, "I beg you to go on."

To the surprise of every body, Sir Patrick addressed himself directly to Blanche—quoting the language in which Lady Lundie had spoken to him, with perfect composure of tone and manner.

"You know me well enough, my dear," he said, "to be assured that I am incapable of willingly harrowing your feelings or misleading your judgment. I have a question to ask you, which you can answer or not, entirely as you please."

Before he could put the question there was a momentary contest between Lady Lundie and her legal adviser. Silencing her ladyship (not without difficulty), the London lawyer interposed. He also begged leave to reserve the right of objection, so far as his client was concerned.

Sir Patrick assented by a sign, and proceeded to put his question to Blanche.

"You have heard what Arnold Brinkworth has said, and what Miss Silvester has said," he resumed. "The husband who loves you, and the sisterly friend who loves you, have each made a solemn declaration. Recall your past experience of both of them; remember what they have just said; and now tell me—do you believe they have spoken falsely?"

Blanche answered on the instant.

"I believe, uncle, they have spoken the truth!"

Both the lawyers registered their objections. Lady Lundie made another attempt to speak, and was stopped once more—this time by Mr. Moy as well as by her own adviser. Sir Patrick went on.

"Do you feel any doubt as to the entire propriety of your husband's conduct and your friend's conduct, now you have seen them and heard them, face to face?"

Blanche answered again, with the same absence of reserve.

"I ask them to forgive me," she said. "I believe I have done them both a great wrong."

She looked at her husband first—then at Anne. Arnold attempted to leave his chair. Sir Patrick firmly restrained him. "Wait!" he whispered. "You don't know what is coming." Having said that, he turned toward Anne. Blanche's look had gone to the heart of the faithful woman who loved her. Anne's face was turned away—the tears were forcing themselves through the worn weak hands that tried vainly to hide them.

The formal objections of the lawyers were registered once more. Sir Patrick addressed himself to his niece for the last time.

"You believe what Arnold Brinkworth has said; you believe what Miss Silvester has said. You know that not even the thought of marriage was in the mind of either of them, at the inn. You know—whatever else may happen in the future—that there is not the most remote possibility of either of them consenting to acknowledge that they ever have been, or ever can be, Man and Wife. Is that enough for you? Are you willing, before this inquiry proceeds any farther to take your husband's hand; to return to your husband's protection; and to leave the rest to me—satisfied with my assurance that, on the facts as they happened, not even the Scotch Law can prove the monstrous assertion of the marriage at Craig Fernie to be true?"

Lady Lundie rose. Both the lawyers rose. Arnold sat lost in astonishment. Geoffrey himself—brutishly careless thus far of all that had passed—lifted his head with a sudden start. In the midst of the profound impression thus produced, Blanche, on whose decision the whole future course of the inquiry now turned, answered in these words:

"I hope you will not think me ungrateful, uncle. I am sure that Arnold has not, knowingly, done me any wrong. But I can't go back to him until I am first certain that I am his wife."

Lady Lundie embraced her step-daughter with a sudden outburst of affection. "My dear child!" exclaimed her ladyship, fervently. "Well done, my own dear child!"

Sir Patrick's head dropped on his breast. "Oh, Blanche! Blanche!" Arnold heard him whisper to himself; "if you only knew what you are forcing me to!"

Mr. Moy put in his word, on Blanche's side of the question.

"I must most respectfully express my approval also of the course which the young lady has taken," he said. "A more dangerous compromise than the compromise which we have just heard suggested it is difficult to imagine. With all deference to Sir Patrick Lundie, his opinion of the impossibility of proving the marriage at Craig Fernie remains to be confirmed as the right one. My own professional opinion is opposed to it. The opinion of another Scottish lawyer (in Glasgow) is, to my certain knowledge, opposed to it. If the young lady had not acted with a wisdom and courage which do her honor, she might have lived to see the day when her reputation would have been destroyed, and her children declared illegitimate. Who is to say that circumstances may not happen in the future which may force Mr. Brinkworth or Miss Silvester—one or the other—to assert the very marriage which they repudiate now? Who is to say that interested relatives (property being concerned here) may not in the lapse of years, discover motives of their own for questioning the asserted marriage in Kent? I acknowledge that I envy the immense self-confidence which emboldens Sir Patrick to venture, what he is willing to venture upon his own individual opinion on an undecided point of law."

He sat down amidst a murmur of approval, and cast a slyly-expectant look at his defeated adversary. "If that doesn't irritate him into showing his hand," thought Mr. Moy, "nothing will!"

Sir Patrick slowly raised his head. There was no irritation—there was only distress in his face—when he spoke next.

"I don't propose, Mr. Moy, to argue the point with you," he said, gently. "I can understand that my conduct must necessarily appear strange and even blameworthy, not in your eyes only, but in the eyes of others. My young friend here will tell you" (he looked toward Arnold) "that the view which you express as to the future peril involved in this case was once the view in my mind too, and that in what I have done thus far I have acted in direct contradiction to advice which I myself gave at no very distant period. Excuse me, if you please, from entering (for the present at least) into the motive which has influenced me from the time when I entered this room. My position is one of unexampled responsibility and of indescribable distress. May I appeal to that statement to stand as my excuse, if I plead for a last extension of indulgence toward the last irregularity of which I shall be guilty, in connection with these proceedings?"

Lady Lundie alone resisted the unaffected and touching dignity with which those words were spoken.

"We have had enough of irregularity," she said sternly. "I, for one, object to more."

Sir Patrick waited patiently for Mr. Moy's reply. The Scotch lawyer and the English lawyer looked at each other—and understood each other. Mr. Moy answered for both.

"We don't presume to restrain you, Sir Patrick, by other limits than those which, as a gentleman, you impose on yourself. Subject," added the cautious Scotchman, "to the right of objection which we have already reserved."

"Do you object to my speaking to your client?" asked Sir Patrick.

"To Mr. Geoffrey Delamayn?"

"Yes."

All eyes turned on Geoffrey. He was sitting half asleep, as it seemed—with his heavy hands hanging listlessly over his knees, and his chin resting on the hooked handle of his stick.

Looking toward Anne, when Sir Patrick pronounced Geoffrey's name, Mr. Moy saw a change in her. She withdrew her hands from her face, and turned suddenly toward her legal adviser. Was she in the secret of the carefully concealed object at which his opponent had been aiming from the first? Mr. Moy decided to put that doubt to the test. He invited Sir Patrick, by a gesture, to proceed. Sir Patrick addressed himself to Geoffrey.

"You are seriously interested in this inquiry," he said; "and you have taken no part in it yet. Take a part in it now. Look at this lady."

Geoffrey never moved.

"I've seen enough of her already," he said, brutally.

"You may well be ashamed to look at her," said Sir Patrick, quietly. "But you might have acknowledged it in fitter words. Carry your memory back to the fourteenth of August. Do you deny that you promised to many Miss Silvester privately at the Craig Fernie inn?"

"I object to that question," said Mr. Moy. "My client is under no sort of obligation to answer it."

Geoffrey's rising temper—ready to resent any thing—resented his adviser's interference. "I shall answer if I like," he retorted, insolently. He looked up for a moment at Sir Patrick, without moving his chin from the hook of his stick. Then he looked down again. "I do deny it," he said.

"You deny that you have promised to marry Miss Silvester?"

"Yes."

"I asked you just now to look at her—"

"And I told you I had seen enough of her already."

"Look at me. In my presence, and in the presence of the other persons here, do you deny that you owe this lady, by your own solemn engagement, the reparation of marriage?"

He suddenly lifted his head. His eyes, after resting for an instant only on Sir Patrick, turned, little by little; and, brightening slowly, fixed themselves with a hideous, tigerish glare on Anne's face. "I know what I owe her," he said.

The devouring hatred of his look was matched by the ferocious vindictiveness of his tone, as he spoke those words. It was horrible to see him; it was horrible to hear him. Mr. Moy said to him, in a whisper, "Control yourself, or I will throw up your case."

Without answering—without even listening—he lifted one of his hands, and looked at it vacantly. He whispered something to himself; and counted out what he was whispering slowly; in divisions of his own, on three of his fingers in succession. He fixed his eyes again on Anne with the same devouring hatred in their look, and spoke (this time directly addressing himself to her) with the same ferocious vindictiveness in his tone. "But for you, I should be married to Mrs. Glenarm. But for you, I should be friends with my father. But for you, I should have won the race. I know what I owe you." His loosely hanging hands stealthily clenched themselves. His head sank again on his broad breast. He said no more.

Not a soul moved—not a word was spoken. The same common horror held them all speechless. Anne's eyes turned once more on Blanche. Anne's courage upheld her, even at that moment.

Sir Patrick rose. The strong emotion which he had suppressed thus far, showed itself plainly in his face—uttered itself plainly in his voice.

"Come into the next room," he said to Anne. "I must speak to you instantly!"

Without noticing the astonishment that he caused; without paying the smallest attention to the remonstrances addressed to him by his sister-in-law and by the Scotch lawyer, he took Anne by the arm, opened the folding-doors at one end of the room—entered the room beyond with her—and closed the doors again.

Lady Lundie appealed to her legal adviser. Blanche rose—advanced a few steps—and stood in breathless suspense, looking at the folding-doors. Arnold advanced a step, to speak to his wife. The captain approached Mr. Moy.

"What does this mean?" he asked.

Mr. Moy answered, in strong agitation on his side.

"It means that I have not been properly instructed. Sir Patrick Lundie has some evidence in his possession that seriously compromises Mr. Delamayn's case. He has shrunk from producing it hitherto—he finds himself forced to produce it now. How is it," asked the lawyer, turning sternly on his client, "that you have left me in the dark?"

"I know nothing about it," answered Geoffrey, without lifting his head.

Lady Lundie signed to Blanche to stand aside, and advanced toward the folding-doors. Mr. Moy stopped her.

"I advise your ladyship to be patient. Interference is useless there."

"Am I not to interfere, Sir, in my own house?"

"Unless I am entirely mistaken, madam, the end of the proceedings in your house is at hand. You will damage your own interests by interfering. Let us know what we are about at last. Let the end come."

Lady Lundie yielded, and returned to her place. They all waited in silence for the opening of the doors.

Sir Patrick Lundie and Anne Silvester were alone in the room.

He took from the breast-pocket of his coat the sheet of note-paper which contained Anne's letter, and Geoffrey's reply. His hand trembled as he held it; his voice faltered as he spoke.

"I have done all that can be done," he said. "I have left nothing untried, to prevent the necessity of producing this."

"I feel your kindness gratefully, Sir Patrick. You must produce it now."

The woman's calmness presented a strange and touching contrast to the man's emotion. There was no shrinking in her face, there was no unsteadiness in her voice as she answered him. He took her hand. Twice he attempted to speak; and twice his own agitation overpowered him. He offered the letter to her in silence.

In silence, on her side, she put the letter away from her, wondering what he meant.

"Take it back," he said. "I can't produce it! I daren't produce it! After what my own eyes have seen, after what my own ears have heard, in the next room—as God is my witness, I daren't ask you to declare yourself Geoffrey Delamayn's wife!"

She answered him in one word.

"Blanche!"

He shook his head impatiently. "Not even in Blanche's interests! Not even for Blanche's sake! If there is any risk, it is a risk I am ready to run. I hold to my own opinion. I believe my own view to be right. Let it come to an appeal to the law! I will fight the case, and win it."

"Are you sure of winning it, Sir Patrick?"

Instead of replying, he pressed the letter on her. "Destroy it," he whispered. "And rely on my silence."

She took the letter from him.

"Destroy it," he repeated. "They may open the doors. They may come in at any moment, and see it in your hand."

"I have something to ask you, Sir Patrick, before I destroy it. Blanche refuses to go back to her husband, unless she returns with the certain assurance of being really his wife. If I produce this letter, she may go back to him to-day. If I declare myself Geoffrey Delamayn's wife, I clear Arnold Brinkworth, at once and forever of all suspicion of being married to me. Can you as certainly and effectually clear him in any other way? Answer me that, as a man of honor speaking to a woman who implicitly trusts him!"

She looked him full in the face. His eyes dropped before hers—he made no reply.

"I am answered," she said.

With those words, she passed him, and laid her hand on the door.

He checked her. The tears rose in his eyes as he drew her gently back into the room.

"Why should we wait?" she asked.

"Wait," he answered, "as a favor to me."

She seated herself calmly in the nearest chair, and rested her head on her hand, thinking.

He bent over her, and roused her, impatiently, almost angrily. The steady resolution in her face was terrible to him, when he thought of the man in the next room.

"Take time to consider," he pleaded. "Don't be led away by your own impulse. Don't act under a false excitement. Nothing binds you to this dreadful sacrifice of yourself."

"Excitement! Sacrifice!" She smiled sadly as she repeated the words. "Do you know, Sir Patrick, what I was thinking of a moment since? Only of old times, when I was a little girl. I saw the sad side of life sooner than most children see it. My mother was cruelly deserted. The hard marriage laws of this country were harder on her than on me. She died broken-hearted. But one friend comforted her at the last moment, and promised to be a mother to her child. I can't remember one unhappy day in all the after-time when I lived with that faithful woman and her little daughter—till the day that parted us. She went away with her husband; and I and the little daughter were left behind. She said her last words to me. Her heart was sinking under the dread of coming death. 'I promised your mother that you should be like my own child to me, and it quieted her mind. Quiet my mind, Anne, before I go. Whatever happens in years to come—promise me to be always what you are now, a sister to Blanche.' Where is the false excitement, Sir Patrick, in old remembrances like these? And how can there be a sacrifice in any thing that I do for Blanche?"

She rose, and offered him her hand. Sir Patrick lifted it to his lips in silence.

"Come!" she said. "For both our sakes, let us not prolong this."

He turned aside his head. It was no moment to let her see that she had completely unmanned him. She waited for him, with her hand on the lock. He rallied his courage—he forced himself to face the horror of the situation calmly. She opened the door, and led the way back into the other room.

Not a word was spoken by any of the persons present, as the two returned to their places. The noise of a carriage passing in the street was painfully audible. The chance banging of a door in the lower regions of the house made every one start.

Anne's sweet voice broke the dreary silence.

"Must I speak for myself, Sir Patrick? Or will you (I ask it as a last and greatest favor) speak for me?"

"You insist on appealing to the letter in your hand?"

"I am resolved to appeal to it."

"Will nothing induce you to defer the close of this inquiry—so far as you are concerned—for four-and-twenty hours?"

"Either you or I, Sir Patrick, must say what is to be said, and do what is to be done, before we leave this room."

"Give me the letter."

She gave it to him. Mr. Moy whispered to his client, "Do you know what that is?" Geoffrey shook his head. "Do you really remember nothing about it?" Geoffrey answered in one surly word, "Nothing!"

Sir Patrick addressed himself to the assembled company.

"I have to ask your pardon," he said, "for abruptly leaving the room, and for obliging Miss Silvester to leave it with me. Every body present, except that man" (he pointed to Geoffrey), "will, I believe, understand and forgive me, now that I am forced to make my conduct the subject of the plainest and the fullest explanation. I shall address that explanation, for reasons which will presently appear, to my niece."

Blanche started. "To me!" she exclaimed.

"To you," Sir Patrick answered.

Blanche turned toward Arnold, daunted by a vague sense of something serious to come. The letter that she had received from her husband on her departure from Ham Farm had necessarily alluded to relations between Geoffrey and Anne, of which Blanche had been previously ignorant. Was any reference coming to those relations? Was there something yet to be disclosed which Arnold's letter had not prepared her to hear?

Sir Patrick resumed.

"A short time since," he said to Blanche, "I proposed to you to return to your husband's protection—and to leave the termination of this matter in my hands. You have refused to go back to him until you are first certainly assured that you are his wife. Thanks to a sacrifice to your interests and your happiness, on Miss Silvester's part—which I tell you frankly I have done my utmost to prevent—I am in a position to prove positively that Arnold Brinkworth was a single man when he married you from my house in Kent."

Mr. Moy's experience forewarned him of what was coming. He pointed to the letter in Sir Patrick's hand.

"Do you claim on a promise of marriage?" he asked.

Sir Patrick rejoined by putting a question on his side.

"Do you remember the famous decision at Doctors' Commons, which established the marriage of Captain Dalrymple and Miss Gordon?"

Mr. Moy was answered. "I understand you, Sir Patrick," he said. After a moment's pause, he addressed his next words to Anne. "And from the bottom of my heart, madam, I respect you."

It was said with a fervent sincerity of tone which wrought the interest of the other persons, who were still waiting for enlightenment, to the highest pitch. Lady Lundie and Captain Newenden whispered to each other anxiously. Arnold turned pale. Blanche burst into tears.

Sir Patrick turned once more to his niece.

"Some little time since," he said, "I had occasion to speak to you of the scandalous uncertainty of the marriage laws of Scotland. But for that uncertainty (entirely without parallel in any other civilized country in Europe), Arnold Brinkworth would never have occupied the position in which he stands here to-day—and these proceedings would never have taken place. Bear that fact in mind. It is not only answerable for the mischief that has been already done, but for the far more serious evil which is still to come."

Mr. Moy took a note. Sir Patrick went on.

"Loose and reckless as the Scotch law is, there happens, however, to be one case in which the action of it has been confirmed and settled by the English Courts. A written promise of marriage exchanged between a man and woman, in Scotland, marries that man and woman by Scotch law. An English Court of Justice (sitting in judgment on the ease I have just mentioned to Mr. Moy) has pronounced that law to be good—and the decision has since been confirmed by the supreme authority of the House of Lords. Where the persons therefore—living in

Scotland at the time—have promised each other marriage in writing, there is now no longer any doubt they are certainly, and lawfully, Man and Wife." He turned from his niece, and appealed to Mr. Moy. "Am I right?"

"Quite right, Sir Patrick, as to the facts. I own, however, that your commentary on them surprises me. I have the highest opinion of our Scottish marriage law. A man who has betrayed a woman under a promise of marriage is forced by that law (in the interests of public morality) to acknowledge her as his wife."

"The persons here present, Mr. Moy, are now about to see the moral merit of the Scotch law of marriage (as approved by England) practically in operation before their own eyes. They will judge for themselves of the morality (Scotch or English) which first forces a deserted woman back on the villain who has betrayed her, and then virtuously leaves her to bear the consequences."

With that answer, he turned to Anne, and showed her the letter, open in his hand.

"For the last time," he said, "do you insist on my appealing to this?"

She rose, and bowed her head gravely.

"It is my distressing duty," said Sir Patrick, "to declare, in this lady's name, and on the faith of written promises of marriage exchanged between the parties, then residing in Scotland, that she claims to be now—and to have been on the afternoon of the fourteenth of August last—Mr. Geoffrey Delamayn's wedded wife."

A cry of horror from Blanche, a low murmur of dismay from the rest, followed the utterance of those words.

There was a pause of an instant.

Then Geoffrey rose slowly to his feet, and fixed his eyes on the wife who had claimed him.

The spectators of the terrible scene turned with one accord toward the sacrificed woman. The look which Geoffrey had cast on her—the words which Geoffrey had spoken to her—were present to all their minds. She stood, waiting by Sir Patrick's side—her soft gray eyes resting sadly and tenderly on Blanche's face. To see that matchless courage and resignation was to doubt the reality of what had happened. They were forced to look back at the man to possess their minds with the truth.

The triumph of law and morality over him was complete. He never uttered a word. His furious temper was perfectly and fearfully calm. With the promise of merciless vengeance written in the Devil s writing on his Devil-possessed face, he kept his eyes fixed on the hated woman whom he had ruined—on the hated woman who was fastened to him as his wife.

His lawyer went over to the table at which Sir Patrick sat. Sir Patrick handed him the sheet of note-paper.

He read the two letters contained in it with absorbed and deliberate attention. The moments that passed before he lifted his head from his reading seemed like hours. "Can you prove the handwritings?" he asked. "And prove the residence?"

Sir Patrick took up a second morsel of paper lying ready under his hand.

"There are the names of persons who can prove the writing, and prove the residence," he replied. "One of your two witnesses below stairs (otherwise useless) can speak to the hour at which Mr. Brinkworth arrived at the inn, and so can prove that the lady for whom he asked was, at that moment, Mrs. Geoffrey Delamayn. The indorsement on the back of the note-paper, also referring to the question of time, is in the handwriting of the same witness—to whom I refer you, when it suits your convenience to question him."

"I will verify the references, Sir Patrick, as matter of form. In the mean time, not to interpose needless and vexatious delay, I am bound to say that I can not resist the evidence of the marriage."

Having replied in those terms he addressed himself, with marked respect and sympathy, to Anne.

"On the faith of the written promise of marriage exchanged between you in Scotland," he said, "you claim Mr. Geoffrey Delamayn as your husband?"

She steadily repented the words after him.

"I claim Mr. Geoffrey Delamayn as my husband."

Mr. Moy appealed to his client. Geoffrey broke silence at last.

"Is it settled?" he asked.

"To all practical purposes, it is settled."

He went on, still looking at nobody but Anne.

"Has the law of Scotland made her my wife?"

"The law of Scotland has made her your wife."

He asked a third and last question.

"Does the law tell her to go where her husband goes?"

"Yes."

He laughed softly to himself, and beckoned to her to cross the room to the place at which he was standing.

She obeyed. At the moment when she took the first step to approach him, Sir Patrick caught her hand, and whispered to her, "Rely on me!" She gently pressed his hand in token that she understood him, and advanced to Geoffrey. At the same moment, Blanche rushed between them, and flung her arms around Anne's neck.

"Oh, Anne! Anne!"

An hysterical passion of tears choked her utterance. Anne gently unwound the arms that clung round her—gently lifted the head that lay helpless on her bosom.

"Happier days are coming, my love," she said. "Don't think of me."

She kissed her—looked at her—kissed her again—and placed her in her husband's arms. Arnold remembered her parting words at Craig Fernie, when they had wished each other good-night. "You have not befriended an ungrateful woman. The day may yet come when I shall prove it." Gratitude and admiration struggled in him which should utter itself first, and held him speechless.

She bent her head gently in token that she understood him. Then she went on, and stood before Geoffrey.

"I am here," she said to him. "What do you wish me to do?"

A hideous smile parted his heavy lips. He offered her his arm.

"Mrs. Geoffrey Delamayn," he said. "Come home."

The picture of the lonely house, isolated amidst its high walls; the ill-omened figure of the dumb woman with the stony eyes and the savage ways—the whole scene, as Anne had pictured it to him but two days since, rose vivid as reality before Sir Patrick's mind. "No!" he cried out, carried away by the generous impulse of the moment. "It shall not be!"

Geoffrey stood impenetrable—waiting with his offered arm. Pale and resolute, she lifted her noble head—called back the courage which had faltered for a moment—and took his arm. He led her to the door. "Don't let Blanche fret about me," she said, simply, to Arnold as they went by. They passed Sir Patrick next. Once more his sympathy for her set every other consideration at defiance. He started up to bar the way to Geoffrey. Geoffrey paused, and looked at Sir Patrick for the first time.

"The law tells her to go with her husband," he said. "The law forbids you to part Man and Wife."

True. Absolutely, undeniably true. The law sanctioned the sacrifice of her as unanswerably as it had sanctioned the sacrifice of her mother before her. In the name of Morality, let him take her! In the interests of Virtue, let her get out of it if she can!

Her husband opened the door. Mr. Moy laid his hand on Sir Patrick's arm. Lady Lundie, Captain Newenden, the London lawyer, all left their places, influenced, for once, by the same interest; feeling, for once, the same suspense. Arnold followed them, supporting his wife. For one memorable instant Anne looked back at them all. Then she and her husband crossed the threshold. They descended the stairs together. The opening and closing of the house door was heard. They were gone.

Done, in the name of Morality. Done, in the interests of Virtue. Done, in an age of progress, and under the most perfect government on the face of the earth.

FIFTEENTH SCENE.—HOLCHESTER HOUSE.

CHAPTER THE FORTY-SEVENTH.

THE LAST CHANCE.

"HIS lordship is dangerously ill, Sir. Her ladyship can receive no visitors."

"Be so good as to take that card to Lady Holchester. It is absolutely necessary that your mistress should be made acquainted—in the interests of her younger son—with something which I can only mention to her ladyship herself."

The two persons speaking were Lord Holchester's head servant and Sir Patrick Lundie. At that time barely half an hour had passed since the close of the proceedings at Portland Place.

The servant still hesitated with the card in his hand. "I shall forfeit my situation," he said, "if I do it."

"You will most assuredly forfeit your situation if you don't do it," returned Sir Patrick. "I warn you plainly, this is too serious a matter to be trifled with."

The tone in which those words were spoken had its effect. The man went up stairs with his message.

Sir Patrick waited in the hall. Even the momentary delay of entering one of the reception-rooms was more than he could endure at that moment. Anne's happiness was hopelessly sacrificed already. The preservation of her personal safety—which Sir Patrick firmly believed to be in danger—was the one service which it was possible to render to her now. The perilous position in which she stood toward her husband—as an immovable obstacle, while she lived, between Geoffrey and Mrs. Glenarm—was beyond the reach of remedy. But it was still possible to prevent her from becoming the innocent cause of Geoffrey's pecuniary ruin, by standing in the way of a reconciliation between father and son.

Resolute to leave no means untried of serving Anne's interests, Sir Patrick had allowed Arnold and Blanche to go to his own residence in London, alone, and had not even waited to say a farewell word to any of the persons who had taken part in the inquiry. "Her life may depend on what I can do for her at Holchester House!" With that conviction in him, he had left Portland Place. With that conviction in him, he had sent his message to Lady Holchester, and was now waiting for the reply.

The servant appeared again on the stairs. Sir Patrick went up to meet him.

"Her ladyship will see you, Sir, for a few minutes."

The door of an upper room was opened; and Sir Patrick found himself in the presence of Geoffrey's mother. There was only time to observe that she possessed the remains of rare personal beauty, and that she received her visitor with a grace and courtesy which implied (under the circumstances) a considerate regard for his position at the expense of her own.

"You have something to say to me, Sir Patrick, on the subject of my second son. I am in great affliction. If you bring me bad news, I will do my best to bear it. May I trust to your kindness not to keep me in suspense?"

"It will help me to make my intrusion as little painful as possible to your ladyship," replied Sir Patrick, "if I am permitted to ask a question. Have you heard of any obstacle to the contemplated marriage of Mr. Geoffrey Delamayn and Mrs. Glenarm?"

Even that distant reference to Anne produced an ominous change for the worse in Lady Holchester's manner.

"I have heard of the obstacle to which you allude," she said. "Mrs. Glenarm is an intimate friend of mine. She has informed me that a person named Silvester, an impudent adventuress—"

"I beg your ladyship's pardon. You are doing a cruel wrong to the noblest woman I have ever met with."

"I can not undertake, Sir Patrick, to enter into your reasons for admiring her. Her conduct toward my son has, I repeat, been the conduct of an impudent adventuress."

Those words showed Sir Patrick the utter hopelessness of shaking her prejudice against Anne. He decided on proceeding at once to the disclosure of the truth.

"I entreat you so say no more," he answered. "Your ladyship is speaking of your son's wife."

"My son has married Miss Silvester?"

"Yes."

She turned deadly pale. It appeared, for an instant, as if the shock had completely overwhelmed her. But the mother's weakness was only momentary The virtuous indignation of the great lady had taken its place before Sir Patrick could speak again. She rose to terminate the interview.

"I presume," she said, "that your errand here is as an end."

Sir Patrick rose, on his side, resolute to do the duty which had brought him to the house.

"I am compelled to trespass on your ladyship's attention for a few minutes more," he answered. "The circumstances attending the marriage of Mr. Geoffrey Delamayn are of no common importance. I beg permission (in the interests of his family) to state, very briefly, what they are."

In a few clear sentences he narrated what had happened, that afternoon, in Portland Place. Lady Holchester listened with the steadiest and coldest attention. So far as outward appearances were concerned, no impression was produced upon her.

"Do you expect me," she asked, "to espouse the interests of a person who has prevented my son from marrying the lady of his choice, and of mine?"

"Mr. Geoffrey Delamayn, unhappily, has that reason for resenting his wife's innocent interference with interests of considerable, importance to him," returned Sir Patrick. "I request your ladyship to consider whether it is desirable—in view of your son's conduct in the future—to allow his wife to stand in the doubly perilous relation toward him of being also a cause of estrangement between his father and himself."

He had put it with scrupulous caution. But Lady Holchester understood what he had refrained from saying as well as what he had actually said. She had hitherto remained standing—she now sat down again. There was a visible impression produced on her at last.

"In Lord Holchester's critical state of health," she answered, "I decline to take the responsibility of telling him what you have just told me. My own influence has been uniformly exerted in my son's favor—as long as my interference could be productive of any good result. The time for my interference has passed. Lord Holchester has altered his will this morning. I was not present; and I have not yet been informed of what has been done. Even if I knew—"

"Your ladyship would naturally decline," said Sir Patrick, "to communicate the information to a stranger."

"Certainly. At the same time, after what you have said, I do not feel justified in deciding on this matter entirely by myself. One of Lord Holchester's executors is now in the house. There can be no impropriety in your seeing him—if you wish it. You are at liberty to say, from me, that I leave it entirely to his discretion to decide what ought to be done."

"I gladly accept your ladyship's proposal."

Lady Holchester rang the bell at her side.

"Take Sir Patrick Lundie to Mr. Marchwood," she said to the servant.

Sir Patrick started. The name was familiar to him, as the name of a friend.

"Mr. Marchwood of Hurlbeck?" he asked.

"The same."

With that brief answer, Lady Holchester dismissed her visitor. Following the servant to the other end of the corridor, Sir Patrick was conducted into a small room—the ante-chamber to the bedroom in which Lord Holchester lay. The door of communication was closed. A gentleman sat writing at a table near the window. He rose, and held out his hand, with a look of surprise, when the servant announced Sir Patrick's name. This was Mr. Marchwood.

After the first explanations had been given, Sir Patrick patiently reverted to the object of his visit to Holchester House. On the first occasion when he mentioned Anne's name he observed that Mr. Marchwood became, from that moment, specially interested in what he was saying.

"Do you happen to be acquainted with the lady?" he asked

"I only know her as the cause of a very strange proceeding, this morning, in that room." He pointed to Lord Holchester's bedroom as he spoke.

"Are you at liberty to mention what the proceeding was?"

"Hardly—even to an old friend like you—unless I felt it a matter of duty, on my part, to state the circumstances. Pray go on with what you were saying to me. You were on the point of telling me what brought you to this house."

Without a word more of preface, Sir Patrick told him the news of Geoffrey's marriage to Anne.

"Married!" cried Mr. Marchwood. "Are you sure of what you say?"

"I am one of the witnesses of the marriage."

"Good Heavens! And Lord Holchester's lawyer has left the house!"

"Can I replace him? Have I, by any chance justified you in telling me what happened this morning in the next room?"

"Justified me? You have left me no other alternative. The doctors are all agreed in dreading apoplexy—his lordship may die at any moment. In the lawyer's absence, I must take it on myself. Here are the facts. There is the codicil to Lord Holchester's Will which is still unsigned."

"Relating to his second son?"

"Relating to Geoffrey Delamayn, and giving him (when it is once executed) a liberal provision for life."

"What is the object in the way of his executing it?"

"The lady whom you have just mentioned to me."

"Anne Silvester!"

"Anne Silvester—now (as you tell me) Mrs. Geoffrey Delamayn. I can only explain the thing very imperfectly. There are certain painful circumstances associated in his lordship's memory with this lady, or with some member of her family. We can only gather that he did something—in the early part of his professional career—which was strictly within the limits of his duty, but which apparently led to very sad results. Some days since he unfortunately heard (either through Mrs. Glenarm or through Mrs. Julius Delamayn) of Miss Silvester's appearance at Swanhaven Lodge. No remark on the subject escaped him at the time. It was only this morning, when the codicil giving the legacy to Geoffrey was waiting to be executed, that his real feeling in the matter came out. To our astonishment, he refused to sign it. 'Find Anne Silvester' (was the only answer we could get from him); 'and bring her to my bedside. You all say my son is guiltless of injuring her. I am lying on my death-bed. I have serious reasons of my own—I owe it to the memory of the dead—to assure myself of the truth. If Anne Silvester herself acquits him of having wronged her, I will provide for Geoffrey. Not otherwise.' We went the length of reminding him that he might die before Miss Silvester could be found. Our interference had but one result. He desired the lawyer to add a second codicil to the Will—which he executed on the spot. It directs his executors to inquire into the relations that have actually existed between Anne Silvester and his younger son. If we find reason to conclude that Geoffrey has gravely wronged her, we are directed to pay her a legacy—provided that she is a single woman at the time."

"And her marriage violates the provision!" exclaimed Sir Patrick.

"Yes. The codicil actually executed is now worthless. And the other codicil remains unsigned until the lawyer can produce Miss Silvester. He has left the house to apply to Geoffrey at Fulham, as the only means at our disposal of finding the lady. Some hours have passed—and he has not yet returned."

"It is useless to wait for him," said Sir Patrick. "While the lawyer was on his way to Fulham, Lord Holchester's son was on his way to Portland Place. This is even more serious than you suppose. Tell me, what under less pressing circumstances I should have no right to ask.

Apart from the unexecuted codicil what is Geoffrey Delamayn's position in the will?"

"He is not even mentioned in it."

"Have you got the will?"

Mr. Marchwood unlocked a drawer, and took it out.

Sir Patrick instantly rose from his chair. "No waiting for the lawyer!" he repeated, vehemently. "This is a matter of life and death. Lady Holchester bitterly resents her son's marriage. She speaks and feels as a friend of Mrs. Glenarm. Do you think Lord Holchester would take the same view if he knew of it?"

"It depends entirely on the circumstances."

"Suppose I informed him—as I inform you in confidence—that his son has gravely wronged Miss Silvester? And suppose I followed that up by telling him that his son has made atonement by marrying her?"

"After the feeling that he has shown in the matter, I believe he would sign the codicil."

"Then, for God's sake, let me see him!"

"I must speak to the doctor."

"Do it instantly!"

With the will in his hand, Mr. Marchwood advanced to the bedroom door. It was opened from within before he could get to it. The doctor appeared on the threshold. He held up his hand warningly when Mr. Marchwood attempted to speak to him.

"Go to Lady Holchester," he said. "It's all over."

"Dead?"

"Dead."

SIXTEENTH SCENE.—SALT PATCH.

CHAPTER THE FORTY-EIGHTH.

THE PLACE.

EARLY in the present century it was generally reported among the neighbors of one Reuben Limbrick that he was in a fair way to make a comfortable little fortune by dealing in Salt.

His place of abode was in Staffordshire, on a morsel of freehold land of his own—appropriately called Salt Patch. Without being absolutely a miser, he lived in the humblest manner, saw very little company; skillfully invested his money; and persisted in remaining a single man.

Toward eighteen hundred and forty he first felt the approach of the chronic malady which ultimately terminated his life. After trying what the medical men of his own locality could do for him, with very poor success, he met by accident with a doctor living in the western suburbs of London, who thoroughly understood his complaint. After some journeying backward and forward to consult this gentleman, he decided on retiring from business, and on taking up his abode within an easy distance of his medical man.

Finding a piece of freehold land to be sold in the neighborhood of Fulham, he bought it, and had a cottage residence built on it, under his own directions. He surrounded the whole—being a man singularly jealous of any intrusion on his retirement, or of any chance observation of his ways and habits—with a high wall, which cost a large sum of money, and which was rightly considered a dismal and hideous object by the neighbors. When the new residence was completed, he called it after the name of the place in Staffordshire where he had made his money, and where he had lived during the happiest period of his life. His relatives, failing to understand that a question of sentiment was involved in this proceeding, appealed to hard facts, and reminded him that there were no salt mines in the neighborhood. Reuben Limbrick answered, "So much the worse for the neighborhood"—and persisted in calling his property, "Salt Patch."

The cottage was so small that it looked quite lost in the large garden all round it. There was a ground-floor and a floor above it—and that was all.

On either side of the passage, on the lower floor, were two rooms. At the right-hand side, on entering by the front-door, there was a kitchen, with its outhouses attached. The room next to the kitchen looked into the garden. In Reuben Limbrick's time it was called the study and contained a small collection of books and a large store of fishing-tackle. On the left-hand side of the passage there was a drawing-room situated at the back of the house, and communicating with a dining-room in the front. On the upper floor there were five bedrooms—two on one side of the passage, corresponding in size with the dining-room and the drawing-room below, but not opening into each other; three on the other side of the passage, consisting of one larger room in front, and of two small rooms at the back. All these were solidly and completely furnished. Money had not been spared, and workmanship had not been stinted. It was all substantial—and, up stairs and down stairs, it was all ugly.

The situation of Salt Patch was lonely. The lands of the market-gardeners separated it from other houses. Jealously surrounded by its own high walls, the cottage suggested, even to the most unimaginative persons, the idea of an asylum or a prison. Reuben Limbrick's relatives, occasionally coming to stay with him, found the place prey on their spirits, and rejoiced when the time came for going home again. They were never pressed to stay against their will. Reuben Limbrick was not a hospitable or a sociable man. He set very little value on human sympathy, in his attacks of illness; and he bore congratulations impatiently, in his intervals of health. "I care about nothing but fishing," he used to say. "I find my dog very good company. And I am quite happy as long as I am free from pain."

On his death-bed, he divided his money justly enough among his relations. The only part of his Will which exposed itself to unfavorable criticism, was a clause conferring a legacy on one of his sisters (then a widow) who had estranged herself from her family by marrying beneath her. The family agreed in considering this unhappy person as undeserving of notice or benefit. Her name was Hester Dethridge. It proved to be a great aggravation of Hester's offenses, in the eyes of Hester's relatives, when it was discovered that she possessed a life-interest in Salt Patch, and an income of two hundred a year.

Not visited by the surviving members of her family, living, literally, by herself in the world, Hester decided, in spite of her comfortable little income, on letting lodgings. The explanation of this strange conduct which she had written on her slate, in reply to an inquiry from Anne, was the true one. "I have not got a friend in the world: I dare not live alone." In that desolate situation, and with that melancholy motive, she put the house into an agent's hands. The first person in want of lodgings whom the agent sent to see the place was Perry the trainer; and Hester's first tenant was Geoffrey Delamayn.

The rooms which the landlady reserved for herself were the kitchen, the room next to it, which had once been her brother's "study," and the two small back bedrooms up stairs—one for herself, the other for the servant-girl whom she employed to help her. The whole of the rest of the cottage was to let. It was more than the trainer wanted; but Hester Dethridge refused to dispose of her lodgings—either as to the rooms occupied, or as to the period for which they were to be taken—on other than her own terms. Perry had no alternative but to lose the advantage of the garden as a private training-ground, or to submit.

Being only two in number, the lodgers had three bedrooms to choose from. Geoffrey established himself in the back-room, over the drawing-room. Perry chose the front-room, placed on the other side of the cottage, next to the two smaller apartments occupied by Hester and her maid. Under this arrangement, the front bedroom, on the opposite side of the passage—next to the room in which Geoffrey slept—was left empty, and was called, for the time being, the spare room. As for the lower floor, the athlete and his trainer ate their meals in the dining-room; and left the drawing-room, as a needless luxury, to take care of itself.

The Foot-Race once over, Perry's business at the cottage was at an end. His empty bedroom became a second spare room. The term for which the lodgings had been taken was then still unexpired. On the day after the race Geoffrey had to choose between sacrificing the money, or remaining in the lodgings by himself, with two spare bedrooms on his hands, and with a drawing-room for the reception of his visitors—who called with pipes in their mouths, and whose idea of hospitality was a pot of beer in the garden.

To use his own phrase, he was "out of sorts." A sluggish reluctance to face change of any kind possessed him. He decided on staying at Salt Patch until his marriage to Mrs. Glenarm (which he then looked upon as a certainty) obliged him to alter his habits completely, once for all. From Fulham he had gone, the next day, to attend the inquiry in Portland Place. And to Fulham he returned, when he brought the wife who had been forced upon him to her "home."

Such was the position of the tenant, and such were the arrangements of the interior of the cottage, on the memorable evening when Anne Silvester entered it as Geoffrey's wife.

CHAPTER THE FORTY-NINTH.

THE NIGHT.

ON leaving Lady Lundie's house, Geoffrey called the first empty cab that passed him. He opened the door, and signed to Anne to enter the vehicle. She obeyed him mechanically. He placed himself on the seat opposite to her, and told the man to drive to Fulham.

The cab started on its journey; husband and wife preserving absolute silence. Anne laid her head back wearily, and closed her eyes. Her strength had broken down under the effort which had sustained her from the beginning to the end of the inquiry. Her power of thinking was gone. She felt nothing, knew nothing, feared nothing. Half in faintness, half in slumber, she had lost all sense of her own terrible position before the first five minutes of the journey to Fulham had come to an end.

Sitting opposite to her, savagely self-concentrated in his own thoughts, Geoffrey roused himself on a sudden. An idea had sprung to life in his sluggish brain. He put his head out of the window of the cab, and directed the driver to turn back, and go to an hotel near the Great Northern Railway.

Resuming his seat, he looked furtively at Anne. She neither moved nor opened her eyes—she was, to all appearance, unconscious of what had happened. He observed her attentively. Was she really ill? Was the time coming when he would be freed from her? He pondered over that question—watching her closely. Little by little the vile hope in him slowly died away, and a vile suspicion took its place. What, if this appearance of illness was a pretense? What, if she was waiting to throw him off his guard, and escape from him at the first opportunity? He put his head out of the window again, and gave another order to the driver. The cab diverged from the direct route, and stopped at a public house in Holborn, kept (under an assumed name) by Perry the trainer.

Geoffrey wrote a line in pencil on his card, and sent it into the house by the driver. After waiting some minutes, a lad appeared and touched his hat. Geoffrey spoke to him, out of the window, in an under-tone. The lad took his place on the box by the driver. The cab turned back, and took the road to the hotel near the Great Northern Railway.

Arrived at the place, Geoffrey posted the lad close at the door of the cab, and pointed to Anne, still reclining with closed eyes; still, as it seemed, too weary to lift her head, too faint to notice any thing that happened. "If she attempts to get out, stop her, and send for me." With those parting directions he entered the hotel, and asked for Mr. Moy.

Mr. Moy was in the house; he had just returned from Portland Place. He rose, and bowed coldly, when Geoffrey was shown into his sitting-room.

"What is your business with me?" he asked.

"I've had a notion come into my head," said Geoffrey. "And I want to speak to you about it directly."

"I must request you to consult some one else. Consider me, if you please, as having withdrawn from all further connection with your affairs."

Geoffrey looked at him in stolid surprise.

"Do you mean to say you're going to leave me in the lurch?" he asked.

"I mean to say that I will take no fresh step in any business of yours," answered Mr. Moy, firmly. "As to the future, I have ceased to be your legal adviser. As to the past, I shall carefully complete the formal duties toward you which remain to be done. Mrs. Inchbare and Bishopriggs are coming here by appointment, at six this evening, to receive the money due to them before they go back. I shall return to Scotland myself by the night mail. The persons referred to, in the matter of the promise of marriage, by Sir Patrick, are all in Scotland. I will take their evidence as to the handwriting, and as to the question of residence in the North—and I will send it to you in written form. That done, I shall have done all. I decline to advise you in any future step which you propose to take."

After reflecting for a moment, Geoffrey put a last question.

"You said Bishopriggs and the woman would be here at six this evening."

"Yes."

"Where are they to be found before that?"

Mr. Moy wrote a few words on a slip of paper, and handed it to Geoffrey. "At their lodgings," he said. "There is the address."

Geoffrey took the address, and left the room. Lawyer and client parted without a word on either side.

Returning to the cab, Geoffrey found the lad steadily waiting at his post.

"Has any thing happened?"

"The lady hasn't moved, Sir, since you left her."

"Is Perry at the public house?"

"Not at this time, Sir."

"I want a lawyer. Do you know who Perry's lawyer is?"

"Yes, Sir."

"And where he is to be found?"

"Yes, Sir."

"Get up on the box, and tell the man where to drive to."

The cab went on again along the Euston Road, and stopped at a house in a side-street, with a professional brass plate on the door. The lad got down, and came to the window.

"Here it is, Sir."

"Knock at the door, and see if he is at home."

He proved to be at home. Geoffrey entered the house, leaving his emissary once more on the watch. The lad noticed that the lady moved this time. She shivered as if she felt cold—opened her eyes for a moment wearily, and looked out through the window—sighed, and sank back again in the corner of the cab.

After an absence of more than half an hour Geoffrey came out again. His interview with Perry's lawyer appeared to have relieved his mind of something that had oppressed it. He once more ordered the driver to go to Fulham—opened the door to get into the cab—then, as it seemed, suddenly recollected himself—and, calling the lad down from the box, ordered him to get inside, and took his place by the driver.

As the cab started he looked over his shoulder at Anne through the front window. "Well worth trying," he said to himself. "It's the way to be even with her. And it's the way to be free."

They arrived at the cottage. Possibly, repose had restored Anne's strength. Possibly, the sight of the place had roused the instinct of self-preservation in her at last. To Geoffrey's surprise, she left the cab without assistance. When he opened the wooden gate, with his own key, she recoiled from it, and looked at him for the first time.

He pointed to the entrance.

"Go in," he said.

"On what terms?" she asked, without stirring a step.

Geoffrey dismissed the cab; and sent the lad in, to wait for further orders. These things done, he answered her loudly and brutally the moment they were alone:

"On any terms I please."

"Nothing will induce me," she said, firmly, "to live with you as your wife. You may kill me—but you will never bend me to that."

He advanced a step—opened his lips—and suddenly checked himself. He waited a while, turning something over in his mind. When he spoke again, it was with marked deliberation and constraint—with the air of a man who was repeating words put into his lips, or words prepared beforehand.

"I have something to tell you in the presence of witnesses," he said. "I don't ask you, or wish you, to see me in the cottage alone."

She started at the change in him. His sudden composure, and his sudden nicety in the choice of words, tried her courage far more severely than it had been tried by his violence of the moment before.

He waited her decision, still pointing through the gate. She trembled a little—steadied herself again—and went in. The lad, waiting in the front garden, followed her.

He threw open the drawing-room door, on the left-hand side of the passage. She entered the room. The servant-girl appeared. He said to her, "Fetch Mrs. Dethridge; and come back with her yourself." Then he went into the room; the lad, by his own directions, following him in; and the door being left wide open.

Hester Dethridge came out from the kitchen with the girl behind her. At the sight of Anne, a faint and momentary change passed over the stony stillness of her face. A dull light glimmered in her eyes. She slowly nodded her head. A dumb sound, vaguely expressive of something like exultation or relief, escaped her lips.

Geoffrey spoke—once more, with marked deliberation and constraint; once more, with the air of repeating something which had been prepared beforehand. He pointed to Anne.

"This woman is my wife," he said. "In the presence of you three, as witnesses, I tell her that I don't forgive her. I have brought her here—having no other place in which I can trust her to be—to wait the issue of proceedings, undertaken in defense of my own honor and good name. While she stays here, she will live separate from me, in a room of her own. If it is necessary for me to communicate with her, I shall only see her in the presence of a third person. Do you all understand me?"

Hester Dethridge bowed her head. The other two answered, "Yes"—and turned to go out.

Anne rose. At a sign from Geoffrey, the servant and the lad waited in the room to hear what she had to say.

"I know nothing in my conduct," she said, addressing herself to Geoffrey, "which justifies you in telling these people that you don't forgive me. Those words applied by you to me are an insult. I am equally ignorant of what you mean when you speak of defending your good name. All I understand is, that we are separate persons in this house, and that I am to have a room of my own. I am grateful, whatever your motives may be, for the arrangement that you have proposed. Direct one of these two women to show me my room."

Geoffrey turned to Hester Dethridge.

"Take her up stairs," he said; "and let her pick which room she pleases. Give her what she wants to eat or drink. Bring down the address of the place where her luggage is. The lad here will go back by railway, and fetch it. That's all. Be off."

Hester went out. Anne followed her up the stairs. In the passage on the upper floor she stopped. The dull light flickered again for a moment in her eyes. She wrote on her slate, and held it up to Anne, with these words on it: "I knew you would come back. It's not over yet between you and him." Anne made no reply. She went on writing, with something faintly like a smile on her thin, colorless lips. "I know something of bad husbands. Yours is as bad a one as ever stood in shoes. He'll try you." Anne made an effort to stop her. "Don't you see how tired I am?" she said, gently. Hester Dethridge dropped the slate—looked with a steady and uncompassionate attention in Anne's face—nodded her head, as much as to say, "I see it now"—and led the way into one of the empty rooms.

It was the front bedroom, over the drawing-room. The first glance round showed it to be scrupulously clean, and solidly and tastelessly furnished. The hideous paper on the walls, the hideous carpet on the floor, were both of the best quality. The great heavy mahogany bedstead, with its curtains hanging from a hook in the ceiling, and with its clumsily carved head and foot on the same level, offered to the view the anomalous spectacle of French design overwhelmed by English execution. The most noticeable thing in the room was the extraordinary attention which had been given to the defense of the door. Besides the usual lock and key, it possessed two solid bolts, fastening inside at the top and the bottom. It had been one among the many eccentric sides of Reuben Limbrick's character to live in perpetual dread of thieves breaking into his cottage at night. All the outer doors and all the window shutters were solidly sheathed with iron, and had alarm-bells attached to them on a new principle. Every one of the bedrooms possessed its two bolts on the inner side of the door. And, to crown all, on the roof of the cottage was a little belfry, containing a bell large enough to make itself heard at the Fulham police station. In Reuben Limbrick's time the rope had communicated with his bedroom. It hung now against the wall, in the passage outside.

Looking from one to the other of the objects around her, Anne's eyes rested on the partition wall which divided the room from the room next to it. The wall was not broken by a door of communication, it had nothing placed against it but a wash-hand-stand and two chairs.

"Who sleeps in the next room?" said Anne.

Hester Dethridge pointed down to the drawing-room in which they had left Geoffrey, Geoffrey slept in the room.

Anne led the way out again into the passage.

"Show me the second room," she said.

The second room was also in front of the house. More ugliness (of first-rate quality) in the paper and the carpet. Another heavy mahogany bedstead; but, this time, a bedstead with a canopy attached to the head of it—supporting its own curtains. Anticipating Anne's inquiry, on this occasion, Hester looked toward the next room, at the back of the cottage, and pointed to herself. Anne at once decided on choosing the second room; it was the farthest from Geoffrey. Hester waited while she wrote the address at which her luggage would be found (at the house of the musical agent), and then, having applied for, and received her directions as to the evening meal which she should send up stairs, quitted the room.

Left alone, Anne secured the door, and threw herself on the bed. Still too weary to exert her mind, still physically incapable of realizing the helplessness and the peril of her position, she opened a locket that hung from her neck, kissed the portrait of her mother and the portrait of Blanche placed opposite to each other inside it, and sank into a deep and dreamless sleep.

Meanwhile Geoffrey repeated his final orders to the lad, at the cottage gate.

"When you have got the luggage, you are to go to the lawyer. If he can come here to-night, you will show him the way. If he can't come, you will bring me a letter from him. Make any mistake in this, and it will be the worst day's work you ever did in your life. Away with you, and don't lose the train."

The lad ran off. Geoffrey waited, looking after him, and turning over in his mind what had been done up to that time.

"All right, so far," he said to himself. "I didn't ride in the cab with her. I told her before witnesses I didn't forgive her, and why I had her in the house. I've put her in a room by herself. And if I must see her, I see her with Hester Dethridge for a witness. My part's done—let the lawyer do his."

He strolled round into the back garden, and lit his pipe. After a while, as the twilight faded, he saw a light in Hester's sitting-room on the ground-floor. He went to the window. Hester and the servant-girl were both there at work. "Well?" he asked. "How about the woman up stairs?" Hester's slate, aided by the girl's tongue, told him all about "the woman" that was to be told. They had taken up to her room tea and an omelet; and they had been obliged to wake her from a sleep. She had eaten a little of the omelet, and had drunk eagerly of the tea. They had gone up again to take the tray down. She had returned to the bed. She was not asleep—only dull and heavy. Made no remark. Looked clean worn out. We left her a light; and we let her be. Such was the report. After listening to it, without making any remark, Geoffrey filled a second pipe, and resumed his walk. The time wore on. It began to feel chilly in the garden. The rising wind swept audibly over the open lands round the cottage; the stars twinkled their last; nothing was to be seen overhead but the black void of night. More rain coming. Geoffrey went indoors.

An evening newspaper was on the dining-room table. The candles were lit. He sat down, and tried to read. No! There was nothing in the newspaper that he cared about. The time for hearing from the lawyer was drawing nearer and nearer. Reading was of no use. Sitting still was of no use. He got up, and went out in the front of the cottage—strolled to the gate—opened it—and looked idly up and down the road.

But one living creature was visible by the light of the gas-lamp over the gate. The creature came nearer, and proved to be the postman going his last round, with the last delivery for the night. He came up to the gate with a letter in his hand.

"The Honorable Geoffrey Delamayn?"

"All right."

He took the letter from the postman, and went back into the dining-room. Looking at the address by the light of the candles, he recognized the handwriting of Mrs. Glenarm. "To congratulate me on my marriage!" he said to himself, bitterly, and opened the letter.

Mrs. Glenarm's congratulations were expressed in these terms:

"MY ADORED GEOFFREY,—I have heard all. My beloved one! my own! you are sacrificed to the vilest wretch that walks the earth, and I have lost you! How is it that I live after hearing it? How is it that I can think, and write, with my brain on fire, and my heart broken! Oh, my angel, there is a purpose that supports me—pure, beautiful, worthy of us both. I live, Geoffrey—I live to dedicate myself to the adored idea of You. My hero! my first, last, love! I will marry no other man. I will live and die—I vow it solemnly on my bended knees—I will live and die true to You. I am your Spiritual Wife. My beloved Geoffrey! she can't come between us, there—she can never rob you of my heart's unalterable fidelity, of my soul's unearthly devotion. I am your Spiritual Wife! Oh, the blameless luxury of writing those words! Write back to me, beloved one, and say you feel it too. Vow it, idol of my heart, as I have vowed it. Unalterable fidelity! unearthly devotion! Never, never will I be the wife of any other man! Never, never will I forgive the woman who has come between us! Yours ever and only; yours with the stainless passion that burns on the altar of the heart; yours, yours, yours—E. G."

This outbreak of hysterical nonsense—in itself simply ridiculous—assumed a serious importance in its effect on Geoffrey. It associated the direct attainment of his own interests with the gratification of his vengeance on Anne. Ten thousand a year self-dedicated to him—

and nothing to prevent his putting out his hand and taking it but the woman who had caught him in her trap, the woman up stairs who had fastened herself on him for life!

He put the letter into his pocket. “Wait till I hear from the lawyer,” he said to himself. “The easiest way out of it is that way. And it’s the law.”

He looked impatiently at his watch. As he put it back again in his pocket there was a ring at the bell. Was it the lad bringing the luggage? Yes. And, with it, the lawyer’s report? No. Better than that—the lawyer himself.

“Come in!” cried Geoffrey, meeting his visitor at the door.

The lawyer entered the dining-room. The candle-light revealed to view a corpulent, full-lipped, bright-eyed man—with a strain of negro blood in his yellow face, and with unmistakable traces in his look and manner of walking habitually in the dirtiest professional by-ways of the law.

“I’ve got a little place of my own in your neighborhood,” he said. “And I thought I would look in myself, Mr. Delamayn, on my way home.”

“Have you seen the witnesses?”

“I have examined them both, Sir. First, Mrs. Inchbare and Mr. Bishopriggs together. Next, Mrs. Inchbare and Mr. Bishopriggs separately.”

“Well?”

“Well, Sir, the result is unfavorable, I am sorry to say.”

“What do you mean?”

“Neither the one nor the other of them, Mr. Delamayn, can give the evidence we want. I have made sure of that.”

“Made sure of that? You have made an infernal mess of it! You don’t understand the case!”

The mulatto lawyer smiled. The rudeness of his client appeared only to amuse him.

“Don’t I?” he said. “Suppose you tell me where I am wrong about it? Here it is in outline only. On the fourteenth of August last your wife was at an inn in Scotland. A gentleman named Arnold Brinkworth joined her there. He represented himself to be her husband, and he staid with her till the next morning. Starting from those facts, the object you have in view is to sue for a Divorce from your wife. You make Mr. Arnold Brinkworth the co-respondent. And you produce in evidence the waiter and the landlady of the inn. Any thing wrong, Sir, so far?”

Nothing wrong. At one cowardly stroke to cast Anne disgraced on the world, and to set himself free—there, plainly and truly stated, was the scheme which he had devised, when he had turned back on the way to Fulham to consult Mr. Moy.

“So much for the case,” resumed the lawyer. “Now for what I have done on receiving your instructions. I have examined the witnesses; and I have had an interview (not a very pleasant one) with Mr. Moy. The result of those two proceedings is briefly this. First discovery: In assuming the character of the lady’s husband Mr. Brinkworth was acting under your directions—which tells dead against you. Second discovery: Not the slightest impropriety of conduct, not an approach even to harmless familiarity, was detected by either of the witnesses, while the lady and gentleman were together at the inn. There is literally no evidence to produce against them, except that they were together—in two rooms. How are you to assume a guilty purpose, when you can't prove an approach to a guilty act? You can no more take such a case as that into Court than you can jump over the roof of this cottage."

He looked hard at his client, expecting to receive a violent reply. His client agreeably disappointed him. A very strange impression appeared to have been produced on this reckless and headstrong man. He got up quietly; he spoke with perfect outward composure of face and manner when he said his next words.

"Have you given up the case?"

"As things are at present, Mr. Delamayn, there is no case."

"And no hope of my getting divorced from her?"

"Wait a moment. Have your wife and Mr. Brinkworth met nowhere since they were together at the Scotch inn?"

"Nowhere."

"As to the future, of course I can't say. As to the past, there is no hope of your getting divorced from her."

"Thank you. Good-night."

"Good-night, Mr. Delamayn."

Fastened to her for life—and the law powerless to cut the knot.

He pondered over that result until he had thoroughly realized it and fixed it in his mind. Then he took out Mrs. Glenarm's letter, and read it through again, attentively, from beginning to end.

Nothing could shake her devotion to him. Nothing would induce her to marry another man. There she was—in her own words—dedicated to him: waiting, with her fortune at her own disposal, to be his wife. There also was his father, waiting (so far as he knew, in the absence of any tidings from Holchester House) to welcome Mrs. Glenarm as a daughter-in-law, and to give Mrs. Glenarm's husband an income of his own. As fair a prospect, on all sides, as man could desire. And nothing in the way of it but the woman who had caught him in her trap—the woman up stairs who had fastened herself on him for life.

He went out in the garden in the darkness of the night.

There was open communication, on all sides, between the back garden and the front. He walked round and round the cottage—now appearing in a stream of light from a window; now disappearing again in the darkness. The wind blew refreshingly over his bare head. For some minutes he went round and round, faster and faster, without a pause. When he stopped at last, it was in front of the cottage. He lifted his head slowly, and looked up at the dim light in the window of Anne's room.

"How?" he said to himself. "That's the question. How?"

He went indoors again, and rang the bell. The servant-girl who answered it started back at the sight of him. His florid color was all gone. His eyes looked at her without appearing to see her. The perspiration was standing on his forehead in great heavy drops.

"Are you ill, Sir?" said the girl.

He told her, with an oath, to hold her tongue and bring the brandy. When she entered the room for the second time, he was standing with his back to her, looking out at the night. He never moved when she put the bottle on the table. She heard him muttering as if he was talking to himself.

The same difficulty which had been present to his mind in secret under Anne's window was present to his mind still.

How? That was the problem to solve. How?

He turned to the brandy, and took counsel of that.

CHAPTER THE FIFTIETH.

THE MORNING.

WHEN does the vain regret find its keenest sting? When is the doubtful future blackened by its darkest cloud? When is life least worth having, and death oftenest at the bedside? In the terrible morning hours, when the sun is rising in its glory, and the birds are singing in the stillness of the new-born day.

Anne woke in the strange bed, and looked round her, by the light of the new morning, at the strange room.

The rain had all fallen in the night. The sun was master in the clear autumn sky. She rose, and opened the window. The fresh morning air, keen and fragrant, filled the room. Far and near, the same bright stillness possessed the view. She stood at the window looking out. Her mind was clear again—she could think, she could feel; she could face the one last question which the merciless morning now forced on her—How will it end?

Was there any hope?—hope for instance, in what she might do for herself. What can a married woman do for herself? She can make her misery public—provided it be misery of a certain kind—and can reckon single-handed with Society when she has done it. Nothing more.

Was there hope in what others might do for her? Blanche might write to her—might even come and see her—if her husband allowed it; and that was all. Sir Patrick had pressed her hand at parting, and had told her to rely on him. He was the firmest, the truest of friends. But what could he do? There were outrages which her husband was privileged to commit, under the sanction of marriage, at the bare thought of which her blood ran cold. Could Sir Patrick protect her? Absurd! Law and Society armed her husband with his conjugal rights. Law and Society had but one answer to give, if she appealed to them—You are his wife.

No hope in herself; no hope in her friends; no hope any where on earth. Nothing to be done but to wait for the end—with faith in the Divine Mercy; with faith in the better world.

She took out of her trunk a little book of Prayers and Meditations—worn with much use—which had once belonged to her mother. She sat by the window reading it. Now and then she looked up from it—thinking. The parallel between her mother's position and her own position was now complete. Both married to husbands who hated them; to husbands whose interests pointed to mercenary alliances with other women; to husbands whose one want and one purpose was to be free from their wives. Strange, what different ways had led mother and daughter both to the same fate! Would the parallel hold to the end? "Shall I die," she wondered, thinking of her mother's last moments, "in Blanche's arms?"

The time had passed unheeded. The morning movement in the house had failed to catch her ear. She was first called out of herself to the sense of the present and passing events by the voice of the servant-girl outside the door.

"The master wants you, ma'am, down stairs."

She rose instantly and put away the little book.

"Is that all the message?" she asked, opening the door.

"Yes, ma'am."

She followed the girl down stairs; recalling to her memory the strange words addressed to her by Geoffrey, in the presence of the servants, on the evening before. Was she now to know what those words really meant? The doubt would soon be set at rest. "Be the trial what it may," she thought to herself, "let me bear it as my mother would have borne it."

The servant opened the door of the dining-room. Breakfast was on the table. Geoffrey was standing at the window. Hester Dethridge was waiting, posted near the door. He came forward—with the nearest approach to gentleness in his manner which she had ever yet seen in it—he came forward, with a set smile on his lips, and offered her his hand!

She had entered the room, prepared (as she believed) for any thing that could happen. She was not prepared for this. She stood speechless, looking at him.

After one glance at her, when she came in, Hester Dethridge looked at him, too—and from that moment never looked away again, as long as Anne remained in the room.

He broke the silence—in a voice that was not like his own; with a furtive restraint in his manner which she had never noticed in it before.

"Won't you shake hands with your husband," he asked, "when your husband asks you?"

She mechanically put her hand in his. He dropped it instantly, with a start. "God! how cold!" he exclaimed. His own hand was burning hot, and shook incessantly.

He pointed to a chair at the head of the table.

"Will you make the tea?" he asked.

She had given him her hand mechanically; she advanced a step mechanically—and then stopped.

"Would you prefer breakfasting by yourself?" he said.

"If you please," she answered, faintly.

"Wait a minute. I have something to say before you go."

She waited. He considered with himself; consulting his memory—visibly, unmistakably, consulting it before he spoke again.

"I have had the night to think in," he said. "The night has made a new man of me. I beg your pardon for what I said yesterday. I was not myself yesterday. I talked nonsense yesterday. Please to forget it, and forgive it. I wish to turn over a new leaf and make amends—make amends for my past conduct. It shall be my endeavor to be a good husband. In the presence of Mrs. Dethridge, I request you to give me a chance. I won't force your inclinations. We are married—what's the use of regretting it? Stay here, as you said yesterday, on your own terms. I wish to make it up. In the presence of Mrs. Dethridge, I say I wish to make it up. I won't detain you. I request you to think of it. Good-morning."

He said those extraordinary words like a slow boy saying a hard lesson—his eyes on the ground, his fingers restlessly fastening and unfastening a button on his waistcoat.

Anne left the room. In the passage she was obliged to wait, and support herself against the wall. His unnatural politeness was horrible; his carefully asserted repentance chilled her to the soul with dread. She had never felt—in the time of his fiercest anger and his foulest language—the unutterable horror of him that she felt now.

Hester Dethridge came out, closing the door behind her. She looked attentively at Anne—then wrote on her slate, and held it out, with these words on it:

"Do you believe him?"

Anne pushed the slate away, and ran up stairs. She fastened the door—and sank into a chair.

"He is plotting something against me," she said to herself. "What?"

A sickening, physical sense of dread—entirely new in her experience of herself—made her shrink from pursuing the question. The sinking at her heart turned her faint. She went to get the air at the open window.

At the same moment there was a ring at the gate bell. Suspicious of any thing and every thing, she felt a sudden distrust of letting herself be seen. She drew back behind the curtain and looked out.

A man-servant, in livery, was let in. He had a letter in his hand. He said to the girl as he passed Anne's window, "I come from Lady Holchester; I must see Mr. Delamayn instantly."

They went in. There was an interval. The footman reappeared, leaving the place. There was another interval. Then there came a knock at the door. Anne hesitated. The knock was repeated, and the dumb murmuring of Hester Dethridge was heard outside. Anne opened the door.

Hester came in with the breakfast. She pointed to a letter among other things on the tray. It was addressed to Anne, in Geoffrey's handwriting, and it contained these words:

"My father died yesterday. Write your orders for your mourning. The boy will take them. You are not to trouble yourself to go to London. Somebody is to come here to you from the shop."

Anne dropped the paper on her lap without looking up. At the same moment Hester Dethridge's slate was passed stealthily between her eyes and the note—with these words traced on it. "His mother is coming to-day. His brother has been telegraphed from Scotland. He was drunk last night. He's drinking again. I know what that means. Look out, missus—look out."

Anne signed to her to leave the room. She went out, pulling the door to, but not closing it behind her.

There was another ring at the gate bell. Once more Anne went to the window. Only the lad, this time; arriving to take his orders for the day. He had barely entered the garden when he was followed by the postman with letters. In a minute more Geoffrey's voice was heard in the passage, and Geoffrey's heavy step ascended the wooden stairs. Anne hurried across the room to draw the bolts. Geoffrey met her before she could close the door.

"A letter for you," he said, keeping scrupulously out of the room. "I don't wish to force your inclinations—I only request you to tell me who it's from."

His manner was as carefully subdued as ever. But the unacknowledged distrust in him (when he looked at her) betrayed itself in his eye.

She glanced at the handwriting on the address.

"From Blanche," she answered.

He softly put his foot between the door and the post—and waited until she had opened and read Blanche's letter.

"May I see it?" he asked—and put in his hand for it through the door.

The spirit in Anne which would once have resisted him was dead in her now. She handed him the open letter.

It was very short. Excepting some brief expressions of fondness, it was studiously confined to stating the purpose for which it had been written. Blanche proposed to visit Anne that afternoon, accompanied by her uncle, she sent word beforehand, to make sure of finding Anne at home. That was all. The letter had evidently been written under Sir Patrick's advice.

Geoffrey handed it back, after first waiting a moment to think.

"My father died yesterday," he said. "My wife can't receive visitors before he is buried. I don't wish to force your inclinations. I only say I can't let visitors in here before the funeral—except my own family. Send a note down stairs. The lad will take it to your friend when he goes to London." With those words he left.

An appeal to the proprieties of life, in the mouth of Geoffrey Delamayn, could only mean one of two things. Either he had spoken in brutal mockery—or he had spoken with some ulterior object in view. Had he seized on the event of his father's death as a pretext for isolating his wife from all communication with the outer world? Were there reasons, which had not yet asserted themselves, for his dreading the result, if he allowed Anne to communicate with her friends?

The hour wore on, and Hester Dethridge appeared again. The lad was waiting for Anne's orders for her mourning, and for her note to Mrs. Arnold Brinkworth.

Anne wrote the orders and the note. Once more the horrible slate appeared when she had done, between the writing paper and her eyes, with the hard lines of warning pitilessly traced on it. "He has locked the gate. When there's a ring we are to come to him for the key. He has written to a woman. Name outside the letter, Mrs. Glenarm. He has had more brandy. Like my husband. Mind yourself."

The one way out of the high walls all round the cottage locked. Friends forbidden to see her. Solitary imprisonment, with her husband for a jailer. Before she had been four-and-twenty hours in the cottage it had come to that. And what was to follow?

She went back mechanically to the window. The sight of the outer world, the occasional view of a passing vehicle, helped to sustain her.

The lad appeared in the front garden departing to perform his errand to London. Geoffrey went with him to open the gate, and called after him, as he passed through it, "Don't forget the books!"

The "books?" What "books?" Who wanted them? The slightest thing now roused Anne's suspicion. For hours afterward the books haunted her mind.

He secured the gate and came back again. He stopped under Anne's window and called to her. She showed herself. "When you want air and exercise," he said, "the back garden is at your own disposal." He put the key of the gate in his pocket and returned to the house.

After some hesitation Anne decided on taking him at his word. In her state of suspense, to remain within the four walls of the bedroom was unendurable. If some lurking snare lay hid under the fair-sounding proposal which Geoffrey had made, it was less repellent to her boldly to prove what it might be than to wait pondering over it with her mind in the dark. She put on her hat and went down into the garden. Nothing happened out of the common. Wherever he was he never showed himself. She wandered up and down, keeping on the side of the garden which was farthest from the dining-room window. To a woman, escape from the place was simply impossible. Setting out of the question the height of the walls, they were armed at the top with a thick setting of jagged broken glass. A small back-door in the end wall (intended probably for the gardener's use) was bolted and locked—the key having been taken out. There was not a house near. The lands of the local growers of vegetables surrounded the garden on all sides. In the nineteenth century, and in the immediate neighborhood of a great metropolis, Anne was as absolutely isolated from all contact with the humanity around her as if she lay in her grave.

After the lapse of half an hour the silence was broken by a noise of carriage wheels on the public road in front, and a ring at the bell. Anne kept close to the cottage, at the back; determined, if a chance offered, on speaking to the visitor, whoever the visitor might be.

She heard voices in the dining-room through the open window—Geoffrey's voice and the voice of a woman. Who was the woman? Not Mrs. Glenarm, surely? After a while the visitor's voice was suddenly raised. "Where is she?" it said. "I wish to see her." Anne instantly advanced to the back-door of the house—and found herself face to face with a lady who was a total stranger to her.

"Are you my son's wife?" asked the lady.

"I am your son's prisoner," Anne answered.

Lady Holchester's pale face turned paler still. It was plain that Anne's reply had confirmed some doubt in the mother s mind which had been already suggested to it by the son.

"What do you mean?" she asked, in a whisper.

Geoffrey's heavy footsteps crossed the dining-room. There was no time to explain. Anne whispered back,

"Tell my friends what I have told you."

Geoffrey appeared at the dining-room door.

"Name one of your friends," said Lady Holchester.

"Sir Patrick Lundie."

Geoffrey heard the answer. "What about Sir Patrick Lundie?" he asked.

"I wish to see Sir Patrick Lundie," said his mother. "And your wife can tell me where to find him."

Anne instantly understood that Lady Holchester would communicate with Sir Patrick. She mentioned his London address. Lady Holchester turned to leave the cottage. Her son stopped her.

"Let's set things straight," he said, "before you go. My mother," he went on, addressing himself to Anne, "don't think there's much chance for us two of living comfortably together. Bear witness to the truth—will you? What did I tell you at breakfast-time? Didn't I say it should be my endeavor to make you a good husband? Didn't I say—in Mrs. Dethridge's presence—I wanted to make it up?" He waited until Anne had answered in the affirmative, and then appealed to his mother. "Well? what do you think now?"

Lady Holchester declined to reveal what she thought. "You shall see me, or hear from me, this evening," she said to Anne. Geoffrey attempted to repeat his unanswered question. His mother looked at him. His eyes instantly dropped before hers. She gravely bent her head to Anne, and drew her veil. Her son followed her out in silence to the gate.

Anne returned to her room, sustained by the first sense of relief which she had felt since the morning. "His mother is alarmed," she said to herself. "A change will come."

A change was to come—with the coming night.

CHAPTER THE FIFTY-FIRST.

THE PROPOSAL.

TOWARD sunset, Lady Holchester's carriage drew up before the gate of the cottage.

Three persons occupied the carriage: Lady Holchester, her eldest son (now Lord Holchester), and Sir Patrick Lundie.

"Will you wait in the carriage, Sir Patrick?" said Julius. "Or will you come in?"

"I will wait. If I can be of the least use to her,, send for me instantly. In the mean time don't forget to make the stipulation which I have suggested. It is the one certain way of putting your brother's real feeling in this matter to the test."

The servant had rung the bell without producing any result. He rang again. Lady Holchester put a question to Sir Patrick.

"If I have an opportunity of speaking to my son's wife alone," she said, "have you any message to give?"

Sir Patrick produced a little note.

"May I appeal to your ladyship's kindness to give her this?" The gate was opened by the servant-girl, as Lady Holchester took the note. "Remember," reiterated Sir Patrick, earnestly "if I can be of the smallest service to her—don't think of my position with Mr. Delamayn. Send for me at once."

Julius and his mother were conducted into the drawing-room. The girl informed them that her master had gone up stairs to lie down, and that he would be with them immediately.

Both mother and son were too anxious to speak. Julius wandered uneasily about the room. Some books attracted his notice on a table in the corner—four dirty, greasy volumes, with a slip of paper projecting from the leaves of one of them, and containing this inscription, "With Mr. Perry's respects." Julius opened the volume. It was the ghastly popular record of Criminal Trials in England, called the Newgate Calendar. Julius showed it to his mother.

"Geoffrey's taste in literature!" he said, with a faint smile.

Lady Holchester signed to him to put the book back.

"You have seen Geoffrey's wife already—have you not?" she asked.

There was no contempt now in her tone when she referred to Anne. The impression produced on her by her visit to the cottage, earlier in the day, associated Geoffrey's wife with family anxieties of no trivial kind. She might still (for Mrs. Glenarm's sake) be a woman to be disliked—but she was no longer a woman to be despised.

"I saw her when she came to Swanhaven," said Julius. "I agree with Sir Patrick in thinking her a very interesting person."

"What did Sir Patrick say to you about Geoffrey this afternoon—while I was out of the room?"

"Only what he said to you. He thought their position toward each other here a very deplorable one. He considered that the reasons were serious for our interfering immediately."

"Sir Patrick's own opinion, Julius, goes farther than that."

"He has not acknowledged it, that I know of."

"How can he acknowledge it—to us?"

The door opened, and Geoffrey entered the room.

Julius eyed him closely as they shook hands. His eyes were bloodshot; his face was flushed; his utterance was thick—the look of him was the look of a man who had been drinking hard.

"Well?" he said to his mother. "What brings you back?"

"Julius has a proposal to make to you," Lady Holchester answered. "I approve of it; and I have come with him."

Geoffrey turned to his brother.

"What can a rich man like you want with a poor devil like me?" he asked.

"I want to do you justice, Geoffrey—if you will help me, by meeting me half-way. Our mother has told you about the will?"

"I'm not down for a half-penny in the will. I expected as much. Go on."

"You are wrong—you are down in it. There is liberal provision made for you in a codicil. Unhappily, my father died without signing it. It is needless to say that I consider it binding on me for all that. I am ready to do for you what your father would have done for you. And I only ask for one concession in return."

"What may that be?"

"You are living here very unhappily, Geoffrey, with your wife."

"Who says so? I don't, for one."

Julius laid his hand kindly on his brother's arm.

"Don't trifle with such a serious matter as this," he said. "Your marriage is, in every sense of the word, a misfortune—not only to you but to your wife. It is impossible that you can live together. I have come here to ask you to consent to a separation. Do that—and the provision made for you in the unsigned codicil is yours. What do you say?"

Geoffrey shook his brother's hand off his arm.

"I say—No!" he answered.

Lady Holchester interfered for the first time.

"Your brother's generous offer deserves a better answer than that," she said.

"My answer," reiterated Geoffrey, "is—No!"

He sat between them with his clenched fists resting on his knees—absolutely impenetrable to any thing that either of them could say.

"In your situation," said Julius, "a refusal is sheer madness. I won't accept it."

"Do as you like about that. My mind's made up. I won't let my wife be taken away from me. Here she stays."

The brutal tone in which he had made that reply roused Lady Holchester's indignation.

"Take care!" she said. "You are not only behaving with the grossest ingratitude toward your brother—you are forcing a suspicion into your mother's mind. You have some motive that you are hiding from us."

He turned on his mother with a sudden ferocity which made Julius spring to his feet. The next instant his eyes were on the ground, and the devil that possessed him was quiet again.

"Some motive I'm hiding from you?" he repeated, with his head down, and his utterance thicker than ever. "I'm ready to have my motive posted all over London, if you like. I'm fond of her."

He looked up as he said the last words. Lady Holchester turned away her head—recoiling from her own son. So overwhelming was the shock inflicted on her that even the strongly rooted prejudice which Mrs. Glenarm had implanted in her mind yielded to it. At that moment she absolutely pitied Anne!

"Poor creature!" said Lady Holchester.

He took instant offense at those two words. "I won't have my wife pitied by any body." With that reply, he dashed into the passage; and called out, "Anne! come down!"

Her soft voice answered; her light footfall was heard on the stairs. She came into the room. Julius advanced, took her hand, and held it kindly in his. "We are having a little family discussion," he said, trying to give her confidence. "And Geoffrey is getting hot over it, as usual."

Geoffrey appealed sternly to his mother.

"Look at her!" he said. "Is she starved? Is she in rags? Is she covered with bruises?" He turned to Anne. "They have come here to propose a separation. They both believe I hate you. I don't hate you. I'm a good Christian. I owe it to you that I'm cut out of my father's will.

I forgive you that. I owe it to you that I've lost the chance of marrying a woman with ten thousand a year. I forgive you that. I'm not a man who does things by halves. I said it should be my endeavor to make you a good husband. I said it was my wish to make it up. Well! I am as good as my word. And what's the consequence? I am insulted. My mother comes here, and my brother comes here—and they offer me money to part from you. Money be hanged! I'll be beholden to nobody. I'll get my own living. Shame on the people who interfere between man and wife! Shame!—that's what I say—shame!"

Anne looked, for an explanation, from her husband to her husband's mother.

"Have you proposed a separation between us?" she asked.

"Yes—on terms of the utmost advantage to my son; arranged with every possible consideration toward you. Is there any objection on your side?"

"Oh, Lady Holchester! is it necessary to ask me? What does he say?"

"He has refused."

"Refused!"

"Yes," said Geoffrey. "I don't go back from my word; I stick to what I said this morning. It's my endeavor to make you a good husband. It's my wish to make it up." He paused, and then added his last reason: "I'm fond of you."

Their eyes met as he said it to her. Julius felt Anne's hand suddenly tighten round his. The desperate grasp of the frail cold fingers, the imploring terror in the gentle sensitive face as it slowly turned his way, said to him as if in words, "Don't leave me friendless to-night!"

"If you both stop here till domesday," said Geoffrey, "you'll get nothing more out of me. You have had my reply."

With that, he seated himself doggedly in a corner of the room; waiting—ostentatiously waiting—for his mother and his brother to take their leave. The position was serious. To argue the matter with him that night was hopeless. To invite Sir Patrick's interference would only be to provoke his savage temper to a new outbreak. On the other hand, to leave the helpless woman, after what had passed, without another effort to befriend her, was, in her situation, an act of downright inhumanity, and nothing less. Julius took the one way out of the difficulty that was left—the one way worthy of him as a compassionate and an honorable man.

"We will drop it for to-night, Geoffrey," he said. "But I am not the less resolved, in spite of all that you have said, to return to the subject to-morrow. It would save me some inconvenience—a second journey here from town, and then going back again to my engagements—if I staid with you to-night. Can you give me a bed?"

A look flashed on him from Anne, which thanked him as no words could have thanked him.

"Give you a bed?" repeated Geoffrey. He checked himself, on the point of refusing. His mother was watching him; his wife was watching him—and his wife knew that the room above them was a room to spare. "All right!" he resumed, in another tone, with his eye on his mother. "There's my empty room up stairs. Have it, if you like. You won't find I've changed my mind to-morrow—but that's your look-out. Stop here, if the fancy takes you. I've no objection. It don't matter to Me.—Will you trust his lordship under my roof?" he added, addressing his mother. "I might have some motive that I'm hiding from you, you know!" Without waiting for an answer, he turned to Anne. "Go and tell old Dummy to put the sheets on the bed. Say there's a live lord in the house—she's to send in something devilish good for supper!" He burst fiercely into a forced laugh. Lady Holchester rose at the moment when Anne was leaving the room. "I shall not be here when you return," she said. "Let me bid you good-night."

She shook hands with Anne—giving her Sir Patrick's note, unseen, at the same moment. Anne left the room. Without addressing another word to her second son, Lady Holchester beckoned to Julius to give her his arm. "You have acted nobly toward your brother," she said to him. "My one comfort and my one hope, Julius, are in you." They went out together to the gate, Geoffrey following them with the key in his hand. "Don't be too anxious," Julius whispered to his mother. "I will keep the drink out of his way to-night—and I will bring you a better account of him to-morrow. Explain every thing to Sir Patrick as you go home."

He handed Lady Holchester into the carriage; and re-entered, leaving Geoffrey to lock the gate. The brothers returned in silence to the cottage. Julius had concealed it from his mother—but he was seriously uneasy in secret. Naturally prone to look at all things on their brighter side, he could place no hopeful interpretation on what Geoffrey had said and done that night. The conviction that he was deliberately acting a part, in his present relations with his wife, for some abominable purpose of his own, had rooted itself firmly in Julius. For the first time in his experience of his brother, the pecuniary consideration was not the uppermost consideration in Geoffrey's mind. They went back into the drawing-room. "What will you have to drink?" said Geoffrey.

"Nothing."

"You won't keep me company over a drop of brandy-and-water?"

"No. You have had enough brandy-and-water."

After a moment of frowning self-consideration in the glass, Geoffrey abruptly agreed with Julius "I look like it," he said. "I'll soon put that right." He disappeared, and returned with a wet towel tied round his head. "What will you do while the women are getting your bed ready? Liberty Hall here. I've taken to cultivating my mind—-I'm a reformed character, you know, now I'm a married man. You do what you like. I shall read."

He turned to the side-table, and, producing the volumes of the Newgate Calendar, gave one to his brother. Julius handed it back again.

"You won't cultivate your mind," he said, "with such a book as that. Vile actions recorded in vile English, make vile reading, Geoffrey, in every sense of the word."

"It will do for me. I don't know good English when I see it."

With that frank acknowledgment—to which the great majority of his companions at school and college might have subscribed without doing the slightest injustice to the present state of English education—Geoffrey drew his chair to the table, and opened one of the volumes of his record of crime.

The evening newspaper was lying on the sofa. Julius took it up, and seated himself opposite to his brother. He noticed, with some surprise, that Geoffrey appeared to have a special object in consulting his book. Instead of beginning at the first page, he ran the leaves through his fingers, and turned them down at certain places, before he entered on his reading.

If Julius had looked over his brother's shoulder, instead of only looking at him across the table, he would have seen that Geoffrey passed by all the lighter crimes reported in the Calendar, and marked for his own private reading the cases of murder only.

CHAPTER THE FIFTY-SECOND.

THE APPARITION.

THE night had advanced. It was close on twelve o'clock when Anne heard the servant's voice, outside her bedroom door, asking leave to speak with her for a moment.

"What is it?"

"The gentleman down stairs wishes to see you, ma'am."

"Do you mean Mr. Delamayn's brother?"

"Yes."

"Where is Mr. Delamayn?"

"Out in the garden, ma'am."

Anne went down stairs, and found Julius alone in the drawing-room.

"I am sorry to disturb you," he said. "I am afraid Geoffrey is ill. The landlady has gone to bed, I am told—and I don't know where to apply for medical assistance. Do you know of any doctor in the neighborhood?"

Anne, like Julius, was a perfect stranger to the neighborhood. She suggested making inquiry of the servant. On speaking to the girl, it turned out that she knew of a medical man, living within ten minutes' walk of the cottage. She could give plain directions enabling any person to find the place—but she was afraid, at that hour of the night and in that lonely neighborhood, to go out by herself.

"Is he seriously ill?" Anne asked.

"He is in such a state of nervous irritability," said Julius, "that he can't remain still for two moments together in the same place. It began with incessant restlessness while he was reading here. I persuaded him to go to bed. He couldn't lie still for an instant—he came down again, burning with fever, and more restless than ever. He is out in the garden in spite of every thing I could do to prevent him; trying, as he says, to 'run it off.' It appears to be serious to me.. Come and judge for yourself."

He led Anne into the next room; and, opening the shutter, pointed to the garden.

The clouds had cleared off; the night was fine. The clear starlight showed Geoffrey, stripped to his shirt and drawers, running round and round the garden. He apparently believed himself to be contending at the Fulham foot-race. At times, as the white figure circled round and round in the star-light, they heard him cheering for "the South." The slackening thump of his feet on the ground, the heavier and heavier gasps in which he drew his breath, as he passed the window, gave warning that his strength was failing him. Exhaustion, if it led to no worse consequences, would force him to return to the house. In the state of his brain at that moment who could say what the result might be, if medical help was not called in?

"I will go for the doctor," said Julius, "if you don't mind my leaving you."

It was impossible for Anne to set any apprehensions of her own against the plain necessity for summoning assistance. They found the key of the gate in the pocket of Geoffrey's coat up stairs. Anne went with Julius to let him out. "How can I thank you!" she said, gratefully. "What should I have done without you!"

"I won't be a moment longer than I can help," he answered, and left her.

She secured the gate again, and went back to the cottage. The servant met her at the door, and proposed calling up Hester Dethridge.

"We don't know what the master may do while his brother's away," said the girl. "And one more of us isn't one too many, when we are only women in the house."

"You are quite right," said Anne. "Wake your mistress."

After ascending the stairs, they looked out into the garden, through the window at the end of the passage on the upper floor. He was still going round and round, but very slowly: his pace was fast slackening to a walk.

Anne went back to her room, and waited near the open door—ready to close and fasten it instantly if any thing occurred to alarm her. "How changed I am!" she thought to herself. "Every thing frightens me, now."

The inference was the natural one—but not the true one. The change was not in herself, but in the situation in which she was placed. Her position during the investigation at Lady Lundie's house had tried her moral courage only. It had exacted from her one of those noble efforts of self-sacrifice which the hidden forces in a woman's nature are essentially capable of making. Her position at the cottage tried her physical courage: it called on her to rise superior to the sense of actual bodily danger—while that danger was lurking in the dark. There, the woman's nature sank under the stress laid on it—there, her courage could strike no root in the strength of her love—there, the animal instincts were the instincts appealed to; and the firmness wanted was the firmness of a man.

Hester Dethridge's door opened. She walked straight into Anne's room.

The yellow clay-cold color of her face showed a faint flush of warmth; its deathlike stillness was stirred by a touch of life. The stony eyes, fixed as ever in their gaze, shone strangely with a dim inner lustre. Her gray hair, so neatly arranged at other times, was in disorder under her cap. All her movements were quicker than usual. Something had roused the stagnant vitality in the woman—it was working in her mind; it was forcing itself outward into her face. The servants at Windygates, in past times, had seen these signs, and had known them for a warning to leave Hester Dethridge to herself.

Anne asked her if she had heard what had happened.

She bowed her head.

"I hope you don't mind being disturbed?"

She wrote on her slate: "I'm glad to be disturbed. I have been dreaming bad dreams. It's good for me to be wakened, when sleep takes me backward in my life. What's wrong with you? Frightened?"

"Yes."

She wrote again, and pointed toward the garden with one hand, while she held the slate up with the other: "Frightened of him?"

"Terribly frightened."

She wrote for the third time, and offered the slate to Anne with a ghastly smile: "I have been through it all. I know. You're only at the beginning now. He'll put the wrinkles in your face, and the gray in your hair. There will come a time when you'll wish yourself dead and buried. You will live through it, for all that. Look at Me."

As she read the last three words, Anne heard the garden door below opened and banged to again. She caught Hester Dethridge by the arm, and listened. The tramp of Geoffrey's feet, staggering heavily in the passage, gave token of his approach to the stairs. He was talking to himself, still possessed by the delusion that he was at the foot-race. "Five to four on Delamayn. Delamayn's won. Three cheers for the South, and one cheer more. Devilish long race. Night already! Perry! where's Perry?"

He advanced, staggering from side to side of the passage. The stairs below creaked as he set his foot on them. Hester Dethridge dragged herself free from Anne, advanced, with her candle in her hand, and threw open Geoffrey's bedroom door; returned to the head of the stairs; and stood there, firm as a rock, waiting for him. He looked up, as he set his foot on the next stair, and met the view of Hester's face, brightly illuminated by the candle, looking down at him. On the instant he stopped, rooted to the place on which he stood. "Ghost! witch! devil!" he cried out, "take your eyes off me!" He shook his fist at her furiously, with an oath—sprang back into the hall—and shut himself into the dining-room from the sight of her. The panic which had seized him once already in the kitchen-garden at Windygates, under the eyes of the dumb cook, had fastened its hold on him once more. Frightened—absolutely frightened—of Hester Dethridge!

The gate bell rang. Julius had returned with the doctor.

Anne gave the key to the girl to let them in. Hester wrote on her slate, as composedly as if nothing had happened: "They'll find me in the kitchen, if they want me. I sha'n't go back to my bedroom. My bedroom's full of bad dreams." She descended the stairs. Anne waited in the upper passage, looking over into the hall below. "Your brother is in the drawing-room," she called down to Julius. "The landlady is in the kitchen, if you want her." She returned to her room, and waited for what might happen next.

After a brief interval she heard the drawing-room door open, and the voices of the men out side. There seemed to be some difficulty in persuading Geoffrey to ascend the stairs; he persisted in declaring that Hester Dethridge was waiting for him at the top of them. After a little they persuaded him that the way was free. Anne heard them ascend the stairs and close his bedroom door.

Another and a longer interval passed before the door opened again. The doctor was going away. He said his parting words to Julius in the passage. "Look in at him from time to time through the night, and give him another dose of the sedative mixture if he wakes. There is nothing to b e alarmed about in the restlessness and the fever. They are only the outward manifestations of some serious mischief hidden under them. Send for the medical man who has last attended him. Knowledge of the patient's constitution is very important knowledge in this case."

As Julius returned from letting the doctor out, Anne met him in the hall. She was at once struck by the worn look in his face, and by the fatigue which expressed itself in all his movements.

"You want rest," she said. "Pray go to your room. I have heard what the doctor said to you. Leave it to the landlady and to me to sit up."

Julius owned that he had been traveling from Scotland during the previous night. But he was unwilling to abandon the responsibility of watching his brother. "You are not strong enough, I am sure, to take my place," he said, kindly. "And Geoffrey has some unreasoning horror of the landlady which makes it very undesirable that he should see her again, in his present state. I will go up to my room, and rest on the bed. If you hear any thing you have only to come and call me."

An hour more passed.

Anne went to Geoffrey's door and listened. He was stirring in his bed, and muttering to himself. She went on to the door of the next room, which Julius had left partly open. Fatigue had overpowered him; she heard, within, the quiet breathing of a man in a sound sleep. Anne turned back again resolved not to disturb him.

At the head of the stairs she hesitated—not knowing what to do. Her horror of entering Geoffrey's room, by herself, was insurmountable. But who else was to do it? The girl had gone to bed. The reason which Julius had given for not employing the assistance of Hester Dethridge was unanswerable. She listened again at Geoffrey's door. No sound was now audible in the room to a person in the passage outside. Would it be well to look in, and make sure that he had only fallen asleep again? She hesitated once more—she was still hesitating, when Hester Dethridge appeared from the kitchen.

She joined Anne at the top of the stairs—looked at her—and wrote a line on her slate: "Frightened to go in? Leave it to Me."

The silence in the room justified the inference that he was asleep. If Hester looked in, Hester could do no harm now. Anne accepted the proposal.

"If you find any thing wrong," she said, "don't disturb his brother. Come to me first."

With that caution she withdrew. It was then nearly two in the morning. She, like Julius, was sinking from fatigue. After waiting a little, and hearing nothing, she threw herself on the sofa in her room. If any thing happened, a knock at the door would rouse her instantly.

In the mean while Hester Dethridge opened Geoffrey's bedroom door and went in.

The movements and the mutterings which Anne had heard, had been movements and mutterings in his sleep. The doctor's composing draught, partially disturbed in its operation for the moment only, had recovered its sedative influence on his brain. Geoffrey was in a deep and quiet sleep.

Hester stood near the door, looking at him. She moved to go out again—stopped—and fixed her eyes suddenly on one of the inner corners of the room.

The same sinister change which had passed over her once already in Geoffrey's presence, when they met in the kitchen-garden at Windygates, now passed over her again. Her closed lips dropped apart. Her eyes slowly dilated—moved, inch by inch from the corner, following something along the empty wall, in the direction of the bed—stopped at the head of the bed, exactly above Geoffrey's sleeping face—stared, rigid and glittering, as if they saw a sight of horror close over it. He sighed faintly in his sleep. The sound, slight as it was, broke the spell that held her. She slowly lifted her withered hands, and wrung them above her head; fled back across the passage; and, rushing into her room, sank on her knees at the bedside.

Now, in the dead of night, a strange thing happened. Now, in the silence and the darkness, a hideous secret was revealed.

In the sanctuary of her own room—with all the other inmates of the house sleeping round her—the dumb woman threw off the mysterious and terrible disguise under which she deliberately isolated herself among her fellow-creatures in the hours of the day. Hester Dethridge spoke. In low, thick, smothered accents—in a wild litany of her own—she prayed. She called upon the mercy of God for deliverance from herself; for deliverance from the possession of the Devil; for blindness to fall on her, for death to strike her, so that she might never see that unnamed Horror more! Sobs shook the whole frame of the stony woman whom nothing human moved at other times. Tears poured over those clay-cold cheeks. One by one, the frantic words of her prayer died away on her lips. Fierce shuddering fits shook her from head to foot. She started up from her knees in the darkness. Light! light! light! The unnamed Horror was behind her in his room. The unnamed Horror was looking at her through his open door. She found the match-box, and lit the candle on her table—lit the two other candles set for ornament only on the mantle piece—and looked all round the brightly lighted little room. "Aha!" she said to herself, wiping the cold sweat of her agony from her face. "Candles to other people. God's light to me. Nothing to be seen! nothing to be seen!" Taking one of the candles in her hand, she crossed the passage, with her head down, turned her back on Geoffrey's open door, closed it quickly and softly, stretching out her hand behind her, and retreated again to her own room. She fastened the door, and took an ink-bottle and a pen from the mantle-piece. After considering for a moment, she hung a handkerchief over the keyhole, and laid an old shawl longwise at the bottom of the door, so as to hide the light in her room from the observation of any one in the house who might wake and come that way. This done, she opened the upper part of her dress, and, slipping her fingers into a secret pocket hidden in the inner side of her stays, produced from it some neatly folded leaves of thin paper. Spread out on the table, the leaves revealed themselves—all but the last—as closely covered with writing, in her own hand.

The first leaf was headed by this inscription: "My Confession. To be put into my coffin, and to be buried with me when I die."

She turned the manuscript over, so as to get at the last page. The greater part of it was left blank. A few lines of writing, at the top, bore the date of the day of the week and month on which Lady Lundie had dismissed her from her situation at Windygates. The entry was expressed in these terms:

"I have seen IT again to-day. The first time for two months past. In the kitchen-garden. Standing behind the young gentleman whose name is Delamayn. Resist the Devil, and he will flee from you. I have resisted. By prayer. By meditation in solitude. By reading good books. I have left my place. I have lost sight of the young gentleman for good. Who will IT stand behind? and point to next? Lord have mercy upon me! Christ have mercy upon me!"

Under this she now added the following lines, first carefully prefixing the date:

"I have seen IT again to-night. I notice one awful change. IT has appeared twice behind the same person. This has never happened before. This makes the temptation more terrible than ever. To-night, in his bedroom, between the bed-head and the wall, I have seen IT behind young Mr. Delamayn again. The head just above his face, and the finger pointing downward at his throat. Twice behind this one man. And never twice behind any other living creature till now. If I see IT a third time behind him—Lord deliver me! Christ deliver me! I daren't think of it. He shall leave my cottage to-morrow. I would fain have drawn back from the bargain, when the stranger took the lodgings for his friend, and the friend proved to be Mr. Delamayn. I didn't like it, even then. After the warning to-night, my mind is made up. He shall go. He may have his money back, if he likes. He shall go. (Memorandum: Felt the temptation whispering this time, and the terror tearing at me all the while, as I have never felt them yet. Resisted, as before, by prayer. Am now going down stairs to meditate against it in solitude—to fortify myself against it by good books. Lord be merciful to me a sinner!)"

In those words she closed the entry, and put the manuscript back in the secret pocket in her stays.

She went down to the little room looking on the garden, which had once been her brother's study. There she lit a lamp, and took some books from a shelf that hung against the wall. The books were the Bible, a volume of Methodist sermons, and a set of collected Memoirs of Methodist saints. Ranging these last carefully round her, in an order of her own, Hester Dethridge sat down with the Bible on her lap to watch out the night.

CHAPTER THE FIFTY-THIRD.

WHAT had happened in the hours of darkness?

This was Anne's first thought, when the sunlight poured in at her window, and woke her the next morning.

She made immediate inquiry of the servant. The girl could only speak for herself. Nothing had occurred to disturb her after she had gone to bed. Her master was still, she believed, in his room. Mrs. Dethridge was at her work in the kitchen.

Anne went to the kitchen. Hester Dethridge was at her usual occupation at that time—preparing the breakfast. The slight signs of animation which Anne had noticed in her when they last met appeared no more. The dull look was back again in her stony eyes; the lifeless torpor possessed all her movements. Asked if any thing had happened in the night, she slowly shook her stolid head, slowly made the sign with her hand which signified, "Nothing."

Leaving the kitchen, Anne saw Julius in the front garden. She went out and joined him.

"I believe I have to thank your consideration for me for some hours of rest," he said. "It was five in the morning when I woke. I hope you had no reason to regret having left me to sleep? I went into Geoffrey's room, and found him stirring. A second dose of the mixture composed him again. The fever has gone. He looks weaker and paler, but in other respects like himself. We will return directly to the question of his health. I have something to say to you, first, about a change which may be coming in your life here."

"Has he consented to the separation?"

"No. He is as obstinate about it as ever. I have placed the matter before him in every possible light. He still refuses, positively refuses, a provision which would make him an independent man for life."

"Is it the provision he might have had, Lord Holchester, if—?"

"If he had married Mrs. Glenarm? No. It is impossible, consistently with my duty to my mother, and with what I owe to the position in which my father's death has placed me, that I can offer him such a fortune as Mrs. Glenarm's. Still, it is a handsome income which he is mad enough to refuse. I shall persist in pressing it on him. He must and shall take it."

Anne felt no reviving hope roused in her by his last words. She turned to another subject.

"You had something to tell me," she said. "You spoke of a change."

"True. The landlady here is a very strange person; and she has done a very strange thing. She has given Geoffrey notice to quit these lodgings."

"Notice to quit?" Anne repeated, in amazement.

"Yes. In a formal letter. She handed it to me open, as soon as I was up this morning. It was impossible to get any explanation from her. The poor dumb creature simply wrote on her slate: 'He may have his money back, if he likes: he shall go!' Greatly to my surprise (for the woman inspires him with the strongest aversion) Geoffrey refuses to go until his term is up. I have made the peace between them for to-day. Mrs. Dethridge very reluctantly, consents to give him four-and-twenty hours. And there the matter rests at present."

"What can her motive be?" said Anne.

"It's useless to inquire. Her mind is evidently off its balance. One thing is clear, Geoffrey shall not keep you here much longer. The coming change will remove you from this dismal place—which is one thing gained. And it is quite possible that new scenes and new surroundings may have their influence on Geoffrey for good. His conduct—otherwise quite incomprehensible—may be the result of some latent nervous irritation which medical help might reach. I don't attempt to disguise from myself or from you, that your position here is a most deplorable one. But before we despair of the future, let us at least inquire whether there is any explanation of my brother's present behavior to be found in the present state of my brother's health. I have been considering what the doctor said to me last night. The first thing to do is to get the best medical advice on Geoffrey's case which is to be had. What do you think?"

"I daren't tell you what I think, Lord Holchester. I will try—it is a very small return to make for your kindness—I will try to see my position with your eyes, not with mine. The best medical advice that you can obtain is the advice of Mr. Speedwell. It was he who first made the discovery that your brother was in broken health."

"The very man for our purpose! I will send him here to-day or to-morrow. Is there any thing else I can do for you? I shall see Sir Patrick as soon as I get to town. Have you any message for him?"

Anne hesitated. Looking attentively at her, Julius noticed that she changed color when he mentioned Sir Patrick's name.

"Will you say that I gratefully thank him for the letter which Lady Holchester was so good us to give me last night," she replied. "And will you entreat him, from me, not to expose himself, on my account, to—" she hesitated, and finished the sentence with her eyes on the ground—"to what might happen, if he came here and insisted on seeing me."

"Does he propose to do that?"

She hesitated again. The little nervous contraction of her lips at one side of the mouth became more marked than usual. "He writes that his anxiety is unendurable, and that he is resolved to see me," she answered softly.

"He is likely to hold to his resolution, I think," said Julius. "When I saw him yesterday, Sir Patrick spoke of you in terms of admiration—"

He stopped. The bright tears were glittering on Anne's eyelashes; one of her hands was toying nervously with something hidden (possibly Sir Patrick's letter) in the bosom of her dress. "I thank him with my whole heart," she said, in low, faltering tones. "But it is best that he should not come here."

"Would you like to write to him?"

"I think I should prefer your giving him my message."

Julius understood that the subject was to proceed no further. Sir Patrick's letter had produced some impression on her, which the sensitive nature of the woman seemed to shrink from acknowledging, even to herself. They turned back to enter the cottage. At the door they were met by a surprise. Hester Dethridge, with her bonnet on—dressed, at that hour of the morning, to go out!

"Are you going to market already?" Anne asked.

Hester shook her head.

"When are you coming back?"

Hester wrote on her slate: "Not till the night-time."

Without another word of explanation she pulled her veil down over her face, and made for the gate. The key had been left in the dining-room by Julius, after he had let the doctor out. Hester had it in her hand. She opened the gate and closed the door after her, leaving the key in the lock. At the moment when the door banged to Geoffrey appeared in the passage.

"Where's the key?" he asked. "Who's gone out?"

His brother answered the question. He looked backward and forward suspiciously between Julius and Anne. "What does she go out for at his time?" he said. "Has she left the house to avoid Me?"

Julius thought this the likely explanation. Geoffrey went down sulkily to the gate to lock it, and returned to them, with the key in his pocket.

"I'm obliged to be careful of the gate," he said. "The neighborhood swarms with beggars and tramps. If you want to go out," he added, turning pointedly to Anne, "I'm at your service, as a good husband ought to be."

After a hurried breakfast Julius took his departure. "I don't accept your refusal," he said to his brother, before Anne. "You will see me here again." Geoffrey obstinately repeated the refusal. "If you come here every day of your life," he said, "it will be just the same."

The gate closed on Julius. Anne returned again to the solitude of her own chamber.

Geoffrey entered the drawing-room, placed the volumes of the Newgate Calendar on the table before him, and resumed the reading which he had been unable to continue on the evening before.

Hour after hour he doggedly plodded through one case of murder after another. He had read one good half of the horrid chronicle of crime before his power of fixing his attention began to fail him. Then he lit his pipe, and went out to think over it in the garden. However the atrocities of which he had been reading might differ in other respects, there was one terrible point of resemblance, which he had not anticipated, and in which every one of the cases agreed. Sooner or later, there was the dead body always certain to be found; always bearing its dumb witness, in the traces of poison or in the marks of violence, to the crime committed on it.

He walked to and fro slowly, still pondering over the problem which had first found its way into his mind when he had stopped in the front garden and had looked up at Anne's window in the dark. "How?" That had been the one question before him, from the time when the lawyer had annihilated his hopes of a divorce. It remained the one question still. There was no answer to it in his own brain; there was no answer to it in the book which he had been consulting. Every thing was in his favor if he could only find out "how." He had got his hated wife up stairs at his mercy—thanks to his refusal of the money which Julius had offered to him. He was living in a place absolutely secluded from public observation on all sides of it—thanks to his resolution to remain at the cottage, even after his landlady had insulted him by sending him a notice to quit. Every thing had been prepared, every thing had been sacrificed, to the fulfillment of one purpose—and how to attain that purpose was still the same impenetrable mystery to him which it had been from the first!

What was the other alternative? To accept the proposal which Julius had made. In other words, to give up his vengeance on Anne, and to turn his back on the splendid future which Mrs. Glenarm's devotion still offered to him.

Never! He would go back to the books. He was not at the end of them. The slightest hint in the pages which were still to be read might set his sluggish brain working in the right direction. The way to be rid of her, without exciting the suspicion of any living creature, in the house or out of it, was a way that might be found yet.

Could a man, in his position of life, reason in this brutal manner? could he act in this merciless way? Surely the thought of what he was about to do must have troubled him this time!

Pause for a moment—and look back at him in the past.

Did he feel any remorse when he was plotting the betrayal of Arnold in the garden at Windygates? The sense which feels remorse had not been put into him. What he is now is the legitimate consequence of what he was then. A far more serious temptation is now urging him to commit a far more serious crime. How is he to resist? Will his skill in rowing (as Sir Patrick once put it), his swiftness in running, his admirable capacity and endurance in other physical exercises, help him to win a purely moral victory over his own selfishness and his own cruelty? No! The moral and mental neglect of himself, which the material tone of public feeling about him has tacitly encouraged, has left him at the mercy of the worst instincts in his nature—of all that is most vile and of all that is most dangerous in the composition of the natural man. With the mass of his fellows, no harm out of the common has come of this, because no temptation out of the common has passed their way. But with him, the case is reversed. A temptation out of the common has passed his way. How does it find him prepared to meet it? It finds him, literally and exactly, what his training has left him, in the presence of any temptation small or great—a defenseless man.

Geoffrey returned to the cottage. The servant stopped him in the passage, to ask at what time he wished to dine. Instead of answering, he inquired angrily for Mrs. Dethridge. Mrs. Dethridge not come back.

It was now late in the afternoon, and she had been out since the early morning. This had never happened before. Vague suspicions of her, one more monstrous than another, began to rise in Geoffrey's mind. Between the drink and the fever, he had been (as Julius had told him) wandering in his mind during a part of the night. Had he let any thing out in that condition? Had Hester heard it? And was it, by any chance, at the bottom of her long absence and her notice to quit? He determined—without letting her see that he suspected her—to clear up that doubt as soon as his landlady returned to the house.

The evening came. It was past nine o'clock before there was a ring at the bell. The servant came to ask for the key. Geoffrey rose to go to the gate himself—and changed his mind before he left the room. Her suspicions might be roused (supposing it to be Hester who was waiting for admission) if he opened the gate to her when the servant was there to do it. He gave the girl the key, and kept out of sight.

"Dead tired!"—the servant said to herself, seeing her mistress by the light of the lamp over the gate.

"Dead tired!"—Geoffrey said to himself, observing Hester suspiciously as she passed him in the passage on her way up stairs to take off her bonnet in her own room.

"Dead tired!"—Anne said to herself, meeting Hester on the upper floor, and receiving from her a letter in Blanche's handwriting, delivered to the mistress of the cottage by the postman, who had met her at her own gate.

Having given the letter to Anne, Hester Dethridge withdrew to her bedroom.

Geoffrey closed the door of the drawing-room, in which the candles were burning, and went into the dining-room, in which there was no light. Leaving the door ajar, he waited to intercept his landlady on her way back to her supper in the kitchen.

Hester wearily secured her door, wearily lit the candles, wearily put the pen and ink on the table. For some minutes after this she was compelled to sit down, and rally her strength and fetch her breath. After a little she was able to remove her upper clothing. This done she took the manuscript inscribed, "My Confession," out of the secret pocket of her stays—turned to the last leaf as before—and wrote another entry, under the entry made on the previous night.

"This morning I gave him notice to quit, and offered him his money back if he wanted it. He refuses to go. He shall go to-morrow, or I will burn the place over his head. All through to-day I have avoided him by keeping out of the house. No rest to ease my mind, and no sleep to close my eyes. I humbly bear my cross as long as my strength will let me."

At those words the pen dropped from her fingers. Her head nodded on her breast. She roused herself with a start. Sleep was the enemy she dreaded: sleep brought dreams.

She unfastened the window-shutters and looked out at the night. The peaceful moonlight was shining over the garden. The clear depths of the night sky were soothing and beautiful to look at. What! Fading already? clouds? darkness? No! Nearly asleep once more. She roused herself again, with a start. There was the moonlight, and there was the garden as bright under it as ever.

Dreams or no dreams, it was useless to fight longer against the weariness that overpowered her. She closed the shutters, and went back to the bed; and put her Confession in its customary place at night, under her pillow.

She looked round the room—and shuddered. Every corner of it was filled with the terrible memories of the past night. She might wake from the torture of the dreams to find the terror of the Apparition watching at her bedside. Was there no remedy? no blessed safeguard under which she might tranquilly resign herself to sleep? A thought crossed her mind. The good book—the Bible. If she slept with the Bible under her pillow, there was hope in the good book—the hope of sleeping in peace.

It was not worth while to put on the gown and the stays which she had taken off. Her shawl would cover her. It was equally needless to take the candle. The lower shutters would not be closed at that hour; and if they were, she could lay her hand on the Bible, in its place on the parlor book-shelf, in the dark.

She removed the Confession from under the pillow. Not even for a minute could she prevail on herself to leave it in one room while she was away from it in another. With the manuscript folded up, and hidden in her hand, she slowly descended the stairs again. Her knees trembled under her. She was obliged to hold by the banister, with the hand that was free.

Geoffrey observed her from the dining-room, on her way down the stairs. He waited to see what she did, before he showed himself, and spoke to her. Instead of going on into the kitchen, she stopped short, and entered the parlor. Another suspicious circumstance! What did she want in the parlor, without a candle, at that time of night?

She went to the book-case—her dark figure plainly visible in the moonlight that flooded the little room. She staggered and put her hand to her head; giddy, to all appearance, from extreme fatigue. She recovered herself, and took a book from the shelf. She leaned against the wall after she had possessed herself of the book. Too weary, as it seemed, to get up stairs again without a little rest. Her arm-chair was near her. Better rest, for a moment or two, to be had in that than could be got by leaning against the wall. She sat down heavily in the chair, with the book on her lap. One of her arms hung over the arm of the chair, with the hand closed, apparently holding something.

Her head nodded on her breast—recovered itself—and sank gently on the cushion at the back of the chair. Asleep? Fast asleep.

In less than a minute the muscles of the closed hand that hung over the arm of the chair slowly relaxed. Something white slipped out of her hand, and lay in the moonlight on the floor.

Geoffrey took off his heavy shoes, and entered the room noiselessly in his stockings. He picked up the white thing on the floor. It proved to be a collection of several sheets of thin paper, neatly folded together, and closely covered with writing.

Writing? As long as she was awake she had kept it hidden in her hand. Why hide it?

Had he let out any thing to compromise himself when he was light-headed with the fever the night before? and had she taken it down in writing to produce against him? Possessed by guilty distrust, even that monstrous doubt assumed a look of probability to Geoffrey's mind. He left the parlor as noiselessly as he had entered it, and made for the candle-light in the drawing-room, determined to examine the manuscript in his hand.

After carefully smoothing out the folded leaves on the table, he turned to the first page, and read these lines.

CHAPTER THE FIFTY-FOURTH.

THE MANUSCRIPT.

1.

"MY Confession: To be put into my coffin; and to be buried with me when I die.

"This is the history of what I did in the time of my married life. Here—known to no other mortal creature, confessed to my Creator alone—is the truth.

"At the great day of the Resurrection, we shall all rise again in our bodies as we have lived. When I am called before the Judgment Seat I shall have this in my hand.

"Oh, just and merciful Judge, Thou knowest what I have suffered. My trust is in Thee."

2.

"I am the eldest of a large family, born of pious parents. We belonged to the congregation of the Primitive Methodists.

"My sisters were all married before me. I remained for some years the only one at home. At the latter part of the time my mother's health failed; and I managed the house in her place. Our spiritual pastor, good Mr. Bapchild, used often to dine with us, on Sundays, between the services. He approved of my management of the house, and, in particular, of my cooking. This was not pleasant to my mother, who felt a jealousy of my being, as it were, set over her in her place. My unhappiness at home began in this way. My mother's temper got worse as her health got worse. My father was much away from us, traveling for his business. I had to bear it all. About this time I began to think it would be well for me if I could marry as my sisters had done; and have good Mr. Bapchild to dinner, between the services, in a house of my own.

"In this frame of mind I made acquaintance with a young man who attended service at our chapel.

"His name was Joel Dethridge. He had a beautiful voice. When we sang hymns, he sang off the same book with me. By trade he was a paper-hanger. We had much serious talk together. I walked with him on Sundays. He was a good ten years younger than I was; and, being only a journeyman, his worldly station was below mine. My mother found out the liking that had grown up between us. She told my father the next time he was at home. Also my married sisters and my brothers. They all joined together to stop things from going further between me and Joel Dethridge. I had a hard time of it. Mr. Bapchild expressed himself as feeling much grieved at the turn things were taking. He introduced me into a sermon—not by name, but I knew who it was meant for. Perhaps I might have given way if they had not done one thing. They made inquiries of my young man's enemies, and brought wicked stories of him to me behind his back. This, after we had sung off the same hymn-book, and walked together, and agreed one with the other on religious subjects, was too much to bear. I was of age to judge for myself. And I married Joel Dethridge."

3.

"My relations all turned their backs on me. Not one of them was present at my marriage; my brother Reuben, in particular, who led the rest, saying that they had done with me from that time forth. Mr. Bapchild was much moved; shed tears, and said he would pray for me.

"I was married in London by a pastor who was a stranger; and we settled in London with fair prospects. I had a little fortune of my own—my share of some money left to us girls by our aunt Hester, whom I was named after. It was three hundred pounds. Nearly one hundred of this I spent in buying furniture to fit up the little house we took to live in. The rest I gave to my husband to put into the bank against the time when he wanted it to set up in business for himself.

"For three months, more or less, we got on nicely—except in one particular. My husband never stirred in the matter of starting in business for himself.

"He was once or twice cross with me when I said it seemed a pity to be spending the money in the bank (which might be afterward wanted) instead of earning more in business. Good Mr. Bapchild, happening about this time to be in London, staid over Sunday, and came to dine with us between the services. He had tried to make my peace with my relations—but he had not succeeded. At my request he spoke to my husband about the necessity of exerting himself. My husband took it ill. I then saw him seriously out of temper for the first time. Good Mr. Bapchild said no more. He appeared to be alarmed at what had happened, and he took his leave early.

"Shortly afterward my husband went out. I got tea ready for him—but he never came back. I got supper ready for him—but he never came back. It was past twelve at night before I saw him again. I was very much startled by the state he came home in. He didn't speak like himself, or look like himself: he didn't seem to know me—wandered in his mind, and fell all in a lump like on our bed. I ran out and fetched the doctor to him.

"The doctor pulled him up to the light, and looked at him; smelled his breath, and dropped him down again on the bed; turned about, and stared at me. 'What's the matter, Sir?' I says. 'Do you mean to tell me you don't know?' says the doctor. 'No, Sir,' says I. 'Why what sort of a woman are you,' says he, 'not to know a drunken man when you see him!' With that he went away, and left me standing by the bedside, all in a tremble from head to foot.

"This was how I first found out that I was the wife of a drunken man."

4.

"I have omitted to say any thing about my husband's family.

"While we were keeping company together he told me he was an orphan—with an uncle and aunt in Canada, and an only brother settled in Scotland. Before we were married he gave me a letter from this brother. It was to say that he was sorry he was not able to come to England, and be present at my marriage, and to wish me joy and the rest of it. Good Mr. Bapchild (to whom, in my distress, I wrote word privately of what had happened) wrote back in return, telling me to wait a little, and see whether my husband did it again.

"I had not long to wait. He was in liquor again the next day, and the next. Hearing this,

Mr. Bapchild instructed me to send him the letter from my husband's brother. He reminded me of some of the stories about my husband which I had refused to believe in the time before I was married; and he said it might be well to make inquiries.

"The end of the inquiries was this. The brother, at that very time, was placed privately (by his own request) under a doctor's care to get broken of habits of drinking. The craving for strong liquor (the doctor wrote) was in the family. They would be sober sometimes for months together, drinking nothing stronger than tea. Then the fit would seize them; and they would drink, drink, drink, for days together, like the mad and miserable wretches that they were.

"This was the husband I was married to. And I had offended all my relations, and estranged them from me, for his sake. Here was surely a sad prospect for a woman after only a few months of wedded life!

"In a year's time the money in the bank was gone; and my husband was out of employment. He always got work—being a first-rate hand when he was sober—and always lost it again when the drinking-fit seized him. I was loth to leave our nice little house, and part with my pretty furniture; and I proposed to him to let me try for employment, by the day, as cook, and so keep things going while he was looking out again for work. He was sober and penitent at the time; and he agreed to what I proposed. And, more than that, he took the Total Abstinence Pledge, and promised to turn over a new leaf. Matters, as I thought, began to look fairly again. We had nobody but our two selves to think of. I had borne no child, and had no prospect of bearing one. Unlike most women, I thought this a mercy instead of a misfortune. In my situation (as I soon grew to know) my becoming a mother would only have proved to be an aggravation of my hard lot.

"The sort of employment I wanted was not to be got in a day. Good Mr. Bapchild gave me a character; and our landlord, a worthy man (belonging, I am sorry to say, to the Popish Church), spoke for me to the steward of a club. Still, it took time to persuade people that I was the thorough good cook I claimed to be. Nigh on a fortnight had passed before I got the chance I had been looking out for. I went home in good spirits (for me) to report what had happened, and found the brokers in the house carrying off the furniture which I had bought with my own money for sale by auction. I asked them how they dared touch it without my leave. They answered, civilly enough I must own, that they were acting under my husband's orders; and they went on removing it before my own eyes, to the cart outside. I ran up stairs, and found my husband on the landing. He was in liquor again. It is useless to say what passed between us. I shall only mention that this was the first occasion on which he lifted his fist, and struck me."

5.

"Having a spirit of my own, I was resolved not to endure it. I ran out to the Police Court, hard by.

"My money had not only bought the furniture—it had kept the house going as well; paying the taxes which the Queen and the Parliament asked for among other things. I now went to the magistrate to see what the Queen and the Parliament, in return for the taxes, would do for me.

"'Is your furniture settled on yourself?' he says, when I told him what had happened.

"I didn't understand what he meant. He turned to some person who was sitting on the bench with him. 'This is a hard case,' he says. 'Poor people in this condition of life don't even know what a marriage settlement means. And, if they did, how many of them could afford to pay the lawyer's charges?' Upon that he turned to me. 'Yours is a common case,' he said. 'In the present state of the law I can do nothing for you.'

"It was impossible to believe that. Common or not, I put my case to him over again.

"'I have bought the furniture with my own money, Sir,' I says. 'It's mine, honestly come by, with bill and receipt to prove it. They are taking it away from me by force, to sell it against my will. Don't tell me that's the law. This is a Christian country. It can't be.'

"'My good creature,' says he, 'you are a married woman. The law doesn't allow a married woman to call any thing her own—unless she has previously (with a lawyer's help) made a bargain to that effect with her husband before marrying him. You have made no bargain. Your husband has a right to sell your furniture if he likes. I am sorry for you; I can't hinder him.'

"I was obstinate about it. 'Please to answer me this, Sir,' I says. 'I've been told by wiser heads than mine that we all pay our taxes to keep the Queen and the Parliament going; and that the Queen and the Parliament make laws to protect us in return. I have paid my taxes. Why, if you please, is there no law to protect me in return?'

"'I can't enter into that,' says he. 'I must take the law as I find it; and so must you. I see a mark there on the side of your face. Has your husband been beating you? If he has, summon him here I can punish him for that.'

"'How can you punish him, Sir?' says I.

"'I can fine him,' says he. 'Or I can send him to prison.'

"'As to the fine,' says I, 'he can pay that out of the money he gets by selling my furniture. As to the prison, while he's in it, what's to become of me, with my money spent by him, and my possessions gone; and when he's out of it, what's to become of me again, with a husband whom I have been the means of punishing, and who comes home to his wife knowing it? It's bad enough as it is, Sir,' says I. 'There's more that's bruised in me than what shows in my face. I wish you good-morning.'"

6.

"When I got back the furniture was gone, and my husband was gone. There was nobody but the landlord in the empty house. He said all that could be said—kindly enough toward me, so far as I was concerned. When he was gone I locked my trunk, and got away in a cab after dark, and found a lodging to lay my head in. If ever there was a lonely, broken-hearted creature in the world, I was that creature that night.

"There was but one chance of earning my bread—to go to the employment offered me (under a man cook, at a club). And there was but one hope—the hope that I had lost sight of my husband forever.

"I went to my work—and prospered in it—and earned my first quarter's wages. But it's not good for a woman to be situated as I was; friendless and alone, with her things that she took a pride in sold away from her, and with nothing to look forward to in her life to come. I was regular in my attendance at chapel; but I think my heart began to get hardened, and my mind to be overcast in secret with its own thoughts about this time. There was a change coming. Two or three days after I had earned the wages just mentioned my husband found me out. The furniture-money was all spent. He made a disturbance at the club, I was only able to quiet him by giving him all the money I could spare from my own necessities. The scandal was brought before the committee. They said, if the circumstance occurred again, they should be obliged to part with me. In a fortnight the circumstance occurred again. It's useless to dwell on it. They all said they were sorry for me. I lost the place. My husband went back with me to my lodgings. The next morning I caught him taking my purse, with the few shillings I had in it, out of my trunk, which he had broken open. We quarreled. And he struck me again—this time knocking me down.

"I went once more to the police court, and told my story—to another magistrate this time. My only petition was to have my husband kept away from me. 'I don't want to be a burden on others' (I says) 'I don't want to do any thing but what's right. I don't even complain of having been very cruelly used. All I ask is to be let to earn an honest living. Will the law protect me in the effort to do that?'

"The answer, in substance, was that the law might protect me, provided I had money to spend in asking some higher court to grant me a separation. After allowing my husband to rob me openly of the only property I possessed—namely, my furniture—the law turned round on me when I called upon it in my distress, and held out its hand to be paid. I had just three and sixpence left in the world—and the prospect, if I earned more, of my husband coming (with permission of the law) and taking it away from me. There was only one chance—namely, to get time to turn round in, and to escape him again. I got a month's freedom from him, by charging him with knocking me down. The magistrate (happening to be young, and new to his business) sent him to prison, instead of fining him. This gave me time to get a character from the club, as well as a special testimonial from good Mr. Bapchild. With the help of these, I obtained a place in a private family—a place in the country, this time.

"I found myself now in a haven of peace. I was among worthy kind-hearted people, who felt for my distresses, and treated me most indulgently. Indeed, through all my troubles, I must say I have found one thing hold good. In my experience, I have observed that people are oftener quick than not to feel a human compassion for others in distress. Also, that they mostly see plain enough what's hard and cruel and unfair on them in the governing of the country which they help to keep going. But once ask them to get on from sitting down and grumbling about it, to rising up and setting it right, and what do you find them? As helpless as a flock of sheep—that's what you find them.

"More than six months passed, and I saved a little money again.

"One night, just as we were going to bed, there was a loud ring at the bell. The footman answered the door—and I heard my husband's voice in the hall. He had traced me, with the help of a man he knew in the police; and he had come to claim his rights. I offered him all the little money I had, to let me be. My good master spoke to him. It was all useless. He was obstinate and savage. If—instead of my running off from him—it had been all the other way and he had run off from me, something might have been done (as I understood) to protect me. But he stuck to his wife. As long as I could make a farthing, he stuck to his wife. Being married to him, I had no right to have left him; I was bound to go with my husband; there was no escape for me. I bade them good-by. And I have never forgotten their kindness to me from that day to this.

"My husband took me back to London.

"As long as the money lasted, the drinking went on. When it was gone, I was beaten again. Where was the remedy? There was no remedy, but to try and escape him once more. Why didn't I have him locked up? What was the good of having him locked up? In a few weeks he would be out of prison; sober and penitent, and promising amendment—and then when the fit took him, there he would be, the same furious savage that he had been often and often before. My heart got hard under the hopelessness of it; and dark thoughts beset me, mostly at night. About this time I began to say to myself, 'There's no deliverance from this, but in death—his death or mine.'

"Once or twice I went down to the bridges after dark and looked over at the river. No. I wasn't the sort of woman who ends her own wretchedness in that way. Your blood must be in a fever, and your head in a flame—at least I fancy so—you must be hurried into it, like, to go and make away with yourself. My troubles never took that effect on me. I always turned cold under them instead of hot. Bad for me, I dare say; but what you are—you are. Can the Ethiopian change his skin, or the leopard his spots?

"I got away from him once more, and found good employment once more. It don't matter how, and it don't matter where. My story is always the same thing, over and over again. Best get to the end.

"There was one change, however, this time. My employment was not in a private family. I was also allowed to teach cookery to young women, in my leisure hours. What with this, and what with a longer time passing on the present occasion before my husband found me out, I was as comfortably off as in my position I could hope to be. When my work was done, I went away at night to sleep in a lodging of my own. It was only a bedroom; and I furnished it myself—partly for the sake of economy (the rent being not half as much as for a furnished room); and partly for the sake of cleanliness. Through all my troubles I always liked things neat about me—neat and shapely and good.

"Well, it's needless to say how it ended. He found me out again—this time by a chance meeting with me in the street.

"He was in rags, and half starved. But that didn't matter now. All he had to do was to put his hand into my pocket and take what he wanted. There is no limit, in England, to what a bad husband may do—as long as he sticks to his wife. On the present occasion, he was cunning enough to see that he would be the loser if he disturbed me in my employment. For a while things went on as smoothly as they could. I made a pretense that the work was harder than usual; and I got leave (loathing the sight of him, I honestly own) to sleep at the place where I was employed. This was not for long. The fit took him again, in due course; and he came and made a disturbance. As before, this was not to be borne by decent people. As before, they were sorry to part with me. As before, I lost my place.

"Another woman would have gone mad under it. I fancy it just missed, by a hair's breadth, maddening Me.

"When I looked at him that night, deep in his drunken sleep, I thought of Jael and Sisera (see the book of Judges; chapter 4th; verses 17 to 21). It says, she 'took a nail of the tent, and took a hammer in her hand, and went softly unto him, and smote the nail into his temples, and fastened it into the ground: for he was fast asleep and weary. So he died.' She did this deed to deliver her nation from Sisera. If there had been a hammer and a nail in the room that night, I think I should have been Jael—with this difference, that I should have done it to deliver myself.

"With the morning this passed off, for the time. I went and spoke to a lawyer.

"Most people, in my place, would have had enough of the law already. But I was one of the sort who drain the cup to the dregs. What I said to him was, in substance, this. 'I come to ask your advice about a madman. Mad people, as I understand it, are people who have lost control over their own minds. Sometimes this leads them to entertaining delusions; and sometimes it leads them to committing actions hurtful to others or to themselves. My husband has lost all control over his own craving for strong drink. He requires to be kept from liquor, as other madmen require to be kept from attempting their own lives, or the lives of those about them. It's a frenzy beyond his own control, with him—just as it's a frenzy beyond their own control, with them. There are Asylums for mad people, all over the country, at the public disposal, on certain conditions. If I fulfill those conditions, will the law deliver me from the misery of being married to a madman, whose madness is drink?'—'No,' says the lawyer. 'The law of England declines to consider an incurable drunkard as a fit object for restraint, the law of England leaves the husbands and wives of such people in a perfectly helpless situation, to deal with their own misery as they best can.'

"I made my acknowledgments to the gentleman and left him. The last chance was this chance—and this had failed me."

7.

"The thought that had once found its way into my mind already, now found its way back again, and never altogether left me from that time forth. No deliverance for me but in death—his death, or mine.

"I had it before me night and day; in chapel and out of chapel just the same. I read the story of Jael and Sisera so often that the Bible got to open of itself at that place.

"The laws of my country, which ought to have protected me as an honest woman, left me helpless. In place of the laws I had no friend near to open my heart to. I was shut up in myself. And I was married to that man. Consider me as a human creature, and say, Was this not trying my humanity very hardly?

"I wrote to good Mr. Bapchild. Not going into particulars; only telling him I was beset by temptation, and begging him to come and help me. He was confined to his bed by illness; he could only write me a letter of good advice. To profit by good advice people must have a glimpse of happiness to look forward to as a reward for exerting themselves. Religion itself is obliged to hold out a reward, and to say to us poor mortals, Be good, and you shall go to Heaven. I had no glimpse of happiness. I was thankful (in a dull sort of way) to good Mr. Bapchild—and there it ended.

"The time had been when a word from my old pastor would have put me in the right way again. I began to feel scared by myself. If the next ill usage I received from Joel Dethridge found me an unchanged woman, it was borne in strongly on my mind that I should be as likely as not to get my deliverance from him by my own hand.

"Goaded to it, by the fear of this, I humbled myself before my relations for the first time.

I wrote to beg their pardon; to own that they had proved to be right in their opinion of my husband; and to entreat them to be friends with me again, so far as to let me visit them from time to time. My notion was, that it might soften my heart if I could see the old place, and talk the old talk, and look again at the well-remembered faces. I am almost ashamed to own it—but, if I had had any thing to give, I would have parted with it all, to be allowed to go back into mother's kitchen and cook the Sunday dinner for them once more.

"But this was not to be. Not long before my letter was received mother had died. They laid it all at my door. She had been ailing for years past, and the doctors had said it was hopeless from the first—but they laid it all at my door. One of my sisters wrote to say that much, in as few words as could possibly suffice for saying it. My father never answered my letter at all."

8.

"Magistrates and lawyers; relations and friends; endurance of injuries, patience, hope, and honest work—I had tried all these, and tried them vainly. Look round me where I might, the prospect was closed on all sides.

"At this time my husband had got a little work to do. He came home out of temper one night, and I gave him a warning. 'Don't try me too far, Joel, for your own sake,' was all I said. It was one of his sober days; and, for the first time, a word from me seemed to have an effect on him. He looked hard at me for a minute or so. And then he went and sat down in a corner, and held his peace.

"This was on a Tuesday in the week. On the Saturday he got paid, and the drinking fit took him again.

"On Friday in the next week I happened to come back late—having had a good stroke of work to do that day, in the way of cooking a public dinner for a tavern-keeper who knew me. I found my husband gone, and the bedroom stripped of the furniture which I had put into it. For the second time he had robbed me of my own property, and had turned it into money to be spent in drink.

"I didn't say a word. I stood and looked round the empty room. What was going on in me I hardly knew myself at the time, and can't describe now. All I remember is, that, after a little, I turned about to leave the house. I knew the places where thy husband was likely to be found; and the devil possessed me to go and find him. The landlady came out into the passage and tried to stop me. She was a bigger and a stronger woman than I was. But I shook her off like a child. Thinking over it now, I believe she was in no condition to put out her strength. The sight of me frightened her.

"I found him. I said—well, I said what a woman beside herself with fury would be likely to say. It's needless to tell how it ended. He knocked me down.

"After that, there is a spot of darkness like in my memory. The next thing I can call to mind, is coming back to my senses after some days. Three of my teeth were knocked out—but that was not the worst of it. My head had struck against something in falling, and some part of me (a nerve, I think they said) was injured in such a way as to affect my speech. I don't mean that I was downright dumb—I only mean that, all of a sudden, it had become a labor to me to speak. A long word was as serious an obstacle as if I was a child again. They took me to the hospital. When the medical gentlemen heard what it was, the medical gentlemen came crowding round me. I appeared to lay hold of their interest, just as a story-book lays hold of the interest of other people. The upshot of it was, that I might end in being dumb, or I might get my speech again—the chances were about equal. Only two things were needful. One of them was that I should live on good nourishing diet. The other was, that I should keep my mind easy.

"About the diet it was not possible to decide. My getting good nourishing food and drink depended on my getting money to buy the same. As to my mind, there was no difficulty about that. If my husband came back to me, my mind was made up to kill him.

"Horrid—I am well aware this is horrid. Nobody else, in my place, would have ended as wickedly as that. All the other women in the world, tried as I was, would have risen superior to the trial."

9.

"I have said that people (excepting my husband and my relations) were almost always good to me.

"The landlord of the house which we had taken when we were married heard of my sad case. He gave me one of his empty houses to look after, and a little weekly allowance for doing it. Some of the furniture in the upper rooms, not being wanted by the last tenant, was left to be taken at a valuation if the next tenant needed it. Two of the servants' bedrooms (in the attics), one next to the other, had all that was wanted in them. So I had a roof to cover me, and a choice of beds to lie on, and money to get me food. All well again—but all too late. If that house could speak, what tales that house would have to tell of me!

"I had been told by the doctors to exercise my speech. Being all alone, with nobody to speak to, except when the landlord dropped in, or when the servant next door said, 'Nice day, ain't it?' or, 'Don't you feel lonely?' or such like, I bought the newspaper, and read it out loud to myself to exercise my speech in that way. One day I came upon a bit about the wives of drunken husbands. It was a report of something said on that subject by a London coroner, who had held inquests on dead husbands (in the lower ranks of life), and who had his reasons for suspecting the wives. Examination of the body (he said) didn't prove it; and witnesses didn't prove it; but he thought it, nevertheless, quite possible, in some cases, that, when the woman could bear it no longer, she sometimes took a damp towel, and waited till the husband (drugged with his own liquor) was sunk in his sleep, and then put the towel over his nose and mouth, and ended it that way without any body being the wiser. I laid down the newspaper; and fell into thinking. My mind was, by this time, in a prophetic way. I said to myself 'I haven't happened on this for nothing: this means that I shall see my husband again.'

"It was then just after my dinner-time—two o'clock. That same night, at the moment when I had put out my candle, and laid me down in bed, I heard a knock at the street door. Before I had lit my candle I says to myself, 'Here he is.'

"I huddled on a few things, and struck a light, and went down stairs. I called out through the door, 'Who's there?' And his voice answered, 'Let me in.'

"I sat down on a chair in the passage, and shook all over like a person struck with palsy. Not from the fear of him—but from my mind being in the prophetic way. I knew I was going to be driven to it at last. Try as I might to keep from doing it, my mind told me I was to do it now. I sat shaking on the chair in the passage; I on one side of the door, and he on the other.

"He knocked again, and again, and again. I knew it was useless to try—and yet I resolved to try. I determined not to let him in till I was forced to it. I determined to let him alarm the neighborhood, and to see if the neighborhood would step between us. I went up stairs and waited at the open staircase window over the door.

"The policeman came up, and the neighbors came out. They were all for giving him into custody. The policeman laid hands on him. He had but one word to say; he had only to point up to me at the window, and to tell them I was his wife. The neighbors went indoors again. The policeman dropped hold of his arm. It was I who was in the wrong, and not he. I was bound to let my husband in. I went down stairs again, and let him in.

"Nothing passed between us that night. I threw open the door of the bedroom next to mine, and went and locked myself into my own room. He was dead beat with roaming the streets, without a penny in his pocket, all day long. The bed to lie on was all he wanted for that night.

"The next morning I tried again—tried to turn back on the way that I was doomed to go; knowing beforehand that it would be of no use. I offered him three parts of my poor weekly earnings, to be paid to him regularly at the landlord's office, if he would only keep away from me, and from the house. He laughed in my face. As my husband, he could take all my earnings if he chose. And as for leaving the house, the house offered him free quarters to live in as long as I was employed to look after it. The landlord couldn't part man and wife.

"I said no more. Later in the day the landlord came. He said if we could make it out to live together peaceably he had neither the right nor the wish to interfere. If we made any disturbances, then he should be obliged to provide himself with some other woman to look after the house. I had nowhere else to go, and no other employment to undertake. If, in spite of that, I had put on my bonnet and walked out, my husband would have walked out after me. And all decent people would have patted him on the back, and said, 'Quite right, good man—quite right.'

"So there he was by his own act, and with the approval of others, in the same house with me.

"I made no remark to him or to the landlord. Nothing roused me now. I knew what was coming; I waited for the end. There was some change visible in me to others, as I suppose, though not noticeable by myself, which first surprised my husband and then daunted him. When the next night came I heard him lock the door softly in his own room. It didn't matter to me. When the time was ripe ten thousand locks wouldn't lock out what was to come.

"The next day, bringing my weekly payment, brought me a step nearer on the way to the end. Getting the money, he could get the drink. This time he began cunningly—in other words, he began his drinking by slow degrees. The landlord (bent, honest man, on trying to keep the peace between us) had given him some odd jobs to do, in the way of small repairs, here and there about the house. 'You owe this,' he says, 'to my desire to do a good turn to your poor wife. I am helping you for her sake. Show yourself worthy to be helped, if you can.'

"He said, as usual, that he was going to turn over a new leaf. Too late! The time had gone by. He was doomed, and I was doomed. It didn't matter what he said now. It didn't matter when he locked his door again the last thing at night.

"The next day was Sunday. Nothing happened. I went to chapel. Mere habit. It did me no good. He got on a little with the drinking—but still cunningly, by slow degrees. I knew by experience that this meant a long fit, and a bad one, to come.

"Monday, there were the odd jobs about the house to be begun. He was by this time just sober enough to do his work, and just tipsy enough to take a spiteful pleasure in persecuting his wife. He went out and got the things he wanted, and came back and called for me. A skilled workman like he was (he said) wanted a journeyman under him. There were things which it was beneath a skilled workman to do for himself. He was not going to call in a man or a boy, and then have to pay them. He was going to get it done for nothing, and he meant to make a journeyman of me. Half tipsy and half sober, he went on talking like that, and laying out his things, all quite right, as he wanted them. When they were ready he straightened himself up, and he gave me his orders what I was to do.

"I obeyed him to the best of my ability. Whatever he said, and whatever he did, I knew he was going as straight as man could go to his own death by my hands.

"The rats and mice were all over the house, and the place generally was out of repair. He ought to have begun on the kitchen-floor; but (having sentence pronounced against him) he began in the empty parlors on the ground-floor.

"These parlors were separated by what is called a 'lath-and-plaster wall.' The rats had damaged it. At one part they had gnawed through and spoiled the paper, at another part they had not got so far. The landlord's orders were to spare the paper, because he had some by him to match it. My husband began at a place where the paper was whole. Under his directions I mixed up—I won't say what. With the help of it he got the paper loose from the wall, without injuring it in any way, in a long hanging strip. Under it was the plaster and the laths, gnawed away in places by the rats. Though strictly a paperhanger by trade, he could be plasterer too when he liked. I saw how he cut away the rotten laths and ripped off the plaster; and (under his directions again) I mixed up the new plaster he wanted, and handed him the new laths, and saw how he set them. I won't say a word about how this was done either.

"I have a reason for keeping silence here, which is, to my mind, a very dreadful one. In every thing that my husband made me do that day he was showing me (blindfold) the way to kill him, so that no living soul, in the police or out of it, could suspect me of the deed.

"We finished the job on the wall just before dark. I went to my cup of tea, and he went to his bottle of gin.

"I left him, drinking hard, to put our two bedrooms tidy for the night. The place that his bed happened to be set in (which I had never remarked particularly before) seemed, in a manner of speaking, to force itself on my notice now.

"The head of the bedstead was set against the wall which divided his room from mine. From looking at the bedstead I got to looking at the wall next. Then to wondering what it was made of. Then to rapping against it with my knuckles. The sound told me there was nothing but lath and plaster under the paper. It was the same as the wall we had been at work on down stairs. We had cleared our way so far through this last—in certain places where the repairs were most needed—that we had to be careful not to burst through the paper in the room on the other side. I found myself calling to mind the caution my husband had given me while we were at this part of the work, word for word as he had spoken it. 'Take care you don't find your hands in the next room.' That was what he had said down in the parlor. Up in his bedroom I kept on repeating it in my own mind—with my eyes all the while on the key, which he had moved to the inner side of the door to lock himself in—till the knowledge of what it meant burst on me like a flash of light. I looked at the wall, at the bedhead, at my own two hands—and I shivered as if it was winter time.

"Hours must have passed like minutes while I was up stairs that night. I lost all count of time. When my husband came up from his drinking, he found me in his room."

10.

"I leave the rest untold, and pass on purposely to the next morning.

"No mortal eyes but mine will ever see these lines. Still, there are things a woman can't write of even to herself. I shall only say this. I suffered the last and worst of many indignities at my husband's hands—at the very time when I first saw, set plainly before me, the way to take his life. He went out toward noon next day, to go his rounds among the public houses; my mind being then strung up to deliver myself from him, for good and all, when he came back at night.

"The things we had used on the previous day were left in the parlor. I was all by myself in the house, free to put in practice the lesson he had taught me. I proved myself an apt scholar. Before the lamps were lit in the street I had my own way prepared (in my bedroom and in his) for laying my own hands on him—after he had locked himself up for the night.

"I don't remember feeling either fear or doubt through all those hours. I sat down to my bit of supper with no better and no worse an appetite than usual. The only change in me that I can call to mind was that I felt a singular longing to have somebody with me to keep me company. Having no friend to ask in, I went to the street door and stood looking at the people passing this way and that.

"A stray dog, sniffing about, came up to me. Generally I dislike dogs and beasts of all kinds. I called this one in and gave him his supper. He had been taught (I suppose) to sit up on his hind-legs and beg for food; at any rate, that was his way of asking me for more. I laughed—it seems impossible when I look back at it now, but for all that it's true—I laughed till the tears ran down my cheeks, at the little beast on his haunches, with his ears pricked up and his head on one side and his mouth watering for the victuals. I wonder whether I was in my right senses? I don't know.

"When the dog had got all he could get he whined to be let out to roam the streets again.

"As I opened the door to let the creature go his ways, I saw my husband crossing the road to come in. 'Keep out' (I says to him); 'to-night, of all nights, keep out.' He was too drunk to heed me; he passed by, and blundered his way up stairs. I followed and listened. I heard him open his door, and bang it to, and lock it. I waited a bit, and went up another stair or two. I heard him drop down on to his bed. In a minute more he was fast asleep and snoring.

"It had all happened as it was wanted to happen. In two minutes—without doing one single thing to bring suspicion on myself—I could have smothered him. I went into my own room. I took up the towel that I had laid ready. I was within an inch of it—when there came a rush of something up into my head. I can't say what it was. I can only say the horrors laid hold of me and hunted me then and there out of the house.

"I put on my bonnet, and slipped the key of the street door into my pocket. It was only half past nine—or maybe a quarter to ten. If I had any one clear notion in my head, it was the notion of running away, and never allowing myself to set eyes on the house or the husband more.

"I went up the street—and came back. I went down the street—and came back. I tried it a third time, and went round and round and round—and came back. It was not to be done The house held me chained to it like a dog to his kennel. I couldn't keep away from it. For the life of me, I couldn't keep away from it.

"A company of gay young men and women passed me, just as I was going to let myself in again. They were in a great hurry. 'Step out,' says one of the men; 'the theatre's close by, and we shall be just in time for the farce.' I turned about and followed them. Having been piously brought up, I had never been inside a theatre in my life. It struck me that I might get taken, as it were, out of myself, if I saw something that was quite strange to me, and heard something which would put new thoughts into my mind.

"They went in to the pit; and I went in after them.

"The thing they called the farce had begun. Men and women came on to the stage, turn and turn about, and talked, and went off again. Before long all the people about me in the pit were laughing and clapping their hands. The noise they made angered me. I don't know how to describe the state I was in. My eyes wouldn't serve me, and my ears wouldn't serve me, to see and to hear what the rest of them were seeing and hearing. There must have been something, I fancy, in my mind that got itself between me and what was going on upon the stage. The play looked fair enough on the surface; but there was danger and death at the bottom of it. The players were talking and laughing to deceive the people—with murder in their minds all the time. And nobody knew it but me—and my tongue was tied when I tried to tell the others. I got up, and ran out. The moment I was in the street my steps turned back of themselves on the way to the house. I called a cab, and told the man to drive (as far as a shilling would take me) the opposite way. He put me down—I don't know where. Across the street I saw an inscription in letters of flame over an open door. The man said it was a dancing-place. Dancing was as new to me as play-going. I had one more shilling left; and I paid to go in, and see what a sight of the dancing would do for me. The light from the ceiling poured down in this place as if it was all on fire. The crashing of the music was dreadful. The whirling round and round of men and women in each other's arms was quite maddening to see. I don't know what happened to me here. The great blaze of light from the ceiling turned blood-red on a sudden. The man standing in front of the musicians waving a stick took the likeness of Satan, as seen in the picture in our family Bible at home. The whirling men and women went round and round, with white faces like the faces of the dead, and bodies robed in winding-sheets. I screamed out with the terror of it; and some person took me by the arm and put me outside the door. The darkness did me good: it was comforting and delicious—like a cool hand laid on a hot head. I went walking on through it, without knowing where; composing my mind with the belief that I had lost my way, and that I should find myself miles distant from home when morning dawned. After some time I got too weary to go on; and I sat me down to rest on a door-step. I dozed a bit, and woke up. When I got on my feet to go on again, I happened to turn my head toward the door of the house. The number on it was the same number an as ours. I looked again. And behold, it was our steps I had been resting on. The door was our door.

"All my doubts and all my struggles dropped out of my mind when I made that discovery. There was no mistaking what this perpetual coming back to the house meant. Resist it as I might, it was to be.

"I opened the street door and went up stairs, and heard him sleeping his heavy sleep, exactly as I had heard him when I went out. I sat down on my bed and took off my bonnet, quite quiet in myself, because I knew it was to be. I damped the towel, and put it ready, and took a turn in the room.

"It was just the dawn of day. The sparrows were chirping among the trees in the square hard by.

"I drew up my blind; the faint light spoke to me as if in words, 'Do it now, before I get brighter, and show too much.'

"I listened. The friendly silence had a word for me too: 'Do it now, and trust the secret to Me.'

"I waited till the church clock chimed before striking the hour. At the first stroke—without touching the lock of his door, without setting foot in his room—I had the towel over his face. Before the last stroke he had ceased struggling. When the hum of the bell through the morning silence was still and dead, he was still and dead with it."

11.

"The rest of this history is counted in my mind by four days—Wednesday, Thursday, Friday, Saturday. After that it all fades off like, and the new years come with a strange look, being the years of a new life.

"What about the old life first? What did I feel, in the horrid quiet of the morning, when I had done it?

"I don't know what I felt. I can't remember it, or I can't tell it, I don't know which. I can write the history of the four days, and that's all.

"Wednesday.—I gave the alarm toward noon. Hours before, I had put things straight and fit to be seen. I had only to call for help, and to leave the people to do as they pleased. The neighbors came in, and then the police. They knocked, uselessly, at his door. Then they broke it open, and found him dead in his bed.

"Not the ghost of a suspicion of me entered the mind of any one. There was no fear of human justice finding me out: my one unutterable dread was dread of an Avenging Providence.

"I had a short sleep that night, and a dream, in which I did the deed over again. For a time my mind was busy with thoughts of confessing to the police, and of giving myself up. If I had not belonged to a respectable family, I should have done it. From generation to generation there had been no stain on our good name. It would be death to my father, and disgrace to all my family, if I owned what I had done, and suffered for it on the public scaffold. I prayed to be guided; and I had a revelation, toward morning, of what to do.

"I was commanded, in a vision, to open the Bible, and vow on it to set my guilty self apart among my innocent fellow-creatures from that day forth; to live among them a separate and silent life, to dedicate the use of my speech to the language of prayer only, offered up in the solitude of my own chamber when no human ear could hear me. Alone, in the morning, I saw the vision, and vowed the vow. No human ear has heard me from that time. No human ear will hear me, to the day of my death.

"Thursday.—The people came to speak to me, as usual. They found me dumb.

"What had happened to me in the past, when my head had been hurt, and my speech affected by it, gave a likelier look to my dumbness than it might have borne in the case of another person. They took me back again to the hospital. The doctors were divided in opinion. Some said the shock of what had taken place in the house, coming on the back of the other shock, might, for all they knew, have done the mischief. And others said, 'She got her speech again after the accident; there has been no new injury since that time; the woman is shamming dumb, for some purpose of her own.' I let them dispute it as they liked. All human talk was nothing now to me. I had set myself apart among my fellow-creatures; I had begun my separate and silent life.

"Through all this time the sense of a coming punishment hanging over me never left my mind. I had nothing to dread from human justice. The judgment of an Avenging Providence—there was what I was waiting for.

"Friday—They held the inquest. He had been known for years past as an inveterate drunkard, he had been seen overnight going home in liquor; he had been found locked up in his room, with the key inside the door, and the latch of the window bolted also. No fire-place was in this garret; nothing was disturbed or altered: nobody by human possibility could have got in. The doctor reported that he had died of congestion of the lungs; and the jury gave their verdict accordingly."

12.

"Saturday.—Marked forever in my calendar as the memorable day on which the judgment descended on me. Toward three o'clock in the afternoon—in the broad sunlight, under the cloudless sky, with hundreds of innocent human creatures all around me—I, Hester Dethridge, saw, for the first time, the Appearance which is appointed to haunt me for the rest of my life.

"I had had a terrible night. My mind felt much as it had felt on the evening when I had gone to the play. I went out to see what the air and the sunshine and the cool green of trees and grass would do for me. The nearest place in which I could find what I wanted was the Regent's Park. I went into one of the quiet walks in the middle of the park, where the horses and carriages are not allowed to go, and where old people can sun themselves, and children play, without danger.

"I sat me down to rest on a bench. Among the children near me was a beautiful little boy, playing with a brand-new toy—a horse and wagon. While I was watching him busily plucking up the blades of grass and loading his wagon with them, I felt for the first time—what I have often and often felt since—a creeping chill come slowly over my flesh, and then a suspicion of something hidden near me, which would steal out and show itself if I looked that way.

"There was a big tree hard by. I looked toward the tree, and waited to see the something hidden appear from behind it.

"The Thing stole out, dark and shadowy in the pleasant sunlight. At first I saw only the dim figure of a woman. After a little it began to get plainer, brightening from within outward—brightening, brightening, brightening, till it set before me the vision of MY OWN SELF, repeated as if I was standing before a glass—the double of myself, looking at me with my own eyes. I saw it move over the grass. I saw it stop behind the beautiful little boy. I saw it stand and listen, as I had stood and listened at the dawn of morning, for the chiming of the bell before the clock struck the hour. When it heard the stroke it pointed down to the boy with my own hand; and it said to me, with my own voice, 'Kill him.'

"A time passed. I don't know whether it was a minute or an hour. The heavens and the earth disappeared from before me. I saw nothing but the double of myself, with the pointing hand. I felt nothing but the longing to kill the boy.

"Then, as it seemed, the heavens and the earth rushed back upon me. I saw the people near staring in surprise at me, and wondering if I was in my right mind.

"I got, by main force, to my feet; I looked, by main force, away from the beautiful boy; I escaped, by main force, from the sight of the Thing, back into the streets. I can only describe the overpowering strength of the temptation that tried me in one way. It was like tearing the life out of me to tear myself from killing the boy. And what it was on this occasion it has been ever since. No remedy against it but in that torturing effort, and no quenching the after-agony but by solitude and prayer.

"The sense of a coming punishment had hung over me. And the punishment had come. I had waited for the judgment of an Avenging Providence. And the judgment was pronounced. With pious David I could now say, Thy fierce wrath goeth over me; thy terrors have cut me off."

Arrived at that point in the narrative, Geoffrey looked up from the manuscript for the first time. Some sound outside the room had disturbed him. Was it a sound in the passage?

He listened. There was an interval of silence. He looked back again at the Confession, turning over the last leaves to count how much was left of it before it came to an end.

After relating the circumstances under which the writer had returned to domestic service, the narrative was resumed no more. Its few remaining pages were occupied by a fragmentary journal. The brief entries referred to the various occasions on which Hester Dethridge had again and again seen the terrible apparition of herself, and had again and again resisted the homicidal frenzy roused in her by the hideous creation of her own distempered brain. In the effort which that resistance cost her lay the secret of her obstinate determination to insist on being freed from her work at certain times, and to make it a condition with any mistress who employed her that she should be privileged to sleep in a room of her own at night. Having counted the pages thus filled, Geoffrey turned back to the place at which he had left off, to read the manuscript through to the end.

As his eyes rested on the first line the noise in the passage—intermitted for a moment only—disturbed him again.

This time there was no doubt of what the sound implied. He heard her hurried footsteps; he heard her dreadful cry. Hester Dethridge had woke in her chair in the pallor, and had discovered that the Confession was no longer in her own hands.

He put the manuscript into the breast-pocket of his coat. On this occasion his reading had been of some use to him. Needless to go on further with it. Needless to return to the Newgate Calendar. The problem was solved.

As he rose to his feet his heavy face brightened slowly with a terrible smile. While the woman's Confession was in his pocket the woman herself was in his power. "If she wants it back," he said, "she must get it on my terms." With that resolution, he opened the door, and met Hester Dethridge, face to face, in the passage.

CHAPTER THE FIFTY-FIFTH.

THE SIGNS OF THE END.

THE servant, appearing the next morning in Anne's room with the breakfast tray, closed the door with an air of mystery, and announced that strange things were going on in the house.

"Did you hear nothing last night, ma'am," she asked, "down stairs in the passage?"

"I thought I heard some voices whispering outside my room," Anne replied. "Has any thing happened?"

Extricated from the confusion in which she involved it, the girl's narrative amounted in substance to this. She had been startled by the sudden appearance of her mistress in the passage, staring about her wildly, like a woman who had gone out of her senses. Almost at the same moment "the master" had flung open the drawing-room door. He had caught Mrs. Dethridge by the arm, had dragged her into the room, and had closed the door again. After the two had remained shut up together for more than half an hour, Mrs. Dethridge had come out, as pale as ashes, and had gone up stairs trembling like a person in great terror. Some time later, when the servant was in bed, but not asleep, she had seen a light under her door, in the narrow wooden passage which separated Anne's bedroom from Hester's bedroom, and by which she obtained access to her own little sleeping-chamber beyond. She had got out of bed; had looked through the keyhole; and had seen "the master" and Mrs. Dethridge standing together examining the walls of the passage. "The master" had laid his hand upon the wall, on the side of his wife's room, and had looked at Mrs. Dethridge. And Mrs. Dethridge had looked back at him, and had shaken her head. Upon that he had said in a whisper (still with his hand on the wooden wall), "Not to be done here?" And Mrs. Dethridge had shaken her head. He had considered a moment, and had whispered again, "The other room will do! won't it?" And Mrs. Dethridge had nodded her head—and so they had parted. That was the story of the night. Early in the morning, more strange things had happened. The master had gone out, with a large sealed packet in his hand, covered with many stamps; taking his own letter to the post, instead of sending the servant with it as usual. On his return, Mrs. Dethridge had gone out next, and had come back with something in a jar which she had locked up in her own sitting-room. Shortly afterward, a working-man had brought a bundle of laths, and some mortar and plaster of Paris, which had been carefully placed together in a corner of the scullery. Last, and most remarkable in the series of domestic events, the girl had received permission to go home and see her friends in the country, on that very day; having been previously informed, when she entered Mrs. Dethridge's service, that she was not to expect to have a holiday granted to her until after Christmas. Such were the strange things which had happened in the house since the previous night. What was the interpretation to be placed on them?

The right interpretation was not easy to discover.

Some of the events pointed apparently toward coming repairs or alterations in the cottage. But what Geoffrey could have to do with them (being at the time served with a notice to quit), and why Hester Dethridge should have shown the violent agitation which had been described, were mysteries which it was impossible to penetrate.

Anne dismissed the girl with a little present and a few kind words. Under other circumstances, the incomprehensible proceedings in the house might have made her seriously uneasy. But her mind was now occupied by more pressing anxieties. Blanche's second letter (received from Hester Dethridge on the previous evening) informed her that Sir Patrick persisted in his resolution, and that he and his niece might be expected, come what might of it, to present themselves at the cottage on that day.

Anne opened the letter, and looked at it for the second time. The passages relating to Sir Patrick were expressed in these terms:

"I don't think, darling, you have any idea of the interest that you have roused in my uncle. Although he has not to reproach himself, as I have, with being the miserable cause of the sacrifice that you have made, he is quite as wretched and quite as anxious about you as I am. We talk of nobody else. He said last night that he did not believe there was your equal in the world. Think of that from a man who has such terribly sharp eyes for the faults of women in general, and such a terribly sharp tongue in talking of them! I am pledged to secrecy; but I must tell you one other thing, between ourselves. Lord Holchester's announcement that his brother refuses to consent to a separation put my uncle almost beside himself. If there is not some change for the better in your life in a few days' time, Sir Patrick will find out a way of his own—lawful or not, he doesn't care—for rescuing you from the dreadful position in which you are placed, and Arnold (with my full approval) will help him. As we understand it, you are, under one pretense or another, kept a close prisoner. Sir Patrick has already secured a post of observation near you. He and Arnold went all round the cottage last night, and examined a door in your back garden wall, with a locksmith to help them. You will no doubt hear further about this from Sir Patrick himself. Pray don't appear to know any thing of it when you see him! I am not in his confidence—but Arnold is, which comes to the same thing exactly. You will see us (I mean you will see my uncle and me) to-morrow, in spite of the brute who keeps you under lock and key. Arnold will not accompany us; he is not to be trusted (he owns it himself) to control his indignation. Courage, dearest! There are two people in the world to whom you are inestimably precious, and who are determined not to let your happiness be sacrificed. I am one of them, and (for Heaven's sake keep this a secret also!) Sir Patrick is the other."

Absorbed in the letter, and in the conflict of opposite feelings which it roused—her color rising when it turned her thoughts inward on herself, and fading again when she was reminded by it of the coming visit—Anne was called back to a sense of present events by the reappearance of the servant, charged with a message. Mr. Speedwell had been for some time in the cottage, and he was now waiting to see her down stairs.

Anne found the surgeon alone in the drawing-room. He apologized for disturbing her at that early hour.

"It was impossible for me to get to Fulham yesterday," he said, "and I could only make sure of complying with Lord Holchester's request by coming here before the time at which I receive patients at home. I have seen Mr. Delamayn, and I have requested permission to say a word to you on the subject of his health."

Anne looked through the window, and saw Geoffrey smoking his pipe—not in the back garden, as usual, but in front of the cottage, where he could keep his eye on the gate.

"Is he ill?" she asked.

"He is seriously ill," answered Mr. Speedwell. "I should not otherwise have troubled you with this interview. It is a matter of professional duty to warn you, as his wife, that he is in danger. He may be seized at any moment by a paralytic stroke. The only chance for him—a very poor one, I am bound to say—is to make him alter his present mode of life without loss of time."

"In one way he will be obliged to alter it," said Anne. "He has received notice from the landlady to quit this cottage."

Mr. Speedwell looked surprised.

"I think you will find that the notice has been withdrawn," he said. "I can only assure you that Mr. Delamayn distinctly informed me, when I advised change of air, that he had decided, for reasons of his own, on remaining here."

(Another in the series of incomprehensible domestic events! Hester Dethridge—on all other occasions the most immovable of women—had changed her mind!)

"Setting that aside," proceeded the surgeon, "there are two preventive measures which I feel bound to suggest. Mr. Delamayn is evidently suffering (though he declines to admit it himself) from mental anxiety. If he is to have a chance for his life, that anxiety must be set at rest. Is it in your power to relieve it?"

"It is not even in my power, Mr. Speedwell, to tell you what it is."

The surgeon bowed, and went on:

"The second caution that I have to give you," he said, "is to keep him from drinking spirits. He admits having committed an excess in that way the night before last. In his state of health, drinking means literally death. If he goes back to the brandy-bottle—forgive me for saying it plainly; the matter is too serious to be trifled with—if he goes back to the brandy-bottle, his life, in my opinion, is not worth five minutes' purchase. Can you keep him from drinking?"

Anne answered sadly and plainly:

"I have no influence over him. The terms we are living on here—"

Mr. Speedwell considerately stopped her.

"I understand," he said. "I will see his brother on my way home." He looked for a moment at Anne. "You are far from well yourself," he resumed. "Can I do any thing for you?"

"While I am living my present life, Mr. Speedwell, not even your skill can help me."

The surgeon took his leave. Anne hurried back up stairs, before Geoffrey could re-enter the cottage. To see the man who had laid her life waste—to meet the vindictive hatred that looked furtively at her out of his eyes—at the moment when sentence of death had been pronounced on him, was an ordeal from which every finer instinct in her nature shrank in horror.

Hour by hour, the morning wore on, and he made no attempt to communicate with her, Stranger still, Hester Dethridge never appeared. The servant came up stairs to say goodby; and went away for her holiday. Shortly afterward, certain sounds reached Anne's ears from the opposite side of the passage. She heard the strokes of a hammer, and then a noise as of some heavy piece of furniture being moved. The mysterious repairs were apparently being begun in the spare room.

She went to the window. The hour was approaching at which Sir Patrick and Blanche might be expected to make the attempt to see her.

For the third time, she looked at the letter.

It suggested, on this occasion, a new consideration to her. Did the strong measures which Sir Patrick had taken in secret indicate alarm as well as sympathy? Did he believe she was in a position in which the protection of the law was powerless to reach her? It seemed just possible. Suppose she were free to consult a magistrate, and to own to him (if words could express it) the vague presentiment of danger which was then present in her mind—what proof could she produce to satisfy the mind of a stranger? The proofs were all in her husband's favor. Witnesses could testify to the conciliatory words which he had spoken to her in their presence. The evidence of his mother and brother would show that he had preferred to sacrifice his own pecuniary interests rather than consent to part with her. She could furnish nobody with the smallest excuse, in her case, for interfering between man and wife. Did Sir Patrick see this? And did Blanche's description of what he and Arnold Brinkworth were doing point to the conclusion that they were taking the law into their own hands in despair? The more she thought of it, the more likely it seemed.

She was still pursuing the train of thought thus suggested, when the gate-bell rang.

The noises in the spare room suddenly stopped.

Anne looked out. The roof of a carriage was visible on the other side of the wall. Sir Patrick and Blanche had arrived. After an interval Hester Dethridge appeared in the garden, and went to the grating in the gate. Anne heard Sir Patrick's voice, clear and resolute. Every word he said reached her ears through the open window.

"Be so good as to give my card to Mr. Delamayn. Say that I bring him a message from Holchester House, and that I can only deliver it at a personal interview."

Hester Dethridge returned to the cottage. Another, and a longer interval elapsed. At the end of the time, Geoffrey himself appeared in the front garden, with the key in his hand. Anne's heart throbbed fast as she saw him unlock the gate, and asked herself what was to follow.

To her unutterable astonishment, Geoffrey admitted Sir Patrick without the slightest hesitation—and, more still, he invited Blanche to leave the carriage and come in!

"Let by-gones be by-gones," Anne heard him say to Sir Patrick. "I only want to do the right thing. If it's the right thing for visitors to come here, so soon after my father's death, come, and welcome. My own notion was, when you proposed it before, that it was wrong. I am not much versed in these things. I leave it to you."

"A visitor who brings you messages from your mother and your brother," Sir Patrick answered gravely, "is a person whom it is your duty to admit, Mr. Delamayn, under any circumstances."

"And he ought to be none the less welcome," added Blanche, "when he is accompanied by your wife's oldest and dearest friend."

Geoffrey looked, in stolid submission, from one to the other.

"I am not much versed in these things," he repeated. "I have said already, I leave it to you."

They were by this time close under Anne's window. She showed herself. Sir Patrick took off his hat. Blanche kissed her hand with a cry of joy, and attempted to enter the cottage. Geoffrey stopped her—and called to his wife to come down.

"No! no!" said Blanche. "Let me go up to her in her room."

She attempted for the second time to gain the stairs. For the second time Geoffrey stopped her. "Don't trouble yourself," he said; "she is coming down."

Anne joined them in the front garden. Blanche flew into her arms and devoured her with kisses. Sir Patrick took her hand in silence. For the first time in Anne's experience of him, the bright, resolute, self-reliant old man was, for the moment, at a loss what to say, at a loss what to do. His eyes, resting on her in mute sympathy and interest, said plainly, "In your husband's presence I must not trust myself to speak."

Geoffrey broke the silence.

"Will you go into the drawing-room?" he asked, looking with steady attention at his wife and Blanche.

Geoffrey's voice appeared to rouse Sir Patrick. He raised his head—he looked like himself again.

"Why go indoors this lovely weather?" he said. "Suppose we take a turn in the garden?"

Blanche pressed Anne's hand significantly. The proposal was evidently made for a purpose. They turned the corner of the cottage and gained the large garden at the back—the two ladies walking together, arm in arm; Sir Patrick and Geoffrey following them. Little by little, Blanche quickened her pace. "I have got my instructions," she whispered to Anne. "Let's get out of his hearing."

It was more easily said than done. Geoffrey kept close behind them.

"Consider my lameness, Mr. Delamayn," said Sir Patrick. "Not quite so fast."

It was well intended. But Geoffrey's cunning had taken the alarm. Instead of dropping behind with Sir Patrick, he called to his wife.

"Consider Sir Patrick's lameness," he repeated. "Not quite so fast."

Sir Patrick met that check with characteristic readiness. When Anne slackened her pace, he addressed himself to Geoffrey, stopping deliberately in the middle of the path. "Let me give you my message from Holchester House," he said. The two ladies were still slowly walking on. Geoffrey was placed between the alternatives of staying with Sir Patrick and leaving them by themselves—or of following them and leaving Sir Patrick. Deliberately, on his side, he followed the ladies.

Sir Patrick called him back. "I told you I wished to speak to you," he said, sharply.

Driven to bay, Geoffrey openly revealed his resolution to give Blanche no opportunity of speaking in private to Anne. He called to Anne to stop.

"I have no secrets from my wife," he said. "And I expect my wife to have no secrets from me. Give me the message in her hearing."

Sir Patrick's eyes brightened with indignation. He controlled himself, and looked for an instant significantly at his niece before he spoke to Geoffrey.

"As you please," he said. "Your brother requests me to tell you that the duties of the new position in which he is placed occupy the whole of his time, and will prevent him from returning to Fulham, as he had proposed, for some days to come. Lady Holchester, hearing that I was likely to see you, has charged me with another message, from herself. She is not well enough to leave home; and she wishes to see you at Holchester House to-morrow—accompanied (as she specially desires) by Mrs. Delamayn."

In giving the two messages, he gradually raised his voice to a louder tone than usual. While he was speaking, Blanche (warned to follow her instructions by the glance her uncle had cast at her) lowered her voice, and said to Anne:

"He won't consent to the separation as long as he has got you here. He is trying for higher terms. Leave him, and he must submit. Put a candle in your window, if you can get into the garden to-night. If not, any other night. Make for the back gate in the wall. Sir Patrick and Arnold will manage the rest."

She slipped those words into Anne's ears—swinging her parasol to and fro, and looking as if the merest gossip was dropping from her lips—with the dexterity which rarely fails a woman when she is called on to assist a deception in which her own interests are concerned. Cleverly as it had been done, however, Geoffrey's inveterate distrust was stirred into action by it. Blanche had got to her last sentence before he was able to turn his attention from what Sir Patrick was saying to what his niece was saying. A quicker man would have heard more. Geoffrey had only distinctly heard the first half of the last sentence.

"What's that," he asked, "about Sir Patrick and Arnold?"

"Nothing very interesting to you," Blanche answered, readily. "I will repeat it if you like. I was telling Anne about my step-mother, Lady Lundie. After what happened that day in Portland Place, she has requested Sir Patrick and Arnold to consider themselves, for the future, as total strangers to her. That's all."

"Oh!" said Geoffrey, eying her narrowly.

"Ask my uncle," returned Blanche, "if you don't believe that I have reported her correctly. She gave us all our dismissal, in her most magnificent manner, and in those very words. Didn't she, Sir Patrick?"

It was perfectly true. Blanche's readiness of resource had met the emergency of the moment by describing something, in connection with Sir Patrick and Arnold, which had really happened. Silenced on one side, in spite of himself, Geoffrey was at the same moment pressed on the other for an answer to his mother's message.

"I must take your reply to Lady Holchester," said Sir Patrick. "What is it to be?"

Geoffrey looked hard at him, without making any reply.

Sir Patrick repeated the message—with a special emphasis on that part of it which related to Anne. The emphasis roused Geoffrey's temper.

"You and my mother have made that message up between you, to try me!" he burst out. "Damn all underhand work is what I say!"

"I am waiting for your answer," persisted Sir Patrick, steadily ignoring the words which had just been addressed to him.

Geoffrey glanced at Anne, and suddenly recovered himself.

"My love to my mother," he said. "I'll go to her to-morrow—and take my wife with me, with the greatest pleasure. Do you hear that? With the greatest pleasure." He stopped to observe the effect of his reply. Sir Patrick waited impenetrably to hear more—if he had more to say. "I'm sorry I lost my temper just now," he resumed "I am badly treated—I'm distrusted without a cause. I ask you to bear witness," he added, his voice getting louder again, while his eyes moved uneasily backward and forward between Sir Patrick and Anne, "that I treat my wife as becomes a lady. Her friend calls on her—and she's free to receive her friend. My mother wants to see her—and I promise to take her to my mother's. At two o'clock to-morrow. Where am I to blame? You stand there looking at me, and saying nothing. Where am I to blame?"

"If a man's own conscience justifies him, Mr. Delamayn," said Sir Patrick, "the opinions of others are of very little importance. My errand here is performed."

As he turned to bid Anne farewell, the uneasiness that he felt at leaving her forced its way to view. The color faded out of his face. His hand trembled as it closed tenderly and firmly on hers. "I shall see you to-morrow, at Holchester House," he said; giving his arm while he spoke to Blanche. He took leave of Geoffrey, without looking at him again, and without seeing his offered hand. In another minute they were gone.

Anne waited on the lower floor of the cottage while Geoffrey closed and locked the gate. She had no wish to appear to avoid him, after the answer that he had sent to his mother's message. He returned slowly half-way across the front garden, looked toward the passage in which she was standing, passed before the door, and disappeared round the corner of the cottage on his way to the back garden. The inference was not to be mistaken. It was Geoffrey who was avoiding her. Had he lied to Sir Patrick? When the next day came would he find reasons of his own for refusing to take her to Holchester House?

She went up stairs. At the same moment Hester Dethridge opened her bedroom door to come out. Observing Anne, she closed it again and remained invisible in her room. Once more the inference was not to be mistaken. Hester Dethridge, also, had her reasons for avoiding Anne.

What did it mean? What object could there be in common between Hester and Geoffrey?

There was no fathoming the meaning of it. Anne's thoughts reverted to the communication which had been secretly made to her by Blanche. It was not in womanhood to be insensible to such devotion as Sir Patrick's conduct implied. Terrible as her position had become in its ever-growing uncertainty, in its never-ending suspense, the oppression of it yielded for the moment to the glow of pride and gratitude which warmed her heart, as she thought of the sacrifices that had been made, of the perils that were still to be encountered, solely for her sake. To shorten the period of suspense seemed to be a duty which she owed to Sir Patrick, as well as to herself. Why, in her situation, wait for what the next day might bring forth? If the opportunity offered, she determined to put the signal in the window that night.

Toward evening she heard once more the noises which appeared to indicate that repairs of some sort were going on in the house. This time the sounds were fainter; and they came, as she fancied, not from the spare room, as before, but from Geoffrey's room, next to it.

The dinner was later than usual that day. Hester Dethridge did not appear with the tray till dusk. Anne spoke to her, and received a mute sign in answer. Determined to see the woman's face plainly, she put a question which required a written answer on the slate; and, telling Hester to wait, went to the mantle-piece to light her candle. When she turned round with the lighted candle in her hand, Hester was gone.

Night came. She rang her bell to have the tray taken away. The fall of a strange footstep startled her outside her door. She called out, "Who's there?" The voice of the lad whom Geoffrey employed to go on errands for him answered her.

"What do you want here?" she asked, through the door.

"Mr. Delamayn sent me up, ma'am. He wishes to speak to you directly."

Anne found Geoffrey in the dining-room. His object in wishing to speak to her was, on the surface of it, trivial enough. He wanted to know how she would prefer going to Holchester House on the next day—by the railway, or in a carriage. "If you prefer driving," he said, "the boy has come here for orders, and he can tell them to send a carriage from the livery-stables, as he goes home."

"The railway will do perfectly well for me," Anne replied.

Instead of accepting the answer, and dropping the subject, he asked her to reconsider her decision. There was an absent, uneasy expression in his eye as he begged her not to consult economy at the expense of her own comfort. He appeared to have some reason of his own for preventing her from leaving the room. "Sit d own a minute, and think before you decide," he said. Having forced her to take a chair, he put his head outside the door and directed the lad to go up stairs, and see if he had left his pipe in his bedroom. "I want you to go in comfort, as a lady should," he repeated, with the uneasy look more marked than ever. Before Anne could reply, the lad's voice reached them from the bedroom floor, raised in shrill alarm, and screaming "Fire!"

Geoffrey ran up stairs. Anne followed him. The lad met them at the top of the stairs. He pointed to the open door of Anne's room. She was absolutely certain of having left her lighted candle, when she went down to Geoffrey, at a safe distance from the bed-curtains. The bed-curtains, nevertheless, were in a blaze of fire.

There was a supply of water to the cottage, on the upper floor. The bedroom jugs and cans usually in their places at an earlier hour, were standing that night at the cistern. An empty pail was left near them. Directing the lad to bring him water from these resources, Geoffrey tore down the curtains in a flaming heap, partly on the bed and partly on the sofa near it. Using the can and the pail alternately, as the boy brought them, he drenched the bed and the sofa. It was all over in little more than a minute. The cottage was saved. But the bed-furniture was destroyed; and the room, as a matter of course, was rendered uninhabitable, for that night at least, and probably for more nights to come.

Geoffrey set down the empty pail; and, turning to Anne, pointed across the passage.

"You won't be much inconvenienced by this," he said. "You have only to shift your quarters to the spare room."

With the assistance of the lad, he moved Anne's boxes, and the chest of drawers, which had escaped damage, into the opposite room. This done, he cautioned her to be careful with her candles for the future—and went down stairs, without waiting to hear what she said in reply. The lad followed him, and was dismissed for the night.

Even in the confusion which attended the extinguishing of the fire, the conduct of Hester Dethridge had been remarkable enough to force itself on the attention of Anne.

She had come out from her bedroom, when the alarm was given; had looked at the flaming curtains; and had drawn back, stolidly submissive, into a corner to wait the event. There she had stood—to all appearance, utterly indifferent to the possible destruction of her own cottage. The fire extinguished, she still waited impenetrably in her corner, while the chest of drawers and the boxes were being moved—then locked the door, without even a passing glance at the scorched ceiling and the burned bed-furniture—put the key into her pocket—and went back to her room.

Anne had hitherto not shared the conviction felt by most other persons who were brought into contact with Hester Dethridge, that the woman's mind was deranged. After what she had just seen, however, the general impression became her impression too. She had thought of putting certain questions to Hester, when they were left together, as to the origin of the fire. Reflection decided her on saying nothing, for that night at least. She crossed the passage, and entered the spare room—the room which she had declined to occupy on her arrival at the cottage, and which she was obliged to sleep in now.

She was instantly struck by a change in the disposition of the furniture of the room.

The bed had been moved. The head—set, when she had last seen it, against the side wall of the cottage—was placed now against the partition wall which separated the room from Geoffrey's room. This new arrangement had evidently been effected with a settled purpose of some sort. The hook in the ceiling which supported the curtains (the bed, unlike the bed in the other room, having no canopy attached to it) had been moved so as to adapt itself to the change that had been made. The chairs and the washhand-stand, formerly placed against the partition wall, were now, as a matter of necessity, shifted over to the vacant space against the side wall of the cottage. For the rest, no other alteration was visible in any part of the room.

In Anne's situation, any event not immediately intelligible on the face of it, was an event to be distrusted. Was there a motive for the change in the position of the bed? And was it, by any chance, a motive in which she was concerned?

The doubt had barely occurred to her, before a startling suspicion succeeded it. Was there some secret purpose to be answered by making her sleep in the spare room? Did the question which the servant had heard Geoffrey put to Hester, on the previous night, refer to this? Had the fire which had so unaccountably caught the curtains in her own room, been, by any possibility, a fire purposely kindled, to force her out?

She dropped into the nearest chair, faint with horror, as those three questions forced themselves in rapid succession on her mind.

After waiting a little, she recovered self-possession enough to recognize the first plain necessity of putting her suspicions to the test. It was possible that her excited fancy had filled her with a purely visionary alarm. For all she knew to the contrary, there might be some undeniably sufficient reason for changing the position of the bed. She went out, and knocked at the door of Hester Dethridge's room.

"I want to speak to you," she said.

Hester came out. Anne pointed to the spare room, and led the way to it. Hester followed her.

"Why have you changed the place of the bed," she asked, "from the wall there, to the wall here?"

Stolidly submissive to the question, as she had been stolidly submissive to the fire, Hester Dethridge wrote her reply. On all other occasions she was accustomed to look the persons to whom she offered her slate steadily in the face. Now, for the first time, she handed it to Anne with her eyes on the floor. The one line written contained no direct answer: the words were these:

"I have meant to move it, for some time past."

"I ask you why you have moved it."

She wrote these four words on the slate: "The wall is damp."

Anne looked at the wall. There was no sign of damp on the paper. She passed her hand over it. Feel where she might, the wall was dry.

"That is not your reason," she said.

Hester stood immovable.

"There is no dampness in the wall."

Hester pointed persistently with her pencil to the four words, still without looking up—waited a moment for Anne to read them again—and left the room.

It was plainly useless to call her back. Anne's first impulse when she was alone again was to secure the door. She not only locked it, but bolted it at top and bottom. The mortise of the lock and the staples of the bolts, when she tried them, were firm. The lurking treachery—wherever else it might be—was not in the fastenings of the door.

She looked all round the room; examining the fire place, the window and its shutters, the interior of the wardrobe, the hidden space under the bed. Nothing was any where to be discovered which could justify the most timid person living in feeling suspicion or alarm.

Appearances, fair as they were, failed to convince her. The presentiment of some hidden treachery, steadily getting nearer and nearer to her in the dark, had rooted itself firmly in her mind. She sat down, and tried to trace her way back to the clew, through the earlier events of the day.

The effort was fruitless: nothing definite, nothing tangible, rewarded it. Worse still, a new doubt grew out of it—a doubt whether the motive which Sir Patrick had avowed (through Blanche) was the motive for helping her which was really in his mind.

Did he sincerely believe Geoffrey's conduct to be animated by no worse object than a mercenary object? and was his only purpose in planning to remove her out of her husband's reach, to force Geoffrey's consent to their separation on the terms which Julius had proposed? Was this really the sole end that he had in view? or was he secretly convinced (knowing Anne's position as he knew it) that she was in personal danger at the cottage? and had he considerately kept that conviction concealed, in the fear that he might otherwise encourage her to feel alarmed about herself? She looked round the strange room, in the silence of the night, and she felt that the latter interpretation was the likeliest interpretation of the two.

The sounds caused by the closing of the doors and windows reached her from the ground-floor. What was to be done?

It was impossible, to show the signal which had been agreed on to Sir Patrick and Arnold. The window in which they expected to see it was the window of the room in which the fire had broken out—the room which Hester Dethridge had locked up for the night.

It was equally hopeless to wait until the policeman passed on his beat, and to call for help. Even if she could prevail upon herself to make that open acknowledgment of distrust under her husband's roof, and even if help was near, what valid reason could she give for raising an alarm? There was not the shadow of a reason to justify any one in placing her under the protection of the law.

As a last resource, impelled by her blind distrust of the change in the position of the bed, she attempted to move it. The utmost exertion of her strength did not suffice to stir the heavy piece of furniture out of its place, by so much as a hair's breadth.

There was no alternative but to trust to the security of the locked and bolted door, and to keep watch through the night—certain that Sir Patrick and Arnold were, on their part, also keeping watch in the near neighborhood of the cottage. She took out her work and her books; and returned to her chair, placing it near the table, in the middle of the room.

The last noises which told of life and movement about her died away. The breathless stillness of the night closed round her.

CHAPTER THE FIFTY-SIXTH.

THE MEANS.

THE new day dawned; the sun rose; the household was astir again. Inside the spare room, and outside the spare room, nothing had happened.

At the hour appointed for leaving the cottage to pay the promised visit to Holchester House, Hester Dethridge and Geoffrey were alone together in the bedroom in which Anne had passed the night.

"She's dressed, and waiting for me in the front garden," said Geoffrey. "You wanted to see me here alone. What is it?"

Hester pointed to the bed.

"You want it moved from the wall?"

Hester nodded her head.

They moved the bed some feet away from the partition wall. After a momentary pause,

Geoffrey spoke again.

"It must be done to-night," he said. "Her friends may interfere; the girl may come back. It must be done to-night."

Hester bowed her head slowly.

"How long do you want to be left by yourself in the house?"

She held up three of her fingers.

"Does that mean three hours?"

She nodded her head.

"Will it be done in that time?"

She made the affirmative sign once more.

Thus far, she had never lifted her eyes to his. In her manner of listening to him when he spoke, in the slightest movement that she made when necessity required it, the same lifeless submission to him, the same mute horror of him, was expressed. He had, thus far, silently resented this, on his side. On the point of leaving the room the restraint which he had laid on himself gave way. For the first time, he resented it in words.

"Why the devil can't you look at me?" he asked

She let the question pass, without a sign to show that she had heard him. He angrily repeated it. She wrote on her slate, and held it out to him—still without raising her eyes to his face.

"You know you can speak," he said. "You know I have found you out. What's the use of playing the fool with me?"

She persisted in holding the slate before him. He read these words:

"I am dumb to you, and blind to you. Let me be."

"Let you be!" he repeated. "It's a little late in the day to be scrupulous, after what you have done. Do you want your Confession back, or not?"

As the reference to the Confession passed his lips, she raised her head. A faint tinge of color showed itself on her livid cheeks; a momentary spasm of pain stirred her deathlike face. The one last interest left in the woman's life was the interest of recovering the manuscript which had been taken from her. To that appeal the stunned intelligence still faintly answered—and to no other.

"Remember the bargain on your side," Geoffrey went on, "and I'll remember the bargain on mine. This is how it stands, you know. I have read your Confession; and I find one thing wanting. You don't tell how it was done. I know you smothered him—but I don't know how. I want to know. You're dumb; and you can't tell me. You must do to the wall here what you did in the other house. You run no risks. There isn't a soul to see you. You have got the place to yourself. When I come back let me find this wall like the other wall—at that small hour of the morning you know, when you were waiting, with the towel in your hand, for the first stroke of the clock. Let me find that; and to-morrow you shall have your Confession back again."

As the reference to the Confession passed his lips for the second time, the sinking energy in the woman leaped up in her once more. She snatched her slate from her side; and, writing on it rapidly, held it, with both hands, close under his eyes. He read these words:

"I won't wait. I must have it to-night."

"Do you think I keep your Confession about me?" said Geoffrey. "I haven't even got it in the house."

She staggered back; and looked up for the first time.

"Don't alarm yourself," he went on. "It's sealed up with my seal; and it's safe in my bankers' keeping. I posted it to them myself. You don't stick at a trifle, Mrs. Dethridge. If I had kept it locked up in the house, you might have forced the lock when my back was turned. If I had kept it about me—I might have had that towel over my face, in the small hours of the morning! The bankers will give you back your Confession—just as they have received it from me—on receipt of an order in my handwriting. Do what I have told you; and you shall have the order to-night."

She passed her apron over her face, and drew a long breath of relief. Geoffrey turned to the door.

"I will be back at six this evening," he said. "Shall I find it done?"

She bowed her head.

His first condition accepted, he proceeded to the second.

"When the opportunity offers," he resumed, "I shall go up to my room. I shall ring the dining room bell first. You will go up before me when you hear that—and you will show me how you did it in the empty house?"

She made the affirmative sign once more.

At the same moment the door in the passage below was opened and closed again. Geoffrey instantly went down stairs. It was possible that Anne might have forgotten something; and it was necessary to prevent her from returning to her own room.

They met in the passage.

"Tired of waiting in the garden?" he asked, abruptly.

She pointed to the dining-room.

"The postman has just given me a letter for you, through the grating in the gate," she answered. "I have put it on the table in there."

He went in. The handwriting on the address of the letter was the handwriting of Mrs. Glenarm. He put it unread into his pocket, and went back to Anne.

"Step out!" he said. "We shall lose the train."

They started for their visit to Holchester House.

CHAPTER THE FIFTY-SEVENTH.

THE END.

AT a few minutes before six o'clock that evening, Lord Holchester's carriage brought Geoffrey and Anne back to the cottage.

Geoffrey prevented the servant from ringing at the gate. He had taken the key with him, when he left home earlier in the day. Having admitted Anne, and having closed the gate again, he went on before her to the kitchen window, and called to Hester Dethridge.

"Take some cold water into the drawing-room and fill the vase on the chimney-piece," he said. "The sooner you put those flowers into water," he added, turning to his wife, "the longer they will last."

He pointed, as he spoke, to a nosegay in Anne's hand, which Julius had gathered for her from the conservatory at Holchester House. Leaving her to arrange the flowers in the vase, he went up stairs. After waiting for a moment, he was joined by Hester Dethridge.

"Done?" he asked, in a whisper.

Hester made the affirmative sign. Geoffrey took off his boots and led the way into the spare room. They noiselessly moved the bed back to its place against the partition wall—and left the room again. When Anne entered it, some minutes afterward, not the slightest change of any kind was visible since she had last seen it in the middle of the day.

She removed her bonnet and mantle, and sat down to rest.

The whole course of events, since the previous night, had tended one way, and had exerted the same delusive influence over her mind. It was impossible for her any longer to resist the conviction that she had distrusted appearances without the slightest reason, and that she had permitted purely visionary suspicions to fill her with purely causeless alarm. In the firm belief that she was in danger, she had watched through the night—and nothing had happened. In the confident anticipation that Geoffrey had promised what he was resolved not to perform, she had waited to see what excuse he would find for keeping her at the cottage. And, when the time came for the visit, she found him ready to fulfill the engagement which he had made. At Holchester House, not the slightest interference had been attempted with her perfect liberty of action and speech. Resolved to inform Sir Patrick that she had changed her room, she had described the alarm of fire and the events which had succeeded it, in the fullest detail—and had not been once checked by Geoffrey from beginning to end. She had spoken in confidence to Blanche, and had never been interrupted. Walking round the conservatory, she had dropped behind the others with perfect impunity, to say a grateful word to Sir Patrick, and to ask if the interpretation that he placed on Geoffrey's conduct was really the interpretation which had been hinted at by Blanche. They had talked together for ten minutes or more. Sir Patrick had assured her that Blanche had correctly represented his opinion. He had declared his conviction that the rash way was, in her case, the right way; and that she would do well (with his assistance) to take the initiative, in the matter of the separation, on herself. "As long as he can keep you under the same roof with him"—Sir Patrick had said—"so long he will speculate on our anxiety to release you from the oppression of living with him; and so long he will hold out with his brother (in the character of a penitent husband) for higher terms. Put the signal in the window, and try the experiment to-night. Once find your way to the garden door, and I answer for keeping you safely out of his reach until he has submitted to the separation, and has signed the deed." In those words he had urged Anne to prompt action. He had received, in return, her promise to be guided by his advice. She had gone back to the drawing-room; and Geoffrey had made no remark on her absence. She had returned to Fulham, alone with him in his brother's carriage; and he had asked no questions. What was it natural, with her means of judging, to infer from all this? Could she see into Sir Patrick's mind and detect that he was deliberately concealing his own conviction, in the fear that he might paralyze her energies if he acknowledged the alarm for her that he really felt? No. She could only accept the false appearances that surrounded her in the disguise of truth. She could only adopt, in good faith, Sir Patrick's assumed point of view, and believe, on the evidence of her own observation, that Sir Patrick was right.

Toward dusk, Anne began to feel the exhaustion which was the necessary result of a night passed without sleep. She rang her bell, and asked for some tea.

Hester Dethridge answered the bell. Instead of making the usual sign, she stood considering—and then wrote on her slate. These were the words: "I have all the work to do, now the girl has gone. If you would have your tea in the drawing-room, you would save me another journey up stairs."

Anne at once engaged to comply with the request.

"Are you ill?" she asked; noticing, faint as the light now was, something strangely altered in Hester's manner.

Without looking up, Hester shook her head.

"Has any thing happened to vex you?"

The negative sign was repeated.

"Have I offended you?"

She suddenly advanced a step, suddenly looked at Anne; checked herself with a dull moan, like a moan of pain; and hurried out of the room.

Concluding that she had inadvertently said, or done, something to offend Hester Dethridge, Anne determined to return to the subject at the first favorable opportunity. In the mean time, she descended to the ground-floor. The dining-room door, standing wide open, showed her Geoffrey sitting at the table, writing a letter—with the fatal brandy-bottle at his side.

After what Mr. Speedwell had told her, it was her duty to interfere. She performed her duty, without an instant's hesitation.

"Pardon me for interrupting you," she said. "I think you have forgotten what Mr. Speedwell told you about that."

She pointed to the bottle. Geoffrey looked at it; looked down again at his letter; and impatiently shook his head. She made a second attempt at remonstrance—again without effect. He only said, "All right!" in lower tones than were customary with him, and continued his occupation. It was useless to court a third repulse. Anne went into the drawing-room.

The letter on which he was engaged was an answer to Mrs. Glenarm, who had written to tell him that she was leaving town. He had reached his two concluding sentences when Anne spoke to him. They ran as follows: "I may have news to bring you, before long, which you don't look for. Stay where you are through to-morrow, and wait to hear from me."

After sealing the envelope, he emptied his glass of brandy and water; and waited, looking through the open door. When Hester Dethridge crossed the passage with the tea-tray, and entered the drawing-room, he gave the sign which had been agreed on. He rang his bell. Hester came out again, closing the drawing-room door behind her.

"Is she safe at her tea?" he asked, removing his heavy boots, and putting on the slippers which were placed ready for him.

Hester bowed her head.

He pointed up the stairs. "You go first," he whispered. "No nonsense! and no noise!"

She ascended the stairs. He followed slowly. Although he had only drunk one glass of brandy and water, his step was uncertain already. With one hand on the wall, and one hand on the banister, he made his way to the top; stopped, and listened for a moment; then joined Hester in his own room, and softly locked the door.

"Well?" he said.

She was standing motionless in the middle of the room—not like a living woman—like a machine waiting to be set in movement. Finding it useless to speak to her, he touched her (with a strange sensation of shrinking in him as he did it), and pointed to the partition wall.

The touch roused her. With slow step and vacant face—moving as if she was walking in her sleep—she led the way to the papered wall; knelt down at the skirting-board; and, taking out two small sharp nails, lifted up a long strip of the paper which had been detached from the plaster beneath. Mounting on a chair, she turned back the strip and pinned it up, out of the way, using the two nails, which she had kept ready in her hand.

By the last dim rays of twilight, Geoffrey looked at the wall.

A hollow space met his view. At a distance of some three feet from the floor, the laths had been sawn away, and the plaster had been ripped out, piecemeal, so as to leave a cavity, sufficient in height and width to allow free power of working in any direction, to a man's arms. The cavity completely pierced the substance of the wall. Nothing but the paper on the other side prevented eye or hand from penetrating into the next room.

Hester Dethridge got down from the chair, and made signs for a light.

Geoffrey took a match from the box. The same strange uncertainty which had already possessed his feet, appeared now to possess his hands. He struck the match too heavily against the sandpaper, and broke it. He tried another, and struck it too lightly to kindle the flame. Hester took the box out of his hands. Having lit the candle, she held it low, and pointed to the skirting-board.

Two little hooks were fixed into the floor, near the part of the wall from which the paper had been removed. Two lengths of fine and strong string were twisted once or twice round the hooks. The loose ends of the string extending to some length beyond the twisted parts, were neatly coiled away against the skirting-board. The other ends, drawn tight, disappeared in two small holes drilled through the wall, at a height of a foot from the floor.

After first untwisting the strings from the hooks, Hester rose, and held the candle so as to light the cavity in the wall. Two more pieces of the fine string were seen here, resting loose upon the uneven surface which marked the lower boundary of the hollowed space. Lifting these higher strings, Hester lifted the loosened paper in the next room—the lower strings, which had previously held the strip firm and flat against the sound portion of the wall, working in their holes, and allowing the paper to move up freely. As it rose higher and higher, Geoffrey saw thin strips of cotton wool lightly attached, at intervals, to the back of the paper, so as effectually to prevent it from making a grating sound against the wall. Up and up it came slowly, till it could be pulled through the hollow space, and pinned up out of the way, as the strip previously lifted had been pinned before it. Hester drew back, and made way for Geoffrey to look through. There was Anne's room, visible through the wall! He softly parted the light curtains that hang over the bed. There was the pillow, on which her head would rest at night, within reach of his hands!

The deadly dexterity of it struck him cold. His nerves gave way. He drew back with a start of guilty fear, and looked round the room. A pocket flask of brandy lay on the table at his bedside. He snatched it up, and emptied it at a draught—and felt like himself again.

He beckoned to Hester to approach him.

"Before we go any further," he said, "there's one thing I want to know. How is it all to be put right again? Suppose this room is examined? Those strings will show."

Hester opened a cupboard and produced a jar. She took out the cork. There was a mixture inside which looked like glue. Partly by signs, and partly by help of the slate, she showed how the mixture could be applied to the back of the loosened strip of paper in the next room—how the paper could be glued to the sound lower part of the wall by tightening the strings—how the strings, having served that purpose, could be safely removed—how the same process could be followed in Geoffrey's room, after the hollowed place had been filled up again with the materials waiting in the scullery, or even without filling up the hollowed place if the time failed for doing it. In either case, the refastened paper would hide every thing, and the wall would tell no tales.

Geoffrey was satisfied. He pointed next to the towels in his room.

"Take one of them," he said, "and show me how you did it, with your own hands."

As he said the words, Anne's voice reached his ear from below, calling for "Mrs. Dethridge."

It was impossible to say what might happen next. In another minute, she might go up to her room, and discover every thing. Geoffrey pointed to the wall.

"Put it right again," he said. "Instantly!"

It was soon done. All that was necessary was to let the two strips of paper drop back into their places—to fasten the strip to the wall in Anne's room, by tightening the two lower strings—and then to replace the nails which held the loose strip on Geoffrey's side. In a minute, the wall had reassumed its customary aspect.

They stole out, and looked over the stairs into the passage below. After calling uselessly for the second time, Anne appeared, crossed over to the kitchen; and, returning again with the kettle in her hand, closed the drawing-room door.

Hester Dethridge waited impenetrably to receive her next directions. There were no further directions to give. The hideous dramatic representation of the woman's crime for which Geoffrey had asked was in no respect necessary: the means were all prepared, and the manner of using them was self-evident. Nothing but the opportunity, and the resolution to profit by it, were wanting to lead the way to the end. Geoffrey signed to Hester to go down stairs.

"Get back into the kitchen," he said, "before she comes out again. I shall keep in the garden. When she goes up into her room for the night, show yourself at the back-door—and I shall know."

Hester set her foot on the first stair—stopped—turned round—and looked slowly along the two walls of the passage, from end to end—shuddered—shook her head—and went slowly on down the stairs.

"What were you looking for?" he whispered after her.

She neither answered, nor looked back—she went her way into the kitchen.

He waited a minute, and then followed her.

On his way out to the garden, he went into the dining-room. The moon had risen; and the window-shutters were not closed. It was easy to find the brandy and the jug of water on the table. He mixed the two, and emptied the tumbler at a draught. "My head's queer," he whispered to himself. He passed his handkerchief over his face. "How infernally hot it is to-night!" He made for the door. It was open, and plainly visible—and yet, he failed to find his way to it. Twice, he found himself trying to walk through the wall, on either side. The third time, he got out, and reached the garden. A strange sensation possessed him, as he walked round and round. He had not drunk enough, or nearly enough, to intoxicate him. His mind, in a dull way, felt the same as usual; but his body was like the body of a drunken man.

The night advanced; the clock of Putney Church struck ten.

Anne appeared again from the drawing room, with her bedroom candle in her hand.

"Put out the lights," she said to Hester, at the kitchen door; "I am going up stairs."

She entered her room. The insupportable sense of weariness, after the sleepless night that she had passed, weighed more heavily on her than ever. She locked her door, but forbore, on this occasion, to fasten the bolts. The dread of danger was no longer present to her mind; and there was this positive objection to losing the bolts, that the unfastening of them would increase the difficulty of leaving the room noiselessly later in the night. She loosened her dress, and lifted her hair from her temples—and paced to and fro in the room wearily, thinking. Geoffrey's habits were irregular; Hester seldom went to bed early.

Two hours at least—more probably three—must pass, before it would be safe to communicate with Sir Patrick by means of the signal in the window. Her strength was fast failing her. If she persisted, for the next three hours, in denying herself the repose which she sorely needed, the chances were that her nerves might fail her, through sheer exhaustion, when the time came for facing the risk and making the effort to escape. Sleep was falling on her even now—and sleep she must have. She had no fear of failing to wake at the needful time. Falling asleep, with a special necessity for rising at a given hour present to her mind, Anne (like most other sensitively organized people) could trust herself to wake at that given hour, instinctively. She put her lighted candle in a safe position, and laid down on the bed. In less than five minutes, she was in a deep sleep.

The church clock struck the quarter to eleven. Hester Dethridge showed herself at the back garden door. Geoffrey crossed the lawn, and joined her. The light of the lamp in the passage fell on his face. She started back from the sight of it.

"What's wrong?" he asked.

She shook her head; and pointed through the dining-room door to the brandy-bottle on the table.

"I'm as sober as you are, you fool!" he said. "Whatever else it is, it's not that."

Hester looked at him again. He was right. However unsteady his gait might be, his speech was not the speech, his eyes were not the eyes, of a drunken man.

"Is she in her room for the night?"

Hester made the affirmative sign.

Geoffrey ascended the stairs, swaying from side to side. He stopped at the top, and beckoned to Hester to join him. He went on into his room; and, signing to her to follow him, closed the door.

He looked at the partition wall—without approaching it. Hester waited, behind him.

"Is she asleep?" he asked.

Hester went to the wall; listened at it; and made the affirmative reply.

He sat down. "My head's queer," he said. "Give me a drink of water." He drank part of the water, and poured the rest over his head. Hester turned toward the door to leave him. He instantly stopped her. "I can't unwind the strings. I can't lift up the paper. Do it."

She sternly made the sign of refusal: she resolutely opened the door to leave him. "Do you want your Confession back?" he asked. She closed the door, stolidly submissive in an instant; and crossed to the partition wall.

She lifted the loose strips of paper on either side of the wall—pointed through the hollowed place—and drew back again to the other end of the room.

He rose and walked unsteadily from the chair to the foot of his bed. Holding by the wood-work of the bed; he waited a little. While he waited, he became conscious of a change in the strange sensations that possessed him. A feeling as of a breath of cold air passed over the right side of his head. He became steady again: he could calculate his distances: he could put his hands through the hollowed place, and draw aside the light curtains, hanging from the hook in the ceiling over the head of her bed. He could look at his sleeping wife.

She was dimly visible, by the light of the candle placed at the other end of her room. The worn and weary look had disappeared from her face. All that had been purest and sweetest in it, in the by-gone time, seemed to be renewed by the deep sleep that held her gently. She was young again in the dim light: she was beautiful in her calm repose. Her head lay back on the pillow. Her upturned face was in a position which placed her completely at the mercy of the man under whose eyes she was sleeping—the man who was looking at her, with the merciless resolution in him to take her life.

After waiting a while, he drew back. "She's more like a child than a woman to-night," he muttered to himself under his breath. He glanced across the room at Hester Dethridge. The lighted candle which she had brought up stairs with her was burning near the place where she stood. "Blow it out," he whispered. She never moved. He repeated the direction. There she stood, deaf to him.

What was she doing? She was looking fixedly into one of the corners of the room.

He turned his head again toward the hollowed place in the wall. He looked at the peaceful face on the pillow once more. He deliberately revived his own vindictive sense of the debt that he owed her. "But for you," he whispered to himself, "I should have won the race: but for you, I should have been friends with my father: but for you, I might marry Mrs. Glenarm." He turned back again into the room while the sense of it was at its fiercest in him. He looked round and round him. He took up a towel; considered for a moment; and threw it down again.

A new idea struck him. In two steps he was at the side of his bed. He seized on one of the pillows, and looked suddenly at Hester. "It's not a drunken brute, this time," he said to her. "It's a woman who will fight for her life. The pillow's the safest of the two." She never answered him, and never looked toward him. He made once more for the place in the wall; and stopped midway between it and his bed—stopped, and cast a backward glance over his shoulder.

Hester Dethridge was stirring at last.

With no third person in the room, she was looking, and moving, nevertheless, as if she was following a third person along the wall, from the corner. Her lips were parted in horror; her eyes, opening wider and wider, stared rigid and glittering at the empty wall. Step by step she stole nearer and nearer to Geoffrey, still following some visionary Thing, which was stealing nearer and nearer, too. He asked himself what it meant. Was the terror of the deed that he was about to do more than the woman's brain could bear? Would she burst out screaming, and wake his wife?

He hurried to the place in the wall—to seize the chance, while the chance was his.

He steadied his strong hold on the pillow.

He stooped to pass it through the opening.

He poised it over Anne's sleeping face.

At the same moment he felt Hester Dethridge's hand laid on him from behind. The touch ran through him, from head to foot, like a touch of ice. He drew back with a start, and faced her. Her eyes were staring straight over his shoulder at something behind him—looking as they had looked in the garden at Windygates.

Before he could speak he felt the flash of her eyes in his eyes. For the third time, she had seen the Apparition behind him. The homicidal frenzy possessed her. She flew at his throat like a wild beast. The feeble old woman attacked the athlete!

He dropped the pillow, and lifted his terrible right arm to brush her from him, as he might have brushed an insect from him.

Even as he raised the arm a frightful distortion seized on his face. As if with an invisible hand, it dragged down the brow and the eyelid on the right; it dragged down the mouth on the same side. His arm fell helpless; his whole body, on the side under the arm, gave way. He dropped on the floor, like a man shot dead.

Hester Dethridge pounced on his prostrate body—knelt on his broad breast—and fastened her ten fingers on his throat.

The shock of the fall woke Anne on the instant. She started up—looked round—and saw a gap in the wall at the head of her bed, and the candle-light glimmering in the next room. Panic-stricken; doubting, for the moment, if she were in her right mind, she drew back, waiting—listening—looking. She saw nothing but the glimmering light in the room; she heard nothing but a hoarse gasping, as of some person laboring for breath. The sound ceased. There was an interval of silence. Then the head of Hester Dethridge rose slowly into sight through the gap in the wall—rose with the glittering light of madness in the eyes, and looked at her.

She flew to the open window, and screamed for help.

Sir Patrick's voice answered her, from the road in front of the cottage.

"Wait for me, for God's sake!" she cried.

She fled from the room, and rushed down the stairs. In another moment, she had opened the door, and was out in the front garden.

As she ran to the gate, she heard the voice of a strange man on the other side of it. Sir Patrick called to her encouragingly. "The police man is with us," he said. "He patrols the garden at night—he has a key." As he spoke the gate was opened from the outside. She saw Sir Patrick, Arnold, and the policeman. She staggered toward them as they came in—she was just able to say, "Up stairs!" before her senses failed her. Sir Patrick saved her from falling. He placed her on the bench in the garden, and waited by her, while Arnold and the policeman hurried into the cottage.

"Where first?" asked Arnold.

"The room the lady called from," said the policeman

They mounted the stairs, and entered Anne's room. The gap in the wall was instantly observed by both of them. They looked through it.

Geoffrey Delamayn's dead body lay on the floor. Hester Dethridge was kneeling at his head, praying.

EPILOGUE.

A MORNING CALL.

I.

THE newspapers have announced the return of Lord and Lady Holchester to their residence in London, after an absence on the continent of more than six months.

It is the height of the season. All day long, within the canonical hours, the door of Holchester House is perpetually opening to receive visitors. The vast majority leave their cards, and go away again. Certain privileged individuals only, get out of their carriages, and enter the house.

Among these last, arriving at an earlier hour than is customary, is a person of distinction who is positively bent on seeing either the master or the mistress of the house, and who will take no denial. While this person is parleying with the chief of the servants, Lord Holchester, passing from one room to another, happens to cross the inner end of the hall. The person instantly darts at him with a cry of "Dear Lord Holchester!" Julius turns, and sees—Lady Lundie!

He is fairly caught, and he gives way with his best grace. As he opens the door of the nearest room for her ladyship, he furtively consults his watch, and says in his inmost soul, "How am I to get rid of her before the others come?"

Lady Lundie settles down on a sofa in a whirlwind of silk and lace, and becomes, in her own majestic way, "perfectly charming." She makes the most affectionate inquiries about Lady Holchester, about the Dowager Lady Holchester, about Julius himself. Where have they been? what have they seen? have time and change helped them to recover the shock of that dreadful event, to which Lady Lundie dare not more particularly allude? Julius answers resignedly, and a little absently. He makes polite inquiries, on his side, as to her ladyship's plans and proceedings—with a mind uneasily conscious of the inexorable lapse of time, and of certain probabilities which that lapse may bring with it. Lady Lundie has very little to say about herself. She is only in town for a few weeks. Her life is a life of retirement. "My modest round of duties at Windygates, Lord Holchester; occasionally relieved, when my mind is overworked, by the society of a few earnest friends whose views harmonize with my own—my existence passes (not quite uselessly, I hope) in that way. I have no news; I see nothing—except, indeed, yesterday, a sight of the saddest kind." She pauses there. Julius observes that he is expected to make inquiries, and makes them accordingly.

Lady Lundie hesitates; announces that her news refers to that painful past event which she has already touched on; acknowledges that she could not find herself in London without feeling an act of duty involved in making inquiries at the asylum in which Hester Dethridge is confined for life; announces that she has not only made the inquiries, but has seen the unhappy woman herself; has spoken to her, has found her unconscious of her dreadful position, incapable of the smallest exertion of memory, resigned to the existence that she leads, and likely (in the opinion of the medical superintendent) to live for some years to come. Having stated these facts, her ladyship is about to make a few of those "remarks appropriate to the occasion," in which she excels, when the door opens; and Lady Holchester, in search of her missing husband, enters the room.

II.

There is a new outburst of affectionate interest on Lady Lundie's part—met civilly, but not cordially, by Lady Holchester. Julius's wife seems, like Julius, to be uneasily conscious of the lapse of time. Like Julius again, she privately wonders how long Lady Lundie is going to stay.

Lady Lundie shows no signs of leaving the sofa. She has evidently come to Holchester House to say something—and she has not said it yet. Is she going to say it? Yes. She is going to get, by a roundabout way, to the object in view. She has another inquiry of the affectionate sort to make. May she be permitted to resume the subject of Lord and Lady Holchester's travels? They have been at Rome. Can they confirm the shocking intelligence which has reached her of the "apostasy" of Mrs. Glenarm?

Lady Holchester can confirm it, by personal experience. Mrs. Glenarm has renounced the world, and has taken refuge in the bosom of the Holy Catholic Church. Lady Holchester has seen her in a convent at Rome. She is passing through the period of her probation; and she is resolved to take the veil. Lady Lundie, as a good Protestant, lifts her hands in horror—declares the topic to be too painful to dwell on—and, by way of varying it, goes straight to the point at last. Has Lady I Holchester, in the course of her continental experience, happened to meet with, or to hear of—Mrs. Arnold Brinkworth?

"I have ceased, as you know, to hold any communication with my relatives," Lady Lundie explains. "The course they took at the time of our family trial—the sympathy they felt with a Person whom I can not even now trust myself to name more particularly—alienated us from each other. I may be grieved, dear Lady Holchester; but I bear no malice. And I shall always feel a motherly interest in hearing of Blanche's welfare. I have been told that she and her husband were traveling, at the time when you and Lord Holchester were traveling. Did you meet with them?"

Julius and his wife looked at each other. Lord Holchester is dumb. Lady Holchester replies:

"We saw Mr. and Mrs. Arnold Brinkworth at Florence, and afterward at Naples, Lady Lundie. They returned to England a week since, in anticipation of a certain happy event, which will possibly increase the members of your family circle. They are now in London. Indeed, I may tell you that we expect them here to lunch to-day."

Having made this plain statement, Lady Holchester looks at Lady Lundie. (If that doesn't hasten her departure, nothing will!)

Quite useless! Lady Lundie holds her ground. Having heard absolutely nothing of her relatives for the last six months, she is burning with curiosity to hear more. There is a name she has not mentioned yet. She places a certain constraint upon herself, and mentions it now.

"And Sir Patrick?" says her ladyship, subsiding into a gentle melancholy, suggestive of past injuries condoned by Christian forgiveness. "I only know what report tells me. Did you meet with Sir Patrick at Florence and Naples, also?"

Julius and his wife look at each other again. The clock in the hall strikes. Julius shudders. Lady Holchester's patience begins to give way. There is an awkward pause. Somebody must say something. As before, Lady Holchester replies "Sir Patrick went abroad, Lady Lundie, with his niece and her husband; and Sir Patrick has come back with them."

"In good health?" her ladyship inquires.

"Younger than ever," Lady Holchester rejoins.

Lady Lundie smiles satirically. Lady Holchester notices the smile; decides that mercy shown to this woman is mercy misplaced; and announces (to her husband's horror) that she has news to tell of Sir Patrick, which will probably take his sister-in-law by surprise.

Lady Lundie waits eagerly to hear what the news is.

"It is no secret," Lady Holchester proceeds—"though it is only known, as yet to a few intimate friends. Sir Patrick has made an important change in his life."

Lady Lundie's charming smile suddenly dies out.

"Sir Patrick is not only a very clever and a very agreeable man," Lady Holchester resumes a little maliciously; "he is also, in all his habits and ways (as you well know), a man younger than his years—who still possesses many of the qualities which seldom fail to attract women."

Lady Lundie starts to her feet.

"You don't mean to tell me, Lady Holchester, that Sir Patrick is married?"

"I do."

Her ladyship drops back on the sofa; helpless really and truly helpless, under the double blow that has fallen on her. She is not only struck out of her place as the chief woman of the family, but (still on the right side of forty) she is socially superannuated, as The Dowager Lady Lundie, for the rest of her life!

"At his age!" she exclaims, as soon as she can speak.

"Pardon me for reminding you," Lady Holchester answers, "that plenty of men marry at Sir Patrick's age. In his case, it is only due to him to say that his motive raises him beyond the reach of ridicule or reproach. His marriage is a good action, in the highest sense of the word. It does honor to him, as well as to the lady who shares his position and his name."

"A young girl, of course!" is Lady Lundie's next remark.

"No. A woman who has been tried by no common suffering, and who has borne her hard lot nobly. A woman who deserves the calmer and the happier life on which she is entering now."

"May I ask who she is?"

Before the question can be answered, a knock at the house door announces the arrival of visitors. For the third time, Julius and his wife look at each other. On this occasion, Julius interferes.

"My wife has already told you, Lady Lundie, that we expect Mr. and Mrs. Brinkworth to lunch. Sir Patrick, and the new Lady Lundie, accompany them. If I am mistaken in supposing that it might not be quite agreeable to you to meet them, I can only ask your pardon. If I am right, I will leave Lady Holchester to receive our friends, and will do myself the honor of taking you into another room."

He advances to the door of an inner room. He offers his arm to Lady Lundie. Her ladyship stands immovable; determined to see the woman who has supplanted her. In a moment more, the door of entrance from the hall is thrown open; and the servant announces, "Sir Patrick and Lady Lundie. Mr. and Mrs. Arnold Brinkworth."

Lady Lundie looks at the woman who has taken her place at the head of the family; and sees—ANNE SILVESTER!

About Author

Early life

Collins was born at 11 New Cavendish Street, Marylebone, London, the son of a well-known Royal Academician landscape painter, William Collins and his wife, Harriet Geddes. Named after his father, he swiftly became known by his middle name, which honoured his godfather, David Wilkie. The family moved to Pond Street, Hampstead, in 1826. In 1828 Collins's brother Charles Allston Collins was born. Between 1829 and 1830, the Collins family moved twice, first to Hampstead Square and then to Porchester Terrace, Bayswater. Wilkie and Charles received their early education from their mother at home. The Collins family were deeply religious, and Collins's mother enforced strict church attendance on her sons, which Wilkie disliked.

In 1835, Collins began attending school at the Maida Vale academy. From 1836 to 1838, he lived with his parents in Italy and France, which made a great impression on him. He learned Italian while the family was in Italy and began learning French, in which he would eventually become fluent. From 1838 to 1840, he attended the Reverend Cole's private boarding school in Highbury, where he was bullied by a boy who would force Collins to tell him a story before allowing him to go to sleep. "It was this brute who first awakened in me, his poor little victim, a power of which but for him I might never have been aware.... When I left school I continued story telling for my own pleasure", Collins later said.

In 1840 the family moved to 85 Oxford Terrace, Bayswater. In late 1840, he left school and was apprenticed as a clerk to the firm of tea merchants Antrobus & Co, owned by a friend of Wilkie's father. He disliked his clerical work but remained employed by the company for more than five years. Collins's first story The Last Stage Coachman, was published in the Illuminated Magazine in August 1843. In 1844 he travelled to Paris with Charles Ward. That same year he wrote his first novel, Iolani, or Tahiti as It Was; a Romance, which was submitted to Chapman and Hall but rejected in 1845. The novel remained unpublished during his lifetime. Collins said of it: "My youthful imagination ran riot among the noble savages, in scenes which caused the respectable British publisher to declare that it was impossible to put his name on the title page of such a novel." It was during the writing of this novel that Collins's father first learned that his assumptions that Wilkie would follow him in becoming a painter were mistaken.

William Collins had intended Wilkie for a clergyman and was disappointed in his son's lack of interest. In 1846 he instead entered Lincoln's Inn to study law, on the initiative of his father, who wanted him to have a steady income. Wilkie showed only a slight interest in law and spent most of his time with friends and on working on a second novel, Antonina, or the Fall of Rome. After his father's death in 1847, Collins produced his first published book, Memoirs of the Life of William Collins, Esq., R. A., published in 1848. The family moved to 38 Blandford Square soon afterwards, where they used their drawing room for amateur theatricals. In 1849, Collins exhibited a painting, "The Smugglers' Retreat", at the Royal Academy summer exhibition. Antonina was published by Richard Bentley in February 1850. Collins went on a walking tour of Cornwall with artist Henry Brandling in July and August 1850. He managed to complete his legal studies and be called to the bar in 1851. Though he never formally practised, he used his legal knowledge in many of his novels.

Early writing career

An instrumental event in his career was an introduction in March 1851 to Charles Dickens by a mutual friend, through the painter Augustus Egg. They became lifelong friends and collaborators. In May of that year, Collins acted with Dickens in Edward Bulwer-Lytton's play Not So Bad As We Seem. Among the audience were Queen Victoria and Prince Albert. Collins's story "A Terribly Strange Bed," his first contribution to Household Words, appeared in April, 1852. In May 1852 he went on tour with Dickens's company of amateur actors, again performing Not So Bad As We Seem, but with a more substantial role. Collins's novel Basil was published by Bentley in November. During the writing of Hide and Seek, in early 1853, Collins suffered what was probably his first attack of gout, which would plague him for the rest of his life. He was ill from April to early July. After that he stayed with Dickens in Boulogne from July to September 1853, then toured Switzerland and Italy with Dickens and Egg from October to December. Collins published Hide and Seek in June 1854.

During this period Collins extended the variety of his writing, publishing articles in George Henry Lewes's paper The Leader, short stories and essays for Bentley's Miscellany, dramatic criticism and the travel book Rambles Beyond Railways. His first play, The Lighthouse, was performed by Dickens's theatrical company at Tavistock House, in 1855. His first collection of short stories, After Dark, was published by Smith, Elder in February 1856. His novel A Rogue's Life was serialised in Household Words in March 1856. Around then, Collins began using laudanum regularly to treat his gout. He became addicted and struggled with that problem later in life.

Collins joined the staff of Household Words in October 1856. In 1856–57 he collaborated closely with Dickens on a play, The Frozen Deep, first performed in Tavistock. Collins's novel The Dead Secret was serialised in Household Words from January to June 1857 and published in volume form by Bradbury and Evans. Collins's play The Lighthouse was performed at the Olympic Theatre in August. The Lazy Tour of Two Idle Apprentices, based on Dickens's and Collins's walking tour in the north of England, was serialised in Household Words in October 1857. In 1858 he collaborated with Dickens and other writers on the story "A House to Let".

1860s

According to biographer Melisa Klimaszewski, "The novels Collins published in the 1860s are the best and most enduring of his career. The Woman in White, No Name, Armadale, and The Moonstone, written in less than a decade, show Collins not just as a master of his craft, but as an innovater and provocateur. These four works, which secured him an international reputation, and sold in large numbers, ensured his financial stability, and allowed him to support many others".

The Woman in White was serialised in All the Year Round from November 1859 to August 1860 and was a great success. The novel was published in book form soon after serial publication ended, and it reached an eighth edition by November 1860. His increased stature as a writer made Collins resign his position with All the Year Round in 1862 to focus on novel writing. During the planning of his next novel, No Name, he continued to suffer from gout, and it now especially affected his eyes. Serial publication of No Name began in early 1862 and finished in 1863. By this time the laudanum he was taking for his continual gout became a serious problem.

At the beginning of 1863, he travelled to German spas and Italy for his health, with Caroline Graves. In 1864, he began work on his novel Armadale, travelling in August to do research for it. It was published serially in The Cornhill Magazine in 1864–66. His play No Thoroughfare, co-written with Dickens, was published as the 1867 Christmas number of All the Year Round and dramatised at the Adelphi Theatre on 26 December. It enjoyed a run of 200 nights before being taken on tour.

Collins's search for background information for Armadale took him to the Norfolk Broads and the small village of Winterton-on-Sea. His novel The Moonstone was serialised in All the Year Round from January to August 1868. His mother, Harriet Collins, died that year.

Later years

In 1870, his novel Man and Wife was published. This year also saw the death of Charles Dickens, which caused him great sadness. He said of their early days together, "We saw each other every day, and were as fond of each other as men could be."

The Woman in White was dramatised and produced at the Olympic Theatre in October 1871.

Collins's novel Poor Miss Finch was serialised in Cassell's Magazine from October to March 1872. His short novel Miss or Mrs? was published in the 1872 Christmas number of the Graphic. His novel The New Magdalen was serialised from October 1872 to July 1873. His younger brother, Charles Allston Collins, died later in 1873. Charles had married Dickens's younger daughter, Kate.

In 1873–74, Collins toured the United States and Canada, giving readings of his work. The American writers he met included Oliver Wendell Holmes, Sr., and Mark Twain, and he began a friendship with the photographer Napoleon Sarony, who took several portraits of him.

His novel The Law and the Lady, serialised in the Graphic from September to March 1875, was followed by a short novel, The Haunted Hotel, which was serialised from June to November 1878. His later novels include Jezebel's Daughter (1880), The Black Robe (1881), Heart and Science (1883) and The Evil Genius (1886). In 1884, Collins was elected Vice-President of the Society of Authors, which had been founded by his friend and fellow novelist Walter Besant.

The inconsistent quality of Collins's dramatic and fictional works in the last decade of his life was accompanied by a general decline in his health, including diminished eyesight. He was often unable to leave home and had difficulty writing. During these last years, he focused on mentoring younger writers, including the novelist Hall Caine, and helped to protect other writers from copyright infringement of their works. His writing became a way for him to fight his illness without allowing it to keep him bedridden. His step-daughter Harriet also served as an amanuensis for several years. His last novel, Blind Love, was finished posthumously by Walter Besant.

Death

Collins died at 82 Wimpole Street, following a paralytic stroke. He is buried in Kensal Green Cemetery, West London. His headstone describes him as the author of The Woman in White. Caroline Graves died in 1895 and was buried with Collins. Martha Rudd died in 1919.

Personal life

In 1858 Collins began living with Caroline Graves and her daughter Harriet. Caroline came from a humble family, having married young, had a child, and been widowed. Collins lived close to the small shop kept by Caroline, and the two may have met in the neighborhood in the mid–1850s. He treated Harriet, whom he called Carrie, as his own daughter, and helped to provide for her education. Excepting one short separation, they lived together for the rest of Collins's life. Collins disliked the institution of marriage, but remained dedicated to Caroline and Harriet, considering them to be his family. Caroline had wanted to marry Collins. She left him while he wrote The Moonstone and was suffering an attack of acute gout. She then married a younger man named Joseph Clow, but returned to Collins after two years.

In 1868, Collins met Martha Rudd in Winterton-on-Sea in Norfolk, and the two began a liaison. She was 19 years old and from a large, poor family. She moved to London to be closer to him a few years later. Their daughter Marian was born in 1869, their second daughter, Harriet Constance, in 1871 and their son, William Charles, in 1874. When he was with Martha he assumed the name William Dawson, and she and their children used the last name of Dawson themselves.

For the last 20 years of his life Collins divided his time between Caroline, who lived with him at his home in Gloucester Place, and Martha who was nearby.

Like his friend Charles Dickens, Collins was a professing Christian.

Works

Collins's works were classified at the time as "sensation novels", a genre seen nowadays as the precursor to detective and suspense fiction. He also wrote penetratingly on the plight of women and on the social and domestic issues of his time. For example, his 1854 Hide and Seek contained one of the first portrayals of a deaf character in English literature. As did many writers of his time, Collins published most of his novels as serials in magazines such as Dickens's All the Year Round and was known as a master of the form, creating just the right degree of suspense to keep his audience reading from week to week. Sales of All The Year Round increased when The Woman in White followed A Tale of Two Cities.

Collins enjoyed ten years of great success following publication of The Woman in White in 1859. His next novel, No Name combined social commentary – the absurdity of the law as it applied to children of unmarried parents (see Illegitimacy in fiction) – with a densely plotted revenge thriller. Armadale, the first and only of Collins's major novels of the 1860s to be serialised in a magazine other than All the Year Round, provoked strong criticism, generally centred upon its transgressive villainess Lydia Gwilt, and provoked in part by Collins's typically confrontational preface. The novel was simultaneously a financial coup for its author and a comparative commercial failure: the sum paid by Cornhill for the serialisation rights was exceptional, eclipsing by a substantial margin the prices paid for the vast majority of similar novels, yet the novel failed to recoup its publisher's investment. The Moonstone, published in 1868, and the last novel of what is generally regarded as the most successful decade of its author's career, was, despite a somewhat cool reception from both Dickens and the critics, a significant return to form and reestablished the market value of an author whose success on the competitive Victorian literary market had been gradually waning in the wake of his first perceived masterpiece. Viewed by many to represent the advent of the detective story within the tradition of the English novel, The Moonstone remains one of Collins's most critically acclaimed productions, identified by T. S. Eliot as "the first, the longest, and the best of modern English detective novels... in a genre invented by Collins and not by Poe," and Dorothy L. Sayers referred to it as "probably the very finest detective story ever written".

After The Moonstone, Collins's novels contained fewer thriller elements and more social commentary. The subject matter continued to be sensational, but his popularity declined. The poet Algernon Charles Swinburne commented: "What brought good Wilkie's genius nigh perdition? / Some demon whispered—'Wilkie! have a mission.'"

Factors most often cited have been the death of Dickens in 1870, and with it the loss of his literary mentoring, Collins's increased dependence upon laudanum, and his penchant for using his fiction to rail against social injustices. His novels and novellas of the 1870s and 1880s are generally regarded as inferior to his previous productions and receive comparatively little critical attention today[when?].

The Woman in White and The Moonstone share an unusual narrative structure, somewhat resembling an epistolary novel, in which different portions of the book have different narrators, each with a distinct narrative voice. Armadale has this to a lesser extent through the correspondence between some characters. (Source: Wikipedia)

Lightning Source UK Ltd.
Milton Keynes UK
UKHW041837050820
367766UK00004B/139